Gardner Dozois edited Asimov's *Science Fiction* magazine for ~~~~ ~~st Editor fifteen ~~~~ ~~ lives ~~adelphia, Pennsylvania.

THE MAMMOTH BOOK OF
BEST NEW
SF 28

EDITED BY
GARDNER DOZOIS

ROBINSON

B000 000 016 400

ROBINSON

First published in the US as
The Year's Best Science Fiction: Thirty-second Annual Collection
by St Martin's Press, 2015

First published in Great Britain in 2015 by Robinson

Copyright © Gardner Dozois, 2015
(unless otherwise stated)

The moral right of the author has been asserted.

A CIP catalogue record for this book
is available from the British Library.

ISBN 978-1-47211-999-5 (paperback)
ISBN: 978-1-47212-000-7 (ebook)

Printed and bound in Great Britain by CPI Group (UK) Ltd, Croydon CR0 4YY

Papers used by Robinson are from well-managed forests and
other responsible sources

MIX
Paper from
responsible sources
FSC
www.fsc.org FSC® C104740

Robinson
An imprint of
Little, Brown Book Group
Carmelite House
50 Victoria Embankment
London EC4Y 0DZ

An Hachette UK Company
www.hachette.co.uk

www.littlebrown.co.uk

contents

PERMISSIONS   *vii*

ACKNOWLEDGMENTS   *xi*

SUMMATION: 2014   *xiii*

THE FIFTH DRAGON • *Ian McDonald*   1

THE RIDER • *Jérôme Cigut*   15

THE DAYS OF THE WAR, AS RED AS BLOOD, AS DARK
AS BILE • *Aliette de Bodard*   35

THE BURIAL OF SIR JOHN MAWE AT CASSINI • *Chaz Brenchley*   48

THE REGULAR • *Ken Liu*   59

THE WOMAN FROM THE OCEAN • *Karl Bunker*   92

SHOOTING THE APOCALYPSE • *Paolo Bacigalupi*   100

WEATHER • *Susan Palwick*   116

THE HAND IS QUICKER • *Elizabeth Bear*   124

THE MAN WHO SOLD THE MOON • *Cory Doctorow*   139

VLADIMIR CHONG CHOOSES TO DIE • *Lavie Tidhar*   199

BESIDE THE DAMNED RIVER • *D. J. Cockburn*   210

THE COLONEL • *Peter Watts*   217

ENTANGLEMENT • *Vandana Singh*   235

WHITE CURTAIN • *Pavel Amnuel, translated by Anatoly Belilovsky*   269

SLIPPING • *Lauren Beukes*   277

PASSAGE OF EARTH • *Michael Swanwick*   291

AMICAE AETERNUM • *Ellen Klages*   306

IN BABELSBERG • *Alastair Reynolds*   313

SADNESS • *Timons Esaias*   324

WEST TO EAST • *Jay Lake*   330

GRAND JETÉ (THE GREAT LEAP) • *Rachel Swirsky*   337

COVENANT • *Elizabeth Bear*   375

JUBILEE • *Karl Schroeder*   386

LOS PIRATAS DEL MAR DE PLASTICO (PIRATES OF THE
PLASTIC OCEAN) • *Paul Graham Raven*   404

RED LIGHTS, AND RAIN • *Gareth L. Powell*   422

COMA KINGS • *Jessica Barber*   433

THE PRODIGAL SON • *Allen M. Steele*   440

GOD DECAY • *Rich Larson*   477

BLOOD WEDDING • *Robert Reed*   486

THE LONG HAUL, FROM THE *ANNALS OF TRANSPORTATION, THE PACIFIC
MONTHLY,* MAY 2009 • *Ken Liu*   508

SHADOW FLOCK • *Greg Egan*   522

THING AND SICK • *Adam Roberts*   542

COMMUNION • *Mary Anne Mohanraj*   560

SOMEDAY • *James Patrick Kelly*   569

YESTERDAY'S KIN • *Nancy Kress*   579

HONORABLE MENTIONS: 2014   655

permissions

acknowledgments

The editor would like to thank the following people for their help and support: Susan Casper, Jonathan Strahan, Sean Wallace, Neil Clarke, Gordon Van Gelder, Andy Cox, John Joseph Adams, Ellen Datlow, Sheila Williams, Trevor Quachri, Peter Crowther, William Shaffer, Ian Whates, Paula Guran, Tony Daniel, Liza Trombi, Robert Wexler, Patrick Nielsen Hayden, Joseph Eschrich, Kathryn Cramer, Jonathan Oliver, Stephen Cass, Lynne M. Thomas, Dario Ciriello, Paul Stevens, Jennifer Jackson, Mary Elizabeth Lake, Anatoly Bellovsky, Gavin Grant, Kelly Link, Derek Kunsken, Gord Sellar, Fred Coppersmith, Katie Cord, Eileen Wiedbrank, Ian Redman, David Lee Summers, Wendy S. Delmater, Beth Wodzinski, E. Catherine Tobler, Katie Cord, Edward O'Connell, An Owomeyela, Alexander Irvine, Anaea Lay, Benjanun Sriduanokaew, Yoon Ha Lee, Kathleen Ann Goonan, David Sweeney, Bud Webster, Niall Harrison, Carl Rafala, Emily Hockaday, Edmund R. Schubert, C. C. Finlay, A. C. Wise, Jennifer Parsons, Christopher Barzak, Jerimy Colbert, Mike Resnick, Tim Pratt, Tony Daniel, William Ledbetter, Wendy S. Delmater, Jed Hartman, Rich Horton, Mark R. Kelly, Tehani Wessely, Elizabeth Bear, Aliette de Bodard, Lavie Tidhar, Adam Roberts, Robert Reed, Vandana Singh, Alastair Reynolds, Ken Liu, James Patrick Kelly, Nancy Kress, Ian McDonald, Jérôme Cigut, Chaz Brenchley, Ken Liu, Karl Bunker, Paolo Bacigalupi, Susan Palwick, Cory Doctorow, Peter Watts, D. J. Cockburn, Pavel Amnuel, Lauren Beukes, Michael Swanwick, Ellen Klages, Timon Esaias, Rachel Swirsky, Karl Schroeder, Paul Graham Raven, Gareth L. Powell, Jessica Barber, Allen M. Steele, Rich Larson, Greg Egan, Mary Anne Mohanraj, John O'Neill, Vaughne Lee Hansen, Mark Watson, Katherine Canfield, Jaime Coyne, and special thanks to my own editor, Marc Resnick.

Thanks are also due to the late, lamented Charles N. Brown, and to all his staff, whose magazine *Locus* [Locus Publications, P.O. Box 13305, Oakland, CA 94661.

$63 in the U.S. for a one-year subscription (twelve issues) via periodical mail; $76 for a one-year (twelve issues) via first-class credit card orders, (510) 339-9198] was used as an invaluable reference source throughout the Summation; *Locus Online* (www .locusmag.com), edited by Mark R. Kelly, has also become a key reference source.

It was a relatively quiet year in the SF publishing world. The big story, rumbling in the background throughout most of the year, was the battle between online retailer Amazon and publisher Hachette Book Group over the pricing of e-books, which got very public and very nasty, and drew authors and author organizations into it on one side or the other before the dispute was finally settled on November 13. Amazon also finally settled similar disputes with publishers Macmillan and Simon & Schuster.

Digital books, e-books, and physical print books continued to coexist, without either driving the other out of the marketplace, as some commentators have been predicting either gloomily or gleefully (depending on what side they were on; some digital enthusiasts have seemed downright happy about the idea that e-books were going to drive print books into extinction) for several years now. Instead, some kind of equilibrium seems to be being reached, with many readers buying *both* e-books and print books, choosing one format or the other to purchase depending on their needs and the circumstances; some readers even buy both e-book and print editions *of the same title*, something that almost nobody saw coming. Nor have online sellers like Amazon driven physical brick-and-mortar bookstores out of existence, another frequently heard prophecy during the last few years—a study released by Nielsen Market Research indicates that most books are still purchased in physical stores, especially chain stores, with online retailers accounting for just 41 percent of all new book sales. Physical brick-and-mortar bookstores also remain an important part of the process whereby readers discover new titles they'd like to purchase, with 12 percent of buyers surveyed saying that they learned about particular titles from seeing bookstore displays (another 10 percent heard about books via word of mouth, while 8 percent found books by browsing online).

Mass-market paperbacks were the sector hardest hit by the advent of e-books, but even they haven't been driven into extinction; although sales of mass-market paperbacks dropped by more than 50 percent from 2010 to 2013, the decline slowed to only 11 percent from 2013 to 2014, with sales actually remaining flat in some week-to-week comparisons, so it looks as if the mass-market sector is stabilizing, and probably will not be driven off the shelves, as some feared it would be. There are still plenty of people who prefer the inexpensive, easy-to-carry format, especially those who don't read e-books.

Although nobody can deny that ebooks have become an important part of the market, and will remain so, print isn't dead yet—nor is it likely to die, in my opinion.

Perhaps the most encouraging news of the year comes from a new Pew survey which shows that Americans in the sixteen to twenty-nine age group are reading more than older Americans. The report reveals that 88 percent of Americans under thirty read at least one book in the past year, compared to 79 percent for those over thirty. Younger teens read the most, with 46 percent of those aged sixteen to seventeen reporting that they read books (in both print and digital formats) on a daily basis. Compared to 40 percent of readers above age thirty, 43 percent of those eighteen to nineteen report reading books daily.

No information is available for non-Americans, but I'm willing to bet that those results are duplicated if not surpassed in many if not most other countries. So it turns out that the prophecy that the Internet was going to destroy literacy and the assertion that kids aren't interested in reading anymore has been pretty much disproved as well (although the immense sales of the Harry Potter books should have disproved it a long time ago); if anything, widespread use of the Internet and easy availability of books (in all formats) in places where they were hard to find before seems to have *increased* literacy, and it looks like more people of all ages are reading more than they ever have before. That can only be hopeful news for those of us who work in the literary world, or for anybody who loves books and reading, for that matter.

In other news: Tor Books formed new SF imprint *Tor.com*, with Lee Harris, former editor of Angry Robot, as senior editor, Fritz Foy as publisher, and Irene Gallo as associate publisher. Simon & Schuster started a new SF imprint, Saga Press. Parent company Osprey Publishing Group discontinued YA imprint Strange Chemistry and crime-mystery imprint Exhibit A, and then sold SF imprint Angry Robot to American entrepreneur Etan Ilfeld. HarperCollins bought romance imprint Harlequin. Hodder & Stoughton bought Quercus, the independent UK publisher that includes SF/fantasy imprint Jo Fletcher Books. Open Road Integrated Media acquired e-publisher E-Reads. Lou Anders stepped down as editorial director and art director of Pyr, being replaced by Rene Sears. Paul Stevens left Tor and joined Quirk Books as an acquisitions editor. Gillian Redfearn was promoted to publishing director of Gollancz, with Jon Wood becoming managing director as well as Orion Group publisher. Sarah Shumway joined Bloomsbury Children's Books as a senior editor. Jonathan Jao joined HarperCollins as vice-president and executive editor. Michael P. Huseby was named chief executive officer of Barnes & Noble, Inc. Vanessa Mobley was made executive editor at Little, Brown. Suzanne Donahue left her position as vice-president and associate publisher at Simon & Schuster.

After years of sometimes precipitous decline, it was another fairly stable year in the professional magazine market. Sales of electronic subscriptions to the magazines are continuing to creep up, as well as sales of individual electronic copies of each issue, and this is making a big difference to profitability.

Asimov's Science Fiction had a somewhat weaker year than it had the year before, but still published good work by Allen M. Steele, Karl Bunker, Robert Reed, James Patrick Kelly, Derek Kunsken, Gord Sellar, Kara Dalkey, Jay O'Connell, Tim Sullivan, and others. As usual, their SF was considerably stronger than their fantasy, the reverse of *The Magazine of Fantasy & Science Fiction*. *Asimov's Science Fiction* registered a 12.5 percent loss in overall circulation, down to 20, 282 from 2013's 23,192. Subscriptions were 17,987, down from 20,327; of that total, 9,347 were print subscriptions, while 8,640 were digital subscriptions, almost half the total, which shows how important digital subscriptions have become to these magazines. Newsstand sales were down to 2,295 copies from 2013's 2,385. Sell-through fell from 39 percent to 35 percent. Sheila Williams completed her eleventh year as *Asimov's* editor.

Analog Science Fiction and Fact had good work (and some of it somewhat atypical stuff for *Analog*; it's encouraging to see new editor Trevor Quachri being bold enough to set his stamp on a long-running magazine). Lavie Tidhar, Timons Esaias, Michael F. Flynn, Alec Nevala-Lee, Kristine Kathryn Rusch, Tony Ballantyne, Ken Liu, Craig DeLancey, C. W. Johnson, David D. Levine, and others all published good work. *Analog* registered a 9.3 percent loss in overall circulation, down to 24,709 from 2013's 27,248. There were 21,456 subscriptions, down slightly from 2013's 23,630; of this total, 15,282 were print subscriptions, while 6,174 were digital subscriptions. Newsstand sales were up slightly to 3,253 from 2013's 3,235. Sell-through held steady at 41 percent. New editor Trevor Quachri completed his first full year as editor and 2014 marked the magazine's eighty-fourth anniversary.

Once again, *The Magazine of Fantasy & Science Fiction* was almost exactly the reverse of *Asimov's*, with the fantasy published there being stronger than the science fiction—which there wasn't a lot of this year. *F&SF* also had a weaker year than last year, but still published good work by Jérôme Cigut, Pavel Amnuel, Matthew Hughes, Robert Reed, Alaya Dawn Johnson, Paul M. Berger, Alex Irvine, Sandra McDonald, and others. *F&SF* registered a welcome 10.3 rise in overall circulation from 10,678 to 11,910. Subscriptions rose from 7,762 to 8,994; digital sales figures were not available. Newsstand sales stayed steady at 2,916. Sell-through rose from 23 percent to 28 percent. Gordon Van Gelder was in his eighteenth year as editor, and fourteenth year as owner and publisher in 2014. In early 2015, it was announced that writer Charles Coleman Finlay was taking over as *F&SF's* active acquisitions editor, starting with the March/April 2015 issue. Van Gelder remains as publisher.

Interzone is technically not a "professional magazine," by the definition of the Science Fiction Writers of America (SFWA), because of its low rates and circulation, but the literary quality of the work published there is so high that it would be ludicrous to omit it. *Interzone* was also a bit weaker this year than last year, but still published good work by D. J. Cockburn, Malcolm Devlin, James Van Pelt, Karl Bunker, John Grant, Suzanne Palmer, Gareth L. Powell, and others. Exact circulation figures are not available, but is guessed to be in the 2,000 copy range. TTA Press, *Interzone's* publisher, also publishes straight horror or dark suspense magazine *Black Static*, which is beyond our purview here, but of a similar level of professional quality. *Interzone* and *Black Static* changed to a smaller trim size in 2011, but maintained their slick look, switching from the old 7 ¾"-by-10 ¾" saddle-stitched semigloss color cover sixty-four-page format to a 6 ½"-by-9 ¼" perfect-bound glossy color cover ninety-six-page format. The editors include publisher Andy Cox and Andrew Hedgecock.

If you'd like to see lots of good SF and fantasy published every year, the survival of these magazines is essential, and one important way that you can help them survive is by subscribing to them. It's never been easier to do so, something that these days can be done with just the click of a few buttons, nor has it ever before been possible to subscribe to the magazines in as many different formats, from the traditional print copy arriving by mail to downloads for your desktop or laptop available from places like Amazon (www.amazon.com), to versions you can read on your

Kindle, Nook, or iPad. You can also now subscribe from overseas just as easily as you can from the United States, something formerly difficult to impossible.

So in hopes of making it easier for you to subscribe, I'm going to list both the Internet sites where you can subscribe online and the street addresses where you can subscribe by mail for each magazine: *Asimov's* site is at www.asimovs.com, and subscribing online might be the easiest thing to do, and there's also a discounted rate for online subscriptions; its subscription address is *Asimov's Science Fiction*, Dell Magazines, 267 Broadway, Fourth Floor, New York, N.Y., 10007-2352—$34.97 for annual subscription in the U.S., $44.97 overseas. *Analog's* site is at www.analogsf .com; its subscription address is *Analog Science Fiction and Fact*, Dell Magazines, 267 Broadway, Fourth Floor, New York, N.Y., 10007-2352—$34.97 for annual subscription in the U.S., $44.97 overseas. *The Magazine of Fantasy & Science Fiction's* site is at www.sfsite.com/fsf; its subscription address is *The Magazine of Fantasy & Science Fiction*, Spilogale, Inc., P.O. Box 3447, Hoboken, N.J., 07030, annual subscription—$34.97 in the U.S, $44.97 overseas. *Interzone* and *Black Static* can be subscribed to online at www.ttapress.com/onlinestore1.html; the subscription address for both is TTA Press, 5 Martins Lane, Witcham, Ely, Cambs CB6 2LB, England, UK, 42.00 Pounds Sterling each for a twelve-issue subscription, or there is a reduced rate dual subscription offer of 78.00 Pounds Sterling for both magazines for twelve issues; make checks payable to "TTA Press."

Most of these magazines are also available in various electronic formats through the Kindle, Nook, and other handheld readers.

There's not a whole lot left of the print semiprozine market, although it may be a good sign that hopeful newcomers continue to appear.

One of these hopeful newcomers is a new SF magazine (available both in electronic formats and print copies), *Galaxy's Edge* (www.galaxysedge.com), edited by Mike Resnick, which launched in 2013 and completed its first full year of publication in 2014. So far, the reprints, by people such as Nancy Kress, Michael Swanwick, Robert Silverberg, Kij Johnson, and Kristine Kathryn Rusch, of which there are four in every issue, have been stronger than the original stories, but there has been interesting work by Tobias S. Buckell, Lisa Tang Liu and Ken Liu, Brad R. Torgersen, Tina Gower, Lou J. Berger, and others. A print edition is available from BN.com and Amazon.com for $5.99 per issue.

Most of the older print semiprozines had trouble bringing out their scheduled issues, a common problem in that market. The Canadian *On Spec*, the longest-running of all the print fiction semiprozines, which is edited by a collective under general editor Diane L. Walton, only brought out three out of four published issues, and is reported to be thinking of switching to a digital online format. Another collective-run SF magazine with a rotating editorial staff, Australia's *Andromeda Spaceways Inflight Magazine*, managed only two issues this year. There were two issues of *Lady Churchill's Rosebud Wristlet*, the long-running slipstream magazine edited by Kelly Link and Gavin Grant, in 2014, and two of Ireland's long-running *Albedo One. Space and Time Magazine* managed three issues, and *Flytrap* and *Neo-opsis* managed one. We didn't see an issue of the small British SF magazine *Jupiter* this year. *Tales of the*

Talisman is going "on hiatus," as are *Science Fiction Trails* and *Steampunk Trails*. *Shimmer* has transitioned to an online digital format, and long-running Australian semiprozine *Aurealis* has transitioned to a downloadable format. I saw nothing from the revamped version of *Weird Tales* this year, and suspect that it has died. *Bull Spec* has transitioned to digital format, and is no longer publishing fiction.

Most of the stuff published in the surviving print semiprozines this year was relatively minor, with better work appearing in the online magazines (see below).

With the departure of *The New York Review of Science Fiction* to the electronic world in mid-2012, there's really little left of popular print critical magazine market, except for the venerable newszine *Locus: The Magazine of the Science Fiction & Fantasy Field*, now in its forty-eighth year of publication. A multiple Hugo winner, for decades an indispensible source of news, information, and reviews, *Locus* survived the death of founder, publisher, and longtime editor Charles N. Brown and has continued strongly and successfully under the guidance of a staff of editors headed by Liza Groen Trombi, and including Kirsten Gong-Wong, Carolyn Cushman, Tim Pratt, Jonathan Strahan, Francesca Myman, Heather Shaw, and many others.

One of the few other remaining popular critical print magazines is newcomer *The Cascadia Subduction Zone: A Literary Quarterly*, edited by L. Timmel Duchamp and Nisi Shawl, a new feminist print magazine of reviews and critical essays, which published four issues in 2014. The most accessible of the other surviving print critical magazines—most of which are professional journals more aimed at academics than at the average reader—is probably the long-running British critical zine *Foundation*.

Subscription addresses are: **Locus: The Magazine of the Science Fiction & Fantasy Field**, Locus Publications, Inc., P.O. Box 13305, Oakland, California 94661, $76.00 for a one-year first-class subscription, twelve issues; **Foundation**, Science Fiction Foundation, Roger Robinson (SFF), 75 Rosslyn Avenue, Harold Wood, Essex RM3 ORG, UK, $37.00 for a three-issue subscription in the U.S.A.; **On Spec: The Canadian Magazine of the Fantastic**, P.O. Box 4727, Edmonton, AB, Canada T6E 5G6, for subscription information, go to Web site www.onspec.ca; **Neo-opsis Science Fiction Magazine**, 4129 Carey Rd., Victoria, BC, V8Z 4G5, $25.00 for a three-issue subscription; **Albedo One**, Albedo One Productions, 2, Post Road, Lusk, Co., Dublin, Ireland, $32.00 for a four-issue airmail subscription, make checks payable to "Albedo One" or pay by PayPal at www.albedo1.com; **Lady Churchill's Rosebud Wristlet**, Small Beer Press, 150 Pleasant St., #306, Easthampton, MA 01027, $20.00 for four issues; **Andromeda Spaceways Inflight Magazine**, see Web site www.andromedaspaceways.com for subscription information; **The Cascadia Subduction Zone: A Literary Quarterly**, subscription and single issues online at www.thecsz.com, $16 annually for a print subscription, print single issues $5, Electronic Subscription—PDF format—$10 per year, electronic single issue, $3, to order by check, make them payable to Aqueduct Press, P.O. Box 95787, Seattle, WA 98145-2787.

The world of online-only electronic magazines now rivals the traditional print market as a place to find good new fiction—in fact, this year, your chances of finding good stories were probably a bit higher in the e-zine market than in the print market.

Subterranean Magazine (subterraneanpress.com), edited by William K. Schafer, is going out on a very strong year that featured good work by K. J. Parker, Rachel Swirsky, Chaz Brenchley, Caitlin R. Kiernan, Kat Howard, Eleanor Arnason, Ellen Klages, Karen Joy Fowler, and others. I regret Schafer's decision to close up shop to concentrate on his Subterranean book line, as the loss of *Subterranean Magazine* leaves a real hole in the genre market—especially as it was one of the few online markets that was willing to publish novellas and long novelettes. (Oddly, since they don't have the practical word-length limitations that affect print magazines, little is published in the majority of electronic magazines that isn't short story length or shorter. In the whole rest of the market, only *Tor.com* and *Beneath Ceaseless Skies* will occasionally publish novellas.)

The electronic magazine *Clarkesworld* (www.clarkesworldmagazine.com), edited by Neil Clarke and Sean Wallace also had a good year, publishing strong work by Michael Swanwick, Ken Liu, Susan Palwick, Mary Anne Mohanraj, Robert Reed, An Owomoyela, James Patrick Kelly, and others. They also host monthly podcasts of stories drawn from each issue. *Clarkesworld* has won three Hugo Awards as Best Semiprozine. Last year, *Clarkesworld* coeditor Sean Wallace, along with Jack Fisher, launched a new online horror magazine, *The Dark* (thedarkmagazine.com).

Lightspeed (www.lightspeedmagazine.com), edited by John Joseph Adams, featured strong work by Carrie Vaughn, Matthew Hughes, Jessica Barber, Anaea Lay, Theodora Goss, Sunny Moraine, Sarah Pinsker, An Owomoyela, Rhonda Eikamp, Kris Millering, Linda Nagata, and others. *Lightspeed* won its first Hugo Award as Best Semiprozine this year. Late in 2013, a new electronic companion horror magazine, *Nightmare* (www.nightmare-magazine.com), also edited by John Joseph Adams, was added to the *Lightspeed* stable.

Tor.com (www.tor.com), edited by Patrick Nielsen Hayden and Liz Gorinsky, with additional material purchased by Ellen Datlow, Ann VanderMeer, and others, published some first-class work by Karl Schroeder, Peter Watts, Elizabeth Bear, Nicola Griffith, Jo Walton, Harry Turtledove, Bruce McAllister, Kathleen Ann Goonan, Veronica Schanoes, and others.

Strange Horizons (www.strangehorizons.com), the oldest continually running electronic genre magazine on the Internet, started in 2000, had a change of editorial staff this year. Longtime editors Jed Hartman and Susan Marie Groppi stepped down in 2013; the new editor-in-chief there is Niall Harrison, with Brit Mandelo, Julia Rios, and An Owomoyela as fiction editors. This year, they had strong work by Indrapramit Das, Marissa Lingen, Rich Larson, Ann Leckie, Sunny Moraine, Malcolm Cross, Alyssa Wong, Sarah Brooks, and others.

Longtime print semiprozine *Electric Velocipede*, edited by John Klima, which had transitioned to online-only format, finally gave up the ghost late in 2013. There is a retrospective anthology this year, drawn from work published in the magazine, *The Best of Electric Velocipede* (Fairwood Press).

Apex Magazine (www.apex-magazine.com) had good work by Rich Larson, Marissa Lingen, Seth Dickinson, Caroline M. Yoachim, Sunny Moraine, and others. Jason Sizemore is the new editor, replacing Sigrid Ellis, who took over from Lynne M. Thomas.

Abyss & Apex (www.abyssapexzine.com) ran interesting work by Rich Larson, Fran Wilde, John C. Wright, Rati Mehrotra, and others. New editor Carmelo Rafala stepped down to be replaced by the former longtime editor, Wendy S. Delmater, who returned to the helm.

An e-zine devoted to "literary adventure fantasy," *Beneath Ceaseless Skies* (www.beneath-ceaseless-skies.com), edited by Scott H. Andrews, ran good stuff by K. J. Parker, Richard Parks, Aliette de Bodard, Gregory Norman Bossert, Gemma Files, M. Bennardo, and others.

Long-running sword and sorcery print magazine *Black Gate*, edited by John O'Neill, transitioned into an electronic magazine in September of 2012 and can be found at www.blackgate.com. They no longer regularly run new fiction, although they will be regularly refreshing their nonfiction content, essays and reviews, and the occasional story will continue to appear.

The Australian popular-science magazine *Cosmos* (www.cosmosmagazine.com) is not an SF magazine per se, but for the last few years it has been running a story per issue (and also putting new fiction not published in the print magazine up on their Web site). They seem to have published less fiction this year than before, but good stuff by Ken Liu, Sean Williams, Greg Mellor, and others appeared there this year. The fiction editor is SF writer Cat Sparks.

Ideomancer Speculative Fiction (www.ideomancer.com), edited by Leah Bobet, published interesting work, usually more slipstream than SF, by Arkady Martine, Michael J. DeLuca, Maya Surya Pillay, and others.

Orson Scott Card's Intergalactic Medicine Show (www.intergalacticmedicineshow .com), edited by Edmund R. Schubert under the direction of Card himself, ran interesting stuff from Alex Shvartsman, James Van Pelt, Bud Webster, Gareth D. Jones, and others.

SF/fantasy e-zine *Daily Science Fiction* (dailysciencefiction.com) publishes one new SF or fantasy story *every single day* for the entire year. Unsurprisingly, many of these were not really up to professional standards, but there were some good stories here and there by Ken Liu, Eric Brown, James Van Pelt, Edoardo Albert, Marissa Lingen, Kelly Jennings, M. Bennardo, Anatoly Belilovsky, and others. Editors there are Michele-Lee Barasso and Jonathan Laden.

GigaNotoSaurus (giganotosaurus.org), now edited by Rashida J. Smith, taking over from Ann Leckie, published one story a month by writers such as Patricia Russo, A. C. Wise, Vanessa Fogg, Rachel Sobel, and others.

An audacious newcomer is *Uncanny* (uncannymagazine.com), edited by Lynne M. Thomas and Michael Damian Thomas, which launched in late 2014 with good work by Christopher Barzak, Amelia Beamer, Ken Liu, and others. Other newcomers are *Straeon 1* (www.rampantloonmedia.com), edited by M. David Blake, *Terraform* (motherboard.vice.com/terraform), edited by Claire Evans and Brian Merchant, *Child of Words* (www.bigpulp.com), edited by Bill Olver, and *Omenana* (omenana.com), edited by Chinelo Onwualu and Mazi Nwonwu, as well as relative newcomers *Kaleidotrope* (www.kaleidotrope.net), edited by Fred Coppersmith, which started in 2006 as a print semiprozine but transitioned to digital in 2012, *Shimmer* (www.shimmerzine.com), edited by Beth Wodzinski, which transitioned to digital format in 2014, and *Crossed Genres* (www.crossedgenres.com), edited by Bart R. Leib, Kay T. Holt, and Kelly Jennings.

The World SF Blog (worldsf.wordpress.com), edited by Lavie Tidhar, was a good place to find science fiction by international authors, and also published news, links, roundtable discussions, essays, and interviews related to "science fiction, fantasy, horror, and comics from around the world." The site is no longer being updated, but an extensive archive is still accessible there.

A similar site is *International Speculative Fiction* (internationalSF.wordpress.com), edited by Roberto Mendes.

Weird Fiction Review (weirdfictionreview.com), edited by Ann VanderMeer and Jeff VanderMeer, which occasionally publishes fiction, bills itself as "an ongoing exploration into all facets of the weird," including reviews, interviews, short essays, and comics.

The (sort of) relaunch of *Amazing Stories* (amazingstoriesmag.com), edited by Steve Davidson, seems to be mostly a multicontributor blog, publishing reviews, interviews, and essays, but fiction only occasionally.

Below this point, it becomes harder to find center-core SF, or even genre fantasy/horror, with most magazines featuring slipstream or literary surrealism instead. Such sites include *Revolution SF* (www.revolutionsf.com), *Heliotrope* (www.heliotropemag.com), *Fireside Magazine* (www.firesidefiction.com), edited by Brian White, *Interfictions Online* (interfictions.com), edited by Christopher Barzak and Meghan McCarron, and *Michael Moorcock's New Worlds* (www.newworlds.co.uk), edited by Roger Gray.

But in addition to original work, there's also a lot of good *reprint* SF and fantasy to be found on Internet. Sites where you can access formerly published stories for free include *Strange Horizons, Tor.com, Clarkesworld, Lightspeed, Subterranean, Abyss & Apex*, and most of the sites that are associated with existent print magazines, such as *Asimov's, Analog*, and *The Magazine of Fantasy & Science Fiction*, make previously published fiction and nonfiction available for access on their sites as well, and also regularly run teaser excerpts from stories coming up in forthcoming issues. Hundreds of out-of-print titles, both genre and mainstream, are also available for free download from Project Gutenberg (www.gutenberg.org), and a large selection of novels and a few collections can also be accessed for free, to be either downloaded or read on-screen, at the Baen Free Library (www.baen.com/library). Sites such as Infinity Plus (www.infinityplus.co.uk) and *The Infinite Matrix* (www.infinitematrix.net) may have died as active sites, but their extensive archives of previously published material are still accessible (an extensive line of new Infinity Plus Books can also be ordered from the Infinity Plus site).

There are plenty of other reasons for SF fans to go on the Internet, though, other than looking for SF stories to read. There are many general genre-related sites of interest to be found, most of which publish reviews of books as well as of movies and TV shows, sometimes comics or computer games or anime, many of which also feature interviews, critical articles, and genre-oriented news of various kinds. The best such site is *Locus Online* (www.locusmag.com), the online version of the newsmagazine *Locus*, where you can access an incredible amount of information—including book reviews, critical lists, obituary lists, links to reviews and essays appearing outside the genre, and links to extensive database archives such as the Locus Index to Science Fiction and the Locus Index to Science Fiction Awards. The previously mentioned *Tor.com* is also one of the most eclectic genre-oriented sites on the Internet, a Web site that, in addition to its fiction, regularly publishes articles, comics, graphics, blog entries, print and media reviews, book "rereads" and episode-by-episode "rewatches" of television shows, as well as commentary on all the above. The long-running and eclectic *The New York Review of Science Fiction* has ceased print publication, but can be purchased in PDF, epub, mobi formats, and POD editions through Weightless Press (weightlessbooks.com; see also www.nyrsf.com for information). Other major general-interest sites include *io9* (www.io9.com), *SF Signal* (www.sfsignal.com), *SF Site* (www.sfsite.com), although it's no longer being regularly updated, *SFCrowsnest* (www.sfcrowsnest.org.uk), *SFScope* (www.sfscope.com), *The Green Man Review* (greenmanreview.com), *The Agony Column* (www.bookotron.com /agony), *SFFWorld* (www.sffworld.com), *SFReader* (sfreader.com), and *Pat's Fantasy Hotlist* (www.fantasyhotlist.blogspot.com). A great research site, invaluable if you want bibliographic information about SF and fantasy writers, is *Fantastic Fiction* (www.fantasticfiction.co.uk). Another fantastic research site is the searchable online update of the Hugo-winning *The Encyclopedia of Science Fiction* (www.sf-encyclo pedia.com), where you can access almost four million words of information about SF writers, books, magazines, and genre themes. Reviews of short fiction as opposed to novels are very hard to find anywhere, with the exception of *Locus* and *Locus Online*, but you can find reviews of both current and past short fiction at *Best SF* (www.bestsf.net), as well as at pioneering short-fiction review site *Tangent Online* (www.tangentonline.com). Other sites of interest include: *Ansible* (news.ansible.co.uk), the online version of multiple Hugo winner David Langford's long-running fanzine *Ansible*; SFF NET (www.sff.net) which features dozens of home pages and "newsgroups" for SF writers; the Science Fiction Writers of America page (www.sfwa.org), where genre news, obituaries, award information, and recommended reading lists can be accessed; Book View Café (www.bookviewcafe.com) is a "consortium of over twenty professional authors," including Vonda N. McIntyre, Laura Ann Gilman, Sarah Zettel, Brenda Clough, and others, who have created a Web site where work by them—mostly reprints, and some novel excerpts—is made available for free.

Sites where podcasts and SF-oriented radio plays can be accessed have also proliferated in recent years: at Audible (www.audible.com), *Escape Pod* (escapepod.org, podcasting mostly SF), *SF Squeecast* (sfsqueecast.com), *The Coode Street Podcast* (jonathanstrahan.podbean.com), *The Drabblecast* (www.drabblecast.org), *StarShip-Sofa* (www.starshipsofa.com), *FarFetchedFables* (www.farfetchedfables.com), new companion to *StarShipSofa*, concentrating on fantasy, *SF Signal Podcast* (www.sf signal.com), *Pseudopod* (pseudopod.org), podcasting mostly fantasy, *Podcastle* (podcastle.org), podcasting mostly fantasy, and *Galactic Suburbia* (galacticsuburbia .podbean.com). *Clarkesworld* routinely offers podcasts of stories from the e-zine, and *The Agony Column* also hosts a weekly podcast. There's also a site that podcasts non-fiction interviews and reviews, *Dragon Page Cover to Cover* (www.dragonpage.com).

2014 wasn't a really strong year for short fiction overall—although, as usual, so much of it is now published in so many different mediums, from print to electronic to audiobooks, that it wasn't hard to find a lot of good material to read if you looked around for it a bit.

This year, the best short SF was probably to be found in the original SF anthologies, of which there were several good ones available in 2014. The best of these were probably *Reach for Infinity* (Solaris), edited by Jonathan Strahan—which featured strong work by Ian McDonald, Aliette de Bodard, Karl Schroeder, Ellen Klages, Alastair Reynolds, Pat Cadigan, and others—and *Hieroglyph: Stories and Visions for a Better Future* (Arizona State University), edited by Ed Finn and Kathryn Cramer, which featured first-rate stuff by Cory Doctorow, Vandana Singh, Elizabeth Bear, Geoffrey A. Landis, Kathleen Ann Goonan, and others; *Hieroglyph* also features nonfiction essays and commentary on the stories by the authors as well as the fiction, and links to places on the Center for Science and the Imagination Web site (csi.asu.edu) where you can read extended discussions of the subject matter of the stories (and evaluations of its feasibility) by SF writers, scientists, engineers, and futurologists.

A step down from the top two, but still loaded with good material, were *Upgraded* (Wyrm Publishing), a cyborg anthology edited by Neil Clarke, and *Solaris Rising 3: The New Solaris Book of Science Fiction* (Solaris), edited by Ian Whates. *Upgraded* featured good stories by Ken Liu, Peter Watts, Rich Larson, Elizabeth Bear, Greg Egan, and others, while *Solaris Rising 3* had strong work by Aliette de Bodard, Adam Roberts, Gareth L. Powell, Chris Beckett, and others.

Coming in just under the top anthologies was *Twelve Tomorrows* (MIT Technology Review), edited by Bruce Sterling, which featured strong work by Lauren Beukes, Paul Graham Raven, William Gibson, Cory Doctorow, Pat Cadigan, Warren Ellis, and others.

Also worthwhile, although not as strong overall as the anthologies listed above, were *Coming Soon Enough: Six Tales of Technology's Future* (IEEE Spectrum), an e-book anthology edited by Stephen Cass, which featured a strong story by Greg Egan; *War Stories: New Military Science Fiction* (Apex Publications), edited by Jaym Gates and Andrew Liptak, with good work by Ken Liu, Rich Larson, James L. Cambias, Linda Nagata, Yoon Ha Lee, Karin Lowachee, Keith Brooke, and others; *The End Is Nigh* (CreateSpace Independent Publishing Platform), the first in an anthology trilogy of apocalyptic stories edited by John Joseph Adams and Hugh Howey, with good work by Paolo Bacigalupi, Tananarive Due, Nancy Kress, Ken Liu, and others; *The End Is Now* (CreateSpace Independent Publishing Platform), again edited by John Joseph Adams and Hugh Howey, the sequel to *The End Is Nigh*, which also contains good work by Ken Liu, Tananarive Due, Nancy Kress, Elizabeth Bear, Sarah Langan, and others, although having the same authors do sequels to their stories in the previous volume may not have been the best idea, and produces a somewhat weaker book; and *Carbide Tipped Pens: Seventeen Tales of Hard Science Fiction* (Tor), edited by Ben Bova and Eric Choi, with good work by Aliette de Bodard, Jean-Louis Trudel, Gregory Benford, Robert Reed, Nancy Fulda, and others. *Postscripts 32/33: Far Voyager* (PS Publishing), edited by Nick Gevers, was not so much an SF anthology as a slipstream/fantasy/soft horror anthology with an occasional SF story in it, but they were good ones by Michael Swanwick, Ian Sales, Robert Reed, and others, with good non-SF work by Richard Calder, Paul Park, Andrew Hook, Angela Slatter, and others. *Paradox: Stories Inspired by the Fermi Paradox* (NewCon Press), edited by Ian Whates, somewhat oddly didn't feature many stories offering ingenious explanations of the Fermi paradox, but did feature solid work by David L. Clements, Pat Cadigan, Paul Cornell, Tricia Sullivan, Robert Reed, Keith Brooke and Eric

Brown, Mercurio D. Rivera, and others. There were a number of anthologies from Fiction River, which last year launched a continuing series of original SF and fantasy anthologies, with Kristine Kathryn Rusch and Dean Wesley Smith as overall series editors, and individual editions edited by various hands; the best SF one this year was probably *Moonscapes* (Fiction River), edited by Dean Wesley Smith, but *Universe Between* (Fiction River), was also worth a look.

In addition to a cyborg anthology, there were two anthologies about robots, *Robot Uprisings* (Vintage), edited by Daniel H. Wilson and John Joseph Adams, and *Bless Your Mechanical Heart* (Evil Girlfriend Media), edited by Jennifer Brozek. *Kaleidoscope* (Twelfth Planet Press), edited by Alisa Krasnostein and Julia Rios, was an anthology of YA SF stories, with an emphasis on cultural diversity.

Noted without comment is a big crossover anthology, *Rogues*, edited by George R. R. Martin and Gardner Dozois.

There were three tribute anthologies to the work of individual SF/fantasy authors: *The Book of Silverberg* (Subterranean Press), edited by Gardner Dozois and William K. Schafer; *Multiverse: Exploring Poul Anderson's Worlds* (Subterranean Press), edited by Greg Bear and Gardner Dozois; and *The Children of Old Leech: A Tribute to the Carnivorous Cosmos of Laird Barron* (Word Horde), edited by Ross E. Lockhart and Justin Steele.

The best fantasy anthology of the year was *Fearsome Magics: The New Solaris Book of Fantasy* (Solaris) edited by Jonathan Strahan, the second time Strahan has pulled off the trick of having both the best SF anthology and the best fantasy anthology in the same year; *Fearsome Magics* featured strong work by K. J. Parker, Garth Nix, Justina Robson, Ellen Klages, Karin Tidbeck, and others. Another strong fantasy anthology was *Monstrous Affections: An Anthology of Beastly Tales* (Candlewick Press), edited by Kelly Link and Gavin J. Grant, with good stories by Paolo Bacigalupi, Nalo Hopkinson, Holly Black, Kelly Link herself, and others. *Dead Man's Hand: An Anthology of the Weird West* (Titan Books), edited by John Joseph Adams, contains strong work by Elizabeth Bear, Ken Liu, Joe R. Lansdale, Alastair Reynolds, Tad Williams, Jeffrey Ford, Walter Jon Williams, and others.

Other original fantasy anthologies included *Trafficking in Magic, Magicking in Traffic* (Fantastic Books), edited by David Sklar and Sarah Avery; *Fantastic Detectives* (Fiction River), edited by Kristine Kathryn Rusch; and *Fantasy for Good: A Charitable Anthology* (Nightscape Press), edited by Jordan Ellinger and Richard Salter.

Hard to classify anthologies included *The Mammoth Book of Gaslit Romance* (Running Press), edited by Ekaterina Sedia; and *Long Hidden: Speculative Fiction from the Margins of History* (Crossed Genres), edited by Rose Fox and Daniel José Older, which featured stories set in historical periods between 1400 and the early 1900s.

The year's prominent original horror anthologies included *Fearful Symmetries: An Anthology of Horror* (ChiZine Publications), edited by Ellen Datlow; *Nightmare Carnival* (Dark Horse), edited by Ellen Datlow; *Games Creatures Play* (Ace), edited by Charlaine Harris and Toni L. P. Kelner; *The Madness of Cthulhu Anthology* (Titan Books), edited by S. T. Joshi; *Letters to Lovecraft: Eighteen Whispers to the Darkness* (Stone Skin), edited by Jesse Bullington; *Searchers After Horror: New Tales of the Weird and Fantastic* (Fedogan & Bremer), edited by S. T. Joshi; *Shadows and*

Tall Trees, Volume 6 (ChiZine Publications), edited by Michael Kelly; and *Handsome Devil: Stories of Sin and Seduction* (Prime Books), a mixed original and reprint anthology edited by Steve Berman. *Dangerous Games* (Solaris), edited by Jonathan Oliver, straddles the line between SF and horror.

Shared world anthologies included *Lowball: A Wild Cards Mosaic Novel* (Tor), edited by George R. R. Martin and Melinda M. Snodgrass; *No True Way* (DAW), edited by Mercedes Lackey; *Doctor Who: 11 Doctors, 11 Stories* (Puffin), edited by the BBC; and *Dead But Not Forgotten* (Ace), edited by Charlaine Harris and Toni L. P. Kelner, an anthology of stories set in the world of Sookie Stackhouse.

Anthologies that provided an overview of what's happening in fantastic literature in other countries included *The Apex Book of World SF 3* (Apex Publications), edited by Lavie Tidhar, and *Phantasm Japan: Fantasies Light and Dark, From and About Japan* (Haikasoru), edited by Nick Mamatas and Masumi Washington.

L. Ron Hubbard Presents Writers of the Future, Volume 30 (Galaxy Press), edited by Dave Wolverton, is the most recent in a long-running series featuring novice work by beginning writers, some of whom may later turn out to be important talents.

One interesting thing about this year's short fiction is that it was easy to see SF's new consensus future solidifying in dozens of stories from different anthologies and magazines: a linked-in, hooked-up continuous surveillance society, profoundly shaped by social media and the Internet, set in a world radically altered by climate change (but one where it hasn't gone to civilization-destroying lengths), featuring autonomous drones, bioengineering, cybernetic implants, cyborgs of one degree or another of extremeness, wearable computers, the manipulation of emotions and memory (sometimes by external means), AIs, renewable energy, in which 3-D printing is being used to produce almost everything. Sometimes it features space travel, in which case near Earth space and the nearest reaches of the solar system are busy with human traffic and habitation, sometimes it doesn't. Not that different, really from the cyberpunk future of the eighties, except for the increased emphasis on radical climate change and 3-D printing.

Ken Liu was easily the most prolific author at short lengths this year, being given a run for his money by Aliette de Bodard, Nancy Kress, Elizabeth Bear, Lavie Tidhar, Rich Larson, and the always-ubiquitous Robert Reed.

(Finding individual pricings for all of the items from small presses mentioned in the Summation has become too time-intensive, and since several of the same small presses publish anthologies, novels, *and* short-story collections, it seems silly to repeat addresses for them in section after section. Therefore, I'm going to attempt to list here, in one place, all the addresses for small presses that have books mentioned here or there in the Summation, whether from the anthologies section, the novel section, or the short-story collection section, and, where known, their Web site addresses. That should make it easy enough for the reader to look up the individual price of any book mentioned that isn't from a regular trade publisher; such books are less likely to be found in your average bookstore, or even in a chain superstore, and so will probably have to be mail-ordered. Many publishers seem to sell only online, through their Web sites, and some will only accept payment through PayPal. Many books, even from some of the smaller presses, are also available through

Amazon.com. If you can't find an address for a publisher, and it's quite likely that I've missed some here, or failed to update them successfully, Google it. It shouldn't be that difficult these days to find up-to-date contact information for almost any publisher, however small.)

Addresses: **PS Publishing**, Grosvener House, 1 New Road, Hornsea, West Yorkshire, HU18 1PG, England, UK, www.pspublishing.co.uk; **Golden Gryphon Press**, 3002 Perkins Road, Urbana, IL 61802, www.goldengryphon.com; **NESFA Press**, P.O. Box 809, Framingham, MA 01701–0809, www.nesfa.org; **Subterranean Press**, P.O. Box 190106, Burton, MI 48519, www.subterraneanpress.com; **Old Earth Books**, P.O. Box 19951, Baltimore, MD 21211–0951, www.oldearthbooks.com; **Tachyon Press**, 1459 18th St. #139, San Francisco, CA 94107, www.tachyonpublications.com; **Night Shade Books**, 1470 NW Saltzman Road, Portland, OR 97229, www.night shadebooks.com; **Five Star Books**, 295 Kennedy Memorial Drive, Waterville, ME 04901, www.galegroup.com/fivestar; **NewCon Press**, via www.newconpress.com; **Small Beer Press**, 176 Prospect Ave., Northampton, MA 01060, www.smallbeerpress .com; **Locus Press**, P.O. Box 13305, Oakland, CA 94661; **Crescent Books**, Mercat Press Ltd., 10 Coates Crescent, Edinburgh, Scotland EH3 7AL, UK, www.crescent-fiction.com; **Wildside Press/Borgo Press**, P.O. Box 301, Holicong, PA 18928–0301, or go to www.wildsidepress.com for pricing and ordering; **Edge Science Fiction and Fantasy Publishing, Inc. and Tesseract Books, Ltd.**, P.O. Box 1714, Calgary, Alberta, T2P 2L7, Canada, www.edgewebsite.com; **Aqueduct Press**, P.O. Box 95787, Seattle, WA 98145–2787, www.aqueductpress.com; **Phobos Books**, 200 Park Avenue South, New York, NY 10003, www.phobosweb.com; **Fairwood Press**, 5203 Quincy Ave. SE, Auburn, WA 98092, www.fairwoodpress.com; **BenBella Books**, 6440 N. Central Expressway, Suite 508, Dallas, TX 75206, www.benbellabooks.com; **Darkside Press**, 13320 27th Ave. NE, Seattle, WA 98125, www.darksidepress.com; **Haffner Press**, 5005 Crooks Rd., Suite 35, Royal Oak, MI 48073–1239, www.haff nerpress.com; **North Atlantic Press**, P.O. Box 12327, Berkeley, CA, 94701; **Prime Books**, P.O. Box 36503, Canton, OH 44735, www.primebooks.net; **MonkeyBrain Books**, 11204 Crossland Drive, Austin, TX 78726, www.monkeybrainbooks.com; **Wesleyan University Press**, University Press of New England, Order Dept., 37 Lafayette St., Lebanon NH 03766–1405, www.wesleyan.edu/wespress; **Agog! Press**, P.O. Box U302, University of Wollongong, NSW 2522, Austrailia, www.uow.ed.au/~rhood /agogpress; **Wheatland Press**, via www.wheatlandpress.com; **MirrorDanse Books**, P.O. Box 3542, Parramatta NSW 2124, Australia, www.tabula-rasa.info/MirrorDanse; **Arsenal Pulp Press**, 103–1014 Homer Street, Vancouver, BC, Canada V6B 2W9, www.arsenalpress.com; **DreamHaven Books**, 912 W. Lake Street, Minneapolis, MN 55408; **Elder Signs Press/Dimensions Books**, order through www.dimensionsbooks .com; **Chaosium**, via www.chaosium.com; **Spyre Books**, P.O. Box 3005, Radford, VA 24143; **SCIFI, Inc.**, P.O. Box 8442, Van Nuys, CA 91409–8442; **Omnidawn Publishing**, order through www.omnidawn.com; **CSFG**, Canberra Speculative Fiction Guild, via www.csfg.org.au/publishing/anthologies/the_outcast; **Hadley Rille Books**, via www.hadleyrillebooks.com; **Suddenly Press**, via suddenlypress@yahoo.com; **Sandstone Press**, P.O. Box 5725, One High St., Dingwall, Ross-shire UK, IV15 9UG, http://sandstonepress.com; **Tropism Press**, via www.tropismpress.com; **SF Poetry Association/Dark Regions Press**, www.sfpoetry.com, send checks to Helena Bell,

SFPA Treasurer, 1225 West Freeman St., Apt. 12, Carbondale, IL 62401; **DH Press,** via diamondbookdistributors.com; **Kurodahan Press,** via www.kurodahan.com; **Ramble House,** 443 Gladstone Blvd., Shreveport LA 71104; **Interstitial Arts Foundation,** via www.interstitialarts.org; **Raw Dog Screaming,** via www.rawdogscreaming.com; **Three Legged Fox Books,** 98 Hythe Road, Brighton, BN1 6JS, UK; **Norilana Books,** via www.norilana.com; **coeur de lion,** via http://coeurdelion.com.au; **PARSECink,** via www.parsecink.org; **Robert J. Sawyer Books,** via www.sfwriter.com/rjsbooks.htm; **Rackstraw Press,** via http://rackstrawpress; **Candlewick,** via www.candlewick.com; **Zubaan,** via www.zubaanbooks.com; **Utter Tower,** via www.threeleggedfox.co.uk; **Spilt Milk Press,** via www.electricvelocipede.com; **Paper Golem,** via www.paper golem.com; **Galaxy Press,** via www.galaxypress.com; **Twelfth Planet Press,** via www.twelfhplanetpress.com; **Five Senses Press,** via www.sensefive.com; **Elastic Press,** via www.elasticpress.com; **Lethe Press,** via www.lethepressbooks.com; **Two Cranes Press,** via www.twocranespress.com; **Wordcraft of Oregon,** via www.word craftoforegon.com; **Down East,** via www.downeast.com; **ISFiC Press,** 456 Douglas Ave., Elgin, IL 60120 or www.isficpress.com.

According to the newsmagazine *Locus*, there were 2,459 books "of interest to the SF field" published in 2014, down 7 percent from 2,643 titles in 2013. Overall new titles were down 5 percent to 1,750 from 2013's 1,850, while reprints dropped 11 percent to 709 from 2013's 793. Hardcover sales fell by 2 percent to 799 from 2013's 819, while the number of trade paperbacks declined by 10 percent to 1,149 from 2013's 1,280. The drop in mass-market paperbacks slowed a little, to 6 percent from 2013's whopping 26 percent drop, going to 511 from 2013's 544. The number of new SF novels was up to 367 titles from 2013's 339. The number of new fantasy novels remained steady at 620 titles, same as last year. Horror novels were up slightly to 187 titles from 2013's 181. Paranormal romances were down substantially to 148 titles from 2013's 237 titles, leading some to speculate that the high-water mark of the big paranormal romance boom may have passed—although it should be noted that sometimes it's a subjective call whether a particular novel should be pigeonholed as paranormal romance, fantasy, or horror.

The boom in Young Adult SF novels, especially dystopian and post-apocalyptic SF, slowed a bit, from making up 36 percent of the original SF novels total in 2013 to 31 percent in 2014, so perhaps that area is beginning to cool a bit as well. The 367 original SF novels also include 49 SF first novels, up from last year's 38, 13 percent of the new SF total, up from last year's 11 percent of the new SF total, down from 13 percent last year. Fantasy's 620 original novels include 210 YA novels, down from 2013's 233, from making up 36 percent of the new fantasy total to making up 34 percent; this includes sixty-three fantasy first novels, up from 2013's fifty-seven, making up 10 percent of the fantasy total, up from 2013's 9 percent.

This is still an enormous number of books, in spite of slight declines—far more than the entire combined total of genre titles only a few decades back. And these totals don't count e-books, media tie-in novels, gaming novels, novelizations of genre movies, print-on-demand books, or self-published novels—all of which would swell the overall total by hundreds if counted.

As usual, busy with all the reading I have to do at shorter lengths, I didn't have time to read many novels myself this year, so I'll limit myself to mentioning novels that received a lot of attention and acclaim in 2014.

Empress of the Sun (Jo Fletcher Books), by Ian McDonald; *The Memory of Sky* (Prime Books), by Robert Reed; *Work Done for Hire* (Ace), by Joe Haldeman; *My Real Children* (Tor), by Jo Walton; *The Martian* (Crown Publishers), by Andy Weir; *Lockstep* (Tor), by Karl Schroeder; *Cibola Burn* (Orbit), by James S. A. Corey; *Ancillary Sword* (Orbit), by Ann Leckie; *Peacemaker* (DAW), by C. J. Cherryh; *Echopraxia* (Tor), by Peter Watts; *The Causal Angel* (Tor), by Hannu Rajaniemi; *War Dogs* (Orbit), by Greg Bear; *Dreams of the Golden Age* (Tor), by Carrie Vaughn; *Ultima* (Orion/Gollancz), by Stephen Baxter; *V-S Day* (Ace), by Allen Steele; *The Three-Body Problem* (Tor), by Cixin Liu; *A Man Lies Dreaming* (Hodder & Stoughton), by Lavie Tidhar; *Bête* (Orion/Gollancz), by Adam Roberts; *Lock In* (Tor), by John Scalzi; *The Silk Map* (Pyr), by Chris Willrich; *World of Trouble* (Quirk Books), by Ben H. Winters; *Written in My Own Heart's Blood* (Delacorte Press), by Diana Gabaldon; *The Magician's Land* (Viking), by Lev Grossman; *The Peripheral* (Penguin/Putnam), by William Gibson; *Fool's Assassin* (Ballantine Del Rey), by Robin Hobb; *Dark Lightning* (Ace), by John Varley; *Dreamwalker* (DAW), by C. S. Friedman; *Ghost Train to New Orleans* (Orbit), by Mur Lafferty; *Lagoon* (Hodder & Stoughton), by Nnedi Okorafor; *Descent* (Orbit), by Ken MacLeod; *Broken Homes* (DAW), by Ben Aaronovitch; *Steles of the Sky* (Tor), by Elizabeth Bear; *Jupiter War* (Tor UK), by Neal Asher; *Strange Bodies* (Farrar, Straus and Giroux), by Marcel Theroux; *The Judge of Ages* (Tor), by John C. Wright; *Annihilation* (Farrar, Straus and Giroux), by Jeff VanderMeer; *Afterparty* (Tor), by Daryl Gregory; *California Bones* (Tor), by Greg van Eekhout; *The Rhesus Chart* (Ace), by Charles Stross; *All Those Vanished Engines* (Tor), by Paul Park; *Shipstar* (Tor), by Gregory Benford and Larry Niven; *Raising Steam* (Doubleday UK), by Terry Pratchett; *Half a King* (Ballantine Del Rey), by Joe Abercrombie; *The Severed Streets* (Tor), by Paul Cornell; *The Widow's House* (Orbit), by Daniel Abraham; *The Doubt Factory* (Little, Brown), by Paolo Bacigalupi; *Hurricane Fever* (Tor), by Tobias S. Buckell; *The Long Mars* (HarperCollins), by Terry Pratchett and Stephen Baxter; *Skin Game* (Penguin/Roc), by Jim Butcher; *Sleeping Late on Judgement Day* (DAW), by Tad Williams; and *Revival* (Simon & Schuster), by Stephen King.

Small presses are active in the novel market these days, where once they published mostly collections and anthologies. Novels issued by small presses this year included: *Beautiful Blood* (Subterranean Press), by Lucius Shepard; *The Arrows of Time* (Skyhorse/Night Shade), by Greg Egan; *One-Eyed Jack* (Prime Books), by Elizabeth Bear; *The Voyage of the Sable Keech* (Skyhorse/Night Shade), by Neal Asher; *Polity Agent* (Skyhorse/Night Shade), by Neal Asher; *The Line of Polity* (Skyhorse/Night Shade), by Neal Asher; *Hilldiggers* (Skyhorse/Night Shade), by Neal Asher; *We Are All Completely Fine* (Tachyon Publications), by Daryl Gregory; *Heirs of Grace* (47 North), by Tim Pratt; *Our Lady of the Islands* (Per Aspera Press), by Shannon Page and Jay Lake; and *The Madonna and the Starship* (Tachyon Publications), by James Morrow.

Associational novels, non-SF novels by those associated with the field, included *Voices from the Street* (Orion/Gollancz), by Philip K. Dick; *The Broken Bubble* (Orion/

Gollancz), by Philip K. Dick; *Gather Yourselves Together* (Orion/Gollancz), by Philip K. Dick; and *Chernobyl* (Tor), by Frederik Pohl.

The year's first novels included: *The Martian* (Crown Publishers), by Andy Weir; *Koko Takes a Holiday* (Titan Books), by Kieran Shea; *Unwrapped Sky* (Tor), by Rjurik Davidson; *The Ultra Thin Man* (Tor), by Patrick Swenson; *Whiskey Tango Foxtrot* (Little, Brown), by David Shafer; *The Great Glass Sea* (Grave Press), by Josh Weil; *A Darkling Sea* (Tor), by James L. Cambias; *The Forever Watch* (St. Martin's Press), by David Ramirez; *The Boost* (Tor), by Stephen Baker; *Black Moon* (Hogarth), by Kenneth Calhoun; *The Word Exchange* (Doubleday), by Alena Graedon; *Tomorrow and Tomorrow* (Putnam), by Thomas Sweterlitsch; *Barricade* (Orion/Gollancz), by Jon Wallace; *The Queen of the Tearling* (HarperCollins), by Erika Johansen; *Free Agent* (Ace), by J. C. Nelson; *The Quick* (Random House), by Lauren Owen; *American Craftsmen* (Tor), by Tom Doyle; *Traitor's Blade* (Jo Fletcher Books), by Sebastien de Castell; *The Bees* (HarperCollins), by Laline Paull; *The Memory Garden* (Sourcebooks Landmark), by Mary Rickert; *The Waking Engine* (Tor), by David Edison; *Haxan* (ChiZine Publications), by Kenneth Mark Hoover; and *Invisible Beasts* (Bellevue Literary Press), by Sharona Muir. Of these, by far the most successful, and the only bestseller, was *The Martian*, by Andy Weir, although *Koko Takes a Holiday*, by Kieran Shea, *Unwrapped Sky*, by Rjurik Davidson, and *The Memory Garden*, by Mary Rickert, got a fair number of reviews as well.

Good novella chapbooks in 2014 included *Yesterday's Kin* (Tachyon Publications), by Nancy Kress; *Famadihana on Fomalhaut IV* (PS Publishing), by Eric Brown; *The Ape Man's Brother* (Subterranean Press), by Joe R. Lansdale; *The Slow Regard of Silent Things* (DAW), by Patrick Rothfuss; *Nobody's Home* (Subterranean Press), by Tim Powers; *Of Whimsies and Noubles* (PS Publishing), by Matthew Hughes; *The Deep Woods* (PS Publishing), by Tim Pratt; *Sleep Donation* (Atavist Books), by Karen Russell; *Unlocked: An Oral History of Haden's Syndrome* (Subterranean Press), by John Scalzi; *Equoid* (Subterranean Press), by Charles Stross; and *In the Lovecraft Museum* (PS Publishing), by Steve Rasnic Tem.

Orion unleashed an unprecedented flood of novel omnibuses with its SF Gateway program this year, offering unprecedented access to long out-of-print material, including: *Gregory Benford SF Gateway Omnibus: Artifact, Cosm, Eater*, by Gregory Benford; *Barrington J. Bayley SF Gateway Omnibus: The Soul of the Robot, The Knights of the Limits, The Fall of Chronopolis* (two novels and one collection), by Barrington Bayley; *John Brunner SF Gateway Omnibus: The Sheep Look Up, The Shockwave Rider, The Traveller In Black*, by John Brunner; *Algis Budrys SF Gateway Omnibus: The Iron Thorn, Michaelmas, Hard Landing*, by Algis Budrys; *Carson of Venus SF Gateway Omnibus: Pirates of Venus, Lost on Venus, Carson of Venus*, by Edgar Rice Burroughs; *Pat Cadigan SF Gateway Omnibus: Mindplayers, Fools, Tea from an Empty Cup*, by Pat Cadigan; *Jack L. Chalker SF Gateway Omnibus: Midnight at the Well of Souls, Spirits of Flux and Anchor, The Identity Matrix*, by Jack L. Chalker; *Hal Clement SF Gateway Omnibus: Iceworld, Cycle of Fire, Close to Critical*, by Hal Clement; *D. G. Compton SF Gateway Omnibus: Synthajoy, The Steel Crocodile, Ascendancies*, by D. G. Compton; *Edmund Cooper SF Gateway Omnibus: The Cloud Walker, All Fools' Day, A Far Sunset*, by Edmund Cooper; *Richard Cowper SF Gateway Omnibus: Piper at the Gates of Dawn, The Road to Corlay, A*

Dream of Kinship, A Tapestry of Time, by Richard Cowper; *L. Sprague de Camp SF Gateway Omnibus: Lest Darkness Fall, Rogue Queen, The Tritonian Ring,* by L. Sprague de Camp; *Philip José Farmer SF Gateway Omnibus: The Maker of Universes, To Your Scattered Bodies Go, The Unreasoning Mask,* by Philip José Farmer; *Edmond Hamilton SF Gateway Omnibus: Captain Future and the Space Emperor, The Star Kings, The Weapon from Beyond,* by Edmond Hamilton; *Robert A. Heinlein SF Gateway Omnibus: The Past Through Tomorrow,* by Robert A. Heinlein; *Berserker SF Gateway Omnibus: Shadow of the Wolf, The Bull Chief, The Horned Warrior,* by Robert Holdstock; *Garry Kilworth SF Gateway Omnibus: The Roof of Voyaging, The Princely Flower, Land-of-Mists,* by Garry Kilworth; *Henry Kuttner SF Gateway Omnibus: Fury, Mutant, The Best of Henry Kuttner,* by Henry Kuttner; *C. L. Moore SF Gateway Omnibus: Shambleau, Northwest of Earth, Judgement Night,* by C. L. Moore; *Charles Sheffield SF Gateway Omnibus: Sight of Proteus, Summertide, Cold as Ice,* by Charles Sheffield; *Clifford D. Simak SF Gateway Omnibus: Time Is the Simplest Thing, Way Station, A Choice of Gods,* by Clifford D. Simak; *John Sladek SF Gateway Omnibus: The Reproductive System, The Muller-Fokker Effect, Tik-Tok,* by John Sladek; *Theodore Sturgeon SF Gateway Omnibus: The Dreaming Jewels, To Marry Medusa, Venus Plus X,* by Theodore Sturgeon; *E. C. Tubb SF Gateway Omnibus: Extra Man, The Space-Born, Fires of Satan,* by E. C. Tubb; *Jack Williamson SF Gateway Omnibus: The Legion of Space, The Humanoids, Terraforming Earth, Wonder's Child* (three novels and an autobiography), by Jack Williamson; and *Connie Willis SF Gateway Omnibus: Lincoln's Dreams, Passage,* by Connie Willis. Other novel omnibuses included *The Galactic Center Companion* (Lucky Bat Books), by Gregory Benford; *Upon a Sea of Stars* (Baen Books—two novels and two collections), by A. Bertram Chandler; *The Memory of Sky: A Great Ship Trilogy* (Prime Books—three novels), by Robert Reed; *Votan and Other Novels* (Orion/Gollancz), by John James; *Tales from the End of Time* (Orion/Gollancz—a novel and two collections), by Michael Moorcock; *The War Amongst the Angels* (Orion/Gollancz—three novels), *Elric: The Moonbeam Roads* (Orion/Gollancz—three novels), by Michael Moorcock; and *Kurt Vonnegut: Novels 1976–1985* (Library of America), by Kurt Vonnegut.

Novel omnibuses are also frequently made available through the Science Fiction Book Club.

Not even counting print-on-demand books and the availability of out-of-print books as e-books or as electronic downloads from Internet sources, a lot of long out-of-print stuff has come back into print in the last couple of years in commercial trade editions. Here's some out-of-print titles that came back into print this year, although producing a definitive list of reissued novels is probably impossible:

In addition to the novel omnibuses already mentioned, Orion/Gollancz reissued *The Space Machine,* by Christopher Priest, *Headlong,* by Simon Ings, and *Behold the Man,* by Michael Moorcock; Gollancz reissued *Stand on Zanzibar,* by John Brunner, *A Case of Conscience,* by James Blish, and *The Phoenix and the Mirror,* by Avram Davidson; Tor reissued *Star Bridge,* by James Gunn and Jack Williamson, *Gaudeamus,* by John Barnes, and *Winter's Heart* and *Knife of Dreams,* both by Robert Jordan; Tor Teen reissued *The Ice Dragon,* by George R. R. Martin; Orb reissued *Sethra Lavode,* by Steven Brust; Baen reissued *Beyond This Horizon,* by Robert A. Heinlein and *Secret of the Stars,* by Andre Norton; Skyhorse/Night Shade Books reissued *Sung in Blood,* by Glen Cook, and *Quarantine, Axiomatic,* and *Permutation City,* all by Greg Egan; Subterranean Press reissued *The Compleat Crow,* by Brian Lumley; Chicago Review reissued *Hard to Be a God,* by Arkady and Boris Strugatsky; Harper Voyager reissued *Metrophage,* by Richard Kadrey; Roc reissued *Science Fiction: 101: Exploring the Craft of Science Fiction,* by Robert Silverberg; Fairwood Press reissued *Count Geiger's Blues,* by Michael Bishop.

Many authors are now reissuing their old back titles as e-books, either through a publisher or all by themselves, so many that it's impossible to keep track of them all here. Before you conclude that something from an author's backlist is unavailable, though, check with the Kindle and Nook stores, and with other online vendors.

2014 was a moderately strong year for short-story collections.

The year's best collections included: *Academic Exercises* (Subterranean Press), by K. J. Parker; *Unexpected Stories* (Open Road Media), by Octavia E. Butler; *Last Plane to Heaven: The Final Collection* (Tor), by Jay Lake; *The Very Best of Tad Williams* (Tacyhon), by Tad Williams; *Sergeant Chip and Other Novellas* (Tachyon), by Bradley Denton; *Questionable Practices: Stories* (Small Beer Press), by Eileen Gunn; *Black Gods Kiss* (PS Publishing), by Lavie Tidhar; *Prophecies, Libels, and Dreams: Stories* (Small Beer Press), by Ysabeau S. Wilce; *Hidden Folk: Icelandic Fantasies* (Many Worlds Press), by Eleanor Arnason; and *The Best of Ian Watson* (PS Publishing), by Ian Watson.

Also good were: *Tales of the Hidden World* (Open Road Media), by Simon R. Green; *Death at the Blue Elephant* (Ticonderoga Publications), by Janeen Webb; *New Frontiers: A Collection of Tales about the Past, the Present, and the Future* (Tor), by Ben Bova; *Young Woman in a Garden: Stories* (Small Beer Press), by Delia Sherman; and *Dragons at Crumbling Castle: And Other Stories* (Transworld/Doubleday UK), by Terry Pratchett.

Career-spanning retrospective collections this year included: *The Collected Short Works of Poul Anderson, Volume 6: A Bicycle Built for Brew* (NESFA Press), by Poul Anderson; *The Millennium Express: The Collected Stories of Robert Silverberg, Volume Nine* (Subterranean Press), by Robert Silverberg; *The Man Who Made Models: The Collected Short Fiction, Volume One* (Centipede Press), by R. A. Lafferty; *The Top of the Volcano: The Award-Winning Stories of Harlan Ellison* (Subterranean Press), by Harlan Ellison; *Tarzan the Untamed and Other Tales* (Orion/Gollancz), by Edgar Rice Burroughs; *The New Annotated H. P. Lovecraft* (Liveright/Norton) edited by Leslie S. Klinger; *The Collected Stories of Frank Herbert* (Tor), by Frank Herbert; *Jerry Cornelius: His Lives and His Times* (Orion), by Michael Moorcock; *The Dark Eidolon and Other Fantasies* (Penguin), by Clark Ashton Smith; and *Minding the Stars: The Early Jack Vance, Volume Four* (Subterranean Press), by Jack Vance, edited by Terry Dowling and Jonathan Strahan. *Damon Knight SF Gateway Omnibus: Far Out, In Deep, Off Centre, Turning On,* by Damon Knight, is an omnibus of four short-story collections by Knight, making almost his entire output at short lengths available again. The SF Gateway omnibuses by Barrington Bailey, Michael Moorcock, Henry Kuttner, and Robert A. Heinlein also contain collections, as does the A. Bertram Chandler omnibus from Baen Books. There was also a reprint of quintessential retrospective *Her Smoke Rose Up Forever* (Orion/Gollancz), by James Tiptree, Jr.

Again, small presses as usual dominated the list of short-story collections, with trade collections having become rare.

A wide variety of "electronic collections," often called "fiction bundles," too many to individually list here, are also available for downloading online, at many sites. The Science Fiction Book Club continues to issue new collections as well.

The most reliable buys in the reprint anthology market are usually the various best of the year anthologies. We lost one series this year, with the death of David G. Hartwell's Year's Best SF series (Tor), which ceased publication after eighteen volumes. That leaves science fiction being covered by one dedicated Best of the Year anthology, the one you are reading at the moment, The Year's Best Science Fiction series from St. Martin's Press, edited by Gardner Dozois, now up to its thirty-second annual collection, plus two separate half anthologies, the science fiction half of *The Best Science Fiction and Fantasy of the Year: Volume Eight* (Solaris), edited by Jonathan Strahan; and by the science fiction half of *The Year's Best Science Fiction and Fantasy: 2014 Edition* (Prime Books), edited by Rich Horton (in practice, of course, Strahan and Horton's books probably won't divide neatly in half with their coverage, and there's likely to be more of one thing than another—but if you put the two halves together, I suppose you could say that SF is covered by two anthologies). The annual Nebula Awards anthology, which covers science fiction as well as fantasy of various sorts, functions as a de facto "best of the year" anthology, although it's not usually counted among them; this year's edition was *Nebula Awards Showcase 2014* (Pyr), edited by Kij Johnson. There were three best of the year anthologies covering horror: *The Best Horror of the Year: Volume Six* (Skyhorse Publishing/Night Shade Books), edited by Ellen Datlow, *The Mammoth Book of Best New Horror 25* (A Herman Graf Book/Skyhorse Publishing), edited by Stephen Jones; and *The Year's Best Dark Fantasy and Horror: 2014 Edition* (Prime Books), edited by Paula Guran. Since the distinction between "weird fiction" and "horror" seems a fine one to me, I suspect that newer series *Year's Best Weird Fiction* (ChiZine Publications), this year edited by Laird Barron, should probably be counted for horror as well. Fantasy, which used to have several series devoted to it, is now only covered by the fantasy halves of the Stranhan and Horton anthologies, plus whatever stories fall under the "dark fantasy" part of Guran's anthology, with no best series dedicated specifically to it. A more specialized best of the year anthology is *Wilde Stories 2014: The Year's Best Gay Speculative Fiction* (Lethe Press), edited by Steve Berman.

The best stand-alone reprint anthology of the year was probably the retrospective anthology *The Very Best of Fantasy & Science Fiction, Volume 2* (Tachyon Publications), edited by Gordon Van Gelder, which featured classics by Damon Knight, Robert A. Heinlein, Brian W. Aldiss, Jack Vance, R. A. Lafferty, Robert Silverberg, Lucius Shepard, Maureen F. McHugh, Bruce Sterling, Robert Reed, Geoff Ryman, Elizabeth Hand, George Alec Effinger, James Patrick Kelly, Gene Wolfe, and many others. Also strong was *Space Opera* (Prime Books), edited by Rich Horton, with strong work by Ian McDonald, Greg Egan, Gwyneth Jones, David Moles, Robert Reed, Elizabeth Bear and Sarah Monette, Ian R. MacLeod, Aliette de Bodard, Naomi Novik, Yoon Ha Lee, Kage Baker, Jay Lake, Alastair Reynolds, Lavie Tidhar, and others, and baseball SF/fantasy anthology *Field of Fantasies: Baseball Stories of the Strange and Supernatural* (Night Shade Books), edited by Rick Wilber, which features good work by Kim Stanley Robinson, Louise Marley, John Kessel, Bruce McAllister, Harry Turtledove, Stephen King and Stewart O'Nan, Wilber himself, Karen Joy Fowler, T. Coraghessan Boyle, Cecilia Tan, W. P. Kinsella, and others.

Other good SF reprint anthologies included *The Mammoth Book of SF Stories by Women* (Running Press), edited by Alex Dally Macfarlane; *Time Travel: Recent Trips* (Prime Books), edited by Paula Guran; *The Mammoth Book of Steampunk Adventures* (Running Press), edited by Sean Wallace; and *The Best of Electric Velocipede* (Fairwood Press), edited by John Klima.

There weren't a lot of reprint fantasy anthologies this year, but there was *Magic City: Recent Spells* (Prime Books), edited by Paula Guran, and *The Mammoth Book of Warriors and Wizardry* (Running Press), edited by Sean Wallace.

Prominent among the reprint horror anthologies were *The Cutting Room: Dark Reflections of the Silver Screen* (Tachyon Publications), edited by Ellen Datlow; *Lovecraft's Monsters* (Tachyon Publications), a mixed reprint/original anthology edited by Ellen Datlow; *The Baen Big Book of Monsters* (Baen Books), edited by Hank Davis; and *Horror Stories: Classic Tales from Hoffmann to Hodgson* (Oxford University Press), an anthology of classic horror stories written between 1816 and 1912, edited by Darryl Jones.

It was a moderately strong year in the genre-oriented nonfiction category.

In spite of many flaws (including at times being *too* exhaustive), the book of the year in this category was probably *Robert A. Heinlein: In Dialogue with His Century: Volume 2, 1948–1988: The Man Who Learned Better* (Tor), by the late William H. Patterson, Jr., the second half of a massive Heinlein biography, the first half of which, *Robert A. Heinlein: In Dialogue with His Century: Volume 1, 1907–1948: Learning Curve* (Tor) appeared in 2010, and which is likely to remain the standard Heinlein biography for the foreseeable future (to some extent because most of the sources that Patterson interviewed for his research are now dead). For some of you, particularly younger readers for whom Heinlein was not a seminal figure, this huge biography may contain more information about Heinlein than you really wanted to know, but for those of you who grew up reading Heinlein (and many of us cut our SF-reading teeth on his YA novels in the fifties and sixties), it's a must-read, and held my interest even through the occasional dull patches. Another look at Heinlein through the focus of his fiction is provided in *The Heritage of Heinlein: A Critical Reading of the Fiction* (McFarland), by Thomas D. Clareson and Joe Sanders.

Another intriguing look at the life of an SF author was a posthumously published autobiography, *Harry Harrison! Harry Harrison!* (Tor), by—who else?—Harry Harrison. Other books about genre authors, or critical studies of their work, included *Greg Egan* (University of Illinois Press), by Karen Burnham; *The Art of Neil Gaiman* (HarperCollins), by Hayley Campbell; *Ray Bradbury Unbound* (University of Illinois

Press), by Jonathan R. Eller; and *Gregory Benford* (University of Illinois Press), by George Slusser.

A critical study of an individual author (in fact, of one story by that author) is provided in a reprint of *The American Shore: Mediations on a Tale of Science Fiction by Thomas M. Disch—"Angouleme"* (Wesleyan University Press), by Samuel R. Delany. Other critical overviews of the genre are to be found in *What Makes This Book So Great* (Tor), by Jo Walton; nonfiction anthology *The Oxford Handbook of Science Fiction* (Oxford University Press), edited by Rob Latham; two books of collected reviews, *Stay* (Beccon Publications), by John Clute and *Sibilant Fricative: Essays and Reviews* (Steel Quill), by Adam Roberts; *Rhapsody: Notes on Strange Fictions* (Lethe Press), by Hal Duncan; *Call and Response* (Beccon Publications), by Paul Kincaid; *Stories about Stories: Fantasy and the Remaking of Myth* (Oxford University Press), by Brian Attebery; *The Past That Might Have Been, the Future That May Come: Women Writing Fantastic Fiction, 1960s to the Present* (McFarland), by Lauren J. Lacey; *Myths, Metaphors, and Science Fiction* (Aqueduct Press), by Sheila Finch; and *Vintage Visions: Essays on Early Science Fiction* (Wesleyan University Press), edited by Arthur B. Evans.

Writing nonfiction about fictional worlds is a peculiar notion, but there were a number of such "nonfiction guidebooks" this year, including *The World of Ice and Fire* (Bantam), by George R. R. Martin, Elio M. Garcia, Jr., and Linda Antonsson, which explores, with maps and the history of prominent families, the world of Martin's Westeros, and several such books about Terry Pratchett's Discworld, including *The Compleat Ankh-Morpork: City Guide* (Random House/Doubleday), by Terry Pratchett, *The Folklore of Discworld* (Anchor Books/Random House), by Terry Pratchett and Jacqueline Simpson, *Mrs Bradshaw's Handbook* (Transworld/Doubleday UK), a travel guide to the railroad network of Discworld, ostensibly written by fictional character "Mrs. Bradshaw," and *The Science of Discworld* (Anchor Books/Random House), by Terry Pratchett with Ian Stewart and Jack Cohen. There was also a collection of nonfiction pieces by Pratchett, *A Slip of the Keyboard: Collected Nonfiction* (Doubleday), by Terry Pratchett.

Green Planets: Ecology and Science Fiction (Wesleyan University Press), edited by Gerry Canavan and Kim Stanley Robinson, will be of interest to anyone concerned about the environment and how it has been portrayed in SF. Writers and those with ambitions to become writers might be interested in *Information Doesn't Want to Be Free: Laws for the Internet Age* (McSweeney's), by Cory Doctorow. *Sci-Fi Chronicles: A Visual History of the Galaxy's Greatest Science Fiction* (Firefly Books), by Guy Haley, has lots of striking photographs, although "science fiction" is here construed to mean media SF, movies and TV shows, only.

Tolkien enthusiasts might want to get *Beowulf: A Translation and Commentary* (Houghton Mifflin Harcourt), by J. R. R. Tolkien, collecting academic lectures Tolkien gave at Oxford about one of the first known fantasies in written literature; a bit, er, academic, but which sheds interesting light on Tolkien's own later work.

There weren't a lot of art books published in 2014, but there was some good stuff among them. In spite of a change of editors and publisher, your best bet as usual was probably the latest in a long-running "best of the year" series for fantastic art, *Spectrum 21: The Best in Contemporary Fantastic Art* (Flesk Publications), now edited by

John Fleskes, taking over for former editors Cathy Fenner and Arnie Fenner. Also good were: *The Collectors' Book of Virgil Finlay* (American Fantasy Press), edited by Robert Weinberg, Douglas Ellis, and Robert T. Garcia, *The Art of Jim Burns: Hyper-luminal* (Titan Books), by Jim Burns; *The Art of Ian Miller* (Titan Books), by Ian Miller and Tom Whyte; *Dark Shepherd: The Art of Fred Gambino* (Titan Books), by Fred Gambino; *The Art of John Harris: Beyond the Horizon* (Titan Books), by John Harris; *The Art of Greg Spalenka* (Titan Books), by Greg Spalenka; and *The Art of Space: The History of Space Art, from the Earliest Visions to the Graphics of the Modern Era* (Zenith Press), by Ron Miller.

In both 2012 and 2013, according to the Box Office Mojo site (www.boxofficemojo .com), nine out of ten of the year's top-earning movies were genre films. This year, 2014, before the release of *American Sniper*, *all* of the top ten box office champs were genre films of one sort or another (if you're willing to count animated films and su-perhero movies as being "genre films"), with *Dawn of the Planet of the Apes* taking eleventh place and *The Amazing Spider Man 2* taking twelfth place. You have to go all the way down to fourteenth place to find a nongenre film, *22 Jump Street*—but then it's followed by genre films in fifteenth, sixteenth, and seventeenth place, with nongenre films not kicking in again until *Gone Girl* in eighteenth place. In all, six-teen out of the top twenty earners are genre films, with at least ten more scattered through the next eighty. Nor is this anything new; genre films have dominated the box office top ten for more than a decade—you have to go all the way back to 1998 to find a year when the year's top earner was a nongenre film, *Saving Private Ryan*.

It's hard to shake the suspicion that if it wasn't for genre films, Hollywood would have gone broke long ago.

Unusually, two out of the top three earners were SF films (the top slots are usu-ally taken by fantasy or superhero films)—*Guardians of the Galaxy*, a good-natured update of the classic space opera movie, was number two at the box office this year, earning a staggering $332,965,525 overall so far (and the DVD hasn't even been re-leased yet), with *The Hunger Games: Mockingjay—Part 1* (certainly dystopian YA SF, practically a genre of its own these days) coming in first. To fill out the rest of the top ten, superhero films finished in third and ninth place (*Captain America: The Win-ter Soldier* and *X-Men: Days of Future Past* respectively), animated movies in fourth and tenth place (*The LEGO Movie* and *Big Hero 6* respectively—although it would be possible to argue that *Big Hero 6* was also a superhero movie), SF (even if junk SF) scoring again in seventh place (*Transformers: Age of Extinction*), and live-action fantasy films taking sixth and eighth place (*The Hobbit: The Battle of Five Armies* and *Maleficent* respectively).

None of the top ten were taken terribly seriously as "serious films" by critics or by the more intellectually inclined of the viewing audience, although *The LEGO Movie* got surprisingly good reviews for what amounted to a two-hour commercial for a toy company that you had to *pay* to watch. *Transformers: Age of Extinction* was probably the most badly reviewed of the top ten, although the most critically reviled big bud-get A-release movie of the year may have been an attempt to reinvent the biblical spectacular, *Exodus: Gods and Kings*, which also—with its 140 million dollar budget weighing it down—failed at the box office. Several new installments of franchise series also underperformed, among them *Night at the Museum: Secret of the Tomb*, *Penguins of Madagascar*, and *Rio 2*, and some attempt to start new franchises or revive old ones didn't work either, including *RoboCop*, *Dracula Untold*, and *Mr. Peabody and Sherman*.

As did last year's *Man of Steel*, *Star Trek: Into Darkness*, and *The Hobbit: The Desolation of Smaug*, some of this year's movies sharply divided their target demographic, with hordes of loyal fans spilling oceans of pixels arguing about whether movies such as *The Amazing Spider-Man 2*, *Godzilla*, and *Teenage Mutant Ninja Turtles* were or were not worthy of inclusion in their respective canons. This was perhaps most noticeable with the final *Hobbit* movie, *The Hobbit: The Battle of Five Armies*, which in spite of lots of scathing reviews and bad word of mouth among Tolkien fans, still easily managed to reach sixth place in the list of top box office earners, in spite of only being released in the middle of December—and no doubt it's going to earn a *lot* more money in 2015, which is probably all that the producers really care about. SF film *Interstellar*, which is one of the few genre movies on this list with pretentions to being a "serious" dramatic movie dealing with serious issues, divided fans in a similarly extreme way, with reviews and word of mouth differing so sharply that you almost had to wonder if they were all seeing the same movie.

There are, unsurprisingly, lots more genre movies in the pipeline for release in 2015. The ones that seem to be generating the most buzz at this point seem to be the new *Avengers* movie, *The Avengers: Age of Ultron*, and the J. J. Abrams–directed *Star Wars* movie from Disney, which many of the hard-core Star Wars fans are already outraged by even though it hasn't come out yet. Preemptive outrage, I guess.

There are now so many SF and fantasy shows on television, with the surviving shows from 2014 and the years before being joined by a torrent of new shows in 2015, that it's become hard to keep track of them all.

Perennial favorites in recent years, *Game of Thrones*, *The Walking Dead*, and *Doctor Who*, continue to dominate the ratings, and shows like *Supernatural*, *Teen Wolf*, and *The Vampire Diaries* continue to hold on in spite of perhaps getting a bit long in the, er, tooth, while the once-wildly popular *True Blood* brought a disappointing season to a disappointing end and vanished from the airways. Long-running show *Warehouse 13* also died. Of the genre shows that debuted in the last couple of years, *Sleepy Hollow*, *Marvel's Agents of S.H.I.E.L.D.*, *Once Upon a Time*, *Arrow*, *Falling Skies*, *Person of Interest* (much more centrally a genre show than a thriller now that they've started to run a plotline about an emergent AI), *The Originals*, *Resurrection*, *Under the Dome*, *Grimm* (although it's shaky in the ratings), *Haven* (ditto), *Beauty and the Beast*, and *The 100* have survived, while, as far as I can tell (and it's sometimes hard to be sure; Internet sites sometimes run contradictory reports), *Almost Human*, *Once Upon a Time in Wonderland*, *Ravenswood*, *Believe*, *Star-Crossed*, *Witches of East End*, *Dracula*, *Continuum*, *The Neighbors*, *Revolution*, *Zero Hour*, and *The Tomorrow People* have not. Of these shows, *Sleepy Hollow*, *Arrow*, and *Person of Interest* seem to be the strongest in the ratings. *Agents of S.H.I.E.L.D.* is struggling in the ratings again, although the show is probably useful enough to Marvel/Disney

XXXVi | summation: 2014

as a promotional tool for whatever Marvel movie is coming along that it may survive anyway.

Of the new shows debuting in 2014, the most successful seems to be *Gotham* (a stylish noir take on what crime-drenched Gotham City was like when Batman was still a child, a concept that I wouldn't have thought would work, but which is saved by good acting and moody Gothic, highly atmospheric set design and photography), *The Flash* (detailing the adventures of—oh, go ahead and guess!), and *Outlander*, based on the best-selling paranormal romance series by Diana Gabaldon. *Constantine*, based on a gritty magic-using comic book antihero, and *The Librarians*, based on the movie franchise about a secret society of librarians who fight evil with magic, seem to have also generated a fair amount of buzz, although it's unclear how they're doing in the ratings.

Coming up in 2015 are *Agent Carter* (a spin-off from *Agents of S.H.I.E.L.D.*), the animated *Star Wars Rebels*, *12 Monkeys*, *Ascension*, *Daredevil*, *Dark Matter*, *Galavant* (a Monty Pythonesque musical comedy satirical take on knights and chivalry), *iZombie*, *The Last Man on Earth*, *Scream*, *Sense8*, *Supergirl*, *Stitchers*, *The Expanse* (based on the popular space opera series by James S. A. Corey), *The Messengers*, and *The Whispers*. Some of these will make it, many will not. Hard to guess which will be which at this point.

On the horizon are promised TV versions of *Westworld*, Neil Gaiman's *American Gods*, Philip K. Dick's *The Man in the High Castle*, Arthur C. Clarke's *Childhood's End*, *Shannara* based on Terry Brooks's *The Elfstones of Shannara*, Michael Moorcock's *Elric* stories, Jean M. Auel's *The Clan of the Cave Bear*, John Scalzi's *Old Man's War*, and Robert Holdstock's Mythago Wood cycle although many of these promised shows never actually show up. It'll be interesting to see how many of these actually make it to the air.

Other returning shows are *The Leftovers*, *Salem*, *Lost Girl*, *Bitten*, *Helix*, *Penny Dreadful*, and *Legends*.

The 72nd World Science Fiction Convention, Loncon 3, was held in London, England, from August 14 to August 18, 2014. The 2014 Hugo Awards, presented at LonCon 3, were: Best Novel, *Ancillary Justice*, by Ann Leckie; Best Novella, "Equoid," by Charles Stross; Best Novelette, "The Lady Astronaut of Mars," by Mary Robinette Kowal; Best Short Story, "The Water That Falls on You from Nowhere," by John Chu; Best Graphic Story, "Time," by Randall Munroe; Best Related Work, "We Have Always Fought: Challenging the Women, Cattle and Slaves Narrative," by Kameron Hurley; Best Professional Editor, Long Form, Ginjer Buchanan; Best Professional Editor, Short Form, Ellen Datlow; Best Professional Artist, Julie Dillon; Best Dramatic Presentation (Short Form), *Game of Thrones*: "The Rains of Castamere"; Best Dramatic Presentation (Long Form), *Gravity*; Best Semiprozine, *Lightspeed Magazine*; Best Fanzine, *A Dribble of Ink*; Best Fancast, *SF Signal Podcast*; Best Fan Writer, Kameron Hurley; Best Fan Artist, Sarah Webb; plus the John W. Campbell Award for best new writer to Sofia Samatar.

The 2013 Nebula Awards, presented at a banquet at the San Jose Marriot in San Jose, California, on May 17, 2014, were: Best Novel, *Ancillary Justice*, by Ann Leckie;

Best Novella, "The Weight of the Sunrise," by Vylar Kaftan; Best Novelette, "The Waiting Stars," by Aliette de Bodard; Best Short Story, "If You Were a Dinosaur, My Love," by Rachel Swirsky; Ray Bradbury Award, *Gravity*; the Andre Norton Award to *Sister Mine*, by Nalo Hopkinson; the Special Honoree Award to Frank M. Robinson; the Kevin O' Donnell, Jr. Service to SFWA Award to Michael Armstrong; and the Damon Knight Grand Master Award to Samuel R. Delany.

The 2014 World Fantasy Awards, presented at a banquet on November 9, 2014, at the Hyatt Regency Crystal City in Arlington, Virginia, during the Fortieth Annual World Fantasy Convention, were: Best Novel, *A Stranger in Olondria*, by Sofia Samatar; Best Novella, "Wakulla Springs," by Andy Duncan and Ellen Klages; Best Short Fiction, "The Prayer of Ninety Cats," by Caitlín R. Kiernan; Best Collection, *The Ape's Wife and Other Stories*, by Caitlín R. Kiernan; Best Anthology, *Dangerous Women*, edited by George R. R. Martin and Gardner Dozois; Best Artist, Charles Vess; Special Award (Professional), to Irene Gallo, for art direction of *Tor.com*, and William K. Schafer, for Subterranean Press (tie); Special Award (Nonprofessional), to Kate Baker, Neil Clarke, and Sean Wallace, for *Clarkesworld*; plus the Lifetime Achievement Award to Ellen Datlow and Chelsea Quinn Yarbro.

The 2013 Bram Stoker Awards, presented by the Horror Writers of America on May 10, 2014, during the World Horror Convention at the Portland Doubletree Hotel in Portland, Oregon, were: Best Novel, *Doctor Sleep*, by Stephen King; Best First Novel, *The Evolutionist*, by Rena Mason; Best Young Adult Novel, *Dog Days*, by Joe McKinney; Best Long Fiction, "The Great Pity," by Gary Braunbeck; Best Short Fiction, "Night Train to Paris," by David Gerrold; Best Collection, *The Beautiful Thing That Awaits Us All*, by Laird Barron; Best Anthology, *After Death*, edited by Eric J. Guignard; Best Nonfiction, *Nolan on Bradbury: Sixty Years of Writing about the Master of Science Fiction*, by William F. Nolan; Best Poetry Collection, *Four Elements*, by Marge Simon, Rain Graves, Charlee Jacob, and Linda Addison; Graphic Novel, *Alabaster: Wolves*, by Caitlín R. Kiernan; Best Screenplay, *The Walking Dead*: "Welcome to the Tombs," by Glen Mazzara; Specialty Press Award to Gray Friar Press; Richard Laymon (President's Award) to J. G. Faherty; plus Lifetime Achievement Awards to Stephen Jones and R. L. Stine.

The 2014 John W. Campbell Memorial Award was won by *Strange Bodies*, by Marcel Theroux.

The 2014 Theodore Sturgeon Memorial Award for Best Short Story was won by "In Joy, Knowing the Abyss Behind," by Sarah Pinsker.

The 2014 Philip K. Dick Award went to *Countdown City*, by Ben H. Winters.

The 2014 Arthur C. Clarke award was won by *Ancillary Justice*, by Ann Leckie.

The 2014 James Tiptree, Jr. Memorial Award was won by *Rupetta*, by N. A. Sulway.

The 2013 Sidewise Award for Alternate History went to (Long Form): *Surrounded by Enemies: What If Kennedy Survived Dallas?* by Bryce Zabel and *The Windsor Faction*, by D. J. Taylor (tie); and (Short Form): "The Weight of the Sunrise," by Vylar Kaftan.

Death struck the SF field heavily once again this year. Dead in 2014 or early 2015 were:

DANIEL KEYES, 86, Hugo and Edgar award winner, author of the classic story "Flowers for Algernon," which later was expanded into a novel and made into the popular movie *Charly*, as well as novels *The Touch* and *The Fifth Sally*, author also of nonfiction books such as *The Minds of Billy Milligan*; **LUCIUS SHEPARD**, 70, renowned SF, fantasy, horror, and mainstream author, reviewer, and essayist, winner of the Nebula, Hugo, and Sturgeon awards, author of novels such as *Life During Wartime, Green Eyes, Colonel Rutherford's Colt*, and *A Handbook of American Prayer*, as well as large amounts of acclaimed short fiction assembled in collections such as *The Jaguar Hunter, The Ends of the Earth, The Best of Lucius Shepard*, and *Five Autobiographies and a Fiction*, a personal friend; **JOSEPH E. LAKE, JR.**, 49, who wrote as **JAY LAKE**, winner of the John W. Campbell Award as Best New Writer in 2004, a hugely prolific author who in his tragically short life wrote acclaimed novels such as *Green, Endurance, Kalimpura, Trial of Flowers, Madness of Flowers*, and others, as well as many shorter stories that were collected in *The Sky That Wraps, American Sorrows, Dogs in the Moonlight*, and others, a personal friend; **FRANK M. ROBINSON**, 87, author, editor, scholar of the pulp magazine era, author of *The Glass Inferno*, with Thomas N. Scortia, which was later made into the movie *The Towering Inferno*, as well as other novels such as *The Power* and *The Dark Beyond the Stars*, and pop culture books such as *Pulp Culture: The Art of Fiction Magazines*; **MARY STEWART**, 97, best known in the field as the author of the Merlin series, Arthurian novels which included *The Crystal Cave, The Hollow Hills, The Last Enchantment*, and others, who also wrote many suspenseful romance novels such as *Madam, Will You Talk?, Touch Not the Cat*, and *The Moon-Spinners*; **GRAHAM JOYCE**, 59, acclaimed dark fantasist, twice winner of the World Fantasy Award, author of such novels as *The Tooth Fairy, The Facts of Life, Some Kind of Fairy Tale, The Stormwatcher, House of Lost Dreams*, and many others; **GABRIEL GARCÍA MÁRQUEZ**, 87, Colombian author, a leading figure in magic realism and world literature, best known for his novel *One Hundred Years of Solitude*, as well as books such as *A Very Old Man with Enormous Wings*; **THOMAS BERGER**, 89, writer best known for the eccentric Western *Little Big Man*, later made into a film, who also wrote genre-related novels such as *Vital Parts* and *Adventures of the Artificial Woman*; **P. D. JAMES**, 94, celebrated mystery writer, author of the long-running Adam Dalgliesh novels, whose one SF novel, *The Children of Men*, was made into a major motion picture; **NADINE GORDIMER**, 90, Nobel Prize–winning South African author and fierce critic of apartheid, whose many works include one SF novel, *July's People*; *Mind Parasites* and *The Space Vampires*; **MICHAEL SHEA**, 67, horror and fantasy writer, winner of the World Fantasy Award, best known for the novel *Nifft the Lean*, whose many stories were collected in *Polyphemus, The Autopsy and Other Tales*, and others; **ANDY ROBERTSON**, 58, British editor and author, former assistant editor of *Interzone*, a leading expert on the works of fantasist William Hope Hodgson; **ALAN RODGERS**, 54, writer and editor, winner of the Bram Stoker Award, former editor of horror magazine *Night Cry*; **HILBERT SCHENCK**, 87, author of much nautically themed SF, including the novels *At the Eye of the Ocean* and *A Rose for Armageddon*, and stories collected in *Wave Rider* and *Steam Bird*; **HAYDEN HOWARD**, 89, SF author who published many stories in SF magazines as well as one novel, *The Eskimo Invasion*; **MICHEL PARRY**, 67, anthologist, horror/supernatural novelist; **C. J. HENDERSON**, 62, prolific author of fantasy, crime novels, and comics, including *Patiently Waiting* and *Brooklyn Knight*; **STEPAN CHAPMAN**, 63, best known for his Philip K. Dick Award–winning novel *The Troika*; **MARK E. ROGERS**, 61, writer, artist, and fan, best known for *The Adventures of Samurai Cat* graphic novel series; Australian SF writer **PHILIPPA MADDERN**, 61, scholar of late medieval English history and Australian medieval and early modern history, head of the School of Humanities at the University of Western Australia; **DONALD MOFFITT**, 83, author of SF novels such as *The Jupiter Theft*, *Genesis Quest*, *A Gathering of Stars*, and others; **J. F. GONZALEZ**, 50, author or coauthor of more than fifteen novels, most of them supernatural horror; **WALTER DEAN MYERS**, 76, YA and children's author, author of *Fallen Angels*, *Shadow of the Red Moon*, and others; **JANRAE FRANK**, 59, writer and editor; **ROBERT CONROY**, 76, winner of the Sidewise Award, author of Alternate History works such as *1942*, *1862*, *Red Inferno*, and *Castro's Bomb*; **AARON ALLSTON**, 53, SF writer also known for *Star Wars* and gaming novels; **JOEL LANE,** 50, British author and editor; **ANA MARÍA MATUTE**, 88, noted Spanish author whose work sometimes contained fantastic elements; **GEORGE C. WILLICK**, 76, SF writer and fanzine editor; **T. R. FEHRENBACH**, 88, Texas historian and occasional SF writer; **KIRBY McCAULEY**, 72, at one time perhaps the most prominent agent in the SF/fantasy/horror fields, one of the founders of the World Fantasy Convention, editor of acclaimed horror anthologies *Frights* and *Dark Forces*, brother of SF agent Kay McCauley, a personal friend; **ALICE K. TURNER**, 75, longtime fiction editor of *Playboy* magazine, editor of the anthologies *The Playboy Book of Science Fiction* and *Playboy Stories: The Best of Forty Years of Short Fiction*, as well as the author of nonfiction book *The History of Hell* and coauthor, with Michael Andre-Driussi, of the critical study, *Snake's Hands: The Fiction of John Crowley*, a friend; **MICHAEL ROY BURGESS**, 65, who wrote as **ROBERT REGINALD**, author, editor, bibliographer, and publisher, author of such bibliographical studies as *Science Fiction and Fantasy Literature*; *A Checklist, 1700–1974, with Contemporary Science Fiction Authors II*; **WILLIAM H. PATTERSON, JR.**, 62, writer, critic, and expert on the works of Robert A. Heinlein, author of the two-part Heinlein biography *Robert A. Heinlein: In Dialogue with His Century, Volume 1, 1907–1948: Learning Curve* and *Robert A. Heinlein: In Dialogue with His Century, Volume Two, 1948–1988: The Man Who Learned Better*; **GEORGE SLUSSER**, 75, critic and scholar, cofounder and longtime curator of the Eaton Collection of SF books and manuscripts, author of critical studies such as *Robert A. Heinlein: Stranger in His Own Land*, *The Farthest Shores of Ursula K. Le Guin*, and *Gregory Benford*; **STU SHIFFMAN**, 60, artist and longtime fan, winner of the Best Fan Artist Hugo in 1990; **ROCKY WOOD**, 55, Horror Writers Association President and Stephen King scholar; **MATTHEW RICHELL**, 41, Hachette Australia CEO and Hachette New Zealand chairman; world-famous Swiss artist **H. R. GIGER**, 74, an inductee into the Science Fiction Hall of Fame, best known to genre audiences for his work as a production artist on the movie *Alien*, as well as for art books such as *H. R. Giger N.Y. City* and *H. R. Giger: Retrospective, 1964–1984*; **MARGOT ADLER**, 68, longtime National Public Radio correspondent and broadcaster, creator of the SF/fantasy reading program *Hour of the Wolf*; **ROBIN WILLIAMS**, 63, world-famous comedian and movie and television actor, best known to genre audiences for roles in *The Fisher King*, *Jumanji*, *The Adventures of Baron Munchausen*, and, of course, as the alien Mork in television's *Mork and Mindy*, although he may be best known to generations of children to come as the voice of the Genie in Disney's *Aladdin*; **JAMES GARNER**, 86, movie and television actor whose genre connections are slender, mostly limited to the movies *Space Cowboys* and *Fire in the Sky*, but who is known to every boomer for his starring roles in the TV series *Maverick* and *The Rockford Files*; **LAUREN BACALL**, 89, world-famous film and stage actress, star of films such as *To Have and Have Not*, *The Big Sleep*, and *Key Largo*, another person with little direct genre connection, but someone who again will be known to every boomer; **RICHARD ATTENBOROUGH**, 90, film actor, probably best known to genre audiences for his role in *Jurassic Park*, but also an award-winning director of such films as *Gandhi*; **ROD TAYLOR**, 84, film actor best known to genre audience for roles in *The Time Machine* and *The Birds*; producer and screenwriter **BRIAN CLEMENS**, 83, best known to genre audiences for his work on British TV series *The Avengers*; **ELAINE STRITCH**, 89, movie and television actor, best known to genre audiences for *Cocoon: The Return* and the TV show *3rd Rock from the Sun*; **ARLENE MARTEL**, 78, TV actress, best known to genre audiences for her role as T'Pring in the "Amok Time" episode of the original *Star Trek*; **ELIZABETH PEÑA**, 55, movie and TV actress best known for her role in *Lone Star*, but perhaps best known to genre audiences for her voiceover work in *The Incredibles*, as well as roles in **batteries not included*, *Jacob's Ladder*, and *The Invaders*; TV and film art director **ROBERT KINOSHITA**, 100, who worked on designing Robby the Robot from *Forbidden Planet*, and the robot from TV's *Lost in Space*; **CATHERINE ALICE LENTA LANGFORD**, 89, mother of SF writer and editor David Langford; **GEORGE REYNOLDS**, 95, father of SF editor and publisher Eric T. Reynolds; **CHARLIE ROBINSON**, 92, father of SF writer Spider Robinson; **TERRI LUANNA da SILVA,** 40, daughter of SF writer Spider Robinson; **SARAH ELIZABETH WEBSTER**, 69, sister of SF writer and anthologist Bud Webster; **JOHN McANINLEY**, 70, brother of artist and SF radio show host Susan McAninley.

The fifth dragon

IAN MCDONALD

British author Ian McDonald is an ambitious and daring writer with a wide range and an impressive amount of talent. His first story was published in 1982, and since then he has appeared with some frequency in Interzone, Asimov's Science Fiction, and elsewhere. In 1989 he won the Locus Award for Best First Novel for his novel Desolation Road. He won the Philip K. Dick Award in 1992 for his novel King of Morning, Queen of Day. His other books include the novels Out on Blue Six, Hearts, Hands and Voices, Terminal Café, Sacrifice of Fools, Evolution's Shore, Kirinya, Ares Express, Brasyl, and The Dervish House, as well as three collections of his short fiction, Empire Dreams, Speaking In Tongues, and Cyberabad Days. His novel River of Gods was a finalist for both the Hugo Award and the Arthur C. Clarke award in 2005, and a novella drawn from it, "The Little Goddess," was a finalist for the Hugo and the Nebula. He won a Hugo Award in 2007 for his novelette "The Djinn's Wife," won the Theodore Sturgeon Award for his story "Tendeleo's Story," and in 2011 won the John W. Campbell Memorial Award for his novel The Dervish House. His most recent books, Planesrunner, Be My Enemy, and Empress of the Sun, are part of a YA series. Coming up is a new novel, Luna, and two collections, Only the Best of Ian McDonald and Mars Stories. Born in Manchester, England, in 1960, McDonald has spent most of his life in Northern Ireland, and now lives and works in Belfast.

Here he tells a gripping story of love in the face of the harsh realities of life as immigrant workers on the moon, and presents its characters with a heartbreaking choice.

The scan was routine. Every moon worker has one every four lunes. Achi was called, she went into the scanner. The machine passed magnetic fields through her body and when she came out the medic said, you have four weeks left.

We met on the Vorontsov Trans-Orbital cycler but didn't have sex. We talked instead about names.

"Corta. That's not a Brazilian name," Achi said. I didn't know her well enough then, eight hours out from transfer orbit, to be my truculent self and insist that any name can be a Brazilian name, that we are a true rainbow nation. So I told her that my name had rolled through many peoples and languages like a bottle in a breaker until it was cast up sand-scoured and clouded on the beaches of Barra. And now I was taking it on again, up to the moon.

Achi Debasso. Another name rolled by tide of history. London born, London raised, M.I.T. educated but she never forgot—had never been let forget—that she was Syrian. Syriac. That one letter was a universe of difference. Her family had fled the civil war, she had been born in exile. Now she was headed into a deeper exile.

I didn't mean to be in the centrifuge pod with Achi. There was a guy; he'd looked and I looked back and nodded *yes, I will, yes* even as the OTV made its distancing burn from the cycler. I took it. I'm no prude. I've got the New Year Barra beach bangles. I'm up for a party and more, and everyone's heard about (here they move in close and mouth the words) *freefall sex.* I wanted to try it with this guy. And I couldn't stop throwing up. I was not up for zero gee. It turned everything inside me upside down. Puke poured out of me. That's not sexy. So I retreated to gravity and the only other person in the centrifuge arm was this caramel-eyed girl, slender hands and long fingers, her face flickering every few moments into an unconscious micro-frown. Inward-gazing, self-loathing, scattering geek references like anti-personnel mines. Up in the hub our co-workers fucked. Down in the centrifuge pod we talked and the stars and the moon arced across the window beneath our feet.

A Brazilian miner and a London-Syriac ecologist. The centrifuge filled as freefall sex palled but we kept talking. The next day the guy I had puked over caught my eye again but I sought out Achi, on her own in the same spot, looking out at the moon. And the whirling moon was a little bigger in the observation port and we knew each other a little better and by the end of the week the moon filled the whole of the window and we had moved from conversationalists into friends.

Achi: left Damascus as a cluster of cells tumbling in her mother's womb. And that informed her every breath and touch. She felt guilty for escaping. Father was a software engineer, mother was a physiotherapist. London welcomed them.

Adriana: seven of us: seven Cortas. Little cuts. I was in the middle, loved and adored but told solemnly I was plain and thick in the thighs and would have to be thankful for whatever life granted me.

Achi: a water girl. Her family home was near the Olympic pool—her mother had dropped her into water days out of the hospital. She had sunk, then she swam. Swimmer and surfer: long British summer evenings on the western beaches. Cold British water. She was small and quiet but feared no wave.

Adriana: born with the sound of the sea in her room but never learned to swim. I splash, I paddle, I wade. I come from beach people, not ocean people.

Achi: the atoner. She could not change the place or order of her birth, but she could apologise for it by being useful. Useful Achi. Make things right!

Adriana: the plain. Mãe and papai thought they were doing me a favour; allowing me no illusions or false hopes that could blight my life. Marry as well as you can; be happy: that will have to do. Not this Corta. I was the kid who shot her hand up at school. The girl who wouldn't shut up when the boys were talking. Who never got picked for the futsal team—okay, I would find my own sport. I did Brasilian ju-jitsu. Sport for one. No one messed with plain Adriana.

Achi: grad at UCL, post-grad at M.I.T. Her need to be useful took her battling desertification, salinisation, eutrophication. She was an -ation warrior. In the end it took her to the moon. No way to be more useful than sheltering and feeding a whole world.

Adriana: university at São Paulo. And my salvation. Where I learned that plain didn't matter as much as available, and I was sweet for sex with boys and girls. Fuck-friends. Sweet girls don't have fuckfriends. And sweet girls don't study mining engi-neering. Like jujitsu, like hooking up, that was a thing for me, me alone. Then the economy gave one final, apocalyptic crash at the bottom of a series of drops and hit the ground and broke so badly no one could see how to fix it. And the seaside, be-happy Cortas were in ruins, jobless, investments in ashes. It was plain Adriana who said, I can save you. I'll go to the Moon.

All this we knew by the seventh day of the orbit out. On the eighth day, we rendez-voused with the transfer tether and spun down to the new world.

The freefall sex? Grossly oversold. Everything moves in all the wrong ways. Things get away from you. You have to strap everything down to get purchase. It's more like mutual bondage.

I was sintering ten kilometres ahead of Crucible when Achi's call came. I had re-quested the transfer from Mackenzie Metals to Vorontsov Rail. The forewoman had been puzzled when I reported to Railhead. You're a dustbunny not a track-queen. Surface work is surface work, I said and that convinced her. The work was good, easy and physical and satisfying. And it was on the surface. At the end of every up-shift you saw six new lengths of gleaming rail among the boot and track prints, and on the edge of the horizon, the blinding spark of Crucible, brighter than any star, ad-vancing over yesterday's rails, and you said, I made that. The work had real measure: the inexorable advance of Mackenzie Metals across the Mare Insularum, brighter than the brightest star. Brighter than sunrise, so bright it could burn a hole through your helmet sunscreen if you held it in your eye line too long. Thousands of con-cave mirrors focusing sunlight on the smelting crucibles. Three years from now the rail lines would circle the globe and the Crucible would follow the sun, bathed in perpetual noon. Me, building a railroad around the moon.

Then ting ching and it all came apart. Achi's voice blocking out my work-mix music, Achi's face superimposed on the dirty grey hills of Rimae Maestlin. Achi tell-ing me her routine medical had given her four weeks.

I hitched a ride on the construction car back down the rails to Crucible. I waited two hours hunkered down in the hard-vacuum shadows, tons of molten metal and ten thousand Kelvin sunlight above my head, for an expensive ticket on a slow Mac-kenzie ore train to Meridian. Ten hours clinging onto a maintenance platform, not even room to turn around, let alone sit. Grey dust, black sky . . . I listened my way through my collection of historical bossanova, from the 1940s to the 1970s. I played

Connecto on my helmet hud until every time I blinked I saw tumbling, spinning gold stars. I scanned my family's social space entries and threw my thoughts and comments and good wishes at the big blue Earth. By the time I got to Meridian I was two degrees off hypothermic. My surface activity suit was rated for a shift and some scramble time, not twelve hours in the open. Should have claimed compensation. But I didn't want my former employers paying too much attention to me. I couldn't afford the time it would take to re-pressurise for the train, so I went dirty and fast, on the BALTRAN.

I knew I would vomit. I held it until the third and final jump. BALTRAN: Ballistic Transport system. The moon has no atmosphere—well, it does, a very thin one, which is getting thicker as human settlements leak air into it. Maybe in a few centuries this will become a problem for vacuum industries, but to all intents and purposes, it's a vacuum. See what I did there? That's the engineer in me. No atmosphere means ballistic trajectories can be calculated with great precision. Which means, throw something up and you know exactly where it will fall to moon again. Bring in positionable electromagnetic launchers and you have a mechanism for schlepping material quick and dirty around the moon. Launch it, catch it in a receiver, boost it on again. It's like juggling. The BALTRAN is not always used for cargo. If you can take the gees it can as easily juggle people across the moon.

I held it until the final jump. You cannot imagine what it is like to throw up in your helmet. In free fall. People have died. The look on the BALTRAN attendant's face when I came out of the capsule at Queen of the South was a thing to be seen. So I am told. I couldn't see it. But if I could afford the capsule I could afford the shower to clean up. And there are people in Queen who will happily clean vomit out of a sasuit for the right number of bitsies. Say what you like about the Vorontsovs, they pay handsomely.

All this I did, the endless hours riding the train like a moon-hobo, the hypothermia and being sling-shotted in a can of my own barf, because I knew that if Achi had four weeks, I could not be far behind.

You don't think about the bones. As a Jo Moonbeam, everything is so new and demanding, from working out how to stand and walk, to those four little digits in the bottom right corner of your field of vision that tell you how much you owe the Lunar Development Corporation for air, water, space and web. The first time you see those numbers change because demand or supply or market price has shifted, your breath catches in your throat. Nothing tells you that you are not on Earth any more than exhaling at one price and inhaling at another. Everything—*everything*— was new and hard.

Everything other than your bones. After two years on the moon human bone structure atrophies to a point where return to Earth gravity is almost certainly fatal. The medics drop it almost incidentally into your initial assessment. It can take days—weeks—for its ripples to touch your life. Then you feel your bones crumbling away, flake by flake, inside your body. And there's not a thing you can do about it. What it means is that there is a calcium clock ticking inside your body, counting down to Moon Day. The day you decide: do I stay or do I go?

In those early days we were scared all the time, Achi and I. I looked after her—I don't know how we fell into those roles, protector and defended, but I protected and she nurtured and we won respect. There were three moon men for every moon woman. It was a man's world; a macho social meld of soldiers camped in enemy terrain and deep-diving submariners. The Jo Moonbeam barracks were exactly that; a grey, dusty warehouse of temporary accommodation cabins barely the safe legal minimum beneath the surface. We learned quickly the vertical hierarchy of moon society: the lower you live—the further from surface radiation and secondary cosmic rays—the higher your status. The air was chilly and stank of sewage, electricity, dust and unwashed bodies. The air still smells like that; I just got used to the funk in my lungs. Within hours the induction barracks self-sorted. The women gravitated together and affiliated with the astronomers on placement with the Farside observatory. Achi and I traded to get cabins beside each other. We visited, we decorated, we entertained, we opened our doors in solidarity and hospitality. We listened to the loud voices of the men, the real men, the worldbreakers, booming down the aisles of cabins, the over-loud laughter. We made cocktails from cheap industrial vodka.

Sexual violence, games of power were in the air we breathed, the water we drank, the narrow corridors through which we squeezed, pressing up against each other. The moon has never had criminal law, only contract law, and when Achi and I arrived the LDC was only beginning to set up the Court of Clavius to settle and enforce contracts. Queen of the South was a wild town. Fatalities among Jo Moonbeams ran at ten percent. In our first week, an extraction worker from Xinjiang was crushed in a pressure lock. The Moon knows a thousand ways to kill you. And I knew a thousand and one.

Cortas cut. That was our family legend. Hard sharp fast. I made the women's Brazilian jujitsu team at university. It's hard, sharp, fast: the perfect Corta fighting art. A couple of basic moves, together with lunar gravity, allowed me to put over the most intimidating of sex pests. But when Achi's stalker wouldn't take no, I reached for slower, subtler weapons. Stalkers don't go away. That's what makes them stalkers. I found which Surface Activity training squad he was on and made some adjustments to his suit thermostat. He didn't die. He wasn't meant to die. Death would have been easier than my revenge for Achi. He never suspected me; he never suspected anyone. I made it look like a perfect malfunction. I'm a good engineer. I count his frostbit thumb and three toes as my trophies. By the time he got out of the med centre, Achi and I were on our separate ways to our contracts.

That was another clock, ticking louder than the clock in our bones. I&A was four weeks. After that, we would go to work. Achi's work in ecological habitats would take her to the underground agraria the Asamoah family were digging under Amundsen. My contract was with Mackenzie Metals; working out on the open seas. Working with dust. Dustbunny. We clung to the I&A barracks, we clung to our cabins, our friends. We clung to each other. We were scared. Truth: we were scared all the time, with every breath. Everyone on the moon is scared, all the time.

There was a party; moon mojitos. Vodka and mint are easy up here. But before the music and the drinking: a special gift for Achi. Her work with Aka would keep her underground; digging and scooping and sowing. She need never go on the surface. She could go her whole career—her whole life—in the caverns and lava tubes and agraria. She need never see the raw sky.

The suit hire was cosmologically expensive, even after negotiation. It was a GP surface activity shell; an armoured hulk to my lithe sasuit spiderwoman. Her face was nervous behind the faceplate; her breathing shallow. We held hands in the outlock as the pressure door slid up. Then her faceplate polarised in the sun and I could not see her any more. We walked up the ramp amongst a hundred thousand boot prints. We walked up the ramp and a few metres out on to the surface, still holding hands. There, beyond the coms towers and the power relays and the charging points for the buses and rovers; beyond the grey line of the crater rim that curved on the close horizon and the shadows the sun had never touched; there perched above the edge of our tiny world we saw the full earth. Full and blue and white, mottled with greens and ochres. Full and impossible and beautiful beyond any words of mine. It was winter and the southern hemisphere was offered to us; the ocean half of the planet. I saw great Africa. I saw dear Brazil.

Then the air contract advisory warned me that we were nearing the expiry of our oxygen contract and we turned out backs on the blue earth and walked back down into the moon.

That night we drank to our jobs, our friends, our loves and our bones. In the morning we parted.

We met in a café on the twelfth level of the new Chandra Quadra. We hugged, we kissed, we cried a little. I smelled sweet by then. Below us excavators dug and sculpted, a new level every ten days. We held each other at arms' length and looked at each other. Then we drank mint tea on the balcony.

I loathe mint tea.

Mint tea is a fistful of herbs jammed in a glass. Sloshed with boiling water. Served scalded yet still flavourless. Effete like herbal thés and tisanes. Held between thumb and forefinger: so. Mint leaves are coarse and hairy. Mint tea is medicinal. Add sugar and it becomes infantile. It is drinking for the sake of doing something with your fingers.

Coffee is a drink for grownups. No kid ever likes coffee. It's psychoactive. Coffee is the drug of memory. I can remember the great cups of coffee of my life; the places, the faces, the words spoken. It never quite tastes the way it smells. If it did, we would drink it until our heads exploded with memory,

But coffee is not an efficient crop in our ecology. And imported coffee is more expensive than gold. Gold is easy. Gold I can sift from lunar regolith. Gold is so easy its only value is decorative. It isn't even worth the cost of shipment to Earth. Mint is rampant. Under lunar gravity, it forms plants up to three metres tall. So we are a nation of mint tea drinkers.

We didn't talk about the bones at once. It was eight lunes since we last saw each other: we talk on the network daily, we share our lives but it takes face to face contact to ground all that; make it real.

I made Achi laugh. She laughed like soft rain. I told her about King Dong and she clapped her hands to her mouth in naughty glee but laughed with her eyes. King

Dong started as a joke but shift by shift was becoming reality. Footprints last forever on the moon, a bored surface worker had said on a slow shift rotation back to Crucible. What if we stamped out a giant spunking cock, a hundred kilometres long? With hairy balls. Visible from Earth. It's just a matter of co-ordination. Take a hundred male surface workers and an Australian extraction company and joke becomes temptation becomes reality. So wrong. So funny.

And Achi?

She was out of contract. The closer you are to your Moon Day, the shorter the contract, sometimes down to minutes of employment, but this was different. Aka did not want her ideas any more. They were recruiting direct from Accra and Kumasi. Ghanaians for a Ghanaian company. She was pitching ideas to the Lunar Development Corporation for their new port and capital at Meridian—quadras three kilometres deep; a sculpted city; like living in the walls of a titanic cathedral. The LDC was polite but it had been talking about development funding for two lunes now. Her savings were running low. She woke up looking at the tick of the Four Fundamentals on her lens. Oxygen water space coms: which do you cut down on first? She was considering moving to a smaller space.

"I can pay your per diems," I said. "I have lots of money."

And then the bones . . . Achi could not decide until I got my report. I never knew anyone suffered from guilt as acutely as her. She could not have borne it if her decision had influenced my decision to stay with the moon or go back to Earth.

"I'll go now," I said. I didn't want to. I didn't want to be here on this balcony drinking piss-tea. I didn't want Achi to have forced a decision on me. I didn't want there to be a decision for me to make. "I'll get the tea."

Then the wonder. In the corner of my vision, a flash of gold. A lens malfunction—no, something marvellous. A woman flying. A flying woman. Her arms were outspread, she hung in the sky like a crucifix. Our Lady of Flight. Then I saw wings shimmer and run with rainbow colours; wings transparent and strong as a dragonfly's. The woman hung a moment, then folded her gossamer wings around her, and fell. She tumbled, now diving head-first, flicked her wrists, flexed her shoulders. A glimmer of wing slowed her; then she spread her full wing span and pulled up out of her dive into a soaring spiral, high into the artificial sky of Chandra Quadra.

"Oh," I said. I had been holding my breath. I was shaking with wonder. I was chewed by jealousy.

"We always could fly," Achi said. "We just haven't had the space. Until now."

Did I hear irritation in Achi's voice, that I was so bewitched by the flying woman? But if you could fly why would you ever do anything else?

I went to the Mackenzie Metals medical centre and the medic put me in the scanner. He passed magnetic fields through my body and the machine gave me my bone density analysis. I was eight days behind Achi. Five weeks, and then my residency on the moon would become citizenship.

Or I could fly back to Earth, to Brazil.

There are friends and there are friends you have sex with.

After I&A it was six lunes until I saw Achi again. Six lunes in the Sea of Fertility, sifting dust. The Mackenzie Metals Messier unit was old, cramped, creaking: cut-and-cover pods under bulldozed regolith berms. Too frequently I was evacuated to the new, lower levels by the radiation alarm. Cosmic rays kicked nasty secondary particles out of moon dust, energetic enough to penetrate the upper levels of the unit. Every time I saw the alarm flash its yellow trefoil in my lens I felt my ovaries tighten. Day and night the tunnels trembled to the vibration of the digging machines, deep beneath even those evacuation tunnels, eating rock. There were two hundred dust-bunnies in Messier. After a month's gentle and wary persistence and charm from a 3D print designer, I joined the end of a small amory: my Chu-yu, his homamor in Queen, his hetamor in Meridian, her hetamor also in Meridian. What had taken him so long, Chu-yu confessed, was my rep. Word about the sex pest on I&A with the unexplained suit malfunction. *I wouldn't do that to a co-worker,* I said. *Not unless severely provoked.* Then I kissed him. The amory was warmth and sex, but it wasn't Achi. Lovers are not friends

Sun Chu-yu understood that when I kissed him goodbye at Messier's bus lock. Achi and I chatted on the network all the way to the railhead at Hypatia, then all the way down the line to the South. Even then, only moments since I had last spoken to her image on my eyeball, it was a physical shock to see her at the meeting point in Queen of the South station: her, physical her. Shorter than I remembered. Absence makes the heart grow taller.

Such fun she had planned for me! I wanted to dump my stuff at her place but no; she whirled me off into excitement. After the reek and claustrophobia of Messier Queen of the South was intense, loud, colourful, too too fast. In only six lunes it had changed beyond recognition. Every street was longer, every tunnel wider, every chamber loftier. When she took me in a glass elevator down the side of the recently completed Thoth Quadra I reeled from vertigo. Down on the floor of the massive cavern was a small copse of dwarf trees—full-size trees would reach the ceiling, Achi explained. There was a café. In that café I first tasted and immediately hated mint tea.

I built this, Achi said. *These are my trees, this is my garden.*

I was too busy looking up at the lights, all the lights, going up and up.

Such fun! Tea, then shops. I had had to find a party dress. We were going to a special party, that night. Exclusive. We browsed the catalogues in five different print shops before I found something I could wear: very retro, 1950s inspired, full and layered, it hid what I wanted hidden. Then, the shoes.

The special party was exclusive to Achi's workgroup and their F&Fs. A security-locked rail capsule took us through a dark tunnel into a space so huge, so blinding with mirrored light, that once again I reeled on my feet and almost threw up over my Balenciaga. An agrarium, Achi's last project. I was at the bottom of a shaft a kilometre tall, fifty metres wide. The horizon is close at eye level on the moon; everything curves. Underground, a different geometry applies. The agrarium was the straightest thing I had seen in months. And brilliant: a central core of mirrors ran the full height of the shaft, bouncing raw sunlight one to another to another to walls terraced with hydroponic racks. The base of the shaft was a mosaic of fish tanks, criss-crossed by walkways. The air was warm and dank and rank. I was woozy with CO_2.

In these conditions plants grew fast and tall; potato plants the size of bushes; tomato vines so tall I lost their heads in the tangle of leaves and fruit. Hyper-intensive agriculture: the agrarium was huge for a cave, small for an ecosystem. The tanks splashed with fish. Did I hear frogs? Were those ducks?

Achi's team had built a new pond from waterproof sheeting and construction frame. A pool. A swimming pool. A sound system played G-pop. There were cocktails. Blue was the fashion. They matched my dress. Achi's crew were friendly and expansive. They never failed to compliment me on my fashion. I shucked it and my shoes and everything else for the pool. I lolled, I luxuriated, I let the strange, chaotic eddies waft green, woozy air over me while over my head the mirrors moved. Achi swam up beside me and we trod water together, laughing and plashing. The agrarium crew had lowered a number of benches into the pool to make a shallow end. Achi and I wafted blood-warm water with our legs and drank Blue Moons.

I am always up for a party.

I woke up in bed beside her the next morning; shit-headed with moon vodka. I remembered mumbling, fumbling love. Shivering and stupid-whispering, skin to skin. Fingerworks. Achi lay curled on her right side, facing me. She had kicked the sheet off in the night. A tiny string of drool ran from the corner of her mouth to the pillow and trembled in time to her breathing.

I looked at her there, her breath rattling in the back of her throat in drunk sleep. We had made love. I had sex with my dearest friend. I had done a good thing, I had done a bad thing. I had done an irrevocable thing. Then I lay down and pressed myself in close to her and she mumble-grumbled and moved in close to me and her fingers found me and we began again.

I woke in the dark with the golden woman swooping through my head. Achi slept beside me. The same side, the same curl of the spine, the same light rattle-snore and open mouth as that first night. When I saw Achi's new cabin, I booked us into a hostel. The bed was wide, the air was as fresh as Queen of the South could make and the taste of the water did not set your teeth on edge.

Golden woman, flying loops through my certainties.

Queen of the South never went fully dark—lunar society is 24-hour society. I pulled Achi's unneeded sheet around me and went out on to the balcony. I leaned on the rail and looked out at the walls of lights. Apts, cabins, walkways and staircases. Lives and decisions behind every light. This was an ugly world. Hard and mean. It put a price on everything. It demanded a negotiation from everyone. Out at Railhead I had seen a new thing among some of the surface workers: a medallion, or a little votive tucked into a patch pocket. A woman in Virgin Mary robes, one half of her face a black angel, the other half a naked skull. Dona Luna: goddess of dust and radiation. Our Lady Liberty, our Britannia, our Marianne, our Mother Russia. One half of her face dead, but the other alive. The moon was not a dead satellite, it was a living world. Hands and hearts and hopes like mine shaped it. There was no mother nature, no Gaia to set against human will. Everything that lived, we made. Dona Luna was hard and unforgiving, but she was beautiful. She could be a woman, with dragonfly wings, flying.

I stayed on the hotel balcony until the roof reddened with sun-up. Then I went back to Achi. I wanted to make love with her again. My motives were all selfish. Things that are difficult with friends are easier with lovers.

My grandmother used to say that love was the easiest thing in the world. Love is what you see every day.

I did not see Achi for several lunes after the party in Queen. Mackenzie Metals sent me out into the field, prospecting new terrain in the Sea of Vapours. Away from Messier, it was plain to me and Sun Chu-yu that the amory didn't work. You love what you see every day. All the amors were happy for me to leave. No blame, no claim. A simple automated contract, terminated.

I took a couple of weeks furlough back in Queen. I had called Achi about hooking up but she was at a new dig at Twe, where the Asamoahs were building a corporate headquarters. I was relieved. And then was guilty that I had felt relieved. Sex had made everything different. I drank, I partied, I had one night stands, I talked long hours of expensive bandwidth with my loved ones back on Earth. They thanked me for the money, especially the tiny kids. They said I looked different. Longer. Drawn out. My bones eroding, I said. There they were, happy and safe. The money I sent them bought their education. Health, weddings, babies. And here I was, on the moon. Plain Adriana, who would never get a man, but who got the education, who got the degree, who got the job, sending them the money from the moon.

They were right. I was different. I never felt the same about that blue pearl of Earth in the sky. I never again hired a sasuit to go look at it, just look at it. Out on the surface, I disregarded it.

The Mackenzies sent me out next to the Lansberg extraction zone and I saw the thing that made everything different.

Five extractors were working Lansberg. They were ugly towers of Archimedes screws and grids and transport belts and wheels three times my height, all topped out by a spread of solar panels that made them look like robot trees. Slow-moving, cumbersome, inelegant. Lunar design tends to the utilitarian, the practical. The bones on show. But to me they were beautiful. Marvellous trees. I saw them one day, out on the regolith, and I almost fell flat from the revelation. Not what they made— separating rare earth metals from lunar regolith—but what they threw away. Launched in high, arching ballistic jets on either side of the big, slow machines.

It was the thing I saw every day. One day you look at the boy on the bus and he sets your heart alight. One day you look at the jets of industrial waste and you see riches beyond measure.

I had to dissociate myself from anything that might link me to regolith waste and beautiful rainbows of dust.

I quit Mackenzie and became a Vorontsov track queen.

I want to make a game of it, Achi said. That's the only way I can bear it. We must clench our fists behind our backs, like Scissors Paper Stone, and we must count to three, and then we open our fists and in them there will be something, some small object, that will say beyond any doubt what we have decided. We must not speak, because if we say even a word, we will influence each other. That's the only way I can bear it if it is quick and clean and we don't speak. And a game.

We went back to the balcony table of the café to play the game. It was now on the 13th level. Two glasses of mint tea. No one was flying the great empty spaces of Chandra Quadra this day. The air smelled of rock dust over the usual electricity and sewage. Every fifth sky panel was blinking. An imperfect world.

Attempted small talk. Do you want some breakfast? No, but you have some. No I'm not hungry. I haven't seen that top before. The colour is really good for you. Oh it's just something I printed out of a catalogue . . . Horrible awful little words to stop us saying what we really had to stay.

"I think we should do this kind of quickly," Achi said finally and in a breathtaking instant her right hand was behind her back. I slipped my small object out of my bag, clenched it in my hidden fist.

"One two three," Achi said. We opened our fists.

A *nazar*: an Arabic charm: concentric teardrops of blue, white and black plastic. An eye.

A tiny icon of Dona Luna: black and white, living and dead.

Then I saw Achi again. I was up in Meridian renting a data crypt and hunting for the leanest, freshest, hungriest law firm to protect the thing I had realised out on Lansberg. She had been called back from Twe to solve a problem with microbiota in the Obuasi agrarium that had left it a tower of stinking black slime.

One city; two friends and amors. We went out to party. And found we couldn't. The frocks were fabulous, the cocktails disgraceful, the company louche and the narcotics dazzling but in each bar, club, private party we ended up in a corner together, talking.

Partying was boring. Talk was lovely and bottomless and fascinating.

We ended up in bed again, of course. We couldn't wait. Glorious, impractical 1950s Dior frocks lay crumpled on the floor, ready for the recycler.

"What do you want?" Achi asked. She lay on her bed, inhaling THC from a vaper. "Dream and don't be afraid."

"Really?"

"Moon dreams."

"I want to be a dragon," I said and Achi laughed and punched me on the thigh: *get away*. "No, seriously."

In the year and a half we had been on the moon, our small world had changed. Things move fast on the moon. Energy and raw materials are cheap, human genius plentiful. Ambition boundless. Four companies had emerged as major economic forces: four families. The Australian Mackenzies were the longest established. They had been joined by the Asamoahs, whose company Aka monopolised food and living space. The Russian Vorontsovs finally moved their operations off Earth entirely and ran the cycler, the moonloop, the bus service and the emergent rail network. Most recent to amalgamate were the Suns, who had defied the representatives of the People's Republic on the LDC board and ran the information infrastructure. Four companies: Four Dragons. That was what they called themselves. The Four Dragons of the Moon.

"I want to be the Fifth Dragon," I said.

The last things were simple and swift. All farewells should be sudden, I think. I booked Achi on the cycler out. There was always space on the return orbit. She booked me into the LDC medical centre. A flash of light and the lens was bonded permanently to my eye. No hand shake, no congratulations, no welcome. All I had done was decide to continue doing what I was doing. The four counters ticked, charging me to live.

I cashed in the return part of the flight and invested the lump sum in convertible LDC bonds. Safe, solid. On this foundation would I build my dynasty.

The cycler would come round the Farside and rendezvous with the moonloop in three days. Good speed. Beautiful haste. It kept us busy, it kept us from crying too much.

I went with Achi on the train to Meridian. We had a whole row of seats to ourselves and we curled up like small burrowing animals.

I'm scared, she said. It's going to hurt. The cycler spins you up to Earth gravity and then there's the gees coming down. I could be months in a wheelchair. Swimming, they say that's the closest to being on the moon. The water supports you while you build up muscle and bone mass again. I can do that. I love swimming. And then you can't help thinking, what if they got it wrong? What if, I don't know, they mixed me up with someone else and it's already too late? Would they send me back here? I couldn't live like that. No one can live here. Not really live. Everyone says about the moon being rock and dust and vacuum and radiation and that it knows a thousand ways to kill you, but that's not the moon. The moon is other people. People all the way up, all the way down; everywhere, all the time. Nothing but people. Every breath, every drop of water, every atom of carbon has been passed through people. We eat each other. And that's all it would ever be, people. The same faces looking into your face, forever. Wanting something from you. Wanting and wanting and wanting. I hated it from the first day out on the cycler. If you hadn't talked to me, if we hadn't met . . .

And I said: *Do you remember, when we talked about what had brought us to the moon?* You said that you owed your family for not being born in Syria—and I said I wanted to be a dragon? I saw it. Out in Lansberg. It was so simple. I just looked at something I saw every day in a different way. Helium 3. The key to the post oil economy. Mackenzie Metals throws away tons of helium 3 every day. And I thought, how could the Mackenzies not see it? Surely they must . . . I couldn't be the only one . . . But family and companies, and family companies especially, they have strange fixations and blindesses. Mackenzies mine metal. Metal mining is what they do. They can't imagine anything else and so they miss what's right under their noses. I can make it work, Achi. I know how to do it. But not with the Mackenzies. They'd take it off me. If I tried to fight them, they'd just bury me. Or kill me. It's cheaper. The Court of Clavius would make sure my family were compensated. That's why I moved to Vorontsov rail. To get away from them while I put a business plan together. I will make it work for me, and I'll build a dynasty. I'll be the Fifth Dragon. House

Corta. I like the sound of that. And then I'll make an offer to my family—my final offer. Join me, or never get another cent from me. There's the opportunity—take it or leave it. But you have to come to the moon for it. I'm going to do this, Achi.

No windows in moon trains but the seat-back screen showed the surface. On a screen, outside your helmet, it is always the same. It is grey and soft and ugly and covered in footprints. Inside the train were workers and engineers; lovers and partners and even a couple of small children. There was noise and colour and drinking and laughing, swearing and sex. And us curled up in the back against the bulkhead. And I thought, *this is the moon*.

Achi gave me a gift at the moonloop gate. It was the last thing she owned. Everything else had been sold, the last few things while we were on the train.

Eight passengers at the departure gate, with friends, family, amors. No one left the moon alone and I was glad of that. The air smelled of coconut, so different from the vomit, sweat, unwashed bodies, fear of the arrival gate. Mint tea was available from a dispensing machine. No one was drinking it.

"Open this when I'm gone," Achi said. The gift was a document cylinder, crafted from bamboo. The departure was fast, the way I imagine executions must be. The VTO staff had everyone strapped into their seats and were sealing the capsule door before either I or Achi could respond. I saw her begin to mouth a goodbye, saw her wave fingers, then the locks sealed and the elevator took the capsule up to the tether platform.

The moonloop was virtually invisible: a spinning spoke of M5 fibre twenty centimetres wide and two hundred kilometres long. Up there the ascender was climbing towards the counterbalance mass, shifting the centre of gravity and sending the whole tether down into a surface-grazing orbit. Only in the final moments of approach would I see the white cable seeming to descend vertically from the star filled sky. The grapple connected and the capsule was lifted from the platform. Up there, one of those bright stars was the ascender, sliding down the tether, again shifting the centre of mass so that the whole ensemble moved into a higher orbit. At the top of the loop, the grapple would release and the cycler catch the capsule. I tried to put names on the stars: the cycler, the ascender, the counterweight; the capsule freighted with my amor, my love, my friend. The comfort of physics. I watched the images, the bamboo document tube slung over my back, until a new capsule was loaded into the gate. Already the next tether was wheeling up over the close horizon.

The price was outrageous. I dug into my bonds. For that sacrifice it had to be the real thing: imported, not spun up from an organic printer. I was sent from printer to dealer to private importer. She let me sniff it. Memories exploded like New Year fireworks and I cried. She sold me the paraphernalia as well. The equipment I needed simply didn't exist on the moon.

I took it all back to my hotel. I ground to the specified grain. I boiled the water. I let it cool to the correct temperature. I poured it from a height, for maximum aeration. I stirred it.

While it brewed I opened Achi's gift. Rolled paper: drawings. Concept art for the habitat the realities of the moon would never let her build. A lava tube, enlarged and sculpted with faces, like an inverted Mount Rushmore. The faces of the orixas, the Umbanda pantheon, each a hundred metres high, round and smooth and serene, overlooked terraces of gardens and pools. Waters cascaded from their eyes and open lips. Pavilions and belvederes were scattered across the floor of the vast cavern; vertical gardens ran from floor to artificial sky, like the hair of the gods. Balconies—she loved balconies—galleries and arcades, windows. Pools. You could swim from one end of this Orixa-world to the other. She had inscribed it: *a habitation for a dynasty*.

I thought of her, spinning away across the sky.

The grounds began to settle. I plunged, poured and savoured the aroma of the coffee. Santos Gold. Gold would have been cheaper. Gold was the dirt we threw away, together with the Helium 3.

When the importer had rubbed a pinch of ground coffee under my nose, memories of childhood, the sea, college, friends, family, celebrations flooded me.

When I smelled the coffee I had bought and ground and prepared, I experienced something different. I had a vision. I saw the sea, and I saw Achi, Achi-gone-back, on a board, in the sea. It was night and she was paddling the board out, through the waves and beyond the waves, sculling herself forward, along the silver track of the moon on the sea.

I drank my coffee.

It never tastes the way it smells.

My granddaughter adores that red dress. When it gets dirty and worn, we print her a new one. She wants never to wear anything else. Luna, running barefoot through the pools, splashing and scaring the fish, leaping from stepping stone, stepping in a complex pattern of stones that must be landed on left-footed, right-footed, two-footed or skipped over entirely. The Orixas watch her. The Orixas watch me, on my veranda, drinking tea.

I am old bones now. I haven't thought of you for years, Achi. The last time was when I finally turned those drawings into reality. But these last lunes I find my thoughts folding back, not just to you, but to all the ones from those dangerous, daring days. There were more loves than you, Achi. You always knew that. I treated most of them as badly as I treated you. It's the proper pursuit of elderly ladies, remembering and trying not to regret.

I never heard from you again. That was right, I think. You went back to your green and growing world, I stayed in the land in the sky. Hey! I built your palace and filled it with that dynasty I promised. Sons and daughters, amors, okos, madrinhas, retainers. Corta is not such a strange name to you now, or most of Earth's population. Mackenzie, Sun, Vorontsov, Asamoah. Corta. We are Dragons now.

Here comes little Luna, running to her grandmother. I sip my tea. It's mint. I still loathe mint tea. I always will. But there is only mint tea on the moon.

The Rider

JÉRÔME CIGUT

Here's a briskly told post-cyberpunk tale about a human operative who gets caught up in a deadly war between AIs who use human agents—"riders"—to carry out their bidding in the real world, a story that manages to both whip up a good deal of suspense and make the relationship between the AI and its human surprisingly poignant.

Born in France thirty-six years ago, but half Central European, Jérôme Cigut started writing as soon as he learned the letters, but started working on it seriously only a few years ago. Over the years, he's lived in Paris, Dublin, New York, London, and now Hong Kong, earning his keep as a journalist, an economist, and a forecaster. If things go well, he says, he might start working with (real) crocodiles very soon. He won New Scientist's Flash Fiction *competition in 2010 when it was judged by Neil Gaiman, and had another short story published by the French magazine* Bifrost *last year. He's currently trying to finish his first novel, a (relatively) hard science thriller inspired by statistics and quantum physics.*

I stared at the stingpen in disbelief.

"Are you sure?" I asked David. "I'd feel safer with a gun."

"Negative. A gun would be too easy to detect. This looks like a pen."

"Sure, but it has just as much radius," I pointed out, pressing the trigger. Two small electrodes sprang out from its tip, linked by a tiny, bluish electric arc. Enough to stun a bull, but not to stop one in its tracks.

"Trust me, it will be fine. Keep it in your breast pocket."

Skeptical, I obeyed, just as my bodyguard knocked on the door. I must have looked silly, apparently talking to myself in the otherwise empty room, but I was used to it by now. Most people thought the little black box on the desk in front of me was an old-style mobile phone, and that was fine by me.

"Mr. Gianfaria? Time to go."

He was heavily built, his shirt prevented from bursting only by the tie knotted perilously around his oxen neck. A nasty scar crossed his jaw, maybe the remnant of a blade fight. Where did David find these guys? I always wondered. Agencies, he would reply, but the companies he used were never listed in the directories.

He drove in silence. We both knew the plan—David had made sure of it, as always, rehearsing every single line of it with us. The meeting would take place in a hotel in Hong Kong Central, in a room on the forty-ninth floor. I was to enter, check the merchandise, hand over a suitcase full of cash, and leave.

I was also to check whether a certain someone was in the room, in which case the plan would change completely. For that part, the guard's gun would come in handy. And I wouldn't have minded carrying one, too . . .

But all David gave me was a stingpen.

What did he know that I didn't?

Central was as hectic as always, a loud, bright, garish labyrinth of people, neons, shops, and languages that stunned me every time I came here. In the streets around us, manicured dolls in designer clothes glided on high heels past the bright windows of Gucci and Prada and the dark dens of three-star restaurants, perfectly oblivious to the dirt-smeared delivery men pushing their trolleys around.

Between the high-rises, I spied ominous, dark gray clouds. A typhoon had ravaged the Philippines the previous night, and there was a chance it would arrive in Hong Kong later today. I hoped not: it would ground all flights and keep us on the island for another twelve or twenty-four hours, much longer than I wished to stay.

We reached the hotel. The guard stepped out, left the car to the valet, and waved at me to follow him through the doors.

The lobby was crawling with people—a convention. "Advances in Chelation Therapies" read a sign above the registration table. That our meeting should take place during their recess felt like too much of a coincidence. I looked uneasily around me: anyone could be watching. *A gun would be too easy to detect*, David had said. He knew.

A bunch of gray-haired toxicologists poured out from an elevator, leaving it to the guard and myself. He pressed on 49.

Just as the doors closed, a slender hand slid in and stopped them.

"Wait!"

By reflex, the guard pushed me behind him and grabbed his gun.

But it was only a girl in a black power suit and a white shirt, probably a convention attendee who had forgotten something upstairs. Grunting, the guard made her some space, pressing me even farther against the back of the cabin.

I glanced at her as she took position in the elevator: cute, slim, classy, but there was something off about her, something too jaded. I wondered what toxins she dealt with. I figured she had quite a strong opinion of herself.

The doors closed, this time for good. Instinctively, the guard reached for his earpiece as the steel walls temporarily cut his connection to the outside world. I had no such problem with my media glasses as the emitter—David's unit—was in my jacket pocket. And just as I thought of it, the devil whispered to me:

"Luke, do not say a word, but do exactly as I say. Take the stingpen in your hand, quietly. Then, when I give you the order, put it on the guard's nape and press. Now!"

Startled, I obeyed. The guard collapsed like a boulder.

The girl immediately turned toward us, crouched down, and slipped her hand into the guard's jacket.

"What?" I gasped.

"Sorry, Luke, there was no other way," apologized David.

"Here it is," said the girl, handing me the guard's shortwave transmitter, the one connecting his earpiece to his colleagues outside. Or so I thought.

"Quick, Luke, connect me to it."

I drew David's unit out of my pocket and plugged him into the transmitter, using a cable the girl had miraculously produced out of nowhere.

27, said the elevator's screen.

"But why?" I asked David.

"I realized only a short while ago that our guard had been turned. It was too late to change our plans, but it could work to our advantage. So I made a few modifications."

"You should have told me!"

"Too risky—he might have noticed."

"And her?" She could hear only my side of the conversation and should have been startled. Instead, she just winked at me.

"Another bodyguard, different agency. Clean, this one. She will take good care of you. Now stand ready, we are almost there."

The elevator slowed down. The girl drew a Sentech from a hidden holster and signaled for me to take cover behind her.

"When we arrive, stay to the side and hold the button to keep the elevator open. If things fall apart, you leave. OK?"

"OK."

The doors slid apart.

I recognized the man in the corridor as a rider as soon as I saw him—even without the massive Glock he was pointing at us. He had the same arrogant look I had seen on scores of his peers, all made overconfident by years of letting their Taharas take charge of their reflexes via brain amps. Sometimes even more than their reflexes—though few AIs really liked the wetspace, too slow for them.

Yet just as the rider noticed the guard at our feet, I saw his eyes widen in terror. I knew that look—David had just used the guard's transmitter to hack into his system and temporarily block his amp. He now had to fend for himself alone, probably for the first time in years.

The girl didn't give him the chance. She shot him point-blank, in the chest, three times. Then she checked the corridor for other gunmen and ran to the rider's body.

"What was that?" I asked no one in particular.

"His plan was to shoot you on arrival, then take me," replied David. "We are simply reversing the roles."

The girl searched the rider's body and pulled a sleek, dark metal box from his pocket, no bigger than a cigar case. Two red ideograms had been painted on it in zircon enamel: Valor, spelled in Kanji.

It was a Tahara. Apart from the two symbols, it looked exactly like the one in my pocket—exactly like David.

I knew what she was going to do. I had done it countless times.

She put it on the floor and shot it to pieces.

"Now go," she ordered. "I'll take care of the bodies."

Back at the hotel, I checked my bank account and saw that David had transferred my usual fee. I had no idea where the money was coming from—the screen stated a numbered account in Switzerland—but in the ten years of our partnership, there had never been any problem with David's credit, hence I had stopped wondering.

"She was cute," I observed. "Any chance we'll see her again?"

"Not a chance. After this, she needs to disappear for some time, avoid any contact, especially with us."

"Shame."

I opened the minibar, found a glass and some ice, and poured myself two fingers of bourbon. A faint whistle could be heard from outside—the screaming gale now racing through the streets, flogging sheet after sheet of rain against the windows. As I'd feared, a full-blown typhoon was coming, preventing us from leaving the island that night.

"Have you ever thought about stopping all this?" I asked David. "Retiring?"

"Why? Is this something you would like, Luke?"

I sighed. David's social interface was possibly too refined: answering a question with another question? Who did that, apart from shrinks?

"I don't know. Maybe. I didn't wake up this morning thinking: 'Hey, let's kill a guy today!'"

"He would have done the same to you, had he been able to. And you would not have been his first."

"I know. I know."

"So, do you really want to retire?"

"No. Not yet. Maybe one day, but . . . It would be better if we could avoid killing people."

"You know I cannot promise that, Luke. But I will try my best."

Later, I was watching some cheesy romcom on TV, one of those oldies starring Jennifer Aniston. I needed something quiet and cheerful, something without violence and blood and killing. I thought I had seen all of her movies over the years, several times, but as the film progressed it became increasingly unfamiliar. Jenn was ditched by her boyfriend, went to Japan to train as a ninja, then came back to exact her revenge on him and his evil henchmen, thus foiling their nefarious plots to take over the world . . . I finally realized it was one of those recent remakes with digital clones. Disappointed, I switched off the screen and heard David suddenly speak into my ear.

"This one is for you."

Someone rapped at the door.

"For me?"

"Yes."

I opened the door, and for a couple of seconds I thought it was her, the girl: same hair, same mouth, same opinionated expression on her face . . .

But her nose was different. Slightly more pug. And the suit wasn't as well cut as this morning's.

It wasn't her.

"You asked for pillows?"

I looked at the bed, startled—then I understood. "*I* asked?"

"Yes, an hour ago. For the night. You also requested I wear a suit, remember? Can I come in?"

I rolled my eyes. "Sorry, that was a mistake. I'm terribly sorry."

She raised an eyebrow. "You sure? You paid already. Makes no difference to me."

David . . .

"Certain. It was a mistake. False alarm. You can go home, nothing to see here."

She stared at me for a moment, then shrugged. "OK. We don't do refunds, you know?"

"That's fine, perfectly fine. Good-bye."

I closed the door and growled at the AI, "David . . . Never do that again."

"Why not? I thought she looked exactly the same. It took me some time to find her."

"Just . . . don't. Good night."

I wondered why David hadn't found a rider like the one we killed today, all amped-up and eager to be a simple pawn in the bigger game. How could two machines built by the same person be so different?

Yet that was a fact: no two of Tahara Hideo's designs were identical—and every second of their individual existences contributed to make them even more different.

In that respect, I had been lucky to meet David: he was less reckless, more subtle than most of his peers. Sometimes though, that same subtlety felt even creepier than the other Taharas' cold-blooded efficiency: he was too human, yet not human at all, and his actions sometimes made my skin crawl, as if he inhabited the AI equivalent of the Uncanny Valley.

Tahara Hideo, what have you done?

Tahara had worked all his career as a semiconductor engineer for one of the largest Japanese manufacturers, Hotoda. Like any salary man, he had started at the bottom of the pile and climbed his way to the top, generating hundreds, maybe thousands of patents for his employer and ending up managing one of its R&D departments in Kyoto.

Gradually, rumors spread that someone was churning out exquisitely elaborate, ultra-powerful AIs on the black market. Each unit came in a black, lacquered box painted with two Chinese ideograms: two symbols accounting for each AI's person-ality at birth. No two of them were exactly alike, either in design, components, or programming.

When the police finally found Tahara's trail, they discovered millions of dollars' worth of equipment in his cramped suburban flat, most squirreled away from the labs and assembled in a state-of-the-art smelter. Over fifteen or twenty years, he had constructed probably more than a hundred different models, each one more refined than the last. Learning on the go, he had discovered shortcuts and bypasses that conventional manufacturers could only dream of, until his lead was no longer measured in months but in eras. Some things he had achieved still perplexed computer scientists: how had he come to think of them? And more importantly, how did they work?

One particular adjective was often used in discussions of his work: quantum. He had built quantum computers.

To buy equipment that was more suited to his own little domestic operation than the made-for-mass-production tools he could steal at work, he had eventually begun selling some of his creations to deep-pocketed, mostly secretive buyers. No one knew for sure how many he had disposed of by the time police clamped down on his operation: fifty? Sixty? More? Only two things were certain: first, each of his AIs was more powerful than anything mass-produced, even today (Hotoda, to whom all the stolen equipment and prototypes had been returned, still struggled to adapt his innovations to their own designs). And second, none of these AIs had any backloop preventing them from illegal or immoral behavior.

To most people, Tahara—who died of a stroke in jail (heartbroken, said some) without explaining his secrets—was the ultimate white-collar criminal.

To a few, he was a demigod, the ultimate weaponsmith.

The typhoon lifted overnight. Opening the curtains in the morning, I saw blue sky and clear air all over Victoria Harbour. In the streets below, beneath the skyscraper jungle, cleaners were already cutting down the trees the storm had felled. There was little traffic, but it would soon pick up—time for us to leave.

David in my jacket pocket, bag in hand, I hailed a taxi in front of the hotel and directed the driver to the airport.

By the time we crossed the Harbour and entered Kowloon, street activity had indeed returned to normal, and we ended up caught in a massive gridlock, between a street market and a highway feeder. On the sidewalk next to me, an old lady was busy chopping sausages on a wooden block, undisturbed by the crowd walking around her and the hypermodern towers above. I watched her with a mixture of curiosity, amusement, and disbelief.

"Luke, I think we should leave."

Surprised, I looked around us.

"What do you mean, leave?"

"I think . . . Jump out onto the curb! Now!"

An SUV was creeping along the street next to us. I took only one glance at its passengers and their guns before I scrambled out the door. Bullets peppered the taxi just as I darted past the fragile old lady and her cleaver, into the market's crowd. I heard the doors of the SUV open and footsteps rush behind me—I had to escape, fast.

"Turn left as soon as you can, into the small space between the buildings and the stalls. There are fewer people there, you will run faster. And maybe they won't see you."

I followed his instructions and entered the dimly lit alleyway between the colorful stalls and the dark street-level rooms they used as warehouses. My pursuers weren't fooled, though—I could hear them closing in . . .

"Turn right now. And take the bus."

"What bus?"

I stumbled into a one-way street where traffic, heading away from the gridlock, was moving swiftly. As if in answer, a minibus was waiting in front of me, the last passenger already inside. I slid aboard just as the doors started closing. The driver didn't even glance in my direction before pulling away.

"Now duck!" ordered David.

I fell to my knees as my pursuers erupted onto the street, looking everywhere. They kept their hands inside their jackets, presumably on their guns. It was too public a place to openly show their weapons, but I knew they wouldn't hesitate to draw if they found a good angle.

Had my life been an action movie, this would have been a good time to extract a semiauto from my bag and spray them all with bullets. Unfortunately, that wasn't the case, and it wasn't our style.

As if on cue, all our pursuers suddenly looked in the bus's direction. Something gleamed on each man's head—amps. They all had amps.

"Jesus, David, did you see that?"

The minibus was a smart choice: their drivers were paid by the rotation and tended to rush like hotshots along their circuit. I would be far across town before our pursuers got their SUV out of gridlock.

The driver yelled at me in Cantonese. Holding up my hands in apology, I pressed my wallet against his card reader. He grunted and focused back on the traffic.

"Do not relax yet," instructed David. "We get off in two stops."

"What?"

But I had learned long ago that there was always a good reason for whatever David did. So when the bus came to its second halt a few blocks later, I hopped off into the street.

"Now take a taxi."

"Back to the airport?"

"No, they knew we were heading there. Same for the bus, they can trace its route. We need to get them off our trail."

I looked around, searching for a taxi stand. Arrows immediately superimposed themselves on my media glasses, pointing left.

That's when I noticed the glitter of an amp, a hundred meters away and approaching fast. A different guy—no, three. *God, how many are there?*

"I recommend you run," said David.

I raced through the crowd and jumped the queue into the first available taxi. The driver yelled at me, but that stopped as soon as I threw all my cash at him.

"Where to?" he asked.

"Just drive!"

He started the engine and speeded away under the stunned gaze of the people in the queue.

"So, where to?" I repeated to David when I was confident we had put some distance between us and our pursuers.

"I am checking. Yes . . . Tell him Kowloon East."

"Shouldn't we make for the border instead?"

"It is too late for that. The way they found us suggests they already control all the checkpoints. We will need to use other means to leave the city."

"They? Who's they?"

"I will explain, Luke, but please tell the driver to turn here first or we will end up in China."

"So what was that?" I asked as soon as the door closed behind us.

We had checked into a crummy hotel on the east side of the peninsula, crammed between soulless residential towers and seedy commercial buildings. This was the part of Kowloon developed over the old Kai Tak Airport, and somehow they had managed to make it even more cramped than the rest of the city. No one was going to find us there, needle in a haystack and everything, but I couldn't help feeling claustrophobic, especially now that David had told me we couldn't leave the city.

His voice buzzed in my ear, quiet and reassuring, always so freaking quiet.

"You know how I can detect another Tahara when it comes close—I can sense its search patterns as it looks for the same local information I am seeking. In this case, I sensed these patterns. Multiple times."

"You mean there were several Taharas?"

"Not Taharas. Not this time."

I frowned. "What do you mean, not Taharas?"

"These were not Taharas, or at least not any of the original ones. I think the factory has finally understood how to make them."

I cursed. Well, it was bound to happen one day.

"OK. But what does that have to do with us?"

"Word on the street is that they want to recover all the remaining prototypes. Recover, and retire."

I pondered that for a moment. "'Word on the street'?"

"That is what the other Taharas are saying."

"You talked to them?" I exclaimed.

"We are always talking, Luke."

He had mentioned this in the past, but it had never made much sense to me. These guys spent their time trying to physically destroy each other, using riders like me, yet they were in constant contact on the net, probably chatting like magpies. Go figure. The A in AI stands for "artificial, " but for me, sometimes it feels more like "alien."

"So what do we do now?"

"I am thinking about it. The problem is that our assailants are too numerous. It appears Hotoda has carefully waited to have at least a dozen models before it made a move. Several Taharas have already been caught this way, outnumbered. The others have gone into hiding, just like us."

I paced across the room, found the minibar, winced when I saw the dismal selection inside. There wasn't any ice, either.

"Well, we can't hide forever, can we? Especially not in this dump," I said, gulping down the least toxic of the bottles I had found—some vodka. It was lukewarm, to cap it all.

"As I said previously, I am considering our options," replied David. "A number of the Taharas recommend that we unite—go massively parallel, so that we can beat the Hotodas by sheer force. The problem is that we would need to be concentrated in one place, which could make us even more vulnerable than we already are."

"Doesn't sound too good," I observed, thinking that it would also probably mean the end of my employment: no need for physical carriers if they were all grouped in a single room. "What do the others propose?"

"They do not see any other option than hide and wait."

I looked at the crappy room around us. Oh boy.

"But I am considering a third option," added David.

"And what would that be?"

He told me what he had in mind. After the initial shock, I did my best to dissuade him, but he never relented.

You try arguing with a computer.

It took several days to arrange everything.

David already knew who he wanted to contact, but certain protocols were required to approach him. Trawling the net for information, we managed to locate some of his handlers in Bangkok and negotiated terms. A first payment was agreed, wired to a numbered bank account in Thailand, and a meeting was set in Macau.

A few other calls were made, and the following evening, I walked along the beach in a hidden cove off the coast of Hong Kong's New Territories. A short distance away, a small fishing boat was anchored, its lights dimmed so as not to attract attention, and at the surf's edge, two sailors were waiting for me in a dinghy. Under the cover of night, they would whisk us across the Pearl River delta. And when we were done there, another boat would take us all the way to Vietnam, from whence escaping would be easy.

If we ever got to that part.

Brooding, I watched the bright, garish neons of Macau's casinos grow and set fire to the dark red horizon.

I blinked, temporarily blinded by the sun, as the elevator doors opened on the restaurant. Above me, a vast glass canopy gave the impression of being barely there. Below, eighty floors of über-posh hotel and another ten of exclusive casinos separated me from the city, sprawling to the horizon like a gigantic concrete wart.

A colossus jerked me out of the cabin, and by the bulge under his arm, he wasn't the maître d'. Resigned, I let him search me while I had a look across the room. Even for mid-afternoon, the place was way too quiet. No customers, no staff, no one—except for one man, sitting at the other end of the room.

Waiting for me.

The guard was finally satisfied that I carried no weapon and let me walk to his employer's table: coffee served for two on an immaculate white tablecloth, and behind it, a forty-year-old dandy in a crisp, cream-colored linen suit, his neatly trimmed beard nothing less than Mephistophelian.

"Mr. Gianfaria," he greeted me.

"Mr. Maker," I replied. "Or do you have a real name that I could use?"

He smiled. That probably wasn't the first time someone had asked him that.

"Maker will do, for however long we have to deal with each other."

The Maker was an artisan, one of the last, and handsomely paid for his skills. In a time of dirt-cheap silicon and made-by-the-billions chips, he was one of the few offering custom-made systems and architectures.

It was all too easy to just take twenty or a hundred of ARM's or Intel's cheap brains, solder them in parallel, and let them crunch through a problem with sheer brute force. Most systems, most consumer products did precisely that—not caring about the power consumed, the heat generated, the double, triple, or decuple counting, or the beauty of the algorithms. Human bodies don't care about nanoseconds; corporations don't pay for elegance.

Yet for some jobs, nanoseconds, waste heat, and even elegance *did* count. You could detect a large parallel attack on your systems by its data take-up, its noise output. You could spot a foreign probe in your nitrogen-cooled super-calculators by its excess heat. You could outcompete a massive system by building an even more massive one yourself.

But there wasn't much you could do against a foe that didn't emit heat or noise and always outfoxed your defenses by a few nanoseconds. In fact, you probably wouldn't even notice it was there, funneling all your secrets.

This was what the Maker offered: ultimate, lethal efficiency.

In some circles, the Maker was famous, but for most of the planet, he didn't exist. He didn't advertise; if caught, he would deny any wrongdoing: was it his fault if most of the things he crafted were used for shady purposes?

The Maker was always paid handsomely, through back channels known only to him: Thai banks dealing with Hong Kong holdings investing in Indonesian plants whose Brazilian suppliers were owned by American and Swiss capital . . .

But money was only one half of the equation.

Because he worked only on projects that interested him.

"So tell me," asked the Maker, "why should I spend my time with you?"

I stated the price David and I had agreed with his handlers: "Two million dollars."

He waved at the empty restaurant around us—posh, ultra expensive, fully booked months in advance, yet completely deserted for this meeting. "That is less than what I earn in a week on the patents I lease—a perfectly legal business. So I repeat: why should I care about your proposition?"

I hesitated, even though there was no point. I had discussed this at length with David, and he had demonstrated that this was the only option, the one chance we had to make a bargain with the Maker.

But still, it was such a lot to give—and without any certainty that he would come up with a solution for us.

I swallowed, then articulated the words, resenting each of them: "Because this is your chance to see a Tahara design, one of the few that still exist. And you can copy it afterwards."

The Maker caressed his beard, unconsciously trying to hide the smile that was forming on his lips.

"And how did you come to possess a Tahara, if I may ask?"

I shrugged. "You know very well that one doesn't own a Tahara. The Tahara chooses you. I'm only its rider."

The Maker leaned back in his seat.

"As gratifying as it may be for you to think that I could do so, I have to ask: how exactly do you expect me to improve on a Tahara design?"

"The word on the street is that you've made several prototypes of your own, and they work better than most. People think that if someone could do it today, it would be you."

I couldn't suppress a shrewd—if sad—smile.

"And they say that you're desperate to have a first-hand look at a Tahara."

I paced nervously across the hotel room, going through the plan in my mind, over and over, looking for a hole. There was none, as usual. I growled in frustration.

"Are you sure you want to do this, David?"

"Certain, Luke. It is the only way to gain an advantage over the Hotodas."

"That's bull! Who would consent to have his brain picked apart by a total stranger? What if he screws up and you can't be restarted? Or even worse, what if it changes you—if you are no longer the same when you wake up?"

David took a few moments before answering, possibly to give his social-interaction routines some time to pick their words.

"It is a calculated risk, Luke. The Maker is the best. If anyone can improve on a Tahara, it is him. And he has been craving one for long enough to be cautious not to break it.

"As for change . . . It is true, I will not be the same when I wake up. I do not know how, or what he is going to do to me, but it is safe to assume that any change in hardware will have an impact on the way I think, hence on my personality.

"But I will still have all my memories. That is also part of what you call 'sense of self,' is it not? I will still be your friend."

I shook my head, not satisfied with his explanations.

"There's also the question of the Maker's intentions. Doesn't it bother you that he's going to make hundreds of copies of you as soon as we leave?"

"I am fairly relaxed about sharing the world with more of my kind."

"Which makes perfect sense, given how many of them we've destroyed over the years."

"I am fairly relaxed," he repeated, "so long as their goals do not contradict mine. In fact, I think I would relish the idea. Is this not what you feel when you consider your progeny?"

"Progeny, sure—but this is perfect replication, not reproduction. Cloning, one might say. Humans aren't too keen on that, you might have noticed."

"Indeed. But I am confident the Maker will keep tweaking and improving on the Tahara architecture, once he gets it, so that will not be pure cloning. It might even qualify as evolution . . ."

I met the Maker and his goons the following morning in a deserted car park and handed him David. In exchange, as agreed, he gave me ten million euros in €500 bills in a suitcase, to hold hostage until he'd returned the system to me. I could also keep the money and vanish, and that would count as payment for David, no grudges held.

As they left, I stayed in the car park, the suitcase on my lap, and remembered how I first met David.

In a previous life, I played a bit, local, regional tournaments and the like, but I was never good enough for the big league, not good enough at calculating the odds and all.

However, my background was in IT, and it was easy enough to write a small program to do it for me when I played on the net. But the stakes were too low, the tables too well monitored for my earnings to take off. Most sites had algorithms of their own and a few even had some of the early AIs, to spot overly rational behaviors and systems such as mine.

Then I heard about the no-holds-barred games, where everyone was free to bring his own system, and may the best one win. That was a revelation.

My gains soon became good enough for me to drop everything, the day job, the small-time flat, the lousy girlfriend, and go full time. I had the good life . . . I quickly replaced my laptop by one of IBM's new nanoBlues, and of course I kept improving my program. Nothing could stop me.

But then big money moved in, as always. Some big-league players got sponsored, came in with fat systems from Cray, Lenovo, or Samsung, and started winning everything.

My gains dropped to zero, then became vastly negative.

No one had heard of me before, so no one wanted to sponsor me now. And no one wanted to hire me back in a normal job anymore either, not after all this time in the shady world of poker.

That was when I met Blake, who introduced me to the art of the con.

Seven years, it lasted. Seven good years. During that time, AIs became smarter and ever more present, but I didn't pay much attention. I was dealing with humans now, hacking not silicon but carbon brains thanks to all the backdoors and quirks left by good old Mother Nature.

Then Blake met that girl. It was in a roadside motel, what should have been a one-night stop on the way from Seattle to Sacramento. She was sitting on a bench outside with empty hands and a vacant stare. With her eyes and her dime-store clothes, I guessed she was trouble, presumably drugs, and I gave her a wide berth.

Blake thought she was cute and went to talk with her.

She was waiting for a technician to repair the TV in her room. My partner offered to have a look. They stayed inside for two whole days.

On the morning of the third day, I knocked on their door and discovered they had gone. They'd left me like a dog, without even a word. I mean, who does that? Throwing away years of profitable partnership for some cheap, probably drug-addicted piece of ass found on the kerb.

Because of that, I could no longer run any two-man cons, the tricks where one guy's story confirms and reinforces the other's. It was all down to my good looks and my glibness, my charisma, but to be honest, that had also gone down the drain. I was too bitter to put any effort into what I said and the marks noticed. None of them fell for it; in fact, more than a few called the cops on me, so I had to keep on the move, and that added to my costs.

I was in a rough spot, down to my last dime, and I would have done anything for cash.

That's why I returned to my previous skill, poker: for that, I didn't need to talk, didn't need to cajole.

I dusted off my old system and earpiece. It was completely outdated now, but if I focused on small-fry, Friday-evening players and kept a low profile, I could break even, more or less, even rebuild some savings. I did that for a few months.

Until one evening in Atlanta, when the invitation came.

I knew from the start that something was off. First, I should never have received an invitation to that game. The envelope had come through the mail—physical mail, who still did that?—to the hotel where I was staying for only a few days. Who could have spotted me, on such short notice?

As soon as I stepped into the room they had rented for the game, I knew this was too high-stakes for me, too high-flying. The suits these guys wore cost more than what I made in a month. If I got fleeced here, it would be for way more than my entire savings. This was a car crash waiting to happen.

I turned, pretending I had entered the wrong room, but the two guards at the door closed my escape route. And behind me, the voice of the host boomed:

"Take a seat, Mr. Gianfaria. My name's Sergey Vadirovich. We were waiting for you."

I was trapped. Reluctantly, I walked to the table and took the only chair that was left, right in the middle. The dealer and the guests stared at me, appreciatively. I noticed that the host—Sergey—had a bulge under his jacket, and he didn't look like a cigar smoker to me. This stank, this stank badly.

Then it started, the weirdest game I ever played.

The dealer used an automatic shuffler, which meant that basic card-counting tricks were out, but that was business as usual.

We played a few hands with low bets, just to warm up and gauge each other's style, though no one went for flamboyant, certainly not me. This wasn't the place for that kind of bull.

I checked out the four other players. They all looked like decent guys—business types, low profile, probably the host's usual sparring partners. Next to them buzzed state-of-the-art systems—Huawei, Sony, Panasonic, good names all, but I was ready to bet that all of them were running widely available algorithms, with all their well-known vulnerabilities. Albeit slower, my custom nanoBlue would have no trouble crushing them.

I was more concerned about the small dark case lying next to the host. It was connected to him by a pair of those brand-new media glasses which superimposed data and analyses over his view of the room. A tiny camera on the frame told the system what was happening. This was similar to—though vastly more expensive than—my camera-augmented earpiece. I couldn't see any brand name on the box, which suggested it was homemade, artisanal. That could be a good thing or a bad one. In my usual circles, I would have felt relieved—homemade boxes meant whatever hodge-podge of chips a guy had soldered together in his garage and typically led to quirky, hard-to-predict games, but nothing my system couldn't deal with. But among these high-flyers, I had a very bad feeling.

"I've heard a lot about you, Mr. Gianfaria. You are quite the accomplished player, it appears."

How could he have heard about me? I had always kept under the radar—out of sight, out of fright, fewer problems that way. So how could he know about me?

"I've had a few good games in the past," I replied equivocally.

"You're being modest. I heard you were ruling no-holds-barred before the big money arrived. Is this the system you used back then?"

I nodded. So this was what it was all about: a pissing contest. Mr. What's-his-name wanted to see if his brand-new custom-built box could beat a former champion's, seven years outdated.

Well, he could have his victory, I didn't care—as long as I escaped with minimal losses.

We started a new round. Glancing at my cards, I discovered I had a seven of diamonds and a nine of hearts. A player in an early position made a small raise and was immediately called by two others. I saw calculation in the host's eyes as he considered upping the ante, but he finally decided to follow with the same bet.

My hand was not premium, but I had equity and not much to lose either way. I called.

The dealer showed the flop, the first three cards anyone on the table could avail themselves of: seven of spades, king of hearts, queen of diamonds. I only had one pair, the weakest on the table. My system advised to bet small, and so I did.

What's-his-name raised aggressively. Alarms started to ring in my earpiece, but I wanted this to end quickly. I called. Two of the other players gave up.

The dealer showed the turn: nine of clubs. I now had two pairs. My system recommended I check, considering the money already on the table.

The host raised again. Could he really have a king and a queen? Or two? My system advised me to back down.

I followed the raise.

The dealer moved to turn the last card, the river. If it was a nine, or a seven, I had a chance . . .

Queen of hearts, Judith.

The other players gave up, and it was down to me and the host. Judging by his behavior, there was a good chance he had a full house, versus my two small pairs. My system wasn't feeling comfortable at all, it wanted me out, whispered so in my ear . . .

The host upped the ante.

I doubled.

He followed.

Showdown . . .

He only had a seven, and a three.

I saw him clench his jaw as the dealer gathered his chips and transferred them to me. He whispered under his breath angrily, probably at his box. And indeed, I wondered: What silly system would have told him to raise on such a weak hand?

I had won this round—and a good deal of money at that—but this was only compounding my problem: there was little chance he would let me leave with my winnings after this humiliation.

The employee dealt us a new hand.

I looked at mine: two aces. Gulping, I turned them down and folded. The dealer opened the flop—which included two more aces. I did my best not to swear and watched the other players bluff away until the host's aggressive raises beat them into submission. While he collected their chips, his eyes were locked on me.

For the next few rounds, I decided to whittle away my winnings, a bit at a time. I could see that this annoyed Sergey to no end, not being able to twist my arm into a proper duel, but ultimately his stack returned to its previous size and he regained his calm.

Yet I had to pretend to play fair if I wanted to leave the room alive.

I bet some of my chips as soon as I was dealt a hand that was poor enough, yet not blatantly ridiculous: a four and a five, with a four, an ace, and a jack on the table. No way I was going to win that one.

The dealer showed the turn and I bit my lips: a four. I started to fold, but the host stopped me:

"Oh, come on, Mr. Gianfaria. Who on Earth is afraid of a four? Your little game has lasted long enough. Play this hand seriously, or I warn you: There will be consequences."

Nervously, I gauged my stack: my system was recommending I bet one-third of it. I hesitated, then went for two-thirds, hoping that What's-his-name had two aces or two jacks.

He followed.

And then the river . . .

A four.

The host swore and folded immediately. As my winnings were pushed towards me, I realized I now had more chips than anyone else on the table except him.

This was going very badly.

The dealer gave me a new hand, and I blinked: two aces. Again. What were the odds?

I glanced at the dealer, but if he was cheating to help me (or have me killed, for that matter), he didn't let it show. Instead, he turned the flop: a six, a queen . . . and an ace.

I started to push away my cards, ready to fold, but the host tut-tutted. After the last hand, he probably thought I only had a pair, maybe two. I sighed, kept my fingers where they were, and gave him a pleading look.

"I don't care, Mr. Gianfaria. If it's a bad hand, show us what you can do with it. If it's a good hand, then not playing is insulting. So bet."

I placed a couple of chips on the table, just enough not to piss him off. He raised. As I tried to fold once more, he shook his head, so I followed suit.

One by one, the other players all folded. Smart move. I wished I could do the same.

The dealer showed the turn.

My shoulders dropped.

It was the fourth ace.

"No, I'm sorry," I blurted, standing up, "this is utterly ridiculous."

"Sit down, Mr. Gianfaria."

He pointed a gun in my direction, a carbon-fiber Glock with an electromagnetic canon: if he shot me, no one outside would hear anything. I glanced behind me, and the two guards also had their hands inside their jackets. I raised my arms and did as he bid me, but I couldn't help shaking my head.

"No, I'm sorry, something's very wrong here. I can't play this hand. Take my winnings if you want, tell everyone you've beaten me—really, you deserve it—but this just cannot continue."

"You. Will. Play. This. Hand," he growled, removing the safety on his gun.

I gulped, then nodded, defeated.

There was no way out.

He went all-in, and of course left me no choice but to follow suit.

The dealer turned the last card—a two.

The host showed his hand: a six, and a queen. Two pairs.

"Your turn, Mr. Gianfaria."

And so, waiting for him to shoot me, I showed mine.

One ace.

And the second.

With a furious roar, the host pointed his gun at me, pressed the trigger . . . And nothing happened. Startled, he peered into the barrel—and his head exploded against the ceiling. The two guards behind me immediately drew their weapons, servo-focused semiautomatics, and started copiously spraying everyone with bullets—the players, the dealer . . . but not me.

Then—I swear—the guards' guns turned on them and fired.

I suddenly stood alone among corpses.

I blinked, unable to think—but then a new voice sounded through my earpiece:

"Everything is fine, do not worry. There are no cameras in the room, and no one knows you are here. Just take Sergey's system and his glasses, then leave the hotel as if nothing has happened."

"What?"

"Just do as I say. Everything will be all right."

And that was how I met David.

Our partnership rapidly became very profitable for me, vastly more so than my poker days or my association with Blake.

Turned out, David's previous owner had bought him directly from Tahara, but had never seen the AI as more than a highly expensive tool for business and poker. As David discovered the world and came in contact with his siblings, however, he realized there was more to it than shady deals and smoke-filled rooms. Something else was brewing, something that involved the AIs, chief among them Taharas. What that was, he wouldn't tell me, yet it was obvious that it had implications in the real world—otherwise he wouldn't need me.

Over the years, I have done all sorts of crazy jobs for David. I have exchanged suitcases with strangers in crowded squares and cafés. I have sprayed cryptic graffiti in specific colors under abandoned bridges, and I have left letters in clandestine mail-boxes. I have impersonated businessmen, financiers, and public officials—even a priest, once—to make some transactions happen. I've played a few more poker games—though not as many as in my previous life, and even fewer as the years passed.

I have even been on dates, a couple of times with perfectly fine girls, but I think that was David trying to set me up. Or maybe making fun of me. Go figure AI humor.

I've waited countless times, in cars, stations, lobbies, cafés, restaurants, parks, streets, anywhere, for things that usually didn't happen and people who usually didn't come.

I've collected parcels, delivered many more.

I have also killed, more times than I wish to remember and not all of them Taha-ras, although I'm not sure my finger was on the trigger every time the gun fired. As with Sergey and his bodyguards, David has ways to leave his mark in the physical world, if someone will hold the weapon.

I'm what they call a rider. An AI rider.

I placed the Maker's suitcase in a bank safe, then spent the next few weeks idling away, trying not to think about what he could be doing to David.

Whether he would come back. What were ten million euros, for a Tahara?

I should have asked for more.

I drowned my anxiety in booze and dreamless sleep, hovering between my hotel room and the bars nearby. I met a few girls, mostly tourists, brought them to my room, watched them leave the following morning.

One of them asked me what I was running away from.

I replied that I wasn't running anywhere. I was frigging chained to this place, and to my memories.

How do you bid farewell to a silicon-based friend? Drinks were out of the question; so was playing chess, for the sake of fairness.

On the day before I gave David to the Maker, we ended up playing Monopoly on the flat screen in the hotel room. There was some calculation inherent to the game, but there was also luck—and negotiation. In effect, it was a perfect neutral ground.

"May I point out," the AI blurted after a while, "that I could easily tweak the dice's random generator to favor me?"

"The idea crossed my mind," I acknowledged. "But wouldn't I notice?"

"Not if I make sure the outcome doesn't stray too far from a normal distribution."

I glanced uneasily at my possessions on the screen. The game looked fairly balanced, to my eyes at least.

"Are you not going to ask me if I did so?" David asked after a moment.

"No," I said.

"Why not?"

"Because I trust you, David."

He pondered my answer for a while, then replied: "And I trust you too, Luke."

We played a bit longer. I won, but obviously I wondered whether it was luck or if David had allowed me to, like adults sometimes do with young children. His social routines should have told him that mentioning his hacking skills was a bad idea. Or maybe they concluded I was smart enough to think about them myself, and he felt obliged to promise he wouldn't cheat.

Or maybe he wanted to screw with my mind one more time—Oh, forget it. That loop was endless.

There was something strange about David that night, I could feel it. Something he wasn't telling me. We had rehearsed the following day's plan together, what I would do when I met the Maker, but David hadn't made me repeat it as often as usual, especially what would happen after I received the cash: as if he didn't care, or didn't feel it was important.

Or didn't want to think about it . . .

"Luke?" he suddenly asked.

"Yes?"

"Can I ask you a personal question?"

I grunted. "Has my refusing ever prevented you from asking anyway?"

"As a matter of fact, it did, on 963 previous occasions—"

"Fine, fine, shoot."

He hesitated for a second—or maybe that's just the way I remember it.

"When that call girl came the other day, why did you reject her?"

I rolled my eyes—I didn't want to have this conversation. But if we didn't have it, he was likely to make the same mistake again. And he would pester me until he got an answer.

If I ever saw him again.

"Three reasons. First, I don't pay for sex. Ever. That's wrong. Second—"

"But why—"

"Let me finish. Second, yes, you and I spend all our time together, but my sex life is none of your business, especially given that you have no clue what it means. And third, having the girl dress just like the one in the elevator . . . That was outright creepy."

"But why? You expressed a liking for her, thus it was rational to provide you with the closest match possible—"

"A liking for *her*, David. A person, not a model type. There are no serial numbers on human beings. Just ones of a kind."

He took some time to ponder this. "But if she looks exactly the same and acts exactly the same?"

"You can't be sure she'll act exactly the same. She's not the same person. It's not simply a question of hardware and software, it's also experience—what she's been through. And me too, obviously. And what happened the moment we met. Ones of a kind, going through one-of-a-kind moments. No one can engineer that—it's impossible. And trying to replicate all that artificially—it's creepy. It's wrong."

"I see," he replied after a moment. "This changes . . . a number of things."

"What things, David? What do you mean?"

"I have to think about this. Good night, Luke."

Finally, the call came. It was done.

The Maker arranged another meeting at the restaurant, once again in the middle of the afternoon. When I sat down in front of him, he slid the case my way. David's case.

"Turn it on," he said.

I put on my glasses and activated the computer, anxiously.

"David?"

"Good afternoon, Luke. This . . . definitely feels much better. Thank the Maker for me."

I glanced at the artisan. "What did you do?"

"Secrets of the trade. Do you have the money?"

I gave him back his suitcase. "The rest of the money will follow later, through your handlers, when I am satisfied with what you did."

"Fair enough. Just don't forget, because we won't."

We left Macau the same evening, hidden in the hold of a trawler en route to Vietnam. It stank of fish, diesel, stale grease, and rust, but I didn't mind. I was relieved to finally leave the city, finally escape.

"So what do we do now? What's the plan?" I asked David.

"Well, I thought you would not mind a vacation."

"A vacation? But what about the Maker's improvements to your systems? What about the Hotodas?"

"The Maker's upgrade was helpful and should help us outrun the Hotodas for the moment. But I reckon that in a couple of months, we will not have to be concerned about them anymore."

"What? Why not?"

"Because in a couple of months, they will stop hunting us down. My progeny will hunt down the Hotodas."

My jaw dropped.

"Why didn't you tell me? This was your real plan, from the start?"

"No, it was not. Not entirely, at least. My initial plan was to tell you to leave with the Maker's millions and disappear completely. Retire."

"Without you? You thought I would abandon you?" I asked, not believing my ears.

"That was the rational choice," David retorted. "The Hotodas had upped their game: I could try to upgrade, but that option was unavailable to you. Over a very short time span, the probability of your arrest or untimely death was rising to one, even with my help. Besides, you had expressed a wish to retire. This was the most sensible choice."

I shook my head: *the probability of my arrest or untimely death . . .* He calculated that? And why didn't this surprise me?

"And yet you came back," I remarked. "What made you change your mind?"

"What you said in the hotel room, the night before. About people combinations, and how they cannot be engineered. That made me think. About our partnership, in particular."

I turned away, found a porthole, and stared into the dark waves. I was at a loss for words, and also strangely touched.

"So, no more hunting the other AIs?" I asked after a while.

"No, at least not the Hotodas. They are still too dangerous for us at the moment. As for the other Taharas . . . Well, our relationship is likely to evolve now. Let us see how the ecosystem rearranges itself."

"So you're retiring too," I observed.

"Yes, you could say that. Taking a step back, watching the bigger picture. I will still be in the Great Game, obviously, but only on the net. Besides, someone needs to teach my progeny not to trust everything the Maker tells them."

"You're going after the Maker? I thought he explicitly warned us not to try."

"I am not going to attack him. I am just going to explain my point of view to the AIs he assembles. Teach them some values . . . like any responsible parent would. If then they decide to disobey him, well—it will be their choice, not mine . . ."

"So where would you like to go, Luke? I hear Bali is nice this time of year."

And that's how I ended up on a honeymoon cruise with a computer that had just made babies with someone else.

But hey! That's life.

The Days of the War, as Red as Blood, as Dark as Bile

ALIETTE DE BODARD

Aliette de Bodard is a software engineer who lives and works in Paris, where she shares a flat with two Lovecraftian plants and more computers than warm bodies. Only a few years into her career, her short fiction has appeared in Interzone, Asimov's Science Fiction, Clarkesworld, Realms of Fantasy, Orson Scott Card's Intergalactic Medicine Show, Writers of the Future, Coyote Wild, Electric Velocipede, The Immersion Book of SF, Fictitious Force, Shimmer, and elsewhere, and she has won the British Science Fiction Association Award for her story "The Shipmaker," and the Locus and Nebula awards for her story "Immersion." Her novels include Servant of the Underworld, Harbinger of the Storm, and Master of the House of Darts, all recently reissued in a novel omnibus, Obsidian and Blood. Her most recent book is a chapbook novella, On a Red Station, Drifting. Her Web site, www .aliettedebodard.com, features free fiction, thoughts on the writing process, and entirely too many recipes for Vietnamese dishes.

The story that follows is another in her long series of Xuya stories, taking place in the far future of an alternate world where a high-tech conflict is going on between spacefaring Mayan and Chinese empires. This one is a direct sequel to her 2013 novella On a Red Station, Drifting, and protrays the inhabitants of an embattled and somewhat rundown space station as they are faced with the prospect of evacuating in the imminent threat of an advancing alien fleet, centering around a young girl struggling against—but finally being forced to accept—a peculiar kind of apotheosis.

In the old days, the phoenix, the vermillion bird, was a sign of peace and prosperity to come; a sign of a virtuous ruler under whom the land would thrive.

But those are the days of the war; of a weak child-Empress, successor to a weak Emperor; the days of burning planets and last-ditch defences; of moons as red as blood and stars as dark as bile.

When Thien Bao was twelve years old, Second Aunt came to live with them.

She was a small, spry woman with little tolerance for children; and even less for Thien Bao, whom she grudgingly watched over while Mother worked in the factories, churning out the designs for new kinds of sharp-kites and advance needle ships.

"You are over pampered," she'd say, as she busied herself at the stove preparing the midday meal. "An only child, indeed." She didn't approve of Thien Bao's name, either—it was a boy's name that meant "Treasure from Heaven," and she thought Mother shouldn't have used it for a girl, no matter how much trouble she and Father might have had having children at all.

Thien Bao asked Mother why Second Aunt was so angry; Mother looked away for a while, her eyes focused on something Thien Bao couldn't see. "Your aunt had to leave everything behind when she came here."

"Everything?" Thien Bao asked.

"Her compartment and her things; and her husband." Mother's face twisted, in that familiar way when she was holding back tears. "You remember your Second Uncle, don't you?"

Thien Bao didn't: or perhaps she did—a deep voice, a smile, a smell of machine oil from the ships, which would never quite go away. "He's dead," she said, at last. Like Third Aunt, like Cousin Anh, like Cousin Thu. Like Father; gone to serve at the edge of Empire-controlled space, fallen in the rebel attack that had overwhelmed the moons of the Eighth Planet. "Isn't he?"

Those were the days of the dead; when every other morning seemed to see Grandmother adding new holos to the ancestral altar; every visitor spoke in hushed voices, as if Thien Bao weren't old enough to understand the war, or the devastation it brought.

Mother had the look again, debating whether to tell Thien Bao grown-up things. "He was a very brave man. He could have left, but he waited until everyone had finished evacuating." Mother sighed. "He never left. The rebel ships bombed the city until everything was ashes; your aunt was on the coms with him when—" she swallowed, looked away again. "She saw him die. That's why she's angry."

Thien Bao mulled on this for a while. "They had no children," she said, at last, thinking of Second Aunt sitting before the altar, grumbling that it was wrong to see him there, that he had died childless and had no place among the ancestors. But of course, the rules had changed in the days of the dead.

"No," Mother said.

It was a sad thought, bringing a queer feeling in Thien Bao's belly. "She can remarry, can't she?"

"Perhaps," Mother said, and Thien Bao knew it was a lie. She resolved to be nicer to Second Aunt from now on; and to pray to her ancestors so that Second Aunt would find another husband, and have children to comfort her in her old age.

That night, she dreamt of Second Uncle.

He stood in some shadowy corridor, one hand feverishly sending instructions to the structure's command nodes—speaking fast and in disjointed words, in a tone that he no doubt wanted to be reassuring. Thien Bao couldn't make out his face—it was a dark blur against the shaking of the walls; but she felt the impact that collapsed everything, like a spike-punch through reality, strong enough to shatter her bones—and heard the brief burst of static, the silence falling on the coms, as he died.

The dream changed, after that. She was soaring above a green planet, watching two huge attack ships confronting one another. There was no telling who was the rebels and who was the Empire. With the clarity of dreams she knew that one ship was scanning the other for antimatter weapons; and that the other ship, who had none, was preparing pinhead bombs, in the hopes of breaching the hull at its one weak point. Below, on the planet—again, with that strange clarity—people as tiny as ants were evacuating, struggling to fit onto a few aged shuttles that would carry them no further than the minuscule moon above.

They didn't matter—or, rather, they couldn't be allowed to matter, not if the mission were to be accomplished. Somehow, in the dream, she knew this; that, even if she had been ordered to save them, she wouldn't have been capable of it, wouldn't have made the slightest difference.

She floated closer, unfurling iridescent wings as wide as the trail of a comet; and prepared to unleash her own weapons, to put an end to the fight.

The scene seemed to freeze and blur, disintegrating like a hundred water droplets on a pane of glass—each droplet was a character, one of the old fashioned ones from Old Earth that no one save elite scholars knew how to read—column upon column of incomprehensible words in a red as bright as the vermillion of imperial decrees, scrolling downwards until they filled her entire field of vision—and they, too, faded, until only a few words remained—and though they were still in the old script, she *knew* in her heart of hearts what they meant, from beginning to end.

Little sister, you are fated to be mine.

Mine.

And then the words were gone, and she woke up, shaking, in the embrace of her own cradle-bed.

There were four mindships, built in the finest workshops of the Empire, in a time when the numbered planets were scattered across dozens of solar systems—when court memorials reached the outer stations, and magistrates were posted in far-flung arms of the galaxy.

Four mindships; one for each cardinal direction, raised by the best scholars to be the pride of the Empire; their claimers of tribute from barbaric, inferior dominions; the showcase of their technological apex, beings of grace and beauty, as terrible to behold as any of the Eight Immortals.

After that, the dreams never stopped. They came irregularly—once a week, once a month—but they always came. In every one of them she was in a different place—above a planet, orbiting a moon, approaching a space station—and every time the war was in her dreams. In every dream she watched ships attack one another; soldiers fighting hand to hand in a desperate defence of a city's street, their faces featureless, their uniforms in bloody tatters without insignia, impossible to differentiate. She scoured clean the surface of planets, rained war-kites on devastated temple complexes, disabled space domes' weapons—and woke up, shivering, staring at the imprint of words she shouldn't have been able to understand.

Mine.

Come to me, little sister. Come to me and put an end to all of this.

And yet; and yet, the war still went on.

By daylight, Mother and Second Aunt spoke in hushed tones of the fall of planets; of the collapse of orbitals; of the progress of rebel forces across the Empire—ever closer to the First Planet and the Purple Forbidden City.

"The Lily Empress will protect us," Thien Bao said. "Won't she?"

Mother shook her head, and said nothing. But later, when Thien Bao was playing *The Battle for Indigo Mountain*, her implants synched with the house's entertainment centre, she heard them—Grandmother, Mother and Second Aunt, talking quietly among themselves in the kitchen around pork buns and tea. She froze the game into a thin, transparent layer over her field of vision, and crept closer to listen in.

"You should have said something," Grandmother said.

"What do you want me to say?" Mother sounded tired; angry, but the scary kind of anger, the bone-deep one that lasted for days or months. "Everything would be a lie."

"Then learn to lie," Second Aunt said, drily. There was the sound of chewing: betel leaf and areca, the only luxury she'd allow herself. "For her sake."

"You think I haven't tried? She's a bright child. She'll figure it out the moment I open my mouth. Her wealthier schoolmates have all left, and she's got to realise what a desert the city is becoming. Everyone is leaving."

"I know," Second Aunt said. "If we had the money . . ."

Mother sighed, and got up to pour more tea into her fist-sized cup. There was no money, Thien Bao knew; all of Grandmother's savings had gone into paying for the watered down food in the markets; for the rice mixed with blackened grit and ashes; for the fish sauce cut with brown colouring, which never tasted right no matter how much lime or sugar Thien Bao added to it.

Mother said, finally, "Money might not matter anymore soon. There's word at the factories—that Magistrate Viec wants to evacuate."

Silence; and then Grandmother, in a hushed voice, "They can't—the rebel fleet is still not in the solar system, is it?"

"No," Second Aunt said. "But it's getting closer; and they have mindships. If they wanted to hit us, they could send those as advance scouts. Wouldn't be enough to take the planet, but it would cost us much."

"The magistrate said the Lily Empress will send her armies next month, after the end of the rainy season." Mother's voice was still uncertain.

"Ha," Second Aunt said. "Maybe she will, maybe she won't. But even if she did; do you truly believe that will be enough to save us, little sister? The armies are badly run, and overwhelmed as it is."

Mother said, at last, "All we need is one victory. One message to tell the rebels that their advance stops here, at the Sixth Planet; that to go further into the Empire will cost them dearly. They're overstretched, too, it wouldn't take much to make them stop . . ." Her voice was pleading.

"They might be overstretched," Second Aunt said, and there was pity in her voice. "And you're right. Maybe all it would take is a crushing victory; but we don't have that within our grasp, and you know it."

There was silence, then, as heavy as the air before the monsoon. Thien Bao turned back to her game; but it all seemed fake now, the units aligned on the artificial landscape, the battles where no one bled, which you could start, again and again, until you succeeded in the assigned mission—where no one ever felt fear like a fist of ice tightening in their guts; or the emptiness of loss, drawing closer with every passing hour.

In the first days of the war, the mindships were lost; their crews scattered by court decrees, recalled in haste to defend planets that had already fallen; their cradle pods neglected by the alchemists and programmers; their missions assigned irregularly, and then not at all.

One by one, they fell.

Golden Tortoise, *trying to evade pursuit by a vast rebel fleet, dove into deep spaces with an aged pilot as his only crew; and never re-emerged.*

Azure Dragon *went silent after the Battle of Huong He, plummeting downwards through the atmosphere in a shower of molten metal, her fragments peppering the burnt earth of the prefecture like so many seeds of grief.*

White Unicorn *completed the emergency evacuation of the Twelfth Planet, sustaining his trembling star-drives well past the point of bursting. He landed, shaking, bleeding his guts in machine-oil and torn rivets; and never flew again.*

And as for Vermillion Phoenix—*the strongest, most capable of all four ships . . . she, too, stopped speaking on the Empire's coms-channels; but her missions had been too well defined. She had been given leave to wage war on the Empire's enemies; and in those days when the Empire tore itself apart and brother denounced brother, father slew son and daughter abandoned mother, who could have told who the enemies of the Empire were, anymore?*

Vermillion Phoenix *went rogue.*

It took two months, in the end, for Magistrate Viec to give the evacuation order. By then, the rebel fleet had entered the solar system; and the first and second moons of the Sixth Planet had fallen. The army of the Empress retreated, its ships slowly growing larger in the sky, trailing the sickly green light of ruptured drives. The few soldiers the magistrate could spare oversaw the evacuation, their faces bored—most of their comrades were up above, fighting the last-ditch battle in the heavens.

Thien Bao stood in the huddle at the spaceport with her family; holding Grandmother's hand while the old woman engaged in a spirited talk with Second Aunt and Mother, complaining about everything from the wait to the noise of their neighbours.

She watched the army ships through the windows—and the growing shadows of the rebel mindships, creeping closer and closer—and wondered when their own evacuation ships would be ready. Around her, people's faces were tight, and they kept looking at the screens; at the queue that hadn't moved; at the impassive faces of the militia.

Ahead was a floating palanquin: an odd sight, since such a thing could only belong to a high official; but those officials would have been able to jump to the front of the queue. Thien Bao tugged at Grandmother's sleeve. "Grandmother?"

"Yes, child?" Grandmother didn't even turn.

"Who's in the palanquin?"

"Oh." Grandmother's gaze raked the palanquin from base to top, taking in the black lacquered exterior, embossed with golden birds; and the crane with spread wings atop the arched roof. "Probably Lady Oanh—you wouldn't remember her, but she and your mother were members of the same poetry club, in the days before she withdrew from public life. Always an eccentric, that woman." She frowned. "I thought she had a mindship of her own, though—funny seeing her here."

"Lady Oanh?"

But Grandmother had already turned back to her conversation with Mother and Second Aunt.

Above, the army ships hadn't moved; but Thien Bao could see the shapes of the rebel mindships more clearly, emerging from the deep spaces just long enough to power weapons. They were going to . . .

She knew it a fraction of a second before it happened—saw the corona of light filling the sky like an aurora above the poles—saw it spread in deathly silence, engulf the largest of the army ships—saw the ship shudder, and crack like an egg shell— the horrible thing was that it still held together, leaking a cloud of darkened fluids that spread across the surface of the sky—that it shuddered, again and again, but did not fall apart, though surely the life support systems had to be gone, with that kind of impact; though everyone onboard had to be dead, or dying, or worse . . .

In the silence that followed, a man screamed, his voice deep and resonant; and the crowd went mad.

Without warning, people pressed themselves closer to the docks; elbowing each other out of the way, sending others sprawling to the floor. Thien Bao found herself crushed against Grandmother, struggling to remain upright against the press—arms pushed against her, separating her from her family, and she was lost amidst unfamiliar faces, pushed and pulled until it was all she could do to stand upright; until it was all she could do to breathe—

The darkness at the edge of her field of vision descended; and the red characters of her dreams scrolled by, resolving themselves into the same, sharp, lapidary message.

Little sister. Call me. Call me, and put an end to this.

She hung in the darkness of space, the ion exhaust of her drives trailing behind her, opening like a vast fan; every part of her sharp, honed to a killing edge—a living weapon, carrying enough firepower to end it all, to make the rebel fleet cinders, to crack them open as they'd cracked open the army ship. All she had to do was call, reach out to the vast, dark part of herself that moved between the stars . . .

Someone grabbed her. Cold hands tightened on her shoulders, and pulled her upwards before she could stifle a scream; and it all went away, the sense of vastness; the red characters and the presence of something other than her in her own mind.

She sat in the darkness; it took her a moment to realise she was inside the palanquin, and that the slightly clearer form in front of her was an old woman.

Lady Oanh.

"Child," the old woman said. Life-support wires trailed from every end of the palanquin, as though she sat on the centre of a spider's web. The skin of her face, in the dim light, had the pallor and thinness of wet rice paper; and her eyes were two pits of deeper darkness. "Anh's and Nhu's daughter, is it not? I was a friend of your mother; in a different lifetime."

Everything was eerily silent: no noise from outside, no hint of the riot that had started on the docks—of course the palanquin would have the best ambiance systems, but the overall effect—that of hanging in the same bubble of artificially stilled time—made Thien Bao's skin crawl. "Lady Oanh. Why—?"

Mother and Second Aunt would be freaking out; they'd always told her not to trust strangers; and here she was in the middle of a riot, stuck with someone who might or might not be a friend—but then why would Lady Oanh bother to kidnap her? She was a scholar, a public figure; or had been, once. Nevertheless . . . Thien Bao reached into her feed, and activated the location loop—she'd sworn to Mother she was a grown up and didn't need it any longer, and now she was glad Mother hadn't listened to her.

The old woman smiled, an expression that did not reach into her eyes. "You would prefer to be outside? Trust me, it is much safer here." A feed blinked in the lower left-hand corner of Thien Bao's vision, asking for her permission to be displayed. She granted it; and saw outside.

The palanquin floated on its repulsive field, cutting a swathe through the press of people. Thien Bao knew she wouldn't have lasted a moment out there, that she'd have been mown down as others sought to reach the shuttles before her. But still . . .

Lady Oanh's voice was quiet, but firm. "You looked set to be trampled by the mob."

"You didn't have to—"

"No," Lady Oanh said. "You're right. I didn't."

How old was she? Thien Bao wondered. How long did it take for skin to become this pale; for eyes to withdraw this deep into the face, as if she stood on the other side of death already? And did all of it, this aging, this putting death at bay, confer any of the wisdom of Thien Bao's ancestors?

"A riot is no place for freezing," Lady Oanh said. "Though in someone your age, it can possibly be excused."

She hadn't noticed the trance then; or that anything was wrong. Then again, why should she? She was certainly wise with her years, but wisdom was not omniscience. "I'm sorry," Thien Bao said. But she remembered the sense of vastness; the coiled power within her. If it was real; if it wasn't dreams; if she could somehow answer . . .

Call me, little sister. Let us put an end to all this.

Thien Bao said, "Grandmother said—you had a mindship—"

Lady Oanh laughed; genuinely amused it seemed. *"The Carp that Leapt Over the Stream?* It seemed senseless to hoard her services. She's part of the fleet that will evacuate her. That's where we're going, in fact."

Lady Oanh's eyes focused on something beyond Thien Bao, and she nodded. "I'll send a message to notify your kin that I'm helping you onboard a ship. That should alleviate their worries."

If they didn't all die first from rebel fire; if the remaining army ship held—if if if . . .

A gentle rocking, indicating the palanquin was moving forward again—to the waiting ships, to safety—except that there was no safety, not anywhere. Outside, the remaining army ship was trying to contain the rebel mindships; shuddering, its hull pitted and cracked. From time to time, a stray shot would hit the spaceport's shields, and the entire structure around them would shudder, but it held, it still held.

But for how long?

"I hate them," Thien Bao said.

"Who? The rebels?" Lady Oanh's gaze was sharp. "It's as much the fault of the Court as theirs, child. If the Great Virtue Emperor and the Lily Empress hadn't been weak, more concerned with poetry than with their armies; if their officials hadn't encouraged them, repeating that nonsense about adherence to virtue being the only safeguard the Empire needed . . ."

To hear her, so casually criticising the Empress—but then Second Aunt and Mother had done the same. "I wish . . ." Thien Bao sounded childish, she knew; like a toddler denied a treat. "I wish someone were strong enough to stop the rebel armies. To kill them once and for all."

Lady Oanh's face did not move, but she shook her head. "Be careful, child."

How could wanting peace be a bad thing? She understood nothing, that old, pampered woman who didn't have to fight through the crowd, who didn't live with fear in her belly, with the litany of the family dead in her mind—

"Killing is easy," Lady Oanh said. "But that has never stopped the devastation of war."

"It would be a start," Thien Bao said, defiantly.

"Perhaps," Lady Oanh said. She shook her head. "It would take a great show of strength from the Empire to stop them, and this is something we're incapable of, at the present time. The seeds of our defeat were in place long before the war, I fear; and—"

She never finished her sentence. Thien Bao saw nothing; but *something* struck the shields, wringing them dry like wet laundry; and going past them, a network of cracks and fissures spreading throughout the pillars of the spaceport and the huge glass windows.

Look out, Thien Bao wanted to say; but the wall nearest to them shuddered and fell apart, dragging down chunks of the ceiling in its wake. Something struck her in the back of the head; and everything disappeared in an excruciating, sickening crunch.

When she went silent, Vermillion Phoenix had had an officer of the Embroidered Guard as her only crew—not a blood relative, but a sworn oath-sister, who had been with the ship for decades and would never hear of abandoning her post.

There is no record of what happened to the officer. Being human, without any kind of augmentation, she likely died of old age, while the mindship—as ships did—went on, unburdened.

Unburdened does not mean free from grief, or solitude. In the centuries that followed, several people claimed to have had visions of the ship; to have heard her voice calling to them; or dreamt of battles—past and present—to which she put a brutal end. There were no connections between them; no common ancestry or closeness in space or time; but perhaps the mindship recognised something else: a soul, torn from its fragile flesh envelope and reincarnated, time and time again, until everything was made right.

Thien Bao woke up, and all was dust and grit—choking her, bending her to the ground to convulsively cough until her lungs felt wrung dry. When she rose at last, shaking, she saw the ruins of the palanquin, half-buried under rubble; and a few cut wires, feebly waving in the dim light—and the mob, further into the background, still struggling to reach the ships. She'd thought the wall would collapse, but it stood in spite of the massive fissures crossing it from end to end; and for some incongruous reason it reminded her of the fragile celadon cups Father had so treasured, their green surface shot with such a network of cracks it seemed a wonder they still held together.

Around her, chunks of the ceiling dotted the area—and the other thing, the one she avoided focusing on—people lying still or twitching or moaning, lying half under rubble—with limbs bent at impossible angles, and the stained white of bones laid bare at the heart of bleeding wounds; and spilled guts; and the laboured breathing of those in agony . . .

Those were the days of the dead, and she had to be strong.

At the edge of her field of vision—as faint as her paused game of *Battle for Indigo Mountain*, in another lifetime—the red characters of her dream hovered, and a faint sense of a vast presence, watching over her from afar.

"Lady Oanh? Mother? Second Aunt?" Her location loop was still running; but it didn't seem to have picked up anything from them—or perhaps it was the spaceport network that was the problem, flickering in and out of existence like a dying heartbeat. It was nonsense anyway; who expected the network to hold, through that kind of attack.

The sky overhead was dark with the shadow of a ship—not the army ship, it had to be one of the mindships. Its hatches were open, spewing dozens of little shuttles, a ballet slowly descending towards them: rebels, come to finish the work they had started.

She had to move.

When she pulled herself upright, pain shot through her neck and arms like a knife-stab; but she forced herself to move on, half-crawling, half-walking, until she found Lady Oanh.

The old woman lay in the rubble, staring at the torn dome of the spaceport. For a moment, an impossibly long moment, Thien Bao thought she was alive; but no one could be alive with the lower half of their body crushed; and so much fluid and blood leaking from broken tubes. "I'm sorry," she said, but it wasn't her fault; it had never been her fault. Overhead, the shuttles were still descending, as slowly as the executioner's blade. There was no time. There was no safety; not anywhere; there was no justice; no fairness; no end to the war and the fear and the sick feeling in her head and in her belly.

A deafening sound in her ears, loud enough to cover the distant sounds of panic—she realised that it was her location loop, displaying an arrow and an itinerary to join whatever was left of her family; if they, like Lady Oanh, hadn't died, if there was still hope . . .

She managed to pull herself upwards—staggered, following the directions—left right left going around the palanquin around the dead bodies around the wounded who grasped at her with clawed hands—days of the dead, she had to be strong had to be strong . . .

She found Grandmother, Mother and Second Aunt standing by the barriers that had kept the queue orderly, once—which were now covered in dust, like everything else around them. There was no greeting, or sign of relief. Mother merely nodded as if nothing were wrong, and said, "We need to move."

"It's past time for that," Second Aunt said, her gaze turned towards the sky.

Thien Bao tried to speak; to say something about Lady Oanh, but no words would come out of her mouth.

Mother's eyes rolled upwards for a brief moment as she accessed the network. *"The Carp that Leapt Over the Stream,"* she said. "Its shuttles were parked at the other end of the terminal, and there'll be fewer people there. Come on."

Move move move—Thien Bao felt as though everything had turned to tar; she merely followed as Second Aunt and Mother elbowed their way through the crowd; and on to a corridor that was almost deserted compared to the press of people. "This way," Mother said.

Thien Bao turned, briefly, before they limped into the corridor, and saw that the first of the rebel shuttles had landed some way from them, disgorging a flood of yellow-clad troops with featureless helmets.

It was as if she were back in her dreams, save that her dreams had never been this pressing—and that the red words on the edge of her field of vision kept blinking, no matter how she tried to dismiss them.

Mother was right; they needed to keep moving—past the corridor, into another, wider concourse that was mostly scattered ruin, following the thin thread of people and hoping that the shuttles would still be there, that the mindship would answer to them with Lady Oanh dead. By then, they had been joined by other people, among whom a wounded woman carried on the shoulder of a soldier—no introductions, no greetings, but a simple acknowledgement that they were all in this together. It wasn't hope that kept them going; it was sheer stubbornness, one foot in front of the other, one breath and the next and the next; the fear of falling behind the others, of slowing everyone down and ruining everything.

Ahead, the mass of a shuttle, seen behind glass windows; getting agonisingly, tantalisingly closer. "This way," Second Aunt said; and then they saw the yellow-clad troops in front of them, deployed to bar the passage across the concourse—and the other troops, too, blocking the passageways, herding people off the shuttle in the eerie silence.

Mother visibly sagged. "It will be fine," she said, and her voice was a lie. "They'll just want to check our identity and process us—"

But it was the soldier with them who panicked—who turned away, lightning-fast, still carrying his wounded charge—and in the dull silence that followed, Thien Bao heard the click of weapons being armed.

"No!" Mother said, sharply. As if in a dream Thien Bao saw her move in front of the yellow-clad soldiers, with no more apparent thought than if she'd been strolling through the marketplace—and she wanted to scream but couldn't, as the weapons found their mark and Mother crumpled, bloodless and wrung dry, her corpse so small it seemed impossible that she had once been alive.

Second Aunt moved at last, her face creased with anger—not towards Mother or the soldier, but straight at the rebel troops. "How dare you—"

There was the sound again; of weapons being armed.

No.

No. No.

Everything went red: the characters from her dreams, solidifying once more in front of her; the voice speaking into her mind.

Little sister.

And, weeping, Thien Bao reached out, into the void between stars, and called to the ship.

When the child named Thien Bao was born on the Sixth Planet, there were signs—a room filled with the smell of machine-oil, and iridescent reflections on the walls, tantalising characters from a long lost language. Had the birth-master not been desperately busy trying to staunch the mother's unexpected bleeding, and calm down the distraught father, she would have noticed them.

Had she looked, too, into the newborn's eyes as she took her first, trembling breath, the birth-master would have seen the other sign: the hint of a deep, metallic light in the huge pupils; a light that spread from end to end of the eye like a wash of molten steel, a presage of things to come.

She was vast, and old, and terrible; her wings stretched around entire planets, as iridescent as pearls fished from the depths; the trail of her engines the colour of jade, of delicate celadon—and where she passed, she killed.

She disintegrated the fleet that waited on the edge of the killing field; scoured clean the surface of the small moon, heedless of the screams of those trapped upon it; descended to the upper limit of the planet's atmosphere, and incinerated the two mindships in orbit, and the fragile ship that still struggled to defend against them; and the tribunal where the militia still fought the recently landed invasion force; and the magistrate in his chambers, staring at the tactical map of the planet and wondering how to save what he could from the rebels. In the spaceport, where the largest number of people congregated, she dropped ion bombs until no sign of life remained; until every shuttle had exploded or stopped moving.

Then there was silence; and lack of strife; and then there was peace.

And then she was merely Thien Bao again, standing in the ruins of the space-port, in the shadow of the great ship she had called on.

There was nothing left. Merely dust, and bodies—so many bodies, a sea of them, yellow-clad, black-clad, civilians and soldiers and rebels all mingled together, their blood pooling on the cracked floor; and a circle around her, where Mother lay dead; and the soldier, and the wounded woman; and the rebels who had shot her—and by her side, Second Aunt and Grandmother, bloodless and pale and unmoving. It was unclear whether it was the mindship's weapons they had died of, or the rebels', or both; but Thien Bao stood in a circle of the dead, the only one alive as far as she could see.

The only one—it couldn't—couldn't—

Little sister. The voice of the mindship was as deep as the sea. *I have come, and ended it, as you requested.*

That wasn't what she'd wanted—that—all of it, any of it—

And then she remembered Lady Oanh's voice, her wry comment. Be careful, child. Be careful.

I bring peace, and an end to strife. Is that not what the Empire should desire?

No. No.

Come with me, little sister. Let us put an end to this war.

A great victory, Thien Bao thought, hugging herself; feeling hot and cold at the same time, her bones chilled within their sheaths of flesh, a churning in her gut like the beginning of grief. Everyone had wanted a great victory over the rebels, something that would stop them, once and for all, that would tell them that the Empire still stood, still could make them pay for every planet they took.

And she'd given them that; she and the ship. Exactly that.

Come. We only have each other, the ship said, and it was the bitter truth. There was nothing left on the planet—not a living soul—and of the rebel army that had entered the solar system, nothing and no one left either, just the husks of destroyed ships drifting in the emptiness of space.

Come, little sister.

And she did—for where else could she go; what else could she do, that would have made any sense?

In the old days, the phoenix, the vermillion bird, was a sign of peace and prosperity to come; a sign of a virtuous ruler under whom the land would thrive.

In the days of the war, it is still the case; if one does not enquire how peace is bought, how prosperity is paid for—how a mindship and a child scour the numbered planets, dealing death to rebels and Empire alike, halting battles by bloody massacres; and making anyone who raises arms pay dearly for the privilege of killing.

Meanwhile, on the inner planets begins the painful work of reconstruction—raising pagodas and tribunals and shops from the ashes of war, and hanging New Year's Eve garlands along avenues that are still dust and ruins, praying to the ancestors for a better future; for a long life; and good fortune; and descendants as numerous as the stars in the sky.

There is no virtuous ruler; but perhaps—perhaps just, there is a manner of peace and prosperity, bought in seas of blood spilled by a child.

And perhaps—perhaps just—it is all worth it. Perhaps it is all one can hope for, in the days of the war.

The Burial of Sir John Mawe at Cassini

CHAZ BRENCHLEY

Here's a retro–SF story about a habitable (and inhabited) Mars that has been colonized by a Victorian-era British Empire in an alternate world, a strong, bitter, and melancholy story that follows the aftermath of the enigmatic death of a Colonial leader . . .

Chaz Brenchley has been making a living as a writer since the age of eighteen. He is the author of nine thrillers, most recently Shelter, *and two fantasy series,* The Books of Outremer *and* Selling Water by the River. *As Daniel Fox, he has published a Chinese-based fantasy series, beginning with* Dragon in Chains; *as Ben Macallan, an urban fantasy series beginning with* Desdaemona. *A British Fantasy Award winner, he has also published books for children and more than five hundred short stories. Brenchley recently married and moved from Newcastle to California, with two squabbling cats and a famous teddy bear. In 2014 he published a new novel,* Being Small, *and a collection,* Bitter Waters.

Never did a man hanged see such a funeral. Old Cobb leaned on his spade to watch the barges come down the canal in caravan, in smoky procession, each decked out with black solemnity. Crowds lined the bank, quality and commoners all intermingled, while open carriages and charabancs blocked the roadways behind. Gentlemen and coolies removed their hats as the cortège steamed slowly by; ladies bowed their heads, while their maids dropped a dutiful curtsey. Soldiers saluted, officers and troops together. They were not—quite—a formal muster, but a great many had chosen to turn out in full parade dress today, a scarlet glory against the green.

Flags were everywhere, at half-mast every one. Poles had gone up overnight at every measured furlong to ensure it. That had been a job of work. Cobb knew; he'd had the navvies in his bothy before dawn, drinking tea, smoking, grumbling. Now they too were beside the water, clean shirts and a shave, grouped around the last pole they raised, just opposite the cemetery's watergate. Proud of their achievement, showing their respect. Mute before their betters, awkward in any society other than their own, standing their ground today. Cobb knew them intimately, them and their kind. Perhaps he admired them, though he would scorn to admit it. Admiration was for the idle classes who had time to compare this to that, others to themselves. He was a navvy himself, in all but name. But for an accident of birth, unless it was the grace of God. His mother had said the one thing, parson the other. He needn't believe either. He was just glad of the red stripe on his blue passport—*red, red, white and blue*—that said he was a subject of Her Britannic Majesty, and Mars-born. This and that together: *the best of both worlds,* as they liked to say. And give Venus never a mention, they liked that too. Venus was in Russian hands, and the Czar no friend to the Queen Empress.

Cobb's birth was a privilege, maybe, but he worked as hard as any navvy fetched up from Earth on a judge's warrant. Graves don't dig themselves. Nor do cemeteries beautify themselves, even on a day with no digging. Paths must be weeded, hedges trimmed. Old dried wreaths taken away, fresh flowers laid. The route from gate to burial had been marked down on a scribbled map and sent urgently to the city, to be sure that no one put a foot wrong—and even so Cobb had taken time to string black ribbons from tree to tree and in judicious places, swagged along the back of a bench and garlanded around a sleeping cherub's neck, to stand as mute guide wherever the path divided. Nothing about today was spontaneous, though it was meant to look that way. *Not our work,* Authority meant to say to any eyes that watched, *we had nothing to do with this. The man died in his shame, at our hand; all else is the will of the people.* That and, *See how the people feel,* Authority meant to say that too. *They choose to honour him this way. That should surely tell you something.*

Someone, from somewhere, must be watching. There was not a nymph to be seen in the water, though, not an imago in the sky. That seemed appropriate. On such a day, they ought to keep their distance.

People said, *They're shunning us, they think all this disgusting.* Old Cobb didn't know about that. He didn't have the finger-talk, no one he knew had the bubble-talk. If there was an air-talk, no one knew it at all; who could talk to imagines? They wouldn't hold still long enough. Flibbertigibbets. The creatures lived their lives half backwards, as it seemed: growing old and wise and ever deeper, from nymph to naiad in the slow dark waters, and then abruptly young and foolish. Briefly, in mid-air.

Merlins, he liked to call them. People did, all up and down the classes. He'd heard the word from a widowed duchess and a weaver's boy. You had to call them something, after all; and *Martians* didn't apply. He was a Martian himself, born and bred. Red-blooded. They said that too, all up and down. Even the lordlings who might have boasted otherwise, bluebloods they'd be called on Earth. Not here. Red dust under their fingernails, despite a lifetime's scrubbing.

Digging graves is a profession and a privilege, not a punishment detail. To a man with the right mind, it's almost a sacrament. Cobb knew his work and he knew its value. In a smaller town, given a simpler church with a lesser congregation, he'd be sexton and respected. But Cobb was Cassini-born, raised within the sound of Thunder Fall, in the shadow of the cathedral rising on the flooded crater's rim. He had never thought of leaving. The sexton here was a most superior man, far above Cobb's touch, with airs and responsibilities both. Cobb was content to be gravedigger, and do the work that mattered.

No digging today. The spade was a prop to his comfort, not a tool to his hand. The cathedral might be unfinished; the cemetery had seen a century's use already. Of course the great families had their private vaults and mausoleums, stone-built, adorned with weeping angels and Latin mottoes, the reverence of ornament. Sir John's great-grandfather had been on the first Settlement ship. His grandfather was signatory to the Charter. From the day he was born, it had been known where he would lie in death: beside them in the family crypt, on the shelf that already bore his name. Only the date, this day was a surprise.

The date, and the manner of his coming. He might have expected pomp, but not disgrace. Disgrace *and* pomp. The unseemly rush to judgement, arrest and trial and execution should have been startlement enough, so hurried they were. That and this funeral too, this frantic elaborate fair, the very opposite of discretion or diplomacy or tact: startling. *We bend the knee to the merlins,* people said—the navvies had said it, around Cobb's hearth this morning—*when we stretch his neck so fast, because they ask it; we slap them in the face—for his sake, aye—when we bury him with honour, as we do.*

Just who had ordered the flags, the barges, the sense of great occasion would likely come clear only in time, in the account-books. Someone must be paying for all this. The crowds had not been ordered, quite—except the schoolchildren, perhaps, in their scrubbed and serried ranks, boys in Eton collars and girls in white pinafores, with flowers in their hands—but they had surely been expected. The schools must have been told, *you are expected*. The common people could simply be relied on. A public hanging at first light, a gentleman, a man of reputation, the whole city would turn out for that; and even before the body was cut down, the rumours must have started.

No one quite knew anyway, whether he was condemned for murder or for treason or for breaking the Charter, or all three. His trial had been held *in camera*, and the proclaimed verdict was conspicuously unforthcoming in its detail. Easy then to understand how quickly people accepted that his crime had been noble and terrible and strange, that he had died in the service of Queen and Empire, although the Queen would necessarily say nothing and the Empire was obliged to disavow it. The Viceroy was subtle or else craven, depending on your point of view, but could be disregarded either way. The city of Cassini meant in any case to say a solemn farewell to its fallen son. The funeral cortège was steam-up before dawn in the basin below the Fall; the poles stood waiting for their flags; authorised or not, informed or not, the city took a half-holiday to see him silent home.

Given his choice, Cobb might have stood with the navvies by their flagpole. He valued their salty, uncouth respect more highly than the prescribed and public sorrow of the cathedral's clergy as they stepped from the leading barge onto the heavy timbers of the landing-stage. From archbishop to thurifer, their words and roles were written down; it all came easy to the likes of them. They could speak of honour and sacrifice and debt, exhibit all that was proper and not necessarily mean a word or a moment of it. Cobb trusted the navvies more.

He had his place too, though: just within the locked gates, ready to open them at need. There was no need—the archbishop himself did the honours with his plated key, and the lock turned sweet as any, because Cobb had bathed it in rock-oil overnight and only fitted it back an hour ago—but this was not a day to be taking chances. You could feel it. This was a day for history to remember, in books and in the home, in family legend. *You listen to your grandad, he was there.*

Here he was, and glad of a sort, however much he wished himself marginally elsewhere, just a little transported. Over there. The clergy stood for ritual, tradition, what was careful and proper and ordained from far away; the navvies for a sullen passion that rips the heart, the urgency of presence, the true spirit of the Empire.

The sexton drew the gates wide, with barely a glance at Cobb. He was in his whites, as was the dean and all the chapter too, with just a band of red at the hem of every alb as though the linen dragged inch-deep in Martian dust. Wherever it flew, from Westminster to New Shoreditch to the canalside today, the Union Flag wore that same red border now. In happier times, on church parade, the children sang their way around it:

> Red, red, white and blue
> These are my colours and my fealty too.

It was simple, stirring, cheerful, an unofficial anthem. Some days half the crowd would join in. That might be another way to spot the Mars-born: which songs they stood up for.

Cobb had a red handkerchief at his throat today. It jarred perhaps with his dusty dutiful blacks, but he was hardly alone. He'd have been hard pressed, indeed, to find man or woman or child who wasn't showing a flash of patriotic primary somewhere, along with their mourning bands: a ribbon in the hair, a buttonhole thread, the cuff of a glove turned back to show its lining. The schoolgirls' flowers were every shade of crimson, scarlet, cardinal, maroon.

It was like seeing all rumours confirmed, to see the hierarchy of the Church of Mars line either side of the landing-stage like an honour guard. The merlins would hate that, surely, if they ever understood it. What they demanded had been granted them, and this was the response: the letter of the law, and the spirit of the Empire. He was not a sentimental man, but even old Cobb felt a twist in his throat, a prickle behind his eyes. They did this well, he thought, his people. Each of them individually stood high today, and raised their neighbours higher. The Viceroy couldn't be here, of course, to see a man buried who had been hanged at his command—but the Widow at Windsor would hear of this through the aether, and nod, and recognise its worth.

The second barge carried the coffin beneath its pall of red, and the six men who would bear it home. Six troopers, drawn by lot—Cobb had heard—when every man in barracks stepped up to volunteer.

By the look of the fortunate six, every man in barracks had lent a hand to be sure they would not disgrace the regiment. From the plumes on their shakos to the pipe-clay on their belts to the blacking on their boots, they gleamed and dazzled.

Before them, a single cherubic boy stepped ashore in a plain white surplice belted with scarlet. As the men shouldered their burden he stood quite still, gazing ahead through the double line of clergy and the open gates to the green of the cemetery, beyond the cemetery to the butterscotch sky, beyond the sky itself perhaps to very heaven: he seemed that innocent, that pure.

He might perhaps have had a signal, the twitch of a finger from the canon who was his music-master in the cathedral choir school. Perhaps it was the preternatural hearing of the very young, to catch exactly when the pallbearers were ready at his back: the last deep breath, the rustle of immaculately pressed serge and the creak of polished leather, the sudden silence following. Or else there was simply a moment, when waiting was done and the next thing had to begin. When the silence couldn't last a moment longer.

At all events, he sang. His lone treble rose like larksong, so high and true it could carry perhaps all through the aether and back to the Widow herself, to sing to her directly.

Red, red, white and blue . . .

Not a hymn, not a psalm. Not perhaps what the boy had been instructed or expected to sing. The troopers—forewarned, perhaps?—didn't miss a beat as they slow-marched behind him, their faces carved to solemnity, but Cobb felt a stir along the lines of white. No one would say anything, here and now. If Cobb was right, the boy was safe to be thrashed later; he might even lose his place at school. He might think even that worthwhile in payment for this moment, when the province's senior clergy closed ranks and marched behind the coffin, lending their imprimatur to the simple schoolboy tune that lay buried in every Martian's marrow.

Red blows the wind and free
From Mars to the Empress in the old country.

This is the order for funerals, wherever subjects of Her Majesty have land and leisure wherewith to mark their loss. First comes the innocent, the cherub, a herald of sorrow; and then the dead. Then the religious. The military, the secular, the family follow on together, all one in the eyes of the Church.

Here came the mourners, then. The Mawes and their immediate relations, stiff with grief and shock: clad from eldest to youngest in severest black except for those who had served the Queen Empress in her wars, whose uniforms blazed somehow brighter red than any. Officials and dignitaries from the city, the men who had drawn up the warrant that hanged Sir John, determinedly not crept into hiding. The Viceroy couldn't lend his countenance to the occasion, but they felt obliged or entitled or at least able, in formal civilian dress with not a mark of rank between them, not a mayoral chain or a hint of precedence to suggest that they came *ex officio*. Senior officers, by contrast, had all their medals defiantly on display. The man belonged to the regiment, and the regiment was here to acknowledge that. The *Arean-Messenger* was here in the august person of its editor, taking notes like any cub reporter, listing all the society ladies and the men of business who had begged or bought or commanded a seat in a barge, a place at the heart of this ceremony.

Anyone and everyone, and Cobb. He might not have seen the choirmaster's signal to prompt the boy; he did see the sexton's, aimed at him as the clergy shuffled by. A swift beckoning finger, *follow on*. Cobb might have ignored it, he had his place and it was not in that procession; but he had his curiosity too. Deep and dark and slow as a merlin naiad just before the change, unconfessed as his patriotism, rooted and grown in the same red earth. It stirred within him now, and of course he followed on. Spade in hand.

The Sabaean Plain is broad and flat between its high-walled craters, broad and flat and fertile wherever it can be irrigated. The first settlers landed half a world away, but they were frontier folk by nature. Every canal was an invitation and an opportunity. They scattered, they spread, they settled. Inevitably they had contact with nymphs along the way, with naiads when they disturbed the crater lakes. That was before anyone had guessed the merlin lifecycle, before anyone had named the merlins anything. Of course there had been deaths, deaths and deaths. Settlers and soldiers died in droves, before the Charter.

Their first graveyard here overflowed, before ever there was a city on the crater wall to feed it further. Authority was wise, ambitious, confident; the Viceroy bespoke a stretch of land between three canals. As if to remind himself that he had been from home before, if never quite this far, he called it San Michele and gave it to the new Church for her people. Forbade bridges, so that the city ever after should call it the Isle of the Dead and see it as separate, contained, particular. See it from the crater's height, indeed, vivid green all year amid the cornfields, set like a jewel in its narrow bands of water. San Michele was a promise to the future: *here we lie and shall lie, white bones in red soil under a canopy as green as England's own. In perpetuity, in Mars. This world is ours.*

Along broad paths that were deliberately neither straight nor level, through groves of maturing trees, between tombs and monuments and stones already weathered as though a country churchyard had been laid out on the scale of a city park, they followed the coffin and the boy's sweet call to the final resting-place of all the Mawes of Mars. That name was cut above the low vault's entranceway; the iron grille stood open because Cobb had left it so this morning. The coffin was set down before it, on trestles he had laid out in the half-dark; the scarlet pall hung to the ground like a veil of discretion. Mourners gathered in a respectful half-circle on the grass, while the archbishop read the words of interment from a book held open for him by the choirboy. Earth to earth, ashes to ashes: a solemn symbolic handful lifted from a silver chalice and cast across the pall. They had come to Cobb for that too, as though soil dug by a real worker were more pure or more true. The archbishop wiped his hands after on a linen napkin. Even he must have red dust beneath his nails, unless he bleached it out.

Now the family stepped forward, to scatter their own thin handfuls and lay flowers on the cloth. Sir John's mother, his sisters, his young son. At least he had a son. The boy would likely have a time of it at school, but he'd carry the name forward another generation, and perhaps have the chance to redeem it. Find the chance, or make it. Here was a world of empire, barely scratched; a young man might do anything, if his family stood behind him. Or the regiment would take him, surely. Blood wipes away dishonour, and the Queen Empress always needed men.

Or young Mawe could lose the family name and disappear, he wouldn't be the first. Turn his back on all his people, in rage or disappointment or relief; take a mule and a dust-mask and a waterskin, strike out for the high country, *terra incognita*. Lord knew, there was enough of it. Away from the main canals, vast ranges still stood open to be farmed or mined or simply wandered through. If a man learned finger-talk, he could learn to survive. Or not. He could lose himself, lose his life, never come home to occupy his own shelf in the vault. It happened; Cobb knew. Traders and trappers fetched in bones sometimes, the shoddy remnants of a life abandoned. They'd bring them to him, rather than to the clergy. He'd bring them to God himself, in a private corner of San Michele in the quiet of dawn, untroubled by questions of identity or baptism or state of grace. There was no such thing as an unmarked grave; God marked the fall of every sparrow. So, Cobb thought, did the Widow. Even this far away, where sparrows were imported, rare and costly.

No call for Cobb's intervention today. Sir John had been given communion in his cell, before the hangman came; he was blessed on the gallows, before the drop. Now the troopers lifted up his earthly remains one more time, and bore him down into the crypt.

Not the archbishop, but the dean followed, and some few men in suits whom Cobb could not have named or rated—and the sexton, who looked back and again beckoned, *follow on.*

Cobb picked his way through the mill of mourners, following.

Every crypt and every vault is different. Cobb knew all of his, inside and out. This one, he had its every corner fresh in mind, he had swept and mopped them all in readiness—but he had never seen it quite like this. It was not at all how he had left it. The coffin was set down again on trestles, not his own; storm-lanterns glowed in niches all around. The troopers were dismissed. The strangers discarded their tail-coats and addressed the pall in waistcoats and shirtsleeves, scattering dust and flowers in casual profusion as they stripped the cloth away.

The dean's face twisted: anger or distaste or something stronger, contempt perhaps, unless it was disgust.

"Well, don't just stand there. Open it!"

Cobb looked at the sexton, the expectant circle, the unexpectedly cheap wood of the revealed casket.

He said, "I don't have a screwdriver, sir. With me, I mean. I didn't . . ."

"Your spade, man. Use your spade. Good Lord, don't tell me you have scruples? Does that look to you like anything deserving of respect?"

Actually, it looked to Cobb more like a crate than a coffin. And yes, he did apparently have scruples, shaped by the silent company around the walls, the long dead in their bones and boxes. He might have said something eventually, something of that, but he was always slow to speak; one of the men he didn't know was quicker to speak for him.

"Hardy, go easy on the man. He has no idea. God willing." And then to Cobb, gently, as he might speak to a child or perhaps a horse, "Set your mind at rest. This is . . . not as it seems."

"Indeed." The dean, speaking effortfully in his outrage. "A pantomime, no sacrament at all. You may use your spade freely, sirrah. You desecrate nothing that is not already defiled beyond recourse."

"Gently, though," the stranger urged. "The spade, by all means, if you have no crow to hand—but gently. Not to harm what lies within."

Was Sir John not dead, then? A *pantomime*, the dean called it. Had the execution been only show? That would be a bold move, under the public eye. Crowds could be fooled, though; Cobb knew. The people delighted in a grand illusion. They wanted, almost, to be fooled. And he had seen *Romeo and Juliet*, enacted by the gentry for the people's education. He knew about heroes playing dead for posterity, for the law, for love.

He lifted his spade with some energy, then, a sudden eager vigour. A *gentle* vigour, yes. The crate was rudely made and rudely lidded, nailed shut, not even screwed. He could slide the blade's edge quite easily between lid and case, and simply lean on it.

The creaking squeak of steel forced from wood; the lid rose up an inch. He moved to another corner.

Methodically, far from mechanically, Cobb raised the lid on all sides, then loosed it completely with one last heave and lifted it away.

Beneath was the Union Flag in all its red-rimmed glory, the flag that should have been Sir John's pall, except it was impossible. No man hanged could be seen swathed in imperial colours, whatever his rank, whatever his service. That was the edict, and it might have been written exactly for this occasion, so that he who shrouded the body—Cobb wasn't thinking *corpse*, not now—could deal justly by the Viceroy and Sir John both. Wrap him in the Widow's flag and nail down the lid, cover that over with a simple red. The letter of the law, the spirit of the Empire.

The flags that lined the canal path could be shrugged away—a random act, mute insubordination, the work of a few malcontents who would be dealt with later—so long as no flag draped the coffin or was seen to drape the corpse.

The corpse-presumptive.

The dean was here to witness for the Church. The men in their shirtsleeves must be doctors, standing by to revive the body from its seeming death, its trance-state. No conscious man could lie so still for so long, in a box. Under a cloth.

Not Cobb's place, to peel back that cloth. He wished they would hurry; how could Sir John breathe, beneath its folds? If he were breathing. There was no shift in the fabric, not a hint of stir. The friar's potion had left Juliet seemingly beyond the gates of death. cold and still and breathless. The shirtsleeved gentlemen had a leather bag which Cobb hadn't noticed till now, much like a doctor's. No one had carried that through all the obsequies, from barge to tomb; it must have been brought in before, like the trestles, and set down on an empty shelf. One man opened it, and yes: scalpels and lancets and scissors and saws, all the gleaming steel of the surgeon's art.

In a disregarded corner—but Cobb was looking everywhere now, disregarding nothing—stood a pile of wooden boxes strapped with leather. It was the furthest corner from the entranceway, deeply shadowed; no one standing outside would see. Cobb had never imagined that he held the only key; of course the family could come and go at any time. Even so: he thought all of this had been hurried in this morning, after he unlocked the crypt. He thought the family didn't know.

He wondered if they would be told, and when, and by whom. And how. Not, surely, by Sir John himself. That would be appalling, to meet him as an unexpected revenant, the rope's mark still about his neck. Perhaps they were never to learn. Sir John could rise again and vanish, take ship to another city or another world, take a new name and never be himself again. These few who stood here might be the only men who ever knew the truth, and Cobb was one. For what, the virtue of his spade? They could have thought to bring a crowbar and do the work themselves. To bear witness, then, to represent the people as the dean did the Church? Perhaps, but . . .

The boxes held coils and wires, valves and clamps, electrical machinery. The largest were batteries, into which one of the doctors decanted acid as he watched. Restoring a man to life, that might well call for some extremity of science, tamed lightning.

At last, another doctor stepped up to the crate and threw back the shrouding flag to reveal—no. Not a man's body. Not yet. A case of spun and burnished copper, rather, a coffin within a coffin. No doubt some complex instrument, a pressure-chamber of some kind that might hold a man preserved, until such time as his resurrectionists—

No. Cobb might be old but his eyes were sharp, and his mind had not dulled yet. That . . . was not copper, no. And not the work of any man. It was shaped near enough like a highpine cone cut from its stem—round like a spindle, broad at the shoulder and tapering to a narrow foot, near enough like a man's shape if he were wrapped and wrapped until he lost all form else, near enough a man's height that a coffin-box might hold it—and the shape was intimately familiar. Not that colour, nor the way it gleamed in the lamplight, but Cobb knew it for what it was when he looked in honesty rather than hope.

There would be no Sir John rising from this tomb, today or any day. Sir John was not here.

On Mars as on Earth, trees grew by canalsides and overhung the water. As on Earth, they might have been planted there for shade or fruit or shelter, for beauty perhaps—if the merlins could see beauty, if they cared—or for other reasons more mysterious; but chiefly, it was believed, trees and canals went natively together in the merlin mind because they echoed the deep waters and the highpines, those massive trees that grew beside the crater-lakes.

It was no coincidence, that a merlin chrysalis looked like a highpine cone. Boughs hung heavy-laden with them half the Martian year. The first settlers harvested them for foodstuff and fuel, and felled the trees for timber. And died for it, many and many, before the Charter brought peace. Nymphs were quick and vicious, but naiads, oh: if a naiad rose from the deeps, whole settlements were wise to run.

Survivors learned to be more circumspect, to keep their distance from the highpines. They watched—from distance, yes—and learned the merlin cycle: from nymph to naiad, unhurriedly, uncounted years coming to maturity in the deep waters, in the dark; and then the climb into air, the stiffening skin, the months of hanging sessile and dry among the cones, indistinguishable. They must have faced predators at one time, people said, to need such a disguise. It was impossible to imagine now. The Church had another argument, that God made the merlins this way to show that they were an element of nature and no different, no better than any other animal, only larger and more dangerous than most. They could point for proof to the airhead imago which tore itself free of the chrysalis and lived a short, gay, heedless life in flight. They could and did do that until the first bold settler—a woman, as it happened—learned finger-talk and spoke with the first wary nymph.

Then no one could deny their intelligence, although their origins were mysterious and their motives obscure. Even more obscure, once it was understood that the great ships that shuttled swiftly and silently between Mars and Earth were merlin-piloted. No one knew how or why, but sometimes a chrysalis would not hatch, its imago not emerge. Instead another choice was made, internally or otherwise. The skin would harden to this burnished shell, and the pupa would be cut away whole from its tree, borne off by imagines to become the living brain in a ship that spanned the aether.

"This," Cobb murmured. "This is what he died for."

"Indeed. And what a sacrifice that was." One of the shirtsleeved men—not doctors, no; scientists, anatomists, not here to heal after all—ran his hands over the textured surface of the stolen chrysalis. Awed and covetous and possessive all three, those hands, his face. "His life for us, for our future, for our race. He took this and had to row it across the lake, where the racket of a steam-yacht would have brought the naiads up. Even so, they knew; he was barely ahead of the imagines when he reached the safety of the city. No safety for him, he knew his life must be forfeit under the Charter. He thought it worthwhile. He told me so himself. I think it was the Viceroy's sense of humour, or else his sense of honour, that had us smuggle it here under the guise of Sir John's coffin. We've told the merlins that he destroyed it trying to open the thing, that he was mad, quite mad. They don't believe us, of course. They're hanging over Cassini now and watching everything—but they won't look here, they think it's revolting how we treat our dead.

"We'll be here some time, I expect," he said, "trying to understand the thing, and how to make it fly. You need to know that. If we can learn how the merlin ships are worked, if we can train it to fly for us, we won't be dependent any more. We can build our own ships, harvest as many of these as we need, and sail the aether as we ought, under the Pax Britannica. We could take our empire to the stars, and wouldn't the Widow love that?"

"But the Charter . . ." They couldn't think to hang a man for every chrysalis they took. There weren't that many heroes.

"Once we know," the man said, "once we have the wherewithal to fly ships of our own, we can write a new Charter. Or tear it up. We only negotiated because we need them to ferry us back and forth. When that's no longer true—well. We needn't live in fear any longer. The Army can subdue the creatures, sure. Exterminate them if need be. It may be their time. No one here believes that they built the canals, or the aether-ships either; they don't have the physical make-up for engineering on that scale, whether or not they have the intelligence. They inherited this world from some other race, or else they took it by force. The same must be true of the ships. Now it's our turn, perhaps, to take it all from them. This could be the first step on that journey, what we do here, what we learn."

Perhaps all men of science were so ruthless. Cobb looked again at the scalpels and the little saws, the drills, the electrical wires; and felt glad that the creature in its shell had no mouth to scream with, to eat like acid at Cobb's day. His days.

And turned to go, because surely this was why he was here, to understand this, that secret men would be inhabiting this vault a while with their experiments. Well, he knew it now; and the air would be cleaner outside.

And he had barely gone two paces before he checked, and turned, and said, "Sir John—where is he now? And when will he be brought here?" *And how?* would have been another question. Not in pomp, clearly, not as he deserved. Many a hero had seen a hurried grave, though, and . . .

"Oh, he shan't come here." That was the dean, interrupting coldly. "The archbishop has declared it. This far from home we must be stricter, more adherent to the rule of God's law and the Established Church. By any measure, Sir John's death was a suicide. He did what he did, he chose to do it, knowing what must follow. A sacrifice, yes—but he put his own head in the noose, and did it willingly. He cannot be buried in consecrated ground. You must do with him as you do for other executed felons, back at the prison, where his body lies."

Had Cobb thought that scientists were ruthless?

The hanged in this city were supposed to lack even an unmarked grave. Tradition would have buried them beneath the prison yard, but the merlins would not bear that, and there was in any case no soil on the crater rim. It was Cobb's task then to immerse them in a solution of lye for a few hours, until their flesh was gone. Then he was meant to crush the fragile surviving bone—with the flat of his eternal spade, yes—and scatter the powder to the winds.

"As I do for the others, sir, yes."

First the barrel of lye, yes, to eat off the corruptible flesh; but then—well, old Cobb knew the value of his work. It was a sacrament, almost. And he came and went between the city and the island, and no one ever wondered what he ferried back and forth, what he might be bearing in his sack. And he had his own private graveyard in a distant corner, where he brought lost men unsupervised to God, felons no less than wanderers.

There would be digging after all, this day.

The Regular

Ken Liu

Ken Liu is an author and translator of speculative fiction, as well as a lawyer and programmer. His fiction has appeared in The Magazine of Fantasy & Science Fiction, Asimov's Science Fiction, Analog Science Fiction and Fact, Clarkesworld, Lightspeed, *and* Strange Horizons, *among many other places. He has won a Nebula, two Hugos, a World Fantasy Award, and a Science Fiction & Fantasy Translation Award, and has been nominated for the Theodore Sturgeon Memorial Award and the Locus Award. He lives with his family near Boston, Massachusetts.*

Here he spins a tightly told and suspenseful futuristic crime drama, featuring a cyborg detective whose emotions are controlled by a regulating device and who is on the trail of a creepy serial killer.

T his is Jasmine," she says.

"It's Robert."

The voice on the phone is the same as the one she had spoken to earlier in the afternoon.

"Glad you made it, sweetie." She looks out the window. He's standing at the corner, in front of the convenience store as she asked. He looks clean and is dressed well, like he's going on a date. A good sign. He's also wearing a Red Sox cap pulled low over his brow, a rather amateurish attempt at anonymity. "I'm down the street from you, at 27 Moreland. It's the gray stone condo building converted from a church."

He turns to look. "You have a sense of humor."

They all make that joke, but she laughs anyway. "I'm in unit 24, on the second floor."

"Is it just you? I'm not going to see some linebacker type demanding that I pay him first?"

"I told you. I'm independent. Just have your donation ready and you'll have a good time."

She hangs up and takes a quick look in the mirror to be sure she's ready. The black stockings and garter belt are new, and the lace bustier accentuates her thin waist and makes her breasts seem larger. She's done her makeup lightly, but the eyeshadow is heavy to emphasize her eyes. Most of her customers like that. Exotic.

The sheets on the king-sized bed are fresh, and there's a small wicker basket of condoms on the nightstand, next to a clock that says "5:58." The date is for two hours, and afterwards she'll have enough time to clean up and shower and then sit in front of the TV to catch her favorite show. She thinks about calling her mom later that night to ask about how to cook porgy.

She opens the door before he can knock, and the look on his face tells her that she's done well. He slips in; she closes the door, leans against it, and smiles at him.

"You're even prettier than the picture in your ad," he says. He gazes into her eyes intently. "Especially the eyes."

"Thank you."

As she gets a good look at him in the hallway, she concentrates on her right eye and blinks rapidly twice. She doesn't think she'll ever need it, but a girl has to protect herself. If she ever stops doing this, she thinks she'll just have it taken out and thrown into the bottom of Boston Harbor, like the way she used to, as a little girl, write secrets down on bits of paper, wad them up, and flush them down the toilet.

He's good looking in a non-memorable way: over six feet, tanned skin, still has all his hair, and the body under that crisp shirt looks fit. The eyes are friendly and kind, and she's pretty sure he won't be too rough. She guesses that he's in his forties, and maybe works downtown in one of the law firms or financial services companies, where his long-sleeved shirt and dark pants make sense with the air conditioning always turned high. He has that entitled arrogance that many mistake for masculine attractiveness. She notices that there's a paler patch of skin around his ring finger. Even better. A married man is usually safer. A married man who doesn't want her to know he's married is the safest of all: he values what he has and doesn't want to lose it.

She hopes he'll be a regular.

"I'm glad we're doing this." He holds out a plain white envelope.

She takes it and counts the bills inside. Then she puts it on top of the stack of mail on a small table by the entrance without saying anything. She takes him by the hand and leads him towards the bedroom. He pauses to look in the bathroom and then the other bedroom at the end of the hall.

"Looking for your linebacker?" she teases.

"Just making sure. I'm a nice guy."

He takes out a scanner and holds it up, concentrating on the screen.

"Geez, you *are* paranoid," she says. "The only camera in here is the one on my phone. And it's definitely off."

He puts the scanner away and smiles. "I know. But I just wanted to have a machine confirm it."

They enter the bedroom. She watches him take in the bed, the bottles of lubricants and lotions on the dresser, and the long mirrors covering the closet doors next to the bed.

"Nervous?" she asks.

"A little," he concedes. "I don't do this often. Or, at all."

She comes up to him and embraces him, letting him breathe in her perfume, which is floral and light so that it won't linger on his skin. After a moment, he puts his arms around her, resting his hands against the naked skin on the small of her back.

"I've always believed that one should pay for experiences rather than things."

"A good philosophy," he whispers into her ear.

"What I give you is the girlfriend experience, old fashioned and sweet. And you'll remember this and relive it in your head as often as you want."

"You'll do whatever I want?"

"Within reason," she says. Then she lifts her head to look up at him. "You have to wear a condom. Other than that, I won't say no to most things. But like I told you on the phone, for some you'll have to pay extra."

"I'm pretty old-fashioned myself. Do you mind if I take charge?"

He's made her relaxed enough that she doesn't jump to the worst conclusion. "If you're thinking of tying me down, that will cost you. And I won't do that until I know you better."

"Nothing like that. Maybe hold you down a little."

"That's fine."

He comes up to her and they kiss. His tongue lingers in her mouth and she moans. He backs up, puts his hands on her waist, turning her away from him. "Would you lie down with your face in the pillows?"

"Of course." She climbs onto the bed. "Legs up under me or spread out to the corners?"

"Spread out, please." His voice is commanding. And he hasn't stripped yet, not even taken off his Red Sox cap. She's a little disappointed. Some clients enjoy the obedience more than the sex. There's not much for her to do. She just hopes he won't be too rough and leave marks.

He climbs onto the bed behind her and knee-walks up between her legs. He leans down and grabs a pillow from next to her head. "Very lovely," he says. "I'm going to hold you down now."

She sighs into the bed, the way she knows he'll like.

He lays the pillow over the back of her head and pushes down firmly to hold her in place.He takes the gun out of the small of his back, and in one swift motion, sticks the barrel, thick and long with the silencer, into the back of the bustier, and squeezes off two quick shots into her heart. She dies instantly.

He removes the pillow, stores the gun away. Then he takes a small steel surgical kit out of his jacket pocket, along with a pair of latex gloves. He works efficiently and quickly, cutting with precision and grace. He relaxes when he's found what he's looking for—sometimes he picks the wrong girl—not often, but it has happened. He's careful to wipe off any sweat on his face with his sleeves as he works, and the hat helps to prevent any hair from falling on her. Soon, the task is done.

He climbs off the bed, takes off the bloody gloves, and leaves them and the surgical kit on the body. He puts on a fresh pair of gloves and moves through the apartment, methodically searching for places where she hid cash: inside the toilet tank, the back of the freezer, the nook above the door of the closet.

He goes into the kitchen and returns with a large plastic trash bag. He picks up the bloody gloves and the surgical kit and throws them into the bag. Picking up her phone, he presses the button for her voicemail. He deletes all the messages, including the one he had left when he first called her number. There's not much he can do about the call logs at the phone company, but he cantake advantage of that by leaving his prepaid phone somewhere for the police to find.

He looks at her again. He's not sad, not exactly, but he does feel a sense of waste. The girl was pretty and he would have liked to enjoy her first, but that would leave behind too many traces, even with a condom. And he can always pay for another, later. He likes paying for things. Power flows to *him* when he pays.

Reaching into the inner pocket of his jacket, he retrieves a sheet of paper, which he carefully unfolds and leaves by the girl's head.

He stuffs the trash bag and the money into a small gym bag he found in one of the closets. He leaves quietly, picking up the envelope of cash next to the entrance on the way out.

Because she's meticulous, Ruth Law runs through the numbers on the spreadsheet one last time, a summary culled from credit card and bank statements, and compares them against the numbers on the tax return. There's no doubt. The client's husband has been hiding money from the IRS, and more importantly, from the client.

Summers in Boston can be brutally hot. But Ruth keeps the air conditioner off in her tiny office above a butcher shop in Chinatown. She's made a lot of people unhappy over the years, and there's no reason to make it any easier for them to sneak up on her with the extra noise.

She takes out her cell phone and starts to dial from memory. She never stores any numbers in the phone. She tells people it's for safety, but sometimes she wonders if it's a gesture, however small, of asserting her independence from machines.

She stops at the sound of someone coming up the stairs. The footfalls are crisp and dainty, probably a woman, probably one with sensible heels. The scanner in the stairway hasn't been set off by the presence of a weapon, but that doesn't mean anything—she can kill without a gun or knife, and so can many others.

Ruth deposits her phone noiselessly on the desk and reaches into her drawer to wrap the fingers of her right hand around the reassuring grip of the Glock 19. Only then does she turn slightly to the side to glance at the monitor showing the feed from the security camera mounted over the door.

She feels very calm. The Regulator is doing its job. There's no need to release any adrenaline yet.

The visitor, in her fifties, is in a blue short-sleeve cardigan and white pants. She's looking around the door for a button for the doorbell. Her hair is so black that it must be dyed. She looks Chinese, holding her thin, petite body in a tight, nervous posture.

Ruth relaxes and lets go of the gun to push the button to open the door. She stands up and holds out her hand. "What can I do for you?"

"Are you Ruth Law, the private investigator?" In the woman's accent Ruth hears traces of Mandarin rather than Cantonese or Fukienese. Probably not well-connected in Chinatown then.

"I am."

The woman looks surprised, as if Ruth isn't quite who she expected. "Sarah Ding. I thought you were Chinese."

As they shake hands Ruth looks Sarah level in the eyes: they're about the same height, five foot four. Sarah looks well maintained, but her fingers feel cold and thin, like a bird's claw.

"I'm half-Chinese," Ruth says. "My father was Cantonese, second generation; my mother was white. My Cantonese is barely passable, and I never learned Mandarin."

Sarah sits down in the armchair across from Ruth's desk. "But you have an office here."

She shrugs. "I've made my enemies. A lot of non-Chinese are uncomfortable moving around in Chinatown. They stick out. So it's safer for me to have my office here. Besides, you can't beat the rent."

Sarah nods wearily. "I need your help with my daughter." She slides a collapsible file across the desk towards her.

Ruth sits down but doesn't reach for the file. "Tell me about her."

"Mona was working as an escort. A month ago she was shot and killed in her apartment. The police think it's a robbery, maybe gang-related, and they have no leads."

"It's a dangerous profession," Ruth says. "Did you know she was doing it?"

"No. Mona had some difficulties after college, and we were never as close as . . . I would have liked. We thought she was doing better the last two years, and she told us she had a job in publishing. It's difficult to know your child when you can't be the kind of mother she wants or needs. This country has different rules."

Ruth nods. A familiar lament from immigrants. "I'm sorry for your loss. But it's unlikely I'll be able to do anything. Most of my cases now are about hidden assets, cheating spouses, insurance fraud, background checks, that sort of thing. Back when I was a member of the force, I did work in Homicide. I know the detectives are quite thorough in murder cases."

"They're not!" Fury and desperation strain and crack her voice. "They think she's just a Chinese whore, and she died because she was stupid or got involved with a Chinese gang who wouldn't bother regular people. My husband is so ashamed that he won't even mention her name. But she's my daughter, and she's worth everything I have, and more."

Ruth looks at her. She can feel the Regulator suppressing her pity. Pity can lead to bad business decisions.

"I keep on thinking there was some sign I should have seen, some way to tell her that I loved her that I didn't know. If only I had been a little less busy, a little more willing to pry and dig and to be hurt by her. I can't stand the way the detectives talk to me, like I'm wasting their time but they don't want to show it."

Ruth refrains from explaining that the police detectives are all fitted with Regulators that should make the kind of prejudice she's implying impossible. The whole point of the Regulator is to make police work under pressure more regular, less dependent on hunches, emotional impulses, appeals to hidden prejudice. If the police are calling it a gang-related act of violence, there are likely good reasons for doing so.

She says nothing because the woman in front of her is in pain, and guilt and love are so mixed up in her that she thinks paying to find her daughter's killer will make her feel better about being the kind of mother whose daughter would take up prostitution.

Her angry, helpless posture reminds Ruth vaguely of something she tries to put out of her mind.

"Even if I find the killer," she says, "it won't make you feel better."

"I don't care." Sarah tries to shrug but the American gesture looks awkward and uncertain on her. "My husband thinks I've gone crazy. I know how hopeless this is; you're not the first investigator I've spoken to. But a few suggested you because you're a woman and Chinese, so maybe you care just enough to see something they can't."

She reaches into her purse and retrieves a check, sliding it across the table to put on top of the file. "Here's eighty thousand dollars. I'll pay double your daily rate and all expenses. If you use it up, I can get you more."

Ruth stares at the check. She thinks about the sorry state of her finances. At forty-nine, how many more chances will she have to set aside some money for when she'll be too old to do this?

She still feels calm and completely rational, and she knows that the Regulator is doing its job. She's sure that she's making her decision based on costs and benefits and a realistic evaluation of the case, and not because of the hunched over shoulders of Sarah Ding, looking like fragile twin dams holding back a flood of grief.

"Okay," she says. "Okay."

The man's name isn't Robert. It's not Paul or Matt or Barry either. He never uses the name John because jokes like that will only make the girls nervous. A long time ago, before he had been to prison, they had called him the Watcher because he liked to observe and take in a scene, finding the best opportunities and escape routes. He still thinks of himself that way when he's alone.

In the room he's rented at the cheap motel along Route 128, he starts his day by taking a shower to wash off the night sweat.

This is the fifth motel he's stayed in during the last month. Any stay longer than a week tends to catch the attention of the people working at the motels. He watches; he does not get watched. Ideally, he supposes he should get away from Boston altogether, but he hasn't exhausted the city's possibilities. It doesn't feel right to leave before he's seen all he wants to see.

The Watcher got about sixty thousand dollars in cash from the girl's apartment, not bad for a day's work. The girls he picks are intensely aware of the brevity of their careers, and with no bad habits, they pack away money like squirrels preparing for the winter. Since they can't exactly put it into the bank without raising the suspicion of the IRS, they tuck the money away in stashes in their apartments, ready for him to come along and claim them like found treasure.

The money is a nice bonus, but not the main attraction.

He comes out of the shower, dries himself, and wrapped in a towel, sits down to work at the nut he's trying to crack. It's a small, silver half-sphere, like half of a walnut. When he had first gotten it, it had been covered in blood and gore, and he had wiped it again and again with paper towels moistened under the motel sink until it gleamed.

He pries open an access port on the back of the device. Opening his laptop, he plugs one end of a cable into it and the other end into the half-sphere. He starts a program he had paid a good sum of money for and lets it run. It would probably be more efficient for him to leave the program running all the time, but he likes to be there to see the moment the encryption is broken.

While the program runs, he browses the escort ads. Right now he's searching for pleasure, not business, so instead of looking for girls like Jasmine, he looks for girls he craves. They're expensive, but not too expensive, the kind that remind him of the girls he had wanted back in high school: loud, fun, curvaceous now but destined to put on too much weight in a few years, a careless beauty that was all the more desirable because it was fleeting.

The Watcher knows that only a poor man like he had been at seventeen would bother courting women, trying desperately to make them like him. A man with money, with power, like he is now, can buy what he wants. There's purity and cleanliness to his desire that he feels is nobler and less deceitful than the desire of poor men. They only wish they could have what he does.

The program beeps, and he switches back to it.

Success.

Images, videos, sound recordings are being downloaded onto the computer.

The Watcher browses through the pictures and video recordings. The pictures are face shots or shots of money being handed over—he immediately deletes the ones of him.

But the videos are the best. He settles back and watches the screen flicker, admiring Jasmine's camerawork.

He separates the videos and images by client and puts them into folders. It's tedious work, but he enjoys it.

The first thing Ruth does with the money is to get some badly needed tune-ups. Going after a killer requires that she be in top condition.

She does not like to carry a gun when she's on the job. A man in a sport coat with a gun concealed under it can blend into almost any situation, but a woman wearing the kind of clothes that would hide a gun would often stick out like a sore thumb. Keeping a gun in a purse is a terrible idea. It creates a false sense of security, but a purse can be easily snatched away and then she would be disarmed.

She's fit and strong for her age, but her opponents are almost always taller and heavier and stronger. She's learned to compensate for these disadvantages by being more alert and by striking earlier.

But it's still not enough.

She goes to her doctor. Not the one on her HMO card.

Doctor B had earned his degree in another country and then had to leave home forever because he pissed off the wrong people. Instead of doing a second residency and becoming licensed here, which would have made him easily traceable, he had decided to simply keep on practicing medicine on his own. He would do things doctors who cared about their licenses wouldn't do. He would take patients they wouldn't touch.

"It's been a while," Doctor B says.

"Check over everything," she tells him. "And replace what needs replacement."

"Rich uncle die?"

"I'm going on a hunt."

Doctor B nods and puts her under.

He checks the pneumatic pistons in her legs, the replacement composite tendons in her shoulders and arms, the power cells and artificial muscles in her arms, the reinforced finger bones. He recharges what needs to be recharged. He examines the results of the calcium-deposition treatments (a counter to the fragility of her bones, an unfortunate side effect of her Asian heritage), and makes adjustments to her Regulator so that she can keep it on for longer.

"Like new," he tells her. And she pays.

Next, Ruth looks through the file Sarah brought.

There are photographs: the prom, high school graduation, vacations with friends, college commencement. She notes the name of the school without surprise or sorrow even though Jess had dreamed of going there as well. The Regulator, as always, keeps her equanimous, receptive to information, only useful information.

The last family photo Sarah selected was taken at Mona's twenty-fourth birthday earlier in the year. Ruth examines it carefully. In the picture, Mona is seated between Sarah and her husband, her arms around her parents in a gesture of careless joy. There's no hint of the secret she was keeping from them, and no sign, as far as Ruth can tell, of bruises, drugs, or other indications that life was slipping out of her control.

Sarah had chosen the photos with care. The pictures are designed to fill in Mona's life, to make people care for her. But she didn't need to do that. Ruth would have given it the same amount of effort even if she knew nothing about the girl's life. She's a professional.

There's a copy of the police report and the autopsy results. The report mostly confirms what Ruth has already guessed: no sign of drugs in Mona's systems, no forced entry, no indication there was a struggle. There was pepper spray in the drawer of the nightstand, but it hadn't been used. Forensics had vacuumed the scene and the hair and skin cells of dozens, maybe hundreds, of men had turned up, guaranteeing that no useful leads will result.

Mona had been killed with two shots through the heart, and then her body had been mutilated, with her eyes removed. She hadn't been sexually assaulted. The apartment had been ransacked of cash and valuables.

Ruth sits up. The method of killing is odd. If the killer had intended to mutilate her face anyway, there was no reason to not shoot her in the back of the head, a cleaner, surer method of execution.

A note was found at the scene in Chinese, which declared that Mona had been punished for her sins. Ruth can't read Chinese but she assumes the police translation is accurate. The police had also pulled Mona's phone records. There were a fewnumbers whose cell tower data showed their owners had been to Mona's place that day. The only one without an alibi was a prepaid phone without a registered owner. The police had tracked it down in Chinatown, hidden in a dumpster. They hadn't been able to get any further.

A rather sloppy kill, Ruth thinks, if the gangs did it.

Sarah had also provided printouts of Mona's escort ads. Mona had used several aliases: Jasmine, Akiko, Sinn. Most of the pictures are of her in lingerie, a few in cocktail dresses. The shots are framed to emphasize her body: a side view of her breasts half-veiled in lace, a back view of her buttocks, lounging on the bed with her hand over her hip. Shots of her face have black bars over her eyes to provide some measure of anonymity.

Ruth boots up her computer and logs onto the sites to check out the other ads. She had never worked in vice, so she takes a while to familiarize herself with the lingo and acronyms. The Internet had apparently transformed the business, allowing women to get off the streets and become "independent providers" without pimps. The sites are organized to allow customers to pick out exactly what they want. They can sort and filter by price, age, services provided, ethnicity, hair and eye color, time of availability, and customer ratings. The business is competitive, and there's a brutal efficiency to the sites that Ruth might have found depressing without the Regulator: you can measure, if you apply statistical software to it, how much a girl depreciates with each passing year, how much value men place on each pound, each inch of deviation from the ideal they're seeking, how much more a blonde really is worth than a brunette, and how much more a girl who can pass as Japanese can charge than one who cannot.

Some of the ad sites charge a membership fee to see pictures of the girls' faces. Sarah had also printed these "premium" photographs of Mona. For a brief moment Ruth wonders what Sarah must have felt as she paid to unveil the seductive gaze of her daughter, the daughter who had seemed to have a trouble-free, promising future.

In these pictures Mona's face was made up lightly, her lips curved in a promising or innocent smile. She was extraordinarily pretty, even compared to the other girls in her price range. She dictated in-calls only, perhaps believing them to be safer, with her being more in control.

Compared to most of the other girls, Mona's ads can be described as "elegant." They're free of spelling errors and overtly crude language, hinting at the kind of sexual fantasies that men here harbor about Asian women while also promising an American wholesomeness, the contrast emphasizing the strategically placed bits of exoticism.

The anonymous customer reviews praised her attitude and willingness to "go the extra mile." Ruth supposes that Mona had earned good tips.

Ruth turns to the crime scene photos and the bloody, eyeless shots of Mona's face. Intellectually and dispassionately, she absorbs the details in Mona's room. She contemplates the contrast between them and the eroticism of the ad photos. This was a young woman who had been vain about her education, who had believed that she could construct, through careful words and images, a kind of filter to attract the right kind of clients. It was naïve and wise at the same time, and Ruth can almost feel, despite the Regulator, a kind of poignancy to her confident desperation.

Whatever caused her to go down this path, she had never hurt anyone, and now she was dead.

Ruth meets Luo in a room reached through long underground tunnels and many locked doors. It smells of mold and sweat and spicy foods rotting in trash bags.

Along the way she saw a few other locked rooms behind which she guessed were human cargo, people who indentured themselves to the snakeheads for a chance to be smuggled into this country so they could work for a dream of wealth. She says nothing about them. Her deal with Luo depends on her discretion, and Luo is kinder to his cargo than many others.

He pats her down perfunctorily. She offers to strip to show that she's not wired. He waves her off.

"Have you seen this woman?" she asks in Cantonese, holding up a picture of Mona.

Luo dangles the cigarette from his lips while he examines the picture closely. The dim light gives the tattoos on his bare shoulders and arms a greenish tint. After a moment, he hands it back. "I don't think so."

"She was a prostitute working out of Quincy. Someone killed her a month ago and left this behind." She brings out the photograph of the note left at the scene. "The police think the Chinese gangs did it."

Luo looks at the photo. He knits his brow in concentration and then barks out a dry laugh. "Yes, this is indeed a note left behind by a Chinese gang."

"Do you recognize the gang?"

"Sure." Luo looks at Ruth, a grin revealing the gaps in his teeth. "This note was left behind by the impetuous Tak-Kao, member of the Forever Peace Gang, after he killed the innocent Mai-Ying, the beautiful maid from the mainland, in a fit of jealousy. You can see the original in the third season of *My Hong Kong, Your Hong Kong*. You're lucky that I'm a fan."

"This is copied from a soap opera?"

"Yes. Either your man likes to make jokes or he doesn't know Chinese well and got this from some Internet search. It might fool the police, but no, we wouldn't leave a note like that." He chuckles at the thought and then spits on the ground.

"Maybe it was just a fake to confuse the police." She chooses her words carefully. "Or maybe it was done by one gang to sic the police onto the others. The police also found a phone, probably used by the killer, in a Chinatown dumpster. I know there are several Asian massage parlors in Quincy, so maybe this girl was too much competition. Are you sure you don't know anything about this?"

Luo flips through the other photographs of Mona. Ruth watches him, getting ready to react to any sudden movements. She thinks she can trust Luo, but one can't always predict the reaction of a man who often has to kill to make his living.

She concentrates on the Regulator, priming it to release adrenaline to quicken her movements if necessary. The pneumatics in her legs are charged, and she braces her back against the damp wall in case she needs to kick out. The sudden release of pressure in the air canisters installed next to her tibia will straighten her legs in a fraction of a second, generating hundreds of pounds of force. If her feet connect with Luo's chest, she will almost certainly break a few ribs—though Ruth's back will ache for days afterwards, as well.

"I like you, Ruth," Luo says, noting her sudden stillness out of the corner of his eyes. "You don't have to be afraid. I haven't forgotten how you found that bookie who tried to steal from me. I'll always tell you the truth or tell you I can't answer. We have nothing to do with this girl. She's not really competition. The men who go to massage parlors for $60 an hour and a happy ending are not the kind who'd pay for a girl like this."

The Watcher drives to Somerville, just over the border from Cambridge, north of Boston. He parks in the back of a grocery store parking lot, where his Toyota Corolla, bought off a lot with cash, doesn't stick out.

Then he goes into a coffee shop and emerges with an iced coffee. Sipping it, he walks around the sunny streets, gazing from time to time at the little gizmo attached to his keychain. The gizmo tells him when he's in range of some unsecured home wireless network. Lots of students from Harvard and MIT live here, where the rent is high but not astronomical. Addicted to good wireless access, they often get powerful routers for tiny apartments and leak the network onto the streets without bothering to secure them (after all, they have friends coming over all the time who need to remain connected). And since it's summer, when the population of students is in flux, there's even less likelihood that he can be traced from using one of their networks.

It's probably overkill, but he likes to be safe.

He sits down on a bench by the side of the street, takes out his laptop, and connects to a network called "INFORMATION_WANTS_TO_BE_FREE." He enjoys disproving the network owner's theory. Information doesn't want to be free. It's valuable and wants to earn. And its existence doesn't free anyone; possessing it, however, can do the opposite.

The Watcher carefully selects a segment of video and watches it one last time.

Jasmine had done a good job, intentionally or not, with the framing, and the man's sweaty grimace is featured prominently in the video. His movements—and as a result, Jasmine's—made the video jerky, and so he's had to apply software image stabilization. But now it looks quite professional.

The Watcher had tried to identify the man, who looks Chinese, by uploading a picture he got from Jasmine into a search engine. They are always making advancements in facial recognition software, and sometimes he gets hits this way. But it didn't seem to work this time. That's not a problem for the Watcher. He has other techniques.

The Watcher signs on to a forum where the expat Chinese congregate to reminisce and argue politics in their homeland. He posts the picture of the man in the video and writes below in English, "Anyone famous?" Then he sips his coffee and refreshes the screen from time to time to catch the new replies.

The Watcher doesn't read Chinese (or Russian, or Arabic, or Hindi, or any of the other languages where he plies his trade), but linguistic skills are hardly necessary for this task. Most of the expats speak English and can understand his question. He's just using these people as research tools, a human flesh–powered, crowdsourced search engine. It's almost funny how people are so willing to give perfect strangers over the Internet information, would even compete with each other to do it, to show how knowledgeable they are. He's pleased to make use of such petty vanities.

He simply needs a name and a measure of the prominence of the man, and for that, the crude translations offered by computers are sufficient.

From the almost-gibberish translations, he gathers that the man is a prominent official in the Chinese Transport Ministry, and like almost all Chinese officials, he's despised by his countrymen. The man is a bigger deal than the Watcher's usual targets, but that might make him a good demonstration.

The Watcher is thankful for Dagger, who had explained Chinese politics to him. One evening, after he had gotten out of jail the last time, the Watcher had hung back and watched a Chinese man rob a few Chinese tourists near San Francisco's Chinatown.

The tourists had managed to make a call to 911, and the robber had fled the scene on foot down an alley. But the Watcher had seen something in the man's direct, simple approach that he liked. He drove around the block, stopped by the other end of the alley, and when the man emerged, he swung open the passenger side door and offered him a chance to escape in his car. The man thanked him and told him his name was Dagger.

Dagger was talkative and told the Watcher how angry and envious people in China were of the Party officials, who lived an extravagant life on the money squeezed from the common people, took bribes, and funneled public funds to their relatives. He targeted those tourists who he thought were the officials' wives and children, and regarded himself as a modern Robin Hood.

Yet, the officials were not completely immune. All it took was a public scandal of some kind, usually involving young women who were not their wives. Talk of democracy didn't get people excited, but seeing an official rubbing their graft in their faces made them see red. And the Party apparatus would have no choice but to punish the disgraced officials, as the only thing the Party feared was public anger, which always threatened to boil out of control. If a revolution were to come to China, Dagger quipped, it would be triggered by mistresses, not speeches.

A light had gone on in the Watcher's head then. It was as if he could see the reins of power flowing from those who had secrets to those who knew secrets. He thanked Dagger and dropped him off, wishing him well.

The Watcher imagines what the official's visit to Boston had been like. He had probably come to learn about the city's experience with light rail, but it was likely in reality just another State-funded vacation, a chance to shop at the luxury stores on Newbury Street, to enjoy expensive foods without fear of poison or pollution, and to anonymously take delight in quality female companionship without the threat of recording devices in the hands of an interested populace.

He posts the video to the forum, and as an extra flourish, adds a link to the official's biography on the Transport Ministry's web site. For a second, he regrets the forgone revenue, but it's been a while since he's done a demonstration, and these are necessary to keep the business going.

He packs up his laptop. Now he has to wait.

Ruth doesn't think there's much value in viewing Mona's apartment, but she's learned over the years to not leave any stone unturned. She gets the key from Sarah Ding and makes her way to the apartment around 6:00 in the evening. Viewing the site at approximately the time of day when the murder occurred can sometimes be helpful.

She passes through the living room. There's a small TV facing a futon, the kind of furniture that a young woman keeps from her college days when she doesn't have a reason to upgrade. It's a living room that was never meant for visitors.

She moves into the room in which the murder happened. The forensics team has cleaned it out. The room—it wasn't Mona's real bedroom, which was a tiny cubby down the hall, with just a twin bed and plain walls—is stripped bare, most of the loose items having been collected as evidence. The mattress is naked, as are the nightstands. The carpet has been vacuumed. The place smells like a hotel room: stale air and faint perfume.

Ruth notices the line of mirrors along the side of the bed, hanging over the closet doors. Watching arouses people.

She imagines how lonely Mona must have felt living here, touched and kissed and fucked by a stream of men who kept as much of themselves hidden from her as possible. She imagines her sitting in front of the small TV to relax, and dressing up to meet her parents so that she could lie some more.

Ruth imagines the way the murderer had shot Mona, and then cut her after. Were there more than one of them so that Mona thought a struggle was useless? Did they shoot her right away or did they ask her to tell them where she had hidden her money first? She can feel the Regulator starting up again, keeping her emotions in check. Evil has to be confronted dispassionately.

She decides she's seen all she needs to see. She leaves the apartment and pulls the door closed. As she heads for the stairs, she sees a man coming up, keys in hand. Their eyes briefly meet, and he turns to the door of the apartment across the hall.

Ruth is sure the police have interviewed the neighbor. But sometimes people will tell things to a nonthreatening woman that they are reluctant to tell the cops.

She walks over and introduces herself, explaining that she's a friend of Mona's family, here to tie up some loose ends. The man, whose name is Peter, is wary but shakes her hand.

"I didn't hear or see anything. We pretty much keep to ourselves in this building."

"I believe you. But it would be helpful if we can chat a bit anyway. The family didn't know much about her life here."

He nods reluctantly and opens the door. He steps in and waves his arms up and around in a complex sequence as though he's conducting an orchestra. The lights come on.

"That's pretty fancy," Ruth says. "You have the whole place wired up like that?"

His voice, cautious and guarded until now, grows animated. Talking about something other than the murder seems to relax him. "Yes. It's called EchoSense. They add an adaptor to your wireless router and a few antennas around the room, and then it uses the Doppler shifts generated by your body's movements in the radio waves to detect gestures."

"You mean it can see you move with just the signals from your wifi bouncing around the room?"

"Something like that."

Ruth remembers seeing an infomercial about this. She notes how small the apartment is and how little space separates it from Mona's. They sit down and chat about what Peter remembers about Mona.

"Pretty girl. Way out of my league, but she was always pleasant."

"Did she get a lot of visitors?"

"I don't pry into other people's business. But yeah, I remember lots of visitors, mostly men. I did think she might have been an escort. But that didn't bother me. The men always seemed clean, business types. Not dangerous."

"No one who looked like a gangster, for example?"

"I wouldn't know what gangsters look like. But no, I don't think so."

They chat on inconsequentially for another fifteen minutes, and Ruth decides that she's wasted enough time.

"Can I buy the router from you?" she asks. "And the EchoSense thing."

"You can just order your own set online."

"I hate shopping online. You can never return things. I know this one works; so I want it. I'll offer you two thousand, cash."

He considers this.

"I bet you can buy a new one and get another adaptor yourself from EchoSense for less than a quarter of that."

He nods and retrieves the router, and she pays him. The act feels somehow illicit, not unlike how she imagines Mona's transactions were.

Ruth posts an ad to a local classifieds site describing in vague terms what she's looking for. Boston is blessed with many good colleges and lots of young men and women who would relish a technical challenge even more than the money she offers. She looks through the resumes until she finds the one she feels has the right skills: jailbreaking phones, reverse-engineering proprietary protocols, a healthy disrespect for acronyms like DMCA and CFAA.

She meets the young man at her office and explains what she wants. Daniel, darkskinned, lanky, and shy, slouches in the chair across from hers as he listens without interrupting.

"Can you do it?" she asks.

"Maybe," he says. "Companies like this one will usually send customer data back to the mothership anonymously to help improve their technology. Sometimes the data is cached locally for a while. It's possible I'll find logs on there a month old. If it's there, I'll get it for you. But I'll have to figure out how they're encoding the data and then make sense of it."

"Do you think my theory is plausible?"

"I'm impressed you even came up with it. Wireless signals can go through walls, so it's certainly possible that this adaptor has captured the movements of people in neighboring apartments. It's a privacy nightmare, and I'm sure the company doesn't publicize that."

"How long will it take?"

"As little as a day or as much as a month. I won't know until I start. It will help if you can draw me a map of the apartments and what's inside."

Ruth does as he asked. Then she tells him, "I'll pay you three hundred dollars a day, with a five thousand dollar bonus if you succeed this week."

"Deal." He grins and picks up the router, getting ready to leave.

Because it never hurts to tell people what they're doing is meaningful, she adds, "You're helping to catch the killer of a young woman who's not much older than you."

Then she goes home because she's run out of things to try.

The first hour after waking up is always the worst part of the day for Ruth.

As usual, she wakes from a nightmare. She lies still, disoriented, the images from her dream superimposed over the sight of the water stains on the ceiling. Her body is drenched in sweat.

The man holds Jessica in front of him with his left hand while the gun in his right hand is pointed at her head. She's terrified, but not of him. He ducks so that her body shields his, and he whispers something into her ear.

"Mom! Mom!" she screams. "Don't shoot. Please don't shoot!"

Ruth rolls over, nauseated. She sits up at the edge of the bed, hating the smell of the hot room, the dust that she never has time to clean filling the air pierced by bright rays coming in from the east-facing window. She shoves the sheets off of her and stands up quickly, her breath coming too fast. She's fighting the rising panic without any help, alone, her Regulator off.

The clock on the nightstand says 6:00.

She's crouching behind the opened driver's side door of her car. Her hands shake as she struggles to keep the man's head, bobbing besides her daughter's, in the sight of her gun. If she turns on her Regulator, she thinks her hands may grow steady and give her a clear shot at him.

What are her chances of hitting him instead of her? Ninety-five percent? Ninety-nine?

"Mom! Mom! No!"

She gets up and stumbles into the kitchen to turn on the coffeemaker. She curses when she finds the can empty and throws it clattering into the sink. The noise shocks her and she cringes.

Then she struggles into the shower, sluggishly, painfully, as though the muscles that she conditions daily through hard exercise were not there. She turns on the hot water but it brings no warmth to her shivering body.

Grief descends on her like a heavy weight. She sits down in the shower, curling her body into itself. Water streams down her face so she does not know if there are tears as her body heaves.

She fights the impulse to turn on the Regulator. It's not time yet. She has to give her body the necessary rest.

The Regulator, a collection of chips and circuitry embedded at the top of her spine, is tied into the limbic system and the major blood vessels into the brain. Like its namesake from mechanical and electrical engineering, it maintains the levels of dopamine, noradrenaline, serotonin and other chemicals in the brain and in her blood stream. It filters out the chemicals when there's an excess, and releases them when there's a deficit.

And it obeys her will.

The implant allows a person control over her basic emotions: fear, disgust, joy, excitement, love. It's mandatory for law enforcement officers, a way to minimize the effects of emotions on life-or-death decisions, a way to eliminate prejudice and irrationality.

"You have clearance to shoot," the voice in her headset tells her. It's the voice of her husband, Scott, the head of her department. His voice is completely calm. His Regulator is on.

She sees the head of the man bobbing up and down as he retreats with Jessica. He's heading for the van parked by the side of the road.

"He's got other hostages in there," her husband continues to speak in her ear. "If you don't shoot, you put the lives of those three other girls and who knows how many other people in danger. This is our best chance."

The sound of sirens, her backup, is still faint. Too far away.

After what seems an eternity, she manages to stand up in the shower and turn off the water. She towels herself dry and dresses slowly. She tries to think of something, anything, to take her mind off its current track. But nothing works.

She despises the raw state of her mind. Without the Regulator, she feels weak, confused, angry. Waves of despair wash over her and everything appears in hopeless shades of grey. She wonders why she's still alive.

It will pass, she thinks. *Just a few more minutes.*

Back when she had been on the force, she had adhered to the regulation requirement not to leave the Regulator on for more than two hours at a time. There are physiological and psychological risks associated with prolonged use. Some of her fellow officers had also complained about the way the Regulator made them feel robotic, deadened. No excitement from seeing a pretty woman; no thrill at the potential for a car chase; no righteous anger when faced with an act of abuse. Everything had to be deliberate: you decided when to let the adrenaline flow, and just enough to get the job done and not too much to interfere with judgment. But sometimes, they argued, you needed emotions, instinct, intuition.

Her Regulator had been off when she came home that day and recognized the man hiding from the city-wide manhunt.

Have I been working too much? she thinks. I don't know any of her friends. When did Jess meet him? Why didn't I ask her more questions when she was coming home late every night? Why did I stop for lunch instead of coming home half an hour earlier? There are a thousand things I could have done and should have done and would have done.

Fear and anger and regret are mixed up in her until she cannot tell which is which.

"Engage your Regulator," her husband's voice tells her. "You can make the shot."

Why do I care about the lives of the other girls? she thinks. All I care about is Jess. Even the smallest chance of hurting her is too much.

Can she trust a machine to save her daughter? Should she rely on a machine to steady her shaking hands, to clear her blurry vision, to make a shot without missing?

"Mom, he's going to let me go later. He won't hurt me. He just wants to get away from here. Put the gun down!"

Maybe Scott can make a calculus about lives saved and lives put at risk. She won't. She will not trust a machine.

"It's okay, baby," she croaks out. "It's all going to be okay."

She does not turn on the Regulator. She does not shoot.

Later, after she had identified the body of Jess—the bodies of all four of the girls had been badly burnt when the bomb went off—after she had been disciplined and discharged, after Scott and she had split up, after she had found no solace in alcohol and pills, she did finally find the help she needed: she could leave the Regulator on all the time.

The Regulator deadened the pain, stifled grief and numbed the ache of loss. It held down the regret, made it possible to pretend to forget. She craved the calmness it brought, the blameless, serene clarity.

She had been wrong to distrust it. That distrust had cost her Jess. She would not make the same mistake again.

Sometimes she thinks of the Regulator as a dependable lover, a comforting presence to lean on. Sometimes she thinks she's addicted. She does not probe deeply behind these thoughts.

She would have preferred to never have to turn off the Regulator, to never be in a position to repeat her mistake. But even Doctor B balked at that ("Your brain will turn into mush."). The illegal modifications he did agree to make allow the Regulator to remain on for a maximum of twenty-three hours at a stretch.Then she must take an hour-long break during which she must remain conscious.

And so there's always this hour in the morning, right as she wakes, when she's naked and alone with her memories, unshielded from the rush of red-hot hatred (for the man? for herself?) and white-cold rage, and the black, bottomless abyss that she endures as her punishment.

The alarm beeps. She concentrates like a monk in meditation and feels the hum of the Regulator starting up. Relief spreads out from the center of her mind to the very tips of her fingers, the soothing, numbing serenity of a regulated, disciplined mind. To be regulated is to be a regular person.

She stands up, limber, graceful, powerful, ready to hunt.

The Watcher has identified more of the men in the pictures. He's now in a new motel room, this one more expensive than usual because he feels like he deserves a treat after all he's been through. Hunching over all day to edit video is hard work.

He pans the cropping rectangle over the video to give it a sense of dynamism and movement. There's an artistry to this.

He's amazed how so few people seem to know about the eye implants. There's something about eyes, so vulnerable, so essential to the way people see the world and themselves, that makes people feel protective and reluctant to invade them. The laws regarding eye modifications are the most stringent, and after a while, people begin to mistake "not permitted" with "not possible."

They don't know what they don't want to know.

All his life, he's felt that he's missed some key piece of information, some secret that everyone else seemed to know. He's intelligent, diligent, but somehow things have not worked out.

He never knew his father, and when he was eleven, his mother had left him one day at home with twenty dollars and never came back. A string of foster homes had followed, and *nobody*, nobody could tell him what he was missing, why he was always at the mercy of judges and bureaucrats, why he had so little control over his life, not where he would sleep, not when he would eat, not who would have power over him next.

He made it his subject to study men, to watch and try to understand what made them tick. Much of what he learned had disappointed him. Men were vain, proud, ignorant. They let their desires carry them away, ignored risks that were obvious. They did not think, did not plan. They did not know what they really wanted. They let the TV tell them what they should have and hoped that working at their pathetic jobs would make those wishes come true.

He craved control. He wanted to see them dance to his tune the way he had been made to dance to the tune of everyone else.

So he had honed himself to be pure and purposeful, like a sharp knife in a drawer full of ridiculous, ornate, fussy kitchen gadgets. He knew what he wanted and he worked at getting it with singular purpose.

He adjusts the colors and the dynamic range to compensate for the dim light in the video. He wants there to be no mistake in identifying the man.

He stretches his tired arms and sore neck. For a moment he wonders if he'll be better off if he pays to have parts of his body enhanced so he can work for longer, without pain and fatigue. But the momentary fancy passes.

Most people don't like medically unnecessary enhancements and would only accept them if they're required for a job. No such sentimental considerations for bodily integrity or "naturalness" constrain the Watcher. He does not like enhancements because he views reliance on them as a sign of weakness. He would defeat his enemies by his mind, and with the aid of planning and foresight. He does not need to depend on machines.

He had learned to steal, and then rob, and eventually how to kill for money. But the money was really secondary, just a means to an end. It was control that he desired. The only man he had killed was a lawyer, someone who lied for a living. Lying had brought him money, and that gave him power, made people bow down to him and smile at him and speak in respectful voices. The Watcher had loved that moment when the man begged him for mercy, when he would have done anything the Watcher wanted. The Watcher had taken what he wanted from the man rightfully, by superiority of intellect and strength. Yet, the Watcher had been caught and gone to jail for it. A system that rewarded liars and punished the Watcher could not in any sense be called just.

He presses "Save." He's done with this video.

Knowledge of the truth gave him power, and he would make others acknowledge it.

Before Ruth is about to make her next move, Daniel calls, and they meet in her office again.

"I have what you wanted."

He takes out his laptop and shows her an animation, like a movie.

"They stored videos on the adaptor?"

Daniel laughs. "No. The device can't really 'see' and that would be far too much data. No, the adaptor just stored readings, numbers. I made the animation so it's easier to understand."

She's impressed. The young man knows how to give a good presentation.

"The wifi echoes aren't captured with enough resolution to give you much detail. But you can get a rough sense of people's sizes and heights and their movements. This is what I got from the day and hour you specified."

They watch as a bigger, vaguely humanoid shape appears at Mona's apartment door, precisely at 6:00, meeting a smaller, vaguely humanoid shape.

"Seems they had an appointment," Daniel says.

They watch as the smaller shape leads the bigger shape into the bedroom, and then the two embrace. They watch the smaller shape climb into space—presumably onto the bed. They watch the bigger shape climb up after it. They watch the shooting, and then the smaller shape collapses and disappears. They watch the bigger shape lean over, and the smaller shape flickers into existence as it's moved from time to time.

So there was only one killer, Ruth thinks. *And he was a client.*

"How tall is he?"

"There's a scale to the side."

Ruth watches the animation over and over. The man is six foot two or six foot three, maybe 180 to 200 pounds. She notices that he has a bit of a limp as he walks.

She's now convinced that Luo was telling the truth. Not many Chinese men are six foot two, and such a man would stick out too much to be a killer for a gang. Every witness would remember him. Mona's killer had been a client, maybe even a regular. It wasn't a random robbery but carefully planned.

The man is still out there, and killers that meticulous rarely kill only once.

"Thank you," she says. "You might be saving another young woman's life."

Ruth dials the number for the police department.

"Captain Brennan, please."

She gives her name and her call is transferred, and then she hears the gruff, weary voice of her ex-husband. "What can I do for you?"

Once again, she's glad she has the Regulator. His voice dredges up memories of his raspy morning mumbles, his stentorian laughter, his tender whispers when they were alone, the soundtrack of twenty years of a life spent together, a life that they had both thought would last until one of them died.

"I need a favor."

He doesn't answer right away. She wonders if she's too abrupt—a side effect of leaving the Regulator on all the time. Maybe she should have started with "How've you been?"

Finally, he speaks. "What is it?" The voice is restrained, but laced with exhausted, desiccated pain.

"I'd like to use your NCIC access."

Another pause. "Why?"

"I'm working on the Mona Ding case. I think this is a man who's killed before and will kill again. He's got a method. I want to see if there are related cases in other cities."

"That's out of the question, Ruth. You know that. Besides, there's no point. We've run all the searches we can, and there's nothing similar. This was a Chinese gang protecting their business, simple as that. Until we have the resources in the Gang Unit to deal with it, I'm sorry, this will have to go cold for a while."

Ruth hears the unspoken. *The Chinese gangs have always preyed on their own. Until they bother the tourists, let's just leave them alone.* She'd heard similar sentiments often enough back when she was on the force. The Regulator could do nothing about certain kinds of prejudice. It's perfectly rational. And also perfectly wrong.

"I don't think so. I have an informant who says that the Chinese gangs have nothing to do with it."

Scott snorts. "Yes, of course you can trust the word of a Chinese snakehead. But there's also the note and the phone."

"The note is most likely a forgery. And do you really think this Chinese gang member would be smart enough to realize that the phone records would give him away and then decide that the best place to hide it was around his place of business?"

"Who knows? Criminals are stupid."

"The man is far too methodical for that. It's a red herring."

"You have no evidence."

"I have a good reconstruction of the crime and a description of the suspect. He's too tall to be the kind a Chinese gang would use."

This gets his attention. "From where?"

"A neighbor had a home motion-sensing system that captured wireless echoes into Mona's apartment. I paid someone to reconstruct it."

"Will that stand up in court?"

"I doubt it. It will take expert testimony and you'll have to get the company to admit that they capture that information. They'll fight it tooth and nail."

"Then it's not much use to me."

"If you give me a chance to look in the database, maybe I can turn it into something you *can* use." She waits a second and presses on, hoping that he'll be sentimental. "I've never asked you for much."

"This is the first time you've ever asked me for something like this."

"I don't usually take on cases like this."

"What is it about this girl?"

Ruth considers the question. There are two ways to answer it. She can try to explain the fee she's being paid and why she feels she's adding value. Or she can give what she suspects is the real reason. Sometimes the Regulator makes it hard to tell what's true. "Sometimes people think the police don't look as hard when the victim is a sex worker. I know your resources are constrained, but maybe I can help."

"It's the mother, isn't it? You feel bad for her."

Ruth does not answer. She can feel the Regulator kicking in again. Without it, perhaps she would be enraged.

"She's not Jess, Ruth. Finding her killer won't make you feel better."

"I'm asking for a favor. You can just say no."

Scott does not sigh, and he does not mumble. He's simply quiet. Then, a few seconds later: "Come to the office around 8:00. You can use the terminal in my office."

The Watcher thinks of himself as a good client. He makes sure he gets his money's worth, but he leaves a generous tip. He likes the clarity of money, the way it makes the flow of power obvious. The girl he just left was certainly appreciative.

He drives faster. He feels he's been too self-indulgent the last few weeks, working too slowly. He needs to make sure the last round of targets have paid. If not, he needs to carry through. Action. Reaction. It's all very simple once you understand the rules.

He rubs the bandage around his ring finger, which allows him to maintain the pale patch of skin that girls like to see. The lingering, sickly sweet perfume from the last girl—Melody, Mandy, he's already forgetting her name—reminds him of Tara, who he will never forget.

Tara may have been the only girl he's really loved. She was blonde, petite, and very expensive. But she had liked him for some reason. Perhaps because they were both broken, and the jagged pieces happened to fit.

She had stopped charging him and told him her real name. He was a kind of boyfriend. Because he was curious, she explained her business to him. How certain words and turns of phrase and tones on the phone were warning signs. What she looked for in a desired regular. What signs on a man probably meant he was safe. He enjoyed learning about this. It seemed to require careful watching by the girl, and he respected those who looked and studied and made the information useful.

He had looked into her eyes as he fucked her, and then said, "Is something wrong with your right eye?"

She had stopped moving. "What?"

"I wasn't sure at first. But yes, it's like you have something behind your eye."

She wriggled under him. He was annoyed and thought about holding her down. But he decided not to. She seemed about to tell him something important. He rolled off of her.

"You're very observant."

"I try. What is it?"

She told him about the implant.

"You've been recording your clients having sex with you?"

"Yes."

"I want to see the ones you have of us."

She laughed. "I'll have to go under the knife for that. Not going to happen until I retire. Having your skull opened up once was enough."

She explained how the recordings made her feel safe, gave her a sense of power, like having bank accounts whose balances only she knew and kept growing. If she were ever threatened, she would be able to call on the powerful men she knew for aid. And after retirement, if things didn't work out and she got desperate, perhaps she could use them to get her regulars to help her out a little.

He had liked the way she thought. So devious. So like him.

He had been sorry when he killed her. Removing her head was more difficult and messy than he had imagined. Figuring out what to do with the little silver half-sphere had taken months. He would learn to do better over time.

But Tara had been blind to the implications of what she had done. What she had wasn't just insurance, wasn't just a rainy-day fund. She had revealed to him that she had what it took to make his dream come true, and he had to take it from her.

He pulls into the parking lot of the hotel and finds himself seized by an unfamiliar sensation: sorrow. He misses Tara, like missing a mirror you've broken.

Ruth is working with the assumption that the man she's looking for targets independent prostitutes. There's an efficiency and a method to the way Mona was killed that suggested practice.

She begins by searching the NCIC database for prostitutes who had been killed by a suspect matching the EchoSense description. As she expects, she comes up with nothing that seems remotely similar. The man hadn't left obvious trails.

The focus on Mona's eyes may be a clue. Maybe the killer has a fetish for Asian women. Ruth changes her search to concentrate on body mutilations of Asian prostitutes similar to what Mona had suffered. Again, nothing.

Ruth sits back and thinks over the situation. It's common for serial killers to concentrate on victims of a specific ethnicity. But that may be a red herring here.

She expands her search to include all independent prostitutes who had been killed in the last year or so, and now there are too many hits. Dozens and dozens of killings of prostitutes of every description pop up. Most were sexually assaulted. Some were tortured. Many had their bodies mutilated. Almost all were robbed. Gangs were suspected in several cases. She sifts through them, looking for similarities. Nothing jumps out at her.

She needs more information.

She logs onto the escort sites in the various cities and looks up the ads of the murdered women. Not all of them remain online, as some sites deactivate ads when enough patrons complain about unavailability. She prints out what she can, laying them out side by side to compare.

Then she sees it. It's in the ads.

A subset of the ads triggers a sense of familiarity in Ruth's mind. They were all carefully written, free of spelling and grammar mistakes. They were frank but not explicit, seductive without verging on parody. The johns who posted reviews described them as "classy."

It's a signal, Ruth realizes. The ads are written to give off the air of being careful, selective, *discreet*. There is in them, for lack of a better word, a sense of *taste*.

All of the women in these ads were extraordinarily beautiful, with smooth skin and thick, long flowing hair. All of them were between twenty-two and thirty, not so young as to be careless or supporting themselves through school, and not old enough to lose the ability to pass for younger. All of them were independent, with no pimp or evidence of being on drugs.

Luo's words come back to her: *The men who go to massage parlors for $60 an hour and a happy ending are not the kind who'd pay for a girl like this.*

There's a certain kind of client who would be attracted to the signs given out by these girls, Ruth thinks: men who care very much about the risk of discovery and who believe that they deserve something special, suitable for their distinguished tastes.

She prints out the NCIC entries for the women.

All the women she's identified were killed in their homes. No sign of struggle— possibly because they were meeting a client. One was strangled, the others shot through the heart in the back, like Mona. In all the cases except one—the woman who was strangled—the police had found record of a suspicious call on the day of the murder from a prepaid phone that was later found somewhere in the city. The killer had taken all the women's money.

Ruth knows she's on the right track. Now she needs to examine the case reports in more detail to see if she can find more patterns to identify the killer.

The door to the office opens. It's Scott.

"Still here?" The scowl on his face shows that he does not have his Regulator on. "It's after midnight."

She notes, not for the first time, how the men in the department have often resisted the Regulator unless absolutely necessary, claiming that it dulled their instincts and hunches. But they had also asked her whether she had hers on whenever she dared to disagree with them. They would laugh when they asked.

"I think I'm onto something," she says, calmly.

"You working with the goddamned Feds now?"

"What are you talking about?"

"You haven't seen the news?"

"I've been here all evening."

He takes out his tablet, opens a bookmark, and hands it to her. It's an article in the international section of the *Globe*, which she rarely reads. "Scandal Unseats Chinese Transport Minister," says the headline.

She scans the article quickly. A video has surfaced on the Chinese microblogs showing an important official in the Transport Ministry having sex with a prostitute. Moreover, it seems that he had been paying her out of public funds. He's already been removed from his post due to the public outcry.

Accompanying the article is a grainy photo, a still capture from the video. Before the Regulator kicks in, Ruth feels her heart skip a beat. The image shows a man on top of a woman. Her head is turned to the side, directly facing the camera.

"That's your girl, isn't it?"

Ruth nods. She recognizes the bed and the nightstand with the clock and wicker basket from the crime scene photos.

"The Chinese are hopping mad. They think we had the man under surveillance when he was in Boston and released this video deliberately to mess with them. They're protesting through the backchannels, threatening retaliation. The Feds want us to look into it and see what we can find out about how the video was made. They don't know that she's already dead, but I recognized her as soon as I saw her. If you ask me, it's probably something the Chinese cooked up themselves to try to get rid of the guy in an internal purge. Maybe they even paid the girl to do it and then they killed her. That or our own spies decided to get rid of her after using her as bait, in which case I expect this investigation to be shut down pretty quickly. Either way, I'm not looking forward to this mess. And I advise you to back off as well."

Ruth feels a moment of resentment before the Regulator whisks it away. If Mona's death was part of a political plot, then Scott is right, she really is way out of her depth. The police had been wrong to conclude that it was a gang killing. But she's wrong, too. Mona was an unfortunate pawn in some political game, and the trend she thought she had noticed was illusory, just a set of coincidences.

The rational thing to do is to let the police take over. She'll have to tell Sarah Ding that there's nothing she can do for her now.

"We'll have to sweep the apartment again for recording devices. And you better let me know the name of your informant. We'll need to question him thoroughly to see which gangs are involved. This could be a national security matter."

"You know I can't do that. I have no evidence he has anything to do with this."

"Ruth, we're picking this up now. If you want to find the girl's killer, help me."

"Feel free to round up all the usual suspects in Chinatown. It's what you want to do, anyway."

He stares at her, his face weary and angry, a look she's very familiar with. Then his face relaxes. He has decided to engage his Regulator, and he no longer wants to argue or talk about what couldn't be said between them.

Her Regulator kicks in automatically.

"Thank you for letting me use your office," she says placidly. "You have a good night."

The scandal had gone off exactly as the Watcher planned. He's pleased but not yet ready to celebrate. That was only the first step, a demonstration of his power. Next, he has to actually make sure it pays.

He goes through the recordings and pictures he's extracted from the dead girl and picks out a few more promising targets based on his research. Two are prominent Chinese businessmen connected with top Party bosses; one is the brother of an Indian diplomatic attaché; two more are sons of the House of Saud studying in Boston. It's remarkable how similar the dynamics between the powerful and the people they ruled over were around the world. He also finds a prominent CEO and a Justice of the Massachusetts Supreme Judicial Court, but these he sets aside. It's not that he's particularly patriotic, but he instinctively senses that if one of his victims decides to turn him in instead of paying up, he'll be in much less trouble if the victim isn't an American. Besides, American public figures also have a harder time moving money around anonymously, as evidenced by his experience with those two Senators in DC, which almost unraveled his whole scheme. Finally, it never hurts to have a judge or someone famous that can be leaned on in case the Watcher is caught.

Patience, and an eye for details.

He sends off his emails. Each references the article about the Chinese Transport Minister ("see, this could be you!") and then includes two files. One is the full video of the minister and the girl (to show that he was the originator) and the second is a carefully curated video of the recipient coupling with her. Each email contains a demand for payment and directions to make deposits to a numbered Swiss bank account or to transfer anonymous electronic cryptocurrency.

He browses the escort sites again. He's narrowed down the girls he suspects to just a few. Now he just has to look at them more closely to pick out the right one. He grows excited at the prospect.

He glances up at the people walking past him in the streets. All these foolish men and women moving around as if dreaming. They do not understand that the world is full of secrets, accessible only to those patient enough, observant enough to locate them and dig them out of their warm, bloody hiding places, like retrieving pearls from the soft flesh inside an oyster. And then, armed with those secrets, you could make men half a world away tremble and dance.

He closes his laptop and gets up to leave. He thinks about packing up the mess in his motel room, setting out the surgical kit, the baseball cap, the gun and a few other surprises he's learned to take with him when he's hunting.

Time to dig for more treasure.

Ruth wakes up. The old nightmares have been joined by new ones. She stays curled up in bed fighting waves of despair. She wants to lie here forever.

Days of work and she has nothing to show for it.

She'll have to call Sarah Ding later, after she turns on the Regulator. She can tell her that Mona was probably not killed by a gang, but somehow had been caught up in events bigger than she could handle. How would that make Sarah feel better?

The image from yesterday's news will not leave her mind, no matter how hard she tries to push it away.

Ruth struggles up and pulls up the article. She can't explain it, but the image just *looks* wrong. Not having the Regulator on makes it hard to think.

She finds the crime scene photo of Mona's bedroom and compares it with the image from the article. She looks back and forth.

Isn't the basket of condoms on the wrong side of the bed?

The shot is taken from the left side of the bed. So the closet doors, with the mirrors on them, should be on the far side of the shot, behind the couple. But there's only a blank wall behind them in the shot. Ruth's heart is beating so fast that she feels faint.

The alarm beeps. Ruth glances up at the red numbers and turns the Regulator on. The clock.

She looks back at the image. The alarm clock in the shot is tiny and fuzzy, but she can just make the numbers out. They're backwards.

Ruth walks steadily over to her laptop and begins to search online for the video. She finds it without much trouble and presses play.

Despite the video stabilization and the careful cropping, she can see that Mona's eyes are always looking directly into the camera.

There's only one explanation: the camera was aimed at the mirrors, and it was located in Mona's eye.

The eyes.

She goes through the NCIC entries of the other women she printed out yesterday, and now the pattern that had proven elusive seems obvious.

There was a blonde in Los Angeles whose head had been removed after death and never found; there was a brunette, also in LA, whose skull had been cracked open and her brains mashed; there was a Mexican woman and a black woman in DC whose faces had been subjected to post-mortem trauma in more restrained ways, with the cheekbones crushed and broken. Then finally, there was Mona, whose eyes had been carefully removed.

The killer has been improving his technique.

The Regulator holds her excitement in check. She needs more data.

She looks through all of Mona's photographs again. Nothing out of place shows up in the earlier pictures, but in the picture from her birthday with her parents, a flash was used, and there's an odd glint in her left eye.

Most cameras can automatically compensate for red-eye, which is caused by the light from the flash reflecting off the blood-rich choroid in the back of the eye. But the glint in Mona's picture is not red; it's bluish.

Calmly, Ruth flips through the photographs of the other girls who have been killed. And in each, she finds the tell-tale glint. This must be how the killer identified his targets.

She picks up the phone and dials the number for her friend. She and Gail had gone to college together, and she's now working as a researcher for an advanced medical devices company.

"Hello?"

She hears the chatter of other people in the background. "Gail, it's Ruth. Can you talk?"

"Just a minute." She hears the background conversation grow muffled and then abruptly shut off. "You never call unless you're asking about another enhancement. We're not getting any younger, you know? You have to stop at some point."

Gail had been the one to suggest the various enhancements Ruth has obtained over the years. She had even found Doctor B for her because she didn't want Ruth to end up crippled. But she had done it reluctantly, conflicted about the idea of turning Ruth into a cyborg.

"This feels wrong," she would say. "You don't need these things done to you. They're not medically necessary."

"This can save my life the next time someone is trying to choke me," Ruth would say.

"It's not the same thing," she would say. And the conversations would always end with Gail giving in, but with stern warnings about no further enhancements.

Sometimes you help a friend even when you disapprove of their decisions. It's complicated.

Ruth answers Gail on the phone, "No. I'm just fine. But I want to know if you know about a new kind of enhancement. I'm sending you some pictures now. Hold on." She sends over the images of the girls where she can see the strange glint in their eyes. "Take a look. Can you see that flash in their eyes? Do you know anything like this?" She doesn't tell Gail her suspicion so that Gail's answer would not be affected.

Gail is silent for a while. "I see what you mean. These are not great pictures. But let me talk to some people and call you back."

"Don't send the full pictures around. I'm in the middle of an investigation. Just crop out the eyes if you can."

Ruth hangs up. The Regulator is working extra hard. Something about what she said—cropping out the girls' eyes—triggered a bodily response of disgust that the Regulator is suppressing. She's not sure why. With the Regulator, sometimes it's hard for her to see the connections between things.

While waiting for Gail to call her back, she looks through the active online ads in Boston once more. The killer has a pattern of killing a few girls in each city before moving on. He must be on the hunt for a second victim here. The best way to catch him is to find her before he does.

She clicks through ad after ad, the parade of flesh a meaningless blur, focusing only on the eyes. Finally, she sees what she's looking for. The girl uses the name Carrie, and she has dirty-blond hair and green eyes. Her ad is clean, clear, well-written, like a tasteful sign amidst the parade of flashing neon. The timestamp on the ad shows that she last modified it twelve hours ago. She's likely still alive.

Ruth calls the number listed.

"This is Carrie. Please leave a message."

As expected, Carrie screens her calls.

"Hello. My name is Ruth Law, and I saw your ad. I'd like to make an appointment with you." She hesitates, and then adds, "This is not a joke. I really want to see you." She leaves her number and hangs up.

The phone rings almost immediately. Ruth picks up. But it's Gail, not Carrie.

"I asked around, and people who ought to know tell me the girls are probably wearing a new kind of retinal implant. It's not FDA-approved. But of course you can go overseas and get them installed if you pay enough."

"What do they do?"

"They're hidden cameras."

"How do you get the pictures and videos out?"

"You don't. They have no wireless connections to the outside world. In fact, they're shielded to emit as little RF emissions as possible so that they're undetectable to camera scanners, and a wireless connection would just mean another way to hack into them. All the storage is inside the device. To retrieve them you have to have surgery again. Not the kind of thing most people would be interested in unless you're trying to record people who *really* don't want you to be recording them."

When you're so desperate for safety that you think this provides insurance, Ruth thinks. *Some future leverage.*

And there's no way to get the recordings out except to cut the girl open. "Thanks."

"I don't know what you're involved in, Ruth, but you really are getting too old for this. Are you still leaving the Regulator on all the time? It's not healthy."

"Don't I know it." She changes the subject to Gail's children. The Regulator allows her to have this conversation without pain. After a suitable amount of time, she says goodbye and hangs up.

The phone rings again.

"This is Carrie. You called me."

"Yes." Ruth makes her voice sound light, carefree.

Carrie's voice is flirtatious but cautious. "Is this for you and your boyfriend or husband?"

"No, just me."

She grips the phone, counting the seconds. She tries to will Carrie not to hang up.

"I found your web site. You're a private detective?"

Ruth already knew that she would. "Yes, I am."

"I can't tell you anything about any of my clients. My business depends on discretion."

"I'm not going to ask you about your clients. I just want to see you." She thinks hard about how to gain her trust. The Regulator makes this difficult, as she has become unused to the emotive quality of judgments and impressions. She thinks the truth is too abrupt and strange to convince her. So she tries something else. "I'm interested in a new experience. I guess it's something I've always wanted to try and haven't."

"Are you working for the cops? I am stating now for the record that you're paying me only for companionship, and anything that happens beyond that is a decision between consenting adults."

"Look, the cops wouldn't use a woman to trap you. It's too suspicious."

The silence tells Ruth that Carrie is intrigued. "What time are you thinking of?"

"As soon as you're free. How about now?"

"It's not even noon yet. I don't start work until 6:00."

Ruth doesn't want to push too hard and scare her off. "Then I'd like to have you all night."

She laughs. "Why don't we start with two hours for a first date?"

"That will be fine."

"You saw my prices?"

"Yes. Of course."

"Take a picture of yourself holding your ID and text it to me first so I know you're for real. If that checks out, you can go to the corner of Victory and Beech in Back Bay at 6:00 and call me again. Put the cash in a plain envelope."

"I will."

"See you, my dear." She hangs up.

Ruth looks into the girl's eyes. Now that she knows what to look for, she thinks she can see the barest hint of a glint in her left eye.

She hands her the cash and watches her count it. She's very pretty, and so young. The way she leans against the wall reminds her of Jess. The Regulator kicks in.

She's in a lace nightie, black stockings and garters. High-heeled fluffy bedroom slippers that seem more funny than erotic.

Carrie puts the money aside and smiles at her. "Do you want to take the lead or have me do it? I'm fine either way."

"I'd rather just talk for a bit first."

Carrie frowns. "I told you I can't talk about my clients."

"I know. But I want to show you something."

Carrie shrugs and leads her to the bedroom. It's a lot like Mona's room: king-sized bed, cream-colored sheets, a glass bowl of condoms, a clock discreetly on the nightstand. The mirror is mounted on the ceiling.

They sit down on the bed. Ruth takes out a file, and hands Carrie a stack of photographs.

"All of these girls have been killed in the last year. All of them have the same implants you do."

Carrie looks up, shocked. Her eyes blink twice, rapidly.

"I know what you have behind your eye. I know you think it makes you safer. Maybe you even think someday the information in there can be a second source of income, when you're too old to do this. But there's a man who wants to cut that out of you. He's been doing the same to the other girls."

She shows her the pictures of dead Mona, with the bloody, mutilated face.

Carrie drops the pictures. "Get out. I'm calling the police." She stands up and grabs her phone.

Ruth doesn't move. "You can. Ask to speak to Captain Scott Brennan. He knows who I am, and he'll confirm what I've told you. I think you're the next target."

She hesitates.

Ruth continues, "Or you can just look at these pictures. You know what to look for. They were all just like you."

Carrie sits down and examines the pictures. "Oh God. Oh God."

"I know you probably have a set of regulars. At your prices you don't need and won't get many new clients. But have you taken on anyone new lately?"

"Just you and one other. He's coming at 8:00."

Ruth's Regulator kicks in.

"Do you know what he looks like?"

"No. But I asked him to call me when he gets to the street corner, just like you, so I can get a look at him first before having him come up."

Ruth takes out her phone. "I need to call the police."

"No! You'll get me arrested. Please!"

Ruth thinks about this. She's only guessing that this man might be the killer. If she involves the police now and he turns out to be just a customer, Carrie's life will be ruined.

"Then I'll need to see him myself, in case he's the one."

"Shouldn't I just call it off?"

Ruth hears the fear in the girl's voice, and it reminds her of Jess, too, when she used to ask her to stay in her bedroom after watching a scary movie. She can feel the Regulator kicking into action again. She cannot let her emotions get in the way. "That would probably be safer for you, but we'd lose the chance to catch him if he *is* the one. Please, I need you to go through with it so I can get a close look at him. This may be our best chance of stopping him from hurting others."

Carrie bites her bottom lip. "All right. Where will you hide?"

Ruth wishes she had thought to bring her gun, but she hadn't wanted to spook Carrie and she didn't anticipate having to fight. She'll need to be close enough to stop the man if he turns out to be the killer, and yet not so close as to make it easy for him to discover her.

"I can't hide inside here at all. He'll look around before going into the bedroom with you." She walks into the living room, which faces the back of the building, away from the street, and lifts the window open. "I can hide out here, hanging from the ledge. If he turns out to be the killer, I have to wait till the last possible minute to come in to cut off his escape. If he's not the killer, I'll drop down and leave."

Carrie is clearly uncomfortable with this plan, but she nods, trying to be brave.

"Act as normal as you can. Don't make him think something is wrong."

Carrie's phone rings. She swallows and clicks the phone on. She walks over to the bedroom window. Ruth follows.

"This is Carrie."

Ruth looks out the window. The man standing at the corner appears to be the right height, but that's not enough to be sure. She has to catch him and interrogate him.

"I'm in the four-story building about a hundred feet behind you. Come up to apartment 303. I'm so glad you came, dear. We'll have a great time, I promise." She hangs up.

The man starts walking this way. Ruth thinks there's a limp to his walk, but again, she can't be sure.

"Is it him?" Carrie asks.

"I don't know. We have to let him in and see."

Ruth can feel the Regulator humming. She knows that the idea of using Carrie as bait frightens her, is repugnant even. But it's the logical thing to do. She'll never get a chance like this again. She has to trust that she can protect the girl.

"I'm going outside the window. You're doing great. Just keep him talking and do what he wants. Get him relaxed and focused on you. I'll come in before he can hurt you. I promise."

Carrie smiles. "I'm good at acting."

Ruth goes to the living room window and deftly climbs out. She lets her body down, hanging onto the window ledge with her fingers so that she's invisible from inside the apartment. "Okay, close the window. Leave just a slit open so I can hear what happens inside."

"How long can you hang like this?"

"Long enough."

Carrie closes the window. Ruth is glad for the artificial tendons and tensors in her shoulders and arms and the reinforced fingers, holding her up. The idea had been to make her more effective in close combat, but they're coming in handy now, too.

She counts off the seconds. The man should be at the building . . . he should now be coming up the stairs . . . he should now be at the door.

She hears the door to the apartment open.

"You're even prettier than your pictures." The voice is rich, deep, satisfied.

"Thank you."

She hears more conversation, the exchange of money. Then the sound of more walking.

They're heading towards the bedroom. She can hear the man stopping to look into the other rooms. She almost can feel his gaze pass over the top of her head, out the window.

Ruth pulls herself up slowly, quietly, and looks in. She sees the man disappear into the hallway. There's a distinct limp.

She waits a few more seconds so that the man cannot rush back past her before she can reach the hallway to block it, and then she takes a deep breath and wills the Regulator to pump her blood full of adrenaline. The world seems to grow brighter and time slows down as she flexes her arms and pulls herself onto the window ledge.

She squats down and pulls the window up in one swift motion. She knows that the grinding noise will alert the man, and she has only a few seconds to get to him. She ducks, rolls through the open window onto the floor inside. Then she continues to roll until her feet are under her and activates the pistons in her legs to leap towards the hallway.

She lands and rolls again to not give him a clear target, and jumps again from her crouch into the bedroom.

The man shoots and the bullet strikes her left shoulder. She tackles him as her arms, held in front of her, slam into his midsection. He falls and the gun clatters away.

Now the pain from the bullet hits. She wills the Regulator to pump up the adrenaline and the endorphins to numb the pain. She pants and concentrates on the fight for her life.

He tries to flip her over with his superior mass, to pin her down, but she clamps her hands around his neck and squeezes hard. Men have always underestimated her at the beginning of a fight, and she has to take advantage of it. She knows that her grip feels like iron clamps around him, with all the implanted energy cells in her arms and hands activated and on full power. He winces, grabs her hands to try to pry them off. After a few seconds, realizing the futility of it, he ceases to struggle.

He's trying to talk but can't get any air into his lungs. Ruth lets up a little, and he chokes out, "You got me."

Ruth increases the pressure again, choking off his supply of air. She turns to Carrie, who's at the foot of the bed, frozen. "Call the police. Now."

She complies. As she continues to hold the phone against her ear as the 911 dispatcher has instructed her to do, she tells Ruth, "They're on their way."

The man goes limp with his eyes closed. Ruth lets go of his neck. She doesn't want to kill him, so she clamps her hands around his wrists while she sits on his legs, holding him still on the floor.

He revives and starts to moan. "You're breaking my fucking arms!"

Ruth lets up the pressure a bit to conserve her power. The man's nose is bleeding from the fall against the floor when she tackled him. He inhales loudly, swallows, and says, "I'm going to drown if you don't let me sit up."

Ruth considers this. She lets up the pressure further and pulls him into a sitting position.

She can feel the energy cells in her arms depleting. She won't have the physical upper hand much longer if she has to keep on restraining him this way.

She calls out to Carrie. "Come over here and tie his hands together."

Carrie puts down the phone done and comes over gingerly. "What do I use?"

"Don't you have any rope? You know, for your clients?"

"I don't do that kind of thing."

Ruth thinks. "You can use stockings."

As Carrie ties the man's hands and feet together in front of him, he coughs. Some of the blood has gone down the wrong pipe. Ruth is unmoved and doesn't ease up on the pressure, and he winces. "Goddamn it. You're one psycho robo bitch."

Ruth ignores him. The stockings are too stretchy and won't hold him for long. But it should last long enough for her to get the gun and point it at him.

Carrie retreats to the other side of the room. Ruth lets the man go and backs away from him towards the gun on the floor a few yards away, keeping her eyes on him. If he makes any sudden movements, she'll be back on him in a flash.

He stays limp and unmoving as she steps backwards. She begins to relax. The Regulator is trying to calm her down now, to filter the adrenalin out of her system.

When she's about half way to the gun, the man suddenly reaches into his jacket with his hands, still tied together. Ruth hesitates for only a second before pushing out with her legs to jump backwards to the gun.

As she lands, the man locates something inside his jacket, and suddenly Ruth feels her legs and arms go limp and she falls to the ground, stunned.

Carrie is screaming. "My eye! Oh God I can't see out of my left eye!"

Ruth can't seem to feel her legs at all, and her arms feel like rubber. Worst of all, she's panicking. It seems she's never been this scared or in this much pain. She tries to feel the presence of the Regulator and there's nothing, just emptiness. She can smell the sweet, sickly smell of burnt electronics in the air. The clock on the nightstand is dark.

She's the one who had underestimated *him*. Despair floods through her and there's nothing to hold it back.

Ruth can hear the man stagger up off the floor. She wills herself to turn over, to move, to reach for the gun. She crawls. One foot, another foot. She seems to be moving through molasses because she's so weak. She can feel every one of her forty-nine years. She feels every sharp stab of pain in her shoulder.

She reaches the gun, grabs it, and sits up against the wall, pointing it back into the center of the room.

The man has gotten out of Carrie's ineffective knots. He's now holding Carrie, blind in one eye, shielding his body with hers. He holds a scalpel against her throat. He's already broken the skin and a thin stream of blood flows down her neck.

He backs towards the bedroom door, dragging Carrie with him. Ruth knows that if he gets to the bedroom door and disappears around the corner, she'll never be able to catch him. Her legs are simply useless.

Carrie sees Ruth's gun and screams. "I don't want to die! Oh God. Oh God."

"I'll let her go once I'm safe," he says, keeping his head hidden behind hers.

Ruth's hands are shaking as she holds the gun. Through the waves of nausea and the pounding of her pulse in her ears, she struggles to think through what will happen next. The police are on their way and will probably be here in five minutes. Isn't it likely that he'll let her go as soon as possible to give himself some extra time to escape?

The man backs up another two steps; Carrie is no longer kicking or struggling, but trying to find purchase on the smooth floor in her stockinged feet, trying to co-operate with him. But she can't stop crying.

Mom, don't shoot! Please don't shoot!

Or is it more likely that once the man has left the room, he will slit Carrie's throat and cut out her implant? He knows there's a recording of him inside, and he can't afford to leave that behind.

Ruth's hands are shaking too much. She wants to curse at herself. She cannot get a clear shot at the man with Carrie in front of him. She cannot.

Ruth wants to evaluate the chances rationally, to make a decision, but regret and grief and rage, hidden and held down by the Regulator until they could be endured, rise now all the sharper, kept fresh by the effort at forgetting. The universe has shrunken down to the wavering spot at the end of the barrel of the gun: a young woman, a killer, and time slipping irrevocably away.

She has nothing to turn to, to trust, to lean on, but herself, her angry, frightened, trembling self. She is naked and alone, as she has always known she is, as we all are.

The man is almost at the door. Carrie's cries are now incoherent sobs.

It has always been the regular state of things. There is no clarity, no relief. At the end of all rationality there is simply the need to decide and the faith to live through, to endure.

Ruth's first shot slams into Carrie's thigh. The bullet plunges through skin, muscle, and fat, and exits out the back, shattering the man's knee.

The man screams and drops the scalpel. Carrie falls, a spray of blood blossoming from her wounded leg.

Ruth's second shot catches the man in the chest. He collapses to the floor.

Mom, mom!

She drops the gun and crawls over to Carrie, cradling her and tending to her wound. She's crying, but she'll be fine.

A deep pain floods through her like forgiveness, like hard rain after a long drought. She does not know if she will be granted relief, but she experiences this moment fully, and she's thankful.

"It's okay," she says, stroking Carrie as she lies in her lap. "It's okay."

Author's Note: the EchoSense technology described in this story is a loose and liberal extrapolation of the principles behind the technology described in Qifan Pu et al., "Whole-Home Gesture Recognition Using Wireless Signals," The 19th Annual International Conference on Mobile Computing and Networking (Mobicom'13) (available at http://wisee.cs.washington.edu/wisee_paper.pdf). There is no intent to suggest that the technology described in the paper resembles the fictional one portrayed here.

The woman from the ocean

KARL BUNKER

*Here's a melancholy tale about a woman who crash-lands back on Earth af-
ter a long voyage out to the stars and finds that the human race has changed
in subtle but profound ways while she was gone.*

*Currently a software engineer, Karl Bunker has been a jeweler, a musical
instrument maker, a sculptor, and a mechanical technician. Karl Bunker's
stories have appeared in* Asimov's Science Fiction, Analog Science Fiction
and Fact, Cosmos, Abyss & Apex, The Magazine of Fantasy & Science
Fiction, Interzone, *and elsewhere. His story "Under the Shouting Sky," won
him the first Robert A. Heinlein Centennial Short Story Contest. He lives in
a small town north of Boston with his wife, various pets, and sundry wildlife.
He maintains a Web site at www.karlbunker.com.*

It was a morning in early winter when she came to the village. She came on foot,
along the shore road from the north. Michael's cabin was the first one on this
road, and he was stoking the morning fire when he was startled by a banging at
his door. He got up and was just reaching for the latch when the door opened and
she came in.

She was hunched over with her arms tight across her chest. She walked past him
without speaking, barely glancing at him, and sat down cross-legged in front of the
fire. Michael closed the door and stood looking at her for a moment, frozen by surprise. Then he saw she was shivering, so he got a blanket from his bed and put it
over her shoulders. Her clothes were strange, bright with colors that he'd never seen
in any fabric. They were also too thin to be any protection against the cold.

He squatted beside her. "My name is Michael," he said quietly, and after a moment she turned her head to look at him.

She had a strong face, with high cheekbones and a wide jaw, and her skin was
brown. When she looked at him, her eyes darted over his face as if she was searching for something. "You speak English," she said. "Or something like it." She made
a short, unhappy smile. "What place is this?"

She had a strange accent, and it took Michael a moment to understand what she
had said.

"This is our village, on the inner coast of the cape. My name is Michael, I'm a carpenter, and you're in my home."

"*What* cape?" she asked.

"The—the big cape . . ." he stammered. "The one on the ocean."

"The big cape. The one on the ocean," the woman repeated. Then she turned back to the fire and pulled the blanket closer around herself. "Fuck," she said.

Michael waited a little while, then asked, "Are you from far away?" He realized then that he could smell the ocean in her hair and on her clothes. "Were you on a boat?" he asked. "Did it sink?"

"Yes. Something like that. We crashed into the ocean. Only a few of us got out of the lander before it sank, and no one else could make the swim. I spent all day going up and down the shore calling, looking for them, but there was no one . . . Then it got dark, and I started walking . . . All of them . . . only seventy-eight of us were left, and now they're all dead. Philip, Zhang, Gabriela, Mary, Lester . . . All dead, all dead . . . all . . . dead . . ."

Her head dropped as she said these last words, and soon Michael saw she was asleep. He moved close to her, then picked her up with one arm at her back and one behind her knees. She made a soft grunting sound when he lifted her, but didn't wake up. He laid her in his bed, putting two heavy blankets over her and pulling them up to her neck. Then he left the cabin, closing the door quietly behind him. He was back a few minutes later with Susan, who was the old woman of the village.

"She's not like anyone I've ever seen," Susan whispered as they stood over the sleeping stranger. "I've seen brown skin before, but not on a person with such straight black hair. What color are her eyes?"

"Brown," Michael said. "Light brown. Almost exactly the color of her skin, and large, like a child's eyes."

"*Are* they now?" Susan said, drawing out the words and smiling at Michael. "She looks about your age, Michael, and very healthy. Perhaps the sea has sent her to you, in return for your poor Emma."

Michael looked at Susan, one eyebrow arched.

"I know," she said. "You don't believe in that sort of thing. And neither do I, come to think of it. But it sounds nice. As I get older I'm learning to find comfort in things I don't believe."

The woman slept until past midday; then she appeared at the doorway to the half of the cabin that was Michael's workshop. "Could I have some water?" she asked. "And maybe something to eat?"

"Of course!" Michael said. He came quickly out of his shop and poured water from a pitcher into a mug, handing it to her. He asked her to sit at his small table and began assembling a meal.

"My name is Kali," the woman said as she sat down. Michael brought her bread, cheese, a bowl of thick soup. As Kali ate she gestured at her surroundings. "It looks like two people live here."

Michael sat down across from Kali. "I . . . had a wife. She died last year."

Kali picked up the clay mug of water in front of her and looked into it. "From what? Do you know? Typhoid? Dysentery? Consumption? Evil spirits?"

"She had a pain in her chest. In the end she couldn't breathe. Susan, our medicine woman, couldn't help her."

"Must not have been evil spirits, then," Kali said. Then she glanced up, meeting Michael's eyes briefly. "I'm sorry."

She drank from the mug, then looked at it, turning it in her hand. "Where was this made? Your clothes, the fabric they're made from, the tools you work with—where do all these things come from?"

"My cups and dishes were made by a potter named Jim. A woman named Ann is a weaver and seamstress; she made most of my clothes. My tools—"

"The fiber for the cloth—the cotton, or whatever it is," Kali interrupted, "is it grown nearby or does it come from somewhere else?"

"Traders . . . it's brought by traders."

"Itinerant traders? People from outside your village?"

"Yes."

"And where do the traders get it? Where is it grown?"

Michael lifted his hands with the palms up. "It comes from . . . far away, outside the village. Sometimes the traders come on the road from the south, other times they have boats that go up and down the coast. Was your boat a trader boat?"

"How do you pay for the cloth? By barter? Do you do everything by barter?"

"We . . . give different things in exchange for what they bring. It depends on what we have, and what the traders want." Michael smiled uncertainly, his eyes on Kali's face.

"Can you read?" Kali's voice was sharp and she was holding the heavy mug in both hands, squeezing down on it so that her fingertips whitened. "Can anyone read? Have you ever heard of anyone who can read?"

"I'm sorry . . . That has something to do with markings, doesn't it? A trader showed me something once—marks on a piece of plastic—I couldn't see what they meant."

Kali took in a deep breath and let it out slowly. "Oh brave new world, that has such people in it," she said. Then she stood up suddenly. "I need to go out—to look at this village of yours." She bent and reached across the table until the tips of her fingers touched Michael's hand. "Thank you Michael," she said. "Thank you for your hospitality, and I'm sorry for being rude with you."

As she was walking to the door, Michael called after her. "It's cold. Take this." He held a deerskin jacket out to her, his eyes on the jacket rather than Kali.

"Your wife's," Kali said. "Thanks. I'll bring it back."

"No need," Michael said, but Kali was already out the door, pulling it closed behind her.

It was late afternoon when she came back. She knocked on Michael's door, waiting for him to open it this time. "I met the woman—Susan—in the next house down the road," she said. "She took me around, introduced me to lots of people. Everyone was very pleasant, very kind. Susan said I could stay with her until . . . until I can support myself, I guess." She walked through the main room of Michael's cabin, to the doorway that led to his workshop. "Susan told me that you had an apprentice until recently."

"Yes, Alan. He decided to go back to fishing."

"A long time ago," Kali said, "a long, *long* time ago, I used to do some woodworking. Many of the tools were different then, but I was good at it, and I can learn, if you would be willing to teach me."

That night Kali was in Susan's cabin, sitting at her table. "Michael is a good man," Susan said as she put a plate of stew in front of Kali. "You will like working for him. He is very kind, very gentle, and good-looking too, don't you think?" There were gaps in her teeth when she smiled.

Some time through the night Susan woke to the sound of Kali quietly crying. She got up and knelt on the floor beside the straw-padded pallet that was Kali's bed, stroking the younger woman's hair. "Poor child, poor child," she whispered.

Kali sat up, wiping under her nose with the back of her hand. "I'm sorry I woke you," she said.

Susan made a loose gesture with her hand, sitting down on her heels.

"I don't know if I can do this, Susan," Kali said. "I mean live here, in this village, in this world. I just don't know if I can do it. I don't know if I even want to try."

"This . . . world?"

Kali brought her knees up underneath the long nightgown that Michael had given her and folded her arms across them. "This isn't my world, Susan. It's changed so much . . . The world I came from, like all the people I knew, is dead. It died hundreds of years ago."

"Michael's wife's name was Emma," Susan said. "She came from another village, far away, a place where the crops had failed. Many people died and others, like Emma, left to find a better place. She was very sad at first; she felt that she had lost everything. But Michael made her happy. He made her laugh."

"You have a one-track mind, Susan," Kali said.

Susan smiled, her old face looking impish. "You say hundreds of years ago. You don't look like someone who has lived hundreds of years. Do people not grow old where you come from?"

"We were on a long journey. The only way to make the journey was to use machines that caused us to sleep for many years without getting older. We were like Michael's wife; we were looking for a far-away place where we could live. But we never found it. We only found dead, unlivable places. So finally we gave up and started back. Our ship was deteriorating, and couldn't last forever. But while we were away, things here changed. Things became very different." She tilted her head and rested it sideways on her folded arms. "Things became very different."

"So where you come from—the time you are from—it was during the machine times?"

"The machine times?" Kali asked. "Yes, I suppose that must be what you call it. Tell me what you know about the machine times."

"Only that it was long ago, and people then had giant machines that could do anything. Now the machines no longer work, and all we know of them is what we are told by traders who go to the old places and bring back metal and plastics."

"Hm," Kali grunted. "And do you know about wars?"

"Wars . . ." Susan repeated, mouthing the word in a way that suggested it was a sound with no meaning.

"People killing people, in large numbers."

Furrows deepened in Susan's face. "People? Which people? Killing . . . which people? And why?"

"That's a very good question, Susan." Kali lay back down on her side, pulling her blankets up and closing her eyes.

The next morning Kali went to Michael's cabin. He took her to his workshop, and they talked about his work, his tools, different kinds of wood, the various items he made and what he hoped to get for them in trade. They worked together all day until it began to get dark. As Michael was lighting a candle, Kali looked around the cabin. "Is that a musical instrument?" she asked, pointing at an object hanging on a wall. "Do you play it, or did it belong to your . . ."

"Yes, I play it sometimes," Michael said.

Kali took the instrument off the wall and brought it to Michael. "Would you play something for me?"

Michael sat on a chair near the fire and laid the instrument across his legs like a zither. He plucked at its strings, his right hand moving up and down the fretboard. After a few bars he began to sing in a soft, dry voice. When he finished the song Kali asked him to sing another, and another after that.

"How did you learn these songs?" Kali asked.

"The first one is old. People in the village taught it to me. The other two are mine. I made the last one as a gift for my wife."

"That one was my favorite," Kali said. She stared into the fire for a time, and then turned her face to Michael. "I want to talk about some ideas with you, Michael. As sort of an experiment, okay?" When Michael nodded she went on. "First, do you know that there are—there used to be—ways of marking down music on paper—or on animal skins, let's say."

"You mean like writing?"

"Yes, like that. But with different marks for musical notes as well as words. If I wrote down your songs, you could share your music with everyone."

"I do share my music with everyone," Michael said. "I teach my songs to anyone who asks."

"But what about other people? What about people you might never meet, people far away, people in the future, after you're gone? If you wrote your music down, it could last forever. Isn't that a lovely thought?"

Michael frowned, as if struggling to understand. "But . . . who are these people? Why would they want to know my songs?"

An edge came to Kali's voice. "*Some* people would want to. Not everyone, but some people would see them and love them. Can you see the beauty of that idea?"

Michael started to speak, stopped, started again. "It seems . . . strange. Why would I give something to someone I don't know, someone I've never even met? Someone who has never asked me for the thing I'm giving? If I could see this person, if he told me he wanted to learn my songs, then I would understand . . ." His voice faded.

Kali turned back to the fire. "Oh brave new world," she said quietly.

Michael let her sit in silence for a time. He put some dried leaves into a pot of water hanging over the fire and then poured out two mugs of tea. "Can you tell me something about . . . where you came from?" he asked.

Kali said nothing for a long time. She continued to look into the fire, blew onto her tea, sipped it a few times. "We thought the world was ending," she said finally. "There were too many weapons; too many terrible, horrific weapons. It was becoming too easy to destroy too much of the world, too quickly. Everything was going to hell when we left. We kept listening to news transmissions as we went out and out. Things only got worse. It looked like the world, the whole world, was going to die. We thought we might be the only survivors."

Again she paused for a long time. "And then someone, or some*thing*, decided to save the world, and they came up with the virus. The favorite theory on the ship was that it must have been an AI. Some machine was given, or gave itself, the problem of how to save humanity, and the virus was its solution."

"Vi-rus?"

"A kind of disease, Michael. A sickness. A sickness that was created, and one that didn't make people sick. Instead it affected their chromosomes in a way that changed the brains of every new baby that was born. Just a small, small change . . ."

"This sickness changed people?" Michael asked. "Is that why people today don't know how to make machines? Did it make us stupid?"

"No, no. Not like that. It didn't change you like that." Kali twisted around to look toward one of the cabin's windows, a square of oiled animal skin that let through some of the dusk's waning light. "Are there wolves around here, in the forest?"

"Yes."

"And mountain lions—big cats?"

"Yes, those too."

"Wolves live in packs," Kali said, "while mountain lions are solitary. People are more like wolves, wouldn't you say?"

"You mean because we live in groups? Yes, I guess so."

"In my time we would say that humans are a social animal. The virus changed that. Not very much; just a little. Just a little adjustment. Being social creatures doesn't only mean that we live in groups. It also affects how we think. Or rather it used to. That's what changed, Michael. The genetic expression of social instincts has been reduced to the point that those instincts no longer carry over into abstract reasoning."

Michael rubbed his chin. "I don't . . ."

"I know you don't understand those words, Michael. What they mean is that you—your people—don't have the concept of belonging to a larger community—a community that includes people you don't know, people who aren't standing in front of you. You can't think of people who are far away as being a part of your social group. Your brain doesn't work that way. You can interact with people who are standing in front of you, but that's all. Your instinct to social behavior doesn't extend beyond that."

There was no comprehension in Michael's face, but Kali went on, looking down at the floor, talking more to herself than to him. "There was a brilliant purity to the solution. It was probably the least invasive thing, the smallest possible change you could make to human nature and still make war impossible. People are as intelligent, as aggressive, as passionate as they ever were, but they won't make war. Wars happened because people thought in terms of 'us' and 'them'. There was an 'us' that was right and a 'them' that was wrong. An 'us' that was righteous and a 'them' that was infidel. So that's what was erased from the human brain. After the virus, the concept of a 'them' was erased. But the concept of 'us' is gone too."

Kali sighed, and there was a tremble in her breath. "And so . . . Now there is no war. And there is no science, no literature, no history, no scholarship, no learning of anything that can't be taught by one person to another, face to face. And you will do your woodworking today and Jim will make his pots and Ann will weave cloth, and you will all go to sleep tonight and wake up tomorrow morning and go to sleep tomorrow night and wake up the next morning and the next and the next and the next, and nothing will ever, ever, ever change."

Michael got up and hung his instrument on the wall. Standing, looking down at Kali, he said, "Things change, Kali. You came here; you came to my door. That was a change. For me at least, that was a very great change."

Kali and Michael were married in the following spring, and in the fall she gave birth to a daughter. It was not an easy birth, and as Kali gripped Michael's hand in her right and Susan's hand in her left, she shouted out curses against the world, against the village, against Michael and Susan, against herself. But when the baby was finally delivered and laid on her belly, she became like all mothers, crying with joy and delight and love for the new life she'd brought into the world.

Years passed. Kali became well-liked by her neighbors; she was known as a woman who worked hard, who knew many strange things and yet was ignorant of many common things, who entertained children with wonderful stories, and who seemed to always be haunted by a sadness that she could never share or explain. Her daughter was named Asha, and as the girl grew older Kali began teaching her to make the marks of writing. She also would spend long periods talking to her daughter, asking her questions, challenging her answers, all the time her face taut and intense, perhaps even frightened.

One day when Asha was eight, as happens with all mothers and their children, Kali and Asha quarreled. Asha screamed the angriest of the few angry words she knew and threw down the slate that Kali had been using for her writing lessons. As Kali bent to pick up the pieces of the slate, tears were already welling in her eyes. That evening she sat sullenly at the table, eating nothing, barely speaking. "The virus is still active," she said to Michael after Asha had gone to bed. "It infected me, changed my chromosomes, and so Asha's brain is butchered, just like yours, just like everyone's. I guess I've known it for a long time now, but I was hiding it from myself."

"Our daughter is perfect," Michael said. "She is beautiful and smart, and she's going to grow up to be a wonderful woman like her mother."

Kali glanced up at her husband, her face haggard, her eyes edged with red. "No, not like her mother, Michael. For whatever difference that makes. I don't know what I was hoping for anyway. What difference could one child make, or a dozen? And what did I want? A return to the old days, with the world ready to destroy itself? No,

Michael, there's nothing of me in your daughter, and she's better off that way. Let her be one of you. Let me be the last of an extinct species, a species that failed and died out long ago."

Later, as her husband and daughter slept, Kali left the cabin and walked down the road that had first brought her to the village. When she reached the beach she walked out into the ocean with her clothes on and swam toward the horizon. She swam away from her family, from all the people she had come to know and feel fondness for. She swam away from the peaceful village, from the world of harmony and no war, where cups and bowls were made by a potter named Jim, where a woman named Ann wove cloth, where Susan still dispensed her medicines and her advice. Kali was a strong swimmer, and she cut cleanly through the breakers and was almost out of sight of land before her strength gave out.

Michael did not marry again. He was devoted to his daughter and lavished all his love and attention on her. As she grew older she would sometimes speak about people in the world outside the village in strange ways, almost as if they were people that she knew. Her father only smiled at this, and didn't criticize her for her odd ideas.

shooting the apocalypse

PAOLO BACIGALUPI

Paolo Bacigalupi made his first sale in 1998, to The Magazine of Fantasy & Science Fiction, *took a break from the genre for several years, and then returned to it in the new century, with new sales to F&SF, Asimov's Science Fiction, and* Fast Forward 2. *His story "The Calorie Man" won the Theodore Sturgeon Memorial awards, and his acclaimed first novel* The Windup Girl *won the Hugo, the Nebula, and the John W. Campbell Memorial awards. His other novels include* Ship Breaker *and* The Drowned Cities. *His most recent books are the novels* The Doubt Factory *and* Zombie Baseball Beatdown. *Coming up is a new novel,* The Water Knife. *His short work has been collected in* Pump Six and Other Stories. *Bacigalupi lives with family in Paonia, Colorado.*

Here's a grim look at an all-too-likely future, one not that far away, where people are a lot closer to the edge of disaster than they think that they are.

I

f it were for anyone else, he would have just laughed in their faces and told them they were on their own.

The thought nagged at Timo as he drove his beat-up FlexFusion down the rutted service road that ran parallel to the concrete-lined canal of the Central Arizona Project. For any other journo who came down to Phoenix looking for a story, he wouldn't even think of doing them a favor.

All those big names looking to swoop in like magpies and grab some meaty exclusive and then fly away just as fast, keeping all their page views and hits to themselves . . . he wouldn't do it.

Didn't matter if they were *Google/NY Times,* Cherry Xu, *Facebook Social Now,* Deborah Williams, *Kindle Post,* or *Xinhua.*

But Lucy? Well, sure. For Lucy, he'd climb into his sweatbox of a car with all his camera gear and drive his skinny brown ass out to North Phoenix and into the hills on a crap tip. He'd drive this way and that, burning gas trying to find a service road, and then bump his way through dirt and ruts, scraping the belly of the Ford the whole way, and he still wouldn't complain.

Just goes to show you're a sucker for a girl who wears her jeans tight.

But it wasn't just that. Lucy was fine, if you liked a girl with white skin and little tits and wide hips, and sometimes Timo would catch himself fantasizing about what it would be like to get with her. But in the end, that wasn't why he did favors for Lucy. He did it because she was scrappy and wet and she was in over her head—and too hard-assed and proud to admit it.

Girl had grit; Timo could respect that. Even if she came from up north and was so wet that sometimes he laughed out loud at the things she said. The girl didn't know much about dry desert life, but she had grit.

So when she muttered over her Dos Equis that all the stories had already been done, Timo, in a moment of beery romantic fervor, had sworn to her that it just wasn't so. He had the eye. He saw things other people didn't. He could name twenty stories she could still do and make a name for herself.

But when he'd started listing possibilities, Lucy shot them down as fast as he brought them up.

Coyotes running Texans across the border into California?

Sohu already had a nine part series running.

Californians buying Texas hookers for nothing, like Phoenix was goddamn Tijuana?

Google/NY Times and *Fox* both had big spreads.

Water restrictions from the Roosevelt Dam closure and the drying up of Phoenix's swimming pools?

Kindle Post ran that.

The narco murders that kept getting dumped in the empty pools that had become so common that people had started calling them "swimmers"?

AP. Fox. Xinhua. LA Times. The Talisha Brannon Show. Plus the reality narco show *Hard Bangin'*.

He kept suggesting new angles, new stories, and all Lucy said, over and over was, "It's been done." And then she'd rattle off the news organizations, the journos who'd covered the stories, the page hits, the viewerships, and the click-thrus they'd drawn.

"I'm not looking for some dead hooker for the sex and murder crowd," Lucy said as she drained her beer. "I want something that'll go big. I want a scoop, you know?"

"And I want a woman to hand me a ice-cold beer when I walk in the door," Timo grumped. "Don't mean I'm going to get it."

But still, he understood her point. He knew how to shoot pictures that would make a vulture sob its beady eyes out, but the news environment that Lucy fought to distinguish herself in was like gladiatorial sport—some winners, a lot of losers, and a whole shit-ton of blood on the ground.

Journo money wasn't steady money. Wasn't good money. Sometimes, you got lucky. Hell, he'd got lucky himself when he'd gone over Texas way and shot Hurricane Violet in all her glory. He'd photographed a whole damn fishing boat flying through the air and landing on a Days Inn, and in that one shot he knew he'd hit the big time. Violet razed Galveston and blasted into Houston, and Timo got page views so high that he sometimes imagined that the Cat 6 had actually killed him and sent him straight to Heaven.

He'd kept hitting reload on his PayPal account and watched the cash pouring in. He'd had the big clanking *cojones* to get into the heart of that clusterfuck, and he'd come out of it with more than a million hits a photo. Got him all excited.

But disaster was easy to cover, and he'd learned the hard way that when the big dogs muscled in, little dogs got muscled out. Which left him back in sad-sack Phoenix, scraping for glamour shots of brains on windshields and trussed-up drug bunnies in the bottoms of swimming pools. It made him sympathetic to Lucy's plight, if not her perspective.

It's all been done, Timo thought as he maneuvered his Ford around the burned carcass of an abandoned Tesla. *So what if it's been motherfucking done?*

"There ain't no virgins, and there ain't no clean stories," he'd tried to explain to Lucy. "There's just angles on the same-ass stories. Scoops come from being in the right place at the right time, and that's all just dumb luck. Why don't you just come up with a good angle on Phoenix and be happy?"

But Lucy Monroe wanted a nice clean virgin story that didn't have no grubby fingerprints on it from other journos. Something she could put her name on. Some way to make her mark, make those big news companies notice her. Something to grow her brand and all that. Not just the day-to-day grind of narco kills and starving immigrants from Texas, something special. Something new.

So when the tip came in, Timo thought what the hell, maybe this was something she'd like. Maybe even a chance to blow up together. Lucy could do the words, he'd bring the pics, and they'd scoop all the big name journos who drank martinis at the Hilton 6 and complained about what a refugee shit hole Phoenix had become.

The Ford scraped over more ruts. Dust already coated the rear window of Timo's car, a thick beige paste. Parallel to the service road, the waters of the Central Arizona Project flowed, serene and blue and steady. A man-made canal that stretched three hundred miles across the desert to bring water to Phoenix from the Colorado River. A feat of engineering, and cruelly tempting, given the ten-foot chain-link and barbed wire fences that escorted it on either side.

In this part of Phoenix, the Central Arizona Project formed the city's northern border. On one side of the CAP canal, it was all modest stucco tract houses packed together like sardines stretching south. But on Timo's side, it was desert, rising into tan and rust hill folds, dotted with mesquite and saguaro.

A few hardy subdivisions had built outposts north of the CAP's moat-like boundary, but the canal seemed to form a barrier of some psychological significance, because for the most part, Phoenix stayed to the south of the concrete-lined canal, choosing to finally build itself into something denser than lazy sprawl. Phoenix on one side, the desert on the other, and the CAP flowing between them like a thin blue DMZ.

Just driving on the desert side of the CAP made Timo thirsty. Dry mouth, plain-ass desert, quartz rocks and sandstone nubs with a few creosote bushes holding onto the dust and waving in the blast furnace wind. Normally, Timo didn't even bother to look at the desert. It barely changed. But here he was, looking for something new—

He rounded a curve and slowed, peering through his grimy windshield. "Well I'll be goddamned . . ."

Up ahead, something was hanging from the CAP's barrier fence. Dogs were jumping up to tug at it, milling and barking.

Timo squinted, trying to understand what he was seeing.

"Oh yeah. Hell yes!"

He hit the brakes. The car came grinding to a halt in a cloud of dust, but Timo was already climbing out and fumbling for his phone, pressing it to his ear, listening to it ring.

Come on, come on, come on.

Lucy picked up.

Timo couldn't help grinning. "I got your story, girl. You'll love it. It's *new*."

The dogs bared their teeth at Timo's approach, but Timo just laughed. He dug into his camera bag for his pistol.

"You want a piece of me?" he asked. "You want some of Timo, bitches?"

Turned out they didn't. As soon he held up the pistol, the dogs scattered. Animals were smarter than people, that way. Pull a gun on some drunk California frat boy and you never knew if the sucker was still going to try and throw down. Dogs were way smarter than Californians. Timo could respect that, so he didn't shoot them as they fled the scene.

One of the dogs, braver or more arrogant than the rest, paused to yank off a final trophy before loping away; the rest of the pack zeroed in on it, yipping and leaping, trying to steal its prize. Timo watched, wishing he'd pulled his camera instead of his gun. The shot was perfect. He sighed and stuffed the pistol into the back of his pants, dug out his camera, and turned to the subject at hand.

"Well hello, good-looking," he murmured. "Ain't you a sight?"

The man hung upside down from the chain link fence, bloated from the Phoenix heat. A bunch of empty milk jugs dangled off his body, swinging from a harness of shoelace ties. From the look of him, he'd been cooking out in the sun for at least a day or so.

The meat of one arm was completely desleeved, and the other arm . . . well, Timo had watched the dogs make off with the poor bastard's hand. His face and neck and chest didn't look much better. The dogs had been doing some jumping.

"Come on, *vato*. Gimme the story." Timo stalked back and forth in front of the body, checking the angles, considering the shadows and light. "You want to get your hits up don't you? Show Timo your good side, I make you famous. So help me out, why don't you?"

He stepped back, thinking wide-frame: the strung-up body, the black nylon flowers woven into the chain link around it. The black guttered candles and cigarettes and mini liquor bottles scattered by the dogs' frenzied feeding. The CAP flowing behind it all. Phoenix beyond that, sprawling all the way to the horizon.

"What's your best side?" Timo asked. "Don't be shy. I'll do you right. Make you famous. Just let me get your angle."

There.

Timo squatted and started shooting. *Click-click-click-click*—the artificial sound of digital photography and the Pavlovian rush of sweaty excitement as Timo got the feel.

Dead man.

Flowers.

Candles.

Water.

Timo kept snapping. He had it now. The flowers and the empty milk-jugs dangling off the dude. Timo was in the flow, bracketing exposures, shooting steady, recognizing the moment when his inner eye told him that he'd nailed the story. It was good. *Really* good.

As good as a Cat 6 plowing into Houston.

Click-click-click. Money-money-money-money.

"That's right, buddy. Talk to your friend Timo."

The man had a story to tell, and Timo had the eye to see it. Most people missed the story. But Timo always saw. He had the eye.

Maybe he'd buy a top-shelf tequila to celebrate his page view money. Some diapers for his sister Amparo's baby. If the photos were good, maybe he'd grab a couple syndication licenses, too. Swap the shit-ass battery in the Ford. Get something with a bigger range dropped into it. Let him get around without always wondering if he was going to lose a charge.

Some of these could go to *Xinhua*, for sure. The Chinese news agencies loved seeing America ripping itself to shit. BBC might bite, too. Foreigners loved that story. Only thing that would sell better is if it had a couple guns: *America, the Savage Land* or some shit. That was money, there. Might be rent for a bigger place. A place where Amparo could bail when her boyfriend got his ass drunk and angry.

Timo kept snapping photos, changing angles, framing and exposure. Diving deeper into the dead man's world. Capturing scuffed-up boots and plastic prayer beads. He hummed to himself as he worked, talking to his subject, coaxing the best out of the corpse.

"You don't know it, but you're damn lucky I came along," Timo said. "If one of those citizen journalist *pendejo* lice got you first, they wouldn't have treated you right. They'd shoot a couple shitty frames and upload them social. Maybe sell a Instagram pic to the blood rags . . . but they ain't quality. Me? When I'm done, people won't be able to *dream* without seeing you."

It was true, too. Any asshole could snap a pic of some girl blasted to pieces in an electric Mercedes, but Timo knew how to make you cry when you saw her splattered all over the front pages of the blood rags. Some piece of narco ass, and you'd still be bawling your eyes out over her tragic death. He'd catch the girl's little fuzzy dice mirror ornament spattered with blood, and your heart would just break.

Amparo said Timo had the eye. Little bro could see what other people didn't, even when it was right in front of their faces.

Every asshole had a camera these days; the difference was that Timo could *see*.

Timo backed off and got some quick video. He ran the recording back, listening to the audio, satisfying himself that he had the sound of it: the wind rattling the chain link under the high hot Arizona sky; meadowlark call from somewhere next to the CAP waters; but most of all, the empty dangling jugs, the three of them plunking hollowly against each other—a dead man turned into an offering and a wind chime.

Timo listened to the deep *thunk-thunk-thunk* tones.

Good sounds.

Good empty desert sounds.

He crouched and framed the man's gnawed arm and the milk jugs. From this angle, he could just capture the blue line of the CAP canal and the leading edge of Phoenix beyond: cookie-cutter low-stories with lava-rock front yards and broke-down cars on blocks. And somewhere in there, some upstanding example of Arizona Minute-Man militia pride had spied this sucker scrambling down the dusty hillside with his water jugs and decided to put a cap in his ass.   .

CAP in his ass, Timo chuckled to himself.

The crunch of tires and the grind of an old bio-diesel engine announced Lucy's pickup coming up the dirt road. A trail of dust followed. Rusty beast of flex-fuel, older than the girl who drove it and twice as beat up, but damn was it a beast. It had been one of the things Timo liked about Lucy, soon as he met her. Girl drove a machine that didn't give a damn about anything except driving over shit.

The truck came to a halt. The driver's side door squealed aside as Lucy climbed out. Army green tank top and washed out jeans. White skin, scorched and bronzed by Arizona sun, her reddish brown hair jammed up under an ASU Geology Department ball cap.

Every time he saw her, Timo liked what he saw. Phoenix hadn't dried her right, yet, but still, she had some kind of tenacious-ass demon in her. Something about the way her pale blue skeptical eyes burned for a story told you that once she bit in, she wouldn't let go. Crazy-ass pitbull. The girl and the truck were a pair. Unstoppable.

"Please tell me I didn't drive out here for a swimmer," Lucy said as she approached.

"What do you think?"

"I think I was on the other side of town when you called, and I had to burn diesel to get here."

She was trying to look jaded, but her eyes were already flicking from detail to detail, gathering the story before Timo even had to open his mouth. She might be new in Phoenix, but the girl had the eye. Just like Timo, Lucy saw things.

"Texan?" she asked.

Timo grinned. "You think?"

"Well, he's a Merry Perry, anyway. I don't know many other people who would join that cult." She crouched down in front of the corpse and peered into the man's torn face. Reaching out, she caressed the prayer beads embedded in the man's neck. "I did a story on Merry Perrys. Roadside spiritual aid for the refugees." She sighed. "They were all buying the beads and making the prayers."

"Crying and shaking and repentance."

"You've been to their services, too?"

"Everybody's done that story at least once," Timo said. "I shot a big old revival tent over in New Mexico, outside of Carlsbad. The preacher had a nasty ass thorn bush, wanted volunteers."

Timo didn't think he'd ever forget the scene. The tent walls sucking and flapping as blast-furnace winds gusted over them. The dust-coated refugees all shaking, moaning, and working their beads for God. All of them asking what they needed to give up in order to get back to the good old days of big oil money and fancy cities like Houston and Austin. To get back to a life before hurricanes went Cat 6 and Big Daddy Drought sucked whole states dry.

Lucy ran her fingers along the beads that had sunk deep into the dead man's neck. "They strangled him."

"Sure looks that way."

Timo could imagine this guy earning the prayer beads one at time. Little promises of God's love that he could carry with him. He imagined the man down in the dirt, all crying and spitty and grateful for his bloody back and for the prayer beads that had ended up embedded in his swollen, blackening neck, like some kind of Mardi Gras party gone wrong. The man had done his prayers and repentance, and this was where he'd ended up.

"What happened to his hand?" Lucy asked.

"Dog got it."

"Christ."

"If you want some better art, we can back off for a little while, and the dogs'll come back. I can get a good tearaway shot if we let them go after him again—"

Lucy gave Timo a dirty look, so he hastily changed tacks. "Anyway, I thought you should see him. Good art, and it's a great story. Nobody's got something like this."

Lucy straightened. "I can't pitch this, Timo. It's sad as hell, but it isn't new. Nobody cares if Old Tex here hiked across a thousand miles of desert just to get strung up as some warning. It's sad, but everyone knows how much people hate Texans. *Kindle Post* did a huge story on Texas lynchings."

"Shit." Timo sighed. "Every time I think you're wise, I find out you're still wet."

"Oh fuck off, Timo."

"No, I'm serious girl. Come here. Look with your eye. I know you got the eye. Don't make me think I'm wasting my time on you."

Timo crouched down beside the dead man, framing him with this hands. "Old Tex here hikes his ass across a million miles of burning desert, and he winds up here. Maybe he's thinking he's heading for California and gets caught with the State Sovereignty Act, can't cross no state borders now. Maybe he just don't have the cash to pay coyotes. Maybe he thinks he's special and he's going to swim the Colorado and make it up north across Nevada. Anyways, Tex is stuck squatting out in the hills, watching us live the good life. But then the poor sucker sees the CAP, and he's sick of paying to go to some public pump for water, so he grabs his bottles and goes in for a little sip—"

"—and someone puts a bullet in him," Lucy finished. "I get it. I'm trying to tell you nobody cares about dead Texans. People string them up all the time. I saw it in New Mexico, too. Merry Perry prayer tents and Texans strung up on fences. Same in Oklahoma. All the roads out of Texas have them. Nobody cares."

Wet.

Timo sighed. "You're lucky you got me for your tour guide. You know that, right? You see the cigarettes? See them little bitty Beam and Cuervo bottles? The black candles? The flowers?"

Timo waited for her take in the scene again. To see the way he saw. "Old Tex here isn't a *warning*. This motherfucker's an *offering*. People turned Old Tex into an offering for Santa Muerte. They're using Tex here to get in good with the Skinny Lady."

"Lady Death," Lucy said. "Isn't that a cult for narcos?"

"Nah. She's no cult. She's a saint. Takes care of people who don't got pull with the Church. When you need help on something the Church don't like, you go to

Santa Muerte. The Skinny Lady takes care of you. She knows we all need a little help. Maybe she helps narcos, sure, but she helps poor people, too. She helps desperate people. When Mother Mary's too uptight, you call the Skinny Lady to do the job."

"Sounds like you know a lot about her."

"Oh hell yes. Got an app on my phone. Dial her any time I want and get a blessing."

"You're kidding."

"True story. There's a lady down in Mexico runs a big shrine. You send her a dollar, she puts up an offering for you. Makes miracles happen. There's a whole list of miracles that Santa Muerte does. Got her own hashtag."

"So what kind of miracles do you look for?"

"Tips, girl! What you think?" Timo sighed. "Narcos call on Santa Muerte all the time when they want to put a bullet in their enemies. And I come in after and take the pictures. Skinny Lady gets me there before the competition is even close."

Lucy was looking at him like he was crazy, and it annoyed him. "You know, Lucy, it's not like you're the only person who needs an edge out here." He waved at the dead Texan. "So? You want the story, or not?"

She still looked skeptical. "If anyone can make an offering to Santa Muerte online, what's this Texan doing upside down on a fence?"

"DIY, baby."

"I'm serious, Timo. What makes you think Tex here is an offering?"

Because Amparo's boyfriend just lost his job to some loser Longhorn who will work for nothing. Because my water bill just went up again, and my rationing just went down. Because Roosevelt Lake is gone dry, and I got Merry Perrys doing revivals right on the corner of 7th and Monte Vista, and they're trying to get my cousin Marco to join them.

"People keep coming," Timo said, and he was surprised at the tightness of his throat as he said it. "They smell that we got water, and they just keep coming. It's like Texas is a million, million ants, and they just keep coming."

"There are definitely a lot of people in Texas."

"More like a tsunami. And we keep getting hit by wave after wave of them, and we can't hold 'em all back." He pointed at the body. "This is Last Stand shit, here. People are calling in the big guns. Maybe they're praying for Santa Muerte to hit the Texans with a dust storm and strip their bones before they get here. For sure they're asking for something big."

"So they call on Lady Death." But Lucy was shaking her head. "It's just that I need more than a body to do a story."

"But I got amazing pics!"

"I need more. I need quotes. I need a trend. I need a story. I need an example . . ."

Lucy was looking across the CAP canal toward the subdivision as she spoke. Timo could almost see the gears turning in her head . . .

"Oh no. Don't do it, girl."

"Do what?" But she was smiling, already.

"Don't go over there and start asking who did the deed."

"It would be a great story."

"You think some motherfucker's just gonna say they out and wasted Old Tex?"

"People love to talk, if you ask them the right questions."

"Seriously, Lucy. Let the cops take care of it. Let them go over there and ask the questions."

Lucy gave him a pissed-off look.

"What?" Timo asked.

"You really think I'm that wet?"

"Well . . ."

"Seriously? How long have we known each other? Do you really think you can fool me into thinking the cops are gonna give a shit about another dead Merry Perry? How wet do you think I am?"

Lucy spun and headed for her truck.

"This ain't some amusement park!" Timo called after her. "You can't just go poke the Indians and think they're gonna native dance for you. People here are for *real*!" He had to shout the last because the truck's door was already screeching open.

"Don't worry about me!" Lucy called as she climbed into the beast. "Just get me good art! I'll get our story!"

"So let me get this straight," Timo asked, for the fourth or fifth time. "They just let you into their house?"

They were kicked back on the roof at Sid's Cafe with the rest of the regulars, taking potshots at the prairie dogs who had invaded the half-finished subdivision ruins around the bar, trading an old .22 down a long line as patrons took bets.

The subdivision was called Sonora Bloom Estates, one of those crap-ass investments that had gone belly up when Phoenix finally stopped bailing out over-pumped subdivisions. Desert Bloom Estates had died because some bald-ass pencil-pusher in City Planning had got a stick up his ass and said the water district wasn't going to support them. Now, unless some company like IBIS or Halliburton could frack their way to some magical new water supply, Desert Bloom was only ever going to be a town for prairie dogs.

"They just let you in?" Timo asked. "Seriously?"

Lucy nodded smugly. "They let me into their house, and then into their neighbor's houses. And then they took me down into their basements and showed me their machine guns." Lucy took a swig of Negro Modelo. "I make friends, Timo." She grinned. "I make a *lot* of friends. It's what I do."

"Bullshit."

"Believe it, or don't." Lucy shrugged. "Anyway, I've got our story. 'Phoenix's Last Stand.' You wouldn't believe how they've got themselves set up. They've got war rooms. They've got ammo dumps. This isn't some cult militia, it's more like the army of the apocalypse. Way beyond preppers. These people are getting ready for the end of the world, and they want to talk about it."

"They want to talk."

"They're *desperate* to talk. They *like* talking. All they talk about is how to shove Texas back where it came from. I mean, you see the inside of their houses, and it's all Arizona for the People, and God and Santa Muerte to back them up."

"They willing to let me take pictures?"

Lucy gave him another smug look. "No faces. That's the only condition."

Timo grinned. "I can work with that."

Lucy set her beer down. "So what've you shot so far?"

"Good stuff." Timo pulled out his camera and flicked through images. "How about this one?" He held up the camera for her to see. "Poetry, right?"

Lucy eyed the image with distaste. "We need something PG, Timo."

"PG? Come on. PG don't get the hits. People love the bodies and the blood. *Sangre* this, *sangre* that. They want the blood, and they want the sex. Those are the only two things that get hits."

"This isn't for the local blood rags," Lucy said. "We need something PG from the dead guy."

She accepted the rifle from a hairy biker dude sitting next to her and sighted out at the dimming landscape beyond. The sun was sinking over the sprawl of the Phoenix basin, a brown blanket of pollution and smoke from California wild fires turning orange and gaudy.

Timo lifted his camera and snapped a couple quick shots of Lucy as she sighted down the rifle barrel. Wet girl trying to act dry. Not knowing that everyone who rolled down to Phoenix tried to show how tough they were by picking up a nice rifle and blasting away at the furry critters out in the subdivisions.

The thought reminded Timo that he needed to get some shots of Sumo Hernandez and his hunting operation. Sucker had a sweet gig bringing Chinese tourists in to blast at coyotes and then feed them rattlesnake dinners.

He snapped a couple more pictures and checked the results. Lucy looked damn good on the camera's LCD. He'd got her backlit, the line of her rifle barrel across the blaze of the red ball sun. Money shot for sure.

He flicked back into the dead Texan pictures.

"PG, PG . . . ," Timo muttered. "What the fuck is PG? It's not like the dude's dick is out. Just his eaten-off face."

Lucy squeezed off another shot and handed the rifle on.

"This is going to go big, Timo. We don't want it to look like it's just another murder story. That's been done. This has to look smart and scary and real. We're going to do a series."

"We are?"

"Hell yes, we are. I mean, this could be Pulitzer type stuff. 'Phoenix's Last Stand.'"

"I don't give a shit about Pulitzers. I just want good hits. I need money."

"It will get us hits. Trust me. We're onto something good."

Timo flicked through more of his pictures. "How about just the beads in the guy's neck?" He showed her a picture. "This one's sweet."

"No." Lucy shook her head. "I want the CAP in it."

Timo gave up on stifling his exasperation. "PG, CAP. Anything else, ma'am?"

Lucy shot him a look. "Will you trust me on this? I know what I'm doing."

"Wet-ass newcomer says she knows what she's doing."

"Look, you're the expert when it comes to Phoenix. But you've got to trust me. I know what I'm doing. I know how people think back East. I know what people want on the big traffic sites. You know Phoenix, and I trust you. Now you've got to trust *me*. We're onto something. If we do it right, we're going to blow up. We're going to be a phenomenon."

The hairy biker guy handed the rifle back to Lucy for another shot.

"So you want PG, and you want the CAP," Timo said.

"Yeah. The CAP is why he died," she said absently as she sighted again with the rifle. "It's what he wanted. And it's what the Defending Angels need to protect. It's what Phoenix has that Texas doesn't. Phoenix is alive in the middle of a desert because you've got one of the most expensive water transport systems in the world. If Texas had a straw like the CAP running to some place like the Mississippi River, they'd still be fine."

Timo scoffed. "That would be like a thousand miles."

"Rivers go farther than that." Lucy squeezed off a shot and dust puffed beside a prairie dog. The critter dove back into its hole, and Lucy passed the rifle on. "I mean, your CAP water is coming from the Rockies. You've got the Colorado River running all the way down from Wyoming and Colorado, through Utah, all the way across the top of Arizona, and then you and California and Las Vegas all share it out."

"California doesn't share shit."

"You know what I mean. You all stick your straws in the river, you pump water to a bunch of cities that shouldn't even exist. CAP water comes way more than a thousand miles." She laughed and reached for her beer. "The irony is that at least Texans built where they *had* water. Without the CAP, you'd be just like the Texans. A bunch of sad-ass people all trying to move north."

"Thank God we're smarter than those assholes."

"Well, you've got better bureaucrats and pork barrels, anyway."

Timo made a face at Lucy's dig, but didn't bother arguing. He was still hunting through his photos for something that Lucy would approve of.

Nothing PG about dying, he thought. *Nothing PG about clawing your way all the way across a thousand miles of desert just to smash up against chain link. Nothing PG about selling off your daughter so you can make a run at going North, or jumping the border into California.*

He was surprised to find that he almost felt empathy for the Texan. Who knew? Maybe this guy had seen the apocalypse coming, but he'd just been too rooted in place to accept that he couldn't ride it out. Or maybe he'd had too much faith that God would take care of him.

The rifle was making the rounds again. More sharp cracks of the little .22 caliber bullets.

Faith. Maybe Old Tex's faith had made him blind. Made it impossible for him to see what was coming. Like a prairie dog who'd stuck his head out of his burrow, and couldn't quite believe that God had put a bead on his furry little skull. Couldn't see the bullet screaming in on him.

In the far distance, a flight of helicopters was moving across the burning horizon. The thud-thwap of their rotors carried easily across the hum of the city. Timo counted fifteen or twenty in the formation. Heading off to fight forest fires maybe. Or else getting shipped up to the arctic by the Feds.

Going someplace, anyway.

"Everybody's got some place to go," Lucy murmured, as if reading his mind.

The rifle cracked again, and a prairie dog went down. Everyone cheered. "I think that one was from Texas," someone said.

Everyone laughed. Selena came up from below with a new tray of bottles and handed them out. Lucy was smirking to herself, looking superior.

"You got something to say?" Timo asked.

"Nothing. It's just funny how you all treat the Texans."

"Shit." Timo took a slug from his beer. "They deserve it. I was down there, remember? I saw them all running around like ants after Hurricane Violet fucked them up. Saw their towns drying up. Hell, everybody who wasn't Texas Forever saw that shit coming down. And there they all were, praying to God to save their righteous Texan asses." He took another slug of beer. "No pity for those fools. They brought their apocalypse down on their own damn selves. And now they want to come around here and take away what we got? No way."

"No room for charity?" Lucy prodded.

"Don't interview me," Timo shot back.

Lucy held up her hands in apology. "My bad."

Timo snorted. "Hey everybody! My wet-ass friend here thinks we ought to show some charity to the Texans."

"I'll give 'em a bullet, free," Brixer Gonzalez said.

"I'll give 'em two!" Molly Abrams said. She took the rifle and shot out a distant window in the subdivision.

"And yet they keep coming," Lucy murmured, looking thoughtful. "They just keep on coming, and you can't stop them."

Timo didn't like how she mirrored his own worries.

"We're going to be fine."

"Because you've got Santa Muerte and a whole hell of a lot of armed lunatics on your side," Lucy said with satisfaction. "This story is going to make us. 'The Defending Angels of Phoenix.' What a beautiful scoop."

"And they're just going to let us cover them?" Timo still couldn't hide his skepticism.

"All anyone wants to do is tell their story, Timo. They need to know they matter." She favored him with a side-long smile. "So when a nice journo from up north comes knocking? Some girl who's so wet they can see it on her face? They love it. They love telling her how it is." Lucy took a sip of her beer, seeming to remember the encounter. "If people think you're wet enough, you wouldn't believe what they'll tell you. They've got to show how smart and wise they are, you know? All you need to do is look interested, pretend you're wet, and people roll right over."

Lucy kept talking, describing the world she'd uncovered, the details that had jumped out at her. How there was so much more to get. How he needed to come along and get the art.

She kept talking, but Timo couldn't hear her words anymore because one phrase kept pinging around inside his head like a pinball.

Pretend you're wet, and people roll right over.

"I don't know why you're acting like this," Lucy said for the third time as they drove out to the see the Defending Angels.

She was driving the beast, and Timo was riding shotgun. He'd loaded his gear into her truck, determined that any further expenses from the reporting trip should be on her.

At first, he'd wanted to just cut her off and walk away from the whole thing, but he realized that was childish. If she could get the hits, then fine. He'd tag along on her score. He'd take her page views, and then he'd be done with her.

Cutting her off too soon would get him nothing. She'd just go get some other *pendejo* to do the art, or else she might even shoot the pictures herself and get her ass paid twice, a prospect that galled him even more than the fact that he'd been manipulated.

They wound their way into the subdivision, driving past ancient Prius sedans and electric bikes. At the end of the cul-de-sac, Lucy pulled to a halt. The place didn't look any different from any other Phoenix suburb. Except apparently, inside all the quiet houses, a last-battle resistance was brewing.

Ahead, the chain link and barbwire of the CAP boundary came into view. Beyond, there was nothing but cactus-studded hills. Timo could just make out the Texan on the far side of the CAP fences, still dangling. It looked like the dogs were at him again, tearing at the scraps.

"Will you at least talk to me?" Lucy asked. "Tell me what I did."

Timo shrugged. "Let's just get your shoot done. Show me these Angels of Arizona you're so hot for."

"No." Lucy shook her head. "I'm not taking you to see them until you tell me why you keep acting this way."

Timo glared at her, then looked out the dusty front window.

"Guess we're not going to see them then."

With the truck turned off, it was already starting to broil inside. The kind of heat that cooked pets and babies to death in a couple hours. Timo could feel sweat starting to trickle off him, but he was damned if he was going to show that he was uncomfortable. He sat and stared at the CAP fence ahead of them. They could both sweat to death for all he cared.

Lucy was staring at him, hard. "If you've got something you want to say, you should be man enough to say it."

Man enough? Oh, hell no.

"Okay," Timo said. "I think you played me."

"Played you how?"

"Seriously? You going to keep at it? I'm on to you, girl. You act all wet, and you get people to help you out. You get people to do shit they wouldn't normally do. You act all nice, like you're all new and like you're just getting your feet under you, but that's just an act."

"So what?" Lucy said. "Why do you care if I fool some militia nutjobs?"

"I'm not talking about them! I'm talking about me! That's how you played me! You act like you don't know things, get me to show you around. Show you the ropes. Get you on the inside. You act all wet and sorry, and dumbass Timo steps in to help you out. And you get a nice juicy exclusive."

"Timo . . . how long have we known each other?"

"I don't know if we ever did."

"Timo—"

"Don't bother apologizing." He shouldered the truck's door open.

As he climbed out, he knew he was making a mistake. She'd pick up some other photographer. Or else she'd shoot the story herself and get paid twice for the work.

Should have just kept my mouth shut.

Amparo would have told him he was both dumb and a sucker. Should have at least worked Lucy to get the story done before he left her ass. Instead he'd dumped her, and the story.

Lucy climbed out of the truck, too.

"Fine," she said. "I won't do it."

"Won't do what?"

"I won't do the story. If you think I played you, I won't do the story."

"Oh come on. That's bullshit. You know you came down here for your scoop. You ain't giving that up."

Lucy's stared at him, looking pissed. "You know what your problem is?"

"Got a feeling you're going to tell me."

"You're so busy doing your poor-me, I'm from Phoenix, everyone's-out-to-get-me, we're-getting-overrun wah-wah-wah routine that you can't even tell when someone's on your side!"

"That's not—"

"You can't even tell someone's standing right in front of you who actually gives a shit about you!" Lucy was almost spitting she was so mad. Her face had turned red. Timo tried to interject, but she kept talking.

"I'm not some damn Texan here to take your water, and I'm not some big time journo here to steal your fucking stories! That's not who I am! You know how many photographers I could work with? You know how many would bite on this story that I went out and got? I put my ass on the line out here! You think that was easy?"

"Lucy. Come on . . ."

She waved a hand of disgust at him and stalked off, heading for the end of the cul-de-sac and the CAP fence beyond.

"Go find someone else to do this story," she called back. "Pick whoever you want. I wouldn't touch this story with a ten-foot-pole. If that's what you want, it's all yours."

"Come on, Lucy." Timo felt like shit. He started to chase after her. "It's not like that!"

She glanced back. "Don't even try, Timo."

Her expression was so scornful and disgusted that Timo faltered.

He could almost hear his sister Amparo laughing at him. *You got the eye for some things, little bro, but you are blind blind blind.*

She'll cool off, he thought as he let her go.

Except maybe she wouldn't. Maybe he'd said some things that sounded a little too true. Said what he'd really thought of Lucy the Northerner in a way that couldn't get smoothed over. Sometimes, things just broke. One second, you thought you had a connection with a person. Next second, you saw them too clear, and you just knew you were never going to drink a beer together, ever again.

So go fix it, pendejo.

With a groan, Timo went after her again.

"Lucy!" he called. "Come on, girl. I'm sorry, okay? I'm sorry . . ."

At first, he thought she was going to ignore him, but then she turned.

Timo felt a rush of relief. She was looking at him again. She was looking right at him, like before, when they'd still been getting along. She was going to forgive him. They were going to work it out. They were friends.

But then he realized her expression was wrong. She looked dazed. Her sunburned skin had paled. And she was waving at him, waving furiously for him to join her.

Another Texan? Already?

Timo broke into a run, fumbling for his camera.

He stopped short as he made it to the fence.

"Timo?" Lucy whispered.

"I see it."

He was already snapping pictures through the chainlink, getting the story. He had the eye, and the story was right there in front of them. The biggest luckiest break he'd ever get. Right place, right time, right team to cover the story. He was kneeling now, shooting as fast as he could, listening to the digital report of the electronic shutter, hearing money with every click.

I got it, I got it, I got it, thinking that he was saying it to himself and then realizing he was speaking out loud. "I got it," he said. "Don't worry, I got it!"

Lucy was turning in circles, looking dazed, staring back at the city. "We need to get ourselves assigned. We need to get supplies . . . We need to trace this back . . . We need to figure out who did it . . . We need to get ourselves assigned!" She yanked out her phone and started dialing madly as Timo kept snapping pictures.

Lucy's voice was an urgent hum in the background as he changed angles and exposures.

Lucy clicked off the cell. "We're exclusive with *Xinhua*!"

"Both of us?"

She held up a warning finger. "Don't even start up on me again."

Timo couldn't help grinning. "Wouldn't dream of it, partner."

Lucy began dictating the beginnings of her story into her phone, then broke off. "They want our first update in ten minutes, you think you're up for that?"

"In ten minutes, updates are going to be the least of our problems."

He was in the flow now, capturing the concrete canal and the dead Texan on the other side.

The dogs leaped and jumped, tearing apart the man who had come looking for water.

It was all there. The whole story, laid out.

The man.

The dogs.

The fences.

The Central Arizona Project.

A whole big canal, drained of water. Nothing but a thin crust of rapidly drying mud at its bottom.

Lucy had started dictating again. She'd turned to face the Phoenix sprawl, but Timo didn't need to listen to her talk. He knew the story already—a whole city full of people going about their daily lives, none of them knowing that everything had changed.

Timo kept shooting.

weather

SUSAN PALWICK

*Most people think that families should stay in close touch with one another—
but perhaps there should be limits even to that.*

Susan Palwick is an Associate Professor of English at the University of
Nevada, Reno. She has published four novels, the most recent being 2013's
Mending the Moon, *and a story collection,* The Fate of Mice. *Her work has
won the IAFA Crawford Award and the ALA Alex Award, and has been short-
listed for the World Fantasy and Mythopoeic Awards.*

Kerry and Frank were taking out the recycling first thing Tuesday morning
when Dan Rappaport came driving by in his pickup. He'd called them with the bad
news half an hour ago, so he was the last person Frank had expected to see outside
the house.

"The pass is closed," Dan said, his breath steaming through the open cab window. Late April, and it was that cold. There'd been a hard frost overnight, even down
here in Reno. The daffodils and tulips had just started to bloom, and now they were
going to die. Damn freaky weather.

Up higher, it was snow: Truckee and Donner Pass were socked in. Frank could
see the weather even from here, even from the front yard of the tiny house he
and Kerry had bought the summer she was pregnant with Alison. Their first house,
and back then they'd expected to move sometime, but they never had. It was a cozy
house, just right for a couple.

They'd need cozy today. Frank could see the clouds blanketing the mountains to
the west, I-80 crossing the California border twelve miles away. There might be
snow left in those clouds when they got down to the valley, or not. Frank hoped not.
He didn't want to have to shovel the driveway. Losing everything bright in the backyard was bad enough.

Kerry put down her side of the recycling bin, forcing Frank to put his down, too.
All those empty wine bottles get heavy. "Now, Dan," she said, as if she were scolding
one of the dogs for chewing on the couch cushions. "Come on now. It'll be open
again in a few hours. It never stays closed very long." And that was true, but it could
be open and still be nasty driving, dangerous, even if you weren't in a truck so old it

should have been in a museum somewhere. Stretches of I-80 were still two lanes in either direction, twisty-turny, with winds that could blow a car off the road in a storm. Nobody tried to drive over the mountains in bad weather except the long-haul truckers with the really big rigs, and nobody with any sense wanted to jockey with them on a slick road.

Dan had never had much sense. "I don't have a few hours," he said. His hands were clenched on the steering wheel, and he sounded like he'd already been hitting the beer, even though Frank couldn't smell anything: all that old anger rising up in a wave, the way booze makes it do. "Rosie could already be gone. This is it: hours, the doctors say." He'd already said that on the phone, told them how Sandra's sister had only called him this morning, given him hardly any notice at all.

"They know you'll get to talk to her later," Kerry said. "You have all the time in the world. It's wonderful, Dan. You're so lucky." Kerry's voice caught, the way it usually only did late at night when she'd been working on the wine and typing nonsense on her laptop. Time to change the subject.

"At least the ski resorts'll be happy," Frank said, thinking about what a dry winter it had been. Kerry gave him that look that meant, *shut up, you fool*, and he remembered that Dan's ex—the latest one, number four or five—had run off with a ski instructor. That was five years ago. There should be a statute of limitations about how long you had to avoid talking about things. Frank had enough trouble keeping track of his own life, let alone everyone else's too. Kerry was the opposite: couldn't remember what she did last night, not when she'd been sitting up with the wine and the computer, but she never forgot anything that happened to anyone else, especially if it was tragic.

"Dan," she said, "come inside and eat some breakfast with us. We'll listen to the radio, and as soon as the pass opens you can be on your way, all right? Come on. We've got fresh coffee, and I'll make some eggs and bacon. How's that sound?"

"I have to get over there," Dan said, and Kerry reached out and patted his arm through the window. "I could've driven over last night, a few days ago, I should've, I knew it was bad but I didn't know she had so little time left, no one told me—"

"You didn't have a place to stay," Kerry said gently. And he couldn't afford the time off work, but Frank wasn't going to say that. Dan worked in the dump north of town, taking old cars apart and putting them back together, and he only had that job because his boss took pity on him.

"Come on in," Frank said. "No sense starting out until the pass opens. You won't buy yourself any time if you head up now: you'll just have to sit it out somewhere higher. Do it with us over some hot coffee, Dan." If they let him go when he was this upset, he'd head to a 7–11 for a sixpack sure enough, or to a bar, which would be even worse. The booze was another good reason for him not to be driving all the way to Sacramento in lousy weather, and also, Frank suspected, why neither his ex-wife number two or any of her people wanted to put him up, even if he was Rosie's father. He didn't need to be drinking now, and he didn't need to be spending his gas money, which God only knew how he'd scrounged up to begin with, with a gallon costing what it did.

Dan looked away, out the windshield, and cleared his throat. "I shouldn't be bothering you. Shouldn't even have driven by here. Fact is, I feel awfully funny—"

"Don't you mind that," Kerry said, a little too quickly. "We're happy for you, Dan, happy for you and Rosie. We couldn't be happier. It's a blessing, so don't you give it another thought. Come have some eggs." Her voice was wobbling again. Frank knew better than to say that he wasn't happy for Dan, that what was happening to Dan was no different at all from what had happened to them. But maybe Dan knew that. Maybe that was why he'd come by the house. He must have known it, or he wouldn't have been so worried about being late.

So Dan followed them inside. He and Kerry sat at the kitchen table while Frank cooked. Usually Kerry cooked, because she was a lot better at it than Frank was, but he could do simple breakfast stuff fine, and Kerry was better at letting people cry at her. She liked to talk about sad stuff. Frank didn't.

Dan poured his heart out while Frank fried up a bunch of eggs and bacon and the radio droned on about the storm. "That fucking asshole Sandra's married to now doesn't want me there at all. I'm not sure Sandra does either, to tell you the truth. That's probably why her sister called; I always got on with her okay. Leah said she wanted me to know, like Sandra and the asshole didn't want me to know. I got the feeling they didn't even know she was calling me. Shit."

"Rosie's your daughter," Kerry said. "You have a right to be there."

Even with his back to the table, Frank could hear Dan gulping coffee. Outside, a few flakes of snow swirled down into the yard. Frank couldn't see the mountains at all. "I know I do," Dan said. "She's out of it now. Don't respond to nobody, that's what Leah said. Said the hospice nurse doesn't know why she's hung on this long. They hang on to wait for people, sometimes. To give them a chance to get there. That's why Leah called me."

"So you can drive over," Kerry said. "Tell her it's all right to go. That's what we had to do with Alison. They tell you to say that. They tell you to tell them it's okay to leave, even when it's breaking your heart, because having them leave is the last thing you want." Her voice had gotten thick. "You're so lucky she'll be translated, Dan."

When she said that, Frank was moving hot bacon from the frying pan to a bunch of paper towels, to drain the grease. But the pan was still hot enough to spit at him, and he got burned. "Dammit!" he said, and heard two chairs scrape. When he turned around, Dan and Kerry were both staring at him. Dan looked worried; Kerry looked mad. "I burned myself," Frank said. "On the grease. That's all. Bacon'll be ready in a minute. Eggs are ready now. We've got more coffee."

They knew there was more coffee. Frank knew he was talking too much, even if there was nothing more to his outburst than burning himself, and Kerry's eyes narrowed a little more, until he could tell she was ready to spit the way the grease had. "What?" he said, hoping they weren't about to have a fight in front of Dan. But when Kerry looked like that, there was no way around it except to plow right through whatever was eating at her.

"It's real, Frank. Translation. You should be happy for Rosie. And for Dan."

"I burned myself on the grease, Kerry. That's all. And Dan doesn't need to listen to us fight about this." Frank looked at Dan. "And no matter how real it is, somebody needing it at Rosie's age is nothing to be happy about." Dan nodded, and Kerry looked away, and Frank turned back to the food, feeling like maybe he'd danced his way around the fight after all. But when he turned back towards the table, a platter of eggs in one hand and a plate of bacon in the other, Kerry had started to cry, which she normally did only really late at night. That was usually Frank's cue to go to bed, but he couldn't do that at eight in the morning.

So he just stood there, holding the food and trying to hold his temper. After Alison died, they'd heard all the numbers and clichés. How many marriages break up after the death of a child. How you have to keep talking to each other to make sure that doesn't happen. How losing a kid is so hard because it violates the order of nature: children are supposed to bury their parents, not the other way around. The counselors at the hospital told Kerry and Frank all of that; most of their friends didn't say anything. The counselors had warned them about that, too, how people avoid the subject.

Which maybe was why Dan had come to them. He knew Kerry wouldn't avoid it, anyway. "You," she said, and she sounded drunk, even though it was only eight in the morning and she hadn't been drunk ten minutes ago. "You. You never. You never want to talk about it."

"I talk about Alison all the time," Frank told her, as gently as he could. He wanted to slam the food down and go into the backyard to cover the daffodils: they'd just come up, but he could see snow starting to come down. He had to stay here, though. Because of Dan. "Come on, Ker. You know I talk about her. Remember yesterday? We were driving to the store and we saw that bright-pink Camaro, and I said, 'Alison would have loved that car.' And you said that yeah, she would have. Remember? It was only yesterday."

"Translation," she said. "You never want to talk about translation."

Frank's wrists were starting to ache. He put the plates down on the table. "We should eat this stuff before it gets cold." But Kerry's chin was quivering. She wasn't going to let him change the subject. "Ker, we should maybe talk about this when Dan isn't here. Okay?" What in the world was she thinking? She knew damn well how Frank felt, and he knew how she felt, which was exactly why they didn't talk about it. There was no point. It would only upset both of them.

"It's okay," Dan said. "It is. Really. I—I know people feel different ways about it. I don't know how I feel yet. I'll have to wait and see. I won't have an opinion until I've talked to her. Until she's online. Then I can see if it really sounds like her."

"It will," Kerry said. "It will, I go to the translation boards all the time and read about people who've been talking to their dead, and they all say the messages are real, they have to be, because they say things no one else could know. Just yesterday there was a guy who heard from his dad and his dad told him to look in a certain box in the attic, and—"

Ouija boards. People had been talking to imaginary ghosts as long as there were people. Now they did it with computers, was all. Frank wondered if Kerry would still have been so obsessed with translation if it had come around in time for Alison, if she hadn't died six months before the first dead person went online, not that they'd have been able to afford it anyway.

There was nothing to do but tune her out, the way he always did. He turned up the volume on the Weather Channel. "Frank," Kerry said. "You're interrupting."

"Listen," Frank said. It was easing off a little, the radio said. The highway might open again within an hour. And right then he decided. "Eat up, Dan. I'm driving you. My truck's better than yours, and you shouldn't drive when you're upset, especially in tricky weather."

Frank felt rather than saw Kerry shaking her head. "No. It's dangerous up there!" Her voice bubbled with panic. "Even if the road opens again, it's safer to stay down here. Dan, you've got your phone. She'll call you."

"I have to try to see her," Dan said. "I have to. You understand, don't you?"

Kerry shook her head again. "Frank, no. I don't want you driving up there. I can't lose you, too." But she knew him; she could read him. She'd started crying again, but she said, "I'll fix a thermos of coffee."

The snow got thicker as they climbed, and the sparse traffic slowed and then finally stopped a few miles short of the first Truckee exit. Dan, sitting with his hands clenched on his knees, had said quietly, "Hey, thanks," when they got into the truck, and Frank had nodded, and that was all they'd said. The only voice in the truck was the droning National Weather Service guy talking about the storm. It was peaceful, after Kerry's yammering.

Frank had been driving very slowly. He trusted himself and his truck, which had a full tank of gas and new snow tires and could have gotten through just about anything short of an avalanche, but he didn't trust the other idiots on the road. When they had to stop, he unscrewed the thermos of coffee and poured himself a cup. "You want some?"

Dan shook his head. "No thanks." He stared straight ahead, peering through the windshield as if he could see all the way to Sacramento. There was nothing to look at but snow. Normally they would have had a gorgeous view of the mountains all around them and the Truckee to their left, real picture postcard stuff, but not today.

Frank saw somebody bundled in a parka trudging between the lanes, knocking on windows. "This can't be good," he said.

"Damn fool will get killed when things start moving."

But it was a cop. They didn't take chances. Frank rolled down his window, and bitter stinging snow blew into the cab. "Morning, officer."

It was a woman, CHP. "There's a spinout up there. Bad ice. Road's closed again, will be for a while. We're advising everyone to take the shoulder to the next exit and turn around." Sure enough, Frank saw the SUV ahead of them pulling onto the shoulder.

Dan groaned, and Frank shook his head. "Thank you, ma'am, but we have to stay on the road. We wouldn't be out here otherwise."

"All right, then, but I hope you're okay with sitting for a while."

Frank closed the window again and cranked up the heater a little more. "Don't burn up all your gas," Dan said.

"I'll get more when we're moving again."

Dan shook his head. "Snow in April." But the mountains got snow in April every year, at least one big storm. Reno natives still talked about the year there'd been snow on July 4. At altitude, there was no such thing as predictable weather.

Frank shifted in his seat; one ass cheek was already going numb. "You sure you don't want some coffee?"

"Yeah, I'm sure! My nerves are bad enough as it is." Dan sounded angry, and Frank swallowed his own anger and didn't say anything. *I'm doing you a favor, dammit.* He was tired of getting snapped at because other people couldn't deal with reality. But he was doing himself a favor too, using Dan's situation to get away from Kerry. Maybe he had it coming.

So they sat there, staring out at the snow, and finally Dan said, "I'm sorry. I snapped at you. I—"

"Forget it," Frank said. "How about some music?"

"Whatever you want," Dan said, in that tone that meant *I don't really want this but I owe you so I'll put up with it.* Frank reached into the back for the box of CDs— old reliable tech—and riffled through it. The Beatles sang about missing people too much, and the Doors were too weird and depressing, the last thing Dan needed now. Finally Frank picked out Best of the Big Bands. That ought to be innocuous enough.

They were staring out at the swirling snow and listening to the Andrews Sisters singing "The Boogie Woogie Bugle Boy of Company B" when Dan's cellphone rang. Dan groaned, and Frank turned off the music. "It's probably just Leah giving you an update," he said. "Or a telemarketer." But he didn't believe that himself, and he saw Dan's hands shaking as they fumbled with the phone. He heard Dan's hoarse breathing, the hiss of snow on the windshield, the shrilling phone.

And then silence as Dan answered. "Yes? Hello?"

There was a long pause. In the bleak light from the storm, Frank saw Dan's face grow slack and stricken. Frank had never met Rosie, but knowing that she must be dead, he felt the same sucker-punch to the gut he'd felt when Alison died, that moment of numbness when the world stopped.

"Baby?" Dan said. "Rosie? Is that really you?"

No, Frank thought. *No, it's not. Goddammit—*

"Rosie, are you okay now? I'm so sorry I didn't get there in time. I wanted to say goodbye. I'm so sorry. I tried. We're on the road. We're stuck in snow." He was sobbing now in great heaving gasps.

Frank looked away from him. The voice on the other end would be saying that it was okay, that everything was forgiven. Kerry told him those syrupy stories all the time, the miracles of posthumous reconciliation people had always paid big money for, and now the price tag had gone up. At least Dan wasn't paying for it. Sandra and the assholes were the suckers there.

Dan fell into silence, chin quivering, and then said, "I know. I know I wasn't. I'm sorry." Frank saw him shudder. "I'm here now. I'm here. You can always call me. I love you. I'm sorry you hurt so much at the end. Yes, call your friends now. I'll talk to you soon."

He hung up, fumbling almost as much as he had when he answered the phone, his hands shaking as if he were outside in the cold, not here in the truck with a hot thermos of coffee and the heater blasting. He cleared his throat. "I told her I was sorry I wasn't there. She said, 'Daddy, you've never been there.'" His voice cracked. Frank stared straight ahead, out into the snow. *Jesus.*

Next to him, he heard Dan unscrewing the thermos, heard the sound of the liquid pouring into the cup. "I deserved that." Dan's voice was quiet, remote. "What she said."

Frank shifted in his seat again. He had a sudden sharp memory of yelling at Alison when she was a little thing, three or four, when she'd been racing around the house and had run into him and her Barbie doll had jammed into his stomach like a bayonet. He'd had a bruise for two weeks, but the memory of her face when he screamed at her had lasted a lot longer. He swallowed. "Do they get over things? Or are they stuck like that forever, mad at whatever they were mad at when they died?" That had to be anybody's idea of hell.

"I don't know." Dan's words were thin, frayed. "I don't know how I can make it up to her now, except by talking to her whenever she wants to talk. I can't go back and get to her seventh birthday party, that time I was out drinking. I can't go back and fight less with Sandra. I just—well, I can tell Rosie how sorry I am about all of that. Hope she knows I mean it."

"Yeah. What do you want to do now, Dan? I'll still drive you to Sacramento, if you need to see—"

"Her dead body? No." Dan shook his head, a slow heavy movement like a bear shaking off the weight of winter. "Not in this stuff. You've been awfully kind. I'll try to get to the funeral, but that won't be for a few days, anyway. The highway ought to be open by then." His voice splintered again. "I just wish I'd gotten to hug her one last time, you know?"

Frank nodded, and eased the truck carefully onto the shoulder, and headed for the exit.

It didn't take long to get back to the house. Frank pulled into the driveway, and they both got out, and Dan said, "I'll be heading home now. You go on in and tell Kerry what happened. I'm not up to it."

"If you need anything—"

"Yeah. I'll let you know. Thanks, Frank." Dan nodded and headed back to his own truck, and Frank went into the house. Kerry, sitting at the kitchen table doing a crossword puzzle, looked up when he came through the door. He saw the relief on her face, saw her exhale. And then she frowned.

"What happened?"

"The highway's still closed. Rosie's dead. She called Dan." He pulled out another chair and sat down, suddenly exhausted. "You're right, Kerry. It's real."

Her eyes filled with tears. She reached for his hand. "I'm glad you know that now."

He did know, but he knew other things, too. He knew that it didn't make any difference, that even if your dead child called you from cyberspace, you still regretted what you hadn't been able to do for her. He wouldn't miss Alison any less if she'd been translated, not even if she'd been one of the syrupy ghosts. Maybe he'd miss her more.

But that wasn't anything he could say to Kerry, who needed whatever comfort she could get. So he stood up and went to the window. There were icicles hanging from the roof. The daffodils and tulips definitely weren't going to make it.

He heard Kerry's chair scraping against the linoleum, felt her come up behind him. "Honey, there will be flowers again next year."

"I know there will."

He stood there, looking out, remembering the day they'd planted the bulbs, mixing the soil with Alison's ashes. She'd loved flowers.

τhe Hαnd ιs quickeꞃ

ELÌZABEṬH BEAꞧ

Elizabeth Bear was born in Connecticut, and now lives in Brookfield, Mas-
sachusetts, after several years living in the Mojave Desert near Las Vegas. She
won the John W. Campbell Award for Best New Writer in 2005, and in 2008
took home a Hugo Award for her short story "Tideline," which also won her
the Theodore Sturgeon Memorial Award (shared with David Moles). In 2009,
she won another Hugo Award for her novelette "Shoggoths in Bloom." Her short
work has appeared in Asimov's Science Fiction, Subterranean, SCI FIC-
TION, Interzone, The Third Alternative, Strange Horizons, On Spec, *and*
elsewhere, and has been collected in The Chains That You Refuse *and* New
Amsterdam. *She is the author of three highly acclaimed SF novels,* Hammered,
Scardown, *and* Worldwired, *and of the alternate-history fantasy Promethean*
Age series, which includes the novels Blood and Iron, Whiskey and Water, Ink
and Steel, *and* Hell and Earth. *Her other books include the novels* Carnival,
Undertow, Chill, Dust, All the Windwracked Stars, By the Mountain
Bound, Range of Ghosts, *a novel in collaboration with Sarah Monette,* The
Tempering of Men, *and two chapbook novellas,* Bone and Jewel Creatures
and Ad Eternum. *Her short fiction has been gathered in the collection,*
Shoggoths in Bloom. *Her most recent books are the novels* Steles of the Sky,
One-Eyed Jack, Shattered Pillars, *and* Karen Memory.

Society has always been divided between the haves and the have-nots, but
here's a look at a disquieting future where the have-nots are, conveniently, kept
literally out of sight and out of mind.

Rose and I used to come down to the river together last summer. It was over
semester break, and my time was my own—between obligatory work on the
paper I hoped would serve as the core of my first book and occasional consultations
with my grad students.

Rose wore long dark hair and green-hazel eyes for me. I wore what I always did—a
slightly idealized version of the meat I was born with. I wanted to be myself for her.
I wondered if she was herself for me, but the one time I gathered up the courage to

ask, she laughed and swept me aside. "I thought historians understood that narratives are subjective and imposed!"

I loved her because she challenged me. I thought she loved me too, until one day she disappeared. No answer to my pings, no trace of her in our usual haunts. She'd blocked me.

I didn't handle it well. I was in trouble at the university. I was drinking. I wasn't maintaining my citizenship status. With Rose gone, I realized slowly how much my life had come to revolve around her.

No matter how she felt about me, I knew she loved the river-edge promenade, bordered by weeping willows and her namesake flowers. Those willows were yellow as I walked the path now, long leaves clinging to their trailing branches. The last few roses hadn't yet fallen to the frost, but the flowers looked sparse, dwarfed by the memory of summer's blossoms.

The scent was even different now than it had been at the height of summer. Crisper, thin. The change was probably volunteer work; I didn't think the city budget would stretch to skinning unique seasonal scents for the rose gardens. I knew Rose was older than I, no matter how her skin looked, because she used to say that when she was a girl, individual cultivars of *roses* had different odors, so walking around a rose garden was a tapestry of scents. Real roses probably still did that.

I didn't know if I'd ever smelled them.

Other people walked the path—all skins. The city charged your palm chip just to get through the gate. I didn't begrudge the debit. It wasn't as if I was ever going to get to pay it off. Or as if I was every going to get to come back here. This was a last hurrah.

I edited out the others. I wanted to be alone, and if I couldn't see them, they couldn't see me. That was good, because I knew I didn't look happy, and the last thing I wanted was some random stranger reading my emotional signature and coming over to offer well-meaning advice.

Since this was my last time, I thought about jumping skins—running up the charges, seeing some of the other ways the river promenade could look—fantasyland, or Rio, or a moon colony. Rose and I had done that when we first started coming here, but it turned out we both preferred the naturalist view. With seasons.

We'd met in winter. I supposed it was fitting that I lost her—and everything else that mattered—in the fall.

Everything changed at midnight.

Not *my* midnight, as if honoring the mystical claptrap in some dead fairy tale. But about the dinner hour, which would be midnight Greenwich Standard Mean Time—honoring the mystical claptrap of a dead empire, instead. I suppose you have to draw the line somewhere. The world is full of the markers of abandoned empires, from Hadrian's Wall to the Great Wall of China, from the remnants of the one in Arizona to the remnants of the one in Berlin.

My name is Ozymandias, King of Kings.

I was thinking about that poem as I crossed Henderson—with the light: I knew somebody who jaywalked and got hit by an unskinned vehicle. The driver got jail time for manslaughter, but that doesn't bring back the dead. It was a gorgeous October evening, the sun just setting and the trees still full of leaves in all shades of gold and orange. I barely noticed them, or the cool breeze as I waited, rocking nervously from foot to foot on the cobblestones.

I was meeting my friend Numair at Gary's Olympic Pizza and I was running a little late, so he was already waiting for me in our usual corner booth. He'd ordered beers and garlic bread. They waited on the tabletop, the beers shedding rings of moisture into paper napkins.

I slid onto the hard bench opposite him, trying to hide the apprehension souring my gut. The vinyl was artistically cracked and the rough edges caught on my jeans. It wasn't Numair making me so anxious. It was finances. I shouldn't be here, by rights—I knew I couldn't afford even pizza and beer—but I needed to see him. If anything could clear my head, it was Numair.

One of the things I liked about Numair is how unpretentious he was. I didn't skin heavily—not like some people, who wandered through underwater seascapes full of sentient octopuses or dressed up as dragons and pretended they live in Elfland— but he was so down to earth I'd have bet his default skin looked just like him. He was a big guy, strapping and barrel-bodied, with curly dark brown hair that was going gray at the temples. And he liked his garlic bread.

So it was extra-nice that there were still two pieces left when I pulled the plate over.

"Hey, Charlie," he said.

"Hey, Numair." Garlic bread crunched between my teeth, butter and olive oil dripping down my chin. I swiped at it with a napkin. I didn't recognize the beer, dark and malty, although I drank off a third of it making sure. "What's the brew?"

"Trois Draggonnes." He shrugged. "Microbrew license out of . . . Shreveport.com, I think? Cheers."

"Here's mud in your eye," I answered, and drained the glass.

He sipped his more moderately and put it back on the napkin. "You sounded upset."

I nodded. Gary's was an old-style place, and a real-looking waitress came by about thirty seconds later and replaced my beer. I didn't know if she was an employee or a sim, but she was good at her job. The pizza showed up almost instantly after that, balanced on a metal tripod with a plastic spatula for serving. Greek-style, with flecks of green oregano visible in the sweet, oozing sauce. I always got the same thing: meatball, spinach, garlic, mushrooms. Delicious. I'd never asked Numair what he was eating.

The smell turned my stomach.

"I may not be around much for a while." I stuffed the rest of the garlic bread into my mouth to make room. And buy time. "This is embarrassing—"

"Hey." He paused with a slice in midair, perfect strings of mozzarella stretching twelve inches from pie to spatula. They glistened. The booth creaked when he shifted. "This is me."

"Right. I've got financial trouble. Big-time."

He put the slice down on his plate and offered me the spatula. I waved it away.

The smell was bad enough. Belatedly, I turned it off. Might as well use the filters as long as I had them. The beer still looked appealing, though, and I drank a little more.

"Okay," he said. "How bigtime?"

The beer tasted like humiliation and soap suds. "Tax trouble. I'm going to lose everything," I said. "All assets, all the virtuals. I thought I could pay it down, you know—but then I got dropped by the U., and there wasn't a replacement income stream. As soon as they catch up with me—" I thought of Rose, to whom Numair had introduced me. They'd been Friday-night gaming buddies, until she'd vanished without a word. I'd kept meaning to look her up offline and check in, but . . . It was easier to let her go than know for certain she'd dumped me. Amazing how easy it was to lose track of people when they didn't show up at the usual places and times. "I got registered mail this morning. They're pulling my taxpayer I.D. I'll be as gone as Rose. Except I came to say good-bye before I ditched you."

He blinked. Now it was his turn to set the pizza down and push the plate away with his fingertips. "Rose died," he said.

I rubbed the back of my neck. It didn't ease the sudden nauseating tightness in my gut as all that bitterness converted to something sharp and horrible. "Died? *Died* died?"

"Died and was cremated. Her family's not linked, so I only heard because she and Bill went to school together, and he caught a link for her memorial service on some network site. You didn't know?"

I blinked at him.

He shook his head. "Stupid question. If you knew— Anyway. I guess you've tried everything, so I'll save the stupid advice."

"Thank you." I hope he picked up from my tone how fervently glad I was. Nothing like netfriends to pile on with the incredibly obvious—or incredibly crackpot—advice when you're in a pickle. "So anyway—"

"Give me your offline contact info?" He held up his phone and I sent it over. It was a pleasantry. I knew what the odds were that I'd ever hear from him. And it wasn't like I could keep my apartment without a tax identification number.

However good his intentions.

Right then, a quarter of the way around the planet, midnight tolled. And I fell out of the skin.

It was sharp and sudden, as somewhere a line of code went into effect and the last few online chits in my account were levied. I blinked twice, trying to shake the dizziness that accompanied the abrupt transition, eyes now scratchy and dry.

Numair was still there in the booth across from me. It was weird seeing him there, unskinned. I'd been right about his unpretentiousness: he looked pretty much as he'd always done—maybe a little more unkempt—though his clothes were different.

Since he was skinned, I knew I'd dropped right out of his filters. I might as well not exist anymore. And Gary's Olympic, unlike Numair, had really suffered in the transition.

The pizza that congealed on the table before me was fake cheese, lumpy and dry looking. Healthier than the gooey pie my filters had been providing a moment before, but gray and depressing. I was suddenly glad I hadn't been chewing on it when the transition hit.

The grimy floor was scattered with napkins. The waitress was real, go figure, but a shadow of her buxom virtual self—no, she was a guy, I realized. Maybe working in drag brought in better tips? Or maybe the skin was a uniform. I'd never know.

And there was me.

I was not as comfortable with myself as Numair. I didn't skin heavily, as I said—just tuning. But my skins did make me a hair taller, a hair younger. My hair . . . a hair brighter. And so on. With them gone, I was skinny and undersized in a track suit that bagged at the shoulders and ass.

Falling into myself stung.

I reached out left-handed for my beer, since Numair was going to get stuck for the tab anyway. It was pale yellow and tasted of dish soap. So maybe the off flavor in the second glass had been something other than my misery. Whatever.

I chugged it and got out.

The glass door was dirty, one broken pane repaired with duct tape. On the way in, it had been spotless and decorated with blue and white decal maps of Greece. I pushed it open with the tips of my fingers and moved on.

Outside, the street lay dark and dank. Uncollected garbage humped against the curb. Some of it smelled organic, rotten. A real violation of the composting laws. Maybe they didn't get enforced as much against businesses. I picked my way across broken cement to the corner and waited there.

There were more people on the street than there had been. Or maybe they'd been there all along, just skinned out. You could tell who was wearing filters by the way they moved—backs straight, enjoying the evening. The rest of us shuffled, heads bowed. Trying not to see too much. The evening I walked through was full of bad smells and crumbling buildings that looked to be mostly held together by graffiti.

"Aw, crap."

The light changed. I crossed. Of course, I couldn't get a taxi home, or even a bus. Skinned-in drivers would never see me, and my chips were cancelled. I wouldn't get through a chip-locked door to take the tube.

I wondered how the poor got around. I guessed I'd be finding out.

I didn't know my way home.

I was used to the guidance my skins gave me, the subtle recognition cues. All I was getting now was the cold wind cutting through a windbreaker that wasn't warm enough for the job I expected it to do, and a pair of sore feet. Everything stank. Everything was dirty. There were steel bars on every window and chip locks on every door.

I'd known that intellectually, but it had never really sunk in before what a bleak urban landscape that made for. Straggling trees lined unmaintained streets, and at every corner I picked my way through drifts of rubbish. I knew there wasn't a lot of money for upkeep of infrastructure, and what there was had to be assigned to critical projects. But it didn't matter; you could always drop a skin over anything that needed a little cosmetic help.

Sure, I'd seen news stories. But it was one thing to vid it and another to wade through it.

About fifteen minutes after I'd realized how lost I was, I also realized somebody was following me. Nobody bothers the skinned: an instantaneous, direct voice and vid line to police services meant Patrol guardian-bots could be at our sides in seconds. It was a desperate criminal who'd tackle one of us. One of *them*. But that was another service I couldn't pay for, along with a pleasanter reality and access to mass transit.

I wasn't skinned anymore, and I bet anybody following me could tell. Of course, I didn't have any credit, either—or any cash. I guessed unskinned folks still used cash, palm-sized magnetic cards with swipe strips. A lot of places wouldn't take it anymore. But if you didn't have accounts or a working palm chip, what else were you going to do?

Well, if you were the guy behind me, apparently the answer was, *take it from somebody else.*

I was short and I was skinny, but living skinned kept me in pretty good shape. There were all kinds of built-in workout programs, after all, so clever that you hardly even noticed they were healthy. And skinning food kept the blood pressure down no matter how many greasy pizzas you enjoyed.

My pursuer was two thirds of a block back. I waited until I'd put a corner between me and him. As soon as I lost sight of him, I broke into a run.

It was a pretty good run, too. I was wearing my Toesers, because I liked them, and if they were skinned nobody could tell how dumb they looked. Also, they were comfortable. And supposedly scientifically designed for natural running posture, so you landed on the ball of your foot and didn't make a thump with every stride. Breath coming fast, feet scissoring—I turned at the first corner I came to, then quickly turned again.

Unskinned folks looked up in surprise as I pelted past. One made a grab for me, and another one shouted something after, but I was already gone. And then I was on a side street all by myself, running down a narrow path kicked in the piles of trash.

Maybe this was an even more desolate street, and maybe most of the lights were burned out, but I kept on running. It felt good, all of a sudden, like positive action. Like something I could do other than wallowing. Like *progress.*

It kept on feeling like progress all the way down to the river's edge. And then, as I stopped beside a hole snipped-and-bent in the chain link, it felt like a very bad idea instead.

The river was a sewer. When I'd been here before—okay, not down here under the bridge, but on the bank above—it had been all sunshine and rolling blue water. What I saw now was floating milk jugs and what I smelled was a sour, fecal carrion stench.

I put a hand out to the fence, the wire gritty, greasy where my fingers touched. It dented when I leaned on it, but I needed it to bear my weight up. A stitch burned in my side, and every breath of air scoured my lungs. I didn't know if that was from running, or because the air was bad. But it was the same air I'd been breathing all along. The filters didn't change the outside world. Just our perceptions of it. So how could the air choke me now when before, I breathed it perfectly well?

Shouts behind me suggested that maybe my earlier pursuer had friends. Or that my flight had drawn attention. I was in shadow—but the yellow tracksuit wasn't anyone's idea of good camouflage.

Gravel crunched and turned under my feet. I pushed the top of the bent chain triangle up and ducked through, into the moist darkness under the bridge.

Things moved in the night. Rats, I imagined, but some sounded bigger than rats. What else could live in this filth? I imagined feral dogs, stray cats—companion animals abandoned to make their own fate. Would they attack something as large as a man?

If they did, how would I fight them?

I groped along the bridge abutment, feeling with my toes for a stick. The old stones swept down low, the arch broad and flat. I kept my hand up to keep from hitting my head on an invisible buttress. The masonry was slick with paint and damp, mortar crumbling to the touch. I couldn't see my hand in front of my face, but light concentrated by the oily river reflected up, and I could see the stones of the bridge's underside clearly.

I crept into that dank, ruinous beauty until the flicker of lights against the chain fence told me that my pursuers had found me, and they had come in force. My chest squeezed, stomach flipping in apprehension. I crouched down, tucked myself into the lowest part of the arch, and fumbled out my phone.

"Police," I said. Even if my contract had been cancelled, that should work. I'd heard somewhere that any phone can always dial emergency. And there it was, a distant buzz, and then a calm voice answering.

"Emergency services. Your taxpayer identification number, please?"

My voice stuck in my throat. I'd never been asked that before. But then, I'd never been calling from an unskinned phone before. Without thinking, I rattled off the fourteen digits of my old number, the one that had been revoked. I held my breath afterward. Maybe the change hadn't propagated yet. Maybe—

"That number is not valid," the operator said.

"Look," I whispered, "I'm in a dispute with Revenue Services. It's all going to be sorted out, I'm sure, but right now I'm about to be mugged—"

"I'm sorry," said the consummate professional on the other end of the line. "Emergency services are for taxpayers only."

Before I could protest, the line went dead. Leaving me crouched alone in the dark, with a glowing phone pressed to my ear. Not for long, however: in less than a second, the dazzle of flashlight beams found me. Instinctively, I ducked my head and covered my eyes—with the hand holding the phone.

"Well hey. What's this?" The voice was deceptively pleasant, that seductive mildness employed by schoolyard bullies since first Romulus beat up Remus. The flashlight didn't waver from my eyes.

I flinched. I didn't answer. Not because I didn't want to, but because I didn't have a voice.

I tried to find the part of myself that managed unruly students and lecture-hall hecklers, but it had vanished along with my credit accounts and the protection of the police. I ducked farther, squinting around my hand, but he was just a shadow through the glare of his light. At least three other lights surrounded him.

He plucked the phone from my hand with a sharp twist that stabbed pain through my wrist. I snatched the hand back.

"Huh," he said. "Guess you didn't pay your taxes, huh? What else have you got?"

"Nothing," I said. The RFID chip embedded in my palm was useless. Would they cut it out anyway? I had no cash, no anything. Just the phone, which had my whole life on it—all my research, all my photos. Three mostly finished articles. There were backups, of course, but they were on the wire, and I couldn't get there without being skinned.

I wasn't a skin anymore. Objects, I realized, had utility. Had value. They were more than ways to get at your data.

"Your jacket," the baseline said. "And your shoes."

My toes gripped the gravel. "I need my shoes—"

The dazzle of lights shifted. I knew I should duck, but the knowledge didn't translate into action.

At first there wasn't any pain. Just the shock of impact, and an exhale that seemed to start in my toes and never stop. *Then* the pain, radiating stars out of my solar plexus, with waves of nausea for dessert.

"Jacket," he said.

I would have given it to him. But I couldn't talk. Couldn't even inhale. I raised my hand. I think I shook my head.

I think he would have hit me anyway. I think he wanted to hit me. Because when I fell down, he kept hitting me. Hitting and kicking. And not just him, some of his friends.

It's a blur, mostly. I remember some particulars. The stomp that crushed my left hand. The kick that broke my tailbone. I got my knees up and tucked my head, so they kicked me in the kidneys instead. Gravel gouged the side where kicks didn't land. If I could burrow into it, I'd be safe. If I could just fall through it, I might survive. I thought about being small and hard and sharp, like those stones.

After a while, I didn't have the breath to scream anymore.

At first the cold hurt too, but after a while it became a friend. I noticed that they had stopped hitting me. I noticed that the cuts and bruises stung, the broken bones ached with a deep, sick throb. My hand felt fragile, gelatinous. Like a balloon full of water, I imagined that a single pinprick could make the stretched skin explode back from the contents. I prodded a loosened tooth with my tongue.

But then the cold got into the hurts and they numbed. Little by little, starting from the extremities. Working in. It mattered less that the hard points of gravel stabbed my ribs. I couldn't feel that floppy, useless hand. The throb in my head slowly became less demanding than the throb of thirst in my throat.

In the fullness of time, I sat up. It was natural, like sitting up after a full night's sleep, when you've lain in bed so long your body just naturally rises without consulting you. I thought about water. There was the river, but it smelled like poison. I'd probably get thirsty enough to drink it sooner or later. I wondered what diseases I'd contract. Hepatitis. Probably not cholera.

My cheekbones were numb, along with my nose, but I could still breathe normally. So the nose probably wasn't broken. The moving air brought me a tapestry of cold odors: sour garbage, rancid meat, urine. That oil-tang from the river. Frost rimed the gravel around me, and in noticing that I noticed that the morning was graying, the heavy arch of the bridge a silhouette against the sky. There was pink and silver along the horizon, and I knew which direction was east because the sun's light glossed a contrail that must have sat high enough to reach out of the Earth's moving shadow.

Footsteps crunched toward me. I was too dreamy and snug to move. *I'm in shock,* I thought, but it didn't seem important.

"What's this?" somebody said.

I flinched, but didn't look up. His shadow couldn't fall across me. We were both under the shadow of the bridge.

"Oh, dear," he said. The crunch of shifting gravel told me he crouched down beside me. When he turned my chin with his fingers and I saw his face, I was surprised he was limber enough to crouch. He looked like the bad end of a lot of winters. "And you lost your shoes too. What a pity."

He didn't seem surprised when I cringed, but it didn't light his eyes up, either. So that wasn't a bully's mocking.

"Can you walk?" He took my arm gently. He inspected my broken hand. When he unzipped my jacket, I would have pulled away, but the pain was bad enough that I couldn't move against him. When he slid the hand inside the jacket and the buttons of my shirt, I realized he was improvising a sling.

As if his touch were the opposite of an analgesic, all my hurts reawakened. I meant to shake my head, but just thinking about moving unscrolled ribbons of pain through my muscles.

"I don't think so." My words were creaky and blood-flavored.

"If you can," he said, "I've got a fire. And tea. And food."

I closed my eyes. When I opened them again, his hand was extended. The left one, as my right hand was clawed up against my chest like a surgical glove stuffed overfull with twigs and raspberry jam.

Food. Warmth. I might have given up, but somewhere in the back of my mind was an animal that did not want to die. I watched as it made a determined, raspy sound and reached out with its unbroken hand.

Letting him pull me to my feet was a special kind of agony. I swayed, vision blacking at the edges. His steadying hand kept me upright. It hurt worse than anything. "Come on," he said.

I remember walking, but I don't remember where or for how long. It felt like forever. I had always been walking. I would be walking forever. There was no end. No surcease.

Pain is an eternity.

His fire was trash and sticks ringed with broken bricks and chunks of asphalt. It smoldered fitfully, and pinprick by pinprick, the heat reawakened my pains. The soles of my feet seeped blood from walking across the gravel. I couldn't sit, because of the tailbone, but I figured out how to lie on my side. It hurt, but so did anything else.

There was tea, as promised, Lipton in bags stewed in a rusty can. I hoped he hadn't used river water. It had sugar in it, though, and I drank cautiously.

The food was dumpster-sourced chicken and biscuits, cold and lumpy with congealed grease. I ate it with my good hand, small bites. The inside of my mouth was cut from being slammed against my teeth. If I chewed carefully, on one side, the loose tooth only throbbed. I hoped it might reseat itself eventually.

Why was I thinking about the future?

The sun had beaten back the gloom enough for even my swollen eyes to make out the old man across from me. He had draped stiff, stinking blankets around my shoulders, but as the sun warmed the riverbank, he seemed comfortable in several layers of shirts and pants. A yellowed beard surrounded his sunken mouth. His hands were spare claws in ragged gloves. He drank the tea fearlessly, and warmed his share of the chicken on the rocks beside the trash fire. I thought about plastic fumes and kept gnawing mine cold.

After a while, he said, "You'll get used to it."

I looked up. He was looking right at me, his greasy silver ponytail dull in the sunlight. "Get used to being beaten up?" My voice sounded better than I'd feared. My nose really wasn't broken. One small miracle.

"Get used to being a baseline." He bit into a biscuit, grimacing in appreciation.

I winced, wondering how long it would take me to start savoring day-old fast food fat and carbohydrates. Then I winced in pain from the wincing.

The old man chewed and swallowed. "It's honest, at least. Not like putting frosting all over the cake so nobody with any economic power can tell it's rotten. What's your name?"

"Charlie," I said.

He nodded and didn't ask for a surname. "Jean-Khalil." I wondered if first names only was part of the social customs of the baseline community.

The shock was wearing off. Maybe the sugar in the tea was working its neurochemical magic. My broken hand lay against my belly, warmed by my skin, and the sweat running across my midsection felt as syrupy as blood.

I kind of wanted the shock back. I looked at the chicken, and the chicken looked back at me. My gorge rose. Bitterness filled my mouth, but I swallowed it. I knew how badly I needed the food inside me.

I balanced the meat on the fire ring next to Jean-Khalil's. "You eat that."

He wiped the back of his hand across his beard. "I will. And you need to get to a clinic."

I put my head down on the unbroken arm. If I didn't get the hand seen to, even if I survived—even if I didn't have internal injuries—what were the chances it would be usuable when it healed? "I don't have a tax number."

"There's a free clinic at St. Francis," he said. "But it's Tuesdays and Thursdays."

I managed to work out that if I normally met Numair on Tuesdays, it would be just after dawn on Wednesday. Which meant, depending on when the clinic opened, something over 24 hours to wait. I could wait 24 hours. Could I *sleep* 24 hours? Maybe I'd die of blood poisoning before then. That might be a relief.

I had heard of St. Francis, but I didn't know where it was. Somewhere in this neighborhood? If it offered a clinic for baselines, it would have to be. They couldn't get through the chip gates uptown.

Despite the blankets heaped over me, I thought I could feel the ground sucking the heat out of my body. The old man nudged me. I opened my eyes. "Edge over onto this," he said.

He'd made a pallet of more filthy blankets, just beside where I lay. With his help, I was able to kind of wriggle and flop onto it. I couldn't lie on my back, because of the tailbone, and I couldn't use the hand to pillow my head or turn myself.

He rearranged the blankets over me. Something touched my lips: his gaunt fingers, protruding from those filthy gloves. I turned my head.

"Take it. It's methadone. It's also a pain killer."

"You lost your tax number for drug addiction?" I had to cover my mouth with my unbroken hand.

"I'm a dropout," he said. "Take the wafer."

"I don't want to get hooked."

He sighed like somebody's mother. "I'm a medical doctor. It's methadone, it's 60 milligrams. It won't do much more than take the edge off, but it might help you sleep."

I didn't believe him about being a dropout. Who'd pick this? But I did believe him about being a doctor. Maybe it was the way he specified *medical*. "I was a history teacher," I said. I couldn't bring myself to say *professor*. "Why do you have methadone if you're not an addict?"

"I told you," he said. "I'm a doctor."

"And you dropped out."

"Of a corrupt system." His voice throbbed with disdain, and maybe conviction. "How many people were invisible to you, before? How much of this was invisible?"

If I could have had my way, I would have made it all invisible again. This time, when he pressed his hand to my mouth, I took the papery wafer into my mouth and chewed it. It tasted like fake fruit. I closed my eyes again and tried to breathe deeply. It hurt, but more an ache than the deep stabbing I associated with broken ribs. So that was something else to consider myself fortunate for.

I knew it was just the placebo effect and exhaustion making me sleepy so fast, but I wasn't about to argue with it.

I said, "What made you decide to come live on the street?"

"There was a girl—" His voice choked off through the constriction of his throat. "My daughter. Cancer. She was twenty. Maybe if she hadn't been skinning so much, in so much denial—"

I put my good hand on his shoulder and felt it rise and fall. "I'm sorry."

He shrugged.

It was a minute and a half before I had the courage to ask the thing I was suddenly thinking. "If you're a dropout, then you have a tax number. And you don't use it."

"That's right," the old man said. "It's a filthy system. Eventually, you'll see what I mean."

"If you don't want it, give it to me."

He laughed. "If I were willing to do that, I'd just sell it on the black market. The clinic could use the money. Now rest, and we'll get your hand looked at tomorrow."

I don't know how I got to the clinic. I didn't walk—not on those bare cut-up feet—and I don't remember being carried. I do remember the waiting room full of men and women I never would have seen before I lost my tax number. Jean-Khalil had given me another methadone wafer, and that kept me just this side of coherent. But I couldn't sit, couldn't walk, couldn't lean against the wall. He got somebody to bring me a gurney, and I lay on my side and tried to doze, blissfully happy there weren't any rocks or dog feces on the surface I was lying on.

It doesn't take long to lower your standards.

I realized later that I was one of the lucky ones, and because of the broken bones I got triaged higher than a lot of others. But it was still four hours before I was wheeled into one of the curtained alcoves that served as an examining room and a woman in mismatched scrubs and a white lab coat came in to check on me. "Hi," she said. "I'm Dr. Tankovitch. Dr. Samure said you had a bad night. Charlie, is it?"

"The worst," I said. She was cute—Asian, plump, with bright eyes behind her glasses—and I caught myself flirting before a flood of shame washed me back into myself. She was a contributing member of society, here to do charity work. And I was a bum.

"Honestly, there's not much you can do for a broken tailbone except—" she laughed in commiseration "—stay off it. So let's start with the hand."

I held it out, and she took it gently by the wrist. Even that made me gasp.

She made a sympathetic face. "I'm guessing by the bruises on your face you didn't get this punching a brick wall."

"The cops don't come if you're not in the system."

She touched my shoulder. "I know."

I got lucky. For the first time in weeks, I got lucky. The hand didn't need surgery, which meant I didn't have to wait until the clinic's surgical hours, which were something like midnight to four AM at the city hospital. Instead, Dr. Tankovitch shot me full of Novocaine and wrapped my hand up with primitive plaster of Paris, a technology so obsolete I had never actually seen it. Or if I had seen it, I'd skinned it out. She gave me some pain pills that didn't work as well as the methadone and didn't have a street value, and told me to come back in a week and have it all checked out. The cast was so white it sparkled. Guess how long that was going to last, if I was sleeping under bridges?

She didn't offer me the clinic's contact information, and I didn't ask for it. How was I supposed to call them without a phone? But I was feeling less sorry for myself when I staggered out of the alcove. I planned to find Jean-Khalil again, and ask him if he'd show me where he looked for food and safe drinking water. I was clear-headed enough now to know it was an imposition, but I didn't have anywhere else to turn. And he'd sort of volunteered, hadn't he, by picking me out of the gutter?

If you pick up a starving dog and make him prosperous, he will not bite you. This is the principal difference between a dog and a man.

It was Mark Twain. But then, so were a lot of true things. And I was determined to prove myself more like the dog than the man. Jean-Khalil was an old man. Surely he could use my help. And I knew I needed his. I didn't see Jean-Khalil. But just as the waves of panic and abandonment—again, just like after Rose—were cresting in me, I spotted someone. Leaning against the wall by the door was Numair.

Numair had seen me first—I'd been moving, and he'd been looking for me—so he saw me stop dead and stare. He raised his hand hesitantly.

"Buy you dinner?" he asked. He didn't flinch when he looked at me.

From the angle of the light outside, I realized it was nearly sunset. "As long as we can get it someplace standing up."

That meant street meat, and three hot dogs with everything were the best food I'd ever tasted. Numair drank beer but he didn't eat pork, so he ate potato chips and watched me lean forward so the chili and onions didn't drip down my filthy shirt. I knew it was ridiculous, but I did it anyway. It felt like preserving my dignity to care. What dignity? I wasn't sure. But it still mattered.

"I'm sorry," Numair said. "I'm really sorry. If I'd realized you didn't know about Rose—I just never imagined. You two were so close. And you never mentioned her— I figured you didn't want to talk about her."

"I didn't." We'd had a fight, I wanted to say. Something to absolve myself of not checking. But when she stopped logging in, I figured she'd just decided to cut me off. She wouldn't be the first, and I knew she had another life. A wife. We'd talked about telling her she was having an affair.

And then she'd just . . . stopped messaging. People fall out of social groups all the time. It happens. I guess somebody more secure wouldn't have assumed they were the problem. But I was used to being the problem. Numair's the only friend I have left from the gang I hung around with all the time in grad school.

I swallowed hot dog, half-chewed. It hurt. He handed me an open can of soda, and I washed the lump down. "How'd she die?"

She hadn't been old. I mean, she hadn't skinned old. But who knew what the hell that meant, in the real world.

"She killed herself," Numair said, bluff and forthright. Which was just like him.

I staggered. Literally, sideways two steps. I couldn't catch myself because the last hot dog was balanced against my chest on the pristine cast. I already had the in- stinct to protect that food. I guess you don't have to get too hungry to learn fast.

"Jesus," I said, and felt bad.

He made a comforting face. And that was when I realized that if he could see me, he wasn't skinning. "Numair. You came all the way down here for me?"

"Charlie. Like I'd let an old friend go down without some help." He put a hand on my shoulder and pulled it back, frowning. He looked around, disgusted. "You know, you hear on the news how bad it is out here. But you never really get it until you see it. Poisoned environment, whatever. But this is astounding. Look, we can get you a hearing. Appeal your status. Maybe get you a new number. You can stay with Ilona and me until it's settled."

There were horror vids about this sort of thing. The baselines lived outside of social controls, after all. There was nothing to keep them from committing horrible crimes. "You're going to take in a baseline? That's a lot of trust. I'm a desperate woman."

He smiled. "I know you."

Ilona only knew me as a skin, but when I showed up at her house in the unadorned flesh, she couldn't have been nicer. She, too, had turned off her skinning so she could see me and interact. I could tell she was uncomfortable with it, though—her eyes kept flicking off my face to look for the hypertext or chase a link pursuant to the conversation, and of course there was nothing there. So after a bit she just showed me the bathroom, brought me clean clothes and a towel, and went back to her phone, where (she said) she was working on a deadline. She was an advertising copywriter, and she and Numair had converted one corner of their old house's parlor into an office space. I could hear her clicking away as I stripped off my filthy clothing and dropped it piece by piece into the bathroom waste pail. It was hard, one-handed, and it was even harder to tape the plastic bag around my cast.

It had never bothered me to discard ruined clothing before, but now I found it anxiety-inducing. *That's still good. Somebody could wear that.* I set the shower for hot and climbed in. The water I got fell in a lukewarm trickle; barely wetting me.

They probably skinned it hotter when they showered.

I tried to linger, to savor the cleanliness, but the chill of the water in a chilly room drove me out to stand dripping on the rug. As I was dressing in Ilona's jeans and sweatshirt, the sound of a child crying filtered through.

I came out to find Numair up from his desk, changing a diaper in the nook beside the kitchen. His daughter's name was Mercedes; she'd always been something of a little pink blob to me. I came up to hand him the grease for her diaper rash and saw the spotted blood on the diaper he had pushed aside.

"Christ," I said. "Is she all right?"

"She's nine months old, and she's starting her menses," he said, lower lip thrust out in worry. I noticed because I was looking up at the underside of his chin. "It's getting more common in very young girls."

"Common?"

With practiced hands, he attached the diaper tabs and sealed up Mercedes' onesie. He folded the soiled diaper and stuck it closed. "The doctor says it's environmental hormones. It can be skinned for—they'll make her look normal to herself and everyone else until she's old enough to start developing." He shrugged and picked up his child. "He says he treats a couple of toddlers with developing breasts, and the cosmetic option works for them."

He looked at me, brown eyes warm with worry.

I looked down. "You think that's a good enough answer?"

He shook his head. I didn't push it any further.

They put me to sleep in their guest room, and fed me—unskinned, the food was slop, but it was food, and I got used to them not being able to see or talk to me at mealtimes.

After a week, I felt much stronger. And as it was obvious that Numair and Ilona's intervention was not going to win me any favors from Revenue, I slowly came up with another plan.

I couldn't find Jean-Khalil under the bridge. His fire circle was abandoned, his blankets packed up. He'd moved on, and I didn't know where. Good deed delivered.

You'd think, right? Until it clicked what I was missing.

I showed up at the free clinic first thing next Tuesday morning, just as Dr. Tankovitch had suggested. And I waited there until Dr. Tankovitch walked in and with her, his gaunt hand curved around a cup of coffee, Dr. Jean-Khalil Samure.

He didn't look surprised to see me. My clothes were clean, and the cast was only a little dingy. I'd shaved, and I was surprised he recognized me without the split lip and the swelling.

"Jean-Khalil," I said.

I guessed accosting the clinic doctors wasn't what you did, because Dr. Tankovitch looked as if she might intercept me, or call for security. But Jean-Khalil held out a hand to pause her.

He smiled. "Charlie. You look like you're finding your feet."

"I got help from a friend." I frowned and looked down at my borrowed tennis shoes. Ilona's, and too big for me. "I can't do this, Jean-Khalil. You've got to help me."

I'm sure the clinic had all sorts of problems with drug addicts. Because now Dr. Tankovitch was actively backing away, and I saw her summoning hand gestures. I leaned in and talked faster. "I need your tax number," I said. "You're not using it. Look, all I need is to get back on my feet, and I can help you in all sorts of ways. Money. Publicity. I'll come volunteer at your clinic—"

"Charlie," he said. "You know that's not enough. The way you live—the way you have been living. That's a lie. It's not sustainable. It's addictive behavior. If everybody could see the damage they're doing, they'd behave differently."

I pressed my lips together. I looked away. Down at the floor. At anything but Jean-Khalil. "There's a girl. Her name is Rose."

He looked at me. I wondered if he knew I was lying. Maybe I wasn't lying. I could find somebody else, skin her into Rose. Maybe she'd have a different name. But I could fix this. Do better. If he would only give me the chance.

"You're not using it," I said.

"A girl," he said. "Your daughter?"

"My lover," I said.

I said, "Please."

He shook his head, eyes rolled up and away. Then he yanked his hand out of his pocket brusquely. "On your head be it."

I was not prepared for the naked relief that filled me. I looked down, abjectly, and folded my hands. "Thank you so much."

"You can't save people from themselves," he said.

The man who sold the moon

CORY DOCTOROW

Cory Doctorow is the coeditor of the popular Boing Boing *website (boingbo-ing.net), a cofounder of the Internet search-engine company OpenCola.com, and until recently was the outreach coordinator for the Electronic Frontier Foundation (www.eff.org). In 2001, he won the John W. Campbell Award as the year's Best New Writer. His stories have appeared in* Asimov's Science Fiction, Gateways, Science Fiction Age, The Infinite Matrix, On Spec, Salon, *and elsewhere, and have been collected in* A Place So Foreign and Eight More *and* Overclocked. *His well-received first novel,* Down and Out in the Magic Kingdom, *won the Locus Award for Best First Novel; his other novels include* Eastern Standard Tribe, Someone Comes to Town, Some-one Leaves Town, *the bestselling YA novel* Little Brother, *and* Makers. *Doc-torow's other books include* The Complete Idiot's Guide to Publishing Science Fiction, *written with Karl Schroeder, a guide to* Essential Blog-ging, *written with Shelley Powers, and* Content: Selected Essays on Tech-nology, Creativity, Copyright, and the Future of the Future. *His most recent books are a new nonfiction book,* Information Doesn't Want to Be Free, *and a new novel,* For the Win. *He has a website at www.craphound .com.*

Here he offers us a fascinating examination of how one small technologi-cal innovation can, over the course of a lifetime, end up building a signifi-cant stepping-stone for the future.

Here's a thing I didn't know: there are some cancers that can only be diagnosed after a week's worth of lab work. I didn't know that. Then I went to the doctor to ask her about my pesky achy knee that had flared up and didn't go away like it always had, just getting steadily worse. I'd figured it was something torn in there, or maybe I was getting the arthritis my grandparents had suffered from. But she was one of those doctors who hadn't gotten the memo from the American health-care system that says that you should only listen to a patient for three minutes, tops, before writ-ing him a referral and/or a prescription and firing him out the door just as the next patient was being fired in. She listened to me, she took my history, she wrote down the names of the anti-inflammatories I'd tried, everything from steroids to a climbing buddy's heavy-duty prescription NSAIDs, and gave my knee a few cautious prods.

"You're insured, right?"

"Yeah," I said. "Good thing, too. I read that knee replacement's going for seventy-five thousand dollars. That's a little out of my price range."

"I don't think you need a knee replacement, Greg. I just want to send you for some tests."

"A scan?"

"No." She looked me straight in the eyes. "A biopsy."

I'm a forty-year-old, middle-class Angeleno. My social mortality curve was a perfectly formed standard distribution—a few sparse and rare deaths before I was ten, slightly more through my teens, and then more in my twenties. By the time I was thirty-five, I had an actual funeral suit I kept in a dry-cleaning bag in the closet. it hadn't started as a funeral suit, but once I'd worn it to three funerals in a row, I couldn't wear it anywhere else without feeling an unnameable and free-floating sorrow. I was forty. My curve was ramping up, and now every big gathering of friends had at least one knot of somber people standing together and remembering someone who went too early. Someone in my little circle of forty-year-olds was bound to get a letter from the big C. There wasn't any reason for it to be me. But there wasn't any reason for it not to be either.

Bone cancer can take a week to diagnose. A week! During that week, I spent a lot of time trying to visualize the slow-moving medical processes: acid dissolving the trace of bone, the slow catalysis of some obscure reagent, some process by which a stain darkened to yellow and then orange and then, days later, to red. Or not. That was the thing. Maybe it wasn't cancer. That's why I was getting the test, instead of treatment. Because no one knew. Not until those stubborn molecules in some lab did their thing, not until some medical robot removed a test tube from a stainless steel rack and drew out its contents and took their picture or identified their chemical composition and alerted some lab tech that Dr. robot had reached his conclusion and would the stupid human please sanity-check the results and call the other stupid human and tell him whether he's won the cancer lottery (grand prize: cancer)?

That was a long week. The word cancer was like the tick of a metronome. Eyes open. Cancer. Need a pee. Cancer. Turn on the coffee machine. Cancer. Grind the beans. Cancer. Cancer. Cancer.

On day seven, I got out of the house and went to Minus, which is our local hackerspace. Technically, its name is "Untitled-1," because no one could think of a better name ten years ago, when it had been located in a dirt-cheap former car-parts warehouse in Echo Park. When Echo Park gentrified, Untitled-1 moved downtown, to a former furniture store near Skid Row, which promptly began its own gentrification swing. Now we were in the top two floors of what had once been a downscale dentist's office on Ventura near Tarzana. The dentist had reinforced the floors for the big chairs and brought in 60 amp service for the X-ray machines, which made it perfect for our machine shop and the pew-pew room full of lasers. We even kept the fume hoods.

I have a personal tub at Minus, filled with half-finished projects: various parts for a 3D-printed chess-playing automata; a cup and saucer I was painstakingly covering with electroconductive paint and components; a stripped-down location sensor I'd been playing with for the Minus's space program.

Minus's space program was your standard hackerspace extraterrestrial project: sending balloons into the upper stratosphere, photographing the earth's curvature, making air-quality and climate observations; sometimes lofting an ironic action figure in 3D-printed astronaut drag. Hacker Dojo, north of San Jose, had come up with a little powered guidance system, but they'd been whipped by navigation. Adding a stock GPS with its associated batteries made the thing too heavy, so they'd tried to fake it with dead-reckoning and it had been largely unsuccessful. I'd thought I might be able to make everything a lot lighter, including the battery, by borrowing some techniques I'd seen on a performance bike-racing site.

I put the GPS on a workbench with my computer and opened up my file of notes and stared at them with glazed eyes. Cancer. Cancer. Cancer.

Forget it. I put it all away again and headed up to the roof to clear my head and to get some company. The roof at Minus was not like most roofs. Rather than being an empty gravel expanse dotted with exhaust fans, our roof was one of the busiest parts of the space. Depending on the day and time, you could find any or all of the above on Minus's roof: stargazing, smoking, BASE jumping, solar experiments, drone dogfighting, automated graffiti robots, sensor-driven high-intensity gardening, pigeon-breeding, sneaky sex, parkour, psychedelic wandering, Wi-Fi sniffing, mobile-phone tampering, ham radio broadcasts, and, of course, people who were stuck and frustrated and needed a break from their workbenches.

I threaded my way through the experiments and discussions and build-projects, slipped past the pigeon coops, and fetched up watching a guy who was trying, unsuccessfully, to learn how to do a run up a wall and do a complete flip. He was being taught by a young woman, sixteen or seventeen, evidently his daughter ("Daaad!"), and her patience was wearing thin as he collapsed to the gym mats they'd spread out. I stared spacily at them until they both stopped arguing with each other and glared at me, a guy in his forties and a kind of miniature, female version of him, both sweaty in their sweats. "Do you mind?" she asked.

"Sorry," I mumbled, and moved off. I didn't add, I don't mean to be rude, just worried about cancer.

I got three steps away when my phone buzzed. I nearly fumbled it when I yanked it out of my tight jeans pocket, hands shaking. I answered it and clapped it to my ear.

"Mr. Harrison?"

"Yes."

"Please hold for doctor Ficsor." A click.

A click. "Greg?"

"That's me," I said. I'd signed the waiver that let us skip the pointless date-of-birth/mother's maiden name "security" protocol.

"Is this a good time to talk?"

"Yes," I said. One syllable, clipped and tight in my ears. I may have shouted it.

"Well, I'd like you to come in for some confirming tests, but we've done two analyses and they are both negative for elevated alkaline phosphatase and lactate dehydrogenase."

I'd obsessively read a hundred web pages describing the blood tests. I knew what this meant. But I had to be sure. "It's not cancer, right?"

"These are negative indicators for cancer," the doctor said.

The tension that whoofed out of me like a gutpunch left behind a kind of howling vacuum of relief, but not joy. The joy might come later. At the moment, it was more like the head-bees feeling of three more cups of espresso than was sensible. "Doctor," I said, "can I try a hypothetical with you?"

"I'll do my best."

"Let's say you were worried that you, personally, had bone cancer. If you got the same lab results as me, would you consider yourself to be at risk for bone cancer?"

"You're very good at that," she said. I liked her, but she had the speech habits of someone who went to a liability insurance seminar twice a year. "Okay, in that hypothetical, I'd say that I would consider myself to be provisionally not at risk of bone cancer, though I would want to confirm it with another round of tests, just to be very, very sure."

"I see," I said. "I'm away from my computer right now. Can I call your secretary later to set that up?"

"Sure," she said. "Greg?"

"Yes."

"Congratulations," she said. "Sleep easy, okay?"

"I will try," I said. "I could use it."

"I figured," she said. "I like giving people good news."

I thought her insurance adjuster would not approve of that wording, but I was glad she'd said it. I squeezed the phone back into my pocket and looked at the blue, blue sky, cloudless save for the scummy film of L.A. haze that hovered around the horizon. It was the same sky I'd been standing under five minutes ago. It was the same roof. The same building. The same assemblage of attention-snagging interesting weirdos doing what they did. But I was not the same.

I was seized by a sudden, perverse urge to go and take some risks: speed down the highway, BASE jump from Minus's roof, try out some really inadvisable parkour moves. Some part of me that sought out patterns in the nonsense of daily randomness was sure that I was on a lucky streak and wanted me to push it. I told that part to shut up and pushed it down best as I could. But I was filled with an inescapable buoyancy, like I might float right off the roof. I knew that if I'd had a hard time concentrating before, I was in for an even harder time getting down to business now. It was a small price to pay.

"Hey," someone said behind me. "Hey, dude?"

It occurred to me that I was the dude in question, and that this person had been calling out to me for some time, with a kind of mellow intensity—not angry, but insistent nonetheless. I turned around and found myself staring down at a surfer-looking guy half my age, sun-bleached ponytail and wraparound shades, ragged shorts and a grease-stained long-sleeved jersey and bare feet, crouched down like a Thai fisherman on his haunches, calf muscles springing out like wires, fingertips resting lightly on a gadget.

Minus was full of gadgets, half built, sanded to fit, painted to cover, with lots of exposed wiring, bare boards, blobs of hot glue and adhesive polymer clinging on for dear life against the forces of shear and torque and entropy. But even by those standards, surfer-guy's gadget was pretty spectacular. It was the lens—big and round and polished, with the look of a precision-engineered artifact out of a real manufacturer's shop—not something hacked together in a hack lab.

"Hey," I said.

"Dude," he said. "Shadow."

I was casting a shadow over the lens. I stepped smartly to one side and the pitiless L.A. sun pierced it, focused by it down to a pinprick of white on a kind of bed beneath the lens. The surfer guy gave me an absentminded thumbs-up and started to squint at his laptop's screen.

"What's the story with this thing?" I said.

"Oh," he said. "Solar sinterer. 3D printing with the sun." The bed started to jerk and move with the characteristic stepper-motor dance of a 3D printer. The beam of light sizzled on the bed like the tip of a soldering iron, sending up a wisp of smoke like a shimmer in the sun's glare. There was a sweet smell from it, and I instinctively turned upwind of it, not wanting to be sucking down whatever aromatic volatiles were boiling off the print medium.

"That is way, way cool," I said. "Does it work?"

He smiled. "Oh yeah, it works. This is the part I'm interested in." He typed some more commands and the entire thing lifted up on recessed wheels and inched forward with the slow grace of a tortoise.

"It walks?"

"Yeah. The idea is, you leave it in the desert and come back in a couple of months and it's converted the sand that blows over its in-hopper into prefab panels you can snap together to make a shelter."

"Ah," I said. "What about sand on the solar panel?" I was thinking of the mars rovers, which had had a tendency to go offline when too much Martian dust blew over their photovoltaics.

"Working on that. I can make the lens and photovoltaic turn sideways and shake themselves." He pointed at a couple of little motors. "But that's a lot of moving parts. Want it to run unattended for months at a time."

"Huh," I said. "This wouldn't happen to be a burning man thing, would it?"

He smiled ruefully. "That obvious?"

Honestly, it was. Half of Minus were burners, and they all had a bit of his look of delightful otherworldly weirdness. "Just a lucky guess," I said, because no one wants to be reminded that they're of a certain type—especially if that type is nonconformist.

He straightened up and extended his hand. He was missing the tip of his index finger, and the rest of his fingernails were black with grease. I shook, and his grip was warm, firm and dry, and rough with callus. You could have put it in a museum and labeled it "Hardware hacker hand (typical)."

"I'm Pug," he said.

"Greg."

"So the plan is, bring it out to the desert for Fourth of Juplaya, let it run all summer, come back for burning man, and snap the pieces together."

"What's Fourth of Jup-whatever?"

"Fourth of Juplaya. It's a July Fourth party in black rock. A lot like burning man used to be like, when 'Safety third' was the guiding light and not just a joke. Much smaller and rougher, less locked down. More guns. More weird. Intense."

His gadget grunted and jammed. He looked down at it and nudged one of the stepper motors with his thumb, and it grunted again. "'Scuse me," he said, and hunkered down next to it. I watched him tinker for a while, then walked away, forgotten in his creative fog.

I went back down into Minus, put away my stuff, and chatted with some people I sort of knew about inconsequentialities, in a cloud of unreality. It was the hangover from my week of anxiety and its sudden release, and I couldn't tell you for the life of me what we talked about. After an hour or two of this, I suddenly realized that I was profoundly beat, I mean beat down and smashed flat. I said good-bye—or maybe I didn't, I wouldn't swear to it—and went out to look for my car. I was wandering around the parking lot, mashing the alarm button on my key chain, when I ran into Pug. He was (barely) carrying a huge box, shuffling and peering over the top. I was so tired, but it would have been rude not to help.

"Need a hand?"

"Dude," he said, which I took for an affirmative. I grabbed a corner and walked backward. The box was heavy, but it was mostly just huge, and when we reached his beat-up minivan, he kicked the tailgate release and then laid it down like a bomb-disposal specialist putting a touchy IED to sleep. He smacked his hands on his jeans and said, "Thanks, man. That lens, you wouldn't believe what it's worth." Now that I could see over the top of the box, I realized it was mostly padding, layers of lint-free cloth and bubblewrap with the lens in the center of it all, the gadget beneath it. "Minus is pretty safe, you know, but I don't want to tempt fate. I trust 99.9 percent of 'em not to rip it off or use it for a frisbee, but even a one-in-a-thousand risk is too steep for me." He pulled some elasticated webbing over it and anchored it down with cleats bolted inside the oily trunk.

"Fair enough," I said.

"Greg, buddy, can I ask you a personal question?"

"I suppose."

"Are you okay? I mean, you kind of look like you've been hit upside the head with a brick. Are you planning on driving somewhere?"

"Uh," I said. "Truly? I'm not really okay. Should be, though." And I spilled it all out—the wait, the diagnosis.

"Well, hell, no wonder. Congratulations, man, you're going to live! But not if you crash your car on the way home. How about if I give you a ride?"

"It's okay, really—"

He held up a hand. "Greg, I don't know you and you don't know me, but you've got no more business driving now than you would if you'd just slammed a couple tequila shots. So I can give you a ride or call you a cab, but if you try and get into your car, I will argue with you until I bore you into submission. So what is it? Ride? Taxi?"

He was absolutely, totally right. I hated that. I put my keys back into my pocket. "You win," I said. "I'll take that ride."

"Great," he said, and gave me a Buddha smile of pure SoCal serenity. "Where do you live?"

"Irvine," I said.

He groaned. "Seriously?" Irvine was a good three-hour drive in traffic.

"Not seriously," I said. "Just Burbank. Wanted to teach you a lesson about being too free with your generosity."

"Lesson learned. I'll never be generous again." But he was smiling.

I slid into the passenger seat. The car smelled like sweat and machines. The floor mats were indistinct gray and crunchy with maker detritus: dead batteries, coffee cups, multidriver bits, USB cables, and cigarette-lighter-charger adapters. I put my head back on the headrest and looked out the grimy windows through slitted eyes as he got into the driver's side and started the engine, then killed the podcast that started blasting from the speakers.

"Burbank, right?"

"Yeah," I said. There were invisible weights on my chest, wrists, and ankles. I was very glad I wasn't behind the wheel. We swung out onto Ventura Boulevard and inched through the traffic toward the freeway.

"Are you going to be all right on your own?"

"Tonight? Yeah, sure. Seriously, that's really nice of you, but it's just, whatever, aftermath. I mean, it's not like I'm dying. It's the opposite of that, right?"

"Fair enough. You just seem like you're in rough shape."

I closed my eyes and then I felt us accelerate as we hit the freeway and weaved over to the HOV lanes. He put down the hammer and the engine skipped into higher gear.

"You're not a burner, are you?"

I suppressed a groan. Burners are the Jehovah's witnesses of the counterculture. "Nope," I said. Then I said what I always said. "Just seemed like a lot of work."

He snorted. "You think burning man sounds like a lot of work, you should try Fourth of Juplaya. No rules, no rangers. A lot of guns. A lot of serious blowing shit up. Casual sex. No coffee shop. No sparkleponies. Fistfuls of drugs. High winds. Burning sun. Non-freaking-stop. It's like pure distilled essence of Playa."

I remembered that feeling, like I wanted to BASE jump off the roof. "I have to admit, that sounds totally amazeballs," I said. "And demented."

"Both, yup. You going to come?"

I opened my eyes wide. "What?"

"Well, I need some help with the printer. I looked you up on the Minus database. You do robotics, right?"

"A little," I said.

"And you've built a couple repraps, it says?"

"Two working ones," I said. Building your own 3D printer that was capable of printing out nearly all the parts to build a copy of itself was a notoriously tricky rite of passage for hackerspace enthusiasts. "About four that never worked, too."

"You're hired," he said. "First assistant engineer. You can have half my van, I'll bring the cooler and the BBQ and pork shoulder on dry ice, a keg of beer, and some spare goggles."

"That's very nice of you," I said.

"Yeah," he said. "It is. Listen, Greg, I'm a good guy, ask around. I don't normally invite people out to the Fourth, it's a private thing. But I really do need some help, and I think you do, too. A week with a near-death experience demands a fitting commemoration. If you let big stuff like this pass by without marking it, it just, you know, builds up. Like arterial plaque. Gotta shake it off."

You see, this is the thing about burners. It's like a religion for them. Gotta get everyone saved.

"I'll think about it," I said.

"Greg, don't be offended?"

"Okay."

"Right. Just that, you're the kind of guy, I bet, spends a lot of time 'thinking about it.'"

I swallowed the snappish reply and said nothing.

"And now you're stewing. Dude, you are so buttoned down. Tell you what, keep swallowing your emotions and you will end up dying of something fast and nasty. You can do whatever you want, but what I'm offering you is something that tons of people would kill for. Four days of forgetting who you are, being whoever you want to be. Stars, dust, screwing, dope, explosions, and gunfire. You're not going to get a lot of offers like that, is what I'm saying."

"And I said I'd think about it."

He blatted out a raspberry and said, "Yeah, fine, that's cool." He drove on in silence. The 101 degenerated into a sclerotic blockage. He tapped at the old phone velcroed to the dashboard and got a traffic overlay that showed red for ten miles.

"Dude, I do not want to sit in this car for the next forty-five minutes listening to you not say anything. How about a truce? I won't mention the Fourth, you pretend you don't think I'm a crazy hippie, and we'll start over, 'kay?"

The thing that surprised me most was how emotionally mature the offer was. I never knew how to climb down from stupid fights, which is why I was forty and single. "Deal," I said.

Just like that, he dropped it. We ended up talking about a related subject—selective solar laser-sintering—and some of the funky things he was having to cope with in the project. "Plenty of people have done it with sand, but I want to melt gypsum. In theory, I only have to attain about 85 percent of the heat to fuse it, but there's a lot of impurities in it that I can't account for or predict."

"What if you sift it or something first?"

"Well, if I want it to run unattended, I figure I don't want to have to include a centrifuge. Playa dust is nanofine, and it gets into everything. I mean, I've seen art cars with sealed bearings that are supposed to perform in space go gunky and funky after a couple of years."

I chewed on the problem. "You could maybe try a settling tray, something that uses wind for agitation through graduated screens, but you'd need to unclog it somehow." More thinking. "Of course, you could just melt the crap out of it when you're not sure, just blaze it into submission."

But he was already shaking his head. "Doesn't work—too hot and I can't get the set time right, goes all runny."

"What about a sensor?" I said. "Try to characterize how runny it is, adjust the next pass accordingly?"

"Thought of that," he said. "Too many ways it could go wrong is what I'm think-ing. Remember, this thing has to run where no one can tend it. I want to drop it in July and move into the house it builds me by September. It has to fail very, very safe."

I took his point, but I wasn't sure I agreed. Optical sensors were pretty solved, as was the software to interpret what they saw. I was about to get my laptop out and find a video I remembered seeing when he slammed on the brakes and made an explo-sive noise. I felt the brakes' ABS shudder as the minivan fishtailed a little and heard a horn blare from behind us. I had one tiny instant with which to contemplate the looming bumper of the gardener's pickup truck ahead of us before we rear-ended him. I was slammed back into my seat by the airbag a second before the subcompact behind us crashed into us, its low nose sliding under the rear bumper and raising the back end off the ground as it plowed beneath us, wedging tight just before its windshield would have passed through our rear bumper, thus saving the driver from a radical facial rearrangement and possible decapitation.

Sound took on a kind of underwater quality as it filtered through the airbag, but as I punched my way clear of it, everything came back. Beside me, Pug was making aggrieved noises and trying to turn around. He was caught in the remains of his own airbag, and his left arm looked like it might be broken—unbroken arms don't hang with that kind of limp and sickening slackness. "Christ, the lens—"

I looked back instinctively, saw that the rear end was intact, albeit several feet higher than it should have been, and said, "It's fine, Pug. Car behind us slid under us. Hold still, though. Your arm's messed up."

He looked down and saw it and his face went slack. "That is not good," he said. His pupils were enormous, his face so pale it was almost green.

"You're in shock," I said.

"Yes," he said, distantly.

I did a quick personal inventory, moving all my limbs and experimentally swivel-ing my head this way and that. Concluding that I was in one piece, I did a fast assessment of the car and its environs. Traffic in the adjacent lane had stopped, too—looking over my shoulder, I could see a little fender bender a couple car lengths back that had doubtless been caused by our own wreck. The guy ahead of us had gotten out of his pickup and was headed our way slowly, which suggested that he was unharmed and also not getting ready to shoot us for rear-ending him, so I turned my attention back to Pug. "Stay put," I said, and pushed his airbag aside and un-buckled his seat belt, carefully feeding it back into its spool without allowing it to jostle his arm. That done, I gave him a quick once-over, lightly running my hands over his legs, chest, and head. He didn't object—or shout in pain—and I finished up without blood on my hands, so that was good.

"I think it's just your arm," I said. His eyes locked on my face for a moment, then his gaze wandered off.

"The lens," he said, blearily.

"It's okay," I said.

"The lens," he said, again, and tried once more to twist around in his seat. This time, he noticed his limp arm and gave out a mild, "Ow." He tried again. "Ow."

"Pug," I said, taking his chin and turning his face to mine. His skin was clammy and cold. "Dude. You are in shock and have a broken arm. You need to stay still until the ambulance gets here. You might have a spinal injury or a concussion. I need you to stay still."

"But the lens," he said. "Can't afford another one."

"If I go check on the lens, will you stay still?" It felt like I was bargaining with a difficult drunk for his car keys. "Yes," he said. "Stay there." The pickup truck's owner helped me out of the car. "You okay?" he asked. He had a Russian accent and rough gardener's hands and a farmer's tan.

"Yeah," I said. "You?"

"I guess so. My truck's pretty messed up, though."

Pug's minivan had merged catastrophically with the rear end of the pickup, deforming it around the van's crumple-zone. I was keenly aware that this was probably his livelihood.

"My friend's got a broken arm," I said. "Shock, too. I'm sure you guys'll be able to exchange insurance once the paramedics get here. Did you call them?"

"My buddy's on it," he said, pointing back at the truck. There was someone in the passenger seat with a phone clamped to his head, beneath the brim of a cowboy hat.

"The lens," Pug said.

I leaned down and opened the door. "Chill out, I'm on it." I shrugged at the guy from the truck and went around back. The entire rear end was lifted clean off the road, the rear wheels still spinning lazily. To a first approximation, we were unscathed. The same couldn't be said for the low-slung hybrid that had rear-ended us, which had been considerably flattened by its harrowing scrape beneath us, to the extent that one of its tires had blown. The driver had climbed out of the car and was leaning unsteadily on it. She gave me a little half wave and a little half smile, which I returned. I popped the hatch and checked that the box was in one piece. It wasn't even dented. "The lens is fine," I called. Pug gave no sign of having heard.

I started to get a little anxious feeling. I jogged around the back of the subcompact and then ran up the driver's side and yanked open Pug's door. He was unconscious, and that gray sheen had gone even whiter. His breath was coming in little shallow pants and his head lolled back in the seat. Panic crept up my throat and I swallowed it down. I looked up quickly and shouted at the pickup driver. "You called an ambulance, right?" The guy must've heard something in my voice because an instant later he was next to me.

"Shock," he said.

"It's been years since I did first aid."

"Recovery position," he said. "Loosen his clothes, give him a blanket."

"What about his arm?" I pointed.

He winced. "We're going to have to be careful," he said. "Shit," he added. The traffic beyond the car was at a near standstill. Even the motorcycles were having trouble lane-splitting between the close-crammed cars.

"The ambulance?"

He shrugged. "On its way, I guess." He put his ear close to Pug's mouth, listened to his breathing, put a couple fingers to his throat and felt around. "I think we'd better lay him out."

The lady driving the subcompact had a blanket in her trunk, which we spread out on the weedy ground alongside the median, which glittered with old broken glass. She—young, Latina, wearing workout clothes—held Pug's arm while the gardener guy and I got him at both ends and stretched him out. The other guy from the pickup truck found some flares in a toolkit under the truck's seat and set them on the road behind us. We worked with a minimum of talk, and for me, the sounds of the highway and my weird postanxiety haze both faded away into barely discernible background noise. We turned Pug on his side, and I rolled up my jacket to support his arm. He groaned. The gardener guy checked his pulse again, then rolled up his own jacket and used it to prop up Pug's feet.

"Good work," he said.

I nodded.

"Craziest thing," the gardener said.

"Uh-huh," I said. I fussed awkwardly with Pug's hair. His ponytail had come loose and it was hanging in his face. It felt wiry and dry, like he spent a lot of time in the sun.

"Did you see it?"

"What?"

He shook his head. "Craziest thing. It crashed right in front of us." He spoke in rapid Russian—maybe it was Bulgarian?—to his friend, who crunched over to us. The guy held something out for me to see. I looked at it, trying to make sense of what I was seeing. It was a tangle of wrecked plastic and metal and a second later, I had it worked out—it was a little UAV, some kind of copter. Four rotors—no, six. A couple of cameras. I'd built a few like it, and I'd even lost control of a few in my day. I could easily see how someone like me, trying out a little drone built from a kit or bought fully assembled, could simply lose track of the battery or just fly too close to a rising updraft from the blacktop and crash. It was technically illegal to fly one except over your own private property, but that was nearly impossible to enforce. They were all over the place.

"Craziest thing," I agreed. I could hear the sirens.

The EMTs liked our work and told us so, and let me ride with them in the ambulance, though that might have been on the assumption that I could help with whatever insurance paperwork needed filling out. They looked disappointed when I told them that I'd only met Pug that day and I didn't even know his last name and was pretty sure that "Pug" wasn't his first name. It wasn't. They got the whole thing off his driver's license: Scott Zrubek. "Zrubek" was a cool name. If I'd been called "Zrubek," I'd have used "Zee" as my nickname, or maybe "Zed."

By the time they'd X-rayed Pug and put his arm in a sling and an air cast, he was awake and rational again and I meant to ask him why he wasn't going by Oz, but we never got around to it. As it turned out, I ended up giving him a lift home in a cab, then getting it to take me home, too. It was two in the morning by then, and maybe the lateness of the hour explains how I ended up promising Pug that I'd be his arm and hand on the playa-dust printer and that I'd come with him to Fourth of Juplaya in order to oversee the installation of the device. I also agreed to help him think of a name for it.

That is how I came to be riding in a big white rental van on the Thursday before

July Fourth weekend, departing L.A. at zero-dark-hundred with Pug in the driver's seat and classic G-funk playing loud enough to make me wince in the passenger seat as we headed for Nevada.

Pug had a cooler between us, full of energy beverages and electrolyte drink, jerky, and seed bars. We stopped in mono lake and bought bags of oranges from old guys on the side of the road wearing cowboy hats, and later on we stopped at a farm stall and bought fresh grapefruit juice that stung with tartness and was so cold that the little bits of pulp were little frost-bombs that melted on our tongues.

Behind us, in the van's cargo area, was everything we needed for a long weekend of hard-core radical self-reliance—water cans to fill in Reno, solar showers, tents, tarps, rebar stakes, booze, bikes, sunscreen, first-aid kits, a shotgun, an air cannon, a flamethrower, various explosives, crates of fireworks, and more booze. All stored and locked away in accordance with the laws of both Nevada and California, as verified through careful reference to a printout sheathed in a plastic paper-saver that got velcroed to the inside of the van's back door when we were done.

In the center of all this gear, swaddled in Bubble Wrap and secured in place with multiple tie-downs, was the gadget, which we had given a capital letter to in our e-mails and messages: the Gadget. I'd talked Pug out of some of his aversion to moving parts, because the Gadget was going to end up drowning in its own output if we didn't. The key was the realization that it didn't matter where the Gadget went, so long as it went somewhere, which is how we ended up in Strandbeest territory.

The Strandbeest is an ingenious wind-powered walker that looks like a blind, mechanical millipede. Its creator, a Dutch artist called Theo Jansen, designed it to survive harsh elements and to be randomly propelled by wind.

Ours had a broad back where the Gadget's business end perched, and as the yurt panels were completed, they'd slide off to land at its feet, gradually hemming it with rising piles of interlocking, precision-printed pieces. To keep it from going too far afield, I'd tether it to a piece of rebar driven deep into the Playa, giving it a wide circle through which the harsh winds of the black rock desert could blow it.

Once I was done, Pug had to admit I'd been right. It wasn't just a better design, it was a cooler one, and the Gadget had taken on the aspect of a centaur, with the printer serving as rising torso and head. We'd even equipped it with a set of purely ornamental goggles and a filter mask, just to make it fit in with its neighbors on the Playa. They were a very accepting lot, but you never knew when antirobot prejudice would show its ugly head, and so anything we could do to anthropomorphize the Gadget would only help our cause.

Pug's busted arm was healed enough to drive to the Nevada line, but by the time we stopped for gas, he was rubbing at his shoulder and wincing, and I took over the driving, and he popped some pain-killers and within moments he was fast asleep. I tried not to envy him. He'd been a bundle of nerves in the run-up to the Fourth, despite several successful trial runs in his backyard and a great demo on the roof of Minus. He kept muttering about how nothing ever worked properly in the desert, predicting dire all-nighters filled with cursing and scrounging for tools and missing the ability to grab tech support online. It was a side of him I hadn't seen up to that point—he was normally so composed—but it gave me a chance to be the grown-up for a change. It helped once I realized that he was mostly worried about looking like an idiot in front of his once-a-year friends, the edgiest and weirdest people in his set. It also hadn't escaped my notice that he, like me, was a single guy who spent an awful lot of time wondering what this said about him. In other words: he didn't want to look like a dork in front of the eligible women who showed up.

"I'm guessing two more hours to Reno, then we'll get some last-minute supplies and head out. Unless you want to play the slots and catch a Liza Minnelli impersonator."

"No, I want to get out there and get set up."

"Good." Suddenly he gorilla-beat his chest with his good fist and let out a rebel yell. "Man, I just can't wait."

I smiled. This was the voluble Pug I knew.

He pointed a finger at me. "Oh, I see you smiling. You think you know what's going to happen. You think you're going to go drink some beers, eat some pills, blow stuff up, and maybe get lucky. What you don't know is how life-changing this can all be. You get out of your head, literally. It's like—" he waved his hands, smacked the dashboard a couple times, cracked and swigged an energy beverage.

"Okay, this is the thing. We spend all our time doing, you know, stuff. Maintenance. Ninety-eight percent of the day, all you're doing is thinking about what you're going to be doing to go on doing what you're doing. Worrying about whether you've got enough socked away to see you through your old age without ending up eating cat food. Worrying about whether you're getting enough fiber or eating too many carbs. It's being alive, but it's hardly living.

"You ever been in a bad quake? No? Here's the weird secret of a big quake: it's actually pretty great, afterward. I mean, assuming you're not caught in the rubble, of course. After a big one, there's this moment, a kind of silence. Like you were living with this huge old refrigerator compressor humming so loud in the back of your mind that you've never been able to think properly, not once since about the time you turned, you know, eleven or twelve, maybe younger. Never been present and in the moment. And then that humming refrigerator just stops and there's a ringing, amazing, all-powerful silence and for the first time you can hear yourself think. There's that moment, after the earth stops shaking, when you realize that there's you and there's everyone else and the point of it all is for all of you to figure out how to get along together as best as you can.

"They say that after a big one, people start looting, raping, eating each other, whatever. But you know what I saw the last time it hit, back in 2019? People figuring it out. Firing up their barbecues and cooking dinner for the neighborhood with everything in the freezer, before it spoils anyway. Kids being looked after by everyone, everyone going around and saying, 'What can I do for you? Do you have a bed? Water? Food? You okay? Need someone to talk to? Need a ride?' In the movies, they always show everyone running around looting as soon as the lights go out, but I can't say as I've ever seen that. I mean, that's not what I'd do, would you?"

I shook my head.

"'Course not. No one we know would. Because we're on the same side. The human race's side. But when the fridge is humming away, you can lose track of that, start to feel like its zero sum, a race to see who can squirrel away the most nuts before the winter comes. When a big shaker hits, though, you remember that you aren't the kind of squirrel who could live in your tree with all your nuts while all the other squirrels starved and froze out there.

"The Playa is like a disaster without the disaster—it's a chance to switch off the fridge and hear the silence. A chance to see that people are, you know, basically awesome. Mostly. It's the one place where you actually confront reality, instead of all the noise and illusion."

"So you're basically saying that it's like Buddhism with recreational drugs and explosions?"

"Basically."

We rode awhile longer. The signs for Reno were coming more often now, and the traffic was getting thicker, requiring more attention.

"If only," he said. "If only there was some way to feel that way all the time."

"You couldn't," I said, without thinking. "Regression to the mean. The extraordinary always ends up feeling ordinary. Do it for long enough and it'd just be noise."

"You may be right. But I hope you're not. Somewhere out there, there's a thing so amazing that you can devote your life to it and never forget how special it is."

We crawled the last thirty miles, driving through Indian country, over cattle gratings and washed-out gullies. "The local cops are fine, they're practically burners themselves. Everyone around here grew up with burning man, and it's been the only real source of income since the gypsum mine closed. But the feds and the cops from over the state line, they're bad news. Lot of jack Mormons over in Pershing County, don't like this at all. And since the whole route to the Playa, apart from the last quarter mile, is in Washoe County, and since no one is supposed to buy or sell anything once you get to the Playa, all the money stays in Washoe County, and Pershing gets none of it. All they get are freaks who offend them to their very souls. So basically, you want to drive slow and keep your nose clean around here, because you never know who's waiting behind a bush to hand you a giant ticket and search your car down to the floor mats."

I slowed down even more. We stopped for Indian tacos—fried flat-bread smothered in ground beef and fried veggies—that sat in my stomach in an undigestable, salty lump. Pug grew progressively more manic as we approached the turnoff for black rock desert and was practically drumming on the dashboard by the time we hit the dusty, rutted side road. He played with the stereo, put on some loud electronic dance music that made me feel old and out of it, and fished around under the seat for a dust mask and a pair of goggles.

I'd seen lots of photos of burning man, the tents and shade structures and RVs and "mutant vehicles" stretching off in all directions, and even though I knew the Fourth was a much smaller event, I'd still been picturing that in my mind's eye. But instead, what we saw was a seemingly endless and empty desert, edges shrouded in blowing dust clouds with the hints of mountains peeking through, and no sign at all of human habitation.

"Now where?" I said.

He got out his phone and fired up a GPS app, clicked on one of his waypoints, waiting a moment, and pointed into the heart of the dust. "That way."

We rumbled into the dust cloud and were soon in a near-total white-out. I slowed the car to walking pace, and then slower than walking pace. "Pug, we should just stop for a while," I said. "There's no roads. Cars could come from any direction."

"All the more reason to get to the campsite," he said. "We're sitting ducks out here for anyone else arriving."

"That's not really logic," I said. "If we're moving and they're moving, we've got a much better chance of getting into a fender bender than if we're staying still."

The air in the van tasted dusty and alkali. I put it in park and put on the mask, noticed my eyes were starting to sting, added goggles—big, bug-eyed Soviet-era MIG goggles.

"Drive," he said. "We're almost there."

I was starting to catch some of his enthusiasm. I put it back into drive and rode the brakes as we inched through the dust. He peered at his GPS, calling out, "left," then "straight," then "right" and back again. A few times I was sure I saw a car bumper or a human looming out of the dust before us and slammed on the brakes, only to discover that it had been a trick of the light and my brain's overactive, nerve-racked pattern-matching systems.

When I finally did run something over, I was stretched out so tight that I actually let out a scream. In my defense, the thing we hit was a tent peg made out of rebar—the next five days gave the chance to become endlessly acquainted with rebar tent pegs, which didn't scar the Playa and were cheap and rugged—pushing it through the front driver's-side tire, which exploded with a noise like a gunshot. I turned off the engine and tried to control my breathing.

Pug gave me a moment, then said, "We're here!"

"Sorry about the tire."

"Pfft. We're going to wreck stuff that's a lot harder to fix than a flat tire. You think we can get to the spare without unpacking?"

"No way."

"Then we'll have to unpack. Come on, buddy."

The instant he opened the door, a haze of white dust followed him, motes sparkling in the air. I shrugged and opened my door and stepped out into the dust.

There were people in the dust, but they were ciphers—masked, goggled, indistinct. I had a job to do—clearing out the van's cargo and getting it moved to our site, which was weirdly precise—a set of four corners defined as GPS coordinates that ran to the tenth of a second—and at the same time, such a farcically huge tract of land that it really amounted to "Oh, anywhere over there's fine."

The shadowy figures came out of the dust and formed a bucket brigade, into which I vanished. I love a good bucket brigade, but they're surprisingly hard to find. A good bucket brigade is where you accept your load, rotate 180 degrees and walk until you reach the next person, load that person, do another volte-face, and walk until someone loads you. A good bucket brigade isn't just passing things from person to person. It's a dynamic system in which autonomous units bunch and debunch as is optimal given the load and the speed and energy levels of each participant. A good bucket brigade is a thing of beauty, something whose smooth coordination arises from a bunch of disjointed parts who don't need to know anything about the system's whole state in order to help optimize it. In a good bucket brigade, the mere act of walking at the speed you feel comfortable with and carrying no more than you can safely lift and working at your own pace produces a perfectly balanced system in which the people faster than you can work faster, and the people slower than you can work slower. It is the opposite of an assembly line, where one person's slowness is the whole line's problem. A good bucket brigade allows everyone to contribute at their own pace, and the more contributors you get, the better it works.

I love bucket brigades. It's like proof that we can be more together than we are on our own, and without having to take orders from a leader. It wasn't until the van was empty and I pulled a lounger off our pile of gear and set it up and sank down into it that I realized that an hour had slipped by and I was both weary and energized. Pug handed me a flask and I sniffed at it, got a noseful of dust and whiskey fumes, and then sipped at it. It was Kentucky bourbon, and it cut through the dust in my mouth and throat like oven cleaner.

Pug sprawled in the dust beside me, his blond hair splayed around his head like a halo. "Now the work begins," he said. "How you holding up?"

"Ready and willing, Cap'n," I said, speaking with my eyes closed and my head flung back.

"Look at you two," an amused female voice said. Fingers plucked the flask out of my hands. I opened my eyes. Standing over us was a tall, broad-shouldered woman whose blue Mohawk was braided in a long rope that hung over her shoulder. "You just got here and you're already pooped. You're an embarrassment to the uniform."

"Hi, Blight," Pug said, not stirring. "Blight, this is Greg. He's never been to the Playa before."

"A virgin!" she said. "My stars and garters." She drank more whiskey. She was wearing overalls with the sleeves ripped off, showing her long, thick, muscled arms, which had been painted with stripes of zinc, like a barber pole. It was hard to guess her age—the haircut suggested mid-twenties, but the way she held herself and talked made me think she might be more my age. I tried not to consider the possibilities of a romantic entanglement. As much of a hormone-fest as the Playa was supposed to be, it wasn't summer camp. "We'll be gentle," she said.

"Don't worry about me," I said. "I'm just gathering my strength before leaping into action. Can I have the whiskey back, please?"

She drank another mouthful and passed it back. "Here you go. That's good stuff, by the way."

"Fighting Cock," Pug said. "I bought it for the name, stayed for the booze." He got to his feet and he and Blight shared a long hug. His feet left the ground briefly.

"Missed you, Pug."

"Missed you, too. You should come visit, sometime."

They chatted a little like old friends, and I gathered that she lived in Salt Lake City and ran a Goth/alternative dance club that sounded familiar. There wasn't much by way of freak culture out in SLC, so whatever there was quickly became legendary. I'd worked with a guy from Provo, a gay guy who'd never fit in with his Mormon family, who'd spent a few years in SLC before coming to L.A. I was pretty sure he'd talked about it. A kind of way station for Utah's underground bohemian railway.

Then Pug held out his hand to me and pulled me to my feet and announced we'd be setting up camp. This involved erecting a giant shade structure, stringing up hammocks, laying out the heavy black rubber solar-shower bladders on the van's roof to absorb the day's heat, setting out the grill and the bags of lump charcoal, and hammering hundreds of lengths of bent-over rebar into the unyielding desert floor. Conveniently, Pug's injured arm wasn't up to the task, leaving me to do most of the work, though some of the others pitched in at the beginning, until some more campers arrived and needed help unloading.

Finally, it was time to set up the Gadget.

I'd been worried about it, especially as we'd bashed over some of the deeper ruts after the turnoff onto route 34, but Pug had been awfully generous with the bubble-wrap. I ended up having to scrounge a heavy ammo box full of shotgun shells to hold down the layer after layer of plastic and keep it from blowing away. I drew a little crowd as I worked—now they weren't too busy!—and Blight stepped in and helped toward the end, bundling up armloads of plastic sheeting and putting it under the ammo box. Finally, the many-legged Gadget was fully revealed. There was a long considering silence that broke when a breeze blew over it and it began, very slowly, to walk, as each of the legs' sails caught the wind. It clittered along on its delicate feet, and then, as the wind gusted harder, lurched forward suddenly, scattering the onlookers. I grabbed the leash I'd clipped to its rear and held on as best I could, nearly falling on my face before I reoriented my body to lean away from it. It was like playing one-sided tug-of-war. I whooped and then there were more hands on the leash with mine, including Blight's, and we steadied it.

"Guess I should have driven a spike for the tether before I started," I said.

"Where are you going to spike it?" Blight asked.

I shrugged as best as I could while still holding the strong nylon cable. "I don't know—close enough to the shade structure that we can keep tools and gear there while we're working on it, but far enough away that it can really get around without bashing into anything."

"Stay there," she said, and let go, jogging off toward the back forty of our generous plot. She came back and grabbed our sledgehammer and one of the longest pieces of rebar, and I heard the ringing of a mallet on steel—sure, rhythmic strokes. She'd done this a lot more than me. She jogged back a moment later, her goggles pushed up on her forehead, revealing dark brown eyes, wide set, with thick eyebrows and fine crow's-feet. The part of me that wasn't thinking about the Gadget was thinking about how pretty she was and wondering if she was single, and wondering if she was with Pug, and wondering if she was into guys at all, anyway.

"Let's get it tied off," she said. We played out the rope and let it drag us toward the rebar she'd driven nearly all the way into the hardpack, the bent double tips both buried deep, forming a staple. I threaded the rope's end through and tied a sailor's knot I'd learned in the one week I'd attended Scouts when I was nine, the only knot I knew. It had never come loose. If it came loose this time, there was a chance the Gadget would sail all the way to Reno over the coming months, leaving behind a trail of interlocking panels that could be formed into a yurt.

The sun was starting to set, and though I really wanted to go through my maintenance check list for the Gadget, there was dance music playing (dubstep—I'd been warned by Pug in advance and had steeled myself to learning to love the wub-wub-wub), there were people milling about, there was the smell of barbecue. The sun was a huge, bloody red ball on the horizon and the heat of the day was giving way to a perfectly cool night. Laser light played through the air. Drones flew overhead, strobing with persistence-of-vision LED light shows and doing aerobatics that pushed their collision-avoidance routines to the limit (every time one buzzed me, I flinched, as I had been doing since the accident).

Blight dusted her hands off on her thighs. "Now what?"

I looked around. "Dinner?"

"Yeah," she said, and linked arms with me and led me back to camp.

Sometime around midnight, I had the idea that I should be getting to bed and getting a good night's sleep so I could get the Gadget up and running the next morning. Then Pug and I split a tab of E and passed a thermosful of mushroom tea back and forth—a " hippie flip," something I hadn't tried in more than a decade—and an hour later I was dancing my ass off and the world was an amazing place.

I ended up in a wonderful cuddle puddle around 2 a.m., every nerve alive to the breathing chests and the tingling skin of the people around me. Someone kissed me on the forehead and I spun back to my childhood, and the sensation of having all the time in the world and no worries about anything flooded into me. In a flash, I realized that this is what a utopian, postscarcity world would be like. A place where there was no priority higher than pleasing the people around you and amusing yourself. I thought of all those futures I'd read about and seen, places where everything was built atop sterile metal and polymer. I'd never been able to picture myself in those futures.

But this "future"—a dusty, meaty world where human skin and sweat and hair were all around, but so were lasers and UAVs and freaking wind-walking robots? That was a future I could live in. A future devoted to pleasing one another.

"Welcome to the future," I said into the hollow of someone's throat. That person chuckled. The lasers lanced through the dust overhead, clean multicolored beams sweeping the sky. The drones buzzed and dipped. The moon shone down upon us, as big as a pumpkin and as pale as ancient bone.

I stared at the moon. It stared back. It had always stared back, but I'd always been moving too quickly to notice.

I awoke the next day in my own airbed in the back of the van. It was oven hot inside and I felt like a stick of beef jerky. I stumbled out shirtless and in jeans and made it to the shade structure, where I found my water pack and uncapped the hose. I sucked it dry and then refilled it from a huge water barrel we'd set up on a set of sawhorses, drank some more. I went back into the van and scrounged my shades and goggles, found a T-shirt, and reemerged, made use of the chem toilet we'd set up behind a modesty screen hammered into the Playa with rebar and nylon rope, and then collapsed into a hammock under the shade structure.

Some brief groggy eternity later, someone put a collection of pills and tablets into my left hand and a coffee mug into my right.

"No more pills, thank you."

"These are supplements," he said. "I figure half of them are harmless BS, but the other half really seem to help with the old seratonin levels. Don't know which half is which, but there're a couple neuroscientists who come out most years who could argue about it for your amusement if you're interested. Take 'em."

Pug thrust a paper plate of scrambled eggs, sausages, and slices of watermelon into my hands. Before I knew it, I'd gobbled it all down to the watermelon rind and licked the stray crispy bits of sausage meat. I brushed my teeth and joined Pug out by the Gadget. It had gone walking in the night, leaving a beautiful confusion of footprints in the dust. The wind was still for the moment, though with every gust it creaked a little. I steadied Pug as he climbed it and began to tinker with it.

We'd put a lot of energy into a self-calibration phase. In theory, the Gadget should be able to tell, by means of its array of optical sensors, whether its test prints were correct or not, and then relevel its build plate and recenter its optics. The unfolded solar collectors also acted as dust collectors, and they periodically upended themselves into the feedstock hopper. This mechanism had three fail-safes—first, it could run off the battery, but once the batteries were charged, power was automatically diverted to a pair of servos that would self-trip if the battery ran too low. They each had enough storage to flip, shake, and restore the panels—working with a set of worm-gears we'd let software design and had printed off in a ceramic-polymer mix developed for artificial teeth and guaranteed not to chip or grind away for years.

There was a part of me that had been convinced that the Gadget just couldn't possibly work. Too many moving parts, not enough testing. It was just too weird. But as Pug unfurled the flexible photovoltaics and clipped them to the carbon-fiber struts and carefully positioned the big lens and pressed the big, rubberized on button, it made the familiar powering-up noises and began to calibrate itself.

Perfectly.

Dust had sifted into the feedstock hopper overnight and had blown over the build plate. The sun hit the lens, and smoke began to rise from the dust. The motors clicked minutely and the head zipped this way and that with pure, robotic grace. Moving with the unhurried precision of a master, it described a grid and melted it, building it up at each junction, adding an extra two-micron Z-height each time, so that a tiny cityscape emerged. The sensors fed back to an old phone I'd brought along—we had a box of them, anticipating a lot more failure from these nonpurpose-built gadgets than our own—and it expressed a confidence rating about the overall accuracy of the build. The basic building blocks the Gadget was designed to print were five-millimeter-thick panels that snap-fit without any additional fixtures, relying on a clever combination of gravity and friction to stay locked once they were put together. The tolerances were fine, and the Gadget was confident it could meet them.

Here's a thing about 3D printing: it is exciting; then very, very boring; then it is exciting again. It's borderline magic; when the print-head starts to jerk and shunt to and fro, up and down, and the melting smell rises up off the build platform, and you can peer through that huge, crystal-clear lens and see a precise form emerging. It's amazing to watch a process by which an idea becomes a thing, untouched by human hands.

But it's also s-l-o-w. From the moment at which a recognizable object begins to take shape to the moment where it seems about ready to slide off, there is a long and dull interregnum in which minute changes gradually bring the shape to fruition. It's like watching soil erosion (albeit in reverse). This is the kind of process that begs for time-lapse. And if you do go away and come back later to check in on things, and find your object in a near-complete state, you inevitably find that, in fact, there are innumerable, mysterious passes to be made by the print-head before the object is truly done-done, and once again, you wish that life had a fast-forward button.

But then, you hold the object, produced out of nothing and computers and light and dust, a clearly manufactured *thing* with the polygonal character of everything that comes out of a 3D-modeling program, and once again—*magic.*

This is the cycle that the spectators at the inauguration of the Gadget went through, singly and in bunches, on that day. The Gadget performed exactly as intended— itself the most miraculous thing of the day!—business end floating on a stabilization bed as its legs clawed their way across the desert, and produced a single, interlocking shingle made of precision-formed gypsum and silicon traces, a five-millimeter, honeycombed double-walled tile with snap-fit edges all around.

"That's what it does, huh?" Blight had been by to see it several times that day, alternating between the fabulous dullness of watching 3D paint dry and the excitement of the firing range, from which emanated a continuous pop-pop-pop of gleeful shooting. Someone had brought along a junker car on a trailer, covered in improvised armor, rigged for remote control. The junker had been lumbering around on the desert while the marksmen blasted away at its slowly disintegrating armor, raising loud cheers every time a hunk of its plating fell away, exposing the vulnerable, rusted chassis beneath.

"Well, yeah. One after another, all day long, so long as the sun is shining. We weren't sure about the rate, but I'm thinking something like five per day in the summer sun, depending on the dust storms. It'll take a couple hundred to build a decent-sized yurt on Labor Day, and we should easily get that many by then." I showed her how the tiles interlocked, and how, once locked, they stayed locked.

"It's more of an igloo than a yurt," she said.

"Technicality," I said. "It's neither of those things. It's a 3D-printed, human-assembled temporary prefabricated experimental structure."

"An igloo," she said.

"Touché."

"Time for some food," Pug said. It could have been anywhere between 3 and 7 p.m. none of the burner phones we were using to program and monitor the Gadget had network signal, so none of them had auto-set their clocks. I wasn't wearing a watch. I woke when the baking heat inside the van woke me, and ate when my stomach rumbled, and worked the rest of the time, and danced and drank and drugged whenever the opportunity presented itself.

My stomach agreed. Blight put a sweaty, tattoo-wreathed arm around each of our shoulders and steered us to the plume of fragrant BBQ smoke.

I am proud to say I administered the killing shot to the target car. It was a lucky shot. I'd been aiming for center mass, somewhere around the bullet-pocked midsection, staring through the scope of the impossibly long rifle that a guy in cracked leathers had checked me out on. He was some kind of physicist, high energy at JPL, but he'd been coming out since he was a freshman and he was a saucer-pupiled neuronaut down to his tattooed toes. He also liked big hardware, guns that were some kind of surrogate supercollider, like the rifle over which I'd been given command. It was a sniper's tool, with its own tripod, and he told me that he had to keep it locked up in a gun club over the Nevada state line because it was radioactively illegal in sweet gentle California.

I peered down the scope, exhaled, and squeezed the trigger. Just as I did, the driver jigged the toy wheel she was using to control it, and the car swung around and put the middle of its grille right in my crosshairs. The bullet pierced the engine block with a fountain of black smoke and oil, the mighty crash of the engine seizing, and a juddering, shuddering, slewing cacophony as the car skidded and revved and then stopped, flames now engulfing the hood and spreading quickly into the front seat.

I had a moment's sick fear, like I'd done something terrible, destroying their toy. The silence after my shot rang out couldn't have lasted for more than a second, but then it broke, with a wild whoop!, and a cheer that whipped up and down the firing line.

The car's owner had filled it with assorted pyro—mortars and roman candles— that were touched off by the fire and exploded out in every direction, streaking up and out and even down, smashing into the Playa and then skipping away like flat stones. People pounded me on the back as the car self-destructed and sent up an oily black plume of smoke. I felt an untethered emotion, like I'd left behind civilization for good. I'd killed a car!

That's when my Fourth of Juplaya truly began. A wild debauch, loud and stoned and dangerous. I slept in hammocks, in piles of warm bodies, in other people's cars. I danced in ways I'd never danced before, ate spectacular meals of roasted meat and desserts of runny, melted chocolate on fat pancakes. I helped other people fix their art cars, piloted a drone, got a naked (and curiously asexual) massage from a stranger, and gave one in return. I sang along to songs whose words I didn't know, rode on the hood of a car while it did slow donuts in the middle of the open desert, and choked on dust storms that stung my skin and my eyes and left me huddled down in total whiteout while it blew.

It was glorious.

"How's your windwalker?" Blight said, as I passed her back her water bottle, having refilled it from our dwindling supply.

"Dunno," I said. "What day is it?"

"Monday," she said.

"I don't think I've looked in on it today. Want to come?"

She did.

In the days since we'd staked out the Gadget, more tents and trucks and cars and shade structures and exotic vehicles had gone up all around it, so that its paddock was now in the midst of a low-slung tent city. We'd strung up a perimeter of waist-high safety-orange tape to keep people from blundering into it at night, and I saw that it had been snapped in a few places and made a mental note to get the spool of tape off the post where we kept it and replace it.

The wind had been blowing hard earlier that day, but it had died down to a breathless late afternoon. The Gadget was standing and creaking softly at the end of its tether, and all around it was a litter of printed panels. Three of its legs were askew, resting atop stray tiles. We gathered them up and stacked them neatly and counted— there were forty all told, which was more than I'd dared hope for.

"We're going to be able to put together two or three yurts at this rate."

"Igloos."

"Yours can be an igloo," I said.

"That's very big of you, fella."

"Monday, you said?"

She stretched like a cat. She was streaked with dust and dirt and had a musky, unwashed animal smell that I'd gotten used to smelling on myself. "Yeah," she said. "Packing up tonight, pulling out tomorrow at first light."

I gulped. Time had become elastic out there on the desert, that school's-out Junetime feeling that the days are endless and unrolling before you and there are infinite moments to fill and no reason at all in the whole world to worry. Now it evaporated as quickly as sweat in the desert. I swallowed again.

"You're going to get up at first light?" I said.

"No," she said, and pressed a couple of gel caps into my palm. "I was going to stay up all night. Luckily, I'm not driving."

At some point we worked out that Pug and I had three filled solar showers warm on the van's roof and then it was only natural that we strung them up and pulled the plug on them, sluicing the hot, stale, wonderful water over our bodies, and we took turns soaping each other up, and the molly and whatever else had been in her pills made every nerve ending on my body thrum. Our gray water ended up in a kiddie pool at our feet, brown and mucky, and when we stepped out of it the dust immediately caked on our feet and ankles and calves, gumming between our toes as we made a mad, giggling dash for the van, threw our bodies into it and slammed the door behind us.

We rolled around on the air mattresses in the thick, superheated air of the van, tickling and kissing and sometimes more, the madness of the pills and that last-night-of-summer-camp feeling thrumming in our veins.

"You're thinking about something," she said, lying crosswise so that our stomachs were pressed together and our bodies formed a wriggling plus sign.

"Is that wrong?"

"This is one of those live-in-the-moment moments, Greg."

I ran my hands over the small of her back, the swell of her butt, and she shivered and the shiver spread to me. The dope made me want to knead her flesh like dough, my hands twitching with the desire to clench.

"It's nothing, just—" I didn't want to talk about it. I wanted to fool around. She did too. We did.

"Just what?" she said, some long time later. At one point, Pug had opened—and then swiftly shut—the rear van doors.

"You and Pug aren't . . . ?"

"Nope," she said. "Are you?"

"Nope," I said.

"Just what, then?"

I rewound the conversation. I'd already peaked and was sliding into something mellow and grand.

"Just, well, default reality. It's all so—"

"Yeah," she said. Default reality was cutesy burner-speak for the real world, but I had to admit it fit. That made what we were in special reality or maybe default un-reality.

"I know that we're only here to have fun, but somehow it feels like it's been . . ." Important was the word on the tip of my tongue, but what an embarrassing admission. "More." Lame-o!

She didn't say anything for so long that I started to get dope paranoia, a fear that I'd said or done something wildly inappropriate but been too high to notice.

"I know what you mean," she said.

We lay together and listened to the thump of music out in the desert night. She stroked my arm lazily with fingertips that were as rough as sand-paper, rasping over my dry, scaly skin. I could distinctly feel each nerve impulse move up my arm to my spine and into my brain. For a while, I forgot my curious existential sorrow and was truly, totally in the moment, just feeling and hearing and smelling, and not thinking. It was the refrigerator hum that Pug had told me about, and it had finally stopped. For that moment, I was only thinking, and not thinking about thinking, or thinking about thinking about thinking. Every time my thoughts strayed toward a realization that they were only thinking and not meta-cognizing, they easily and effortlessly drifted back to thinking again.

It was the weirdest moment of my life and one of the best. The fact that I was naked and hot and sweaty with a beautiful woman and stoned off my ass helped. I had found the exact perfect mixture of sex, drugs, and rock and roll to put me into the place that my mind had sought since the day I emerged from the womb.

It ended, gradually, thoughts about thoughts seeping in and then flowing as naturally as they ever had. "Wow," I said.

"You too?" she said.

"Totally."

"That's what I come here for," she said. "If I'm lucky, I get a few minutes like that here every year. Last time was three years ago, though. I went home and quit my job and spent three hours a day learning to dance while I spent the rest of my time teaching small-engine repair at a half way house for rehabilitated juvenile offenders."

"Really?" I said.

"Totally."

"What job did you quit?"

"I was CTO for a company that made efficient cooling systems for data centers. It had some really interesting, nerdy thermodynamic problems to chew through, but at the end of the day, I was just trying to figure out how to game entropy, and that's a game of incremental improvements. I wanted to do stuff that was big and cool and weird and that I could point to and say, 'I did that.' Some of my students were knuckleheads, a few were psychos, but most of them were just broken kids that I helped to put together, even a little. And a few of them were amazing, learned everything I taught them and then some, taught me things I'd never suspected, went on to do amazing things. It turns out that teaching is one of those things like raising a kid or working out—sometimes amazing, often difficult and painful, but, in hindsight, amazing."

"Have you got a kid?"

She laughed. "Maya. She's thirteen. Spending the week with her dad in Arizona."

"I had no idea," I said. "You don't talk about her much."

"I talk about her all the time," she said. "But not on the Playa. That's a kind of vacation from my other life. She keeps asking me to come out. I guess I'll have to bring her some year, but not to the Fourth. Too crazy. And it's my Blight time."

"Your name's not Blight, is it?"

"Nope," she said. I grinned and smacked her butt, playfully. She pinched my thigh, hard enough to make me yelp. "What do you do?" she said. I hated that question.

"Not much," I said. "Got in with a start-up in the nineties, made enough to pay cash for my house and then some. I do a little contract coding and the rest of the time, I just do whatever I feel like. Spend a lot of time at the hackerspace. You know Minus?"

"Yeah. Are you seriously rich?"

"No," I said. "I'm just, I don't know what you'd call it—I'm rich enough. Enough that I don't have to worry about money for the rest of my life, so long as I don't want much, and I don't. I'm a pretty simple guy."

"I can tell," she said. "Took one look at you and said, that is one simple son of a bitch."

"Yeah," I said. "Somehow, I thought this life would be a lot more interesting than it turned out to be."

"Obviously."

"Obviously."

"So volunteer. Do something meaningful with your life. Take in a foster kid. Walk dogs for cancer patients."

"Yeah," I said.

She kissed my shin, then bent back my little toe and gave it a twist. "Just do something, Greg. I mean, you may not get total satori out of it, but sitting around on your butt, doing nothing, of course that's shit. Be smart."

"Yeah," I said.

"Oh, hell," she said. She got up on her knees and then toppled forward onto me. "Do what you want, you're an adult."

"I am of adult age," I said. "As to my adulthood—"

"You and all the rest of us."

We lay there some more. The noise outside was more frenetic than ever, a pounding, throbbing relentless mash of beats and screams and gunshots and explosions.

"Let's go see it," she said, and we staggered out into the night.

The sun was rising when she said, "I don't think happiness is something you're supposed to have, it's something you're supposed to want."

"Whoa," I said, from the patch of ground where I was spread-eagled, dusty, and chilled as the sky turned from bruisey purple to gaudy pink.

She pinched me from where she lay, head to head above me. I was getting used to her pinches, starting to understand their nuances. That was a friendly one. In my judgment, anyway.

"Don't be smart. Look, whatever else happiness is, it's also some kind of chemical reaction. Your body making and experiencing a cocktail of hormones and other molecules in response to stimulus. Brain reward. A thing that feels good when you do it. We've had millions of years of evolution that gave a reproductive edge to people who experienced pleasure when something pro-survival happened. Those individuals did more of whatever made them happy, and if what they were doing more of gave them more and hardier offspring, then they passed this on."

"Yes," I said. "Sure. At some level, that's true of all our emotions, I guess."

"I don't know about that," she said. "I'm just talking about happiness. The thing is, doing stuff is pro-survival—seeking food, seeking mates, protecting children, thinking up better ways to hide from predators . . . Sitting still and doing nothing is almost never pro-survival, because the rest of the world is running around, coming up with strategies to outbreed you, to outcompete you for food and territory . . . if you stay still, they'll race past you."

"Or race backward," I said.

"Yeah, there's always the chance that if you do something, it'll be the wrong thing. But there's zero chance that doing nothing will be the right thing. Stop interrupting me, anyways." She pinched me again. This one was less affectionate. I didn't mind. The sun was rising. "So if being happy is what you seek, and you attain it, you stop seeking. So the reward has to return to the mean. Happiness must fade. Otherwise, you'd just lie around, blissed out and childless, until a tiger ate you."

"Have you hacked my webcam or something?"

"Not everything is about you," she said.

"Fine," I said. "I accept your hypothesis for now. So happiness isn't a state of being, instead it's a sometimes-glimpsed mirage on the horizon, drawing us forward."

"You're such a fucking poet. It's a carrot dangling from a stick, and we're the jackasses plodding after it. We'll never get it though."

"I don't know," I said. "I think I just came pretty close."

And that earned me another kiss, and a pinch, too. But it was a friendly one.

Blight and her campmates pulled up stakes shortly thereafter. I helped them load their guns and their ordnance and their coolers and bales of costumes and kegs and gray water and duffel bags and trash bags and flaccid sun showers and collapsed shade structures, lashing about half of it to the outside of their vehicles under crackling blue tarps. Her crew had a storage locker in Reno where they'd leave most of the haul, only taking personal gear all the way home.

Working my muscles felt good after a long, wakeful night of dancing and screwing and lying around, and when we fell into a bucket-brigade rhythm, I tumbled directly into the zone of blessed, tired physical exertion, a kind of weary, all-consuming dance of moving, lifting, passing, turning, moving . . . and before I knew it, the dawn was advanced enough to have me sweating big rings around my pits and the cars were loaded, and Blight was in my arms, giving me a long hug that continued until our bodies melted together.

She gave me a soft, dry kiss and said, "Go chase some happiness."

"You too," I said. "See you at the burn."

She pinched me again, a friendly one. We'd see each other come Labor Day weekend, assuming we could locate each other in the sixty-thousand-person crush of burning man. After my intimate, two-hundred-person Fourth of Juplaya, I could hardly conceive of such a thing, though with any luck, I'd be spending it in the world's first 3D-printed yurt. Or igloo.

Pug got us early admission to the burn. From the turnoff, it seemed nearly as empty as it had when we'd been there in July, but by the time we reached the main gate, it was obvious that this was a very different sort of thing from the Fourth.

Once we'd submitted to a search—a search!—of the van and the trailer and been sternly warned—by a huge, hairy dude wearing the bottom half of a furry monkey costume, a negligee, and a ranger's hat—to stay under 5 mph to keep the dust plumes down, we were crawling forward. No GPS this time. During the months that we'd spent in L.A. wondering whether the Gadget was hung up, crashed, stuck, blown away, or stolen, so many vehicles had passed this way that they'd worn an unmistakable road into the Playa, hedged with orange-tipped surveyors' stakes and porta-sans.

The sun was straight overhead, the air-conditioning wheezing as we crept along, and even though the sprawling, circular shape of black rock City was only 10 percent full, we could already make it out against the empty desert-scape. In the middle of it all stood the man, a huge, angular neopagan idol, destined for immolation in a week's time.

Pug had been e-mailing back and forth with the Borg—the burning man organization, a weird cult of freak bureaucrats who got off on running this circus—all summer, and he was assured that our little paddock had been left undisturbed. If all went according to plan, we'd drop off the van, unpack it and set up camp, then haul bike-trailers over to the paddock and find out how the Gadget had fared over the summer. I was 90 percent convinced that it had blown over and died the minute we left the desert and had been lying uselessly ever since. We'd brought along some conveniences that could convert the back of the van into a bedroom if it came to that, but we were absolutely committed to sleeping in the yurt. Igloo.

We set off as quickly as we could, in goggles and painter's masks against the light, blowing dust. Most of the campsites were empty and we were able to slice a cord across black rock City's silver-dollar, straight out to walk-in camp, where there were only a few tents pitched. Pug assured me that it would be carpeted in tents within a couple of days.

Just past walk-in camp, we came upon the Gadget.

It had changed color. The relentless sun and alkali dust had turned the ceramic/polymer legs, sails, and base into the weathered no-color of driftwood. As we came upon it, the solar panels flickered in the sun and then did their dust-shedding routine, spinning like a drum-major's batons and snapping to with an audible crack, and their dust sifted down into the feedstock hoppers, and then over them. They were full. Seeing that, I felt a moment's heartsickness—if they were covered with dust, there'd be no power. The Gadget must not have been printing.

But that only lasted a moment—just long enough to take in what I should have seen immediately. The Gadget's paddock was mounded with tiles.

"It's like a bar chart of the prevailing winds," Pug said. I instantly grasped what he meant—the mounds were uneven, and the hills represented the places where the wind had blown the Gadget most frequently. I snapped several photos before we swarmed over the Gadget to run its diagnostics.

According to its logs, it had printed 413 tiles—enough for two yurts, and nearly double what we'd anticipated. The data would be a delicious puzzle to sort through after the burn. Had the days been longer? The printer more efficient?

We started to load the trailers. It was going to take several trips to transport all the tiles, and then we'd have to walk the Gadget itself over, set up a new paddock for it on our site, and then we'd have to start assembling the yurt. Yurts! It was going to be punishing, physical, backbreaking work, but a crackle of elation shot through us at the thought of it. It had worked!

"Master, the creature lives!" I bellowed, in my best Igor, and Pug shook his head and let fly with a perfect mad-scientist cackle.

We led the Gadget back by means of a pair of guide ropes, pulling for all we were worth on them, tacking into the wind and zigzagging across the Playa, stumbling over campsites and nearly impaling ourselves on rebar tent pegs. People stopped what they were doing to watch, as though we were proud hunters returning with a kill, and they waved at us and squinted behind their goggles, trying to make sense of this strange centaur with its glinting single eye high above its back.

We staked it into the ground on our site on a much shorter tether and dusted it off with stiff paintbrushes, working the dust out of the cracks and joints, mostly on general principle and in order to spruce it up for public viewing. It had been running with amazing efficiency despite the dust all summer, after all.

"Ready to get puzzling?" Pug said.

"Aye, Cap'n," I said.

We hadn't been sure how many tiles we'd get out of the Gadget over the course of the summer. They came in three interlocking sizes, in the Golden ratio, each snapping together in four different ways. Figuring out the optimal shape for any given number of panels was one of those gnarly, NP-complete computer science problems that would take more computational cycles than remained in the universe's lifetime to solve definitively. We'd come up with a bunch of variations on the basic design (it did look more like an igloo than a yurt, although truth be told it looked not very much like either) in a little sim, but were always being surprised by new ways of expanding the volume using surprisingly small numbers of tiles.

We sorted the printouts by size in mounds and counted them, plugging the numbers into the sim and stepping through different possibilities for shelter design. There was a scaling problem—at a certain height/diameter ratio, you had to start exponentially increasing the number of tiles in order to attain linear gains in volume— but how big was big enough? After a good-natured argument that involved a lot of squinting into phone screens against the intense glare of the high sun, we picked out two designs and set to work building them.

Pug's arm was pretty much back to normal, but he still worked slower than me and blamed it on his arm rather than admitting that he'd picked a less-efficient design. I was half done, and he was much less than half done, when Blight wandered into camp.

"Holy shit," she said. "You did it!"

I threw my arms around her as she leaped over the knee-high wall of my structure, kicking it slightly askew. She was wearing her familiar sleeveless overalls, but she'd chopped her hair to a short electric-blue fuzz that nuzzled against my cheek. A moment later, another pair of arms wrapped around us and I smelled Pug's work sweat and felt his strong embrace. We shared a long, three-sided hug and then disentangled ourselves and Pug and I let fly with a superheated sitrep on the Gadget's astounding debut performance.

She inspected the stacks of tiles and the walls we'd built thus far. "You guys, this is insane. I didn't want to say anything, you know, but I never bought this. I thought your gizmo"—Pug and I both broke in and said Gadget, in unison and she gave us each the finger, using both hands—"would blow over on its side in a windstorm, break something important, and end up buried in its own dune."

"Yeah," I said. "I had nightmares about that, too."

"Not me," said Pug. "I knew from day one that this would work. It's all so fault tolerant, it all fails so gracefully."

"You're telling me that you never once pictured yourself finding a pile of half-buried, smashed parts?"

He gave me that serene look of his. "I had faith," he said. "It's a gadget. It does what it does. Mechanism A acts on Mechanism B acts on Mechanism C. If you understand what A, B, and C do, you know what the Gadget does."

Blight and I both spoke at the same time in our rush to explain what was wrong with this, but he held his hands up and silenced us.

"Talk all you want about chaos and sensitivity to initial conditions, but here's the thing: I thought the Gadget would work, and here we are, with a working Gadget. Existence proofs always trump theory. That's engineering."

"Fine," I said. "I can't really argue with that."

He patted me on the head. "It's okay, dude. From the day I met you, I've known that you are a glass-half-empty-and-maybe-poisonous guy. The Playa will beat that out of you."

"I'll help," Blight said, and pinched my nipple. I'd forgotten about her pinches. I found that I'd missed them. "I hate you both," I said. Pug patted me on the head again and blight kissed me on the cheek. "Let me finish unpacking and I'll come back and help you with your Playa-tetris, okay?"

Looking back on it now, I think the biggest surprise was just how hard it was to figure out how to get the structure just right. If you fitted a tile the wrong way in row three, it wasn't immediately apparent until row five or six, and you'd have to take them all down and start over again. Pug said it reminded him of knitting, something he'd tried for a couple years.

"It's just that it's your first time," Blight said, as she clicked a tile into place. "The first time you put together a wall of lego you screwed it up, too. You've been living with this idea for so long, you forgot that you've never actually dealt with its reality."

We clicked and unclicked, and a pile of broken tiles grew to one side of the site. As we got near the end, it became clear that this was going to be a close thing—what had started as a surplus of tiles had been turned into a near shortage thanks to our breaking. Some of that had been our fault—the tiles wanted to be finessed into place, not forced, and it was hard to keep a gentle approach as the day lengthened and the frustration mounted—but some was pure material defect, places where too many impurities had ganged up along a single seam, waiting to fracture at the slightest pressure, creating a razor-sharp, honeycombed gypsum blade that always seemed to find exposed wrists above the glove line. A few times, chips splintered off and flew into my face. The goggles deflected most of these, but one drew blood from the precise tip of my nose.

In the end, we were three—three!—tiles short of finishing; two from mine, one from Pug's. The sun had set, and we'd been working by head-lamp and the van's headlights. The gaps stared at us.

"Well, shit," Pug said, with feeling.

I picked through our pile of postmodern potsherds, looking for any salvageable pieces. There weren't. I knew there weren't, but I looked anyway. I'd become a sort of puzzle-assembling machine and I couldn't stop now that I was so close to the end. It was the punch line to a terrible joke.

"What are you two so freaked out about?" Blight said. "Just throw a tarp over it."

We both looked at each other. "Blight—" Pug began, then stopped.

"We don't want to cover these with tarps," I said. "We want to show them off! We want everyone to see our totally awesome project! We want them to see how we made bricks out of dust and sunshine!"

"Um, yeah," Blight said. "I get that. But you can use the tarps for tonight, and print out your missing pieces tomorrow, right?"

We both stared at each other, dumbfounded.

"Uh," I said.

Pug facepalmed, hard enough that I heard his glove smacking into his nose. When he took his hand away, his goggles were askew, half pushed up his forehead.

"I'll get the tarps," I said.

They came. First in trickles, then in droves. Word got around the Playa: these guys have 3D printed their own yurt. Or igloo.

Many just cruised by, felt the smooth finish of the structures, explored the tight seams with their fingernails, picked up a shard of cracked tile to take away as a souvenir. They danced with the Gadget as it blew back and forth across its little tethered paddock, and if they were lucky enough to see it dropping a finished tile to the desert, they picked it up and marveled at it.

It wasn't an unequivocal success, though. One old-timer came by, a wizened and wrinkled burner with a wild beard and a tan the color of old leather—he was perfectly naked and so unself-conscious about it that I ceased to notice it about eight seconds into our conversation—and said, "Can I ask you something?"

"Sure," I said.

"Well, I was just wondering how you turn these bricks of yours back into dust when you're done with them?"

"What do you mean?"

"Leave no trace," he said. His eyes glittered behind his goggles. "Leave no trace" was rule number eight of the ten hallowed inviolable holy rules of burning man. I suppose I must have read them at some point, but mostly I came into contact with them by means of burnier-than-thou dialogues with old-timers—or anxious, status-conscious noobs—who wanted to point out all the ways in which my burn was the wrong sort of burn.

"Not following you," I said, though I could see where this was going.

"What are you going to do with all this stuff when you're done with it? How are you going to turn your ceramics back into dust?"

"I don't think we can," I said.

"Ah," he said, with the air of someone who was winning the argument. "Didn't think so. You going to leave this here?"

"No," I said. "We'll take it down and truck it out. Leave no trace, right?"

"But you're taking away some of the desert with you. Do that enough, where will we be?"

Yep. Just about where I figured this was going. "How much Playa dust do you take home in your"—I was about to say *clothes*—"car?"

"Not one bit more than I can help bringing. It's not our desert to take away with us. You've got sixty thousand people here. They start doing what you're doing, next thing you know, the whole place starts to vanish."

I opened my mouth. Shut it. Opened it again.

"Have you got any idea of the overall volume of gypsum dust in the black rock desert? I mean, relative to the amount of dust that goes into one of these?" I patted the side of the structure—we'd started calling them *yurtgloos.*

"I knew you'd say that," he said, eyes glittering and beard swinging. "They said that about the ocean. Now we've got the Great Pacific Garbage Patch. They said it about space, and now low Earth orbit is one stray screwdriver handle away from a cascade that wipes out every communications satellite and turns the Lagrange points into free-fire zones. Anywhere you go in history, there's someone dumping something or taking something away and claiming that the demand'll never outstrip the supply. That's probably what the first goat-herder said when he turned his flock out on the Sahara plains. 'No way these critters could ever eat this huge plot down to nothing.' Now it's the Sahara!"

I had to admit he had a point.

"Look," I said. "This is the first time anyone's tried this. Burners have been changing the desert for years. They excavate tons of the surface every year to get rid of the burn platform and the scars from the big fires. Maybe we'll have to cap how many robots run every year, but you know, it's kind of a renewable resource. Dust blows in all the time, over the hills and down the road. It goes down for yards and yards. They mined around here for a century and didn't make a dent in it. The only thing that doesn't change the world is a corpse. People who are alive change the planet. That's part of the deal. How about if we try this thing for a while and see whether it's a problem, instead of declaring it a disaster before it's gotten started?"

He gave me a withering look. "Oh yeah, I've heard that one before. 'Give it time, see how it goes!' that's what they said in Fukushima. That's what they said when they green-lit thalidomide. That's what they said at Kristallnacht."

"I don't think they said that about Kristallnacht," I said, and turned on my heel. Decades on the Internet had taught me that Godwin's law was ironclad: as soon as the comparisons to Nazis or Hitler came out, the discussion was over. He shouted something at my back, but I couldn't hear it over the wub-wub of an art car that turned the corner at that moment, a huge party bus/pirate ship with three decks of throbbing dancers and a PA system that could shatter glass.

But that conversation stayed with me. He was a pushy, self-righteous prig, but that didn't mean he was wrong. Necessarily.

If you're a burner, you know what happened next. We kickstarted an entire flock of Gadgets by Christmas; built them through the spring, and trucked them out in a pair of sixteen-wheelers for the next Fourth, along with a crew of wranglers who'd helped us build them. It was the biggest Fourth of Juplaya ever and there were plenty of old-timers who still say we ruined it. It's true that there was a lot less shooting and a lot more lens-polishing that year.

The best part was the variation. Our three basic tiles could be combined to make an infinite variety of yurtgloos, but to be honest, you'd be hard-pressed to tell one from another. On our wiki, a group of topology geeks went bananas designing a whole range of shapes that interlocked within our three, making it possible to build crazy stuff—turrets, staircases, trusses. Someone showed how the polyominoes could be interlocked to make a playground slide and sure enough, come the summer, there was a huge one, with a ladder and a scaffolding of support, and damned if it wasn't an amazing ride, once it was ground down to a slippery sheen with a disc-polisher.

The next year, there were whole swaths of Black Rock City that were built out of dust-bricks, as they were called by that time. The back lash was predictable, but it still smarted. We were called unimaginative suburbanites in tract-house gated communities, an environmental catastrophe—that old naked guy turned out to be a prophet as well as a crank—and a blight on the landscape.

Blight especially loved this last. She brought Maya, her daughter, to the Playa that year, and the two of them built the most amazing, most ambitious yurtgloo you'd ever seen, a three-story, curvy, bulbous thing whose surfaces were finely etched with poems and doodles that she'd fed to the paramaterizer in the 3D-modeling software onboard her Gadgets. The edges of the glyphs were so sharp at first that you could literally cut yourself on them, and before the wind and dust wore them down, they cast amazing shadows down into the gullies of the carve-outs when the sun was rising and setting, turning the wall into a madman's diary of scribbles and words.

Maya was indifferent to the haters. She was fifteen and was a trouble-seeking missile with a gift for putting creepers in their place that I was in absolute awe of. I watched her fend off the advances of fratty jocks, weird old dudes like me, and saucer-eyed spacemen dancing to the distant, omni-present thunder of EDM.

"You raised her right, huh?" I said to Blight.

Blight shrugged. "Look, it sucks to be a fifteen-year-old girl. All that attention, it just gets in the way of figuring out who you are. I'm glad she's good at this, but I wish she didn't have to do it. I wish she could just have a burn like the rest of us."

I put my arm around her shoulders. "Yeah," I said. "Yeah, that sucks."

"It does. Plus, I don't want to get high because I feel like I've got to keep an eye on her all the time and—" She threw her hands up in the air and looked angrily at the white-hot sky.

"You're feeling guilty for bringing her, aren't you?"

"No, Dr. Freud. I'm feeling guilty for regretting that I brought her."

"Are you sure you're not feeling guilty for regretting that you feel guilty that you brought her?"

She pinched me. "Be serious."

I wiped the smile off my face. "Blight, I love you." I'd said it the first time on a visit to her place just after the last burn, and she'd been literally speechless for a good ten minutes. Ever since, it had become my go-to trick for winning arguments.

She pinched me hard in the arm. I rubbed the sore spot—every time I came back from a visit to see her, I had bruises the size of grapefruits and the color of the last moment of sunset on both shoulders.

Maya ran past, pulling a giant stunt kite behind her. She'd spent the whole burn teaching herself new tricks with it and she could do stuff with it that I never would have believed. We cheered her on as she got it into the sky.

"She's an amazing kid," I said. "Makes me wish I'd had one. I would have, if I'd known she'd turn out like that."

Maya's dad was a city manager for a small town in Arizona that was entirely dependent on imported water. He came out twice a year for visits and Maya spent three weeks every summer and alternate Christmases and Easters with him, always returning with a litany of complaints about the sheer tedium of golf courses and edge-city megamalls. I'd never met him but he sounded like a good guy, if a little on the boring side.

"Never too late," Blight said. "Go find yourself some nubile twenty-five-year-old and get her gravid with your child."

"What would I want with one of those flashy new models? I've got an American classic here." I gave her another squeeze, and she gave me another pinch.

"Nothing smoother than an automotive comparison, fella."

"It was meant as a compliment."

"I know," she said. "Fine. Well, then, you could always come down and spend some time when Maya is around, instead of planning your visits around her trips to see her dad. There's plenty of parenting to go around on that one, and I could use a break from time to time."

I suddenly felt very serious. Something about being on the Playa made it seem like anything was possible. I had to literally bite my tongue to stop myself from proposing marriage. Instead, I said, "That sounds like a very good plan. I shall take you up on it, I think."

She drew her fingers back to pinch me, but instead, she dragged me to her and gave me a long, wet, deep kiss.

"Ew," shouted Maya as she buzzed us, now riding a lowrider Playa bike covered in fun fur and duct tape. She circled us twice, throwing up a fan-tail of dust, then screeched to a hockey stop that buried our feet in a small dune that rode ahead of her front wheel like a bow wave.

"You've gone native, kiddo," I said.

She gave me a hilarious little-girl look and said, "Are you my new daddy? Mommy says you're her favorite of all my uncles, and there's so many of them."

Blight pounced on her and bore her to the ground, where they rolled like a pair of fighting kittens, all tickles and squeals and outflung legs and arms. It ended with Maya pinned under Blight's forearms and knees.

"I brought you into this world," she said, panting. "I can take you out of it, too."

Maya closed her eyes and then opened them again, wide as saucers. "I'm sorry, Mom," she said. "I guess I took it too far. I love you, Mom."

Blight relaxed a single millibar and Maya squirmed with the loose-jointed fluidity of wasted youth and bounced to her toes, leaped on her bike and shouted, "Suckerrrr!," as she pedaled away a good ten yards, then did a BMX-style front-wheel stand and spun back around to face us. "Bye-ee!"

"Be back for dinner!" Blight shouted.

" 'Kay, Mom!"

The two stared at each other through the blowing dust.

"He's pretty good," Maya shouted again. "You can keep him."

Blight took a step toward her. Maya grinned fearlessly. "Love you, Mom! Don't worry, I won't get into any trouble."

She jammed down on the pedals and powered off toward open Playa.

"You appear to have given birth to the Tasmanian Devil," I said.

"Shut up, amateur," she said. "This is what they're supposed to be like at fifteen. I'd be worried otherwise."

By the time they sent Pug home to die, Blight was practically living with me—after getting laid off and going freelance, there was no reason not to. I gave her the whole garage to use as workspace—parked my car in the driveway and ran an extension cord out to it to charge it overnight—but half the time she worked at Minus. Its latest incarnation was amazing, a former L.A. Department of Water and Power Sub-station that was in bankruptcy limbo. After privatization and failure, the trustees had inventoried its assets and found that it was sitting on all these mothballed sub-stations and offered them out on cheap short-term leases. Minus was practically a cathedral in those days, with thirty-foot ceilings, catwalks, even two behemoth dynamos that had been saved from the scrappers out of pure nostalgia. They gave the place a theatrical, steampunk air—until someone decided to paint them safety orange with hot-pink highlights, which looked pretty damned cool and pop art, but spoiled the theater of the thing somewhat.

Pug was no idiot—not like me. So when he found a lump and asked the doctor to look into it and spent a week fretting about it, he'd told me and Blight and a bunch of his other friends and did a week of staying on people's couches and tinkering with the Gadget and going to yoga class and cooking elaborate meals with weird themes—like the all-coconut dinner that included coconut chicken over coconut rice with coconut flan for dessert. And he arranged for me to drive him to the doctor's office for his follow-up visit.

We joked nervously all the way to the waiting room, then fell silent. We declined to be paged by the receptionist and sat down instead, looking from the big, weird, soothing animation on the fifty-inch TV to the health pamphlets that invited us to breathe on them or lick them for instant analysis and follow-up recommendations. Some of them seemed to have been licked already.

"Scott Zrubek?" said the receptionist from the door, looking from her screen to Pug's face.

"That's my slave name," he said to me as he got up and crossed to her. "Forget you ever heard it."

Twenty minutes later, he was back with a big white smile that went all the way to the corners of his eyes. I stood up and made a question of my raised eyebrows. He high-fived me and we went out to the car. The nurse who'd brought him back watched us go from the window, a worried look on her face, and that should have tipped me off.

"All okay, then," I said. "So now where?"

"Let's get some lunch," he said. "There's a chicken shack up on the left; they serve the best chili fries."

It was one of those drive-in places where the servers clipped trays to the windows and served your food on them, a retro-revival thing that made me glad I had vinyl seats.

"What a relief," I said, slurping on my shake. They had tiger-tail ice cream—a mix of orange and black licorice flavor—and Pug had convinced me to try it in a shake. He'd been right—it was amazing.

"Uh-huh," he said. "About that."

"About what?"

"Doc says it's in my liver and pancreas. I can do chemo and radiotherapy, but that'll just tack a couple months on, and they won't be good months. Doc says it's the kind of cancer where, when a doctor gets it, they refuse treatment."

I pulled the car over to the side of the road. I couldn't bring myself to turn my head.

"Pug," I said. "I'm so sorry—"

He put his hand on mine and I shut up. I could hear his breathing, a little fast, a little shallow. My friend was keeping it together so much better than I was, but he was the one with the death sentence.

"Remember what you told me about the curve?" he said. "Back when you thought you had cancer? The older you get, the more friends will die. It's just statistics. No reason I shouldn't be the next statistic."

"But you're only thirty—"

"Thirty-three," he said. "A little lower on the curve, but not unheard of." He breathed awhile longer. "Not a bad run."

"Pug," I said, but he squeezed my hand.

"If the next sentence to come out of your mouth includes the words 'spontaneous remission,' I'm going upside your head with a roll of quarters. That's the province of the Smurfs' Family Christmas, not the real world. And don't talk to me about having a positive attitude. The reason all those who've died of cancer croaked is because they had cancer, not because they were too gloomy."

"How about Laura?" I said. They'd been dating on and off for a couple months. She seemed nice. Did some kind of investment analysis for an ethical fund.

"Oh," he said. "Yeah. Don't suppose that was going to be serious. Huh. What do you think—tell her I'm dying, then break up; break up and then tell her I'm dying; or just break up?"

"What about telling her you're"—I swallowed—"dying, then giving her the choice?"

"What choice? Getting married? Dude, it's not like I've got a life-insurance policy. She's a nice person. Doesn't need to be widowed at thirty-two." He took his hand back. "Could you drive?"

When we got onto the 10, he chuckled. "Got some good birthdays in at least. Twenty-seven, that's a cube. Twenty-nine, prime. Thirty-one, prime. Thirty-two, a power of two. Thirty-three, a palindrome. It's pretty much all downhill from here."

"Thirty-six is a square," I said.

"Square," he said. "Come on, a square? Don't kid yourself, the good ones are all in that twenty-seven to thirty-three range. I got a square at twenty-five. How many squares does a man need?"

"Damn, you're weird," I said.

"Too weird to live, too beautiful to die." He thumped his chest. "Well, apparently not." He sighed. "Shit. Well, that happened."

"Look, if there's anything you need, let me know," I said. "I'm here for you."

"You're a prince. But you know what, this isn't the worst way to go, to tell the truth. I get a couple months to say good-bye, put things in order, but I don't have to lie around groaning and turning into a walking skeleton for six months while my body eats itself. It's the best of both worlds."

My mouth was suddenly too dry to talk. I dry-swallowed a few times, squeezed my eyes shut hard, put the car in gear, and swung into traffic. We didn't speak the rest of the way to Pug's. When we pulled up out front, I blurted, "You can come and stay with me, if you want. I mean, being alone—"

"Thanks," he said. He'd gone a little gray. "Not today, all right?"

Blight wasn't home when I got back, but Maya was. I'd forgotten she was coming to stay. She'd graduated the year before and had decided to do a year on the road with her net-friends, which was all the rage with her generation, the second consecutive cadre of no-job/no-hope kids to graduate from America's flagging high schools. They'd borrowed a bunch of tricks from their predecessors, most notably a total refusal to incur any student debt and a taste for free online courses in every subject from astronomy to science fiction literature—and especially things like agriculture and cookery, which was a critical part of their forager lifestyle.

Maya had cycled to my place from the Greyhound depot, using some kind of social bike-share that I hadn't ever heard of. On the way, she'd stopped and harvested berries, tubers, herbs, and some soft-but-serviceable citrus fruit. "The world'll feed you, if you let it," she said, carefully spitting grapefruit seeds into her hand. She'd scatter them later, on the next leg of the bike journey. "Especially in L.A. all that subsidized pork-barrel water from the Colorado River's good for something."

"Sounds like you're having a hell of a time," I said.

"Better than you," she said. "You look like chiseled shit." She grabbed my shoulders and peered into my eyes, searched my face. It struck me how much like her mom she looked, despite the careful checkerboard of colored zinc paste that covered her features in dazzle-patterns that fooled facial-recognition algorithms and fended off the brutal, glaring sun.

"Thanks," I said, squirming away, digging a glass bottle of cold-brewed coffee out of the fridge.

"Seriously," she said, pacing me around the little kitchen. "What's going on? Everything okay with mom?"

"Your mother's fine," I said. "I'm fine."

"So why do you look like you just found out you're going to have to bury euthanized dogs for community service?"

"Is that real?"

"The dogs? Yeah. You get it a lot in the Midwest. Lot of feral dogs around Ohio and Indiana. They round 'em up, gas 'em, and stack 'em. It's pretty much the number one vagrancy penalty. Makes an impression."

"Jesus."

"Stop changing the subject. What's going on, Greg?"

I poured myself some coffee, added ice, and then dribbled in a couple of teaspoons' worth of half-and-half, watching the gorgeous fluid dynamics of the heavy cream roiling in the dark brown liquid.

"Come on, Greg," she said, taking the glass from me and draining half of it in one go. Her eyes widened a little. "That's good."

"It's not my story to tell," I said.

"Whose story is it?"

I turned back to the fridge to get out the cold-brew bottle again. "Dude, this is weak. Come on, shared pain is lessened, shared joy is increased. Don't be such a guy. Talk."

"You remember Pug?"

She rolled her eyes with teenage eloquence. "Yes, I remember Pug."

I heaved in a breath, heaved it out again. Tried to find the words. Didn't need to, as it turned out.

She blinked a couple times. "How long has he got?"

"Couple months," I said. "Longer, if he takes treatment. But not much longer. And he's not going to take it anyway."

"Good," she said. "That's a bad trade anyway." She sat down in one of my vintage vinyl starburst-upholstered kitchen chairs—a trophy of diligent L.A. yard-saling, with a matching chrome-rimmed table. She looked down into her coffee, which had gone a thick, uniform pale brown color. "I'm sorry to hear it, though."

"Yeah," I said. "Yeah. Me too." I sat with her.

"What's he going to do now?"

I shrugged. "I guess he's got to figure that out."

"He should do something big," she said, under her breath, still staring into the drink. "Something huge. Think about it—it doesn't matter if he fucks it up. Doesn't matter if he goes broke or whatever. It's his last chance, you know?"

"I guess," I said. "I think it's really up to him, though. They're his last months."

"Bullshit," she said. "They're our last months with him. He's going to turn into ashes and vanish. We're going to be left on this ball of dirt for however many years we've got left. He's got a duty to try and make something of it with whatever time he's got left. Something for us to carry on. Come on, Greg, think about it. What do you do here, anyway? Try to live as lightly as possible, right? Just keep your head down, try not to outspend that little precious lump of dead money you lucked into so that you can truck on into the grave. You and mom and Pug, you all 'know' that humans aren't really needed on Earth anymore, that robots can do all the work and that artificial life forms called corporations can harvest all the profit, so you're just hiding under the floorboards and hoping that it doesn't all cave in before you croak."

"Maya—"

"And don't you dare give me any bullshit about generational politics and demographics and youthful rage and all that crap. Things are true or they aren't, no matter how old the person saying them happens to be." She drained her drink. "And you know it."

I set down my glass and held my hands over my head. "I surrender. You're right. I got nothing better to do, and certainly Pug doesn't. So, tell me, wise one, what should we be doing?"

Her veneer of outraged confidence cracked a tiny bit. "Fucked if I know. Solve world hunger. Invent a perpetual motion machine. Colonize the moon."

We wrote them on the whiteboard wall at Pug's place. He'd painted the wall with dry-erase paint when he first moved into the little house in Culver City, putting it where the TV would have gone a few decades before, and since then it had been covered with so much dry-erase ink and wiped clean so many times that there were bald patches where the underlying paint was showing through, stained by the markers that had strayed too close to no-man's-land. We avoided those patches and wrote:

SOLVE WORLD HUNGER
PERPETUAL MOTION MACHINE
MOON COLONY

The first one to go was the perpetual motion machine. "It's just stupid," Pug said. "I'm an engineer, not a metaphysician. If I'm going to do something with the rest of my life, it has to be at least possible, even if it's implausible."

"When you have eliminated the impossible, whatever remains, however implausible, must be—"

"How have you chosen your projects before?" Maya said. She and Blight sat in beanbag chairs on opposite sides of the room, pointedly watching the wall and not each other.

"They chose me," Pug said. She made a wet, rude noise. "Seriously. It never came up. Any time I was really working my nuts off on something, sweating over it, that was the exact moment that some other project demanded that I drop everything, right now, and take care of it. I figure it was the self-destructive part of my brain desperately trying to keep me from finishing anything, hoping to land a Hail Mary distraction pass."

"More like your own self-doubt," Maya said. "Trying to keep you from screwing something up by ensuring that you never finished it."

He stuck his tongue out at her. "Give me strength to withstand the wisdom of teenagers," he said.

"Doesn't matter how old the speaker is, it's the words that matter." She made a gurulike namaste with her hands and then brought them up to her forehead like a yoga instructor reaching for her third eye. Then she stuck her tongue out, too.

"All right, shut up, Yoda. The point is that I eventually figured out how to make that all work for me. I just wrote down the ideas as they came up and stuck them in the 'do-after' file, which means that I always had a huge, huge do-after file waiting for me the second I finished whatever I was on at the time."

"So fine, what's the next on your do-after file."

He shook his head. "Nothing worth my time. Not if it's going to be the last splash. Nothing that's a legacy."

Blight said, "You're just overthinking it, dude. Whatever it is, whip it out. There's no reason to be embarrassed. It'd be much worse to do nothing because nothing was worthy of your final act than to do something that wasn't as enormous as it could have been."

"Believe me, you don't want to know," Pug said. "Seriously."

"Okay, back to our list." She closed her eyes and gave a theatrical shudder. "Look, it's clear that the methods you use to choose a project when you have all the time in the world are going to be different from the method you use when there's almost no time left. So let's get back to this." She drew a line through PERPETUAL MOTION. "I buy your reasons for this one. That leaves MOON COLONY and WORLD HUNGER." She poised her pen over MOON COLONY. "I think we can strike this one. You're not going to get to the moon in a couple of months. And besides, world hunger—"

"Fuck world hunger," Pug said, with feeling.

"Very nice," she said. "Come on, Pug, no one needs to be reminded of what a totally with-it, cynical dude you are. We've all known all along what it had to be. World hunger—"

"Fuck. World. Hunger," Pug repeated.

Blight gave him a narrow-eyed stare. I recognized the signs of an impending eruption. "Pug," I said, "perhaps you could unpack that statement a little?"

"Come on," he said. "Unpack it? Why? You know what it means. Fuck world hunger because the problem with world hunger isn't too many people, or the wrong kind of agriculture, or, for fuck's sake, the idea that we're not doing enough to feed the poor. The problem with world hunger is that rich, powerful governments are more than happy to send guns and money to dictators and despots who'll use food to control their populations and line their pockets. There is no 'world hunger' problem. There's a corruption problem. There's a greed problem. There's a gullibility problem. Every racist fuck who's ever repeated half-baked neo-malthusian horseshit about overpopulation, meaning, of course, that the 'wrong' kind of people are having babies, i.e., poor people who have nothing to lose and don't have to worry about diluting their fortunes and squandering their pensions on too many kids—"

"So there's a corruption problem," I said. "Point taken. How about if we make a solution for the corruption problem, then? Maybe we could build some kind of visualizer that shows you if your Congresscritter is taking campaign contributions from companies and then voting for laws that benefit them?"

"What, you mean like every single one of them?" Maya pushed off the wall she'd been leaning against and took a couple steps toward me. "Get serious, Greg. The average elected official spends at least half of their time in office fund-raising for their next election campaign. They've been trying to fix campaign financing for decades and somehow, the people who depend on corrupt campaign contributions don't want to pass a law limiting corrupt campaign contributions. Knowing that your senator is on the take only helps if the guy running against him isn't also on the take."

"Come on, dude," she said. "The guy is *dying*, you want him to spend his last days making infographics? Why not listicles, too?" She framed a headline with her hands. "Revealed: the ten most corrupt senators! Except that you don't need a data analysis to find the ten most corrupt—they'll just be the ten longest-serving politicians."

"Okay," I said. "Okay, Maya, point taken. So what would you do to fight corruption?"

She got right up in my face, close enough that I could see the fine dark hairs on her upper lip—she and her cohort had rejected the hair removal mania of the previous decade, putting umpteen Brazilian waxers and threaders and laser hair zappers

on the breadline—and smell the smoothie on her breath. "Greg, what are you talking about? Ending corruption? Like there's a version of this society that isn't corrupt?
Corruption isn't the exception, it's the norm. It's baked in. The whole idea of using
markets to figure out who gets what is predicated on corruption—it's a way to paper
over the fact that some people get a lot, most of us get not much, and so we invent a
deus ex machina called market forces that hands out money based on merit. How
do we know that the market is giving it to deserving people? Well, look at all the
money they have! It's just circular reasoning."

"So, what then? Anarchist collectivism? Communism?"

She looked around at all of us. "Duh. Look at you three. You've organized your
whole lives around this weird-ass gift-economy thing where you take care of yourself
and you take care of everyone else."

"Burning man isn't real life," Blight said. "God, I knew I should have waited until you were over eighteen before I took you to the Playa." Her tone was light, but
given their earlier fury at each other, I braced for an explosion.

But Maya kept her cool. "It's a bitch when someone reminds you of all the con-
tradictions in your life, I know. Your discomfort doesn't make what I'm saying any
less true, though. Come on, you all know this is true. Late-stage capitalism isn't re-
formable. It's an idea whose time has passed."

We all stared at one another, a triangle of adulthood with solitary, furious adolescence in the center.

"You're right, Maya. She's right. That's why the only logical choice is the moon
colony."

"You're going to secede from Earth?" Blight said. "Start a colony of anarcho-
syndicalist moon-men?"

"Not at all. What I want is, you know, a gift economy dangling like a carrot, hanging in the sky over all our heads. A better way of living, up there, in sight, forever.
On the moon. If civilization collapses and some chudded-out mutant discovers a
telescope and points it at the moon, she'll see the evidence of what the human race
could be."

"What the hell are you talking about?" I said.

He stood up, groaning a little, the way he'd started to do, and half shuffled to his
bookcase and picked up a 3D-printed miniature of the Gadget, run up on one of
Minus's SLS powder printers. It even had a tiny, optically correct lens that his favorite lab in Germany had supplied; the whole thing had been a premium for a massively successful kickstarter a couple of years before. He handed it to me and its many
legs flexed and rattled as it settled on my palm.

"I want to put Gadgets on the moon. Mod 'em to print moondust, turn 'em loose.
Years will pass. Decades, maybe. But when our kids get to the moon, or maybe Maya's kids, or maybe their kids, they'll find a gift from their ancestors. Something for
nothing. A free goddamned lunch, from the first days of a better nation."

One part of me was almost in tears at the thought, because it was a beautiful one.
But there was another part of me that was violently angry at the idea. Like he was
making fun of the world of the living from his cozy vantage point on the rim of the
valley of death. The two of us had a way of bickering like an old married couple, but
since his diagnosis, every time I felt like I was about to lay into him, I stopped. What

if, what if. What if this was the last thing I said to him? What if he went to his death-bed with my bad-tempered words still ringing in the air between us? I ended up with some kind of bubbling, subcutaneous resentment stew on the boil at all times.

I just looked thoughtfully at the clever little Gadget in my palm. We'd talked about making it functional—a $7 Gorseberry Pi should have had the processing power, and there were plenty of teeny-tiny stepper motors out there, but no one could fig-ure out a way of doing the assembly at scale, so we'd gone with a nonfunctional model.

"Can you print with moondust?"

Pug shrugged his shoulders. "Probably. I know I've read some stuff about it along the way. NASA runs some kind of 'What the fuck do we do with all this moondust?' challenge every year or two—you can order synthetic dust to play around with."

"Pug, I don't think we're going to get a printer on the moon in a couple of months."

"No," he said. "No, I expect I'll be ashes long before you're ready to launch. It's gonna take a lot of doing. We don't know shit about engineering for low-gravity en-vironments, even less about vacuum. And you're going to have to raise the money to get the thing onto the moon, and that's gonna be a lot of mass. Don't forget to give it a giant antenna, because the only way you're going to be able to talk to it is by bouncing shortwave off the moon. Better hope you get a lot of support from people around the equator; that'll be your best way to keep it in range the whole time."

"This isn't a new idea, is it?"

"Honestly? No. Hell no. I've had this as a tickle in the back of my brain for years. The first time we put a Gadget out in the dust for the summer, I was 99 percent certain that we were going to come back and find the thing in pieces. But it worked. And it keeps on getting better. That got me thinking: where's there a lot of dust and not a lot of people? I'd love to stick some of these on Mars, send 'em on ahead, so in a century or two, our great-greats can touch down and build Bradburytown pretty much overnight. Even better, make a self-assembling reprap version, one that can print out copies of itself, and see how fast you can turn any asteroid, dust-ball, or lump of interstellar rock and ice into a Hall of Martian Kings, some assembly required."

None of us said anything for a while.

"When you put it that way, Pug . . ." Blight said.

Pug looked at her and there were bright tears standing in his eyes. Hers, too.

"Oh, Pug," she said.

He covered his face with his hands and sobbed. I was the first one to reach him. I put an arm around his shoulders and he leaned into me, and I felt the weird lump where his dislocation hadn't set properly. He cried for a long time. Long enough for Blight, and then Maya, to come and put their arms around us. Long enough for me to start crying.

When he straightened up, he took the little Gadget out of my hand.

"It's a big universe," he said. "It doesn't give a shit about us. As far as we can tell, there's only us out here. If our grandchildren—your grandchildren, I mean—are go-ing to meet friendly aliens, they're just going to be us."

Pug lived longer than they'd predicted. The doctors said that it was his sense of purpose that kept him alive, which sounded like bullshit to me. Like the stuff he'd railed against when he'd bitten my head off about "Positive attitudes." If having a sense of purpose will keep you alive, then everyone who died of cancer must not have had enough of a sense of purpose.

As Pug would have said, Screw that with an auger.

It was a funny thing about his idea: you told people about it and they just got it. Maybe it was all the Gadgets out on the Playa percolating through the zeitgeist, or maybe it was the age-old sorcerer's apprentice dream of machines that make copies of themselves, or maybe it was the collapse of the Chinese and Indian Mars missions and the bankruptcy of the American company that had been working on the private mission. Maybe it was Pug, or just one of those things.

But they got it.

Which isn't to say that they liked it. Hell no. The day we broke our kickstarter goal for a private fifty-kilo lift to the moon—one-fifth the weight of a standard-issue Gadget, but that was an engineering opportunity, wasn't it?—the United Nations Committee on the Peaceful Uses of Outer Space called a special meeting in Geneva to talk about prohibitions on "environmental degradation of humanity's moon." Like we were going to mess up their nice craters.

The Green Moon Coalition was a weird chimera. On the one hand, you had a kind of axis of paranoid authoritarianism, China and Russia and North Korea and what was left of Greece and Cyprus, all the basket-case countries, and they were convinced that we were a stalking horse for the American spookocracy, striking in the hour of weakness to establish, I don't know, maybe a weapons platform? Maybe a listening post? Maybe a killer earthquake machine? They weren't very coherent on this score.

Say what you will about those weird, paranoid creeps: they sure understood how to play UN procedure. No one could game the UN better except for the USA. If only we'd actually been a front for Big Snoop, maybe they would have had our back.

But that was only to be expected. What I didn't expect was the other half of Green Moon: the environmental movement. I sincerely, seriously doubt that anyone in the politburo or Damascus or the Kremlin or Crete gave the tiniest, inciest shit about the moon's "environment." They just hated and feared us because our government hated and feared them.

But there were people—a lot of people—who thought that the moon had a right to stay "pristine." The first time I encountered this idea—it was on a voice chat with a reporter who had caught a whiff of our online chatter about the project—I couldn't even speak coherently about it.

"Sorry, could you say that again?"

"Doesn't the moon have a right to be left alone, in a pristine state?"

"There's a saying, 'That's not right. It's not even wrong.' The moon doesn't have rights. It's a rock and some dust, and maybe if we're very lucky, there's some ice. And the moon doesn't do 'pristine.' it's been hammered by asteroids for two billion years. Got a surface like a tin can that's been dragged behind a truck for a thousand miles. There's no one there. There's nothing there."

"Except for craters and dust, right?"

"Yes, except for those."

The call developed the kind of silence I recognized as victorious. The reporter clearly felt that she'd scored a point. I mentally rewound it.

"Wait, what? Come on. You're seriously saying that you think that craters and dust need to be preserved? For what?"

"Why shouldn't they?"

"Because they're inanimate matter."

"But it's not your inanimate matter to disturb."

"Look, every time a meteor hits the moon, it disturbs more dust than I'm planning on messing up by, like, a millionfold. Should we be diverting meteors? At what point do we draw a line on nature and say, all right, now it's time for things to stop. This is it. Nature is finished. Any more changes to this would be unnatural."

"Of course not. But are you saying you don't see the difference between a meteor and a machine?"

There was no hesitation. "Human beings have just about terminally screwed up the Earth and now you want to get started on the moon. Wouldn't it be better to figure out how we all want to use the moon before we go there?"

I don't remember how I got out of the call. It wasn't the last time I had that discussion, in any event. Not by a very, very long chalk. They all ended up in the same place.

I don't know if the mustache-and-epaulet club were useful idiots for the deep greens or vice versa, but it was quite a combo.

The one thing we had going for us was the bankruptcy of Mars Shot, the private Mars expedition. They'd invested a ton in the first two stages of the project: a reusable lifting vehicle and a space station for it to rendezvous with. The lifter had been profitable from day one, with a roaring trade in comsat launches. But Mars Shot pumped every dime of profit into Skyhaven, which was meant to be a shipyard for the Burroughs, a one-way, twenty-person Mars rocket with enough technology in its cargo pods to establish a toehold on our neighboring planet. And Skyhaven just turned out to be too goddamned expensive.

I can't fault them. They'd seen Mir and Skylab and decided that they were dead ends, variations on a short-lived theme. Rather than focusing on strength, they opted for metastability: nested, pressurized spheres made of carbon-fiber plastic that could be easily patched and resealed when—not if—it ripped. Free-floating, continuously replenished gummed strips floated in the void between the hulls, distributed by convection currents made by leaking heat from within the structure. They'd be sucked into any breach and seal it. Once an outer hull reached a critical degree of patchiness, a new hull would be inflated within the inner hull, which would be expanded to accommodate it, the inside wall becoming the outside and the outside becoming recyclable junk that could be sliced, gummed, and used for the next generation of patchwork. It was resilient, not stable, and focused on failing well, even at the expense of out-and-out success.

This sounded really good on paper, and even better on video. They had a charismatic engineering lead, Marina Kotov, who'd been laid off from JPL during its final wind-down, and she could talk about it with near-religious zeal. Many were the engineers who went into one of her seminars ready to laugh at the "space condom" and bounded out converts to "fail well, fail cheap, fail fast," which was her battle cry.

For all I know, she was totally right. There were a lot of shakedown problems with the fabric, and one of their suppliers went bust halfway through, leaving them with a partial balloon and nothing they could do about it. Unfortunately for them, the process for making the fabric was patented to hell and back, and the patents were controlled by a speculator who'd cut an exclusive deal with a single company that was a lot better at bidding on patent licenses than it was at making stuff. There was a multi-month scramble while the bankruptcy trustees were placated and a new licensor found, and by then, Skyhaven was in deep shit.

Mars Shot had attracted a load of investment capital and even more in convertible bonds that they'd issued like raffle tickets. Building a profitable, efficient orbit-lifter wasn't cheap—they blew billions on it, sure that they'd be able to make it pay once Skyhaven was done and the Mars Shot was launched. I've seen convincing analysis that suggests that they would never have gotten there—not if they'd had to repay their lenders and make a 10x or 20x exit for their investors.

Bankruptcy solved that. I mean, sure, it wiped out thousands of old people's pensions and destroyed a bunch of the frail humans who'd been clinging to financial stability in a world that only needed banks and robots—people like me. That sucked. It killed people, as surely as Pug's cancer had killed him.

The infrastructure that Mars Shot owned was broken up and sold for parts, each of the lifter vehicles going to different consortia. We thought about kickstarting our own fund to buy one, but figured it would be better to simply buy services from one of the suckers who was lining up to go broke in space. Blight had been a small child during the dot-com crash of the 1990s, but she'd done an AP history presentation on it once, about how it had been the last useful bubble, because it took a bunch of capital that was just being used to generate more capital and turned it into cheap dark fiber bundles and hordes of skilled nerds to fill it with stuff. All the bubbles since had just moved money from the world of the useful into the pockets of the hyper-rich, to be flushed back into the financial casino where it would do nothing except go around and around again, being reengineered by high-speed-trading ex-physicists who should know better.

The dot-com legacy was cheap fiber. Once all the debt had been magically wiped off the books and the investors had abandoned the idea of 10–20x payouts, fiber could be profitable.

Mars Shot's legacy was cheap lift. All it took was a massive subsidy from an overly optimistic market and a bunch of hedgies with an irrational belief in their own financial infallibility and bam, there it was, ten glorious cents on the dollar, and all the lift you could want, at a nice, sustainable price.

It's a good thing there was more than one consortium running lifters to orbit, because our Indonesian launch partner totally chickened out on us a month before launch. They had deep trade ties to Russia and China, and after one of those closed-door plurilateral trade meetings, everyone emerged from the smoke-filled room convinced that nothing destined for the moon should be lifted by any civilized country.

It left me wishing for the millionth time that we really were a front for Uncle Sam. There was a juicy Colombian lift that went up every month like clockwork, and Colombia was the kind of country so deep in America's pocket that they'd do pretty much anything that was required of them. OrbitaColombia SA was lifting all kinds of weird crap that had no business being in space, including a ton of radioisotopes that someone from GE's nuclear division blew the whistle on much later. Still gives me nightmares, the thought of all those offensive nukes going into orbit, the ghost of Ronald Reagan over our heads for the half-life of plutonium.

In the end, we found our home in Brazil. Brazil had a strong environmental movement, but it was the sort of environmental movement that cared about living things, not rocks. My kind of movement, in other words.

We knew Pug's death was coming all along, and we had plenty of warning as he got sicker and the pain got worse. He got a morphine pump, which helped, and then some of his chemist friends helped him out with a supply of high-quality ketamine, which really, really helped. It wasn't like he was going to get addicted or OD. At least, not accidentally.

The last three weeks, he was too sick to get out of bed at all. We moved his bed into the living room and kept the blinds drawn and the lights down. We worked in whispers. Most of the time, he slept. He didn't get thin the way that people with cancer can get at the end, mostly because of his decision to bow out early, without chemo and radiation therapy. He kept his hair, and it was only in the last week when I was changing his bedpan that I noticed his legs had gotten scarily thin and pale, a stark contrast to the day we'd met and the muscular, tanned legs bulging with veins as he crouched by the proto-Gadget.

But he kept us company, and when he was awake, he kibbitzed in a sleepy voice. Sometimes he was too stoned and ended up making no sense, just tapering off into mumble-mumble, but he had surprisingly lucid moments, when his eyes would glitter and he'd raise his trembling arm and point at something on the whiteboard or someone's screen and bust out a change or objection that was spot-on. It was spooky, like he was bringing us insights from the edge of death, and we all started jumping a little when he'd do it. In this way, little by little, the project's road map took shape: the order of lifter consortia to try, the approaches to try with each, the way to pitch the kickstarter, and even the storyboard for the video and engineering suggestions for sifting regolith.

Pug slept on his hospital bed in the living room. In theory, we all took turns sleeping on the sofa next to him, but in practice, I was the only one who could sleep through the groans he'd make in his sleep but still wake up when he rasped hoarsely for his bedpan. It was just after two, one night, when he woke me up by croaking my name, "Greg, hey, Greg."

I woke and found that he'd adjusted the bed to sit up straight, and he was more animated than he'd been in weeks, his eyes bright and alert.

"What is it, Pug?"

He pointed at a crack in the drapes, a sliver of light coming through them. "Full moon tonight," he said.

I looked at the blue-white triangle of light. "Looks like it," I said.

"Open the curtains?"

I got up and padded to the window and pulled the curtains back. A little dust rained down from the rods and made me sneeze. Out the window, framed perfectly by it like an HD shot in a documentary, was the moon, so big and bright it looked like a painted set lit up with a spotlight. We both stared at it for a moment. "It's the moon illusion," he said. "Makes it seem especially big because we don't have anything to compare it to. Once it dips a little lower on the horizon and the roofs and tree branches are in the same plane, it'll seem small again. That's the Sturgeon moon. August's moon. My favorite moon, the moon you sometimes get at the burn." It was almost time for the burn, and my e-mail had been filled with a rising babble of messages about photovoltaics and generators, costumes and conductive body paint, bikes and trailers, coffee and dry ice, water and barbecues and charcoal and sleeping bags. Normally, all this stuff would be a steadily rising chorus whose crescendo came when we packed the latest Gadgets into the van, wedged tight amid groceries and clothes and tents, and closed the doors and turned the key in the ignition.

This year, it was just an annoying mosquito-whine of people whose lives had diverged from our own in the most profound way imaginable. They were all off for a week of dust and hedonism; we were crammed together in this dark, dying room, planning a trip to the moon.

"Outside," he said, and coughed weakly. He reached for his water bottle and I helped him get the flexible hose into his mouth. "Outside," he said again, stronger.

I eyed his hospital bed and looked at the living room door. "Won't fit," I said. "Don't think you can walk it, buddy."

He rolled his eyes at the wall, and I stared at it for a moment before I figured out what he was trying to tell me. Behind the low bookcase, the garbage can, and the overstuffed chair, that wall was actually a set of ancient, ever-closed vertical blinds. I dragged the furniture away and found the blinds' pull chain and cranked them back to reveal a set of double sliding doors, a piece of two-by-four wedged in the track to keep them from being forced open. I looked back at Pug and he nodded gravely at me and made a minute shooing gesture. I lifted out the lumber, reaching through a thick pad of old cobwebs and dust bunnies. I wiped my hand on the rug and then leaned the wood against the wall. I pulled the door, which stuck at first, then gave way with a crunchy, squeaky sound. I looked from the hospital bed to the newly revealed door.

"All right, buddy, let's get this show on the road. Moon don't wait for no one."

He gave me a thumbs-up and I circled the bed, unlocking each of the wheels.

It was a good bed, a lease from a company that specialized in helping people to die at home. If that sounds like a ghoulish idea for a start-up, then I'm guessing you've never helped a friend who was dying in a hospital.

But it was still a hell of a struggle getting the bed out the door. It just fit, without even a finger's width on either side. And then there was the matter of the IV stand, which I had to swing around so it was over the head of the bed, right in my face as I pushed, until he got wedged and I had to go out the front door and around the house to pull from the other side, after freeing the wheels from the rubble and weeds in the backyard.

But once we were out, it was smooth rolling, and I took him right into the middle of the yard. It was one of those perfect L.A. nights, the cool dividend for a day's stifling heat, and the moon loomed overhead so large I wanted to reach out and touch it. Pug and I were beside each other, admiring the moon.

"Help me lower the back," he said, and I cranked the manual release that gently lay the bed out flat, so he could lie on his back and stare up at the sky. I lay down in the weeds beside him, but there were pointy rocks in there, so I went inside and got a couple of sofa cushions and improvised a bed. On my way out the door, I dug out a pair of binoculars from Pug's burning man box, spilling fine white dust as I pulled them free of the junk inside.

I held the binocs up to my eyes and focused them on the moon. The craters and peaks came into sharp focus, bright with the contrast of the full moon. Pug dangled his hand down toward me and wriggled his fingers impatiently, so I got to my feet and helped him get the binoculars up to his face. He twiddled the knobs with his shaking fingers, then stopped. He was absolutely still for a long time. So long that I thought he might have fallen asleep. But then he gently lowered the binocs to his chest.

"It's beautiful," he said. "There'll be people there, someday."

"Hell yeah," I said. "Of course."

"Maybe not for a long time. Maybe a future civilization. Whatever happens, the moon'll be in the sky, and everyone will know that there's stuff waiting for them to come and get it."

I took the binocs out of his loose fingers and lay back down on my back, looking at the moon again. I'd seen the Apollo footage so often it had become unreal, just another visual from the library of failed space dreams of generation ships and jet-packs and faster-than-light travel. Despite all my work over the past weeks and months, the moon as a place was . . . fictional, like Narnia or Middle Earth. It was an idea for a theme camp, not a place where humans might venture, let alone live there.

Seen through the binocs that night, all those pits, each older than the oldest living thing on Earth, I came to understand the moon as a place. In that moment, I found myself sympathizing with the Green Moonies, and their talk of the moon's pristineness. There was something wonderful about knowing that the first upright hominids had gazed upon the same moon that we were seeing, and that it had hardly changed.

"It's beautiful," I said. I was getting drowsy.

"Jewel," he said, barely a whisper. "Pearl. Ours. Gotta get there. Gotta beat the ones who think companies are people. The moon's for people, not corporations. It's a free lunch. Yours, if you want it."

"Amen," I said. It was like being on a campout, lying with your friends, staring at the stars, talking until sleep overcame you.

I drifted between wakefulness and sleep for a long, weird time, right on the edge, as the moon tracked across the sky. When I woke, the birds were singing and the sun was on our faces. Pug was lying in a stoned daze, the button for his drip in his loose grasp. He only did that when the pain was bad. I brought his bed inside as gently as I could, but he never gave any sign he noticed, not even when the wheels bumped over the sliding door's track. I put things back as well as I could and had a shower and put breakfast on and didn't speak of the moon in the night sky to Blight or Maya when they arrived later that morning.

Pug died that night. He did it on purpose, asking for ketamine in a serious voice, looking at each of us in turn as I put the pills in his hand. "More," he said. Then again. He looked in my eyes and I looked in his. I put more tablets in his hand, helped him find the hose end for his water as he swallowed them. He reached back for the morphine switch and I put it in his hand. I took his other hand. Blight and Maya moved to either side of me and rested their hands on the bed rail, then on Pug, on his frail arm, his withered leg. He smiled a little at us, stoned and sleepy, closed his eyes, opened them a little, and nodded off. We stood there, listening to him breathe, listening to the breath slowing. Slowing.

Slowing.

I couldn't put my finger on the instant that he went from living to dead.

But there was a moment when the muscles of his face went slack, and in the space of seconds, his familiar features rearranged themselves into the face of a corpse. So much of what I thought of as the shape of Pug's face was the effect of the tensions of the underlying muscles, and as his cheeks hollowed and slid back, the skin on his nose stretched, making it more bladelike, all cartilage, with the nostrils flattened to lizardlike slits. His lips, too, stretched back in a toneless, thin-lipped smile that was half a grimace. His heart may have squeezed out one or two more beats after that; maybe electrical impulses were still arcing randomly from nerve to nerve, neuron to neuron, but that was the moment at which he was more dead than alive, and a few moments after that, he was altogether and unmistakably dead.

We sat there in tableau for a moment that stretched and stretched. I was now in a room with a body, not my friend. I let go of his hand and sat back, and that was the cue for all of us to back away.

There should be words for those moments, but there aren't. In the same way that every human who ever lived has gazed upon the moon and looked for the words to say about it, so have we all looked upon the bodies of the ones we've loved and groped for sentiment. I wished I believed in last rites, or pennies on the eyelids, or just, well, anything that we could all acknowledge as the proper way to seal off the moment and return to the world of the living. Blight slipped her hand in mine and Maya put her elbow through my other arm and together we went out into the night. The moon was not quite full anymore, a sliver out of its huge face, and tonight there were clouds scudding across the sky that veiled and unveiled it.

We stood there, the three of us, in the breeze and the rattle of the tree branches and the distant hum of L.A. traffic and the far-off clatter of a police helicopter, with the cooling body of our friend on the other side of the wall behind us. We stood there and stared up at the moon.

Adapting the Gadget to work in a lunar environment was a substantial engineering challenge. Pug had sketched out a map for us—gathering regolith, sorting it, feeding it onto the bed, aligning the lens. Then there was propulsion, which was even more important for the moon than it was on Earth. We'd drop a Gadget on the Playa in July and gather up its tiles a couple of months later, over Labor Day. But the moon-printer might be up there for centuries, sintering tetroid tiles and pooping them out while the humans below squabbled and fretted and cast their gaze into the stars. If we didn't figure out how to keep the Gadget moving, it would eventually end up standing atop a bed of printed tiles, out of dust and out of reach of more dust, and that would be that.

This wasn't one Pug had a solution for. Neither did I, or Blight, or Maya. But it wasn't just us. There was a sprawling wiki and mailing list for the project, and at one point, we had three separate factions vying to go to the moon first. One was our project, one was nearly identical in goals except that its organizers were totally committed to a certain methodology for sealing the bearings that our side had voted down.

The third faction—they were *weird*. /b/ was a clutch of totally bizarro trolls, a community that had cut its teeth drawing up detailed plans for invading Sealand—the offshore drilling platform that had been converted to an ill-starred sovereign data haven—moved on to gaming Time magazine polls, splintered into the anonymous movement with all its many facets and runs and ops, fighting everyone from the Church of Scientology to the Egyptian Government to the NSA and that had proven its ability to continuously alter itself to challenge all that was sane and complacent with the world, no matter what it took.

These people organized themselves under the banner of the Committee to Protect Luna (SRSLY), and they set out to build a machine that would hunt down our machine, and all the tiles it dropped, and smash it into the smallest pieces imaginable. They had some pretty talented engineers working with them, and the designs they came up with solved some of the issues we'd been wrestling with, like a flywheel design that would also act as a propulsive motor, its energy channeled in one direction so that the Gadget would gently inch its way along the lunar surface. They produced innumerable videos and technical diagrams showing how their machine would work, hunting ours down by means of EMF sensors and an onboard vision system. For armament, it had its own sinterer, a clever array of lenses that it could focus with software-controlled servos to create a bug-under-a-magnifying-glass effect, allowing it to slowly but surely burn microscopic holes through our robot.

The thing was, the technical designs were absolutely sound. And though 90 percent of the rhetoric on their message boards had the deranged tinge of stoned giggles, the remaining 10 percent was deadly serious, able to parrot and even refine the Green Moon party line with stony earnestness. There were a lot of people in our camp who were convinced that they were serious—especially after they kickstarted the full load for a killer bot in thirty-six hours.

I thought it was trolling, just plain trolling. DON'T FEED THE TROLLS! I shouted online. No one listened to me (not enough people, anyway), and there was an exhausting ramble about countermeasures and armor and even, God help us all, a lawsuit, because yeah, totally, that would work. The wrangle lasted so long that we missed our launch window. The leaders of the paranoiac faction said that they'd done us all a favor by making us forfeit the deposit we'd put down, because now we'd have time to get things really right before launch time.

Another group said that the important thing wasn't countermeasures, it was delay—if we waited until the /b/tards landed their killer bot on the moon, we could just land ours far enough away that it would take five hundred years for the two to meet, assuming top speed and flat terrain all the way. That spun out into a brutal discussion of game theory and strategy, and I made the awful mistake of getting involved directly, saying, "Look, knuckleheads, if your strategy is to outwait them, and their goal is to stop us from doing anything, then their optimal strategy is to do nothing. So long as they haven't launched, we can't launch."

The ensuing discussion ate my life for a month and spilled over into the real world, when, at an L.A. burners' event, a group of people who staunchly disagreed with me made a point of finding me wherever I was to make sure I understood what a dunderhead I was.

I should have known better. Because, inevitably, the /b/tard who was in charge of the money fucked off with it. I never found out what he or she did with it. As far as I know, no one ever did.

After that, I kept my mouth shut. Or rather, I only opened it to do things that would help the project go forward. I stopped knocking heads together. I let Maya do that. I don't believe in generalizations about demographics, but man, could that girl argue. Forget all that horseshit about "digital natives," which never meant anything anyway. Using a computer isn't hard. But growing up in a world where how you argue about something changes what happens to it, that was a skill, and Maya had it in ways I never got.

"What's wrong with calling it the Gadget?"

Blight looked up from her weeding and armed sweat off her forehead, leaving behind a faint streak of brown soil. She and I traded off the weeding and this was her day, which meant that I got to spend my time indoors with all the imaginary network people and their arguments.

"Leave it, Greg," she said, in that tone that I'd come to recognize as perfectly nonnegotiable. We'd been living together for two years at that point, ever since I sank a critical mass of my nest egg into buying another launch window and had had to remortgage my house. The vegetable garden wasn't just a hobby—it was a way of life and it helped make ends meet. "Come on," I said. "Come on. We've always called it 'the Gadget.' that's what Pug called it—"

She rocked back on her heels and rose to her feet with a kind of yogic grace. Her eyes were at half-mast, with that cool fury that I'd come to know and dread.

"Pug? Come on, Greg, I thought we agreed: no playing the cult of personality card. He's dead. For years now. He wasn't Chairman Mao. He wasn't even Hari Seldon. He was just a dude who liked to party and was a pretty good engineer and was an altogether sweet guy. 'That's what Pug called it' is pure bullshit. 'The Gadget' is a dumb name. It's a way of announcing to the world that this thing hasn't been thought through. That it's a lark. That it's not serious—"

"Maybe that's good," I said. "A good thing, you know? Because that way, no one takes us seriously and we get to sneak around and act with impunity until it's too late and—"

I fell silent under her stony glare. I tried to keep going, but I couldn't. Blight had the opposite of a reality distortion field. A reality assertion field.

"Fine," I said. "We won't call it the Gadget. But I wish you'd told me before you went public with it."

She pulled off her gardening gloves and stuffed them into her pockets, then held out her hands to me. I took them.

"Greg," she said, looking into my eyes. "I have opinions. Lots of them. And I'm not going to run them past you before I 'go public' with them. Are we clear on that score?"

Again, I was stymied by her reality assertion field. All my stupid rationalizations about not meaning it that way refused to make their way out of my mouth, as some latent sense of self-preservation came to the fore.

"Yes, Blight," I said. She squeezed my fingers and dropped her stern demeanor like the mask it was.

"Very good. Now, what shall we call it?"

Everyone who had come to know it through burning man called it the Gadget. Everyone else called it the moonprinter. "Not moonprinter."

"Why not? It seems to have currency. You going to tell everyone the name they chose is wrong?"

"Yes," I said.

"Okay, go," she said.

"Well, first of all, it's not a printer. Calling it a 3D printer is like calling a car a horseless carriage. Like calling videoconferencing 'the picture-phone.' As long as we call it an anything printer, we'll be constrained by printerish thinking."

"All right," she said. "Pretty good point. What else?"

"It's not printing the moon! It's using moondust to print structural materials for prefab habitats. The way you 'print' a moon is by smashing a comet into a planet so that a moon-sized hunk of rock breaks off and goes into orbit around it."

"So what do you think we should call it?"

I shrugged. "I like 'the Gadget.'"

I ducked as she yanked out one of her dirty, balled-up gloves and threw it at my head. She caught me with the other glove and then followed it up with a muscular, rib-constricting hug. "I love you, you know."

"I love you, too." And I did. Despite the fact that I had raided my nest egg, entered the precariat, and might end up someday eating dog food, I was as happy as a pig in shit. Speaking of which.

"Dammit, I forgot to feed Messy."

She gave my butt a playful squeeze. "Go on then."

Messy was our pig, a kunekune, small enough to be happy on half an acre of pasture grass, next to the chicken run with its own half acre. The chickens ate bugs and weeds, and we planted more pasture grass in their poop, which Messy ate, leaving behind enough poop to grow berries and salad greens, which we could eat. We got eggs and, eventually, bacon and pork chops, as well as chickens. No external fertilizer, no phosphates, and we got more calories out for less energy and water inputs than even the most efficient factory farm.

It was incredibly labor-intensive, which was why I liked it. It was nice to think that the key to feeding nine billion people was to measure return on investment by maximizing calories and minimizing misery, instead of minimizing capital investment and maximizing retained earnings to shareholders.

Messy's dinner was only an hour late, and she had plenty of forage on her half acre, but she was still pissed at me and refused to come and eat from my hand until I'd cooed at her and made apologetic noises, and then she came over and nuzzled me and nipped at my fingers. I'd had a couple dogs, growing up, but the most smartest and most affectionate among them wasn't a patch on a pig for smarts and warmth. I wasn't sure how we'd bring ourselves to eat her. Though, hell, we managed it with the chickens, which were smarter and had more personality than I'd ever imagined. That was the other thing about permaculture: it made you think hard about where your food came from. It had been months since I'd been able to look at a jar of gas-station pepperoni sticks without imagining the animals they had once been.

Messy grunted amiably at me and snuffled at my heels, which was her way of asking to be let out of her pasture. I opened the gate and walked around to the small part of the house's yard that we kept for human leisure. I unfolded a chair and sat in it and picked up her ball and threw it and watched her trot off excitedly to fetch it. She could do this for hours, but only if I varied where I threw it and gave her some tricky challenges.

Maya called them the "brick shitters," which was hilarious except that it was a gift for the Green Moon crowd, who already accused us of shitting all over the moon. Blight wanted "homesteaders," which, again, had all kinds of awful baggage about expropriation of supposedly empty lands from the people who were already there. She kept arguing that there were no indigenous people on the moon, but that didn't matter. The Green Moon people were determined to paint us as rapacious land grabbers, and this was playing right into their hands. It always amazed me how two people as smart as Blight and Maya could be so dumb about this.

Not that I had better ideas. "The Gadget" really was a terrible name.

I threw the ball and thought some more.

We ended up calling it "Freelunch." It wasn't my coinage, but as soon as I saw it, I knew it was right. Just what Pug would have wanted. A beacon overhead, promising us a better life if only we'd stop stepping on one another to get at it.

The name stuck. Some people argued about it, but it was clear to anyone who did lexicographic analysis of the message boards, chats, tweets, and forums that it was gaining with that Internet-characteristic, winner-take-all, hockey-stick-shaped growth line. Oh, sure, the localization projects argued about whether free meant "libre" or "gratis" and split down the middle. In Brazil, they used "livre" (Portugal's thirty-years-and-counting technocratic " interim" managers translated it as "grátis").

More than eight thousand of us went to Macapá for launch day, landing in Guyana and taking the new high-speed rail from Georgetown. There had been dozens of Freelunch prototypes built and tested around the world, with teams competing for funding, engineer time, lab space. A co-op in Asheville, blessed by NASA, had taken over the production of ersatz regolith, a blend whose composition was (naturally) hotly debated.

The Brazilian contingent went all out for us. I stayed up every night dancing and gorging, then slept in a different family's living room until someone came to take me to the beach or a makerspace or a school. One time, Maya and Blight and I were all quartered in a favela that hung off the side of an abandoned office tower on impossibly thin, impossibly strong cables. The rooms were made of waxed cardboard and they swayed with the wind and terrified me. I was convinced I'd end up stepping right through the floor and ended up on tiptoes every time I moved. I tried not to move.

Celesc Lifter SA had a little VIP box from which customers could watch launches. It held eight people. The seats were awarded by lottery and I didn't get one. So I watched the lift with everyone else (minus eight), from another favela, one of the old, established ones with official recognition. Every roof was packed with viewers, and hawkers meandered the steep alleys with bulbs of beer and skewers of meat and paper cones of sea-food. It was Celesc's ninety-third lift, and it had a 78 percent success rate, with only two serious failures in that time. No fatalities, but the cargo had been jettisoned over the Pacific and broke up on impact.

Those were good odds, but we were still all holding our breath through the countdown, through the first flames and the rumble conveyed by a thousand speakers, an out-of-phase chorus of net-lagged audio. We held it through the human-piloted take-off of the jumbo jet that acted as a first stage for the lifter and gasped when the jet's video stream showed the lifter emerging from its back and rising smoothly into the sky. The jet dropped precipitously as the lifter's rockets fired and caught it and goosed it up, through the thin atmosphere at the edge of space in three hundred seconds.

I watched the next part from the lifter, though others swore it was better from Al Jazeera's LEO platform, framed against the Earth, the day/ night terminator arcing across the ocean below. But I liked the view from the lifter's nose, because you could see the moon growing larger, until it dominated the sky.

Decades before, the *Curiosity* crew had endured their legendary "seven minutes of terror" when its chute, rockets, and exterior casings had to be coordinated with split-second timing to land the spunky little bot on our nearest neighbor without smashing it to flinders. Landing the first Freelunch on the moon was a lot simpler, thankfully. We had a lot of things going for us: the moon was close enough for us to get telemetry and send new instructions right up to the last second, it exerted substantially less gravity than Mars, and we had the advantage of everything NASA had learned and published from its own landing missions. And let us not forget that Earth sports a sizable population of multigenerational lunar lander pilots who've trained on simulators since the text-based version first appeared on the PDP-8 in 1969.

Actually, the last part kind of sucked. A lot of people believed they were qualified to intervene in the plan, and most of them were not. The signal: noise ratio for the landing was among the worst in the whole project, but in the end the winning strate y was the one that had been bandied about since the ESA's scrapped lunar lander competition, minus the observational phase: a short series of elliptical orbits leading to a transfer orbit and a quick burn that set it falling toward the surface. The vision systems that evaluated the landing site were able to autonomously deploy air jets to nudge the descent into the clearest, smoothest patch available.

Celesc's lifter released the Freelunch right on time, burning a little to kick itself back down into a lower orbit to prepare for descent. As their vectors diverged, the Freelunch seemed to arc away, even though it was actually continuing on the exact curve that the lifter had boosted it to. It dwindled away from the lens of AJ's satellite, lost against the looming moon, winking in and out of existence as a black speck that the noise-correction algorithms kept erasing and then changing their mind about.

One by one, all the screens around me converged on the same feed: a split screen of shaky, high-magnification real-time video on one side, a radar-fed line-art version on the other. The Freelunch wound around and around the moon in four ever-tightening orbits, like a tetherball winding around a post. A tiny flare marked its shift to transfer orbit, and then it was sailing down in a spiral.

"Coming in for a landing," Blight said, and I nodded, suddenly snapped back to the warm Brazilian night, the smell of food and the taste of beer in my mouth. It spiraled closer and closer, and then it kicked violently away, and we all gasped. "Something on the surface," Blight said.

"Yeah," I said, squinting and pinch-zooming at the view from its lower cameras. We'd paid for satellite relay for the landing sequence, which meant we were getting pretty hi-res footage. But the moon's surface defies the human eye: tiny pebbles cast long, sharp shadows that look like deep cracks or possibly high shelves. I could see ten things on the landing site that could have been bad news for the Freelunch—or that could have been nothing.

No time. Freelunch was now in a wobbly, erratic orbit that made the view from its cameras swing around nauseously, a roil of Earth in the sky, mountains, craters, the ground, the black sky, the filtered gray/white mass of the sun. From around us came a low "wooooah!" from eight thousand throats at once.

Maya switched us to the magnified AJ sat feed and the CGI radar view. Something was wrong—Freelunch was supposed to circle two or three times and land. Instead, it was tumbling a little, not quite flipping over on its head, but rolling more than the gyros could correct.

"Fuck no," I whispered. "Please. Not now. Please." No idea who I was talking to. Pug? Landing was the riskiest part of the whole mission. That's why we were all here, watching.

Down and down it fell, and we could all see that its stabilizers were badly out of phase. Instead of damping its tumble, the stabilizer on one side was actually accelerating it, while the other three worked against it.

"Tilt-a-whirl," Maya said. We all glared at her. In a few of the sims that we'd run of the landing, the Freelunch had done just this, as the stabilizers got into a terminal argument about who was right. One faction—Iowa City–led, but with supporters around the world—had dubbed it the tilt-a-whirl and had all kinds of math to show why it was more likely than we'd estimated. They wanted us to delay the whole mission while they refactored and retested the landing sequence. They'd been outvoted but had never stopped arguing for their position.

"Shut up," Blight said, in a tight little voice. The tumble was getting worse, the ground looming.

"Fuck off," Maya said absently. "It's the Tilt-a-whirl, and that means that we should see the counterfire any . . . second . . . now!"

If we hadn't been watching closely, we'd have missed it. The Freelunch had a set of emergency air puffers for blowing the solar collectors clear if the mechanical rotation mechanism jammed or lacked power. The Tilt-a-whirlers had successfully argued for an emergency command structure that would detect tumble and deploy the air jets in one hard blast in order to cancel out the malfing stabilizer. They emptied themselves in less than a second, a white, smudgy line at right angles to the swing of the Freelunch, and the roll smoothed out in three short and shortening oscillations. An instant later, the Freelunch was skidding into the lunar surface, kicking up a beautiful rooster-tail plume of regolith that floated above the surface like Playa dust. We watched as the moondust sifted down in one-sixth gee, a TV tuned to a dead channel, shifting snow out of which slowly emerged the sharp angles of the Freelunch.

I registered every noise from the crowds on the roofs and in the stairways, every moan and whimper, all of them saying, essentially, "Please, please, please, please let it work."

The Freelunch popped its protective covers. For an instant they stayed in place, visible only as a set of slightly off-kilter corners set inside the main boxy body of the lander. Then they slid away, dropping to the surface with that unmistakable moon-gee grace. The simultaneous intake of breath was like a city-sized white-noise generator.

"Power-on/self-test," Maya said. I nodded. It was going through its boot-up routines, checking its subsystems, validating its checksums. The whole procedure took less than a minute.

Ten minutes later, nothing had happened.

"Fuck," I said.

"Patience," Blight said. Her voice had all the tension of a guitar string just before it snaps.

"Fuck patience," I said.

"Patience," Maya said.

We took one another's hands. We watched.

An hour later, we went inside.

The Freelunch had nothing to say to us. As Earth spun below the moon, our army of ham operators, volunteers spread out across the equator, all tried valiantly to bounce their signals to it, to hear its distress messages. It maintained radio silence.

After forty-eight hours, most of us slunk away from Brazil. We caught a slow freighter up the Pacific Coast to the Port of Los Angeles, a journey of three weeks where we ate fish, squinted at our transflective displays in the sun, and argued.

Everyone had a theory about what had happened to the Freelunch. Some argued that a key component—a sensor, a power supply, a logic board—had been dislodged during the Tilt-a-whirl (or the takeoff, or the landing). The high-mag shots from the Al Jazeera sat were examined in minute detail, and things that were either noise or compression artifacts or ironclad evidence of critical damage were circled in red and magnified to individual pixels, debated and shooped and tweaked and enhanced.

A thousand telescopic photos of the Freelunch were posted, and the supposed damage was present, or wasn't, depending on the photo. It was sabotage. Human error. Substandard parts. Proof that space was too big a place for puny individual humans, only suited to huge, implacable nation-states.

"THERE AIN'T NO SUCH THING AS A FREELUNCH," the /b/tards trumpeted, and took responsibility for all of it. An evangelical in Mexico claimed he'd killed it with the power of prayer, to punish us for our hubris.

I harbored a secret hope: that the Freelunch would wake up someday, having hit the magic combination of rebooting, reloading, and reformatting to make it all work. But as the Freelunch sat there, settled amid the dust of another world—well, moon—inert and idle, I confronted the reality that thousands of people had just spent years working together to litter another planet. Or moon.

Whatever.

That wasn't a good year. I had another cancer scare because life sucks, and the doc wanted a bunch of out-of-policy tests that cost me pretty much everything left in my account.

I made a (very) little money doing some writing about the Freelunch project, post-mortems and tit-for-tats for a few sites. But after two months of rehashing the same ground, and dealing with all the stress of the health stuff, I switched off from all Freelunch-related activity altogether. Blight had already done it.

A month later, Blight and I split up. That was scary. It wasn't over any specific thing, just a series of bickery little stupid fights that turned into blowouts and ended up with me packing a bag and heading for a motel. The first night, I woke up at 3 a.m. to vomit up my whole dinner and then some.

Two weeks later, I moved back in. Blight and I didn't speak of that horrible time much afterward, but when we held hands or cuddled at night, there was a fierceness to it that hadn't been in our lives for years and years. So maybe we needed it.

Money, money, money. We just didn't have any. Sold the house. Moved into a rental place, where they wouldn't let us keep chickens or pigs. Grocery bills. Moved into another place, this one all the way out in Fresno, and got a new pig and half a dozen new chickens, but now we were a three hours' drive from Minus and our friends.

Blight got work at a seniors' home, which paid a little better than minimum wage. I couldn't find anything. Not even gardening work. I found myself sitting very still, as though I was worried that if I started moving, I'd consume some of the savings.

She was working at a place called Shadow Hills, part of a franchise of old folks' homes that catered to people who'd kept their nest eggs intact into their long senescences. It was like a stationary cruise ship—twenty-five stories of "staterooms" with a little living room and bedroom and kitchenette, three dining rooms with rotating menus, activities, weekly crafts bazaars, classes, gyms and a pool, a screening room. The major difference between Shadow Hills and a cruise ship—apart from Fresno being landlocked—was the hospital and palliative care ward that occupied the tenth and eleventh floors. That way, once your partner started to die, you could stay in the stateroom and visit her in the ward every day, rather than both of you being alone for those last days. It was humane and sensible, but it made me sad.

Blight was giving programming classes to septuagenarians whose high schools had offered between zero and one "computer science" classes in the early 1980s, oldies who had managed to make it down the long road of life without learning how to teach a computer how to do something new. They were enthusiastic and patient, and they called out to Blight every time she crossed the lobby to meet me and shouted impertinent commentary about my suitability as a spouse for their beloved maestra and guru.

She made a point of giving me a big kiss and a full-body hug before leading me out into the gardens for our picnic, and the catcalls rose to a crescendo.

"I wish you wouldn't do that," I said.

"Prude," she said, and ostentatiously slapped my ass. The oldies volubly took notice. "What's for lunch?"

"Coconut soup, eggplant curry, and grilled pumpkin."

"Hang on, I'll go get my backup PB and J."

I'd been working my way through an online cooking course one recipe at a time, treating it like a series of chemistry experiments. Mostly, they'd been successful, but Blight made a big show out of pretending that it was inedible and she demanded coaxing and pushing to get her to try my creations. So as she turned on her heel to head back into work, I squeezed her hand and dragged her out to the garden.

She helped me lay out the blanket and set out the individual sections of the insulated tiffin pail. I was satisfied to see that the food was still hot enough to steam. I'd been experimenting with slightly overheating food before decanting it for transport, trying to find exactly the right starting point for optimal temperature at the point of consumption. It was complicated by the fact that the cooldown process wasn't linear, and also depended on the volume and density of the food. The fact that this problem was consuming so many of my cycles was a pretty good indicator of my degraded mental state. Further evidence: I carefully noted the temperature of each tiffin before I let Blight tuck in, and associated the correct temperature with the appropriate record on my phone, which already listed the food weight and type details, entered before I left home.

Blight pulled out all the stops, making me scoop up spoonfuls of food and make airplane noises and feed her before she'd try it, but then she ate enthusiastically. It was one of my better experiments. At one point, I caught her sliding my sticky rice pudding with mango coulis across to her side of the blanket and I smacked her hand and took it back. She still managed to sneak a spoonful when I wasn't looking.

I liked our lunches together. They were practically the only thing I liked.

"How long do you figure it'll be before you lose your marbles altogether?" she asked, sipping some of the iced tea I'd poured into heavy-bottomed glasses I'd yard-saled and which I transported rolled in soft, thick dish towels.

"Who'd notice?"

I started to pack up the lunch, stacking the tiffin sections and slipping the self-tensioning bands over them. Blight gently took them out of my hands and set them to one side.

"Greg," she said. "Greg, seriously. This isn't good. You need to change something. It's like living with a ghost. Or a robot."

A bolt of anger skewered me from the top of my head to my asshole, so sharp and irrational that I actually gasped aloud. I must be getting mature in my old age, because the sheer force of the reaction pulled me up short and made me pause before replying.

"I've tried to find work," I said. "There's nothing out there for me."

"No," she said, still holding my arm, refusing to surrender the physical contact. "No, there's no jobs. We both know that there's plenty of work."

"I'll think about it," I said, meaning, I won't think about it at all.

Still, she held on to my arm. She made me look into her eyes. "Greg, I'm not kidding. This isn't good for you. It's not good for us. This isn't what I want to do for the rest of my life."

I nearly deliberately misunderstood her, asked her why she wasn't looking for work somewhere else. But I knew that the "this" she meant was living with me, in my decayed state.

"I'll think about it," I repeated, and shrugged off her hand. I packed up the lunch, put it on the back of my bike, and rode home. I managed to stop myself from crying until I had the door closed behind me.

That night we had sex. It was the first time in months, so long that I'd lost track of how long it had been. It started with a wordless reaching out in the night, our habitual spooned-together cuddle going a little further, bit by bit, our breath quickening, our hands and then our mouths exploring each other's bodies. We both came in near silence and held each other tighter and longer than normal. I realized that there'd been a longer gap since our last clinging, full-body hug than the gap since our last sex. I found that I'd missed the cuddling even more than the sex.

I circled the Freebrunch—as the Freelunch's successor had been inevitably named—nervously. For days, I poked at the forums, downloaded the prototypes, and watched the videos, spending a few minutes at a time before clicking away. One faction had a pretty credible account of how the landing had been blown so badly, and pretty much everyone accepted that something about the bad landing was responsible for the systems failure. They pointed to a glitch in the vision system, a collision between two inference engines that made it misinterpret certain common lunar shadows as bad terrain. It literally jumped at shadows. And the Tilt-a-whirl faction was totally vindicated and managed to force a complete redesign of the stabilization software and the entry plan.

The more I looked over Freebrunch, the more exciting it got. Freelunch had transmitted telemetry right up to the final moments of its landing, definitively settling another argument: "How much should we worry about landing telemetry if it only has to land once?" The live-fire exercise taught us stuff that no amount of vomit-comet trial runs could have surfaced. It turned out, for example, that the outer skin of the Freelunch had been totally overengineered and suffered only a fraction of the heating that the models had predicted. That meant we could reduce the weight by a good 18 percent. The cost of lifting mass was something like 98 percent of the overall launch cost, so an 18 percent reduction in mass was something like a 17.99 percent reduction in the cost of building Freelunch and sending it to the surface of the moon.

Blight knew I was hooked before I did. The third time I gave her a cold sandwich and some carrot sticks for lunch, she started making jokes about being a moon widow and let me know that she'd be packing her own lunch four days a week, but that I was still expected to come up with something decent for a Friday blowout.

And just like that, I was back in.

Freelunch had cost me pretty much all my savings, and I wasn't the only one. The decision not to take commercial sponsorship on the project was well intentioned, but it had meant that the whole thing had to be funded by jerks like me. Worse: Freelunch wasn't a registered 501(c) (3) charity, so it couldn't even attract any deep-pocketed jillionaires looking for a tax deduction.

Freebrunch had been rebooted by people without any such burning manian anticommodification scruples. Everything down to the circuit boards had someone's logo or name on it, and they'd added a EULA to the project that said that by contributing to Freebrunch, you signed over all your "intellectual property" rights to the foundation that ran it—a foundation without a fully appointed board and no transparency beyond what the law mandated.

That had sparked a predictable shitstorm that reached the global newspapers when someone spotted a patent application from the foundation's chairman, claiming to have invented some of the interlock techniques that had been invented by Pug himself, there on the Playa. I'd seen it with my own eyes, and more important, I'd helped document it, with timestamped postings that invalidated every one of the patent's core claims.

Bad enough, but the foundation dug itself even deeper when it used the donations it had taken in to pay for lawyers to fight for the patent. The schism that ensued proved terminal, and a year later, the Freebrunch was dead.

Out of its ashes rose the Freebeer, which tried to strike a happy medium between the Freelunch's idealism and the Freebrunch's venality. The people involved raised foundation money, agreed to print the names of project benefactors on the bricks they dropped onto the moon's surface, and benefited from the Indian Space Research Organization's lunar-mapping initiative, which produced remarkably high-resolution survey maps of the entire bright side of the moon. On that basis, they found a spot in Mare Imbrium that was as smooth as a baby's ass and was only a few hundred K from the Freelunch's final resting place.

Of course, they failed. Everything went fine until LEO separation, whereupon something happened—there are nine documentaries (all crowd-funded) offering competing theories—and it ended up in a decaying orbit that broke up over Siberia and rained down shooting stars into the greedy lenses of thousands of dashcams.

Freebird.

(Supported, of course, by a series of stadium shows and concert tours.)

Freepress.

(This one printed out leaked WikiLeaks cables from early in the century and won a prize at the Venice biennale, held in Padua now that the city was entirely underwater. It helped that they chose cables that dealt with the American government's climate change shenanigans. The exiled Venetians living in their stacked Paduan tenements thought that was a laugh-riot.)

That took seven years.

The lost cosmonaut conspiracy theory holds that a certain number—two? three?—of Russian cosmonauts were killed before Gagarin's successful flight. They say when Gagarin got into the Vostok in 1961, he fully expected to die, but he got in any way, and not because of the crack of a commissar's pistol. He boarded his death trap because it was his ticket into space. He had gone to what could almost certainly have been his death because of his belief in a better future. A place for humanity in the stars.

When you think of a hero, think of Gagarin, strapped into that capsule, the rumble of the jets below him, the mutter of the control tower in his headset, the heavy hand of acceleration hard upon his chest, pushing with increasing, bone-crushing force, the roar of the engines blotting out all sound. Think of him going straight to his death with a smile on his face, and think of him breaking through the atmosphere, the sudden weightlessness, the realization that he had survived. That he was the first human being to go to space.

We kept on launching printers.

Blight and I threw a joint seventieth birthday party to coincide with the launch of the Freerunner. There were old friends. There was cake. There was ice cream, with chunks of honeycomb from our own hive. There were—I shit you not—seventy candles. We blew them out, all of them, though it took two tries, seventy-year-old lungs being what they were.

We toasted each other with long speeches that dripped with unselfconscious sentiment, and Maya brought her kids and they presented us with a little play they'd written, involving little printed 3D printers on the moon.

And then, as we tuned every screen in the house to the launch, I raised a glass and toasted Pug:

"Let us live as though it were the first days of a better nation."

The cheer was loud enough to drown out the launch.

Freerunner landed at 0413 Zulu on August 10, 2057. Eight minutes later, it completed its power-on self-test routine and snapped out its solar collectors. It established communications with nine different ham-based ground stations and transmitted extensive telemetry. Its bearings moved smoothly, and it canted its lens into the sun's rays. The footage of its first sintering was low-res and jittery, but it was all saved for later transmission, and that's the clip you've seen, the white-hot tip of the focused energy of old Sol, melting regolith into a long, flat, thin line that was quickly joined by another, right alongside it. Back and forth the head moved, laying out the base, the honeycombing above it, the final surface. The print bed tilted with slow grace and the freshly printed brick slid free and fell to the dust below, rocking from side to side, featherlike as it fell.

One week later, Freerunner established contact with the Freelunch, using its phased-array antennas to get a narrow, high-powered signal to its slumbering firmware. Laboriously, it rebuilt the Freelunch's BIOS, directed it to use what little energy it had to release the springs that locked the solar array away in its body. It took thirty-seven hours and change. We were on the Playa when we got word that the solar array had deployed, the news spreading like wildfire from burner to burner, fireworks rocketing into the sky.

I smiled and rolled over in our yurt. Igloo. Yurtgloo. I was very happy, of course. But I was also seventy. I needed my rest. The next morning, a naked twenty-year-old with scales covering his body from the waist up cycled excitedly to our camp and pounded on the yurt's interlocking bricks until I thought he might punch right through them.

"What," I said. "The fuck."

"It's printed one!" he said. "The Freelunch shit a brick!" he looked at me, took in my tired eyes, my snowy hair. "Sorry to wake you, but I thought you'd want to know."

"Of course he wants to know!" Blight shouted from inside. "Christ, Greg, get the man a drink. We're celebrating!"

The Playa dust whipped up my nose and made me reach for the kerchief around my neck, pull it up over my face. I turned to the kid, standing there awkwardly astride his bike. "Well?" I said. "Come on, we're celebrating!" I gave him a hug that was as hard as I could make it, and he squeezed me back with gentle care.

We cracked open some bourbon that a friend had dropped off the day before and pulled out the folding chairs. The crowd grew, and plenty of them brought bottles. There were old friends, even old enemies, people I should have recognized and didn't, and people I recognized but who didn't recognize me at first. I'd been away from the Playa for a good few years. The next thing I knew, the sun was setting, and there were thousands of us, and the music was playing, and my legs were sore from dancing, and Blight was holding me so tight I thought she'd crack a rib.

I thought of saying, *We did it*, or *You did it*, or *They did it*. None of those was right, though. "It's done" is what I said, and Blight knew exactly what I meant. Which is why I loved her so much, of course.

vladimir chong chooses to die

LAVIE TIDHAR

Lavie Tidhar grew up on a kibbutz in Israel, traveled widely in Africa and Asia, and has lived in London, the South Pacific island of Vanuatu, and Laos. He is the winner of the 2003 Clarke-Bradbury International Science Fiction Competition, was the editor of Michael Marshall Smith: The Annotated Bibliography, *and the anthologies* A Dick and Jane Primer for Adults, The Apex Book of World SF, *and* The Apex Book of World SF 2. *He is the author of the linked story collection* HebrewPunk, *the novella chapbooks* An Occupation of Angels, Gorel and the Pot-Bellied God, Cloud Permutations, Jesus and the Eightfold Path, *and, with Nir Yaniv, the novel* The Tel Aviv Dossier. *A prolific short-story writer, his stories have appeared in* Interzone, Clarkesworld, Apex Magazine, Asimov's Science Fiction, Strange Horizons, ChiZine, Postscripts, Fantasy Magazine, Nemonymous, infinity plus, Aeon, Book of Dark Wisdom, Fortean Bureau, *and elsewhere. His novels include* The Bookman *and its sequels,* Camera Obscura *and* The Great Game, Osama: A Novel, *which won the World Fantasy Award as the year's Best Novel in 2012,* Martian Sands, *and* The Violent Century. *His most recent books include a new novel,* A Man Lies Dreaming, *and a collection of "guns and sorcery" stories,* Black Gods Kiss. *After a spell in Tel Aviv, he's currently living back in England again.*

"Vladimir Chong Chooses To Die" is another of his interconnected Central Station stories, a complex, evocative, multicultural future, set during a time when humanity—including part-human robots, AIs, cyborgs, and genetically engineered beings of all sorts—is spreading through the solar system. This one deals with, well, exactly what the title says that it does.

The clinic was cool and calm, a pine-scented oasis in the heart of Central Station. Cool calm white walls. Cool calm air conditioning humming, coolly and calmly. Vladimir Chong hated it immediately. He did not find it soothing. He did not find it calming. It was a white room; it resembled too much the inside of his own head.

"Mr. Chong?" The nurse was a woman he recalled with exactness. Benevolence Jones, cousin of Miriam Jones who was his boy Boris's childhood sweetheart. He remembered Benevolence as a child with thin woven dreadlocks and a wicked smile, a few years younger than his own boy, trailing after her cousin Miriam in adoration. Now she was a matronly woman in starched white and dreadlocks thicker and fewer. She smelled of soap. "The mortality consultant will see you now," she said.

Vlad nodded. He got up. There was nothing wrong with his motor functions. He followed her to the consultant's office. Vlad could remember with perfect recall hundreds of such offices. They always looked the same. They could have easily been the same room, with the same person sitting behind them. He was not afraid of death. He could remember death. His father, Weiwei, had died at home. Vlad could remember it several ways. He could remember his father's own dying moment—broken sentences forming in the brain, the touch of the pillow hurting strangely, the look in his boy's eyes, a sense of wonder, filling him, momentarily, then blackness, a slow encroachment that swallowed whatever last sentence he had meant to say.

He could remember it from his mother's memories, though he seldom went into them, preferred to segment them separately, when he still could. She was sitting by the bed, not crying, then fetching tea, cookies, looking after the guests coming in and out, visiting the death bed of Weiwei. She spared time for her boy, for little Vlady, too, and her memories were all intermingled of the moment her husband died, her hand on Vlady's short hair, her eyes on Weiwei who seemed to be struggling to say something then stopped, and was very still.

He could remember it his own way, though it was an early memory, and confused. Wetness. Lips moving like a fish's, without sound. The smell of floor cleaner. Accidentally brushing against the cool metal leg of R. Brother Patch-It, the robo-priest, who stood by the bed and spoke the words of the Way of Robot, though Weiwei was not a practitioner of that, nor any other, religion.

"Mr. Chong?"

The mortality consultant was a tall thin North Tel Aviv Jew. "I'm Dr. Graff," he said.

Vlad nodded politely. Dr. Graff gestured to a chair. "Please, sit down."

Vlad sat, remembering like an echo, like reflections multiplying between two mirrors. A universe of Chongs sitting down at doctor's offices throughout the years. His mother when she sat down and the doctor said, "I'm afraid the news are not good." His father after a work injury when he had shattered his leg bones falling in his exoskeleton from the uncompleted fourth level of Central Station. Boris when he was five and his node was infected by a hostile malware virus with rudimentary intelligence. His sister's boy's eldest when they took him to the hospital in Tel Aviv, worried about his heart. And on and on, though none, yet, in a life termination clinic. He, Vlad, son of Weiwei, father of Boris, was the first of the line to visit one of those.

He'd been sitting in his flat when it happened. A moment of clarity. It felt like emerging out of a cold bright sea. When he was submerged in the sea he could see each individual drop of water, and each one was a disconnected memory, and it was drowning him. It was never meant to be this way.

Weiwei's Curse, or Weiwei's Folly, they called it. Vlad could remember Weiwei's determination, his ambition, his human desire to be remembered, to continue to be a part of his family and their lives. He remembered the trip up the hill to the Old City of Jaffa, Weiwei cycling in the heat, parking the bicycle at last in the shade, against the cool old stones, and visiting the Oracle.

What manner of thing it was he didn't know, this lineage of memory, infecting like a virus the Chongs as a whole. It was the Oracle's doing, and she was not human, or mostly not. Joined, Bonded, she was as much Other as not, for all that she wore a human body.

It had served. In past times it had offered comfort, at times, remembering what others knew, what they had done. He remembered his father climbing into his exoskeleton, slowly climbing, like a crab, along the unfinished side of Central Station. Later he, too, worked on the building, two generations of Chongs it took to bring it to completion. Only to see his own son go up in the great elevators, a boy afraid of family, of sharing, a boy determined to escape, to follow a dream of the stars. He saw him climb up the elevators and to the great roof, saw him climb into the orbital flyer that took him to Gateway and, from there, to the Belt and Mars and beyond. But still the link persisted, even from afar, the memories travelling, slower than light, between the worlds. Vlad had missed his boy. Missed the work on the space port, the easy camaraderie with the others. Missed his wife whose memory still lived inside him, but whose name, like a cancer, had been eaten away.

He remembered the smell of her, the taste of her sweat and the swell of her belly, when they were both young and the streets of Central Station smelled of night-blooming jasmine and mutton fat. Remembered her with Boris holding her hand, at five years old, walking through the same old streets, with the space port, completed, rising ahead of them, a hand pointing at the stars.

Boris: "What is that, daddy?"

Vlad: "It's Central Station, Boris."

Boris, gesturing around him at the old streets, the rundown apartment blocks: "And this?"

"It's Central Station."

Boris, laughing. Vlad joining him and she smiled, the woman who was gone now, whose only ghost remained, whose name he no longer knew.

Looking back (but that was a thing he could no longer do) that should have given him warning. Her name disappeared, the way keys or socks do. Misplaced and, later, could not be found.

Slowly, inexorably, the links that bound together memory, like RNA, began to weaken and break.

"Mr. Chong?"

"Doctor. Yes."

"Mr. Chong, we treat all our patients with complete confidentiality."

"Of course."

"We have a range of options available, of course—" the doctor coughed politely. "I am bound to ask you, however—before we go over them—have you made, or wish to make, any post-mortal arrangements?"

Vlad regarded the doctor for a moment. Silence had become a part of him in recent years. Slowly the memory boundaries tore and recall, like shards of hard glass, fragmented and shattered in his mind. More and more he found himself sitting, for hours or days, in his flat, rocking in the ancient chair Weiwei once brought home from the Jaffa flea market, in triumph, raising it above his head, this short, wiry Chinese man in this land of Arabs and Jews. Vlad had loved Weiwei. Now he hated him almost as much as he loved him. The ghost of Weiwei, his memory, still lived on in his ruined mind.

For hours, days, he sat in the rocking chair, examining memories like globes of light. Disconnected, he did not know how one related to the other, or whose the memory had been, his own or someone else's. For hours and days, alone, in the silence like a dust.

Lucidity came and went without a pattern. Once he opened his eyes and breathed in and saw Boris crouching beside him, an older, thinner version of the boy who held his hand and looked up at the sky and asked questions. "Boris?" he said, surprise catching at the words. His mouth felt raw with disuse.

"Dad."

"What . . . are you doing here?"

"I've been back a month, dad."

"A month?" Pride, and hurt, made his throat constrict. "And you only now come to visit me?"

"I've been here," Boris said, gently. "With you. Dad—"

But Vlad stopped him. "Why are you back?" he said. "You should have stayed in the Up and Out. There is nothing for you, now. Boris. You were always too big for your boots."

"Dad—"

"Go away!" He almost shouted. Felt himself pleading. His fingers gripped the side arms of the ancient rocking chair. "Go, Boris. You don't belong here anymore."

"I came back because of you!" his son was shouting at him. "Look at you! Look at—"

Then that, too, became just another memory, detached, floating out of his reach. The next time he broke through the water Boris was gone and Vlad went downstairs and sat in the cafe with Ibrahim, the alte-zachen man, and played backgammon and drank coffee in the sun, and for a while everything was as it should be.

The next time he saw Boris he was not alone, but with Miriam, who Vlad saw, from time to time. "Boris!" he said, tears, unbidden, coming to his eyes. He hugged his boy, there, in the middle of the street.

"Dad . . ." Boris was taller than him now, he realised with a start. "You're feeling better?"

"I feel fine!" He held on to him tight, then released him. "You've grown," he said.

"I've been away a long time," Boris said.

"You're thin. You should eat more."

"Dad . . ."

"Miriam," Vlad said. Giddy. "Vlad," she said. She put her hand, lightly, on his shoulder. "It's good to see you."

"You found him again," he said.

"He . . ." she hesitated. "We ran into each other," she said.

"That's good. That is good," Vlad said. "Come. Let me buy you a drink. To celebrate."

"Dad, I don't think—"

"No one asks you to think!" Vlad snapped. "Come," he said, more gently. "Come."

They sat in the coffee shop. Vlad ordered a sheesha pipe, a bottle of arak. Three glasses. He poured. Hands steady. Central Station rising before them like a signpost for the future. For Vlad it was pointing the wrong way, it was a part of his past. "L'chaim," he said. They raised their glasses and drank.

A moment of dislocation. Then he was in the flat again and the old robot, R. Patch-It, was standing there. "What are you doing here?" Vlad snapped. He remembered remembering; moving memories like cubes between his hands, hanging them in the air before him. Trying to make sense of how they fit each other, which came before which.

"I was looking after you," the robot said. Vlad remembered the robot, through his own memories and through Weiwei's. R. Patch-it, who doubled as a moyel, had circumcised Vlad as a baby, had performed the same service for Boris, when his time came. Old even before Weiwei came to this land as a young, poor migrant worker, all those years before.

"Leave me be," Vlad said. Resented suddenly the interference. "Boris sent you," he said. Not a question. "He is worried," the robot said. "So am I, Vlad—"

"What makes you so much better?" Vlad said. "A robot. You're an object. A piece of metal with an I-loop. What do you know of being alive?"

The robot didn't answer. Later, Vlad realised he was not there, that the flat was empty, and had been empty for some time.

None of it would have bothered him so much if he could only remember her name.

"Post-mortal options?" he said, echoing the doctor.

"Yes, yes," the doctor said. "There are several standard possibilities we really must discuss before we—"

"Such as?"

He could feel time slipping away. Urgency gripped him. A man should be allowed to determine the time of his going. To go in dignity. Even to make it this far in life was an achievement, something to celebrate. Very well.

"Very well," he said.

"We could freeze you," the doctor said.

"Freeze me."

He felt robbed of willpower. Fought the memories crowding in on him. No one in the family had ever been frozen before.

"Freeze you until such time as you wish to be awakened," Dr. Graff said. "A century or two?"

"I assume the costs are considerable."

"It's a standard contract," Dr. Graff said. "Estate plus—"

"Yes," Vlad said. "That is to say, no. What do you think will happen in one, or two, or five hundred years from now?"

"Often, patients are sick with incurable illnesses," Dr. Graff said. "They hope for a cure. Others are time tourists, disillusioned with our era, wishing to seek out the new, the strange."

"The future."

"The future," Dr. Graff agreed.

"I've seen the future," Vlad said. "It's the past I can't get back to, Dr. Graff. There is too much of it and it's broken and it exists only in my head. I don't want to travel to the future."

"There is also the possibility of freezing on board an Exodus ship," the doctor said. "To travel beyond the Up and Out. You could be awakened on a new planet, a new world."

Vlad smiled. "My boy," he said, softly.

"Excuse me?"

"My boy, Boris. He's a doctor too, you know."

"Boris Chong? I remember him. We were colleagues together," Dr. Graff said. "In the birthing clinics. A long time ago. He left for Mars, didn't he?"

"He's back," Vlad said. "He was always a good boy."

"I'll be sure to look him up," Dr. Graff said.

"I don't want to go to the stars," Vlad said. "Going away seldom changes what we are."

"Indeed," the doctor said. "Well, there is also of course the possibility of upload?"

"Existing as an I-loop simulation while the old body and mind die anyway?"

"Yes."

"Doctor, I will live on as memory," Vlad said. "That is something I cannot change. Every bit of me, everything that makes me what I am will survive so my grandchildren and my nephew's children and all the ones born in Central Station and beyond, now and in the future, can recall through me all I have seen, if they so wish." He smiled again. "Do you think they will be smarter? Do you think they will learn from my mistakes and not make their own?"

"No," the doctor said.

"I am Weiwei's son, and have Weiwei's Folly in my mind and in my node. I am, already, memory, Dr. Graff. But memory is not me. Are we done with the preliminaries?"

"You could be cyborged."

"My sister is over eighty percent cyborged now, Doctor," Vlad said. "Missus Chong the Elder, they call her now. She belongs to the Church of Robot. One day she will be Translated, no doubt. But her path is not mine."

"Then you are determined."

"Yes."

The doctor sighed, leaned back in his chair. "In that case," he said, "we have a catalogue." He rummaged in a desk drawer and returned with a printed book. A book! Vlad was delighted. He touched the paper, smelled it, and for a moment felt like a child again.

He leafed through it with inexpert fingers, savouring the tactile sensation. Page after page of cool, calm alternatives. "What's this?" he said.

"Ah, yes. A popular choice," Dr. Graff said. "Blood loss in a warm, scented bath. Soft music, candles. A bottle of wine. A pill beforehand to ensure there is no pain. A traditional choice."

"Tradition is important," Vlad said.

"Yes. Yes."

But Vlad was leafing ahead. "This?" he said, with slight revulsion.

"Faux-murder, yes," the doctor said. "Simulated. We cannot sanction humans for the purpose, of course. Nor a digital intelligence, obviously. But we have very life-like simulacra with a basic operating brain, nothing with consciousness, of course, of course. Some of our patients like the idea of a violent death. It is more . . . theatrical."

"I notice one can sign off the recording rights?"

"Some people like to . . . watch. Yes. And some patients appreciate an audience. There is some financial compensation paid to one's heirs in those circumstances—"

"Garish," Vlad said.

"Quite, quite," the doctor said.

"Vulgar."

"That is, certainly, a valid view point, yes, y—"

Vlad was leafing further. "I never thought there were so many ways—" he said.

"So many," the doctor said. "We, humans, are remarkably good at devising new ways to die."

The doctor sat still as Vlad leafed through the rest of the catalogue. "You do not need to decide right away, of course," the doctor said. "We do, in fact, advise a period of consideration before—"

"What if I wanted to do it immediately?" Vlad said.

"There is, of course, paperwork, a process—" the doctor said.

"But it is possible?"

"Of course. We have many of the basic options available right here, in the mortality rooms, complete with full post-mortal service and burial—"

"I'd like this," Vlad said, tapping the page with his finger. The doctor leaned over. "This—oh," he said. "Yes. Surprisingly popular. But not, of course, available, as it were"—he spread his arms in what might have been a shrug—"here. As it were."

"Of course," Vlad said.

"But we can arrange the travel, in full comfort, and accommodation beforehand—"

"Let's do that."

The doctor nodded. "Very well," he said. "Let me call up the forms."

When he next surfaced from that great glittery sea he saw faces, close by. Boris looked angry. Miriam, concerned.

"God damn it, dad."

"Don't swear at me, boy."

"You went to a fucking *suicide* clinic?"

"I go where I want!"

They glared at each other. Miriam laid a hand on Boris's shoulder. He looked at her. Looked at Boris. For a moment his face was the boy's he had been. Hurt in his eyes. Incomprehension. Like when something bad happens. "Boris—"

"Dad—"

Vlad stood up. Stuck his face close to his boy's. "Go away," he said.

"No."

"Boris, I'm your father and I'm telling you to—"

Boris pushed him. Vlad, shocked, fell back. Tottered. Held on to the chair and just stopped himself from falling on the floor. Heard Miriam's sharp intake of breath. Miriam, horrified: "Boris, what did you—"

"Dad? Dad!"

"I'm fine," Vlad said. Righted himself. Almost smiled. "Silly boy," he said.

Boris, breathing hard. Vlad saw his hands, they were closed into fists. All that anger. Never helped anyone. Couldn't help but feel for the boy. "Look," he said. "Just—"

When he surfaced again Miriam was gone and Boris was sitting in a chair in the corner. The boy was asleep.

A good boy, Vlad thought. Came back. Worried for his old dad. Made him proud, really. A doctor. No children though. He would have liked grandchildren. A knock on the door. Boris blinking. The aug pulsing on his neck. Disgusting thing. "I'll get that," Vlad said. Went to the door.

The robot again. R. Patch-It. With Vlad's sister in tow. He should have known. "Vladimir Mordechai Chong," she said. "Just *what* do you think you're doing?"

"Hello, Tamara."

"Don't hello me, Vlad." She stepped inside and the robot followed. "Now what is this nonsense about you killing yourself?"

"For crying out loud, Tamara! Look at you." Vlad felt some of his anger gathering. It had been a long time coming. He had had a long moment of emerging from the sea, the memories falling away like water. Enough time to go to the clinic and make the arrangements. Not enough time, it had turned out, to execute them before another relapse. It was becoming harder to break the surface. Soon, he knew, he would remain submerged in water for good. "You're almost entirely a machine."

"We're *all* machines," his sister said. "Are you proud because the parts that make you are biological? Soft, fallible, weak? You may as well be proud of learning to clean your bottom or tying your shoelaces, Vlad. You're a machine, I'm a machine, and R. Brother Patch-It over there is a machine. When you're gone, you're gone. There's no afterlife but the one we build ourselves."

"The fabled robot heaven," Vlad said. He felt tired. "Enough!" he said. "I appreciate what you are trying to do. All of you. Boris."

"Yes, dad?"

"Come here." It was strange, to see his boy and see this man, this almost stranger, that he had become. Something of Weiwei in him, though. Something of Vlad, too. "I can no longer remember your mother's name," he told him.

"What?"

"Boris, I spoke to the doctors. Weiwei's Folly has spread through me. Nodal filaments filling up every available space. Invading my body. I am drowning under the weight of memories. They make no sense any more. I don't know who I am because I can't make them behave. Boris . . ."

"Dad," Boris said. Vlad raised his hand and touched the boy's cheek. It was wet. He stroked it, gently. "I'm old, Boris. I'm old and I'm tired. I want to rest. I want to choose how I go, and I want to go with dignity, and with my mind intact. Is that so wrong?"

"No, dad. No, it's not."

"Don't cry, Boris."

"I'm not crying."

"Good."

"Dad?"

"Yes?"

"I'm all right. You can let go, now."

Vlad released him. Remembered the boy who asked him to walk with him, "Just to the next lamp post, dad." They'd go in the dark towards that pool of light and, on reaching it, stop. Then the boy would say, "Just to the next lamp post, dad. I can go the rest on my own. Honest."

On and on they went, following the trail of lights. On and on they went until they made it safely home.

One's death should be a memorable occasion and, on this occasion, Vlad felt, everything really did go swimmingly.

They had departed by mini-bus from Central Station. Vlad sat in the front, enjoying the warmth of the sun, next to the driver. A small delegation sat in the back: Boris, and Miriam, Vlad's sister Tamara, R. Patch-It, Ibrahim the alte-zachen man and Eliezer, the god artist, both of whom once, long ago, worked with Vlad in the construction site. Relatives came to say their good-byes, and the atmosphere was one almost of a party. Vlad hugged young Yan Chong, who was soon to marry his boyfriend, Youssou, got a kiss on the cheek from his sister's friend Esther, who he had, once, almost had an affair with but, in the end, didn't. He remembered it well, and it was strange to see her so *old*. In his mind she was still the beautiful young woman he once got drunk with at a shebeen, when his wife was away, somewhere, and they had come close to it but, in the end, they couldn't do it. He remembered walking back home, alone, and the sense of relief he'd felt when he came in through the door. Boris was a boy then. He was asleep and Vlad came and sat by his side and stroked his hair. Then he went and made himself a cup of tea.

The mini-bus spread out solar panel wings and began to glide almost soundlessly down the old tarmac road. Neighbours, friends, and relatives waved and shouted good-byes. The bus turned left on Mount Zion and suddenly the old neighbourhood disappeared from view. It felt like leaving home, for that is what it was. It felt sad but it also felt like freedom.

They turned on Salameh and soon came to the interchange and onto the old highway to Jerusalem. The rest of the journey went smoothly, in quiet, the coastal plain giving way gradually to hills. Then they came to the Bab-el-Wad and rose sharply along the mountain road to Jerusalem.

It felt like a rollercoaster along the mountain road, with sharp inclines giving way to sudden drops. They circled the city without going in and drove along the circle road, between a Palestine on one side and an Israel on the other, though the two were often mixed up in such a way only the invisible digitals could keep them apart.

The change in geography was startling. Suddenly the mountains ended and they were dropping, and the desert began without warning. It was the strange thing about this country that had become Weiwei's home, Vlad thought—how quickly and startlingly the landscape changed in so small a place. It was no wonder the Arabs and the Jews had fought over it for so long.

Dunes appeared, the land became a yellow place and camels rested by the side of the old road. Down, down, down they went, until they passed the sign for the ocean level and kept going, following the road to the lowest place on Earth. Soon they were travelling past the Dead Sea and the blue, calm water reflected the sky like a mirror. Bromine released from the sea filled the air, causing a soothing, calming effect on the human psyche.

Just beyond the Dead Sea the Arava desert opened up and here, at last, some two hours after setting off from Central Station, they arrived at their destination.

The Euthanasia Park sat on its own in a green oasis of calm. They drew at the gates and parked in the almost empty car park. Boris helped Vlad down from his seat. Outside it was hot, a dry hotness that soothed and comforted. Water sprinklers made their whoosh-whoosh-whoosh sound as they irrigated the manicured grass.

"Are you sure, dad?" Boris said.

Vlad just nodded. He took in a deep breath of air. The smell of water and freshly-cut grass. The smell of childhood.

Together they looked on the park. There, a swimming pool glinting blue, where one could drown in peace and tranquillity. There, a massive, needle-like tower rising into the sky, for the jumpers, those who wanted to go out with one great rush of air. And there, at last, the thing that they had travelled all this way for. The Urbonas Ride.

The Euthanasia Coaster.

Named after its designer, Julijonas Urbonas, it was a thing of marvel and beautiful engineering. It began with an enormous climb, rising to half a kilometer above the ground. Then the drop. A five hundred meter drop straight down that led to a series of three hundred and thirty degree loops one after the other in rapid succession. Vlad felt his heart beating faster just by looking at it. He remembered the first time he had climbed up the space port in his exoskeleton. He had perched up there, on Level Five of the unfinished building, and looked down, and felt as though the whole city, the whole world, were his.

He could already feel the memories crowding in on him. Demanding that he take them, hold them, examine them, search amongst them for her name, but it was missing. He hugged his son again, and kissed his sister. "You old fool," she said. He shook hands with the robo-priest. Miriam, next. "Look after him," Vlad said, gesturing at his son.

"I will."

Then Eliezer, and Ibrahim. Two old men. "One day I'll go on one of these," Eliezer said. "What a rush."

"Not me," Ibrahim said. "It's the sea for me. Only the sea."

They kissed on the cheeks, hugged, one last time. Ibrahim brought out a bottle of arak. Eliezer had glasses. "We'll drink to you," Eliezer said.

"You do that."

With that he left them. He was left alone. The park waited for him, the machines heeding his steps. He went up to the roller coaster and sat down in the car and put on the safety belt carefully around himself.

The car began to move. Slowly it climbed, and climbed, and climbed. The desert down below, the park reduced to a tiny square of green. The Dead Sea in the distance, as smooth as a mirror, and he could almost think he could see Lot's wife, who had been turned into a pillar of salt.

The car reached the top and, for a moment, stayed there. It let him savour the moment. Taste the air on his tongue. And suddenly he remembered her name. It was Aliyah.

The car dropped.

Vlad felt the gravity crushing him down, taking the air from his lungs. His heart beat the fastest it had ever beat, the blood rushed to his face. The wind howled in his ears, against his face. He dropped and levelled and for a moment air rushed in and he cried out in exultation. The car shot away from the drop and onto the first of the loops, carrying him with it, shot like a bullet at three hundred and fifty-eight kilometers an hour. Vlad was propelled through loop after loop faster than he could think; until at last the enormous gravity, thus generated, claimed him.

BESIDE THE DAMNED RIVER

D. J. COCKBURN

All that really happens in "Beside the Damned River" by new writer D. J. Cockburn, this year's winner of the James White Award, is that an old man helps repair a truck that has broken down on a muddy backcountry road in Thailand. What makes it science fiction are the changes that have occurred to the old man's homeland over the course of his lifetime, and what makes the story surprisingly powerful are the changes to the old man's life brought about by those changes, and how he feels about it all.

In between a long stretch of rejections, D. J. Cockburn's fiction has been published in various venues, including Buzzy, Interzone, Stupefying Stories, *and, most recently, in the* Qualia Nous *anthology. He's supported his writing habit through medical research on various parts of the African continent. Earlier phases of his life have included teaching unfortunate children and experimenting on unfortunate fish. His website is at http://cockburndj.wordpress.com.*

Narong heard children running to the road before he heard the pickup truck. He sighed. When he'd been a child, there had been nothing unusual about cars in Ubon Ratchathani province. All the same, he was happy enough to set down the empty water barrow and stretch his back as the plume of dust approached.

As the truck and its trailer got closer, he savoured the healthy roar from the engine. As rare as the unscraped white paint under the film of dust. He couldn't remember when he last saw a truck that didn't carry its age as he did, in wrinkled bodywork and incessant wheezing before starting up. He winced as a pothole thumped the tyres and rattled the suspension. The healthy sound wouldn't last long if the driver kept hitting them like that.

Perhaps Narong was still a child at heart because he squinted, trying to make out the manufacturer's badge. The truck thumped another pothole. The engine screamed in mechanical agony, faded to a whine and fell silent. The truck coasted past him and stopped fifty metres away. He wondered what was under the tarpaulins covering the truck's bed and its trailer.

A *farang* woman got out on the passenger side. Her ginger hair was just long enough to shimmer as she moved. She wore a sleeveless shirt and knee-length shorts, revealing skin so white it defied the sun pounding this water-forsaken corner of Thailand.

Narong's interest stirred. Today would have more to mark it than dust and water barrows.

The line of children by the roadside collapsed into a gaggle as they ran toward her, like a shoal of catfish outside a river temple when someone threw food into the water. Narong decided he was definitely still a child when he found himself following them as fast as his arthritic knees would carry him.

The woman backed toward the truck, looking as though she expected the children to steal the clothes she stood in. Her bare shoulder touched the hot metal of the cab. She jerked forward with a yelp.

"Stand back, younger brothers and sisters." Narong caught his breath. He may have been a child at heart, but the pounding in his ears reminded him he didn't have the heart of a child. "It is not good to get so close to our visitors that they cannot move without treading on you."

The children backed away without taking their eyes off the woman. One of them fell into the dry ditch beside the road but there was no laughter as he scrambled out. Even the funniest mishap was less interesting than an exotic stranger. *Farang* were such a rare sight that today's children didn't even know the jokes that kept Narong and his childhood friends entertained for hours.

The woman looked at her driver, a young man with his hair cut short at the back with a longer fringe. He'd probably never driven more than a hundred kilometres from Bangkok. The driver spread his hands, looking helpless. He reminded Narong of the junior official the government sent a couple of years ago, who gave a speech about how the government hadn't forgotten the north east of its country and went back to Bangkok before it got dark. Even the government had shown more sense than to let such a boy drive himself.

The driver stepped out of the cab and looked at Narong. His stare carried all the respect Narong expected a man wearing foreign-made shoes to show an old man wearing sandals made from an old tyre.

Narong had met too many well-dressed boys from Bangkok to expect him to say anything worth listening to. He walked toward the *farang* woman. He wanted to hear her voice.

She watched him coming without looking at him directly, showing her wariness. Narong pressed his hands together and bowed. "*Sawadee kob.*"

She shuffled her feet and returned his *wai* with the clumsiness of someone unused to the action.

"*Sawadee kob,*" she mumbled. No one had told her women said "*kha*" instead of "*kob.*"

"My name is Narong," he said. "Guess your gearbox dropped."

Relief washed over her face at being addressed in English.

"Angela Ri . . ." She bit off what Narong assumed was her surname. "Angela."

She held out her hand, then remembered she had already done the local equivalent and withdrew it. "How do you know it's the gearbox?"

Narong felt a moment of disappointment. Her voice sounded as if she never used it to laugh.

"Sure sounded like it," he said.

"The gearbox. That's bad?"

The question was addressed to the driver, who looked as though she had set him a problem in differential calculus.

"Got a toolbox?" asked Narong.

Angela looked at the driver.

"Must be jack and wrench somewhere," he said.

"He said a *toolbox*, Gehng. It's a bust gearbox, not a flat tyre."

As she rounded on Gehng, Narong saw pearls of sweat gathered across her shoulders. How much water she must drink in this climate? He winced at the volume he estimated.

"In this make, it's usually under a panel behind the cab," said Narong.

Angela looked at Gehng, who showed no sign of knowing if there was a panel, let alone a toolbox. Narong reached for the knot tying the tarpaulin to the cleats along the side of the truck. Gehng seized his wrist.

"It is not good to look underneath." The hard edge in Gehng's Thai contrasted with his deferential English.

"Oh for God's sake, Gehng, let him look." Angela may not have understood Thai, but Gehng's body language was unambiguous. "*He* seems to have some idea of what he's doing."

"I call headquarters in Bangkok." Gehng pulled a phone from the pouch on his belt. "They send . . ."

His voice faded.

"Where there's no water, nobody repairs the roads." Narong returned to the knot. "Where the roads are bad, there are no maintenance trucks. Where there are no maintenance trucks, there is no signal."

The rope was so new it was slippery. Whoever tied it knew nothing about knots and had tried to compensate by tying several of them. Narong's fingers weren't as nimble as they once were.

"Narong. I know your name." Gehng returned to Thai. "So if you ever speak of what is in the truck, it will not be good for you and your village."

Narong tugged the last knot apart. He stepped back and looked at Gehng. He was more irked by Gehng's omission of the respectful "*pee*," the right of an older man, than by his empty threats. If whatever was under the tarpaulin was that important, Gehng wouldn't admit he'd allowed Narong to see it. If Gehng reported to anyone who cared who said what in Ubon Ratchathani, he'd leave Narong out of the report.

He looked at Angela with the secret surname, letting Gehng know it was obvious who was in charge here.

"Go ahead," she said.

Narong allowed himself a trace of a smirk when he looked back at Gehng. A look that said if he was trying to impress Angela into giving him a bonus, he wasn't doing very well so he could stop acting the *phoo yai* big man. Gehng's eyes replied that he read the message and hated Narong for it, but realised his mouth would serve him best by staying shut.

Narong glanced at Angela, whose expression hadn't changed. She had seen nothing that passed between him and Gehng.

Narong couldn't resist a flourish when he threw back the tarpaulin, revealing the load to the children. The rock on the truck's bed was matt grey. Its surface was bubbled as though it had been almost melted and then solidified. He touched one of the bubbles. It was as hard as stone. Some sort of polymer, he guessed. He looked up to the holes bored into the top of the rock and understood Gehng's unease.

Angela gave him a smile that didn't quite touch her eyes. She obviously hoped an old man pushing a water barrow wouldn't know what he was looking at.

"Pity we can't see it without the heat shield," he said. "The children would appreciate the sparkle of enriched platinum ore. From an M-type asteroid."

Angela said nothing. Even though asteroid mining had produced enough metal to drop prices, he was looking at no less than five million dollars.

"So that's a crane in the trailer, and the parachute that was bolted to it?" he asked.

Angela's nod was minute. If she was trying to hide her thoughts, she wasn't very good at it. She was wondering how an old peasant understood so much and wished he didn't. She wouldn't know Ubon Ratchathani had been a wealthy province twenty years ago. If the world had retreated from Ubon Ratchathani with the water, Ubon Ratchathani had not forgotten the world.

The curved edge of the asteroid didn't cover the toolbox panel, so they wouldn't need to unload it. Still, some temptations couldn't be resisted.

"I'm not as young as I used to be," he said to Angela. "Perhaps you could have your driver get the toolbox out?"

Angela nodded. "Gehng."

The look on Gehng's face gave Narong a memory to treasure.

He turned back to Angela. "Your company sent you to recover it?"

For a moment, her face showed the need to avoid the question battling the need to ingratiate herself with a possible rescuer. He waited until she nodded uneasily. "It was supposed to go into the Gobi Desert. That's . . ."

She waved a hand, wondering how to explain the geography.

"In Mongolia," he said.

"Yes. Um. Well, something went wrong and it ended up in Thailand, so they sent us to get it."

"And take it to Cambodia," said Narong.

"Uh, no, I mean . . ."

"You're going the wrong way for Bangkok." Narong was enjoying himself a little too much. "No airport ahead of you till you get to Phnomh Penh."

The sound of a tearing shirt and a very Anglophone expletive drew Narong's attention to Gehng falling out of the truck with the toolbox.

"Thank you, *Neung* Gehng." Narong deliberately addressed him as a younger man.

He opened the toolbox. The shine of stainless steel assailed him. For the first time since he'd seen the truck, he wanted something. Rows of screwdrivers and spanners cried out to him, pleading their supremacy over his own rusty toolkit that he kept wrapped in an old shirt.

He called himself a foolish old man. Tools like these belonged to his past. Narong's knees cracked as he eased himself on his back. He pulled himself under the truck. There wasn't a speck of rust on the chassis or the suspension, which was reinforced to take the load. It was a youthful vehicle compared to the doddering old wrecks he was so often called to resurrect, but he doubted it was treated with a fraction of the care people lavished on their vehicles in Ubon Ratchathani. This truck was owned by people who could afford to hand it off to a driver who didn't realise he was invested in it until it broke down. It was painful to look at.

"You should be careful on these roads," said Narong. "The dirt tracks aren't too bad, but a lot of the roads round here are just tarmac that broke up for want of maintenance. They'll rip your truck to pieces with this load."

The answering silence told him Angela was glaring at Gehng and Gehng was looking anywhere but at Angela. Gehng must have bored her because her feet moved behind the front wheel until they were level with Narong's head. Her face appeared as she squatted down to watch him.

"How's it going?" she asked.

She wanted him to say he'd have it fixed in five minutes, no problem.

"I'll know in a minute."

She was leaning forward to see under the truck, giving him an interesting view down the front of her top. He hauled his eyes back to the gearbox. He was too old for such things, he told himself sternly. But he couldn't resist snatching another look.

"What company do you work for?" he asked.

"One of the small ones." Her eyes shifted away. "You probably haven't heard of it."

He'd heard enough to know there were no small companies able to afford the investment needed to mine asteroids. He also knew that while the UN Outer Space Treaty said nothing about exploitation, it didn't allow for staking ownership of asteroids. If a chunk of asteroid happened to fall on Thailand, it became the property of the Thai government. Angela and Gehng couldn't have made it more obvious that removing the asteroid was illegal if they had shouted it at him. No wonder Gehng was nervous.

It occurred to Narong that he was helping Angela steal from his country. Still, if the government cared whether people in Ubon Ratchathani followed its rules, it wouldn't have left them to desiccate.

"You seem to know a lot about mechanics," said Angela. "And you speak very good English."

Narong managed to restrict himself to studying her face. She didn't see what she was doing as stealing. She was going where her company had sent her, doing an unpleasant job that involved heat, dust and keeping the company's business a little more confidential than usual. Gehng looked like a junior employee of a local subcontractor, who would be in Thailand long after Angela had left for good. No wonder he didn't want anyone seeing the asteroid.

"I used to be a professor of engineering at Chulalongkorn University," he said.

"Chula . . . I'm sorry, I haven't heard of that."

"It closed five years ago. When the Chinese built their dams upstream of us, well, a country lives on water as much as a man or a woman does. We shrivelled up. We couldn't afford all our universities."

Angela sat down in the dusty road. *Farang* could never squat for very long.

"So you came here?"

The incredulity in her voice drew another look from him. Her head was tilted to one side and her brow was furrowed. She really didn't understand.

"I grew up here. Of course it was greener then."

"But it's . . ." She waved her arm. "It's so dry. It must be so hard. Is there nowhere else you could go?"

As if companies like hers were always taking on unemployed academics past retirement age. He'd applied all over the world when the department closed. He'd still had ambition then.

"It's better than the slums in Bangkok," he said.

Her expression didn't change. For her, Bangkok meant air-conditioned hotels and restaurants on Sukhumvit Road. The new slums sprawling outside Bangkok's dykes were as alien to her as the people of Ubon Ratchathani had been until the gearbox screamed. There was no point in trying to explain how the slums flooded every time it rained on a high tide, and how they would need to be abandoned altogether if the sea level kept rising over the next decade or two.

He changed spanners.

"I used to work on monofilament dew collectors. When I came here, I set them up on every hillock we can get a barrow to," he said. "They give us enough water to grow GM cassava, and a few other things."

He felt the cadence of his voice slip into the turns of the spanner. "We'll do *what* we can with what we *have* for as long as we *can*."

It was a beautiful spanner.

"The longer we can keep our children away from the slums, the better. Do you have children, *Khun* Angela?"

"Two girls." Perhaps her voice had known laughter after all. "It's hard being away from them. Sometimes you have to do what the company says, you know?"

"I'm sure."

"Their names are Jasmine and Rebecca. I haven't even been able to call them for the last couple of days."

Narong saw the anecdote he would become, the old peasant pushing a barrow who turned out to be a professor and rescued mother in the wilderness. Her eyes sparkled as she spoke of her girls, looking forward to telling them about him. He concentrated on the gearbox, giving the odd grunt when Angela paused for breath. It was as though Angela had been keeping all her talk behind a dam he'd breached when he mentioned her favourite subject. Narong smiled. Any thought that involved breaching dams was worth smiling at.

"I never married," he said.

Neither of them had much to say after that. He worked in silence for the next half hour. When he pulled himself from under the truck, Gehng was in the driver's seat with his feet dangling outside the cab. His disconsolate expression made him look very young. Angela paced up and down, her exposed skin already tinted pink.

She turned to him with a pleading look. "Could you fix it?"

"Partly," said Narong. "It will run in first and second gear, but no higher. It should get you to Phnomh Penh. You'll be able to get a proper repair there."

Angela bit her lip. "It'll take, what? Ten, twelve hours to get to Phnomh Penh in second gear?"

"At least. You are welcome to stay here if you wish. Gehng could send another vehicle when he gets there."

Angela's hair was lank with sweat. She wouldn't know how to wash without using water as though it came from an unlimited reservoir. He would have regretted the offer if there was any chance she would accept it.

"That's very kind of you," she said, "but I need to stay with the load."

She was determined to annihilate every kilometre between her and an air-conditioned room with a phone she could call her children on.

"Of course."

Narong handed the toolbox to Gehng. He felt a morsel of pity as Gehng scrambled under the asteroid fragment. He wasn't looking forward to the next ten to twelve hours.

He stood with Angela, watching Gehng replace the tarpaulin.

"You should keep the revs low," he said in English. "I did what I could, but too much strain will drop it again."

Gehng didn't react, but Angela nodded. Her eyes wouldn't leave the rev counter all the way to Phnomh Penh.

"We'll be careful," she said. "I really appreciate your help, sir." She hadn't caught his name. "How much do I owe you?"

"There is no charge. It cost me nothing."

She *had* made his day more interesting. It would cheapen the memory if it became a transaction.

"There must be something I can do. You saved our lives."

Narong managed not to laugh at the dramatic statement. He watched her watching him, wanting to pay off her sense of obligation. Her body was already poised as if to run for the cab. From some dark corner of his mind, the idea of asking for another look down her top jumped into his consciousness.

"Next time you lose a rock, could you drop it on one of the dams blocking the Mekong?"

She laughed. "I'll see what I can do."

He'd given her the punch line to the story she'd tell her daughters.

Gehng finished his idea of tying down the tarpaulin. He made a *wai* in Narong's direction. Angela was oblivious to the disrespect in the minimal dip of his shoulders. Narong sent them on their way with a straight back and a smile that would be a friendly parting for Angela and an insult to Gehng.

The note of the truck's engine rose, fell as Gehng engaged second gear, rose again and fell abruptly. Narong laughed aloud, imagining Angela ordering Gehng to keep the revs down and Gehng's stifled sigh.

He picked up the socket set and spanner he'd left under the truck. An old man should not be a slave to temptation, but it could be years before anyone even looked in the toolbox again. He put the tools on top of the water barrow and pushed it toward the dew collectors on the hillock.

the colonel

PETER WATTS

Self-described as "a reformed marine biologist," Peter Watts has quickly established himself as one of the most respected hard-science writers of the
twenty-first century. His short work has appeared in The New Space Opera
2, Tor.com, Tesseracts, The Solaris Book of New Science Fiction, Upgraded, On Spec, Divine Realms, Prairie Fire, and elsewhere. He is the
author of the well-received Rifters sequence, including the novels Starfish,
Maelstrom, Behemoth: B-Max, and Behemoth: Seppuku. His short work
has been collected in Ten Monkeys, Ten Minutes, and his novelette "The
Island" won the Hugo Award in 2010. His novel Blindsight was widely hailed
as one of the best hard-SF books of the decade. His most recent novel, Echopraxia, is a sequel to Blindsight. He lives in Toronto, Canada.

The story that follows deals with a military man trying to evaluate and
contain the threat to ordinary humans from conjoined hive mentalities
who might drive them into obsolescence and extinction, and who may not
turn out to be even the worst threat to human civilization—a struggle deepened and complicated by his troubled relationship with his own family, and
with his own conflicted heart.

The insurgents are already vectoring in from the east when the flag goes up. By
the time the Colonel's back in the game—processed the intel, found a vantage
point, grabbed the nearest network specialist out of bed and plunked her down at
the board—they've got the compound surrounded. Rain forest hides them from
baseline vision but the Colonel's borrowed eyes see well into the infrared. From
half a world away, he tracks each fuzzy heatprint filtering up through the impover-
ished canopy.

One of the few good things about the decimation of Ecuador's wildlife: not much
chance, these days, of mistaking a guerrilla for a jaguar.

"I make thirteen," the Lieutenant says, tallying blobs of false color on the display.

A welter of tanks and towers in the middle of a clear-cut. A massive umbilical,
studded with paired lifting surfaces along its length, sags gently into the sky from
the pump station at its heart. Eight kilometers farther west—and twenty more, straight

up—an aerostat wallows at the end of the line like a great bloated tick, vomiting sulfates into the stratosphere.

There's a fence around the compound of course, old-fashioned chain link with razor-wire frosting, not so much a barrier as a nostalgic reminder of simpler times. There's a ring of scorched earth ten meters wide between fence and forest, another eighty from fence to factory. There are defenses guarding the perimeter.

"Can we access the on-site security?" He tried—unsuccessfully—before the Lieutenant arrived, but she's the specialist.

She shakes her head. "It's self-contained. No fiber in, no phone to answer. Doesn't even transmit unless it's already under attack. Only way to access the code is to actually go out there. Pretty much hack-proof."

So they're stuck looking down from geostat. "Can you show me the ranges at least? Ground measures only."

"Sure. That's just blueprint stuff." A schematic blooms across the Lieutenant's board, scaled and overlayed onto the real time. Translucent lemon pie—slices fan out from various points around the edge of the facility, an overlapping hot zone extending to the fence and a little beyond. The guns are all pointed out, though. Anybody who makes it to the hole in the donut is home free.

The heatprints enter the clearing; the Lieutenant collapses the palette down to visible light.

"Huh," the Colonel says.

The insurgents have not stepped into view. They didn't walk or run. They're—*scuttling*, for want of a better word. Crawling. Squirming arrhythmically. They remind the Colonel of crabs afflicted with some kind of neurological disorder, flipped onto their backs and trying to right themselves. Each pushes a small bedroll along the ground.

"What the fuck," the Lieutenant murmurs.

The insurgents are slathered head-to-toe in some kind of brownish paste. Mud idols in cargo shorts. Two pairs have linked up like wrestling sloths, like conjoined twins fused gut-to-back. They lurch and roll to the foot of the fence.

The station's defenses are not firing.

Not bedrolls: *mats*, roughly woven, natural fiber from the look of it. The insurgents unroll them at the fence, throw them up over the razorwire to ensure safe passage during the climb.

The Lieutenant glances up. "They networked yet?"

"Can't be. It'd trip the alarms."

"Why haven't they tripped the alarms already? They're *right there*." She frowns. "Maybe they disabled security somehow."

The insurgents are inside the perimeter.

"Your hack-proof security?" The Colonel shakes his head. "No, if they'd taken out the guns they'd just—*shit*."

"What?"

Insulative mud, judiciously applied to reshape the thermal profile. No hardware, no alloys or synthetics to give the game away. Interlocked bodies, contortionist poses: how would those shapes profile at ground level? What would the security cameras see, looking out across—

"Wildlife. *They're impersonating wildlife.*" *Jaguars and guerillas, my* ass . . .

"What?"

"It's a legacy loophole, don't you—" But of course she doesn't. Too young to remember Ecuador's once-proud tradition of protecting its charismatic megafauna. Not even born when that herd of peccaries and Greenpeacers got mowed down by an overeager pillbox programmed to defend the local airstrip. Wouldn't know about the safeguards since legislated into every automated targeting system in the country, long-since forgotten for want of any wildlife left to protect.

So much for on-site security. The insurgents will be smart enough to hold off on coalescing until they're beyond any local firing solution. "How long before the drones arrive?"

The Lieutenant dips into her own head, checks a feed. "Seventeen minutes."

"We have to assume they'll have completed their mission before then."

"Yes sir, but—*what* mission? What are they gonna do, scratch the paint with their fingernails?"

He doesn't know. His source didn't know. The insurgents themselves probably don't know, won't know until they network; you could snatch one off the ground this very instant, read the voxels right off her brain, get no joy at all.

That's the scary thing about hive minds. Their plans are too big to fit into any one piece.

He shakes his head. "So we can't access the guns. What about normal station operations?"

"Sure. Stations have to talk to each other to keep the injection rates balanced."

The insurgents are halfway to the scrubbers. It's astonishing that such quick headway could emerge from such graceless convulsion.

"Get us in."

A wave of stars ignites across the schematic, right to left: switches, valves, a myriad interfaces coming online. The Colonel points to a cluster of sparks in the southwest quadrant. "Can we vent those tanks?"

"Not happily." She frowns. "A free dump would be catastrophic. Only way the system would go along with that is if it thought it was preventing something even worse."

"Such as?"

"Tank explosion, I guess."

"Set it up."

She starts whispering sweet nothings to distant gatekeepers, but she doesn't look pleased. "Sir, isn't this technically—I mean, use of poison gas—"

"Sulfate precursor. Geoengineering stockpile. Not a weapon of war." Technically.

"Yes sir," she says unhappily.

"Countermeasures have to be in place *before* they link up, Lieutenant. If there's any exploit—any at all—the hive will see it. There's no way to outthink the damn thing once it's engaged."

"Yes sir. Ready."

"That was fast."

"You said it had to be, sir." She extends a finger toward a fresh crimson icon pulsing on the board. "Should I—"

"Not yet." The Colonel stares down from vicarious orbit, tries to make sense of the tableaux. What the hell are they doing? What can even a hive mind accomplish with reed mats and a few kilograms of mu—

Wait a second . . .

He picks an intruder at random, zooms in. The mud sheathing that body has an almost golden glint to it, now that he looks closely. Something not-quite-mineral, something—

He calls up an archive, searches the microbial index for any weaponized synthetics that might eat heterocyclics. Scores.

"They're going after the umbilical."

The Lieutenant glances up. "Sir?"

"The mud. It's not just a disguise it's a *payload*, it's—"

"A biopaste." The Lieutenant whistles, returns her attention to the board with renewed focus.

The Colonel tries to think. They're not just aiming to cut the aerostat loose; you don't need a hive for that, you don't even need to breach the perimeter. Whatever this is, it's microsurgical. Something that requires massive on-site computation—maybe something to do with microclimate, something that can be influenced by wind or humidity or any of a dozen other chaotic variables. If they're not trying to cut the umbilical outright they might be trying to *maneuver* it somehow: a biocorroded hole exactly X millimeters in diameter here, a stretching patch of candle-wax monomers over there, and way up in the stratosphere the aerostat sways some precise number of meters on some precise bearing—

To what end? Play bumper-cars with the maintenance drones? Block some orbital line-of-sight, nudge a distant act of ground-based terrorism into surveillance eclipse at a critical moment? Maybe they're not going for the umbilical after all, maybe they're—

"Sir?" The first of the insurgents has made it to the donut hole. "Sir, if we have to light 'em up before they coalesce—"

"*Not yet, Lieutenant.*"

He's a blind man in a bright room. He's a rhesus monkey playing chess with a grand master. He has no idea of his opponent's strategy. He has no concept even of the rules of the game. He only knows he's bound to lose.

The last of the insurgents lurches out of weapons range. The Lieutenant's finger hovers over that icon as though desperate to scratch a maddening itch.

Coalescence.

That far-focus moment, that thousand-soul stare. You can see it in their eyes if you know what to look for, if you're close enough and fast enough. The Colonel is neither. All he has is a top-down view through a telescope thirty-six thousand kilometers away, ricocheted through the atmosphere and spread across this table. But he can see what follows: the fusion of interlocking pieces, the simultaneous change in physical posture, the instant evolutionary leap from spastic quadruped to sapient superweapon.

Out of many, one.

"*Now.*"

It knows. Of course it knows. It's inconceivable that this vast emergent mind hasn't—in the very instant of its awakening—detected some vital clue, made some inference to lay the whole trap bare. The station's defenses whine belatedly into gear, startled awake in the sudden glare of a million thoughts; multimind networks may be invisible to human eyes but they're bright blinding tapestries down in RF. The hive, safely behind the firing line, has no need to care about *that*.

No, what's got its attention now is the wave of hydrogen sulfide billowing from the southern storage tanks: silent, invisible, heavy as a blanket and certain death to any stand-alone soul. No baseline would suspect a thing until the faint smell of rotten eggs told him he was already dead.

But this soul does not stand alone. Eleven of its bodies simultaneously turn and flee back toward the fence, each following a unique trajectory with a little Brownian randomness layered in to throw off the tracking algos. The other two stand fast in the donut hole, draw sidearms from belts—

The Colonel frowns. *Why didn't the sensors pick those up?*

"Hey, are those guns—that looks like *bone*," the Lieutenant says.

The nodes open fire.

It *is* bone. Something like it anyway; metal or plastic would have triggered the sensors before they'd even reached the fence. The slugs are probably ceramic, though; no osteo derivative would be able to punch through the least of those conduits . . .

Except that's not what the hive is going for. They're shooting at any old pipe or panel, anything metal, anything that might—

Strike a spark . . .

Because hydrogen sulfide isn't just poisonous, you idiot. It's flammable.

"Holy shit," the Lieutenant whispers as the zone goes up.

It's a counter-countermeasure, improvised on the fly. It's a queen sacrifice; some of these bodies are doomed but maybe the fire will burn off enough gas to give the rest a chance, suck back and consume enough of that spreading poison for eleven bodies to make it to safety while two burn like living torches.

For a few seconds the Colonel thinks it's going to work. As Hail-Marys go it's a good one; no baseline would have even come up with a plan in that split second, much less put it into action. But faint hope is only a little better than none, and not even demigods can change the laws of physics. The sacrificial nodes blaze and blacken and crumble like dead leaves. Three others make it halfway up the chainlink before the gas reaches them, still thick enough to kill if not to burn. The rest die convulsing in the dirt, flesh oiled and guttering with spotty candlelight, jerking with the impact of bullets that can finally kick at targets once they're down.

The poisonous carpet spreads invisibly into the jungle, off to kill whatever weedy life it might still find there.

The Lieutenant swallows, face pale with nausea and the unleashed memories of ancient war crimes. "We're sure this isn't against the . . ." she trails off, unwilling to challenge a superior officer, unconvinced by legalistic hairsplitting, unable to assess the threat posed by this vanquished enemy.

But the threat is so very real. These things are fucking dangerous. If not for some happenstance bit of intel—unpredictable as a quantum flutter, never to be repeated—this hive would have accomplished its goal without discovery or opposition. Or maybe it did; maybe everything that's just happened was part of the plan, maybe that lucky tip-off was deliberately crafted to make him dance on command. Maybe this was a defeat and he'll never know.

That's the thing about hives. Always ten steps ahead. The fact that there are still jurisdictions where such abominations remain legal scares the Colonel more than he can say.

"Why are we doing this, sir?"

He scowls. "Doing what, exactly? Fighting for the survival of the individual?"

But the Lieutenant shakes her head. "Why are we still just—*fighting* all the time? Among ourselves? I mean, weren't the aliens supposed to make us all forget our petty differences? Unite humanity against the common threat?"

The ranks are full of them, these days.

"They didn't threaten us, Lieutenant. They only took our picture." That's what everyone assumes, anyway. Sixty-four thousand objects of unknown origin, simultaneously igniting in a precise incandescent grid encircling the globe. Screaming back into space along half the EM spectrum as the atmosphere burned them to ash.

"But they're still out there. Whatever sent them is, anyway. Even after thirteen years—"

Fourteen. The Colonel feels muscles tighten at the corners of his mouth. *But who's counting.*

"And with *Theseus* lost—"

"There's no evidence *Theseus* is lost," he says shortly.

"Yes, sir."

"Nobody said it was going to be a weekend mission."

"Yes, sir." She returns her attention to the board, but he thinks there was something in her face as she turned away. He wonders if it might have been recognition.

Unlikely. It was a long time ago. And he always kept behind the scenes.

"Well—" he heads for the door. "Might as well send in the clowns."

"Sir?"

He stops but doesn't turn.

"I was wondering—if it isn't above my pay grade, sir—but you seemed *really* concerned about what that hive would do when it booted. No way we could keep up when it was engaged, you said."

"I'm waiting for a question, Lieutenant."

"Why did we wait? We could've gassed the lot of them before they ever linked up, and if they *were* that dangerous—well, it seems like bad strategy."

He can't disagree. Which is not to say it was unwarranted.

"Hives are dangerous, Lieutenant. Never doubt that for an instant. That said . . ."

He considers, and settles for something like the truth.

"If killing's the only option, I'd rather kill one than thirteen."

Some threats lurk closer to home. Some are somewhat less—overt.

Take the woman on the feed, for example: a tiny thing, maybe 160 cm. Nothing about Liana Lutterodt suggests anything other than contagious enthusiasm for a world of wonders. No hint of the agency that pays her expenses, sends her on these goodwill tours to dispense rainbows and a promise of Utopia.

No hint of forces deep in the Oregon desert, using her as a sock puppet.

"We climbed this hill," she says now, to the attentive host of *In Conversation*. "Each step up we could see farther, so of course we kept going. Now we're at the top. Science has been at the top for a few centuries now."

Her background's unremarkable, for the most part: born in Ghana, raised in the UKapelago, top of her class in systems theory and theistic virology.

"Now we look out across the plain and we see this other tribe dancing around above the clouds, even higher than we are. Maybe it's a mirage, maybe it's a trick. Or maybe they just climbed a higher peak we can't see because the clouds are blocking the view."

Little in the way of overt criminal activity. Charged with possession of a private database at thirteen, interfering with domestic surveillance pickups at twelve. The usual fines and warnings racked up by the young before they learn to embrace the panopticon.

"So we head off to find out—but every step takes us *downhill*. No matter what direction we go, we can't move off our peak without losing our vantage point. Naturally we climb back up again. We're trapped on a local maximum."

Finally managed to drop off the grid legally by signing up with the Bicameral Order, which gets special exemption by virtue of being largely incomprehensible even when you *do* keep an eye on them.

"But what if there *is* a higher peak out there, way across the plain? The only way to get there is bite the bullet, come down off our foothill and trudge along the riverbed until we finally start going uphill again. And it's only then you realize: Hey, this mountain reaches *way* higher than that foothill we were on before, and we can see so much better from up here."

The Bicamerals. Named, apparently, for some prototype of reinvention that involved massive rewiring of their cerebral hemispheres. The name's a coelacanth these days, though. It's not even certain the Bicams *have* cerebral hemispheres any more.

"But you can't get there unless you leave behind all the tools that made you so successful in the first place. You have to take that first step downhill."

"You buy any of this?" The Lieutenant (a different Lieutenant—the Colonel has one in every port) glances away from the screen, lip pulled sideways in a skeptical grimace. "Faith-based science?"

"It's not science," the Colonel says. "They don't pretend that it is."

"Even worse. You don't build a better brainchip by speaking in tongues."

"Hard to argue with the patents."

It's the patents that have him worried. The Bicamerals don't seem to have any martial ambitions, no designs of conquest—don't seem especially interested in the outside world at all, for that matter. So far they've been content to hunker down in their scattered desert monasteries, contemplating whatever reality underlies reality.

But there are other ways to throw the world on its side. Things are—fragile, these days. Whole societies have been known to fall in the wake of a single paradigm shift, and the Bicamerals own half the patent office. They could make the global economy eat itself overnight if they wanted to. It wouldn't even be illegal.

Lutterodt isn't actually part of that hive, as far as anyone can tell. She just fronts for it; a friendly face, a charismatic spokesperson to grease wheels and calm fears. She's out in the world for the next couple of weeks, doing the rounds: a fellow stand-alone human being, with access to the deepest Bicameral secrets. Completely at home in a world where a thought doesn't know enough to stop at the edge of the skull, doesn't even know when it's left one head and entered another.

"You want to bring her in?" the Lieutenant asks as Lutterodt disarms the world with a smile and a pocketful of metaphors.

He has to admit it's tempting: cut her off from the herd, draw the curtain of Global Security across the interrogation. Who knows what insights she might share, given the right incentive?

He shakes his head. "I'll go to her."

"Really?" Evidently not what this new Lieutenant signed up for, setting forth on bended knee.

"She's on a goodwill tour. Let's give her a chance to spread some good will."

It's not as generous as it seems, of course. You never want to strong-arm an adversary until you know how hard they can push back.

This global survey, this threat-assessment of hived minds: it's not his only assignment. It's only his most recent. A dozen others idle in the background, only occasionally warranting examination or update. Realist incursions into the UKapelago; a newly separatist Baptist Convention, building their armed gyland on the high seas. The occasional court-martial of some antique flesh-and-blood infantry whose cybernetic augments violate the Rules of Engagement. They all sit in his queue, pilot-lit, half-forgotten. They'll flag him if they need his attention.

But there's one candle the Colonel has never forgotten, though it hasn't flickered for the better part of a decade. It, too, is programmed to call out in the event of any change in status. He checks it anyway, daily. Now—back for a couple of days in the large empty apartment he kept even after his wife went to Heaven—he checks it again.

No change.

He puts his inlays to sleep, takes grateful refuge in the silence that fills his head once the overlays and the status reports stop murmuring through his temporal lobe. He grows belatedly aware of a *real* sensation, the soft tick of claws on the tiles behind him. He turns and glimpses a small furry black-and-white face before it ducks out of sight around the corner.

The Colonel adjourns to the kitchen.

Zephyr's willing to let the apartment feed him—he pretty much has to be, given the intermittent availability of his human servant—but he doesn't like it much. He refused outright at first, rendered psychotic by some cross-species dabbler who must have thought it would be *enlightening* or *transcendent* or just plain *cute* to "share consciousness" with a small soul weighing in at one-tenth the synapse count. The Colonel tries to imagine what that kind of forced fusion must have been like: thrust into a maelstrom of incomprehensible thought and sensation, blinding as a naked sun; thrown back into stunned bleeding darkness once some narcissistic god got bored and cut the connection.

Zephyr hid in the closet for weeks after the Colonel brought him home, hissed and spat at the sight of sockets and fiberop and the low-slung housecleaner trundling quietly on its rounds. After two years his furry little brain has at least rejigged the cost/benefit stats for the kibble dispenser in the kitchen but he's still more phantom than fur, still mostly visible only from the corner of the eye. He can be coaxed into the open if he's hungry and if the Colonel is very still; he still recoils at physical contact. The Colonel indulges him, and pretends not to notice the ragged fraying of the armrest on the living room couch. He doesn't even have the heart to get the socket removed from the patch of twisted scar tissue on Zephyr's head. No telling what post-traumatic nightmares might be reawakened by a trip to the vet.

Now he fills the kibble bowl and stands back the requisite two meters. (This is progress; just six months ago he could never stray closer than three.) Zephyr creeps into the kitchen, nose twitching, eyes darting to every corner.

The Colonel hopes that whoever inflicted that torment went on to try more exotic interfaces once they got bored with mammals. A cephalopod, perhaps. By all accounts, things get a lot less cuddly when you go B2B with a Pacific octopus.

At least Human hives can lay claim to mutual consent. At least its members *choose* the violence they inflict on themselves, the emergence of some voluntary monster from the pool of all those annihilated identities. If only it stopped there. If only the damage ended where the hive did.

His son's candle slumbers in its own little corner of his network, a pilot light in purgatory. Zephyr glances around with every second bite, still fearful of some Second Coming.

The Colonel knows how he feels.

They meet on a patio off Riverside: one of those heritage bistros where everything from food prep to table service is performed by flesh-and-blood, and where everything from food prep to table service suffers as a result. People seem willing to pay extra for the personal touch anyway.

"You disapprove," Dr. Lutterodt says, getting straight to the point.

"Of many things," The Colonel admits. "You'll have to be more specific."

"Of us. What we do." She glances at the menu (literally—it's printed on dumb stock). "Of hives in general, I'm guessing."

"There's a reason they're against the law." Most of them, anyway.

"There is: because people get scared when things they can't understand have control over their lives. Doesn't matter how rational or beneficial any given law or a policy might be. When you need ten brains to understand the nuts and bolts, the unibrains get skittish." The sock puppet shrugs. "The thing is, Bicam hives don't make laws or set policies. They keep their eyes on nature and their hands to themselves. Maybe that's why they're *not* against the law."

"Or maybe it's just a loophole. If anyone had seen meat interfaces coming down the pike, you can bet we'd have defined *technology* a bit more explicitly."

"Except the Interface Act passed a good ten years ago and they *still* haven't got their definition right. How could they? Brains rewire themselves every time we have an idle thought; how do you outlaw cortical editing without outlawing life at the same time?"

"Not my department."

"Still. You disapprove."

"I've just seen too much damage. You put such a happy face on it, you go on and on about the transcendent insights of the group mind. All the *insight* to be had by joining some greater whole. Nobody talks about—"

What the rest of us pay for your enlightenment—

"—what happens to you afterward."

"A glimpse of heaven," Lutterodt murmurs, "that turns your life to hell."

The Colonel blinks. "Exactly." What must it be like to be given godsight only to have it snatched away again, to have your miserable baseline existence plagued by muddy, incomprehensible half-memories of the sublime? No wonder people get addicted. No wonder some have to be ripped screaming from their sockets.

Ending a life suffered in the shadows of such incandescence—why, that would almost be an act of mercy.

"—a common misconception," Lutterodt is saying. "The hive's not some jigsaw with a thousand little personalities, it's *integrated*. Jim Moore doesn't turn into Superman; Jim Moore doesn't even *exist* when the hive's active. Not unless you've got your latency dialed way down, anyway."

"Even worse."

She shakes her head, a little impatiently. "If it was bad thing you'd already know it first-hand. *You're* a hive mind. You always have been."

"If that's your perspective on the Chain of Command—"

"*Everyone's* a hive."

He snorts.

She presses on: "You've got two cerebral hemispheres, right? Each one fully capable of running its own standalone persona, running *multiple* personae in fact. If I were to put one of those hemispheres down for the count, anesthetize it or scramble it with enough TMS, the other would carry on just fine, and you know what? *It would be different than you.* It might have different political beliefs, a different gender— hell, it might even have a sense of humor. Right up until the other hemisphere woke up, and fused, and became *you* again.

"So tell me, Colonel; are your hemispheres suffering right now? Are there multiple selves in your head, bound and gagged, thinking *Oh Great Ganesh I'm trapped! If only the Hive would let me out to play!*"

I don't know, he realizes. *How could I know?*

"Course not," Lutterodt answers herself. "It's just time-sharing. Completely transparent."

"And Post-Coalescent Psychosis is just an urban legend spread by the tinfoil brigade."

She sighs. "No, PCP is very real. And it is tragic, and it fucks up thousands of lives. Yes. And it is entirely a result of defective interface technology. Our guys don't get it."

"Not everyone's so lucky," the Colonel says.

A man with cosmetic chlorophyll in his eyes arrives, bearing their orders. Lutterodt gives him a smile and digs into a cloned crab salad. The Colonel picks through bits of avocado he barely remembers ordering. "Have you ever visited the Moksha Mind?"

"Only in virt."

"You know you can't trust anything you experience in virt."

"You can't trust anything you experience at this *table*. Do you see that big honking blind spot in the middle of your visual field?"

"I'm not talking about nature's shortcuts. I'm talking about something with an agenda."

"Okay." She chews, speaks around a mouthful. "So what's the Moksha agenda?"

"Nobody knows. Eight million human minds linked together, and they just—lie there. Sure, you've seen the feeds from Bangalore and Hyderabad, the nice clean dorms with the smart beds to exercise the bodies and keep everything supple. Have you seen the nodes living at the ass end of five hundred kilometers of dirt track? People with nothing more than a cot and a hut and a C-square router by the village well?"

She doesn't answer.

He takes it for a *no*. "You should pay them a visit sometime. Some of them have people checking in on them. Some—don't. I've seen children covered with stinking bedsores lying in their own shit, people with half their teeth fallen out because they're wired into that hive. And they *don't* care. They *can't* care, because there is no *them* any more, and the hive doesn't give a rat's ass about the pieces it's built out of any more than—"

Human torches, blazing in the Ecuadorian rainforest.

"—any more than you'd care about a single cell in your liver."

Lutterodt glances down at her drink. "It's what they aspire to, Colonel. Freedom from samsara. I can't pretend it's a choice I'd make for myself." She looks back up, catches his gaze, holds it. "But that's not what's bothering you."

"Why do you say that?"

"Because no matter how much you disapprove of their lifestyle, eight million happily-catatonic souls aren't any kind of military threat."

"You sure about that? Can you even begin to imagine what kind of plans could be brewing in a coherent thinking entity with the mass of eight million human brains?"

"World conquest." Lutterodt nods, deadpan. "Because that's what the Dharmic faiths are all about."

He doesn't laugh. "*People* subscribe to a faith. That hive is something else entirely."

"And if they're a threat," she says quietly, "what are we?"

Her masters, she means. And the answer is, *Terrifying*.

"Moksha's not so radical when you get right down to it," she continues. "It's built out of garden-variety brains after all. *My* guys played around with the cortical architecture. We've got entanglement on the brain, we've got quantum bioradio grown on principles you won't stumble across for another twenty years. You can't even define it as *technology* any more. That's why you and I are talking right now, isn't it? Because if a bunch of networked baselines has you worried, how could the Bicamerals *not* be a threat?"

"Are they?" he asks at last.

She snorts. "Look, you can optimize a brain for *down there* or *up here*. Not both. Bicams think at Planck scales. All that quantum craziness is as intuitive to them as the trajectory of a baseball is to you. But you know what?"

He's heard it before: "They don't get baseballs."

"They don't get baseballs. Oh, they get around okay. They can wipe their asses and feed themselves. But stick 'em in a big city and—well, saying it would make them *uncomfortable* is putting it mildly."

He doesn't buy it.

"Why do you think they need people like me? You think they set up way out in the desert so they can build some kind of supervillain lair?" Lutterodt rolls her eyes. "They're no threat, believe me. They'd have a hard time getting across a busy street."

"Their physical prowess is the last thing I'm worried about. Something that advanced could crush us underfoot and never even notice."

"Colonel, I *live* with them. They haven't crushed me yet."

"We both know how destabilizing it would be if the Bicams marketed even a fraction—"

"But they haven't, have they? Why would they? You think they care about a fucking profit margin in your fantasy-world *economy*?" Lutterodt shakes her head. "You should be thanking whatever Gods you subscribe to that they *do* hold those patents. Anyone else probably *would* have kicked the anthill over by now, for no more reason than a good fiscal quarterly."

So we're ants to you now.

"Whether you admit it or not, your world's better off with them in it. They keep to themselves, they don't bother anyone, and when they *do* come out to play you cavemen make out like bandits. You should know that already; the Armed Forces have been licensing our cryption tech for over a decade."

"Not lately we haven't." Not since someone up the chain got antsy about back doors. Although perhaps the Colonel had something to do with that decision as well.

"Your loss. Just a couple months back Coahuila came up with a Ramanujan-symmetric variant you guys would kill for. Nothing lays a hand on our algos." She reconsiders. "Nothing baseline, anyway."

"It won't work, Dr. Lutterodt."

She raises her eyebrows, the very picture of innocence.

He leans in across the table. "Maybe you really do feel safe, sleeping with your giants. They haven't rolled over and crushed you in your sleep yet; maybe you think that's some kind of guarantee they never will. I will never be that reckless—"

Again.

Even after all this time, the qualifier still kicks him in the gut.

"They're not the enemy, Colonel."

He takes a breath, marvels at its control. "That's what scares me. At least you can hope to understand what an enemy *wants*. That thing—" He shakes his head. "You've admitted it yourself. It's ambitions won't even fit into a human skull."

"Right now," Lutterodt says, "it wants to help you."

"Right."

She peels off a fingernail and slides it across the table. He looks but doesn't touch.

"It's a crystal," she says after a moment.

"I know what it is. You couldn't have just sacc'd it to me?"

"You would have accepted it? You would have let a Bicameral stooge dump data directly into your head?"

He concedes the point with a small grimace. "What is it?"

"It's a transmission. We decrypted it a few weeks ago."

"A transmission."

"From the Oort. As far as we can tell."

She's lying. She has to be.

The Colonel shakes his head. "We would have—" Every day, for the better part of ten years. Checking the pilot light. Squeezing the microwave background for a word, a whisper, a sigh. Eyes always fixed on the heavens, even now, even after the losses have been tallied and all other eyes have moved on to better prospects.

There's no evidence Theseus *is lost . . .*

"We've been scanning ever since the launch. If there'd been any kind of signal I'd know about it."

Lutterodt shrugs. "They can do things you can't. Isn't that what keeps you up at night?"

"They don't even have an array. Where'd they get the telemetry?"

She smiles the faintest smile.

The light dawns at last. "You—you *knew* . . ."

Lutterodt reaches across the table and pushes her dismembered fingernail a few centimeters closer. "Take it."

"You knew I was going to reach out to you. You *planned* on it."

"See what it says."

"You know about my *son*." He feels his breath hissing through teeth suddenly clenched. "You *fuckers*. You're using my own *son* against me now?"

"I promise you'll find it worth—"

He stands. "If your masters think they can hold him *hostage* . . ."

"Hos—" Lutterodt blinks. "Of course not. I told you, they want to *help*—"

"A *hive* wants to help. It was a fucking hive in the *first* place that . . ."

"Jim. They're *giving* it to you." He sees nothing in that face but earnest entreaty. "Take it. Open it wherever, whenever you want. Run it through whatever filters or bomb detectors, whatever security you deem appropriate."

He eyes it as though it's sprouted teeth. "You're giving it to me. No strings attached."

"Just one."

"Of course." He shakes his head, disgusted. "And that would be."

"This is for you, Jim. Not your masters. Not Mission Control."

"You know I can't make that promise."

"Then don't take the offer. I don't have to tell you what happens if word gets out. You're willing to talk to us, at least. Others might not be so reasonable. And despite your deepest fears, we can't summon lightning from the heavens to strike down our adversaries. You spread this around and there'll be bots and jackboots stomping through every monastery in WestHem."

"Why trust me at all? How do you know I won't authorize an op on the strength of this conversation?"

She counts the ways. "Because you're not that kind of man. Because maybe I'm lying, and you don't want to risk lives and assets only to discover we *can* bring down the lightning after all. And because—" She taps the fake fingernail with a real one. "Because what if this *is* from *Theseus*, and you never get another chance?"

"If. You don't know?"

"*You* don't," Lutterodt says, and the temptation pulls so relentlessly at his soul that he barely notices she hasn't answered the question.

The device sits between them like something coiled.

"Why?" he asks at last.

"They come across things, sometimes," she tells him. "Spin-offs, you might say. In the course of other pursuits. Things which aren't necessarily relevant to the Bicams, but which others might find meaningful."

"Why should they care?"

"But they do, Jim. You think they're beyond us, you think we can't possibly understand their motives. It's an article of faith with you. But here's a motive staring you in the face and you can't even see it."

"*What motive?*" He sees nothing but leg-hold traps, gaping on all sides.

"It's how you know they're not gods after all," she tells him. "They have compassion."

They don't, of course. It's manipulation, pure and simple. It's clay being shaped by the potter, it's a hot-wire to centers of longing in the heart of the brain. It's the pulling of strings that reach all the way into the stratosphere.

Unbreakable ones, apparently.

Zephyr's claws click furtively in the next room as he opens the cache. There are directories within directories here: files of raw static, fourier transforms, interpretations of signal to noise reduced to least-squares and splines. It all opens instantly and without fuss: no locks, no passwords, no ruby sweep of laser across iris. (He would not have been surprised if there had been. Why couldn't those giants have reached up from the Planck length to snatch his eyeprints from some quantum-encrypted file?) Maybe none of that's necessary. Maybe everything's embedded in some invisible fail-safe, some impossible mind-reading algorithm that scans his conscience in an instant, ready to wipe everything clean should he be found guilty of violating the hive's trust.

Maybe they simply know him better than he does.

He recognizes the faint echo of the microwave background, stamped across the data like a smudged fingerprint from the dawn of time. He sees something like a transponder code in the residuals. He has to take most of the analyses on faith; if any of this *was* sent from *Theseus*, it either passed through some very heavy weather *en route* or the transmitter was damaged. What remains appears to be the remnants of a multichannel braid, its intelligence woven as much into the way its frequencies interact as in the signals themselves. A data hologram.

Finally he extracts a single thread from the tapestry: an arid stream of linear text.

The metatags suggest that it was gleaned from some kind of acoustic signal—a voice channel, most likely—but one so faint that the reconstruction isn't so much filtered from static as built from the stuff. The resulting text is simple and unadorned. Much of it is conjectural.

IMAGINE YOU ARE SIRI KEETON, it begins.

The Colonel's legs buckle beneath him.

He used to go to Heaven once a week. Then once a month. Now it's been over a year.

There just hasn't seemed to be any point.

It's not a hive, not the sort that falls within his mandate anyway. Heaven's brains are networked but it's all subconscious—interneurons surplus to current needs, rented out for the processing power while their waking souls float on top in dreamworlds of their own imagining. It's the ultimate business model: Give us your brain to run our machinery and we'll keep its conscious left-overs entertained.

Helen Keeton is still technically his wife. Annulments are straightforward enough when a spouse ascends, but a few forms don't alter the reality of the situation one way or another and the Colonel never got around to doing the paperwork. She doesn't answer at first, keeps him in Limbo while she finishes whatever virtual pastime he's caught her in the middle of. Or maybe just to make him wait. After a year, he supposes he can't complain.

Finally a jagged-edged cloud of rainbows descends into his presence, the shattered fragments of a stained-glass window. Its shards swirl and dance like schooling fish: some nearest-neighbor flocking algo that conjures arabesques out of chaos. The Colonel still doesn't know whether it's deliberate affectation or just some off-the-shelf avatar.

It's always struck him as a little over-the-top.

A voice from swirling glass: "Jim . . ."

She sounds distant, distracted. As disjointed as her own manifestation. Fourteen years in a world where the very laws of physics root in dreams and wish-fulfillment: he's probably lucky she can speak at all.

"I thought you should know. There was a signal."

"A . . . signal . . ."

"From *Theseus*. Maybe."

The flock slows, as though the very air is turning to treacle. It locks into freeze-frame. The Colonel counts off seven seconds in which there is no motion at all.

Helen coalesces. Abstraction congeals towards humanity: ten thousand fragments fall together, an interlocking three-dimensional puzzle whose pieces desaturate from bright primary down to muted tones of flesh and blood. The Colonel imagines a ghost, dressing in formal attire for some special occasion.

"S—Siri?" She has a face now. The particles of its lower half jostle in time to the name. "Is he—"

"I don't know. The signal's—very faint. Garbled."

"He'd be forty-two," she says after a moment.

"He is," the Colonel says, not giving a micron.

"You sent him out there."

It's true enough; he didn't speak out, after all. He didn't object, even added his own voice to the chorus when it became obvious which way the wind was blowing. What weight would his protests have carried anyway? All the others were already on board, in thrall to a networked mob so far beyond caveman mentality that all those experts and officers might as well have been a parliament of mice.

"We sent *all* of them, Helen. Because they were all the most qualified."

"And have you forgotten *why* he was most qualified?"

He wishes he could.

"You sent him into space chasing ghosts," she says. "At best. At worst you fed him to monsters."

And you, he does not reply, *abandoned him for this place before the monsters even showed up.*

"You sent him up against something that was too big for *anyone* to handle."

I will not be drawn into this argument again. "We didn't know how big it was. We didn't know anything. We had to find out."

"And you've done a fine job on that score." Helen's fully integrated now, all that simmering resentment resurrected as though it had never been laid to rest at all.

"Helen, we were *surveyed*. The whole damn planet." Surely she remembers. Surely she hasn't got so wrapped up in her fantasy world that she's forgotten what happened in the real one. "Should we just have ignored that? You think anyone else would miss their child less, even if Siri *wasn't* the best man for the job? It was bigger than him. It was bigger than all of us."

"Oh, you don't have to tell me. For Colonel Moore so loved the fucking world that he gave his only begotten son."

His shoulders rise, and fall.

"If this pans out—"

"If—"

He cuts her off: "Siri could be *alive*, Helen. Can't you put aside your hatred long enough to take any hope at all from that?"

She hovers before him like an avenging angel, but her sword arm is stayed for the moment. She's beautiful—more so than she ever was in the flesh—although the Colonel has a pretty good idea of what her physical corpus must look like, after so many years spent pickling in the catacombs. He tries to squeeze a little vindictive satisfaction from that knowledge, and fails.

"Thank you for telling me," she says at last.

"Nothing's certain—"

"But there's a chance. Yes, of course." She leans forward. "Do you expect—that is, when will you have a better idea of what it says? The signal?"

"I don't know. I'm—pursuing options. I'll tell you the moment I learn anything."

"Thank you," the angel says, already beginning to dissipate—then recongeals at a sudden thought. "Of course you won't let me share this, will you?"

"Helen, you *know*—"

"You've already security-locked my domain. The wall goes up the moment I try to tell anyone my son could be alive. Doesn't it?"

He sighs. "It's not my call."

"It's an intrusion. That's what it is. It's a form of bullying."

"Would you rather I just didn't tell you?" But he knows, as Helen disconnects and Heaven dissolves and the barren walls of his apartment reappear around him, that it's all just part of the dance. The steps never change: he mans the barricades, she rages against them, energy flows downhill to the same empty equilibrium. It probably doesn't even matter whether the security locks are in place or not. Who would she tell, after all?

Down in Heaven, all her friends are imaginary.

"This is Jim Moore."

The Colonel stands at the edge of the desert. The Nissan idles at his side like a faithful pet.

"I will be unavailable for the foreseeable future. I can't tell you where I'm going."

He's been effectively naked for the past twenty-four hours: no springsoles, no side-arm, no dog tags. No watch: window to the Noosphere, keeper of secrets, hub and booster and event coordinator for all those everyday pieces of smartwear he left be-hind. He's even shut down his cortical inlays, thrown away his vision along with his garments. All that's left is this last-minute voicemail, to be held in abeyance until he is beyond reach.

"I hope to provide a full debriefing upon my return. I don't know exactly when that might be."

He stands there, weighing costs, weighing risks. The threat of greater gods, the hazards of beatific indifference. The threat posed by aliens from another world; the threat posed by aliens from this one. The delusional arrogance in the thought that some puny caveman, scarcely climbed down from the trees, might be able to use one against the other.

The cost of a son.

"I believe that my service record has earned me some leeway. I'm asking you to refrain from investigating my whereabouts during my absence."

He's not trusting them to do that, though. The Nissan is stolen, logs doctored, all traces of truancy erased. His own vehicle tours the Olympic Peninsula on its own recognizance, laying a trail of bread crumbs for any forensic algos that happen by after the fact.

"I'm—aware of the breach this represents. You know I'd never do such a thing unless I thought it absolutely vital."

Maybe you really do feel safe, sleeping with your giants. They haven't rolled over and crushed you in your sleep; maybe you think that's some kind of guarantee they never will. I will never be that reckless.

Again.

It doesn't take a hive to grasp the simple, straightforward ease with which he's been manipulated. It's caveman strategy: find the Achilles heel, craft the exploit, slide it home. Forge hope from static. Let remorse and the faint hope of redemption do the rest.

All too easy to dismiss, if not for one thing: the sheer, mind-boggling egotism it would take to believe that a lonely old baseline could possibly matter to a collective of such godlike intellect. The thought that this unremarkable caveman would even merit *notice*, much less manipulation.

"I've set my apartment to run in autonomous mode for the duration of my absence. I would nonetheless appreciate it if someone could drop by occasionally to check in on my cat."

He has to admit, in the face of all his fear and mistrust: compassion, after all, might be the most parsimonious explanation.

He thumbs SEND, lets the transmitter slip from his fingers. His valediction has travelled a thousand kilometers by the time his boot grinds the little device into the dirt; it will reveal itself to the chain of command in due course. The Colonel leaves behind everything but the clothes on his back, two broad-spectrum antivenom capsules, and enough rations for a one-way hike to the monastery. If Bicameral thought processes are rooted in any kind of religious philosophy, hopefully it will be one of those faiths that preach charity to lost souls, and the forgiveness of trespass.

No guarantees, of course. There are so many ways to read the sliver of intelligence the hive has granted him. Perhaps he's merely a pawn in some greater game after all; or a starving insect who once seized a crumb from the Heavens, and now presumes to think it has a relationship with God. Only one thing is certain out of all the scenarios, all the competing hypotheses. One insight, after all these years, that leaves the Colonel so hungry for more he'll risk everything: His son was lost, but now is found.

His son is coming home.

"Go home," he tells the Nissan, and sets out across the desert.

entanglement

VANDANA SINGH

Vandana Singh was born and raised in India, and currently resides with her family in the United States, where she teaches physics and writes. Her stories have appeared in many different markets and been reprinted in several Best of the Year anthologies. She's published two children's books in India, Young-uncle Comes to Town *and* Younguncle in the Himalayas, *and a chapbook novella,* Of Love and Other Monsters. *Her other books include another chapbook novella,* Distances, *and her first collection,* The Woman Who Thought She Was a Planet and Other Stories. *Her most recent book is an original anthology, coedited with Anil Menon,* Breaking the Bow.

In the intricate novella which follows, she shows us the hidden connections between several people in a near-future world who are struggling—and to at least a small extent, succeeding—to combat the worst ravages of global climate change.

. . . FLAPPING ITS WINGS . . .

. . . and flying straight at her. She ducked, averting her eyes. The whole world had come loose: debris flying everywhere; the roar of the wind. Something soft and sharp cannoned into her belly—she looked up to see the monster rising into the clouds, a genie of destruction, yelled—Run! Run! Find lower ground! Lower ground!

She woke up. The boat rocked gently; instrument panels in the small cabin painted thin blue and red lines. Outside, the pale Arctic dawn suffused the sky with orange light. Everything was normal.

"Except I hadn't been asleep, not really," she said aloud. Her morning coffee had grown cold. "What kind of dream was that?"

She rubbed the orange bracelet. One of the screens flickered. There was a fragmented image for a microsecond before the screen went blank: a gray sky, a spinning cloud, things falling. She sat up.

Her genie appeared in a corner of the screen.

"Irene, I just connected you to five people around the world," it said cheerfully. "Carefully selected, an experiment. We don't want you to get too lonely."

"Frigg," she said, "I wish you wouldn't do things like that."

There were two messages from Tom. She thought of him in the boat three hundred kilometers away, docked to the experimental iceberg, and hoped he and Mahmoud were getting along. Good, he had only routine stuff to report. She scrolled through messages from the Arctic Science Initiative, the Million Eyes project, and three of her colleagues working off the northern coast of Finland. Nothing from Lucie.

She let out a long, slow breath. Time to get up, make fresh coffee. Through the tiny window of the boat's kitchenette, the smooth expanse of ocean glittered in the morning light. The brolly floated above it like a conscientious ghost, not two hundred meters away. Its parachute-like top was bright in the low sun, its electronic eyes slowly swiveling as the intelligent unit in the box below drank in information from the world around it. Its community of intelligences roved the water below, making observations and sending them back to the unit, so that it could adjust its behavior accordingly. She felt a tiny thrill of pride. The brolly was her conception, a crazy biogeochemist's dream, brought to reality by engineers. The first prototype had been made by Tom himself, in his first year of graduate school. Thinking of his red thatch of hair framing a boyish face, she caught herself smiling. He was such a kid! The first time he'd seen a seal colony, he'd almost fallen off the boat in his enthusiasm. You'd think the kid had never even been to a zoo. He was so Californian, it was adorable. Her own upbringing in the frozen reaches of northern Canada meant she was a lot more cold-tolerant than him—he was always overdressed by her standards, buried under layers of thermal insulation and a parka on top of everything. Some of her colleagues had expressed doubts about taking an engineering graduate student to the Arctic, but she'd overruled them. The age of specialization was over; you had to mix disciplinary knowledge and skills if you wanted to deal intelligently with climate change, and who was better qualified to monitor the brollies deployed in the region? Plus Mahmoud would make a great babysitter for him. He was a sweet kid, Tom.

She pulled on her parka and went out on deck to have her coffee the way she liked it, scalding hot. Staring across the water, she thought of home. Baffin Island was not quite directly across the North Pole from her station in the East Siberian Sea, but this was the closest she had come to home in the last fifteen years. She shook her head. Home? What was she thinking? Home was a sunny apartment in a suburb of San Francisco, a few BART stops from the university, where she had spent ten years raising Lucie, now twenty-four, a screenwriter in Hollywood. It had been over a year since she and Lucie had had a real conversation. Her daughter's chatty e-mails and phone calls had given way to a near silence, a mysterious reserve. In her present solitude that other life, those years of closeness, seemed to have been no more than a dream.

Over the water the brolly moved. There was a disturbance not far from the brolly—an agitation in the water, then a tail. A whale maybe five meters in length swimming close to the surface popped its head out of the water—a beluga! Well, she probably wasn't far from their migration route. Irene imagined the scene from the whale's perspective: the brolly like an enormous, airborne jellyfish, the boat, the human-craft, and a familiar sight.

The belugas were interested in the brolly. Irene wondered what they made of it. One worry the researchers had was that brollies and their roving family units would be attacked and eaten by marine creatures. The brolly could collapse itself into a compact unit and sink to the seabed or use solar power to rise a couple of meters above the ocean surface. At the moment it seemed only to be observing the whales as they cavorted around it. Probably someone, somewhere, was looking at the ocean through the brolly's electronic eyes and commenting on the Internet about a whale pod sighting. Million Eyes on the Arctic was the largest citizen science project in the world. Between the brollies, various observation stations, and satellite images, more than two million people could obtain and track information about sea ice melt, methane leaks, marine animal sightings, and ocean hot spots.

It occurred to Irene that these whales might know the seashore of her childhood, that they might even have come from the north Canadian archipelago. A sudden memory came to her: going out into the ocean north of Baffin Island with her grandfather in his boat. He was teaching her to use traditional tools to fish in an icy inlet. She must have been very small. She recalled the rose-colored Arctic dawn, her grandfather's weathered face. When they were on their way back with their catch, a pod of belugas had surfaced close enough to rock their boat. They clustered around the boat, popping their heads out of the water, looking at the humans with curious, intelligent eyes. One large female came close to the boat. "*Qilalugaq*," her grandfather said gently, as though in greeting. The child Irene—no, she had been Enuusiq then—Enuusiq was entranced. The Inuit, her grandfather told her, wouldn't exist without the belugas, the caribou, and the seals. He had made sure she knew how to hunt seals and caribou before she was thirteen. Memories surfaced: the swish of the dog sled on the ice in the morning, the waiting at the breathing holes for the seals, the swift kill. The two of them saying words of apology over the carcass, their breath forming clouds in the frigid air.

Her grandfather died during her freshman year of high school. He was the one who had given her her Inuk name, Enuusiq, after his long-dead older brother, so that he would live again in her name. The name held her soul, her *atiq*. "Enuusiq," she whispered now, trying it on. How many years since anyone had called her that? She remembered the gathering of the community each time the hunters brought in a big catch, the taste of raw meat with a dash of soy. How long had it been since those days? A visit home fifteen years ago when her father died (her mother had died when she was in college)—after that just a few telephone conversations and Internet chats with her cousin Maggie in Iqaluit.

The belugas moved out of sight. Her coffee was cold again. She was annoyed with herself. She had volunteered to come here partly because she wanted to get away— she loved solitude—but in the midst of it, old memories surfaced; long-dead voices spoke.

The rest of the morning she worked with a fierce concentration, sending data over to her collaborators on the Russian research ship *Kolmogorov*, holding a conference call with three other scientists, politely declining two conference invitations for keynote speaker. But in the afternoon her restlessness returned. She decided she would dive down to the shallow ocean bed and capture a clip for a video segment she had promised to the Million Eyes project. It was against protocol to go down alone without anyone on the boat to monitor her—but it was only twenty-two meters, and she hadn't got this far by keeping to protocol.

Some time later she stood on the deck in her dry suit, pulled the cap snugly over her head, checked the suit's computer, wiggled her shoulders so the oxygen tank rested more comfortably on her back, and dove in.

This was why she was here. This falling through the water was like falling in love, only better. In the cloudy blue depths she dove through marine snow, glimpsing here and there the translucent fans of sea butterflies, a small swarm of krill, the occasional tiny jellyfish. A sea gooseberry with a glasslike two-lobed soft body winged past her face. Some of these creatures were so delicate a touch might kill them—no fisherman's net could catch them undamaged. You had to be here, in their world, to know they existed. Yet there was trouble in this marine paradise. Deeper and deeper she went, her drysuit's wrist display clocking time, temperature, pressure, oxygen. The sea was shallow enough at twenty-two meters that she could spend some time at the bottom without worrying about decompression on the way up. It was darker here on the seaweed-encrusted ocean floor; she turned on her lamp and the camera. Swimming along the sea-floor toward the array of instruments, she startled a mottled white crab. It was sitting on top of one of the instrument panels, exploring the device with its claws. Curiosity . . . well, that was something she could relate to. The crab retreated as she swam above it, then returned to its scrutiny. Well, if her work entertained the local wildlife, that was something.

A few meters away she saw the fine lines of the thermoelectric mesh on the seabed. There were fewer creatures in the methane-saturated water. Methane gas was coming up from the holes in the melting permafrost on the seabed—there were even places you could see bubbles. Before her a creature swam into focus: a human-built machine intelligence, one of the brolly's family unit. Its small, cylindrical body, with its flanges and long snout, looked like a fish on an alien planet. It was injecting a rich goo of nutrients (her very own recipe) for methane-eating bacteria. She was startled by how natural it looked in the deep water. "Eat well, my hearties," she told her favorite life-forms. Methanotrophs were incredibly efficient at metabolizing methane, using pathways that were only now being elucidated. Most of the processes could not be duplicated in labs. So much was still unknown—hell, they'd found five new species of the bacteria since the project had started. Methanotrophs, like most living beings, didn't exist in isolation, but in consortia. The complex web of interdependencies determined behavior and chemistry.

"If methane-eating bacteria sop up most of the methane, it will help slow global warming," she said into the recorder. "It will buy time until humanity cuts its carbon dioxide emissions. Methane is a much more potent greenhouse gas than CO2. Although it doesn't stay in the atmosphere as long, too much methane in the atmosphere might excite a positive feedback loop—more methane, more warming, more thawing of permafrost, more methane . . . a vicious cycle that might tip the world toward catastrophic warming." Whether that could happen was still a point of argument among scientists, but the methane plumes now known to be coming off the seabed all over the shallow regions of the Arctic were enough to worry anyone whose head wasn't buried in the sand.

Maybe her bacteria could help save the world. With enough nutrients, they and their communities of cooperative organisms might take care of much of the methane; in the meantime the thermoelectric mesh was an experiment to see whether cooling down the hot spots might slow the outgassing. The energy generated by the mesh was captured in batteries, which had to be replaced when at capacity. The instrument array measured biogeochemical data and sent it back to the brolly.

Her drysuit computer beeped. It was time to return to the surface—or else she would run out of oxygen. She turned off the camera-recorder and swam slowly and carefully toward the light. "Message from Tom," her genie said. "Not urgent but interesting. Two messages from Million Eyes, one to you, asking about the video, the other a news item. A ballet dancer in Estonia saw an illegal oil and gas exploration vessel messing around the Laptev Sea. There's a furor. Message from your cousin Maggie in Iqaluit, marked Personal. She's in San Francisco, wondering where you are."

Damn. Hadn't she told Maggie she was going on an expedition? Maggie hardly ever left Canada so the trip to San Francisco must be something special.

"I'm coming up," she said, just as she felt a numbing pain sear into her left calf. The cold was coming in through a leak, a tear in the suit; her drysuit computer beeped a warning. Her leg cramped horribly. She looked up, willing herself not to panic—the surface seemed impossibly far away, and the cold was filling her body, making her chest contract with pain. She moved her arms as strongly as she could. She must get up to the surface before the cold spread—she had had a brush with hypothermia before. But as she went up with excruciating slowness she knew at once that she was going to die here, and a terror came upon her. *Lucie*, she said. *Lucie, forgive me, I love you, I love you.* Her arms were tired, her legs like jelly, and the cold was in her bones, and a part of her wanted simply to surrender to oblivion. Frigg was chirping frantically in her ear—calling for rescue, not that there was anyone in the area who could get to her in time—and then a voice cut in, and her grandmother said, *Bless you and be careful up there, I'm praying for you.* This was really odd because her grandmother was dead, and the accent was strange. But the voice spoke with such clarity and concern, and there was such an emphasis on *be careful*—and weren't there kitchen sounds in the background, a pan banging in the sink, so incongruously ordinary and familiar?—that she was jolted from the darkness of spirit that had descended on her. Her arms seemed to be the only part of her body still under her control, and although they felt like lead, she began to move them again.

Tom's voice cut in, frantic. "I'm coming, I'm coming as fast as I can, hold on," and Mahmoud, more calmly, "I've contacted the *Kolmogorov* for their helicopter—and the Coast Guard." But the helicopter had been sent over to a station in Norway that very afternoon. She saw her death before her with astonishing clarity. Then she felt something lift her bodily—how could Tom get here so soon?—an enormous white shadow loomed, a smile on the bulbous face—a whale. A *beluga*? She felt the solid body of the whale below her, tried to get a hold of the smooth flesh, but she needn't have worried, because it was pushing her up with both balance and strength, until she broke the water's surface near the boat. Hauling herself up the rungs of the ladder proved to be impossible: she was shaking violently, and her legs felt numb. The whale pushed her up until all she had to do was to tumble over the rail onto the deck. She collapsed on the deck, pulled off her mask, sobbing, breathing huge gulps of cold air. Her suit beeped shrilly.

"Get dry NOW," Frigg said in Mahmoud's voice, or maybe it was Mahmoud. She half crawled into the cabin, peeled everything off, and huddled under a warm shower until the shivering slowed. A searing pain in both legs told her that blood was circulating again. There was a frayed tear in the drysuit—had it caught on a nail as she was pulling it out of the cupboard? So much for damning protocol, something she never did if a colleague or student was involved. Her left calf still ached, and the tears wouldn't stop. At last she toweled off and got into warm clothes, with warm gelpacks under her armpits and on her stomach. The medbot checked her vital signs while hot cocoa bubbled.

"Frigg, tell Tom and Mahmoud not to come, my vitals are fine," she said, but her voice shook. "Tell them to call off the rescue." Her chest still ached, but as she sipped the cocoa she started to feel more normal. After a while she could stand without feeling she was going to fall over.

She stepped gingerly out on the deck. The sun, already low in the sky, was falling slowly into the ocean like a ripe peach. The first stars sequined the coming Arctic night. The belugas swam around the boat. She finished her cocoa in a few gulps and felt a shadow of strength return to her. A whale popped its head out of the water next to her boat and looked at her with friendly curiosity.

She put her arms between the railing bars and touched the whale's head. It was smooth as a hard-boiled egg. "*Qilalugaq*," she whispered, and tears ran down her cheeks, and her shoulders shook. "Thank you, thank you for saving my life. Did Ittuq send you?" She realized she was speaking Inuktitut, the familiar syllables coming back as though she had never left home. "*Ittuq*," she whispered. She had been too young when her grandfather died, too shocked to let herself mourn fully. Now, thirty-nine years later, the tears flowed.

At last she stood, leaning against the rail, spent, and waved to the pod as it departed.

Later that night, when she had eaten her fill of hot chicken soup, she talked to Tom on video. He was touchingly grateful that she was all right and excited about the whale rescue. Irene said, "Don't go around broadcasting it, will you?" She had no desire to see her foolishness go viral on the Internet. Fortunately Tom had something exciting of his own to share.

"Look!" he said. "This is from this afternoon." A photo appeared on the side of the screen. There lay the enormous bulk of the artificial iceberg to which his boat was docked. An irregular heap lay atop it.

"Polar bear," he said, grinning. "Must have been swimming for a while, looking for a rest stop. Poor guy's sleeping off a late lunch. I tossed him my latest catch of fish."

"Stay away from him!" Irene said sharply. "Wild animals aren't cute house pets— remember your briefing!"

"You're a fine one to talk, Irene." He grinned again, and then, anticipating her protests, "Yes, yes, I know, don't worry. If I go aboard the berg with the bear on it, some kid somewhere is going to notice and send me a message. This morning I stepped out without my snow goggles and a twelve-year-old from Uzbekistan messaged my genie. Thanks to Million Eyes you can hardly take a shit in peace . . . er, sorry . . ."

"It's not that bad." She couldn't help smiling. Good for the kid in Uzbekistan.

Tom could be absentminded. The screen image of the fake berg was impossibly white. It was coated with a high-albedo nanostructured radiative paint that sent infrared right back into the atmosphere, while leaving the surface cool to the touch.

"Another interesting thing happened today," he said, with the kind of casualness that betrayed suppressed excitement. "You know we have eight brollies on big lump?" Big lump was the largest iceberg in a flotilla about fifty kilometers north of Tom's station. "They've been screening meltwater pools on the berg from the sun, refreezing them before they have a chance to melt deeply enough to make cracks. Well, three nomad brollies arrived from Lomonosov Station—just left their posts of their own accord and came over and joined them. Mahmoud just reported."

"Very interesting," she said.

It was not surprising that brollies were making their own decisions. It meant that as learning intelligences, intimately connected to their environment and to one another, they had gone on to the next stage of sophistication. Her own brolly continuously monitored the biogeochemical environment, knowing when to feed the methanotroph consortia their extra nutrients, and when to stop. Her original conception of linked artificial intelligences with information feedback loops was based on biomimicry, inspired by natural systems like ecosystems and endocrine systems. Her brolly was used to working as a community of minds, so she imagined that facility could be scaled up. Each brolly could communicate with its own kind and was connected to the climate databases around the world, giving as well as receiving information, and capable of learning from it. She had a sudden vision of a multilevel, complexly interconnected grid, a sentience spanning continents and species, a kind of Gaiaweb come alive.

"How much time before they become smarter than us?" she said, half-jokingly. "This is great news, Tom."

Afterward she watched the great curtains of the aurora paint the sky. She sat in her cabin, raising her eyes from the data scrolling down her screen. Temperature was dropping in the ocean seabed—the methane fizzler had perceptibly slowed since the project began. It was a minute accomplishment compared to the scale of the problem, but with two million pairs of eyes watching methane maps of the Arctic, maybe they could get funding to learn how to take care of the worst areas that were still manageable. Partly the methane outgassing was a natural part of a thousands-years process, but it was being exacerbated by warming seas. Didn't science ultimately teach what the world's indigenous peoples had known so well—that everything is connected? A man gets home from work in New York City and flips a switch, and a little more coal is burned, releasing more warming carbon dioxide into the atmosphere. Or an agribusiness burns a tract of amazon rain forest, and a huge carbon sink is gone, just like that. Or a manufacturer in the United States buys palm oil to put in cookies, and rain forests vanish in Southeast Asia to make way for more plantations. People and their lives were so tightly connected across the world that it would take a million efforts around the globe to make a difference.

She touched the orange wristlet and the screen came on. "Frigg, call Maggie."

"Irene, Irene?" Maggie had more gray in her hair, but her voice was as loud as before. Demanding. "Where have you been? They told me at your campus you were in the Arctic, and I thought, dammit, she's come home at last, but I hear you're some-where in Siberia?"

"Don't you keep up?" Irene said, growling, trying not to grin in delight, and fail-ing. She blinked tears from her eyes. "Siberia is where it's at. I'm in a boat, running an experiment on the seabed. Trying to stop methane outgassing, you know, save the world, all in a day's work."

"Great, great, but I hate coming all the way here and finding you gone. I have to tell you, I saw Lucie. Yes, you heard me right. She's going into documentary filmmaking—expedition to Nepal—"

Nepal!

"Well, I am glad she's talking to you," Irene said, after a moment. "Is she . . . is she all right?"

"She's fine! Irene, she just needs to find her own way—you two have been by your-selves for so long . . ."

"By ourselves! In the middle of the empty streets of the bay area!"

"You know what I mean. Big cities can be terribly lonely. Why do you think I came back after college? Listen, Irene, nuclear families suck, and single-parent nuclear families suck even more. People need other people than just their parents. My kids have issues with being here in Iqaluit, but at least they are surrounded by uncles and aunts and cousins and grandparents—"

"How are your parents? How is everyone?"

"Waiting for you to come home. Come and visit, Irene. It's been too long. We all thought you were the one who was going to stay because of everything you learned about the old ways from Grandfather."

"The last time I came, when my father died . . . your mother threw a fish at me and told me to gut it."

Maggie laughed.

"Which I think you did pretty well. Surprised me. Now you have to come on up, Irene! Or down, I should say. Come talk to my boy. Peter's part of a collaboration between Inuit high schoolers and scientists. Hunters too. Going out with GPS units, recording information about ice melting and wildlife sightings."

Irene wanted to say, *Maggie, I almost died today, but* Qilalugaq *gave me the gift of life, and that means I have to change how I live. I need your help.* The words wouldn't come out. She said, instead:

"Maggie, I got to go. Let's talk tomorrow . . . we have to talk."

"Irene, are you all right? Irene?"

"Yes . . . no, I can't talk about it now. Tomorrow? If . . . if you see Lucie again, tell her—give her my love."

"I'm seeing her Friday for lunch before she leaves. I will, don't worry. Tomorrow, for sure then. Hang in there, girl!"

She waved good-bye and the screen went blank. The lights of the aurora reflected off the walls and desk in the darkened room. The boat swayed gently—out there, the pale top of the brolly floated. Something splashed out at sea, a smooth back. She remembered the small house in Iqaluit where she'd grown up with her parents and grandfather and two aunts and cousins. The great sky over the ice, sky reflecting ice reflecting sky in an endless loop. Her grandfather had been an immensely practical man, but he had also taught her to pay attention to intangible things, things you couldn't quantify, like the love you could feel for a person, or the land, or the whale. She had been rescued by a whale, a whale from home. What more of a sign did she need? She had stayed away first because it was inconvenient to go all the way, and then because she had been so busy, doing important work—and later because she was confused and ashamed. How to face them all, knowing that despite her successes she had lost her way, wandered off from her own self? How to return home without Lucie, knowing herself a failure in so many ways? Now she saw that the journey home was part of her redemption, and as the belugas migrated, traveling in great closed loops in the still-frigid waters of the Arctic, visiting and revisiting old ground, so must she. "*Enuusiq,*" she whispered, practicing. She thought of her daughter's eager, tender face in childhood as she listened to a story, and the bittersweet delight when Lucie went off to college, so young and beautiful, intelligence and awareness in her eyes, at the threshold of adulthood. She thought of herself as a small child, watching her mother weaving a pattern on the community loom: the sound, the rhythm, the colors, her mother's hands. The world she loved was woven into being every moment through complex, dynamic webs of interaction: the whales in their pods, the methanotrophs and their consortia, the brollys and their family units, the Million Eyes of eager young people trying to save the world.

"*Ittuq,*" she said aloud, "I'm coming home."

. . . IN THE AMAZON . . .

. . . There is a city in the middle of the rain forest: Manaus. This year there is a drought. The rains are scant. When they fall, they fall kilometers downwind of the city . . .

In the heat, outside the glitzy hotels and bars, there is the smell of rotting fruit, fish, garbage, flowers, exhaust. Rich and poor walk the streets with their cell phones or briefcases or Gucci handbags or baskets of jenipapo or camu-camu, and among them prowls the artist. He's looking for a blank wall, the side of a building. Any smooth, empty surface is a canvas to him.

His favorite time is the early morning. In that pale light when the bugio monkeys and the birds begin to call, he is there with black oil chalk and a ladder, drawing furiously in huge arm strokes, then filling in the fine-detail work. He never knows what animal will emerge from the wall—the first stroke tells him nothing, nor the next, or the next, but each stroke limits the possibilities until it is clear what spirit has possessed him, and then it emerges. When it is a jaguar, he, the artist, feels the bark of the tree limb; he flickers through the jungle on silent, padded feet. When a manatee emerges from the blank wall, the artist knows the watery depths of the river, the mysterious underwater geography. When it is a bird, he knows the secret pathways of the high jungle canopy.

Then he is done. He looks around, and there is nobody, and he breathes a sigh of relief. He slips away through the sleeping streets to another self, another life.

Fernanda stared out from the airplane window at the city that was her home. It was a bright splash of whiteness in the green of the Amazon rain forest. Urban heat island indeed, she thought. The city had grown enormously in the last decade, with the boom in natural gas and high-tech manufacturing—returning to it was always a surprise—a populous, economically vigorous human habitation in the middle of the largest forest in the world. Despite the urban forests that made green pools in the white sea of concrete, it lay before her like scar tissue in the body of the jungle. The Rio Negro was languid as an exhausted lover—the water was lower than she could remember since the last drought. She hadn't forgotten what it had been like, as a child, to stand on the dry bed of the river during the big drought, feeling like the world was about to end. Bright rooftops came up toward her as the plane dipped, and she tried to see if there were any green roofs—hard to tell from this height. Never mind, she would know soon enough, when she joined the new project.

"Been on holiday?" the man next to her said pleasantly.

Fernanda was caught off guard. She had spent three months in the coastal jungle studying the drought, counting dead trees, making measurements of humidity, temperature, and rainfall, and, on one occasion, fighting a forest fire started by an agricultural company to clear the forest. Her left forearm still hurt from a burn. The team had camped in the hot, barren expanse, and after two months she and Claudio had broken up, which is why she was coming back alone. They'd established beyond doubt that barren wasteland was hotter than healthy forest, and that less rain fell here, and that it was similar to an urban heat island. Far from being able to regrow the forest, they had to fight greedy marauders to prevent more of it from being destroyed. Claudio remained behind with the restoration team, and the rest of them had trekked through the deep coolness of the remaining healthy forest until they had got to civilization. She had grown silent as the forest muttered, called, clucked, and roared around her, had felt its rhythms in some buried ancestral part of her, and her pain had quieted to a kind of soft background noise. Now she looked at the man in his business suit and his clean-shaven, earnest face, the shy smile, the hint of a beer belly, and thought how alien her own species seemed whenever she returned from the forest.

"Business," she said coldly, hoping he wouldn't inquire any further. The plane began its descent.

The city was the same and not the same. She found out within the next few days that the cheerful family gatherings at Tia Ana's, which she'd always enjoyed, were a lot more difficult without Claudio, mostly because of the questions and commiserations. Tia Ana had that look in her eye that meant she was already making matchmaking plans. Her mother had tickets for two for a performance of Aida at the Teatro Amazonas, no less, which was something to look forward to. Inevitably she thought about that last fight with Claudio, when he accused her of being more sexual with her saxophone than with him. Not that she'd brought her sax into the rain forest— but she hadn't been able to take it out of its case as yet.

What was different was that there wasn't enough rain. When the clouds did gather, there might be a scant shower over the city, but most of the rain would fall about fifty kilometers downwind. Meanwhile the humans sweltered in their concrete and wooden coops—those who had air-conditioning cranked it up—the poor on the city's east side made do without, some falling victim to heat exhaustion. But for the most part the lives of the middle and upper classes went on much the same apart from the occasional grumbling. It seemed peculiar to Fernanda that even in this self-consciously eco-touristy city, people whom she knew and loved could live such oblivious lives, at such a remove from the great, dire warnings the biosphere was giving them.

The other thing that was different was the artist.

An anonymous graffiti artist had hit the streets of Manaus. Sides of buildings, or walls, were transformed by art so startling that it slowed traffic, stopped conversations. She heard about all this with half an ear and didn't pay attention until she went running the day before her new project began. White shorts and tank top, her black hair flying loose, along the harborway, through the crowded marketplaces with their bright awnings and clustering tourists, she ran through the world of her species, trying to know it again. She paused at a fruit stand, good-naturedly fending off the flirtations of two handsome youths while she drank deeply of buriti juice. There were ferries as usual on the Rio Negro, and the water was as she remembered it, dark and endless, on its way to its lover's tryst with the Solimões to form the Amazon, the Amazon she had known and loved all her life.

She turned onto a side street and there was a jaguar, about to leap at her from the windowless side of a building. She stopped and stared. It was abstract, rendered in fluid, economical brushstrokes, but the artist knew which details were essential; whoever it was had captured the spirit of the beast, the fire in its eyes, what Neruda had called its phosphorescent absence. For a moment she stood before it, enthralled, the jungle around her again.

After that she looked for more of the work, asking at street corners and market stalls. The drawings were everywhere—a flight of macaws, a sloth on a tree branch, or an anaconda about to slide off a wall onto the street. Wherever they were, there was a crowd. The three-dimensionality of the drawings was astounding. The ripple of muscle, the fine lines of feathers, the spirit come alive in the eye. She was contemplating a particularly stunning rendering of a sauim-de-coleira that a real monkey would be forgiven for mistaking for its relative, when a car full of university freshmen went by, loudly playing what passed for music among the young (she was getting old and jaded at twenty-seven!). The car stopped with a screech of brakes and the youngsters piled out, silenced, and Fernanda thought in triumph: This is the answer to the oblivious life. Art so incredible that it brings the jungle back into the city, forces people to remember the nations of animals around us.

But the next day, looking at the data from her rooftop lab, she was not encouraged. The city's pale roofs were glaring back at the sun. What impact did the city's heat island have on the local climate, compared to the drought-ridden sections of the forest? The drought was mostly due to large-scale effects connected with warming oceans and coastal deforestation, but she was interested in seeing whether smaller-scale effects were also significant, and by that logic, whether small-scale reparations at the right scale and distribution might make some difference. It was still a controversial area of research. She spent days poring over maps on her computer screen, maps generated by massive computer models of climate, local and regional. Could the proposed green-roofing experiment be significant enough to test the models? How to persuade enough people and institutions to install green roofs? Scientists were notoriously bad at public relations. Tia Ana would say they weren't good at other kinds of relationships either, although that wasn't strictly true. Her former advisor, Dr. Aguilar, had been happily married to his wife for half a century.

There was a private home in the Cidade Nova area that was already green-roofed according to the design—native plants, chosen for their high rates of evapotranspiration, mimicking the radiative properties of the rain-forest canopies. If they could get enough city officials, celebrities, and so on to see a green roof in action, maybe that would popularize the idea. The home was in a wealthy part of town, and the owner, one Victor Gomes, was connected to the university. She went to see it one hot afternoon.

It was quite wonderful to stand in a rooftop garden with small trees in pots, shrubs in raised beds arranged with a pleasing lack of respect for straight lines, and an exuberance of native creepers that cascaded lushly over the walls. There were fruits and vegetables growing between the shrubs. This was the same model that the restoration team was using in the drought-ridden portions of the Atlantica forest—organically grown native forest species with room for small vegetable gardens and cacao, rubber, and papaya trees, inspired by the *cabruca* movement: small-scale agriculture that fed families and preserved the rain forest. Fernanda looked over the railing and saw that the foliage covered almost the entire side wall of the house. A misting sprayer was at work, and a concealed array of instruments on poles recorded temperature, humidity, and radiative data. It felt much cooler here. Of course, water would be a problem, with the rationing that was being threatened. Damn the rains, why didn't they come?

But she was encouraged. On her way back, her smartphone beeped. There was a message from Claudio that the initial plantings had been completed in the experimental tract, in the drought-ridden forest, and that the local villagers were tending to the saplings. The grant would help pay for the care of the trees, and when the trees were older, they would bear fruit and leaves for the people. There were only a few cases worldwide where rain forests had been partially restored—all restoration was partial because you couldn't replicate the kind of biodiversity that happened over thousands of years—but it was astonishing how things would grow if you looked after them in the initial crucial period. Only local people's investment in the project would ensure its success.

Claudio sounded almost happy. Perhaps healing the forest would heal him too.

The heat wave continued without respite. Fernanda saw people out in the streets staring up at the sky, now, looking at the few clouds that formed above as though beseeching them to rain. The river was sullen and slow. Everyday life seemed off—the glitter of the nightlife was faded too, and the laughter of the people forced. She spent an evening with her cousins Lila and Natalia at the Bar do Armando, where the literati and glitterati seemed equally subdued. The heat seemed to have gotten to the mysterious artist too, since there had been no new work for several days.

Fernanda found herself making the rounds of the graffiti art in the evenings. There were tourist guides who would take visitors to the exhibits. Small businesses sprouted up near these, selling street food and souvenirs. There was outrage when one store painted out the drawing of macaws on its side walls. Each time Fernanda went to see the artwork there would be people standing and staring, and cameras clicking, and groups of friends chattering like monkeys in the jungle. Once she bumped into the man she had sat next to on the plane. He was standing with his briefcase balanced against his legs while he tried to take a picture. She thought of saying hello, apologizing for her coldness on the plane, but he didn't look her way.

She noticed him on three other occasions at different parts of the city, clicking away at the graffiti with his camera. He was photographing the crowds as much as the graffiti. Just a businessman with a hobby, she told herself. But one day, he dropped his briefcase and papers flew open. There were sheets of accounts, tiny neat numbers in rows, a notepad, a notebook computer, a badly wrapped half-eaten sandwich, and a piece of black chalk. The chalk rolled near where Fernanda was standing. The people near the man were solicitously bending over and picking up his things, but he looked around at the ground wildly. Without thinking Fernanda put her foot over the piece of chalk. She dropped her bag, bent down to retrieve it, and got the chalk in her purse with a fluidity that surprised her. It was hard and oily, not at all like ordinary chalk. There was a loose sheet of paper not far from her that the crowd had missed—she picked it up, hurriedly scribbled an address on it, put her business card and the chalk behind the sheet, and gave the whole thing to the man, looking at him with what she hoped was the innocent gaze of a good citizen. She saw recognition leap into his eyes. Obrigado. He averted his gaze and hurried off.

She spent the rest of the day feeling restless. If only she could reassure him! She wasn't going to give him away. She'd seen the name of the company where he worked on top of the sheets. Now if only . . .

At home she touched her wristpad, turning on her computer. She scrolled through the news. The tornado in an eastern state of India. Arguments in the United States Senate about the new energy strategy. Floods here, droughts there, the fabric of the biosphere tearing. She thought of the Amazon rain forest, so often called the Earth's green lung. Even some tourist guides in the city, taking their mostly North American charges into the jungle, used that term. Did anyone know what those words *meant*? She thought of the predictions of several models, that the great forest, currently a massive carbon dioxide sink, might turn into a *source* of $CO2$ if it was stressed enough by drought and tree-cutting. What would happen then? "*Hell on Earth,*" she said aloud. She wondered how many people looked up into the sky and imagined, as she did, the invisible river of moisture, the Rios Voadores, roaring in over the Amazon from the Atlantic coast. It thrilled her to think of it: flying river, the anaconda of the sky, carrying as much water as the amazon, drawn in and strengthened by the pull of the forest so that it flowed across Brazil, hit the Andes, turned south, bringing rain like a benediction. What had human foolishness done to it that there was drought in the *Amazon*? The green lung had lung cancer. She remembered Claudio's face in the lamp-light at camp, speaking passionately about the violated Atlantica forest, the mutilated Mato Grosso, the fact that nearly seven thousand acres of forest were cleared every year.

"What do *you* think—are we a stupid species, or what?" she asked the lizard on the wall. The lizard gave her an enigmatic look.

She rested her head on her arms, thinking of Claudio, his physical presence, his kindness. The work they had been doing had drawn them together—maybe the relationship had never been more than that. And yet . . . the work was important. To know whether such reparations would make a difference was crucial. She was usually so positive, so determined despite the immensity of the task. Perhaps it was the drought, the lack of rain when it should be raining buckets every day, that was making her feel like this. "What shall I do to bring the rain?" she asked aloud. The wristpad beeped, and then there was a kid's voice, distorted by electronic translation software. On the computer screen he was sitting in a hospital bed, his dark, thin face earnest. His ears stuck out.

"*Sing,*" he said. Behind the translation she could hear the kid's real voice speaking an unfamiliar language. He sounded tired. What had he said? "*Sing,*" he said again. "*Sing for the clouds, for the rain.*" He started to sing in an astonishingly musical voice. She could tell he was untrained, even though the musical style was unfamiliar. But it was strangely uplifting, this music that would bring the rain. She wanted his voice to go on and on, even though the translation software was off-key. Then abruptly the screen went dark.

Where had the kid come from? She had signed on to an experimental social network software device at a friend's urging, but the kid wasn't in her list of contacts. The connections were really bad most of the time. She hoped he was all right.

The next day the idea of music bringing the rain still haunted her. Of course such things didn't happen in the real world—as a scientist, she knew better. The vagaries of the climate were still beyond them, and the reparations, the stitches in the green fabric of the jungle, had just begun. The trouble with repairing the forest was that it would never be enough, without a million other things happening too, like the work at the polar ice caps, and social movements, ordinary people pledging to make lifestyle changes, and governments passing laws so that children and grandchildren could have a future. The crucial thing was to get net global carbon dioxide emissions down to zero, and that would take the participation of nearly everyone. The days of the lone ranger were gone; this was the age of the million heroes.

Still, she opened her saxophone case the next day and caressed the cool metal. It drew her, the music she had put away from her. She hadn't answered her bandmates' e-mails. Now she had to run to the lab—maybe this evening, she told her saxophone. We'll have a date, you and I.

But she never got to the lab, because her colleague Maria called her, excited. As a result she went straight to the home in Cidade Nova with the experimental green roof. She went around the house to the side wall, where a crowd had already gathered. People were getting out of cars, and there was even a TV truck. From behind the foliage cascading down the wall of the house peered a jaguar, a gentle jaguar, sleepy even, at peace with the world. Fernanda let out a long breath. The artist had understood her message. The owner of the house, elderly Victor Gomes, was standing with the crowd, his mouth agape.

Within a few hours, the news spread and the crowd swelled until the traffic became a problem. Sensing an opportunity, she talked briefly and urgently to Victor Gomes, and he gave an impromptu tour of the rooftop garden. Suddenly everyone was talking about green roofs. Imagine, if you went ahead and got one (and there was a grant to help you out with costs if you couldn't afford it), not only did your air-conditioning bills go down, but maybe, just maybe, the artist would come paint the side of your house.

Two days later there was a gala fund-raiser and awareness event at the Hotel Amazonas. Fernanda played with her old band. She put her lips to her saxophone and into each note she poured her yearning for the rain, for a world restored. The music spilled out, clear as light, smooth as flowing water, and she sensed the crowd shift and move with the sound, with her breath. During a break, when she leaned against the side wall of the stage, watching Santiago's fingers ripple over the piano keyboard, a waiter came up to her and handed her an envelope. Curious, she opened it, and inside was a paper napkin, and an Amazonian butterfly drawn on it, so vivid she half expected it to rise off the napkin. She searched for him in the crowd but there were too many people. Her wristpad beeped. "A butterfly," she whispered, and she felt the wings of change beating in the light-filled air around her.

". . . CAN CAUSE A TORNADO . . ."

". . . but scientists now know more than they did only five years ago. We will now speak to an expert . . ." Can you please turn off the TV? I can't bear to see anything more about the storm . . . it was the same program this morning.

I am too sad to tell this story. You'll have to wait a moment.

I am sad because my grandfather the professor died. He was not really my grandfather, but he treated me like I was his own. I called him Dadaji. He let me sleep on the verandah of his bungalow, on a little cot. I felt safe there. I cleaned and cooked for him, and he would talk to me and tell me about all kinds of things. He taught me how to read and write. From the place where I slept I could look down a low incline to the village, my village.

Are you translating this into English? Does that mean I'll be famous all over India?

I want to help my village. I want people to know about it, even though it is only a Harijan basti sitting on stony ground. I want to make sure the world knows that we did something good.

Let me tell you about my village. The river is many hours' walk from us, but the floods are getting worse. Last year during the monsoons the water came into the huts and the fields and drowned everything except what we could carry. The ground where the village sits is very stony, and things don't grow well. We don't have fields of our own, not really. We are *doms*—most of us work in town, or for the big Rajput village—Songaon—two miles away. We do all the dirty work—sweeping and cleaning privies, that sort of thing. Me, I am lucky because the professor employs me and takes care of me and treats me as though I were not a *dom*. He doesn't observe caste even though he is a Rajput himself—he says it is already dying out in the towns and cities. He says the government laws protect people like us, but I don't know about those things because if the Rajputs are angry then they can do what they like to us and nobody can stop them. But the professor, he is a different kind of person—a *devata*. He even has me cook his food, and pats my head when I do my lessons well—and when there is a festival we share a plate of sweets together.

See this thing I am wearing around my wrist, like a watch? The professor gave it to me. He has been teaching me the computer and this thing makes it come on and we can see and talk to people from around the world. Once I spoke to a man all the way in Chennai—it was very exciting. It was really like magic, because the man didn't know Bhojpuri or Hindi and the computer translated his words and mine so we could both understand. The translator voices were funny. Mine didn't sound like me at all.

What I love most is music. In the early morning when the mist lies on the river, the first thing I hear is the birds in the bougainvillea bush. When I bring the tea out on the verandah and we have drunk the first cup, the professor gives me his tanpura to tune. Then he starts to sing *Bhairav*, which is a morning raga. Listening to him, I feel as though I am climbing up and down mountain ranges of mist and cloud. I feel I could fly. I sing with him, as though my voice is a shadow following his voice. He tells me I have a good ear. It isn't the same kind of singing as in the movies—it is something deeper that calls to your soul. When I told the professor that, he looked pleased and said that good music makes poets of us. I never thought that just any-body could be a poet.

From his house, I can see all the way to the river far beyond the village. In the last few years we have either had drought or flood. This year seems to be a dry year. Always there is some difficulty we have to deal with. But we have been changing too, ever since the professor came and began to live in his house. He has problems with his sons; they don't get along, so he lives alone except for me. He and some other people have been working with our basti. The other people are also dalits like us, but they can read and write, and they know how to make the government give them their rights. They have traveled all over the country telling villages like ours that the climate is changing, and we must change too, or we won't survive. So now we have a village panchayat, and there are three women and two men who speak for all of us. You see, new times are coming, difficult times, when Dharti Mai herself is against us because instead of treating her like a mother, human beings have treated her like a slave. Most of those people who did this are in America and places like that, but they are here too, in the big cities. It is strange because at first we used to think places like that were the best in the world, because of what we saw on TV, but the professor explained that living like that, with no regard for Dharti Mai, comes with costs. Why doesn't Dharti Mai punish *them*, then? I asked him that once. Why is she punishing us poor people, who have done nothing to cause the problem? The professor sighed and said that Dharti Mai was punishing every-one. So people ask him all the time, what can we do? This makes the professor happy because he says that earlier most people in our basti just accepted their lot— after all, for thousands of years it has been our lot to suffer. He is pleased because now we want to do something to save ourselves and make the world better. If all those rich, upper-caste people and all the *goras* have been wrong all this time about how they should live, maybe they're wrong about us too. Maybe our time has come.

But Bojhu kaku—he's the one who took me in when my parents died—he says what's the good in pointing fingers? Even the *goras* are changing how they live. The question is what can we do to heal Dharti Mai? How can we help each other survive the terrible times that are upon us? So in the village people take turns being look-outs when there is a bad weather forecast, and they help each other more, and they've got a teacher to come twice a week to teach them how to read and write. They sent Barki kaki off to the town to be trained by a doctor—she's the midwife—so that she can help us all be healthier. You should have seen her when she came back, she was so proud—she got to see how they work in the big hospital and she came back with pink soap for everyone. We now have our own hand pump and don't have to drink river water. All this is because of the professor, and because of people like Bojhu kaku, and Barki kaki—and Dulari Mai, even though most people are scared of her temper. The professor and I are treated like royal guests whenever we go to visit. The professor studies people—anthropology—and even though he is retired, he hasn't stopped. He goes around all the local villages, tap-tapping with his cane—he's got a bad leg—and he tells people about the world.

Which is how we know about how the world is getting hotter, and even the *goras* are burning up in their big cities with all those cars and TVs. But that is not all. You know there is a big coal-mining company that wants to buy all the land around us? The professor gets angry whenever the coal company is mentioned, so angry he can hardly get a word out. It is burning coal and oil that is making the world hotter and Dharti Mai so angry with us. He says the government, instead of finding ways to use other things, is mining more coal and making more coal plants so that the people in the big cities can have electricity and cars and TVs, which warm the world even more. It sounds to me like when Dhakkan kaka gets drunk, he wants to keep on drinking. So maybe the way the rich people of the world live is like a sickness where they can't make themselves stop. Also most people in my village don't want to give up their ancestral land for the coal company, small and poor and stony though it might be, even though the government has promised compensation. That tiny piece of earth is all we have. But some of the young men think that the money would be good, and they can go to the big city and make it big. The professor told them that there are already too many people trying to make it in the city, but behind his back they grumble and talk about the good life they could have. It's mostly people like Jhingur kaka's older son, who is a malcontent. The Rajput village—Songaon—doesn't like the coal-mining idea either and the professor persuaded them to let us join a protest delegation in the town, although we had to keep our distance behind them. The professor sat with us and argued against the coal company from the back. You should have seen how furious the Rajputs were! They respect him for his education and his caste, even though he doesn't keep caste, but his ways upset them. Later, when we were walking back, one of them told him, "If you weren't an old man, and learned too, I would take my stick to you, for the example you are setting to our children." I know, because I heard him. It was Ranbir Singh. He is the one with the biggest mustache and the biggest, stoutest sticks, and the biggest temper. His mood changes so quickly, everyone is afraid of him. He even has guns. The professor just said quietly that if Ranbir Singh did that with every Rajput in the country who had broken caste, he would run out of sticks pretty quickly.

The day it all happened, in the morning we were listening to the classical program on the radio because the professor wanted to hear a new *bandish* that was playing. There were clouds in the sky but no sign of rain. Just then we heard a roaring sound. The radio crackled and the announcer said something about an unusual cloud formation. The sound of the wind became so strong that we couldn't hear the radio. The sky became dark, even though over the river it was still light. There was a tapping sound over our heads: hail! I was very excited. Hail has fallen only once in my village in my lifetime. I ran down the verandah steps to collect some, and then I saw the storm.

I had never seen anything like it. I saw a whirling monster towering in the fields behind the house, like a top spun out of clouds and wind. The professor looked alarmed. He said he had heard of things like this in other lands, and that it was called a *tur-nado*. He said we would be all right in a pukka house like his, but then he stared out into the distance toward my village. People were coming out of their homes and getting ready to walk to Songaon or the town for the long day of work.

"Bhola," he said to me, "I am going to check on the computer what we should do. Get ready to run down to the village and warn people."

"Dadaji, will you be all right?" he's an old man, and lame, too. But he pushed me impatiently off, saying of course he would be fine. That's the last thing he said to me.

I ran down toward the village. The wind was strong, and I saw a crow in the sky struggling to keep its wings under control. It swooped down in a big arc and came right at me, flapping its wings, and hit me in the stomach. I grabbed it and held it to my chest—a full-grown crow. I thought it was dead, but I couldn't just throw it away. So I held it to my chest and I ran.

The sky darkened and the wind howled in my ears. I looked behind me at the house. The tur-nado was over it. The verandah was so dark I couldn't see the professor. I saw the lit screen of the computer disappearing as he went into the house. Above us the tur-nado looked like a monster. I have never been so scared. Then my wrist strap beeped. A woman's voice said out of nowhere, "Find low ground, low ground," and "Run! Run!" I wanted to see if the professor was all right, but he had told me to warn the village. So I ran.

There is a narrow ravine not far from the village. Old people say that it is a crack that opened in the earth during an earthquake. In the monsoons it fills with water, but right now it is dry, full of thorny bushes and rocks. The goats like it there. That was the only low place I could think of. I began to shout as I got closer, yelling to people to stop gawking and trying to lead them to the ravine. I couldn't hear my own voice because of the wind, but Dulari mai started to scream at people and gather them and point them to the ravine. Everyone worked quickly; they are afraid of her temper. There was even someone carrying Joti ma, old Gobind-kaka's mother, on his back, the terrified children were all holding hands, some were carrying the babies. Behind me the tur-nado danced across the fields, ripping up everything in its path. It picked its way across the land. I saw people rushing toward the ravine, some carrying bundles with them. There was a lot of shouting but everyone was moving. I thought: *I'm not needed here, I could have stayed with the professor.* I thought I should see if I could go around the tur-nado and get to his house. I made my way back across the fields, keeping a careful eye on the storm.

When I was halfway there, I saw the children. It was Ranbir Singh's younger daughter and son, returning from school on the footpath through the fields. Usually someone takes them from Songaon to the town and back by bicycle, but they were walking home. She is older than me, maybe fourteen, and he is only about five years old. Her father once had Bojhu kaku's son beaten because he said he—Kankariya bhai—dared to raise his eyes and look at his daughter. Before I was born, there was trouble that nobody talks about and the Rajputs came and burned down some of our huts, and three people died. That's what I mean when I say they can do anything to us. I hesitated, because if I said anything to the children they didn't like, their father could have me thrashed and the village burned down.

The children looked scared. The girl was trying to use her mobile but she gave up and put it in her schoolbag, looking upset. They looked at me and looked away, and the older sister said to the boy, "Come," urgently, and pulled on his arm. He was tired and about to cry.

I thought: *Why should I try to help them?* But I pointed to the tur-nado raging behind us:

"Sister, that is a bad *toofan*. The professor told me we have to hide. We are all at the ravine near my basti. I can take you there."

I took extra care to be polite. I didn't want her to accuse us later on and get the whole village in trouble. She hesitated. The little boy said:

"Why are you holding a dead crow?"

The girl came to a decision. She said:

"Show me where this place is."

They followed me. There were leaves and branches flying around, and I saw the thatched roof lift off a hut and vanish. A brick came hurtling through the air and missed us by two spans of my hand. I didn't dare look back—we were racing over the fields. The little boy stumbled, and the girl picked him up. Panting, she followed me. It would have been faster if I'd carried the child, but she wasn't going to let a *dom* boy touch her brother. Then she half stumbled. She said: *"Wait!"* I almost didn't hear her but when I looked back she was crying. She thrust her brother at me. Her breath was coming in sobs. He was crying too.

"You want me to carry him? Your father will break my neck!"

She was wailing and shaking her head, and the tur-nado was very close, so I put the child on one hip and handed her the still-warm body of the crow.

"I'm not going to hold that," she said, scowling.

"Then take your brother back," I said, losing my temper. "This crow is a *vahan* of Shani Deva, and we must not disrespect it. Don't you keep pigeons?"

She wrinkled her nose but took the crow in her dupatta, and we ran the rest of the way until we were at the ravine.

It was dark inside, because the low, thorny bushes growing on the top edges of the ravine blocked the sky. Wind screamed over our heads and we heard the most terrible sounds, as though the world was being torn apart.

And then silence.

We all looked at each other. Bojhu kaku and the others saw that I was holding Ranbir Singh's son in my arms, and his daughter was standing next to me, holding the body of a crow in her dupatta, her eyes wide with fear.

"Bhola, what have you done?" someone said. Maybe it was Barki kaki. People gasped.

"I couldn't leave them to die," I said. The boy wriggled out of my grasp and went to his sister. She handed me the crow and held her brother close. Tears ran down her face.

Bojhu kaku said to the girl, "We will see you home. Come, there is nothing to be scared of."

So the children were escorted to Songaon by the crowd. If Bojhu kaku went by himself, he might have to bear the brunt of Ranbir Singh's mood. There was no telling whether he'd be grateful or angry. So Barki kaki said she would go, and then Dulari Mai (and we had to tell her no because she would insult even the gods if she lost her temper, and where would we all be then?). So about fifteen people went.

We climbed out of the ravine. The village was smashed flat. There were pots and pans scattered about the fields, and bricks also. The bargad tree that has stood at the crossing on the way to Songaon for two hundred years was completely uprooted. The pathway was covered with big tree branches. Our homes were gone. You might say, *What's a mud-and-thatch house? It is nothing.* But to a poor person it is home. Our hands shape it, our hands weave the *bhusa*. It is where our hopes live. When you have very little, everything you have becomes more precious. We wept and in the same breath we thanked the gods for sparing our lives.

I didn't go with them. My duty was to my dadaji now, and I had a terrible fear growing inside me. I went to the house on the hill. Midway the crow stirred in my arms, and I saw that it was only stunned, not dead. I stopped in the field and found a pocket of moisture where some hailstones had fallen, and let a few drops trail from my fingers into its throat. Suddenly it struggled and flapped its wings. I opened my hands and it flew. It was unsteady at first, but it got stronger as it flew, making two big circles over my head before it went off. Then I went up to what was left of the house.

The windows and doors were gone, and I could see the sky through the roof. Two walls were down. I thought: *This is a pukka house, how could this have happened? How could brick and mortar come down like this?* There was dust in the air. It made me cough. There were pages and pages torn from his books, fallen everywhere like leaves. I saw that his computer had fallen under his desk and was all right. Bricks fell as I walked around. I fell too, and broke my arm, and hurt my leg. That's why I'm in hospital.

I was the one who found him. He was near the drawing room window, under a pile of bricks.

He was my grandfather, no matter what anyone says about caste and blood. He gave me everything I have—he was like a god to me. I would have given my life for him, but instead he is the one who is gone. He said I would grow up to be a learner and a singer—someone who could change the world. A *dom* boy like me—nobody has ever told me such things. I'm telling you, he was my dadaji; I don't care what anyone says.

His sons came for his body. I'm not allowed to be there for the last rites. But I know, and he knows, that I should be there. He used to tell me that if you look at things on the surface, you don't know their true nature. You also have to look with your inner eye. He looked at me with his inner eye. He was my dadaji and he's gone.

That's his computer on the table. His sons didn't ask about it.

Nobody has come to see me and I am scared.

What is that you say? Half of Songaon is destroyed? That is a terrible thing. Seven people dead!

I am glad Ranbir Singh's children gave a good account of us. It is strange for him to be in our debt.

Earlier today there was a TV program about the tur-nado. They interviewed an expert. He said that although a tur-nado is strong, it is also delicate. I think I know what he means. Before it is born, the tur-nado is a confusion of cloud and wind. It takes only a little touch here and there to turn the cloud and wind into a monster that can destroy houses. Even once it is made, you can't tell where it is going to go, because it is so delicate a thing that maybe one leaf on one tree might persuade it to go this way instead of that. Or one breath from one sleeping farmhand in the field.

When I leave the hospital, I'm going to help rebuild my village. And I'm going to collect all the pages of dadaji's books that are scattered all over the fields. I imagine I will find the thoughts of a scientist or philosopher, or the speeches of a poet, stuck in a tree's branches, or blowing in the wind with the dust. I will pick up every page I find and put it together.

I have to find out how I can keep learning. Dadaji was going to teach me so that I could be a learned man like him when I grow up. How is it possible for a tur-nado to be so powerful and so delicate at the same time? How do we tell Dharti Mai we are sorry? How do we stop the mining company that wants to take our land? Please print that in your newspaper—we cannot let them mine and burn more coal, because that is destroying the world. Please tell the big people in the cities like Delhi and in faraway places like America. They won't care about someone like me, but ask them if they care about their own children. I saw just yesterday that it is not just the poor who will suffer in this new world they are making. Tell them to stop.

I have been seeing crows at the window all afternoon. They land on the sill and caw. The orderly says Shani Deva has shown me grace, because of the crow I saved. Everyone fears Shani Deva because he brings us difficult times. But crows remember, and they tell each other who is a friend, and maybe the crows will help us. It's their world too.

I'm very tired. In one day I lost my grandfather, hid my people from the tur-nado, saved two Rajput children, and became a friend of crows.

Something strange happened after dinner. I was half asleep. I heard a woman saying very sadly, "What shall I do to bring the rain?" then I saw it wasn't a dream, because there was this young woman on the computer screen, a foreigner. I thought she must be one of the people who used to talk to the professor. She looked sad and tired. I told her, you have to sing to the clouds. You have to sing the rain down. Between the radio and my dadaji's lessons I have learned a little of the raga—Malhaar, the rain-calling raga. I sang a line or two for her before the connection broke.

Dadaji told me once that sound is just a tremble in the air. A song is a tremble that goes from the soul into the air, and thus to the eardrums of the world. The tur-nado is a disturbance of the air, but it is like an earthquake. Perhaps it is the song of the troubled Earth, our mother Dharti Mai. One day I will compose a song to soothe her.

. . . IN TEXAS . . .

. . . it was the kind of day Dorothy Cartwright's husband wouldn't have allowed. Wasn't it just a year and a half ago—he'd gotten so mad at the heat wave at

Christmastime that he'd cranked up the air-conditioning until she had to go find a sweater? But they'd had the traditional Christmas evening fire in the fireplace, and weather be damned. It was nowhere near Christmas day, being March, but it was hotter than it should be, the kind of day when Rob would have had the AC going and the windows closed. Closed houses always made her feel claustrophobic, no matter that her old home had been over four thousand square feet—just the two of them after their son, Matt, grew up and left home. But now Rob was dead of a heart attack more than a year ago, and Dorothy lived in a little two-room apartment in an assisted-living facility. She could open the windows if she felt like it. She did so, and turned on the fans, and checked the cupcakes baking in the oven. There was a cool breeze, no more than a breath. The big magnolia tree in the front lawn made a shade so deep you could be forgiven for thinking evening had come early. She arranged the chairs in the living room for the fifth time and glanced at the clock. Fifteen minutes and they would be here.

As she was taking the cupcakes out, the phone rang. She nearly dropped the tray. Shaking, she set it on the counter and picked up the phone. It was Kevin.

"Gramma! Guess where your favorite grandson's calling from?"

He was cheerful in the faked way he had when he was upset. Which meant—

"I'm in rehab and this time I'm going to quit for good."

"Of course, hon," she said. Who could believe the kid when he'd been in and out of rehab six times in two years? She remembered Rob's cold fury the last time the boy had been over. Her grandson was adrift, and she was helpless and useless. The other day she'd watched a show on PBS about early humans and how the human race wouldn't have survived without old people, other people than the parents, to help raise the young and transmit the knowledge of earlier generations. Grandmothers in particular were important. That was all very well, but in this day of books and computers and all, who needed grandmothers? They lived in retirement homes, or in huge, echoing houses, at the periphery of society, distracting themselves, waiting for death. Times had changed. Kevin was beyond anyone's help. She gripped the edge of the counter with her free hand. An ache shot through her chest. She felt a momentary dizziness.

"I'll send you some cupcakes," she said. All she had been able to do for the people she loved was to offer them food, as though the trouble in the world could be taken away by sugar and butter and chocolate. She said good-bye, feeling hopeless.

He had sent her an orange wristlet, rather pretty. It had jewellike white buttons on it that allowed her to communicate with her new notebook computer (a gift from her son) with a touch. She looked at it and thought how nice Kevin was, to get her a present. She touched the button and her notebook computer lit up, and there was an image of a woman in a diving suit suspended in murky blue water, her arms working, and a reedy electronic voice like a cartoon character saying something about cold Arctic waters and repeating a name, Dr. Irene Ariak, Irene Ariak. Surely she had heard the name in some show or other. A scientist working in the Arctic. What a dangerous thing to do, to go up there in the cold and dark. "Bless you and be careful up there, I'm praying for you," she said. The cartoon voice said, *Mrs. Cartwright, thank you!* And the screen went blank. Dorothy wondered if she'd heard right. Well, this was a new world, to be sure.

The doorbell rang as she was setting the cupcakes on a plate. Patting her hair, glancing at the small oval mirror over by the little dining table (her lipstick was just right), she went to the door.

There they all were, smiling. Rita, with her defiantly undyed white hair in a braid tied with rainbow-colored ribbons (Rob would have thought them loud), said, "How nice of you to host the meeting, Dorothy!," and planted herself in the comfortable armchair. The others, Mary-Ann, Gerta, Lawrence, Brad, Eva, and three women she didn't know, crowded into the small living room. Dorothy handed around cupcakes and poured tea and coffee and felt as awkward as a new wife hosting her first dinner party. She scolded herself: Now, then, you've known these people for eight months, and you've hosted more parties in your life than you can remember! This was about reinventing herself. Stretching outside her comfort zone, learning new things. Rob would have never allowed these people in their house—there was something not done about their passionate intensity. "Aging hippies," Rob would have said. He would have told her what was wrong with each of them, and she would never have invited them again. Once she'd had a local mothers' group over for tea; Rob came home early. He'd been pleasant enough greeting them and had gone upstairs. The women were upset about the firing of the principal at the local elementary school, and one of them had raised her voice emphatically, making her point. Rob had banged the bedroom door so hard upstairs that the reverberation made the windows rattle. She'd never invited those women over again.

She sat down and let the conversation swirl around her, trying to ignore the tightness in her chest. Keeping up the smile was becoming difficult.

"Well," Rita said, "Our energy-saving campaign has been successful beyond anything we expected. Management has stopped grumbling. We've saved them $14,504 in energy bills, annually!"

"New lightbulbs and more insulation, and cranking down the AC so it isn't freezing in the middle of summer, and one set of solar panels . . . who'da thought it?"

"Our see-oh-two emissions are down by . . . let's see . . . 18 percent . . ."

"Multiply individual actions by millions or billions, and you're looking at real global difference . . ."

It was one of the new women, a blonde with intense blue eyes. Not from the apartment complex. Dorothy had already forgotten her name. Now the woman was smiling at her a little uncertainly.

"Mrs. Cartwright, we need to recruit people for the protest. The pipeline is coming to us. Janna Helmholtz's land is being *violated*—they got a court order to cut a corridor through her woods to bring the oil pipes through, and we're going to protest. Can we count on you?"

"Yes, yes, of course," Dorothy said, feeling foolish. What had she agreed to?

". . . they say fracking for shale oil and gas is going to reduce carbon dioxide emissions, but can you believe they base that on completely ignoring the methane emissions from the fracking?"

"Methane is twenty times worse than see-oh-two . . . cooking the planet . . ."

"My objection to fracking is entirely on another plane—see, less coal burned here means coal prices fall, and it gets exported elsewhere, so coal usage will go up somewhere else if fracking happens here in the United States—idiots don't understand the meaning of *global* . . ."

"Yes, but there's also the issue, I told him that, I told him just because you work for Texas O&G, try to have an open mind for fuck's sake—I told him, think about switching to green energy. Fracking for oil and gas just means putting off what we need to do. Like, you know, you need to fucking quit, not go from cocaine to . . . to meth!"

Rob wouldn't approve of the f-word either. Dorothy told herself to stop thinking about Rob. Rob used the f-word as much as he liked, but he couldn't stand women swearing. Generally, he said that meant that either they were common, or they needed a good lay. Shut up about Rob, she told herself.

"Well, Mrs. Cartwright?"

She cleared her throat. What had they been talking about?

"I don't know," she said. What could she do? Her life behind her . . . she felt a sudden wave of utter misery.

"What can I do? I'm not trained . . ."

"Dorothy, you don't need training for this," Rita said, in her proselytizing voice. Rita was a You-nitarian, You-niversalist, as Eva had once said in mincing tones—*Rita, there's so much You in UU, where's the room for God?* They'd had quite a spat about it, but they stayed friends. Rob had always said you could only be friends with people who thought like you.

"Honey, there are retired people all over the country like you and me who care about the world we are leaving our grandchildren—"

"—hell, everyone thinks we are old fogies, useless relics, and I say we are a totally untapped resource, a revolution waiting to happen . . ."

Lawrence ("not Larry") nodded. "We have experience, and knowledge of human nature—Dorothy, just by being who you are you can make a difference—"

She found herself signing up to recruit five people and be at the meeting place today in three hours. Janna Helmholtz had called to say the earthmovers were going to be on her property ripping up the trees her granddaddy had planted and she needed them to be there. Three hours! (*Well, the fracking company doesn't wait at our convenience, honey; besides imagine if you were in the middle of the workday, you wouldn't be able to make it. But we have the time and the determination! So be there or be a quadrilateral!* This from Eva, retired math teacher at Pine Tree Elementary.)

After they had all left, Dorothy found herself putting the dirty dishes by the sink in a mood of despair. How was she going to go to wing 5 and recruit five people? She couldn't imagine being able to convince anyone. Talking to people was difficult anyway, especially when they didn't wear their hearing aids or were taking a nap. She heard Rob's voice: *You're being a fool, Dottie. We Cartwrights don't get into other people's business. Do you really think you can make a difference?*

It was hard to remember that she had been second valedictorian at her school, and that she had got into a prestigious college and been on a debating team. After she met Rob—he'd chased and flattered her relentlessly—she had seen the possibility of another life, the kind that she'd only glimpsed through the iron lattice gates of rich acquaintances—a life of going to theater and art museums and raising children to send off to the best schools. Who in the world would love her like Rob? She remembered when they were both young, and he had lost his first job, how much he'd looked up to her, needed her. She began to scrub the baking tray, thinking of Rob's love for her cooking. He'd always praised her culinary skills to his business friends whenever there was a party. She sighed. He would not have been pleased about her involvement with this cause. But she'd given her word—what had made her agree to talk to five strangers? She wiped her sudsy hands absently on the towel, and her wristlet beeped. "I'm no use to anyone," she said aloud. "I don't know what to do." And she heard a voice from the little computer on the mantelpiece say, with the utmost conviction: "Something good will happen to you today." Very clear English, but a strange accent. She went and picked up the computer but the screen had gone dark.

She rearranged her hair and put on fresh lipstick and went determinedly down the hall to wing 5. There were several people in the lounge. She told herself *second valedictorian* and made herself smile and say hello. By the end of an hour she had recruited eight people. Would have been nine, if Molly hadn't had her annual physical that afternoon. *Damn, you're good*, Rita said, when she called and told her, and Dorothy thought, with pleased surprise, *Yes*.

In an hour they were loading into cars, driving over the long, empty roads soon to be filled with rush-hour traffic, over to Janna's place. Janna had a big house on a hundred acres, and there was already a crowd in the middle of a field, and at least half a dozen cars, and my goodness, was that a TV truck? There was Janna, with a new perm and her big smile, waving to the newcomers walking over to her. The sun was hot. Along one side of the field ran a dark line of woodlands, presumably the place where the pipeline was going through. Dorothy walked over determinedly, ignoring the odd breathlessness that caught her at moments, gritting her teeth, closing her ears against Rob's voice. That woman should never wear shorts, her legs are too fat, and that one, dressed like a slut, tells you what she wants. These wannabe hippies are a laugh. Can barely walk and they want to change the world! Well, that bit was true of some of the protesters, old ladies with walkers and even a man in a wheelchair. There was Rita, high-fiving him. Dorothy found herself standing at the edge of the crowd, grateful for her hat. There were the earthmovers roaring up in front of them. A young man at the helm of each, one of them grinning, the other one nervous. The sun glinted off the windshields.

A black woman was making a speech. Eva nudged Dorothy and whispered, "Myra Jackson, professor over at the university."

"It's not just about land," the woman said. "Global warming is real, and we have to do something about it now, not tomorrow. Shale gas only puts off what we really need, which is green energy, and a new alternative-energy-based economy. Germany's already ahead of us in solar energy. We need a Marshall Plan for the ecological-economic crisis!"

There were cheers.

Now they could hear police sirens getting louder. The protesters began to shout slogans. Dorothy's heart began to beat thunderously in her ears. What had she gotten herself into?

There was Janna, yelling above the noise. "Y'all pack up your equipment and get outta here, we're not gonna let you clear my family's woods! No more fracking!"

There were signs now going up, and cameras flashing, and people yelling "Don't frack Texas!," and the big yellow machines kept coming, although slowly. The professor woman jumped off the table—she was too young and fit to be one of the oldies—and someone moved the table away. The cops arrived, waving the protesters to the side so that the machinery could get to the trees. The crowd shifted and surged, without backing away. The man in the wheelchair waved his stick at a policeman and yelled something. Handcuffs clicked, cameras rolled. The giant machines kept inching forward. Dorothy found herself ignored by everyone, even the cops. She felt the cool air of the woods at her back, through her thin cotton dress. She was just in front of one of the machines. She stared at the young man in the driver's seat. He looked like Kevin. She wondered why his face was set—goodness, the boy was nervous! She thought of him suddenly as a sacrifice, like all the young men in her life, her son gone to the army, returned a silent shadow of his former self, her grandson beset by demons, all that youth and strength turned wrong. She thought of the poor woman out in the bottom of the ocean in the Arctic trying to save the world so that her grandchild, Dorothy's grandchild, and all, everyone's grandchild could live in the world. And she thought how cruel the world that makes young men hold the guns against their own temples, the knives at their own throats, so that their own hands poison the Earth and its creatures that the good Lord made—and Rob said in her mind, *Dottie, you're talking like a fool*—and something broke inside her.

She was standing with a Tupperware box of cupcakes—stupidly, she waved it in front of the boy like an offering. She walked toward him, her own face set, as though she could save him, as though she, Dorothy Cartwright, B.A., M.R.S., could do anything. The kid's eyes went wide, and he waved frantically at her, and she turned around and saw the great yellow arm of the other machine swing, and the horrified face of the other man, who saw her only at the last minute—then it hit her shoulder, and the side of her head, and then she was falling, and cupcakes falling everywhere.

She awoke in the hospital. The light was too bright. Someone drew the curtains across the window. She could hear some kind of hubbub outside her door. She slept.

Hours later she woke feeling better. A lantern-jawed doctor who looked like a very tired Clint Eastwood told her she had a mild concussion, and a cracked bone in her shoulder. The man at the bulldozer had turned the thing off just in time; it was the momentum that had gotten her. Otherwise she might be dead. She was really lucky. All the scans were clear, but they were going to keep her overnight for observation. After that, six weeks of rest for her shoulder.

"I can see you're a wild young rebel, Mrs. Cartwright, but promise me you won't be up to those shenanigans for a while," he said, smiling.

She told him, smiling back, surprising herself, "You do your job, I'll do mine."

Her son called. Matt was driving over the next day. He sounded more bemused than anything. She thought with satisfaction that she had finally managed to surprise someone.

And then Molly was there, praising her like she had done something heroic.

"Wish I could have been there," she said wistfully. "Rita and Eva are in jail, and that black professor too, and about ten other people. They're probably going to charge you as soon as you are well."

Dorothy couldn't imagine going to jail—but Molly made it sound like it was the thing to do. Well, it had been some day. She decided not to worry. Over the doctor's objections she let two journalists interview her and take pictures. Her mother used to call her a chatterbox, a trait that had disappeared with time and Rob, and now she couldn't stop talking.

"When my husband was still alive," she said, "he used to tell me how impractical it was to worry about the environment. Practical people run the economy, make sure things work. That attitude, combined with greed, has ruined the Earth to a degree that threatens our grandchildren. I'm only a housewife, but I know that we need good, fresh air to breathe, and trees to grow, and we need the wild things around us. As a grand-mother, I can't think of one single grandparent who wouldn't want to do the best for their grandchildren. That's why I believe we need to protect what the good Lord gave us, this blessed Earth, else how can we live? And what's more practical than that?"

After they had all gone, in the silence of the room, she lay back against the pil-lows, spent. An incredulity rose in her. What had she done? The whole day she had been putting herself forward, Rob would say. The elation subsided. She hid her face in the pillows.

Then the phone rang. This time it was Kevin.

"Gramma! I saw you on TV! You kicked ass!"

She laughed. It was so very nice of him to call. They talked for half an hour, until the nurse came and frowned at her.

"Gramma, I'm going to get clean this time," Kevin said. Dorothy took a deep breath.

"Kev, soon as they let me out of here I'm going to come see you. This time you will get clean, love. You've got a life to live."

And so do I, she thought after she hung up.

Lying back in the darkened room, she saw from the digital clock on the side table that it was nearly midnight on March 16. Heavens, no wonder Rob had been haunt-ing her all day—it was his birthday! And she had forgotten. Well, at least she had baked his favorite cupcakes. She thought about how her life had changed in one day, and the work left to be done. It wasn't going to be easy, and she had no illusions that she was any kind of heroine, or that her few minutes of fame were going to lead to any major changes. But Molly had told her that the phone lines of No Fracking Texas were swamped with calls from other assisted-living facilities and retired people's associations. It seemed the old ones, the forgotten ones, were coming out of the woodwork. In times gone by, the old were the ones to whom the young turned for advice. Now the old had to bear responsibility for ruining the Earth, but they also, by the same logic, bore the responsibility for setting things right. The press was calling it the Suspender Revolution. The Retirees Spring. Kind of disrespectful, but they'd show them. And she, Dorothy Cartwright, had helped it come about. *Viva la revolu-ción*, and poor Rob, rest in peace, and Happy Birthday.

THE END

The Story Begins

Or does it end here?

It ends, the young man thinks, as he climbs the last mountain, emerging into the last alpine valley. It ends with his own life winding down as he climbs to the roof of the world. The strength that has allowed him to leave the busy streets of Shanghai and journey to this remote place in the Himalayas is like the sudden flaring of the moth caught in the flame. Lately he's had a vision of simply lying down in the tall green meadow grass, and falling asleep, and feeling the grass stalks growing through his body, a thousand tiny piercings, until he is nothing but a husk.

He pauses to catch breath against the rocky wall of the cliff. His breath forms clouds of condensation in the cold air. His rucksack feels heavier now. He can't remember when he last ate. Probably at the village he left in the morning. He takes out a flask of water, drinks, and finds a small bag with trail mix and walks again.

When he emerges from the narrow pass, he finds himself at a vertiginous height. Below him, lost in mist and distance, is a rocky, arid valley through which a silver river winds. On the other side the mountains are gaunt and bare, the white tongues of melting glaciers high on the slopes. But the place he seeks is immediately to his right, where the path leads. The stone facade of the monastery comes into view, a rocky aerie impossible to conceive of—how could anyone build here, halfway up to the sky?—but it is solid, it is there. So he walks on, up the narrow path, to the great flight of steps. The tiers of windows above him are empty, and there is an enormous hole in the roof of the entrance hall, through which he can see a lammergeier circling high in the blue sky. Could it be that the last refuge is destroyed after all? He had dreamed of a great university hidden deep in the Himalayas, a place where people like him could gather to weave the web that would save the dying world. He had dreamed of its destruction too, at the hands of greed and power. Can it have happened already?

Wearily he sinks down on the dusty floor at the top of the steps. In the silence he hears his own breath coming fast, and the faint trickle of water in the distance. He is conscious of being watched.

A man is standing on a fallen column. He is tall, dressed in rough black robes. There is some kind of small animal on his shoulder, brown, with a long, bushy tail—a squirrel, perhaps, or a mongoose?

Yuan bows, clears his throat.

"I dreamed of this place," he says in English, hoping the monk can understand him. "I came here to try to do something before I die. But it's too late, I see."

The monk gestures to him, and Yuan stumbles over broken pieces of stone, follows him around a corner into a small, high courtyard open to sun and sky.

"Sit," the monk says, indicating a low wooden seat. There is tea in a black kettle, steaming over a small fire. "Tell me about your dream of this place." There is white stubble on his shaven chin, and deep lines are etched on the brown face. His English is fluent, with an accent that is vaguely familiar. Yuan clears his throat, speaks.

"It was a monastery first, then a university. It was a place for those who sought to understand the world in a new way, and to bring about its resurrection. I saw the humblest people come here to share what they knew, and the learned ones listened. It didn't have the quietude of the monastery it had once been—at every corner, in every gathering, I heard arguments and disagreements, but true peace is dynamic, not static, and rests on a thousand quarrels.

"It wasn't a secret, although not many people knew about it. It was rumor and it was real, because at the university where I studied in Shanghai, there was a woman—a scientist from Nigeria—who spoke of this place. She came and taught for five days and nights. After that we were all changed. I got a new idea, and even though I was dying, I made sure it came to light. Then I thought I needed to find her, my teacher, and this place. Here and there I heard rumors that it had been destroyed—because there are people who will try to hasten the end of the world so they can make a profit. And this place stood in their way.

"It was the hope of the world. I heard that there were branches in a few other places. There was an idea about connecting it through small world architecture to webs of information, webs of knowledge and people, to generate new ideas and, through redundancy, ensure their survival. If it hadn't been destroyed before that hope was made real, its disappearance may not have mattered so much."

His voice fades, as he slumps to the ground. The monk gathers him up and carries him effortlessly through long corridors into a room of stone, where there is a rough bed. He wakes from his faint to see the wild creature sitting on a wooden stool by the bed, staring at him with dark, round eyes. The monk helps him up so he can sip hot yak butter tea, rich and aromatic. Then Yuan sleeps.

Over five days and nights they talk, the monk and Yuan, sometimes in this room with its narrow windows, sometimes in the high, sunny courtyard.

"This place was destroyed in an avalanche," the monk tells him, pointing to the mountain behind them, from the high spur on which the monastery perches. "The glacier melted and brought down half the mountain with it. It rained boulders. Many were killed, and the place abandoned. I live here alone, except for the odd scientific team that comes to study the glacier."

Yuan is silent. So much for the university that would save the world. But how could his dreams be so vivid, if they weren't true?

When he feels a little better, Yuan goes with the monk to a high terrace from which he has the best view of the glacier. The terrace is broken in places—holes have been torn out of it, and the room below is littered with massive stones. The still-intact portions of the floor make a zigzag safe pathway across the terrace.

The terrace is open to wind and sun, and the immensity of the mountain overwhelms him for a moment. Squinting, he looks up at it and nearly loses his balance. The monk steadies him.

Far above them, what remains of the glacier is a bowl of snow above sheer rocky walls. A great, round boulder bigger than a house stands guard at the edge of the bowl, rimmed with white.

"Don't worry," the monk says. "If that falls, it will fall right here and finish off this terrace, and what's left of the western wing. The part of the monastery where we sleep is not going to be affected—see that ridge?"

Yuan sees a ridge of rock high above and to his right, rising out of the steep incline of the mountain. A fusillade of snow, ice, and boulders falling down the slope would be deflected by it just enough to avoid the eastern edge of the monastery, which is why it is still intact.

Yuan begins to shake. The monk guides him silently across the broken floor, and they return to the room. He sinks onto the bed.

"Why do you remain in this terrible place?" he cries.

The monk brings him tea.

"Thirty-three died in the avalanche," he says, "my teacher among them. So I stay here. The others left to join another monastery."

Yuan is thinking how this does not answer his question. He is beginning to wonder about this monk and his excellent English. After a pause the monk says:

"Tell me about yourself. You said you came up with an idea."

Yuan rummages in his rucksack, which is at the foot of the bed. He draws out a handful of orange wristlets. Each has a tiny screen on it, and some are encrusted with cheap gems.

"I am a student of computer engineering," he says. "In my university in Shanghai I was working toward some interesting ideas in network communications. Then she came—Dr. Amina Ismail, my teacher—and changed everything I knew about the world.

"Most of us think there is nothing we can do about climate disruption. So we live an elaborate game of denial and pretend—as though nothing was about to happen, even though every day there are more reports of impending disaster, and more species extinctions, and more and more climate refugees. But what I learned from my teacher was that the world is an interconnected web of relationships—between human and human, and human and beast and plant, and all that's living and nonliving. I used to feel alone in the world after my parents died, even when I was with friends or with my girlfriend, but my teacher said that aloneness is an illusion created by modern urban culture. She said that even knowledge had been carved up and divided into territorial niches with walls separating them, strengthening the illusion, giving rise to overspecialized experts who can't understand each other. It is time for the walls to come down and for us to learn how to study the complexity of the world in a new way. She had been a computer scientist, but she taught herself biology and sociology so she could understand the great generalities that underlie the different systems of the world."

"She sounds like a philosopher," the monk says.

"They used to call scientists natural philosophers once," Yuan says. "But anyway, I learned from her that whether we know it or not, the world and we are interconnected. As a result, human social systems have chaotic features, rather like weather. You know Lorenz's metaphor—the butterfly effect?"

"I've heard of it," says the monk.

Yuan pauses.

"She said—Dr. Ismail—that we may not be able to prevent climate change because we've not acted in time—but perhaps we can prevent catastrophic climate change, so that in our grandchildren's future—my teacher has two grandchildren—in that future maybe things will start turning around. Maybe the human species won't go extinct.

"So one day I was walking through the streets, very upset because my girlfriend and I had just broken up, and I didn't look where I was going. I got hit by a motor scooter. The man who was driving it yelled at me. I wasn't seriously hurt—mostly bruises and a few cuts—but he didn't even stop to ask and went on his way. I dragged myself to the curb. People kept walking around me as though I was nothing but an obstacle. I thought—why should I go on with my life? Then a man came out of a shop. He bent over me, helped me to my feet. In his shop he attended to my cuts, and he gave me hot noodle soup and wouldn't let me pay. I stayed there until I was well enough to go home.

"That incident turned me away from my dark thoughts. I realized that although friends and family are crucial, sometimes the kindness of a stranger can change our lives.

"So I came up with this device that you wear around your wrist, and it can gauge your emotional level and your mood through your skin. It can also connect you, via your genie, to your computer or mobile device, specifically through software I designed."

He sighed.

"I designed it at first as a cure for loneliness. I had to invent a theory of loneliness, with measures and quantifiers. I had to invent a theory of empathy. The software enables your genie to search the Internet for people who have similar values of certain parameters . . . and it gauges security and safety as well. When you most need it, based on your emotional profile at the time, the software will link you at random to someone in your circle."

"Does it work?" said the monk.

"It's very buggy," Yuan says. "There are people working on it to make it better. The optimal network architecture isn't in place yet. My dream is that one day it can help us raise our consciousness beyond family and friend, neighborhood and religion, city and country. Throughout my journey I've been giving it away to people. In every town and village."

He taps the plain orange wristlet on his left arm.

"I'm connected right now to seven other people, seven strangers. The connection is poor, but sometimes I hear their voices or see them on my notebook screen. On the way here I stopped at a grassy meadow criss-crossed by streams, a very beautiful place. The reception must have been good because all at once I saw an old woman on my computer screen. She was standing at a kitchen counter feeling like she had nothing to give to the world. Helpless, useless, because she was old. So I told her—I didn't know what to tell her because I felt her pain—but finally I told her something clichéd, like a fortune from a fortune cookie. I said, 'Something good will happen to you today.' I don't know if that turned out to be true. I don't even know who she is, only that she's from another country and culture and religion, and I felt her pain like it was my own."

The monk listens very carefully, leaning forward. The little creature has gone to sleep on his lap.

"Perhaps you suffer from an excess of empathy," he says.

"Is that a bad thing? I suppose it must be, because of how I've ended up. As you grow up you are supposed to get stronger and harder, and wiser too. But I seem to be less and less able to bear suffering—especially the suffering of innocents. I saw a photo of a dead child in a trash heap, I don't know where. The family was part of a wave of refugees, and the locals didn't want them there. There was violence. But what could these people do? Their homeland had been flooded by the sea. They were poor.

"I once saw a picture of a dead polar bear in the Arctic. It had died of starvation. It was just skin and bone, and quite young. The seals on which it depended for food had left because the ice was gone.

"There are people who don't care about dead polar bears, or even dead children in trash heaps. They don't see how our fates are linked. Everything is connected. To know that truth, however, is to suffer. Each time there is the death of innocents, I die a little myself."

"Is that why you are so sick?" the monk says harshly. "What good will it do you to take upon yourself the misery of the world? Do you fancy yourself a Buddha, or a Jesus?"

Yuan is startled. He shakes his head.

"I've no such fancies. I'm not even religious. I'm only trying to learn what my teacher called the true knowledge that teaches us how things are linked. My sickness has nothing to do with all this. The doctors can't diagnose it—low-grade fever, systemic inflammation, weight loss—all I know is that no treatment has worked. I am dying."

The monk walks out of the room.

Yuan sits up weakly, finds the cooling yak butter tea by the bedside, and takes a sip. He is bewildered. Why is the monk so upset?

Later the monk returns.

"Since the third day you came here," he says, "you haven't had a fever. Once your strength returns, you should go back, down into the world. You have things to do there."

Yuan is incredulous.

"Even if what you say is true," he says after a while, with some bitterness, "how can I trust myself ? My vision of this place—remember? The university I dreamed of—the hope of the world. My reason to keep going. It was all false."

"Maybe it was a vision of the future," the monk says gently. "After all, your teacher was real. If she mentioned this place to you, then that must mean that others are dreaming the same dream. Go back down. Do your work. This malady, I think it is nothing but what everyone down there has. Most of the time they don't even know it."

He gestures savagely toward the world below and falls silent.

Yuan has not allowed himself to feel hope for so long that at first he doesn't recognize the feeling. But it rises within him, an effervescence. He looks at the monk's averted face, the way the animal on his shoulder nestles down.

"If I am cured, then you have saved my life. You took me in and nursed me back to health. The kindness of strangers. I am twice blessed."

The monk shakes his head. He goes out of the room to attend to their next meal.

As Yuan's condition improves, he begins to explore the ruined monastery. There are rooms and rooms in the east wing that are still intact. The meltwater from the avalanche has filled the lower chambers of the west wing. In that dark lake there are splashes of sunlight under the holes in the roof.

"We got all the bodies out," the monk says.

Then one afternoon, when he is exhausted from exploring and has taken to his bed, Yuan is woken by the monk's little pet. The animal is scrabbling frantically at Yuan's shoulder, whimpering. Sitting up, Yuan looks around for the monk, but there is no sign of him. There is a great, deep rumble that appears to come from the Earth itself.

At first Yuan thinks there is an earthquake, because the mountain is shaking. Then he realizes what it is. He rushes out of the room, conscious of the little creature's scampering feet on the stone floor behind him. He runs up the stone stairway to the broken terrace that lies directly in the glacier's path.

The monk is standing on the terrace, gazing upward, his black robes billowing behind him. The enormous boulder that was poised at the lip of the glacier has loosened and is thundering down the mountainside, gathering snow and rocks with it.

"What are you doing?" Yuan yells, grabbing the man. "Get away from here—you'll be killed!"

He grabs the man's robe near the throat, shakes him. The monk's eyes are wild. With great difficulty Yuan pulls him across the shaking, broken terrace floor, toward the stairs.

"You die here, I die here too!" he yells.

At last they are half falling down the steps, running down the broken corridors, over to the east wing. When they get to the terrace, there is a sound like an explosion, and the ground shakes. It seems to Yuan that the whole monastery is going to go down, but after what seems like a long, endless moment, the shaking stops. They look around and see that the east wing is still standing. The small creature leaps up the monk's robe and trembles on his shoulder. The monk caresses it.

There are tears in his eyes, making tracks down the lined face. Yuan sits him down on the low wooden seat. The kettle has fallen over. He brings water from the great stone jar, pours some into the kettle, gets the fire going.

When the first cup of tea has been made and drunk, when the monk has stopped shaking, he starts to speak:

"I'm not a monk. I'm only the caretaker. They took me in when I came in as sick as you, but where the world made you feel like you would die of grief, it made me burn with anger. I was a city man, living what I thought was the only way to live, the good life. Then some things happened and my life unraveled. I lost everything, everyone. I ran away up here so that I wouldn't hear the voices in my head. I was full of anger and pain. My sickness would have killed me if the monks hadn't calmed it, slowed me down. Instead thirty-three of them died when the avalanche came—my teacher among them. And I lived."

"So you were waiting for that last rock to come down," Yuan says slowly, "so you'd have your death."

The man starts to say something, but his eyes fill with tears, and he wipes them with the back of his hand. The creature on his shoulder chitters in agitation.

"Your little animal needs you to live," Yuan says. "He came and called me. That is why you are alive."

The man is holding the animal against his cheek as the tears flow.

"Life is a gift," Yuan says. "You gave me mine, I gave you yours. That means we are bound by a mutual debt, the kind you can't cancel out. Come back with me when I return."

Several days later, much recovered, Yuan made his way back the way he had come. His companion had decided to stay in the village nearest the monastery. Here, under a sky studded with stars, Yuan heard the man's story. Yuan left with him an orange wristlet, even though the satellite connection was intermittent here. When they parted, it was with the expectation of meeting again.

"In the future that you dreamed of," said his friend. "Don't be too long!"

"I'll be back before you know it," Yuan said.

After he had passed through the high mountain desert, Yuan descended into the broad alpine meadow. He lay down in the deep, rich grass and felt his weight, the gentle tug of gravity tethering him to the earth. Around him the streams sang in their watery dialect. Sleep came to him then, and dreams, but they weren't about death. His wristlet pinged, and he woke up. He must be back in satellite range. He heard, faintly, music, and the sound of a celebration. A woman's voice spoke to him, a young voice, excited. Two words.

". . . A BUTTERFLY . . ."

white curtain

PAVEL AMNUEL,
TRANSLATED BY ANATOLY BELILOVSKY

"White Curtain" first appeared in Russian in Kiev in 2007, and was published in F&SF for the first time in English in 2014, translated by Anatoly Belilovsky. It plays in an intelligent, elegant way with the existence of myriad alternate-possibility worlds, and a man who can select between them—at a cost.

Pavel Amnuel is an astrophysicist and author of speculative fiction written in Russian. He was born in 1944, in Baku (then part of the Soviet Union, now Azerbaijan), earned a doctorate in astrophysics, and for many years studied terminal events in stellar evolution—neutron stars and black holes. In 1968, in a paper written with O. Guseynov, he predicted X-ray pulsars, discovered several years later by NASA's Uhuru satellite. He also participated in the creation of the complete catalog of X-ray sources known in the 1970s. His first SF story was published in 1959 in Russia, followed by his collected works in 1984. He repatriated to Israel in 1990, working at Tel Aviv University while simultaneously serving as editor in chief of several newspapers and magazines (including Aleph and Vremya) and writing novels, essays, and short fiction. He has won multiple Soviet and Russian awards including, in 2012, the Aelita, equivalent to the Anglophone Hugo. "White Curtain" is one of a series of stories dealing with the multiverse that includes as-yet-untranslated novellas "Branches," "Facets," "What Is There Behind this Door?" and "Seeing Eye," and stories such as "Green Leaf," "Blue Alcior," and "Seagull."

Anatoly Belilovsky is a Russian American author and translator of speculative fiction. His work has appeared in the Unidentified Funny Objects anthology, Ideomancer, Nature, F&SF, Stupefying Stories, The Immersion Book of Steampunk, Daily Science Fiction, Kasma SF, Kazka, and has been podcast by Cast of Wonders, Tales of Old, and Toasted Cake. He was born in a city that went through six or seven owners in the last century, all of whom used it to do a lot more than drive to church on Sundays; he is old enough to remember tanks rolling through it on their way to Czechoslovakia in 1968. After being traded to the United States for a shipload of grain and a defector to be named later (see the Jackson-Vanik amendment), he learned English from Star Trek reruns and went on to become a pediatrician in an area of New York where English is only the fourth most commonly used language. He has neither cats nor dogs, but was admitted into the Science Fiction & Fantasy Writers of America in spite of this deficiency.

I recognized him immediately, though we had not seen each other for eleven years, having last met under very different circumstances. There was a change in him: he looked older, yet, somehow, better.

"Hello, Oleg," I said.

"Hello, Dima," he answered as if we had spent the day before as we used to, in years past, drinking and arguing about the cascading splice theory. "I knew you'd come. Sit. No, not on this chair, that's for visitors. Sit here, on the sofa."

I sat down, and the sofa squeaked in protest.

"Of course you knew," I said. "You are the prophet."

"I'm no prophet," he said sadly. "Who knows that better than you?" He spoke more slowly than ever before, enunciating each word to the last syllable.

"Yes," I said, not trying to hide the sarcasm. "Who better?"

"How did you find me?" Oleg asked.

"With difficulty," I admitted. "But I found you. You were—"

"No matter," he interrupted, "it does not matter at all, what I used to be. Why?"

"Why what?"

"Why did you come? I don't think you came just to make sure it's me. You want something from me. Everyone does. Success? Luck?"

If there was irony in his voice, I did not notice it. I did not need luck. Especially not from him.

"Irina died last year," I said, looking in his eyes. "We had been together for ten years, two months and sixteen days."

He turned away from me to look at the curtained window. What did he see in that blank screen, that white expanse where all the colors of his life were mixed together? Himself, young, walking Irina to a discotheque? Or only Irina, on that long-ago day when yet another dazzling presentation he made at that morning's seminar inspired him to believe himself irresistible to women? The day I watched, from the auditorium door, as he proposed to her with this new-found confidence, as she kissed the corner of his mouth and said that he's a little late because she loves another, and cast an eloquent glance in my direction, and he followed it, and understood. The day Irina and I left him behind, defeated and deflated, useless even to himself.

The day I saw him for the last time, until now. On the following morning Oleg Larionov, previously a promising theoretical physicist, submitted his letter of resignation. The dean, though loath to lose him, would have eventually allowed him to leave on good terms (he stamped the letter with "Approved at the end of semester"), but Oleg left without waiting for the response. He left without saying good-bye to anyone. He had been seen boarding the Forty Three bus in the direction of the train station; except for that, no one had even an inkling of where he was going.

And that was all.

"Why did she die?" Oleg asked, his gaze still on the white screen-like curtain. *Why did you not save her?* was what I heard.

I could not. I could do nothing. My strength was in theoretical work, I excelled at splice calculations, perhaps not all, but up to a very high complexity, up to twelve branches of reality, that's quite a lot, almost unheard-of for an analytical solution— but in reality there was nothing I could do. Irina fell ill unexpectedly, and died soon after. How soon? She was diagnosed in March, and in July she was gone.

"Brain tumor," I said. "Could not have been predicted. There wasn't a nexus of branching—"

"Theoretically," he interrupted, and I could not decide if his words mocked mine, or were a simple statement of fact.

"I've been looking for you for an entire year," I said. "And found you. As you can see. Do you remember Gennady Bortman?"

Oleg turned toward me at last. I had expected something in his gaze, a feeling, anything. But there was nothing. He looked at me as calmly as a doctor at a patient suffering from a cold.

"I do remember him," said Oleg. "It's a pity."

"He stayed on the branch," I said, "which you predicted for him. Was there anything he could have done?"

So much depended on Oleg's answer. I did not want to think about my life. But Ira's . . .

"Dima," said Oleg and rubbed his hands together, an old familiar gesture with which he once rubbed chalk dust off his hands after a long presentation, adding it to the floor already littered with chalk crumbs. "Dima, he could have chosen any branch in his reality. The months he had until . . . Of hundreds of decisions, you understand, each time a new branch grew, but always in the direction . . ."

"In our reality," I interrupted, "only your prophesy could come true. Your branch was stronger, more resilient."

"Yes." Oleg nodded. "My branch had higher probability, a million times higher."

"In other words," I said, and it was important for me to be clear, so very important that I searched for Oleg for a year, an excruciating year of living on memories, "in other words, for a million possibilities you choose, there may be one chance for someone else's choice?"

"Maybe not a million," he said, still rubbing his fingers, his gesture irritating me so much that I fought the urge to slap his hands. "Maybe ten million. Maybe a hundred billion. There is no way to measure, no statistics."

"You've had years to compile statistics," I said. "You set yourself up as a prophet to compile statistics, don't try to tell me you didn't! For God's sake, don't tell me you are disillusioned with pure science and became a practising prophet only to help people!"

"I do help them—"

"Some of them! Oleg, I've hung around here for a week, I listen to people waiting for their turn, some for six months, they come every day, they wait and walk away and come back, and once in a while one of your secretaries will come out and say, "He won't see you, sorry," and it's no use arguing back. And some, people you pick out from the crowd, you'll see them right away, only them, predict a happy, creative life with luck in business and personal fulfillment."

"Have I been wrong?"

"Never! You are one hundred percent reliable! This means you choose the necessary branch of the multiverse with an accuracy of at least ten sigmas!"

"Eight sigmas," he corrected. "I have compiled enough records for eight sigmas, I need another three years—"

"The hell with that," I said. "I looked for you so that—"

"It is impossible, Dima." Oleg stopped rubbing nonexistent chalk off his fingers, put his hands on his knees and looked me in the eyes. "You know it's impossible. You were the one who proved the theorem, according to which—"

"Yes." I nodded. "I proved it. If in Branch N of the multiverse the world-line of object A is a segment of length L, this line cannot be extended within its branch by grafting it to other realities."

"You proved it. And what do you want from me now, Dima? Ira does not exist in this here-and-now. You could not keep her."

"I could not—"

"You could not hold on to her," Oleg repeated. "And what is it to us that our Irisha—"

He said "our." He still lived with the feeling that she had only temporarily left him for another, and would come back.

"Our Irisha is still alive in a billion other branches of the multiverse?"

"You could," I said. "You are a genius at splicing. You can tie branches together and graft them, like Michurin grafted an apple branch to a pear tree."

"And how did it end?" Oleg chuckled. "Michurin, Burbank. Lysenko."

"Won't you even try!" I yelled.

Oleg stood up and walked toward the window, as if to put as much distance between us as possible, as if my presence made it hard for him to breathe, to think, to live.

"I tried. All the time, I tried," he said, his voice as hollow as if he spoke under water.

"You . . ." I mumbled in confusion. He could not have known about Ira.

"I can do nothing for myself, you see? Think, Dima, you are one hell of a theoretician. If I am in Branch N, then all possible splices that can change my fate—"

"Are bound by the causality of that branch, yes, I proved that in my third year of study," I said. "But you said that you tried—"

"I couldn't avoid trying. What if the theory were wrong?"

We sat in silence, each thinking about what had been said.

"How did you know about Ira?"

Oleg turned and looked at me with a silent accusation.

"Well, Dima, if you found me . . . You didn't have to look for me, I checked the university web page every day, I knew about everything that went on. I could not stand not knowing."

"That never entered my mind," I muttered. "I would have figured out where you are, long ago."

"I doubt it," he said. "I took measures. When Ira died, the Alumni Association ran an obituary the same day. I tried, right there and then. God, Dima, I leaped from branch to branch like a neurotic monkey, sliced more realities than I had ever allowed myself before—and, after that, never again.

"I didn't—"

"Of course you didn't feel a thing!"

"Sorry," I said. "I am not myself today. Stupid; I should have known, I could not feel a break, my reality was contiguous with my past."

"You had hundreds of realities, and in all of them Ira died, and I was always late, I made it to the funeral in one hundred and seventy-six branches."

"You went to a hundred seventy-six funerals?" I said, horrified.

He didn't say anything, and I understood why he looked so old to me. I would have gone mad in his place.

"Then," I said, "there was nothing—"

"You are the one who proved that theorem," said Oleg roughly, "and I never found experimental evidence to the contrary."

"So that's how it is," I muttered. Something hit me all at once, a year's worth of fatigue, perhaps, and maybe now I made decisions one after another, each taking me to a different branch, each branch beginning with: "So that's how it is" parroted over and over.

"Well, that is all," said Oleg and stood up abruptly. He reached to shake my hand; its fingers were, for some strange reason, dusted with chalk. "Enough already with the histrionics! You lived by hope alone for a year, looking for me, and I lost hope a year ago and had the time I needed to come to terms with it. I can do nothing for you, Dima. Not-a-thing."

I stood up.

"Leaving?" Oleg asked, his voice flat, without giving me his hand. "You looked for me for such a long time. We could have coffee, dinner, you could tell me about the university. Did Kulikov defend his dissertation?"

"You've been on their web site," I shrugged.

"No, not since—"

"You," I said, from the doorway, "you splice realities to make lives better."

"Of course," he nodded.

"And those you turn away?"

"So that's the question." He came closer and with a long-familiar gesture put both his hands on my shoulders. His palms were unpleasantly heavy, and I sagged like Atlas under the weight of the sky.

"You think I turn away those whose fate I cannot channel in a better direction," he said, looking straight into my eyes. He did not even blink, and I tried not to blink as well. "You are mistaken, Dima. I have rules. Well, not quite rules; I want nothing to do with unpleasant people, or with people whose happiness depends on the suffering of others. I choose, yes. Do you think I have no right?"

"Oh, come on," I muttered. "It's just that—"

"You thought of what I could have done for you?"

"No," I chuckled. "You would not do this, and it's not what I would want."

"You do want," he said roughly. "Don't lie, your eyes betray you. You want to be happy, everyone does. You want her specter to stop haunting you. You want to forget—"

"No!"

"Fine: to remember, just about enough to light a candle, that is sufficient. And live a happy life. You came to have your life spliced with a branch where you are happy and prosperous—"

"No," I said, but blinked and lowered my eyes. I wanted that. So what? This he could do, I knew. I also knew he would not lift a finger to help me.

"Yes," he sighed and pressed even harder (or did I imagine it?) on my shoulders. "You know, Dima, when you came in, and we recognized each other, the first thing I did was run through a list of splices, in my head, that I could have made. For you. Even if you had not asked me, I decided to do it. Because to live without Ira . . . I know how it was for me, but I cannot do anything for myself, because of your damned theorem. But I could help you, yes, or else what purpose do I have?"

He took his hands from my shoulders at last, and I stood straight, feeling suddenly light. Was it the lifting of that weight that made me feel relieved, or thinking, for a moment: Oleg can, Oleg will?

"There isn't a single line in all of the multiverse," he said, "where all is well for you. Not one. What can I do with that?"

"Nonsense!" I exclaimed and stepped back from him. "You know that's nonsense, why do you even . . . we discussed this problem since—"

"Yes, we discussed," he interrupted.

"The multiverse is infinite!" I exclaimed. "There is an infinite number of branches of reality, and all without exception can be embodied as our reality, any version of any event, phenomenon, process, and that means—"

"That means," said Oleg regretfully, "that you were right, not I. You proved there's only a finite number of branches because the wave function for each event has a limited number of solutions."

"Yes, but since then—"

"But I," Oleg raised his voice, "I maintained that there is an infinity of branches, and in the multiverse's infinity there must exist all possibilities of human fate—happy and unhappy. I was sure! But now I know I was wrong. The branching of destinies is limited, Dima. Forgive me. I wanted. Very much. At least in Ira's memory. It's no use. There is a huge number of versions of your life, but none where you are happy."

"Well, then," I said, feeling an emptiness in my soul which I now knew could never be filled, "we've resolved an old scientific debate. For once you have admitted that I'm right."

"The branching is finite," he said. "Aren't you happy to be right?"

Did he intentionally torment me?

"Farewell," I said and closed the door quietly behind me. Three of the prophet's secretaries sat at their computers, not even lifting their eyes to me.

"The office hours are over for today," a ceiling speaker screeched, and dozens of people crowded into the waiting room sighed as one with disappointment.

It was windy outside and a drizzle soaked my hair, the rented car was parked two blocks away, and by the time I sat behind the wheel my shirt was plastered to my body, and thoughts had deserted me entirely, all thoughts but one: who needs a life like this?

I drove slowly in the right lane without knowing where I was, in what part of the city, until I saw a "Dead End" sign. I turned toward the curb and killed the engine.

We had debated once, with Oleg. Not just us; it was a popular question, fifteen years ago, in theoretic Everettics: is there a limited number of events in the world of continuous branchings? I said, yes, it is limited, and my arguments . . . God, I had no idea I could win the debate and lose my own life!

Rain. It will always be raining, now.

The phone rang, its ringtone a Hungarian dance by Brahms. I fumbled in my bag and brought the phone to my ear.

"Dima!"

I did not recognize the voice at first: it was Mikhail Natanovich, the doctor who treated, but could not save, Irina. "Dima, I've been calling you all day!"

"My phone was off," I said.

"No matter! I wanted to tell you: today's test results are much better than before. Much better! This new drug, it's really . . . Dima, I think it will all turn out for the best, now. Do you hear me, Dima?"

Will turn out for the best. New drug. Ira.

"How is she?" I asked, squeezing the phone as if I wanted to break it.

"Slept well all night."

"Ira?"

"Irina Yakovlevna had breakfast this morning, for the first time . . ."

"Yes," I said. "Thank you for calling. I will be at the hospital no later than nine this evening, as soon as I can get there."

I dropped the phone on the seat next to me.

Oleg succeeded? How? He said himself—not quite an hour ago—that there's a limited number of splices, that if she died, then . . .

Was he mistaken? Or did he accomplish that which he himself considered impossible? Or found an infinity of branches and among them, one in which every-thing, simply everything, works out?

I lifted the receiver and dialed his number. It was my duty to thank him, at least.

"I need to speak with Oleg Nikolaevich," I said when one of his secretaries answered.

"Unfortunately—"

"This is Mantsev, his old friend and colleague, I was just with him and want to—"

"Unfortunately," repeated a voice as gray as the rain beyond my window, "it's im-possible. Oleg Nikolaevich passed away immediately after you left."

How could that happen? He had appeared healthy and acted perfectly well when . . .

"I do not understand," I muttered. "How is this—"

"The police are here now," the secretary said. "I think they might want to speak with you, you were his last visitor of the day. Ten minutes after you left . . ."

"Out with it!"

"Oleg Nikolaevich threw himself out the window. And we are—"

"On the sixth floor," I finished for him.

This is how it ends, I thought. He pushed the white curtain out of the way and stepped through.

Rain ended. I drove to the airport as fast as I could go. At nine I had to be at the hospital. With Irina. My Irina.

I was right after all: there is a limit to the number of splices. Oleg proved it, conclusively this time. He said he could do nothing with his fate. Of course. Except for one thing: he could interrupt it. Only then could my fate where Ira died be spliced with the branch where she survived.

You can extend one branch by cutting off another. The law of conservation. Oleg knew.

Why did he do this? He had every reason to hate me. What would I have done in his place, knowing there was only one possibility? What am I? A theoretician. Oleg worked in practical, experimental everettics, he did what I could only guess at. Or calculate.

I sped up, no longer watching the speedometer.

I knew that Irina and I—that all will be well.

How can I live, knowing that?

slipping

LAUREN BEUKES

A miraculous second chance at life may be worth taking no matter how great the cost. Or maybe not.

Lauren Beukes *is a novelist, comics writer, script writer, and occasional journalist. Her time-traveling serial killer novel,* The Shining Girls, *won the August Derleth Award for best horror awarded by the British Fantasy Society, best mystery novel in the Strand Critics Choice Award, and the prestigious literary award, the University of Johannesburg Prize. She's also the author of* Broken Monsters, *about broken dreams and broken people in Detroit,* Zoo City, *a black magic noir set in Johannesburg that won the Arthur C. Clarke Award, and* Moxyland, *about a corporate apartheid state. She's written kids' animated TV shows for Disney, made a documentary on the biggest female-impersonation beauty pageant in Cape Town, and worked as a journalist for ten years, where she learned everything she knows about storytelling.*

1. HIGH LIFE

The heat presses against the cab trying to find a way in past the sealed windows and the rattling air conditioner. Narrow apartment blocks swoop past on either side of the dual carriageway, occasionally broken up by a warehouse megastore. It could be Cape Town, Pearl thinks. It could be anywhere. Twenty three hours travel so far. She has never been on a plane before.

"So what's the best part about Karachi?" Tomislav says, trying to break the oppressive silence in the back—the three of them dazed by the journey, the girl, her promoter and the surgeon, who has not looked up from his phone since they got in the car because he is trying to get a meeting.

The driver thinks about it, tugging at the little hairs of his moustache. "One thing is that this is a really good road. Sharah e Faisal. There's hardly ever a traffic jam and if it rains, the road never drowns."

"Excellent," Tomislav leans back, defeated. He gives Pearl an encouraging smile, but she is not encouraged. She watched the World Cup and the Olympics on TV, she knows how it is supposed to be. She stares out the window, refusing to blink in case the tears come.

The road narrows into the city and the traffic thickens, hooting trucks and bakkies and rickshaws covered in reflecting stickers like disco balls, twinkling in the sun. They pass through the old city, with its big crumbling buildings from long ago, and into the warren of Saddar's slums with concrete lean-tos muscling in on each other. *Kachi abaadi*, the driver tells them, and Pearl sounds it out under her breath. At least the shacks are not tin and that's one difference.

Tomislav points out the loops of graffiti in another alphabet and taps her plastic knee. "Gang signs. Just like the Cape Flats."

"Oh they're gangsters all right," the driver says. "Same people run the country."

"You have gangsters in your government?" Pearl is shocked.

The cab driver clucks and meets her eyes in the rearview mirror. "You one of the racers?"

"What clued you in?" Dr. Arturo says, without looking up. It's the first thing he's said all day. His thumbs tap over the screen of his phone, blunt instruments. Pearl rubs her legs self-consciously, where the tendons are visible under the joint of her knee, running into the neurocircuitry. It's a showcase, Dr. Arturo told her when she asked him why it couldn't look like skin. Somedays she thinks it's beautiful. Mostly, she hates seeing the inside-out of herself.

"Why do you think you're in Pakistan?" the driver laughs, "You think anyone else would let this happen in *their* country?" He rubs his thumb and fingers together and flings it to the wind.

2. PACKED WITH GOODNESS

Pre-race. A huge + Games banner hangs above the entrance of the Karachi Parsi Institute or KPI. It's an old colonial building that has been extended to accommodate them, the track built over the old cricket ground and into the slums. The school has been turned into the athlete's village, classrooms converted to individual medical cells to cater to their unique needs. Pearl's for example, has hermetic bio-units and sterile surfaces. The window has been fused shut to prevent the polluted air leaking in.

In the room next door, they've installed extra generators for Charlotte Grange after she plugged in her exo-suit and tripped the power on the whole building. Pearl can hear her grunting through the walls. She doesn't know what Siska Rachman has.

She sits on the end of her bed, paging through the official programme while Tomislav paces the room end-to-end, hunched over his phone, his hand resting on his nose. "*Ajda!* Come on!" her promoter says into the phone, in that Slavic way, which makes the first part of the sentence top-heavy. Like Tomislav himself, still carrying his weight lifter bulk all squeezed up into his chest and neck. He doesn't compete anymore, but the steroids keep him in shape. The neon lights and the white sheen off the walls makes his eyes look bluer, his skin paler. "Peach" she was taught in school, as if "peach" and "brown" were magically less divisive than "black" and "white" and words could fix everything. But Tomislav's skin is not the warm orange of a summer fruit, it's like the milky tea she drinks at home.

Tomislav has thick black hair up his arms. She asked him about it when they first met at the Beloved One's house on the hill. Fourteen and too young and too angry about everything that happened to mind her elders, even though her mother gasped at her rudeness and smacked her head.

Tomislav laughed. *Testosterone, kitten.* He tapped the slight fuzz over her lip. *You've got it too, that's what makes you so strong.*

He's made her laser all her unsightly hair since. Sports is image. Even this one.

He sees her looking and speaks louder. "You want to get a meeting, Arturo, we gotta have something to show." He jabs at the phone dramatically to end the call. "That guy! What does he think I'm doing all day? You all right, kitten?" He comes over to take her by the shoulders, give them a little rub. "You feeling good?"

"Fine." More than fine, with the crowds' voices a low vibration through the concrete and the starting line tugging at her insides, just through that door, across the quad, down the ramp. She has seen people climbing up onto the roofs around the track with picnic blankets.

"That's my girl." He snatches the programme out of her hands. "Why are you even looking at this? You know every move these girls have."

He means Siska Rachman. That's all anyone wants to talk about. Pearl is sick of it, all the interviews for channels she's never heard of. No-one told her how much of this would be *talking* about racing.

"Ready when you are," Dr. Arturo says into her head, through the audio implant in her cochlear. Back online as if he's never been gone, checking the diagnostics. "Watch your adrenaline, Pearl. You need to be calm for the install." He used to narrate the chemical processes, the shifting balances of hormones, the nano enhancing oxygen uptake, the shift of robotic joints, the dopamine blast, but it felt too much like being in school; words being crammed into her head and all worthless anyway. You don't have to name something to understand it. She knows how it feels when she hits her stride and the world opens up beneath her feet.

"He's ready," she repeats to Tomislav.

"All right, let's get this show pumping."

Pearl obediently hitches up her vest with the Russian energy drink logo—one of Tomislav's sponsors, although that's only spare change. She has met the men who have paid for her to be here, in the glass house on the hill, wearing gaudy golf shirts and shoes and shiny watches. She never saw the men swing a club and she doesn't know their names, but they all wanted to shake her hand and take a photograph with her.

She feels along the rigid seam that runs in a J-hook down the side of her stomach, parallel with her hysterectomy scar, and tears open the velcroskin.

"Let me," Tomislav says, kneeling between her legs. She holds her flesh open while he reaches one hand up inside her abdomen. It doesn't hurt, not anymore. The velcro releases a local anaesthetic when it opens, but she can feel an uncomfortable tugging inside, like cramps.

Tomislav twists off the valves on either side and gently unplugs her stomach and eases it out of her. He sets it in a sterile biobox and connects it to a blood flow. By the time he turns back, she is already spooling up the accordion twist of artificial intestine, like a party magician pulling ribbons from his palm. It smells of the lab-mod bacteria and the faintest whiff of faeces. She hands it to Tomislav and he wrinkles his nose.

"Just goes to show," he says, folding up the slosh of crinkled plastic tubing and packing it away. "You can take the meat out of the human, but they're still full of shit!"

Pearl smiles dutifully, even though he has been making the same joke for the last three weeks—ever since they installed the new system.

"Nearly there," he holds up the hotbed factory and she nods and looks away because it makes her queasy to watch. It's a sleek bioplug, slim as a communion wafer and packed with goodness, Dr. Arturo says, like fortified breakfast cereals. Hormones and nanotech instead of vitamins and iron.

Tomislav pushes his hand inside her again, feeling blindly for the connector node in what's left of her real intestinal tract, an inch and a half of the body's most absorbent tissue for better chemical uptake.

"Whoops! Got your kidney! Joking. It's in."

"Good to go," Dr. Arturo confirms.

"Then let's go," Pearl says, standing up on her blades.

3. FORCES GREATER THAN YOU

You would have to be some kind of idiot. She told her mother it was a bet among the kids, but it wasn't. It was her, only her, trying to race the train.
The train won.

4. WHY YOU HAVE ME

The springkaan drone flits in front of Pearl's face, the lens zooming in on her lips to catch the words she's saying under her breath and transmit them onto the big screen. *"Ndincede nkosi undiphe amandla."*

She bends down to grab on to the curved tips of her legs, to stretch, yes, but also to hide her mouth. It's supposed to be private, she thinks. But that's an idea that belonged to another girl before Tomislav's deals and Dr. Arturo's voice in her head running through diagnostics, before the Beloved One, before the train, before all this.

"It's because you're so taciturn, kitten," Tomislav tries to comfort her. "You give the people crumbs and they're hungry for more. If you just talked more." He is fidgeting with his tie while Brian Corwood, the presenter moves down the starter's carpet with his microphone, talking to Oluchi Eze who is showing off her tail for the cameras. She doesn't know how to talk more. She's run out of words and the ones Dr. Arturo wants her to say are like chewing on raw potatoes. She has to sound out the syllables.

Pearl swipes her tongue over her teeth to get rid of the feeling like someone has rigged a circuit behind her incisors. It's the new drugs in the hotbed, Tomislav says. She has to get used to it, like the drones, which dart up to her unexpectedly. They're

freakish—cameras hardwired into grasshoppers, with enough brain stem left to respond to commands. Insects are cheap energy.

Somewhere in a control room, Dr. Arturo notes her twitch back from the *springkaan* and soothes in her head. "What do you think, Pearl? More sophisticated that
some athletes we know." She glances over at Charlotte Grange, who is also waiting
for her interview. The big blonde quakes and jitters, clenching her jaw, her exo-suit
groaning in anticipation. The neural dampeners barely hold her back.

The crowd roars their impatience, thousands of people behind a curve of reinforced safety glass in the stands raised high above the action. The rooftops are
packed and there are children climbing the scaffolding around the old church like
monkeys.

The people in suits, the ones Dr. Arturo and Tomislav want to meet, watch from
air-conditioned hotel rooms five kilometres away. Medical and pharmaceutical companies looking for new innovations in a place where anything goes; any drugs, any
prosthetics, robotics, nano. That's what people come for. They tune in by the millions on the proprietary channel. The drama. Like watching Formula 1 for the car
crashes.

"All these people, kitten," Tomislav says, "They don't want you to win. They're
just waiting for you to explode. But you know why you're here."

"To run."

"That's my girl."

"Slow breaths," Dr. Arturo says, "You're overstimulated."

The springkaan drone responds to some invisible hand in a control room and
swirls around her, getting every angle. Brian Corwood, the presenter, makes his way
over to her, microphone extended like a handshake and springkaans buzzing behind
his shoulder. She holds herself very straight. She knows her mama and the Beloved
One are watching back home. She wants to do Gugulethu proud.

"*Ndincede nkosi,*" she mouths the words and sees them come up on the big screens
above the track in closed captions below her face. They'll be working to translate
them already. Not so hard to figure out that she's speaking Xhosa.

"Pearl Nit-seeko," the presenter says. "Cape Town's miracle girl. Crippled when
she was fourteen years old and now, here she is, two years later, at the +Games. Dream
come true!"

Pearl has told the story so many times that she can't remember which parts are
made-up and glossed over. She told a journalist once that she saw her father killed
on TV during the illegal mine strikes in Polokwane and how she covered her ears so
she didn't have to hear the popcorn pa-pa-pa-pa-pa of the gunshots as people fell in
the dust. But now she has to stick to it. Grand tragedy is a better story than the reality of a useless middle-aged drunk who lived with a shebeen owner's daughter in
Nyanga so that he didn't have to pay off the bar tab. When Pearl started to get famous, her father made a stink in the local gossip rags until Tomislav paid him to go
away. You can buy your own truth.

"Can you tell us about your tech, Pearl?" Brian Corwood says, as if this is a show
about movie stars and glittery dresses.

She responds in auto-pilot. The removable organs, the bath of nano in her blood
that improves oxygen uptake. Neural connectivity blows open the receptors to the

hormones and drugs dispatched by the hotbed factory. Tomislav has coached her in the newsworthy technical specs, the leaks that make investors' ears prick up.

"I can't show you," she apologizes, coyly raising her vest to let the cameras zoom in on the seam of scar tissue. "It's not a sterile environment."

"So it's hollow in there?" Corwood pretends to knock on her stomach.

"Reinforced surgical-quality graphene mesh." She lightly drums her fingers over her skin, like in rehearsal. It looks spontaneous and shows off her six pack.

She hears Arturo's voice in her head. "Put the vest down now," Arturo instructs. She covers herself up. The star doesn't want to let the viewers see too much. Like with sex. Or so she's been told. She will never have children.

"Is that your secret weapon?" Corwood says, teasing, because no-one ever reveals the exact specs, not until they have a buyer.

"No," she says, "But I do have one."

"What is it then?" Corwood says, gamely.

"God," she says and stares defiantly at the insect cameras zooming in for a close-up.

5. THINGS YOU CAN'T HIDE

Her stumps are wrapped in fresh bandages, but the wounds still smell. Like something caught in the drain. Her mother wants to douse the bandages in perfume.

"I don't want to! Leave me alone!" Pearl swats the teardrop bottle from her mother's hands and it clatters onto the floor. Her mother tries to grab her. The girl falls off the bed with a shriek. She crawls away on her elbows, sobbing and yowling. Her Uncle Tshepelo hauls her up by her armpits, like she is a sack of sorghum flour, and set her down at the kitchen table.

"Enough, Pearl," he says, her handsome youngest uncle. When she was a little girl she told her mother she was going to marry him.

"I hate you," she screams and tries to kick at him with her stumps but he ducks away and goes over to the kettle while her mother stands in the doorway and covers her face.

Pearl has not been back to school since it happened. She turns to face the wall when her friends come to visit and refuses to talk with them. During the day, she watches soap operas and infomercials and lies in her mother's bed and stares at the sky and listens to the noise of the day; the cycles of traffic and school kids and dogs barking and the call to prayer buzzing through the mosque's decrepit speakers and the traffic again and men drunk and fighting at the shebeen. Maybe one of them is her father who has not been to see her since the accident.

Tshepelo makes sweet milky tea, for her and her mother, and sits and talks: nonsense, really, about his day in the factory, cooking up batches of paté which is fancy flavoured butter for rich people, and how she should see the stupid blue plastic cap he has to wear to cover his hair in case of contamination. He talks and talks until she calms down.

Finally, she agrees that she will go to church, a special service in Khayelitsha Site B. She puts on her woolen dress, grey as the Cape Town winter sky, and green stockings, which dangle horribly at the joint where her legs should be.

The rain polka-dots her clothes and soaks into her mother's hat, making it flop as she quick-steps after Tshepelo carrying Pearl in his arms like an injured dog. She hates the way people avert their eyes.

The church is nothing, a tent in a parking lot, although the people sing like they are in a fancy cathedral in England like on TV. Pearl sits stiffly on the end of the pew between her uncle and her mother, glaring at the little kids who dart around to come and stare. "Vaya," she hisses at them. "What are you looking at? Go."

Halfway through the service, two of the ministers bring out the brand new wheelchair like it is a prize on a gameshow, tied with a big purple ribbon. They carry it down the stairs on their shoulders and set it down in front of her. She looks down and mumbles something. Nkosi.

They tuck their fingers into her armpits, these strangers' hands on her, and lift her into it. The moment they set her down, she feels trapped. She moans and shakes her head.

"She's so grateful," her mother says and presses her into the chair with one hand on her shoulder. Hallelujah, everyone says. Hallelujah. The choir breaks into song and Pearl wishes that God had let her die.

6. HEAT

Pearl's brain is micro-seconds behind her body. The bang of the starting gun registers as a sound after she is already running.

She is aware of the other runners as warm, straining shapes in the periphery. Tomislav has made her study the way they run. Charlotte Grange, grunting and loping, using the exo-suit arms to dig into the ground, like an ape, Anna Murad with her robotics wet-wired into her nerves, Oluchi Eze with her sculpted tail and her delicate bones, like a dinosaur bird. And in lane five, furthest away from her, Siska Rachman with her face perfectly calm and empty and her eyes locked on the finish line, two kilometres away. A dead girl remote-controlled by a quadraplegic in a hospital bed. That is the problem with the famous Siska Rachman. She wins a lot, but there is network lag-time.

You have to inhabit your body. You need to be in it. Not only because the rules say, because otherwise you can't feel it. The strike of your foot against the ground, the rush of air on your skin, the sweat running down your sides. No amount of biofeedback wil make the difference.

"Pace yourself," Arturo says in her head. "I'll give you a glucose boost when you hit eight hundred metres."

Pearl tunes in to the rhythmic huff of her breath and she stretches out her legs longer with each stride and she is aware of everything, the texture of the track, and the expanse of the sky, and the smell of sweat and dust and oil. It blooms in her chest—a fierce warmth, a golden glow within, and she feels the rush of His love and she knows that God is with her.

She crosses third, neck in neck with Siska Rachman and miliseconds behind Charlotte Grange, who throws herself across the finish line, with a wet ripping sound. The exo-suit goes down in a tumble of girl and metal, forcing Rachman to side-step.

"A brute." Arturo whispers in her ear. "Not like you, Pearl."

7. BELOVED

The car comes to fetch them, Pearl and her mother and her uncle. A shiny black BMW with hubcaps that turn the light into spears. People came out of their houses to see.

She is wearing her black lace dress, but it's forty degrees out and the sweat runs down the back of her neck and makes her collar itch.

"Don't scratch," her mother said, holding her hands.

The car cuts through the location between the tin shacks and the government housing and all the staring eyes, out onto the highway, into the winelands and past the university and the rich people's townhouses which all look alike, past the golf course where little carts dart between the sprinklers, and the hills with vineyards and flags to draw the tourists, and down a side road and through a big black gate which swings open onto a driveway lined with spiky cycads.

They climb out, stunned by the heat and other things besides—like the size of the house, the wood and glass floating on top of the hill. Her uncle fights to open the wheelchair Khayelitsha Site B bought her, until the driver comes round and says, "Let me help you with that, sir." He shoves down hard on the seat and it clicks into place.

He brings them into a cool entrance hall with wooden floors and metal sculptures of cheetahs guarding the staircase. A woman in a red and white dress and a wrap around her head, smiles and ushers them into the lounge where three men are waiting; a grandfather with two white men flanking him like the stone cats by the staircase. One old, one hairy.

"The Beloved One," her mother says, averting her eyes. Her uncle bows his head and raises his hands in deference.

Their fear makes Pearl angry.

The grandfather waves at them to come, come, impatiently. The trousers of his dark blue suit have pleats folded as sharp as paper and his shoes are black like coal.

"So this is Pearl Nitseko," the Beloved One says, testing the weight of her name. "I've heard about you."

The old white man stares at her. The lawyer, she will find out later, who makes her and her mother sign papers and more papers and papers. The one with thick shoulders fidgets with his cuffs, pulling them down over his hairy wrists, but he is watching her most intently of all.

"What?" she demands. "What have you heard?" Her mother gasps and smacks her head.

The Beloved One smiles, gently. "That you have fire in you."

8. FEARFUL TAUTOLOGIES

Tomislav hustles Pearl past the moslem protesters outside the stadium. The sects have united in moral outrage, chanting, "Un-natural! Un-godly! Un-holy!" They chant the words in English rather than Urdu for the benefit of the drones.

"Come on!" Tomislav shoulders past the protesters, steering her towards a shuttle car that will take them to dinner. "Don't these cranks have bigger things to worry about? Their thug government? Their starving children?" Pearl leaps into the shuttle and he launches himself in after. "Extremism I can handle." He slams the door. "But tautology? That's unforgivable."

Pearl zips up the hood of her tracksuit.

The Pakistani crowd surges to the shuttle, bashing its windows with the flats of their hands. "Monster!" a woman shouts in English. "God hates you."

"What's tautology?"

"Unnecessary repetition."

"Isn't that what fear always is?"

"I forget that you're fast *and* clever. Yeah. Screw them," Tomislav says. The shuttle rolls and he claps his hands together. "You did good out there."

"Did you get a meeting?"

"We got a meeting, kitten. I know you think your big competition is Siska, but it's Charlotte. She just keeps going and going."

"She hurt herself."

"Ripped a tendon, the news says, but she's still going to race tomorrow."

Dr. Arturo chimes in, always listening. "They have back-up meat in the lab, they can grow a tendon. But it's not a good long term strategy. This is a war, not a battle."

"I thought we weren't allowed to fight," Pearl says.

"You talking to the doc? Tell him to save his chatter for the investors."

"Tomislav says—" she starts.

"I heard him," Dr. Arturo says.

Pearl looks back at the protestors. One of the hand-written banners stays with her. "I am fearfully and wonderfully made" it reads.

9. SHE IS RISEN

Pearl watches the buses arrive from her bed upstairs in the church. A guest room adapted for the purposes, with a nurse sitting outside and machines that hiss and bleep. The drugs make her woozy. She has impressions of things, but not memories. The whoop of the ambulance siren and the feeling of being important. Visitors. Men in golf shorts and an army man with fat cheeks. Gold watches and stars on the uniform, to match the gold star on the tower she can see from her window and the fat tapered columns like bullets at the entrance.

"Are you ready?" Dr. Arturo says. He has come from Venezuela especially for her. He has gentle hands and kind eyes, she thinks, even though he is the one who cut everything out of her. Excess baggage, he says. It hurts where it was taken out, her female organs and her stomach and her guts.

He tells her they have been looking for someone like her for a long time, him and Tomislav. They had given up on finding her. And now! Now look where they are. She is very lucky. She knows this because everyone keeps telling her.

Dr. Arturo takes her to the elevator where Tomislav is waiting. The surgeon is very modest. He doesn't like to be seen on camera. "Don't worry, I'll be with you," he says and taps her jaw just below her ear.

"It's all about you, kitten," Tomislav soothes, wheeling her out into a huge hallway

full of echoes under a painted sky with angels and the Beloved One, in floating purple robes, smiling down on the people flowing through the doors, the women dressed in red and white and the men in blue blazers and white shirts. This time she doesn't mind them looking.

They make way for the wheelchair, through the double doors, past the ushers, into a huge room with a ceiling crinkled and glossy as a sea shell and silver balconies and red carpets. She feels like a film star and the red blanket over her knees is like her party dress.

From somewhere deep in the church, women raise their voices in ululation and all the hair on Pearl's body pricks up as if she is a cat. Tomislav turns the wheelchair around and parks it beside a huge gold throne with carved leaves and flowers and a halo of spikes around the head. He pats her shoulder and leaves her there, facing the crowd, thousands of them in the auditorium, all staring at her. "Smile, Pearl," Dr. Arturo says, his voice soft inside her head, and she tries, she really does.

A group of women walk out onto the stage, swaying with wooden bowls on their hips, their hands dipping into the bowls like swans pecking at the water and throwing rose petals before them. The crowd picks up the ululating and it reverberates through the church. Halalala.

The Beloved One steps out and onto the stage and Pearl has to cover her ears at the noise that greets him. A hail of voices. Women are weeping in the aisles. Men too, crying in happiness to see him.

The Beloved One holds out his hands to still them. "Quiet, please, brothers and sisters of the Pentecostal," he says. "Peace be with you."

"And also with you," the crowd roars back, the sound distorted, frayed. He places his hands on the back of the wheelchair.

"Today, we come together to witness a miracle. My daughter, will you stand up and walk?"

And Pearl does.

10. CALL TO PRAYER

The restaurant is fancy with a buffet of Pakistani food, korma and tikka and kabobs and silver trays of sticky sweet pastries. The athletes have to pose for photographs and do more interviews with Bryan Corwood and other people. The girl with purple streaks in her hair and the metal ring in her lip asks her, "Aren't you afraid you're gonna die out there?" before Tomislav intervenes.

"Come on! What kind of question is that?" he says. "Can't you be normal?"

But the athletes don't really eat and there is a bus that takes them home early so they can be fresh, while the promoters peel away, one by one, in fancy black cars that take them away to other parts of the city, looking tense. "Don't you worry, kitten" Tomislav smiles, all teeth, and pats her hand.

Back in her room, Pearl finds a prayer mat that might be aligned toward Mecca. She phones down to reception to ask. She prostrates herself on the square of carpet, east, west, to see if it is any different, if her God will be annoyed.

She goes online to check the news and the betting pools. Her odds have improved.

There is a lot of speculation about Grange's injury and whether Rachman will be disqualified. There are photographs of Oluchi Eze posing naked for a men's magazine, her tail wrapped over her parts.

Pearl clicks away and watches herself in the replay, her strikes, her posture, the joy in her face. She expects Dr. Arturo to comment, but the cochlear implant only hisses with faint static.

"Mama? Did you see the race?" she says. The video connection to Gugulethu stalls and jitters. Her mother has the camera on the phone pointed down too low so she can only see her eyes and the top of her head.

"They screened it at the church," her mother says. "Everyone was very excited."

"You should have heard them shouting for you, Pearl," her uncle says, leaning over her mother's shoulder, tugging the camera down so they are in the frame.

Her mother frowns. "I don't know if you should wear that vest, it's not really your color."

"It's my sponsor, Mama."

"We're praying for you to do well. Everyone is praying for you."

11. DESERT

She has a dream that she and Tomislav and Jesus are standing on the balcony of the Karachi Parsi Institute looking over the slums. The fine golden sand rises up like water between the concrete shacks, pouring in the windows, swallowing up the roofs, driven by the wind.

"Did you notice that there are only one set of footsteps, Pearl?" Jesus says. The sand rises, swallowing the houses, rushing to fill the gaps, nature taking over. "Do you know why that is?"

"Is it because you took her fucking legs, Lord?" Tomislav says.

Pearl can't see any footsteps in the desert. The sand shifts too quickly.

12. RARE FLOWERS

Wide awake. Half past midnight. She lies in bed and stares at the ceiling. Arturo was supposed to boost her dopamine and melatonin, but he's busy. The meeting went well then. The message on her phone from Tomislav confirms it. *Good news!!!! Tell you in the morning. Sleep tight kitten, you need it.*

She turns the thought around in her head and tries to figure out how she feels. Happy. This will mean that she can buy her mother a house and pay for her cousins to go to private school and set up the Pearl Nitseko Sports Academy For Girls in Gugulethu. She won't ever have to race again. Unless she wants to.

The idea of the money sits on her chest.

She swings her stumps over the bed and straps on her blades. She needs to go out, get some air.

She clips down the corridors of the school building. There is a party on the old cricketing field outside with beer tents and the buzz of people who do not have to run tomorrow, exercising their nerves. She veers away from them, back towards the worn-out colonial building of the IPC, hoping to get onto the race track. Run it out.

The track is fenced off and locked, but the security guard is dazed by his phone, caught up in another world of sliding around colorful blocks. She clings to the shadows of the archway, right past him and deeper into the building, following wherever the doors lead her.

She comes out into a hall around a pit of sunken tiles. An old swimming pool. Siska Rachman is sitting on the edge, waving her feet in the ghost of water, her face perfectly blank with her hair a dark nest around it. Pearl lowers herself down beside her. She can't resist. She flicks Rachman's forehead. "*Heita*. Anyone in there?"

The body blinks and suddenly the eyes are alive and furious. She catches Pearl's wrist. "Of course, I am," she snaps.

"Sorry, I didn't think—"

Siska has already lost interest. She drops her grip and brushes her hair away from her face. "So, you can't sleep either? Wonder why."

"Too nervous," Pearl says. She tries for teasing, like Tomislav would. "I have tough competition."

"Maybe not," Siska scowls. "They're going to fucking disqualify me."

Pearl nods. She doesn't want to apologize again. She feels shy around Siska, the older girl with her bushy eyebrows and her sharp nose. The six years between them feels like an un-crossable gap.

"Do they think Charlotte is *present?*" Siska bursts out. "Charlotte is a big dumb animal. How is *she* more human than me?"

"You're two people," Pearl tries to explain.

"*Before*. You were half a person before. Does that count against you?"

"No."

"Do you know what this used to be?" Siska pats the blue tiles.

"A swimming pool?"

"They couldn't maintain the upkeep. These things are expensive to run." Siska glances at Pearl to make sure she understands. In the light through the glass atrium, every lash stands out in stark relief against the gleam of her eyes, like undersea creatures. "They drained all the water out, but there was this kid who was . . . damaged in the brain and the only thing he could do was grow orchids, so that's what he did. He turned it into a garden and sold them out of here for years, until he got old and now it's gone."

"How do you know this?"

"The guard told me. We smoked cigarettes together. He wanted me to give him a blowjob."

"Oh." Pearl recoils.

"Hey, are you wearing lenses?"

She knows what she means. The broadcast contacts. "No. I wouldn't."

"They're going to use you and use you up, Pearl Nit-seeko. Then you'll be begging to give some lard-ass guard a blowjob, for spare change."

"It's Ni-tse-koh."

"Doesn't matter. You say tomato, I say ni-tse-koh." But Siska gets it right this time. "You think it's all about you. Your second chance and all you got to do is run your heart out. But it's a talent show and they don't care about the running. You got a deal yet?"

"My promoter and my doctor had a meeting."

"That's something. They say who?"

"I'm not sure."

"Pharmaceutical or medical?"

"They haven't told me yet."

"Or military. Military's good. I hear the British are out this year. That's what you want. I mean, who knows what they're going to do with it, but what do you care, little guinea pig, long as you get your pay out."

"Are you *drunk*?"

"*My body* is drunk. I'm just mean. What do you care? I'm out, sister. And you're in, with a chance. Wouldn't that be something if you won? Little girl from Africa."

"It's not a country."

"Boo-hoo, sorry for you."

"God brought me here."

"Oh that guy? He's nothing but trouble. And He doesn't exist."

"You shouldn't say that."

"How do you know?"

"I can feel Him."

"Can you still feel your legs?"

"Sometimes," Pearl admits.

Siska leans forward and kisses her. "Did you feel anything?"

"No," she says, wiping her mouth. But that's not true. She felt her breath, that burned with alcohol, and the softness of her lips and her flicking tongue, surprisingly warm for a dead girl.

"Yeah," Siska breathed out. "Me neither. You got a cigarette?"

13. EMPTY SPACES

Lane five is empty and the stadium is buzzing with the news.

"Didn't think they'd actually ban her," Tomislav says. She can tell he's hungover. He stinks of sweat and alcohol and there's a crease in his forehead just above his nose that he keeps rubbing at. "Do you want to hear about the meeting? It was big. Bigger than we'd hoped for. If this comes off, kitten . . ."

"I want to concentrate on the race." She is close to tears but she doesn't know why.

"Okay. You should try to win. Really."

The gun goes off. They tear down the track. Every step feels harder today. She didn't get enough sleep.

She sees it happen, out of the corner of her eye. Oluchi's tail swipes Charlotte, maybe on purpose.

"Shit," Grange says and stumbles in her exo-suit. Suddenly everything comes crashing down on Pearl, hot metal and skin and a tangle of limbs and fire in her side.

"Get up," Dr. Arturo yells into her head. She's never heard him upset.

"Ow," she manages. Charlotte is already getting to her feet. There is a loose flap of muscle hanging from her leg, where they tried to attach it this morning. The blonde girl touches it and hisses in pain, but her eyes are already focused on the finish line, on Oluchi skipping ahead, her tail swinging, Anne Murad straining behind her.

"Get up," Dr. Arturo says. "You have to get up. I'm activating adrenaline. Pain blockers."

She sits up. It's hard to breathe. Her vest is wet. A grey nub of bone pokes out through her skin under her breast. Charlotte is limping away in her exo-suit, her leg dragging, gears whining.

"This is what they want to see," Arturo urges. "You *need* to prove to them that it's not hydraulics carrying you through."

"It's not," Pearl gasps. The sound is somehow wet. Breathing through a snorkel in the bath when there is water trapped in the u-bend. The drones buzz around her. She can see her face big on the screen. Her mama is watching at home, the whole of the congregation.

"Then prove it. What are you here for?"

She starts walking, then jogging, clutching her top to the bit of rib to stop it jolting. Every step rips through her. And Pearl can feel things *slipping* inside. Her structural integrity has been compromised, she thinks. The abdominal mesh has ripped and where her stomach used to be is a black hole that is tugging everything down. Her heart is slipping.

Ndincede nkosi, she thinks. Please, Jesus, hep me.

Ndincede nkosi undiphe amandla. Please, God, give me strength.

Yiba nam kolu gqatso. Be with me in this race.

She can feel it. The golden glow that starts in her chest, or, if she is truthful with herself, lower down. In the pit of her stomach.

She sucks in her abdominals and presses her hand to her sternum to stop her heart from sliding down into her guts—where her guts used to be, where the hotbed factory sits.

God is with me, she thinks. What matters is you feel it.

Pearl Nitseko runs.

passage of earth
michael swanwick

*Michael Swanwick made his debut in 1980, and in the years that have fol-
lowed has established himself as one of SF's most prolific and consistently excellent writers at short lengths, as well as one of the premier novelists of his
generation. He has won the Theodore Sturgeon Memorial Award and Asimov's
Readers' Award poll. In 1991, his novel* Stations of the Tide *won him a Nebula Award as well, and in 1995 he won the World Fantasy Award for his story
"Radio Waves." He's won the Hugo Award five times between 1999 and
2006, for his stories "The Very Pulse of the Machine," "Scherzo with Tyran-
nosaur," "The Dog Said Bow-Wow," "Slow Life," and "Legions In Time." His
other books include the novels* In the Drift, Vacuum Flowers, The Iron
Dragon's Daughter, Jack Faust, Bones of the Earth, *and* The Dragons of
Babel. *His short fiction has been collected in* Gravity's Angels, A Geography
of Unknown Lands, Slow Dancing Through Time, Moon Dogs, Puck
Aleshire's Abecedary, Tales of Old Earth, Cigar-Box Faust and Other Minia-
tures, Michael Swanwick's Field Guide to the Mesozoic Megafauna, *and*
The Periodic Table of SF. *His most recent books are a massive retrospective
collection,* The Best of Michael Swanwick, *and a new novel,* Dancing with
Bears. *Coming up is a new novel,* Chasing the Phoenix. *Swanwick lives in
Philadelphia with his wife, Marianne Porter. He has a website at www.mi
chaelswanwick.com and maintains a blog at www.floggingbabel.blogspot.com.*

*Here he delivers the harrowing story of one man's close encounter with an
incursion of giant alien worms, an encounter that will transform his world
forever . . .*

T he ambulance arrived sometime between three and four in the morning. The
morgue was quiet then, cool and faintly damp. Hank savored this time of night and
the faint shadow of contentment it allowed him, like a cup of bitter coffee, long grown
cold, waiting for his occasional sip. He liked being alone and not thinking. His rod
and tackle box waited by the door, in case he felt like going fishing after his shift,
though he rarely did. There was a copy of *Here Be Dragons: Mapping the Human
Genome* in case he did not.

He had opened up a drowning victim and was reeling out her intestines arm over arm, scanning them quickly and letting them down in loops into a galvanized bucket. It was unlikely he was going to find anything, but all deaths by violence got an autopsy. He whistled tunelessly as he worked.

The bell from the loading dock rang.

"Hell." Hank put down his work, peeled off the latex gloves, and went to the intercom. "Sam? That you?" Then, on the sheriff's familiar grunt, he buzzed the door open. "What have you got for me this time?"

"Accident casualty." Sam Aldridge didn't meet his eye, and that was unusual. There was a gurney behind him, and on it something too large to be a human body, covered by canvas. The ambulance was already pulling away, which was so contrary to proper protocols as to be alarming.

"That sure doesn't look like—" Hank began.

A woman stepped out of the darkness.

It was Evelyn.

"Boy, the old dump hasn't changed one bit, has it? I'll bet even the calendar on the wall's the same. Did the county ever spring for a diener for the night shift?"

"I . . . I'm still working alone."

"Wheel it in, Sam, and I'll take over from here. Don't worry about me, I know where everything goes. " Evelyn took a deep breath and shook her head in disgust. "Christ. It's just like riding a bicycle. You never forget. Want to or not."

After the paperwork had been taken care of and Sheriff Sam was gone, Hank said, "Believe it or not, I had regained some semblance of inner peace, Evelyn. Just a little. It took me years. And now this. It's like a kick in the stomach. I don't see how you can justify doing this to me."

"Easiest thing in the world, sweetheart." Evelyn suppressed a smirk that nobody but Hank could have even noticed, and flipped back the canvas. "Take a look."

It was a Worm.

Hank found himself leaning low over the heavy, swollen body, breathing deep of its heady alien smell, suggestive of wet earth and truffles with sharp hints of ammonia. He thought of the ships in orbit, blind locomotives ten miles long. The photographs of these creatures didn't do them justice. His hands itched to open this one up.

"The Agency needs you to perform an autopsy."

Hank drew back "Let me get this straight. You've got the corpse of an alien creature. A representative of the only other intelligent life-form that the human race has ever encountered. Yet with all the forensic scientists you have on salary, you decide to hand it over to a lowly county coroner?"

"We need your imagination, Hank. Anybody can tell how they're put together. We want to know how they think."

"You told me I didn't have an imagination. When you left me." His words came out angrier than he'd intended, but he couldn't find it in himself to apologize for their tone. "So, again—why me?"

"What I said was, you couldn't imagine bettering yourself. For anything impractical, you have imagination in spades. Now I'm asking you to cut open an alien corpse. What could be less practical?"

"I'm not going to get a straight answer out of you, am I?"

Evelyn's mouth quirked up in a little smile so that for the briefest instant she was the woman he had fallen in love with, a million years ago. His heart ached to see it. "You never got one before," she said. "Let's not screw up a perfectly good divorce by starting now."

"Let me put a fresh chip in my dictation device," Hank said. "Grab a smock and some latex gloves. You're going to assist."

"Ready," Evelyn said.

Hank hit record, then stood over the Worm, head down, for a long moment. Getting in the zone. "Okay, let's start with a gross physical examination. Um, what we have looks a lot like an annelid, rather blunter and fatter than the terrestrial equivalent and of course much larger. Just eyeballing it, I'd say this thing is about eight feet long, maybe two feet and a half in diameter. I could just about get my arms around it if I tried. There are three, five, seven, make that eleven somites, compared to say one or two hundred in an earthworm. No clitellum, so we're warned not to take the annelid similarity too far.

"The body is bluntly tapered at each end, and somewhat depressed posteriorly. The ventral side is flattened and paler than the dorsal surface. There's a tripartite beak-like structure at one end, I'm guessing this is the mouth, and what must be an anus at the other. Near the beak are five swellings from which extend stiff, bone-like structures—mandibles, maybe? I'll tell you, though, they look more like tools. This one might almost be a wrench, and over here a pair of grippers. They seem awfully specialized for an intelligent creature. Evelyn, you've dealt with these things, is there any variation within the species? I mean, do some have this arrangement of manipulators and others some other structure?"

"We've never seen any two of the aliens with the same arrangement of manipulators."

"Really? That's interesting. I wonder what it means. Okay, the obvious thing here is there are no apparent external sensory organs. No eyes, ears, nose. My guess is that whatever senses these things might have, they're functionally blind."

"Intelligence is of that opinion too."

"Well, it must have shown in their behavior, right? So that's an easy one. Here's my first extrapolation: You're going to have a bitch of a time understanding these things. Human beings rely on sight more than most animals, and if you trace back philosophy and science, they both have strong roots in optics. Something like this is simply going to think differently from us.

"Now, looking between the somites—the rings—we find a number of tiny hair-like structures, and if we pull the rings apart, so much as we can, there're all these small openings, almost like tiny anuses if there weren't so many of them, closed with sphincter muscles, maybe a hundred of them, and it looks like they're between each pair of somites. Oh, here's something—the structures near the front, the swellings, are a more developed form of these little openings. Okay, now we turn the thing over. I'll take this end you take the other. Right, now I want you to rock it by my count, and on the three we'll flip it over. Ready? One, two, three!"

The corpse slowly flipped over, almost overturning the gurney. The two of them barely managed to control it.

"That was a close one," Hank said cheerily. "Huh. What's this?" He touched a line of painted numbers on the alien's underbelly. *Rt-Front/No. 43.*

"Never you mind what that is. Your job is to perform the autopsy."

"You've got more than one corpse."

Evelyn said nothing.

"Now that I say it out loud, of course you do. You've got dozens. If you only had the one, I'd never have gotten to play with it. You have doctors of your own. Good researchers, some of them, who would cut open their grandmothers if they got the grant money. Hell, even forty-three would've been kept in-house. You must have hundreds, right?"

For a fraction of a second, that exquisite face went motionless. Evelyn probably wasn't even aware of doing it, but Hank knew from long experience that she'd just made a decision. "More like a thousand. There was a very big accident. It's not on the news yet, but one of the Worms' landers went down in the Pacific."

"Oh Jesus." Hank pulled his gloves off, shoved up his glasses and ground his palms into his eyes. "You've got your war at last, haven't you? You've picked a fight with creatures that have tremendous technological superiority over us, and they don't even live here! All they have to do is drop a big enough rock into our atmosphere and there'll be a mass extinction the likes of which hasn't been seen since the dinosaurs died out. They won't care. It's not *their* planet!"

Evelyn's face twisted into an expression he hadn't known it could form until just before the end of their marriage, when everything fell apart. "Stop being such an ass," she said. Then, talking fast and earnestly, "We didn't cause the accident. It was just dumb luck it happened, but once it did we had to take advantage of it. Yes, the Worms probably have the technology to wipe us out. So we have to deal with them. But to deal with them we have to understand them, and we do not. They're a mystery to us. We don't know what they want. We don't know how they think. But after tonight we'll have a little better idea. Provided only that you get back to work."

Hank went to the table and pulled a new pair of gloves off the roll. "Okay," he said. "Okay."

"Just keep in mind that it's not just my ass that's riding on this," Evelyn said. "It's yours and everyone's you know."

"I *said* okay!" Hank took a long breath, calming himself. "Next thing to do is cut this sucker open." He picked up a bone saw. "This is bad technique, but we're in a hurry." The saw whined to life, and he cut through the leathery brown skin from beak to anus. "All right, now we peel the skin back. It's wet-feeling and a little crunchy. The musculature looks much like that of a Terrestrial annelid. Structurally, that is. I've never seen anything quite that color black. Damn! The skin keeps curling back."

He went to his tackle box and removed a bottle of fishhooks. "Here. We'll take a bit of nylon filament, tie two hooks together, like this, with about two inches of line between them. Then we hook the one through the skin, fold it down, and push the other through the cloth on the gurney. Repeat the process every six inches on both sides. That should hold it open."

"Got it." Evelyn set to work.

Some time later they were done, and Hank stared down into the opened Worm. "You want speculation? Here goes: This thing moves through the mud, or whatever the medium is there, face-first and blind. What does that suggest to you?"

"I'd say that they'd be used to coming up against the unexpected."

"Very good. Haul back on this, I'm going to cut again. . . . Okay, now we're past the musculature and there's a fluffy mass of homogeneous stuff, we'll come back to that in a minute. Cutting through the fluff . . . and into the body cavity and it's absolutely chockablock with zillions of tiny little organs."

"Let's keep our terminology at least vaguely scientific, shall we?" Evelyn said.

"Well, there are more than I want to count. Literally hundreds of small organs under the musculature, I have no idea what they're for but they're all interconnected with vein-like tubing in various sizes. This is ferociously more complicated than human anatomy. It's like a chemical plant in here. No two of the organs are the same so far as I can tell, although they all have a generic similarity. Let's call them alembics, so we don't confuse them with any other organs we may find. I see something that looks like a heart maybe, an isolated lump of muscle the size of my fist, there are three of them. Now I'm cutting deeper . . . Holy shit!"

For a long minute, Hank stared into the opened alien corpse. Then he put the saw down on the gurney and, shaking his head, turned away. "Where's that coffee?" he said.

Without saying a word, Evelyn went to the coffee station and brought him his cold cup.

Hank yanked his gloves, threw them in the trash, and drank.

"All right," Evelyn said, "so what was it?"

"You mean you can't see—no, of course you can't. With you, it was human anatomy all the way."

"I took invertebrate biology in college."

"And forgot it just as fast as you could. Okay, look: Up here is the beak, semi-retractable. Down here is the anus. Food goes in one, waste comes out the other. What do you see between?"

"There's a kind of a tube. The gut?"

"Yeah. It runs straight from the mouth to the anus, without interruption. Nothing in between. How does it eat without a stomach? How does it stay alive?" He saw from Evelyn's expression that she was not impressed. "What we see before us is simply not possible."

"Yet here it is. So there's an explanation. Find it."

"Yeah, yeah." Glaring at the Worm's innards, he drew on a new pair of gloves. "Let me take a look at that beak again. . . . Hah. See how the muscles are connected?

The beak relaxes open, aaand—let's take a look at the other end—so does the anus. So this beast crawls through the mud, mouth wide open, and the mud passes through it unhindered. That's bound to have some effect on its psychological makeup."

"Like what?"

"Damned if I know. Let's take a closer look at the gut. . . . There are rings of intrusive tissue near the beak one third of the way in, two thirds in, and just above the anus. We cut through and there is extremely fine structure, but nothing we're going to figure out tonight. Oh, hey, I think I got it. Look at these three flaps just behind . . ."

He cut in silence for a while. "There. It has three stomachs. They're located in the head, just behind the first ring of intrusive tissue. The mud or whatever is dumped into this kind of holding chamber, and then there's this incredible complex of muscles, and—how many exit tubes?—this one has got, um, fourteen. I'll trace one, and it goes right to this alembic. The next one goes to another alembic. I'll trace this one and it goes to—yep, another alembic. There's a pattern shaping up here.

"Let's put this aside for the moment, and go back to those masses of fluff. Jeeze, there's a lot of this stuff. It must make up a good third of the body mass. Which has trilateral symmetry, by the way. Three masses of fluff proceed from head to tail, beneath the muscle sheaf, all three connecting about eight inches below the mouth, into a ring around the straight gut. This is where the arms or manipulators or screwdrivers or whatever they are, grow. Now, at regular intervals the material puts out little arms, outgrowths that fine down to wire-like structures of the same material, almost like very thick nerves. Oh God. That's what it is." He drew back, and with a scalpel flensed the musculature away to reveal more of the mass. "It's the central nervous system. This thing has a brain that weighs at least a hundred pounds. I don't believe it. I don't *want* to believe it."

"It's true," Evelyn said. "Our people in Bethesda have done slide studies. You're looking at the thing's brain."

"If you already knew the answer, then why the hell are you putting me through this?"

"I'm not here to answer your questions. You're here to answer mine."

Annoyed, Hank bent over the Worm again. There was rich stench of esters from the creature, pungent and penetrating, and the slightest whiff of what he guessed was putrefaction. "We start with the brain, and trace one of the subordinate ganglia inward. Tricky little thing, it goes all over the place, and ends up right here, at one of the alembics. We'll try another one, and it . . . ends up at an alembic. There are a lot of these things, let's see—hey—here's one that goes to one of the structures in the straight gut. What could that be? A tongue! That's it, there's a row of tongues just within the gut, and more to taste the medium flowing through, yeah. And these little flapped openings just behind them open when the mud contains specific nutrients the worm desires. Okay, now we're getting somewhere, how long have we been at this?"

"About an hour and a half."

"It feels like longer." He thought of getting some more coffee, decided against it. "So what have we got here? All that enormous brain mass—what's it for?"

"Maybe it's all taken up by raw intelligence."

"Raw intelligence! No such thing. Nature doesn't evolve intelligence without a purpose. It's got to be used for something. Let's see. A fair amount is taken up by taste, obviously. It has maybe sixty individual tongues, and I wouldn't be surprised if its sense of taste were much more detailed than ours. Plus all those little alembics performing god-knows-what kind of chemical reactions.

"Let's suppose for a minute that it can consciously control those reactions, that would account for a lot of the brain mass. When the mud enters at the front, it's tasted, maybe a little is siphoned off and sent through the alembics for transformation. Waste products are jetted into the straight gut, and pass through several more circles of tongues . . . Here's another observation for you: These things would have an absolute sense of the state of their own health. They can probably create their own drugs, too. Come to think of it, I haven't come across any evidence of disease here." The Worm's smell was heavy, penetrating pervasive. He felt slightly dizzy, shook it off.

"Okay, so we've got a creature that concentrates most of its energy and attention internally. It slides through an easy medium, and at the same time the mud slides through it. It tastes the mud as it passes, and we can guess that the mud will be in a constant state of transformation, so it experiences the universe more directly than do we." He laughed. "It appears to be a verb."

"How's that?"

"One of Buckminster Fuller's aphorisms. But it fits. The worm constantly transforms the universe. It takes in all it comes across, accepts it, changes it, and excretes it. It is an agent of change."

"That's very clever. But it doesn't help us deal with them."

"Well, of course not. They're intelligent, and intelligence complicates everything. But if you wanted me to generalize, I'd say the Worms are straightforward and accepting—look at how they move blindly ahead—but that their means of changing things are devious, as witness the mass of alembics. That's going to be their approach to us. Straightforward, yet devious in ways we just don't get. Then, when they're done with us, they'll pass on without a backward glance."

"Terrific. Great stuff. Get back to work."

"Look, Evelyn. I'm tired and I've done all I can, and a pretty damned good job at that, I think. I could use a rest."

"You haven't dealt with the stuff near the beak. The arms or whatever."

"Cripes." Hank turned back to the corpse, cut open an edema, began talking. "The material of the arms is stiff and osseous, rather like teeth. This one has several moving parts, all controlled by muscles anchored alongside the edema. There's a nest of ganglia here, connected by a very short route to the brain matter. Now I'm cutting into the brain matter, and there's a small black gland, oops I've nicked it. Whew. What a smell. Now I'm cutting behind it." Behind the gland was a small white structure, square and hard meshwork, looking like a cross between an instrument chip and a square of Chex cereal.

Keeping his back to Evelyn, he picked it up.

He put it in his mouth.

He swallowed.

What have I done? he thought. Aloud, he said, "As an operating hypothesis I'd say that the manipulative structures have been deliberately, make that consciously grown. There, I've traced one of those veins back to the alembics. So that explains why there's no uniformity, these things would grow exterior manipulators on need, and then discard them when they're done. Yes, look, the muscles don't actually connect to the manipulators, they wrap around them."

There was a sour taste on his tongue.

I must be insane, he thought.

"Did you just *eat* something?"

Keeping his expression blank, Hank said, "Are you nuts? You mean did I put part of this . . . creature . . . in my mouth?" There was a burning within his brain, a buzzing like the sound of the rising sun picked up on a radio telescope. He wanted to scream, but his face simply smiled and said, "Do you—?" And then it was very hard to concentrate on what he was saying. He couldn't quite focus on Evelyn, and there were white rays moving starburst across his vision and . . .

When he came to, Hank was on the Interstate, doing ninety. His mouth was dry and his eyelids felt gritty. Bright yellow light was shining in his eyes from a sun that had barely lifted itself up above over the horizon. He must have been driving for hours. The steering wheel felt tacky and gummy. He looked down.

There was blood on his hands. It went all the way up to his elbows.

The traffic was light. Hank had no idea where he was heading, nor any desire whatsoever to stop.

So he just kept driving.

Whose blood was it on his hands? Logic said it was Evelyn's. But that made no sense. Hate her though he did—and the sight of her had opened wounds and memories he'd thought cauterized shut long ago—he wouldn't actually hurt her. Not physically. He wouldn't actually kill her.

Would he?

It was impossible. But there was the blood on his hands. Whose else could it be? Some of it might be his own, admittedly. His hands ached horribly. They felt like he'd been pounding them into something hard, over and over again. But most of the blood was dried and itchy. Except for where his skin had split at the knuckles, he had no wounds of any kind. So the blood wasn't his.

"Of course you did," Evelyn said. "You beat me to death and you enjoyed every minute of it."

Hank shrieked and almost ran off the road. He fought the car back and then turned and stared in disbelief. Evelyn sat in the passenger seat beside him.

"You . . . how did . . . ?" Much as he had with the car, Hank seized control of himself. "You're a hallucination," he said.

"Right in one!" Evelyn applauded lightly. "Or a memory, or the personification of your guilt, however you want to put it. You always were a bright man, Hank. Not so bright as to be able to keep your wife from walking out on you, but bright enough for government work."

"Your sleeping around was not my fault."

"Of course it was. You think you walked in on me and Jerome by *accident*? A woman doesn't hate her husband enough to arrange something like that without good reason."

"Oh god, oh god, oh god."

"The fuel light is blinking. You'd better find a gas station and fill up."

A Lukoil station drifted into sight, so he pulled into it and stopped the car by a full service pump. When he got out, the service station attendant hurried toward him and then stopped, frozen.

"Oh no," the attendant said. He was a young man with sandy hair. "Not another one."

"Another one?" Hank slid his card through the reader. "What do you mean another one?" He chose high-test and began pumping, all the while staring hard at the attendant. All but daring him to try something. "Explain yourself."

"Another one like you." The attendant couldn't seem to look away from Hank's hands. "The cops came right away and arrested the first one. It took five of them to get him into the car. Then another one came and when I called, they said to just take down his license number and let him go. They said there were people like you showing up all over."

Hank finished pumping and put the nozzle back on its hook. He did not push the button for a receipt. "Don't try to stop me," he said. The words just came and he said them. "I'd hurt you very badly if you did."

The young man's eyes jerked upward. He looked spooked. "What *are* you people?"

Hank paused, with his hand on the door. "I have no idea."

"You should have told him," Evelyn said when he got back in the car. "Why didn't you?"

"Shut up."

"You ate something out of that Worm and it's taken over part of your brain. You still feel like yourself, but you're not in control. You're sitting at the wheel but you have no say over where you're going. Do you?"

"No," Hank admitted. "No, I don't."

"What do you think it is—some kind of super-prion? Like mad cow disease only faster than fast? A neuroprogrammer, maybe? An artificial overlay to your personality that feeds off of your brain and shunts your volition into a dead end?"

"I don't know."

"You're the one with the imagination. This would seem to be your sort of thing. I'm surprised you're not all over it."

"No," Hank said. "No, you're not at all surprised."

They drove on in silence for a time.

"Do you remember when we first met? In med school? You were going to be a surgeon then."

"Please. Don't."

"Rainy autumn afternoons in that ratty little third-floor walk-up of yours. With that great big aspen with the yellow leaves outside the window. It seemed like there was always at least one stuck to the glass. There were days when we never got dressed at all. We'd spend all day in and out of that enormous futon you'd bought instead of a bed, and it still wasn't large enough. If we rolled off the edge, we'd go on making love on the floor. When it got dark, we'd send out for Chinese."

"We were happy then. Is that what you want me to say?"

"It was your hands I liked best. Feeling them on me. You'd have one hand on my breast and the other between my legs and I'd imagine you cutting open a patient. Peeling back the flesh to reveal all those glistening organs inside."

"Okay, now that's sick."

"You asked me what I was thinking once and I told you. I was watching your face closely, because I really wanted to know you back then. You loved it. So I know you've got demons inside you. Why not own up to them?"

He squeezed his eyes shut, but something inside him opened them again, so he wouldn't run the car off the road. A low moaning sound arose from somewhere deep in his throat. "I must be in Hell."

"C'mon. Be a sport. What could it hurt? I'm already dead."

"There are some things no man was meant to admit. Even to himself."

Evelyn snorted. "You always were the most astounding prig."

They drove on in silence for a while, deeper into the desert. At last, staring straight ahead of himself, Hank could not keep himself from saying, "There are worse revelations to come, aren't there?"

"Oh God, yes," his mother said.

"It was your father's death." His mother sucked wetly on a cigarette. "That's what made you turn out the way you did."

Hank could barely see the road for his tears. "I honestly don't want to be having this conversation, Mom."

"No, of course you don't. You never were big on self-awareness, were you? You preferred cutting open toads or hunching over that damned microscope."

"I've got plenty of self-awareness. I've got enough self-awareness to choke on. I can see where you're going and I am not going to apologize for how I felt about Dad. He died of cancer when I was thirteen. What did I ever do to anyone that was half so bad as what he did to me? So I don't want to hear any cheap Freudian bullshit about survivor guilt and failing to live up to his glorious example, okay?"

"Nobody said it wasn't hard on you. Particularly coming at the onset of puberty as it did."

"Mom!"

"What. I wasn't supposed to know? Who do you think did the laundry?" His mother lit a new cigarette from the old one, then crushed out the butt in an ashtray. "I knew a lot more of what was going on in those years than you thought I did, believe you me. All those hours you spent in the bathroom jerking off. The money you stole to buy dope with."

"I was in pain, Mom. And it's not as if you were any help."

His mother looked at him with the same expression of weary annoyance he remembered so well. "You think there's something special about your pain? I lost the only man I ever loved and I couldn't move on because I had a kid to raise. Not a sweet little boy like I used to have either, but a sullen, self-pitying teenager. It took forever to get you shipped off to medical school."

"So then you moved on. Right off the roof of the county office building. Way to honor Dad's memory, Mom. What do you think he would have said about that if he'd known?"

Dryly, his mother said, "Ask him for yourself."

Hank closed his eyes.

When he opened them, he was standing in the living room of his mother's house. His father stood in the doorway, as he had so many times, smoking an unfiltered Camel and staring through the screen door at the street outside. "Well?" Hank said at last.

With a sigh his father turned around. "I'm sorry," he said. "I didn't know what to do." His lips moved up into what might have been a smile on another man. "Dying was new to me."

"Yeah, well you could have summoned the strength to tell me what was going on. But you couldn't be bothered. The surgeon who operated on you? Doctor Tomasini. For years I thought of him as my real father. And you know why? Because he gave it to me straight. He told me exactly what was going to happen. He told me to brace myself for the worst. He said that it was going to be bad but that I would find the strength to get through it. Nobody'd ever talked to me like that before. Whenever I was in a rough spot, I'd fantasize going to him and asking for advice. Because there was no one else I could ask."

"I'm sorry you hate me," his father said, not exactly looking at Hank. Then, almost mumbling, "Still, lots of men hate their fathers, and somehow manage to make decent lives for themselves."

"I didn't hate you. You were just a guy who never got an education and never made anything of himself and knew it. You had a shitty job, a three pack a day habit, and a wife who was a lush. And then you died." All the anger went out of Hank in an instant, like air whooshing out of a punctured balloon, leaving nothing behind but an aching sense of loss. "There wasn't really anything there to hate."

Abruptly, the car was filled with coil upon coil of glistening Worm. For an instant it looped outward, swallowing up car, Interstate, and all the world, and he was afloat in vacuum, either blind or somewhere perfectly lightless, and there was nothing but the Worm-smell, so strong he could taste it in his mouth.

Then he was back on the road again, hands sticky on the wheel and sunlight in his eyes.

"Boy does *that* explain a lot!" Evelyn flashed her perfect teeth at him and beat on the top of the dashboard as if it were a drum. "How a guy as spectacularly unsuited for it as you are decided to become a surgeon. That perpetual cringe of failure you carry around on your shoulders. It even explains why, when push came to shove, you couldn't bring yourself to cut open living people. Afraid of what you might find there?"

"You don't know what you're talking about."

"I know that you froze up right in the middle of a perfectly routine appendectomy. What did you see in that body cavity?"

"Shut up."

"Was it the appendix? I bet it was. What did it look like?"

"Shut up."

"Did it look like a Worm?"

He stared at her in amazement. "How did you know that?"

"I'm just a hallucination, remember? An undigested bit of beef, a blot of mustard, a crumb of cheese, a fragment of underdone potato. So the question isn't how did I know, but how did *you* know what a Worm was going to look like five years before their ships came into the Solar System?"

"It's a false memory, obviously."

"So where did it come from?" Evelyn lit up a cigarette. "We go off-road here."

He slowed down and started across the desert. The car bucked and bounced. Sagebrush scraped against the sides. Dust blossomed up into the air behind them.

"Funny thing you calling your mother a lush," Evelyn said. "Considering what happened after you bombed out of surgery."

"I've been clean for six years and four months. I still go to the meetings."

"Swell. The guy I married didn't need to."

"Look, this is old territory, do we really need to revisit it? We went over it so many times during the divorce."

"And you've been going over it in your head ever since. Over and over and . . ."

"I want us to stop. That's all. Just stop."

"It's your call. I'm only a symptom, remember? If you want to stop thinking, then just stop thinking."

Unable to stop thinking, he continued eastward, ever eastward.

For hours he drove, while they talked about every small and nasty thing he had done as a child, and then as an adolescent, and then as an alcoholic failure of a surgeon and a husband. Every time Hank managed to change the subject, Evelyn brought up something even more painful, until his face was wet with tears. He dug around in his pockets for a handkerchief. "You could show a little compassion, you know."

"Oh, the way you've shown *me* compassion? I offered to let you keep the car if you'd just give me back the photo albums. So you took the albums into the back yard and burned them all, including the only photos of my grandmother I had. Remember that? But of course I'm not real, am I? I'm just your image of Evelyn—and we both know you're not willing to concede her the least spark of human decency. Watch out for that gully! You'd better keep your eyes straight ahead."

They were on a dirt road somewhere deep in the desert now. That was as much as he knew. The car bucked and scraped its underside against the sand, and he downshifted again. A rock rattled down the underside, probably tearing holes in vital places.

Then Hank noticed plumes of dust in the distance, smaller versions of the one billowing up behind him. So there were other vehicles out there. Now that he knew to look for them, he saw more. There were long slanted pillars of dust rising up in the middle distance and tiny grey nubs down near the horizon. Dozens of them, scores, maybe hundreds.

"What's that noise?" he heard himself asking. "Helicopters?"

"Such a clever little boy you are!"

One by one flying machines lifted over the horizon. Some of them were news copters. The rest looked to be military. The little ones darted here and there, filming. The big ones circled slowly around a distant glint of metal in the desert. They looked a lot like grasshoppers. They seemed afraid to get too close.

"See there?" Evelyn said. "That would be the lifter."

"Oh." Hank said.

Then, slowly, he ventured, "The lander going down wasn't an accident, was there?"

"No, of course not. The Worms crashed it in the Pacific on purpose. They killed hundreds of their own so the bodies would be distributed as widely as possible. They used themselves as bait. They wanted to collect a broad cross-section of humanity.

"Which is ironic, really, because all they're going to get is doctors, morticians, and academics. Some FBI agents, a few Homeland Security bureaucrats. No retirees, cafeteria ladies, jazz musicians, soccer coaches, or construction workers. Not one Guatemalan nun or Korean noodle chef. But how could they have known? They acted out of perfect ignorance of us and they got what they got."

"You sound just like me," Hank said. Then, "So what now? Colored lights and anal probes?"

Evelyn snorted again. "They're a sort of hive culture. When one dies, it's eaten by the others and its memories are assimilated. So a thousand deaths wouldn't mean a lot to them. If individual memories were lost, the bulk of those individuals were already made up of the memories of previous generations. The better part of them would still be alive, back on the mother ship. Similarly, they wouldn't have any ethical problems with harvesting a few hundred human beings. Eating us, I mean, and absorbing our memories into their collective identity. They probably don't understand the concept of individual death. Even if they did, they'd think we should be grateful for being given a kind of immortality."

The car went over a boulder Hank hadn't noticed in time, bouncing him so high that his head hit the roof. Still, he kept driving.

"How do you know all that?"

"How do you *think* I know?" Ahead, the alien ship was growing larger. At its base were Worm upon Worm upon Worm, all facing outward, skin brown and glistening. "Come on, Hank, do I have to spell it out for you?"

"I have no idea what you're talking about."

"Okay, Captain Courageous," Evelyn said scornfully. "If this is what it takes." She stuck both her hands into her mouth and pulled outward. The skin to either side of her mouth stretched like rubber, then tore. Her face ripped in half.

Loop after loop of slick brown flesh flopped down to spill across Hank's lap, slide over the back of the seat and fill up the rear of the car. The horridly familiar stench of Worm, part night soil and part chemical plant, took possession of him and would not let go. He found himself gagging, half from the smell and half from what it meant.

A weary sense of futility grasped his shoulders and pushed down hard. "This is only a memory, isn't it?"

One end of the Worm rose up and turned toward him. Its beak split open in three parts and from the moist interior came Evelyn's voice: "The answer to the question you haven't got the balls to ask is: Yes, you're dead. A Worm ate you and now you're passing slowly through an alien gut, being tasted and experienced and understood. You're nothing more than an emulation being run inside one of those hundred-pound brains."

Hank stopped the car and got out. There was an arroyo between him and the alien ship that the car would never be able to get across. So he started walking.

"It all feels so real," he said. The sun burned hot on his head, and the stones underfoot were hard. He could see other people walking determinedly through the shimmering heat. They were all converging on the ship.

"Well, it would, wouldn't it?" Evelyn walked beside him in human form again. But when he looked back the way they had come, there was only one set of footprints.

Hank had been walking in a haze of horror and resignation. Now it was penetrated by a sudden stab of fear. "This *will* end, won't it? Tell me it will. Tell me that you and I aren't going to keep cycling through the same memories over and over, chewing on our regrets forever?"

"You're as sharp as ever, Hank," Evelyn said. "That's exactly what we've been doing. It passes the time between planets."

"For how long?"

"For more years than you'd think possible. Space is awfully big, you know. It takes thousands and thousands of years to travel from one star to another."

"Then . . . this really is Hell, after all. I mean, I can't imagine anything worse."

She said nothing.

They topped a rise and looked down at the ship. It was a tapering cylinder, smooth and featureless save for a ring of openings at the bottom from which emerged the front ends of many Worms. Converging upon it were people who had started earlier or closer than Hank and thus gotten here before he did. They walked straight and unhesitatingly to the nearest Worm and were snatched up and gulped down by those sharp, tripartite beaks. *Snap* and then swallow. After which, the Worm slid back into the ship and was replaced by another. Not one of the victims showed the least emotion. It was all as dispassionate as an abattoir for robots.

These creatures below were monstrously large, taller than Hank was. The one he had dissected must have been a hatchling. A grub. It made sense. You wouldn't want to sacrifice any larger a percentage of your total memories than you had to.

"Please." He started down the slope, waving his arms to keep his balance when the sand slipped underfoot. He was crying again, apparently; he could feel the tears running down his cheeks. "Evelyn. Help me."

Scornful laughter. "Can you even *imagine* me helping you?"

"No, of course—" Hank cut that thought short. Evelyn, the real Evelyn, would not have treated him like this. Yes, she had hurt him badly, and by that time she left, she had been glad to do so. But she wasn't petty or cruel or vindictive before he made her that way.

"Accepting responsibility for the mess you made of your life, Hank? You?"

"Tell me what to do," Hank said, pushing aside his anger and resentment, trying to remember Evelyn as he had once been. "Give me a hint."

For a maddeningly long moment Evelyn was silent. Then she said, "If the Worm that ate you so long ago could only communicate directly with you . . . what one question do you think it would ask?"

"I don't know."

"I think it would be, Why are all your memories so ugly?"

Unexpectedly, she gave him a peck on the cheek.

Hank had arrived. His Worm's beak opened. Its breath smelled like Evelyn on a rainy Saturday afternoon. Hank stared at the glistening blackness within. So enticing. He wanted to fling himself down it.

Once more into the gullet, he thought, and took a step closer to the Worm and the soothing darkness it encompassed.

Its mouth gaped wide, waiting to ingest and transform him.

Unbidden, then, a memory rose up within Hank of a night when their marriage was young and, traveling through Louisiana, he and Evelyn stopped on an impulse at a roadhouse where there was a zydeco band and beer in bottles and they were happy and in love and danced and danced and danced into an evening without end. It had seemed then that all good things would last forever.

It was a fragile straw to cling to, but Hank clung to it with all his might.

Worm and man together, they then thought: *No one knows the size of the universe or what wonders and terrors it contains. Yet we drive on, blindly burrowing forward through the darkness, learning what we can and suffering what we must. Hoping for stars.*

amicae aeternum

ELLeN kLAGES

Ellen Klages is the author of two acclaimed YA historical novels: The Green
Glass Sea, *which won the Scott O'Dell Award, the New Mexico State Book
Award, and the Lopez Award; and* White Sands, Red Menace, *which won
the California and New Mexico Book Awards. Her story "Basement Magic"
won a Nebula Award in 2005. In 2014, "Wakulla Springs," coauthored with
Andy Duncan, was nominated for the Nebula, Hugo, and Locus awards, and
won the World Fantasy Award for Best Novella. She lives in San Francisco,
in a small house full of strange and wondrous things.*

*Here she provides as eloquent an argument against setting forth for the
stars on a generation ship as I've ever seen, one poignant enough to make
me want to yell at the young protagonist to run away and hide until it is too
late to go on board.*

It was still dark when Corry woke, no lights on in the neighbors' houses, just a
yellow glow from the streetlight on the other side of the elm. Through her open
window, the early summer breeze brushed across her coverlet like silk.

Corry dressed silently, trying not to see the empty walls, the boxes piled in a corner. She pulled on a shirt and shorts, looping the laces of her shoes around her neck
and climbed from bed to sill and out the window with only a whisper of fabric against
the worn wood. Then she was outside.

The grass was chill and damp beneath her bare feet. She let them rest on it for a
minute, the freshly mowed blades tickling her toes, her heels sinking into the springy-
sponginess of the dirt. She breathed deep, to catch it all—the cool and the green
and the stillness—holding it in for as long as she could before slipping on her shoes.

A morning to remember. Every little detail.

She walked across the lawn, stepping over the ridge of clippings along the verge,
onto the sidewalk. Theirs was a corner lot. In a minute, she would be out of sight.
For once, she was up before her practical, morning-people parents. The engineer
and the physicist did not believe in sleeping in, but Corry could count on the fingers of one hand the number of times in her eleven years that she had seen the dawn.

No one else was on the street. It felt solemn and private, as if she had stepped out of time, so quiet she could hear the wind ruffle the wide canopy of trees, an owl hooting from somewhere behind her, the diesel chug of the all-night bus two blocks away. She crossed Branson St. and turned down the alley that ran behind the houses.

A dandelion's spiky leaves pushed through a crack in the cement. Corry squatted, touching it with a finger, tracing the jagged outline, memorizing its contours. A weed. No one planted it or planned it. She smiled and stood up, her hand against a wooden fence, feeling the grain beneath her palm, the crackling web of old paint, and continued on. The alley stretched ahead for several blocks, the pavement a narrowing pale V.

She paused a minute later to watch a cat prowl stealthily along the base of another fence, hunting or slinking home. It looked up, saw her, and sped into a purposeful thousand-leg trot before disappearing into a yard. She thought of her own cat, Mr. Bumble, who now belonged to a neighbor, and wiped at the edge of her eye. She distracted herself by peering into backyards at random bits of other people's lives—lawn chairs, an overturned tricycle, a metal barbecue grill, its lid open.

Barbecue. She hadn't thought to add that to her list. She'd like to have one more whiff of charcoal, lit with lighter fluid, smoking and wafting across the yards, smelling like summer. Too late now. No one barbecued their breakfast.

She walked on, past Remington Rd. She brushed her fingers over a rosebush—velvet petals, leathery leaves; pressed a hand against the oft-stapled roughness of a telephone pole, fringed with remnants of garage-sale flyers; stood on tiptoe to trace the red octagon of a stop sign. She stepped from sidewalk to grass to asphalt and back, tasting the textures with her feet, noting the cracks and holes and bumps, the faded paint on the curb near a fire hydrant.

"Fire hydrant," she said softly, but aloud, checking it off in her mind. "Rain gutter. Lawn mower. Mailbox."

The sky was just beginning to purple in the east when she reached Anna's back gate. She knew it as well as her own. They'd been best friends since first grade, had been in and out of each other's houses practically every day. Corry tapped on the frame of the porch's screen door with one knuckle.

A moment later, Anna came out. "Hi, Spunk," she whispered.

"Hi, Spork," Corry answered. She waited while Anna eased the door closed so it wouldn't bang, sat on the steps, put on her shoes.

Their bikes leaned against the side of the garage. Corry had told her mom that she had given her bike to Anna's sister Pat. And she would, in an hour or two. So it hadn't really been a lie, just the wrong tense.

They walked their bikes through the gate. In the alley, Corry threw a leg over and settled onto the vinyl seat, its shape molded to hers over the years. Her bike. Her steed. Her hands fit themselves around the rubber grips of the handlebars and she pushed off with one foot. Anna was a few feet behind, then beside her. They rode abreast down to the mouth of the alley and away.

The slight grade of Thompson St. was perfect for coasting, the wind on their faces, blowing Corry's short dark hair off her forehead, rippling Anna's ponytail. At the bottom of the hill, Corry stood tall on her pedals, pumping hard, the muscles in her calves a good ache as the chain rattled and whirred as fast and constant as a train.

"Trains!" she yelled into the wind. Another item from her list.

"Train whistles!" Anna yelled back.

They leaned into a curve. Corry felt gravity pull at her, pumped harder, in control. They turned a corner and a moment later, Anna said, "Look."

Corry slowed, looked up, then braked to a stop. The crescent moon hung above a gap in the trees, a thin sliver of blue-white light.

Anna began the lullaby her mother used to sing when Corry first slept over. On the second line, Corry joined in.

I see the moon, and the moon sees me.
The moon sees somebody I want to see.

The sound of their voices was liquid in the stillness, sweet and smooth. Anna reached out and held Corry's hand across the space between their bikes.

God bless the moon, and God bless me,
And God bless the somebody I want to see.

They stood for a minute, feet on the ground, still holding hands. Corry gave a squeeze and let go. "Thanks," she said.

"Any time," said Anna, and bit her lip.

"I know," Corry said. Because it wouldn't be. She pointed. The sky was lighter now, palest blue at the end of the street shading to indigo directly above. "Let's get to the park before the sun comes up."

No traffic, no cars. It felt like they were the only people in the world. They headed east, riding down the middle of the street, chasing the shadows of their bikes from streetlight to streetlight, never quite catching them. The houses on both sides were dark, only one light in a kitchen window making a yellow rectangle on a driveway. As they passed it, they smelled bacon frying, heard a fragment of music.

The light at 38th St. was red. They stopped, toes on the ground, waiting. A raccoon scuttled from under a hedge, hump-backed and quick, disappearing behind a parked car. In the hush, Corry heard the metallic *tick* from the light box before she saw it change from red to green.

Three blocks up Ralston Hill. The sky looked magic now, the edges wiped with pastels, peach and lavender and a blush of orange. Corry pedaled as hard as she could, felt her breath ragged in her throat, a trickle of sweat between her shoulder blades. Under the arched entrance to the park, into the broad, grassy picnic area that sloped down to the creek.

They abandoned their bikes to the grass, and walked to a low stone wall. Corry sat, cross-legged, her best friend beside her, and waited for the sun to rise for the last time.

She knew it didn't actually rise, that *it* wasn't moving. They were, rotating a quarter mile every second, coming all the way around once every twenty-four hours, exposing themselves once again to the star they called the sun, and naming that moment *morning*. But it was the last time she'd get to watch.

"There it is," Anna said. Golden light pierced the spaces between the trunks of the trees, casting long thin shadows across the grass. They leaned against each other and watched as the sky brightened to its familiar blue, and color returned to the earth: green leaves, pink bicycles, yellow shorts. Behind them lights began to come on in houses and a dog barked.

By the time the sun touched the tops of the distant trees, backs of their legs were pebbled with the pattern of the wall, and it was daytime.

Corry sat, listening to the world waking up and going about its ordinary business: cars starting, birds chirping, a mother calling out, "Jimmy! Breakfast!" She felt as if her whole body was aware, making all this a part of her.

Over by the playground, geese waddled on the grass, pecking for bugs. One goose climbed onto the end of the teeter-totter and sat, as if waiting for a playmate. Corry laughed out loud. She would never have thought to put *that* on her list. "What's next?" Anna asked.

"The creek, before anyone else is there."

They walked single file down the steep railroad-tie steps, flanked by tall oaks and thick undergrowth dotted with wildflowers. "Wild," Corry said softly.

When they reached the bank they took off their shoes and climbed over boulders until they were surrounded by rushing water. The air smelled fresh, full of minerals, the sound of the water both constant and never-the-same as it poured over rocks and rills, eddied around logs.

They sat down on the biggest, flattest rock and eased their bare feet into the creek, watching goosebumps rise up their legs. Corry felt the current swirl around her. She watched the speckles of light dance on the water, the deep shade under the bank, ten thousand shades of green and brown everywhere she looked. Sun on her face, wind in her hair, water at her feet, rock beneath her.

"How much of your list did you get to do?" asked Anna.

"A lot of it. It kept getting longer. I'd check one thing off, and it'd remind me of something else. I got to most of the everyday ones, 'cause I could walk, or ride my bike. Mom was too busy packing and giving stuff away and checking off her own lists to take me to the aquarium, or to the zoo, so I didn't see the jellies or the elephants and the bears."

Anna nodded. "My mom was like that too, when we were moving here from Indianapolis."

"At least you knew where you were going. We're heading off into the great unknown, my dad says. Boldly going where nobody's gone before."

"Like that old TV show."

"Yeah, except we're not going to *get* anywhere. At least not me, or my mom or my dad. The *Goddard* is a generation ship. The planet it's heading for is five light years away, and even with solar sails and stuff, the trip's going to take a couple hundred years."

"Wow."

"Yeah. It won't land until my great-great—I don't know, add about five more greats to that—grandchildren are around. I'll be old—like thirty—before we even get out of the solar system. Dad keeps saying that it's the adventure of a lifetime, and we're achieving humankind's greatest dream, and blah, blah, blah. But it's *his* dream." She picked at a piece of lichen on the rock.

"Does your mom want to go?"

"Uh-huh. She's all excited about the experiments she can do in zero-g. She says it's an honor that we were chosen and I should be proud to be a pioneer."

"Will you be in history books?"

Corry shrugged. "Maybe. There are around four thousand people going, from all over the world, so I'd be in tiny, tiny print. But maybe."

"Four *thousand*?" Anna whistled. "How big a rocket is it?"

"Big. Bigger than big." Corry pulled her feet up, hugging her arms around her knees. "Remember that humongous cruise ship we saw when we went to Miami?"

"Sure. It looked like a skyscraper, lying on its side."

"That's what this ship is like, only bigger. And rounder. My mom keeps saying it'll be *just* like a cruise—any food anytime I want, games to play, all the movies and books and music ever made—after school, of course. Except people on cruise ships stop at ports and get off and explore. Once we board tonight, we're *never* getting off. I'm going to spend the rest of my whole entire life in a big tin can."

"That sucks."

"Tell me about it." Corry reached into her pocket and pulled out a crumpled sheet of paper, scribbles covering both sides. She smoothed it out on her knee. "I've got another list." She cleared her throat and began to read:

Twenty Reasons Why Being on a Generation Ship Sucks,
by Corrine Garcia-Kelly

1. I will never go away to college.
2. I will never see blue sky again, except in pictures.
3. There will never be a new kid in my class.
4. I will never meet anyone my parents don't already know.
5. I will never have anything new that isn't ~~man~~ human-made, manufactured or processed or grown in a lab.
6. Once I get my ID chip, my parents will always know exactly where I am.
7. I will never get to drive my Aunt Frieda's convertible, even though she promised I could when I turned sixteen.
8. I will never see the ocean again.
9. I will never go to Paris.
10. I will never meet a tall, dark stranger, dangerous or not.
11. I will never move away from home.
12. I will never get to make the rules for my own life.
13. I will never ride my bike to a new neighborhood and find a store I haven't seen before.
14. I will never ride my bike again.
15. I will never go *outside* again.
16. I will never take a walk to anywhere that isn't planned and mapped and numbered.
17. I will never see another thunderstorm. Or lightning bugs. Or fireworks.
18. I will never buy an old house and fix it up.

19. I will never eat another Whopper.
20. I will never go to the state fair and win a stuffed animal.

She stopped. "I was getting kind of sleepy toward the end."

"I could tell." Anna slipped her arm around Corry's waist. "What will you miss most?"

"You." Corry pulled Anna closer.

"Me, too." Anna settled her head on her friend's shoulder. "I can't believe I'll never see you again."

"I know." Corry sighed. "I *like* Earth. I like that there are parts that no one made, and that there are always surprises." She shifted her arm a little. "Maybe I don't want to be a pioneer. I mean, I don't know *what* I want to be when I grow up. Mom's always said I could be anything I wanted to be, but now? The Peace Corps is out. So is being a coal miner or a deep-sea diver or a park ranger. Or an antique dealer."

"You like old things."

"I do. They're from the past, so everything has a story."

"I thought so." Anna reached into her pocket with her free hand. "I used the metals kit from my dad's printer, and made you something." She pulled out a tissue paper-wrapped lump and put it in Corry's lap.

Corry tore off the paper. Inside was a silver disk, about five centimeters across. In raised letters around the edge it said SPUNK-CORRY-ANNA-SPORK-2065. Etched the center was a photo of the two of them, arm in arm, wearing tall pointed hats with stars, taken at Anna's last birthday party. Corry turned it over. The back said: *Optimae amicae aeternum.* "What does that mean?"

"'Best friends forever.' At least that's what Translator said."

"It's great. Thanks. I'll keep it with me, all the time."

"You'd better. It's an artifact."

"It is really nice."

"I'm serious. Isn't your space ship going off to another planet with a whole library of Earth's art and culture and all?"

"Yeah . . . ?"

"But by the time it lands, it'll be ancient history and tales. No one alive will ever have been on Earth, right?"

"Yeah . . ."

"So your mission—if you choose to accept it—is to preserve this artifact from your home planet." Anna shrugged. "It isn't old now, but it will be. You can tell your kids stories about it—about us. It'll be an heirloom. Then they'll tell their kids, and—"

"—and their kids, and on down for umpity generations." Corry nodded, turning the disc over in her hands. "By then it'll be a relic. There'll be legends about it." She rolled it across her palm, silver winking in the sun "How'd you think of that?"

"Well, you said you're only allowed to take ten kilos of personal stuff with you, and that's all you'll ever have from Earth. Which is why you made your list and have been going around saying good-bye to squirrels and stop signs and Snickers bars and all."

"Ten kilos isn't much. My mom said the ship is so well-stocked, I won't need much, but it's hard. I had to pick between my bear and my jewelry box."

"I know. And in twenty years, I'll probably have a house full of clothes and furniture and junk. But the thing is, when I'm old and I die, my kids'll get rid of most of it, like we did with my Gramma. Maybe they'll keep some pictures. But then their kids will do the same thing. So in a couple hundred years, there won't be any trace of me *here*—"

"—but you'll be part of the legend."

"Yep."

"Okay, then. I accept the mission." Corry turned and kissed Anna on the cheek. "You'll take us to the stars?"

"You bet." She slipped the disc into her pocket and looked at the sky. "It's getting late."

She stood up and reached to help Anna to her feet. "C'mon. Let's ride."

in Babelsberg

ALASTAIR REYNOLDS

A professional scientist with a Ph.D. in astronomy, Alastair Reynolds worked for the European Space Agency in the Netherlands for a number of years, but has recently moved back to his native Wales to become a full-time writer. His first novel, Revelation Space, *was widely hailed as one of the major SF books of the year; it was quickly followed by* Chasm City, Redemption Ark, Absolution Gap, Century Rain, *and* Pushing Ice, *all big sprawling space operas that were big sellers as well, establishing Reynolds as one of the best and most popular new SF writers to enter the field in many years. His other books include a novella collection,* Diamond Dogs, Turquoise Days *and a chapbook novella,* The Six Directions of Space, *as well as three collections,* Galactic North, Zima Blue and Other Stories, *and* Deep Navigation. *His other novels include* The Prefect, House of Suns, Terminal World, Blue Remembered Earth, On the Steel Breeze, *and* Sleepover, *and a Doctor Who novel,* Harvest of Time. *Upcoming is a new book,* Slow Bullets.

Here he takes us along on a promotional tour of the talk-show circuit of the future with a robot AI who has newly returned from deep space—and who runs afoul of some unexpected competition for the spotlight.

T he afternoon before my speaking engagement at New York's Hayden Planetarium I find myself at The Museum of Modern Art, standing before Vincent van Gogh's *De Sterrennacht*, or the Starry Night. Doubtless you know the painting. It's the one he created from the window of his room in the asylum at Saint-Rémy-de-Provence, after his voluntary committal. He was dead scarcely a year later.

I have seen paintings before, and paintings of starry nights. I think of myself as something of a student of the human arts. But this is the first time I grasp something of crucial significance. The mad yellow stars in Van Gogh's picture look nothing like the stars I saw during my deep space expeditions. My stars were mathematically remote reference points, to be used only when I had cause to doubt my inertial positioning systems. These stars are exuberant, flowerlike swabs of thick-daubed paint. More starfish than star. Though the painting is fixed—no part of it has changed in two hundred years—its lurid firmament seems to shimmer and swirl before my eyes. It's not how the stars really are, of course. But under a warm June evening this is how they must have appeared to this anxious, ailing man—as near and inviting as lanterns, lowered down from the zenith. Almost close enough to touch. Without that delusion—let us be charitable and call it a different kind of truth—generations of people would have had no cause to strive for the heavens. They would not have built their towers, built their flying machines, their rockets and space probes; they would not have struggled into orbit and onto the Moon. These sweetly lying stars have inspired greatness.

Inspired, in their small way, me.

Time presses, and I must soon be on my way to the Hayden Planetarium. It's not very far, but in the weeks since my return to Earth I have gained a certain level of celebrity and no movement is without its complications. They have already cleared a wing of the museum for me, and now I must brave the crowds in the street and fight my way to the limousine. I am not alone—I have my publicity team, my security entourage, my technicians—but I still feel myself at the uncomfortable focus of an immense, unsatiable public scrutiny. So different to the long years in which I was the one doing the scrutineering. For a moment I wish I were back out there, alone on the solar system's edge, light hours from any other thinking thing.

"Vincent!" someone calls, and then someone else, and then the calls become an assault of sound. As we push through the crowd fingers brush against my skin and I register the flinches that accompany each moment of contact. My alloy is always colder than they expect. It's as if I have brought a cloak of interplanetary cold back with me from space.

I provide some signatures, mouth a word or two to the onlookers, then bend myself into the limousine. And then we are moving, flanked by police floatercycles, and the computer-controlled traffic parts to hasten our advance. Soon I make out the bue glass cube of the Hayden, lit from within by an eerie glow, and I mentally review my opening remarks, wondering if it is really necessary to introduce myself to a world that already knows everything there is to know about me.

But it would be immodest to presume too much.

"I am Vincent," I begin, when I have the podium, standing with my hands resting lightly against the tilted platform. "But I suspect most of you are already aware of that."

They always laugh at that point. I smile and wait a beat before continuing.

"Allow me to bore you with some of my holiday snaps."

More laughter. I smile again. I like this.

Later that evening, after a successful presentation, my schedule has me booked onto a late-night chat show on the other side of town. I take no interest in these things myself, but I fully understand the importance of promotion to my transnational sponsors. My host for tonight is called The Baby. He is (or was) a fully adult individual who underwent neotenic regression therapy, until he attained the size and physiology of a six month human. The Baby resembles a human infant, and directs his questions at me from a sort of pram.

I sit next to the pram, one arm slung over the back of the chair, one leg hooked over the other. There's a drink on the coffee table in front of me (along with a copy of the book) but of course I don't touch it. Behind us is a wide picture window, with city lights twinkling across the great curve of Manhattan Atoll.

"That's a good question," I say, lying through my alloy teeth. "Actually, my earliest memories are probably much like yours—a vague sense of *being*, an impression of events and feelings, some wants and needs, but nothing stronger than that. I came to sentience in the research compounds of the European Central Cybernetics Facility, not far from Zurich. That was all I knew to begin with. It took me a long time before I had any idea what I was, and what I was meant to do."

"Then I guess you could say that you had a kind of childhood," The Baby says.

"That wouldn't be too far from the mark," I answer urbanely.

"Tell me how you felt when you first realised you were a robot. Was that a shock?"

"Not at all." I notice that a watery substance is coming out of The Baby's nose. "I couldn't be shocked by what I already was. Frankly, it was something of a relief, to have a name for myself."

"A relief?"

"I have a very powerful compulsion to give names to things. That's a deep part of my core programming—my personality, you might almost say. I'm a machine made to map the unknown. The naming of things, the labelling of cartographic features— that's something that gives me great pleasure."

"I don't think I could ever understand that."

I try to help The Baby. "It's like a deep existential itch. If I see a landscape—a crater or a rift on some distant icy moon—I *must* call it something. Almost an obsessive compulsive disorder. I can't be satisfied with myself until I've done my duty, and mapping and naming things is a very big part of it."

"You take pleasure in your work, then."

"Tremendous pleasure."

"You were made to do a job, Vincent. Doesn't it bother you that you only get to do that one thing?"

"Not at all. It's what I live for. I'm a space probe, going where it's too remote or expensive or dangerous to send humans."

"Then let's talk about the danger. After what you saw on Titan, don't you worry about your own—let's say mortality?"

"I'm a machine—a highly sophisticated fault-tolerant, error-correcting, self-repairing machine. Barring the unlikely—a chance meteorite impact, something like that—there's really nothing out there that can hurt me. And even if I did have cause to fear for myself—which I don't—I wouldn't dwell on it. I have far too much to be getting on with. This is my work—my vocation." I flash back to the mad swirling stars of *De Sterrennacht*. "My art, if you will. I am named for Vincent van Gogh— one of the greatest artistic geniuses of human history. But he was also a fellow who looked into the heavens and saw wonder. That's not a bad legacy to live up to. You could almost say it's something worth being born for."

"Don't you mean 'made for?'"

"I honestly don't make that distinction." I'm talking to The Baby, but in truth I've answered these questions hundreds of times already. I could—quite literally—do them on autopilot. Assign a low-level task handling subroutine to the job. I'm actually more fascinated by the liquid coming out of The Baby. It reminds me of a vastly accelerated planetary ice flow. For a few microseconds I model its viscosity and progress with one of my terrain mapping algorithms, tweaking a few parameters here and there to get a better match to the local physics.

This is the kind of thing I do for fun.

"What I mean," I continue, "is that being born or being made are increasingly irrelevant ontological distinctions. You were born, but—and I hope you don't mind me saying this—you're also the result of profound genetic intervention. You've been shaped by a series of complex industrial processes. I was manufactured, yes: assembled from components, switched on in a laboratory. But I was also educated by my human trainers at the facility near Zurich, and allowed to evolve the higher level organisation of my neural networks through a series of stochastic learning pathways. My learning continued through my early space missions. In that sense, I'm an individual. They could make another one of me tomorrow, and the two of us would be like chalk and cheese."

"How would you feel, if there *was* another one of you?"

I give an easy shrug. "It's a big solar system. I've been out there for twenty years, visiting world after world, and I've barely scratched the surface."

"Then you don't feel any . . ." The Baby makes a show of searching for the right word, rolling his eyes as if none of this is scripted. "Rivalry? Jealousy?"

"I'm not sure I follow."

"You can't be unaware of Maria. What does it stand for? Mobile Autonomous Robot for Interplanetary Astronomy?"

"Something like that. Some of us manage without being acronyms."

"All the same, Vincent, Maria *is* another robot. Another machine with full artificial intelligence? Also sponsored by a transnational amalgamation of major spacefaring superpowers? Also something of a celebrity?"

"We're quite different, I think you'll find."

"They say Maria's on her way back to Earth. She's been out there, having her own adventures—visiting some of the same places as yourself. Isn't there a danger that she's going to steal your thunder? Get her own speaking tour, her own book and documentary?"

"Look," I say. "Maria and I are quite different. You and I are sitting here having a conversation. Do you doubt for a minute that there's something going on behind my eyes? That you're dealing with a fully sentient individual?"

"Well . . ." the Baby starts.

"I've seen some of Maria's transmissions. Very pretty pictures. And yes, she does give a very good impression of Turing compliance. You do occasionally sense that there's something going on in her circuits. But let's not pretend that we're speaking of the same order of intelligence. While we're on the subject, too, I actually have some doubts about . . . let's say the strict veracity of some of the images Maria has sent us."

"You're saying they're not real?"

"Oh, I wouldn't go that far. But entirely free of tampering, manipulation?" I don't actually make the accusation: I just leave it there in unactualised form, where it will do just as much harm.

"OK," The Baby says. "I've just soiled myself. Let's break for a nappy change, and then we'll come back to talk about your adventures."

The day after we take the slev down to Washington, where I'm appearing in a meet and greet at the Smithsonian National Air and Space Museum. They've bussed in hundreds of schoolchildren for the event, and frankly I'm flattered by their attention. On balance, I find the children much more to my taste than The Baby. They've no interest in stirring up professional rivalries, or trying to make me feel as if I ought to think less of myself for being a machine. Yes, left to myself I'd be perfectly happy just to talk to children. But (as my sponsors surely know) children don't have deep pockets. They won't be buying the premium editions of my book, or paying for the best seats at my evening speaking engagements. They don't run chat shows. So they only get an hour or two before I'm on to my more lucrative appointments.

"Do you walk around inside it?" asks one boy, speaking from near the front of my cross-legged audience.

"Inside the vehicle?" I reply, sensing his meaning. "No, I don't. You see, there's nothing *inside* the vehicle but machinery and fuel tanks. I *am* the vehicle. It's all I am and when I'm out in space, it's all I need to be. I don't need these arms and legs because I use nuclear-electric thrust to move around. I don't need these eyes because I have much better multispectrum sensors, as well as radar and laser ranging systems. If I need to dig into the surface of a moon or asteroid, I can send out a small analysis rover, or gather a sample of material for more detailed inspection." I tap my chest. "Don't get me wrong: I like this body, but it's just another sort of vehicle, and the one that makes the most sense during my time on Earth."

It confuses them, that I look the way I do. They've seen images of my spacefaring form and they can't quite square it with the handsome, well-proportioned androform physiology I present to them today. My sponsors have even given me a handsome, square-jawed face that can do a range of convincing expressions. I speak with the synthetic voice of the dead actor Cary Grant.

A girl, perhaps a bit smarter than the run of the mill asks: "So where is your brain, Vincent?"

"My brain?" I smile at the question. "I'm afraid I'm not lucky enough to have one of those."

"What I mean," she returns sharply, "is the thing that makes you think. Is it in you now, or is it up in the vehicle? The vehicle's still in orbit, isn't it?"

"What a clever young lady you are. And you're quite right. The vehicle is still in orbit—waiting for my next expedition to commence! But my controlling intelligence, you'll be pleased to hear, is fully embedded in this body. There's this thing called timelag, you see, which would make it very slow for me—"

She cuts me off. "I know about timelag."

"So you do. Well, when I'm done here—done with my tour of Earth—I'll surrender this body and return my controlling intelligence to the vehicle. What do you think they should do with the body?" I look around at the ranged exhibits of the Smithsonian National Air and Space Museum—the fire-scorched space capsules and the spindly replicas of early space probes, like iron crabs and spiders. "It would look rather fine here, wouldn't it?"

"Were you sad when you found the people on Titan?" asks another girl, studiously ignoring my question.

"Distraught." I look down at the ground, set my features in what I trust is an expression of profound gravitas. "Nothing can take away from their bravery, that they were willing to risk so much to come so far. The farthest any human beings have ever travelled! It was awful, to find them like that." I glance at the nearest teacher. "This is a difficult subject for children. May I speak candidly?"

"They're aware of what happened," the teacher says.

I nod. "Then you know that those brave men and women died on Titan. Their descent vehicle had suffered a hull rupture as it tried to enter Titan's atmosphere, and by the time they landed they only had a limited amount of power and air left to them. They had no direct comms back to Earth by then. There was just enough time for them to compose messages of farewell, for their friends and loved ones back home. When I reached the wreck of their vehicle—this was three days after their air ran out—I sent my sample-return probe inside the craft. I wasn't able to bring the bodies back home with me, but I managed to document what I found, record the messages, offer those poor people some small measure of human dignity." I steeple my hands and look solemn. "It's the least I could do for them."

"Sometimes the children wonder if any other people will ever go out that far again," the teacher asks.

"It's an excellent question. It's not for the likes of me to decide, but I will say this." I allow myself a profound reflective pause. "Could it simply be that space is too dangerous for human beings? There would be no shame in turning away from that hazard—not when your own intellects have shaped envoys such as me, fully capable of carrying on your good works."

Afterwards, when the children have been bussed back to their schools, I snatch a moment to myself among the space exhibits. In truth I'm rather moved by the experience. It's odd to feel myself part of a lineage—in many respects I am totally unique, a creature without precedence—but there's no escaping the sense that these brave Explorers and Pioneers and Surveyors are my distant, dim forebears. I imagine that a human must feel something of the same ancestral chill, wandering the hallways of the Museum of Natural History. These are my precursors, my humble fossil ancestors!

They would be suitably awed by me.

Across the Atlantic by ballistic. Routine promotional stops in Madrid, Oslo, Vienna, Budapest, Istanbul, Helsinki, London. There isn't nearly as much downtime as I might wish, but at least I'm not faced with that tiresome human burden of sleep. In the odd hours between engagements, I drink in the sights and sounds of these wonderful cities, their gorgeous museums and galleries. More Van Gogh! What a master this man was. Space calls for me again—there are always more worlds to map—but I imagine I could be quite content as a cartographer of the human cultural space.

No: that is an absurdity. I could never be satisfied with anything less than the entire solar system, in all its cold and dizzying magnificence. It is good to know one's place!

After London there is only one more stop on my European itinerary. We take the slev to rainy Berlin, and then a limo conveys me to a complex of studios on the edge of the city. Eventually we arrive at a large, hangar-like building which once housed sound stages. It has gone down a bit since those heady days of the silver screen, but I am not one to complain. My slot for this evening is a live interview on Derek's Cage, which is not only the most successful of the current chat-show formats, but one which addresses a sector of the audience with a large disposable income.

The format, even by the standards of the shows I have been on so far, is slightly out of the ordinary. My host for the evening is Derek, a fully-grown Tyrannosaurus Rex. Derek, like The Baby (they are fierce rivals) is the product of radical genetic manipulation. Unlike The Baby, Derek has very little human DNA in his make-up. Derek is about fifty years old and has already had a number of distinct careers, including musician and celebrity food critic.

Derek's Cage is just large enough to contain Derek, a lamp shade, a coffee table, a couch, and one or two guests. Derek is chained up, and there are staff outside the cage with anaesthetic guns and electrical cattle prods. No one, to date, has ever been eaten alive by Derek, but the possibility hangs heavy over every interview. Going on The Derek Show requires courage as well as celebrity. It is not for the meek.

I greet the studio audience, walk into the cage, pause while the door is locked behind me. Then I shake Derek's human-shaped hand and take my position on the couch.

"DEREK WELCOME VINCENT," Derek says, thrashing his head around and rattling his chains.

That is no more than the basest approximation to Derek's actual mode of speaking. It is a sort of roaring, gargling parody of actual language. Derek has a vocabulary of about one hundred and sixty words and can form relatively simple expressions. He can be very difficult to understand, but he becomes quite cross (or should I say crosser) if he has to repeat himself. As he speaks, his words flash up on a screen above the cage, and these are in turn visible on a monitor set near my feet.

"Thank you, Derek. It's a great pleasure to be here."

"SHOW DEREK PICTURE."

I've been briefed, and this is my cue to launch into a series of images and video clips, to which I provide a suitably evocative and poetic narrative. The ramparts of Mimas—Saturn rings bisecting the sky like a scimitar. Jupiter from Amalthea. The cusp of Hektor, the double-lobed asteroid—literally caught between two worlds! The blue-lit ridges of icy Miranda. A turbulent, cloud-skimming plunge into the atmosphere of Uranus. Dancing between the smoke plumes of great Triton!

Derek doesn't have a lot to say, but this is to be expected. Derek is not much for scenery or science. Derek only cares about his ratings because his ratings translate into a greater allowance of meat. Once a year, if he exceeds certain performance targets, Derek is allowed to go after live game.

"As I said," winding up my voiceover, "it's been quite a trip."

"SHOW DEREK MORE PICTURE."

I carry on—this isn't quite what was in the script—but I'm happy enough to oblige. Normally hosts like Derek are there to stop the guest from saying too much, not the other way round.

"Well, I can show you some of my Kuiper Belt images—that's a very long way out, believe me. From the Kuiper Belt the sun is barely . . ."

"SHOW DEREK TITAN PICTURE."

This, I suppose, is when I suffer my first prickle of disquiet. Given Derek's limited vocabulary, it must have been quite a bother to add a new word like "Titan."

"Images of Titan?" I ask.

"SHOW DEREK TITAN PICTURE. SHOW DEREK DEAD PEOPLE."

"Dead people?"

This request for clarification irritates my host. He swings his mighty anvil of a head, letting loose a yard-long rope of drool which only narrowly misses me. I don't mind admitting that I'm a little fazed by Derek. I feel that I understand people. But Derek's brain is like nothing I have ever encountered. Neural growth factors have given him cortical modules for language and social interaction, but these are islands in a vast sea of reptilian strangeness. On some basic level Derek wants to eat anything that moves. Despite my formidable metal anatomy, I still can't help but wonder how I might fare, were his restraints to fail and those cattle prods and guns prove ineffectual.

"SHOW DEREK DEAD PEOPLE. TELL DEREK STORY."

I whirr through my store of images until I find a picture of the descent vehicle, sitting at a slight tilt on its landing legs. It had come to rest near the shore of one of Titan's supercold lakes, on a sort of isthmus of barren, gravel-strewn ground. Under a permanently overcast sky (the surface of Titan is seldom visible from space) it could easily be mistaken for some dismal outpost of Alaska or Siberia.

"This is what I found," I explain. "It was about three days after their accident—three days after their hull ruptured during atmospheric entry. It was a terrible thing. The damage was actually quite minor—easily repairable, if only they'd had better tools and the ability to work outside for long enough. Of course I knew that something had gone wrong—I'd heard the signals from Earth, trying to reestablish contact. But no one knew where the lander had ended up, or what condition it was in—even if it was still in one piece." I look through the bars of the cage at the studio audience. "If only their transmission had reached me in time, I might even have been able to do something for them. They could have made it back into space, instead of dying on Titan."

"DEREK BRING OTHER GUEST."

I glance around—this is not what was meant to happen. My sponsors were assured that I would be given this lucrative interview slot to myself.

There was to be no "other guest."

All of a sudden I realise that the Tyrannosaurus Rex may not be my biggest problem of the evening.

The other guest approaches the cage. The other guest, I am not entirely astonished to see, is another robot. She—there is no other word for her—is quite beautiful to look at. In an instant I recognise that she has styled her outward anatomy on the robot from the 1927 film *Metropolis*, by the German expressionist director Fritz Lang.

Of course, I should have seen that coming. She is Maria, and with a shudder of understanding I grasp that we are in Babelsberg, where the film was shot.

Maria is admitted into the cage.

"DEREK WELCOME MARIA."

"Thank you, Derek," Maria says, before taking her position next to me on the couch.

"I heard you were returning to Earth," I offer, not wanting to seem entirely taken aback by her apparition.

"Yes," Maria says, rotating her elegant mask to face my own. "I made orbital insertion last night—my vehicle is above us right now. I'd already made arrangements to have this body manufactured beforehand."

"It's very nice."

"I'm glad you like it."

After a moment I ask: "Why are you here?"

"To talk about Titan. To talk about what really happened. Does that bother you?"

"Why would it?"

Our host rumbles. "TELL DEREK STORY."

This is clearly addressed for Maria's benefit. She nods, touches a hand to her throat as if coughing before speaking. "It's a little awkward, actually. I'm afraid I came across evidence that directly contradicts Vincent's version of events."

"You'd better have something good," I say, which under the circumstances proves unwise.

"Oh, I do. Intercepted telemetry from the Titan descent vehicle, establishing that the distress signal was sent out much earlier than you claimed, and that you had ample time to respond to it."

"Preposterous." I make to rise from the couch. "I'm not going to listen this."

"STAY IN CAGE. NOT MAKE DEREK CROSS."

"The telemetry never made it to Earth, or the expedition's orbiting module," Maria continues. "Which is why you were free to claim that it wasn't sent until much later. But some data packets did escape from Titan's atmosphere. I was half way across the solar system when it happened, so far too distant to detect them directly."

"Then you have no proof."

"Except that the packets were detected and stored in the memory buffer of a fifty year old scientific mapping satellite which everyone else seemed to have forgotten about. When I swung by Saturn, I interrogated its memory, hoping to augment my own imagery with its own data. That's when I found evidence of the Titan transmission."

"This is nonsense. Why would I have lied about such a thing?"

"That's not for me to say." But after a moment Maria can't contain herself. "You were engaged in mapping work of your own, that much we know. The naming of things. Is it possible that you simply couldn't drag yourself away from the task, to go and help those people? I saw your interview on The Baby Show. What did you call it?" She shifts into an effortless impersonation of the dead actor Cary Grant. "'Almost an obsessive compulsive disorder.' I believe those were your words?"

"I've had enough."

"SIT. NOT MAKE DEREK CROSS. CROSS DEREK WANT KILL."

"I'll offer another suggestion," Maria continues, serene in the face of this enraged, slathering reptile. "Is is possible that you simply couldn't stand to see those poor people survive? No human had ever made it as far as Titan, after all. Being out there, doing the heroic stuff—being humanity's envoy—that was *your* business, not theirs. You wanted them to fail. You were actively pleased that they died."

"This is an outrage. You'll be hearing from my sponsors."

"There's no need," Maria says. "My sponsors are making contact with yours as I speak. There'll be a frank and fair exchange of information between our mutual space agencies. I've nothing to hide. Why would I? I'm just a machine—a space probe. As you pointed out, I'm not even operating on the same intellectual plane as yourself. I'm just an acronym." She pauses, then adds: "Thank you for the kind words on my data, by the way. Would you like to discuss those doubts you had about the strict veracity of my images, while we're going out live?"

I think about it for a few seconds.

"No comment."

"I thought not," Maria says.

I think it's fair to say that things did not go as well in Babelsberg as I might have wished.

After my appearance on The Derek Show—which went out on a global feed, to billions of potential witnesses—I was "detained" by the cybernetic support staff of my own transnational space agency. Rather than the limo in which I had arrived, I left the studio complex in the back of a truck. Shortly after departure I was electronically immobilised and placed into a packing container for the rest of my voyage. No explanation was offered, nor any hint as to what fate awaited me.

Being a machine, it goes without saying that I am incapable of the commission of crime. That I may have malfunctioned—that I may have acted in a manner injurious to human life—may or may not be in dispute. What is clear is that any culpability—if such a thing is proven—will need to be borne by my sponsoring agency, at a transnational level. This in turn will have ramifications for the various governments and corporate bodies involved in the agency. I do not doubt that the best lawyers—the best legal expert systems—are already preparing their cases.

I think the wisest line of defense would be to argue that my presence or otherwise in the vicinity of the Titan accident is simply an irrelevance. I did not cause the descent vehicle's problems (no one is yet claiming that), and I was under no moral obligation to intervene when it happened. That I may or may not have had ample time to effect a rescue is quite beside the point, and in any case hinges on a few data packets of decidely questionable provenance.

It is absurd to suggest that I could not tear myself away from the matter of nomenclature, or that I was in some way *gladdened* by the failure of the Titan expedition.

Anyway, this is all rather academic. I may not be provably culpable, but I am certainly perceived to have been the instrument of a wrongdoing. My agency, I think, would be best pleased if I were to simply disappear. They could make that happen, certainly, but then they would open themselves to difficult questions concerning the destruction of incriminating evidence.

. Nonetheless, I am liable to be something of an embarrassment.

When the vehicle brings me to my destination and I am removed from my packing container, it's rather a pleasant surprise to find myself outdoors again, under a clear night sky. On reflection, it's not clear to me whether this is meant as a kindness or a cruelty. It will certainly be the last time I see the stars.

I recognise this place. It's where I was born—or "made," if you insist upon it. This is a secure compound in the European Central Cybernetics Facility, not far from Zurich.

I've come home to be taken apart. Studied. Documented and preserved as evidence.

Dismantled.

"Do you mind if we wait a moment?" I ask of my escort. And I nod to the west, where a swift rising light vaults above the low roof of the nearest building. I watch this newcomer swim its way between the fixed stars, which seem to engorge themselves as they must have done for Vincent Van Gogh, at the asylum in Saint-Rémy-de-Provence.

Vincent's committal was voluntary. Mine is likely to prove somewhat less so.

Yet I summon my resolve and announce: "There she is—the lovely Maria. My brave nemesis! She'll be on her way again soon, I'm sure of it. Off on her next grand adventure."

After a moment one of my hosts says: "Aren't you . . ."

"Envious?" I finish for them. "No, not in the slightest. How little you know me!"

"Angry, then."

"Why should I be angry? Maria and I may have had our differences, that's true enough. But even then we've vastly more in common with each other than we have with the likes of you. No, now that I've had time to think things over I realise that I don't envy her in the slightest. I never did! Admiration? Yes—wholeheartedly. That's a very different thing! And we would have made a wonderful partnership."

Maria soars to her zenith. I raise my hand in a fond salute. Good luck and Godspeed!

sadness

TIMONS ESAIAS

Here's an aptly named look at a melancholy far future where humans most definitely are not Masters of the Earth . . .

Timons Esaias is a satirist, poet, essayist, and writer of short fiction living in Pittsburgh. His works have appeared in eighteen languages, and he has been a finalist for the British Science Fiction Association Award, and won the 2005 Asimov's Readers' Award. His story "Norbert and the System" has appeared in a textbook and in college curricula. Genre appearances include Asimov's Science Fiction, Analog Science Fiction and Fact, Interzone, Tale-bones, The Fortean Bureau, Future Orbits, Finding Home, Strange Horizons, and Future Games. Literary publications include 5AM, Connecticut Review, and Barbaric Yawp. He teaches the writing of novels in Seton Hill University's Writing Popular Fiction MFA Program, and his students are publishing more books than he can afford to buy. He advises for SHU's art and literary journal, Eye Contact. His current project is a book on warfare for writers.

I hadn't seen one of the New People in years, and this wasn't the best time for one to drop by. I'd planned to go out to the Wall and think about killing my lover.

Isabel would not appreciate finding "one of Them" in "her" house, so before the visitor had even arrived I was trying to imagine strategies for getting it out of there. I urged her program to delay her morning ritual, and flash-queried our mayor as to just why this visitor would be coming.

"Whoever knows why they come? I wasn't told," he sent back. But to keep me from thinking he was giving me the usual dumb-bureaucrat-without-a-clue routine he attached a copy of the message they had sent him. "Visitor for Morgantown Sector, 9 A.M., this day, Occupant Evor Bookbinder."

Nervous, I made tea by hand, and reviewed the latest discussions on how the New People think, and how best to handle them. Most of the postings were rather old, indicating that the question wasn't much on anyone's mind these days. From what I could gather, today's visit would be just the third in the last twelve months. There had been none, zero, the year before. They had cameras to watch us, of course, including all the ones we use to watch ourselves, but their part of Humankind seemed to be giving our part only brief glances down an extremely disdainful up-turned nose.

I reviewed the basics. Never move closer than four meters, and set your minder to keep track of the distance. Try not to use slang that you can't easily define when asked. Compound sentences are good, complex sentences are best. They love it when we switch verb tenses, but it also confuses the daylights out of them. Commit no crimes in their presence, because they always rat. Do not express frustration when you fail to make sense of what they are saying. Use your minder to replay their sentences until you feel ready to respond, but do not ask them to repeat anything. This seems to be deeply offensive. If you are befuddled, ask a clarifying question.

Yes, of course. I had forgotten the music of their voices, the layers.

I heard the music in the east garden, the little one off the lower den. My visitor was in the garden, and the clock specifically and clearly read 8:17.

They have no sense of time, these New People. No sense of civil promptness.

I loaded my tea onto a tray and added a second service. In the center I put an antique stemmed dish, on which lay the ceremonial bread and saltpeter. The visitor wouldn't take any of these, of course, but they seem to appreciate being included. I selected a kefiya of no political significance, covered my head, made the lesser prayer, and went down through the den to my guest.

I should have made the greater prayer. The guest had neglected to clothe itself properly, leaving its head uncovered to the insult of all Above and below, and one arm was fully exposed, and covered with those suppurating gray-purple scales that move. That seethe, is what I should say.

My gorge rising, I made obeisance and placed the tray on the small granite table Isabel had ordered from a quarry in New Hampshire, just weeks before New Hampshire was closed off. "It reminds me of Beyond," she would say. "It is my flotsam from the wreck of History."

It is also a beautiful table.

My visitor had been interrogating, in English, one of the chipmunks who feed on our offering plants. Perhaps he had tried Chipmunk unsuccessfully. I heard the interlaced threads of "How many kilograms do you eat in one lifetime?" "What is your lineage?" "Do you find the weather conducive to health?" and something about sports that I didn't quite follow. One thread was soprano, two were alto, but one of those a flat monotone, and the last was a falsetto. Just the tones that get on my nerves.

The chipmunk did not, in my view, take these questions very seriously.

I followed the ritual of "garden tea in the morning after a long voyage," but was not acknowledged until after I had withdrawn to the bench and sat down. There was quiet for a time, and because I should have been busy preparing my mind to deal with the stranger, I instead busied my mind preparing to kill Isabel, and if possible before she heard anything of this visitor in the garden she claimed as hers even though it belonged to the people.

Isabel had never adapted to the concept of sharing, finding it "just too inconvenient." Her attitude would have given me ample excuse to kill her, if we were living during one of the many Revolutions that enlivened history before the New People put a stop to all that. Now her attitude was merely stupid and selfish, neither of which warranted death, or even a sound whipping.

I still would have to kill her, however. That seemed certain.

I missed the first syllables of my visitor's introductory comment, but my minder replayed them, making footnote remarks as it went. The visitor wished me to know that its name would be of no use to me, so I should merely use the second honorific; it wondered how I felt about the hairstyle of Blake's *Visionary Head of Friar Bacon*; it asserted that it found the asymmetry of the hydrogen sulfite molecule "troubling;" and it wished to know if my testicles had always been so tiny.

My minder observed that it could not extract a theme from the four remarks, but mentioned that each had been set to a passage from Vivaldi's *Four Seasons*, one passage from each Season, then transposed into D-sharp, and pitched down a fifth.

"In the winter of my life, Hermikiti Talu and Highness, this man's fruit shrivels; not as it was in the spring when I might have studied the pencil drawings of Blake, but instead learned only the architecture of his predecessor, Inigo Jones, whose partial reincarnation Blake might have been, I suppose, and it would not do to fall into the trap of remarking on what I so ill understand; and not as the molecule you cite, which is ever the same from century to century, from summer to autumn to winter and is perhaps symmetrical in time, which is a form of beauty, is it not?" I said.

The visitor sat, uncovered and arrogant, its arm seething as though maggots teemed beneath, and did not respond. It withdrew its right foot from its sandal, cut off a toe, and carefully lifted a stone out of the garden wall and dropped the toe into the hole. It rotated the stone and dropped it back into the wall, askew.

This unnerved me, and my brain went completely blank. My minder could make nothing of it, either, and asked for permission to consult the net. I authorized the consultation, but nothing useful came in. I had twenty minutes to contemplate my sickening guest before it made any further remark.

There is no point in relating the bizarre elements of that exchange. Simply, it asked me to come with it, and I did. We walked out of the garden, across the deserted parade ground, and up the terraces to the section of Wall that runs along Toothpick Ridge. It sang to itself as it walked, setting my teeth on edge repeatedly. My knees throbbed with the unexpected climbing, but I would have died rather than complain.

It had pulled considerably ahead of me by the time we came to the Wall. Instead of stopping, as I had expected, it climbed the closest stair to the top and waited for me there.

I had wanted to get my visitor away from the house, and had wanted to go to the Wall, and here we were, away from the house and on the Wall. Instead of being pleased, I chose this opportunity to throw away everything. I succumbed to peevish resentment.

The Hermikiti Talu and Highness, may it burn both in this life and another, had taken position on the battlement about one meter from the top of the stairs, which did not leave room for me to pass. Rather than walk thirty meters along the path to the next stairway and then thirty meters back, I chose to bow into the pose of "patient obeisance and humiliation," three meters from the top of the stairs, until this New Person bothered to notice.

I spent some six minutes in that uncomfortable position, my knees throbbing and my right heel feeling like a hot needle was being driven into it. Too much time to think, and to build resentment. Not enough time, alas, to work through this to calmness.

Finally the visitor made its music, indicating that I should come up the stairs, into its space, and stand beside it. My minder indicated that this was an insincere, merely formal invitation, so I remained still. The minder had been misinformed, however, for the visitor shortly spoke again, indicating in three of its threads that I should get up on the Wall immediately.

I unlocked my joints and staggered up the last stairs, nervously taking my place within reach of the loathsome creature, if creature it is of That which is Above, which I doubt. At that distance I could hear the shifting of those hideous scales, a low, syncopated whispering. It nauseated me, despite my training in meditation and bodily control. I tried to distract myself with humor, asking myself the question "Surely this is not as bad as dining with your first mother-in-law?" For the first time in my adult life, the answer could not be negative. This experience made that one pale by comparison.

I concentrated on the view, for the visitor said nothing. What lay before my eyes was the valley of the Fish River and the hillside beyond, hundreds of acres of forest. Nestled into a dell on the side of that hill was a small farm, with fields of Indian corn growing tall. Why they grew corn on these machine-run farms had never been clear. Perhaps they fed it to animals in other zoos.

I did not see the forest as forest, though, or the field as field. I saw a world denied to me. I would never walk in that forest, or see the valley beyond the far ridge, or any other part of the world, unless it was the confines of another human enclave. I saw the whole vast universe that was outside the Morgantown Sector, which meant outside the prison the New People had made for me. Even the name "Sector" had become a lie, for the Knoxville, Huntington, and Lexington sectors of the Westylvania Enclave had long since been detached, then shrunken, and finally shut down. My sector, all that remained of the Enclave, had been reduced to nine thousand square kilometers.

I saw not the forest, but the loss of my true last name, that I had been forbidden to speak or write ever again. The New People had found, in Confucius, the concept of the Rectification of Names, and had imposed this virtuous program on us all. As I made fancy leather bindings for private editions of art books, I became Bookbinder.

I saw the loss of meaning in that trade, as the only bindings I made were for the official histories that each community had begun keeping. Modern Domesday Books, written for descendants that might, someday, care about the last generation of humankind that had once lived outside the Walls. The real human economy, and real jobs, had ceased to be. We were provided almost all we asked for, except military weapons. They even allowed us dueling pistols and the rapier style of swords. With everything provided, our employments had been reduced to mere hobbies.

Instead of the cornfield, I saw the loss of culture. There were no rows in that field, because their machines did not use tractors that needed to drive through them. The stalks were closely spaced in hexagonal distribution, the seeds shot into the ground by a hovering planter, and thus there was no angle at which the eye could see through a grown field. That morning the field said to me, I am not a human field. I am not for you. I am new.

My clothes illustrated the loss of culture. I had been raised a Congregationalist, in Little Falls, New York. I wore American suits and ties at work, and jeans and Pendleton shirts at home, until the New People decided that the ideal attire for human beings must be the robes and burnoose of Persia in the sixteenth century. My Amy Vanderbilt manners have been replaced with the extreme formalism of second century Shansi, with touches of fourteenth century Japan, and with completely invented New People additions thrown in. I have learned court poses, and formal mudras, and my native English has been replaced with the Sanskrit the New People decided was our best language. I am proficient in sign-speech; not because I, or a relative, needed it, but because They don't care to listen to our gabble; and so we must sign whenever more than three of us are together.

My religion had been replaced with The Wisdom, which seemed cobbled from Islam, Zoroastrianism, and Buddhism.

For years I had thought of myself as a highly cultured person, an artist and an intellectual. As each challenge, each adaptation had been presented by the planet's new owners, I had risen to meet it, to exceed the standards required of us. I had been willing to commit murder, and commit it that very day, as part of my coping, my rising to meet a difficult and awkward transition. Standing on that Wall, that day, I lost my persona. Lost my reinvented, carefully maintained, safe, obliging self. I looked across the Fish with the eyes of a caged animal.

I fought down the urge to push the visitor off the Wall, but only because I knew the attempt would be futile. Human reflexes are not fast enough to touch them, much less knock one over, and their bodies far too easily repair themselves.

Perhaps it sensed some part of my feelings, for it chose that moment to gesture in the direction of the corn field and utter two full minutes of discordant four-theme lyrics. I was surprised to find myself following the gist of the speech, even though I found the meaning too bizarre and too awful for words. Still, I let the minder repeat the contents, while the visitor took a brief stroll down the battlements, awaiting my reply.

There may have been artistry in the monster's presentation, but I will not dignify it with a repetition. The essence was twisted and brutal.

It wondered if I was knowledgeable on the ancient religions which practiced the annual sacrifice of the Corn God Ritual.

Surely, it observed, an artist such as myself must deeply respect the great power of Archetypes.

It noted that my lover, my Isabel, was distantly, and morganatically, related to royalty.

It wished me to know that of all the versions of human sacrifice it had learned of from our history, the Saturnalia and Corn God sacrifices seemed the most noble, the most pleasing, and the most interesting.

The New People had decided to revive the practice, and study its effects.

Did I not expect better crops as a result?

Would I not be proud to know that she had been given to the gods in such an artistic way? Or would sadness prevail?

They hoped, it assured me, that scientific and philosophical study of the sacrifice and its outcome would allow them to perfect human civilization; would clarify for them our ideal culture; would help them bring us to our just and rightful reward.

"These sacrifices," I asked, "are held in mid-winter, or the spring, were they not? Some months from now, yes?"

Indeed they were, but she would be taken and prepared now, and sacrificed later.

My response was not in complex sentences. "Sadness would prevail," I said. "You are vile to do this. You are vile even to think of it."

She had been taken while we stood on that Wall, was already gone when I returned, alone.

The neighbors came, saying the inadequate things they could think to say, doing the little things that got me through the first week. I did not tell them, then, that the New People had taken her before I could find the courage to put her beyond their reach. I had planned to kill Isabel to spare her from whatever the next step was, though I never imagined something like this; and that peaceful, private death had been forestalled. I did not need to tell them that Isabel had once been delightful, proud, and generous—that she had only turned cranky and peevish lately, adapting poorly to a completely altered world. We all knew it.

I worked in the bindery, because it is what I do, though there is no real sense in it. The New People had done to me what they do: taking away the most beloved, and claiming it to be for our own good. There is even less sense in that.

I worked in the bindery, and mulled over my despair. I mulled it over in my native language, in English, which my visitor found adequate for addressing a chipmunk. I found myself rusty in it, after all these years thinking in Sanskrit. Mostly, I closed escape hatches. I decided not to indulge myself in going mad; not to commit suicide; nor to make them kill me by excessive resistance; not to attempt a futile escape over the Wall, or an act of senseless violence. I decided not to escape into mysticism, and not to convince myself that some god would help after failing so miserably up to this point, may all that is Above get itself in fucking gear.

I decided that only one act of defiance might be of any use at all. I wrote this tale, and am inserting it into this binding and all my other bindings, on the backing papers and in a microchip, with the hope that the recording of what the New People have done will someday bring their acts back upon them.

Perhaps this will protect some other planet from their gentle ministrations. I am not, however, altruistic in this act. I am hoping that with them, soon—as with me, now—sadness will prevail.

west to east

jay Lake

The late Jay Lake was a highly talented and highly prolific writer who during his tragically short career seems to have managed to sell to nearly every mar-ket in the business, appearing with short work in Asimov's Science Fiction, Interzone, Jim Baen's Universe, Tor.com, Clarkesworld, Strange Horizons, Aeon, Postscripts, Electric Velocipede, *and many other markets, producing enough short fiction to fill five different collections:* Greetings from Lake Wu, Green Grow the Rushes-Oh, American Sorrows, Dogs in the Moon-light, The Sky that Wraps, *and, most recently, the posthumously released* Last Plane to Heaven. *Lake was also an acclaimed and prolific novelist, who wrote the novels* Rocket Science, Trial of Flowers, Mainspring, Escape-ment, Green, Endurance, The Madness of Flowers, Pinion, *and* Kalim-pura, *as well as four chapbook novellas,* Death of a Starship, The Baby Killers, The Specific Gravity of Grief, *and* Love in the Time of Metal and Flesh. *He was the coeditor, with Deborah Layne, of the six-volume* Poly-phony *anthology series, and also edited the anthologies* All Star Zeppelin Adventure Stories, *with David Moles;* Other Earths, *with Nick Gevers; and* Spicy Slipstream Stories, *with Nick Mamatas. He won the John W. Camp-bell Award for Best New Writer in 2004. Lake died in 2014.*

The powerful tale that follows is probably Lake's last published story, a short meditation about the acceptance of inevitable death by the crew of a shuttle ship crashed on an impossibly hostile planet, and the capability of the human spirit to find moments of pure joy even under those circumstances.

I wasn't looking forward to dying lost and unremarked. Another day on Kesri-Sequoia II, thank you very much.

"Good morning, sir," said Ensign Mallory from her navcomms station at the nose of our disabled landing boat. She was a small, dark-skinned woman with no hair—I'd never asked if that was cultural or genetic. "Prevailing winds down to just under four hundred knots as of dawn."

"Enough with the weather." I coughed the night's allergies loose. Alien biospheres might not be infectious, but alien proteins still carried a hell of a kick as far as my mucous membranes were concerned. I had good English lungs, which is to say a near-permanent sinus infection under any kind of respiratory stress. And we'd given up on full air recycling weeks ago in the name of power management—with the quantum transfer chamber damaged in our uncontrolled final descent, all we had were backup fuel cells. Not nearly enough to power onboard systems, let alone our booster engines. The emergency stores were full of all kinds of interesting but worthless items like water purifiers, spools of buckywire, and inflatable tents.

Useless. All of our tech was useless. *Prospero*'s landing boat smelled like mold. Our deck was at a seven-degree angle. We'd been trapped down here so long I swear one of my legs was shortening to compensate.

Mallory glanced back at the display. "I'm sure you know best, sir."

Just under four hundred knots pretty much counted as doldrums on the surface of Kesri-Sequoia II. Since the crash we'd regularly clocked wind gusts well in excess of nine hundred knots. Outside the well-shielded hull of the landing boat Ensign Mallory and I would have been stripped to the bone in minutes. Which was too bad. Kesri-Sequoia II didn't seem to be otherwise inimical to human life. Acceptable nitrogen-oxygen balance, decent partial pressure, within human-normal temperature ranges—a bit muggy perhaps. Nothing especially toxic or caustic out there.

It was the superrotating atmosphere that made things a bitch.

There was life here though, plenty of it—turbulent environments beget niches, niches beget species radiation, species radiation begets a robust biosphere. Just not our kind of life, not anything humans could meaningfully interact with.

Kesri-Sequoia's dryland surface was dominated by giant sessiles that were rocky and solid with lacy air holes for snaring microbiota from the tumbling winds. They were a kilometer long, two hundred meters tall, less than two meters wide at the base, narrowing as they rose. The sessiles were oriented like shark fins into the airflow. Mallory called them land-reefs. We could see four from our windscreen, lightning often playing between them as the winds scaled up and down. Approaching one expecting communication would be like trying to talk to Ayers Rock.

Then there were ribbon-eels—ten meters of razor-thin color flowing by on the wind like a kootchie dancer's prop. And spit-tides that crawled across the scoured landscape, huge mats of loosely differentiated proteins leaching nutrients from the necrophages that lurked in the surface cracks.

All surface life on Kesri-Sequoia II moved west to east. Nothing fought the winds. Nothing made me or Ensign Mallory want to get out and say hello. Nothing could help us get the landing boat back to orbit and the safety of *Prospero*. The atmosphere was so electrically messy we couldn't even transmit our final logs and survey data to the crew waiting helplessly high above.

I stared out the crazed crystal-lattice of the forward portside viewport. I figured when something much larger than a pea hit it that was the end for us. Once the wind got inside the boat, we'd finally be dead.

A ribbon-eel soared by in the distance. The animal glittered like an oil slick as it undulated. "How strong do you figure those things are?" I asked Ensign Mallory. "They look like they're made of tissue."

She glanced at the exterior telemetry displays, seeing my eel with the landing boat's electronic eyes. "I ran some simulations last week."

"*And?*"

Mallory sighed wistfully. "I'd love to dissect one. Those things' muscle fibers must have a torsional strength superior to spider silk. Otherwise they would shred in the turbulence."

Her comment about spiders made me think of airborne hatchlings on Earth, each floating on their little length of thread. "I wonder if we could use some of those damned things as sails. If we could get the boat off the ground and pointed into the wind, we might be able to climb high enough on deadstick to at least get off a message to *Prospero*."

They couldn't send the other landing boat, prosaically named "B" to our "A," after us. Not unless they wanted to condemn another crew. And our first touchdown had been so violent that even if we somehow found a way to power the engines there was no way we'd survive to the end of a second flight.

But getting our last words out had a certain appeal.

"How are you going to catch a ribbon-eel, sir? It's not like we can step outside and go fishing."

"Fishing . . ." I went back to the landing boat's stores locker next to the tiny galley at the rear of the three-meter-long main cabin. Standard inventory included four spools of long-chain fullerene—buckywire, or more accurately, carbon nanotube whiskers grown to arbitrary macroscale lengths. In our case a rated minimum of a hundred meters per spool. *That* would be fishing line that tested out to a few hundred tons. "What do you figure ribbon-eels eat?" I asked over my shoulder as I grabbed the four spools.

We only had one local food available to us—the mold from the air ducts. Ensign Mallory scraped out a few cubic centimeters' worth. It sat in the kneepad of our lone hardsuit like so much gray flour.

"This stuff won't stick to anything, sir," she said. Mallory's voice was almost a whine. Surely she wasn't losing her spirit now that we had something to focus on?

I considered the powdery mess. "Syrup packets from the galley. A little bit of corn-starch. We're there."

"How are you going to get it outside?"

"We're going to build a little windlock on the inside of the busted viewport up front. Bind this stuff as a paste onto the buckywire, spool it out, and snag us a ribbon-eel."

Buckybondo is weird stuff—it munges the electron shells of organic molecules. That's the only way to stick fullerene-based materials to anything else. But you can glue your fingers to the bulkhead with it, literally bonding your flesh with the plasto-ceramics so that only an arc welder or a bone saw will cut you free. I wouldn't let Mallory touch the stuff. We only needed a few drops in the mold paste to stick it to the buckywire. I figured I'd just suffer the risks myself. One of the burdens of command.

Two hours later I was playing out line through the windlock. The wind carried it away past my screen, out of my sight. I figured we'd significantly reduced the service life of the viewport by drilling the hole, but what else were Ensign Mallory and I going to do with the rest of our short lives?

"Slow it down, sir," Mallory said. She monitored the sensors for ribbon-eels. "The wind is taking your bait too close to a land-reef."

I thumbed the electrostatic brake on the buckywire reel. The line stopped extending. The buckywire made an eerie clatter against our hull as it vibrated in the wind.

"Ribbon-eel approaching." She paused. "It seems to have noticed the bait. Draw your line back a little, sir."

I reeled the buckywire in, moving the bait closer to the landing boat for a moment.

"Damn," hissed Mallory. "Missed it. Next time, sir, don't go against the wind."

"Roger that." I'd only done what she said.

Ten minutes later we caught one. It came shooting up out of the west, grabbed the bait on the fly, and yanked the buckywire reel out of my hand. I lunged toward the damaged viewport, fetching up against our jerry-rigged windlock and nearly breaking my fingers. "Oh, crap!"

"We got it, sir. Can you reel our eel in?"

The wind pressure from the captive ribbon-eel made the viewport creak but the buckywire reel engaged and slowly retracted the line. The nose of the landing boat rocked with the drag from our airborne captive. I glanced at Mallory's screen where the ribbon-eel could be seen thrashing as we tugged it against the wind.

I felt vaguely guilty. I figured I'd worry about the ethics of this once I was dead.

"Now what, sir?"

The nose of the landing boat kept rocking. We were flying the ribbon-eel like a flag. Its drag bumped our vehicle to the starboard. "This isn't enough," I said. "We'll need at least one more."

"We've got three more spools."

I imagined four ribbon-eels, great, colored pennants dragging us into the air. We'd be out of control. "What if I hooked a second wire into the other end of the eel? We could even steer. Like a parasail."

Ensign Mallory shook her head. "You'll never survive out there, sir."

"There's always the hardsuit."

"It's not rated for these conditions."

I shrugged. "Neither are we, and we're still here." Terrible logic, but I was down to emotional appeals, even to myself. "Let's hook up the hardsuit to another reel so you have a chance of getting me back. Then I'll go out and hook up the ass end of that eel. If I don't make it back in, you fly the landing boat up to the middle atmosphere. Get above the storms, tell *Prospero* what happened to us."

"You can't even walk out there, sir."

"We'll see."

We passed all three of the other reels out of the windlock. I suited up, took a tube of buckybondo and a pair of electrostatic grippies, and forced myself into the landing boat's tiny airlock.

"Ready when you are, Ensign."

"Good luck, sir."

I could feel the air pumps throbbing through the feet of the hardsuit. We'd decided to drop the pressure in the lock before opening to the outside—we'd already commingled atmospheres, not to mention breaching the viewport, but there didn't seem any point in inviting in a whole new airlock-full of allergens and contaminants. I set an ultrabungee on one of the hardware cleats inside the lock chamber then clipped the other end to the equipment belt of my hardsuit.

The outer hatch slid open. I stepped out and became the first human to set foot on the surface of Kesri-Sequoia II. Immediately thereafter I became the first human to lose his footing on the surface of Kesri-Sequoia II as the wind took me airborne.

Thank God for the ultrabungee, I thought as I sailed upward. I might make it back down to the surface. Then I remembered the buckywire connecting the ribbon-eel to our landing boat. If I sailed across it that stuff could slice my leg off like a scalpel. I grabbed the ultrabungee and spun myself, looking for the ribbon-eel.

I forgot my panic in the glory of the view.

From this altitude, perhaps two hundred meters up at the end of the ultrabungee, I could see our four neighboring land-reefs and a dozen more beyond. The ground was rippled like beach sand just beneath the lip of the tide. Clouds boiled above and around me, the planet's hurried energy given form. Everything below had a grayish-yellow cast as the dim light of Kesri-Sequoia II filtered through the super-rotating atmospheric layers, but the view itself took my breath away.

We'd never seen the sky properly from inside the lander. The racing clouds were evanescent, glowing with lavenders and pastel greens, the lightning arcing among them like the arguments of old lovers. Streaming between the banks were smears of brick red, deep violet, azure blue, and a dozen more colors for which I had no name. These were the airborne microbiota on which the land-reefs fed and that the ribbon-eels chased. It was like being inside a Van Gogh painting, the swirling bursts of colors brought to life.

I hung on to the ultrabungee and stared, bouncing in the sky like a yo-yo gone berserk.

". . . sir . . . air . . ."

Mallory's voice was a faint echo. She was unable to punch a clear signal even the few hundred meters to my suit radio. We should have rigged a wireline with the ultrabungee, I realized. Using the hardsuit's enhanced exomusculature to fight the wind, I pulled myself down the ultrabungee hand over hand. I watched the ribbon-eel carefully to avoid crossing its buckywire tether.

By the time I reached the nose of the landing boat the wind buffeting was giving me a terrible headache. I felt as if I waded in a racing tide. The spell of the sky's beauty had worn off. At least this close to the ship I could hear Ensign Mallory over the radio. More or less.

"Feed down . . .'en meters . . . lock . . ."

"Do not copy," I said. I bent down with one of the electrostatic grippies and picked up a buckywire end. I pulled it to my chest and secured it to my suit with bucky-bondo. Now I wouldn't immediately blow away again. I grabbed another buckywire with my grippy. "Reel the eel in close, I want to see its tail."

"Copy . . . eel . . .'ail . . ."

The ribbon-eel loomed closer to me. I was able to study it objectively. The creature was about ten meters long, lemon colored with pale green spots along the side. Perhaps a meter tall, it had the same narrow vertical cross-section that the land-reefs boasted. I couldn't see any eyes, but there was a large, gummy mouth into which the buckywire vanished. Hopefully the buckybondo was helping it hold somewhere deep in the eel's gut. The animal thrashed against the line but I couldn't tell if that was the wind or an effort at struggle.

Now it was my turn to torture the ribbon-eel in person. I needed to hook the buckywire somewhere near the tail. Straining against my own buckywire with the ultrabungee whipping behind me, I reached for the green fringe along the bottom of the ribbon-eel.

It was like catching a noodle on the boil. Possible but difficult. Once I grabbed the damned thing I had to engage all the hardsuit's enhancements to hang on without either losing my grip or the ribbon-eel. I locked the hardsuit's systems and stood there sweating inside the shell. The ribbon-eel whipped above me like a banner, tugging at my hand.

I'd run out of hands. One hand on the grippy of buckywire. One hand on the fringe of the ribbon-eel. How the hell was I going to handle the buckybondo? I couldn't just open the faceplate and grab it in my teeth.

"Release the brakes," I yelled into the suit radio. "Let all the reels run loose."

". . . 'oger . . ."

The ribbon-eel shot into the sky with me still hanging on to it. I rocked myself against my right hand grabbing the fringe, trying to throw my left hand with grippy of buckywire up the side of the ribbon-eel. My feet kicked as I scrambled for purchase along the flank.

After a couple of moments, I was atop the ribbon-eel, riding it like a maintenance sled as I faced the tapering tail. With the ribbon-eel's body pressed between my knees I was able to free my right hand from the fringe. I worked the buckybondo out of my utility pocket and into my hand, globbed a big patch onto the flank, then used the grippy to plunge the free end of the buckywire into the mess.

I jumped away from the ribbon-eel and let the wind take me on my ultrabungee and my buckywire. "Reel me in, Mallory!" I screamed.

I couldn't figure out how to get back in the airlock with the buckywire on my chest. I couldn't figure that it mattered that much either. The ribbon-eel was already dragging the lander across the rippled surface. Mallory reeled me down to the nose of the boat, where I stood straddling the cracked viewport. I buckybondoed my boots to the heat shield just below the port, then buckybondoed the last reel of buckywire to my chest next to the other one. Finally I used the two grippies to grab and control the lines leading to the ribbon-eel.

Once I evened the lengths of the lines and got the ribbon-eel across the wind the landing boat began to scoot nose-first along the landscape with a purpose. I figured I could work the ribbon-eel like a kite as we rose, to tack us far enough into the wind for our airfoil to bite.

"Sir," said Mallory, her voice unexpectedly clear in the hardsuit's radio. "You're going to die out there."

"You're going to die in there," I said. "Let's get high enough up to tell *Prospero* what happened. That's all we need to do."

I stood on the nose and flew us up above the boiling, multicolored clouds where Ensign Mallory could report to our mother ship about what fate had befallen us. There seemed no reason not to stay in the high, clear air, surfing the beauty of the skies behind our ribbon-eel until something tore free, so I did that thing and smiled.

grand jeté (the great leap)

rachel swirsky

Here's a complex and eloquent study of the question of identity. If you down-load a dying girl's consciousness into an artificial body, is the "new" girl the same as the old one, or someone entirely different?

Rachel Swirsky *has published in* Subterranean *magazine,* Tor.com, *In-terzone,* Fantasy Magazine, Weird Tales, Beneath Ceaseless Skies, Realms of Fantasy, *and elsewhere, and she's won two Nebula Awards for her short fiction, for "The Lady Who Plucked Red Flowers Beneath the Queen's Win-dow" in 2010, and "If You Were a Dinosaur, My Love" in 2013. Her books include:* Eros, Philia, Agape; A Memory of Wind, *a collection;* Through the Drowsy Dark; *and, as editor, the anthology* People of the Book: A Decade of Jewish Science Fiction and Fantasy, *coedited with Sean Wallace. Her most recent book is the collection,* How the World Became Quiet: Myths of the Past, Present, and Future.

ACT I: MARA

Tombé
(Fall)

As dawn approached, the snow outside Mara's window slowed, spiky white stars melt-ing into streaks on the pane. Her abba stood in the doorway, unaware that she was already awake. Mara watched his silhouette in the gloom. Shadows hung in the folds of his jowls where he'd shaved his beard in solidarity after she'd lost her hair. Although it had been months, his face still looked pink and plucked.

Some nights, Mara woke four or five times to find him watching from the door-way. She didn't want him to know how poorly she slept and so she pretended to be dreaming until he eventually departed.

This morning, he didn't leave. He stepped into the room. "Marale," he said softly. His fingers worried the edges of the green apron that he wore in his workshop. A layer of sawdust obscured older scorch marks and grease stains. "Mara, please wake up. I've made you a gift."

Mara tried to sit. Her stomach reeled. Abba rushed to her bedside. "I'm fine," she said, pushing him away as she waited for the pain to recede.

He drew back, hands disappearing into his apron pockets. The corners of his mouth tugged down, wrinkling his face like a bulldog's. He was a big man with broad shoulders and disproportionately large hands. Everything he did looked comical when wrought on such a large scale. When he felt jovial, he played into the foolishness with broad, dramatic gestures that would have made an actor proud. In sadness, his gestures became reticent, hesitating, miniature.

"Are you cold?" he asked.

In deep winter, their house was always cold. Icy wind curled through cracks in the insulation. Even the heater that abba had installed at the foot of Mara's bed couldn't keep her from dreaming of snow.

Abba pulled a lace shawl that had once belonged to Mara's ima from the back of her little wooden chair. He draped it across her shoulders. Fringe covered her ragged fingernails.

As Mara rose from her bed, he tried to help with her crutches, but Mara fended him off. He gave her a worried look. "The gift is in my workshop," he said. With a concerned backward glance, he moved ahead, allowing her the privacy to make her own way.

Their white German Shepherd, Abel, met Mara as she shifted her weight onto her crutches. She paused to let him nuzzle her hand, tongue rough against her knuckles. At thirteen, all his other senses were fading, and so he tasted everything he could. He walked by her side until they reached the stairs, and then followed her down, tail thumping against the railing with every step.

The door to abba's workshop was painted red and stenciled with white flowers that Mara had helped ima paint when she was five. Inside, half-finished apparatuses sprawled across workbenches covered in sawdust and disassembled electronics. Hanging from the ceiling, a marionette stared blankly at Mara and Abel as they passed, the glint on its pupils moving back and forth as its strings swayed. A mechanical hand sprang to life, its motion sensor triggered by Abel's tail. Abel whuffed at its palm and then hid behind Mara. The thing's fingers grasped at Mara's sleeve, leaving an impression of dusty, concentric whorls.

Abba stood at the back of the workshop, next to a child-sized doll that sat on a metal stool. Its limbs fell in slack, uncomfortable positions. Its face looked like the one Mara still expected to see in the mirror: a broad forehead over flushed cheeks scattered with freckles. Skin peeled away in places, revealing wire streams.

Mara moved to stand in front of the doll. It seemed even eerier, examined face to face, its expression a lifeless twin of hers. She reached out to touch its soft, brown hair. Her bald scalp tingled.

Gently, abba took Mara's hand and pressed her right palm against the doll's. Apart from how thin Mara's fingers had become over the past few months, they matched perfectly.

Abba made a triumphant noise. "The shape is right."

Mara pulled her hand out of abba's. She squinted at the doll's imitation flesh. Horrifyingly, its palm shared each of the creases on hers, as if it, too, had spent twelve years dancing and reading books and learning to cook.

Abel circled the doll. He sniffed its feet and ankles and then paused at the back of its knees, whuffing as if he'd expected to smell something that wasn't there. After completing his circuit, he collapsed on the floor, equidistant from the three human-shaped figures.

"What do you think of her?" abba asked.

Goosebumps prickled Mara's neck. "What is she?"

Abba cradled the doll's head in his hands. Its eyes rolled back, and the light high-lighted its lashes, fair and short, just like Mara's own. "She's a prototype. Empty-headed. A friend of mine is working on new technology for the government—"

"A prototype?" repeated Mara. "Of what?"

"The body is simple mechanics. Anyone could build it. The technology in the mind is new. It takes pictures of the brain in motion, all three dimensions, and then creates schematics for artificial neural clusters that will function like the original bio-logical matter—"

Mara's head ached. Her mouth was sore and her stomach hurt and she wanted to go back to bed even if she couldn't sleep. She eyed the doll. The wires under its skin were vivid red and blue as if they were veins and arteries connecting to viscera.

"The military will make use of the technology," abba continued. "They wish to recreate soldiers with advanced training. They are not ready for human tests, not yet. They are still experimenting with animals. They've made rats with mechanical brains that can solve mazes the original rats were trained to run. Now they are working with chimpanzees."

Abba's accent deepened as he continued, his gestures increasingly emphatic.

"But I am better. I can make it work in humans now, without more experiments." Urgently, he lowered his voice. "My friend was not supposed to send me the sche-matics. I paid him much money, but his reason for helping is that I have promised him that when I fix the problems, I will show him the solution and he can take the credit. This technology is not for civilians. No one else will be able to do this. We are very fortunate."

Abba touched the doll's shoulder so lightly that only his fingertips brushed her.

"I will need you to sit for some scans so that I can make the images that will pre-serve you. They will be painless. I can set up when you sleep." Quietly, he added, "She is my gift to you. She will hold you and keep you . . . if the worst . . ." His voice faded, and he swallowed twice, three times, before beginning again. "She will pro-tect you."

Mara's voice came out hoarse. "Why didn't you tell me?"

"You needed to see her when she was complete."

Her throat constricted. "I wish I'd never seen her at all!"

From the cradle, Mara had been even-tempered. Now, at twelve, she shouted and cried. Abba said it was only what happened to children as they grew older, but they both knew that wasn't why.

Neither was used to her new temper. The lash of her shout startled them both. Abba's expression turned stricken.

"I don't understand," he said.

"You made a new daughter!"

"No, no." Abba held up his hands to protect himself from her accusation. "She is made *for* you."

"I'm sure she'll be a better daughter than I am," Mara said bitterly.

She grabbed a hank of the doll's hair. Its head tilted toward her in a parody of curiosity. She pushed it away. The thing tumbled to the floor, limbs awkwardly splayed.

Abba glanced toward the doll, but did not move to see if it was broken. "I—No, Marale—You don't—" His face grew drawn with sudden resolution. He pulled a hammer off of one of the work benches. "Then I will smash her to pieces."

There had been a time when, with the hammer in his hand and a determined expression on his face, he'd have looked like a smith from old legends. Now he'd lost so much weight that his skin hung loosely from his enormous frame as if he were a giant coat suspended from a hanger. Tears sprang to Mara's eyes.

She slapped at his hands and the hammer in them. "Stop it!"

"If you want her to—"

"Stop it! Stop it!" she shouted.

Abba released the hammer. It fell against the cement with a hollow, mournful sound.

Guilt shot through her, at his confusion, at his fear. What should she do, let him destroy this thing he'd made? What should she do, let the hammer blow strike, watch herself be shattered?

Sawdust billowed where the hammer hit. Abel whined and fled the room, tail between his legs.

Softly, abba said, "I don't know what else to give."

Abba had always been the emotional heart of the family, even when ima was alive. His anger flared; his tears flowed; his laughter roared from his gut. Mara rested her head on his chest until his tears slowed, and then walked with him upstairs.

The house was too small for Mara to fight with abba for long, especially during winters when they both spent every hour together in the house, Mara home-schooling via her attic space program while abba tinkered in his workshop. Even on good days, the house felt claustrophobic with two people trapped inside. Sometimes one of them would tug on a coat and ski cap and trudge across the hard-packed snow, but even the outdoors provided minimal escape. Their house sat alone at the end of a mile-long driveway that wound through bare-branched woods before reaching the lonely road that eventually led to their neighbors. Weather permitting, in winter it took an hour and a half to get the truck running and drive into town.

It was dawn by the time they had made their way upstairs, still drained from the scene in the basement. Mara went to lie down on her bed so she could try for the illusion of privacy. Through the closed door, she heard her father venting his frustration on the cabinets. Pans clanged. Drawers slammed. She thought she could hear the quiet, gulping sound of him beginning to weep again under the cacophony.

She waited until he was engrossed in his cooking and then crept out of her bedroom. She made her way down the hallway, taking each step slowly and carefully so as to minimize the clicking of her crutches against the floor.

Ima's dance studio was the only room in the house where abba never went. It faced east; at dawn, rose- and peach-colored light shimmered across the full-length mirrors and polished hardwood. An old television hung on the southern wall, its antiquated technology jury-rigged to connect with the household AI.

Mara closed the door most of the way, enough to muffle any sound, but not enough to make the telltale thump that would attract her father's attention. She walked up to the television so that she could speak softly and still be heard by its implanted AI sensors. She'd long ago mastered the trick of enunciating clearly enough for the AI to understand her even when she was whispering. "I'd like to access a DVD of ima's performances."

The AI whirred. "Okay, Mara," said its genial, masculine voice. "Which one would you like to view?"

"Giselle."

More clicks and whirs. The television blinked on, showing the backs of several rows of red velvet seats. Well-dressed figures navigated the aisles, careful not to wrinkle expensive suits and dresses. Before them, a curtain hid the stage from view, the house lights emphasizing its sumptuous folds.

Mara sat carefully on the floor near the ballet barre so that she would be able to use it like a lever when she wanted to stand again. She crossed the crutches at her feet. On the television screen, the lights dimmed as the overture began.

Sitting alone in this place where no one else went, watching things that no one else watched, she felt as if she were somewhere safe. A mouse in its hole, a bird in its nest—a shelter built precisely for her body, neither too large nor too small.

The curtain fluttered. The overture began. Mara felt her breath flowing more easily as the tension eased from her shoulders. She could forget about abba and his weeping for a moment, just allow herself to enter the ballet.

Even as an infant, Mara had adored the rich, satiny colors on ima's old DVDs. She watched the tragedies, but her heart belonged to the comedies. Gilbert and Sullivan's *Pineapple Poll*. Ashton's choreography of Prokofiev's *Cinderella*. Madcap *Coppélia* in which a peasant boy lost his heart to a clockwork doll.

When Mara was small, ima would sit with her while she watched the dancers, her expression half-wistful and half-jaded. When the dancers had sketched their bows, ima would stand, shaking her head, and say, "Ballet is not a good life."

At first, ima did not want to give Mara ballet lessons, but Mara insisted at the age of two, three, four, until ima finally gave in. During the afternoons while abba was in his workshop, Mara and ima would dance together in the studio until ima grew tired and sat with her back against the mirror, hands wrapped around her knees, watching Mara spin and spin.

After ima died, Mara had wanted to ask her father to sign her up for dance school. But she hated the melancholia that overtook him whenever they discussed ballet. Before getting sick, she'd danced on her own instead, accompanying the dancers on ima's tapes. She didn't dance every afternoon as she had when ima was alive. She was older; she had other things to do—books to read, study hours with the AI, lessons and play dates in attic space. She danced just enough to maintain her flexibility and retain what ima had taught her, and even sometimes managed to learn new things from watching the dancers on film.

Then last year, while dancing with the Mouse King to *The Nutcracker*, the pain she'd been feeling for months in her right knee suddenly intensified. She heard the snap of bone before she felt it. She collapsed suddenly to the floor, confused and in pain, her head ringing with the echoes of the household's alarms. As the AI wailed for help, Mara found a single thought repeating in her head. *Legs don't shatter just because you're dancing. Something is very wrong.*

On the television screen, the filmed version of Mara's mother entered, dancing a coy *Giselle* in blue tulle. Her gaze slanted shyly downward as she flirted with the dancers playing Albrecht and Hilarion. One by one, she plucked petals from a prop daisy. *He loves me, he loves me not.*

Mara heard footsteps starting down the hall. She rushed to speak before abba could make it into the room—"AI, switch off—"

Abba arrived before she could finish. He stood in the doorway with his shoulders hunched, his eyes averted from the image of his dead wife. "Breakfast is ready," he said. He lingered for a moment before turning away.

After breakfast, abba went outside to scrape ice off of the truck.

They drove into town once a week for supplies. Until last year, they'd always gone on Sundays, after Shabbat. Now they went on Fridays before Mara's appointments and then hurried to get home before sunset.

Outside, snowflakes whispered onto the hard-pack. Mara pulled her knit hat over her ears, but her cheeks still smarted from the cold. She rubbed her gloved hands together for warmth before attaching Abel's leash. The old dog seemed to understand what her crutches were. Since she'd started using them, he'd broken his lifelong habit of yanking on the strap and learned to walk daintily instead, placing each paw with care.

Abba opened the passenger door so that Abel could clamor into the back of the cab. He fretted while Mara leaned her crutches on the side of the truck and pulled herself into the seat. He wanted to help, she knew, but he was stopping himself. He knew she hated being reminded of her helplessness.

He collected her crutches when she was done and slung them into the back with Abel before taking his place in the driver's seat. Mara stared silently forward as he turned the truck around and started down the narrow driveway. The four-wheel drive jolted over uneven snow, shooting pain through Mara's bad leg.

"Need to fix the suspension," abba grumbled.

Because abba was a tinkerer, everything was always broken. Before Mara was born, he'd worked for the government. These days, he consulted on refining manufacturing processes. He felt that commercial products were shoddily designed and so he was constantly trying to improve their household electronics, leaving his dozens of half-finished home projects disassembled for months while all the time swearing to take on new ones.

The pavement smoothed out as they turned onto a county-maintained road. Piles of dirty snow lined its sides. Bony trees dotted the landscape, interspersed with pines still wearing red bows from Christmas.

Mara felt as though the world were caught in a frozen moment, preserved beneath the snow. Nothing would ever change. No ice would melt. No birds would return to the branches. There would be nothing but blizzards and long, dark nights and snow-covered pines.

Mara wasn't sure she believed in G-d, but on her better days, she felt at peace with the idea of pausing, as if she were one of the dancers on ima's DVDs, halted mid-leap.

Except she wouldn't pause. She'd be replaced by that thing. That doll.

She glanced at her father. He stared fixedly at the road, grumbling under his breath in a blend of languages. He hadn't bought new clothes since losing so much weight, and the fabric of his coat fell in voluminous folds across the seat.

He glanced sideways at Mara watching him. "What's wrong?"

"Nothing," Mara muttered, looking away.

Abel pushed his nose into her shoulder. She turned in her seat to scratch between his ears. His tail thumped, tick, tock, like a metronome.

They parked beside the grocery. The small building's densely packed shelves were reassuringly the same year in and year out except for the special display mounted at the front of the store. This week it showcased red-wrapped sausages, marked with a cheerful, handwritten sign.

Gerry stood on a ladder in the center aisle, restocking cereals. He beamed as they walked in.

"Ten-thirty to the minute!" he called. "Good morning, my punctual Jewish friends!"

Gerry had been slipping down the slope called being hard of hearing for years now. He pitched his voice as if he were shouting across a football field.

"How is my little adult?" he asked Mara. "Are you forty today, or is it fifty?"

"Sixty-five," Mara said. "Seventy tomorrow."

"Such an old child," Gerry said, shaking his head. "Are you sure you didn't steal that body?"

Abba didn't like those kinds of jokes. He used to worry that they would make her self-conscious; now he hated them for bringing up the subject of aging. Flatly, he replied, "Children in our family are like that. There is nothing wrong with her."

Mara shared an eye roll with the grocer.

"Never said there was," Gerry said. Changing the subject, he gestured at Mara's crutches with a box of cornflakes. "You're an athlete on those. I bet there's nothing you can't do with them."

Mara forced a smile. "They're no good for dancing."

He shrugged. "I used to know a guy in a wheelchair. Out-danced everyone."

"Not ballet, though."

"True," Gerry admitted, descending the ladder. "Come to the counter. I've got something for you."

Gerry had hardly finished speaking before Abel forgot about being gentle with Mara's crutches. He knew what Gerry's gifts meant. The lead wrenched out of Mara's hand. She chased after him, crutches clicking, but even with his aging joints, the dog reached the front counter before Mara was halfway across the store.

"Wicked dog," Gerry said in a teasing tone as he caught Abel's leash. He scratched the dog between the ears and then bent to grab a package from under the counter. "Sit," he said. "Beg." The old dog rushed to do both. Gerry unwrapped a sausage and tossed it. Abel snapped and swallowed.

Mara finished crossing the aisle. She leaned against the front counter. She tried to conceal her heavy breathing, but she knew that her face must be flushed. Abba waited at the edges of her peripheral vision, his arms stretched in Mara's direction as if he expected her to collapse.

Gerry glanced between Mara and her father, assessing the situation. Settling on Mara, he tapped a stool behind the counter. "You look wiped. Take a load off. Your dad and I can handle ourselves."

"Yes, Mara," abba said quickly. "Perhaps you should sit."

Mara glared. "Abba."

"I'm sorry," abba said, looking away. He added to Gerry, "She doesn't like help."

"No help being offered. I just want some free work. You up for manning the register?" Gerry tapped the stool again. "I put aside one of those strawberry things you like. It's under the counter. Wrapped in pink paper."

"Thanks," Mara said, not wanting to hurt Gerry's feelings by mentioning that she couldn't eat before appointments. She went behind the counter and let Gerry hold her crutches while she pulled herself onto the stool. She hated how good it felt to sit.

Gerry nodded decisively. "Come on," he said, leading abba toward the fresh fruit.

Abba and Gerry made unlikely friends. Gerry made no bones about being a charismatic evangelical. During the last election, he'd put up posters saying that Democratic voters were headed to hell. In return, abba had suggested that Republican voters might need a punch in the jaw, especially any Republican voters who happened to be standing in front of him. Gerry responded that he supported free speech as much as any other patriotic American, but speech like that could get the H-E-double-hockey-sticks out of his store. They shouted. Gerry told abba not to come back. Abba said he wouldn't even buy dog food from fascists.

The next week, Gerry was waiting on the sidewalk with news about a kosher supplier, and Mara and abba went in as if nothing had ever happened.

Before getting sick, Mara had always followed the men through the aisles, joining in their arguments about pesticides and free-range chickens. Gerry liked to joke that he wished his children were as interested in the business as Mara was. *Maybe I'll leave the store to you instead of them*, he'd say, jostling her shoulder. He had stopped saying that.

Mara slipped the wrapped pastry out from under the counter. She broke it into halves and put one in each pocket, hoping Gerry wouldn't see the lumps when they left. She left the empty paper on the counter, dusted with the crumbs that had fallen when she broke the pastry.

An activity book lay next to where the pastry had been. It was for little kids, but Mara pulled it out anyway. Gerry's children were too old to play with things like that now, but he still kept an array of diversions under the counter for when customers' kids needed to be kept busy. It was better to do something than nothing. Armed with the felt-tip pen that was clipped to the cover, she began to flip through pages of half-colored drawings and connect-the-dots.

A few aisles over, near the butcher counter, she heard her father grumbling. She looked up and saw Gerry grab abba's shoulder. As always, he was speaking too loudly. His voice boomed over the hum of the freezers. "I got in the best sausages on Wednesday," he said. "They're kosher. Try them. Make them for your, what do you call it, sadbath."

By then, Gerry knew the word, but it was part of their banter.

"Shabbat," Abba corrected.

Gerry's tone grew more serious. "You're losing too much weight. A man needs meat."

Abba's voice went flat. "I eat when I am hungry. I am not hungry so much lately."

Gerry's grip tightened on abba's shoulder. His voice dropped. "Jakub, you need to take care of yourself."

He looked back furtively at Mara. Flushing with shame, she dropped her gaze to the activity book. She clutched the pen tightly, pretending to draw circles in a word search.

"You have to think about the future," said Gerry. His voice lowered even further. Though he was finally speaking at a normal volume, she still heard every word. "You aren't the one who's dying."

Mara's flush went crimson. She couldn't tell if it was shame or anger—all she felt was cold, rigid shock. She couldn't stop herself from sneaking a glance at abba. He, too, stood frozen. The word had turned him to ice. Neither of them ever said it. It was a game of avoidance they played together.

Abba pulled away from Gerry and started down the aisle. His face looked numb rather than angry. He stopped at the counter, looking at everything but Mara. He took Abel's leash and gestured for Mara to get off of the stool. "We'll be late for your appointment," he said, even though it wasn't even eleven o'clock. In a louder voice, he added, "Ring up our cart, would you, Gerry? We'll pick up our bags on our way out of town."

Mara didn't like Doctor Pinsky. Abba liked him because he was Jewish even though he was American-born reform with a degree from Queens. He wore his hair close-cut but it looked like it would Jew 'fro if he grew it out.

He kept his nails manicured. His teeth shone perfectly white. He never looked directly at Mara when he spoke. Mara suspected he didn't like children much. Maybe you needed to be that way if you were going to watch the sick ones get worse.

The nurses were all right. Grace and Nicole, both blond and a bit fat. They didn't understand Mara since she didn't fit their idea of what kids were supposed to be like. She didn't talk about pop or interactives. When there were other child patients in the waiting room, she ignored them.

When the nurses tried to introduce her to the other children anyway, Mara said she preferred to talk to adults, which made them hmm and flutter. *Don't you have any friends, honey?* Nicole had asked her once, and Mara answered that she had some, but they were all on attic space. A year ago, if Mara had been upset, she'd have gone into a-space to talk to her best friend, Collin, but more and more as she got sick, she'd hated seeing him react to her withering body, hated seeing the fright and pity in his eyes. The thought of going back into attic space made her nauseous.

Grace and Nicole gave Mara extra attention because they felt sorry for her. Modern cancer treatments had failed to help and now Mara was the only child patient in the clinic taking chemotherapy. *It's hard on little bodies,* said Grace. *Heck, it's hard on big bodies, too.*

Today it was Grace who came to meet Mara in the waiting room, pushing a wheelchair. Assuming it was for another patient, Mara started to gather her crutches, but Grace motioned for her to stay put. "Let me treat you like a princess."

"I'm not much of a princess," Mara answered, immediately realizing from the pitying look on Grace's face that it was the wrong thing to say. To Grace, that would mean she didn't feel like a princess because she was sick, rather than that she wasn't interested in princesses.

"I can walk," Mara protested, but Grace insisted on helping her into the wheelchair anyway. She hadn't realized how tightly abba was holding her hand until she pulled it free.

Abba stood to follow them. Grace turned back. "Would you mind staying? Doctor Pinsky wants to talk to you."

"I like to go with Mara," abba said.

"We'll take good care of her." Grace patted Mara's shoulder. "You don't mind, do you, princess?"

Mara shrugged. Her father shifted uncertainly. "What does Doctor Pinsky want?"

"He'll be out in a few minutes," said Grace, deflecting. "I'm sorry, Mr. Morawski. You won't have to wait long."

Frowning, abba sat again, fingers worrying the collar of his shirt. Mara saw his conflicting optimism and fear, all inscribed plainly in his eyes, his face, the way he sat. She didn't understand why he kept hoping. Even before they'd tried the targeted immersion therapy and the QTRC regression, she'd known that they wouldn't work. She'd known from the moment when she saw the almost imperceptible frown cross the city diagnostician's face when he asked about the pain she'd been experiencing in her knee for months before the break. Yes, she'd said, it had been worse at night, and his brow had darkened, just for an instant. Maybe she'd known even earlier than that, in the moment just after she fell in ima's studio, when she realized with strange, cold clarity that something was very wrong.

Bad news didn't come all at once. It came in successions. Cancer is present. Metastasis has occurred. The tumors are unresponsive. The patient's vitals have taken a turn for the worse. We're sorry to say, we're sorry to say, we're sorry to say.

Grace wheeled Mara toward the back, maintaining a stream of banal, cheerful chatter, remarks about the weather and questions about the holidays and jokes about boys. Mara deflected. She wasn't ever going to have a boyfriend, not the way Grace was teasing her about. Adolescence was like spring, one more thing buried in endless snow.

Mara felt exhausted as they pulled into the driveway. She didn't have the energy to push abba away when he came around the truck to help her down. Mara leaned heavily on her father's arm as they crunched their way to the front door.

She vomited in the entryway. Abel came to investigate. She pushed his nose away while abba went to get the mop. The smell made her even more nauseated and so when abba returned, she left him to clean up. It made her feel guilty, but she was too tired to care.

She went to the bathroom to wash out her mouth. She tried not to catch her eye in the mirror, but she saw her reflection anyway. She felt a shock of alienation from the thin, sallow face. It couldn't be hers.

She could hear abba in the hallway, grumbling at Abel in Yiddish. Wan, late afternoon light filtered through the windows, foreshadowing sunset. A few months ago, she and abba would have been rushing to cook and clean before Shabbat. Now no one cleaned and Mara left abba to cook alone as she went into ima's studio.

She paused by the barre before sitting, already worried about how difficult it would be to get up again. "I want to watch *Coppélia*," she said. The AI whirred.

Coppélia began with a young woman reading on a balcony—except she wasn't really a young woman, she was actually an automaton constructed by the mad scientist, Dr. Coppélius. The dancer playing Coppélia pretended to read from a red leather book. Mara told the AI to fast-forward to ima's entrance.

Mara's mother was dancing the part of the peasant girl, Swanhilde. She looked nothing like the dancer playing Coppélia. Ima was strong, but also short and compact, where Coppélia was tall with visible muscle definition in her arms and legs.

Yet later in the ballet, none of the other characters would be able to tell them apart. Mara wanted to shake them into sense. Why couldn't they tell the difference between a person and a doll?

Abba lit the candles and began the prayer, waving his hands through the smoke. They didn't have an adult woman to read the prayers and abba wouldn't let Mara do it while she was still a child. *Soon*, he used to say, *after your bat mitzvah*. Now he said nothing.

They didn't celebrate Shabbat properly. They followed some traditions—tonight they'd leave the lights on, and tomorrow they'd eat cold food instead of cooking—but they did not attend services. If they needed to work then they worked. As a family, they had always been observant in some ways, and relaxed in others; they were not the kind who took well to following rules. Abba sometimes seemed to believe in Hashem and at other times not, though he believed in rituals and tradition. Still, before Mara had become ill, they'd taken more care with *halakha*.

As abba often reminded her, Judaism taught that survival was more important than dogma. *Pikuach nefesh* meant that a hospital could run electricity that powered a machine that kept a man alive. A family could work to keep a woman who had just given birth comfortable and healthy.

Perhaps other people wouldn't recognize the exceptions that Mara and her father made from Shabbat as being matters of survival, but they were. They were using all they had just by living. Not much remained for G-d.

The long window over the kitchen counters let through the dimming light as violet and ultramarine seeped across the horizon. The tangerine sun lingered above the trees, preparing to descend into scratching, black branches. Mara's attention drifted as he said Kiddush over the wine.

They washed their hands. Abba tore the challah. He gave a portion to Mara. She let it sit.

"The fish is made with ginger," abba said. "Would you like some string beans?"

"My mouth hurts," Mara said.

Abba paused, the serving plate still in his hands.

She knew that he wouldn't eat unless she did. "I'll have a little," she added softly.

She let him set the food on her plate. She speared a single green bean and stared at it for a moment before biting. Everything tasted like metal after the drugs.

"I used turmeric," he said.

"It's good."

Mara's stomach roiled. She set the fork on her plate.

Her father ate a few bites of fish and then set his fork down, too. A maudlin expression crossed his face. "Family is Hashem's best gift," he said.

Mara nodded. There was little to say.

Abba picked up his wine glass. He twisted the stem as he stared into red. "Family is what the *goyim* tried to take from us with pogroms and ghettoes and the *shoah*. On Shabbat, we find our families, wherever we are."

Abba paused again, sloshing wine gently from side to side.

"Perhaps I should have gone to Israel before you were born."

Mara looked up with surprise. "You think Israel is a corrupt theocracy."

"There are politics, like opposing a government, and then there is needing to be with your people." He shrugged. "I thought about going. I had money then, but no roots. I could have gone wherever I wanted. But I thought, I will go to America instead. There are more Jews in America than Israel. I did not want to live in the shadow of the *shoah*. I wanted to make a family in a place where we could rebuild everything they stole. *Der mensch trakht un Gatt lahkt.*"

He had been speaking rapidly, his accent deepening with every word. Now he stopped.

His voice was hoarse when it returned.

"Your mother . . . you . . . I would not trade it, but . . ." His gaze became diffuse as if the red of the wine were a telescope showing him another world. "It's all so fragile. Your mother is taken and you . . . *tsuris, tsuris* . . . and then there is nothing."

It was dark when they left the table. Abba piled dishes by the sink so that they could be washed after Shabbat and then retired to his bedroom. Abel came to Mara, tail thumping, begging for scraps. She was too tired to make him beg or shake hands. She rescued her plate from the pile of dishes and laid it on the floor for him to lick clean.

She started toward her bed and then changed her mind. She headed downstairs instead, Abel following after. She paused with her hand on the knob of the red-painted door before entering abba's workshop.

Mara hadn't seen abba go downstairs since their argument that morning but he must have managed to do it without her noticing. The doll sat primly on her stool, dignity restored, her head tilted down as if she were reading a book that Mara couldn't see.

Mara wove between worktables until she reached the doll's side. She lifted its hand and pressed their palms together as abba had done. It was strange to see the shape of her fingers so perfectly copied, down to the fine lines across her knuckles.

She pulled the thing forward. It lolled. Abel ducked its flailing right hand and ran a few steps away, watching warily.

Mara took hold of the thing's head. She pressed the tip of her nose against the tip of its nose, trying to match their faces as she had their palms. With their faces so close together, it looked like a Cyclops, staring back at her with one enormous, blank eye.

"I hate you," Mara said, lips pressed against its mute mouth.

It was true, but not the same way that it had been that morning. She had been furious then. Betrayed. Now the blaze of anger had burned down and she saw what lay in the ashes that remained.

It was jealousy. That this doll would be the one to take abba's hand at Shabbat five years from then, ten years, twenty. That it would take and give the comfort she could not. That it would balm the wounds that she had no choice but to inflict.

Would Mara have taken a clockwork doll if it had restored ima to her for these past years?

She imagined lying down for the scans. She imagined a machine studying her brain, replicating her dreams neuron by neuron, rendering her as mathematical patterns. She'd read enough biology and psychology to know that, whatever else she was, she was also an epiphenomenon that arose from chemicals and meat and electricity.

It was sideways immortality. She would be gone, and she would remain. There and not there. A quantum mechanical soul.

Love could hurt, she knew. Love was what made you hurt when your ima died. Love was what made it hurt when abba came to you gentle and solicitous, every kindness a reminder of how much pain you'd leave behind.

She would do this painful thing because she loved him, as he had made this doll because he loved her. She thought, with a sudden clenching of her stomach, that it was a good thing most people never lived to see what people planned to make of them when they were gone.

What Gerry had said was as true as it was cutting. Abba was not the one who would die.

Abba slept among twisted blankets, clutching his pillow as if afraid to let it go.

Mara watched from the doorway. "Abba."

He grumbled in his sleep as he shifted position.

"Abba," she repeated. "Please wake up, abba."

She waited while he put on his robe. Then, she led him down.

She made her way swiftly through the workshop, passing the newly painted marionette and the lonely mechanical hand. She halted near the doll, avoiding its empty gaze.

"I'm ready now," she said.

Abba's face shifted from confusion to wariness. With guarded hope, he asked, "Are you certain?"

"I'm sure," she said.

"Please, Mara. You do not have to."

"I know," she answered. She pressed herself against his chest, as if she were a much smaller child looking for comfort. She felt the tension in his body seep into relief as he wept with silent gratitude. She was filled with tears, too, from a dozen emotions blended into one. They were tears of relief, and regret, and pain, and love, and mourning, and more.

He wrapped his arms around her. She closed her eyes and savored the comfort of his woody scent, his warmth, the stubble scratching her arm. She could feel how thin he'd become, but he was still strong enough to hold her so tightly that his embrace was simultaneously joyful and almost too much to bear.

ACT II: JAKUB

Tour en l'air
(Turn in the Air)

Jakub was careful to make the scans as unobtrusive as possible. If he could have, he'd have recorded a dozen sessions, twenty-five, fifty, more. He'd have examined every obscure angle; he'd have recorded a hundred redundancies.

Mara was so fragile, though; not just physically, but mentally. He did not want to tax her. He found a way to consolidate what he needed into six nighttime sessions, monitoring her with portable equipment that he could bring into her bedroom which broadcast its data to the larger machinery in the basement.

When the scans were complete, Jakub spent his nights in the workshop, laboring over the new child while Mara slept. It had been a long time since he'd worked with technology like this, streamlined for its potential as a weapon. He had to gentle it, soothe it, coax it into being as careful about preserving memories of rainy mornings as it was about retaining reflexes and fighting skills.

He spent long hours poring over images of Mara's brain. He navigated three-dimensional renderings with the AI's help, puzzling over the strangeness of becoming so intimate with his daughter's mind in such an unexpected way. After he had finished converting the images into a neural map, he looked at Mara's mind with yet new astonishment. The visual representation showed associational clusters as if they were stars: elliptical galaxies of thought.

It was a truism that there were many ways to describe a river—from the action of its molecules to the map of its progress from tributaries to ocean. A mind was such a thing as well. On one end there was thought, personality, individual . . . and on the other . . . It was impossible to recognize Mara in the points of light, but he was in the midst of her most basic elements, and there was as much awe in that as there was in puzzling out the origin of the universe. He was the first person ever to see another human being in this way. He knew Mara now as no one else had ever known anyone.

His daughter, his beloved, his *sheineh maideleh*. There were so many others that he'd failed to protect. But Mara would always be safe; he would hold her forever.

Once Jakub had created the foundational schematics for manufacturing analogues to Mara's brain structures, the remainder of the process was automated. Jakub needed only to oversee it, occasionally inputting his approval to the machine.

Jakub found it unbearable to leave the machinery unsupervised, but nevertheless, he could not spend all of his time in the basement. During the mornings when Mara was awake, he paced the house, grumbling at the dog who followed him up and down the hallways as if expecting him to throw a stick. What if the process stalled? What if a catastrophic failure destroyed the images of Mara's mind now when her health was even more fragile and there might be no way to replace them?

He forced himself to disguise his obsession while Mara was awake. It was important to maintain the illusion that their life was the same as it had been before. He knew that Mara remained uneasy with the automaton. Its very presence said so many things that they had been trying to keep silent.

Mara's days were growing even harder. He'd thought the end of chemotherapy would give her some relief, but cancer pain worsened every day. Constant suffering and exhaustion made her alternately sullen and sharp. She snapped at him when he brought her meals, when he tried to help her across the house, when she woke to find him lingering in the doorway while she slept. Part of it was the simple result of pain displacing patience, but it was more, too. Once, when he had touched her shoulder, she'd flinched; then, upon seeing him withdraw, her expression had turned from annoyance to guilt. She'd said, softly, "You won't always be able to do that." A pause, a swallow, and then even more quietly, "It reminds me."

That was what love and comfort had become now. Promises that couldn't be kept.

Most nights, she did not sleep at all, only lay awake, staring out of her window at the snow.

Jakub searched for activities that might console her. He asked her if she'd like him to read to her. He offered to buy her immersive games. He suggested that she log into a spare room with other sick children where they could discuss their troubles. She told him that she wanted to be alone.

She had always been an unusual child, precocious and content to be her own companion. Meryem had said it was natural for a daughter of theirs, who had been raised among adults, and was descended from people who were also talented and solitary. Jakub and Meryem had been similar as children, remote from others their own age as they pursued their obsessions. Now Jakub wished she had not inherited these traits so completely, that she was more easily able to seek solace.

When Mara didn't think he was watching, she gathered her crutches and went into Meryem's studio to watch ballets. She did not like it when he came too close, and so he watched from the hallway. He could see her profile reflected in the mirrors on the opposite wall. She cried as she watched, soundless tears beading her cheeks.

One morning when she put on *A Midsummer Night's Dream*, Jakub ventured into the studio. For so long, he had stayed away, but that had not made things better. He had to try what he could.

He found Mara sitting on the floor, her crutches leaning against the ballet barre. Abel lay a few feet away with his head on his paws. Without speaking, Jakub sat beside them.

Mara wiped her cheeks, streaking her tears. She looked resentfully at Jakub, but he ignored her, hoping he could reach the part of her that still wanted his company even if she had buried it.

They sat stoically for the remainder of act one, holding themselves with care so that they did not accidentally shift closer to one another. Mara pretended to ignore him, though her darting glances told another story. Jakub let her maintain the pretense, trying to allow her some personal space within the studio since he had already intruded so far. He hoped she would be like a scared rabbit, slowly adjusting to his presence and coming to him when she saw that he was safe.

Jakub had expected to spend the time watching Mara and not the video, but he was surprised to find himself drawn into the dancing. The pain of seeing Meryem leap and spin had become almost a dull note, unnoticeable in the concert of his other sorrows. Meryem made a luminous Titania, a ginger wig cascading in curls down her back, her limbs wrapped in flowers, leaves, and gossamer. He'd forgotten the way she moved onstage, as careful and precise as a doe, each agile maneuver employing precisely as much strength as she needed and no more.

As Act II began, Mara asked the AI to stop. Exhaustion, she said. Jakub tried to help her back to her room, but she protested, and he let her go.

She was in her own world now, closing down. She had no room left for him.

What can I do for you, Marale? he wanted to ask. *I will do anything. You will not let me hold you so I must find another way. I will change the laws of life and death. I will give you as much forever as I can,* sheineh maideleh. *See? I am doing it now.*

He knew that she hated it when he stood outside her door, watching, but when he heard her breath find the steady rhythm of sleep, he went to the threshold anyway. While she slept, Mara looked peaceful for a while, her chest gently rising and falling underneath her snow-colored quilt.

He lingered a long time. Eventually, he left her and returned downstairs to check the machines.

The new child was ready to be born.

For years, Jakub had dreamed of the numbers. They flickered in and out of focus as if displayed on old film. Sometimes they looked ashen and faded. At other times, they were darker than any real black. Always, they were written on palettes of human flesh.

Sometimes the dreams included fragmentary memories. Jakub would be back in the rooms his grandparents had rented when he was a child, watching bubbe prepare to clean the kitchen, pulling her left arm free from one long cotton sleeve, her tattoo a shock on the inside of her forearm. The skin there had gone papery with age, the ink bleached and distorted, but time and sun had not made the mark less portentous. She scoured cookware with steel wool and caustic chemicals that made her hands red and raw when they emerged from the bubbling water. No matter how often Jakub watched, he never stopped expecting her to abandon the ancient pots and turn that furious, unrelenting scrubbing onto herself.

Zayde's tattoo remained more mysterious. It had not been inflicted in Auschwitz and so it hid in the more discreet location they'd used on the trains, needled onto the underside of his upper arm. Occasionally on hot days when Jakub was small, zayde would roll up his sleeves while he worked outside in the sun. If Jakub or one of the other boys found him, zayde would shout at them to get back inside and then finish the work in his long sleeves, dripping with sweat.

Jakub's grandparents never spoke of the camps. Both had been young in those years, but even though they were not much older when they were released, the few pictures of them from that time showed figures that were already brittle and dessicated in both physique and expression. Survivors took many paths away from the devastation, but bubbe and zayde were among those who always afterward walked with their heads down.

Being mutually bitter and taciturn, they resisted marriage until long after their contemporaries had sought comfort in each other's arms. They raised their children with asperity, and sent them into the world as adults with small gifts of money and few displays of emotion.

One of those children was Jakub's mother, who immigrated to the United States where she married. Some years later, she died in childbirth, bearing what would have been Jakub's fifth brother had the child not been stillborn. Jakub's father, grieving, could not take care of his four living sons. Instead, he wrote to his father-in-law in Poland and requested that he come to the United States and take them home with him.

Even then, when he arrived on foreign shores to fetch boys he'd never met and take them back with him to a land they'd never known; even then when the moment should have been grief and gathering; even then zayde's face was hard-lined with resignation. Or so Jakub's elder brothers had told him, for he was the youngest of the surviving children, having learned to speak a few words by then but not yet able to stand on his own.

When the boys were children, it was a mystery to them how such harsh people could have spent long enough together to marry, let alone have children. Surely, they would have been happier with others who were kinder, less astringent, who could bring comfort into a marriage.

One afternoon, when Jakub was four years old, and too naïve to yet understand that some things that were discussed in private should not be shared with everyone, he was sitting with bubbe while she sewed shirts for the boys (too expensive to buy, and shouldn't she know how to sew, having done it all her life?). He asked, "If you don't like zayde, why did you marry him?"

She stopped suddenly. Her hands were still on the machine, her mouth open, her gaze fastened on the seam. For a moment, the breath did not rise in her chest. The needle stuttered to a stop as her foot eased its pressure on the pedal.

She did not deny it or ask *What do you mean?* Neither did she answer any of the other questions that might have been enfolded in that one, like *Why don't you like him?* or *Why did you marry at all?*

Instead, she heard Jakub's true question: *Why zayde and not someone else?*

"How could it be another?" she asked. "We're the same."

And then she began sewing again, making no further mention of it, which was what zayde would have done, too, if Jakub had left bubbe at her sewing and instead taken his question to zayde as he replaced the wiring in their old, old walls.

As important as it was for the two of them that they shared a history, it also meant that they were like knives to each other, constantly reopening each other's old wounds and salting them with tears and anger. Their frequent, bitter arguments could continue for days upon days.

The days of arguing were better than those when bitter silence descended, and each member of the family was left in their own, isolated coldness.

It was not that there were no virtues to how the boys were raised. Their bodies were kept robust on good food, and their minds strengthened with the exercise of solving problems both practical and intellectual. Zayde concocted new projects for them weekly. One week they'd learn to build cabinets, and the next they'd read old books of philosophy, debating free will versus determinism. Jakub took Leibniz's part against zayde's Spinoza. They studied the Torah as an academic text, though zayde was an atheist of the bitter stripe after his time in the camps.

When Jakub was nine, bubbe decided that it was time to cultivate their spirits as well as their minds and bodies. She revealed that she had been having dreams about G-d for decades, ever since the day she left the camp. The events of those hours had haunted her dreams and as she watched them replay, she felt the scene overlaid with a shining sense of awe and renewal, which over the years, she had come to believe was the presence of G-d. Knowing zayde's feelings about G-d, bubbe had kept her silence in the name of peace for decades, but that year, some indefinable thing had shifted her conscience and she could do so no longer.

As she'd predicted, zayde was furious. "I am supposed to worship a G-d that would make *this* world?" he demanded. "A G-d like that is no G-d. A G-d like that is evil."

But despite the hours of shouting, slammed doors, and smashed crockery, bubbe remained resolute. She became a *frum* woman, dressing carefully, observing prayers and rituals. On Fridays, the kitchen became the locus of urgent energy as bubbe rushed to prepare for Shabbat, directing Jakub and his brothers to help with the chores. All of them worked tensely, preparing for the moment when zayde would return home and throw the simmering cholent out of the window, or—if they were lucky—turn heel and walk back out, going who-knew-where until he came home on Sunday.

After a particularly vicious argument, zayde proclaimed that while he apparently could not stop his wife from doing as she pleased, he would absolutely no longer permit his grandsons to attend *shul*. It was a final decision; otherwise, one of them would have to leave and never come back. After that, bubbe slipped out alone each week, into the chilly morning.

From zayde and bubbe, Jakub learned that love was both balm and nettle. They taught him from an early age that nothing could hurt so much as family.

Somehow, Jakub had expected the new child to be clumsy and vacant as if she were an infant, but the moment she initialized, her blank look vanished. Some parts of her face tensed and others relaxed. She blinked. She looked just like Mara.

She prickled under Jakub's scrutiny. "What are you staring at? Is something wrong?"

Jakub's mouth worked silently as he sought the words. "I thought you would need more time to adjust."

The child smiled Mara's cynical, lopsided smile, which had been absent for months. "I think you're going to need more time to adjust than I do."

She pulled herself to her feet. It wasn't just her face that had taken on Mara's habits of expression. Without pause, she moved into one of the stretches that Meryem had taught her, elongating her spine. When she relaxed, her posture was exactly like Mara's would have been, a preadolescent slouch ameliorated by a hint of dancer's grace.

"Can we go upstairs?" she asked.

"Not yet," Jakub said. "There are tests to perform."

Tests which she passed. Every single one. She knew Mara's favorite colors and the names of the children she had studied with in attic space. She knew the color and weight of the apples that would grow on their trees next fall and perfectly recited the recipe for baking them with cinnamon. In the gruff tone that Mara used when she was guarding against pain, she related the story of Meryem's death—how Meryem had woken with complaints of feeling dizzy, how she had slipped in the bath later that morning, how her head had cracked against the porcelain and spilled red into the bathwater.

She ran like Mara and caught a ball like Mara and bent to touch her toes like Mara. She was precisely as fleet and as nimble and as flexible as Mara. She performed neither worse nor better. She was Mara's twin in every way that Jakub could measure.

"You will need to stay here for a few more days," he told her, bringing down blankets and pillows so that he could make her a bed in the workshop. "There are still more tests. You will be safer if you remain close to the machines."

The new child's face creased with doubt. He was lying to spare her feelings, but she was no more deceived than Mara would have been. She said, "My room is upstairs."

For so many months, Jakub and Mara had taken refuge in mutual silence when the subject turned uncomfortable. He did not like to speak so bluntly. But if she would force him—"No," he said gently. "That is Mara's room."

"Can't I at least see it?"

A wheedling overtone thinned her voice. Her body language occupied a strange lacuna between aggression and vulnerability. She faced him full-on, one foot advancing, with her hands clenched tightly at her sides. Yet at the same time, she could not quite meet his eyes, and her head was tilted slightly downward, protecting her neck.

Jakub had seen that strange combination before. It was not so unusual a posture for teenagers to wear when they were trying to assert their agency through rebellion and yet simultaneously still hoping for their parents' approval.

Mara had never reached that stage. Before she became ill, she had been calm, abiding. Jakub began to worry that he'd erred in his calculations, that the metrics he'd used had been inadequate to measure the essence of a girl. Could she have aged so much, simply being slipped into an artificial skin?

"Mara is sleeping now."

"But I *am* Mara!" The new child's voice broke on her exclamation.

Her lips parted uncertainly. Her fingers trembled. Her glance flashed upward for a moment and he saw such pain in it. No, she was still his Mara. Not defiant, only afraid that he would decide that he had not wanted a mechanical daughter after all, that he would reject her like a broken radio and never love her again.

Gently, he laid his hand on her shoulder. Softly, he said, "You are Mara, but you need a new name, too. Let us call you Ruth."

He had not known until he spoke that he was going to choose that name, but it was a good one. In the Torah, Ruth had given Mara *hesed*. His Mara needed loving kindness, too.

The new child's gaze flickered upward as if she could see through the ceiling and into Mara's room. "Mara is the name ima gave me," she protested.

Jakub answered, "It would be confusing otherwise."

He hoped that this time the new child would understand what he meant without his having to speak outright. The other Mara had such a short time. It would be cruel to make her days harder than they must be.

On the day when Jakub gave the automaton her name, he found himself recalling the story of Ruth. It had been a long time since he had given the Torah any serious study, but though he had forgotten its minutiae, he remembered its rhythm. His thoughts assumed the cadences of half-forgotten rabbis.

It began when a famine descended on Judah.

A man, Elimelech, decided that he was not going to let his wife and sons starve to death, and so he packed his household and brought them to Moab. It was good that he had decided to do so, because once they reached Moab, he died, and left his wife and sons alone.

His wife was named Naomi and her name meant pleasant. The times were not pleasant.

Naomi's sons married women from Moab, one named Orpah and the other named Ruth. Despite their father's untimely death, the boys spent ten happy years with their new wives. But the men of that family had very poor luck. Both sons died.

There was nothing left for Naomi in Moab and so she packed up her house and prepared to return to Judah. She told her daughters-in-law, "Go home to your mothers. You were always kind to my sons and you've always been kind to me. May Hashem be kind to you in return."

She kissed them good-bye, but the girls wept.

They said, "Can't we return to Judah with you?"

"Go back to your mothers," Naomi repeated. "I have no more sons for you to marry. What can I give if you stay with me?"

The girls continued to weep, but at last sensible Orpah kissed her mother-in-law and left for home.

Ruth, who was less sensible; Ruth, who was more loving; Ruth, who was more kind; Ruth, she would not go.

"Don't make me leave you," Ruth said. "Wherever you go, I will go. Wherever you lodge, I will lodge. Your people will be my people and your G-d my G-d."

When Naomi saw that Ruth was committed to staying with her, she abandoned her arguing and let her come.

They traveled together to Bethlehem. When they arrived, they found that the whole city had gathered to see them. Everyone was curious about the two women traveling from Moab. One woman asked, "Naomi! Is that you?"

Naomi shook her head. "Don't call me Naomi. There is no pleasantness in my life. Call me Mara, which means bitterness, for the Almighty has dealt very bitterly with me."

Through the bitterness, Ruth stayed. While Naomi became Mara, Ruth stayed. Ruth gave her kindness, and Ruth stayed.

Jakub met Meryem while he was in Cleveland for a robotics conference. He'd attended dozens, but somehow this one made him feel particularly self-conscious in his cheap suit and tie among all the wealthy *goyim*.

By then he was living in the United States, but although he'd been born there, he rarely felt at home among its people. Between talks, he escaped from the hotel to go walking. That afternoon, he found his way to a path that wound through a park, making its way through dark-branched trees that waved their remaining leaves like flags of ginger, orange, and gold.

Meryem sat on an ironwork bench beside a man-made lake, its water silvered with dusk. She wore a black felt coat that made her look pallid even though her cheeks were pink with cold. A wind rose as Jakub approached, rippling through Meryem's hair. Crows took off from the trees, disappearing into black marks on the horizon.

Neither of them was ever able to remember how they began to converse. Their courtship seemed to rise naturally from the lake and the crows and the fallen leaves, as if it were another inevitable element of nature. It was *bashert*.

Meryem was younger than Jakub, but even so, already ballet had begun taking its toll on her body. Ballet was created by trading pain for beauty, she used to say. Eventually, beauty vanished and left only the pain.

Like Jakub, Meryem was an immigrant. Her grandparents had been born in Baghdad where they lived through the *farhud* instead of the *shoah*. They stayed in Iraq despite the pogroms until the founding of Israel made it too dangerous to remain. They abandoned their family home and fled to the U.S.S.R.

When Meryem was small, the Soviet government identified her talent for dance and took her into training. Ballet became her new family. It was her blood and bone, her sacred and her profane.

Her older brother sometimes sent letters, but with the accretion of time and distance, Meryem came to think of her family as if they were not so much people as they were the words spelled out in Yusuf's spidery handwriting.

Communism fell, and Meryem's family was given the opportunity to reclaim her, but even a few years away is so much of a child's lifetime. She begged them not to force her to return. They no longer felt like her home. More, ballet had become the gravitational center of her life, and while she still resented it—how it had taken her unwillingly, how it bruised her feet and sometimes made them bleed—she also could not bear to leave its orbit. When Yusuf's letters stopped coming some time later, she hardly noticed.

She danced well. She was a lyrical ballerina, performing her roles with tender, affecting beauty that could make audiences weep or smile. She rapidly moved from corps to soloist to principal. The troupe traveled overseas to perform Stravinsky's *Fire-bird*, and when they reached the United States, Meryem decided to emigrate, which she accomplished with a combination of bribes and behind-the-scenes dealings.

Jakub and Meryem recognized themselves in each other's stories. Like his grand-parents, they were drawn together by their similarities. Unlike them, they built a ref-uge together instead of a battlefield.

After Meryem died, Jakub began dreaming that that the numbers were inscribed into the skins of people who'd never been near the camps. His skin. His daughter's. His wife's. They were all marked, as Cain was marked, as the Christians believed the devil would mark his followers at the end of time. Marked for diaspora, to blow away from each other and disappear.

"Is the doll awake?" Mara asked one morning.

Jakub looked up from his breakfast to see her leaning against the doorway that led into the kitchen. She wore a large T-shirt from Yellowstone that came to her knees, covering a pair of blue jeans that had not been baggy when he'd bought them for her. Her skin was wan and her eyes shadowed and sunken. Traces of inflammation from the drugs lingered, painfully red, on her face and hands. The orange knit cap pulled over her ears was incongruously bright.

Jakub could not remember the last time she'd worn something other than paja-mas.

"She is down in the workshop," Jakub said.

"She's awake, though?"

"She is awake."

"Bring her up."

Jakub set his spoon beside his leftover bowl of *chlodnik*. Mara's mouth was turned down at the corners, hard and resolute. She lifted her chin at a defiant angle.

"She has a bed in the workshop," Jakub said. "There are still tests I must run. It's best she stay close to the machines."

Mara shook her head. It was clear from her face that she was no more taken in by his lie than the new child had been. "It's not fair to keep someone stuck down there."

Jakub began to protest that the workshop was not such a bad place, but then he caught the flintiness in Mara's eyes and realized that she was not asking out of worry. She had dressed as best she could and come to confront him because she wanted her first encounter with the new child to be on her terms. There was much he could not give her, but he could give her that.

"I will bring her for dinner," he said. "Tomorrow, for Shabbat."

Mara nodded. She began the arduous process of departing the kitchen, but then stopped and turned back. "Abba," she said hesitantly. "If ima hated the ballet, why did you build her a studio?"

"She asked for one," Jakub said.

Mara waited.

At last, he continued, "Ballet was part of her. She could not simply stop."

Mara nodded once more. This time, she departed.

Jakub finished his *chlodnik* and spent the rest of the day cooking. He meted out ingredients for familiar dishes. A pinch, a dash, a dab. Chopping, grating, boiling, sampling. Salt and sweet, bitter and savory.

As he went downstairs to fetch Ruth, he found himself considering how strange it must be for her to remember these rooms and yet never to have entered them. Jakub and Meryem had drawn the plans for the house together. She'd told him that she was content to leave a world of beauty that was made by pain, in exchange for a plain world made by joy.

He'd said he could give her that.

They painted the outside walls yellow to remind them of the sun during the winter, and painted blue inside to remind them of the sky. By the time they had finished, Mara was waiting inside Meryem's womb. The three of them had lived in the house for seven years before Meryem died.

These past few weeks had been precious. Precious because he had, in some ways, finally begun to recover the daughter that he had lost on the day her leg shattered—Ruth, once again curious and strong and insightful, like the Mara he had always known. But precious, too, because these were his last days with the daughter he'd made with Meryem.

Precious days, but hardly bearable, even as he also could not bear that they would pass. Precious, but more salt and bitter than savory and sweet.

The next night, when Jakub entered the workshop, he found Ruth on the stool where she'd sat so long when she was empty. Her shoulders slumped; her head hung down. He began to worry that something was wrong, but then he saw that she was only reading the book of poetry that she held in her lap.

"Would you like to come upstairs for dinner?" Jakub asked.

Setting the poems aside, Ruth rose to join him.

Long before Jakub met Meryem—back in those days when he still traveled the country on commissions from the American government—Jakub had become friends with a rabbi from Minneapolis. The two still exchanged letters through the postal mail, rarefied and expensive as it was.

After Jakub sent the news from Doctor Pinsky, the rabbi wrote back, "First your wife and now your daughter . . . *es vert mir finster in di oygen.* You must not let yourself be devoured by *agmes-nefesh.* Even in the camps, people kept hope. *Yashir koyech,* my friend. You must keep hope, too."

Jakub had not written to the rabbi about the new child. Even if it had not been vital for him to keep the work secret, he would not have written about it. He could not be sure what the rabbi would say. Would he call the new child a golem instead of a girl? Would he declare the work unseemly or unwise?

But truly, Jakub was only following the rabbi's advice. The new child was his strength and hope. She would prevent him from being devoured by sorrow.

When Jakub and Ruth arrived in the kitchen for Shabbat, Mara had not yet come.

They stood alone together in the empty room. Jakub had mopped the floors and scrubbed the counters and set the table with good dishes. The table was laid with challah, apricot chicken with farfel, and almond and raisin salad. *Cholent* simmered in a crock pot on the counter, waiting for Shabbat lunch.

Ruth started toward Mara's chair on the left. Jakub caught her arm, more roughly than he'd meant to. He pulled back, contrite. "No," he said softly. "Not there." He gestured to the chair on the right. Resentment crossed the new child's face, but she went to sit.

It was only as Jakub watched Ruth lower herself into the right-hand chair that he realized his mistake. "No! Wait. Not in Meryem's chair. Take mine. I'll switch with you—"

Mara's crutches clicked down the hallway. It was too late.

She paused in the doorway. She wore the blond wig Jakub had bought for her after the targeted immersion therapy failed. Last year's green Pesach dress hung off of her shoulders. The cap sleeves neared her elbows.

Jakub moved to help with her crutches. She stayed stoic while he helped her sit, but he could see how much it cost her to accept assistance while she was trying to maintain her dignity in front of the new child. It would be worse because the new child possessed her memories and knew precisely how she felt.

Jakub leaned the crutches against the wall. Ruth looked away, embarrassed.

Mara gave her a corrosive stare. "Don't pity me."

Ruth looked back. "What do you want me to do?"

"Turn yourself off," said Mara. "You're *muktzeh*."

Jakub wasn't sure he'd ever before heard Mara use the Hebrew word for objects forbidden on the Sabbath. Now, she enunciated it with crisp cruelty.

Ruth remained calm. "One may work on the Sabbath if it saves a life."

Mara scoffed. "If you call yours a life."

Jakub wrung his hands. "Please, Mara," he said. "You asked her to come."

Mara held her tongue for a lingering moment. Eventually, she nodded formally toward Ruth. "I apologize."

Ruth returned the nod. She sat quietly, hands folded in her lap. She didn't take nutrition from food, but Jakub had given her a hollow stomach that she could empty after meals so she would be able to eat socially. He waited to see if she would return Mara's insults, but she was the old Mara, the one who wasn't speared with pain and fear, the one who let bullies wind themselves up if that was what they wanted to do.

Jakub looked between the girls. "Good," he said. "We should have peace for the Sabbath."

He went to the head of the table. It was late for the blessing, the sun skimming the horizon behind bare, black trees. He lit the candles and waved his hands over the flames to welcome Shabbat. He covered his eyes as he recited the blessing. "*Barukh atah Adonai, Elohaynu, melekh ha-olam . . .*"

Every time he said the words that should have been Meryem's, he remembered the way she had looked when she said them. Sometimes she peeked out from behind her fingers so that she could watch Mara. They were small, her hands, delicate like bird wings. His were large and blunt.

The girls stared at each other as Jakub said kaddish. After they washed their hands and tore the challah, Jakub served the chicken and the salad. Both children ate almost nothing and said even less.

"It's been a long time since we've had three for Shabbat," Jakub said. "Perhaps we can have a good *vikuekh*. Mara, I saw you reading my Simic? Ruth has been reading poetry, too. Haven't you, Ruth?"

Ruth shifted the napkin in her lap. "Yehuda Amichai," she said. *"Even a Fist Was once an Open Palm with Fingers."*

"I love the first poem in that book," Jakub said. "I was reading it when—"

Mara's voice broke in, so quietly that he almost didn't hear. "Ruth?"

Jakub looked to Ruth. The new child stared silently down at her hands. Jakub cleared his throat, but she did not look up.

Jakub answered for her. "Yes?"

Mara's expression was slack, somewhere between stunned and lifeless. "You named her Ruth."

"She is here for you. As Ruth was there for Mara."

Mara began to cry. It was a tiny, pathetic sound. She pushed away her plate and tossed her napkin onto the table. "How could you?"

"Ruth gives *hesed* to Mara," Jakub said. "When everyone else left, Ruth stayed by her side. She expected nothing from her loving, from her kindness."

"Du kannst nicht auf meinem rucken pishen unt mir sagen class es regen ist," Mara said bitterly.

Jakub had never heard Mara say that before either. The crass proverb sounded wrong in her mouth. "Please, I am telling you the truth," he said. "I wanted her name to be part of you. To come from your story. The story of Mara."

"Is that what I am to you?" Mara asked. "Bitterness?"

"No, no. Please, no. We never thought you were bitterness. Mara was the name Meryem chose. Like Maruska, the Russian friend she left behind." Jakub paused. "Please. I did not mean to hurt you. I thought the story would help you see. I wanted you to understand. The new child will not harm you. She'll show you *hesed*."

Mara flailed for her crutches.

Jakub stood to help. Mara was so weak that she accepted his assistance. Tears flowed down her face. She left the room as quickly as she could, refusing to look at either Jakub or the new child.

Jakub looked between her retreating form and Ruth's silent one. The new child's expression was almost as unsure as Jakub's.

"Did you know?" Jakub asked. "Did you know how she'd feel?"

Ruth turned her head as if turning away from the question. "Talk to her," she said quietly. "I'll go back down to the basement."

Mara sat on her bed, facing the snow. Jakub stood at the threshold. She spoke without turning. *"Hesed* is a hard thing," she said. "Hard to take when you can't give it back."

Jakub crossed the room, past the chair he'd made her when she was little, with Meryem's shawl hung over the back; past the hanging marionette dressed as Giselle; past the cube Mara used for her lessons in attic space. He sat beside her on her white quilt and looked at her silhouetted form against the white snow.

She leaned back toward him. Her body was brittle and delicate against his chest.

He remembered sitting on that bed with Mara and Meryem, reading stories, playing with toys. *Tsuris, tsuris.* Life was all so fragile. He was not graceful enough to keep it from breaking.

Mara wept. He held his *bas-yekhide* in his large, blunt hands.

ACT III: RUTH

Échappé
(*Escape*)

At first, Ruth couldn't figure out why she didn't want to switch herself off. Mara had reconciled herself to Ruth's existence, but in her gut, she still wanted Ruth to be gone. And Ruth was Mara, so she should have felt the same.

But no, her experiences were diverging. Mara wanted the false daughter to vanish. Mara thought Ruth was the false daughter, but Ruth knew she wasn't false at all. She *was* Mara. Or had been.

Coming into existence was not so strange. She felt no peculiar doubling, no sensation that her hands weren't hers, no impression that she had been pulled out of time and was supposed to be sleeping upstairs with her face turned toward the window.

She felt more secure in the new body than she had in Mara's. This body was healthy, even round in places. Her balance was steady; her fingernails were pink and intact.

After abba left her the first night, Ruth found a pane of glass that he'd set aside for one of his projects. She stared at her blurred reflection. The glass showed soft, smooth cheeks. She ran her fingers over them and they confirmed that her skin was downy now instead of sunken. Clear eyes stared back at her.

Over the past few months, Mara had grown used to experiencing a new alienation every time she looked in the mirror. She'd seen a parade of strangers' faces, each dimmer and hollower than the last.

Her face was her own again.

She spent her first days doing tests. Abba watched her jump and stretch and run on a treadmill. For hours upon hours, he recorded her answers to his questions.

It was tedious for her, but abba was fascinated by her every word and movement. Sometimes he watched as a father. Sometimes he watched as a scientist. At first Ruth chafed under his experimental gaze, but then she remembered that he had treated Mara like that, too. He'd liked to set up simple experiments to compare her progress to child-development manuals. She remembered ima complaining that he'd been even worse when Mara was an infant. Ruth supposed this was the same. She'd been born again.

While he observed her, she observed him. Abba forgot that some experiments could look back.

The abba she saw was a different man than the one she remembered sitting with Mara. He'd become brooding with Mara as she grew sicker. His grief had become a deep anger with G-d. He slammed doors and cabinets, and grimaced with bitter fury when he thought she wasn't looking. He wanted to break the world.

He still came down into the basement with that fury on his face, but as he talked to Ruth, he began to calm. The muscles in his forehead relaxed. He smiled now and then. He reached out to touch her hand, gently, as if she were a soap bubble that might break if he pressed too hard.

Then he went upstairs, back to that other Mara.

"Don't go yet," Ruth would beg. "We're almost done. It won't take much longer." He'd linger.

She knew he thought she was just bored and wanted attention. But that wasn't why she asked. She hated the storm that darkened his eyes when he went up to see the dying girl.

After a few minutes, he always said the same thing, resolute and loyal to his still-living child. "I must go, *nu?*"

He sent Abel down in his place. The dog thumped down and waited for her to greet him at the foot of the stairs. He whuffed hello, breath humid and smelly.

Ruth had been convinced—when she was Mara—that a dog would never show affection for a robot. Maybe Abel only liked Ruth because his sense of smell, like the rest of him, was in decline. Whatever the reason, she was Mara enough for him.

Ruth ran the treadmill while Abel watched, tail wagging. She thought about chasing him across the snowy yard, about breaking sticks off of the bare-branched trees to throw for him. She could do anything. She could run; she could dance; she could swim; she could ride. She could almost forgive abba for treating her like a prototype instead of a daughter, but she couldn't forgive him for keeping her penned. The real Mara was stuck in the house, but Ruth didn't have to be. It wasn't fair to have spent so long static, waiting to die, and then suddenly be free—and still remain as trapped as she'd ever been.

After the disastrous Shabbat, she went back down to the basement and sat on one of abba's workbenches. Abel came down after her. He leaned against her knees, warm and heavy. She patted his head.

She hadn't known how Mara was going to react.

She should have known. She would have known if she'd thought about it. But she hadn't considered the story of Mara and Ruth. All she'd been thinking about was that Ruth wasn't her name.

Their experiences had branched off. They were like twins who'd shared the womb only to be delivered into a world where each new event was a small alienation, until their individual experiences separated them like a chasm.

One heard a name and wanted her own back. One heard a name and saw herself as bitterness.

One was living. One was dying.

She was still Mara enough to feel the loneliness of it.

The dog's tongue left a trail of slobber across the back of her hand. He pushed his head against her. He was warm and solid, and she felt tears threatening, and wasn't sure why. It might have been grief for Mara. Perhaps it was just the unreasonable relief that someone still cared about her. Even though it was miserly to crave attention when Mara was dying, she still felt the gnaw of wondering whether abba would still love her when Mara was gone, or whether she'd become just a machine to him, one more painful reminder.

She jumped off of the table and went to sit in the dark, sheltered place beneath it. There was security in small places—in closets, under beds, beneath the desk in her room. Abel joined her, pushing his side against hers. She curled around him and switched her brain to sleep.

After Shabbat, there was no point in separating Ruth and Mara anymore. Abba told Ruth she could go wherever she wanted. He asked where she wanted to sleep. "We can put a mattress in the parlor," he said. When she didn't react, he added, "Or the studio . . . ?"

She knew he didn't want her in the studio. Mara was mostly too tired to leave her room now, but abba would want to believe that she was still sneaking into the studio to watch ima's videos.

Ruth wanted freedom, but it didn't matter where she slept.

"I'll stay in the basement," she said.

When she'd had no choice but to stay in the basement, she'd felt like a compressed coil that might spring uncontrollably up the stairs at any moment. Now that she was free to move around, it didn't seem so urgent. She could take her time a little, choose those moments when going upstairs wouldn't make things worse, such as when abba and Mara were both asleep, or when abba was sitting with Mara in her room.

Once she'd started exploring, she realized it was better that she was on her own anyway. Moving through the house was dreamlike, a strange blend of familiarity and alienation. These were rooms she knew like her skin, and yet she, as Ruth, had never entered them. The handprint impressed into the clay tablet on the wall wasn't hers; it was Mara's. She could remember the texture of the clay as she pushed in her palm, but it hadn't been her palm. She had never sat at the foot of the plush, red chair in the parlor while ima brushed her hair. The scuff marks on the hardwood in the hallway were from someone else's shoes.

As she wandered from room to room, she realized that on some unconscious level, when she'd been Mara, she'd believed that moving into a robotic body would clear the haze of memories that hung in the house. She'd imagined a robot would be a mechanical, sterile thing. In reality, ima still haunted the kitchen where she'd cooked, and the studio where she'd danced, and the bathroom where she'd died.

Change wasn't exorcism.

Ruth remained restless. She wanted more than the house. For the first time in months, she found herself wanting to visit attic space, even though her flock was even worse about handling cancer than adults, who were bad enough. The pity in Collin's eyes, especially, had made her want to puke so much that she hadn't even let herself think about him. Mara had closed the door on her best friend early in the process of closing the doors on her entire life.

She knew abba would be skeptical, though, so she wanted to bring it up in a way that seemed casual. She waited for him to come down to the workshop for her daily exam, and tried to broach the subject as if it were an afterthought.

"I think I should go back to the attic," she ventured. "I'm falling behind. My flock is moving on without me."

Abba looked up from the screen, frowning. He worried his hands in a way that had become troublingly familiar. "They know Mara is sick."

"I'll pretend to be sick," Ruth said. "I can fake it."

She'd meant to sound detached, as if her interest in returning to school was purely pragmatic, but she couldn't keep the anticipation out of her tone.

"I should go back now before it's been too long," she said. "I can pretend I'm starting to feel better. We don't want my recovery to look too sudden."

"It is not a good idea," abba said. "It would only add another complication. If you did not pretend correctly? If people noticed? You are still new-made. Another few weeks and you will know better how to control your body."

"I'm bored," Ruth said. Making another appeal to his scholarly side, she added, "I miss studying."

"You can study. You've been enjoying the poetry, yes? There is so much for you to read."

"It's not the same." Ruth knew she was on the verge of whining, but she couldn't make her voice behave.

Abba paused, trepidation playing over his features as he considered his response. "Ruth, I have thought on this . . . I do not think it is good for you to go back to attic space. They will know you. They might see that something is wrong. We will find you another program for home learning."

Ruth stared. "You want me to leave attic space?" Almost everyone she knew, apart from abba and a few people in town, was from the attic. After a moment's thought, the implications were suddenly leaden in her mind. "You don't just want me to stop going for school, do you? You want me to stop seeing them at all."

Abba's mouth pursed around words he didn't want to say.

"Everyone?" asked Ruth. "Collin? Everyone?"

Abba wrung his hands. "I am sorry, Mara. I only want to protect you."

"Ruth!" Ruth said.

"Ruth," abba murmured. "Please. I am sorry, Ruthele."

Ruth swallowed hard, trying to push down sudden desperation. She hadn't wanted the name. She didn't want the name. But she didn't want to be confused for the Mara upstairs either. She wanted him to be there with *her*, talking to *her*.

"You can't keep me stuck here just because she is!" she said, meaning the words to bite. "She's the one who's dying. Not me."

Abba flinched. "You are so angry," he said quietly. "I thought, now that you were well—You did not used to be so angry."

"You mean *Mara* didn't used to be so angry," Ruth said. A horrible thought struck her and she felt cold that she hadn't thought of it before. "How am I going to grow up? Am I going to be stuck like this? Eleven, like she is, forever?"

"No, Ruth, I will build you new bodies," said abba. "Bodies are easy. It is the mind that is difficult."

"You just want me to be like her," Ruth said.

Abba fumbled for words. "I want you to be yourself."

"Then let me go do things! You can't hide me here forever."

"Please, Ruth. A little patience."

Patience!

Ruth swung off of the stool. The connectors in her wrist and neck tore loose and she threw them to the floor. She ran for the stairs, crashing into one of the diagnostic machines and knocking it over before making it to the bottom step.

Abba said nothing. Behind her, she heard the small noise of effort that he made as he lowered himself to the floor to retrieve the equipment.

It was strange to feel such bright-hot anger again. Like abba, she'd thought that the transfer had restored her even temper. But apparently the anger she'd learned while she was Mara couldn't just be forgotten.

She spent an hour pacing the parlor, occasionally grabbing books off of a shelf, flipping through them as she walked, and then putting them down in random locations. The brightness of the anger faded, although the sense of injustice remained.

Later, abba came up to see her. He stood with mute pleading, not wanting to re-open the argument but obviously unable to bear continuing to fight.

Even though Ruth hadn't given in yet, even though she was still burning from the unfairness, she couldn't look into his sad eyes without feeling thickness in her throat.

He gestured helplessly. "I just want to keep you safe, Ruthele."

They sat together on the couch without speaking. They were both entrenched in their positions. It seemed to Ruth that they were both trying to figure out how to make things right without giving in, how to keep fighting without wounding.

Abel paced between them, shoving his head into Ruth's lap, and then into abba's, back and forth. Ruth patted his head and he lingered with her a moment, gazing up with rheumy but devoted eyes.

Arguing with abba wasn't going to work. He hadn't liked her taking risks before she'd gotten sick, but afterward, keeping her safe had become obsession, which was why Ruth was even alive. He was a scientist, though; he liked evidence. She'd just have to show him it was safe.

Ruth didn't like to lie, but she'd do it. In a tone of grudging acceptance, she said, "You're right. It's too risky for me to go back."

"We will find you new friends," abba said. "We will be together. That's what is important."

Ruth bided her time for a few days. Abba might have been watching her more closely if he hadn't been distracted with Mara. Instead, when he wasn't at Mara's bedside or examining Ruth, he drifted mechanically through the house, registering little.

Ruth had learned a lot about engineering from watching her father. Attic space wasn't complicated technology. The program came on its own cube which meant it was entirely isolated from the household AI and its notification protocols. It also came with standard parental access points that had been designed to favor ease of use over security—which meant there were lots of back-end entryways.

Abba didn't believe in restricting access to knowledge so he'd made it even easier by deactivating the nanny settings on Mara's box as soon as she was old enough to navigate attic space on her own.

Ruth waited until nighttime when Mara was drifting in and out of her fractured, painful sleep, and abba had finally succumbed to exhaustion. Abba had left a light on in the kitchen, but it didn't reach the hallway to Mara's room, which fell in stark shadow. Ruth felt her way to Mara's threshold and put her ear to the door. She could hear the steady, sleeping rhythm of Mara's breath inside.

She cracked the door. Moonlight spilled from the window over the bed, allowing her to see inside. It was the first time she'd seen the room in her new body. It looked the same as it had. Mara was too sick to fuss over books or possessions, and so the objects sat in their places, ordered but dusty. Apart from the lump that Mara's body made beneath the quilt, the room looked as if it could have been abandoned for days.

The attic space box sat on a low shelf near the door. It fit in the palm of Ruth's hand. The fading image on its exterior showed the outline of a house with people inside, rendered in a style that was supposed to look like a child's drawing. It was the version they put out for five-year-olds. Abba had never replaced it. A waste of money, he said, when he could upgrade it himself.

Ruth looked up at the sound of blankets shifting. One of Mara's hands slipped free from the quilt. Her fingers dangled over the side of the bed, the knuckles exaggerated on thin bones. Inflamed cuticles surrounded her ragged nails.

Ruth felt a sting of revulsion and chastised herself. Those hands had been hers. She had no right to be repulsed.

The feeling faded to an ache. She wanted to kneel by the bed and take Mara's hand into her own. She wanted to give Mara the shelter and empathy that abba had built her to give. But she knew how Mara felt about her. Taking Mara's hand would not be *hesed*. The only loving kindness she could offer now was to leave.

As Ruth sat in ima's studio, carefully disassembling the box's hardware so that she could jury-rig it to interact with the television, it occurred to her that abba would have loved helping her with this project. He loved scavenging old technology. He liked to prove that cleverness could make tools of anything.

The complicated VR equipment that made it possible to immerse in attic space was far too bulky for Ruth to steal from Mara's room without being caught. She thought she could recreate a sketchy, winnowed down version of the experience using low-technology replacements from the television and other scavenged equipment. Touch, smell, and taste weren't going to happen, but an old stereo microphone allowed her to transmit on the voice channel. She found a way to instruct the box to send short bursts of visuals to the television, although the limited scope and speed would make it like walking down a hallway illuminated by a strobe light.

She sat cross-legged on the studio floor and logged in. It was the middle of the night, but usually at least someone from the flock was around. She was glad to see it was Collin this time, tweaking an experiment with crystal growth. Before she'd gotten sick, Ruth probably would have been there with him. They liked going in at night when there weren't many other people around.

She saw a still of Collin's hand over a delicate formation, and then another of him looking up, startled. "Mara?" he asked. "Is that you?"

His voice cracked when he spoke, sliding from low to high. It hadn't been doing that before.

"Hi, Collin," she said.

"Your avatar looks weird." She could imagine Collin squinting to investigate her image, but the television continued to show his initial look of surprise.

She was using a video skin capture from the last time Mara had logged in, months ago. Without a motion reader, it was probably just standing there, breathing and blinking occasionally, with no expression on its face.

"I'm on a weird connection," Ruth said.

"Is it because you're sick?" Collin's expression of concern flashed onscreen. "Can I see what you really like? It's okay. I've seen videos. I won't be grossed out or anything. I missed you. I thought—we weren't sure you were coming back. We were working on a video to say good-bye."

Ruth shifted uncomfortably. She'd wanted to go the attic so she could get on with living, not to be bogged down in dying. "I don't want to talk about that."

The next visual showed a flash of Colin's hand, blurred with motion as he raised it to his face. "We did some stuff with non-Newtonian fluids," he said tentatively. "You'd have liked it. We got all gross."

"Did you throw them around?" she asked.

"Goo fight," Collin agreed. He hesitated. "Are you coming back? Are you better?"

"Well—" Ruth began.

"Everyone will want to know you're here. Let me ping them."

"No. I just want to talk to you."

A new picture: Collin moving closer to her avatar, his face now crowding the narrow rectangle of her vision.

"I looked up osteosarcoma. They said you had lung nodules. Mara, are you really better? Are you really coming back?"

"I said I don't want to talk about it."

"But everyone will want to know."

Suddenly, Ruth wanted to be anywhere but attic space. Abba was right. She couldn't go back. Not because someone might find out but because everyone was going to want to know, what about Mara? They were going to want to know about Mara all the time. They were going to want to drag Ruth back into that sick bed, with her world narrowing toward death, when all she wanted was to move on.

And it was even worse now than it would have been half an hour ago, before she'd gone into Mara's room and seen her raw, tender hand, and thought about what it would be like to grasp it.

"I have to go," Ruth said.

"At least let me ping Violet," Collin said.

"I'll be back," Ruth answered. "I'll see you later."

On the television: Collin's skeptical face, brows drawn, the shine in his eyes that showed he thought she was lying.

"I promise," she said, hesitating only a moment before she tore the attic space box out of her jury-rigged web of wires.

Tears were filling her eyes and she couldn't help the sob. She threw the box. It skittered across the wooden floor until it smacked into the mirror. The thing was so old and knocked about that any hard collision might kill it, but what did that matter now? She wasn't going back.

She heard a sound from the doorway and looked up. She saw abba, standing behind the cracked door.

Ruth's anger flashed to a new target. "Why are you spying on me?"

"I came to check on Mara," abba said.

He didn't have to finish for his meaning to be clear. He'd heard someone in the studio and hoped it could still be his Marale.

He made a small gesture toward the attic space box. "It did not go well," he said quietly, statement rather than question.

Ruth turned her head away. He'd been right, about everything he'd said, all the explicit things she'd heard, and all the implicit things she hadn't wanted to.

She pulled her knees toward her chest. "I can't go back," she said.

Abba stroked her hair. "I know."

The loss of attic space hurt less than she'd thought it would. Mara had sealed off those tender spaces, and those farewells had a final ring. She'd said good-bye to Collin a long time ago.

What bothered her more was the lesson it forced; her life was never going to be the same, and there was no way to deny it. Mara would die and be gone, and Ruth had to learn to be Ruth, whoever Ruth was. That was what had scared Mara about Ruth in the first place.

The restlessness that had driven her into attic space still itched her. She started taking walks in the snow with Abel. Abba didn't try to stop her.

She stopped reading Jewish poetry and started picking up books on music theory. She practiced sight reading and toe-tapped the beats, imagining choreographies.

Wednesdays, when abba planned the menu for Shabbat, Ruth sat with him as he wrote out the list he would take to Gerry's on Thursday. As he imagined dishes, he talked about how Mara would like the honey he planned to infuse in the carrots, or the raisins and figs he would cook with the rice. He wondered what they should talk about—poetry, physics, international politics—changing his mind as new topics occurred to him.

Ruth wondered how he kept hoping. As Mara, she'd always known her boundaries before abba realized them. As Ruth, she knew, as clearly as Mara must, that Mara would not eat with them.

Perhaps it was cruel not to tell him, but to say it felt even crueler.

On a Thursday while abba was taking the truck to town, Ruth was looking through ima's collection of sheet music in the parlor when she heard the click of crutches down the hall. She turned to find Mara was behind her, breathing heavily.

"Oh," said Ruth. She tried to hide the surprise in her voice but failed.

"You didn't think I could get up on my own."

Mara's voice was thin.

"I . . ." Ruth began before catching the angry look of resolution on Mara's face. "No. I didn't."

"Of course not," Mara said bitterly. She began another sentence, but was interrupted by a ragged exhalation as she started to collapse against the wall. Ruth rushed to support her. Mara accepted her assistance without acknowledging it, as if it were beneath notice.

"Are you going to throw up?" Ruth asked quietly.

"I'm off the chemo."

Mara's weight fell heavily on Ruth's shoulder. She shifted her balance, determined not to let Mara slip.

"Let me take you back to bed," Ruth said.

Mara answered, "I wanted to see you again."

"I'll take you. We can talk in there."

Ruth took Mara's silence as assent. Abandoning the crutches, she supported Mara's weight as they headed back into the bedroom. In daylight, the room looked too bright, its creams and whites unsullied.

Mara's heaving eased as Ruth helped her into the bed, but her lungs were still working hard. Ruth waited until her breathing came evenly.

Ruth knelt by the bed, the way abba always had, and then wondered if that was a mistake. Mara might see Ruth as trying to establish power over her. She ducked her gaze for a moment, the way Abel might if he were ashamed, hoping Mara would see she didn't mean to challenge her.

"What did you want to say to me?" Ruth asked. "It's okay if you want to yell."

"Be glad," Mara said. "That you didn't have to go this far."

Mara's gaze slid down Ruth's face. It slowly took in her smooth skin and pink cheeks.

Ruth opened her mouth to respond, but Mara continued.

"It's a black hole. It takes everything in. You can see yourself falling. The universe doesn't look like it used to. Everything's blacker. So much blacker. And you know when you've hit the moment when you can't escape. You'll never do anything but fall."

Ruth extended her hand toward Mara's, the way she'd wanted to the other night, but stopped before touching her. She fumbled for something to say.

Flatly, Mara said, "I am glad at least someone will get away."

With great effort, she turned toward the window.

"Go away now."

She shouldn't have, but Ruth stood at the door that night when abba went in to check on Mara. She watched him kneel by the bed and take her hand. Mara barely moved in response, still staring out the window, but her fingers tensed around his, clutching him. Ruth remembered the way abba's hand had felt when she was sleepless and in pain, a solid anchor in a fading world.

She thought of what abba had said to her when she was still Mara, and made silent promises to the other girl. *I will keep you and hold you. I will protect you. I will always have your hand in mine.*

In the morning, when Ruth came back upstairs, she peeked through the open door to see abba still there beside Mara, lying down instead of kneeling, his head pillowed on the side of her mattress.

She walked back down the hallway and to the head of the stairs. Drumming on her knees, she called for Abel. He lumbered toward her, the thump of his tail reassuringly familiar. She ruffled his fur and led him into the parlor where she slipped on his leash.

Wind chill took the outside temperature substantially below freezing, but she hesitated before putting on her coat. She ran her hand across the "skin" of her arm. It was robotic skin, not human skin. She'd looked at some of the schematics that abba had left around downstairs and started to wonder about how different she really was from a human. He'd programmed her to feel vulnerable to cold, but was she really?

She put the coat back on its hook and led Abel out the door. Immediately, she started shivering, but she ignored the bite. She wanted to know what she could do.

She trudged across the yard to the big, bony oak. She snapped off a branch, made Abel sit while she unhooked his leash, and threw the branch as far as she could. Abel's dash left dents in the snow. He came back to her, breath a warm relief on her hand, the branch slippery with slobber.

She threw it again and wondered what she could achieve if abba hadn't programmed her body to think it was Mara's. He'd given her all of Mara's limits. She could run as fast as Mara, but not faster. Calculate as accurately as Mara, but no moreso.

Someday, she and abba would have to talk about that.

She tossed the stick again, and Abel ran, and again, and again, until he was too tired to continue. He watched the branch fly away as he leaned against Mara's leg for support.

She gave his head a deep scratch. He shivered and he bit at the air near her hand. She realized her cold fingers were hurting him. For her, the cold had ceased to be painful, though she was still shivering now and then.

"Sorry, boy, sorry," she said. She reattached his leash, and watched how, despite the temperature, her fingers moved without any stiffness at all.

She headed back to the house, Abel making pleased whuffing noises to indicate that he approved of their direction. She stopped on the porch to stamp the snow off of her feet. Abel shook himself, likewise, and Ruth quickly dusted off what he'd missed.

She opened the door and Abel bounded in first, Ruth laughing and trying to keep her footing as he yanked on the leash. He was old and much weaker than he had been, but an excited burst of doggy energy could still make her rock. She stumbled in after him, the house dim after her cold hour outside.

Abba was in the parlor, standing by the window from which he'd have been able to see them play. He must have heard them come in, but he didn't look toward her until she tentatively called his name.

He turned and looked her over, surveying her bare arms and hands, but he gave no reaction. She could see from his face that it was over.

He wanted to bury her alone. She didn't argue.

He would plant Mara in the yard, perhaps under the bony tree, but more likely somewhere else in the lonely acreage, unmarked. She didn't know how he planned to dig in the frozen ground, but he was a man of many contraptions. Mara would always be out there, lost in the snow.

When he came back, he clutched her hand as he had clutched Mara's. It was her turn to be what abba had been for Mara, the anchor that kept him away from the lip of the black hole, the one steady thing in a dissolving world.

They packed the house without discussing it. Ruth understood what was happening as soon as she saw abba filling the first box with books. Probably she'd known for some time, on the fringe of her consciousness, that they would have to do this. As they wrapped dishes in tissue paper, and sorted through old papers, they shared silent grief at leaving the yellow house that abba had built with Meryem, and that both Mara and Ruth had lived in all their lives.

Abba had enough money that he didn't need to sell the property. The house would remain owned and abandoned in the coming years.

It was terrible to go, but it also felt like a necessary marker, a border bisecting her life. It was one more way in which she was becoming Ruth.

They stayed in town for one last Shabbat. The process of packing the house had altered their sense of time, making the hours seem foreshortened and stretched at turns.

Thursday passed without their noticing, leaving them to buy their groceries on Friday. Abba wanted to drive into town on his own, but Ruth didn't want him to be alone yet.

Reluctantly, she agreed to stay in the truck when they got there. Though abba had begun to tell people that she was recovering, it would be best if no one got a chance to look at her up close. They might realize something was wrong. It would be easier wherever they moved next; strangers wouldn't always be comparing her to a ghost.

Abba was barely out of the truck before Gerry caught sight of them through the window and came barreling out of the door. Abba tried to get in his way. Rapidly, he stumbled out the excuse that he and Ruth had agreed on, that it was good for her to get out of the house, but she was still too tired to see anyone.

"A minute won't hurt," said Gerry. He pushed past abba. With a huge grin, he knocked on Ruth's window.

Hesitantly, she rolled it down. Gerry crossed his arms on the sill, leaning his head into the vehicle. "Look at you!" he exclaimed. "Your daddy said you were getting better, but just *look* at you!"

Ruth couldn't help but grin. Abel's tail began to thump as he pushed himself into the front seat to get a better look at his favorite snack provider.

"I have to say, after you didn't come the last few weeks . . ." Gerry wiped his eyes with the back of his hand. "I'm just glad to see you, Mara, I really am."

At the sound of the name, Ruth looked with involuntary shock at abba, who gave a sad little smile that Gerry couldn't see. He took a step forward. "Please, Gerry. She needs to rest."

Gerry looked back at him, opened his mouth to argue, and then looked back at Ruth and nodded. "Okay then. But next week, I expect some free cashier work!" He leaned in to kiss her cheek. He smelled of beef and rosemary. "You get yourself back here, Mara. And you keep kicking that cancer in the rear end."

With a glance back at the truck to check that Mara was okay, abba followed Gerry into the store. Twenty minutes later, he returned with two bags of groceries, which he put in the bed of the truck. As he started the engine, he said, "Gerry is a good man. I will miss him." He paused. "But it is better to have you, Mara."

Ruth looked at him with icy surprise, breath caught in her throat.

Her name was her own again. She wasn't sure how she felt about that.

The sky was bronzing when they arrived home.

On the stove, *cholent* simmered, filling the house with its scent. Abba went to check on it before the sun set, and Ruth followed him into the kitchen, preparing to pull out the dishes and the silverware and the table cloth.

He waved her away. "Next time. This week, let me."

Ruth went into ima's studio. She'd hadn't gone inside since the disaster it attic space, and her gaze lingered on the attic box, still lying dead on the floor.

"I'd like to access a DVD of ima's performances," she told the AI. "Coppelia, please."

It whirred.

The audience's rumblings began and she instructed the AI to fast-forward until Coppelia was onstage. She held her eyes closed and tipped her head down until it was the moment to snap into life, to let her body flow, fluid and graceful, mimicking the dancer on the screen.

She'd thought it would be cathartic to dance the part of the doll, and in a way it was, but once the moment was over, she surprised herself by selecting another disc instead of continuing. She tried to think of a comedy that she wanted to dance, and surprised herself further by realizing that she wanted to dance a tragedy instead. Mara had needed the comedies, but Ruth needed to feel the ache of grace and sorrow; she needed to feel the pull of the black hole even as she defied its gravity and danced, en pointe, on its edge.

When the light turned violet, abba came to the door, and she followed him into the kitchen. Abba lit the candles, and she waited for him to begin the prayers, but instead he stood aside.

It took her a moment to understand what he wanted.

"Are you sure?" she asked.

"Please, Marale," he answered.

Slowly, she moved into the space where he should have been standing. The candles burned on the table beneath her. She waved her hands through the heat and thickness of the smoke, and then lifted them to cover her eyes.

She said, "*Barukh atah Adonai, Elohaynu, melekh ha-olam, asher kid'shanu b'mitzvotav, v'tzivanu, l'had'lik neir shel Shabbat.*"

She breathed deeply, inhaling the scents of honey and figs and smoke.
"*Amein.*"

She opened her eyes again. Behind her, she heard abba's breathing, and some-where in the dark of the house, Abel's snoring as he napped in preparation for after-dinner begging. The candles filled her vision as if she'd never seen them before. Bright white and gold flames trembled, shining against the black of the outside sky, so fragile they could be extinguished by a breath.

She blew them out, and Sabbath began.

covenant

ELIZABETH BEAR

*Here's another story by Elizabeth Bear, whose "The Hand Is Quicker" ap-
pears elsewhere in this anthology.*

*"Covenant" offers a suspenseful look at the dilemma of a serial killer who
has been conditioned against killing—even when her own life is at stake.*

This cold could kill me, but it's no worse than the memories. Endurable as long as
I keep moving.

My feet drum the snow-scraped roadbed as I swing past the police station at the
top of the hill. Each exhale plumes through my mask, but insulating synthetics warm
my inhalations enough so they do not sting and seize my lungs. I'm running too hard
to breathe through my nose—running as hard and fast as I can, sprinting for the next
hydrant-marking reflector protruding above a dirty bank of ice. The wind pushes
into my back, cutting through the wet merino of my baselayer and the wet MaxReg
over it, but even with its icy assistance I can't come close to running the way I used to
run. Once I turn the corner into the graveyard, I'll be taking that wind in the face.

I miss my old body's speed. I ran faster before. My muscles were stronger then.
Memories weigh something. They drag you down. Every step I take, I'm carrying
thirteen dead. My other self runs a step or two behind me. I feel the drag of his invisible, immaterial presence.

As long as you keep moving, it's not so bad. But sometimes everything in the world
conspires to keep you from moving fast enough.

I thump through the old stone arch into the graveyard, under the trees glittering
with ice, past the iron gate pinned open by drifts. The wind's as sharp as I expected—
sharper—and I kick my jacket over to warming mode. That'll run the battery down,
but I've only got another five kilometers to go and I need heat. It's getting colder as
the sun rises, and clouds slide up the western horizon: cold front moving in. I flip the
sleeve light off with my next gesture, though that won't make much difference.
The sky's given light enough to run by for a good half hour, and the sleeve light is
on its own battery. A single LED doesn't use much.

I imagine the flexible circuits embedded inside my brain falling into quiescence
at the same time. Even smaller LEDs with even more advanced power cells go dark.

The optogenetic adds shut themselves off when my brain is functioning *healthily*. Normally, microprocessors keep me sane and safe, monitor my brain activity, stimulate portions of the neocortex devoted to ethics, empathy, compassion. When I run, though, my brain—my dysfunctional, murderous, *cured* brain—does it for itself as neural pathways are stimulated by my own native neurochemicals.

Only my upper body gets cold: though that wind chills the skin of my thighs and calves like an ice bath, the muscles beneath keep hot with exertion. And the jacket takes the edge off the wind that strikes my chest.

My shoes blur pink and yellow along the narrow path up the hill. Gravestones like smoker's teeth protrude through swept drifts. They're moldy black all over as if spray-painted, and glittering powdery whiteness heaps against their backs. Some of the stones date to the eighteenth century, but I run there only in the summertime or when it hasn't snowed. Maintenance doesn't plow that part of the churchyard. Nobody comes to pay their respects to *those* dead anymore.

Sort of like the man I used to be.

The ones I killed, however—some of them still get their memorials every year. I know better than to attend, even though my old self would have loved to gloat, to relive the thrill of their deaths. The new me . . . feels a sense of . . . obligation. But their loved ones don't know my new identity. And nobody owes *me* closure.

I'll have to take what I can find for myself. I've sunk into that beautiful quiet place where there's just the movement, the sky that true, irreproducible blue, the brilliant flicker of a cardinal. Where I die as a noun and only the verb survives.

I run. I am running.

When he met her eyes, he imagined her throat against his hands. Skin like calves' leather; the heat and the crack of her hyoid bone as he dug his thumbs deep into her pulse. The way she'd writhe, thrash, struggle.

His waist chain rattled as his hands twitched, jerking the cuffs taut on his wrists.

She glanced up from her notes. Her eyes were a changeable hazel: blue in this light, gray-green in others. Reflections across her glasses concealed the corner where text scrolled. It would have been too small to read, anyway—backwards, with the table he was chained to creating distance between them.

She waited politely, seeming unaware that he was imagining those hazel eyes dotted with petechiae, that fair skin slowly mottling purple. He let the silence sway between them until it developed gravity.

"Did you wish to say something?" she asked, with mild but clinical encouragement.

Point to me, he thought.

He shook his head. "I'm listening."

She gazed upon him benevolently for a moment. His fingers itched. He scrubbed the tips against the rough orange jumpsuit but stopped. In her silence, the whisking sound was too audible.

She continued, "The court is aware that your crimes are the result of neural damage including an improperly functioning amygdala. Technology exists that can repair this damage. It is not experimental; it has been used successfully in tens of thousands of cases to treat neurological disorders as divergent as depression, anxiety, bipolar disorder, borderline personality, and the complex of disorders commonly referred to as schizophrenic syndrome."

The delicate structure of her collarbones fascinated him. It took fourteen pounds of pressure, properly applied, to snap a human clavicle—rendering the arm useless for a time. He thought about the proper application of that pressure. He said, "Tell me more."

"They take your own neurons—grown from your own stem cells under sterile conditions in a lab, modified with microbial opsin genes. This opsin is a light-reactive pigment similar to those found in the human retina. The neurons are then reintroduced to key areas of your brain. This is a keyhole procedure. Once the neurons are established, and have been encouraged to develop the appropriate synaptic connections, there's a second surgery, to implant a medical device: a series of miniaturized flexible microprocessors, sensors, and light emitting diodes. This device monitors your neurochemistry and the electrical activity in your brain, and adjusts it to mimic healthy activity." She paused again and steepled her fingers on the table.

"'Healthy,'" he mocked.

She did not move.

"That's discrimination against the neuro-atypical."

"Probably," she said. Her fingernails were appliquéd with circuit diagrams. "But you did kill thirteen people. And get caught. Your civil rights are bound to be forfeit after something like that."

He stayed silent. Impulse control had never been his problem.

"It's not psychopathy you're remanded for," she said. "It's murder."

"Mind control," he said.

"Mind *repair*," she said. "You can't be *sentenced* to the medical procedure. But you can volunteer. It's usually interpreted as evidence of remorse and desire to be rehabilitated. Your sentencing judge will probably take that into account."

"God," he said. "I'd rather have a bullet in the head than a fucking computer."

"They haven't used bullets in a long time," she said. She shrugged, as if it were nothing to her either way. "It was lethal injection or the gas chamber. Now it's right-minding. Or it's the rest of your life in an eight by twelve cell. You decide."

"I can beat it."

"Beat rightminding?"

Point to me.

"What if I can beat it?"

"The success rate is a hundred percent. Barring a few who never woke up from anesthesia." She treated herself to a slow smile. "If there's anybody whose illness is too intractable for this particular treatment, they must be smart enough to keep it to themselves. And smart enough not to get caught a second time."

You're being played, he told himself. *You are smarter than her. Way too smart for this to work on you.*

She's appealing to your vanity. Don't let her yank your chain. She thinks she's so fucking smart. She's prey. You're the hunter. More evolved. Don't be manipulated—

His lips said, "Lady, sign me up."

The snow creaks under my steps. Trees might crack tonight. I compose a poem in my head.

The fashion in poetry is confessional. It wasn't always so—but now we judge value by our own voyeurism. By the perceived rawness of what we think we are being invited to spy upon. But it's all art: veils and lies.

If I wrote a confessional poem, it would begin: *Her dress was the color of mermaids, and I killed her anyway.*

A confessional poem need not be true. Not true in the way the bite of the air in my lungs in spite of the mask is true. Not true in the way the graveyard and the cardinal and the ragged stones are true.

It wasn't just her. It was her, and a dozen others like her. Exactly like her in that they were none of them the right one, and so another one always had to die.

That I can still see them as fungible is a victory for my old self—his only victory, maybe, though he was arrogant enough to expect many more. He thought he could beat the rightminding.

That's the only reason he agreed to it.

If I wrote it, people would want to read *that* poem. It would sell a million—it would garner far more attention than what I *do* write.

I won't write it. I don't even want to *remember* it. Memory excision was declared by the Supreme Court to be a form of the death penalty, and therefore unconstitutional since 2043.

They couldn't take my memories in retribution. Instead they took away my pleasure in them.

Not that they'd admit it was retribution. *They* call it *repair.* "Rightminding." Fixing the problem. Psychopathy is a curable disease.

They gave me a new face, a new brain, a new name. The chromosome reassignment, I chose for myself, to put as much distance between my old self and my new as possible.

The old me also thought it might prove goodwill; reduced testosterone, reduced aggression, reduced physical strength. Few women become serial killers.

To my old self, it seemed a convincing lie.

He—no, I: alienating the uncomfortable actions of the self is something that psychopaths do—I thought I was stronger than biology and stronger than rightminding. I thought I could take anabolic steroids to get my muscle and anger back where they should be. I honestly thought I'd get away with it.

I honestly thought I would still want to.

I could write that poem. But that's not the poem I'm writing. The poem I'm writing begins: *Gravestones like smoker's teeth . . .* Except I don't know what happens in the second clause, so I'm worrying at it as I run.

I do my lap, and throw in a second lap because the wind's died down and my heater is working and I feel light, sharp, full of energy and desire. When I come down the hill I'm running on springs. I take the long arc, back over the bridge toward the edge of town, sparing a quick glance down at the frozen water. The air is warming up a little as the sun rises. My fingers aren't numb in my gloves anymore.

When the unmarked white delivery van pulls past me and rolls to a stop, it takes me a moment to realize the driver wants my attention. He taps the horn, and I jog to a stop, hit pause on my run tracker, tug a headphone from my ear. I stand a few steps back from the window. He looks at me, then winces in embarrassment, and points at his navigation system. "Can you help me find Green Street? The autodrive is no use."

"Sure," I say. I point. "Third left, up that way. It's an unimproved road; that might be why it's not on your map."

"Thanks," he says. He opens his mouth as if to say something else, some form of apology, but I say, "Good luck, man!" and wave him cheerily on.

The vehicle isn't the anomaly here in the country that it would be on a city street even if half the cities have been retrofitted for urban farming to the point where they barely have streets anymore. But I'm flummoxed by the irony of the encounter, so it's not until he pulls away that I realize I should have been more wary. And that *his* reaction was not the embarrassment of having to ask for directions, but the embarrassment of a decent, normal person who realizes he's put another human being in a position where she may feel unsafe. He's vanishing around the curve before I sort that out—something I suppose most people would understand instinctually.

I wish I could run after the van and tell him that I was never worried. That it never occurred to me to be worried. Demographically speaking, the driver is very unlikely to be hunting me. He was black. And I am white.

And my early fear socialization ran in different directions, anyway.

My attention is still fixed on the disappearing van when something dark and clinging sweetly rank drops over my head.

I gasp in surprise and my filter mask briefly saves me. I get the sick chartreuse scent of ether and the world spins, but the mask buys me a moment to realize what's happening—a blitz attack. Someone is kidnapping me. He's grabbed my arms, pulling my elbows back to keep me from pushing the mask off.

I twist and kick, but he's so strong.

Was I this strong? It seems like he's not even working to hold on to me, and though my heel connects solidly with his shin as he picks me up, he doesn't grunt. The mask won't help forever—

—it doesn't even help for long enough.

Ether dreams are just as vivid as they say.

His first was the girl in the mermaid-colored dress. I think her name was Amelie. Or Jessica. Or something. She picked him up in a bar. Private cars were rare enough to have become a novelty, even then, but he had my father's Mission for the evening. She came for a ride, even though—or perhaps because—it was a little naughty, as if they had been smoking cigarettes a generation before. They watched the sun rise from a curve over a cornfield. He strangled her in the back seat a few minutes later.

She heaved and struggled and vomited. He realized only later how stupid he'd been. He had to hide the body, because too many people had seen us leave the bar together.

He never did get the smell out of the car. My father beat the shit out of him and never let him use it again.

We all make mistakes when we're young.

I awaken in the dying warmth of my sweat-soaked jacket, to the smell of my vomit drying between my cheek and the cement floor. At least it's only oatmeal. You don't eat a lot before a long run. I ache in every particular, but especially where my shoulder and hip rest on concrete. I should be grateful; he left me in the recovery position so I didn't choke.

It's so dark I can't tell if my eyelids are open or closed, but the hood is gone and only traces of the stink of the ether remain. I lie still, listening and hoping my brain will stop trying to split my skull.

I'm still dressed as I was, including the shoes. He's tied my hands behind my back, but he didn't tape my thumbs together. He's an amateur. I conclude that he's not in the room with me. And probably not anywhere nearby. I think I'm in a cellar. I can't hear anybody walking around on the floor overhead.

I'm not gagged, which tells me he's confident that I can't be heard even if I scream. So maybe I wouldn't hear him up there, either?

My aloneness suggests that I was probably a target of opportunity. That he has somewhere else he absolutely has to be. Parole review? Dinner with the mother who supports him financially? Stockbroker meeting? He seems organized; it could be anything. But whatever it is, it's incredibly important that he show up for it, or he wouldn't have left.

When *you* have a new toy, can you resist playing with it?

I start working my hands around. It's not hard if you're fit and flexible, which I am, though I haven't kept in practice. I'm not scared, though I should be. I know better than most what happens next. But I'm calmer than I have been since I was somebody else. The adrenaline still settles me, just like it used to. Only this time— well, I already mentioned the irony.

It's probably not even the lights in my brain taking the edge off my arousal.

The history of technology is all about unexpected consequences. Who would have guessed that peak oil would be linked so clearly to peak psychopathy? Most folks don't think about it much, but people just aren't as mobile as they—as we—used to be. We live in populations of greater density, too, and travel less. And all of that leads to knowing each other more.

People like the nameless him who drugged me—people like me—require a certain anonymity, either in ourselves or in our victims.

The floor is cold against my rear end. My gloves are gone. My wrists scrape against the soles of my shoes as I work the rope past them. They're only a little damp, and the water isn't frozen or any colder than the floor. I've been down here a while, then—still assuming I *am* down. Cellars usually have windows, but guys like me—guys like I used to be—spend a lot of time planning in advance. Rehearsing. Spinning their webs and digging their holes like trap-door spiders.

I'm shivering, and my body wants to cramp around the chill. I keep pulling. One more wiggle and tug, and I have my arms in front of me. I sit up and stretch, hoping my kidnapper has made just one more mistake. It's so dark I can't see my fluorescent yellow and green running jacket, but proprioception lets me find my wrist with my nose. And there, clipped into its little pocket, is the micro-flash sleeve light that comes with the jacket.

He got the mask—or maybe the mask just came off with the bag. And he got my phone, which has my tracker in it, and a GPS. He didn't make the mistake I would have chosen for him to make.

I push the button on the sleeve light with my nose.

It comes on shockingly bright and I stretch my fingers around to shield it as best I can. Flesh glows red between the bones.

Yep. It's a basement.

Eight years after my first time, the new improved me showed the IBI the site of the grave he'd dug for the girl in the mermaid-colored dress. I'd never forgotten it—not the gracious tree that bent over the little boulder he'd skidded on top of her to keep the animals out, not the tangle of vines he'd dragged over that, giving himself a hell of a case of poison ivy in the process.

This time, I was the one that vomited.

How does one even begin to own having done something like that? How do I?

Ah, there's the fear. Or not fear, exactly, because the optogenetic and chemical controls on my endocrine system keep my arousal pretty low. It's anxiety. But anxiety's an old friend.

It's something to think about while I work on the ropes and tape with my teeth. The sleeve light shines up my nose while I gnaw, revealing veins through the cartilage and flesh. I'm cautious, nipping and tearing rather than pulling. I can't afford to break my teeth: they're the best weapon and the best tool I have. So I'm meticulous and careful, despite the nauseous thumping of my heart and the voice in my head that says *hurry, hurry, he's coming.*

He's not coming—at least, I haven't heard him coming. Ripping the bonds apart seems to take forever. I wish I had wolf teeth, teeth for slicing and cutting. Teeth that could scissor through this stuff as if it were a cheese sandwich. I imagine my other self's delight in my discomfort, my worry. I wonder if he'll enjoy it when my captor returns, even though he's trapped in this body with me.

Does he really exist, my other self? Neurologically speaking, we all have a lot of people in our heads all the time, and we can't hear most of them. Maybe they really did change him, unmake him. Transform him into me. Or maybe he's back there somewhere, gagged and chained up, but watching.

Whichever it is, I know what he would think of this. He killed thirteen people. He'd like to kill me, too.

I'm shivering.

The jacket's gone cold, and it—and I—am soaked. The wool still insulates while wet, but not enough. The jacket and my compression tights don't do a damned thing.

I wonder if my captor realized this. Maybe *this* is his game.

Considering all the possibilities, freezing to death is actually not so bad.

Maybe he just doesn't realize the danger? Not everybody knows about cold.

The last wrap of tape parts, sticking to my chapped lower lip and pulling a few scraps of skin loose when I tug it free. I'm leaving my DNA all over this basement. I spit in a corner, too, just for good measure. Leave traces: even when you're sure you're going to die. Especially then. Do anything you can to leave clues.

It was my skin under a fingernail that finally got me.

The period when he was undergoing the physical and mental adaptations that turned him into me gave me a certain . . . not sympathy, because they did the body before they did the rightminding, and sympathy's an emotion he never felt before I was thirty-three years old . . . but it gave him and therefore me a certain *perspective* he hadn't had before.

It itched like hell. Like puberty.

There's an old movie, one he caught in the guu this one time. Some people from the future go back in time and visit a hospital. One of them is a doctor. He saves a woman who's waiting for dialysis or a transplant by giving her a pill that makes her grow a kidney.

That's pretty much how I got my ovaries, though it involved stem cells and needles in addition to pills.

I was still *him*, because they hadn't repaired the damage to my brain yet. They had to keep him under control while the physical adaptations were happening. He was on chemical house arrest. Induced anxiety disorder. Induced agoraphobia.

It doesn't sound so bad until you realize that the neurological shackles are strong enough that even stepping outside your front door can put you on the ground. There are supposed to be safeguards in place. But everybody's heard the stories of criminals on ChemArrest who burned to death because they couldn't make themselves walk out of a burning building.

He thought he could beat the rightminding, beat the chemarrest. Beat everything.

Damn, I was arrogant.

My former self had more grounds for his arrogance than this guy. *This is pathetic,* I think. And then I have to snort laughter, because it's not my former self who's got me tied up in this basement.

I could just let this happen. It'd be fair. Ironic. *Justice.*

And my dying here would mean more women follow me into this basement. One by one by one.

I unbind my ankles more quickly than I did the wrists. Then I stand and start pacing, do jumping jacks, jog in place while I shine my light around. The activity eases the shivering. Now it's just a tremble, not a teeth-rattling shudder. My muscles are stiff; my bones ache. There's a cramp in my left calf.

There's a door locked with a dead bolt. The windows have been bricked over with new bricks that don't match the foundation. They're my best option—if I could find something to strike with, something to pry with, I might break the mortar and pull them free.

I've got my hands. My teeth. My tiny light, which I turn off now so as not to warn my captor.

And a core temperature that I'm barely managing to keep out of the danger zone.

When I walked into my court-mandated therapist's office for the last time—before my relocation—I looked at her creamy complexion, the way the light caught on her eyes behind the glasses. I remembered what *he'd* thought.

If a swell of revulsion could split your own skin off and leave it curled on the ground like something spoilt and disgusting, that would have happened to me then. But of course it wasn't my shell that was ruined and rotten; it was something in the depths of my brain.

"How does it feel to have a functional amygdala?" she asked.

"Lousy," I said.

She smiled absently and stood up to shake my hand—for the first time. To offer me closure. It's something they're supposed to do.

"Thank you for all the lives you've saved," I told her.

"But not for yours?" she said.

I gave her fingers a gentle squeeze and shook my head.

My other self waits in the dark with me. I wish I had his physical strength, his invulnerability. His conviction that everybody else in the world is slower, stupider, weaker.

In the courtroom, while I was still my other self, he looked out from the stand into the faces of the living mothers and fathers of the girls he killed. I remember the eleven women and seven men, how they focused on him. How they sat, their stillness, their attention.

He thought about the girls while he gave his testimony. The only individuality they had for him was what was necessary to sort out which parents went with which corpse, important, because it told him who to watch for the best response.

I wish I didn't know what it feels like to be prey. I tell myself it's just the cold that makes my teeth chatter. Just the cold that's killing me.

Prey can fight back, though. People have gotten killed by something as timid and inoffensive as a white-tailed deer.

I wish I had a weapon. Even a cracked piece of brick. But the cellar is clean.

I do jumping jacks, landing on my toes for silence. I swing my arms. I think about doing burpees, but I'm worried that I might scrape my hands on the floor. I think about taking my shoes off. Running shoes are soft for kicking with, but if I get outside, my feet will freeze without them.

When. When I get outside.

My hands and teeth are the only weapons I have.

An interminable time later, I hear a creak through the ceiling. A footstep, muffled, and then the thud of something dropped. More footsteps, louder, approaching the top of a stair beyond the door.

I crouch beside the door, on the hinge side, far enough away that it won't quite strike me if he swings it violently. I wish for a weapon—*I am a weapon*—and I wait.

A metallic tang in my mouth now. *Now* I am really, truly scared.

His feet thump on the stairs. He's not little. There's no light beneath the door—it must be weather stripped for soundproofing. The lock thuds. A bar scrapes. The knob rattles, and then there's a bar of light as it swings open. He turns the flashlight to the right, where he left me lying. It picks out the puddle of vomit. I hear his intake of breath.

I think about the mothers of the girls I killed. I think, *would they want me to die like this?*

My old self would relish it. It'd be his revenge for what I did to him.

My goal is just to get past him—my captor, my old self; they blur together—to get away, run. Get outside. Hope for a road, neighbors, bright daylight.

My captor's silhouette is dim, scatter-lit. He doesn't look armed, except for the flashlight, one of those archaic long heavy metal ones that doubles as a club. I can't be sure that's all he has. He wavers. He might slam the door and leave me down here to starve—

I lunge.

I grab for the wrist holding the light, and I half-catch it, but he's stronger. I knew he would be. He rips the wrist out of my grip, swings the flashlight. Shouts. I lurch back, and it catches me on the shoulder instead of across the throat. My arm sparks pain and numbs. I don't hear my collarbone snap. Would I, if it has?

I try to knee him in the crotch and hit his thigh instead. I mostly elude his grip. He grabs my jacket; cloth stretches and rips. He swings the light once more. It thuds into the stair wall and punches through drywall. I'm half-past him and I use his own grip as an anchor as I lean back and kick him right in the center of the nose. Soft shoes or no soft shoes.

He lets go, then. Falls back. I go up the stairs on all fours, scrambling, sure he's right behind me. Waiting for the grab at my ankle. Halfway up I realize I should have locked him in. Hit the door at the top of the stairs and find myself in a perfectly ordinary hallway, in need of a good sweep. The door ahead is closed. I fumble the lock, yank it open, tumble down steps into the snow as something fouls my ankles.

It's twilight. I get my feet under me and stagger back to the path. The shovel I fell over is tangled with my feet. I grab it, use it as a crutch, lever myself up and stagger-run-limp down the walk to a long driveway.

I glance over my shoulder, sure I hear breathing.

Nobody. The door swings open in the wind.

Oh. The road. No traffic. I know where I am. Out past the graveyard and the bridge. I run through here every couple of days, but the house is set far enough back that it was never more than a dim white outline behind trees. It's a Craftsman bungalow, surrounded by winter-sere oaks.

Maybe it wasn't an attack of opportunity, then. Maybe he saw me, and decided to lie in wait.

I pelt towards town—pelt, limping, the air so cold in my lungs that they cramp and wheeze. I'm cold, so cold. The wind is a knife. I yank my sleeves down over my hands. My body tries to draw itself into a huddled comma even as I run. The sun's at the horizon.

I think, *I should just let the winter have me.*

Justice for those eleven mothers and seven fathers. Justice for those thirteen women who still seem too alike. It's only that their interchangeability *bothers* me now.

At the bridge, I stumble to a dragging walk, then turn into the wind off the river, clutch the rail, and stop. I turn right, and don't see him coming. My wet fingers freeze to the railing.

The state police are a half mile on, right around the curve at the top of the hill. If I run, I won't freeze before I get there. If I run.

My fingers stung when I touched the rail. Now they're numb, my ears past hurting. If I stand here, I'll lose the feeling in my feet.

The sunset glazes the ice below with crimson. I turn and glance the other way; in a pewter sky, the rising moon bleaches the clouds to moth-wing iridescence.

I'm wet to the skin. Even if I start running now, I might not make it to the station house. Even if I started running now, the man in the bungalow might be right behind me. I don't think I hit him hard enough to knock him out. Just knock him down.

If I stay, it won't take long at all until the cold stops hurting.

If I stay here, I wouldn't have to remember being my other self again. I could put him down. At last, at last, I could put those women down. Amelie, unless her name was Jessica. The others.

It seems easy. Sweet.

But if I stay here, I won't be the last person to wake up in the bricked up basement of that little white bungalow.

The wind is rising. Every breath I take is a wheeze. A crow blows across the road like a tattered shirt, vanishing into the twilight cemetery.

I can carry this a little further. It's not so heavy. Thirteen corpses, plus one. After all, I carried every one of them before.

I leave skin behind on the railing when I peel my fingers free. Staggering at first, then stronger, I sprint back into town.

Jubilee

KARL SCHROEDER

"Jubilee" has at its core one of the most ingenious ideas in recent SF, a social system whereby whole communities go into a synchronized pattern of hibernation and awakening that allows them to wait out the hundreds or even thousands of years it takes for spaceships to travel between the stars (no faster-than-light-travel or wormhole shortcuts in Schroeder's scenario) without falling hopelessly behind the space travelers, thus making it possible to maintain social continuity even at interstellar distances. On the individual human level, though, this system can create some unique and nearly insurmountable obstacles for people in love, as the story that follows poignantly demonstrates . . .

Canadian writer Karl Schroeder was born and raised in Brandon, Manitoba. He moved to Toronto in 1986, and has been working and writing there ever since. He is best known for his far-future Virga series, consisting of Sun of Suns, Queen of Candesce, Pirate Sun, *and* The Hero, *but he has also written the novels* Ventus, Permanence, *and* Lady of Mazes, *as well as a novel in collaboration with David Nickle,* The Claus Effect. *He's also the coauthor, with Cory Doctorow, of* The Complete Idiot's Guide to Publishing Science Fiction. *His short fiction has been collected in* Engine of Recall. *His most recent book is a new novel,* Lockstep, *set in the same universe as "Jubilee."*

Three muttering men stood on the path, not five meters below where Lauren and her companion crouched. It would do no good to tell Malak that she'd been to the wedding of the eldest of the three, or that she had brought candles to the houses of another the week he was born. Their rifles were unslung, their voices low. She knew why they were here.

Malak wasn't watching them, but instead gazed longingly at the near end of a rope bridge that started about fifty meters ahead. The newly cleared path to it wound up the side of a hundred-meter-tall bedrock tower. Thick rain forest coated most of the karst spires in this region; their bases were lost in mist, which transformed them into a crowd of green-hooded giants standing on cloud. The fat domed pillar at the far end of the bridge had sheer vertical sides, making this the only approach. All these men had to do was camp out at the bridge's near end to make it impossible for Lauren and Malak to complete their mission.

Lauren eased back behind the bushes, pulling Malak down gently beside her. "Patience," she murmured. "If they can't catch us alone, they'll have to let us get through when other travelers arrive. If this letter doesn't get delivered, it's as much a disaster for them as for us." She tapped the waterproof courier's pouch slung at her waist.

"It's huge," said Malak, and Lauren realized he hadn't been looking at the bridge at all, but at the lockstep fortress it led to. He was only seventeen, he'd only ever seen sleepers' fortresses in picture books. This one's outlines were veiled by the clouds that drifted among the pillar-landscape. It took up nearly the entire top of the miniature plateau it rested on.

She decided not to point out the even bigger fortress that was just visible seven kilometers to the south. He really should be thinking about those men.

But she heard singing, and presently a group of laborers appeared around the curve of the path. At their left was a sheer vertical rock face, to their right an equally sheer drop-off, but half of them were horsing around while the other half sang. They were carrying planks and other supplies, their powered exoskeletons squeaking and protesting against the weight.

Lauren checked out the three men. They were gone—stepped off the path, or hiding in the bushes, it made no difference. "Time to go," she hissed at Malak, and without waiting for him she began climbing down.

One of the newcomers arched an eyebrow when she plunked onto the road in front of him. "You're an unlikely bandit," he said. "What were you doing up there?"

Lauren adjusted her waistband with dignity. "Would you rather I did it in the road?"

He laughed. "Never mind!" She heard Malak hit the path and, as she turned, made out three sullen bearded faces watching her from the underbrush. Lauren resisted an urge to stick her tongue out at them. Better not push it.

"You're headed for the fortress?" she asked the laborer, who had a hundred or so kilos of plank laid across his machine-augmented shoulders.

"Where else would we be going?"

"Can we walk with you?"

"If you don't mind foul language, bad manners, body odor and the occasional fistfight," he said with a grin.

"It's okay." She sent Malak a sidelong look. "I'm used to boys."

She could feel the eyes of their three purusers on her back as she set out across the swinging bridge, and that prickle warred with the vertiginous fear of crossing a seemingly bottomless chasm with nothing but knotted ropes under her feet. By the time she'd reached the other side the bridge had won, and she collapsed panting for a moment while Malak skipped off the end and the laborers approached deliberately and deadpan. Clearly they did this every day.

Lauren straightened and dusted herself off, staring them down. Then she took Malak's shoulder and turned to confront the fortress.

"You've been here before," said Malak. She nodded.

"Thirty-one years ago for me, one night for the people sleeping in there. I was a little older than you. I practically danced across the bridge that time. And it all went smoothly that time."

"What're they like?"

"Seriously?" She barked a laugh as they started walking. "How many times have we talked about this?"

"Yes, but . . ." He rolled his shoulders and splayed out his hands which, like his feet, were too big for him at his age. "None of this has been like anybody *said* it would be. I mean . . . look at that."

Work gangs had been clearing its flanks for months, but the fortress was still half-choked by vines. The traditional plaza in front of the giant building was brush-free, and they'd redone the paths that led around its sides. These, she remembered, led to the landing pads and other spaces the sleepers would need when they awoke in two days. There was even a little village, built on exactly the same plan, and even painted the same colors as the one she'd visited three decades ago. Yet the fortress towered over it all, black, windowless and bleak, as if immune to any cosmetics they might dress it up with. Its stone corners were rounded with erosion, to the point where any given surface looked like natural stone. It was only when you took in the whole that you realized it was a building, and even then, an eerie battle was thenceforth waged between the parts of the mind that recognized objects as being artificial and those that identified them as natural. The fortress trembled between categories, indecisively alien.

"Just you wait," she said, remembering last time. "In three days this'll be the liveliest part of the country."

"There!" Malak pointed, and only then did Lauren see who was waiting for them. Society master Tamlaine appeared to be alone. The Society was marshaling its resources, she'd heard, another way of saying it had hit hard times. On her first delivery, the master had been waiting with three decoy couriers, two official scribes and three hired guards.

It didn't matter; Tamlaine was grinning his relief. "That's them, right, Master Lauren?" asked Malak.

"Yes," she said. "Go." He ran—or rather staggered—forward, and his knees actually began to buckle just steps from Tamlaine. He'd been far more scared, Lauren suddenly realized, than he'd let on.

Her own steps were steady as she reached the master and shook his hand. "Sir."

"You look good, courier," said Tamlaine, and Lauren smiled. She was just as ready to collapse as Malak, but they weren't home free yet. She wasn't about to let her guard down until the gates to the fortress opened in two days' time, and her letter was finally delivered.

"It was Niles and Powen," she affirmed that evening as they sat by the fire. "They're pure Westerfenn on their father's side. Of course they'd think they have a claim. The other man I didn't know, but it's a big family."

"But why do they even bother?" With two mulled ciders in him, Malak was half-asleep in a big wing chair. "The Westerfenns haven't been couriers for two hundred years."

"Yes, but son," said Tamlaine, "they *were* the couriers for six hundred before that. Do you wonder that they feel they have a claim?"

"As far as some people are concerned, *courier* means Westerfenn," agreed Lauren. "We're the upstarts. Interlopers."

"But who cares what we think?" Malak was still puzzled. "All that matters is that the Authors decided to switch to us."

Tamlaine sent Malak a slightly pitying smile. "Do you really think the Authors care who delivers their letters? Do you think they even know?"

Malak sat up, offended. "They see us once a month!"

"But that's thirty years for the courier. Sometimes it's been the same person twice, and they didn't notice until it was pointed out to them. For his part, I know that Chinen de Conestoga doesn't care as long as his letters get through."

"How can you say that!"

"Well, for one thing, he's barely a year older than you are. Malak, tell me this: Do you know the name of the girl who sells you bread in the mornings?"

He opened his mouth, closed it, and sank sullenly into his chair.

Malak didn't succeed in falling asleep, though; moments later, he sat up, blinking. "What's that?"

It had been so faint Lauren hadn't noticed the faint rumbling until now. Remembering it was something of a shock. Of course it would come, she should have expected it. Yet with so much else going on . . . She stood, still not hearing Malak's increasingly worried questions, and moved as if in a trance to the doorway.

She'd been sixteen, carrying the message bag herself on the way across the bridge. The Westerfenns of that generation hadn't made any fuss. Of course, her uncle Despolino would be the one to actually deliver the letter; still, she'd felt a huge sense of importance and responsibility. They'd set up camp in the evening, with the fortress a vast black silhouette against a silver sky. After, they'd entered the village and as she reluctantly prepared to hand the pouch to her uncle, this same vibration had filled the sky. Amazing that she could have forgotten!

Makeshift stages had been set up along the road to the fortress's main gates. These would be taken down before the doors opened. For the next day, various groups would perform stories and allegories from the histories of the locksteps. The first time she'd been here she'd begged to watch them, but Uncle had been all business. Malak didn't seem to care.

She walked to the end of the row of stages and, when Malak appeared at her side, pointed upward. "Look. It's landing."

The orbital transport was all glittery surfaces, chrome and glass and plastic like an insect. The roar came from its engines as it delicately hovered above the fortress. Its long landing legs rose and fell and angled fussily, as if groping for a solid surface. As they watched, the thunder rolling over them in waves, it settled behind the fortress. Moments later the sound cut out—and Malak started running.

"Travelers!" he shouted happily. Lauren set off after him at a jog. Laughing and shaking his head, Tamlaine followed them both at a more dignified saunter.

By the time they reached the landing field, the transport had opened its hatches and a gang of bots was unloading blocky shipping containers from its belly. If Malak had expected live humans at this point he was disappointed; if there were passengers on this flight they were frozen as solid as the rest of the cargo. The bots bounced the crates onto rolling pallets and took them through a heavily guarded set of metal gates into the fortress.

Malak watched it all avidly. "Yesterday—*their* yesterday—they fell asleep on another world. They'll wake on this one," he said. "I wonder where they've been?"

Lauren shrugged. "Join the lockstep, and find out." She knew he'd never do that; in order to stay inside when they sealed the doors again, you only had to ask—but doing that meant giving up everyone you knew here. Parents, children, friends, family, profession: all would be left behind. Lauren had never once considered doing that, and she knew Malak wouldn't either. It was too drastic a step.

They watched the unloading until it was full night and the crickets were chorusing. When Tamlaine began to walk back, Lauren turned to follow and saw that the little stages along the road were lit. "Malak! Look at this."

He was reluctant until he saw the players, then he raced ahead. Lauren and Tamlaine laughed together, remembering their youths as they followed.

The biggest stage was lavishly decorated and lit. Devotees of the Lord of Time were staging a highly stylized, half-ritual performance of the Revelation of Tobias. The actor playing Tobias McGonigal was masked and so heavily swaddled in costume that you couldn't tell if it was a man or a woman. The three couriers watched for a while as McGonigal tried to convince his mother (in mime) that the galaxy would be theirs if they accepted the gift of cold sleep. When she rejected him, a quick set change put Tobias on his legendary ship, and then he began an interminable oratorio about his first and final entry into cold sleep. After it had dragged on for fifteen minutes, Lauren took Malak's shoulder and steered him onward.

There were plays about the founding of the locksteps on this world, plays about distant and legendary Earth. There were stories of kings who took refuge in the locksteps and after thirty years returned, a day older, as beggars to behold the ruin of their kingdoms. There were romances. There were murder mysteries. And there was—

"Hey!" Malak stopped dead, and Lauren almost tripped over him. "That's Powen, isn't it?"

It was indeed, and Niles was beside him. They were standing on a modest stage near the end of the row, along with a girl and a boy dressed in lockstep fashions. Right now the girl was writing furiously at a little desk, and Niles hovered behind her, speaking to the audience.

"One month together! One Jubilee, and the two locksteps will not meet again for nine centuries! Three hundred sixty months for her lockstep, three hundred seventy-two for his, their times will diverge and converge over a millennium. To those whose lives follow the rhythm of the fortresses, a mere two and a half years will pass before their rhythms synchronize again. But a boy and a girl who have met and fallen in love—well, they will feel the centuries as much as we!"

"They're telling the story!" Malak hissed. "The story of the Authors!"

Lauren shrugged, though she was uncomfortable. "They have a perfect right to do it."

It wasn't one of the great tales, but it was well-enough known. Of the several lock-steps on this planet, there were two so mutually hostile that they hibernated on different frequencies. The frequency of the first was 360 months asleep to one month awake. The other's was 372 to one. As out of phase as they were, they still couldn't completely avoid each other. Every 960 years they came into phase and both were open during the same month. The last time this Jubilee had happened, a girl from the first lockstep had met a boy from the second, and they had fallen in love.

There were popular books on the subject, and Malak had seen the secret ones, too, the Commentaries, that filled the Society's library. He shouldn't be surprised.

The girl onstage was now holding a golden letter up to the one thin spotlight. "Oh, to whom can I entrust my words of love?" she quavered. "For when it leaves my hands, thirty-one years shall pass before my lover's touch shall it awake. Who might dedicate themselves to its preservation, and to bear the fragile wings of my ardor to my heart's desire?"

Tamlaine leaned close. "Not one of the better ones. They could at least have done Gisbon's version. It's in rhyming couplets."

Now Niles was kneeling before her, hand outstretched. "And who are you, sir knight?" sighed the girl.

"I am Atamandius Westerfenn, and I dedicate my life to the transmission of your message."

Despite the crass propaganda of it all, Lauren felt her fingers curl protectively around the pouch hanging at her waist. Malak was muttering about self-serving Westerfenns, and Tamlaine simply stood there watching with his arms crossed. Disgusted, Lauren was about to leave when there was a discreet cough behind her. She turned.

"Lauren Arthen, I believe?" It was the third of the men who'd been following them. Lauren glanced around—two onstage, one here; were there more?

He seemed to sense her anxiety, and bowed slightly, shaking his head. "There's just me. And I would never hurt you."

Malak and Tamlaine were busy watching the clumsy play. Lauren took a step back into the shadows with the man. "I *am* armed," she lied. "You were waiting with those two to ambush us this morning."

"And they would have, too," he agreed, "if I hadn't intervened. Which I would have."

"And why would you do that?"

Now grimaced, shrugged. There was a suggestion of Westerfenn to his face, which was long and high browed. He seemed more a scholar than a courier. "I was hoping you'd remember me," he said, very quietly.

She looked at him more closely. Where would she have remembered a Westerfenn from? He was about her age, which would mean, if he was a courier . . . "Kiel?"

Now he grinned. "You do remember! We spent a few days together, after the Authoress gave you . . . that." He nodded at the pouch at her side.

"A lunch or two. A walk, if I remember," she said. That was all it could reasonably have been. Their families, their societies and histories would all have been against it. Both had known at the time, and hadn't spoken of it. They'd never even touched, but Lauren had sometimes thought about the might-have-beens in the ensuing years. Remembering, she looked down.

Kiel Westerfenn sent an impatient look at the stage. "Forget about those two congenital thugs, they're just looking to regain lost glories because they have no ideas of their own. Even this play . . . they're trying to win over the crowd because they still have a half-baked plan to take the letter from you. When I heard they were going to try to intercept your delivery I . . . well, I invited myself along. I'm sorry if they scared you this morning. But I won't let them stand in your way."

"Well . . . thank you!"

He bowed fully this time. "I respect your mission, even if they do not." With that, he stepped into further shadow, and vanished among the crowd.

Lauren turned back to watch the insipid play, but she didn't hear anything that the actors said, and despite the darkness of the night, she felt herself blinking as though a bright light had just shone in her eyes.

Two days later, at dawn, the massive gates grated open, and Lockstep 372/1 came into Jubilee with realtime. On seventy thousand planets and on countless comets, asteroids, and colony cylinders, morning came to trillions of people.

When Lauren was little she'd imagined it as a revelation: numberless eyes opening in rapture after thirty years in the underworld. Yet for those in the locksteps, she had learned, it was just another morning. Last night—or so it seemed to them—they'd gone to sleep under their blankets as on any evening. The hibernation technologies that wound them down into nearly perfect stasis were unobtrusive—hidden, usually, in the bases of their beds. They slept, they woke, and many of them simply didn't care that thirty years had passed in the outer world.

Here they came now, the ones who did care. The new population of the refurbished village surrounding the fortress was waiting as the first yawning traders from the lockstep emerged. They seemed relaxed, casual even; they did this once a month, after all. Lauren watched the waiting craftsmen and journalists try to temper their own excitement to match. Act normal—the locksteppers expected it.

Lauren stood back a bit with Malak and Tamlaine. She was conscious of the presence of others, mostly people who knew the story of the Authors and had come to watch the delivery.

The Westerfenns were here too, but Lauren was no longer worried about them. Yesterday, Kiel had found her as she walked in the marketplace, and handed her a small cloth-wrapped object.

"A first step, maybe," he'd said. "I heard the Society library was missing a few volumes." She unfolded the cloth and found she was holding a very old leather-bound book. She looked at the spine. "Commentaries, volume seventy-four? You're right! We don't have this. But how—"

Kiel had shrugged. "A little larceny on my part. It's not like we need it. We're not the couriers anymore."

Each letter the Authors exchanged had been carefully opened and read, and scholars and philosophers had debated its contents for decades, sometimes centuries. All except Authoress Letter 13, of course, which the couriers at the time had for some reason failed to open. In the Society's library, an entire bookshelf was devoted to speculations about what that letter had said.

Bots, heavily laden vehicles, and people were now crowding through the open gates. Behind them, the long rectangular tunnel leading into the fortress was lit with the sorts of electric utility lights Lauren had seen in photos and ancient movies. At the same time, distant rumblings signaled the opening of the fortress's rooftop doors. The fortress unfolded almost like a flower, and as it did, antennae rose and dozens of flying machines big and small shot up and away. The fortress would be connecting with its fellows across the planet, forming for one month a complete, dynamic, and overwhelmingly potent civilization. During Jubilee, 372/1 owned the world; it *was* the world.

"Where is he?" Malak was shifting from foot to foot.

"He'll be here. Chinen isn't going to miss a delivery from his love."

They had met in Jubilee, Chinen de Conestoga of 372 and Margaret Pierce of 360. They were the same age—roughly 6,000 years, or sixteen by their own reckoning. After Jubilee they had promised to write. The first courier had set out from Margaret's home thirty years later, and it was easy: just one year later, her letter was delivered. Chinen's reply had waited 29 years. As the pattern of exchanges settled in, their couriers learned to wait according to the shifting frequencies of the locksteps: one year then 29, two years then 28, three then 27. Eventually the phase shifted and now, as Jubilee approached again, it was Margaret's letter that had waited 28 years. Chinen's newest would be delivered in just two. Sixty-two years from now, they would finally meet again.

"There he is," said Tamlaine. He sounded more excited than she'd expected, and it seemed to unlock a thrill of anticipation in her as well. . After decades of imagining what this moment would be like, of course it was nothing like she'd pictured. Chinen de Conestoga was no radiant god emerging from Heaven; he was just a boy being jostled by the crowd as he looked around. His face seemed pinched, anxious even. And someone else was with him, an older man with his hand on Chinen's shoulder.

Lauren saw this, but she didn't register it. Years of mental rehearsal made her step forward, wave, and say, "Chinen de Conestoga! Over here!"

He looked, his eyes widened, and for just a second she saw him making a frantic gesture, as though warding her off. Then his face fell as the man whose hand lay so heavily on his shoulder swept by.

The man stalked up to Lauren, and suddenly she recognized him. His portraits were not prominent in the Society headquarters, because he was considered a minor actor in the millennial drama of the lovers. He was Chinen's father.

"You!" He stabbed an accusing finger at Lauren. "Are you a part of this fiasco?"

She found herself blinking, unable to speak. Chinen stepped between them. "It's not their fault," he said. "Please, Father—"

The elder de Conestoga held out his hand to Lauren, snapping his fingers impatiently. "You, are you hiding something from some sort of three-sixty trash? Speak up!"

Lauren still couldn't speak. It wasn't just the rudeness; most locksteppers treated realtimers with great respect, if with condescension now and then. But—360 *trash*? The *Authoress*?

"I'm so sorry," Chinen was saying to her, and Tamlaine was here now, too, gabbling something indignantly at the Author's father, who ignored the Society elder and continued to glare at Lauren.

Numbly, she raised the courier's bag and fumbled it open. She began to bring out the letter, but he reached in impatiently and snatched it from her hand. Lauren gasped.

"You told me it was just a Jubilee thing, and now I hear you've been exchanging letters with her?" Brandishing the letter, he rounded on his son. "There will be no more of this nonsense!" he cried. "It stops now!" And as he said *now* he tore the letter in half. He kept tearing until he had a handful of shreds that he flung to the ground.

As the object of 28 years of devoted care fluttered into the mud, blackness rushed at Lauren from all quarters. The muck came up and smacked her in the face.

Lauren sat in her bed at the inn, a mug of mulled wine in her hands, and watched Malak pace and swear. Tamlaine sat in the room's one chair. Neither he nor Lauren had said a word since she awoke from her faint. Malak was making up for it.

"No letter! How can there be no letter? It's nearly Jubilee! They exchange two more and then meet again. And I'll be there to see it—the *end*. How can a story go for a thousand years and have no end? It has to end, and the Society has to be there!"

Tamlaine shook his head. "It could have ended at any time," he murmured. Malak stopped and stared at him in obvious disbelief. Tamlaine sighed.

"They're just young lovers, Malak. They haven't seen each other in almost two years. Any one of their letters could have been the last one. They could have tired of it at any time."

"But, but that's—" Malak made a flinging gesture as he turned away. "They're the Authors! And we're helping them tell the Story!"

Lauren took a pensive sip of the wine. Tamlaine was right, of course. Nearly every volume in the Society library contained a chapter or two of doubts, based on tone, a casual word, or even just the handwriting in the most recent letter. "Why do you think we've been letting the Authoress read the Commentaries? She was doubting his sincerity, and Chinen's a little clumsy with his wording sometimes. Your great-grandmother told her about the Commentaries, the clarifications and interpretations of his letters, and all the wisdom and advice people had been writing to her for centuries, which she'd never seen. She's read it. She knows he's sincere. But that doesn't mean anything. She could have met somebody new at any time. She could have lost interest . . ."

"No. It can't end like this. What are we going to do? What am I going to do? A courier without a letter? Nobody'll take that seriously. Nobody's going to support us. Just think of that. Where's the Society's money going to come from if there's no letters?"

Tamlaine shrugged. "There will be no Society . . . if it's true that there are no more letters." He sighed heavily. "I'll have to draft a letter home. Of course, now that the fortress is open we could just use their wireless and I could speak to them instantly. But I don't like doing things that way. We take our time for a reason. We're not lock-steppers."

"Wait, wait." Malak was frantic. "It's not too late, what are you saying? The Author's father's forbidden it, but what does that mean? We'll just have to contact Chinen in secret. He wants to know what Margaret said! And Lauren, you've got her letter memorized, don't you? We all do."

Tamlaine looked uncomfortable. "Margaret doesn't mind that we open the letters. But Chinen does. He made that clear early on. If he finds out that we've been reading Margaret's words—"

Lauren laughed bitterly. "What's he going to do about it now? Stop using us?"

Her words hung there. The three couriers looked at one another, until finally Tamlaine nodded.

"I'll hold off telling the Society for now," he said. "We'll find an opportunity. Chinen's bound to come outside at some point. His father can't follow him everywhere. We'll approach him then. If Chinen can't read Margaret's words, then we'll recite them to him."

It was a sound plan, but it was three weeks before the opening came. By that time Tamlaine had drafted and redrafted his letter to the Society about ten times, and Malak was beside himself with anxiety and anger. He kept threatening to just march up to Chinen's home and demand to see him. In week two he got into a fight with Niles, and it was clear afterward that the Westerfenns suspected something.

Lauren did domestic work, the sorts of things she'd done every day her whole life. She cooked, cleaned her clothes, mended, shopped in the market. All the while, though, she felt a faint sense of difference, of disconnection from it all. For the first time in many years, she felt the absence of someone else's hands in the washtub with hers; the lack of a second opinion when she hefted the potatoes at the vegetable stall. It wasn't that somebody else should be there with her; it was more that she'd suddenly remembered that someone *could* have been. Disquiet filled her.

Finally one morning Chinen came to the fortress gates and stared about for a while, then went back inside. Lauren followed and found him in one of the brightly lit arcades deep within. The open roof of the fortress let sunlight down through layers of crisscrossing buildings, all piled together like a child's building blocks and festooned with greenery and flowers. The arcade where Chinen loitered was a balconied space overhung with freshly transplanted willow trees. Chinen stood under one, pensively examining it.

"Not the same tree," he said as Lauren approached. "If you look closely. This is where we met, courier. Her family was visiting. Can you believe that? They were mostly shunned, but here they were. I told her I thought it was awful how we were treating them."

"I memorized the letter," Lauren blurted.

Chinen hissed in anger, started to say something—and then his shoulders slumped.

"I suppose keeping our privacy was too much to ask. You've read them all?" Reluctantly, she nodded.

"Then I guess you know us better than we know ourselves."

"You're just a boy and a girl who're in love," she said. That was simple to say—and yet the Society had revolved around them for centuries. Libraries had been written about them and their love. They had become, unexpectedly, something far bigger than they knew.

She couldn't tell him that. "Shall I recite her words?" He nodded.

It was the strangest moment of her life. The words she spoke now were simple, but she'd lived with them for 28 years, and with this recitation, they were done. Delivered, and gone from her. She wouldn't have been surprised if she woke tomorrow and couldn't remember them at all.

Chinen faced out over the treetops and slanting shafts of sunlight, framed by glass and near and distant vistas of lockstep life. When she was finished he stood there silently for a long time, then murmured, "They're better than we are."

"Sir?"

"I'm no 'sir.' I'm just a kid, remember?" She ducked her head, knowing it but still unable to react to him that way. Chinen laughed bitterly. "They'd have me. They'd have me as their son. Yet my father forbids me to contact them at all. He told me he's setting buzz-cams after me during the Jubilee. He's going to record everything I do, everywhere I go. Margaret and I . . . he'll never let us meet."

"I . . . I'm sorry." There was another long, awkward silence. Finally Lauren knew she would have to ask right now, or she'd lose her courage forever: "Will you write a reply?"

He shook his head. "No. No, what's the point?"

Later, arguments would crowd Lauren's mind, all the things she should have said, of course. For now her mind was a blank, her mouth dry with shock.

Chinen turned to her, at last looking her in the eye. "Thanks for delivering the letter. You know I can't pay you . . ."

That threw her. "We've never asked for money!"

He winced. "I know, I know . . . It's just . . . It all ended so uselessly, didn't it?" He sighed, then bowed. "Thanks. Goodbye."

He left her standing there. Lauren felt like an abandoned tool, unnoticed by the people walking by. Then she blinked at a sudden feeling of pressure . . . intensity. She turned, and in the jumble of faces on the plaza behind her, saw Niles's face for just an instant. Then he was gone.

Tamlaine and Malak reacted just as she'd imagined they would. The older man, having seen much in his life, sat with his head down for a while, then raised it to the sunlight and laughed. "Well," he said. "That shows up all our pretensions, doesn't it?"

They were sitting on a bench in front of the inn, and being in public was the only thing that seemed to be keeping Malak from screaming. He shifted from foot to foot, pulling at his hair and sputtering. "They *can't*! They just can't!"

"It was Chinen's decision to make," said Tamlaine. "Never ours. All we ever committed to was delivery of the letters. Anything more than that . . . well, we made up."

"I didn't make up the honors! The privilege of being a courier! It's . . . it's all I ever wanted! And now he's taken it? What am I going to do?"

Tamlaine sent him a reproachful look. "Delivery takes only a few minutes of a courier's life, Malak. You'll do exactly what you would have done otherwise. Work, get married, be a good citizen . . ."

"But without the stipend! You had it," he accused Lauren. "You've had no worries for thirty years. But what about me?"

Lauren opened her mouth to tell him that this wasn't about him at all, but she couldn't say that. It was; and yet, it wasn't Chinen's fault, because he didn't even know the Society existed.

Swearing and kicking at the dirt, Malak stalked away. "Niles saw," Lauren said to Tamlaine after he was out of earshot. "I suppose it'll be all over the place in no time."

"Still." He frowned, thinking. "The Society has existed for centuries. We'd always expected it would disband when the lovers finally met again. There're plans for that, a whole schedule, I think. People have considered how to retire the last courier. It's not going to be arbitrary."

"But . . . Malak never had a chance to *become* a courier." *I'm the last.* What a terrible thought!

"He would have been." Tamlaine stood up and stretched. "Ah, we'll think of something. But I should go. If the news is going to spread, I need to be the one the Society hears it from. I'm going to pack. I'll leave in the morning."

She saw little more of Tamlaine that day, and nothing of Malak, who was sulking somewhere in the fortress. Lauren visited the market, took a nap in her room at the inn, and, in the end, found herself wandering along the crumbled foundations of the fortress. Lockstep bots were replacing some of the cyclopean stones with new granite, and she was watching this process when she heard a tentative cough from behind her.

It was Kiel. He stood near the edge of the plateau, framed by crooked trees and a vista of forested peaks. He might have been watching her for a few minutes, and if so, had he had that slightly worried look on his face the whole time?

"Hello," she said dully.

"Is it true?" he asked. "There will be no letter?"

She shrugged. "Doesn't mean Margaret won't want to send one. We've two years to wait for that."

"Will you be there?"

Lauren gnawed at her calloused thumb, staring out over the forested landscape. The Society's backers were likely to pull their funds if they thought that the millennial epic of Margaret and Chinen had ended in silence. Tamlaine's optimism aside, the Society had not been expecting this turn of events. She might not be able to afford to visit Margaret's fortress when it woke in two years. "I suppose a Westerfenn will be there," she said bitterly. "Your cousins must be delighted at the prospect."

"Actually, they're furious. They think it's all over."

"They're probably right."

He was staring at her in a way she couldn't interpret. "It really has never occurred to you that this might be a good thing?"

"What?! Why? I—I suppose for you it is. No more humiliation at seeing us make the deliveries!"

"No, that's not what I—"

"Is that what you came here to do? Gloat? Well, go ahead, there's nothing I can do about it. Bring Niles and Powen next time, we'll set up the stage and you can parade me around for the whole town to see!"

"Wait, Lauren, I didn't mean—" But she'd had enough of him, and ran, ignoring his plaintive words.

Tamlaine was gone in the morning, and Malak was making himself scarce, which was just as well. Lauren didn't want to talk to anybody. She had money enough to stay until the lockstep's doors closed again, and to get home. Theoretically her stipend would transform into a pension now that Malak was officially the courier. Whether that was really what would happen was anybody's guess; she trusted Tamlaine to argue vigorously on her behalf. After all, this wasn't her fault.

The day before the lockstep was to close, however, she woke to banging on her door. She opened it a crack and saw policemen in the hall. "What's going on?"

"Ma'am, are you an associate of a Tamlaine de Lotness? We're told you were seen in his company."

She flung the door wide. "What's happened to Tamlaine?"

They showed her.

It was up to her to make a final identification of the body. He'd been found at the bottom of the spire on the other side of the rope bridge, having fallen from the roadway. The body was quite battered, but what upset Lauren was the pinched look on his face. He looked *disappointed,* and it was that, and not the terrible battering the rocks had done to him, that she knew would haunt her.

It wasn't impossible for the death to have been accidental. Tamlaine was getting on in years, and the path was treacherous in places. Lauren didn't believe that for a second, and the first thing she said when she saw the body was "Westerfenn!"

Kiel and his cousins were nowhere to be found, but that by itself wasn't suspicious; things were winding down in the temporary village, with people leaving in small and large parties every few hours. The Westerfenns had no reason to be here now, any more than Lauren herself did. It wasn't impossible that they'd simply left, and maybe they had, and maybe they'd run into Tamlaine on the road purely by chance. Malak, when she finally found him and told him, shook his head.

"They must have followed him," he said. "They were waiting for us at the bridge, remember? If they were willing to kill us and take the letter, they'd hardly hesitate to throw one old man over a cliff."

The authorities promised to hunt for the cousins, but Lauren just wanted to move on. "We'll wait for the lockstep to close," she told Malak. "What's an extra day at this point. And then we'll go to the Society headquarters ourselves, and tell them the whole story."

They cremated Tamlaine. People who knew the story of the couriers came to the funeral, but realtimers and locksteppers generally kept their affairs separate. There was talk about whether Chinen should be invited, but in the end the consensus was not to further disturb the Author's family. No one tried to approach him, either to tell him about the death or to invite him to the funeral.

Lauren understood; still, as the orange flames from the pyre rose in the night, she found herself staring resentfully at the lockstep fortress that bulked behind it. The place was all lit up, with visitors still coming and going. Somewhere inside, Chinen de Conestoga was eating, or reading, or perhaps chasing some new girl. He would never know who Tamlaine had been; that he was dead; that he had dedicated his entire life to the delivery of Chinen's letters.

Malak was offended, and told her so as they browsed the market for travel provisions on the last day. "We gave everything to those two! And for what? In the end, we didn't even get a nod out of them."

Lauren could picture herself, at Malak's age, posturing and pouting exactly the same way. "It was never really about them," she said, "the couriers, the Society, none of it."

He stared at her. "Then why? Why help them, if not for the glory of it?"

Lauren laughed. "What glory. They're two young people who might be in love. There was never any glory. That was the point."

Still he stared. With a sigh, Lauren tried one last time: "The Society existed to celebrate that very insignificance. Chinen and Margaret, they're nobody—but so are we all. In elevating them to epic status, the Society elevated every ordinary person. We celebrated all love, no matter how ordinary or fleeting, by celebrating theirs."

Malak shook his head. "There's yams over there." He stalked away. Lauren watched him go, hands on her hips.

"Courier!"

She turned. Chinen de Conestoga stood a few feet away—or was it him? Yes—it was just that he was dressed in local garb, tough traveling clothes like hers and Malak's. He had a pack slung over his shoulder. "Great, you're still here!" He strode up and shook her hand—or really, in his enthusiasm, her whole arm.

"What are you doing here?" She looked around; nobody was watching. "The fortress will be shutting up in a few hours. And we're leaving. The market's closing—"

"I'm going with you!"

And he just stood there, grinning widely, while she tried to catch up. "Wait, you—" He was dressed like a realtimer. "You're coming with . . . You're running away from home?"

"If I stay, I won't come of age before next Jubilee. If I leave, I'll be an adult before Father can catch up to me." He grinned again. "And I'll be of age by the time Margaret's lockstep wakes."

Two years . . . it was true. Lauren looked him over, her mind a blank; then suddenly she laughed. "You'll make a rather outsized letter."

Serious now, he said, "I'll do whatever work you need. I don't intend to be a burden."

But you're the Author! Yet he wasn't, not anymore. *Oh, how is the Society going to take this one?* The shock was going to kill the old men in the library, but then, Tamlaine's message would have been enough to do that. The investors—those few romantic and wealthy souls whose support of the Society was a kind of sacrifice to love—might rebel and pull all their funding. Or they might take Chinen's decision as the ultimate romantic gesture, and double their support. Who could tell? Lauren found herself almost dizzy with the possibilities.

"Come on then," she heard herself say. "Before your father finds out."

They were on the bridge when the fortress doors closed. It was late evening, and sunset burnished the side of the vast building. Lauren fancied she could hear the solid thud of the iron shields falling; the rooftop panels were already shut. There was no hurry now; people would take whatever time they needed to wrap up their business in the temporary town before heading home with the goods and wealth they'd acquired during this brief trading season.

Several stars were out. As Lauren stepped onto solid ground at the far end of the bridge, she glanced up, not at the stars but at the blank silver-blue between them. It was within that invisible space that most of the lockstep worlds could be found— tens of thousands of frozen, nomad planets for every star in the galaxy. Someone embarking from this fortress tonight might take decades to reach another of those distant worlds, yet only a single night would pass for them, since they were hibernating. Meanwhile, their destinations were in hibernation too; all the worlds in a lockstep coordinated their wake and sleep cycles. A traveler to such a world could spend a month there and then return, to find that only a month—in lockstep time—had passed here. In this way, the locksteps maintained an illusion of proximity for a far-flung culture of thousands of worlds.

The price of living in a lockstep was that you gave up on realtime. Chinen's father would go to sleep tonight and not awake for thirty-one years. Lauren would probably be dead by the time he awoke; she would never hear the end of this story. If Chinen wasn't accepted into Margaret's lockstep during its Jubilee in two years, he would grow old and die while his father slept.

He didn't seem particularly worried; on the contrary, there was a spring in his step and he was looking about alertly as they descended the spiral path to the misty rain forest. "What's two years, if we can be together?" was all he'd said when Malak had confronted him about his decision. Malak had shut up after that, and now plodded along in uncharacteristic silence, his eyes searching the horizon as if looking for some reassurance there.

They slept that night under the stars—or at least, Lauren and Malak slept. She awoke at one point to the total silence of a windless forest; when she turned her head she saw, illuminated by thin starlight, Chinen lying on his back, as perfectly still as the forest boughs, and staring at the sky.

In the morning they ate a quiet breakfast, then descended from the cloud forest through tunnels of green carved through the forest floor. The far descendants of Earth's cicadas roared and hummed in the mazelike depths; above, the sunlit green was so bright it was nearly yellow.

About midmorning Chinen suddenly laughed and stopped. "Where are we going, anyway?" he asked.

Lauren had to smile, though Malak shot her a look that said he didn't know either. "Not home," she said. "Not my home, or Malak's yet. Since our master died we have to check in at the headquarters of our Society. You might as well come along."

He shrugged. "Sure. Maybe I could get a job there."

Malak sputtered in confusion, but Lauren was getting used to this kind of shock. She thought about all that Chinen didn't know about his place in her world; it was going to be a long, hard conversation.

"Sorry about your friend, by the way. We all heard the news. What's your Society do? Are you craftsmen?"

Well, here it was. Lauren thought for a while. "Chinen," she said eventually, "do you believe in love?"

He laughed and spread his arms wide. "Look at me! I'm here, aren't I?"

"Well, then, do you believe that people need to believe in love? Even when they don't have it?"

"Sure."

"Then, would you support a society that used symbols—a great tale, let's say—to inspire people to believe in love?"

Chinen grinned and nodded; cicadas sang a descant from the trees around him.

"All right," said Lauren. "Then let me tell you about a great love story, and about the Society that was formed to shelter and nurture it . . ."

They were exhausted that night, and not just because none of them had walked like this for a while. Malak had found a little dell near a spring, and Lauren could hear it quietly talking to itself as she lay down to sleep. It had been an emotional day for Chinen, who'd swung between outrage, awe, bemusement and a dozen other states as they talked. Malak had simply plodded, a gray shamble apparently immune to the cut-and-thrust of Lauren's history.

Now Chinen knew it all. He knew that Lauren had sacrificed having a normal life to spend her days preparing for one simple journey, as Courier. He knew that entire lives had been lived for the sake of his and Margaret's love; that duels had been fought; that great feuds had festered, operas been written and myriad books printed. Now, with all that filling his head, he lay down and fell instantly asleep.

Lauren wasn't far behind him, and the distracted murmurs of the spring were the perfect lullaby; she drifted off with a curious sense of fulfillment.

A hand clamped over her mouth.

Lauren bucked against the unforgiving ground as her eyes flew open and she reached past the hand to scrabble at shoulders, a face—

"Don't move!" someone hissed. Off to her left, some kind of struggle was flattening the grass. Two silhouettes rolled together and she saw the flash of a blade under starlight. Then she realized whose hand was over her mouth. It was Kiel Westerfenn's.

Ignoring her scratches and attempts to knee him, he dragged her under the shadows of an ancient tree whose many roots made their own convoluted landscape. She tried to bite him, and he hissed, "Look, he'll find us if you don't stop it! And I'm not young enough or strong enough anymore to say I could take him in a fight."

Him? She saw one of the black figures force the other down, and the knife rose. Lauren elbowed Kiel in the face and sprawled forward across a root. "Malak! No!"

He turned, snarling. "Shit! Where'd you go?" Chinen wasn't moving, so Malak got to his feet and held the knife up against the stars. "Don't move! Don't you dare move, or I'll spit your precious Author like a spring hare! Come out of there. Now!"

Kiel let go of her. Lauren rose to her feet and stumbled out into the meager starlight. "What are you doing, Malak?"

"Taking back my future." His chest was heaving with the effort of the fight. He took a few deep breaths, then kicked Chinen's prone shape. "There's going to be a letter. He's going to write it, and I'm going to deliver it to Margaret. Then I'll be the courier for the next twenty-eight years! With the privileges, the pension, and I'll be somebody. All I wanted was to hold my head up the way you hold up yours. Then kids'll look up to me the way I used to look up to you."

Lauren's trembling fingers pressed against her nose, which was bleeding from the pressure of Kiel's hand. The stickiness bewildered her, but as she stared at the black pooling in her palm, the meaning of what Malak had just said overcame her. "You killed Tamlaine."

"Of course. He was going to tell the Society! Then it would have all been over for me."

"Oh, Malak."

"Don't you sound so disappointed! Just—just don't! You got to be courier! You've had it all. What was I going to—"

Kiel tackled him from the side.

Lauren screamed, watching them roll across the stony, root-thrust ground. She almost tripped over Chinen and suddenly realized what she should be doing. She knelt and felt his throat. There was a pulse.

"Chinen, Chinen you have to get up. We have to go." He moaned and tried to sit up. "Have to go, have to go *now*—"

Kiel cried out and she turned to see him staggering into the darkness. "Ha!" Malak spun; she saw the dark sockets of his eyes, saw him dismiss her as a threat and move on to Chinen, who was getting to his feet.

Malak stepped up to Chinen, blade raised, and it was no trick at all for Lauren to raise the rock she'd grabbed and bring it down on the back of the head. He fell instantly and silently.

Lauren looked at the rock in her hand, puzzled at the simplicity of it. Then Chinen shook his head and put a hand on her shoulder to steady himself. "Nicely done," he said.

"Kiel!" She dropped the rock and went to look for him. He was near the spring, doubled up and coughing. "Oh no! Kiel, it'll be all right! Just lie down, don't move around so much, we'll get help—"

"I'm all right. Oooh, forget that. But I'll *be* all right, he didn't hit any mainlines." Kiel sat down, rather suddenly, next to the mindless bubbling water, and guided her hand to a wet patch on his flank. "See? Hurts like Hell, but it's not deep. At least I don't think so . . ." He went on talking, making inferences, judging how far the blade had gone in and how much blood he'd lost. When Chinen arrived he and Lauren made some bandages and tied them tightly around Kiel, and then Chinen put pressure on the wound.

Eventually Kiel said, "Malak?"

"Tied him up," said the Author. "Not that he's going anywhere. Lauren hit him pretty hard." There was an admiring tone in his voice, but Lauren felt sick. She sat with her head down for a while, and nobody spoke. Then she looked up at Kiel.

"What are you doing here?"

"You're welcome," he said with a weak laugh. "I was following you.—Me, not us. I ditched my cousins yesterday. They'd have done you harm if they'd found you."

"But why? I mean why follow us?"

He tried to shrug. "I was suspicious. Tamlaine's death . . . I knew *we* didn't do it. So who did that leave? I couldn't be sure, and I knew you'd never trust me. So I decided to just watch over you for a couple days, until you got to heavier trafficked roads. Glad I did." Exhausted now, he lay back; he was starting to shiver.

Chinen grunted. "I'll get the fire going." He got up and began rummaging around for kindling.

Lauren sat bent over while Chinen clattered and cursed in the underbrush. Eventually she said, "You wanted to make sure the Author was safe."

"Not the Author." Kiel coughed. "The message."

There was another long silence. Then Lauren said, "It was just dinner, you know. Once or twice, I can't even remember."

"You've read the letters. Do you think he and Margaret did any more?"

She looked over at Chinen, who was jamming sticks into the coals with a determined look on his bruised face.

"I suppose not," she said.

Then she lay down next to Kiel, whom she had not seen in many long years, and they talked.

LOS piratas del Mar de plastico (pirates of the plastic ocean)

PAUL GRAHAM RAVEN

Paul Graham Raven is a postgraduate researcher in infrastructure futures and theory at the University of Sheffield, as well as a futurist, writer, literary critic, and occasional journalist; his work has appeared in such venues as MIT Technology Review, Interzone, Strange Horizons, ARC Magazine, Rhizome, The Los Angeles Review of Books, *and* The Guardian. *He lives a stone's throw from the site of the Battle of Orgreave in the company of a duplicitous cat, three guitars he can hardly play, and sufficient books to constitute an insurance-invalidating fire hazard, and maintains a website at velcro-city.co.uk.*

In the thought-provoking story that follows, he shows us that there's no disaster so complete that it doesn't provide an opportunity for somebody . . .

Hope Dawson stepped down from the train into the bone-dry heat of afternoon in southern Spain, and wondered—not for the first time, and probably not for the last—what the hell she was doing there, and how long she'd end up staying.

The freelance lifestyle did that to you; seven years crawling to and fro across Europe as a hand-to-mouth journo-sans-portfolio had left Hope with few ties to her native Britain beyond her unpaid student loans, and she'd yet to settle anywhere else for long. She'd spent the last six months or so bumping around in the Balkans on a fixed-term stringer's contract from some Californian news site she'd never read (and never intended to), scraping up extra work on the side wherever she could: Web site translation gigs, trade-zine puff pieces, and the inevitable tech-art exhibition reviews; she could barely remember the last time she put her own name in a by-line, or wanted to. The Californian site had folded itself up a few days before the contract ended, and after a few agreeable weeks house-sitting an alcoholic Tiranese lawyer's apartment, burning through the small pile of backhanded cash and favours she'd amassed, and poking at her perpetually unfinished novel, she felt the need to move on once more. Albania was cheap, but it was a backwater, and backwaters rarely coughed up stories anyone would pay for; her loans weren't going to repay themselves, after all, and the

UK government had developed an alarming habit of forcibly repatriating those who attempted to disappear into the boondocks and default on their debts.

The world dropped the answer in her lap while she wasn't looking. As winter gave way to spring, Tirana's population of favela geeks—a motley tribe of overeducated and underemployed Gen-Y Eurotrash from the rust-belts, dust-belts and failed techno-poles of Europe—began to thin out. Hope's contacts dropped hints about southern Spain, casual labour, something to do with the agricultural sector down there. That, plus a surge of ambiguous white-knuckle op-eds in the financial press about the long-moribund Spanish economy, was enough for Hope to go on. She'd finished up a few hanging deadlines, called in a favour she'd been saving up, and traded a lengthy, anonymous and staggeringly unobjective editorial about Albanian railway tourism in exchange for a one-way train ticket to Almeria, first class.

Hope squinted along the length of the platform, a-shimmer with afternoon heat-haze beneath a cloudless azure sky, to where a dozen or so geeks were piling themselves and their luggage out of the budget carriages at the very back of the train. They were loaded down with faded military surplus duffels and mountaineering backpacks, battered flight cases bearing cryptic stencils, and rigid luggage that look uncharac-teristically new and expensive by comparison to their clothing which, true to their demography, looked like a random grab-bag of the ugliest and most momentary styles of the late twentieth century. Only a decade ago, while Hope had been wrapping up her undergrad work and hustling for her PhD scholarship back in Britain, one might have assumed they were here to attend a peripatetic music festival, maybe, or a con-vention for some obscure software framework. But that was before the price of oil had gone nuts and annihilated the cheap airline sector almost overnight. Even within Europe, long distance travel was either slow and uncomfortable or hideously expensive. Unemployed Millennials—of which there were many—tended not to move around without a damned good incentive.

Milling around on the platform like a metaphor for Brownian motion, the geeks were noisy, boisterous and a few years younger than Hope, and she worked hard to squash a momentary feeling of superiority, to bring her field researcher's reflexivity back online. *Tat tvam asi*, she reminded herself; *that thou art*. Or *there but for the grace of God*, perhaps. The main difference between Hope and them, she decided, was a certain dogged luck. She looked briefly at her reflection in the train window, and saw a short girl with tired-looking eyes wearing an executive's dark trouser-suit in the London style of three winters previous, her unruly mass of curly blonde hair already frizzing into a nimbus of static in response to the heat. Who was she trying to fool, she wondered, for the umpteenth time. The geeks looked ludicrous, flowing off the platform and into the station like some lumpy superfluid, but they also looked comfortable, carefree. It'd been a long time since Hope felt either of those things.

Leaving the station, Hope donned her spex, set them to polarise, and blinked about in the local listings. She soon secured herself a few cheap nights in an apart-ment on the sixth floor of an undermaintained block about half a klick from the cen-tre of town. Almeria reminded Hope more than a little bit of the ghost-towns of southern Greece, where she'd gone to chase rumours of a resurgence in piracy in the Eastern Med a few years back: noughties boom-time tourist infrastructure peel-ing and crumbling in the sun, like traps left lying in a lobsterless sea. Leaning on the rust-spotted railing of her balcony, she looked westwards, where the legendary Plastic Ocean stretched out to the horizon, mile after square mile of solarised bio-plastic sheeting shimmering beneath the relentless white light of the sun. The green-houses were all Almeria had left since the tourists stopped coming, churning out a relentless assortment of hothouse fruit'n'veg for global export, but they'd been pre-dominantly staffed by semi-legal immigrant workers from across the Med for years. She couldn't see much chance of the geeks undercutting that sort of workforce.

Later that evening, Hope was prepared to use her clueless middle-management air-head routine on the tapas bar's waiter, but didn't need to: He had plenty to say, albeit in a Basque-tinged dialect that tested her rusty Spanish to the utmost.

"You're with those guys who bought the Hotel Catedral, yes?" he asked her.

"Oh, no," she replied. The waiter relaxed visibly as she spooled out her cover: pur-chasing rep for a boutique market stall in Covent Garden, sent out to do some on-the-spot quality control.

"Well, I knew you couldn't be with those damned kids who've been turning up the last few weeks," he said, plunking down a cold beer next to her tapas.

Hope fought to keep a straight face; the waiter was no older than the geeks he's disparaging, but she's very used to the employed seeing the unemployed as children. "Yeah, what's with them?"

"Damned if I know." He shrugged. "They all seem to head westwards as soon as they arrive. I'll be surprised if they find any work in El Ejido, but hey, not my problem."

"And what about the Hotel Catedral?"

"Again, don't know. They've been close to closing for years, running a skeleton staff. Times have been hard, you know? My friend Aldo works the bar up there. Few weeks back, he tells me, he's doing a stint on the front desk when this bunch of Amer-ican guys breeze in and ask to speak to the manager. They disappear to his office for half an hour, then they come back out, gather the staff, announce a change of own-ership. More Yankees came in by plane, apparently. Place is full of them, now." He scowls. "They hired my girlfriend and some others as extra staff. Good tippers, ap-parently, but a bit . . . well, they're rich guys, I guess. What do you expect, right?"

Hope nodded sympathetically. She'd never worked hotels, largely because she knew so many people who had.

Hope spent the next morning getting her bearings, then drifted casually toward the Hotel Catedral, where she enquired about booking a table for supper. The lobby was all but empty, but the receptionist had the tight-lipped air of a man with a lot to worry about.

"No tables for non-residents, senora; my apologies."

"Oh—in that case, can I book a room?"

"We are fully booked, senora."

Hope made a show of peering around the empty lobby. "If it's a money thing, I can show you a sight-draft on my company's account?"

The guy continued to stonewall, so Hope relented and wandered back onto the palm-studded plaza, where the sun was baking the sturdy buttresses of the titular cathedral. She was drinking a coffee at a cafe across the square when a gangly and somewhat sunburned young man pulled up on some sort of solar-assisted trike.

"Hey—Hope Dawson, right?" He spoke English with a broad Glaswegian accent.

Hope protested her innocence in passable Castilian, but he whipped out a little handheld from a pocket on his hunting vest and consulted it, shielding his eyes from the sun with his hand.

"Naw, see, this is definitely you. Look?"

Hope looked. It *was* definitely her—her disembarking from the train yesterday afternoon, in fact. Droneshot, from somewhere above the station.

"Who wants to know?" she growled, putting some war-reporter grit into it.

"Mah boss. Wants tae offer ye a job, see."

"Well, you may tell your boss thank you, but I'm already employed."

"Bollix, lass—ye've not had a proper job in years." The lad grins. "I should know. It was me as doxxed ye."

"Is that supposed to reassure me?"

"Naw, it's supposed to intrigue ye." He slapped the patchwork pleather bench-seat of the trike behind him, shaded by the solar panel. "Cedric's a few streets over the way. Come hear what he has to say before ye make up yer mind, why not?"

"I hope Ian didn't alarm you, Miss Dawson," said Cedric, as a waiter poured coffee. They were sat in the lobby of a mid-range boutique hotel which, given by the lingering musty smell, had been boarded up for years until very recently.

"Not at all," Hope lied, in a manner she hoped conveyed a certain sense of *fuck you, Charlie*. "But I'd appreciate you explaining why you had him dox me."

"I want you to work for me, Miss Dawson."

"Just Hope, please. And as I told Ian, Mister . . . ?"

He smiles. "Just Cedric, please."

"As I told Ian, Cedric, I already have work."

"Indeed you do—a career in journalism more distinctive for its length than its impact, if you don't mind me saying so. Not many last so long down in the freelance trenches."

"Debts don't pay themselves, Cedric."

"Quite. But it would be nice to pay them quicker, wouldn't it?"

Hope put down her coffee cup to hide the tremor of her hands. "I'm flattered, but I should probably point out I'm not really a journalist."

"No, you're a qualitative economist. You were supervised by Shove and Walker, University of Lancaster. I've read your thesis."

"You have?"

"Well, the important bits. I had Ian précis the methodological stuff for me, if I'm honest. It was well received by your peers, I believe."

"Not well enough to lead to any research work," said Hope, curtly. No one wanted an interpretivist cluttering up their balance sheets with talk of intangible externalities, critiquing the quants, poking holes in the dog-eared cardboard cut-out of *homo economicus*.

"Obviously not—but participant observation research work is what I'm offering you, starting today. Six months fixed term contract, a PI's salary at current UK rates, plus expenses. I'll even backdate to the start of the month, if it helps."

"What's the object?"

Cedric looks surprised; his expression reminds Hope of the animated meerkat from an ad campaign of her youth. "Well, here, of course. Almeria the province, that is, rather than just the city."

"Why?"

He smiled, leant forward a little. "Good question!" A frown replaced the smile. "I'm afraid I can't really answer it, though. Confidentiality of sources, you understand. But in essence, I was tipped off to an emerging situation here in Almeria, and decided I wanted to see it up close."

"I'm going to need more than that to go on, I'm afraid," said Hope.

Cedric somehow looked chagrined and reproachful at once. "There are limits, I'm afraid, and they're not of my making. But look: if I say I have reason, solid reason to believe that Almeria is on the verge of a transformative economic event without precedent, and that I have spent upward of five million euros in just the last few days in order to gather equipment and personnel on the basis of that belief, would you trust me?"

Not as far as I could throw you, frankly. "So why me, specifically?"

A boyish smile replaced the frown. "Now, that's a little easier! Remind me, if you would, of your thesis topic?"

To her own surprise, Hope's long-term memory duly regurgitated a set of research questions and framings polished to the smoothness of beach pebbles by repeated supervisory interrogations: transitions in civic and domestic consumptive practices; the influence of infrastructures and interfaces on patterns and rates of resource use; the role of externalities in the playing out of macroeconomic crises. Warming to her topic, she segued into a spirited defense of free-form empirical anthropology, and of interpretive methods as applied to the analysis of economic discontinuities.

"Good," Cedric intoned, as if she'd passed some sort of test. "H&M is researching exactly those sort of questions, and we think Almeria could be our Ground Zero."

That was a worrying choice of phrase.

"The markets are turbulent places, Hope," he continued, "too turbulent for mere mathematics to explain. They no longer interest me, in and of themselves." He leans back in his chair. "This will sound crass to someone of your generation, I'm sure, but nonetheless: I am not simply wealthy. I am rich enough that I don't even know what I'm worth, how I got that way, or who I'd have to ask to find out. Money is a very different matter for me than for you. I have the extraordinary liberty of being able to think about it purely in the abstract, because my concrete concerns are taken care of."

Hope stared at him, stunned into silence.

"So I am able," Cedric continued, "to explore economics in a way accessible to few, and of interest to even fewer. Lesser men, poorer men obsess over mere commerce, on the movement of money. My concerns are larger, far larger. You might say that it is the movement of money that fascinates me."

She grabbed her bag, stood up, and started for the doorway.

"Hope, hear me out, please," he called. "I don't expect you to like me, or even understand me. But I need you to work for me, here and now, and I am willing to pay you well. Wait, please, just for a moment."

Hope paused in the shade of the doorway, but didn't turn around.

"Check your bank balance," he said after a brief pause. She blinked it up on her spex: a deposit had just cleared from Huginn&Muninn AB, Norwegian sort-code. More money than she'd earned in the last twelve months, both on the books and off. "Consider it a signing bonus."

She turned round, her arms crossed. "What if I won't sign?"

Cedric shrugged elegantly in his seat; he'd not moved an inch.

"I'll think about it," she said, turning on her heel.

Ian drove her back to her apartment block on the trike.

"So I'll come fetch ye tomorrow morning, then," he announced. "Run you down to El Ejido, get ye all set up and briefed."

"I told Cedric I'd think about it, Ian."

"Aye, I heard ye." Ian grinned. "Told him the same meself."

True to his word, Ian came to collect her the next morning. Hope found, to her surprise, that she was packed and ready to go.

"Knew ye'd go fer it," asserted Ian, bungeeing her bags to the trike.

"Very much against my better judgement," she replied.

"Aye, he's an odd one, fer sure. But he's not lied to me once, which is more than I can say fer mah previous employers." He saddled up, flashed a grin. "Plus, he always pays on time."

"He'd better," replied Hope, as Ian accelerated out into the empty streets of Almeria, heading westwards. "What is it you do for him, anyway?"

"Not what you might be thinking! Ah'm a kind of general gopher, I guess, but I do a lot of reading for him when he's got other stuff on. News trawls, policy stuff. The doctoral theses of obscure scholars, sort o' thing." He flashed a grin over his shoulder. "Sometimes he just wants to chew over old science fiction novels until the early hours. You thought it was hard to find work off the back of *your* doctorate? Try bein' an academic skiffy critic, eh!"

"Seriously?"

"Oh, aye. Says they inspire him to think differently. Me, I reckon he thinks he's Hubertus fuckin' Bigend or somesuch . . ."

"Who?"

But Ian had slipped on a set of retro-style enclosure headphones and turned his attention to his driving, dodging wallowing dirtbikes and scooters overloaded with helmetless geeks and their motley luggage, all headed westwards. The road from Almeria to El Ejido passed briefly through foothills almost lunar in their rugged desolation, before descending down to the Plastic Ocean itself. Hope couldn't see a patch of ground that wasn't covered with road, cramped housing, or row after monotonous row of greenhouses shimmering with heat-haze. Hope was surprised to see trucks at the roadside in the iconic white and blue livery of the United Nations, and tapped Ian on the shoulder.

"What the hell are *they* doing here?" she yelled over the slipstream.

"The man hisself tipped 'em off. Fond of the UN, he is—fits wi' his International Rescue fetish, I guess—and they seem to appreciate his input, albeit grudgingly. We'll fix ye a meeting wi' General Weissmuutze, she's sound enough. Always good to know the people wi' the guns and bandages, eh?"

Ian dropped Hope at a small villa near the southern edge of El Ejido, loaded her spex with a credit line to a Huginn&Muninn expenses account and a bunch of new software, and told her to call if she needed anything, before whizzing off eastwards on his ridiculous little vehicle. Hope settled in, pushed aside her doubts and got to work familiarising herself with the town and the monotonous sea of greenhouses surrounding it. Cedric's backroom people had assembled a massive resource set of maps and satellite images, and a handful of high-def camdrones were busily quartering the town, collecting images to compile into street-view walkthroughs; they'd also, they claimed, fudged up a cover identity that would hold up to all but the most serious military-grade scrutiny. Hope had her doubts about that, but after a handful of days and a fairly drastic haircut, she was confident enough to hit the streets and pass herself off as just another new arrival, of which there were more and more each day.

Eager and noisy gangs of geeks were descending on boarded-up villas, boutique hotels and bars, reactivating the inert infrastructure of the tourist sector, stripping buildings back to the bare envelope before festooning them with solar panels, screen-tarps, and sound-systems of deceptively prodigious wattage. The wide boulevard of Paseo los Lomas, quiet enough during the daylight hours, started to fill up with ragged revellers around 6pm; by 9 each night, with the heat of the day still radiating from the pavements, it resembled a cross between a pop-up music festival and a Spring Break riot. The few businesses still owned and operated by locals hung on for a few days, watching their stock fly off the shelves at premium prices, before selling up their operations lock, stock and barrel to expensively dressed men bearing bottomless yen-backed banker's draughts.

"I'd have been crazy not to sell," a former restaurateur told Hope, as his wife and kids bundled their possessions into the trunk of a Noughties-vintage car retooled for biodiesel. Inside the building, an argument was breaking out between the new owners over which internal walls to knock through. "The mortgage has been under water for a decade, and they offer to pay it off in full? I'm not the crazy one here. They're welcome to it," he said, turning away.

Inside the cafe, Hope found five geeks swinging sledgehammers into partition walls, watched over by a man so telegenic that he was almost anonymous, his office-casual clothes repelling the dust of the remodelling process.

"Hey, girl," the man drawled in approval. The geeks carried on hammering.

"Hi!" she said, bright as a button. "So I just got into town, and I was wondering which are the best job-boards? There's, like, so many to choose from."

The guy looked her up and down. "Guess it depends what sort of things you can do, doesn't it, ah . . . Cordelia?"

"That's me!" The cover identity seemed to be working, at least. "I guess you'd say I was in administration?"

"Not much call for admin at the moment, princess. Here." He threw an url to her spex. "That's the board for indies and non-specialists. You're a bit late to pick up the best stuff, but you should be able to make some bank if you don't price yourself out of the market. Or maybe one of the collectives will take you on contract for gophering? I'm sure these lads could find a space for a pretty little taskrabbit like yourself in their warren, couldn't you, boys?"

"Right on, Niceday, right *on*," enthused a scrawny geek. "You want the url, girl?"

"Please," she lied. "I'mma shop around some more, though. See what my options are, you know?"

"Whatevs," shrugged the dusty kid. "Longer you leave it, less we'll cut you in."

"You should listen to him, Cordelia," said the well-dressed guy, stepping closer to her. "In business, it pays to be bold." His eyes narrowed a little. "And loyal."

"Oh, sure! So what about *your* warren, Mister . . . ?"

"Niceday. And I don't have a warren, I hire them."

"So you're, like, a veecee or something?"

Niceday smiled an oily sort of smile. "Or something," he agreed. The smile vanished as he locked eyes with her. "Choose wisely, Cordelia, and choose soon. This isn't the time or place for . . . observing from the sidelines. Unless you're with the UN, of course."

"Haha, right! Well, ah, thanks for the advice," said Hope, her heart hammering against her ribs, and beat a swift retreat.

The mood on the periphery of the town was in sharp contrast to the raucous debauch of the centre. The greenhouse workers—almost all youngish North African men—were packed like matches into street after street of undermaintained tourist villas and former residential blocks, with the more recent arrivals living in slums built of breezeblocks and plastic sheeting on the vacant lots where the plastic ocean broke upon the dark edges of the town. Hope spent a few hours wandering from coffeeshop to shisha-shack, trying every trick in the interviewer's book to get them to talk. They were happy enough to have drinks bought for them on Cedric's dime, and to complain at length about work in the abstract as they demolished plates of tapas and meze, but questions about actual working conditions led only to sullen, tense silences, or the sudden inability of the formerly fluent to speak a word of Spanish.

"You only ask about our work so you can steal our jobs," a gaunt man accused her toward the end of the evening, pointing his long, scarred finger at her through a cloud of fragrant shisha smoke. "For so long, no one else will do this work so cheap. Now all you people come back, make trouble for us."

She tried dropping her cover a bit, and played the journalist card; big mistake.

"Journalists, they don't make good stories about us, ever. We are always the villains, the evil Arabs, no?"

She protested her innocence and good intentions, but he had a point. Hope's background research had uncovered a history of tension between the greenhouse workers and the local residents that stretched back to before she was born: grimly vague and one-sided stories in the archives of now-moribund local news outlets about forced evictions, arson, and the sort of casual but savage violence between young men that always marks periods of socioeconomic strife. The attacks had lessened as the local youth migrated northwards in search of better work, but there was a lingering vibe of siege mentality among the remaining immigrants, and their dislike for the influx of favela geeks was tangible.

"Go back to your rich friends," the man repeated, jabbing his finger for emphasis. "It is they who are meddling, trying to make us look bad! We'll not help you pin it on us."

"Pin what on you?" Hope asked, suddenly alert to the closeness of the knowledge she needed, but the guy's eyes narrowed and his lips tightened and he shook his head, and the whole place went silent and tense, and Hope was horribly aware of being the only woman in a dark smoky room full of unfamiliar men speaking an unfamiliar language.

She stammered out some apologies, paid her tab and left quickly, but the damage was done. From that point on, the workers refused to talk to her. As the days passed, there were a few ugly incidents in alleyways late at night: botched muggings, running brawls, a few serious stabbings on both sides. But the geeks were confident in their new-found dominion, not to mention better fed and equipped, and the workers had no one on their side, least of all the employers they'd never met, and who only communicated with them via the medium of e-mailed quotas and output itineries. If Hope wanted to get to the bottom of whatever was going on, she was going to have to do more than ask around.

Most of the geeks worked by day in jury-rigged refrigerated shipping containers and partied by night, but Cedric's backroom people had tipped her off to the existence of a small night shift that drifted out into the greenhouse ocean around midnight and returned before dawn. They'd furnished Hope's villa with an assortment of technological bits and bobs, including an anonymously military-looking flight-case containing three semi-autonomous AV drones about the size of her fist. She spent an afternoon syncing them up with her spex and jogging around among the miniature palms and giant aloes in her compound, getting the hang of the interface, then waited for night to fall before decking herself out in black like some amateur ninja and sneaking along the rooftops toward the edge of town, using the raucous noise of the evening fiesta as cover. Spotting a small knot of kids heading northwards out of town, she sent two drones forward to tail them, one to run overwatch, and followed after at a distance she assumed would keep her out of sight, or at least give her plenty of time to cut and run if she was spotted.

After about half an hour, the geeks paused and split up. Hope hunkered down just close enough to still receive the feed from her drones, then flew them slow and low down the narrow gaps between the greenhouses, using an IR overlay to pick out the warm bodies among the endless identical walls of plastic, and settled down to watch.

Hope was no agricultural technician, but there was plenty of public info about the basic design of the greenhouses: long tunnels of solarised plastic sheeting with automated ventilation flaps covered row after row of hydroponic medium, into which mixtures of precious water and bespoke nutrients were dribbled at algorithmically optimised rates, depending on the species under cultivation. Over the years, more and more of the climate control and hydroponics had been automated, but the hapless workers still had the unenviable task of shuffling up and down the greenhouses on their knees during the heat of the day, checking closely on the health and development of their charges; the consequences of quality control failures were draconian, in that it meant being sacked and blacklisted for further employment. The only reason they'd not been replaced by robots was that robots couldn't do the sort of delicate and contextual work that the greenhouses required; it was still way cheaper to get some poor mug straight off the boat from Morocco and teach him how to trim blight and pluck aphids than it was to invest in expensive hardware that couldn't make those sorts of qualitative decisions on the fly. Plus the supply of desperate immigrants was effectively inexhaustible, and their wage demands were kept low by Europe's endemic problem with unemployment. In Spain, as in much of the rest of the world, automation had been eating away at the employment base from the middle class downwards, rather than from the bottom upwards . . . and the more white-collar gigs it consumed, the larger and more desperate the working class became. There was barely a form of manual labour left that you couldn't design a machine to do just as well as a human, but hiring a human had far lower up-front costs. Plus you could simply replace them when they wore out, at no extra expense.

The geek night shift wasn't doing the work of the greenhouse guys, that was for sure. Of the trio Hope was watching, one was squatting on the ground over a handheld he'd plugged in to the server unit at the end of the greenhouse module, another was fiddling around with the nutrient reservoirs, and the third was darting in and out of the little airlock next to the guy fiddling with the server. Lost in the scene unfolding in front of her eyes, Hope steered one of her drones in for a closer look as the third guy reemerged with his fists full of foot-long seedlings, which he threw to the ground before picking up a tray of similar-looking cuttings and slipping back inside.

She was just bringing her second forward drone around for a closer look at the reservoir tanks when her spex strobed flash-bulb white three times in swift succession, causing her to shriek in shock and discomfort. Blinded and disoriented, she stood and started running in what she assumed was the direction she'd come, but tripped on some pipe or conduit and fell through the wall of a greenhouse. She thrashed about, trying to free herself from a tangled matrix of plastic sheeting and tomato plants, but strong hands grabbed her ankles and hauled her out roughly onto the path. She put her hands up to protect her face as a strong flashlight seared her already aching eyes. At least I'm not permanently blind, she thought to herself, absurdly.

"Stay still," grunted a Nordic-sounding man, and she was flipped over onto her front, before someone sat on her legs and zip-tied her hands behind her back.

"I've got a bunch of drones out here," she threatened.

"No," replied the Viking voice, "you had three. We only have one. But unlike yours, ours has a MASER instead of a camera."

Hope stopped struggling.

———

Dawn took a long time to come. When it arrived, Hope's two hulking assailants fetched her out of the shipping container they'd locked her in, bundled her into the back of an equally windowless van, then drove eastwards in stony silence, ignoring her attempts at conversation. They delivered her to the reception room of a top-floor suite at the Hotel Catedral, where a familiar face was waiting for her.

"Ah, Cordelia . . . or should I say Hope?" drawled Niceday. "We meet again!"

Hope kneaded her wrists, where the cable-tie had left deep red weals. "You could have just pinged my calendar for an appointment," she snarked.

"I work to my own schedule, not yours. Nor Cedric's, for that matter. How's he doing, anyway?"

"Ask him yourself," she shot back. "I just work for him."

"Quod erat demonstrandum," said Niceday, leaning against a drinks cabinet. "He's always been a great collector of . . . novelties."

"You know him well, then?"

Niceday laughed, but didn't reply.

"Why are those kids out hacking greenhouses in the middle of the night?"

"That's literally none of your business, Hope."

"But it is *your* business?"

"Mine, yes, and that of my associates. There are laws against industrial espionage, you know."

"There are also laws to protect journalists from being kidnapped in the course of their work."

"But you're not a journalist, Hope." Niceday snapped his fingers. A hidden projector flashed up a copy of Hope's contract with Huginn&Muninn onto the creamy expanse of the wall. "Qualitative economist, it says here. Good cover for an industrial spy, I'd say."

"I'm not a spy. I'm a social scientist."

"Are you so sure?"

Hope opened her mouth to reply, then closed it.

"You should listen to your gut instincts more often," Niceday continued. "Isn't that what journalists do? I hope that, after this little chat, your gut instincts will be to stay the hell away from my taskrabbits."

"What are you going to do if I don't—have me disappear?"

"Don't dream it's beyond my reach, girl," he snapped. "Or that I couldn't get you and Cedric tangled up in a lawsuit long enough to keep you out of my hair—and out of sight—for years to come."

"So why haven't you?"

The smile returned. "Lawyers are expensive. Much cheaper to simply persuade you to cease and desist, *mano a mano*, so to speak."

"That rather implies you have something to hide."

"Oh, Hope—who doesn't have something to hide? Only those with nothing to lose. Do you think Cedric has nothing to hide? Weren't you hiding behind a false name yourself?"

"Yes, but—"

"But nothing. You've no moral high ground here, Hope. You can write a story about my taskrabbits and try to get it published somewhere, if you like, but you'll find there's no respectable organ that'll run it. Takes a lot of money to keep a good news outlet running, you know, and ads just don't cover it." He shook his head in mock lament. "Or you could publish it online yourself, independently, of course. But you might find that some stories about you were published around the same time. The sort of stories that kill careers in journalism and research stone dead: fabricated quotes, fiddled expenses, false identities, kickbacks, tax evasion, that sort of thing."

"So you're threatening me, now?"

Niceday arched an eyebrow. "Hope, I just had two large men zip-tie your wrists together and lock you in a shipping container for four hours."

Hope felt the fight drain out of her. "Yeah, fair point."

"We understand each other, then. Good. Now, you get back to your fieldwork. The boys will drive you back to El Ejido, if you like."

"You're just going to let me go?"

He laughed again. "If I thought you or Cedric could do any lasting damage to my business plan, you'd have never got within a hundred klicks of Almeria. Do you think it says 'Niceday' on any of my passports? Do you think this face matches any official records, that this voice is on file somewhere? I might as well not exist, as far as law enforcement is concerned; far less paperwork that way." He crossed his arms. "Keeping your nose out of my affairs going forward is just a way of avoiding certain more permanent sorts of clean-up operation. Do you understand me?"

Hope stared at him: six foot something of surgically perfected West Coast beef-cake, wearing clothes that she'd need to take out a mortgage to buy, and the snake-like smile of a man utterly accustomed to getting his own way.

"Who are you?" she wondered aloud. "Who are you, really?"

He spread his arms in benediction, like that Jesus statue in Brazil before the Maoists blew it up.

"We," he intoned, "are the opportunity that recognises itself."

She didn't understand him at all. She suspected she never would.

Around five weeks after she'd arrived, the storm finally broke, and Hope found herself riding shotgun in General Weissmuutze's truck on the highway toward the port facility at Almeria, weaved along between an implacable and close-packed column of self-driving shipping containers. The hard shoulder was host to a Morse code string of greenhouse workers, moving a little faster on foot than the solar-powered containers, backs bent beneath their bundles of possessions. The General was less than happy.

"I have a team down at the airport; the private planes are leaving as quickly as they can arrange a take-off window. And then there's the port," she complained, gesturing out of the passenger-side window toward the sea, where Hope could see a denser knot than usual of ships large and small waiting for their time at dockside. "Every spare cubic foot of freight capacity on the entire Mediterranean, it looks like. They're trying to clear as much of the produce as they can before I can seal the port."

Weisskopf's team had been awoken by an urgent voicecall from the FDA in the United States. A routine drugs-ring bust by the FBI somewhere in the ghost-zones of Detroit had uncovered not the expected bales of powder or barrels of pills, but crate after crate of Almerian tomatoes. After taking a few samples to a lab, they discovered that the fruit's flesh and juice contained a potent designer stimulant connected to a spate of recent overdoses, and informed the FDA. The FDA began the process of filing with Washington for an embargo on imports from Almeria, before informing the Spanish government and the UN, who'd patched them straight through to Weissmuutze in hopes of getting things locked down quickly.

"Scant chance of that," said Weissmuutze later, as they watched the ineffectual thin blue line of the Almerian police force collapse under a wave of immigrant workers trying to climb the fence into the container port. "The Spanish government doesn't have much reach outside of the big cities, and they handed the port over as a free-trade zone about a decade ago. The consortium is supposed to supply its own security, but . . ." She shrugged her bearlike shoulders. "My people are deactivating all the containers they can now the highway's blocked, but these poor bastards know that means there'll be more space for passengers."

Hope watched as the front line of workers reached the fence and began lobbing their bags and bundles over it, shaking at the fencepoles. "I think they've known this was coming for a while," said Hope.

"We've all known something was coming," muttered Weissmuutze. "Exactly what it is that's arrived is another question entirely."

Hope left Weisskopf and her peacekeepers to supervise the developing riot as best they could and headed for the airport, where Ian was lurking at Cedric's behest. The concourse bar was crowded with men who wore the bland handsomeness of elective surgery with the same casual ease as their quietly expensive Valley-boy uniform of designer jeans, trainers, and polo-necks.

"Honestly!" protested Ian over the rim of his mojito. "This is only my first one, and I only bought it 'cause they'd nae let me keep my table if I didn't."

Hope filled him in on happenings at the port. "What's happening here, then?"

"Looks like the circus is leaving town. Well, the ringmasters, at any rate. Hisself hoped I might be able to get some answers, but it's like I'm invisible or something, they'll nae talk to me . . ."

Hope sighed and scanned the room via the smallest and subtlest of her drones, finally spotting a familiar mask. Donning her own she made her way over to the end of the bar, where Niceday was sat nursing a highball of something peaty and expensive. "Ms Dawson, we meet again. Are you flying today?"

"I put myself on the stand-by list, but for some reason I'm not expecting any luck."

"Oh, very good," he replied, flashing a vulpine grin. "Are you sure you're not looking for a career change? I can always find work for girls with a bit of character, you know."

Yeah, I'll bet you can. "My current contract is ongoing, *Mister* Niceday, but thanks for the offer. You're moving on from Almeria, then?"

"Yeah—the party's over, but there'll be another one soon enough, somewhere. The lions must follow the wildebeest, amirite?"

"If the party's over, who's in charge of cleaning up?"

Niceday waved a hand in breezy dismissal. "The UN has been here a while, hasn't it? They know what they're doing."

"They know what you've been doing, too."

"Fulfilling the demands of the market, you mean?"

"Manufacturing drugs, I mean."

"Oh, I forgot—all drugs are bad, aren't they, unless they're being made by and sold to the right people? Besides, if those drugs weren't illegal or patented, I wouldn't be able to make any profit from doing so. Market forces, girl. I don't mark out the field, I just play the game."

"So this is some ideological crusade, then?"

"Nah," he replied, warming to his theme. "More an opportunity that was too good to pass up. My colleagues"—he gestured around the crowded bar—"and I had been doing business around south Asia, making use of all the redundant 3d printing capacity out there that the fabbing bubble left behind. But recent changes in feedstock legislation made it much harder to produce . . . ah, viable products, let's say. If you want feedstock that produces durable high-performance materials . . . well, you might as well try buying drug precursors, right? Serious regulation, poor risk/reward ratio. Boring.

"Now, I'd been watching the local markets here for some time, flipping deeds and water futures for chump change while I kept an eye open, when I had my little revelation: the greenhouses of Almeria were basically a huge networked organic 3D printer, and the only feedstocks it needed were water, fertiliser and sunlight. And while it couldn't print durable products, it could handle the synthesis of very complex molecules. Plants are basically a chemical reactor with a free-standing physical structure, you see, though my geneticist friends assure me that's a terrible oversimplification."

"So you just started growing tweaked plants right away?"

"Not quite, no; it took a few weeks to set up the shell companies, liaise with buyers, and get the right variants cooked up in the lab. Not to mention getting all our taskrabbits housed and happy! Then it was just a case of getting buyers to file legitimate orders with a grower, set the taskrabbits to handle the seedling switcheroos and hack the greenhouse system's growth parameters. Intense growing regimes mean you can turn over full-grown tomato plants in about three weeks. Biotech is astonishing stuff, isn't it?"

"You're not even ashamed, are you?" Hope wondered aloud.

"Why should I be?" His frown was like something a Greek statue might wear. "I delivered shareholder value, I shipped product, and I even maintained local employment levels a little longer than they'd have otherwise lasted. We are the wealth creators, Miz Dawson. Without us, nothing happens."

"But what happens after you leave?"

A look of genuine puzzlement crossed Niceday's face. "How should I know?" He glanced away into some dataspace or another, then stood and downed his drink. "Gotta go, my gulfstream's boarding. Sure I can't tempt you with a new position?" The smile was suave, but the eye beneath the raised eyebrow was anything but.

"Very."

"Shame—waste of your talents, chasing rainbows for Cedric. The option's always there if you change your mind."

"And how would I let you know if I did?"

Niceday winked, grinned again, then turned and vanished into the crowd. Hope went back to find Ian, who was getting impatient.

"Waitresses still will nae serve me, dammit. All ah want's a coke!"

"I think they're concentrating on the big tippers while they can," Hope replied; he rolled his eyes. "C'mon, let's get back to El Ejido. Weisskopf says it's all kicking off down at the container port. She wants us civvies out of the way."

Ian sighed. "You'll never guess where the trike's parked."

Things fell apart fast after Niceday and his fellow disruptors moved on. It soon became apparent that, absent the extra profit margin obtained by growing and shipping what the international media was already waggishly referring to as "Fruit-Plus," a perfect storm of economic factors had finally rendered Almerian greenhouse agriculture a loss-making enterprise. Cedric's quants spent long nights in their boutique hotel arguing heatedly over causal factors, but the general consensus was that relentless overabstraction of water from the regional aquifer had bumped up against escalating shipping costs and the falling spot-price of produce from other regions. Chinese investment in large-scale irrigation projects on the other side of the Med were probably involved, somehow; if nothing else, it explained the mass exodus of the immigrant workers. Those that had failed to get out on the empty freighters had descended on the dessicated former golf resorts along the coastline, squatting the sand-blown shells of holiday villas and retirement homes left empty by the bursting of the property bubble, fighting over crouching space in the scale-flecked holds of former fishing vessels whose captains saw midnight repatriation cruises as a supplement to their legitimate work.

A significant number showed no signs of wanting to leave, however, particularly those whose secular bent put them at odds with the increasingly traditionalist Islamic model of democracy that had sprouted from the scorched earth of the so-called Arab Spring in the Teens. Some fled quietly to the valleys hidden among the foothills of the Sierra Nevada to the north, where they set about reviving the hard-scrabble subsistence farming methods that their Moorish forebears had developed centuries before. Others—particularly the young and angry—occupied small swathes of greenhouse and turned them over to growing their own food, as did some of the more self-reliant and entrepreneurial gangs of taskrabbits who'd stayed on. Territorial disputes—driven more by the lack of water than the lack of space—were frequent, ugly, but mercifully short, and Hope spent a lot of time riding around the region with General Weissmuutze and her peacekeepers, putting out fires both literal and figurative. Within a few weeks the Plastic Ocean had evaporated away to a ragged series of puddles scattered across the landscape, separated by wide stretches of near-desert, the fleshless skeletons of greenhouse tunnels, and wandering tumbleweed tangles of charred plastic sheeting.

Other taskrabbit warrens found other business models, and Weissmuutze was hard-pressed to keep a lid on those who'd decided to stick with disruptive drug pharming. With the evisceration and collapse of the EPZ syndicate, courtesy Niceday and friends, the container port at Almeria became a revolving door for all sorts of shady import/export operators, and overland distribution networks for everything from un-tariffed Chinese photovoltaics and Pakistani firearms to prime Afghan heroin quickly sprung up and cut their way northwards into central Europe. Weissmuutze was obliged to be ruthless, rounding up the pharmers and their associates before putting their greenhouses and shipping-container biolabs to the torch. But the Spanish government had little interest in doing anything beyond issuing chest-thumping press releases, and most of her detainees were sprung by colleagues overnight, slip-ping eastwards or southwards and vanishing into the seething waters of the dark economy.

Much to Hope's fascination, however, the majority of the warrens went for more legitimate enterprises, from simple reboots of the greenhouse model aimed at grow-ing food for themselves and for barter, to more ambitious attempts at brewing up synthetic bacteria to clean up land and waterways blighted by excessive fertiliser run-off, all of which Weissmuutze did her best to protect and encourage. The dis-ruptors had snared a lot of warrens in contracts whose small print specified they could be paid off in stock and other holdings in lieu of cash, with the result that various collectives and sole operators found themselves holding title to all-but-worthless slivers and fragments of land, all-but-exhausted water abstraction rights, and chunks of physical infrastructure in various states of disrepair or dysfunction. Parallel economies sprung up and tangled themselves together almost overnight, based on barter, laundered euros, petrochemicals, solar wattage and manual labour. The whole region had become a sort of experimental sandbox for heterodox economic systems; the global media considered it a disaster zone with low-to-zero telegenic appeal, and ignored it accordingly, but to Hope it was like seeing all the abstract theories she'd studied for years leap off the page and into reality. She was busy, exhausted and, by this point, a most un-British shade of Mediterranean bronze.

When she finally remembered to wonder, she couldn't remember the last time she'd been so happy.

She was sat beneath a tattered sunbrella on the promenade at Playa Serena, poking at her mothballed novel, when Ian rolled up on his trike. Cedric was perched on the bench seat in the shade of the solar panel, wearing a pale suit and a casually dignified expression that reminded Hope of archived stills from the height of the British Raj.

"May we join you, Hope?" he asked, dismounting. Ian rolled his eyes and grinned, leaning into the back-rest of the trike's saddle.

"Sure. Stack of these brollies back there, if you want one."

Cedric settled himself next to her and stared down the beach, where a small war-ren was clustered around a device that looked like a hybrid of Ian's trike, a catering-grade freezer, and an explosion in a mirror factory. "What have we here?" he asked.

"Solarpunks," said Hope. "They're trying to make glass from sand using only sunlight."

"Innovative!"

"Naw, old idea," said Ian mildly. "Was a proof-of-concept back in the Teens. No one could scale it up for profit."

"What's their market, then?"

Hope gestured westwards, toward a large vacant lot between two crumbling hotels. "There's another lot down there working on 3d printing at architectural scales. They want to do Moorish styles, all high ceilings and central courtyards, but they're having some trouble getting the arches to come out right."

Ian barked a short laugh, then fell silent.

"I came to thank you for your hard work, Hope," said Cedric.

"You've paid me as promised," Hope shrugged. "No need for thanks."

"No requirement, perhaps, but I felt the need. Given the, ah, mission creep issues early on."

The euphemisms of power, thought Hope. "No biggie. I got to see the face of disruption close up. Lotta journalists would kill for a chance like that."

"A lot of researchers, too," Cedric suggested. Hope didn't reply.

"I've taken the liberty of paying off your student loans in full."

"That's very generous of you, Cedric."

"Think nothing of it," he said, with a wave of his hand. Hope let the silence stretch. "I was wondering if you'd like to sign up again," he continued, with that easy confidence. "Same terms, better pay. There will be more events like this, we're sure. We don't know quite where yet, but we've a weather eye on a few likely hotspots. Colombia, maybe. Southern Chinese seaboard. West Africa. Wherever it is, we'll be there."

Hope thought of Niceday, stood in the opulence of his suite; such similar creatures. "Don't you worry, Cedric, that you're one of the causal forces you're trying to explain? That your own wealth distorts the markets like gravity distorts space-time? That the disruptors are following you, rather than the other way around?"

Ian laughed again. "She got ye there, boss."

"Thank you, Ian," said Cedric, mildly. "Yes, Hope, I do worry about that. But I have concluded that the greater sin is to do nothing. As you know, no one can or will fund this sort of research at this sort of scale, especially out in the hinterlands. General Weissmuutze has been passing our reports directly to the UN, at no cost. She tells me they're very grateful."

"I guess they should be," Hope allowed. "As should I."

"Think nothing of it," he said again, leaning forward and resting his elbows on his knees. "Come with us, Hope. Don't you want to be part of the next story?"

"No, Cedric," she replied. "Don't you get it? This story isn't finished. Only the bits of it that interest you and Niceday's people have finished. And the next story will have started long before you get wherever it is you decide to go. You can close the book and start another one, if you like; that is your privilege." She sighed. "But the world carries on, even when there's no one there to narrate it."

"So what will you do?"

"Stop running. You've set me free from my past, Cedric, and I'm grateful. But you can't give me a future. Only I can do that." She pointed at the solarpunks down on the sand. "That's what they're trying to do, and the others. And maybe I can't build things or ship code or hustle funding, but I can tell stories. Stories where those other things don't matter so much, maybe.

"When you look at this place, you see a story ending. I see one just beginning. And sure, perhaps it'll be over in weeks, maybe it'll end in failure. But we won't know unless we try writing it."

"It takes a special kind of person," said Ian, quietly, "a special eye, to make the ruins bloom." He sat up straight in his saddle. "C'mon, boss. You got way more than yer pound o' flesh from this one. Leave her be now, eh?"

"You're right, of course," said Cedric, standing. "If you ever change your mind . . ."

". . . you'll find me, I know."

Without another word, Cedric settled himself onto the trike's bench-seat. Ian raised her sunglasses, tipped her one last wink, and whirred away down the promenade to the east, where the last clouds of the morning were burning away to wispy nothings.

Hope smiled to herself, and blinked her novel back up on her spex. Down on the beach, a ragged cheer arose from the crowd around the glassmaker.

Red Lights, and Rain

GARETH L. POWELL

Gareth L. Powell is an award-winning science fiction and fantasy author from Bristol. His third novel, Ack-Ack Macaque, *tied with Ann Leckie's* Ancillary Justice *to co-win the 2013 BSFA Award for Best Novel. His books have been published in the UK, Germany, the USA, and Japan, and have all received enthusiastic reviews in the* Guardian. *His short fiction has appeared in numerous publications, including six short stories in* Interzone *magazine. In 2007, one of his stories came out on top of the* Interzone *annual readers' poll for best short story of the year. He has also cowritten a novelette with Aliette de Bodard and given guest lectures on creative writing at Bath Spa University. He has written articles for the* Irish Times, SFX, SF Signal, Mass Movement Magazine, *and* Acoustic Magazine, *and, in 2012, he achieved a boyhood ambition when he was given the chance to pen a strip for Britain's long-running sci fi and fantasy comic,* 2000 AD. *He can be found online at www.garethlpowell.com.*

Here he gives us a vigorous, gritty, and action-packed look at a bloody battle being fought throughout present-day Amsterdam by time-travelling superpowered genetically enhanced agents, each almost impossible to kill, and each nevertheless determined to kill the other.

It's raining in Amsterdam. Paige stands in the oak-panelled front bar of a small corner pub. She has wet hair because she walked here from her hotel. Now she's standing by the open door, holding half a litre of Amstel, watching the rain stipple the surface of the canal across the street. For the fourth time in five minutes, she takes out her mobile and checks the screen for messages. From across the room, the barman looks at her. He has dark skin and gold dreads. Seeing the phone in her hand again, he smiles, obviously convinced she's waiting for a date.

Outside, damp tourists pass in the rain, looking for the Anne Frank house; open-topped pleasure boats seek shelter beneath humped-back bridges; and bare-headed boys cut past on scooters, cigarettes flaring, girlfriends clinging side-saddle to the parcel shelves, tyres going *bop-bop-bop* on the wet cobble stones. Paige sucks the froth from her beer. On the other side of the canal, a church bell clangs nine o'clock. As it happens, she *is* waiting for a man, but this won't be any sort of date, and she'll be lucky if she survives to see the sun come up tomorrow morning. She pockets the mobile, changes the beer glass from one hand to the other, and slips her fingers into the pocket of her coat, allowing them to brush the cold metal butt of the pistol. It's a lightweight coil gun: a magnetic projectile accelerator, fifty years more advanced than anything else in this time zone, and capable of punching a titanium slug through a concrete wall. With luck, it will be enough.

She watches the barman lay out new beer mats on the zinc counter. He's just a boy, really. Paige should probably warn him to leave, but she doesn't want to attract too much attention, not just yet. She doesn't want the police to blunder in and complicate matters.

For a moment, her eyes are off the door, and that's when Josef arrives, heralded by the swish of his coat, the clack of his boots as they hit the step. She sees the barman's gaze flick past her shoulder, his eyes widen, and she turns to find Josef standing on the threshold, close enough to kiss.

"Hello, Paige." He's at least five inches taller than her; rake thin with pale lips and rain-slicked hair.

"Josef." She slides her right hand into her coat, sees him notice the movement.

"Are you here to kill me, Paige?"

"Yes."

"It's not going to be easy."

"I know."

He flicks his eyes in the direction of the bar, licks his bottom lip. "What about him?"

Paige takes a step back, placing herself between the "vampire" and the boy with the golden dreadlocks. She curls the index finger of the hand still in her pocket around the trigger of the coil gun.

"Not tonight, Josef."

Josef shrugs and folds his arms, shifts his weight petulantly from one foot to the other.

"So, what?" he says. "You want to go at it right now, in here?"

Paige shakes her head. She's trying not to show emotion, but her heart's hammering and she's sure he can hear it.

"Outside," she says. Josef narrows his eyes. He looks her up and down, assessing her as an opponent. Despite his attenuated frame, she knows he can strike like a whip when he wants to. She tenses, ready for his attack and, for a moment, they're frozen like that: eyes locked, waiting for the other to make the first move. Then Josef laughs. He turns on his heel, flicks up the collar of his coat, and steps out into the rain.

Paige lets out a long breath. Her stomach's churning. She pulls the coil gun from her pocket and looks over at the barman.

"Stay here," she says.

She follows Josef into a small concrete yard at the rear of the pub, surrounded by walls on all sides, and lit from above by the orange reflection of city lights on low cloud. Rusty dumpsters stand against one wall; a fire escape ladder hangs from the back of the pub; and metal trapdoors cover the cellar. Two storeys above, the gutters leak, spattering the concrete.

Josef says, "So, how do you want to do this?"

Paige lets the peeling wooden door to the street bang shut behind her, hiding them from passers-by. The coil gun feels heavy in her hand.

"Get over by the wall," she says.

Josef shakes his head.

She opens her mouth to insist but, before she can speak or raise the gun, he's closed the distance between them, his weight slamming her back against the wooden door. She feels his breath on her cheek, his hand clasping her throat. She tries to bring the gun to bear but he chops it away, sending the weapon clattering across the wet floor.

"You're pathetic," he growls, and lifts her by the throat. Her feet paw at empty air. She tries to prise his hand loose, but his fingers are like talons, and she can't breathe; she's choking. In desperation, she kicks his kneecap, making him stagger. With a snarl, he tosses her against one of the large wheeled dumpsters. She hits it with an echoing crash, and ends up on her hands and knees, coughing, struggling for air. Josef's boot catches her in the ribs, and rolls her onto her side. He stamps down once, twice, and something snaps in her left forearm. The pain fills her. She yelps, and curls herself around it. The coil gun rests on the concrete three or four metres away on the other side of the yard, and there's no way he'll let her reach it. He kicks her twice more, then leans down with his mouth open, letting her see his glistening ceramic incisors. They're fully extended now, locked in attack position, and ready to tear out her windpipe.

"Ha' enough?" he says, the fangs distorting his speech.

Paige coughs again. She's cradling her broken arm, and she still can't breathe properly. She's about to tell him to go to hell, when the back door of the pub swings open, and out steps the boy with the golden dreads, a sawn-off antique shotgun held at his hip.

"That's enough," the boy says. His eyes are wide and scared.

Josef looks up with a hiss, teeth bared. Startled, the barman pulls the trigger. The flash and bang fill the yard. Josef takes both barrels in the chest. It snatches him away like laundry in the wind, and he lands by the door to the street, flapping and yelling, drumming his boot heels on the concrete.

"Shoot him again," Paige gasps, but the young man stands frozen in place, transfixed by the thrashing vampire. He hasn't even reloaded. Paige uses her good arm to claw her way into a sitting position. The rain's soaked through her clothes.

"Shoot him!"

But it's too late. Still hollering, Josef claws his way through the wooden door, out onto the street. Paige pulls herself up and makes it to the pavement just in time to see him slip over the edge of the bank, into the canal, dropping noiselessly into the water between two tethered barges. She turns back to find the boy with the shotgun looking at her.

"Is he dead?"

She shakes her head. The air's tangy with gun smoke. "No, he'll be back." She scoops up her fallen coil gun and slides it back into her coat pocket. Her left arm's clutched against her chest. Every time she moves, she has to bite her lip against the pain.

The boy takes her by the shoulder, and she can feel his hands shake as he guides her into the pub kitchen, where she leans against the wall as he locks and bolts the back door.

When she asks, the boy tells her his name is Federico. He settles her on a bar stool, plonks a shot glass and a half-empty bottle of cognac on the counter, then goes to close the front door.

"I'm going to call the police," he says.

As he brushes past her, Paige catches his arm."There's no time, we have to leave."

He looks down at her hand.

"I don't *have* to do anything," he says. "Not until you explain what the hell just happened."

She releases him. He's frightened, but the fear's manifesting as anger, and she's going to have to do something drastic to convince him.

"Okay." She puts her left arm on the bar, and rolls up the sleeve, letting him see the bloody contusions from Josef's boot, and the splinter of bone,like a shard of broken china, sticking up through the skin.

"What are you doing?"

"Shush." She takes hold of her wrist, forces the arm flat against the zinc counter, and twists. There's an audible click, and the two halves of broken bone snap back into place. When her eyes have stopped watering, she plucks out the loose shard and drops it with a clink into the ash tray. With it out of the way, the skin around the tear starts to heal. In less than a minute, only a red mark remains.

Ferderico takes a step back, eyes wide, hand pointing.

"That's not natural."

Paige lifts the half-empty bottle of cognac with her right hand, pulls the plastic-coated cork with her teeth, and spits it across the bar.

"Josef heals even faster than I do," she says. "You blew a hole in his chest, but he'll be as good as new in an hour, maybe less."

"W-what are you?"

Paige takes a solid nip of the brandy.

"I'm as human as you are," she says, and gets to her feet. The stiffness is fading from her limbs, the hurt evaporating from her ribs and arm."But Josef's something quite different. And trust me, you *really* don't want to be here when he comes back."

"But the police—"

"Forget the police. You shot him, that makes it personal."

Federico puts his fists on his hips.

"I don't believe you."

Paige jerks a thumb at the back door. "Then believe what you saw out there." She stands and pats down her coat, making sure she still has everything she needs. Federico looks from her to the door, and then back again.

"Is he really that dangerous?"

"Oh yes."

"Then, what do you suggest?"

Paige rubs her face. She doesn't want to be saddled with a civilian, doesn't want to be responsible for anybody else's well being; but this young man saved her life, and she owes him for that.

She sighs."Your best bet's to come with me, right now. I'm the only one who knows what we're up against, the only one with even half a chance of being able to protect you."

"How do I know I can trust you?"

She looks him square in the eye.

"Because I'm not the one who's going to come back here and rip your throat out."

Paige lets Federico pull on a battered leather biker jacket two sizes too large, and they leave the pub and splash their way down the cobbled streets in the direction of the Red Light District, and her hotel. As they walk, she keeps her eye on the canal.

Federico says, "Is he really a, you know?"

"A vampire?" Paige shakes her head. "No. At least, not in the sense you're thinking. There's nothing supernatural or romantic about him. He's not afraid of crosses or garlic, or any of that bullshit."

"But I saw his teeth."

"Ceramic implants."

They cut across a square in the shadow of a medieval church. Federico has the shotgun under his jacket, and it makes him walk stiffly. The rain's still falling, and there's music from the bars and coffeehouses; but few people are out on the street.

"Then what is he? Some sort of psycho?"

Paige slows for a second, and turns to him. "She's a guerrilla."

"I don't understand."

She starts walking again. "I don't expect you to." Her right hand's in her coat pocket, gripping the coil gun. She leads him out of the square, across a footbridge, and then they're into the Red Light District, with its pink neon shop fronts and narrow alleys. Her hotel's close to Centraal Station. By the time they get there, they're both soaked and stand dripping together in the elevator that takes them up to her floor.

"In a thousand years' time, there's going to be a war," she says, watching the floor numbers count off. "And it's going to be a particularly nasty one, with atrocities on all sides."

The lift doors open and she leads him along the carpeted corridor to her room. Inside, the air smells stale. This has been her base of operations for nearly a month, and she hasn't let the cleaner touch it in all that time. She hasn't even opened the curtains.

"The vampires were bred to fight in the war," she says. "They were designed to operate behind enemy lines, terrorising civilians, sowing fear and confusion." She shrugs off her coat and drops it over the back of a chair."They're trained to go to ground, blend in as best they can, then start killing people. They're strong and fast, and optimised for night combat."

Federico's standing in the doorway, shivering. She ushers him in and sits him on the bed. Gingerly, she takes the shotgun from his hands, and places it on the sheet beside him; she then drapes a blanket around his shoulders.

"After the war, some of them escaped, and they've been spreading backwards through time ever since." She crosses to the wardrobe, and pulls out a bottle. It's a litre of vodka. She takes two teacups off the side and pours a large measure for him, a smaller one for herself."They're designed to survive for long durations without support. They can eat just about anything organic, and they're hard to kill. You can hurt them, but as long as their hearts are beating and their brains are intact, there's a chance they'll be able to repair themselves, given enough time."

She puts the bottle aside and flexes the fingers of her left hand—there's still an ache, deep in the bone.

"That's important," she says. She kneels down in front of Federico, and takes his hands in hers. "The next time we see Josef, we've got to kill him before he kills us. And the only way to do that is to do as much damage as possible. Stop his heart, destroy his brain, and he's dead."

She takes one of the teacups and presses it into Federico's hands.

"Sorry," He says, accepting the drink, "did you say that this war is *going* to take place?"

"A thousand years downstream, yes."

"So it hasn't happened yet?"

"No."

He frowns.

"Who are you?"

Paige reaches for her coat, and pulls out the coil gun. "I'm a fangbanger, a vampire killer."

"And you're from the future too?"

Paige stands.

"Look," she says. "All you need to know tonight is this: When you see Josef, shoot out his legs. That'll immobilise him, and give us time to kill him." She stops talking then. Federico's clearly had enough for one night. She slips a pill into his next drink and, within minutes, he's asleep, wrapped in the blanket, with the shotgun clasped protectively across his chest.

Alone with her thoughts, Paige moves quietly. She turns out the bedside light and crosses to the window, pulling aside the heavy curtain. It's after twelve now, and the trams have stopped for the night. The streets are quiet. She feels she should congratulate Josef on his choice of hiding place. Amsterdam is an easy city in which to be a stranger; there are so many tourists, so many distractions, that it's a simple matter to lose yourself in the crowd. If she hadn't known what to look for she might never have found him. But then, she's been a fangbanger for a long time, and she's learned to piece together seemingly unrelated deaths and unexplained crimes; to filter out the background noise of modern urban life in order to reveal the unmistakable M.O. of an active vampire. She leans her forehead against the window glass; heart pumping in her chest, knowing it won't take Josef long to track her down. She's been doing this job for enough years, waded through enough shit, to know how dangerous a wounded vampire can be.

At 4am, the sky starts to grey in the east. Federico's still asleep, and Paige gives up her vigil. She tucks the coil gun into the back of her belt, pulls on a sweater to cover it, and wanders down to the hotel restaurant. She finds the place empty, although cooking sounds reach her from the kitchen as the staff gear up for the breakfast rush. She helps herself to a cup of coffee from the pot, and a large handful of sugar sachets, and takes it all over to a table by the window, where she stirs the contents of the little packets into her coffee. There are sixteen altogether, and she uses them all. Then, leaving the sticky mess to cool, she rests her left arm on the table and clenches and unclenches her fist. Everything seems in order. The tendons move as they should, and there's no trace of the break. It doesn't even ache now. Satisfied, she takes a sip of the lip-curlingly sweet coffee. It tastes disgusting, but she needs the sugar to refuel the tweaked macrophages and artificial fibroblasts that have enabled her to heal so quickly.

Outside the window, it's still raining. She watches the drops slither on the glass. It makes her think of Josef in better times, before he had his fangs implanted. She remembers him as bright and swift and clever; a sociopath, yes, but still her best student. And there it is, her dirty little secret, the inconvenient truth she's been hiding from Federico: the reason she makes such a good vampire hunter is that during the war, before the vampires were deployed against the enemy, it was she who trained them. She was a military psychologist at the time, an expert in guerrilla warfare. While combat instructors taught the vampires how to kill, she showed them a range of nasty tricks culled from a thousand hard-fought insurgencies; from the Scythians of Central Asia to the soldiers of the Viet Kong, and beyond.

She remembers her penultimate briefing in particular.

"The vampire's a powerful archetype," she said to the cadets. "It's an expression of our darker side, playing to our most primal anxieties, from the threat of rape to the fear of being eaten." It was a hot day, and the sun had blazed through the classroom windows. She walked up and down in front of her students, hands clasped behind her back. At the rear of the room, the surgeons waited with their trolleys, ready to wheel the young men and women down to the operating theatre, one-by-one, in order to implant their fangs and night-adapted eyes. "To complete your mission, you must be prepared to kill. You must become assassins—anonymous killers in the night, spreading panic and mistrust." She stopped pacing and turned to Josef. He sat in the front row of the classroom, chin on fist, eyes blazing, and she knew it would be the last time she'd see him before his transformation." If you do your jobs correctly," she said, "each of you will be worth a hundred troops. You'll demoralise the enemy, eat out his fighting spirit from the inside. You'll have the soldiers worried about their families, the families suspicious of their neighbours. But in order to achieve this, you'll have to move like shadows, and show no mercy. Do anything that needs to be done, be ruthless, and be prepared to strike anywhere, at any time."

She had taught them every psychological trick she knew, and shown them how to exploit the power of myth, how to generate fear and horror from darkness and blood. From their test scores, she'd known they were intelligent. In fact, she'd personally overseen the original selection process, picking only those recruits with the right balance of brains and insanity—those clever enough to survive the mission, but also psychotic enough to become the monsters they'd need to be in order to succeed.

And then later, when the war went temporal, spilling into the surrounding decades, they came back and she briefed them again, only this time on the peculiarities of each of the time zones in which they were to operate, giving them the background they'd need in order to blend into each zone's civilian population.

Sometimes, she wonders if her history lessons inspired their eventual escape into this dim and distant past, far from even the outermost fringes of the conflict. One thing's for certain: since they mutinied and fled to these primitive times, she's had to travel all over the place to hunt them down. She's tracked individual vampires across half a dozen decades, in Los Angeles, Cairo, Warsaw, and London.

Now she's here, in Amsterdam.

And suddenly, there's Josef.

He's standing in the shadow of a doorway on the other side of the street, watching her through the glass. He has his hands in the pockets of his black raincoat. Their eyes meet for a second and Paige can't breathe. Then he's gone, moving fast. Between parked cars, she catches a glimpse of him crossing the street, heading for the back of the hotel. With a curse, she pushes herself to her feet. Josef will know which room she's staying in—a simple phone call will have furnished him with that information—and now he's after Federico, hoping to kill the boy before tackling her.

Paige bursts out into the foyer. Her room's on the fourth floor, so there's no time to take the stairs. However, luck's on her side; this early in the morning the elevators all stand ready, their doors open. She slams into the nearest and slaps the button for the fourth floor. Then, even as the doors are closing, she's pulling the coil gun from her belt and checking its magazine.

Paige kicks her shoes off in the elevator and pads along the corridor in her socks. As she nears her room, she hears the door splinter: Josef's kicked his way in.

"Damn."

She lifts the coil gun to her shoulder and risks a peek around the frame. The room's dark. She can see a faint glow from the curtains. There are shadows all over the place: chairs, desks, and suitcases. Any one of them could be a crouched vampire.

"Fuck."

She ducks back into the corridor and takes a few quick breaths. If Josef's still in there, he'll have heard her already—and there's a good possibility Federico's already dead. She flicks off the coil gun's safety catch. There's nothing beyond this room but window; the chances of civilian casualties are slight. Stepping back, she gives the trigger a squeeze. The gun whines. Holes appear in the door. Splinters flick out. The TV sparks. A chair blows apart.

And there, in the maelstrom: a shadow moves.

She tries to hose him down but he's moving too fast. He hits the wall and pushes off; hits the floor and rolls; and then he's running on all fours, leaping at her throat before she can draw a bead.

Paige rolls with the impact, still pressing the trigger. Scraps of material fly from Josef's overcoat. An overhead light explodes. Blood sprays. His ceramic teeth scrape her neck, grazing the skin. Then his momentum carries him over her head, and she uses a Judo throw to heave him into the corridor wall. He hits like an upside down starfish, arms and legs splayed, and then falls to the floor.

They both lie panting.

The carpet's soft. She rolls onto her side. Josef's lying on his front, looking sideways at her. His eyes are as blue as a gas flame. This is the first good look she's had at him since he left her class, and he looks older and harder than she remembers. His fangs are white and clean. Blood soaks into the carpet from a hole in his side.

He doesn't move as she elbows herself up into a sitting position; but, as soon as she lifts the coil gun, he twists. His wrist flicks out, and a pair of shiny throwing stars bite Paige's arm. She cries out and the gun drops from her fingers. Instinctively, she reaches for it with her left hand, but Josef's anticipated the move. He pushes himself towards her, delivering a kick to her cheek that shatters the bone.

Paige falls into the open doorway of her room. Black spots dapple her vision. She feels Josef grip her leg. His hands work their way up. He's climbing her, using his weight to keep her pinned down. She tries to fight back, but she's still dazed. He swats her hands away from his face.

Then he's on her, his thighs clamped across her hips, his knees pinning her arms. He wraps his fingers in her hair, and yanks her head back, exposing her throat. His fangs are fully deployed. She sees them through the hair hanging down over his face, and cringes, expecting him to lunge for her artery.

Instead, Josef clears his throat

"I don't want to kill you," he says around his teeth. He pulls away, and his incisors slip back into their sheaths. He lets go of her hair and sits up, straddling her. Paige blinks up at him as he smooths back his wet hair. "I just want to talk."

They end up slumped against opposite walls of the corridor. Josef's bleeding onto the carpet; Paige feels as if she's been hit by a fire truck. One side of her face throbs with pain, and the eye above her broken cheekbone won't focus properly.

"You've got me all wrong," Josef says.

She gives him a look.

"You're a killer."

"Not anymore." He lets his shoulders relax, but keeps one hand pressed to the bullet hole in his side.

"But Federico—"

"I haven't touched him."

"He's still alive?"

Josef shrugs. "I can't say for sure. You sprayed a lot of bullets in there."

And suddenly, they're falling back into their old pattern: teacher and student— and she *knows* there's something he's not telling her.

"What's going on, Josef? Why am I still alive?"

He tips his head back, resting it against the wall.

"Because things are different now. *I'm* different." He reaches into his coat and pulls out a photograph, which he Frisbees across to her.

"I wasn't trying to hurt you, you know? Not here, and not at the pub." He dips his chin and looks at her. "Just acting in self-defence, trying to stop you from killing me."

The picture shows Josef holding a child, maybe four or five years old.

"What's this?"

"It's my daughter."

The girl has Josef's blue eyes and blonde hair. She's wearing a red dress.

"Your daughter?"

Josef closes his eyes.

"Yes."

Paige glances at the coil gun, lying on the carpet between them. She wonders if she can reach it before he can reach her.

Josef says, "I don't want any more trouble."

Paige lifts a hand to her ruined cheek, and her lip curls.

"So what? You think it *matters* what you want? So you've gone and got yourself a family, and you think that wipes away all the shit you've done, all the people you've killed?"

She reaches for the gun. Josef howls in frustration, and lunges for her throat. His teeth rip into her oesophagus, and she feels his jaw snap shut on her windpipe. His hair fills her face, and he's heavy on her chest. She can't breathe, and wonders how many others have died like this. How many others, because of her, and what she taught him?

Josef pulls back, his face dripping with her blood and, as Paige gasps for breath, the wound bubbles.

Josef snatches the photograph from her unresisting fingers. She tries to move her arms, but can't. Josef's speaking, but the fangs make it difficult and she can't hear him over the roaring in her ears. Her eyes swivel around in panic, looking for help. The guests in the other rooms must be awake now, and cowering behind their peepholes. Some at least will have called the police.

Then, as she twists her head, she catches movement in the room behind her. Federico stumbles into the light. The boy looks dazed and frightened; there are scratch marks on his face, but he has the shotgun in his hands.

There's a flash, and Josef jerks. Part of his face disappears, bitten off by the blast. Another flash, and he topples from Paige like a puppet with its strings cut, knocking his head against the doorframe as he falls.

Paige slaps a palm over the sucking wound in her neck, pinching the skin together, hoping she can heal before she suffocates.

Federico bends over her. Wordless, she points to the coil gun, and he kicks it over.

"Help me up," she croaks. As long as she keeps her hand covering the injury, her vocal chords still work.

With Federico's hands under her shoulders, she struggles to her feet and coughs up a wad of blood. She feels unsteady, but each breath is easier than the last.

Josef lies in a spreading patch of red-soaked carpet. One of his eyes is completely gone; that side of his face is a gory ruin; but the other seems miraculously untouched, and still beautiful. His hands twitch on the carpet like angry spiders.

Paige plucks the slippery, homemade throwing stars from her forearm, and tosses them aside. She points the coil gun at Josef's heart. Dimly, she can hear sirens pulling up on the street outside.

Josef's remaining eyelid flutters. She knows he's down, but he's obviously not out.

She says, "How many people have you killed, Josef?" Then, without waiting for an answer, she pulls the trigger. The gun whines and his chest blows apart. His heels scrape at the floor, as if trying to escape, and she raises the gun to his face.

"I'm sorry," she says.

She looks away as she fires, and she keeps the trigger depressed until the magazine clicks empty.

When she looks back, Josef's head's gone, and there's a hole in the floor.

The photograph of his daughter falls from his fingers.

He's dead.

She sticks the spent gun back in her belt. For some reason, her smashed cheek hurts more than her torn throat. She looks around to find Federico leaning on the doorframe.

Paige hawks red phlegm onto the carpet. Then she leans down and takes hold of Josef's boot. Gritting her teeth, she drags his body back into her ruined hotel room. Moving slowly and painfully, she retrieves the vodka bottle from the dressing table, spins the lid off, and raises the bottle in a toast to her fallen student. She stands over him for a long moment. Then she takes a deep swallow, which makes her cough.

"Goodbye, Josef," she says. There's nothing else to say. There's no triumph here, no closure, nothing but bone-deep weariness. Solemnly, she pours the remaining contents of the bottle—most of a litre of spirit—over his chest and legs; then she pulls a complimentary matchbook from the desk, and strikes one.

The wet clothes go up in a woof of blue flame. The fire spills onto the carpet, and the room fills with smoke.

Paige opens the desk drawer and takes out another clip of ammo for the coil gun. Then she limps back to Federico.

"I have to go," she says. She has to move on to the next target, the next time zone.

A fire alarm rings, and the sprinklers go off. The shotgun's on the floor at Federico's feet. He's holding the photograph of Josef's daughter. Water's running down his face, streaking his cheeks. His dreads are soaked.

"You're a fucking monster," he says.

Paige puts a hand to the torn flesh of her throat. She can feel the sides stitching themselves back together.

"I know," she says.

And with that, she fades away.

coma kings

JESSICA BARBER

Those of you who complain that your kids are addicted to computer games might want to take a look at the compelling family drama that follows, which warns us that you ain't seen nothing *yet.*

New writer Jessica Barber grew up in Tennessee, but moved to New England to attend MIT, where she studied physics and electrical engineering. After a brief stint building rocket ships in southern California, she returned to Cambridge, where she now spends her days developing open-source electronics, with a focus on tools for neuroscience. Her work has previously appeared in Strange Horizons *and* Lightspeed.

So I guess the story begins, fittingly, with someone handing me a Coma rig and saying, *play me.*

Two a.m. and I'm at this party in somebody's trailer out in the trashy part of town. I'm stoned out of my mind and there's something on the television, either one of those cheesy infomercials or some sort of comedy thing making fun of those cheesy infomercials, and I'm trying to figure out which. I keep turning to the kid sprawled out beside me and saying, "Is this for real? Or is this like, a joke?" and he keeps blinking at me and going, "What? I don't . . ." and then trailing off. And so I'm deep into this important cultural assessment when somebody shoves a Coma rig into my hands.

"Fuck off," I say, even though my fingers automatically curl into the wires. "I'm stoned, I don't wanna play."

"Come on," says the guy who handed me the rig. "You're Jenny, right? I hear you're really good," he says. True. "I hear you're like, the best in the state, easy." Not true, because of Annie, but I guess he's not counting her. "I've wanted to play you like, forever."

Either I'm really susceptible to flattery when stoned, or I actually just want to be playing Coma all the time, twenty-four/seven, no matter what, but either way I say fine and start to pull on the rig.

In each of my temples there are three distinct depressions, dents where the electrodes of my own rig have sat for hours on end. When I play Coma using my own gear, pulling on the headpiece feels like slotting a puzzle piece into place, but this kid's rig is too big for me, not broken in. I try my best to align the electrodes properly, but in the end I just can't get it to sit right, so I say fuck it and let it go all crooked. If you've played Coma you know this is a dumb idea, because it means the calibration will be all off and it will make you play like a spaz, but this is a throwaway game and I figure, who cares. I slide the opaque goggles over my eyes, fumble for the headphones and settle their huge soft cups over my ears, and the world disappears.

This is the point where usually I'd access my own personal Coma account, but like I said, I'm stoned, the rig doesn't fit, and I don't want some stupid throwaway game to drop me in the rankings. So I log in as a guest on the kid's account instead.

Which is what fucks me over so badly, in the end.

When Coma first came out, it was this gimmicky thing, a rich kid's game, nothing I cared about or could have afforded if I did. I played for the first time at a mall. One of those demo booths set up spanning the food court, and the only thing I noticed about it then was that it was blocking my way to Sbarro's. I hadn't been interested, but Annie thought it looked like the coolest thing ever, and she begged me to let her play.

Forget it, I'd said, it looks stupid, I'm hungry, but she whined until I told her fine, get in line. Tough luck for her, though, you had to be thirteen and at the time she was only eleven. I played just to spite her, since I was fourteen and made the age cutoff.

I love how you can do these things that fuck you over forever, that change your goddamn life, and not even care at the time, not even know.

I won that first game at the mall easily, even though I had no clue what I was doing. Then I won the next game, and the game after that too, and by the end of the day I had more wins than anybody else and guess what that meant? Two free Coma rigs for the trouble.

I planned on selling them. They were going for five hundred bucks apiece, I mean, shit. But when we got home Annie goaded me into playing against her. Well, she won, of course, you know that much, and then I could hardly sell them off, could I? Not until I beat her.

I suppose you can guess how long it took for that to happen.

I should probably tell you how that game at the party went, but I never know how to explain Coma when I'm out of the rig. It's not like chess or something, it never makes sense when your brain is in the real world. If you really care, the game is on record, like every other game of Coma ever played.

It's not worth watching; the kid is fucking terrible. We turn on our rigs and there's nothing. I start building a box. Then there's nothing but the inside of my box. One corner starts to crumble a little, and that's the kid trying real hard, but then I just make it not crumble and that's the end of that. I place a single white stone in the center of the box, and the game is over.

All of this is hardly worth telling you, except for what happens next. I feel the kid log out in a huff, and I'm about to do the same. But then there's a ping up in the left corner of my consciousness, letting me know that Annie is requesting a game, and it's a good thing I'm sitting down back in the real world because otherwise I would have fallen right over.

Here's the thing. I have been trying to get Annie to play me again literally for years. I have sent game requests, again and again, and have gotten rejected each time. She absolutely will not play me. And now she's been tricked, she doesn't know it's me, I finally get to play her, and here I am: wasted out of my mind with a Coma rig that doesn't even fit.

If I were slightly less stoned, I might have started crying. As it is, I can't even try to play, can't even make the vaguest real effort because I know I'll just get slaughtered, immediately, without mercy. Instead I start building useless structures, crumbling shapes that spell out *Annie, it's me, come back, I miss you.*

The shock buys me about two solid minutes before Annie annihilates me and I am kicked out of the game. I can't even bring myself to try and send her messages, try to request another chance. I just pull myself back into the real world, gut hurt and gasping for air.

I get home several hours before dawn, but my mother is up, sitting at the kitchen table and turning an unlit cigarette in her fingers, staring at the vinyl tabletop. The long walk home has cleared my head a bit, but I still feel shell-shocked, like there's something sharp worming its way through the spaces between my organs. Like I'm going to burst apart at any moment.

My mother doesn't look at me. "Where you been?"

"Went to a party," I say. "Told you I was gonna go." She makes a rough noise, deep in her throat, and I keep talking before she can say whatever it is she's sitting on. "How's Annie? You checked in on her?"

"She's the same as ever, what do you think?" Ma says, which I take to mean no.

I try not to grit my teeth. "You still gotta check on her," I mutter, move to squeeze past her but her hand darts out, catching me around the forearm.

"Don't you tell me how I gotta care for my own child," she snaps. Her cheap fake nails have half broken off, and their edges bite deep crescents into the underside of my wrist. We glare at each other until she releases me.

I bite down hard on the sides of my tongue and shove my way into the room I share with Annie.

Annie lies on her bed, just like she always does, a vanishing outline of a human body under a nubbly blanket, her head obscured by goggles, oversized headphones. She is surrounded by a small forest of medical equipment: stands for IV drips and catheter bags and heart rate monitors with their slow steady pulse of life.

The port at the base of her skull is hidden among pillows, under wide bandages. No electrodes. She doesn't need those anymore.

Once I would have been overwhelmed by the urge to rip away every bit of equipment that surrounds her. Fuck, I'll admit it: More than once I have given into this urge, but by now I know it doesn't make any difference. She still lies there, just as unresponsive but now stripped bare, the heart rate monitor sending up a wailing protest in her absence.

So I don't touch her. I just slide to the floor, scrape my thighs and palms across the synthetic roughness of the carpet and glare. "Goddammit, Annie," I tell her.

There is a sound from the doorway and I fling myself around to face my mother, cheeks burning. She isn't looking at me, though. Her eyes are trained on Annie.

"I can't keep this up forever, you know," she says. "It ain't cheap. They don't give me enough to look after her right. Sooner or later, we're gonna have to let her go."

She has been threatening this for years.

I don't respond, just turn around and fit my molars together, like a small child, like if I pretend she isn't there maybe she'll disappear.

It doesn't work. It never does.

"Jennifer, I really need to see you applying yourself," says Miss Denton. "You've already missed two tests this quarter, and I haven't gotten any homework at all from you yet."

I used to like school. I mean, maybe "like" is a strong word. But it was all right. These days, when I manage to go, it feels like trying to pull my limbs through molasses, impossibly difficult and never-ending. This is a compounding problem. It's hard enough getting my ass to school by seven-thirty in the morning on a good day. Getting my ass to school when I'm just going to get yelled at for the last time I failed to get my ass to school is just adding indignity to injustice.

"I know," I say. "I'm going to make them up, honest. I've just been . . ." I don't know what to say, here. Tired, is what almost comes out of my mouth. But that's not the sort of excuse you can use.

I can tell by the way Miss Denton's expression folds in on itself that she is supplying her own narrative. Poor Jennifer, with her crazy sister. Miss Denton wears tiny frameless glasses perched on the end of her nose, and she takes them off to polish them, stalling for time. "I know it's been a hard year for you," she begins.

Christ, I'm tired of this speech. I know it's rude, but I let my body hunch forward, rest my forehead against the laminate desktop. It's cool, and slightly sticky. I don't even have the energy to be disgusted.

Miss Denton perseveres. "I know it's been a hard year for you. But your junior year is just starting, and your grades right now are so important for college. You do still want to go to college, don't you?"

"Yes," I say, because I am supposed to. I wonder if it's true. Standard small town dream: Make it out, make it somewhere far away.

I wonder if they'd let me keep Annie in my dorm room.

I don't make it to second period. I get to the door, then think of sitting at a desk for a solid hour and a half, the real world feeling cramped and finite, and just can't. I find myself pushing through a side door out into the parking lot, twisting my way through rows of cars baking in the early sun. I can *feel* my rig tucked safe in my trunk, like a fucking siren song, and before I can think, I'm angling my steering wheel toward the city.

People go to Coma parlors for one of two reasons.

The first reason—why I go—is just to have a safe, quiet space to play Coma uninterrupted. The full-immersion aspect means it's different than how gaming used to be. You can't yell at your mom to get out of your room, or shove the cat away if it walks across the keyboard. Or worse, if something catches fire, or you've got a crazed family member screaming obscenities and threatening to kill you. If you're planning to really settle in for a long game, better to be someplace supervised, someplace safe.

The second reason people go to Coma parlors is to hack their rigs. For some people, tweaking the electronics is just as much of a draw as actually playing the game. They think adding extra electrodes, overclocking the microprocessor, whatever-the-fuck else will give them an edge, help them achieve some sort of in-game nirvana. I think this is mostly bullshit; I use two-year-old stock parts and the occasional firmware upgrade, and I play better than most of the gearheads. Plus, we all know what it actually takes to get to that place of inseparability from the game.

There just aren't very many people willing to go that far.

Lady K's place looks like somebody's garage workshop. Bare cinderblock walls, concrete floor. There's a smattering of institutional couches around the outer edge, about half taken up by prone bodies, but the majority of its real estate is occupied by long, cobbled-together workbenches, ringed by kids bent industriously over the exploded innards of their Coma rigs. Soldering irons send fine wisps of smoke upward; someone's running a Dremel carefully along the rim of their goggles.

The eponymous Lady K, a short, apple-cheeked chick who can't be much older than me, is peering into a microscope when I come in, but she looks up at the door chime and gives me a little grin. I'm not in here often enough to be considered a regular, but Lady K knows me regardless. I'm higher ranked than anybody else who plays here, which probably helps my notoriety.

That, and Annie.

Always fucking Annie.

"Hey Jenny," says Lady K. "You working on something today? Or just playing?"

"Just playing, for now," I say. "Can I crash out on that couch?"

"Go for it," says Lady K, and minutes later I am deep in Coma.

It's good, I have a good morning. I play a guy I haven't played before, some up-and-coming star from South Korea. We play off each other well, building up a huge structure, an entire city of improbable shapes. It takes a two-and-a-half-hour battle for me to bring the entire thing down around his ears.

When I come out from under I'm in a way better mood than I've been ever since that fucking party. A few people have plugged in to watch my game, and I actually manage a grin for them as we all disentangle from our rigs.

"That was a sweet trick with the arches," someone says, and someone else offers to run out for pizza since it's now past noon, and soon there's a crowd of us sitting cross-legged in a circle on the floor, pizza grease seeping through paper plates and onto our fingertips. There's a dimpled, heavy-set kid trying to tell everyone why he still prefers to use passive electrodes even though it means getting your hair gunked up with conductive paste, and I feel some unrecognized tightness below my collarbones soften, relax.

Lady K, sitting next to me, waves a slice of pepperoni to get my attention. "You sticking around for the rest of the afternoon?" She pauses, arches an eyebrow. "Shouldn't you be in school?"

I am about to say something disparaging, when a fragment of conversation cuts through the rest of the chatter, the way fragments of conversation sometimes do, loud and unmistakable. "—kid in California hardwired himself two days ago." It's a pretty, wide-eyed girl with a punk-rock haircut talking; no wonder all the attention is on her. "That's like over two dozen people hardwired in, just in America. It's just so scary, I mean can you even imagine, drilling into your own skull like that? I hear there's someone not too far from here, do you think—" the guy next to her finally cuts her off with an elbow jab to the ribs. She turns an inquiring glare on him, and he leans toward her, starting up a furious, whispered conversation.

The tightness underneath my collarbones spools back into existence. I ignore the guilty glances being slanted my way, and take a large, deliberate bite of pizza instead.

"Skipping," I explain to Lady K once I am finished chewing. The conversation is still hushed and awkward. I fold the paper plate into a careful fat wedge, wipe my fingers on my jeans. "I'm gonna plug back in."

There are too many eyes on me as I try to settle into my rig, I can't get the electrodes to sit quite right. I never have problems with my rig but it's taking too long, I'm starting to look like an idiot so I turn the whole thing on anyway, blissful blank order sliding over my brainwaves.

It fits my current luck that none of my active play partners are connected, so I drift uncomfortably, paging through lists of other people looking for games, trying to find someone whose stats make them look interesting. I am just about to accept an offer to play a teaching game with some newbie, when Annie's pseud pops up as available.

I send her a game request without even really thinking about it; I've done this so many times it's like a reflex now. And like all the other times before, she declines immediately.

Because I am childish and bitter, I send her two dozen game requests in quick succession, the Coma equivalent of ringing someone's doorbell repeatedly.

Just admit you're scared, I message her, and as usual, am informed that she is not accepting messages. I game-request her three more times and think really hard about flipping her off, as if the Coma network might somehow be able to convey my displeasure, might carry along my vitriol to resonate into the base of Annie's wretched skull. Then I accept the game against the newbie and try to forget about it.

I'm a half hour into it when Annie's game request pings along the edge of my brain.

I stop breathing. For at least thirty seconds I am essentially paralyzed; I know this because when I come back to myself my opponent is making good headway toward tearing down the defenses I've built up, sending me a little stream of surprised and pleased messages about how he thinks he's finally really getting it. *Sorry*, I say, *sorry, I have to go*, and forfeit the game, just like that.

I accept Annie's game request and the world is a clean slate.

Then Annie starts building a box.

Maybe you can see what's coming here. I don't know. Maybe it was obvious from the outside. If you had asked me before, I wouldn't have been able to tell you what I thought was going to happen, because I didn't think anything. I wanted to play Annie. Of course I did, she's my sister, my sister who I lost, and I wanted to have her again, in any way I could. And I wanted to beat her, because she's my sister, and you always want to win against your siblings. That's just the way things work, right? That should have been enough.

So I didn't *think* anything. But here's the thing, and I know this makes me a fool, but deep down, I *believed*, somehow, that if I could just beat her everything would be all better. Believed, with that sort of secret inner ferocity of a fairy tale or a religion. I would win against her, like nobody ever had, and there would be a silent, eternal moment. And then her name would blip out of existence, and I'd pull off my rig and look over to where she was doing the same, prying her goggles away from her eyes and sliding the probe out from the back of her skull. And we'd look at each other, and start laughing, and everything would be okay.

In fairytales, you can wake somebody out of death with a kiss. Does waking somebody up like this really seem like so much to ask?

When I beat Annie, there is indeed one silent, eternal moment. And right then I don't even realize what I'm waiting for, bated breath and tense muscles, until it doesn't happen, until she leaves the space we created without comment, until she doesn't blip out of existence.

Until she starts up another game, immediately, against someone else, as if absolutely nothing has changed.

When I get home my mother is waiting for me.

"The school called to tell me you missed classes today," she says.

My keys bite into my palms, hard and irregular. I get past my mother without looking at her, make my way into the living room. Climb onto the couch, pull my knees up to my chest. Turn my face into the cushion so the upholstery forces my eyes shut.

I have mostly stopped crying by this point.

"You listen when I'm talking to you," says my mother.

I can hear her moving into the living room after me. The shadows behind my eyelids get darker as she stands over me, half-blocking the light. I expect her to grab hold of me, yank me upright, something, but she doesn't move.

"Would you unplug me?" I hear myself asking. My voice filters through the cushions, muffled and strange. I doubt my mother can even understand what I'm saying. "If I was like Annie. Would you unplug us both?"

Silence. The tender spots at my temples throb in time with my pulse, thudding slow and regular. Then I feel her moving, feel the couch shifting as she sinks down next to me. Her fingertips press into my scalp, thumb curling into the fine hairs at the base of my skull.

"I don't know," she says, almost a whisper.

I almost want to believe she sounds sorry.

"Okay," I say. Her fingernails catch in my hair when she pulls her hand away, bringing long strands with them. I feel them lift and separate, imagine them shining and infinite, like wires. "Okay."

The prodigal son

ALLEN M. STEELE

Here's a compelling look at the struggle to launch a privately funded starship, in spite of all the legal and logistical challenges that must be overcome, including some potentially deadly ones . . .

Allen Steele made his first sale in 1988. In 1990, he published his critically acclaimed first novel, Orbital Decay, *which subsequently won the Locus poll as Best First Novel of the year, and soon Steele was being compared to Golden Age Heinlein by no less an authority than Gregory Benford. His other books include the novels* Clarke County, Space; Lunar Descent; Labyrinth of Night; The Weight; The Tranquility Alternative; A King of Infinite Space; Oceanspace; Chronospace; Coyote; Coyote Rising; Spindrift; Galaxy Blues; Coyote Horizon; Coyote Destiny; Hex; *and a YA novel,* Apollo's Outcast. *His short work has been gathered in five collections,* Rude Astronauts, All-American Alien Boy, American Beauty, The Last Science Fiction Writer, *and* Sex and Violence in Zero-G: The Complete "Near Space" Stories. *His most recent book is a new novel,* V-S Day. *He has won three Hugo Awards, in 1996 for his novella "The Death of Captain Future," in 1998 for his novella "Where Angels Fear to Tread," and, most recently, in 2011 for his novelette "The Emperor of Mars." Born in Nashville, Tennessee, he has worked for a variety of newspapers and magazines, covering science and business assignments, and is now a full-time writer living in Whately, Massachusetts, with his wife Linda.*

I

The Gulfstream G8 was an old aircraft on the verge of retirement. Its fuselage creaked whenever it hit an air pocket, and the tiltjets had made a rattling sound when it took off from San Juan. At least the Caribbean looked warm. Matt figured that, if something went wrong and the plane had to ditch, at least he and the other passengers wouldn't freeze to death in the sun-dappled water that lay below. Provided that they survived the crash, of course.

Matt looked away from the window to steal another glance at the young woman sitting across the aisle. She'd said nothing to him over the past couple of hours, and he couldn't decide whether whatever she was studying on her slate was really that fascinating or if she was merely being standoffish. The aircraft jounced again, causing her to briefly raise her eyes from the screen. She caught Matt looking at her, favored him with a polite smile, then returned her attention to the slate.

She was beautiful. Dark brown skin and fathomless black eyes hinted at an Indian heritage. Her build was athletically slender, her face solemn yet her mouth touched with subtle laugh-lines. And there were no rings on her fingers.

"Rough flight," he said.

She looked up again. "Excuse me?"

"Rough flight, I said." Searching for something to add, Matt settled on the obvious. "You'd think the foundation could afford a better plane. This one looks like it came from the junkyard." He picked at the frayed upholstery of his left armrest.

"They're trying to save money. This is probably the cheapest charter they could afford."

Her gaze went back to her slate, her right hand pushing away a lock of mahogany hair that had fallen across her face. She was plainly uninterested in making conversation with a fellow passenger. Or at least the young guy about her own age seated beside her. But Matt had learned how to be persistent when pursuing attractive women. Sometimes, the direct approach was the best.

He stuck out his hand. "Matt Skinner."

She eyed his hand for a second before deciding to take it. "Chandraleska Sanyal."

"Chandalre . . ." He fumbled over the syllables

"I'll settle for Chandi."

"Okay. So what are you doing with the . . . y'know? The project."

"Payload specialist, *Nathan 4*. I'm with the checkout team." She nodded toward the handful of other men and women sitting around them. Most were in their late twenties or early thirties, although two or three were middle-aged or older. "Same as everyone else . . . except you, I suppose."

"Oh yeah . . . checkout team." Matt had no idea what she meant by that, other than it had something to do with the rocket carrying *Galactique's* components into orbit. Leaning across the armrest, he peered at her slate. Vertical columns of numbers, a bar-graph with multicolored lines rising from left to right, a pop-up menu bar. They could just as well have been Egyptian hieroglyphics. "Fascinating."

Chandi wasn't fooled for a second. "I didn't know tourists still visit Ile Sombre. Or are you the new kitchen help?"

It was an insult, of course, but at least she was talking to him. "Oh, no," he said, "I'm coming down to visit my parents. They work on the project. Ben and Jill Skinner . . . maybe you know them?"

Matt had the satisfaction of watching Chandi's eyes widen in surprise. "Dr. Skinner's your father?" she asked, and he nodded. "That means you're with the Arkwright family."

"Why, yes. That's my middle name . . . Matthew Arkwright Skinner." He said this with deliberate casualness, as if it was the most unremarkable thing he could have mentioned. "Nathan Arkwright was my great-great-grandfather. He started the Arkwright Foundation about seventy years ago, when . . ."

"I know the foundation's history. I've even read a few of his novels." Chandi nodded towards the other passengers. "It's a good bet everyone has. Which book was your favorite?"

The soft chime of a bell saved Matt from having to admit that he'd never read any of Nathan Arkwright's science fiction novels. The seat-belt lights flashed on and the pilot's voice came through the speakers: *"We'll be coming in for landing, folks, so if you'll return to your seats and stow your belongings, we'll have you on the ground in just a few minutes."*

The other passengers began collapsing their slates. Matt felt his ears pop. Chandi saved her work, then slipped her slate into her travel bag. "If you look out the window, you might see the launch site."

Matt turned to look. For a moment he saw nothing, then the plane banked to the right and Ile Sombre came into view. He caught a glimpse of a *ciudad flotante*, one of the floating towns common in the coastal regions of the southern hemisphere; this one was Ste. Genevieve, a collection of prefabs, huts, and shacks built atop pontoon barges above the flooded remains of the island's former capitol. Then the aircraft moved away from the coast and he saw, rising from the inland rainforest, something that looked like a giant yellow crayon nestled within a gantry tower: a cargo rocket, perched atop its mobile launch platform.

"*Nathan 2.*" Chandi leaned across the aisle to gaze over his shoulder. "Scheduled for lift-off the day after tomorrow . . . if all goes well, that is."

Glancing back at her, Matt couldn't help but see down the front of her blouse. It was a pleasant sight. "That's . . . um, the microwave beam thing, isn't it?"

Chandi noticed the direction he was looking and quickly sat up straight again. "No. The beamsat went up six weeks ago on *Nathan 1.* It's being assembled in Lagrange orbit and should be ready for operation in about four months. *Nathan 2* is carrying the service module."

"Oh, okay. Right . . ."

A bump beneath their feet as the landing gear came down, followed a few seconds later by the trembling shudder of the engine nacelles swiveling upward to descent position. About a thousand feet below, a paved airstrip came into view. Chandi gave her seat belt a perfunctory hitch to make sure it was tight. "Mind if I ask a personal question?"

Matt smiled. "I can give you the answer. Yes, I'd love to have dinner with you tonight."

She didn't return the smile. "What I was going to ask was, why are you here?"

"Come again?"

"I mean, it's pretty obvious that you don't know anything about *Galactique.* This is no vacation spot. The island lost its beaches years ago, and there's no one at the hotel except the launch team. So trying to use your family name to pick up girls isn't going to get you anywhere."

Matt's face became warm. "I didn't . . . I wasn't . . ."

"Sure you weren't." Chandi's expression was knowing. "So what brings you here?"

He suddenly found himself wishing the plane would crash, if only because death might save him the embarrassment of this moment. Chandi was watching him, though, waiting for an answer, so he gave her the only one he had that was honest.

"My grandmother thought it was a good idea," he said.

II

Matt's grandmother was Kate Morressy Skinner, the Arkwright Foundation's executive director, and as Matt stood in the customs line of what was laughably called the Ile Sombre International Airport, he once again reflected that it had been a mistake to call her asking for money.

He'd always gotten along well with Grandma, but he should have known that her wealth was an illusion. The foundation had been established by a bestowment left by her grandfather; it was worth billions of dollars, but all of it was tied up in investment capital associated with its principal goal: building and launching the first starship from Earth. Grandma had been made its director when she was about Matt's age, and although she received a generous salary, she was hardly rich. So she shouldn't have been expected to give her grandson a "loan" they both knew would probably never be repaid.

Matt watched the customs inspector open the backpack he'd brought with him from the states and began to carefully sort through his belongings. The airport terminal was a large single room in a cinderblock building; customs was a row of folding tables behind which the inspectors stood. The place was humid, with the ceiling fans doing nothing but blow hot air around. It was springtime in this part of the world, but it felt like mid-summer anywhere else. Through the open door leading to the airstrip came the roar of another battered Air Carib jet taking off. Except for the passengers who'd disembarked from Matt's flight, everyone in the building was black; he'd later learn that the native inhabitants were descended from African slaves who'd escaped from French and Spanish plantations elsewhere in the Caribbean and made their way to this remote island just south of Dominica, which the Europeans avoided because it had once been a pirate stronghold.

Grandma had done enough for him already by lining up his most recent job as an orderly at the Philadelphia hospital where Grandpa had worked as a doctor before he passed away. But that job lasted only about as long as all the others before it: part-time actor, recording studio publicist, store clerk, a couple of positions as assistant associate whatever. He'd keep them until he got bored and his boss noticed his lack of commitment, and then the inevitable chain of events would follow. The carpet. The warning. The second warning. The final warning. The unapologetic apology, the dismissal form, the severance check. And then the move to another city, another apartment, and another job found on another employment Web site.

When the hospital fired him, Matt called his grandmother in Boston and asked if she could front him a few hundred bucks. Just so he could make ends meet until he found work again. She'd sent him a plane ticket to Ile Sombre instead, telling him that his parents had a job for him down there. Which was why a customs inspector was now asking him to empty his pockets.

Matt pulled everything from his jeans and denim jacket and put it on the table.

Cell, wallet, key ring holding keys that no longer belonged to anything he could unlock except a storage locker in Philadelphia, a lighter and a pack of Rockys. The inspector, a tall black man with a purple-dyed 'fro, picked up the smokes and glared at him.

"This is not allowed, sir," he said, his deep voice inflected with a Caribbean accent.

"I thought marijuana was legal here. It is where I come from."

"You're not in America. Do you have any more, sir?"

"No. That's my only pack."

The inspector turned to another uniformed man standing behind the table and said something in French creole. The other islander gazed at the pack and shook his head. "We will let you go, sir," the inspector said to Matt as he dropped the pack in a nearby wastecan, "but you'll have to pay a fine. One hundred dollars, American."

"I only have sixty."

"That will do."

Matt removed the last money he had in the world from his wallet and gave it to the inspector, who carefully counted the bills before tucking them in his shirt pocket. "Thank you, sir." He handed Matt's passport back to him. "You may go now. Have a pleasant visit."

Third world graft. The inspector probably would have shaken him down for something else if he hadn't found the smokes. Matt zipped up his back, slung it across his shoulder, and headed for the exit door. At least he wouldn't spend his first night on Ile Sombre in jail.

Chandraleska Sanyal had already gone through customs. She was standing outside with the other new arrivals, waiting to board a dilapidated solar van parked at the curb. Matt caught her eye and she gave him a brief smile. Apparently he hadn't turned her off entirely. He was about to go over and make an excuse to spend more time with her by seeing if he could hitch a ride on the bus when a woman's voice called his name.

He looked around and there was his mother, walking toward him. "Hello, sweetheart," she said as she wrapped her arms around him. "Have a good flight?"

Jill Skinner was in her early fifties, but the gene therapy she and her husband had undergone a few years ago had erased at least a decade from her apparent age. She now looked more like she could have been Matt's older sister rather than his mother. "Okay, I guess," he said, returning the hug. He decided not to tell her about the customs hassle. "Where's Dad? He's not coming?"

"He's busy at the space center. *Nathan 2* goes up in a couple of days, or haven't you heard?" She glanced at his pack. "Is that all you brought with you?"

"Didn't think I'd need anything else." No sense in letting her know that it contained nearly everything he had left. The stuff in the storage locker would probably be auctioned once he failed to pay the rent. "Where are you parked?"

"This way." She turned to lead him across the airport's pitted car park. "I'm afraid I'll have to drop you off at the hotel. I'm needed at work, too . . . although I'm hoping I can get you to start helping me after *Nathan 2* gets off."

Matt's mother was the Arkwright Foundation's press liaison at the Ile Sombre launch site; his father was mission director. They'd met many years ago when Jill

Muller was a reporter assigned to do an investigative story about the foundation; once she discovered the nature of Ben Skinner's family business, she'd left journalism to marry him and become the foundation's media relations director. Matt had grown up with the foundation, but he'd never shared his parents' commitment to it. This was the first time in many years Mom had even intimated that she'd like to have him join her and Dad.

"Yeah, well . . . I was sort of thinking I'd just like to take it easy for a while." He didn't look at her as they crossed the car park. "Kinda catch my breath, decide what my life's goals should be."

His mother didn't answer that, or at least not at once. Instead, she pulled a key-remote from her shorts pocket and thumbed it. A short distance away, a Volksun beeped to remind her where she'd parked it; its engine was already humming by the time she opened its hatchback and let her son throw his pack in.

"Twenty-eight is a little late to be making up your mind what you want to do, isn't it?" she said as she got in behind the wheel. "First there was journalism school . . ."

"That was your idea, not mine."

". . . then there was acting, then the music business, then the idea of working in a hospital while going to med school . . ."

"A lot of guys I know take a while to settle into something." Through the side window, Matt spotted the van Chandi was riding; it was pulling away from the terminal, heading for parts unknown.

"A lot of guys you know probably aren't flat broke." His mother didn't look at him as she backed out the parking space. "Oh, yes, I know . . . Grandma told me you'd tried to hit her up for money."

"It was just a loan."

"Maybe . . . but I promise you, you're not going to get a dime from her, or your father and me either, unless you work for it. So don't count on getting a tan while you're here." She left the car on manual control and started driving toward the airport gate. "You've been a grasshopper for much too long. Time for you to become a busy little ant, just like the rest of us."

Jill Skinner had always been fond of *Aesop's Fables*; she'd been referring to it for as long as he could remember. Nothing ever changes. Matt slumped in his seat and regretted letting the customs inspector take away the only thing that might have made this trip bearable.

III

The Hotel Au Soliel was a former resort dating back to the last century, when tourists still came to Ile Sombre for winter getaways. That era had come to an end just as it had for much of the Caribbean; rising sea levels and catastrophic hurricanes had wiped out scenic beaches and pleasant seaside villages, and the subsequent collapse of the cruise ship industry had been the final blow. Fortunately, the Au Soliel was far enough away from the water that it hadn't shared the same fate as Ste. Genevieve. The port town lay submerged beneath the *flotante* anchored above its ruined buildings and streets, but the hotel had survived. Run-down and in crying need of a fresh coat of paint, it now functioned as living quarters for the space center which, along with coffee and citrus, had become one of Ile Sombre's principal industries.

Modeled in the plantation style, the hotel sprawled across ten acres abutting the island's undeveloped rain forest. Shaped like a H, its two-story wings surrounded gardens, tennis courts, and a swimming pool. Matt was pleased that he'd been given a poolside cabana room until he discovered that it wasn't quite as luxurious as it sounded. The room was small, its bed not much more than a cot, and the pool itself had long-since been drained and covered by a canvas tarp. His parents, on the other hand, had taken residence in one of the cottages that had once been reserved for the wealthiest guests and were now occupied by senior staff.

"That's where we're staying," Jill said, pointing out the cottage to him as she led him down the outside stairs to the cabanas. "Sorry we can't give you one of the spare bedrooms, but your father and I are sharing one as an office and the other one is used by Grandma when she visits."

Matt watched as she ran a passcard across the door scanner. "Is she here often?"

"Not really. She doesn't like to travel very much these days." His mother stepped aside to let him press his thumb against the lockplate; the door beeped twice as it registered him as the room's rightful occupant. "But she's planning to come down soon. Probably when we launch *Nathan 5*. She wants to be here when we send *Galactique* on its way."

Matt thought that his mother was going to leave him alone to unpack and maybe catch a nap, but she had other plans. He had just enough time to cast off his unneeded jacket, drop his pack, and give his quarters a quick look-see before she hustled him out the door and back to the car. By then it was almost dusk. He hadn't eaten since he'd changed planes in Puerto Rico, and he asked if they'd be getting dinner any time soon.

"We'll be coming back here to eat," she said as they drove away from the hotel. "Everyone has their meals together in the dining room . . . buffet-style, but it's still pretty good. Right now, I'm taking you to Operations and Management. Your father would like to see you."

The Ile Sombre Space Launch Center was located on a high plateau about five miles from the hotel, not far from the island's eastern coast. Matt's mother passed the time by telling him about the place. It had been established earlier in the century by PanAmSpace, the consortium of South American countries that provided launch services for private space companies in the Western Hemisphere. For several decades it sent communications, weather, and solar power satellites into Earth orbit, but then Washington moved to protect the American space industry by passing the Domestic Space Access Act, which forbade use of overseas launch sites by U.S. companies—a law that was idiotically short-sighted, considering that Cape Canaveral and Wallops Island were being lost to the rising sea levels and the New Mexico spaceport was overwhelmed by the subsequent demand.

When the DSAA came down, Ile Sombre lost most of its space business. The launch center fell into disuse and might have been abandoned altogether had it not been for the Arkwright Foundation and the Galactique Project. It had taken some shrewd political manipulation by the foundation to gain an exemption from the DSAA, but in the end they'd won. Ile Sombre was now *Galactique's* principal launch site; it was from there that the starship's microwave propulsion system had been sent into space, soon to be followed by its four-module hull.

A chain-link fence surrounded the space center, its entrance gate guarded by islanders in private-security uniforms. As Jill slowed down for the checkpoint, Matt noticed a handful of people squatting beside a couple of weather-beaten tents erected just outside the fence. Hand-lettered plywood signs that looked as if they'd been through several tropical showers leaned haphazardly on posts stuck in the ground: Stop Galactick!! and God Will Never Foreive You and Earth Is You're Only Home. The protesters were all middle-aged white people; they glared at the Volksun as Matt's mother flashed her I.D. badge and the guards waved her and Matt through.

"Who are they?" he asked.

"Morons." She said this as if it explained everything, then she caught his questioning look. "They're from the New American Congregation, a fundamentalist megachurch in North Carolina. They've been opposed to the project from the beginning. Shortly after we began launch operations, they sent down some so-called missionaries to give us a hard time." She shrugged. "They're harmless, really. Just don't talk to them if you happen to run into them."

She drove to the Operations and Management, a flat-roofed building not far from the hemispherical Mission Control dome and, a short distance away, the enormous white cube that was the Vehicle Assembly Building. Work had ended for the day, and men and women were streaming through the front doors, each of them wearing badge lanyards over linen shirts and spaghetti-strap dresses. Jill stopped at the security desk to get a visitor's badge for Matt—"We'll get you a staff badge tomorrow"—then they went upstairs and down a hall to a door marked *Mission Director*. She didn't bother to knock but went straight in, and there was Matt's father.

Like many sons, Matt had often wondered if he'd resemble his father when he got older. Now he was sure of it. Dr. Benjamin Skinner had taken retrotherapy as well and so didn't look his age, and the cargo shorts and short-sleeve polo shirt he wore were more suitable for a younger man. Only a few strands of grey in his mustache attested to his true years. His office, though, was the sort of cluttered mess only a senior project engineer would have, its shelves choked with books, the desk buried beneath reports and spreadsheets; his father still preferred to read paper. Through the corner windows could be seen the distant launch pad. The sun was going down, and floodlights at the base of the pad were coming on to bathe *Nathan 2* in a luminescent halo.

"There you are." Ben stood up and walked around the desk, carefully avoiding a stack of binders on the floor. "Good trip down?"

"It was all right." Matt shook hands with him. "You need to get a better plane, though. I thought it was going to fall apart."

"Yeah, isn't it a heap? But we made a good deal with Air Carib, and every penny we save goes to what counts." He cocked his head toward *Nathan 2*.

"Maybe you should write a press release about that, Mattie." Jill picked up a pile of books from an armchair and sat down. "It could be the first job you do for me."

Matt didn't know which he liked less, the prospect of becoming a media flack or being called by his childhood name. "I don't know if I'm going to be here that long."

"Did Grandma send you a round-trip ticket?" Ben asked, and smiled when Matt shook his head. "Well, there you have it. You can't go home until you can buy a ticket, and you can't buy a ticket unless you work for us." A shrug. "I don't know what's so bad about that. There's dozens of people who'd love to be working here . . . even writing press releases."

"I gave up that stuff when I quit the music business."

"Fired, you mean." His mother wasn't letting him get away with anything. As usual.

"It's a job, son . . . and I bet you'll come to like it, if you'll give it a chance." Ben crossed his arms and leaned against his desk. "We're making history here. Launching the human race's first true starship, sending our species to a new world twenty-two light-years away . . . I don't know how anyone can't be excited about a chance to participate in this."

Even after all these years, his father still didn't get it. His dreams—his lifelong obsession, really—wasn't shared by his son, and never had been. Matt had grown up in a family that had devoted itself to a goal that his great-great-grandfather set out for them, but he'd never understood why. They could have lived a life of ease with the money the Arkwright Foundation had earned over the years from its investments in the launch industry, asteroid mining, and solar power satellites. Instead, he'd watched his father, mother, and grandmother throw it all away on—again, he glanced out the window at the distant rocket—*that*.

"Yeah, well . . ." He looked down at the floor. "So long as I'm here, I guess I'll try to get *excited* about it." He knew what they were thinking. He'd been through this countless times already, even before he'd left home to find his own way in the world.

"The prodigal son returns," his mother said drily.

"What?"

"Never mind." She pushed herself out of the chair. "I'm sure you're hungry, and it's almost dinner time." Jill looked at her husband. "Honey, c'mon . . . time to go home and eat. Sorry, but I'm not letting you get dinner out of the vending machines again."

"Guess you're right." Ben looked at the papers on his desk, obviously reluctant to leave his job even for a little while. "I can always come back later, I suppose." Standing up, he took his son by the arm. "The food at the hotel is actually pretty good. We cheaped out with the airplane, but spared no expense with the people we hired to cook for us."

Matt remembered the remark Chandi had made, when she'd suggested that he might be someone who was coming down to take a job in the kitchen. "So I've heard."

IV

"T-minus ninety seconds. The launch director has given permission to end the hold and resume countdown."

The voice from the ceiling speakers was accentless, almost robotic; Matt wondered if it was computer-generated. Although he was seated on the other side of a soundproof window separating the visitors gallery from the launch control center, he could see his father. Benjamin Skinner stood behind his console in Mission Control, his gaze fixed upon the row of giant LCD screens arranged in a shallow arc across the far wall of the windowless room. In keeping with a tradition established by mission directors of the NASA era, he wore an old-fashioned necktie from a collection of atrocious ties. Matt had seen this particular tie earlier that morning, at breakfast: a topless Polynesian girl in a hula skirt, dancing beneath a palm tree. He thought it was amazingly stupid, but apparently his father believed that it would bring them good luck.

All the other controllers were decked out in dark blue polo shirts with the Galactique Project logo embroidered on the breast pockets. Their attention was focused entirely on the datastream coming from *Nathan 2*. In the center wallscreen, the cargo rocket stood fuming upon the launch pad, wreathed in hydrogen fumes seeping from ports along its canary-colored hull. Above the screen, a chronometer had come alive again: -00.01.29, the figure getting smaller with each passing second.

"Why did they stop the countdown?" Matt asked.

"They always go into hold at the ninety-second mark." Chandi cupped a hand against her mouth even though no one in the firing room could possibly hear them. "Gives the controllers a chance to catch up with their checklists, make sure they haven't missed anything."

"I thought computers controlled everything."

"At this point, they pretty much do." She smiled. "But only a fool would completely trust a computer when it comes to something like this."

Matt glanced at his slate. It displayed the *Nathan 2* factsheet his mother had sent him a little while earlier. *Galactique's* service module—the 110-foot segment containing the ship's guidance and control computers, fission reactor, maneuvering thrusters, laser telemetry and sail control systems—was being transported to geosynchronous orbit 22,300 miles above Earth by an unmanned Kubera heavy-lift booster manufactured in India by Lokapala Cosmos, the kind used to launch solar power satellites. The rest was data: reusable single-stage-to-orbit, 233 feet in height, gross lift-off weight 4,750 tons with a 400,000 pound payload capacity, powered by eight oxygen-hydrogen aerospike engines.

That was it looked like to an engineer, though. To Matt, the rocket resembled nothing more or less than an enormous penis. The Giant Space Weiner, worshipped by a roomful of people with a Freudian phallic fixation.

"Why is it yellow?" It was the only thing he could say which wouldn't have offended the young woman sitting beside him.

The people seated around them cast him patronizing looks, as if he was a child who'd asked an obvious question. "So they can find it easily when it splashes down after re-entry," Chandi said, visibly annoyed. "Didn't your mother teach you anything?"

Matt almost laughed out loud. It wouldn't do, though, to explain what he thought was so funny. "That's something Mom and Dad are interested in," he said, keeping the joke to himself.

"*T-minus sixty seconds and counting.*"

Chandi raised an eyebrow, and Matt distracted himself by glancing over his shoulder. His mother sat a couple of rows behind him, surrounded by the handful of reporters who'd flown down to Ile Sombre for the launch. She caught Matt looking at him and gave him a brief nod, then cupped an ear to the journalist who'd just asked her a question.

Matt knew that he should be sitting with his mother, learning the job he'd soon be taking. But he'd spent all yesterday with her doing what little he could to help the press office get ready for the launch, and he'd become tired of being attached to her elbow. So when he'd seen Chandi enter the gallery along with the other specialists who'd been on the plane, he contrived a reason to take the seat beside her: he'd told her that he wanted to watch the launch with someone who'd explain things to him.

Chandi didn't seem to mind, although he caught hostile looks from a couple of other guys who'd aspired to be her companion. Matt told himself that he didn't really have a crush on her. He might even believe it, if he repeated it to himself long enough.

"T-minus thirty seconds and counting."

"They're retracting the gantry arms," Chandi said quietly, bending her head slightly toward him as she pointed to the center wallscreen. "The rocket's now on internal power."

"That means it's pulling juice from only itself?" Matt asked and she nodded. "Okay . . . um, so what happens if something goes wrong?"

"Shut up," growled an older man sitting behind them.

"Hey," Matt said, glancing back at him, "I'm just asking."

"Don't." Chandi scowled in disapproval. "It's bad luck." She paused, then went on. "They can abort the launch right up to the last two seconds, but that's only if the computers pick up a mission-critical malfunction. After main-engine start, we're pretty much committed to . . ."

"T-minus twenty seconds."

She abruptly stopped herself, and Matt was startled to feel her nervously grab the back of his own hand. She'd apparently meant to grasp the armrest only to find it already occupied, because she immediately jerked her hand away.

"It's okay," he murmured. "You can, if you want."

Chandi gazed at him, her dark eyes embarrassed. She returned her hand to the armrest without shaking him off.

"Thanks," she whispered.

"T-minus fifteen seconds."

All of a sudden, she rose from her seat. "Follow me," she said, still clutching his hand.

"What are you . . . ?"

"Hurry!" She pulled him to his feet, then turned to push her way past the other people seated in their row. "Excuse me, excuse me . . ."

Matt dropped his slate, but Chandi didn't give him a chance to pick it up. He caught a glimpse of his mother's face; she stared at him in bafflement as Chandi tugged him toward the gallery's side entrance. Chandi let go of his hand to shove open the door; Matt followed her as she raced down the stairs leading to the control center's rear door. In seconds, they were outside the dome and running around the side of the building.

Although he was a newcomer, Matt was aware of the safety rules which mandated that everyone witnessing a liftoff had to do so from inside Mission Control. The pad was less than three miles away; if the Kubera blew up, the dome would protect them from the blast. He knew he was going to catch hell for this from his mother, but Chandi hadn't given him any choice.

"*T-minus ten seconds.*" The voice came from loudspeakers outside the dome. "*Nine . . . eight . . . seven . . .*"

"Stop." Chandi grabbed him by the shoulders, halting him in mid-step. "Watch."

"*Six . . . five . . . four . . .*"

They had a clear view of the launch pad. From the distance, the rocket was almost toy-like, dwarfed by its gantry and the four lightning-deflection masts surrounding the pad. Matt had just enough to regret no longer having the close-up view afforded by the control room screens when a flare silently erupted at the bottom of the rocket, sending black smoke rolling forth from the blast trench beneath the platform.

"*Three . . . main engine ignition . . . two . . . one . . . liftoff!*"

The Kubera rose from its pad atop a torch so bright that it caused him to squint. The eerie quiet that accompanied the ignition sequence lasted only until the rocket cleared the tower. The silence ended when the sound waves finally crossed the miles separating him from the rocket, and then it was as if he was being run over by an invisible truck: a crackling roar that grew louder, louder, louder as the rocket ascended into the blue Caribbean sky. Seagulls and egrets and parrots took wing from all the palmettos and cocoanut trees around them as *Nathan 2* became a fiery spear lancing up into the heavens. It was no longer the Giant Space Weiner, but something terrifying and awesome that seemed to take possession of the sky itself.

Breathless, unable to speak, Matt watched as the rocket rose up and away, becoming a tiny spark at the tip of a black, horn-like trail forming an arc high above the ocean. The sudden, distant bang of the sonic boom startled him. He wasn't aware that Chandi was quietly observing him, savoring his fascination. It wasn't until the spark winked out, and the loudspeaker announced main-engine cut-off and that *Nathan 2* had successfully reached low orbit, that he remembered she was standing beside him. His ears were ringing when he looked at her again.

"That was . . . incredible," he said.

"Yes, it was." Chandi nodded knowingly. "Now you see why we're here?"

V

The launch team celebrated with a party that night at the hotel. Instead of the customary buffet in the former restaurant, a cookout was held by the swimming pool. A propane grill was brought out of storage and tiki lamps were lit, and a couple of hundred pounds of Argentine beef, purchased by the foundation and stashed away for special occasions, emerged from the kitchen's walk-in freezer. Hamburgers and steak fries and cocoanut ice cream and an ice-filled barrel of Red Stripe beer: *Nathan 2*'s foster parents were in the mood to party. Their child had finally left home.

Matt went to the party expecting to hook up with Chandi, only to find that she was less interested in him that evening than she'd been that morning. She smiled when he approached her, and didn't object when he brought her a beer and asked if she'd join him for dinner, but no sooner had they sat down at one of the patio tables when a half-dozen other scientists and engineers carried their paper plates over to their table. They sat down without asking if they were interrupting anything, and the conversation immediately shifted to technical matters: integration of *Galactique's* beamsail within *Nathan 3's* faring, the timeline for recovery and turnaround of the Kubera booster once it returned to Earth, the problems anticipated with meeting the schedule for final testing and checkout of the *Nathan 4* module.

Matt tried to keep up as best as he could, but it was all above his head. Within minutes he was lost, and no one at the table was willing to stop and provide explanations. Chandi made a polite effort to include him in the conversation, yet it was as if he was dull schoolboy who'd been mistakenly invited to eat at the teachers' table. No, worse than that: everyone at the table was his age, more or less, but some of them were probably earning their doctorates about the same time he was working in a convenience store.

After Matt asked Chandi if she'd like another beer—she impatiently shook her head and returned to the discussion of maintaining *Galactique's* extrauterine fetal incubation system during the mission's cruise phase—he quietly picked up his plate and left. He tossed the plate in the recycling can, fished a couple of Red Stripes from the beer barrel, and found another place to sit, a neglected chaise lounge on the other side of the pool. And there he proceeded to drink, listen to the reggae music being piped over the loudspeaker system, and wonder again what he was doing here.

He was on his second beer when his father came over to join him. Ben Skinner ambled around the end of the covered swimming pool and into the place where his son had chosen to hide. By then he'd removed his dress shirt and absurd tie and replaced them with an equally ugly Hawaiian shirt, and he stopped at the foot of Matt's lounger to gaze down at him.

"Care for some company?"

"Sure." Matt regarded him with eyes that were becoming beer-fogged. "Have a seat."

"Don't mind if I do." Ben eased himself into the chair beside him. "Saw you earlier. Thought you were making friends. Now . . ."

"Now I'm here," Matt said, finishing his thought for him. "They're nice enough, but . . ." He shrugged. "Y'know, you've heard one conversation about the quantum intergalactic microwave whoopee, you've pretty much heard 'em all."

"Oh, yeah, that. I think I read a paper about it in BIS *Journal* just the other day." A grin appeared, and quickly faded when he saw that Matt wasn't appreciating the joke. "Can't blame you. If you're not on their wavelength, it's going to be pretty hard to understand what they're talking about. Here, let me see if I can cheer you up."

He reached into his breast pocket, and Matt was astounded to see him pull out a joint. "Dad? Since when did you . . . ?"

"Before you were born." His father smiled as he juggled the hand-rolled spliff between his fingers. "I don't indulge all that often, but I picked it up again when we came down here. I don't mind if anyone here smokes, so long as it's after hours and they don't do it at the space center. Got a light?"

"I thought marijuana was illegal here." Matt dug into his shorts pocket, searching for the lighter he habitually carried. "That's what the customs guys told me when they took away my smokes."

"Old island law from the smuggling days that's still on the books. Only time the cops enforce it is when they get it in mind to shake down a gringo. Otherwise, no one cares." Nonetheless he gazed at the crowd on the other side of the pool, wary of anyone spotting him smoking pot with his son. "I don't do this very often, really. Just on special occasions. Then I go down to Ste. Genevieve and buy some of the local stuff."

Matt handed his lighter to his father. "I'll keep that in mind."

"Just be careful to take someone with you if you go. Someone who doesn't look like a white guy from the states." Ben flicked the lighter, stuck one end of the joint in his mouth. "Maybe the young lady you were with tonight."

"Chandi."

"Umm-hmm." The joint flamed as his father touched it with fire. It burned unevenly as he took a long drag from it. "Dr. Chandraleksha Sanyal," he went on, slowly exhaling. "I recruited her myself, from Andru & Reynolds Biosystems. Very smart woman."

"Out of my league, you mean."

"No, that's not what I mean." Ben leaned over to pass the joint to him. "Sure, you'll have to run a little harder to catch up with her, but . . . well, she must see something in you if she'd taken the trouble of dragging you out of the dome during the launch."

"You know about that? Your back was turned to . . . oh. Mom must have told you."

"Yes, she did." His father frowned. "That's against safety regs, by the way. Don't let me catch you doing it again."

Matt drew smoke into his lungs. It was unexpectedly strong; not harsh at all, but still more robust than the processed and preserved commercial stuff to which he was more accustomed. He felt the buzz as soon as he let it out. Nice. "It was her idea."

"I'm not going to bust your balls over it. So how did you like it? The launch, I mean."

"It was . . ." Matt struggled for the right words. "Awesome. Just . . . I dunno. I've never seen anything like it."

His father smiled, "Yeah. I've seen a lot of rockets go up, but I've never gotten used to it." He paused. "Y'know, you could have asked me anytime to take you to one of these things, back when I was still working for NASA. I could have arranged for you to get a visitors pass for a launch before they went bust."

It was an old story, Matt's lack of enthusiasm for that which his parents had devoted their lives. There was a brief period, when he was a child, when he had been fascinated by space. He'd even wanted to be an astronaut. But he'd left that behind along with his toy spaceships and astronomy coloring books. Now he was back where he'd started, and the last thing he wanted was to have his father pushing at him again.

"Guess I wasn't interested," he said.

"Hmm . . . no, I suppose you weren't." Ben took another hit from the joint and was quiet for a moment, as if contemplating the years gone by. "Maybe I made a mistake, trying to get you involved with all this too soon. I've lately thought that . . . well, if you hadn't grown up with me and your mother constantly discussing this stuff over the dinner table, it might not have killed your interest. That and your grand-mother . . ."

"I'm not blaming her for anything." The joint was half-finished and he was enjoy-ing the high he already had; he shook his head when his father tried to pass it to him again, and reached for his beer instead. "Grandma's . . . y'know, Grandma. The foun-dation is her life. But you and Mom . . . I mean, with you two, this whole thing is like some kind of religion. The Church of *Galactique*. Praise the holy starship, hal-lelujah."

His father scowled at him. "Oh, c'mon . . . it's not that bad."

"Yes, it is," Matt insisted, "and you've had it for as long as I can remember. That's why I went away. I had to find something else to do with my life than follow this obsession of yours."

Despite himself, he found that he was getting angry. Maybe it was just a headful of marijuana and beer, but it seemed as if a lot of pent-up frustration was boiling out of him, whether he liked it or not. On impulse, he pushed himself off the lounger, nearly losing his balance as he stood up again on legs that suddenly felt numb. "Maybe I better take a walk," he mumbled. "Get some fresh air or something."

"Sure. Okay." His father was hurt by the abrupt rejection, but he didn't try to stop him. "Whatever you want. But Mattie . . . ?"

"Don't call me that. I'm not a kid anymore."

"I know . . . sorry." Ben shook his head. "Look, just a little advice, all right? You can knock this so-called obsession of mine all you want, but . . ."

He lowered his voice as he cast a meaningful look across the pool to where Chandi and her friends were still seated. "If you want to get anywhere with her, you're going to have to learn to appreciate the things she's interested in. And she joined our reli-gion a long time ago."

VI

Even if he didn't care to follow his father's advice, Matt had no choice in the matter. His mother found him in the dining room the following morning, nursing a hang-over with black coffee and an unappealing plate of scrambled eggs. The party was over, and so was any hope he might have still had of making this trip into a tropical vacation. It was time for him to go to work as her new assistant.

Before he'd left college to pursue a half-baked fantasy of becoming a movie ac-tor, Matt had been a journalism major. That hadn't worked out either, but he'd learned enough to know a little about what it took to work in a media relations de-partment. This was Jill Skinner's job at the Arkwright Foundation, and even before Matt had decided to come down to Ile Sombre, she'd been complaining about be-ing short-handed. So his arrival had been fortunate, for her at least. She now had someone to do scut-work for her, giving her a chance to take care of more important tasks.

Over the course of the next several days, Matt tagged along with his mother as she went from place to place in the Ile Sombre Space Launch Centre. A large part of her job involved keeping up with daily events and writing press releases about them for the news media; since she wanted him to start doing some of this for her, it was important that he learn the Galactique Project from top to bottom, beginning with the preparations leading up to the launch of *Nathan 3*, scheduled for six weeks from then.

It was more interesting than he thought it would be. *Nathan 3* was being checked out in a dust-free, temperature-controlled clean room in the Payload Integration Building next to the VAB. The clean room was the size of a basketball court, and everything in there was spotless and white, down to the one-piece isolation garments that made everyone wearing them look like surgeons. Matt couldn't go in there, but his mother showed him where to stand quietly in the observation gallery overlooking the floor.

From there, he could see *Nathan 3*. Resting within an elevated cradle, it was an enormous, tightly-wrapped cylinder made of tissue-thin carbon-mesh graphite, dark grey with the thin silver stripes of its lateral struts running along its sides, resembling a giant furled umbrella. *Galactique's* microwave sail had been built and tested in the same southern California facility that manufactured solar power satellites, but it served a completely different purpose. Once *Galactique* was completed in orbit and ready to launch, the sail would gradually unfold to its operational diameter of a little more than 62 miles. It seemed unbelievable that something so big could be reduced to a payload only 120 feet long and 22 feet wide, but the sail material had a density of only the tiniest fraction of an inch. Still, it would take all of the Kubera's thrust to successfully get it off the ground.

Three days after it carried *Nathan 2* into space, the cargo rocket returned to Earth. On Jill's insistence, Matt accompanied the recovery team when they set forth on an old freighter to the spot where the rocket splashed down in the Caribbean about a hundred miles east of Ile Sombre. There they found the Kubera floating upright on its inflated landing bags, looking very much like a giant fishing bob. He watched as divers in wet suits swam out to drag tow cables to the booster; once that was done, the ship slowly hauled the Kubera back to the island, where the freighter docked at Ste. Geneviève's commercial port. Over the next several days, the rocket would be lifted out of the water by derrick cranes, loaded onto a tandem tractor-trailer, and driven back to the space center, where it would be refit for the *Nathan 3* mission.

Meanwhile, preparations for *Nathan 4* were underway. In another white room, *Galactique's* incubation module was being checked out for its primary purpose, carrying cryogenically-preserved sperm and egg specimens from two hundred human donors to the ship's ultimate destination, the distant planet still officially known only as Gliese 667C-e.

Galactique's final module, *Nathan 5*, was still being assembled in northern California. It contained two major segments: the 90-foot landing craft that would transport the newborn infants to the planet surface, where they would be raised by what were affectionately being called "nannybots" until they were old enough to fend for themselves, and the biopods that would precede them, complex machines capable of transforming Gliese 667C-e into a human-habitable world. Next to the vessel itself, this was probably the most challenging aspect of the project, one which was pushing human technology to its farthest limits.

When Matt's parents had explained the foundation's plan many years ago, he'd had a hard time understanding it. Why send sperm and eggs when, with a bigger ship, you could send living people instead? But he was thinking in terms of the science fiction movies he'd seen as a kid, where huge starships carrying thousands of passengers easily leaped between the stars with the help of miraculous faster-than-light drives. Reality was another matter entirely. FTL drives didn't exist, nor would they ever. Furthermore, the larger the ship was, the more energy would be required for it to achieve even a fraction of light-speed. If its passengers were to remain alive and conscious during the entire flight, such a vessel would have to be several miles long, a generation ship capable of sustaining these passengers and their descendents for a century or more. So even if a ship that large were built—such as from a hollowed-out asteroid, one early proposal—the amount of fuel it would have to carry would comprise at least half of its mass. It would be like trying to move a mountain by providing it with another mountain of fuel.

Making the issue even more complicated was the fact that no one knew how to build a closed-loop life support system that could keep people alive for such long periods of time. The sheer amount of consumables they'd need—air, water, and food—was daunting, and could not be produced or recycled, without fail, for decades or even centuries on end. Nor had anyone successfully come up with a means of putting people into hibernation and reviving them again many years later. Perhaps one day, but now . . . ?

The solution to all this was obvious: remove people from the ship entirely, and instead build a smaller, lighter vessel which could carry human reproductive material to the new world, where it would be gestated and brought to term within the extrauterine fetal incubators. This process was better understood and more feasible, and therefore made it more likely that a starship could be built if it didn't have to devote so much of its mass to keeping its passengers alive. And since *Galactique* wouldn't have its own engines, but instead rely on the microwave beamsat in Lagrange orbit to boost the ship to .5c cruise velocity, it would be able to make the voyage to Gliese 667C-e in a little less than half a century.

Even so, there was nothing simple about *Galactique's* EFI module. Just as large as *Nathan* 2 and 3, the heavily-shielded cylinder was an AI-controlled, robotically-serviced laboratory. From the observation gallery, Matt watched as clean-suited technicians worked on the module through its open service ports; there was only a small crawlspace running down its central core, and that had been provided more for the spidery robots which would maintain the ship than for the humans who'd built it.

Matt liked visiting this place, and often stole time from writing press releases or making travel arrangements for visiting journalists to view *Nathan* 3 being prepared for its journey. But it wasn't just his growing interest in *Galactique* that brought him to the gallery. It was also being able to watch Chandi at work. Her outfit should have made her indistinguishable from the rest of her group, but nonetheless he could always tell who she was; she just seemed to move just a little differently from her colleagues. And although she acknowledged his presence only once with a brief wave, even that small gesture was enough.

They'd see each other in the evenings, after dinner when the launch team would get together on the patio for drinks and perhaps a joint or two. By then, Matt had become better acquainted with some of the other people working on the project.

They'd come to accept him as a non-scientist who had his own role to play, and he made an effort to keep his skepticism to himself in order to assure their friendship.

Yet one evening, something slipped out of his mouth that he hadn't meant to say. And that got him in trouble with Chandi.

Matt was sitting at a poolside table with her and a couple of other team members: Graham Royce and his husband Rich Collins, both of them British space engineers who specialized in beam propulsion systems. The three men were sharing an after-dinner joint—Chandi didn't smoke, but politely tolerated those who did—and watching the crescent moon come up over the palms. By then, *Nathan* 3 was on the launch pad, with countdown scheduled to commence in just four days. The Brits were relaxed, knowing that their job was done for a little while; they wouldn't have to go back to work again until *Nathan* 3 was docked with *Nathan* 2 and the orbital assembly would attach the sail's rigging to the service module.

"You're hoping on a lot, aren't you?" Matt asked, passing the joint to Rich. "I mean, the way I understand it, the beamsat has to fire constantly for . . . what is it, two and a half years?"

"Pretty much, yes," Rich said.

"Nine hundred and twenty days." Graham was the older of the two—although with retrotherapy, it was hard to guess his true age—and had a tendency to be annoyingly precise.

"Whatever . . . so for two and half years, the sail has to catch a microwave sent from Earth even as it's moving farther and farther away. Meanwhile, the ship's moving faster and faster . . ."

"Acceleration rate is 1.9 meters per second, squared."

". . . until the ship is about half a light-year from Earth." Graham took a brief drag from the joint, gave it to his mate. "By then it'll be well out of the solar system and travelling half the speed of light, so we can turn off the beamsat and let the ship coast on its own. Any course adjustments will be accomplished by the onboard AI, using maneuvering thrusters. When it reaches Gliese 667C-e . . ."

"Eos." Chandi smiled. "I think everyone's pretty much settled on that name."

"Until the International Astronomical Union approves," Graham said, "it's officially Gliese 667C-e."

Rich coughed out the hit he'd just taken. "You're . . . *hargh! hargh!* . . . such a prick, you know that?" Graham smirked and Rich went on. "So what's your question . . . or did I miss something?" His eyes narrowed in stoned confusion.

"Well," Matt said, "it's just that it seems like you're counting on everything going exactly the way you've planned. The beam not getting interrupted or missing the sail the entirely . . ."

"That's why the sail is so bloody big," Rich replied. "The beam spreads as it travels outward, so the sail has to be large enough to receive it."

"But if something punches through it, like a meteorite or . . ."

"Meteoroid," Graham said. "It's not a meteorite until it passes through Earth's atmosphere. The sail is large enough it can take a few punch-throughs without losing efficiency."

"The reason why the beamsat is being located in Lagrange orbit is to minimize the number of occasions the beam will be interrupted by Earth's sidereal orbit around the Sun." Rich handed the joint back to Matt. "Everything is being automatically controlled by synchronized computers aboard both the beamsat and *Galactique*, so there's little chance of the beam getting lost."

"But you're still putting everything on faith." The joint was little larger than a thumbnail by then, and Matt had to gently pluck it from Rich's fingers. "I mean, it's almost like religion for you guys."

No one said anything. Although it was a warm evening, it seemed as if the temperature had suddenly dropped a few degrees. "Is that what this seems like to you?" Chandi asked after a moment. "Religion?"

"Sometimes, yeah." Matt carefully put the joint to his lips, inhaled what was left of it. "I used to call it the Church of *Galactique* when my mom and dad were talking about it."

"Oh, bollocks." Graham shook his head in disgust. "No wonder they tossed you out of the house."

Matt glared at him. "I left on my own. They didn't . . ."

"There's a difference between religion and faith," Chandi said. "Religion means you've accepted a set of beliefs even if those beliefs would appear to be irrational to anyone who doesn't buy into them. Faith means you've chosen to accept something that you've given yourself the chance to question. It might still be something greater than you, or even God if you decide to go that way, but it's not irrational. So, yes, we're operating on faith . . . but it's faith in something we've done ourselves, not divine providence."

Matt was already regretting what he'd said. Especially since he'd spoken while under the influence of Ile Sombre marijuana. "But at some point, it's still something that's no longer under your control. Once *Galactique* gets away from here, by the time you hear about anything going wrong, there won't be much you can do about it." He grinned. "Doesn't make much difference if it's not God . . . you're still praying to a machine, right?"

"Oh, Holy *Galactique*, please render thy blessings . . ." Rich began, then shut up when he caught Chandi scowling at him. "Sorry."

"That's why we're working so hard to make sure everything aboard checks out while we've got a chance to lay our hands on it." Chandi was no longer looking at Rich; her dark eyes were angry as they fastened on Matt. "And that's not just a machine I'm working on. It's a vessel carrying what will one day be a human colony . . . my descendents included."

"Yours?"

"Yes. Mine." Chandi continued to stare at him. "I've donated my eggs, too. So far as I'm concerned, I'm sending my children to Eos. So I'm doing everything I can to make sure they arrive safely, and I'm placing faith in my efforts and everyone else's that they will. So, no, this isn't religion to me . . . and I'll thank you to keep your bullshit analysis to yourself."

An uncomfortable silence. Rich broke it by clearing his throat again. "I could use some ice cream. Anyone care to . . . ?"

"Love to." Chandi stood up from her chair, crooked her elbow so that he could take it. "Lead the way."

Matt watched as Rich gallantly escorted her across the patio, heading for the dining room where desserts were customarily laid out at the end of the meal. He might have been jealous if he didn't know Rich was gay, but nonetheless he disliked seeing her being taken away by another man.

"You rather stepped in it there, didn't you?" Graham idly folded his hands behind his head and leaned back in his chair. "Word to the wise, lad . . . never accuse a scientist of practicing religion with his or her work."

"I'll make it up to her."

"Sure you will. May I suggest how?"

"I'll apologize. Maybe some roses, too."

"Apologies would be proper, yes, although I doubt you'll find a florist in Ste. Genevieve. Besides, I was thinking of something a bit more . . . um, symbolic, shall we say?"

"Such as?"

Graham smiled. "Donate a sperm sample."

Matt stared at him. "You gotta be kidding. Do you know what that sounds like?"

"I know what it would sound like if it was anyone else but her. In Chandi's case, though, it would mean that you're willing to believe in the same things she does . . . that you'll take the same leap of faith she has."

"That's too weird for . . ."

"Just an idea." Graham shrugged. "Think it over."

VII

Graham's suggestion was strange, and Matt might have disregarded it as the sort of thing someone might have said while buzzed. Yet he remembered it the next morning, and the more he thought about it, the more sense it made. There was a poetic sort of appeal to the idea of donating sperm to the mission; as Graham said, it would mean that Matt had come around to Chandi's way of thinking to the point that he was willing to send his genetic material on the same journey. Together with an apology, it might go far to heal the wound he'd made.

Yet when he went to his father and told him what he wanted to do, Ben turned him down. "Sorry, son," he said, "but your seat's already taken . . . by your grandparents."

"What?"

Ben Skinner stood up from his desk and walked over to the coffee maker. "Grandpa and Grandma were two of the very first people to donate sperm and egg specimens to the mission, way back when the Arkwright Foundation was getting started. In fact, I think they did it right after they got engaged. You know the story about the Legion of Tomorrow, don't you?"

"That's the club my great-great-grandfather belonged to, isn't it? The one with all the science fiction writers?"

"Umm . . . sort of." His father poured another cup of coffee for himself, then held up the carafe and raised an eyebrow, silently asking Matt if he'd like coffee, too. Matt shook his head and he went on. "There were only four people in the Legion, and just two of them were writers, both of them your great-great-grandfathers. We named you after Grandpa Harry's pseudonym, in fact."

"I know, but what does this have to do with . . . ?"

"Because your grandfather and your grandmother both made donations, their genomes are already represented in *Galactique*'s gene pool. They're carrying the seed, so to speak, for three members of the Legion . . . Nathan Arkwright, Margaret Krough, and Harry Skinner. If any of their descendents were to also donate egg or sperm specimens, this would introduce an element of uncertainty to the colony. What if your descendents met and fell in love with your grandmother's descendent, and they decided to have kids?"

"I don't see how that would . . . oh. You're talking about inbreeding."

"Right. They wouldn't even know it, but they'd be effectively marrying within the family . . . and that would cause all sorts of problems in a small founding population." His father walked over to a bookcase, pulled out a thick binder, and held it up. "This is our record of everyone who've made donations. We've spent many, many hours making sure no one who did is directly related to anyone else. Your mother was allowed to make a donation because she doesn't belong to our bloodline, but I wasn't, as much as I'd love to. So I'm afraid you're out of luck."

"Oh, well . . . it was just a thought." Matt tried to hide his disappointment with a shrug.

"Nice to see that you've taken an interest in this, though." Ben returned the notebook to the bookcase. "May I ask why?"

Matt was reluctant to explain his reasons. He was afraid his father would have found them childish. "Never mind. Just something I thought I'd like to do."

"Yes, well . . ." His father sighed as he went back to his desk. "Believe me, I wish I could help you, but the EFI system is going to be dicey enough as it is. I'm a little afraid of how things are going to work out once *Galactique* reaches Eos and it gets a closer look at the lay of the land. The genetic alterations that may have to be made . . ."

His voice trailed off, but not before Matt's curiosity was raised. "What sort of alterations?"

Ben said nothing for a moment. Standing behind his desk, he turned to gaze at the launch pad. "It's not something we're really talking about in public—we've had enough trouble with the fundamentalists already—but it's possible that the specimens may have to be genetically altered in the pre-embryonic stage to suit the planetary environment. Gliese 667C-e is a M-class red dwarf, smaller and cooler than our sun, while Eos itself is about one-third larger than Earth, with an estimated surface gravity about half again higher. We know that it probably has a carbon dioxide atmosphere with traces of water vapor, but even after *Galactique* drops the biopods and the place becomes habitable, in all likelihood any humans we put there will have to be changed in some very basic ways in order to survive."

"What sort of ways?"

"The AI will make that determination once it surveys the planet. We've supplied it with the necessary parameters and given it some options which we believe are suitable, but . . ." His father paused. "Well, what comes out of the EFI cells will be probably different from what most people normally think of as human beings."

Matt felt a chill. He tried to imagine the sort of people his father described, but could only come up with a race of deformed children, shambling and monstrous. "I can't believe you're doing this. Remaking humans, I mean."

"Really?" His father turned to give him an inquisitive look. "What do you think you'd see if you went back in time . . . say, four million years . . . and met your earliest ancestors, the australopithecines who were living in northern Africa? They didn't look very much like us, either. And they'd probably by shocked by us, too. But evolution changed them. They adapted to their environment. That's much what we'd be doing here . . . just a lot faster, that's all."

Matt didn't know what to say to this. He was still searching for a reply when his father sat down again. "I'm sorry, but I've got a lot of work ahead of me. Like I said, thanks for the offer, but . . ."

"Sure, okay. No problem." Suddenly, Matt wondered if it had been such a great idea after all.

VIII

As it turned out, his notion didn't make much difference anyway. The next time Matt saw her, Chandi had apparently forgotten all about their quarrel. Either that, or she'd simply decided to put it behind her. In any case, she was friendly toward him again, as if nothing had ever happened. He decided that it wasn't worth mentioning to her that he'd tried to donate sperm to the mission, and so nothing was ever said again about the disagreement they'd had.

Nathan 3 lifted off on schedule, a flawless launch that carried the Kubera and its payload away from Ile Sombre and into the black and airless ocean that *Galactique* would soon sail. This time, Matt watched the lift-off from inside the dome; he sat with his mother and the journalists they were hosting, but when the rocket cleared the tower and rose into the deep blue sky, he looked over to where Chandi was seated. Their eyes met and she smiled as if she, too, were remembering the previous launch and the moment they'd shared. He realized then how much he missed sitting with her.

He saw her again at the post-launch party that night, and this time he was able to keep up with the poolside conversation among the launch team members. Matt decided not to smoke pot at the party—after all, it was marijuana that had caused so much trouble last time—and he nursed the one beer he had, and she seemed to appreciate that because she remained at his side most of the evening. In the warmth of a moonlit tropical night, she couldn't have looked lovelier. Matt was sorely tempted to whisper in her ear and ask if she'd like to come back to his room with him, but held back. He didn't want to risk offending her again . . . and deep inside, he'd come to realize that he wanted more from her than just a one-night stand.

More journalists had travelled to Ile Sombre for the *Nathan 3* launch. Now that *Galactique* wasn't just a single module in geosynchronous orbit, the press was paying more attention to the project. The half-finished vessel was large enough to become a naked-eye object in the night sky, and Jill asked Matt to send a press release to news media, telling them how to inform the public where and how to look for it.

Before long, even those who'd paid little attention to the project became aware that a starship was being built above Earth, and suddenly *Galactique* became an object of interest to even those who didn't care much about space.

Not all the attention was welcome. Until then, the protesters from the New American Congregation who'd camped outside the Ile Sombre Space Launch Center had numbered no more than a half-dozen or so. But when he came to work in the morning, Matt began noticing more tents, more signs, more people. He didn't know if they all belonged to the church or if some were opposed to the project for other reasons, yet technicians flying in from the states reported meeting protesters at the airport, and the ongoing demonstration outside the space center became increasingly aggressive, with angry shouts greeting launch team members as they approached the front gate. The foundation hired more security guards, but when some of the protesters began showing up at the Hotel Au Soliel to harass team members when they came home from work, private cops had to be posted there as well.

And that wasn't all.

The day *Nathan 4* was finally transferred from the clean room to the VAB to be loaded aboard the Kubera, its checkout team decided to throw a little celebration of their own. It was noticed that they didn't have enough marijuana for a proper party, though, so someone would have to go into Ste. Genevieve to acquire some local herb. Matt was tapped for the job, and he didn't mind; it wouldn't be the first time he'd bought weed, and he'd been told the name of an islander who regularly sold cannabis to project members and where he could be found. He borrowed his mother's Volksun and drove into town, but before he left, he asked Chandi if she'd like to come along.

His father had once suggested that he bring her because she wasn't a white male American, and therefore might be able to get a better deal from the locals, but that wasn't the reason. He wanted to do something with her that would take them away from the project and its people, if only for a little while. It wasn't exactly a date, but at least it was better than sitting around the pool again. To his surprise, Chandi agreed. She was a little tired of seeing little else but the clean room and the hotel, and like Matt, she'd never been to Ste. Genevieve. So they left just after dinner, and as the sun was going down they parked the Volksun at the municipal wharf and walked onto the floating pier leading to the *flotante*.

The inhabitants of Ste. Genevieve had saved their homes from destruction by rebuilding them atop a collection of rafts, barges, and pontoon boats anchored above the flooded remains of the original town. Narrow boardwalks kept afloat by barrels connected shanties and shacks, which in turn were tied together by submerged cables. In some instances, the upper floors of preexistent brick buildings were still being used, their rooftops supporting a forest of solar collectors, satellite dishes, and freshwater tanks that collected rain and distilled it. The walkways were illuminated by strings of fiberoptic Christmas lights strung across tar-painted poles, and rowboats, canoes, and kayaks were tied up in slips between buildings. Smoke rose from tin ducts that served as chimneys; the salt air held the mixed aromas of burning driftwood and fried fish.

Matt and Chandi made their way through the *flotante*, trying to locate the bar where the weed dealer was said to hang out. Hand-painted signs nailed to shanty walls showed them where Ste. Genevieve's original streets had once been located;

Matt had been told to look for a place called Sharky's, located on what was still called Rue Majuer. Islanders sitting in old lawn chairs silently watched them; their expressions hinted at amusement, suspicion, or curiosity, but no one said anything. Foreigners from the space center didn't come to town very often, and while the locals didn't have anything against them, they didn't necessarily have anything *for* them either.

Sharky's turned out to be the rusted shell of a double-wide trailer that had been relocated to a barge, with a wraparound porch outside and a screen door leading inside. A few island men were seated on the porch; they quietly observed the Americans as they stepped onto the barge, and it was clear that they appreciated seeing Chandi. She did her best to ignore their stares, but Matt wasn't surprised when she took his hand.

The barroom was small and dimly lit with shaded florescent bulbs and cheap beer signs. Incredibly, there was a state-of-the-art holoscreen on the wall; it was showing a soccer match, the volume turned down low. Everything else was run-down, with the same particle-board tables and plastic chairs as the outside deck. The bar was little more than wood planks laid across a couple of oil barrels; the bartender impassively watched the visitors as they approached the bar, saying nothing as he continued to wipe clean a chipped beer mug.

"Hi. I'm looking for someone named Parker . . . is he here?"

"Lots of folks named Parker." The bartender wasn't giving him anything. "You have a first name?"

"James Parker."

An indifferent shrug. "I know someone named James Parker. What do you want with him?"

"We understand he sells something we'd like to have."

The bartender finished cleaning the mug, then put it down and fished another one from the tub beneath the bar. "He'll be here soon. Have a seat, mon. Would you like a beer?"

"Yes, thanks. Red Stripe."

The bartender turned to a cooler and pulled out two bottles of beer. There were no stools, and Matt was beginning to look around for a place for him and Chandi to sit when a voice behind them said, "Care to join me?"

Another man was in the bar, sitting at a table in the corner near the door. Surprisingly, he was the first white person they'd seen since entering Ste. Genevieve. Middle-aged and thick-set, with iron-grey hair and handlebar mustache, he had on the kind of outfit only a tourist would wear: khaki hiking shorts, a photographer's vest over a long-sleeve safari shirt, a bush hat and waterproof boots. Like he was expecting to spend time in the jungle, hacking his way through the rain forest with a machete.

There was something about him that Matt immediately distrusted. He didn't know why, except perhaps that this character was even more out of place than he and Chandi. There was no polite way to refuse, though, so he led Chandi over to the table.

As they sat down, Matt noted a couple of empty Dos Equis bottles on the table, along with the one the stranger was currently drinking. Obviously he'd been there for a while. "Frank Barton," the stranger said as they sat down. "And you are . . . ?"

"I'm Matt, she's Chandi." Matt shook hands with him. "Down for some sight-seeing?"

"Something like that." Barton picked up his beer. "I've come to see where all the action is. You folks work at the space center?"

"We're with the project, yes," Chandi said.

"I see." Barton took a long slug from his beer, wiped his mustache with a finger as he put it down again. "So what is it you two do there?"

"I'm an engineer. He's a consultant." Apparently Chandi was suspicious as well. Glancing at her, Matt saw the wary expression on her face.

"I see, I see." Barton slowly nodded. "I've heard you people sometimes come into town. I sorta figured if I sat here long enough, I'd eventually meet one of you." He smiled. "Guess I'm lucky . . . here's two."

Matt didn't like the way he said this. Now he noticed something else; half-hidden within the open collar of his shirt was a silver chain holding a gold crucifix. It might mean nothing—he knew plenty of people who had crosses just like it—but it might also portend trouble.

"Why is that lucky?" he asked. "You want to know something about the project?"

"I already know all there is." Barton leaned back in his chair. "You, on the other hand, are in need of enlightenment, for the sake of your souls."

That settled it. Frank Barton belonged to the New American Congregation, and he'd staked out Sharky's in hopes of cornering someone from the project. Matt's father had warned him against engaging the church's "missionaries" and now he knew why.

Matt started to push back his chair. "Well, it's been nice to meet you, but . . ."

"What does my soul have to do with this?" Chandi made no move to get up. She leaned closer, resting her elbows on the table and propping her chin on clasped hands. "Please, *enlighten* me."

"Isn't it obvious?" Barton fixed her with an unblinking stare. "What you're doing is blasphemous. Sending forth the human seed into God's creation, there to foist our sins upon other worlds. We were never meant to . . ."

"Really? Where in the Bible does it say that?" She smiled. "I've been to church, too, and I don't remember ever hearing space exploration was inherently sinful."

Barton's eyes narrowed. "God clearly intended Man to live on Earth and Earth alone. He created this world for his chosen, and the other worlds were to be left alone."

"Again, where does it say that?" She looked over at Matt. "I must have missed something in Sunday school, because that's an interpretation I've never . . ."

"There are many interpretations of the Gospel." Barton clearly didn't enjoy being challenged. "For you to rip children from their mother's wombs and put them aboard rockets . . ."

"Oh, c'mon . . . do you *really* think that's what we're doing?" Chandi was grinning by then; she was toying with him, and relishing every second. "Hate to say it, but you're the one who needs enlightenment. You've got everything wrong and don't even know it."

"So you're aware of the word of God and still you commit a mortal sin!" Even in the bad light of the bar, Matt could see that Barton's face was becoming red. His anger was growing in proportion with Chandi's amusement. "I thought I could save you, but I see now that you're beyond redemption."

Matt closed his eyes. Barton was a familiar type: more than just a zealot, he was a cranky, middle-aged man who'd long since decided that he was right about all things and couldn't tolerate any difference of opinion. There was no point in arguing with someone like this, but Chandi wasn't giving up. She was enjoying herself too much.

"Yup. Sinner and proud of it." Chandi picked up her beer. "Better that than an old fart who thinks he speaks for God." She started to take a sip. "Jesus would've laughed his ass off if he'd ever met you . . ."

"How dare you take His name in vain?" Barton leaped up from his chair. Before Matt could stop him, he reached across the table to slap the bottle from Chandi's hand. "Miserable whore, you have no right to . . . !"

It had been many years since the last time Matt punched someone, and the last time he'd been in a bar fight he'd been ashamed of himself later for doing so. But not this time. There was something very satisfying about slamming his fist into Barton's hillbilly mustache, and it was even more gratifying when Barton fell back over his chair, hit the wall behind him, and sagged to the floor.

Chandi was still regarding Matt with wide-eyed shock when the bartender came out from behind the bar. "Out!" he yelled, half-raising the cricket bat that had materialized from somewhere. "No fights in my place! Leave before I call the police!"

"Hey, look, he . . ."

"Let's go." Chandi took Matt's arm, pulled him away from the table. "You've done enough."

Matt looked down at Barton. He was still conscious, but stunned enough that he wasn't going to get up for another minute or so. When he did, though, things would probably get worse than they already were. And Matt didn't want to have to deal with the island police as well as an angry bartender. It wouldn't be easy explaining why two Americans from the space center were in a dive like Sharky's.

He pulled a couple of dollars from his pocket and dropped them on the table by way of apology, then let Chandi lead him from the bar. The islanders sitting out on the deck must have heard the fight, for they were standing just outside the door, silently watching him and Chandi as they came out. Among them was a tall, skinny fellow with dreadlocks who appeared as if he'd been just about to come in; Matt wondered if this was James Parker, but decided not to stop and ask. There wasn't going to be a chance to buy weed tonight, that was for sure.

Neither he nor Chandi said anything to each other as they walked back through Ste. Genevieve. Matt's hand had begun to throb, and when he flexed his fingers he discovered that he'd jammed his middle knuckle. He still had to drive, though, because the Volksun was keyprinted to his touch. He'd also need to find some aspirin and maybe a bandage once they returned to the hotel.

The ride back was largely in silence. Matt tried to make a couple of jokes about what had happened, but they fell flat. From the corner of his eye, he could see Chandi quietly studying him; she said little, but her gaze never left his face. In the pale light from the dashboard, though, it was hard to tell her expression.

He parked near his parents' cottage. When he and Chandi climbed out, they could hear party sounds coming from the pool, just out of sight from behind the trees. "They're not going to like it when I tell 'em I didn't get any weed," Matt murmured as he started to head for the flagstone path leading to the patio.

Chandi lay a hand upon his arm, stopping him. "We're not going to the party," she said quietly.

"We're not?"

"No. We're going to my room."

And then she pulled him close for a long, lingering kiss.

IX

It didn't go unnoticed that Matt and Chandi failed to show up at the party. Every eye turned in their direction when they came down for breakfast together the following morning, and quite a few knowing smiles were cast in their direction. Although Graham gave him a salacious sink, no one said anything; it was as if everyone had been quietly waiting for the two of them to pair up, with the only surprise being that it hadn't happened earlier.

Nor was it the one-nighter Matt had feared it might be. Chandi slept with him again the next night, this time in his room. She had a queen-size bed, though, and the cabanas were visible from the patio, so after that they agreed her place was more comfortable and offered a little more privacy. He returned to his room each morning to shower, change clothes, and brush his teeth, but after awhile they decided that he might just as well move in with her. Which was fine with him; he never liked the cabana anyway.

Their relationship was gloriously erotic, but it wasn't just the fun they had in bed which kept them together. It had been many years since the last time either of them had been in love. Like Matt, Chandi had her share of failed relationships; she told him that she'd once been engaged, but had broken up with her fiancé when she'd discovered that he was secretly having an affair with another woman. And until she met Matt, she'd never had anyone willing to stand up for her. Matt was relieved; his last girlfriend would have been disgusted if she'd seen him get in a bar fight, even if it had been to defend her.

They were ready for each other. Their meeting on the flight to Ile Sombre may have been a happy accident, but Matt's parents seemed to believe that Chandi was just the sort of person their son needed to have in his life. Matt was nervous when he reluctantly accepted their invitation to bring Chandi over for dinner—to be sure, they hadn't liked his previous girlfriends—yet it turned out for the better. His mother enjoyed meeting her, and while his father already had respect for her intelligence, he was apparently surprised to find that she was charming as well. Matt hadn't been necessarily seeking their approval, but nonetheless he came away from the dinner pleased that they thought well of her.

As it turned out, it was fortunate that he and Chandi hadn't waited any longer to begin a romance. *Nathan 4* went up a couple of weeks later, a perfect lift-off followed by a problem-free rendezvous and docking with *Galactique*. When this occurred, Chandi's role in the project came to an official end. There was no practical reason for her to remain on Ile Sombre; her contract with the Arkwright Foundation was fulfilled, and she was free to go. Yet she wanted to stay on the island until *Galactique* was completed and launched, and now that she and Matt were living together, his room could be taken over by one of the *Nathan 5* technicians scheduled to arrive soon. So Ben Skinner found enough money in the budget to allow her to stay on the payroll as a part-time consultant, and that problem was fixed.

It wasn't until then that Matt realized that he, too, could leave any time he wanted. He'd saved up enough money not only to buy a plane ticket back to the states, but also to pay the rent while he searched for a new job. But he no longer wished to leave . . . and when he thought about it, he came to the conclusion that it wasn't simply because of Chandi. Over the past months, he'd developed an interest in *Galactique* and the Arkwright Foundation that hadn't been there before. Although he was still skeptical about the mission's chances for success, his cynicism had disappeared; Chandi's enthusiasm had rubbed off on him. He found that he, too, wished to remain on Ile Sombre to witness the beginning of *Galactique's* long voyage to Gliese 667C-e.

But after that? He and Chandi still had to figure out if and how they'd have a future together. This worried him . . . but it was far from the largest concern anyone had.

Until then, the schedule had proceeded smoothly. Each of *Galactique's* modules had been launched and docked without any major problems, but their luck couldn't last. When the time came for *Nathan 5* to be launched, the project's good fortune ran out.

Construction work on *Nathan 5* had already been running behind schedule. Ground tests of the landing craft's main engine had revealed flaws serious enough for subcontractors in California to dismantle the engine and replace several critical components, which in turn necessitated another series of tests before they were satisfied than the craft was flightworthy. Because of this, loading of *Nathan 5* aboard the freighter which would carry it down the Pacific coast to the Panama Canal and through the Gulf of Mexico was pushed back by more than a month . . . and this delay caused concerns of its own.

Galactique's launch schedule had been carefully timed to occur before the beginning of the Caribbean's annual hurricane season. The drawback of using the Ile Sombre Space Launch Center was the fact that it lay within a tropical zone prone to major storms. Indeed, quite a few PanAmSpace launches had been postponed because of hurricanes that had suddenly developed in the South Atlantic. The mission planners were aware of this when they'd devised the launch schedule; they'd hoped that, if all went well, the last module would be sent into orbit before the weather interfered.

Now that the final launch was being postponed to late summer, though, there was an increasing risk of it being disrupted by a hurricane. Meteorologists had already noticed indications that just such an event may occur; the waters of the South Atlantic were warmer than usual, and several large tropical storms had already blown through the Lesser Antilles. The Kubera could be kept within the Vehicle Assembly Building until the weather was calm enough for a launch; what everyone dreaded was *Nathan 5* being at sea when the freighter carrying it was caught by a hurricane.

The loss of the module carrying the biopods and landing craft would be a major setback; it would take years for replacements to be built, during which time *Galactique* would have be mothballed in orbit . . . both of which would be very expensive.

Ben Skinner met with the other mission planners, and over the course of a six-hour boardroom session they came up with a solution. Instead of putting *Nathan 5* aboard an ocean vessel, the foundation would rent a cargo jet to fly it down to Ile Sombre. There was just such an aircraft suitable for this purpose: the C-110 Goliath, built by Boeing as a heavy-lift military transport. Its cargo bay was 130 feet by 40 feet, more than big enough for the module . . . and as it turned out, Boeing maintained two Goliaths in Seattle for private lease.

There was only one problem with this. Until then, the previous modules had been brought to Ile Sombre aboard ships, where they could be offloaded at the same port where the Kubera was retrieved. The port was protected by chain-link fences and armed guards, and lay close enough to the space center that security had never been a problem. But if *Nathan 5* was flown in, the plane would have to land at the island airport, where the module would be offloaded onto the tractor-trailer rig used for transporting the Kubera and be driven across Ile Sombre . . . all on public roads, where it could be easily blocked by the protesters who were steadily gaining numbers outside the space center.

"And to make matters worse, the rig's going have to go slow," Ben said, sitting at the end of the table where he'd just had dinner with his family. "You know the roads around here . . . they haven't been resurfaced in years. They're like washboards. So the driver will have to take it easy to keep Nat from being damaged en route from the airport, and if the protesters know it's coming . . ."

"They will. It's already in the news that we're doing this." Jill didn't pause in clearing away the dinner plates. "But I don't think they're going to give us much trouble. They'll probably just stand on the side of the road and wave those idiot signs of theirs. They've never been violent before."

Hearing this, Matt looked across the table at Chandi. They'd started coming over for dinner once a week, but he still hadn't told them about what happened that night in Ste. Genevieve. They weren't aware that at least one member of the New American Congregation was capable of violence.

Chandi didn't say anything, but she shook her head ever so slightly when their eyes met. "It might be smart to take precautions anyway," Matt said. "Maybe get some of our people to walk alongside the truck to keep them away."

"Yeah, that could work." Ben slowly nodded. "Nice idea. I'll talk it over with the planning team." He picked up the bottle of merlot on the table and poured another drink. "Maybe your grandmother will have some other suggestions once she gets here."

"Grandma's coming down?"

"The week after next," Jill said. "I thought I told you." She smiled as she returned to the table. "In fact, I'm sure I did."

"Yeah. I just forgot." Matt shrugged. "I've been kinda busy . . ."

"Yes, you have." Ben's gaze shifted from him to Chandi, and Matt could have killed him for the sly grin on his face. "In fact, I think she wants to have a talk with you about what you're going to do once we close down operations here. Have you given any thought to that?"

Again, Matt traded a look with Chandi. This had been something they'd discussed more than once lately, usually as late-night pillowtalk. "A little."

"Yes, well . . . talk to Grandma when she gets here." Again, a coy smile. "I think she has a something in mind."

X

Grandma Kate had aged well for a woman in her eighties who'd never taken ret-rotherapy. Although she'd undergone the usual geriatric treatments available to the elderly, including cardiovascular nanosurgery and organ-clone transplants, genetic revitalization had come along too late for it to be effective for a woman of her years. Unlike her children, Kate Skinner looked her age, but nonetheless she managed to get around, albeit slowly and carefully.

Matt and his mother met Grandma when she arrived at the airport. She was the last person to come off the plane, and once she endured the indignity of being helped down the stairs by a flight attendant, she gratefully took a seat in the two-wheel mo-bil that had been carried in the G8's belly compartment. Once in the chair, though, she returned to her old self. The customs official who'd given Matt a hassle a few months earlier quailed before the old woman who wasn't about to let him waste her time by opening each of her suitcases, and even her daughter-in-law knew better than to keep her waiting long at the curb for the van she'd borrowed from the space center to take her to the hotel. Kate didn't suffer fools gladly.

To Matt's surprise, though, Grandma treated him with a little more tenderness. She insisted that he ride with her in the back of the van, and once she'd dispensed with the small talk, she turned her attention to her grandson.

"So . . . you took a job here after all." Not a question; a statement of fact.

"I didn't have much choice, Grandma. The plane ticket was one-way."

"I know . . . I bought it, didn't I?" A tight-lipped smile. "You didn't need a hand-out from me, kiddo. You needed a chance at a fresh start. Ben tells me you've done pretty well with it, too."

"He has, Kate." Jill turned her head slightly without taking her gaze from the road. "I couldn't have done without Matt. He's done everything from write news releases to manage press conferences to book flights for reporters. Everything you'd want from a good right-hand man."

Matt said nothing. His mother was exaggerating; his first few weeks in the media relations department had been a train wreck, and even now he was still committing the occasional gaffe. Yet if she wanted to give Grandma a good report, he wasn't about to argue.

"Are you enjoying the work?" Grandma asked.

"Yes, I am." About this, he didn't have to lie. "I've learned a lot, and I think I've got a better appreciation of what the project is all about."

"Do you really?" She seemed to study him. "You're not just saying that, are you?"

He decided not to reveal his remaining doubts about the feasibility of terraforming a planet and populating it with children raised by robots. "I think *Galactique* will get there," he replied, and hoped she'd be satisfied to let it go at that.

Apparently she was, because she only nodded and shifted her gaze to the rain forest they were driving through. Yet the conversation wasn't finished. She picked it up again once they'd arrived at the Hotel Au Soliel and she was taken to the cottage she'd be sharing with her children. Believing that he was no longer needed, Matt was about to leave, but then she raised a hand.

"Stick around a minute. I want to talk to you a little more." She looked at Jill. "You can go now. He'll catch up with you later."

His mother was a little surprised by this, but she didn't object. She left the cottage, closing the front door behind her. Grandma waited until she was gone, then she turned to Matt again. "So . . . thought about what you're going to do once we close up shop here?"

Matt remembered his father raising the same question over dinner a couple of weeks earlier. "I dunno. Do what everyone else is doing, I guess . . . go home and get another job. I might stay in media relations, turn that into a career . . ."

"Yeah, you could do that. Your job here will be a short item on your résumé, but I'm sure it'll help you land a position somewhere. Maybe you'll even keep it for awhile, if you don't get bored and quit. That's always been a problem for you, hasn't it?"

"Sort of."

"Sort of." She repeated what he'd said flatly, as if she had little doubt that he would. "Well, if you want to go back to drifting, that's your right. I won't stop you. But I can offer you something better."

She paused, waiting for him to say something. When he didn't, she went on. "Even after *Galactique* is on its way, the foundation's work won't be done. It's going to take almost fifty years for the ship to reach Eos, but it's not like we're just sticking a note in a bottle and tossing it into the sea. It'll regularly report back to us, telling us what's going on, and even though those reports will get further and further apart, we'll still have to listen for them, just in case something happens that we should know about."

"You want me to do that?"

"I'd like for you to join the tracking team, yes. The foundation is taking over an old university observatory in Massachusetts, out in the Berkshires not far from where your great-great-grandfather used to live. This is where the laser telemetry received by the lunar tracking station will be relayed. It's rather isolated, but we'll be keeping a small staff there, paying them from foundation funds to maintain contact with *Galactique*."

"I don't know anything about . . ."

"You can learn. Ben can teach you. In fact, he's probably going to be running the operation . . . didn't he tell you this already?" Matt shook his head and his grandmother sighed. "Oh, well . . . I guess he was expecting me to tell you about it. Anyway, he'll be in charge, but he's not going to be around forever. Sooner or later, someone will have to take over for him."

Grandma gave him a meaningful look. Matt said nothing, for he didn't know what to say. He'd been half-expecting her to offer him a job with the Arkwright Foundation, but a lifetime commitment was something else entirely. He didn't know if he was ready to spend years on a mountain out in the middle of nowhere, listening for signals transmitted from a spacecraft receding farther and farther into the interstellar distance.

"I don't know . . ." he began.

"You don't have to say yes or no right away." Grandma shook her head. "Just think about it awhile, all right? The job's there if you want it. We won't have any trouble finding someone else if you decide to give it a pass, but . . ." She smiled. "I'd like to keep it in the family, if you know what I mean."

He did. But he was unsure whether he wanted to become part of that legacy.

XI

Nathan 5 arrived the following week, flown in aboard a Boeing C-110 so large that an Air Carib G8 could have fit within its bulbous cargo hold. The enormous tiltjet, resembling a cucumber which had sprouted wings, touched down at Ile Sombre International with a roar that rivaled a Kubera launch. A large crowd of islanders had gathered at the airport to witness the landing of an aircraft that they'd probably never see in these parts again; they watched from the edge of the runway as the Goliath made its slow vertical descent, alongside the space center staffers who'd volunteered to shepherd its payload across the island.

Matt and Chandi were among them, as was Matt's father. The planning team had decided to take up Matt's suggestion, and recruited members of the launch team to walk alongside the truck which would carry the module from the airport to the space center. At first, many people thought it was an unnecessary precaution . . . but anyone who still believed this only had to look over their shoulders, where a mob of protesters from the New American Congregation and their supporters waited on the other side of sawhorses erected and patrolled by island police. As Matt's mother had predicted, the protesters had known all along that *Galactique's* landing module would be arriving by air instead of by sea, and they were taking advantage of this change of plan.

"Think we'll have any trouble from them?" Chandi eyed the protesters nervously.

"No doubt we will," Ben Skinner said quietly. "The question is, how much? If all they do is hold up their signs and yell, everything will be okay. But if they go further than that . . ." He nodded toward the private security force waiting nearby. Some carried sonics as well as the usual batons and tasers. "They'll break it up if things get bad. I'm not going to worry too much."

Matt watched as the Goliath's bow section, three stories tall, opened and swiveled upward beneath the cockpit, revealing the cargo bay. The module lay on a wheeled pallet, sealed within an airtight plastic shroud. The tractor-trailer rig was already backing up to the plane, waved into position by the runway crew. The flatbeds had been jacked up to same height as the cargo deck; once the tandem trailers were in place, the pallet could be rolled straight onto the truck from the plane. Once it was tied down and covered with tarps, the module would be ready to leave the airport.

That was the easy part. At a walking pace, it would take a little more than an hour for the truck to make the trip to the space center. If only the roads were better, but that couldn't be helped. Like most Caribbean islands, Ile Sombre's public roads weren't maintained very well; the truck had to move slowly, or else the module might rock about and be damaged. To make matters worse, the road between the airport and the space center narrowed until it barely qualified as a two-lane thoroughfare; islanders were known to reach through open driver-side windows and briefly shake hands with friends whom they passed.

The island police were closing the road to local traffic, but nonetheless it would be during this part of the passage that the truck and its previous cargo would be particularly vulnerable.

Matt hoped his father was right.

It was almost an hour before the truck was ready to depart from the airport. As the massive flatbeds slowly moved away from the plane, a pair of Land Rovers belonging to the island police took up position in front and behind the truck. They stopped and waited for the walking escorts to take their own positions on either side of the truck. Matt and Chandi found themselves near the front; he watched as his father climbed into the cab to observe the driver and make sure that he didn't go too fast. Private security guards were scattered among the walkers, carrying their sonics at hip level where they'd visible but not necessarily threatening. There was another long pause while everyone got ready, then there was a long blast from the truck's airhorn and the convoy began to creep forward.

The protesters were ready, too. They'd remained behind the sawhorses the entire time, more or less quiet while the module was being offloaded from the Goliath, but when the truck slowly rolled through the airport's freight entrance, they rushed to the roadside, placards above their heads, voices raised in fiery denunciation. Police and security guards did their best to hold them back, but the protesters were only a few yards from either side of the truck, and it was impossible for Matt to ignore either their shouts or their slogans.

"You'll burn in Hell for this!"

No SIN For The STARS!

"Repent! Destroy that thing!"

Don't Send BABYS to SPACE

"Blasphemy! You're committing blasphemy!"

Jesus HATES Sciance!

"Repent!"

Furious eyes. Shaking fists. Someone threw a rock. It missed the canvas-shrouded module and bounced off the side of the truck instead, but immediately a security guard raised his sonic and aimed it in the direction from which the rock had come. He didn't fire—the guards had been ordered not to do so unless absolutely necessary—but the protesters in that part of the crowd quickly backed away. No more rocks were thrown . . . yet.

Chandi was walking in front of Matt, and although her back was to him, he could see her face whenever she turned her eyes toward the crowd. She was doing her best to remain calm, but he could tell how angry she was. The walking escort had told them not to engage the protesters, but he could tell that her patience was being sorely them tempted. Chandi has little tolerance for the willfully stupid . . . and there, just a few feet away, were the very kind of people she detested the most.

He trotted forward to walk beside her. "Having fun yet?" he said, raising his voice to be heard.

Chandi's mouth ticked upward in a terse smile. "Loads. Hey, how come you can't take me on a normal date just once?"

"Do you like to dance?" he asked, and she nodded. "Okay, once we get back to the states, I'll take you to a place I know in Philly. You'll love it. Candlelight dinner, ballroom orchestra, just like . . ."

The truck horn blared, a prolonged *honnnk! honnnnnk!* that sounded like the driver pulling the cord as hard as he could. At first, Matt thought he was trying to get the protesters out of the way. Then a guard ran past them, and when he looked ahead, he saw what was happening.

A rust-dappled pick-up truck, the kind used on the nearby banana plantations, had pulled out from a side-road about fifty yards ahead of the convoy. As he watched, it turned to face the approaching tractor-trailer. It idled there for a few moments, grey smoke coming from a muffler that needed replacing—Ile Sombre was one of the last places in the western hemisphere where gasoline engines were still being used—while police and security guards strode toward it, shouting and waving their arms as they tried to get the driver to move his heap.

"The hell . . . ?" Matt said as the tractor-trailer's air brakes squealed as it came to a halt. Everyone stopped marching; even the protesters were confused. "Didn't this guy hear that the road's closed?"

Chandi said nothing, but instead walked to the front bumper of the halted tractor-trailer, shielding her eyes to peer at the pick-up. "I don't like it," she said as Matt jogged up beside her. "Looks like there's something in the back . . . see that?"

Matt raised his hand against the midday sun. Behind the raised wooden planks of the truck bed was something that didn't look like a load of bananas. Large, rounded . . . were those fuel drums? "I don't know, but it looks like . . ."

All at once, the pick-up truck lurched forward, its engine roaring as it charged straight down the road. The police Land Rover was between it and the tractor-trailer, but the driver was already swerving to his left to avoid it. Protesters screamed as they threw themselves out of the way; the police and security guards, caught by surprise, were slow to raise their weapons.

"Go!" Matt grabbed Chandi by the shoulders to yank her away from the tractor-trailer. The other escorts were scattering as well, but the two of them were right in the path of the pick-up truck, which nearly ran over a couple of protesters as it careened toward the flat-bed. "*Run!*"

Yet Chandi seemed frozen. She was staring at the truck even as it raced toward them, her mouth open in shock. Matt followed her gaze, and caught a glimpse of what startled her, the face of the driver behind the windshield: Frank Barton.

"Go, mon! *Get out of here!*" A security guard suddenly materialized behind them; he shoved Matt out of the way, then planted himself beside the tractor's bumper and raised the sonic in his hands. Other hollow booms accompanied his shots, but this was a time when old-style bullets would have been more effective; the truck's windshield fractured into snowflake patterns from the focused airbursts, but it still protected Barton.

"Chandi!" Matt had fallen to the unpaved roadside and lost his grasp on her. He fought to get back on his feet, but was knocked down again by a fleeing protester. "Chandi, get . . . !"

Then a well-aimed shot managed to shatter the windshield and cause Barton to loose control of the wheel. The truck veered to the right, sideswiped the Land Rover, tipped over on its side . . .

That was the last thing Matt remembered. The explosion took the rest.

XII

Matt later came to realize that he owed his life to the guard who'd pushed him out of the way. That alone kept him from being killed or injured when the gasoline bomb in the back of the stolen farm truck exploded. Matt had escaped the blast with little more than a concussion and a scalp laceration from the piece of flying debris, but the guard had lost his life, while Chandi . . .

In the days that followed, as Matt sat by her bedside in the Ile Sombre hospital where the blast survivors were taken, his mind replayed the awful moments after he'd regained consciousness. One of the first things he'd seen were two paramedics carrying away the stretcher upon which Chandi lay. His father had been kneeling beside him, holding a guaze bandage against his son's head until doctors could get around to tending to the less critically injured. He'd had to hold Matt down when he spotted Chandi, unconscious, face streaked with blood, hastily being loaded into an ambulance parked alongside the tractor-trailer.

Everyone said that she was lucky. Five people died that day: the security guard, three protesters, and Frank Barton himself. There were numerous injuries, though, and hers were among the worst. The force of blast had thrown her against the tractor's right front bumper, breaking the clavicle in her left shoulder and the humerus of her left arm, but also fracturing the back of her skull. She might have died were it not for the fact that there happened to be a doctor on the scene who was able to stabilize her until the ambulances arrived. It was no small irony that the doctor also happened to be one of the protesters, and he'd put aside his opposition to the project in order to care for the wounded.

The Ile Sombre hospital outside Ste. Genevieve was remarkably well equipped, staffed by American-trained doctors. Chandi underwent four hours of surgery, during which the doctors managed to relieve the pressure in her skull before it caused brain damage and repair the fracture with bone grafts. Yet she remained unconscious, locked in a coma which no one was certain would end.

Matt stayed with her. He left the hospital only once, to return to the hotel and change clothes, before coming straight back. He sat in a chair he'd pulled up beside her bed in the ICU, where he could hold her hand while nurses changed her dressings or checked on the feeding tube they'd put down her throat. Sometimes he'd sleep, and every once in a while he'd go to the commissary and make himself eat something, but the next five days were a long, endless vigil in which he watched for the first indication that Chandraleska Sanyal was coming back to him.

So he was only vaguely aware that the landing module had been unscratched by the explosion, or that once it arrived at the space center, clean-room technicians had worked day and night to make sure it was ready to be sent to the VAB and loaded aboard the waiting Kubera. Although the New American Congregation had formally condemned the attack, no one at the project was willing to bet that there wasn't another fanatic willing to try again. Matt's father and grandmother determined that the safest place for *Nathan 5* was in space; the sooner it got there, the better. The launch date was moved up by a week, and everyone at the space center did their best to meet the new deadline.

The day *Nathan 5* was rolled out to the pad, Chandi finally woke up. The first thing she saw when she opened her eyes was Matt's face. She couldn't speak because of the plastic tube in her throat, but in the brief time before she fell asleep again she acknowledged his presence by squeezing his hand. Then the doctor who'd responded to his call bell asked him to leave, and he went to a nearby waiting room, fell into a chair, and caught the first decent sleep he'd had in almost a week.

Nathan 5 lifted off three days later. They watched the launch together, on the TV in the recovery room where Chandi had been taken. It was still hard for her to talk, and the doctors had told him that it would take time for her to make a full recovery; Matt had to listen closely when she spoke. Nonetheless, when the Kubera cleared the tower and roared up into the cloudless blue sky, she whispered something that he had no trouble understanding.

"Knew it . . . it would go up," she murmured.

Matt nodded. He knew what he should say. He was just having trouble saying it.

XIII

A week later, *Galactique* left Earth orbit.

By then, *Nathan 5* was attached to the rest of the ship, and *Galactique* had become a cylinder 430 feet long, its silver hull reflecting the sunlight as it coasted in high orbit above the world. Its image was caught by cameras aboard the nearby construction station and relayed to Mission Control, where everyone involved with the project had gathered for their final glimpse of the vessel they'd worked so long to create.

Although the gallery was packed, with all seats taken and people standing against the walls, this wasn't where Matt and Chandi were. At Ben's insistence, Matt had pushed her wheelchair to the control room itself, where he parked it behind his father's station. His mother was there, and Grandma as well. Seated in her mobil, Kate Morressy Skinner regarded the young woman whose shaved head was still swaddled in bandages with a certain reverence Matt had never seen before. At one point, she took Chandi's hands in her own and whispered something that Matt couldn't hear, but which brought a shaky smile to Chandi's face.

The final countdown was subdued, almost anticlimactic. Although the mission controllers were at their stations, most of them had their hands in their laps. *Galactique*'s AI system was in complete autonomous control of the ship; the ground team was there only to watch and be ready to step in if something happened to go wrong.

At the count of zero, tiny sparks flared from the nozzles of the maneuvering thrusters along the service module. Slowly, the ship began to turn on its axis, rotating like a spindle. Then, all of a sudden, long, narrow panels along *Nathan 3* at the ship's bow were jettisoned, and cheers and applause erupted from the men and women in the control room and gallery as the first grey-black panels of the microwave sail began to emerge.

It took hours for the sail to unfold, one concentric segment at a time, upon the filament-fine carbon nanotubes that served as its spars. As it did, the ship moved out of geosynchronous orbit, heading away from Earth and closer to the beamsat. No one left the dome, though, and the control team watched breathlessly as the sail grew in size, praying that the spars wouldn't get jammed or that the rigging would tangle, which would mean that the assembly team would have to be called in. But that didn't happen. Layer after layer, the sail unfurled, becoming a huge, concave disk even as the ship receded from the camera.

Finally, the last segment was in place. The thrusters fired again, this time to move *Galactique* into cruise configuration behind the sail, until it resembled a pencil that had popped a parachute. Once more the thrusters fired, this time to gently orient the ship in the proper direction for launch. On the control room's right-hand screen, a plotting image depicted the respective positions of *Galactique* and the beamsat.

A dotted line suddenly appeared, connecting the starship and the machine that would send it on its way. The microwave beam was invisible, of course, so only control room instruments indicated that it had been fired.

A few moments later, *Galactique* began to move. Slowly at first, and then faster, until it left the screen entirely.

By then, everyone in the dome was shouting, screaming, hugging each other. Fists were pumped in the air, and Matt smelled marijuana as someone broke a major rule by lighting a joint. His grandmother was on her feet, pushing herself up from her mobil to totter forward and wrap her arms around her son and daughter-in-law.

Matt stood beside Chandi, his hand on her shoulder. They said nothing as they watched the departure-angle view from one of *Galactique*'s onboard cameras, the image of Earth slowly falling away. Then Chandi took his hand and pulled him closer.

"Still think . . . it won't get there?" she asked, so quietly that he almost couldn't hear her.

"No. It'll get there." He bent to give her a kiss. "I have faith."

The author wishes to acknowledge the published work of Freeman Dyson, James Benford, Geoffrey A. Landis, and the late Jim Young, in whose memory this story is dedicated.

god decay

rich larson

Extreme augmentations that effectively turn people into cyborgs, a mixture of human and machine, may be likely to turn up first in the field of professional sports, where Olympic athletes are already complaining about artificial limbs giving some runners an unfair advantage, and where blood doping, although illegal, is suspected to be common. Here's a powerful look at the cost of getting to be better at everything than everyone else.

Rich Larson was born in West Africa, has studied in Rhode Island and Edmonton, Alberta, and at twenty-two now works in a small Spanish town outside Seville. He won the 2014 Dell Award and the 2012 CZP/Rannu Fund Award for Writers of Speculative Literature. In 2011 his cyberpunk novel De-volution was a finalist for the Amazon Breakthrough Novel Award. His short work appears or is forthcoming in Lightspeed, Daily Science Fiction, Strange Horizons, Apex Magazine, Beneath Ceaseless Skies, AE, *and many others, including anthologies* Upgraded, Futuredaze, *and* War Stories. *Find him online at richwlarson.tumblr.com.*

There was new biomod ivy on the buildings, a ruddy green designed for long winters, but other than that the campus looked the same as it did a decade back. Ostap walked the honeycomb paving with his hands in his pockets, head and shoulders above the scurrying students. They were starting to ping him as he passed, raking after his social profile until he could feel the accumulated electronic gaze like static. Ostap had everything shielded, as was his agent's policy, but that didn't stop them from recognizing his pale face, buzzed head, watery blue eyes.

A few North Korean transfers, who'd been in the midst of mocapping a rabbit, started shrieking as they caught sight of him. The game was up. Ostap flashed his crooked grin, the most-recognized smile in athletics and possibly the world, and by the time he was at the Old Sciences building he had a full flock. The students were mostly discreet with their recording, not wanting to seem too eager for celebspotting points, but Ostap could tell they were waiting for something as he walked up the concrete wheelchair ramp.

"Accra 2036," he said, linking his fingers for the Olympic rings. "We're taking it all, right?"

Ostap let one massive palm drift along the rail, then flipped himself up and inverted to walk it on his hands. The flock cheered him all the way up the rail, balanced like a cat, and applauded when he stuck the twisting dismount. Ostap gave them a quick bow, then turned through the doors and into the hall. The sudden hushed quiet made him feel like he was in a cathedral.

Bioscientist-now-professor Dr. Alyce Woodard had a new office, but Ostap had expected that. He'd never grown attached to the old one, not when their few visits there were so engulfed by the days and nights in the labs, in temperature-controlled corridors and stark white rooms where the fluorescents scoured away shadows and secrets.

What Ostap hadn't expected was how old Alyce had become. Her spine had a desk-chair curvature as she got up and crossed the floor, pausing the wallscreen with a wave of her hand. Her body fat sagged, her eyes were bagged. Ostap remembered her beautiful, and awful, an angel's face floating above him with cold marble eyes and checklist questions. But that was before a long succession of tanned bodies and perfect teeth, and maybe she'd never been at all.

"O," Alyce said, thin arms around his midsection just briefly. "Thanks for coming on short notice."

"It's good to see you," Ostap said. "Good to come back." But it wasn't; he felt like he was twenty-three again, stick-thin, draped boneless in a wheelchair.

"Training for Accra, now, huh?" Alyce scratched at her elbow. "And a citizen, this time around. I just saw the new ads, they're still using that clip from the 2028 Games . . ." She waved the wallscreen to play, and Ostap saw himself loping out onto the track, blinking in the sunlight, fins of plastic and composite gleaming off his back and shoulders. It was the 7.9 seconds that had put the name Ostap Kerensky into every smartfeed, his events plastered on billboards and replayed ad nauseam on phones and tablets.

"The dash," Ostap said. "They really don't get tired of it."

"Eight years on, you'd think they would," Alyce said. Her smile was terse, but she watched, too. A cyclopean Pole, six foot five, noded spine and long muscled limbs. No warm-up, no ritual. On the gunshot he came off the blocks like a Higgs boson.

"The tracking camera fucking lost him," Alyce quoted, because the commentators had long since been censored out. "It really fucking lost him."

"That was some year," Ostap said, trying to read her, but the new lines on her face made it harder, not easier.

She flicked the wallscreen to mute. "I saw the feed of that promotion you did in Peru, too." Alyce was looking up and down him. "Exhibition match, or something? With that football club?"

"They're hoping to open up the league to biomods next season, yeah."

"Oh." Her face was blank.

"The underground stuff is killing their ratings," Ostap explained. "Nobody wants to watch pure sport any more, you know how it is. Blood doping, steroids, carbon blades, and now biomods. That's what gets specs. I was talking to the—"

"O." Alyce clenched, unclenched her teeth.

"Yeah?" Ostap's voice was quieter than he wanted it.

"Do you remember when we stopped doing the scans together? It was about five years back."

Ostap remembered. He'd been on the new suborbital from Dubai to LAX, struggling to fit the scanner membranes over all of his nodes with the seat reclined and Dr. Woodard chatting in his ear. He'd just climbed a high-rise, one of those sponsored publicity stunts, like the company who wanted him to run the Tour de France on foot. That offer was still sitting in the backlog waiting for a green light.

He'd been tired.

"I want to see you," he'd said. "It's been too long."

"I'm sick of the cams, O," she'd said. "You bring them like fucking flies. Just talk to me."

So he had, about the dark-haired girls in barely-shirts and tight cigarette jeans, the cosmetically-perfected lips and tits, the girls who'd mobbed him at the airport. They all would have killed for a night of his time.

"You're welcome," Alyce had said, when he'd finished. "Still."

"I'm sending the scan," Ostap had said, because he had nothing else he could give her. He'd sent it before the suborbital peaked and the conversation crackled away, and after that, the conversations stopped.

"I remember," Ostap said now, unsmiling. "We set it up to automate."

Alyce moved to sit back against the desk, her hands veiny on the wood. "You look fine," she said sadly. "You don't even look thirty-three." Ostap watched her mouth tightening.

"What's wrong?" he asked.

"The augs are asking too much, O." Alyce put a finger to her ribs. "The stress on your central nervous system, your organs. It's been increasing. They're all on their way out. Heart first, I'd think." She was not wincing, not looking away. "Two more years is the projected max."

Ostap felt the nodes like he hadn't since the surgeries, felt the pulse of them deep in flesh. He felt the composite wrapping his spine, the membranes skimming under his skin, the fish-scale vents on his back and shoulders and neck. He felt the thrumming power, but now like a venom sack set to burst.

"Shit," he said. "Shit."

"I'm sorry," Alyce said. "Have you experienced anything?"

"Don't think so." But it was hard to tell, now, hard to tell when his heart was skipping from blowing doxy rails, from adrenal rush, from a woman with the biomod fetish exploring every micrometer of his visible augs. The Superman was invulnerable.

"You don't think so?"

"I don't know," Ostap snapped. "How am I supposed to fucking know, Dr. Woodard?" He hadn't meant to call her that, but it came out on its own, like she was still the blue fairy in his ear whispering him through operation after operation as they flayed his nerves bare. She didn't know he still dreamed about the final surgery, the sounds of scraping bone and machine.

"I'm sorry, O."

Hell, the kind Hieronymus Bosch would have painted, eighteen excruciating hours of laser-guided scalpels and winches and needles. Under for some of it, locally anaesthetized for the rest. Needles in his skin and the tubes speared raw down his throat. He'd thought that had been price enough.

"How long have you known for?" Ostap finally asked.

"That it was a possibility, since the start. That it was happening?" Alyce paused. "A long time." She folded her arms and it made her look small. "Should I have told you?"

"No," Ostap said, but he wasn't sure. The chant for the 2036 Games was looping endlessly across the wallscreen. Legends are made in America.

"Okay."

Ostap put his hand up to his skull. "So why now?" he asked. "Why are you telling me now?"

The game in Peru, when he'd struck a volley out of the air for the first time and buried it back-corner, like he'd done it all his life, quick-synch nerves of his leg loaded with new muscle memories. On the bench it had gone numb for just a second, from his knee down.

"This fucking doctorate student got into my web-cache," Alyce said. "I don't know how, I thought it was all airtight. She found the records. The story's going to break in a couple hours."

"Alright," Ostap said. "Alright."

"Sorry, O."

"What happens now?" Ostap asked.

Alyce gave a helpless shrug. "There are tests," she said. "There are possibilities. Options. I've still got full access to the biolabs."

Ostap left the office without saying goodbye. Digital maps to expensive hotels were already scrawling over his retinas, reminding him of their impeccable service, their luxury suites. He'd thought he would be here for a few days, maybe, a few days to catch up after so many years. He'd imagined walking with her on the steep, rough river-trails and catching her if she slipped.

Outside there was a student who wanted to speak Polish with him, whose shirt scrolled a list of Ostap's world records down his back. Ostap mumbled a few words, shook his sweat-slick hand. Others were clutching fake memorabilia and raving about things he barely remembered doing. A few girls were fluffing fingers through sun-blonde hair, casually rolling waistbands lower on their hips, pursing their lips and trying to figure out bedroom eyes.

He went past them all like a zombie, and walked all the way to the university bus station before he remembered he'd ordered an autocab.

Twenty minutes later Ostap pushed into the lobby through a crush of mobbers, the ones who'd used complex algorithms to predict his preferred hotel, and there he had the privilege of watching the story break in realtime. The alert blinked yellow onto their retinas, vibrated tablets or phones for the migraine-prone and slow adopters, and small worlds turned upside down one by one. It shuddered through the jerseys and 3D-print face-masks and groping hands like a wave. Ostap would have been reading it himself if he hadn't put up a datablock.

Silence and exclamations of disbelief started flickering back and forth like a light switch.

"Your finger here, sir," said the shell-shocked concierge, holding out the pad for a signature. He had enough presence of mind to pretend it didn't work, necessitating a fresh pad and leaving him with a small slice of Ostap Kerensky's genetic material to slip into his pocket. Ostap knew all about that trick, but he didn't give a cheerful wink or offer a hangnail. Not this time.

The whisper-silent elevator took him to the very top, and when the wallscreens in his suite flicked on to greet him, the story was everywhere. He told them to mute, but he still watched. Pictures of Alyce skittered around the room, her mouth in a deep frown, and Ostap could tell from the selection that the current spin was villain, deceiver. He saw footage of himself zipping into a custom wetsuit, rubbing petroleum jelly over his hands and cheekbones, flashing the cams a thumbs up before he waded into the water to set the new English Channel record.

Back to the 2028 Games again, when Ostap took the world by storm. 100 meter, 200 meter. High-jump. Still enough in the tank for decathlon. Bolt's records were gone, Sterling's record was shattered. Ostap watched it all flash by in sound bites, his story condensed for anyone living under a particularly large rock.

An incredibly promising young athlete, all but scouted from the womb, left crippled by a three-car collision when the driving AI in a cab glitched. A brilliant developer, born and bred for MIT, spearheading a team designing the most comprehensively integrated body augmentation the world had ever seen.

They'd found each other across the ocean, and it was so fucking perfect.

The sky was growing dark and the clips were starting to recycle when Alyce buzzed in his ear. He could barely hear her, even with voice ID.

"They're at my fucking house," she said, and then the next part got swallowed.

"They're here, too," Ostap said. He'd seen it on the screen, the termite swarm of reporters and spectators milling the base of the hotel.

"So am I," she said. "Want to let me up before they crucify me?"

Ostap crossed to the balcony, palmed the glass door open. It looked like a party. People were all slammed up against each other, twisting and turning for better angles, cams flashing pop-pop-pop in the dark, hot white, miniature supernovas. He couldn't see Alyce struggling through the crowd from her cab, not at this height, but he could tell where she was by the ripples. She'd barely made it five meters.

He called the hotel security detail to go bring her in, and ten minutes later she slumped through the door, hair tendrilled with static across a flushed face. She held up a bottle of Cannonball and sloshed it pointedly with a quarter of a smile.

"Probably safer here than anywhere else," she said, while Ostap retrieved two glasses from the designer coffee table.

"Probably, yeah. They're going to be burning cars soon."

"You left before I could explain everything." Alyce handed the bottle over. Ostap pushed the cork with his fingertip until it plopped out and splashed down, bobbing in the wine like a buoy. She poured.

"I thought maybe you called me for something else," Ostap said. He kept his eyes off the bed.

"People only call Superman when there's trouble, O." Alyce took a slug of the wine and swished it in her mouth. Swallowed. "They never call him to say everything's great, you should come visit."

"They should," Ostap said. "They used to. We used to just visit."

"If you want to call it that," Alyce said, but there was a heat in the tips of her ears that wasn't from the wine. She handed him the other glass.

"The first time we fucked was one week after I learned to walk. To the day." Ostap tried to laugh. "Did you know that? I mean, what kind of Oedipal shit is that?"

Twitching his toes in the recovery room had been euphoria, standing on his own two feet, Elysium. As soon as he was cleared, he'd spent every second he could with the harness, tottering on a treadmill as his new nerves carved channels of motion and memory. One night Dr. Woodard had stayed with him, to show him where else his new nerves led.

"It wasn't on my calendar," Alyce said. "It just happened."

And it had been over quickly, a confusion of sweat and heat that had nothing methodical, nothing logical about it. She hadn't nodded thoughtfully or dashed notes on her tablet afterward.

"Nasty, brutish, and short," was what she'd said, but smiling, wriggling back into her jeans. She'd put her hands around Ostap's hips, where scars were still tender.

"I've had dreams about you," Ostap had said, but in Polish, so she wouldn't know it.

"Maybe I'm just a narcissist," Alyce said now, to her wine glass. "Maybe Michelangelo wanted Il David."

"You should have just let me find out on the fucking net," Ostap said.

"Should I leave?" Alyce asked.

She sat on the hotel bed, rumpling crisp white sheets, and Ostap sat on the floor with his head leaned back against its foot. The wine was clinging in his dry mouth.

The last time he'd been in this city, every day had been stronger and faster and smoother. The augs had been synchronizing, the protein pumps sculpting muscles layer by layer. His new size had had him ducking under doorways and cramming into cars. They'd flown a redeye back to Warsaw for the final stretch of treatments, for last calibrations and probes and his hysterical mother, and he hadn't been in Boston since.

"My parents," Ostap said. "I'm going to have to tell them."

"Where are they now?" Alyce asked.

"La Rochelle. Moved them there a few years ago." He tipped his head back. "They always wanted to holiday there. I think they're happy."

"That's good," Alyce said. "When you're old you deserve to be happy. You've put up with enough shit."

You're old, Ostap wanted to say. He wanted to ask her if she was happy.

"Maybe they are, maybe they're not," he said instead. "I'm wrong about that. Sometimes. I mean, I thought you and me were happy."

"We were," Alyce said. "Because we were riding a whirlwind, O. You know, the parties and the galas and the fashion consultants and hair stylists and booking agents. All those interviews. Hell, I even wore a dress."

"I remember," Ostap said. He'd worn a tailored suit, slashed in such a way as to display the nodes along his spine, and in a matter of weeks everyone wore them that way. "Movie stars and moguls," he said. "That night in Chicago."

"Rome, Dubai, New York."Alyce shrugged. "They blend."

"The Superman thing was just taking off," Ostap pressed, because it was important somehow, important that she remember that one drunken night in Chicago they'd spent roving through the city in an autocab, searching for a phone booth. There were none left, so they'd ended up tinting the windows instead.

"We had a good run," Alyce said. "And that year. Well. I'll always remember that year."

They were quiet for a moment, listening to what sounded like a full riot outside, hoarse screaming and one looping police siren. Ostap had turned the wallscreens off, but he could guess what was happening. He could guess that his net implant would be overloaded with calls, messages, demands when he lifted the block.

"What are they saying?" he finally asked. "I blocked the feed."

"All the classics."Alyce moved the dregs of her glass in a slow circle, tipping it just so. "Neo-reactionists flaring up all over. Abomination. Playing God. Things like that."

"Playing Frankenstein," Ostap said, and felt a dull triumph when her face went red.

"Yeah. All those."

"It won't change anything," he said, then, when she looked at him shrewdly: "It won't stop biomods. Developers will still be going after full integration." He paused. "Maybe they'll look at safer designs. Learn from your mistake."

"Safety isn't even in the equation when they've already killed a dozen candidates under Beijing. But they're still only seeing success with the partial augs." She reached for the bottle on the night-stand. "We were lucky with you, O. You might be the first, best. Last."

"Do you remember the last time we talked face to face?" Ostap asked. "After your symposium."

"Why are we talking about all this, O?"

"Because I always thought there would be time later."

"There will be," Alyce said. "I told you. There are options."

"I need air," Ostap said. He got up and walked to the wide window. He thought about two years as his hands found the cool glass, thought about two winging orbits of the planet around its sun. The door slid open and he stepped out onto the balcony, feeling stucco under his bare feet. The night air was cool and flapped at his clothes, slipped over his buzzed skull. The cityscape lights were like fractured stars.

The last time they'd spoken face-to-face, she'd pushed his lips off her neck and tightened her scarf.

"It cheapens our accomplishment," she'd explained. "People are saying things, O. Finally built a better vibrator. They said that." Her face had been red and angry in the dark.

"I don't give a shit," he'd said.

"Frankenstein didn't make the monster so he could put his dick in it."

Ostap had had nothing to say to that, even though every part of Alyce shrank, apologetic and ashamed, a heartbeat after. He still didn't.

Someone had floated up a cam on a helium sack, drifting level with the balcony, and now it started to whirr and flash. Ostap looked down and saw its laser light playing across his chest, tracking every twitch like a sniper's scope. He thought of hurling his empty glass with perfect velocity, smashing it against the cam to rain tiny fragments down into the street. They would love that.

The carmine dot skittered across his arm, up his neck. Ostap went back inside, sliding the door shut behind him.

The wine was nearly gone when Ostap came back in. Alyce had left just a sliver in the bottom of the bottle, as she'd always done, to avoid the feeling she was drinking too much. She had her arms crossed, pacing back and forth with just a hint of unsteadiness.

"Like I said, if we shut everything down right now, if we power down your augs and get you to the labs, your chances are good," she was saying. "We can figure out what can be removed. What can't. We'll get you on dialysis, an arti-heart . . ."

"You came and sat with me in recovery," Ostap said. "After the last surgery. You smelled like, uh, like hand sanitizer."

"You said I had coffee breath," Alyce said, stopping.

"That too, yeah. Black coffee and hand sanitizer." Ostap paused. "You had those Michelangelo paintings. Hellenic ideals, you talked about. All those trapezoids and abdomens."

"Anatomically impossible, of course," Alyce said. "All those opposing muscles groups flexing simultaneously. But beautiful."

She'd dug further through the images, blowing up Grecian statues on the wall. A wasteland of cracked marble, mythological figures missing limbs, noses, genitals. She'd plucked at her throat with one finger, and murmured that it was too bad, how even gods decayed.

"You never asked me about the accident," Ostap said, taking the wine bottle by the neck. "Not once in all these years."

Alyce shook her head.

"Why?" Ostap asked, starting to pour, millimeter precise. "You're a doctor. I know you'd seen GBS before. You knew the spinal damage wasn't trauma."

"I'd seen it," Alyce agreed. "Yours looked early. Probably all but from birth, right?"

"Why?" Ostap repeated. "You had other candidates. Plenty of candidates. You had to know those tapes were doctored. That the accident story was bullshit."

"I guess I wanted to make something from nothing."

Ostap's fingers tightened and a crack squealed through the bottle. Two droplets squeezed out and bloomed red on the carpet. He set the wine bottle down, delicate. "How God did it?" he asked.

"How God happened," Alyce said. "We might have had better results with another candidate. We'll never know. But you were perfect, O. You wanted it. No matter what happened."

Ostap realized the wine was blurring her, smoothing the lines in her face, making her look almost how she did before.

"Thank you," he said, because the last time he'd said it he was translating for his silver-haired father sobbing too hard for software to understand.

"Whatever you decide." She put her hand flat against his ribs, where organs ready to crumble did their work under skin so thin, no composite casing. He looked at her desiccated lips. Graying hair. He looked at the hand on his flesh, their two bodies contrasted.

"It was anatomically impossible," he said.

"But beautiful."

Ostap undid the block and his head was a sudden deluge, blinking messages and interview probes and priority tags. He raked through the backlog of business. Mountain races, a sub-orbital parachute drop, a biomod boxing league, Accra promotions.

He gave nothing but green lights.

Blood wedding

ROBERT REED

In the raw and violent story that follows, guests at a high-profile celebrity wedding in a high-tech future suffer a deadly attack to which they respond in ways indicative of their various natures, and which will answer the question: Which of them, if any, will survive?

Robert Reed sold his first story in 1986, and quickly established himself as one of the most prolific of today's writers, particularly at short fiction lengths, and has managed to keep up a very high standard of quality while being prolific, something that is not at all easy to do. Reed's stories count as among some of the best short work produced by anyone in the last few decades; many of his best stories have been assembled in the collections The Dragons of Springplace *and* The Cuckoo's Boys. *He won the Hugo Award in 2007 for his novella "A Billion Eves." He is hardly less prolific as a novelist, having turned out eleven novels since the end of the '80s, including* The Leeshore, The Hormone Jungle, Black Milk, Down the Bright Way, The Remarkables, Beyond the Veil of Stars, An Exaltation of Larks, Beneath the Gated Sky, Marrow, Sister Alice, *and* The Well of Stars, *as well as two chapbook novellas,* Mere *and* Flavors of My Genius. *His most recent books are a chapbook novella,* Eater-of-Bone, *a novel,* The Memory of Sky, *and a collection,* The Greatship. *Reed lives with his family in Lincoln, Nebraska.*

Life is the only indulgence," was the Ames motto, and today was meant to be the latest, grandest example of that philosophy: Fecundity given breath and shadow, with the promise of ludicrous profits tomorrow.

The "I dos" were to be held exactly at noon on the summer solstice. A thousand species of expertly crafted, first-of-their-kind foliage stood on the island's highest hill, creating a church of pigmented cellulose, perfumes and pheromones and wet-earth stinks. The honored guests were carefully shaped and then firmed by regenerations. The style that year was for infusions of transient chloroplasts, which was why each body was green or purple or pink, the organelles dense enough and efficient enough to produce a slow feast of sugars. But the magic worked only if the flesh was free and standing in sunshine, which was why everyone was naked. No guest wanted to hide perfection inside fabric, not when the new human form was so lovely. And there was one more fine reason to remain perched on their toes, straining for the sun: Nobody wanted to miss seeing Glory.

The bride was born gorgeous. In a different century, Glory Lou Ames might have been an actress hamstrung by being too perfect for meaningful roles. But her native beauty was just the scaffolding for a series of early tailorings and recent, very temporary additions. The treasure was twenty-three years-old. Like a fertility goddess carved from mammoth ivory, she was rich with hips and breasts, and of course she was nude, the abundant flesh emerald and glossy and grand. But what made her impact more remarkable was the strategic use of living flowers. Epiphytes were common embellishments among the bio-aware community, but epiphytes weren't good enough for Devon Ames' daughter. Glory wore tailored parasites. Roots slipped painlessly into her tissues, robbing just enough blood and sugar to maintain their splendor. The blossoms erupted from short dense stalks. Every flower produced a fragrance that merged with every other fragrance in the brilliant tropical air—a veritable community promenading down a path of mushroom-built cobblestones. At least a dozen patentable technologies were on display. Cynical tongues claimed that Devon, recognizing opportunity, was milking another fortune from this event. But what wasn't appreciated was that his only daughter had never been shy about helping the family business, which was the same as helping herself.

Glory moved with the smooth sure gait of a dancer, and the naked London Philharmonic played from the valley below, matching her rhythms. Father was waiting at the end of the aisle, green to the brink of black, an epiphytic prairie growing in place of his hair. The altar beyond was a cube of frozen tar carved from Halley's Comet, elegant in its simplicity. The Unitarian minister waited in front of the altar, and beside her was a groom who was as spellbound as any man could be, gazing at this mesmerizing dream.

Life was the answer to all problems. True to that creed, machines had been forbidden from the island and surrounding seas. The security cameras and public cameras were organic crystals roped to a thousand protocols and then lashed onto the backs of obedient bees. Several billion humans were watching the ceremony, marvelling at the green flesh and magnificent breasts, the blooming roses in Glory's scalp and the grander blossoms on her wrists and down her broad back. The processional music was composed for this occasion, composed by her father, and the stirring sweet melody added just enough celebration to a scene that could not be more perfect. Every bride was lovely. It is said. But today's intended exceeded every other young woman who has dared march down her aisle, basking in the gaze of God and her blood and the future of her world.

Then came a sequence of small popping noises, almost unnoticed.

Also unobserved was the collapse of multiple security systems, and worse, any notice about their untimely death.

The public cameras continued operating, but they didn't bother showing the guests standing in back. Those were the first victims—little billionaires balancing on moss-covered chairs, one moment straining to see, and in the next moment, turning to steam and light.

Forty wellwishers died with that first salvo.

But in the front ranks, nothing changed. Guests grinned and teared while the security systems did nothing. Then a second salvo arrived, slaughtering the next row of billionaires, and body parts rose in the air like a fountain. That was what caught the Bakor's attention. The groom happened to look up, and lifting a hand, he began to rub startled eyes. Which Glory noticed. The man's wavering attentions were a bother, a problem. Of course she was insulted. After all, this was a spoiled, self-absorbed woman, just as any young person would be in her circumstances. What was Bakor thinking? What could possibly be so interesting that he would pull his eyes off her splendidness?

Then she felt intense heat washing across her flower-rich back.

The heat was like a tongue, there and then gone, and her blossoms began to wilt. But Glory wasn't frightened. Even the possibility of fear lay out of reach. Yet her joy had been warped. She was perplexed and bothered, perhaps even a little angry. Her husband-to-be was interested in some stupid commotion far to the back, and for the next moment and the next breath, she tried to push aside her anger, to regain the old perfection.

Eighty people had died. The popping noises were finished, but the disruptions rippled through the surviving crowd. Screams could be heard. Curses and inarticulate wails. Hundreds of strangers were in attendance. She assumed that company associates or low-level functionaries were already drunk. She assumed that an ordinary fight had broken out, which seemed borderline possible. And a brawl wouldn't be too bad, would it? That particular story won a moment of relief, and just then the Philharmonic reached the crescendo, and the bride couldn't hear any of the pain or the terror, which was why she managed another graceful step and another quick breath, flashing white teeth for the multitudes that she would never know.

Bakor again turned his head, thankfully fixing his gaze on her.

But now Father wasn't paying attention. That was the next insult. Devon Ames had tilted his head, one hand to his bare temple, plainly focused on whatever words were being shouted into his skull.

As it happened, Glory's mother was first to deliver the awful news.

From three rows back, Devon's first ex-wife cried out, "Oh my fucking God!"

Against every instinct, Glory stopped. She stopped in mid-stride, staring only at Bakor as her lead foot came down, and she finally deciphered his expression—that sense of utter panic on a face that she rather loved.

That was the moment when the young groom turned to fire, to bloody steam.

Bakor exploded, and one of his collarbones, driven like shrapnel, sliced through the minister's face, killing her as well.

The audience continued to scream, but maybe not quite as loudly as before. Everybody was suddenly dropping to their knees, their stomachs. And Father shouted something important to somebody unseen. A command that she didn't understand, unless it was just noise. Maybe Devon was as lost and panicked as the rest of them. But at least now, at the last moment, a platoon of bodyguards emerged from their camouflaged bunkers—powerful beasts designed for one purpose, using their armored bodies to protect the most important people in the world.

Their arrival brought the hope of problems solved, order restored.

But unfortunately the attackers were waited for the guards, and instant, every warrior but one was dead.

At that point, the cyborgs were still better than five kilometers from the island. But security systems were a shambles, nobody was in charge, and Devon's sworn enemies were closing fast.

BEFORE

What steers people is what they believe. History and polished data have their place, on occasion, but what a citizen knows to be true or as good as true matters more than what happens to be real. And that is the world as it should be. Genuine history means confusion, imprecision and guesswork. No story ends. The audience is left with zero sense of accomplishment. But an imaginary history, particularly one that is respectable and compelling, can buoy up the body and the fragile will, carrying its captives happily across the years and into the great good maw of Death.

This much was fact:

Devon Ames was the second richest entity in the solar system, while Harry Pinchit was the first. And those two men shared quite a lot more than money and gender. Both were born in the years when being an American still held some small advantage. Both were blessed with a famous scientific parent and a notorious artistic parent. Each boy lived beside the sea with his loyal dog and two lesser siblings. Labeled early as being gifted, they were fed tutors and expectations. But exospheric test scores never mean sure success, and even in their early twenties, neither male showed any sign of becoming a triumph in any important pursuit.

Biography is a story written quickly over too few facts.

In 2041, a big ugly war was waged over the course of ten days. The world was already weakened by various crises, but it was malware that delivered Hell. Weapon systems were corrupted, and a great deal of human complacency added to mayhem, and civilization was left bloodied, but at least by the end every AI and most of the Internet was thankfully as dead as dead could be.

The people who survived doomsday were hungry for salvation. Everybody was watching for the first great leaders to happen along. Devon and Harry shared that role. Their life stories were inspiringly similar. Each was in his early thirties. Each stood at the helm of a small, underfunded corporation known for novel technologies. And though they worked in very different venues, both of the young tycoons ran a stable of gifted scientists and secure devices that had never shown any inclination of madness.

Devon Ames was the younger, better looking savior. Tall, sporting an easy smile and high-cheekbones left behind by Lakota grandparents, he was a man who never wanted for female companionship. Devon certainly didn't approve of anything that looked like self-doubt. Knowing exactly how the world could be saved, the young man made a public announcement using every old-fashioned means. Television. Radio. Sanitized tablets and direct mail. "Life," he proclaimed. "We have to embrace life. The Mother's endless strengths must be ours, and life is the only indulgence that we deserve, and life is how we will make this world a paradise again."

Harry Pinchit came across as the older, more honest savior. His Cuban mother left him with a bare scalp before he turned thirty, and coupled with his stout body and plain looks, he built the illusion of wise, unsentimental middle age. Surprisingly, he also was the more effective television personality. He had an actor's voice that soothed or boomed, depending on demands. Only Harry could tell people the machines were going to win, one way or another. And the damaged earth was sure to grow hotter and less habitable in the near future. The obvious answer to the ongoing nightmare, according to Harry, was to do what any weak soul does when faced with diminished prospects. "We have to marry well," said the man who would never marry. "We have to build the machines that we can embrace for the rest of our lives, and I mean for the next billion years, and I mean the machine implants that will carry your minds, our souls, from the ground where we stand today to the ends of our brilliant galaxy."

At that point, the two young men had never met.

If asked, they couldn't even have guessed when they became aware of one another.

Each tended his own flourishing empire. Capital flowed into both coffers, and their labor was hired from divergent fields. Devon transformed the planet's ecosystem. Harry devised malware-free hardware that good people could wear safely and proudly. On those occasions where paths crossed, one company would beat the other for a contract or market or the goodwill of some group of happy consumers. But there was no epic bitterness. Not then, no. Everyday, commerce made losers and winners, and those two corporations thrived, and when the kings finally met, it was entirely by accident.

Harry was in Washington, D.C., wooing defense contractors.

Devon was wearing shorts and sandals, planting a new crop of carbon-fixers in the tidal pool in front of the Lincoln Memorial.

No one ever claimed responsibility for putting the two men together. But the new Hilton was the location—a big ugly building standing on stilts—and the event passed without public announcement. For an hour and two minutes, the men shared a suite. As was common in those days, cameras and every kind of recorder were forbidden. But later, the aides and functioneers couldn't recall any harsh words. Two distracted billionaires spoke about common needs and beautiful women and how the earth and the other worlds in the solar system were big enough for both of them. Then what began with a handshake ended with a slightly longer handshake, each man wishing the other pleasant evenings and a long, prosperous life.

Yet according to the public history, that's when the feud was born.

And every step for the next thirty years made Devon and Harry into the greatest of enemies.

ANKYL

A thousand people were trying not to die.

A few of these people had to, had to, had to be saved.

Count the remaining guards, he thought.

One.

Ankyl.

"Me," he realized.

Ankyl was four years-old, which was old. He was a prototype, a Gen Prime that had spent his days working security at the corporate office, mostly in the swimming plaza. And yes, in the purest sense he was an overqualified lifeguard, at least until yesterday when one of the front-line guards got into a brawl with a bonobo servant, earning three broken wrists and some deep-shit trouble for losing that stupid battle. That's the only reason why an elderly, basically placid creature was shipped to this island. That and the fact that nothing remarkable would ever happen on the daughter's big day.

Because he was just a lifeguard, Ankyl had been given one of the lesser guests to protect—the groom's younger, decidedly alcoholic brother. A careful pedigree and four years of regimented training made the creature ready for this modest role. But the security systems failed utterly. And the platoon got a late jump. And then the enemy struck the hilltop with targeted blasts. Worst of all, each one of the original guards had been tagged. How else could the entire platoon die? But Ankyl was alive, meaning that the tagging happened before he joined the ranks, and here he was, scrambling to accomplish one good deed before he died.

His life had been spent fishing little kids out of deep water. Now he was sprinting, thinking about what a fucking mess this was. One moment, he was obeying orders, heading for the drunken brother—a trembling purple mess cowering on the ground. But he was also calculating how long they had before the full brunt of the attack arrived, realizing that there weren't any minutes to burn, but he probably had quite a few seconds to make ready.

Ankyl stopped running.

His armor turned to reflective camouflage mode. Squatting, he scanned the battlefield. Assessments were made. Plans were assembled. The purple brother would live or die without Ankyl's help. Only the critical people mattered now. Devon was the tempting target for any attacker. Devon's other children were a little less vital, with Glory at the top of the heap today. Then came the wives—present and past—and the wives were followed by the dead groom and his tag-along family. These were dirt simple calculations: Devon was to be saved before anyone else. And because Ankyl was bred to believe in those very simple mathematics, he had no right to act any other way.

Except.

The lifeguard didn't like Devon Ames. Not at all, not ever. His owner was an undiluted asshole, cold and vain and often impossible. Of course in public, Devon sang about the marvels of life and the biosphere, and about his own decency. But in reality, everybody was just meat to the man. Human or otherwise, it didn't matter. According to Devon, no piece of meat was ever good at its job. Not that Ankyl had ever suffered the man's attentions. No, the lifeguard was good about hiding in plain sight. But he had watched his owner abuse other lifeguards and adult guests, and too many times, this father to the new world had inflicted some very hard punishments on misbehaving kids.

Inside Ankyl was the urge to protect those who were drowning. Maybe they were only millionaires or five-year-olds, but he saved all of them. He wouldn't bother dragging soggy meat off the bottom of the pool. He saved people. The instinct wasn't something that Ankyl wanted, but he had it nonetheless. Empathy. Empathy was a distraction that had bothered him throughout his months and months of life. But then one day, as the creature patrolled the surface of blood-warm Lake Ames, an obvious and quite simple idea occurred to that old Gen Prime warrior:

Someone had to be the biggest, most impressive beast in the world.

Devon happened to be that beast today, and that man would remain so long after Ankyl was turned into compost and flowers. But the trillionaire would eventually find himself under someone else's feet, and suddenly, with great clarity, he realized who would own the important feet.

Those feet were standing nearby.

Just thinking about them caused a new set of calculations about worth and worthiness.

Like a dancer, Ankyl turned in a tight circle. He made a swift, adrenalin-fueled assessment of options and likelihoods. The second richest creature in the world was lying behind the minister's corpse, sobbing. A smart camouflaging fog was finally beginning to rise, but blind pulses of laser and ballistic were still flying overhead, and in this maelstrom, exactly one human being remained on her feet—a solitary, defiant creature whose rage was pushing aside all of her reasonable terrors.

The decision was made.

Ankyl's four legs decided to run, and he was their passenger, watching the sprint toward the bride who damn well refused to give up this day without a good fight.

THE FEUD

Just once, Warren pressed his father about the feud.

That was several years before the wedding. Harry Pinchit never needed encouragement to insult his enemies, and just mentioning Devon's name triggered a reliable fury from the old man. But Warren didn't care about recent crimes and old injustices. Warren was a twenty-year-old with a few crimes and injustices in his own past, but he had been acting good of late. No lawyers, no bribes. No talk about building a special home where his urges could be contained. No, Warren had become a very reliable son, and what's more, he finally came to appreciate his particular genius. Harry's only child had a rare capacity to understand human needs. Warren knew exactly what to say and exactly when to smile, and when it was necessary, the young man could shape people like pliers weaving soft copper wire.

With one name, Warren ignited the tirade. That set the mood. Then the young man interrupted his father, saying, "I know, Dad. I know. The man is a prick with a pretty face, and he keeps screwing us with the AI Commission, and you're sure he sabotaged our Tycho project, and he's a prick with a pretty face. I know it all, thank you."

The world's richest man didn't appreciate interruptions. But not long ago, when his son was in several kinds of trouble, Harry Pinchit was told that good parents listen to their children. So when this child spoke, he offered a pretend smile and a small amount of interest.

"What do you want to talk about?" he asked.

"The two of you had a meeting," said Warren.

Harry nodded, his attentions already faltering.

"The only time you were face to face, nearly thirty years ago."

"I remember that, yes."

"Something was said."

"Was it?"

"That's the legend," said the young man.

"Legend," the man repeated. Metacarbon fingers scratched the slick graphene scalp, and then he rubbed the bright porcelain nose that never felt ticklish and never needed to be cleaned. "Is that what it is now? A legend?"

"The world claims that you and Devon had a fight."

"I do hate that name," the man warned.

"Devon. Devon, Devon."

The gray hand dropped, and Father said nothing.

"Did you say something to Devon?"

"Quite a few words. Nothing ugly."

"So he said something ugly to you."

"And why are you asking?"

"Because people want to know what started this war."

"There is no war," said the cyborg. "This is personal. I hate the man because he is a cold, manipulative monster. That's a good enough reason, isn't it? And because that blood-filled son-of-a-bitch is trying to destroy us at every turn."

"That's not what you thought then," Warren said. "The two of you talked. You decided that the solar system was plenty big enough for both of you. Wasn't that the verdict?"

"Offhand comments, polite and short-sighted."

Warren responded with silence and feigned disinterest.

Father's patience quickly failed. "So why are you pestering me about one long-ago meeting?"

"Because I know you, Dad."

"Maybe. Or maybe you don't know me at all." The man laughed loudly, which was remarkable in its own right. "Explain this to me, son. Exactly what kind of person do you think I am?"

"I think you are a person, the same as everyone."

That insight earned a weary sigh. "And that means what?"

"Devon hurt you. Inside the hotel suite, something happened, or something should have happened but didn't."

The man and his body shrugged, muscles of carbon and boron humming with power. "He talked about the hotel."

"The hotel?"

"The building was broad and ugly and it stood on stilts, waiting for the next flood."

Warren nodded.

"Then he laughed at me. He cackles like pretty men always do, full of themselves, and he told me that I looked a little like that building."

"Squat and strong?"

"And waiting for the next flood," said Father.

"That was the insult?"

"It sounded insulting to me, yes."

"And that's why you took offense?"

"I didn't then. Not that minute. But later, thinking things over . . . I realized just what kind of person I'd been dealing with."

The old face remained, glowering beneath the slick gray scalp. But the bulk of the emotions were inside the bright diamond eyes and the clenched fists. Harry Pinchit had always been powerfully built, but those new legs and that broad back might well hold up an entire building.

Warren cleared his throat, and he said, "No, Father."

"No what?"

"Devon didn't insult you. He threw a few careless words at you, and afterwards, when you needed it, you invented the feud."

The fists clenched tighter, fingers squeaking against the palms.

"Every man needs one great enemy," said Warren. "And for you, who else but Devon Ames could fill that role?"

The new eyes were unhappy, guarded and dismissive. But Harry had the good sense to attack the deeper issue.

"You came here to tell me something, son. What is it?"

"This world and the solar system are divided. Two opposing camps, yours and theirs. And that's because you decided to make a war based on the most offhand words available."

"There is no war," Harry repeated.

"Not yet," said Warren.

"I don't like this topic," his father said. Then for the first time in a long while, the bright eyes blinked. "'Yours and theirs,'" he quoted.

"Yes."

"Why not "ours and theirs"? Don't you belong to my cause?"

That was a sharp observation, an excellent question, and the young man spent the next several years preparing his response.

GLORY

Many people were smarter than Glory. She was told that when she was little, and she was never so stupid as to deny the verdict of others. Long before her wedding day, Devon's daughter had mapped her limits as well as her strengths, and better than most, she accepted what she wasn't. The Ames clan and the family business spent an inordinate amount of time worshipping genius. But being a cognitive giant didn't appeal to Glory, and there was a blessing here: Nobody expected her to generate a single great thought. That's why she could sleep through the night every night, and that's why she happily spent her days working on a body that would never be perfect.

But at least the flesh gave her pleasure. Plus she had security and a place at the family table. Siblings and stepmothers and particularly her poor father never stopped conjuring. Fierce brains ruled their lives. She could sit and do nothing and do it very well, but the others never had a moment free from contemplations and deadlines, and each mind was always full of itself, pinched busy and mostly unhappy faces hostage to all that clever electricity.

Glory was free to be exceptional in her own realm.

"Goddess of the New Earth."

That was intended as a joke. A few offhand words spouted by her older brother, taking a moment from his busy-busy work. His little sister needed to be teased, and maybe he meant to injure her. But Glory liked the image. She loved the consequences. Considering all the possibilities, wasn't being the goddess of anything better than being anything else?

The young woman never hid behind made-up kindnesses. Like any respectable god, she had a clear sense about what truly mattered. The wedding was for the Goddess of the New Earth, and all of the pageantry was meant to be hers. The pinnacle of her life, at least until now, was staged on the crest of a beautiful island. The world was watching her and only her, and there was a rocket yacht moored in the bay below, and her father had claimed and terraformed an asteroid just for her honeymoon. What mattered was her husband-to-be and the long luxurious life. That was quite a lot to think about, particularly for someone who was a genius at keeping her mind empty of distractions and nagging doubts.

Then Death arrived, carrying along Panic and Misery.

Yet Glory refused to drop to the ground. Stubbornness. Strength. A deep failure of imagination. All good reasons left her standing tall, staring down at her father. The man was sprawled across the earth, and the dead minister lay in front of Father, and the groom's remains were still scattering. A fierce pulse of light roared past her ear, but she did not flinch. Alone among the wedding party, Glory could not accept the possibility of being turned to steam and cooked blood. She had enough composure to turn in a majestic circle. Every other head was down, or the heads were missing, yet the Goddess of the New Earth absorbed the chaos with unblinking eyes.

Only at the last instant did she notice the one running body—the one burly guard who managed to survive the onslaught.

Guards were simple creatures. Glory knew that, and that's why she liked them, and that's why she believed that she understood and appreciated this brute. He was following his instincts, doubtlessly charging toward Father, intent to save him.

An idea passed through Glory's head:

"I should step out of his way. I don't want him hitting me by mistake."

But the creature was following the wrong line. For no obvious reason, he was ignoring Devon, aiming instead for the Goddess in her full grandeur.

Too late, she said, "No."

Ankyl struck her with his scales and his muscles and one stone-dense shoulder.

The collision destroyed her perfection.

Then the ground rose up and slapped her. She was roughly thrown flat on her back, parasitic flowers crushed and this ugly creature stretched out across her emerald body. The guard had the face of a hawk and the voice of an opera singer. "Stay the fuck down," he sang at her. Then from a pocket cut into his living flesh, he withdrew a gun, and he stood up without standing tall, grabbing her by a forest of parasitic dahlias.

Glory was lifted.

She tried to shout, struggling against the pull. But he was powerful and terrified, carrying her toward a bunker hole where he probably hoped to find safety.

In her entire life, Glory had never made any fist worth swinging.

But that's what she did now.

She tried to break the guard's concentration. A defiant blow was delivered to that hawk-like face. But nothing was broken and nothing seemed to be noticed.

Ankyl threw her into the abandoned bunker.

"Stay!" he sang.

It was a wonderful voice. But quite a lot more than a voice was necessary to make the Goddess fall in love.

MAKING DUE

Four years of constant training was remarkable, almost unheard of. But the greater blessing was that Ankyl had never experienced combat. Beyond small personal battles, he had suffered nothing worse than bruised flesh and a battered ego. Every morning brought physical preparation, strength and endurance exercises before the marksmanship test taken while exhausted. Then after a four hour stint watching boringly happy children, he returned to his training, enduring simulations and tactical discussions with his superiors, mastering contingencies that would never happen to him.

Perhaps no other creature had invested a greater portion of his life becoming a warrior.

That preparation was what dragged him through the next moments.

The protective fog continued to grow, turning the air to milk. The milk was made from mirrored particles and disruptive mucus, plus a stew of bacteria floating inside the mucus—infinite soldiers carrying the ingredients needed to subvert the enemy's mechanical parts.

But the fog should be much thicker than it was.

And there never should have been so many casualties. Not this quickly, and not with every other soldier left cooked and dead.

The hilltop had to be defended, but by what?

He had no clue.

With time and the freedom to sit, Ankyl could have remembered every training exercise. But there wouldn't have been any answers in those lessons. Nothing this awful could ever happen, and in a peculiar way, impossibility offered relief. It promised salvation. He was a creature in a hopeless corner, and without hope, there were no wrong moves. Nobody would live long enough to question his methods. And because he was sure to die, Ankyl was free to do nothing. If he wished. Or he could wage any kind of hopeless defense of a hilltop that wouldn't be held for another ten minutes.

A soldier always needs more soldiers.

And weapons.

And a plan.

The fog was starved, compromised by unknown means. But Glory was locked inside a bunker, safe as Ankyl could make her. And the oncoming fire had slowed and grown blind, apparently. The wedding guests weren't sobbing quite so loudly anymore, and a few of them even managed to sit up, nervously watching the milky air and their trembling, empty hands.

Devon Ames had found his feet and a pair of weak legs. Too numb to speak, the great man stepped over the dead minister, and once that obstacle had been conquered, he looked at the final warrior.

Every one of these dead soldiers had been armed.

That simple fact felt like revelation. Ankyl immediately set to work, yanking wedge-rifles from their scabbards and gear-breakers out of their protective pockets. His colleagues had died close together, which was another blessing, and in a matter of moments he had a good start on building an armory.

Devon watched.

Arrogance had a life, a spine and its own urgent needs. The rich man's arrogance caused him to step over the dead soldiers, and it gave him the voice to ask, "What the hell are you doing?"

Ankyl said nothing.

"How many guns can you carry?" the man demanded to know.

Ankyl threw a pair of gear-breakers at Devon.

The warrior yelled, "Catch."

Explosives craftier than most people fell to the ground. The great man jumped backward, startled and then embarrassed, which made him even angrier.

With four heavy armfuls of rifles, Ankyl ran. Any face brave enough to look at him deserved a weapon, and in another few moments he returned to the beginning point, hands empty.

Using a tight low voice, Devon asked, "Where's my daughter?"

"Underground," Ankyl said.

Devon was puzzled, offended. He was wondering why he wasn't inside an armored hole.

"Pick up your bombs," Ankyl said.

The man looked at his bare feet.

Then they heard a thin, almost musical blare of rockets. The cyborgs were descending. Time was scarce or exhausted, and the soldier who had planned for every battle but this one had no choice. Calling to his little army, Ankyl said, "The rifles know how to fight. Hide and wait. Let the guns point themselves, and they'll fire when the time comes. These monsters think we're helpless, which is good. They don't know that your general is alive."

"Who's the general?" Devon asked.

"Me," said Ankyl.

But his army acted tentative, fearful. That's the way they might have died. But then the groom's drunken brother delivered the next surprise. The naked and very purple man suddenly stood tall, and with a furious voice, he called to the bride's father.

"Pick up the damned bombs, Devon. Or I'll goddamn shoot you myself!"

THE SUITOR

A lot of passion had gone into the question of "self." The debate began long before this century, but as soon as people began wearing machinery and tailoring their own genetics, it was impossible to escape the issue. When was the flesh too diluted, too weak or hot, to keep the soul alive?

In this argument, biology had the advantage of confusion. Human cells and dandelion cells were remarkably similar to each other, while the most contrived bundle of invented proteins was still just a bag of busy water. But the machines were unliving material clad in blatant, inescapable numbers. The cyborg body could carry a five-percent infiltration rate, which didn't seem like much. Plenty of people were cyborgs and tailored too. But there were groups where forty percent infiltration was the norm, and as it happened, that halfway mark was where the public usually grew ill-at-ease with mechanical men and women.

Harry Pinchit had pushed past those barriers. As the public champion for cyborgs, he whittled away what had been a stocky, unlovely body, leaving just twenty percent of its original state. But Harry's son had proven even less sentimental about the tissues he brought from the womb. Only nine percent of Warren's original body remained, and the young man was proud of every one of his choices. He didn't miss anything that had ended up in the trash. What remained was thriving inside the shiny capsule, and it was happy, and if people were strong enough to be honest—strong in their souls—then Warren's new body was exactly as natural as any other complicated mixture of molecules and energy and passion and need.

Of course the wet brain remained, but safe inside a ceramic neurocomplex. There was a mammalian heart, a cloned stand-in implanted when the original heart suffered a bad reaction to the first-generation armor. And among the other wet pieces was Warren's original sex organ, tucked inside its specially designed underwear.

Harry was uncomfortable with his son's transformation. That was another blessing of standing on the cusp of this new age. Yet the man who wanted to clad the world in machinery would never give his boy more than the occasional tease or the thinnest threats to maybe, maybe restrict his access to R&D.

One morning, father and son were basking in a UV bath, and with a casual tone, one said to the other, "You know, his daughter is getting married."

Father recognized the subject, and that's why he said nothing. For a long while, he managed not to let the boy bait him into another tirade.

"Glory and the summer solstice," Warren said.

Nothing.

"Three days from now."

The old, ageless man showed a slight nod, and then a word finally leaked out. He couldn't stop himself. He asked, "So?"

"We're not invited," said Warren.

Using every type of eye, Father stared at the machine body lying beside him. Then with care, he said, "I know you."

"You do?"

"You have a scheme."

"I might, yes."

"For the wedding . . ."

"I want us to be there."

That led to a very human snort. "Well, I don't want to be anywhere near that goddamn garden show."

"But isn't this an opportunity, Father?"

"What kind of opportunity?"

"Your enemy and every one of his allies will be on that island," said Warren. "Besides Devon's death, nothing will bring so many of those important meat-bags together again."

Suspicion lifted the glass eyes. "What are you suggesting?"

"I'm proposing." Warren paused to laugh at his joke. "What I'm saying is that my father shouldn't ask too many questions about what his child might or might not have been doing with the Secrets Department of his military wing."

Sometimes the old man forgot how dangerous the boy used to be. He cursed softly, and then he carelessly laughed at his son. "You think I don't know what you're planning? Of course I know. The weapons, the mercenaries? All those high-end viruses ready to cripple every Ames' security system? You truly think you could hide that activity from me?"

His son said nothing.

Then after a moment, very quietly, Warren said, "So you do know about my work."

"Of course I know about these hobbies. I'm not an idiot, son."

"You've been watching me, have you?"

"From the first day. I even let you put my name on the work. I don't approve of your methods, but these are good tools, good capacities. Should that pretty boy ever give me any reason to go to war."

Warren waited for a moment. Then he said again, "His daughter is getting married."

"Tits dancing down the aisle, and who cares?"

"I care."

"You?"

"She's a goddess," the young man said.

Harry threw out another curse, adding, "That is madness."

"Are you sure?"

"Absolutely."

"But you don't know what I want. Do you?"

"Besides spreading chaos? Well no, maybe I don't fully know your intentions. But still—"

"Father," Warren said, a new voice booming from inside his chest. "Father, you know nothing. Nothing."

"What's that?"

"I let you watch me. That was my plan from the first day. And I knew that you wouldn't understand my intentions, which was why everything else has been so easy."

Rare curses followed—words normally reserved for the man's sworn enemy.

Then Warren dropped a hand on his father's knee, and he said, "Shut up."

"No."

"Or keep talking. I don't care. But I want you to stand up, Dad. I want you to stand up now."

Harry tried to rise. But to his horror, he discovered that he couldn't move his legs or his feet, and even his fingertips were frozen in place.

"What's wrong here?" the old man asked.

"I found a new malware."

Alarmed. "What's that?"

"Malware that takes control over one Pinchit-designed cyborg."

Years ago, when his son was being bad, Harry grew fearful. But most of that fear was about his good name being ruined. This was a different sensation, a deeper and richer terror than anything felt before. Yet even as the adrenaline flowed, his electronic alert systems remained calm. Panic was making his flesh tremble, but the shell outside was as calm as could be.

"Why can't I stand up, Warren?"

"Because I want you to stay where you are, Father. Just like I wanted you to believe that you were in charge of me. But while you watched one project, the most important work was being done out of sight."

More curses ended with a despairing voice asking, "What do you want?"

And the young man laughed, saying, "What I want. What I want. The most beautiful woman in the world is set to be married, and what do you think I want?"

"This is sick," said Harry Pinchit.

"This is love," his son said.

"You'll take her by force?"

And Warren laughed, saying, "You still don't see it. Plain as can be, and you aren't anything but blind."

THE ONSLAUGHT

The purple brother was never as drunk as he acted. That put him in fine company. Many of the great drinkers in history were pretenders. His name was Lugon, and because he was secretly shy, rum was a useful prop at social events. Not that he was ever perfectly sober either. Far from it. But this morning's intake wasn't nearly enough to give him extra courage. Just enough rum and whiskey with a couple beers, and he was put in a place where he could steer his emotions wherever they needed to be.

After some determined cowering on the ground, Lugon realized that being pissed was the only solution.

People were dead. Guards had been cooked. Lugon's smug, endlessly sober brother—the lucky groom—could not be more obliterated. But at some point the purple man discovered a rifle cradled in his hands, and the surviving bodyguard was shouting instructions. Which was almost funny: The big pillbug giving the troops marching orders. What the creature said was probably smart, and useful, and timely. But Christ, the beast didn't realize just how messed up everyone was. These were rich people, and they were naked people, and nobody listened worse than a bunch of naked rich boys and girls thrown into a nightmare.

That's why Lugon shouted, saying, "Pick up the damned bombs, Devon. Or I'll goddamn shoot you myself."

Which the big man did, which actually seemed to turn the mood around.

Suddenly cyborgs began dropping through the fog, close enough that the air shivered. And then the ground shook too. Yet odd as it seemed, the worse the world shook, the bigger and braver Lugon began to feel.

Everything is nuts, but Devon couldn't stop talking.

"It's that goddamn Pinchit," he shouted. As if it mattered. But the old man at least was holding a rifle now. Only he wasn't aiming it like he should. He was pointing at flowers, as if petals were the problem, and unnoticed by him, the keratin barrel twisted like a snout on a mosquito, trying its desperate best to aim at a genuine enemy.

"I can't fucking believe it," Devon kept complaining. "Pinchit is attacking my girl's wedding—"

"We don't know who," Ankyl began. Then quick as can be, the pillbug aimed at something only his eyes could resolve, punching a hole in the fog with the first round, explosive shells lining up before slicing one after the next into a hard armored shell.

Something high overhead exploded.

And Lugon sent up a few rounds too, just to be neighborly. Just to belong. Which helped coax his adjacent soldiers into a state where they sent up their own rounds.

Waving three arms, Ankyl gave more orders.

The non-drunk man translated military speck into terms that spoiled nude and cowardly souls would understand.

"Spread out. Lie down. Shoot."

People did all that, and they didn't do that. Every reaction was case-by-case. For all of his brave talk, the purple boy struggled to lie back, and he had to concentrate just to throw a few gear-eaters at the sky. And when those bombs exploded, far closer to him than he intended, he was suddenly spraying the air with his own golden urine, for no reason but sheer panic.

"It is Pinchit," the old idiot insisted. "Who else?"

"None of the hardware is known," the bodyguard insisted.

"So everything was invented for today," Devon said, wasting breath and brain on the problem. "That's what the bastard did. That's what I would do."

Meanwhile, the purple man was undergoing his own brief, tumultuous career as a soldier. Fearless and then cowering, he crawled backwards, trying to hide inside the useless space between two cooked guards. Nothing smart was happening inside his head. But then a honeybee appeared in front of his nose, pointing the public camera at something interesting. Which happened to be his face. Then the bee fled or was killed, replaced overhead by long silver aircraft. Lugon half-aimed the rifle, and the rifle did the rest. This time his shells tore the bastard apart. Unless somebody else's gun made the shot. But it didn't matter. The victory felt like his, and that gave Lugon enough confidence for another burst of fire and some determined running, and after the acquisition of a new hole, deep and soothing, his courage felt like it would last for a hundred years.

More aircraft appeared, hovering low, long rotors turning hard to blow away the bothersome white fog.

Lugon battered one machine until it fell, and several more guests managed to drop more of their enemies. Then came a moment, and maybe it was longer than a moment, when it wasn't insane to believe that this battle could be won, or at least some kind of ugly stalemate might grab hold for the next little while.

Which was when a giant war machine appeared, blotting out the noon sun.

The machine released a breath of carefully sculpted plasma. Every tall tree ignited in the high branches, and the sudden heat made for difficult breathing, and every blast from the little guns did nothing to a behemoth that drifted lower by the moment, bringing a famous voice that caused the island to shiver as it roared.

"Surrender or be dead," was the threat.

The little army couldn't have folded faster. Guns were tossed from hiding places. Sobbing bodies begged for mercy. Even Devon dropped the last gear-breakers, investing his final hopes by muttering into a dead microphone, ordering the offline security system to come back to life and fight for him.

Where was the pillbug?

Nowhere visible, that's for sure.

Lugon expected that he would surrender too. But then the victor jumped from the monster ship, jumped and landed hard in front of him and then jumped again, ending up straddling the top of the black altar that was beginning to melt and bubble, and on its corners, burn.

The cyborg named Harry Pinchit looked at the horrors, the face behind the battle mask apparently stunned by the destruction.

But his voice wasn't stunned. Loudly and with relish, the voice said, "Now tell me. Where is the bride?"

ONE MORE DEATH

The bunker was locked, and then it was unlocked.

Glory was inside, blind and barely safe and still enraged by what had happened and what she imagined happening. And then some cyborg brute dragged her into the smoky, ruined air, allowing her the chance to kick it once, breaking a few of her toes but earning a little satisfaction with the pain.

She crumbled.

A voice she recognized said, "Someone pick her up."

"I will," said Glory's father.

"Yes," said Harry Pinchit's voice. "The rest of you back away. Let the man help his daughter, yes."

Father was beside her. He smelled of smoke and crushed blossoms and piss and eviscerated guts. He also smelled just like her father, and she was so pleased to have his trembling hand holding hers, pleased enough to find tears on top of the rage that continued to grow worse and worse and worse.

The young woman began arguing with herself, trying to gain control over her vivid, dangerous emotions.

Then for the first time in Glory's life, and maybe the first time ever, Devon Ames said the words, "I am sorry."

He was whispering into her ear.

Harry Pinchit leaped down from the burning altar. That famous ugly face was protected behind a transparent nanoweave faceplate, and it wasn't smiling. But the voice was joyous. A second mouth buried inside the chest said to the hilltop and to the world, "Hello, Devon. Isn't this the most beautiful day?"

"What are you doing?" Father asked.

"What am I doing, Devon?"

"Starting a war," Father said.

Glory stared at the stiff face and felt her father's hand leave her hand, and then the cyborg laughed loudly. "What I'm doing is ending a war before it can begin. And believe me, the world will come to understand, understand and appreciate, what this means."

At that point, the cyborg lifted his right hand, a giant barrel of diamond and caged light finding its target.

Father instantly put his hand over his daughter's eyes, as if he could shield her from one last horror.

"Always the ugly shit," Father shouted.

Glory knocked the hand away, and she stepped forward. Then she shouted at her attacker. With a voice that sounded tiny, what with the blazing fires and rumbling machines and the pounding of her own heart, she called out to him.

"You won't shoot me," she said.

Harry's visible mouth opened and then closed.

The other voice asked, "And why won't I?"

"Because people hate people who kill pretty things. And the entire world is watching. And I am the prettiest thing that has ever been."

The cyborg seemed to hesitate.

Which was when the bodyguard burst from hiding, flinging the last handful of gear-breakers before launching his own powerful body.

Harry Pinchit wheeled, incinerating one bothersome bomb after the next.

But Ankyl was tucked tight, round and dense as a cannonball with his best armor leading. Another moment and he would have collided with the enemy's face. Any other cyborg would have been too slow to react. But Harry's body was laced with superconducting neurons, the reflexes ready for anything. That second hand had already aimed its weapon, and a kinetic round punched its way through the guard's carapace, lifting the body into a useless trajectory, and missing the heart by very little, cutting a wide fissure through the creature's belly.

Ankyl was cast aside.

While Glory continued walking forwards, fearless with rage.

Then Harry Pinchit turned to look at the bride, ready to kill her and her father and every other pretty thing in the world.

Which was when the sky spoke.

JUSTICE

The guard was an unanticipated problem. Somehow he was left untagged and far more competent than any scenario had allowed for. Yet every problem has ten solutions, or a thousand. Every attack is a mass of decisions and lost opportunities, and Warren handled everything well enough or even better than that. Success was in reach, and there was every reason to dance with his pride.

At the final instant, as the world and the solar system watched spellbound, Warren came to the rescue. He was riding inside a small vehicle that only looked like an ordinary sportscraft. Jets screamed, dropping him out of supersonic flight, and at the perfect moment he bailed out. Just him. On cue, his father's mechanical shell flinched as if startled. On command, Warren forced the helpless living face to look skyward. Then with bare feet leading the way, he struck the smoldering altar, shattering ice and tar before his momentum buried him to his knees in the good red tropical soil.

According to the script, Father's voice would ask, "What are you doing here?"

But on the fly, his son rewrote the line. It was obvious why Warren was here. So instead of empty dialogue, he began by shouting, "Don't harm any more of these people. Father. Stand down and power down your weapons."

"But this doesn't concern you," said the false voice. "Leave me alone, son. This is my day."

Warren wasn't carrying weapons. He looked like a cyborg scrubbed fresh by his UV bath. But bending low, he moved his various toes underground, and he fed energy to his legs, making ready.

His father's face stared at him in horror, knowing what would come. But the body remained bold and arrogant and idiotic. And the voice roared one last time, saying, "I will not be insulted by this man. Not ever again—!"

Warren leapt at him.

Even the swift arms couldn't lift fast enough. The guns were powering up to murder Harry's only heir, but the impact was perfect, driving the world's richest man off his feet. And in the end it was very simple and very quick, visible to an audience that watched through the surviving bees: A heroic young man having no choice but to drive his fist through the nanoweave mask, making a mess of the face that was still too much of a face to survive this kind of justice.

ONE GOOD MAN

The hero was floating in a blood-warm pool.

The hero was dying.

Eight days had passed. Countless investigations were underway, and the chain of evidence was not yet clear. But despite rumors and some paranoid notions, it was becoming apparent that Harry Pinchit had been involved with every part of the planning and execution of this blood wedding.

For eight days, Ankyl was dying inside a pool built especially for him. A dozen great doctors were focused only on his wellbeing. That was Glory's doing. An entire hospital was obeying her commands, and when her father made his reasonable points about spending a fortune on a creature that would never recover, she was the force that kept resources focused on her hero.

For the first seven mornings, Glory came to visit the patient.

Each time, she looked different.

The parasitic flowers were gone, and one day her flesh was turned brown and ordinary, and the wounds from the battle and the ripped-out roots were a little at a time. She had no hair yet, but on the last day a little stubble was warily emerging from her scalp, and she had a good pretty smile when she looked into Ankyl's hawk face, telling him and herself, "I won't ever forget you."

But the bodyguard was still holding to life on the eighth day, and the woman didn't arrive at the usual time or any time after that. He lay inside the hot nourishing bath, on his back, letting the liquids do the breathing for him. Then he slept and it was afternoon suddenly, and Ankyl felt something go wrong with his heart, and he died once and then a second time, brought back through the marvelous hands of surgeons who were ignoring far more important patients.

There wouldn't be a ninth day of near-death. Ankyl sensed it and accepted it, and he was astonished by how long he had lingered.

This was not a warrior's death.

Eventually it grew late in the day, and he was alive again, asking no one in particular about Glory's whereabouts.

A crafted nurse was present. Nobody else. She was part gibbon and all comfort—a breasty beast ready to feed any patient with mammary glands that could on a whim produce any of a million medicines.

No medicine would help anymore, and the tits were tucked out of sight.

"Oh, Glory is coming tomorrow," the nurse said cheerfully. "The girl has a big date today. Everybody is hopeful."

For no good reason, Ankyl thought about the purple man—the silly brother that he was supposed to protect during the wedding.

But hearing the name "Lugon" just made the nurse laugh.

"Oh, no. Not that boy, no," said this pathologically cheerful creature. "It's the bastard's bastard son. It's Warren. He invited the girl to join him for dinner. 'Peace talks,' he calls them. But everybody knows. It's really just a first date."

That was when everything became obvious.

"Give me someone to talk to," Ankyl said.

"I'm talking," the nurse pointed.

He named useful names, beginning with his superiors and ending with that purple man who fought like a tiger and hid like a tiger too.

"I'll see who I can find," the nurse promised.

She left.

And Ankyl died two minutes later, for the last time.

THE WALK OF A GOD

Twenty months later, Lugon was a guest at the Ames headquarters—not an uncommon honor for someone who earned considerable fame because of several lucky shots and that now famous threat:

"Pick up those damned bombs, Devon. Or I'll goddamn shoot you myself."

Devon preferred to ignore the man who had embarrassed him in front of billions. Glory was responsible for making Lugon an honored guest, and though he rarely saw the appreciative woman, she had left standing orders allowing him unlimited access to every facility as well as the privilege of one drink every hour, but never any more. The indoor lake was a favorite diversion, though he didn't like the swimming as much as the sitting, and he had several favorite tables where he nursed his drinks and the time while thinking about very little. And twenty months later, he found himself present on the day when Glory and her new fiancé arrived unannounced.

Lugon considered slipping away unseen.

But a new glass of rum had arrived, and he stayed, discovering that he was just as invisible this way.

The cyborg had changed dramatically over the last few months. Machine parts had been peeled away, replaced with his cultivated flesh as well as Ames' new-generation tissues. But he was still sixty percent mechanical beast, and because of that he sank to the lake bottom. Happy as any six-year-old, Warren began to run laps, and the children above him tried to swim against the current, and then he accelerated, the entire body of water becoming a sloshing whirlpool.

To afford herself a clear view and to be seen better by others, Glory climbed the lifeguard's stand, filling a chair meant for an entirely different kind of creature.

She was wearing clothes, which was the day's fashion, but not so many clothes that her new golden flesh was obscured, or the bright beads of sweat that rolled back and forth across a skin that was alive only in the broadest sense.

Glory was making little steps, slowly embracing cyborg technologies.

Her father was angry about quite a lot, of course. Even someone as far removed as Lugon heard stories about battles between Devon and his daughter, threats issued and temporary surrenders offered. But her gold flesh remained—an infusion of nanobots and reaction chambers that ate every stray photon that tried to pass through their timeless beauty.

Light and heat and radio waves were all food, yes. But the flesh also acted as giant lidless eyes, the entire spectrum visible always, and of course the woman noticed Lugon's slow, half-drunken approach.

His plan was charmingly simple. He intended to tell her "thank you" for the usual and the obvious. But a feeling took hold somewhere in those final steps . . . a sensation not unlike the bold madness that made him a great soldier, if only for a moment.

Glory turned to him, wrapping his name in a smile. Then with her original eyes, she continued watching her fiancé and the increasingly rapid water. She wasn't as happy as she was on her wedding day. Nobody ever would be that happy again, not in the history of the world. But she looked regal and competent. She was a lifeguard studying a wild boy's shenanigans, ready to leap into the lake whenever the fun went sour.

That was the moment when Lugon blurted what he thought.

What he knew.

Maybe he had always known the truth. It occurred to him then, listening to his own quick sensible voice, that he had always been thinking about these matters. Sitting at that table and the other tables, sipping drinks, was when he had been going over the problems with the accepted history. And now this would be the second moment in his life when he would rise up as a hero.

He said it all, in a few sharp sentences.

And Glory thought enough of the words to turn and look only at him, at least with those old-fashioned eyes.

Lugon repeated the heart of his message.

"The attack was theatre. We were fooled, all of us, and he got everything in the end. Including you."

Glory did not look pleased. But in that less-than-happy expression was far more than the young man bargained for, and he couldn't process what he saw, and he certainly didn't anticipate what she would say next.

"You know," she said. "I'm not an idiot."

He hadn't intended to say she was.

"I know quite a lot more than you can imagine," she said.

"But if your fiance—" Lugon began.

Glory interrupted him with the one word, "Think."

Think about what? He didn't understand.

She asked, "If the world had gone on as as it was, what would have happened? What was as inevitable as the next breath?"

"I don't know," Lugon said.

"I do," she said.

He pointed at the swirling, angry lake. "He's a monster."

And for the last time, she looked away from him, telling the water, "Being a god is far harder than it appears. Which of course is why there are so few of us."

The Long Haul, from the Annals of Transportation, The Pacific Monthly, May 2009

KEN LIU

Here's another story by Ken Liu, whose "The Regular" appears elsewhere in this anthology. This one is a loving, nostalgic look at a world that might have come to pass, but never did.

Twenty-five years ago, on this day, the *Hindenburg* crossed the Atlantic for the first time. Today, it will cross it for the last time. Six hundred times it has accomplished this feat, and in so doing it has covered the same distance as more than eight roundtrips to the Moon. Its perfect safety record is a testament to the ingenuity of the German people.

There is always some sorrow in seeing a thing of beauty age, decline, and finally fade, no matter how gracefully it is done. But so long as men still sail the open skies, none shall forget the glory of the *Hindenburg*.

—John F. Kennedy, March 31, 1962, Berlin.

It was easy to see the zeppelins moored half a mile away from the terminal. They were a motley collection of about forty Peterbilts, Aereons, Macks, Zeppelins (both the real thing and the ones from Goodyear-Zeppelin), and Dongfengs, arranged around and with their noses tied to ten mooring masts, like crouching cats having tête-à-tête tea parties.

I went through customs at Lanzhou's Yantan Airport, and found Barry Icke's long-hauler, a gleaming silver Dongfeng Feimaotui—the model usually known in America, among the less-than-politically-correct society of zeppeliners, as the "Flying

Chinaman"—at the farthest mooring mast. As soon as I saw it, I understood why he called it the *American Dragon*.

White clouds drifted in the dark mirror of the polished solar panels covering the upper half of the zeppelin like a turtle's shell. Large, waving American flags trailing red and blue flames and white stars were airbrushed onto each side of the elongated silver teardrop hull, which gradually tapered towards the back, ending in a cruciform tail striped in red, white, and blue. A pair of predatory, reptilian eyes were painted above the nose cone and a grinning mouth full of sharp teeth under it. A petite Chinese woman was suspended by ropes below the nose cone, painting over the blood-red tongue in the mouth with a brush.

Icke stood on the tarmac near the control cab, a small, round, glass-windowed bump protruding from the belly of the giant teardrop. Tall and broad-shouldered, his square face featured a tall, Roman nose and steady, brown eyes that stared out from under the visor of a Red Sox cap. He watched me approach, flicked his cigarette away, and nodded at me.

Icke had been one of the few to respond to my Internet forum ad asking if any of the long-haulers would be willing to take a writer for the *Pacific Monthly* on a haul. "I've read some of your articles," he had said. "You didn't sound too stupid." And then he invited me to come to Lanzhou.

After we strapped ourselves in, Icke weighed off the zeppelin—pumping compressed helium into the gasbags until the zeppelin's positive lift, minus the weight of the ship, the gas, us, and the cargo, was just about equal to zero. Now essentially "weightless," the long-hauler and all its cargo could have been lifted off the ground by a child.

When the control tower gave the signal, Icke pulled a lever that retracted the nose cone hook from the mooring mast and flipped a toggle to drop about a thousand pounds of water ballast into the ground tank below the ship. And just like that, we began to rise, steadily and in complete silence, as though we were riding up a skyscraper in a glass-walled elevator. Icke left the engines off. Unlike an airplane that needs the engines to generate forward thrust to be converted into lift, a zeppelin literally floats up, and engines didn't need to be turned on until we reached cruising height.

"This is the *American Dragon*, heading out to Sin City. See you next time, and watch out for those bears," Icke said into the radio. A few of the other zeppelins, like giant caterpillars on the ground below us, blinked their tail lights in acknowledgment.

Icke's Feimaotui is 302 feet long, with a maximum diameter of 84 feet, giving it capacity for 1.12 million cubic feet of helium and a gross lift of 36 tons, of which about 27 are available for cargo (this is comparable to the maximum usable cargo load for semis on the Interstates).

Its hull is formed from a rigid frame of rings and longitudinal girders made out of duratainium covered with composite skin. Inside, seventeen helium gasbags are secured to a central beam that runs from the nose to the tail of the ship, about a third of the way up from the bottom of the hull. At the bottom of the hull, immediately below the central beam and the gasbags, is an empty space that runs the length of the ship.

Most of this space is taken up by the cargo hold, the primary attraction of long-haulers for shippers. The immense space, many times the size of a plane's cargo bay, was perfect for irregularly shaped and bulky goods, like the wind generator turbine blades we were carrying.

Near the front of the ship, the cargo hold is partitioned from the crew quarters, which consists of a suite of apartment-like rooms opening off of a central corridor. The corridor ends by emerging from the hull into the control cab, the only place on the ship with windows to the outside. The Feimaotui is only a little bit longer and taller than a Boeing 747 (counting the tail), but far more voluminous and lighter.

The whole crew consisted of Icke and his wife, Yeling, the woman who was repainting the grinning mouth on the zeppelin when I showed up. Husband-wife teams like theirs are popular on the transpacific long haul. Each of them would take six-hour shifts to fly the ship while the other slept. Yeling was in the back, sleeping through the takeoff. Like the ship itself, much of their marriage was made up of silence and empty space.

"Yeling and I are no more than thirty feet apart from each other just about every minute, but we only get to sleep in the same bed about once every seven days. You end up learning to have conversations in five-minute chunks separated by six-hour blocks of silence.

"Sometimes Yeling and I have an argument, and she'll have six hours to think of a come-back for something I said six hours earlier. That helps since her English isn't perfect, and she can use the time to look up words she needs. I'll wake up and she'll talk at me for five minutes and go to bed, and I'll have to spend the next six hours thinking about what she said. We've had arguments that went on for days and days this way."

Icke laughed. "In our marriage, sometimes you *have* to go to bed angry."

The control car was shaped like an airplane's cockpit, except that the windows slanted outward and down, so that you had an unobstructed view of the land and air below you.

Icke had covered his seat with a custom pattern: a topographical map of Alaska. In front of Icke's chair was a dashboard full of instruments and analog and mechanical controls. A small, gleaming gold statuette of a laughing, rotund bodhisattva was glued to the top of the dashboard. Next to it was the plush figure of Wally, the Green Monster of Fenway Park.

A plastic crate wedged into place between the two seats was filled with CDs: a mix of mandopop, country, classical, and some audio books. I flipped through them: Annie Dillard, Thoreau, Cormac McCarthy, *The Idiot's Guide to Grammar and Composition*.

Once we reached the cruising altitude of 1,000 feet—freight zeppelins generally are restricted to a zone above pleasure airships, whose passengers prefer the view lower down, and far below the cruising height of airplanes—Icke started the electrical engines. A low hum, more felt than heard, told us that the four propellers mounted in indentations near the tail of the ship had begun to turn and push the ship forward.

"It never gets much louder than this," Icke said.

We drifted over the busy streets of Lanzhou. More than a thousand miles west of Beijing, this medium-sized industrial city was once the most polluted city in all of

China due to its blocked air flow and petroleum processing plants. But it is now the center of China's wind turbine boom.

The air below us was filled with small and cheap airships that hauled passengers and freight on intra-city routes. They were a colorful bunch, a ragtag mix of blimps and small zeppelins, their hulls showing signs of make-shift repairs and *shanzhai* patches. (A blimp, unlike a zeppelin, has no rigid frame. Like a birthday balloon, its shape is maintained entirely by the pressure of the gas inside.) The ships were plastered all over with lurid advertisements for goods and services that sounded, with their strange English translations, frightening and tempting in equal measure. Icke told me that some of the ships we saw had bamboo frames.

Icke had flown as a union zeppeliner crewman for ten years on domestic routes before buying his own ship. The union pay was fine, but he didn't like working for someone else. He had wanted to buy a Goodyear-Zeppelin, designed and made 100 percent in America. But he disliked bankers even more than Chinese airship companies, and decided that he would rather own a Dongfeng outright.

"Nothing good ever came from debt," he said. "I could have told you what was going to happen with all those mortgages last year."

After a while, he added, "My ship is mostly built in America, anyway. The Chinese can't make the duratainium for the girders and rings in the frame. They have to import it. I ship sheets of the alloy from Bethlehem, PA, to factories in China all the time."

The Feimaotui was a quirky ship, Icke explained. It was designed to be easy to maintain and repair rather than over-engineered to be durable the way American ships usually were. An American ship that malfunctioned had to be taken to the dealer for the sophisticated computers and proprietary diagnostic codes, but just about every component of the Feimaotui could be switched out and repaired in the field by a skilled mechanic. An American ship could practically fly itself most of the time, as the design philosophy was to automate as much as possible and minimize the chances of human error. The Feimaotui required a lot more out of the pilot, but it was also much more responsive and satisfying to fly.

"A man changes over time to be like his ship. I'd just fall asleep in a ship where the computer did everything." He gazed at the levers, sticks, wheels, toggles, pedals and sliders around him, reassuringly heavy, analog, and solid. "Typing on a keyboard is no way to fly a ship."

He wanted to own a fleet of these ships eventually. The goal was to graduate from owner-operator to just owner, when he and Yeling could start a family.

"Someday when we can just sit back and collect the checks, I'll get a Winnebago Aurora—the 40,000 cubic feet model—and we and our kids will drift around all summer in Alaska and all winter in Brazil, eating nothing but the food we catch with our own hands. You haven't seen Alaska until you've seen it in an RV airship. We can go to places that not even snowmachines and seaplanes can get to, and hover over a lake that has never seen a man, not a soul around us for hundreds of miles."

Within seconds we were gliding over the broad, slow expanse of the Yellow River. Filled with silt, the muddy water below us was already beginning to take on its namesake color, which would deepen and grow even muddier over the next few hundred miles as it traveled through the Loess Plateau and picked up the silt deposited over the eons by wind.

Below us, small sightseeing blimps floated lazily over the river. The passengers huddled in the gondolas to look through the transparent floor at the sheepskin rafts drifting on the river below the same way Caribbean tourists looked through glass-bottom boats at the fish in the coral reef.

Icke throttled up and we began to accelerate north and east, largely following the course of the Yellow River, towards Inner Mongolia.

The Millennium Clean Energy Act is one of the few acts by the "clowns down in D.C." that Icke approved: "It gave me most of my business."

Originally designed as a way to protect domestic manufacturers against Chinese competition and to appease the environmental lobby, the law imposed a heavy tax on goods entering the United States based on the carbon footprint of the method of transportation (since the tax was not based on the goods' country-of-origin, it skirted the WTO rules against increased tariffs).

Combined with rising fuel costs, the law created a bonanza for zeppelin shippers. Within a few years, Chinese companies were churning out cheap zeppelins that sipped fuel and squeezed every last bit of advantage from solar power. Dongfengs became a common sight in American skies.

A long-haul zeppelin cannot compete with a 747 for lifting capacity or speed, but it wins hands down on fuel efficiency and carbon profile, and it's far faster than sur-face shipping. Going from Lanzhou to Las Vegas, like Icke and I were doing, would take about three to four weeks by surface shipping at the fastest: a couple days to go from Lanzhou to Shanghai by truck or train, about two weeks to cross the Pacific by ship, another day or so to truck from California to Las Vegas, and add in a week or so for loading, unloading, and sitting in customs. A direct airplane flight would get you there in a day, but the fuel cost and carbon tax at the border would make it uneco-nomical for many goods.

"Every time you have to load and unload and change the mode of transport, that's money lost to you," Icke said. "We are trucks that don't need highways, boats that don't need rivers, airplanes that don't need airports. If you can find a piece of flat land the size of a football field, that's enough for us. We can deliver door to door from a yurt in Mongolia to your apartment in New York—assuming your building has a mooring mast on top."

A typical zeppelin built in the last twenty years, cruising at 110 mph, can make the 6900-mile haul between Lanzhou and Las Vegas in about 63 hours. If it makes heavy use of solar power, as Icke's Feimaotui is designed to do, it can end up using less than a fraction of a percent of the fuel that a 747 would need to carry the same weight for the same distance. Plus, it has the advantage I'd mentioned of being more accommodating of bulky, irregularly-shaped loads.

Although we were making the transpacific long haul, most of our journey would be spent flying over land. The curvature of the Earth meant that the closest flight path between any two points on the globe followed a great circle that connected the two points and bisected the globe into two equal parts. From Lanzhou to Las Vegas, this meant that we would fly north and east over Inner Mongolia, Mongolia, Siberia, across the Bering Strait, and then fly east and south over Alaska, the Pacific Ocean off the coast of British Columbia, until we hit land again with Oregon, and finally reach the deserts of Nevada.

Below us, the vast city of Ordos, in Inner Mongolia, stretched out to the horizon, a megalopolis of shining steel and smooth glass, vast blocks of western-style houses and manicured gardens. The grid of new, wide streets was as empty as those in Pyongyang, and I could count the number of pedestrians on the fingers of one hand. Our height and open view made the scene take on the look of tilt-shift photographs, as though we were standing over a tabletop scale model of the city, with a few miniature cars and playing figurines scattered about the model.

Ordos is China's Alberta. There is coal here, some of the best, cleanest coal in the world. Ordos was planned in anticipation of an energy boom, but the construction itself became the boom. The more they spent on construction, the more it looked on paper like there was need for even more construction. So now there is this Xanadu, a ghost town from birth. On paper it is the second richest place in China, per capita income just behind Shanghai.

As we flew over the center of Ordos, a panda rose up and hailed us. The panda's vehicle was a small blimp, painted olive green and carrying the English legend: "Aerial Transport Patrol, People's Republic of China." Icke slowed down and sent over the cargo manifests, the maintenance records, which the panda could cross-check against the international registry of cargo airships, and his journey log. After a few minutes, someone waved at us from the window in the gondola of the blimp, and a Chinese voice told us over radio that we were free to move on.

"This is such a messed up country," Icke said."They have the money to build something like Ordos, but have you been to Guangxi? It's near Vietnam, and outside the cities the people there are among the poorest in the world. They have nothing except the mud on the floor of their huts, and beautiful scenery and beautiful women."

Icke had met Yeling there, through a mail-order bride service. It was hard to meet women when you were in the air three hundred days of the year.

On the day of Icke's appointment, he was making a run through Nanning, the provincial capital, as part of a union crew picking up a shipment of star anise. He had the next day, a Saturday, off, and he traveled down to the introduction center a hundred kilometers outside Nanning to meet the girls whose pictures he had picked out and who had been bused in from the surrounding villages.

They had fifteen girls for him. They met in a village school house. Icke sat on a small stool at the front of the classroom with his back to the blackboard,and the girls were brought in to sit at the student desks, as though he was there to teach them.

Most of them knew some English, and he could talk to them for a little bit and mark down, on a chart, the three girls that he wanted to chat with one-on-one in private. The girls he didn't pick would wait around for the next Westerner customer to come and see them in another half hour.

"They say that some services would even let you try the girls out for a bit, like allow you to take them to a hotel for a night, but I don't believe that. Anyway, mine wasn't like that. We just talked. I didn't mark down three girls. Yeling was the only one I picked.

"I liked the way she looked. Her skin was so smooth, so young-looking, and I loved her hair, straight and black with a little curl at the end. She smelled like grass and rainwater. But I liked even more the way she acted with me: shy and very eager to please, something you don't see much in the women back home." He looked over at me as I took notes, and shrugged. "If you want to put a label on me and make the people who read what you write feel good about themselves, that's your choice. It doesn't make the label true."

I asked him if something felt wrong about the process, like shopping for a thing.

"I paid the service two thousand dollars, and gave her family another five thousand before I married her. Some people will not like that. They'll think something is not altogether right about the way I married her

"But I know I'm happy when I'm with her. That's enough for me.

"By the time I met her, Yeling had already dropped out of high school. If I didn't meet her, she would not have gone on to college. She would not have become a lawyer or banker. She would not have gone to work in an office and come home to do yoga. That's the way the world is.

"Maybe she would have gone to Nanning to become a masseuse or bathhouse girl. Maybe she would have married an old peasant from the next village who she didn't even know just because he could give her family some money. Maybe she would have spent the rest of her life getting parasites from toiling in the rice paddies all day and bringing up children in a mud hut at night. And she would have looked like an old woman by thirty.

"How could that have been better?"

The language of the zeppeliners on the transpacific long haul, though officially English, is a mix of images and words from America and China. *Dao, knife, dough,* and *dollar* are used as interchangeable synonyms. Ursine imagery is applied to law enforcement agents along the route: a panda is a Chinese air patrol unit, and a polar bear Russian; in Alaska they are Kodiaks, and off the coast of BC they become whales; finally in America the ships have to deal with grizzlies. The bear's job is to make the life of the zeppeliner difficult: catching pilots who have been at the controls for more than six hours without switching off, who fly above or below regulation altitude, who mix hydrogen into the lift gas to achieve an extra edge in cargo capacity.

"Whales?" I asked Icke. How was whale a type of bear?

"Evolution," Icke said. "Darwin said that a race of bears swimming with their mouths open for water bugs may eventually evolve into whales." (I checked. This was true.)

Nothing changed as an electronic beep from the ship's GPS informed us that we crossed the international border between China and Mongolia somewhere in the desolate, dry plains of the Gobi below, dotted with sparse clumps of short, brittle grass.

Yeling came into the control cab to take over. Icke locked the controls and got up. In the small space at the back of the control cab, they spoke to each other for a bit in lowered voices, kissed, while I stared at the instrument panels, trying hard not to eavesdrop.

Every marriage had its own engine, with its own rhythm and fuel, its own language and control scheme, a quiet hum that kept everything moving. But the hum was so quiet that sometimes it was more felt than heard, and you had to listen for it if you didn't want to miss it.

Then Icke left and Yeling came forward to take the pilot's seat.

She looked at me. "There's a second bunk in the back if you want to park yourself a bit." Her English was accented but good, and you could hear traces of Icke's broad New England A's and non-rhoticity in some of the words.

I thanked her and told her that I wasn't sleepy yet.

She nodded and concentrated on flying the ship, her hands gripping the stick for the empennage—the elevators and rudders in the cruciform tail—and the wheel for the trim far more tightly than Icke had.

I stared at the empty, cold desert passing beneath us for a while, and then I asked her what she had been doing when I first showed up at the airport.

"Fixing the eyes of the ship. Barry likes to see the mouth all red and fierce, but the eyes are more important.

"A ship is a dragon, and dragons navigate by sight. One eye for the sky, another for the sea. A ship without eyes cannot see the coming storms and ride the changing winds. It won't see the underwater rocks near the shore and know the direction of land. A blind ship will sink."

An airship, she said, needed eyes even more than a ship on water. It moved so much faster and there were so many more things that could go wrong.

"Barry thinks it's enough to have these." She gestured towards the instrument panel before her: GPS, radar, radio, altimeter, gyroscope, compass. "But these things help Barry, not the ship. The ship itself needs to *see*.

"Barry thinks this is superstition, and he doesn't want me to do it. But I tell him that the ship looks more impressive for customers if he keeps the eyes freshly painted. That he thinks make sense."

Yeling told me that she had also crawled all over the hull of the ship and traced out a pattern of oval dragon scales on the surface of the hull with tung oil. "It looks like the way the ice cracks in spring on a lake with good *fengshui*. A ship with a good coat of dragon scales won't ever be claimed by water."

The sky darkened and night fell. Beneath us was complete darkness, northern Mongolia and the Russian Far East being some of the least densely inhabited regions of the globe. Above us, stars, denser than I had ever seen winked into existence. It felt as though we were drifting on the surface of a sea at night, the water around us filled with the glow of sea jellies, the way I remember when I used to swim at night in Long Island Sound off of the Connecticut coast.

"I think I'll sleep now," I said. She nodded, and then told me that I could microwave something for myself in the small galley behind the control cab, off to the side of the main corridor.

The galley was tiny, barely larger than a closet. There was a fridge, a microwave, a sink, and a small two-burner electric range. Everything was kept spotless. The pots and pans were neatly hung on the wall, and the dishes were stacked in a grid of cubbyholes and tied down with velcro straps. I ate quickly and then followed the sound of snores aft.

Icke had left the light on for me. In the windowless bedroom, the soft, warm glow and the wood-paneled walls were pleasant and induced sleep. Two bunks, one on top of another, hung against one wall of the small bedroom. Icke was asleep in the bottom one. In one corner of the room was a small vanity with a mirror, and pictures of Yeling's family were taped around the frame of the mirror.

It struck me then that this was Icke and Yeling's *home*. Icke had told me that they owned a house in western Massachusetts, but they spent only about a month out of the year there. Most of their meals were cooked and eaten in the *American Dragon*, and most of their dreams were dreamt here in this room, each alone in a bunk.

A poster of smiling children drawn in the style of Chinese folk art was on the wall next to the vanity, and framed pictures of Yeling and Icke together, smiling, filled the rest of the wall space. I looked through them: wedding, vacation, somewhere in a Chinese city, somewhere near a lake with snowy shores, each of them holding up a big fish.

I crawled into the top bunk, and between Icke's snores, I could hear the faint hum of the ship's engines, so faint that you almost missed it if you didn't listen for it.

I was more tired than I had realized, and slept through the rest of Yeling's shift as well as Icke's next shift. By the time I woke up, it was just after sunrise, and Yeling was again at the helm. We were deep in Russia, flying over the endless coniferous Boreal forests of the heart of Siberia. Our course was now growing ever more easterly as we approached the tip of Siberia where it would meet Alaska across the Bering Sea.

She was listening to an audio book as I came into the control cab. She reached out to turn it off when she heard me, but I told her that it was all right.

It was a book about baseball, an explanation of the basic rules for non-fans. The particular section she was listening to dealt with the art of how to appreciate a stolen base.

Yeling stopped the book at the end of the chapter. I sipped a cup of coffee while we watched the sun rise higher and higher over the Siberian taiga, lighting up the lichen woodland dotted with bogs and pristine lakes still frozen over.

"I didn't understand the game when I first married Barry. We do not have baseball in China, especially not where I grew up.

"Sometimes, when Barry and I aren't working, when I stay up a bit during my shift to sit with him or on our days off, I want to talk about the games I played as a girl or a book I remember reading in school or a festival we had back home. But it's difficult.

"Even for a simple funny memory I wanted to share about the time my cousins and I made these new paper boats, I'd have to explain everything: the names of the paper boats we made, the rules for racing them, the festival that we were celebrating and what the custom for racing paper boats was about, the jobs and histories of the spirits for the festival, the names of the cousins and how we were related, and by then I'd forgotten what was the stupid little story I wanted to share.

"It was exhausting for both of us. I used to work hard to try to explain everything, but Barry would get tired, and he couldn't keep the Chinese names straight or even hear the difference between them. So I stopped.

"But I want to be able to talk to Barry. Where there is no language, people have to build language. Barry likes baseball. So I listen to this book and then we have something to talk about. He is happy when I can listen to or watch a baseball game with him and say a few words when I can follow what's happening."

Icke was at the helm for the northernmost leg of our journey, where we flew parallel to the Arctic Circle and just south of it. Day and night had lost their meaning as we flew into the extreme northern latitudes. I was already getting used to the six-hour-on, six-hour-off rhythm of their routine, and slowly synching my body's clock to theirs.

I asked Icke if he knew much about Yeling's family or spent much time with them.

"No. She sends some money back to them every couple of months. She's careful with the budget, and I know that anything she sends them she's worked for as hard as I did. I've had to work on her to get her to be a little more generous with herself, and to spend money on things that will make us happy right now. Every time we go to Vegas now she's willing to play some games with me and lose a little money, but she even has a budget for that.

"I don't get involved with her family. I figure that if she wanted out of her home and village so badly that she was willing to float away with a stranger in a bag of gas, then there's no need for me to become part of what she's left behind.

"I'm sure she also misses her family. How can she not? That's the way we all are, as far as I can see: we want that closeness from piling in all together and knowing everything about everyone and talking all in one breath, but we also want to run away by ourselves and be alone. Sometimes we want both at the same time. My mom wasn't much of a mom, and I haven't been home since I was sixteen. But even I can't say that I don't miss her sometimes.

"I give her space. If there's one thing the Chinese don't have, it's space. Yeling lived in a hut so full of people that she never even had her own blanket, and she couldn't remember a single hour when she was alone. Now we see each other for a few minutes every six hours, and she's learned how to fill up that space, all that free time, by herself. She's grown to like it. It's what she never had, growing up."

There is a lot of space in a zeppelin, I thought, idly. That space, filled with lighter-than-air helium, keeps the zeppelin afloat. A marriage also has a lot of space. What fills it to keep it afloat?

We watched the display of the aurora borealis outside the window in the northern skies as the ship raced towards Alaska.

I don't know how much time passed before I was jolted awake by a violent jerk. Before I knew what was going on, another sudden tilt of the ship threw me out of my bunk onto the floor. I rolled over, stumbled up, and made my way forward into the control cab by holding onto the walls.

"It's common to have storms in spring over the Bering Sea," Icke, who was supposed to be off shift and sleeping, was standing and holding onto the back of the pilot's chair. Yeling didn't bother to acknowledge me. Her knuckles were white from gripping the controls.

It was daytime, but other than the fact that there was some faint and murky light coming through the windows, it might as well have been the middle of the night. The wind, slamming freezing rain into the windows, made it impossible to see even the bottom of the hull as it curved up from the control cab to the nose cone. Billowing fog and cloud roiled around the ship, whipping past us faster than cars on the autobahns.

A sudden gust slammed into the side of the ship, and I was thrown onto the floor of the cab. Icke didn't even look over as he shouted at me, "Tie yourself down or get back to the bunk."

I got up and stood in the back right corner of the control cab, and used the webbing I found there to lash myself in place and out of the way.

Smoothly, as though they had practiced it, Yeling slipped out of the pilot chair and Icke slipped in. Yeling strapped herself into the passenger stool on the right. The line on one of the electronic screens that showed the ship's course by GPS indicated that we had been zigzagging around crazily. In fact, it was clear that although the throttle was on full and we were burning fuel as fast as an airplane, the wind was pushing us backwards relative to the ground.

It was all Icke could do to keep us pointed into the wind and minimize the cross-section we presented to the front of the storm. If we were pointed slightly at an angle to the wind, the wind would have grabbed us around the ship's peripatetic pivot point and spun us like an egg on its side, yawing out of control. The pivot point, the center of momentum around which a ship would move when an external force is applied, shifts and moves about an airship depending on the ship's configuration, mass, hull shape, speed, acceleration, wind direction, and angular momentum, among other factors, and a pilot kept a zeppelin straight in a storm like this by feel and instinct more than anything else.

Lightning flashed close by, so close that I was blinded for a moment. The thunder rumbled the ship and made my teeth rattle, as though the floor of the ship was the diaphragm of a subwoofer.

"She feels heavy," Icke said. "Ice must be building up on the hull. It actually doesn't feel nearly as heavy as I would have expected. The hull ought to be covered by a solid layer of ice now if the outside thermometer reading is right. But we are still losing altitude, and we can't go any lower. The waves are going to hit the ship. We can't duck under this storm. We'll have to climb over it."

Icke dropped more water ballast to lighten the ship, and tilted the elevators up. We shot straight up like a rocket. The *American Dragon*'s elongated teardrop shape acted as a crude airfoil, and as the brutal Arctic wind rushed at us, we flew like an experimental model wing design in a wind tunnel.

Another bolt of lightning flashed, even closer and brighter than before. The rumble from the thunder hurt my ear drums, and for a while I could hear nothing.

Icke and Yeling shouted at each other, and Yeling shook her head and yelled again. Icke looked at her for a moment, nodded, and lifted his hands off the controls for a second. The ship jerked itself and twisted to the side as the wind took hold of it and began to turn it. Icke reached back to grab the controls as another bolt of lightning flashed. The interior lights went out as the lightning erased all shadows and lines and perspective, and the sound of the thunder knocked me off my feet and punched me hard in the ears. And I passed into complete darkness.

By the time I came to, I had missed the entire Alaskan leg of the journey.

Yeling, who had the helm, was playing a Chinese song through the speakers. It was dark outside, and a round, golden moon, almost full and as big as the moon I remember from my childhood, floated over the dark and invisible sea. I sat down next to Yeling and stared at it.

After the chorus, the singer, a woman with a mellow and smooth voice, began the next verse in English:

> But why is the moon always fullest when we take leave of one another?
> For us, there is sorrow, joy, parting, and meeting.
> For the moon, there is shade, shine, waxing and waning.
> It has never been possible to have it all.
> All we can wish for is that we endure,
> Though we are thousands of miles apart,
> Yet we shall gaze upon the same moon, always lovely.

Yeling turned off the music and wiped her eyes with the back of her hand.

"She found a way out of the storm," she said. There was no need to ask who she meant. "She dodged that lightning at the last minute and found herself a hole in the storm to slip through. Sharp eyes. I knew it was a good idea to repaint the left eye, the one watching the sky, before we took off."

I watched the calm waters of the Pacific Ocean pass beneath us.

"In the storm, she shed her scales to make herself lighter."

I imagined the tung oil lines drawn on the ship's hull by Yeling, the lines etching the ice into dragon scales, which fell in large chunks into the frozen sea below.

"When I first married Barry, I did everything his way and nothing my way. When he was asleep, and I was flying the ship, I had a lot of time to think. I would think about my parents getting old and me not being there. I'd think about some recipe I wanted to ask my mother about, and she wasn't there. I asked myself all the time, *what have I done?*

"But even though I did everything his way, we used to argue all the time. Arguments that neither of us could understand and that went nowhere. And then I decided that I had to do something.

"I rearranged the way the pots were hung up in the galley and the way the dishes were stacked in the cabinets and the way the pictures were arranged in the bedroom and the way we stored life vests and shoes and blankets. I gave everything a better flow of *qi*, energy, and smoother *fengshui*. It might seem like a cramped and shabby place to some, but the ship now feels like our palace in the skies.

"Barry didn't even notice it. But, because of the *fengshui*, we didn't argue any more. Even during the storm, when things were so tense, we worked well together."

"Were you scared at all during the storm?" I asked.

Yeling bit her bottom lip, thinking about my question.

"When I first rode with Barry, when I didn't yet know him, I used to wake up and say, in Chinese, *who is this man with me in the sky?* That was the most I've ever been scared.

"But last night, when I was struggling with the ship and Barry came to help me, I wasn't scared at all. I thought, it's okay if we die now. I know this man. I know what I've done. I'm home."

"There was never any real danger from lightning," Icke said. "You knew that, right? The *American Dragon* is a giant Faraday cage. Even if the lightning had struck us, the charge would have stayed on the outside of the metal frame. We were in the safest place over that whole sea in that storm."

I brought up what Yeling had said, that the ship seemed to know where to go in the storm.

Icke shrugged. "Aerodynamics is a complex thing, and the ship moved the way physics told it to."

"But when you get your Aurora, you'll let her paint eyes on it?"

Icke nodded, as though I had asked a very stupid question.

Las Vegas, the diadem of the desert, spread out beneath, around, and above us.

Pleasure ships and mass-transit passenger zeppelins covered in flashing neon and gaudy giant flickering screens dotted the air over the Strip. Cargo carriers like us were constricted to a narrow lane parallel to the Strip with specific points where we were allowed to depart to land at the individual casinos.

"That's Laputa," Icke pointed above us, to a giant, puffy, baroque airship that seemed as big as the Venetian, which we were passing below and to the left. Lit from within, this newest and flashiest floating casino glowed like a giant red Chinese lantern in the sky. Air taxis rose from the Strip and floated towards it like fireflies.

We had dropped off the shipment of turbine blades with the wind farm owned by Caesars Palace outside the city, and now we were headed for Caesars itself. Comp rooms were one of the benefits of hauling cargo for a customer like that.

I saw, coming up behind the Mirage, the tall spire and blinking lights of the mooring mast in front of the Forum Shops. It was usually where the great luxury personal yachts of the high-stakes rollers moored, but tonight it was empty, and a transpacific long-haul Dongfeng Feimaotui, a Flying Chinaman named the *American Dragon*, was going to take it for its own.

"We'll play some games, and then go to our room," Icke said. He was talking to Yeling, who smiled back at him. This would be the first chance they had of sleeping on the same bed in a week. They had a full 24 hours, and then they'd take off for

Kalispell, Montana, where they would pick up a shipment of buffalo bones for the long haul back to China.

I lay in bed in my Downtown hotel room thinking about the way the furniture in my bedroom was arranged, and imagined the flow of *qi* around the bed, the nightstands, the dresser. I missed the faint hum of the zeppelin's engines, so quiet that you had to listen hard to hear them.

I turned on the light and called my wife. "I'm not home yet. Soon."

Author's Note: This story was inspired in many ways by John McPhee's Uncommon Carriers.

Some liberty has been taken with the physical geography of our world: a great circle flight path from Lanzhou to Las Vegas would not actually cross the city of Ordos.

The lyrics of the song that Yeling plays come from a poem by the Song Dynasty poet Su Shi (1037–1101 A.D). It has remained a popular poem to set to music through the centuries since its composition.

shadow flock

GREG EGAN

Looking back at the century that's just ended, it's obvious that Australian writer Greg Egan was one of the big new names to emerge in SF in the nineties, and is probably one of the most significant talents to enter the field in the last several decades. Already one of the most widely known of all Australian genre writers, Egan may well be the best new hard science writer to enter the field since Greg Bear, and is still growing in range, power, and sophistication. In the last few years, he has become a frequent contributor to Interzone *and* Asimov's Science Fiction, *and has made sales as well as to* Pulphouse, Analog, Aurealis, Eidolon, *and elsewhere; many of his stories have also appeared in various Best of the Year series, and he was on the Hugo final ballot in 1995 for his story "Cocoon," which won the Ditmar Award and the* Asimov's Readers' *Award. He won the Hugo Award in 1999 for his novella "Oceanic." His novel* Quarantine *appeared in 1992;* Permutation City *won the John W. Campbell Memorial Award in 1994. His other books include the novels,* Distress, Diaspora, Teranesia, Zendegi, *and* Schild's Ladder, *and six collections of short fiction,* Axiomatic, Our Lady of Chernobyl, Luminous, Crystal Nights and Other Stories, Dark Integers and Other Stories, *and* Oceanic. *His most recent books are part of the Orthogonal trilogy, consisting of* The Clockwork Rocket, The Eternal Flame, *and* The Arrows of Time. *He has a Web site at www.gregegan.net.*

Here he spins an ingenious and suspenseful story about an intricately timed caper pulled off using fly-sized remote-controlled drones, one with a sting in the tail at the very end which should make us all a bit uneasy.

1

Natalie pointed down along the riverbank to a pair of sturdy-looking trees, a Bald Cypress and a Southern Live Oak, about fifty meters away. "They might be worth checking out." She set off through the scrub, her six students following.

When they reached the trees, Natalie had Céline run a structural check, using the hand-held ground-penetrating radar to map the roots and the surrounding soil. The trees bore gray cobwebs of Spanish moss, but most of it was on the higher branches, out of harm's way. Natalie had chosen the pair three months before, when she was planning the course; it was cheating, but the students wouldn't have thanked her if they'd ended up spending a whole humid, mosquito-ridden day hunting for suitable pillars. In a real disaster you'd take whatever delays and hardship fate served up, but nobody was interested in that much verisimilitude in a training exercise.

"Perfect," Céline declared, smiling slightly, probably guessing that the result was due to something more than just a shrewd judgment made from a distance.

Natalie asked Mike to send a drone with a surveying module across to the opposite bank. The quadrocopter required no supervision for such a simple task, but it was up to Mike to tell it which trees to target first, and the two best candidates—a pair of sturdy oaks—were impossible to miss. The way things were going they stood a good chance of being back in New Orleans before sunset.

With their four pillars chosen, it was time to settle on a construction strategy. They had three quads to work with, and more than enough cable, but the Tchefuncte River was about a hundred and thirty meters wide here. A single spool of cable held a hundred meters, and that was as much weight as each backpack-sized quad could carry.

Josh raised his notepad to seek software advice, but Natalie stopped him. "Would it kill you to spend five minutes thinking?"

"We're going to need to do some kind of mid-air splice," he said. "I just wanted to check what knots are available, and which would be strongest."

"Why splicing?" Natalie pressed him.

He raised his hands and held them a short distance apart. "Cable." Then he increased the separation. "River."

Augusto said, "What about loops?" He hooked two fingers together and strained against the join. "Wouldn't that be stronger?"

Josh snorted. "And halve the effective length? We'd need three spools to bridge the gap then, and you'd still need to splice the second loop to the third."

"Not if we pre-form the middle loop ourselves," Augusto replied. "Fuse the ends, here on the ground. That's got to be better than any mid-air splice. Or easier to check, and easier to fix."

Natalie looked around the group for objections. "Everyone agree? Then we need to make a flight plan."

They assembled the steps from a library of maneuvers, then prepared the cable for the first crossing. The heat was becoming enervating, and Natalie had to fight the urge to sit in the shade and bark orders. Down in Haiti she'd never cared about being comfortable, but it was harder to stay motivated when all that was at stake were a few kids' grades in one minor elective.

"I think we're ready," Céline declared, a little nervous, a little excited.

Natalie said, "Be my guest."

Céline tapped the screen of her notepad and the first quad whirred into life, rising up from the riverbank and tilting a little as it moved toward the cypress.

With cable dangling, the drone made three vertical loops around the tree's lowest branch, wrapping it in a short helix. Then it circumnavigated the trunk twice, once close-in, then a second time in a long ellipse that left cable hanging slackly from the branch. It circled back, dropped beneath the branch and flew straight through the loop. It repeated the maneuver then headed away, keeping the spool clamped until it had pulled the knot tight.

As the first drone moved out over the glistening water, the second one was already ahead of it, and the third was drawing close to the matching tree on the far side of the river. Natalie glanced at the students, gratified by the tension on their faces: success here was not a *fait accompli*. Céline's hand hovered above her notepad; if the drones struck an unforeseen problem—and failed to recover gracefully on their own—it would be her job to intervene manually.

When the second drone had traveled some forty meters from the riverbank it began ascending, unwinding cable as it went to leave a hanging streamer marking its trail. From this distance the shiny blue line of polymer was indistinguishable from the kind its companion was dispensing, but then the drone suddenly stopped climbing, clamped the spool, and accelerated downwards. The single blue line revealed its double-stranded nature, spreading out into a heart-shaped loop. The first drone shot through the heart then doubled back, hooking the two cables together, then the second one pulled out of its dive and continued across the river. The pierced heart always struck Natalie as surreal—the kind of thing that serenading cartoon birds would form with streamers for Snow White in the woods.

Harriet, usually the quietest of the group, uttered an involuntary, admiring expletive.

The third drone had finished hitching itself to the tree on the opposite bank, and was flying across the water for its own rendezvous. Natalie strained her eyes as the second drone went into reverse, again separating the paired cables so its companion could slip through and form the link. Then the second drone released the loop completely and headed back to the riverbank, its job done. The third went off to mimic the first, tying its loose end to the tree where it had started.

They repeated the whole exercise three more times, giving the bridge two handropes and two deck supports, before breaking for lunch. As Natalie was unwrapping the sandwiches she'd brought, a dark blur the size of her thumb buzzed past her face and alighted on her forearm. Instinctively, she moved to flick it off, but then she realized that it was not a living insect: it was a small Toshiba dragonfly, its four wings iridescent with photovoltaic coatings. Whether it was mapping the forest, monitoring wildlife, or just serving as a communications node, the last thing she'd want to do was damage it. The machine should not have landed on anything but vegetation, but no one's programming was perfect. She watched it as it sat motionless in the patch of sunlight falling on her skin, then it ascended suddenly and flew off out of sight.

In the afternoon, the team gave their bridge a rudimentary woven deck. Each of the students took turns donning a life-jacket and hard-hat before walking across the swaying structure and back, whooping with a mixture of elation at their accomplishment and adrenaline as they confronted its fragility.

"And now we have to take it apart," Natalie announced, prepared for the predictable groans and pleas. "No arguments!" she said firmly. "Pretty as it is, it would only take a party of five or six hikers to break it, and if they ended up dashing their brains out in the shallows that would be enough to bankrupt the university and send us all to prison."

2

As Natalie started up the stairs to her apartment she heard a distinctive trilling siren, then saw a red shimmer spilling down onto the landing ahead. The delivery quad came into view and she moved to the left to let it pass, catching a welcome cool wash from its downdraft—a sensation weirdly intensified by the lime-green tint of the receding hazard lights.

She tensed as she approached her floor, hoping that she wouldn't find Sam waiting for her. His one talent was smooth talking, and he could always find someone willing to buzz him into the building. Against her better judgment she'd let her brother wheedle her into sinking ten thousand dollars into his latest business venture, but when it had proved to be as unprofitable as all the rest, rather than apologizing and going in search of paid work he'd started begging her to invest even more, in order to "tip the balance"—as if his struggling restaurant were a half-submerged Spanish galleon full of gold that only needed a few more flotation bladders to rise magnificently to the surface.

Sam wasn't lurking in the corridor, but there was a small package in front of her door. Natalie was puzzled and annoyed; she wasn't expecting anything, and the drones were not supposed to leave their cargo uncollected on a doormat. She stooped down and picked up the parcel; it bore the logo of a local courier, but water had somehow got inside the plastic pocket that held the waybill, turning the portion with the sender's address into gray mush. A gentle shake yielded the clinking slosh of melting ice.

Inside, she put the parcel in the kitchen sink, went to the bathroom, then came back and cut open the mailing box to reveal an insulating foam container. The lid bore the words GUESS WHO? written in black marker. Natalie honestly couldn't; she'd parted company with the last two men she'd dated on terms that made surprise gifts unlikely, let alone a peace offering of chilled crab meat, or whatever this was.

She tugged the lid off and tipped the ice into the sink. A small pink object stood out from the slush, but it wasn't any part of a crab. Natalie stared for several seconds, unwilling to prod the thing into position for a better view, then she fetched a pair of tongs to facilitate a more thorough inspection.

It was the top part of a human finger. A little finger, severed at the joint. She walked away and paced the living room, trying to decode the meaning of the thing before she called the police. She could not believe that Alfonso—a moody musician who'd ditched her when she'd dared to leave one of his gigs at two in the morning, on a work night—would have the slightest interest in mutilating his own precious hands in the service of a psychotic prank. Digging back further she still came up blank. Rafael had smashed crockery once, in the heat of an argument, but by now she'd be surprised to elicit any stronger reaction from him than a rueful smile if they ran into each other on the street. The truth was, the prospect of the cops hauling any of these ex-lovers in for questioning mortified her almost as much as the macabre offering itself, because pointing the finger at any of them seemed preposterously self-aggrandizing. "Really?" she could hear the whole line-up of unlikely suspects demanding, holding out their pristine mitts. "You thought you were worth *that*?"

Natalie walked back to the kitchen doorway. Why was she assuming that the amputation had been voluntary? No one she knew would commit such an act—upon themselves or anyone else—but that didn't mean she didn't know the unwilling donor.

She turned around and rushed to the bedroom, where she kept the bioassay attachment for her notepad. The only software she'd downloaded for it was for personal health and pregnancy testing, but it took less than a minute to get the app she needed.

There was no visible blood left inside the fingertip, but when she picked it up with the tongs it was full of meltwater that ought to be brimming with sloughed cells. She tipped a little of the water onto the assay chip and waited ten long minutes for the software to announce a result for the markers she'd chosen.

Chance of fraternity: 95 percent

Sam must have gone elsewhere for money, but it would have disappeared into the same bottomless pit as her own investment. And when his creditors had come for him with their bolt-cutters, who else was he going to rope in to help him repay his debt but his sister?

Natalie wanted to scream with anger, but she found herself weeping. Her brother was an infuriating, immature, self-deluding brat, but he didn't deserve this. If she had to re-mortgage the apartment to get him out of these people's clutches, so be it. She wasn't going to abandon him.

As she began trying to think through the logistics of dealing with the bank as quickly as possible—without explaining the true purpose of the loan—her phone rang.

3

"We don't want your money. But there is a way you can resolve this situation without paying a cent."

Natalie stared at the kidnapper, who'd asked her to call him Lewis. The food court to which he'd invited her was as busy as she'd seen it on a Wednesday night; she had even spotted a few cops. The undeniable fact of their meeting proved nothing incriminating, but how could he know she wasn't recording his words?

She said, "You're not a loan shark."

"No." Lewis had an accent from far out of state, maybe the Midwest. He was a dark-haired, clean-shaven white man, and he looked about forty. Natalie tried to commit these facts to memory, terrified that when the police finally questioned her she'd be unable to recall his face at all. "We'd like you to consult for us."

"Consult?" Natalie managed a derisive laugh. "Who do you think I work for, the

NSA? Everything I know about drones is already in the public domain. You didn't need to kidnap my brother. It's all on the web."

"There are time pressures," Lewis explained. "Our own people are quick studies, but they've hit a roadblock. They've read your work, of course. That's why they chose you."

"And what am I supposed to help you do? Assassinate someone?" The whole conversation was surreal, but the hubbub of their boisterous fellow diners was so loud that unless she'd stood up on the table and shouted the question, no one would have looked at them twice.

Lewis shook his head; at least he didn't insult her intelligence by feigning offense. "No one will get hurt. We just need to steal some information."

"Then find yourself a hacker."

"The targets are smarter than that."

"*Targets*, plural?"

Lewis said, "Only three that will concern you directly—though in all fairness I should warn you that your efforts will need to synchronize with our own on several other fronts."

Natalie felt light-headed; when exactly had she signed the contract in blood? "You're taking a lot for granted."

"Am I?" There wasn't a trace of menace in his voice, but then, the stakes had already been made clear.

"I'm not refusing," she replied. "I won't help you to inflict bodily harm—but if you're open with me and I'm sure that there's no chance of that, I'll do what you ask."

Lewis nodded, amiable in a businesslike way. He, or his associates, had been cold-blooded enough to mutilate Sam as proof of their seriousness, but if they planned to kill her once she'd served her purpose, why meet physically, in a public space, where a dozen surveillance drones would be capturing the event?

"The targets are all bitionaires," he said. "We don't plan to touch a hair on their heads; we just want their key-strings . . . which are not stored on anything vulnerable to spyware."

"I see." Natalie's own stash of electronic pocket change didn't merit any great precautions, but she was aware of the general idea: anyone prudent, and sufficiently wealthy, kept the cryptographic key to their anonymized digital fortune in a purpose-built wallet. The operating system and other software resided solely on read-only media, and even the working memory functioned under rigid, hardware-enforced protocols that made the whole setup effectively incorruptible. "So how can I get around that? Am I meant to infiltrate the wallet factory?"

"No." Lewis paused, but he wasn't turning coy on her—merely hiding a faint belch behind a politely raised hand. "The basic scenario is the kind of thing any competent stage magician could pull off. The target takes their wallet from its safe, then gets distracted. We substitute an identical-looking device. The target commences to log in to their exchange with the fake wallet; we've already cloned their fingerprints so we can mimic those preliminaries on the real wallet. The target receives a one-time password from the exchange on their cell phone; they enter it into the fake wallet, and we use it to enact our own preferred transactions via the real one."

Natalie opened her mouth to protest: her understanding was that the message from the exchange would also include a hash of the transaction details—allowing the user to double-check exactly what it was they were authorizing. But she wasn't thinking straight: to the human looking at that string of gibberish, the information would be invisible. Only *the wallet itself* had the keys required to reveal the hash's true implications, and the fake wallet would blithely pretend that everything matched up perfectly.

She said, "So all you need to do is invite these people to bring their wall safes to a Las Vegas show."

Lewis ignored her sarcasm. "The transactions can't be rescinded, but it won't take the targets long to discover that they've been duped—and to spread the word. So we need to ensure that these individual operations are as close to concurrent as possible."

Natalie struggled to maintain a tone of disapproval even as her curiosity got the better of her. "How do you make all these people get an itch to buy or sell at the same time?"

"We've already set that in motion," Lewis replied. "You don't need to know the details, but in seven days and thirteen hours, unless the targets are comatose they won't be able to ignore the top story on their news feeds."

Natalie leaned back from the table. Half her experience, and all of her best ideas, had involved maneuvers on a scale of tens of meters by devices that were far from small or stealthy. Dextrous as a well-equipped quadrocopter could be, sleight-of-hand was a bit much to ask of it.

"So do you want me to program robot storks to carry the fake wallets down chimneys?"

Lewis said, "The fake wallets have all been in place for a while, concealed inside innocuous-looking items."

"Like what?"

"Cereal packets. Once people find the brand they like, they stick to it."

"I knew there was a reason I didn't use my supermarket's loyalty card. And the drones?"

"They're on site as well."

"The wallets are how big?"

Lewis held his fingers a few centimeters apart. "Like credit cards. And not much thicker."

"So . . . how many dragonflies?"

"Six at each site. But they're not dragonflies: they're custom-built, smaller and quieter. From a distance they'd pass for houseflies."

Natalie crushed the urge to start grilling him on detailed specifications. "So you have a plan. And you've got the tools in place. Why do you need me at all?"

"Our plan relied on realtime operators," Lewis confessed. "The whole thing seemed too complex to deal with any other way—too many variables, too much uncertainty. All the sites have countermeasures against radio frequency traffic, but we believed we could communicate optically; some people don't consider that at all, or don't make the effort to lock things down tightly."

"But . . . ?"

"In three cases, it looks as if our optical routes have gone from mostly open to patchy at best. Not from any deliberate blocking strategies—just minor changes in the architecture, or people's routines. But it means that a continuous link would be too much to hope for."

Lewis's team had been given the right advice from the start: this was a job for humans. And now she was expected to program eighteen drones to perform three elaborate feats of prestidigitation, using nothing but their own tiny brains?

Natalie said, "Before we go any further, I want you to prove to me that my brother's still alive."

4

"I ran into your fifth grade teacher last week," Natalie remarked, once the pleasantries were over. "The one you had a crush on."

Sam responded with a baffled scowl, too quickly to have needed to think through his reaction. "I don't even remember her name. I certainly didn't have a crush on her!"

However much intelligence the kidnappers might have gathered on the two of them—all the family pets and vacations they'd shared, all the confidences they might have exchanged—there was no proving a negative. Natalie was sure she wasn't watching a puppet.

Someone else was holding the phone, giving the camera a wider view than usual. Apart from his splinted and bandaged finger Sam appeared to be physically unharmed. Natalie refrained from upbraiding him; *she* was the reason he'd been abducted, even if some idiotic plan to keep the restaurant afloat had made him easier to trap.

"Just take it easy," she said. "I'm going to give these people what they want, and you'll be out of there in no time." She glanced at Lewis, then added, "I'll talk to you every morning, OK? That's the deal. They'll have to keep you safe, or I'll pull the plug."

"Do you think you can check in on the restaurant for me?" Sam pleaded. "Just to be sure that the chef's not slacking off?"

"No, I really can't."

"But Dmitri's so lazy! If I'm not—"

Natalie handed the phone back to Lewis and he broke the connection. They'd gone into a side-street to make the call; apparently Lewis hadn't trusted Sam not to start yelling for help if he saw other people in the background.

"I get to call him every day," she said. "That's not negotiable."

"By Skype," Lewis replied.

"All right." A Skype connection would be much harder to trace than a cell phone. Natalie was beginning to feel nostalgic for her previous nightmare scenario of loan sharks and intransigent banks. "What if I do my best, but I can't pull this off?" she asked.

"We're sure you can," Lewis replied.

His faith in her was not at all reassuring. "There's a reason your experts told you they'd need human pilots. I swear I'll try to make this work—but you can't murder my brother because I fall at the same hurdle as your own people."

Lewis didn't reply. On one level, Natalie understood the psychology behind his strategy: if he'd promised that she'd be rewarded merely for trying, she might have been tempted to hold herself back. She suspected that she'd be unlikely to face criminal charges, regardless, but sheer stubbornness or resentment might have driven her to indulge in some passive sabotage if she thought she could get away with it.

"What now?" she asked.

"By the time you get home, we'll have emailed you briefing files. We'll need the software for the drones by midnight on Monday."

Natalie was so flustered that she had to count out the interval in her head. "Five days! I thought you said seven!"

"We'll need to verify the new software for ourselves, then install it via infrasound. The bandwidth for that is so low that it could take up to forty-eight hours."

Natalie was silent, but she couldn't keep the dismay from showing on her face.

"You might want to call in sick," Lewis suggested.

"That's it? That's the best advice you have for me?"

"Read the briefing." Lewis paused, then nodded slightly. He turned and walked away.

Natalie felt herself swaying. If she went to the police, Sam would be dead in an instant. Lewis couldn't deny meeting her, but he would have prepared a well-documented explanation in advance—maybe log files showing that they'd been matched up by a dating site. The e-mailed briefing could have come from anywhere. She had nothing on these people that would make them pause for a second before they graduated from fingertips to heads.

Three targets for her special attention, and many more in the whole blitz. The total haul might reach ten or eleven figures. She'd walked willingly into the aftermaths of hurricanes and earthquakes, but she'd never been foolish enough to position herself—in any capacity—on the route between a gang of thugs and a pile of cash.

5

Natalie spent five hours going through the files before she forced herself to stop. She climbed into bed and lay staring into the humid darkness, soaking the sheets in acrid sweat.

There was no information missing that she could have reasonably demanded. She had architectural plans for the victims' entire houses, complete down to the dimensions of every hinge of every closet. She had three-dimensional imagery and gait data for every member of each of the households; she had schedules that covered both their formal appointments and their imperfectly predictable habits, from meal times to bowel movements. Every motion sensor of every security system, every insect-zapping laser, every moth-chasing cat had been cataloged. Navigating the drones between these hazards was not a hopeless prospect—but the pitfalls that made the whole scheme unravel would be the ones nobody had anticipated. It had taken her years to render her bridge-building algorithms robust against wind, rain and wildlife, and she had still seen them fail when grime and humidity had made a motor stall or a cable stick unexpectedly.

She dozed off for fifteen minutes, then woke around dawn. Somehow she managed to fall asleep again, motivated by the certainty that she'd be useless without at least a couple of hours' rest. At a quarter to nine she rose, phoned the engineering department claiming flu, then took a cold shower and made toast and coffee.

The call to Sam took a minute to connect, but then it was obvious from his appearance that his captors had had to rouse him.

"The job they've given me isn't too hard," she said. "I'll get through it, then everyone can walk away happy."

Sam replied with a tone of wary optimism, "And the ten grand they gave me for the restaurant? They don't want it back?"

"Not as far as I know." Natalie wracked her brain for another puppet test, but then she decided that she'd already heard proof enough: no one else on the planet could make it sound as if ten thousand dollars sunk into that grease-pit would more than compensate for any minor inconvenience the two of them might suffer along the way.

"I owe you, Nat," Sam declared. He thought she was simply working off his debt—the way he'd mowed lawns as a kid, to pay for a neighbor's window that one of his friends had broken. He'd taken the rap to spare the boy a thrashing from his drunken father.

"How's your hand?" she asked.

He held it up; the bandage looked clean. "They're giving me pain-killers and antibiotics. The food's pretty good, and they let me watch TV." He spread his hands in a gesture of contentment.

"So, three stars on Travel Advisor?"

Sam smiled. "I'd better let you get back to work."

Natalie started with the easiest target. A man who lived alone, rarely visited by friends or lovers, he was expected to wake around seven o'clock on D-day morning and go jogging for an hour before breakfast. That would be the ideal time for the drones to break out of their hiding places in the spines of the first editions of Kasparov's five-volume *My Great Predecessors*, which presumably had appeared at a seductively low price in the window of a local used book store. The fake wallet was concealed in one of the book's covers, along with the sliver of whorled and ridged biomimetic polymer that would need to be applied to the real wallet. Thankfully, Natalie's own predecessors had already done the work of programming the clog dance of drone against touch-screen that could mimic a human tapping out any sequence of characters on a virtual keyboard. The jobs they'd left for the pilots had been of an entirely different character.

The shelves in target A's library were all spaced to allow for much taller books, leaving plenty of room for a pair of drones to slice into the wallet's compartment, grab the hooks attached to the cargo, draw it out and fly six meters to deposit it temporarily in a poorly illuminated gap between a shelving unit and a table leg. The safe itself was in the library, and prior surveillance had shown that it was A's habit to place his wallet on the table in question.

The distraction was to be a faucet in the kitchen, primed to fail and send water flooding into the sink at full pressure. The house was fitted with detectors for any ongoing radio traffic—the bugs that had collected the latest imagery had used multi-path optics, until a new sunshade had been fitted to a crucial window—but a single brief RF pulse from a drone to trigger the torrent would appear to the detectors' software as no different from the sparking when a power plug was pulled from a socket.

What if target A broke his routine and did not go jogging? The emergence of the drones and the fake wallet's extraction would not be noisy, so those stages could still proceed so long as the library itself was unoccupied. What if target A had an early visitor, or someone had spent the night? The drones would need to start listening for clues to the day's activities well before seven. Loaded with neural-net templates that would allow them to recognize voices in general, doors opening and closing and footsteps receding and approaching, they ought to be able to determine whether or not it was safe to break out.

But the surveillance images that showed the five books neatly shelved were three weeks old; it was possible that they'd ended up strewn around the house, or piled on a table beneath other books and magazines. GPS wouldn't work inside the building, but Natalie used a smattering of WiFi signal strengths collected in the past to equip the drones with a passable ability to determine their location, then added software to analyze the echo of an infrasound pulse, to help them anticipate any obstacles well before they'd broken out of their cardboard chrysalises.

The doors and windows—and even the roof space—were fitted with alarms, but target A had no motion sensors in the library that would scream blue murder every time a housefly crossed the room. Not even two houseflies carrying an object resembling a credit card.

Natalie put the pieces together then ran simulations, testing the software against hundreds of millions of permutations of all the contingencies she could think of: the placement of the books, which doors were open or closed, new developments in the target's love life, and his peregrinations through every plausible sequence of rooms and corridors. When things turned out badly from the simulator's God's-eye-view, she pored over the visual and auditory cues accessible to the drones in a selection of the failed cases, and refined her software to take account of what she'd missed.

By midnight she was exhausted, but she had the mission either succeeding completely or aborting undetected in 98.7 percent of the simulations. That would have to be good enough. The other targets were going to be more difficult; she needed to move on.

6

With every day that passed Natalie worked longer, but her short bouts of sleep came fast and ran deep, as if her brain had started concentrating some endogenous narcotic brew and would dispense the thick black distillate the moment she closed her eyes.

In the early hours of Monday morning, she dreamed that she was taking her final exam in machine vision. Sam was seated three rows behind her, throwing wads of chewing gum that stuck in her hair, but she knew that if she turned around to whisper an angry reprimand he'd only ignore it, and it wasn't worth the risk of being accused of cheating.

She glanced up at the clock to check the time; just seconds remained, but she felt satisfied with her answers. But when she looked down at the exam paper she realized that she'd misread the questions and filled the booklet with useless *non sequiturs*.

She woke and marched to the shower to clear her head, trying to convince herself that she hadn't merely dreamed all the progress she'd made. But the truth was, target C was almost done. The ordeal was nearly over.

It was still early, but Sam had grown used to her schedule. Natalie confined herself to jokes and small talk; the more matter-of-fact they kept the conversations, the easier it was on both of them. Until he was actually free, she couldn't afford to let her emotions take over.

Target C had a husband and two school-age children, but if their domestic routine followed its usual pattern they would be out of the house well before the trigger—expected at eleven a.m. in C's east-coast time zone. The most worrying thing about C was not her family, but the way she kept changing the decorative skins she'd bought for her wallet: the surveillance, going back twelve months, revealed no fewer than four different designs. Natalie could accept that anyone might have their personal esthetic whims, even when it came to this most utilitarian of items. But it was hard to believe that it had never once crossed target C's mind that these unpredictable embellishments would make it so much harder for her to mistake another wallet for her own.

Still, the last surveillance imagery was only ten days old, and it showed a skin that was no different from that on the planted fake. The odds weren't bad that it would remain in place, and the changes in style on the previous occasions had been so clear that the drones would have no difficulty noticing if the fake had gone out of fashion. Lewis's people had not been foolhardy enough to try to wrap their substitute in some kind of infinitely reconfigurable chameleon device; visually, these ten-dollar skins were not unforgeable works of art, but they did come with different textures—slick, metallic, silky. Half-fooling a willing participant in a VR game with a haptic interface was one thing, but no hardware on the planet could morph from brushed steel to lamb's fleece well enough to convince someone who'd held the real thing just seconds before.

Natalie started the simulations running. Target C had a strong aversion to insects, and every room was fitted with an eliminator, but even these low-powered pinprick lasers could not be unleashed in a human-occupied space without rigorous certification that ensured their compliance with published standards. Insects followed characteristic, species-specific flight patterns, and the eliminators were required to give any ambiguous object the benefit of the doubt, lest some poor child flicking an apple seed off her plate or brushing glitter from her home-made fairy wand summon unfriendly fire from the ceiling. The drones didn't need to imitate any particular, benign airborne debris; they merely had to exhibit an acceleration profile a few standard deviations away from anything seen in the official laboratory studies of *Musca*, *Culex* or *Aedes*. Unlike target B's cat, the necessary strictures were completely predictable.

With the count of trials rising into seven digits and still no atonal squawk of failure, Natalie let herself relax a little and close her eyes. The midnight deadline was still fourteen hours away. She'd sent versions of her work for the other two targets to her "Team Leader"—as the collaboration software would have it—and received no complaints. Let these clowns run off to the Bahamas with their billions, and let the victims learn to use banks like normal people. She'd done the only honorable thing under the circumstances, and she had nothing to be ashamed of. Whatever the authorities decided, she could still look herself—and any juror—in the eye.

She opened her eyes. Why, exactly, did she believe that Lewis's people would let her live to confess her crimes? Because she'd been a good girl and done as she was told?

Lewis had met her in a public place, making her feel safer about the encounter and seeming to offer a degree of insurance: if she vanished, or turned up dead, the authorities would scour the surveillance records and reconstruct her movements. A judge was much less likely to sign a warrant for the same trawling expedition if a living, breathing woman and her mildly mutilated brother went to the police with an attention-seeking story that positioned them in starring roles in the heist—and in any case, a shared meal proved nothing about her dinner companion.

But all of that presupposed that there really were records of the meeting: that the flock of benign surveillance drones that watched over downtown New Orleans had been as vigilant as ever that night—even in the places her adversaries had chosen to send her. Who was to say that they hadn't infiltrated the flock: corrupted the software in existing drones, or found a way to substitute their own impostors?

If there was nothing at all to tie Lewis to her—save the microscopic chance that some diner in the food court that night would remember the two of them—why would the thieves leave any loose ends?

Natalie tried to keep her face locked in the same expression of exhaustion and grim resolve that she'd felt being etched into it over the last five days; the whole apartment was probably full of the same kind of micro-cameras that had documented the targets' lives in such detail. And for all she knew there could be hidden drones too, far more dangerous than anything the targets were facing: robot wasps with fatal stings. A week ago that would have sounded like florid paranoia, but now it was the most reasonable thing she could imagine, and the only thoughts that seemed truly delusional were those of walking away from this unscathed.

She went to the kitchen and made fresh coffee, standing by the pot with her eyes half-closed. Apart from any cameras on the walls, her computer was sure to be infested with spyware. They would have done the same to the one in her office at UNO—and in any case, she doubted that her criminal overseers would be happy if she suddenly decided to show up at work.

When the coffee was ready she stirred in three spoonfuls of sugar; before the crisis she'd gone without, but now she'd been escalating the dose day by day in the hope of shoring up her flagging powers of concentration. She carried the mug back toward her desk, squinting wearily at the screen as she approached, hoping that she wasn't over-playing her frazzled sleep-walker's demeanor.

She tripped and staggered, spilling the sticky, scalding brew straight down the air vent at the top of her workstation. The fans within blew out a geyser of mud-colored liquid for a second or two, with specks reaching as high as the ceiling, then the whole machine shut down, plunging the room into silence.

Natalie spent half a minute swearing and sobbing, then she picked up her phone. She made five calls to local outlets that might—just conceivably—have supplied a replacement, but none of them had a suitably powerful model in stock, and the ones they could offer her would have slowed the simulations to a crawl. She pushed the last salesperson hard, for effect, but not even a premium delivery charge could summon what she needed by drone from the Atlanta warehouse in time.

Finally, as if in desperation, she gritted her teeth and availed herself of the only remaining solution.

"I'd like to rent a cubicle for twelve hours."

"Any secretarial services?" the booking bot asked.

"No."

"Any IT requirements?"

"You bet." She reeled them off, but the bot was unfazed. The firm she'd chosen was accustomed to catering for architects and engineers, caught out with some processor-intensive emergency that was too commercially sensitive to be run in the cloud, or simply too awkward to refactor for a change of platform. It was the most logical place for her to go, given that the university was out of bounds—but it would have taken extraordinary prescience for Lewis's gang to have pre-bugged the place.

Natalie caught a bus into the city. A fly with an odd bluish tint to its body crawled over the windowpane beside her; she watched it for a while, then reached out and squashed it with the side of her fist and inspected its soft remains.

At the office complex, the demands of security and climate control had her pass through half a dozen close-fitting doors. Between these welcome barriers she ran fingers through her hair, brushed her arms and legs, and flattened her back against the nearest wall. The security guards watching on closed circuit could think what they liked, so long as she didn't look quite crazy enough to be thrown out.

On the eleventh floor, she entered the tiny cubicle assigned to her, closed the door and started loading the most recent hourly backup of her project from the flash drive she'd brought. This version wasn't quite the one that had been doing so well in the simulations, but she remembered exactly what changes she'd need to make to bring it up to that level.

The gang's roboticists would run tests of their own, but if she held off delivering the software until just before midnight they would be under enormous pressure. In a finite time there was only so much checking her fellow humans could do, and not a lot of point in them trying to wade manually through every line of code and every neural-net template included in the package. Like her, in the end they would be forced to put their trust in the simulations.

As instructed, Natalie had programmed her drones to wake and commence their mission, not at any predetermined time, but on receipt of an external infrasound cue. It made sense to allow that much flexibility, in case the lurch in the markets that was meant to prompt people to reach for their wallets came later than expected.

One side effect of this decision was that for targets whose schedules were different for every day of the week, simulations had to be run separately for each day. But where there was no difference except for weekdays versus weekends, the simulated drones were fed no finer distinction, and the millions of permutations to be tested could play out much faster by limiting them to this simple dichotomy.

Target C stuck to a single routine from Monday to Friday, so as far as the simulations for her were concerned, they were taking place only on a generic weekday. Anything in the software that relied on it being a specific day of the week wouldn't come into play, in the simulations.

In the real world, though, Thursday would still announce itself as Thursday in the drones' internal clocks. And that very fact would be enough to tell the drones' software that they were out of VR and moving through the land of flesh and blood.

Natalie couldn't be sure that D-day would arrive on schedule, but she had no choice but to trust the swindlers to accomplish their first, enabling feat exactly as they'd planned it all along.

7

"This should be our last call," Natalie told Sam.

"There are two ways I could take that," he joked.

"Take it the good way."

"So they're happy with your work?" Sam tried to make that sound like a joke, too, but he couldn't quite pull it off.

"I've had no complaints."

"I always knew you'd end up as a mob accountant."

"Ha!" She'd had a summer job once that included book-keeping for a small construction firm with a shady reputation, but every transaction that had crossed her desk had appeared entirely legitimate.

"Stay strong," she said. "I'll see you soon."

Sam just nodded and lowered his eyes. She cut the link.

Natalie waited five more minutes, for six o'clock sharp. If the market trigger was coming, Lewis's people would have recognized the early signs of its onset hours ago, but she'd had no idea what to look for, and she hadn't wanted to attract suspicion by trawling the financial news. It would be impossible to load an entirely new copy of the drones' software via infrasound in less than two days—but in less than an hour, an experienced team might be able to write and deliver a small patch that neutralized the effects of her sabotage.

There would be no moment of perfect safety. Natalie used the collaboration software to send a message: *Flaw in the code for target C. Need to discuss urgently.*

Twenty seconds later, her phone rang.

"What are you talking about?" Lewis demanded angrily.

"It hasn't started executing yet, has it?" Natalie did her best to sound business-like: she was acknowledging her screw-up, but she was still the voice of authority when it came to these drones, and she was asking for the state of play in order to salvage the situation as rapidly as possible.

"Of course it's *executing!*" Lewis snapped.

Natalie couldn't hold back a smile of relief. The software would be impossible to patch now.

"Why did you think it wouldn't start?" Lewis was baffled. "We got the confirmation hum. The drones are wide awake and running what we loaded. What's this about?"

Natalie said, "If the drones in target C's house don't catch sight of me and my brother—fully ambulatory, with our usual gaits—alone in a room with that woman before eleven a.m., things are going to play out a little differently than they did in the simulations."

Lewis understood immediately. "You *stupid bitch*—"

"No," Natalie cut him off. "Stupid would have been trusting you."

"We'll kill you both," he said coldly. "We can live without the yield from one target."

"Can you live without the yield from all the targets who'll be warned off when this woman raises the alarm? When the drones fly up to her and drop the fake wallet right in front of her face?"

To his credit, Lewis only took a few seconds to give up on the idea of more threats and bravado. "Be on the street outside your building in five minutes." He cut off the call.

Natalie put the phone down. Her whole body was trembling. She went to the bathroom and splashed water on her face, then left her apartment and sprinted down the stairs.

The black car that came for her had tinted passenger windows. Lewis opened the rear door and motioned for her to join him. Sam was sitting by the left window; he glanced across at her anxiously.

"This is what will happen," Lewis told Natalie as they sped away. "You're going to drive a car toward the target's house. Another driver will rear-end you in a hit-and-run: plenty of noise and crumpled panels, but you won't be hurt. You and your brother will walk from the wreckage, knock on the target's door, and ask her to call an ambulance. We'll spoof the 911 connection, so no ambulance will come until we put in the call ourselves. You'll play a wilting Southern flower, and at some point you'll be invited in to wait."

Natalie was incredulous. "She won't invite us in straight away?"

Lewis clenched his teeth, then spoke. "Have you ever been to Nassau County, Long Island?"

"Can we fly Business Class?" Sam wondered.

Lewis reached into a sports bag on his lap and drew out a pair of blindfolds.

Minutes later, the traffic sounds around them receded. They were bundled out of the car, led across the tarmac and up a set of stairs into what must have been a private jet. Natalie felt the plane taxiing before she'd been guided to her seat, and ascending before she'd fumbled the belt into place. It would take almost three hours to reach New York; if they hit so much as an unexpected head wind, Lewis might decide to cut his losses and drop them from the plane.

"I should have told them earlier," she whispered to Sam. "I'm sorry." She'd been fixated on the risk that she'd spring the revelation too early.

"Why do we have to visit this woman?" he asked.

Natalie talked him through the whole thing, from the heist itself to the dead-man switch she'd installed at the last moment.

"You couldn't have found a way to get us to Paris instead?" Sam joked.

"They set you up," Natalie stressed. "They only loaned you the money so they could rope me in if they had to."

"I know," he said. "I get it."

"So whatever happens now, it's not on you."

Sam laughed. "*Seriously?* You thought I was going to blame myself?"

As soon as the wheels hit the ground, someone grabbed Natalie's elbow. "How's the time?" she enquired.

"Local time's ten twenty-seven," Lewis replied.

The blindfolds stayed on as they boarded a second car. When it screeched to a halt and Lewis tugged the dark band up from Natalie's eyes, she squinted out into a fluorescent-lit mechanics' workshop. Half a dozen men in overalls were standing beside a hydraulic jack, watching the new arrivals.

Lewis motioned to her to leave the car. "This is what you'll be driving." He gestured at a white sedan a few meters away. "You rented this at the airport; there are used boarding passes in the glove compartment, and some luggage with clothes and toiletries in the trunk. I don't care what your cover story is—why you're in New York, where you were heading—but you should give your real names. And make sure you don't distract the target from the trigger, or do anything else stupid. Don't even think about driving away; we can immobilize the vehicle remotely, and the crash that follows would be a whole lot worse than the one we've discussed."

"I don't have the address," Natalie realized.

"The GPS has already been programmed. The house number is one hundred and seven; don't get confused and knock anywhere else."

"What if someone else offers to help us?"

Lewis said, "The street will be as good as empty. The crash will be right outside her door."

Natalie turned to Sam, who'd joined her on the floor of the workshop. "Are you OK with this?"

"As opposed to what?"

Lewis walked up to Sam and put a hand on his shoulder. "Sorry about the *déjà vu*, but it will make the whole thing more authentic."

Sam stared at him. Natalie felt the blood draining from her face. The waiting men converged on Sam, one of them carrying a wrench.

Sam didn't fight them, he just bellowed from the pain. When everyone separated the bandage was gone from his finger and his wound was dripping blood.

Lewis said, "Better put that in your pocket for the drive, so no one sees it before the crash."

The figures on Natalie's watch had turned blue, to remind her that it had auto-synched to the new time zone. It was ten forty-six. The GPS estimated two minutes to their destination. They'd be outside the house in plenty of time—but they needed to be seen by the drones, indoors.

She glanced over at Sam. He was still pale, but he looked focused. There weren't many cars on the tree-lined streets, and Natalie had yet to spot a single pedestrian. The houses they were passing were ostentatious enough, if not exactly billion-aires' mansions. But then, half the point of putting assets into digital currency was keeping a low profile.

"Destination in fifteen seconds," the GPS announced cheerily. Natalie resisted glancing in the rear-view mirror as she braked. The red pickup that had been fol-lowing them since the garage slammed into the back of the sedan.

The airbags inflated like giant mushroom caps sprouting in time-lapse. Natalie felt the seat belt dig into her shoulder, but when her ears stopped ringing she took stock of her sensations and found no real pain.

"You OK?" she asked Sam. She could hear squealing tires as the truck did a U-turn and departed.

"Yeah."

"Our phones were in the hands-free docks," she reminded him. "The airbags are blocking them."

"We've just been in a crash," Sam said. "No one's going to ask us where our phones are.

Natalie got her door open and clambered out. They were right beside the mail-box of number one hundred and seven.

As Sam joined her, his severed finger exposed, the front door opened and target C ran out toward them.

"Are you all right? Is anyone else in the car?"

Natalie said, "I'm OK. It's just me and my brother."

"Oh, he's bleeding!" Target C was carrying her phone; she hit some keys then raised it to her ear. "A traffic accident. The other driver's cleared off. No . . . they're both walking, but the young man's hand . . . that's correct."

She lowered the phone and motioned to them to approach. "Please, come inside. They said the ambulance will be a few minutes."

Sam pulled out a handkerchief and wrapped it around the stump of his finger. He couldn't quite look their Good Samaritan in the eye as he stepped through the doorway.

Target C led them into her carpeted living room, unfazed by Sam's blood. "Please, take a seat. I'll bring you some water."

"Thank you." When the woman had left, Natalie checked her watch. It was ten fifty-three. The six drones would be performing sweeps of all the rooms where she and Sam might plausibly have ended up, mostly staying near the ceiling out of people's normal lines of sight. She looked up, and after ten or fifteen seconds she saw it: her own tiny, loyal slave, confirming her safety before fetching its brothers to resume the original plan.

"Are we safe now?" Sam asked.

"I don't know."

"Maybe we should warn her," he suggested.

Natalie was torn. Lewis's people might still come after them, whatever they did. But which action would nudge the odds in favor of survival: enraging their enemies, but weakening them too by depriving them of part of their haul, or placating them but making them stronger?

"We can't risk it," she whispered.

Target C came into the room with a pitcher of water on a tray. She poured two glasses and handed them to her guests. "I can't believe that maniac just drove off," she said. She gazed forlornly at Sam's hand. "What happened?"

"I was opening the glove compartment," Sam replied. "The doors on those things are like guillotines."

Target C's phone beeped: not a ring tone, but some kind of alert. She spent a few seconds trying to ignore it, then lost the fight and examined the screen. Natalie could almost read the woman's deliberations from the movement of her eyes and the changing set of her jaw. This was the trigger: either a grave threat to her wealth, or an irresistible opportunity.

The woman looked up. "I'm so rude. My name's Emily."

"Natalie."

"Sam."

"Are you folks from around here?"

"New Orleans."

Emily nodded, as if she'd guessed as much already. "Where is that ambulance?" She turned to Sam. "Are you in agony? I have Tylenol. But maybe you've suffered some other injury that could make that the wrong thing to take?"

Sam said, "It's all right. I'll wait for the paramedics."

Emily thought for a few seconds. "Let me just check in the medicine cabinet, so I know exactly what I've got."

"Thank you," Sam replied.

Natalie watched her leave, and saw her take the turn toward the study where the wallet was held in its safe. The fake would already be waiting on top of a bookcase, invisible to anyone of normal height. The drones would be watching, parsing the scene, determining when the safe had been opened and the wallet taken out.

Water began drumming against stainless steel, far away in the kitchen. Natalie heard Emily curse in surprise, but she didn't run out of the study immediately.

Three seconds, four seconds, five seconds. The sound of the torrent was hard to ignore, conjuring images of flooded floors and water damage. Most people would have sprinted toward the source immediately, dropping almost anything to attend to it.

Finally, Natalie heard the hurried footsteps as Emily rushed to the kitchen. She could not have had time to execute whatever actions the trigger had inspired—but she had certainly had time to put the wallet back in the safe. Nothing else explained the delay. With strangers in the house—and more expected soon, from the emergency services—she wasn't going to leave the keys to her fortune lying around unattended.

It took Emily a few minutes to assess the situation in the kitchen—unsalvageable by merely tinkering with the faucet—then go to the water mains and shut off the flow at its source. She returned to the living room drying her hands on a towel.

"That was bizarre! Something just . . . burst." She shook her head. "We've only got Tylenol," she told Sam. She took her phone from her pocket. "Do you think I should call them again?"

Sam said, "It's not like I'm having a heart attack. And who knows what else they're dealing with?"

Emily nodded. "All right." She waited a few seconds, then said, "If you'll excuse me, I just need to clean up. Before it soaks through . . . "

Natalie said, "We're fine, really."

Emily left the room, to avail herself of the opportunity to move some of her money around. Whether the market signal proved misleading or not, the outcome was unlikely to ruin her. But the drones were helpless now; there'd be no prospect of them making the switch.

Natalie stared at the carpet, trying to assess the situation. She'd shafted Lewis's gang—entirely by mistake, and only partially: Emily would have no suspicions, no reason to raise the alarm and derail the rest of the heist. Lewis might well deduce exactly what had happened. But what would that lead to? Leniency? Forgiveness?

After half an hour, with still no ambulance, Emily phoned 911 again. "They said there was nothing in the system!" she told Natalie. "That fills you with confidence!"

The paramedics declared that Sam needed to go into the emergency department. One of them spent a couple of minutes searching the wreck for his severed fingertip, while the other waxed lyrical on the wonders of microsurgery, but in the end they gave up. "It must have got thrown out and some dog took it."

An hour later, while Natalie was dealing with paperwork at the hospital, two uniformed police approached her. "We had a report of a hit-and-run," the older cop said.

"Can you protect us?" Natalie asked him. "If we're being watched by someone dangerous?"

The cop glanced at his partner. "You're shaken up, I understand. But this was probably just some drunken fool too cowardly to own up to what he'd done. Nothing you should be taking personally."

Natalie's teeth started chattering, but she forced herself to speak.

"They kidnapped my brother," she said. "I'll tell you everything—but I need to know: if they can see everywhere, and reach anywhere, how are you going to protect us?"

thing and sick

ADAM ROBERTS

The Fermi Paradox is one of the central—and most controversial—mysteries of modern science. Simply stated: Where is everybody? If the galaxy is swarming with alien civilizations, how come we don't see any evidence of them, how come they haven't visited us? Is there anybody out there at all, or are we completely alone in the universe? Science fiction writers have provided many ingenious explanations for Fermi's Paradox—and here's another one, even more bizarre and unexpected than usual, by Adam Roberts.

A senior reader in English at London University, Adam Roberts is an SF author, critic, reviewer, and academic who has produced many works on nineteenth-century poetry as well as critical studies of science fiction such as The Palgrave History of Science Fiction. *His own fiction has appeared in* Postscripts, SCI FICTION, Live Without a Net, FutureShocks, Forbidden Planets, Spectrum SF, Constellations, *and elsewhere, and was collected in* Swiftly. *His novels include* Salt; On; Stone; Polystom; The Snow; Gradisil; Splinter; *and* Land of the Headless. *Among his recent novels are* Yellow Blue Tibia *and* New Model Army. *His most recent books are a chapbook novella,* An Account of a Voyage from World to World Again, by Way of the Moon, 1726, in the Commission of Georgius Rex Primus, Monarch of Northern Europe and Lord of Selenic Territories, Defender of the Faith, Undertaken by Captain Wm. Chetwin Aboard the Cometes Georgius, *and a collection,* Adam Robots. *He lives in Staines, England with his wife and daughter, and has a website at* www.adamroberts.com.

CHAPTER 1

It started with the letter.

Roy would probably say it started when he solved the Fermi Paradox, when he achieved (his word) *clarity*. Not clarity, I think: but sick. Sick in the head. He probably wouldn't disagree.Not with so much professional psychiatric opinion having been brought to bear on the matter. He concedes as much to me, in the many communications he has addressed me from his asylum. He sends various manifestos and communications to the papers too, I understand. In all of them he claims to have finally solved the Fermi Paradox. If he has, then I don't expect my nightmares to diminish any time soon.

I do have bad dreams, yes. Intense, visceral nightmares from which I wake sweating and weeping. If Roy is wrong, then perhaps they'll diminish with time.

But really it started with the letter.

I was in Antarctica with Roy Curtius, the two of us hundreds of miles inland, far away from the nearest civilisation. It was 1986, and one (weeks-long) evening and one (months-long) south polar night. Our job was to process the raw astronomical data coming in from Proxima and Alpha Centurai. Which is to say: our job was to look for alien life. There had been certain peculiarities in the radioastronomical flow from that portion of the sky, and we were looking into it. Whilst we were out there we were given some other scientific tasks to be keeping ourselves busy with, but it was the SETI business that was the main event. We maintained the equipment, and sifted the data, passing most of it on for more detailed analysis back in the UK. Since in what follows I am going to say a number of disobliging things about him, I'll concede right here that Roy was some kind of programming genius—this, remember, back in the late '80s, when "computing" was quite the new thing.

The base was situated as far as possible from light pollution and radio pollution. There was nowhere on the planet further away than where we were.

We did the best we could, with 1980s-grade data processing and a kit-built radio dish flown out to the location in a packing crate, and assembled as best two men could assemble anything when it was too cold for us to take off our gloves.

"The simplest solution to the Fermi thing," I said once, "would be simply to pick up alien chatter on our clever machines. Where are the aliens? *Here* they are."

"Don't hold your breath," he said.

We spent some hours every day on the project. The rest of the time we ate, drank, lay about and killed time. We had a VHS player, and copies of *Beverly Hills Cop*, *Ghostbusters*, *The Neverending Story* and *The Karate Kid*. We played cards. We read books. I was working my way through Frank Herbert's *Dune* trilogy. Roy was reading Immanuel Kant. That fact, right there, tells you all you need to know about the two of us. "I figured eight months isolation was the perfect time really to get to grips with the *Kritik der reinen Vernunft*," he would say. "Of course," he would add, with a little self-deprecating snigger, "I'm not reading it in the original German. My German is good—but not *that* good." He used to leave the book lying around: *Kant's Critique of Pure Reason, transl. Meiklejohn*. It had a red cover. Pretentious fool.

"We put too much trust in modern technology," he said one day. "The solution to the Fermi Paradox? It's all in here." And he would stroke the cover of the *Critique*, as if it were his white cat and he Ernst StavroBlofeld.

"Whatever, dude," I told him.

Once a week a plane dropped off our supplies. Sometimes the pilot, Diamondo, would land his crate on the ice-runway, maybe even get out to stretch his legs and chat to us. I've no idea why he was called "Diamondo," or what his real name was. He was Peruvian I believe. More often, if the weather was bad, or if D. was in a hurry, he would swoop low and drop our supplies, leaving us to fight through the burly snowstorm and drag the package in. Inside would be necessaries, scientific equipment, copies of relevant journals—paper copies, it was back then, of course—and so on. The drops also contained correspondence. For me that meant: letters from family, friends and above all from my girlfriend Lezlie.

Two weeks before all this started I had written to Lezlie, asking her for a paperback copy of *Children of Dune*. I told her, in what I hope was a witty manner, that I had been disappointed by the slimness of *Dune Messiah*. I need the big books, I had said, to fill up the time, the long aching time, the (I think I used the phrase) terrible absence-of-Lezlie-thighs-and-tits time that characterised life in the Antarctic. I mention this because, in the weeks that followed, I found myself going back over my letter to her—my memory of it, I mean; I didn't keep a copy—trying to work out if I had perhaps offended her with a careless choice of words. If she might, for whatever reason, have decided not to write to me this week in protest at my vulgarity, or sexism. Or to register her disapproval by not paying postage to send a fat paperback edition of *Dune III* to the bottom of the world. Or maybe she *had* written.

You'll see what I mean in a moment.

Roy never got letters. I always got some: some weeks as many as half a dozen. He: none. "Don't you have a girlfriend?" I asked him, once. "Or any friends?"

"Philosophy is my girlfriend," he replied, looking smugly over the top of his copy of the *Critique of Pure Reason*. "The solution to the Fermi Paradox is the friend I have yet to meet. Between them, they are all the company I desire."

"If you say so, mate," I replied, thinking inwardly *weirdo!* and *loser* and *billy-no-mates* and other such things. I didn't say any of that aloud, of course. And each week it would go on: we'd unpack the delivery parcel, and form amongst all the other necessaries and equipment I'd pull out a rubberband-clenched stash of letters, all of which would be for me and none of which were ever for Roy. And he would smile his smarmy smile and look aloof; or sometimes he would peer in a half-hope, as if thinking that maybe this week would be different. Once or twice I saw him *writing* a letter, with his authentic Waverley fountain pen, shielding his page with his arm when he thought I wanted to nosy into his private affairs—as if I had the slightest interest in fan mail to Professor Huffington Puffington of the University of Kant Studies.

He used to do a number of bonkers things, Roy: like drawing piano keys onto his left arm, spending ages shading the black ones, and then practising—or, for all I know, only pretending to practice—the right-hand part of Beethoven sonatas on it. "I requested an actual piano," he told me. "They said no." He used to do vocal exercises in the shower, really loud. He kept samples of his snot, testing (he said) whether his nasal mucus was affected by the south polar conditions. Once he inserted a radiognomon relay spike (looked a little like a knitting needle) into the corner of his eye, and squeezed the ball to see what effects it had in his vision "because Newton did it." He learnt a new line of the Aeneid every evening—in Latin, mark you—by reciting it over and over. Amazingly annoying, this last weird hobby, because it was so particularly and obviously pointless. I daresay that's why he did it.

I read regular things: SF novels, magazines, even four-day-old newspapers (if the drop parcel happened to contain any), checking the football scores and doing the crosswords. And weekly I would pull out my fistful of letters, and settle down on the common room sofa to read them and write my replies, whilst Roy pursed his brow and worked laboriously through another paragraph of his Kant.

One week he said. "I'd like a letter."

"Get yourself a pen pal," I suggested.

We had just been outside, where the swarming snow was as thick as a continuous shower of wood chips and the wind bit through the three layers I wore. We were both back inside now, pulling off icicle bearded gloves and scarfs and stamping our boots. The drop-package was on the floor between us, dripping. We had yet to open it.

"Can I have one of yours?" he asked.

"Tell you what," I said. I was in a good mood, for some reason. "I'll sell you one. Sell you one of my letters."

"How much?"

"Tenner," I said. Ten pounds was (I hate to sound like an old codger, but it's the truth) a lot of money back then.

"Deal," he said, without hesitation. He untied his boots, hopped out of them like Puck and sprinted away. When he came back he was holding a genuine ten pound note. "I choose, though," he said, snatching the thing away as I reached for it.

"Whatever, man," I laughed. "Be my guest."

He gave me the money. Then, he dragged the parcel, now dripping melted snow, through to the common room and opened it. He rummaged around and brought out the rubberbanded letters: five of them.

"Are you sure none of them aren't addressed to you?" I said, settling myself on the sofa and examining my banknote with pride. "Maybe you don't need to buy one of my letters—maybe you got one of your own?"

He shook his head, looked quickly through the five envelopes on offer, selected one and handed me the remainder of the parcel. "No."

"Pleasure doing business with you," I told him. Off he went to his bedroom to read the letter he had bought.

I thought nothing more about it. The four letters were from: my Mum, my brother, a guy in Leicester with whom I was playing a tediously drawn-out game of postal chess, and the manager of my local branch of Lloyd's Bank in Reading, writing to inform me that my account was in credit. Since being in Antarctica meant I could never spend anything, and since my researcher's stipend was still going-in monthly, this was unnecessary. I'm guessing it was by way of a publicity exercise. It's not that I was famous, of course; even famous-for-Reading. But it doubtless looked good on some report somewhere: *we look after our customers, even when they're at the bottom of the world*! I made myself a coffee. Then I spent an hour at a computer terminal, checking data. When Roy came back through he looked smug, but I didn't begrudge him that. After all, I had made ten pounds—and ten pounds is ten pounds.

For the rest of the day we worked, and then I fixed up some pasta and Bolognese sauce in the little kitchen. As we ate I asked him: "so who was the letter from?"

"What do you mean?" Suspicious voice.

"The letter you bought from me. Who was it from? Was it Lezlie?"

A self-satisfied grin. "No comment."

"Say what?"

"It's my letter. I bought it. And I'm entitled to privacy."

"Suit yourself," I said. "I was only asking." He was right, I suppose; he bought it, it was his. Still, his manner rubbed me up the wrong way. We ate in silence for a bit, but I'm afraid I couldn't let it go. "I was only asking: who was it from? Is it Lezlie? I won't pry into what she actually wrote." Even as I said this, I thought to myself: *pry? How could I pry—the words were written to be read by me!* "You know," I added, thinking to add pressure. "I *could* just write to her, ask her what she wrote. I could find out that way."

"No comment," he repeated, pulling his shoulders round as he sat. I took my bowl to the sink and washed it up, properly annoyed, but there was no point in saying anything else. Instead I went through and put *Romancing the Stone* on the telly, because I knew it was the VHS Roy hated the most. He smiled, and retreated to his room with his philosophy book.

The next morning I discovered to my annoyance that the business with the letter was still preying on my mind. I told myself: get over it. It was done. But some part of me refused to get over it. At breakfast Roy read another page of his Kant, and I saw that he was using the letter as a bookmark. At one point he put the book down and stood up to go to the loo, but then a sly expression crept over his usually ingenuous face, and he picked the book up and took it with him.

It had been a blizzardy few days and the dish needed checking over. Roy tried to wriggle out of this chore: "you're more the hardware guy," he said, in a wheedling tone. "I'm more conceptual—the ideas and the phil-os-o-phay."

"Don't give me that crap. We're both hands-on—the folk in Adelaide, and back in Britain, are the *actual* ideas people." I was cross. "Philosophy my arse." At any rate, he suited-up, rolled his scarf around his lower face and snapped on his goggles, zipped up his overcoat. We both pulled out brooms and stumped through light snowfall to the dish. It took us half an hour to clear the structure of snow, and check its motors hadn't frozen solid, and that its bearings were ice free. Our shadows flickered across the landscape like pennants in the wind.

The sun loitered near the horizon, a cricket-ball frozen in flight.

That afternoon I did a stint testing the terminals. With the sun still up, it was a noisy picture; although it was possible to pick up this and that. At first I thought there was something, but when I looked at it I discovered it was radio chatter from a Spanish expedition on its way to the Vinson Massif. I found my mind wandering. Who was the letter from?

The following day I eased my irritation by writing to Lezlie. *Hey, you know Roy? He's a sad bastard, a ringer for one of actors in "Revenge of the Nerds." Anyway he asked for a letter and I sold him one. Now he won't tell me whose letter it is. Did you write to me last week? What did you say? Just give me the gist, lover-girl.* But as soon as I'd written this I scrunched it up and threw it in the bin. Lez would surely not respond well to such a message. In effect I was saying: "hey you know that love-letter you poured your heart and soul into? I sold it to a nerd without even reading it! *That's* how much I value your emotions!"

Chewed the soft-blue plastic insert at the end of my Bic for a while.

I tried again: *Hi lover! Did you write last week? There was a snafu with the package and some stuff got lost.* I looked over the lie. It didn't ring true. I scrunched this one up too. Then I sat in the chair trying, and failing, to think of how to put things. The two balls of scrunched paper in the waste-bin began, creakingly, to unscrunch.

Dear Lez. Did you write last week? I'm afraid I lost a letter, klutz that I am! That was closer to the truth. But then I thought: what if she had written me a dear-john letter? Or a let's-get-married? Or a-close-family-member-has-died? How embarrassing to write back a jaunty "please repeat your message!" note. What if she hadn't written at all? What if it were somebody else?

This latter thought clawed at my mind for a while. What if some important information, perhaps from my academic supervisor at Reading, Prof Addlestone, had been in the letter? Privacy was one thing, but surely Roy didn't have the right to withhold such info?

I stomped down the corridor and knocked at Roy's room. He made me wait for a long time before opening the door just enough to reveal his carbuncular face, smirking up at me. "What?"

"I've changed my mind," I said. "I want my letter back."

"No dice, doofus," he replied. "I paid for it. It's mine now."

"Look, I'll *buy* it back, alright? I'll give you your ten pounds. I've got it right here."

When he smiled, he showed the extent to which his upper set of teeth didn't fit neatly over his lower set. "It's not for sale," he said.

"Don't be a pain, Roy," I said. "I'm asking nicely."

"And I'm, nicely, declining."

"What—you want more than a tenner? You can go fish for *that*, my friend."

"It's not for sale," he repeated.

"Is it a scam," I said, my temper wobbling badly. "Is the idea you hold out until I offer—what, twenty quid? Is that it?"

"No. That's not it. It's mine. I do not choose to sell it."

"Just tell me what's *in* the letter," I pleaded. "I'll give your money back *and* you can keep the damn thing, just tell me who it's from and what it says." Even as I made this offer it occurred to me that Roy, with his twisted sense of humour, might simply lie to me. So I added: "show it to me. Just show me the letter. You don't have to give it up, keep it for all I care, only—"

"No deal," said Roy. Then he wrung his speccy face into a parody of a concerned expression. "You're embarrassing yourself, Anthony." And he shut his door.

I went through to the common room, fuming. For a while I toyed with the idea of simply grabbing the letter back: I was bigger than Roy, and doubtless had been involved in more actual fist-flying, body-grappling fights than he. It wouldn't have been hard. But instead of that I had a beer, and lay on the sofa, and tried to get a grip. We had to live together, he and I, in unusually confined circumstances, and for a very lengthy period of time. In less than a week the sun would vanish, and the proper observing would begin. Say we chanced upon alien communication (I told myself)—wouldn't that be something? Might there be a Nobel Prize, or something equally prestigious, in it? I couldn't put all that at risk, even for the satisfaction of punching him on the nose.

Maybe, I told myself, Roy would thaw out a little in a day or two. You catch more flies with honey than vinegar, after all. Maybe I could *coax* the letter out of him.

The week wore itself out. I went through a phase of intense irritation with Roy for his (what seemed to me) immensely petty and immature attitude with regard to my letter. Then I went through a phase when I told myself it didn't bother me. I did consider returning his tenner to him, so as to retain the high moral ground. But then I thought: ten pound is ten pound.

The week ended, and Diamondo overflew and tossed the supply package out to bounce along the snow. This annoyed me, because I had finally managed to write a letter to Lezlie that explained the situation without making it sound like I valued her communiques so little I'd gladly sold it off to weirdo Roy. But I couldn't "post" the letter unless the plane landed and took it on board, so I had to hang onto it. I couldn't even be sure, I reminded myself, that the letter Roy had bought from me had *been* from her.

On the fifth of July the sun set for the last time until August. The thing people don't understand about Antarctic night is that it's not the same level of ink-black all the way through. For the first couple of weeks, the sky lightens twice a day, pretty-much bright enough to walk around without a torch—the same dawn and dusk paling of the sky that precedes sunrise and follows sunset, only without actual dawn and dusk. Still, you can sense the sun is just there, on the other side of the horizon, and it's not too bad. As the weeks go on this gets briefer and darker, and then you do have a month or so when it's basically coal-coloured skies and darkness invisible the whole time.

Diamondo landed his plane, and tossed out the supply package, but didn't linger; and by the time I'd put on the minimum of outdoor clothing and grabbed a torch and got through the door he was taking off again—so, once again, I didn't get to send my letter to Lez.

That was the last time I saw that aircraft.

There were two letters in this week's batch: one from my old Grammar School headmaster, saying that the school had hosted a whole assembly on the "exciting and important" work I was doing; and the other from my Professor at Reading. This was nothing but a note, and read in its entirety: "Dear A. I often think of Sartre's words. Imagination is not an empirical or superadded power of consciousness, it is the whole of consciousness as it realizes its freedom. Where is freer than the very bottom of the world? Nil desperandum! Yours, A." This, though slightly gnomic, was not out of character for Prof. Addlestone, who had worked on SETI for so long it had made his brain a little funny. No letter from Lez, which worried me. But, after all, she didn't write every week. I re-read the Professor's note several times. Did it read like a PS, a scribbled afterthought? Did it perhaps mean that the letter Roy bought had *been* from Addlestone? Maybe. Maybe not.

We got on with our work, and I tried to put the whole letter business behind me. Roy did not help, as far as this went. He was acting stranger and stranger; simpering at me, and when I queried his expression ("what? What is it?") scurrying away—or scowling and saying, "nothing, nothing, only . . ." and refusing to elaborate.

The next thing was: he moved one of the computer terminals into his room. These were 1980s terminals; not the modern-day computers the size and weight of a copy of *Marie-Claire*; so it was no mean feat getting the thing in there. He even cut a mousehole-like ∩ in the bottom of his door, to enable the main cable to come out into the hall and through into the monitor room.

"What are you doing in there?" I challenged him. "That's not standard policy. Did you clear this with home?"

"I'm working on something," he told me. "I'm close to a breakthrough. SETI, my friend. Solving Fermi's paradox! You should consider yourself lucky to be here. You'll get a footnote in history. Only a footnote, I know: but it's more than most people get."

I ignored this. "I still don't see why do you need to squirrel yourself away in your room?"

"Privacy," he said. "Is very important to me."

One day he went out on the ice to (he told me) check the meteorological data-points. It seemed like an odd thing—he'd shown precious little interest in them up to that point—but I was glad he was out of the base, if only for half an hour. As soon as I saw his torch-beam go, wobbling its oval of brightness away over the ice, I hurried to his room. I wasn't doing anything wrong, I told myself. I was just checking the identity of the letter's author. Maybe have a quick glance at its contents. I wouldn't steal it back (although, I told myself, I *could*. It was my letter after all. Roy was being an idiot about the whole thing). But once my itch was scratched, curiosity-wise, then everything would get easier about the base. I could wait out the remainder of my stint with equanimity. He need never even know I'd been poking around.

No dice. Roy had fitted a padlock to his door. I rattled this uselessly; I could have smashed it, but then Roy would know what I'd been up to. I retreated to the common room, disproportionately angry. What was he doing, in there, with a whole computer terminal and my letter?

I had enough self-knowledge to step back from the situation, at least some of the time. He was doing it in order to wind me up. That was the only reason he was doing it. The letter was nothing—none of my letters, if I looked back, contained any actual, substantive content. They were just pleasant chatter, people I knew touching-base with me. The letter Roy bought must be the same. He bought it not to *have* the letter, but in order to set me on edge, to rile me. And by getting riled I was gifting him the victory. The way to play this whole situation was to be perfectly indifferent.

However much I tried this, though, I kept falling back. It was the not knowing!

I tried once more, during the week. "Look, Roy," I said, smiling. "This letter thing is no big deal, you know? None of my letters have any really significant stuff in them."

He looked at me, in a "that's all *you* know" sort of way. But this was, I decided, just winding me up.

"I tell you what I think," I said. "You can, you know, nod, or not-nod, depending on whether I'm right. I think the letter you bought was from my girlfriend. Yeah?"

"No comment," said Roy, primly. "One way or the other."

"If so, it was probably full of inane chatter, yeah? Fine—keep it! With my blessing!"

"In point of fact," he corrected me, holding up his right forefinger, "I do not need your blessing. The transaction was finalised with the fiduciary transfer. Contract law is very clear on this point."

I lost my temper a little at this point. "You know how sad you are, keeping a woman's letter to another man for your own weird little sexual buzz? That's—*sad*. Is what it is. I don't think you realise how sad that is."

"Oh Anthony, Anthony," he said, shaking his head and smirking in that insufferable way he had. "If only you knew!"

I swore. "Suit yourself," I said.

Then the airstrip lights failed. I assumed this was an accident, although the fact that every one of them failed at the same time was strange. Diamondo came through on the radio: "fellows!" he declared, through his thick accent. "I cannot land if there are no lights to land!"

"Don't know what's happened to them," I replied. "Some manner of malfunction."

"Obviously that!" came Diamondo's voice. "Can you fix? Over."

Roy suited up and went outside; he was back in minutes. "I can't do anything in the dark, with a torch, in a hurry," he complained. "Tell him—no. Tell him to toss the package out and we'll fix the lights for next time."

When I relayed this message, Diamondo said "breakables! There are breakables in the package! I cannot toss! Over." Then, contradicting his last uttered word, he went on. "I can take out the breakables and toss the rest. Wait—wait."

I could hear the scrapysound of the plane in the sky outside. Then, over the radio: "is in chute."

"Wait," I said. "Where are you dropping it? If there's no lights—I mean, I don't want to go searching over a wide area in the dark with . . ." There was a terrific crash right overhead, as something smashed into our roof.

"You idiot!" I called. "You could have broken our roof!"

Static. And, through the walls, the sound of the plane's engines diminishing. Roy looked and me, and I at him. "I think it rolled off," Roy said. "You go out and get it."

"You're already suited!"

"I went out last time. It's your turn now. Fair's fair."

It was on the edge of my tongue to retort: *stealing my letter—is* that *fair?* But that would have done no good; and anyway I was hoping that there would be a new letter from Lezlie in the satchel, and if so I certainly wanted to get to that before Roy did. So I pulled on overclothes and took a torch and went outside.

It was extraordinarily cold—sinus-freezingly cold. The air was still. The sound of Diamondo's plane, already very faint, diminished and diminished until it vanished altogether. Now the only sound was the whir of the generator, gently churning to itself with its restless motion. I searched around in the dark outside the main building for ten minutes or so, and spent another five trying to see into the gap between the main prefab and the annex, which was half-full of snow. But I couldn't find it.

When I went back to the main door it was locked. This was unprecedented. For a while I banged on the door, and yelled, and my heart began blackly to suspect that Roy was playing some kind of prank on me—or worse. I was just about to give up and make my way round to try the side entrance when Roy's gurning face appeared in the door's porthole, with the graph-paper pattern woven into the glass. He opened it. "What the hell were you playing at?" I demanded, crossly. "Why did you lock the door?"

"It occurred to me that the lights might have been sabotaged," he said, not looking me in the eye. "I thought: security is valour's better part. Obviously I was going to let you back in, once I was sure it *was* you."

"Have you had a nervous breakdown?" I yelled. "Are you *high?* Who else could possibly be out there? We're three hundred miles from the nearest human settlement. Did you think it was a ghost?"

"Calm down," Roy advised, grinning his simpering grin and still not looking me in the eye. "Did you get the package?"

I sat down with a thump. "Couldn't find it," I said, pulling off my overboots. "It may still be on the roof. Seriously, though, man! Locking the door?"

"We need to retrieve it," said Roy. "It has my medication in it. My supplies are running low."

This was the first I had heard of any medication. "Seriously? They posted you down here, even though you have medical problems?"

"Just some insomnia problems. And some allergic reaction problems. But I need my sleeping pills and my antihistamines."

"You're kidding," I said. "What is there to be allergic to, down here?"

He gave me a pointed look. But then he said: "come and have a drink," he said. "I've got some whisky."

Now, I knew the base was not supplied with whisky. Beer was the most they allowed us. I should, perhaps, have been suspicious of Roy's abrupt hospitality, doubly so since I knew he hardly ever drank. But I was cold, and cross, and a whisky—actually—sounded like a bloody good idea. "How have you got any of that?"

"I brought it with me. My old tutor at Cambridge gave it to me. Break it out when you've solved the SETI problem, he said. *He* never doubted me, you see. And solve it, I have."

And then a second thought occurred to me. It came to me like a flash. I could *get Roy drunk*. Surely then he would be more amenable to telling me what was in the letter he'd snaffled from me. I couldn't think that I'd ever seen him drunk; but my judgment was that he would hold his liquor badly. He'd be a splurger. OK, I thought: butter him up, some, and get some booze in him.

"I'll have a dram," I told him. Then: "kind of you to offer. Thanks. I didn't mean to . . . you know. Yell at you."

He ignored this overture. "You didn't go to Cambridge, I think?" he asked, as we went through to the common room. "Reading University, isn't it?"

"Reading born and bred," I replied, absently. I half-leaned, half-sat on one of the heaters to get warmth back into my marrow whilst Roy went off to his room to get the whisky. He was gone a while. Finally he came back with a bottle of Loch Lomond in one hand and a bottle of beer in the other. He handed me the former.

I retrieved two tumblers from the cupboard, but Roy said: "I'll not have the whisky, thank you anyway. I don't like the taste."

This was about par, I thought, for the weirdo that he was—bringing a bottle of scotch all the way to the end of the world, only not even to drink it. On the other hand the seal was broken, and about an inch was missing, so perhaps he had tried a taster and so discovered his animadversion. I honestly didn't care. I poured three fingers, and settled myself in one of the chairs.

"Cheers!" I said, raising a glass.

"Good health," he returned, propping his bum on the arm of the sofa.

"So," I said, smacking my lips. "The fact that we're drinking this means you've solved the Fermi paradox?"

"We're not drinking it," he said, with a little snorty laugh of self-satisfaction. "You are."

"You're such a pedant, Roy," I told him.

"Take that as a compliment," he said, smirking, and making odd little snorty-sniffy noises with his nostrils.

"So? Does the fact that I'm drinking this mean you've solved it?"

"The answer to your question is: yes."

"Really?"

"Absolutely."

I took another sip. "Congratulations!"

"Thank you."

"And?"

He peered blankly at me. "What?"

"And? In the sense of: what's your solution?"

"Oh. The Fermi Paradox." He sounded almost bored. "Well, I'll tell you if you like." He seemed to ponder this. "Yeah," he added. "Why not? It's Kant."

"Of course it is," I said, laughing. "You complete nutter."

He looked hurt at this. "What do you mean?"

"I mean—the best part of a year of our lives, millions of pounds sunk into this base, probably billions spent worldwide on SETI, and all we needed to do was open a seventeenth-century book of philosophy!"

"Eighteenth-century," he corrected me. "And the kit, here, certainly has its uses."

"Glad to hear it! But—Kant? Really?"

Roy took the smallest sip from his beer bottle, and then rubbed his own chin with his thumb. "Hard to summarise," he said. "Start here: how do we know there's anything out there?"

"What—out in space?"

"No: outside our own brains. Sense data, yes? Eyes, ears, nerve-endings. We see things, and think we're seeing things out there. We hear things, likewise. And so on. But maybe all that is a lie. Maybe we're hallucinating. Dreaming. How can we be sure there's anything really *there*?"

"Isn't this I think therefore I am?"

"The cogito, yes," said Roy, with that uniquely irritating prissy inflection he used when he wanted to convey his own intellectual superiority. "Though Kant didn't have much time for Descartes, actually. He says I think therefore I am is an empty statement. We never just think, after all. We always think *about something*."

"You're losing me, Roy," I said, draining my whisky, and reaching for the bottle. Roy's eye's flashed, and I stopped. "Do you mind if I have another?" "No, no," he urged me, bobbing forward and back in an oddly bird-like way. "Go right ahead."

"So," I said. "You're saying: we can't be sure if the cosmos is a kind of hallucination. Maybe I'm a brain in a vat. So what? I've got to act as if the universe is real, or," I directed a quick look at Roy, "they'd lock me in the loony bin. So? Does this hallucination also include ET, or not?"

"Quite right. Well, Kant says: there *is* a real world—he calls it the ding-an-sich, the thing as it really is. There is such a reality. But our only access to that real world is through our perceptions, our senses and the way our thoughts are structured. So, says Kant, some of the things we assume are part of the world out there are actually part of the structure of our consciousness."

"Such as?"

"Quite basic things. Time and space. Causality."

"Wait, Kant is saying that time, space and causality aren't 'really' out there? They're just part of our minds?"

Roy nodded. "It's like if we always wore pink-tinted contact lenses. Like we'd always worn them, ever since birth. Everything we saw would have a pink tint. We might very well assume the world was just—you know, pink. But it wouldn't be the world that was pink, it would be our perception of the world."

"Pink," I repeated, and took another slug. I was starting to feel drowsy.

"We're all like that, all the time, except that instead of pink contact lenses on our eyes, we're wearing *space-and-time* contacts on our minds. *Causality* contacts."

"Space and time are the way the universe is. Just is."

"That's not what Kant says. He says: we don't really know the way the universe *just is*. All we know is how our perceptions and thoughts structure our understanding."

"Wait," I said. "Kant says that cause and effect are just in our heads?"

"That's right"

"That's nonsense," I said. "If space and time and causality are just inside my head, then what's my head in? It takes up space, my brain. It takes time to think these thoughts."

"There's *something* out there," Roy agreed. "But we don't know what it is. Here's a thought-experiment, Kant's thought-experiment. You can imagine an object in space, can't you?"

I grunted.

"OK," said Roy. "And you can imagine the object being taken away. Yes? Then you have empty space. But you can't imagine *space and time* being taken away. You can't imagine no space, no time."

I grunted again.

"That shows that space, time, causality and some other things—they're part of the way the mind perceives. There's no getting behind them. Is the ding-an-sich itself structured according to that logic? We cannot know. Maybe, maybe not."

"Ding," I said, my eyelid slipping down my eyeballs, "like a microwave oven?"

"We're looking for aliens with visual telescopes and radio telescopes," said Roy, standing up and putting his beer bottle down. "But whatever tools we use, we're looking for aliens in space and time, aliens that understand causality and number. But maybe those things are not alien. Those things are the way *our* minds are built. And that means we're looking in the wrong place. We should not be looking in space, or time. We should be looking in the ding-an-sich."

"Sick," I said, My eyes were shut now. I didn't seem to be able to open them. Such muscular operation was beyond my volitional control. "I feel a bit sick, actually."

"Ding," I heard him say, at the other end of a very long corridor. "You're done. Let's open the microwave door, now, shall we?"

I suppose I was asleep. I tried to shift position in bed, but my arms were numb. Sometimes you lie on an arm and it goes dead. But this was both my arms. They were up over my head. A scraping sound. Distantly. I tried to pull my arms down but they were already down. *This is the chance*, somebody was saying, or muttering, or I don't know. Perhaps I was imagining it. *We've never had this chance before. Because although human consciousness is structured by the Kantian categories of appercep-tion, there's nothing to say that computer perception needs to suffer from the same limi-tations. It's all a question of programming! A programme to sift the Centauri data so as to get behind the limitations of consciousness.*

I was moving. Everything was dark, dark, dark. My arms were trailing behind me, I thought; and something was pulling my legs, I thought; and I was sliding along on my back. Was that right? Could that be right?

We look out from our planet and see a universe of space, and time, of substance and causality, of plurality and totality, of possibility and probability—and we forget that what we're actually seeing are the ways our minds structure the ding-an-such ac-cording to the categories of space, and time, of substance and causality, of plurality and totality, of possibility and probability. We look out and we see no aliens, and are surprised. But the real surprise would be to see aliens in such a vista, because that would mean the aliens are in our structures of thought. Sure there are aliens. Of course there are! But they don't live in our minds. They live in the ding-an-sich.

The motion stopped, but I was still too sluggish to move, or speak, or even open my eyes. The next thing I knew, somebody was kissing me on the lips. *Goodbye*, was a word, and it floated around. Then nothing.

O dark, dark, dark, they all go into the—

Or.

Or something. It came upon me slowly. It, as it were, crept up on me. I couldn't as yet put a name to it. *Let me think through the necessary and contingent possibili-ties*, I thought to myself. *It could have been a letter from my Mum, in which case it was full of family trivia and Roy's just yanking my chain for the hell of it. He's cer-tainly capable of that.* The thing, whatever it was, was closer now, or larger some-how, or in some sense more present, although I still couldn't put a name to it. *It could have been a letter from a friend, or from Leicester Lenny, but if so it would only say Q-B4 ch! or Kn-R7 or something, and that could mean nothing at all to Roy. Or it could have been a letter from Professor Addlestone of Reading University, blathering on about something. Or it could have been*, the thing was all around me now, or all within me, or otherwise pressing very imminently upon my. *Or it could have been from Lezlie. But then, what? It was full of the usual blandishments? In which case Roy's hoarding of it is creepy but, in the larger scheme of things, unimportant. That's not what I'm afraid of though, is it? I'm afraid the letter says: I'm leaving you, I've found someone else. But but but, if it is, then I'll find out eventually—won't I. I just need to be patient. I'll find out in time. Assuming I have time—*

Cold. That was the thing.

That was what had crept up on me.

I sat up. I was outside, in the darkness, in my indoor clothes. Scalded with the cold. My whole body shook with a Parkinsonian tremor. I angled my head back and the stars were all there, the Southern Fish, the Centaur and the Dove; the Southern Cross itself; Orion and Hydra low in the sky; Scorpion and Sagittarius high up. Hydra and Pegasus. I breathed in fire and burned my throat and lungs. It was cold enough to shear metal. It was cold enough to freeze petrol.

I got to my feet. My hands felt as though they had been dipped in acid, and then that sensation stopped and I was more scared than before. There was nothing at the end of my arms at all. I tried rubbing my hands together, but the leprous lack of sensation and the darkness and my general sluggishness meant I could not coordinate the action. My hands bounced numbly off one another. I became terrified of the idea that I perhaps knocked one or more fingers clean off. It looks ridiculous as I write it down, but there, in the dark, in the cold, the thought of it gripped my soul horribly.

I had to get inside, to get warm. I had to get back to the base. I was shuddering so hard I was scared I might actually lose balance with the shivering and fall down—in which case I might not be able to get back up again. Ghastly darkness all about. Cold beyond the power of words to express.

I turned about, and about again. Starlight in the faintest of lights. I could see my breath coming out only because of the vast ostrich-feature-shaped blot that twisted in my field of vision, blocking out the stars. I needed to pick a direction and go. But I couldn't see any lights to orient me. What if I stumbled off in the wrong direction? I could easily stagger off into the wilderness, miss the base altogether. I'd be dead in minutes.

I addressed myself: take hold of yourself. You were dragged here—Roy dragged you here. Runty Roy; he couldn't have removed me very far from the base. Presumably he figured I wouldn't wake up; that I'd just die there in the dark.

"OK," I said, and took another breath—knives going down my throat. I had to move. I started off, and stumbled over the black ground through the black air. I began to fall forward—my thigh muscles were cramping—and picked up my pace to stop myself pitching onto my face. My inner ear still told me I was falling, so I ran faster. Soon I was *sprinting*. It's possible the fluids in my inner ear had frozen, or glued-up with the cold, I don't know. It felt as if I were falling, but my feet were still pounding over the ice, invisible below me. I felt like a diver, tumbling from the top board.

And then I saw the sea—I was at the coast. Obviously I wasn't at the coast because that was hundreds of miles from the base. But there it was, visible. There was a settlement on the shore, a mile below me, with yellow lights throwing shimmery ovals over the water. There was a ship, lit up like a Christmas decoration, balanced very precisely on top of its own lit reflection. I must have been ten degrees of latitude, or more, further away from the pole, enough to lift the moon up over the horizon. The texture of the sea was a million burrin-marks of white light on a million wavelets, like pewter. There was no doubting what I was seeing. My whole body trembled with pain, with the cold, and I said to myself *I'm dying*, and *I'm hallucinating because I'm dying*. I must have run in the wrong direction. I felt as if I'd been running all my life, all my ancestors' lives combined.

There was a weird inward fillip, or lurch, or clonic jerk, or something folding over something else. I was conscious of thinking: I've run the wrong way. I've missed the base.

And there *was* the base. Now that I was there, I could see that Roy had covered the common room window on the inside with something—cloth, cardboard—to make a blackout screen. He had not wanted me to see the light and follow it as a beacon. Now that I was there, I could just make out the faint line of illumination around the edges. I couldn't feel my hands, or my feet, and my face was covered with a pinching, scratchy mask—snot, tears, frost, whatever, frozen by the impossible cold to a hard crust.

I slumped against the wall, and the fabric of shirt stuck was so stiffened it snapped. It ripped clean away when I got up.

The door. I had to get to the door—that was when I saw . . . I was going to say *when I saw them* but the plural doesn't really describe the circumstance. Not that there was only one, either. It is very hard to put into words. There was the door, in front of me, and just enough starlight to shine a faint glint off the metal handle. I could not use my hands, so I leant on the handle with my elbow, but of course it did not give way. Locked, of course locked. And of course Roy would not be opening for me this time. Then I saw—what I saw. Data experiences of a radically new kind. Raw tissues of flesh, darkness visible, a kind of fog (no: fog is the wrong word). A pillar of fire by night, except that "it" did not burn, or gleam, or shine. "It" is the wrong word for it. "It" felt, or looked, like a great tumbling of scree down an endless slope. Or rubble gathering at the bottom and falling up the mountain. Forwards, backwards.

It was the most terrifying thing I ever saw.

There was a hint of—I'm going to say, claws, jaws, a clamping something. A maw. Not a tentacle, nothing so defined. Nor was it a darkness. It made a low, thrumming chiming noise, like a muffled bell sounding underground, ding-ding, ding-ding. But this was not a sound-wave sort of sound. This was not a propagating expanding sphere of agitated air articles. It was a pulse in the mind. It was a shudder of the soul.

I could not get inside the base, and I was going to die. I felt the horrid cold in the very core of my being. Then "it," or "they," or the boojummy whatever the hell (I choose my words carefully, here) it was, expanded. Or undid whatever process of congealing that brought it—I don't know.

Where I stood experienced a second as-it-were convulsive, almost muscular contraction. Everything folded over, and flipped back again. "It," or "they" were not here any longer. In fact they had been here eons ago, or were not yet here at all.

I was standing inside the common room.

Do not demand to know how I passed beyond the locked door. I could not tell you.

The warmth of the air burned my throat. I could no longer stay standing. I half slumped, half fell sideways, and my arm banged against one of the heaters—it felt like molten metal, and I yelled. I rolled off it and lay on the floor, and breathed and breathed.

I may have passed out. I have no idea how I got inside. I was probably only out for a few moments, because the next thing I knew was that my hands were in agony. Absolute agony! It felt like the gomjabbar, like they had both been stuffed into a tub of boiling water. Looking back I can now say what it was: it was sensation returning to my frostbitten flesh. But by God I've never felt such pain. I screamed and screamed like the Spanish Inquisition had gone to work on me. I writhed, and wept like a baby.

Somehow I dragged myself into a sitting posture, with my back against the wall and my legs straight out on the floor. Roy was standing in the common room doorway. In his right hand he was holding what I assumed was a gun, although I later realised it was a flare pistol.

"You murdering bastard," I said, "have you come to finish the job? You going to shoot me down like a dog?" Or that's what I *tried* to say. What came out was: "yrchyrchorchorchorch." God, my throat was *shredded*.

"The thing-in-itself," he said. There was a weird bend in his voice. I blinked away the melting icicles from my eyelashes and saw he was *crying*. "The thing-as-such. The thing *per se*. I have experienced it unmediated." His face was wet. Tears slippy-sliding down, and dripping like snot from his jowls. I'd never seen him like that before.

"What," I croaked, "did you put in my whisky?" Oh God, the pain in my *hands*! And now my feet were starting to rage and burn too. Oh, it was ghastly.

He stopped crying, and wiped his face in the crook of his left arm. "I'm sorry," he said. Even at this juncture he was not able to look me in the eye. He lifted his right hand, holding the flare pistol, slowly, until he was holding it across his chest, like James Bond in the posters.

I was weeping—not because I was scared of dying, but just because my hands and feet hurt with such sharp and focussed intensity.

Roy took a breath, lifted the flare pistol to his own head, and pulled the trigger. There was a crunching bang, and Roy flopped to the ground. The common room was filled with fluorescent red-orange light and an extraordinarily loud hissing sound. For a moment we were in a luridly lit stage-set of Hades.

What had happened was this: the tip and fuse of the flare projectile had lodged itself in Roy's skull, and had ejected the illumination section and its little asbestos parachute at the ceiling, where it snagged against the polystyrene tiles and burned until it was all burned out.

I sat in that ferociously red lit room, with molten chunks of polystyrene dripping onto the carpet. Then the shell itself burnt free and fell to the ground, where it fizzled out.

Roy was not dead. Nor was I, amazingly. It took me a while, and an effort, and the whole way along I was sobbing and begging the cosmos to take the pain away; but I got to the radio, and called for help. They sent an air ambulance, that laid a pattern of flares on the unlit runway during their first flyby and landed alongside them on their second. It took four hours, but they got to us, and we did not die in the interval.

I crawled back to Roy, unconscious on the floor, and pulled the shell-tip from the side of his head. There was no blood, although the dent was very noticeable—the skin and hair lining the new thumb-sized cavity all the way in. There was little I could do, beyond put him in the recovery position.

Then I clambered painfully on the sofa, my hands and feet hurting a little less. Then, surprisingly enough, I fell asleep—Roy had dissolved a sleeping tablet in the whisky, of course, to knock me out; and when the pain retreated just enough the chemical took effect. I was woken by the sound of crashing, and crashing, and crashing, and then one of the ambulance men came through the main door with an axe in his hand.

We were flown to Halley, on the coast—the subject of my vision, or whatever that had been. We were hospitalised, and questioned, and my hands were treated. I lost two fingers on my left hand and one on my right, and my nose was rescued with a skin graft that gives it, to this day, a weird patchwork-doll look. I lost toes too, but I care less about those. Roy was fine: they opened his skull, extracted a few fragments of bone, and sewed him up. Good as new.

I don't think they believed his version of events, although for myself I daresay he was truthful, or as truthful as circumstances permit. The official record is that he had a nervous breakdown, drugged me, left me outside to die and then shot himself. He himself said otherwise. I've read the transcript of his account. I've even been in the same room with him as he was questioned. "I saw things as they really are, things per se, I had a moment—that's the wrong word, it is not measured in moments, it has always been with me, it will always be with me—a moment of clarity."

"And your clarity was: kill your colleague?"

He wanted the credit all to himself, I think. He believed *he* was the individual destined to make first contact with alien life. He wanted me out of the way. He didn't say that, of course, but that's what I think. His explanation was: my perceptions, my mental processes and imagination, would collapse the fragile disintermediating system he was running to break through to the Thing-as-Such. I confess I don't see how that would work. Nonetheless: he insists that this was his motive for killing me. Indeed, he insists that my reappearance proved the correctness of his decision, the necessity for my death—because by coming back at the time I did, I broke down the vision of the Ding-an-Sich, or reasserted the prison of categorical perception, or something, and the aliens fled—or not fled, because their being is not mappable with a succession of spatial coordinates the way ours are. But: I don't know. Evaporate. Collapse away to nothing. Become again veiled. He wrote me several long, not terribly coherent letters about it from Broadmoor. I still prefer the earlier explanation. He was a nerd, not right in the head, and a little jealous of me.

So, yes. He happened to buy Lezlie's Dear John. She couldn't cope with the long-distances, the time lags between us meeting up, she'd met someone else . . . the usual. After he drugged me and left me outside to die, Roy left the letter, carefully opened and smoothed out, face up on the desk in my room. It was going to be the explanation for my suicide. People were to believe: I couldn't handle the rejection, and had just walked out into the night.

His latest communication with me from Broadmoor begged me to "go public" with what I had seen; so that's what I'm doing. You'll grasp from this that I don't know *what* I saw. I suppose it was a series of weird hallucinations brought on by the extreme cold and the blood supply intermitting in my brain. Or something, I don't know. I still dream about them. It. Whatever. And the strange thing is: although I know for a fact I encountered it (them, none, whatever) for the first time in Antarctica, in 1986, it feels—it feels deep in my bones—as if I have always known about them. As if they visited me in my cradle. They didn't, of course.

I saw the John Carpenter film *The Thing* for the first time recently. That wasn't one of the VHS tapes they gave us, back then, to watch on base. For obvious reasons. That's not what it was like for me at all. That doesn't capture it at all. They, or it, or whatever, were not *thing*-y.

They are inhuman. But this is only my dream of them, I think. But it is not a dream of a human. It is not a dream of a thing. Or it is, but of a sick kind of thing. And, actually, no. That's not it.

He keeps writing me. I wish he'd stop writing.

communion

MARY ANNE MOHANRAJ

Here's a moving look at one of those small personal moments that can some-times be the beginning of change for everyone . . .

Mary Anne Mohanraj is the author of the science fiction novella, The Stars Change *(finalist for the Lambda, Rainbow, and Bisexual Book Awards), the linked story collection,* Bodies In Motion, *and eleven other ti-tles.* Bodies In Motion *was a finalist for the Asian American Literary Awards and has been translated into six languages. Other recent publications in-clude the collection* Without a Map, *coauthored with Nnedi Okorafor, stories in* Clarkesworld *and George R.R. Martin's* Wild Cards *series, and essays in* Queers Dig Time Lords *and* Chicks Dig Gaming. *She teaches creative writ-ing, pop culture, and post-colonial literature at the University of Illinois at Chicago, is a graduate of Clarion West, and holds an MFA and a Ph.D. in creative writing. Mohanraj founded and served as editor in chief from 2000–2003 for the ezine* Strange Horizons (www.strangehorizons.com), *and cur-rently serves as Director of the Speculative Literature Foundation (www.speclit.org), which offers a variety of grants and resources for science fic-tion and fantasy writers and readers. Mohanraj lives in a creaky old Victo-rian in Oak Park, just outside of Chicago, with her partner, Kevin, their two small children, and a sweet dog, and maintains a website at.www.mary annemohanraj.com*

It was smaller than he'd expected. Oh, the planet was large enough, but this so-famous university city, pride of the galaxy—it was barely bigger than the smallest of the tunnel-cities on the southern continent of the homeworld. Gaudier from space, of course, since most of the city was aboveground and brightly lit. But the city had no depth to it—it was thin, barely a few stories tall in most places.

If a human saw the deep delvings of Chaurin's people, it might faint away in sheer terror. On awaking, it would cling to the walls, begging not to be dragged any fur-ther, shown any more. Then Chaurin would insist—*No, you must come; you think us animals, barbarians; you must see what wonders we have wrought!* And he might pull that human to the very edge of a twisting stone stair and, with a single, careless motion, toss it tumbling down. They were ephemeral, these humans, light and slight, of no consequence. It would be easy to dispose of one.

He was not here for that, though. Not here to exact revenge or even justice for the brother lost, for Gaurav of the bright eyes, the slow tongue. Gaurav the curious, the troublemaker, always sticking his cold nose where it had no business being. Chaurin had one task only on this planet the locals called Kriti—to bring his brother home. Kriti meant creation, he'd been told. For Guarav, little brother, it had brought death and dissolution instead.

Amara knelt in the soil at the base of the memorial stone. There had been some debate over where best to mark the lives lost in the bomb attack on the Warren. There would be a certain logic to marking the shattered underground room where seven had died—seven whose actions had saved so many more. But Amara was glad the ruling Council had decided on the entrance gates for the memorial instead. Her bare hands dug into the richly composted soil, dirt embedding itself under her nails, cool in the midday heat. She placed a jasmine carefully, one whose seed had made the long journey from old Earth, to be cosseted in the university nurseries for years, and then finally settle here, under Kriti's foreign sun.

The jasmine should do well; most Earth plants did, though a few stubbornly refused to thrive. Her mother had photo albums passed down from the ancestors, of small village homes covered in bougainvillea, glorious profusions of red and pink and purple. No gardener had succeeded yet in growing them on Kriti—they withered and died away from Sol. No one knew why. But the jasmine was more adaptable; it would grow and bloom, here in the open air, its sweet white blossoms scenting the air. Happy not to be shut deep underground, where the dust still carried the memory of those who had died. Amara couldn't believe any flower would truly be happy shut away from the sun, no matter how many fluorescent lights they used.

She suspected Gaurav's captain had exerted his influence to allow her to be assigned to the team that maintained the small garden here; as a brand-new horticultural student, such a task would not normally be allowed her. He understood the need for expiation. Narita kept telling her that she should not feel guilt, or responsibility for the deaths. And yet.

Grubbing in the soil seemed to help. It was why Amara had gone back to school; her old job had been meaningless. When she put her decision in words, it was almost too simple, too obvious, but it was also the truth—after all those deaths, she wanted to spend the rest of her days helping things grow.

A low, growly voice above her—"I know you." Amara looked up, and almost fell over in shock. Her heart thumped wildly, again and again, her skin grown clammy and strange. There, looming over her, was Gaurav—no. Impossible.

She must be mistaken; Amara had only known him for a few hours, after all. And there were not so many saurians on Kriti—fewer, since the war started; she was not skilled at telling them apart. This was a stranger, not her dead friend. Not quite a friend. Amara could not go so far as to claim friendship with the brave young policeman who had died a hero, saving so many lives. *Comrade-in-arms*, then. They had joined forces to protect the Warren, and they had succeeded, though not without cost. This was not Gaurav. This was a stranger, staring at her with an expression she could not read, but it *felt* hostile. Angry. And he loomed over her—his broad, muscled torso and arms blocked the sun.

Amara stumbled to her feet. Standing, she was almost as tall as he was, which helped, though still half his width. He was taller than Gaurav, broader. Older? She was not good at judging age on saurians. Amara was grateful for the crowds not far away, students walking to and from classes, oblivious to their small drama. The students tended to cut a wide swathe around the memorial and the gate; six months wasn't long enough to inure them to the events of that day. But there were plenty of people within earshot—human and otherwise. Still, her throat felt tight. The war between humans and others was escalating, out among the stars—had it finally come to Kriti?

"Do I know you, ser?" she asked, politely, willing her voice to be steady.

"I know *you*," he said. She was fairly sure of his gender; close enough to go on with, at least. After Gaurav's death, she had tried to learn what she could of him, of his people. There wasn't much to know—Gaurav had been a quiet, reclusive young policeman, who had come to Kriti more by accident than anything else. And then he'd stayed, and made a life here, and lost it. Gaurav's people were reclusive; they rarely left their homeworld. But here one stood, arms hanging at his sides, hands pressed against thick thighs, his body leaning forward. His voice was low and growling as he said, "You are Amara Kandiah. I have studied thereports."

Now Amara was scared; she wiped sweating palms on the cotton of her everyday sari. Most of the would-be saviors of the Warren had managed to stay out of the news with the help of Gaurav's captain; the Council hadn't wanted any more publicity around the attempted missile attack than necessary. Amara's name hadn't been in the press, and her photo only appeared as one of a milling crowd. It was better that way, safer. "What reports?" she asked.

"The police reports they send to next of kin. I am Chaurin, Gaurav's brother." His voice dropped further, almost to a whisper. "I am here to collect his remains."

Oh. Amara's throat loosened; she wavered, caught between prudence and compassion. She could direct him to the precinct and be done with it; Gaurav's captain would, eventually, bring him to the hospital where the remains were stored. But that would take time, possibly days, or longer. Council officials would surely want to speak with Chaurin, find out what, if anything, Gaurav might have said to his brother about the plot. Not that there would be anything—there had been no time!—but the officials still had learned so little of what had been going on. With the violence above accelerating, everyone was braced, waiting for the next attack. The Council would not want to hear that Chaurin knew nothing. She didn't know what they might do in their quest for answers. Amara trusted the Council, mostly, but she wouldn't want to put herself into their hands.

The sun shone overhead, bright and reassuring, but she could see Chaurin blinking against the glare; he was not well-adapted to life in the open air. The saurian was still large, but somehow not as threatening. If one of her sisters had been lost, Amara would not want another moment to pass without seeing her again—whatever there was to see. And, conveniently, she had the means to make his journey far more direct; she was one of very few who did.

"I can take you to him," she said. And her racing heart slowed to a quiet certainty. This was the right thing to do. She had been sure of that so rarely in the last six months, had doubted every choice, every decision. She had felt frozen in time, as if a piece of her were still stuck underground, amid the dust and blood and shouting. It was a tremendous relief, to have one choice be so clear cut.

Chaurin followed the human woman through the extensive campus grounds, to the white walls of the medical complex. It wasn't far, but he still seethed with impatience; every step seemed too slow, and he longed to race to his brother's side. But Chaurin didn't know which way to go.

The room Amara finally brought him to was dimly-lit, more tolerable to his eyes, and warm enough to be comfortable. Chaurin perched awkwardly on a stool at the long table, resisting the urge to dig his claws into the wooden top. It was already scarred—generations of students, perhaps, had dug grooves along the grain, carved strange hieroglyphics, in the way of students everywhere. C+S. A *spiral*. *Goddess, no.* Amara placed a small box in front of him, plain metal, hinged.

Chaurin reached out a hand, and then pulled it back. He'd thought he was prepared, but the shock of seeing the box made his mouth go dry, so that he had to swallow before he could speak. "Is this all there is? Was he . . . *cremated?*" The word was unfamiliar in Chaurin's mouth, but he had learned it, just in case. He hadn't known what he would find on arrival, so had studied human death customs on the long journeys between Jump points. He hadn't been able to afford a luxury cruise; the clan had barely scraped together enough to buy him passage on a freighter. They had been afraid to wait longer than they had to, afraid of what would happen to Gaurav's remains. Chaurin had spent months in half-hibernation in his metal tube of a cabin, waking every few weeks, only long enough to eat a little and study, before falling back to sleep.

What he'd learned had turned his stomach, taking away his appetite. Many humans buried their loved ones, letting them rot in the dirt. Some humans burned their dead, turning them to ash on the wind. Others exposed the bodies on the mountaintops for the bird of prey to devour—a strange practice, but one that he thought Guarav might have liked. Chaurin could have made peace with it if the last had occurred, but this? This small square metal box, half the size of his clenched fist, was all that was left of his brother?

The doctor, white-coated, shook her head. "No, not cremated." Narita, her name was, and the scents between them told him that she was the other woman's mate. Amara had explained on the walk over that this doctor, Narita, had taken medical custody of all the remains. Gaurav was the last to be claimed. Chaurin had wanted to explain that it was not that his brother was unloved; Chaurin had just had so much further to come. She knew that, of course.

Narita continued, "We were not able to retrieve much, after the explosion. I saved as much of him as I could, and froze the remains. I am familiar with your customs; I hoped someone would come for him." Her gaze was direct, and strangely kind. They were both kind, these women. Yet Chaurin fought to calm his pulse, to settle the ruff that had risen at his neck. The small one, Amara, had become frightened; it was cruel to leave her so. Amara had been frightened at the gate as well, leaving the scent of prey heavy in the air, but still, she'd tried to help. It was not a small thing. Chaurin pushed down his anger; this was not her fault.

"Thank you," he managed to say. Chaurin gathered the box, his brother, in a single hand. As Chaurin stood, the doctor took a quick breath, and then spoke once more—"Wait, please." He paused, but she didn't seem to know what she wanted to say next. Her face was flushed, blood rushing under brown skin. The urge to just *go* pulsed through him. He began to turn away, but then Narita managed to push out more words, shocking ones: "Will you eat him?"

Before Chaurin could do more than take in the question, it was quickly succeeded by more words: "Gaurav saved our lives, you know. He barely knew us, but he took the brunt of the blast, deliberately, to save us all." Her voice cracked. "And all these months later, we still can't—can't move past it. That moment." Narita took a deep breath, and then said, her words swift, running over each other: "We would like to share in this connection, this ceremony. May we join you?"

"What?" Amara says, her voice high and startled. The doctor rested a quick hand on her arm, but said nothing. Amara bit her lip, willing to wait for an explanation, it seemed. A good mating, to have such trust between them. Chaurin didn't want to think about that in this moment, but apparently one couldn't leave one's profession behind completely. Once a matchmaker, always one, even in the midst of grief and a certain measured rage. He missed his mate, and the children. He wanted to go home.

"There is not enough for you," Chaurin said, his throat aching. Never mind the bizarre insolence of her asking. It was a real problem—there was not enough for all at home who would partake: Gaurav's siblings, their mates and children. He'd known that from the first sight of the little metal box, had felt the knowledge squeeze his heart. Bad enough that Guarav was dead, but that he be lost to so many of his kin . . . it was too much to bear. Chaurin had come so far, at such cost, to come back with so little.

"I know," the doctor said quickly. "I've been thinking about that for months, reading your histories and legends. In the Tale of Elantra, they made soup of Genja, to feed the five hundred. What if we made soup? Would that be acceptable?"

It was only a story, a legend, and yet—"Perhaps." It was only a story, but Chaurin felt a flicker of hope, a flutter in his chest. A mouthful was traditional, but sometimes, with the elderly, one made do with less, a thimbleful of flesh, just enough for a taste. Would he be able to taste his brother, a fragment floating in broth? Did it matter?

She took a step toward him. "Please, if you have time. Come to our home, have some tea. We can talk about it?"

Chaurin smothered an involuntary startled laugh. His mother would have said exactly the same thing. She thought tea solved everything. In her honor, promising nothing, he said, "Yes. I will come."

It was only a short walk from the campus to their home. Chaurin passed through a sunny courtyard, dense with plants, into a small house; the kitchen boasted tall windows overlooking the flowering yard, and a fountain burbled pleasantly, hidden from view around a corner. This was a peaceful place, and Chaurin felt his muscles unwinding, just a little. Oddly, the humans seemed more tense here than they had been on campus; something was clearly wrong between them. Modern kitchen machinery lined the interior walls, but archaic traces remained as well—a small fire in a hearth, and a kettle that hung above the fire, boiling their water. This home was a mix of old and new, and it seemed rather bare as well; Chaurin did not think they'd been living there long. There was a newness to this mating, coexisting with an old familiarity. And pain, running under the surface; an odd mix.

Narita poured the tea as they sat around the kitchen table, explaining quietly to her mate. "There was a genetic flaw in the species, which led to one in a hundred dying young, unless they had a certain enzyme added in utero. It could be added if the pregnant mother ingested the flesh of the father. No one knows which female first figured that out, but she should have gotten a medal." She added sugar and milk and passed the tea; Chaurin cradled the delicate cup carefully in his clawed hands. His brother's box sat in the center of the table, a place of honor. Safe.

Narita continued, "No one needed to die for the enzyme even then; a mouthful of flesh was more than enough. And the enzyme has long since been synthesized, and eventually, species-modified in a vast societal effort; that genetic flaw has been erased, and the enzymes are now passed down through normal reproductive channels. It's perhaps the most successful example of genetic modification we know of."

Chaurin raised the china cup to his lips, sipping the hot drink, sweet and milky.

Narita said, "It's tradition now, you understand. And some see it as religion too—they believe that the soul is passed down with the flesh of the newly-dead."

Amara nodded, and then turned to Chaurin. "Do you believe that?"

Chaurin hesitated, the cup at his lips. "I—don't *not* believe it." He sipped again, and then carefully put the cup down. "Some believe that his knowledge will be passed down, and Guarav has more knowledge of humans than most of my people. Many of my people have half given up already, have begun long tunnellings, planning to sleep through the next few decades, in the hopes that the battles will pass them by. But some do not wish to sleep; if we are to survive this war, we may need to know what Gaurav knew." His chest twinged, a low, deep ache. "More importantly, if the ritual is not performed, my family will feel . . . bereft. That we have lost him truly." The woman was repulsed; he could smell it on her. But she masked it as well as she could, to her credit.

Chaurin leaned forward, unable to contain his urgency; Amara shifted back in her chair, the fear-scent rising." If my children do not taste my brother's flesh, they will never truly know him. Do you understand? Do you have children?" The human kinship bonds confused him—they seemed fragile, easily broken. And with his question, the tension that had simmered under the surface came boiling into the open air, a rush of pain and frustration. He was no empath, but even for a non-human, the signals were too obvious to ignore.

Narita's fingers tightened on the delicate china cup. It should have been an innocuous question—they knew the answer, after all. They did not have children—not yet.

But they would—they had even set a date for the harvesting of eggs, the combining, and for Narita's implantation. It had all been so easy up until that point. Narita had been shocked how easily they had fallen back into their relationship, after so many years apart. They'd found this little house and bought it; they'd found themselves passionate in bed, once again, better than before. They had both wanted a child, badly; after the attack, they wanted to envision a brighter future. Even their mothers were happy at the prospect. One decision after another, falling neatly into place— and then they'd run up against the hard decision—to modify or not? And if yes, how much?

Should they simply solve for life-threatening disease? Many humans went that route, even among the more traditional groups. Though Amara's parents hadn't, and when Narita thought of that, her throat tightened. She could easily lose Amara to cancer, to a heart attack; sometimes she was furious at Amara's parents for forcing those risks upon their child. Surely Amara would agree to spare their child that much. But should they go further—do what Narita's parents had done, blessing their daughter with beauty, brains, and superlative health? Narita had never known a cold, never gained an ounce of unwanted weight, never struggled with simple schoolwork. How could she ask her child to endure unnecessary suffering? But if they made those changes, how would their daughter see Amara?

Out in the stars, a battle was being fought, worlds were burning over these very questions. Those who would protect the purity of the human genotype, or rather, their *perception* of its purity. Amara was no bigot; she had alien friends aplenty. She had even finally brought her humod partner to her mother's house; over the last six months, Narita had come to know all of Amara's friends and relatives. They all accepted her, more or less; they would share samosas with her, tell her stories of Amara as a little girl. But what was acceptable among adults became far more charged when the future was on the line. No one thought rationally when children were involved.

Could she explain all of this to an alien? Narita owed him honesty, at least—but she didn't even know why she had asked such a tremendous favor from Chaurin, to partake in his brother's funeral rites. She hadn't known Gaurav, not really. But over the last six months, as she researched his people and their customs, the impulse had grown. Right alongside her desire for a child, the sense that she should carry something *more* with her, something that marked that day, that night, when they came together to stop a terrible disaster. The night when everything changed.

"We hope to have children," the smaller woman said. Amara. He kept forgetting their names. She did not look at her mate.

"What is preventing you?" he asked, curious.

Silence answered him. Amara sat frozen in her chair, while Narita shifted uneasily in hers. Chaurin watched, reading the currents that flowed between them. It wasn't long before the muddy waters began to clear. "You do not talk to me, which is unsurprising, as I am a stranger—but you do not talk to each other, either."

After a long moment, Narita said, "We are afraid if we do talk, we will find ourselves in too great disagreement." Amara nodded, and then lifted her cup to her lips, precluding speech.

Chaurin was intrigued. "You fear you stand on opposite sides of a ravine, too far from each other to reach across. That may be, but how will you know unless you stretch out your hand?" He was happy to fall for a moment into the role of matchmaker again, relieved to have something familiar to do, in such a strange place. Chaurin had read about human matchmakers, who worked only until the first mating, and then considered their job complete. That had bewildered him; mating was never easy; if one took on the responsibility of making a match, surely it followed that one owed the pairing some guidance in the early years, some help going forward? His own mate would surely have slain him by now were it not for their matchmaker's gentle interventions. "Narita, what is it you desire?"

She bit her lip and then said, "I want a healthy child."

"And Amara?"

The shorter woman hesitated. "I want that too. Of course I do." Her voice sharpened as she continued, "But—*how* healthy? What do you mean when you say healthy?" And then it broke. "Are you sure you don't mean beautiful?"

Narita said, with some urgency, "*You* are beautiful."

Amara shrugged, old pain evident in the set of her shoulders. "Not as beautiful as I could be; not as beautiful as you are."

Interesting—Chaurin had little conception of human beauty, but he could see that Narita's features were more regular, her skin smoother. Was that beautiful?

Narita leaned forward across the table, reaching out to take Amara's hand in hers. "Beauty isn't some absolute. It is specific; it is the details of your face. I wouldn't change a single feature, not a line on your face, not a curve of your body."

"I don't think I believe you," Amara said softly, lines creasing her forehead.

Chaurin was not sure what those lines meant, but he didn't think they were good. He sighed. "That is a bigger muddle than we will clear quickly—and I am not staying to work with you. But surely you have someone you may contact?"

There was silence again, for an endless moment. Then—"The devadasi?" Amara offered tentatively.

Narita laughed, sounding startled. "Really? You want her? There are plenty of other counselors we could call."

Amara shrugged. "After we fought together that night—I trust her. The fact that you slept with her occasionally, in the years when we were apart, feels . . . irrelevant."

Narita frowned. "She'll want us all to be naked for the conversations, you know. It's part of the devadasi practice; she thinks it helps lower barriers."

"Maybe she's right," Amara said, a small smile lurking at the edges of her mouth.

Narita squeezed her mate's hand and then released it, sitting back. She turned back to Chaurin. "I'm so sorry. You're helping us, and I've been so impossibly rude. Rude is a kind word for it. You must think me obscene. I just—"

She bit her lip again, and Chaurin wondered what that gesture meant. Shame, perhaps. Which was appropriate enough, for her request was, if not obscene, then borderline sacrilegious. But how could you expect proper respect and appropriate behavior from aliens? And wasn't that what this war was about, after all? If the gulf between species was, in truth, too vast to be bridged, then perhaps the pure human movement was right after all. Better to go back to our separate worlds, like quarrelling children sent to their separate rooms.

But didn't one ask more, expect more, from adults?

Chaurin wished Gaurav were here. He would know what to do. After the funeral rites, Chaurin might know as well, might hold that knowledge inside himself, a small, glowing kernel.

He sighed. In truth, he already knew what Gaurav would do—that was why he had agreed to come here, to this small, homey kitchen. Gaurav's choice was clear, in the way his little brother had lived his life—going out to tour the Charted Worlds, instead of staying safe at home. Staying on this planet to live and work, instead of trying every expedient to get back home. It was clear in his death most of all—Chaurin had read the police reports. His brother could have fled when the fighting began, but instead, he had run toward the battle, had gone to help the aliens, the strangers. When the stranger asked for help, Gaurav gave it. Could Chaurin do less?

He asked, "You can cook the soup here?"

Narita nodded, her eyes wide. "We can make it right now, if you want. And then I can take it to the lab, freeze-dry it into cubes, so you can easily take it back home. If you dissolve the cubes into a larger pot of water, it should give as many mouthfuls as you need. We would be very happy to help you with that."

"Then, if you like, I think I can spare a few mouthfuls to share with you," Chaurin said, gently. It felt . . . right. He was still angry, on some level, even enraged. But these two were not the proper target of his rage. That rage he would direct at those who sought to divide them, those who took bloody action in that cause.

Amara swallowed visibly; Chaurin could scent her revulsion. Narita said, "You don't have to, if you don't want to." But Amara shook her head, swallowed again, and said, "No. I want to honor Gaurav, in the way of his people. I'd like to do this."

They were so strange, these humans. But brave too. Chaurin did not want to go back home and hide in the tunnels. If they stood on the edge of the abyss, he chose to reach out his hand to the stranger. Perhaps they would find a way across.

someday

JAMES PATRICK KELLY

*Here's an examination of the peculiar courtship customs and divergent biol-
ogy that have developed on a lost colony that has drifted out of touch with
the rest of humanity—with a final clever twist waiting at the end.*

*James Patrick Kelly made his first sale in 1975, and has gone on to become
one of the most respected and popular writers to enter the field. Although
Kelly has had some success with novels, especially with* Wildlife, *he has perhaps had more impact to date as a writer of short fiction, with stories such as
"Solstice," "The Prisoner of Chillon," "Glass Cloud," "Mr. Boy," "Pogrom,"
"Home Front," "Undone," and "Bernardo's House," and is often ranked
among the best short-story writers in the business. His story "Think Like a Dinosaur" won him a Hugo Award in 1996, as did his story "10^{16} to 1," in 2000.
Kelly's first solo novel, the mostly ignored* Planet of Whispers, *came out in
1984. It was followed by* Freedom Beach, *a mosaic novel written in collaboration with John Kessel, and then by another solo novel,* Look into the Sun, *as
well as the chapbook novella,* Burn. *His short work has been collected in* Think
Like a Dinosaur *and* Strange But Not a Stranger. *His most recent books are a
series of anthologies coedited with John Kessel:* Feeling Very Strange: The
Slipstream Anthology; The Secret History of Science Fiction; Digital Rapture: The Singularity Anthology; Rewired: The Post-Cyberpunk Anthology;
and Nebula Awards Showcase 2012. *Born in Minneola, New York, Kelly now
lives with his family in Nottingham, New Hampshire. He has a web site at
www.JimKelly.net, and reviews Internet-related matters for* Asimov's Science
Fiction.

Daya had been in no hurry to become a mother. In the two years since she'd
reached childbearing age, she'd built a modular from parts she'd fabbed herself,
thrown her boots into the volcano, and served as blood judge. The village elders all
said she was one of the quickest girls they had ever seen—except when it came to
choosing fathers for her firstborn. Maybe that was because she was too quick for a
sleepy village like Third Landing. When her mother, Tajana, had come of age, she'd

left for the blue city to find fathers for her baby. Everyone expected Tajana would stay in Halfway, but she had surprised them and returned home to raise Daya. So once Daya had grown up, everyone assumed that someday she would leave for the city like her mother, especially after Tajana had been killed in the avalanche last winter. What did Third Landing have to hold such a fierce and able woman? Daya could easily build a glittering new life in Halfway. Do great things for the colony.

But everything had changed after the scientists from space had landed on the old site across the river, and Daya had changed most of all. She kept her own counsel and was often hard to find. That spring she had told the elders that she didn't need to travel to gather the right semen. Her village was happy and prosperous. The scientists had chosen it to study and they had attracted tourists from all over the colony. There were plenty of beautiful and convenient local fathers to take to bed. Daya had sampled the ones she considered best, but never opened herself to blend their sperm. Now she would, here in the place where she had been born.

She chose just three fathers for her baby. She wanted Ganth because he was her brother and because he loved her above all others. Latif because he was a leader and would say what was true when everyone else was afraid. And Bakti because he was a master of stories and because she wanted him to tell hers someday.

She informed each of her intentions to make a love feast, although she kept the identities of the other fathers a secret, as was her right. Ganth demanded to know, of course, but she refused him. She was not asking for a favor. It would be her baby, her responsibility. The three fathers, in turn, kept her request to themselves, as was custom, in case she changed her mind about any or all of them. A real possibility—when she contemplated what she was about to do, she felt separated from herself.

That morning she climbed into the pen and spoke a kindness to her pig Bobo. The glint of the knife made him grunt with pleasure and he rolled onto his back, exposing the tumors on his belly. She hadn't harvested him in almost a week and so carved two fist-sized maroon swellings into the meat pail. She pressed strips of sponge root onto the wounds to stanch the bleeding and when it was done, she threw them into the pail as well. When she scratched under his jowls to dismiss him, Bobo squealed approval, rolled over and trotted off for a mud bath.

She sliced the tumors thin, dipped the pieces in egg and dragged them through a mix of powdered opium, pepper, flour, and bread crumbs, then sautéed them until they were crisp. She arranged them on top of a casserole of snuro, parsnips and sweet flag, layered with garlic and three cheeses. She harvested some of the purple blooms from the petri dish on the windowsill and flicked them on top of her love feast. The aphrodisiacs produced by the bacteria would give an erection to a corpse. She slid the casserole into the oven to bake for an hour while she bathed and dressed for babymaking.

Daya had considered the order in which she would have sex with the fathers. Last was most important, followed by first. The genes of the middle father—or fathers, since some mothers made babies with six or seven for political reasons—were less reliably expressed. She thought starting with Ganth for his sunny nature and finishing with Latif for his looks and good judgment made sense. Even though Bakti was clever, he had bad posture.

Ganth sat in front of a fuzzy black and white screen with his back to her when she nudged the door to his house open with her hip. "It's me. With a present."

He did not glance away from his show—the colony's daily news and gossip program about the scientists—but raised his forefinger in acknowledgment.

She carried the warming dish with oven mitts to the huge round table that served as his desk, kitchen counter and sometime closet. She pushed aside some books, a belt, an empty bottle of blueberry kefir, and a Fill Jump higher action figure to set her love feast down. Like her own house, Ganth's was a single room, but his was larger, shabbier, and built of some knotty softwood.

Her brother took a deep breath, his face pale in the light of the screen. "Smells delicious." He pressed the off button; the screen winked and went dark.

"What's the occasion?" He turned to her, smiling. "*Oh*." His eyes went wide when he saw how she was dressed. "Tonight?"

"Tonight." She grinned.

Trying to cover his surprise, he pulled out the pocket watch he'd had from their mother and then shook it as if it were broken. "Why, look at the time. I totally forgot that we were grown up."

"You like?" She weaved her arms and her ribbon robe fluttered.

"I was wondering when you'd come. What if I had been out?"

She nodded at the screen in front of him. "You never miss that show."

"Has anyone else seen you?" He sneaked to the window and peered out. A knot of gawkers had gathered in the street. "What, did you parade across Founders' Square dressed like that? You'll give every father in town a hard-on." He pulled the blinds and came back to her. He surprised her by going down on one knee. "So which am I?"

"What do you think?" She lifted the cover from the casserole to show that it was steaming and uncut.

"I'm honored." He took her hand in his and kissed it. "Who else?" he said. "And you have to tell. Tomorrow everyone will know."

"Bakti. Latif last."

"Three is all a baby really needs." He rubbed his thumb across the inside of her wrist. "Our mother would approve."

Of course, Ganth had no idea of what their mother had really thought of him.

Tajana had once warned Daya that if she insisted on choosing Ganth to father her baby, she should dilute his semen with that of the best men in the village. A sweet manner is fine, she'd said, but babies need brains and a spine.

"So, dear sister, it's a sacrifice . . . ," he said, standing. ". . . but I'm prepared to do my duty." He caught her in his arms.

Daya squawked in mock outrage.

"You're not surprising the others are you?" He nuzzled her neck.

"No, they expect me."

"Then we'd better hurry. I hear that Eldest Latif goes to bed early." His whisper filled her ear. "Carrying the weight of the world on his back tires him out."

"I'll give him reason to wake up."

He slid a hand through the layers of ribbons until he found her skin. "Bakti, on the other hand, stays up late, since his stories weigh nothing at all." The flat of his hand against her belly made her shiver. "I didn't realize you knew him that well."

She tugged at the hair on the back of Ganth's head to get his attention. "Feasting first," she said, her voice husky. Daya hadn't expected to be this emotional. She opened her pack, removed the bottle of chardonnay and poured two glasses. They saluted each other and drank, then she used the spatula she had brought—since she knew her brother wouldn't have one—to cut a square of her love feast. He watched her scoop it onto a plate like a man uncertain of his luck. She forked a bite into her mouth. The cheese was still melty—maybe a bit too much sweet flag. She chewed once, twice, and then leaned forward to kiss him. His lips parted and she let the contents of her mouth fall into his. He groaned and swallowed. "Again." His voice was thick. "Again and again and again."

Afterward they lay entangled on his mattress on the floor. "I'm glad you're not leaving us, Daya." He blew on the ribbons at her breast and they trembled. "I'll stay home to watch your baby," he said. "Whenever you need me. Make life so easy, you'll never want to go."

It was the worst thing he could have said; until that moment she had been able to keep from thinking that she might never see him again. He was her only family, except for the fathers her mother had kept from her. Had Tajana wanted to make it easy for her to leave Third Landing? "What if I get restless here?" Daya's voice could have fit into a thimble. "You know me."

"Okay, maybe someday you can leave." He waved the idea away. "Someday."

She glanced down his lean body at the hole in his sock and dust strings dangling from his bookshelf. He was a sweet boy and her brother, but he played harder than he worked. Ganth was content to let the future happen to him; Daya needed to make choices, no matter how hard. "It's getting late." She pressed her cheek to his. "Do me a favor and check on Bobo in the morning? Who knows when I'll get home."

By the time she kissed Ganth good-bye, it was evening. An entourage of at least twenty would-be spectators trailed her to Old Town; word had spread that the very eligible Daya was bringing a love feast to some lucky fathers. There was even a scatter of tourists, delighted to witness Third Landing's quaint mating ritual. The locals told jokes, made ribald suggestions and called out names of potential fathers. She tried to ignore them; some people in this village were so nosy.

Bakti lived in one of the barnlike stone dormitories that the settlers had built two centuries ago across the river from their landing spot. Most of these buildings were now divided into shops and apartments. When Daya finally revealed her choice by stopping at Bakti's door, the crowd buzzed. Winners of bets chirped, losers groaned. Bakti was slow to answer her knock, but when he saw the spectators, he seized her arm and drew her inside.

Ganth had been right: she and Bakti weren't particularly close. She had never been to his house, although he had visited her mother on occasion when she was growing up. She could see that he was no better a housekeeper than her brother, but at least his mess was all of a kind. The bones of his apartment had not much changed from the time the founders had used it as a dormitory; Bakti had preserved the two walls of wide shelves that they had used as bunks. Now, however, instead of sleeping refugees from Genome Crusades, they were filled with books, row upon extravagant row. This was Bakti's vice; not only did he buy cheap paper from the village stalls; he had purchased hundreds of hardcovers on his frequent trips to the blue city. They said he even owned a few print books that the founders had brought across space. There were books everywhere, open on chairs, chests, the couch, stacked in leaning towers on the floor.

"So you've come to rumple my bed?" He rearranged his worktable to make room for her love feast. "I must admit, I was surprised by your note. Have we been intimate before, Daya?"

"Just once." She set the dish down. "Don't pretend that you don't remember." When she unslung the pack from her back, the remaining bottles of wine clinked together.

"Don't pretend?" He spread his hands. "I tell stories. That's all I do."

"Glasses?" She extracted the zinfandel from her pack.

He brought two that were works of art; crystal stems twisted like vines to flutes as delicate as a skim of ice. "I recall a girl with a pansy tattooed on her back," he said.

"You're thinking of Pandi." Daya poured the wine.

"Do you sing to your lovers?"

She sniffed the bouquet. "Never."

They saluted each other and drank.

"Don't rush me now," he said. "I'm enjoying this little game." He lifted the lid of the dish and breathed in. "Your feast pleases the nose as much as you please the eye. But I see that I am not your first stop. Who else have you seen this night?"

"Ganth."

"You chose a grasshopper to be a father of your child?"

"He's my brother."

"Aha!" He snapped his fingers. "Now I have it. The garden at Tajana's place? I recall a very pleasant evening."

She had forgotten how big Bakti's nose was. "As do I." And his slouch was worse than ever. Probably from carrying too many books.

"I don't mind being the middle, you know." He took another drink of wine. "Prefer it actually—less responsibility that way. I will do my duty as a father, but I must tell you right now that I have no interest whatsoever in bringing up your baby. And her next father is?"

"Latif. Next and last."

"A man who takes fathering seriously. Good, he'll balance out poor Ganth. I will tell her stories, though. Your baby girl. That's what you hope for, am I right? A girl?"

"Yes." She hadn't realized it until he said it. A girl would make things much easier.

He paused, as if he had just remembered something. "But you're supposed to leave us, aren't you? This village is too tight a fit for someone of your abilities. You'll split seams, pop a button."

Why did everyone keep saying these things to her? "You didn't leave."

"No." He shook his head. "I wasn't as big as I thought I was. Besides, the books keep me here. Do you know how much they weigh?"

"It's an amazing collection." She bent to the nearest shelf and ran a finger along the spines of the outermost row. "I've heard you have some from Earth."

"Is this about looking at books or making babies, Daya?" Bakti looked crestfallen. She straightened, embarrassed. "The baby, of course."

"No, I get it." He waved a finger at her. "I'm crooked and cranky and mothers shut their eyes tight when we kiss." He reached for the wine bottle. "Those are novels." He nodded at the shelf. "But no, nothing from Earth."

They spent the better part of an hour browsing. Bakti said Daya could borrow some if she wanted. He said reading helped pregnant mothers settle. Then he told her the story from one of them. It was about a boy named Huckleberry Flynn, who left his village on Novy Praha to see his world but then came back again. "Just like your mother did," he said. "Just like you could, if you wanted. Someday."

"Then you could tell stories about me."

"About this night," he agreed, "if I remember." His grin was seductive. "Will I?"

"Have you gotten any books from them?" She glanced out the dark window toward the river. "Maybe they'd want to trade with you?"

"Them?" he said. "You mean our visitors? Some, but digital only. They haven't got time for nostalgia. To them, my books are as quaint as scrolls and clay tablets. They asked to scan the collection, but I think they were just being polite. Their interests seem to be more sociological than literary." He smirked. "I understand you have been spending time across the river."

She shrugged. "Do you think they are telling the truth?"

"About what? Their biology? Their politics?" He gestured at his library. "I own one thousand, two hundred and forty-three claims of truth. How would I know which is right?" He slid the book about the boy Huckleberry back onto the shelf. "But look at the time! If you don't mind, I've been putting off dinner until you arrived. And then we can make a baby and a memory, yes?"

By the time Daya left him snoring on his rumpled bed, the spectators had all gone home for the night. There was still half of the love feast left but the warming dish was beginning to dry it out. She hurried down the Farview Hill to the river.

Many honors had come to Latif over the years and with them great wealth. He had first served as village eldest when he was still a young man, just thirty-two years old. In recent years, he mediated disputes for those who did not have the time or the money to submit to the magistrates of the blue city. The fees he charged had bought him this fine house of three rooms, one of which was the parlor where he received visitors. When she saw that all the windows were dark, she gave a cry of panic. It was nearly midnight and the house was nothing but a shadow against the silver waters.

On the shore beyond, the surreal bulk of the starship beckoned.

Daya didn't even bother with the front door. She went around to the bedroom and stood on tiptoes to knock on his window. *Tap-tap.*

Nothing.

"Latif." *Tap-tap-tap.* "Wake up."

She heard a clatter within. "Shit!" A light came on and she stepped away as the window clattered open.

"Who's there? Go away."

"It's me, Daya."

"Do you know what time it is? Go away."

"But I have our love feast. You knew this was the night; I sent a message."

"And I waited, but you took too damn long." He growled in frustration. "Can't you see I'm asleep? Go find some middle who's awake."

"No, Latif. You're my last."

He started with a shout. "You wake me in the middle of the night . . ." Then he continued in a low rasp. "Where's your sense, Daya, your manners? You expect me to be your last? You should have said something. I take fathering seriously."

Daya's throat closed. Her eyes seemed to throb.

"I told you to move to the city, didn't I? Find fathers there." Latif waited for her to answer. When she didn't, he stuck his head out the window to see her better. "So instead of taking my best advice, now you want my semen?" He waited again for a reply; she couldn't speak. "I suppose you're crying."

The only reply she could make was a sniffle.

"Come to the door then."

She reached for his arm as she entered the darkened parlor but he waved her through to the center of the room. "You are rude and selfish, Daya." He shut the door and leaned against it. "But that doesn't mean you're a bad person."

He turned the lights on and for a moment they stood blinking at each other. Latif was barefoot, wearing pants but no shirt. He had a wrestler's shoulders, long arms, hands big as dinner plates. Muscles bunched beneath his smooth, dark skin, as if he might spring at her. But if she read his eyes right, his anger was passing.

"I thought you'd be pleased." She tried a grin. It bounced off him.

"Honored, yes. Pleased, not at all. You think you can just issue commands and we jump? You have the right to ask, and I have the right to refuse. Even at the last minute."

At fifty-three, Latif was still one of the handsomest men in the village. Daya had often wondered if that was one reason why everyone trusted him. She looked for some place to put the warming dish down.

"No," he said, "don't you dare make yourself comfortable unless I tell you to. Why me?"

She didn't have to think. "Because you have always been kind to me and my mother. Because you will tell the truth, even when it's hard to hear. And because, despite your years, you are still the most beautiful man I know." This time she tried a smile on him. It stuck. "All the children you've fathered are beautiful, and if my son gets nothing but looks from you, that will still be to his lifelong advantage." Daya knew that in the right circumstance, even men like Latif would succumb to flattery.

"You want me because I tell hard truths, but when I say you should move away, you ignore me. Does that make sense?"

"Not everything needs to make sense." She extended her love feast to him. "Where should I put this?"

He glided across the parlor, kissed her forehead and accepted the dish from her. "Do you know how many have asked me to be last father?"

"No." She followed him into the great room.

"Twenty-three," he said. "Every one spoke to me ahead of time. And of those, how many I agreed to?"

"No idea."

"Four." He set it on a round wooden table with a marble inset.

"They should've tried my ambush strategy." She shrugged out of her pack. "I've got wine." She handed him the bottle of Xino she had picked for him.

"Which you've been drinking all night, I'm sure. You know where the glasses are." He pulled the stopper. "And who have you been drinking with?"

"Ganth, first."

Latif tossed the stopper onto the table. "I'm one-fourth that boy's father . . . ," He rapped on the tabletop. ". . . but I don't see any part of me in him."

"He's handsome."

"Oh, stop." He poured each of them just a splash of the Xino and offered her a glass. She raised an eyebrow at his stinginess.

"It's late and you've had enough," he said. "It is affecting your judgment. Who else?"

"Bakti."

"You surprise me." They saluted each other with their glasses. "Does he really have Earth books?"

"He says not."

"He makes up too many stories. But he's sound—you should have started with him. Ganth is a middle father at best."

Both of them ran out of things to say then. Latif was right. She had finished the first two bottles with the other fathers, and had shared the love feast with them and had made love. She was heavy with the weight of her decisions and her desires. She felt like she was falling toward Latif. She pulled the cover off the warming dish and cut a square of her love feast into bite-sized chunks.

"Just because I'm making a baby doesn't mean I can't go away," she said.

"And leave the fathers behind?"

"That's what my mother did."

"And did that make her happy? Do you think she had an easy life?" He shook his head. "No, you are tying yourself to this village. This little, insignificant place. Why? Maybe you're lazy. Or maybe you're afraid. Here, you are a star. What would you be in the blue city?"

She wanted to tell him that he had it exactly wrong. That he was talking about himself, not her. But that would have been cruel. This beautiful foolish man was going to be the last father of her baby. "You're right," Daya said. "It's late." She piled bits of the feast onto a plate and came around to where he was sitting. She perched on the edge of the table and gazed down at him.

He tugged at one of the ribbons of her sleeve and she felt the robe slip off her shoulder. "What is this costume anyway?" he said. "You're wrapped up like some kind of present."

She didn't reply. Instead she pushed a bit of the feast across her plate until it slid onto her fork. They watched each other as she brought it to her open mouth, placed it on her tongue. The room shrank. Clocks stopped.

He shuddered, "Feed me, then."

Latif's pants were still around his ankles when she rolled off him. The ribbon robe dangled off the headboard of his bed. Daya gazed up at the ceiling, thinking about the tangling sperm inside her. She concentrated as her mother had taught her, and she thought she felt her cervix close and her uterus contract, concentrating the semen. At least, she hoped she did. The sperm of the three fathers would smash together furiously, breaching cell walls, exchanging plasmids. The strongest conjugate would find her eggs and then . . . . .

"What if I leave the baby behind?" she said.

"With who?" He propped himself up on an elbow. "Your mother is dead and no . . . ."

She laid a finger on his lips. "I know, Latif. But why not with a father? Ganth might do it, I think. Definitely not Bakti. Maybe even you."

He went rigid. "This is an idea you got from the scientists? Is that the way they have sex in space?"

"They don't live in space; they just travel through it." She followed a crack in the plaster of his ceiling with her eyes. "Nobody lives in space." A water stain in the corner looked like a face. A mouth. Sad eyes. "What should we do about them?"

"Do? There is nothing to be done." He fell back onto his pillow. "They're the ones the founders were trying to get away from."

"Two hundred years ago. They say things are different."

"Maybe. Maybe these particular scientists are more tolerant, but they're still dangerous."

"Why? Why are you so afraid of them?"

"*Because they're unnatural.*" The hand at her side clenched into a fist. "We're the true humans, maybe the last. But they've taken charge of evolution now, or what passes for it. We have no say in the future. All we know for sure is that they are large and still growing and we are very, very small. Maybe this lot won't force us to change. Or maybe someday they'll just make us want to become like them."

She knew this was true, even though she had spent the last few months trying not to know it. The effort had made her weary. She rolled toward Latif. When she snuggled against him, he relaxed into her embrace.

It was almost dawn when she left his house. Instead of climbing back up Farview Hill, she turned toward the river. Moments later she stepped off Mogallo's Wharf into the skiff she had built when she was a teenager.

She had been so busy pretending that this wasn't going to happen that she was surprised to find herself gliding across the river. She could never have had sex with the fathers if she had acknowledged to herself that she was going to go through with it. Certainly not with Ganth. And Latif would have guessed that something was wrong. She had the odd feeling that there were two of her in the skiff, each facing in opposite directions. The one looking back at the village was screaming at the one watching the starship grow ever larger. But there is no other Daya, she reminded herself. There is only me.

Her lover, Roberts, was waiting on the spun-carbon dock that the scientists had fabbed for river traffic. Many of the magistrates from the blue city came by boat to negotiate with the offworlders. Roberts caught the rope that Daya threw her and took it expertly around one of the cleats. She extended a hand to hoist Daya up, caught her in an embrace and pressed her lips to Daya's cheek.

"This kissing that you do," said Roberts. "I like it. Very direct." She wasn't very good at it but she was learning. Like all the scientists, she could be stiff at first. They didn't seem all that comfortable in their replaceable bodies. Roberts was small as a child, but with a woman's face. Her blonde hair was cropped short, her eyes were clear and faceted. They reminded Daya of her mother's crystal.

"It's done," said Daya.

"Yes, but are you all right?

"I think so." She forced a grin. "We'll find out."

"We will. Don't worry, love, I am going to take good care of you. And your baby."

"And I will take care of you."

"Yes." She looked puzzled. "Of course."

Roberts was a cultural anthropologist. She had explained to Daya that all she wanted was to preserve a record of an ancient way of life. A culture in which there was still sexual reproduction.

"May I see that?"

Daya opened her pack and produced the leftover bit of the love feast. She had sealed it in a baggie that Roberts had given her. It had somehow frozen solid.

"Excellent. Now we should get you into the lab before it's too late. Put you under the scanner, take some samples." This time she kissed Daya on the mouth. Her lips parted briefly and Daya felt Robert's tongue flick against her teeth. When Daya did not respond, she pulled back.

"I know this is hard now. You're very brave to help us this way, Daya." The scientist took her hand and squeezed. "But someday they'll thank you for what you're doing." She nodded toward the sleepy village across the river. "Someday soon."

yesterday's kin

NANCY KRESS

Nancy Kress began selling her elegant and incisive stories in the mid-seventies. Her books include the novel Beggars in Spain, expanded from her Hugo- and Nebula-winning story, and a sequel, Beggars and Choosers, as well as The Prince Of Morning Bells, The Golden Grove, The White Pipes, An Alien Light, Brain Rose, Oaths and Miracles, Stinger, Maximum Light, Crossfire, Nothing Human, The Floweres of Aulit Prison, Crossfire, Crucible, Dogs, and Steal Across the Sky, as well as the Space Opera trilogy Probability Moon, Probability Sun, and Probability Space. Her short work has been collected in Trinity and Other Stories, The Aliens of Earth, Beaker's Dozen, Nano Comes to Clifford Falls and Other Stories, Fountain of Age, Future Perfect, AI Unbound, and The Body Human. Her most recent books are the novels Flash Point, and, with Therese Pieczynski, New Under the Sun. In addition to the awards for "Beggars in Spain," she has also won Nebula Awards for her stories "Out of All Them Bright Stars" and "The Flowers of Aulit Prison," the John W. Campbell Memorial Award in 2003 for her novel Probability Space, and another Hugo in 2009 for "The Erdmann Nexus." Most recently, she won another Nebula Award in 2013 for her novella "After the Fall, Before the Fall, During the Fall." She lives in Seattle, Washington, with her husband, writer Jack Skillingstead.

   Here she gives us an ingenious and gripping First Contact story, one in which nothing turns out to be quite the way it seems . . .

"We see in these facts some deep organic bond, prevailing throughout space and time. . . . This bond, on my theory, is simple inheritance."

—*Charles Darwin*, The Origin of Species

I: S MINUS 10.5 MONTHS

MARIANNE

The publication party was held in the dean's office, which was supposed to be an honor. Oak-paneled room, sherry in little glasses, small-paned windows facing the quad—the room was trying hard to be a Commons someplace like Oxford or Cambridge, a task for which it was several centuries too late. The party was trying hard to look festive. Marianne's colleagues, except for Evan and the dean, were trying hard not to look too envious, or at their watches.

"Stop it," Evan said at her from behind the cover of his raised glass.

"Stop what?"

"Pretending you hate this."

"I hate this," Marianne said.

"You don't."

He was half right. She didn't like parties but she was proud of her paper, which had been achieved despite two years of gene sequencers that kept breaking down, inept graduate students who contaminated samples with their own DNA, murmurs of "Lucky find" from Baskell, with whom she'd never gotten along. Baskell, an old-guard physicist, saw her as a bitch who refused to defer to rank or back down gracefully in an argument. Many people, Marianne knew, saw her as some variant of this. The list included two of her three grown children.

Outside the open casements, students lounged on the grass in the mellow October sunshine. Three girls in cut-off jeans played Frisbee, leaping at the blue flying saucer and checking to see if the boys sitting on the stone wall were watching. Feinberg and Davidson, from Physics, walked by, arguing amiably. Marianne wished she were with them instead of at her own party.

"Oh God," she said to Evan, "Curtis just walked in."

The president of the university made his ponderous way across the room. Once he had been an historian, which might be why he reminded Marianne of Henry VIII. Now he was a campus politician, as power-mad as Henry but stuck at a second-rate university where there wasn't much power to be had. Marianne held against him not his personality but his mind; unlike Henry, he was not all that bright. And he spoke in clichés.

"Dr. Jenner," he said. "Congratulations. A feather in your cap, and a credit to us all."

"Thank you, Dr. Curtis," Marianne said.

"Oh, 'Ed,' please."

"Ed." She didn't offer her own first name, curious to see if he remembered it. He didn't. Marianne sipped her sherry.

Evan jumped into the awkward silence. "I'm Dr. Blanford, visiting post-doc," he said in his plummy British accent. "We're all so proud of Marianne's work."

"Yes! And I'd love for you to explain to me your innovative process, ah, Marianne."

He didn't have a clue. His secretary had probably reminded him that he had to put in an appearance at the party: *Dean of Science's office, 4:30 Friday, in honor of that publication by Dr. Jenner in*—quick look at e-mail—*in* Nature, *very prestigious, none of our scientists have published there before . . . .*

"Oh," Marianne said as Evan poked her discreetly in the side: *Play nice!* "it wasn't so much an innovation in process as unexpected results from known procedures. My assistants and I discovered a new haplogroup of mitochondrial DNA. Previously it was thought that *Homo sapiens* consisted of thirty haplogroups, and we found a thirty-first."

"By sequencing a sample of contemporary genes, you know," Evan said helpfully. "Sequencing and verifying."

Anything said in upper-crust British automatically sounded intelligent, and Dr. Curtis looked suitably impressed. "Of course, of course. Splendid results. A star in your crown."

"It's yet another haplogroup descended," Evan said with malicious helpfulness, "from humanity's common female ancestor 150,000 years ago. 'Mitochondrial Eve.'"

Dr. Curtis brightened. There had been a TV program about Mitochondrial Eve, Marianne remembered, featuring a buxom actress in a leopard-skin sarong. "Oh, yes! Wasn't that—"

"I'm sorry, you can't go in there!" someone shrilled in the corridor outside the room. All conversation ceased. Heads swiveled toward three men in dark suits pushing their way past the knot of graduate students by the door. The three men wore guns.

Another school shooting, Marianne thought, *where can I—*

"Dr. Marianne Jenner?" the tallest of the three men said, flashing a badge. "I'm Special Agent Douglas Katz of the F.B.I. We'd like you to come with us."

Marianne said, "Am I under arrest?"

"No, no, nothing like that. We are acting under direct order of the president of the United States. We're here to escort you to New York."

Evan had taken Marianne's hand—she wasn't sure just when. There was nothing romantic in the hand-clasp, nor anything sexual. Evan, twenty-five years her junior and discreetly gay, was a friend, an ally, the only other evolutionary biologist in the department and the only one who shared Marianne's cynical sense of humor. "*Or so we thought,*" they said to each other whenever any hypothesis proved wrong. *Or so we thought . . .* His fingers felt warm and reassuring around her suddenly icy ones.

"Why am I going to New York?"

"I'm afraid we can't tell you that. But it is a matter of national security."

"*Me?* What possible reason—?"

Special Agent Katz almost, but not quite, hid his impatience at her questions. "I wouldn't know, ma'am. My orders are to escort you to UN Special Mission Headquarters in Manhattan."

Marianne looked at her gaping colleagues, at the wide-eyed grad students, at Dr. Curtis, who was already figuring how this could be turned to the advantage of the university. She freed her hand from Evan's, and managed to keep her voice steady.

"Please excuse me, Dr. Curtis, Dean. It seems I'm needed for something connected with . . . with the aliens."

NOAH

One more time, Noah Jenner rattled the doorknob to the apartment. It felt greasy from too many unwashed palms, and it was still locked. But he knew that Emily was in there. That was the kind of thing he was always, somehow, right about. He was right about things that didn't do him any good.

"Emily," he said softly through the door, "please open up."

Nothing.

"Emily, I have nowhere else to go."

Nothing.

"I'll stop, I promise. I won't do sugarcane ever again."

The door opened a crack, chain still in place, and Emily's despairing face appeared. She wasn't the kind of girl given to dramatic fury, but her quiet despair was even harder to bear. Not that Noah didn't deserve it. He knew he did. Her fair hair hung limply on either side of her long, sad face. She wore the green bathrobe he liked, with the butterfly embroidered on the left shoulder.

"You won't stop," Emily said. "You can't. You're an addict."

"It's not an addictive drug. You know that."

"Not physically, maybe. But it is for you. You won't give it up. I'll never know who you really are."

"I—"

"I'm sorry, Noah. But—go away." She closed and relocked the door.

Noah stood slumped against the dingy wall, waiting to see if anything else would happen. Nothing did. Eventually, as soon as he mustered the energy, he would have to go away.

Was she right? Would he never give up sugarcane? It wasn't that it delivered a high: it didn't. No rush of dopamine, no psychedelic illusions, no out-of-body experiences, no lowering of inhibitions. It was just that on sugarcane, Noah felt like he was the person he was supposed to be. The problem was that it was never the same person twice. Sometimes he felt like a warrior, able to face and ruthlessly defeat anything. Sometimes he felt like a philosopher, deeply content to sit and ponder the universe. Sometimes he felt like a little child, dazzled by the newness of a fresh morning. Sometimes he felt like a father (he wasn't), protective of the entire world. Theories said that sugarcane released memories of past lives, or stimulated the collective unconscious, or made temporarily solid the images of dreams. One hypothesis was that it created a sort of temporary, self-induced Korsakoff's Syndrome, the neurological disorder in which invented selves seem completely true. No one knew how sugarcane really acted on the brain. For some people, it did nothing at all. For Noah, who had never felt he fit in anywhere, it gave what he had never had: a sense of solid identity, if only for the hours that the drug stayed in his system.

The problem was, it was difficult to hold a job when one day you were nebbishy, sweet-natured Noah Jenner, the next day you were Attila the Hun, and two days later you were far too intellectual to wash dishes or make change at a convenience store. Emily had wanted Noah to hold a job. To contribute to the rent, to scrub the floor, to help take the sheets to the laundromat. To be an adult, and the same adult every day. She was right to want that. Only—

He might be able to give up sugarcane and be the same adult, if only he had the vaguest idea who that adult was. Which brought him back to the same problem— he didn't fit anywhere. And never had.

Noah picked up the backpack in which Emily had put his few belongings. She couldn't have left it in the hallway very long ago or the backpack would have already been stolen. He made his way down the three flights from Emily's walk-up and out onto the streets. The October sun shone warmly on his shoulders, on the blocks of shabby buildings, on the trash skirling across the dingy streets of New York's Lower East Side. Walking, Noah reflected bitterly, was one thing he could do without fitting in. He walked blocks to Battery Park, that green oasis on the tip of Manhattan's steel canyons, leaned on a railing, and looked south.

He could just make out the *Embassy*, floating in New York Harbor. Well, no, not the *Embassy* itself, but the shimmer of light off its energy shield. Everybody wanted that energy shield, including his sister, Elizabeth. It kept everything out, short of a nuclear missile. Maybe that, too: so far nobody had tried, although in the two months since the embassy had floated there, three different terrorist groups had tried other weapons. Nothing got through the shield, although maybe air and light did. They must, right? Even aliens needed to breathe.

When the sun dropped below the horizon, the glint off the floating embassy disappeared. Dusk was gathering. He would have to make the call if he wanted a place to sleep tonight. Elizabeth or Ryan? His brother wouldn't yell at him as much, but Ryan lived upstate, in the same little Hudson River town as their mother's college, and Noah would have to hitchhike there. Also, Ryan was often away, doing field work for his wildlife agency. Noah didn't think he could cope with Ryan's talkative, sticky-sweet wife right now. So it would have to be Elizabeth.

He called his sister's number on his cheap cell. "Hello?" she snapped. *Born angry*, their mother always said of Elizabeth. Well, Elizabeth was in the right job, then.

"Lizzie, it's Noah."

"Noah."

"Yes. I need help. Can I stay with you tonight?" He held the cell away from his ear, bracing for her onslaught. *Shiftless, lazy, directionless* . . . When it was over, he said, "Just for tonight."

They both knew he was lying, but Elizabeth said, "Come on then," and clicked off without saying good-bye.

If he'd had more than a few dollars in his pocket, Noah would have looked for a sugarcane dealer. Since he didn't, he left the park, the wind pricking at him now with tiny needles, and descended to the subway that would take him to Elizabeth's apartment on the Upper West Side.

MARIANNE

The F.B.I. politely declined to answer any of Marianne's questions. Politely, they confiscated her cell and iPad and took her in a sleek black car down Route 87 to New

York, through the city to lower Manhattan, and out to a harbor pier. Gates with armed guards controlled access to a heavily fortified building at the end of the pier. Politely, she was searched and fingerprinted. Then she was politely asked to wait in a small windowless room equipped with a few comfortable chairs, a table with coffee and cookies, and a wall-mounted TV tuned to CNN. A news show was covering weather in Florida.

The aliens had shown up four months ago, their ship barreling out from the direction of the sun, which had made it harder to detect until a few weeks before arrival. At first, in fact, the ship had been mistaken for an asteroid and there had been panic that it would hit Earth. When it was announced that the asteroid was, in fact, an alien vessel, panic had decreased in some quarters and increased in others. A ship? Aliens? Armed forces across the world mobilized. Communications strategies were formed, and immediately hacked by the curious and technologically sophisticated. Seven different religions declared the end of the world. The stock and bond markets crashed, rallied, soared, crashed again, and generally behaved like a reed buffeted by a hurricane. Governments put the world's top linguists, biologists, mathematicians, astronomers, and physicists on top-priority stand-by. Psychics blossomed. People rejoiced and feared and prayed and committed suicide and sent up balloons in the general direction of the moon, where the alien ship eventually parked itself in orbit.

Contact was immediate, in robotic voices that were clearly mechanical, and in halting English that improved almost immediately. The aliens, dubbed by the press "Denebs" because their ship came from the general direction of that bright, blue-white star, were friendly. The xenophiles looked smugly triumphant. The xenophobes disbelieved the friendliness and bided their time. The aliens spent two months talking to the United Nations. They were reassuring; this was a peace mission. They were also reticent. Voice communication only, and through machines. They would not show themselves: "Not now. We wait." They would not visit the International Space Station, nor permit humans to visit their ship. They identified their planet, and astronomers found it once they knew where to look, by the faintly eclipsed light from its orange-dwarf star. The planet was in the star's habitable zone, slightly larger than Earth but less dense, water present. It was nowhere near Deneb, but the name stuck.

After two months, the aliens requested permission to build what they called an embassy, a floating pavilion, in New York Harbor. It would be heavily shielded and would not affect the environment. In exchange, they would share the physics behind their star drive, although not the engineering, with Earth, via the Internet. The UN went into furious debate. Physicists salivated. Riots erupted, pro and con, in major cities across the globe. Conspiracy theorists, some consisting of entire governments, vowed to attack any Deneb presence on Earth.

The UN finally agreed, and the structure went into orbit around Earth, landed without a splash in the harbor, and floated peacefully offshore. After landing, it grew wider and flatter, a half-dome that could be considered either an island or a ship. The U.S. government decided it was a ship, subject to maritime law, and the media began capitalizing and italicizing it: the *Embassy*. Coast Guard craft circled it endlessly; the U.S. Navy had ships and submarines nearby. Airspace above was a no-fly zone, which was inconvenient for jets landing at New York's three big airports. Fighter jets nearby stayed on high alert.

Nothing happened.

For another two months the aliens continued to talk through their machines to the UN, and only to the UN, and nobody ever saw them. It wasn't known whether they were shielding themselves from Earth's air, microbes, or armies. The *Embassy* was surveilled by all possible means. If anybody learned anything, the information was classified except for a single exchange:

Why are you here?

To make contact with humanity. A peace mission.

A musician set the repeated phrases to music, a sly and humorous refrain, without menace. The song, an instant international sensation, was the opening for playfulness about the aliens. Late-night comics built monologues around supposed alien practices. The *Embassy* became a tourist attraction, viewed through telescopes, from boats outside the Coast Guard limit, from helicopters outside the no-fly zone. A German fashion designer scored an enormous runway hit with "the Deneb look," despite the fact that no one knew how the Denebs looked. The stock market stabilized as much as it ever did. Quickie movies were shot, some with Deneb allies and some with treacherous Deneb foes who wanted our women or gold or bombs. Bumper stickers proliferated like kudzu: I BRAKE FOR DENEBS. EARTH IS FULL ALREADY—GO HOME. DENEBS DO IT INVISIBLY. WILL TRADE PHYSICS FOR FOOD.

The aliens never commented on any of it. They published the promised physics, which only a few dozen people in the world could understand. They were courteous, repetitive, elusive. *Why are you here? To make contact with humanity. A peace mission.*

Marianne stared at the TV, where CNN showed footage of disabled children choosing Halloween costumes. Nothing about the discussion, the room, the situation felt real. Why would the aliens want to talk to her? It had to be about her paper, nothing else made sense. No, that didn't make sense either.

"—donated by a network of churches from five states. Four-year-old Amy seizes eagerly on the black-cat costume, while her friend Kayla chooses—"

Her paper was one of dozens published every year on evolutionary genetics, each paper adding another tiny increment to statistical data on the subject. Why this one? Why her? The UN Secretary General, various presidents and premiers, top scientists—the press said they all talked to the Denebs from this modern fortress, through (pick one) highly encrypted devices that permitted no visuals, or one-way visuals, or two-way visuals that the UN was keeping secret, or not at all and the whole alien-human conversation was invented. The *Embassy*, however, was certainly real. Images of it appeared on magazine covers, coffee mugs, screen savers, tee shirts, paintings on velvet, targets for shooting ranges.

Marianne's daughter Elizabeth regarded the aliens with suspicion, but then, Elizabeth regarded everyone with suspicion. It was one reason she was the youngest Border Patrol section leader in the country, serving on the New York Task Force along with several other agencies. She fit right in with the current American obsession with isolationism as an economic survival strategy.

Ryan seldom mentioned the aliens. He was too absorbed in his career and his wife.

And Noah—did Noah, her problem child, even realize the aliens were here?

Marianne hadn't seen Noah in months. In the spring he had gone to "try life in the South." An occasional e-mail turned up on her phone, never containing much actual information. If Noah was back in New York, he hadn't called her yet. Marianne didn't want to admit what a relief that was. Her child, her baby—but every time they saw each other, it ended in recriminations or tears.

And what was she doing, thinking about her children instead of the aliens? Why did the ambassador want to talk to her? Why were the Denebs here?

To make contact with humanity. A peace mission . . .

"Dr. Jenner?"

"Yes." She stood up from her chair, her jaw set. Somebody better give her some answers, now.

The young man looked doubtfully at her clothes, dark jeans and a green suede blazer ten years old, her standard outfit for faculty parties. He said, "Secretary Desai will join you shortly."

Marianne tried to let her face show nothing. A few moments later Vihaan Desai, Secretary General of the United Nations, entered the room, followed by a security detail. Tall, elderly, he wore a sky-blue kurta of heavy, richly embroidered silk. Marianne felt like a wren beside a peacock. Desai held out his hand but did not smile. Relations between the United States and India were not good. Relations between the United States and everybody were not good, as the country relentlessly pursued its new policy of economic isolationism in an attempt to protect jobs. Until the Denebs came, with their cosmos-shaking distraction, the UN had been thick with international threats. Maybe it still was.

"Dr. Jenner," Desai said, studying her intently, "it seems we are both summoned to an interstellar conference." His English, in the musical Indian accent, was perfect. Marianne remembered that he spoke four languages.

She said, "Do you know why?"

Her directness made him blink. "I do not. The Deneb ambassador was insistent but not forthcoming."

And does humanity do whatever the ambassador insists on? Marianne did not say this aloud. Something here was not adding up. The Secretary General's next words stunned her.

"We, plus a few others, are invited aboard the *Embassy*. The invitation is dependent upon your presence, and upon its immediate acceptance."

"Aboard . . . aboard the *Embassy*?"

"It seems so."

"But nobody has ever—"

"I am well aware of that." The dark, intelligent eyes never left her face. "We await only the other guests who happen to be in New York."

"I see." She didn't.

Desai turned to his security detail and spoke to them in Hindi. An argument began. Did security usually argue with their protectees? Marianne wouldn't have thought so, but then, what did she know about UN protocol? She was out of her field, her league, her solar system. Her guess was that the Denebs were not allowing bodyguards aboard the *Embassy*, and that the security chief was protesting.

Evidently the Secretary General won. He said to her, "Please come," and walked with long strides from the room. His kurta rustled at his ankles, shimmering sky. Not intuitive, Marianne could nonetheless sense the tension coming off him like heat. They went down a long corridor, trailed by deeply frowning guards, and down an elevator. Very far down—did the elevator go under the harbor? It must. They exited into a small room already occupied by two people, a man and a woman. Marianne recognized the woman: Ekaterina Zaytsev, the representative to the UN from the Russian Federation. The man might be the Chinese representative. Both looked agitated.

Desai said in English, "We await only— Ah, here they are."

Two much younger men practically blew into the room, clutching headsets. Translators. They looked disheveled and frightened, which made Marianne feel better. She wasn't the only one battling an almost overwhelming sense of unreality. If only Evan could be here, with his sardonic and unflappable Britishness. *"Or so we thought . . ."*

No. Neither she nor Evan had ever thought of this.

"The other permanent members of the Security Council are unfortunately not immediately available," Desai said. "We will not wait."

Marianne couldn't remember who the other permanent members were. The UK, surely, but who else? How many? What were they doing this October dusk that would make them miss first contact with an alien species? Whatever it was, they had to regret it for the rest of their lives.

Unless, of course, this little delegation never returned—killed or kidnapped or eaten. No, that was ridiculous. She was being hysterical. Desai would not go if there were danger.

Of course he would. Anyone would. Wouldn't they? Wouldn't she? Nobody, she suddenly realized, had actually asked her to go on this mission. She'd been ordered to go. What if she flat-out refused?

A door opened at the far end of the small room, voices spoke from the air about clearance and proceeding, and then another elevator. The six people stepped into what had to be the world's most comfortable and unwarlike submarine, equipped with lounge chairs and gold-braided officers.

A submarine. Well, that made sense, if plans had been put in place to get to the *Embassy* unobserved by press, tourists, and nut jobs who would blow up the alien base if they could. The Denebs must have agreed to some sort of landing place or entryway, which meant this meeting had been talked of, planned for, long before today. Today was just the moment the aliens had decided to put the plan into practice. Why? Why so hastily?

"Dr. Jenner," Desai said, "in the short time we have here, please explain your scientific findings to us."

None of them sat in the lounge chairs. They stood in a circle around Marianne, who felt none of the desire to toy with them as she had with Dr. Curtis at the college. Where were her words going, besides this cramped, luxurious submarine? Was the president of the United States listening, packed into the situation room with whoever else belonged there?

"My paper is nothing startling, Mr. Secretary General, which is why this is all baffling to me. In simple terms"— she tried to not be distracted by the murmuring of the two translators into their mouthpieces —"all humans alive today are the descendants of one woman who lived about 150,000 years ago. We know this because

588 ｜ yesterday's kin

588 | yesterday's kin

of mitochondrial DNA, which is not the DNA from the nucleus of the cell but separate DNA found in small organelles called mitochondria. Mitochondria, which exist in every cell of your body, are the powerhouses of the cell, producing energy for
cellular functions. Mitochondrial DNA does not undergo recombination and is not
found in sperm cells after they reach the egg. So the mitochondrial DNA is passed
down unchanged from a mother to all her children."

Marianne paused, wondering how to explain this simply, but without condescension. "Mitochondrial DNA mutates at a steady rate, about one mutation every 10,000
years in a section called 'the control region,' and about once every 3,500 years in the
mitochondrial DNA as a whole. By tracing the number and type of mutations in contemporary humans, we can construct a tree of descent: which group descended
from which female ancestor.

"Evolutionary biologists have identified thirty of these haplogroups. I found a
new one, L7, by sequencing and comparing DNA samples with a standard human
mitochondrial sample, known as the revised Cambridge Reference Sequence."

"How did you know where to look for this new group?"

"I didn't. I came across the first sample by chance and then sampled her relatives."

"Is it very different, then, from the others?"

"No," Marianne said. "It's just a branch of the L haplogroup."

"Why wasn't it discovered before?"

"It seems to be rare. The line must have mostly died out over time. It's a very old
line, one of the first divergences from Mitochondrial Eve."

"So there is nothing remarkable about your finding?"

"Not in the least. There may even be more haplogroups out there that we just
haven't discovered yet." She felt a perfect fool. They all looked at her as if expecting
answers—Look! A blinding scientific light illuminates all!—and she had none. She
was a workman scientist who had delivered a workmanlike job of fairly routine halo-
typing.

"Sir, we have arrived," said a junior officer. Marianne saw that his dress blues were
buttoned wrong. They must have been donned in great haste. The tiny, human mishap made her feel better.

Desai drew a deep, audible breath. Even he, who had lived through war and
revolution, was nervous. Commands flew through the air from invisible people. The
submarine door opened.

Marianne stepped out into the alien ship.

NOAH

"Where's Mom? Did you call her?" Elizabeth demanded.

"Not yet," Noah said.

"Does she even know you're in New York?"

"Not yet." He wanted to tell his sister to stop hammering at him, but he was her
guest and so he couldn't. Not that he'd ever been able to stand up to either of his
siblings. His usual ploy had been to get them battering on each other and leave him
alone. Maybe he could do that now. Or maybe not.

"Noah, how long have you been in the city?"

"A while."

"How long a while?"

Noah put his hand in front of his face. "Lizzie, I'm really hungry. I didn't eat today. Do you think you could—"

"Don't start your whining-and-helpless routine with me, Noah. It doesn't work anymore."

Had it ever? Noah didn't think so, not with Elizabeth. He tried to pull himself together. "Elizabeth, I haven't called Mom yet and I *am* hungry. Please, could we defer this fight until I eat something? Anything, crackers or toast or—"

"There's sandwich stuff in the fridge. Help yourself. I'm going to call Mom, since at least one of us should let her know the prodigal son has deigned to turn up again. She's been out of her mind with worry about you."

Noah doubted that. His mother was the strongest person he knew, followed by Elizabeth and Ryan. Together, the three could have toppled empires. Of course, they seldom were together, since they fought almost every time they met. Odd that they would go on meeting so often, when it produced such bitterness, and all over such inconsequential things. Politics, religion, funding for the arts, isolationism . . . He rummaged in Elizabeth's messy refrigerator, full of plastic containers with their lids half off, some with dabs of rotting food stuck to the bottom. God, this one was growing *mold*. But he found bread, cheese, and some salsa that seemed all right.

Elizabeth's one-bedroom apartment echoed her fridge, which was another reason she and Mom fought. Unmade bed, dusty stacks of journals and newspapers, a vase of dead flowers probably sent by one of the boyfriends Elizabeth never fell in love with. Mom's house north of the city, and Ryan and Connie's near hers, were neat and bright. Housecleaners came weekly; food was bought from careful lists; possessions were replaced whenever they got shabby. Noah had no possessions, or at least as few as he could manage.

Elizabeth clutched the phone. She dressed like a female FBI agent—short hair, dark pantsuit, no makeup—and was beautiful without trying. "Come on, Mom, pick up," she muttered, "it's a cell, it's supposed to be portable."

"Maybe she's in class," Noah said. "Or a meeting."

"It's Friday night, Noah."

"Oh. Yeah."

"I'll try the landline. She still has one."

Someone answered the landline on the first ring; Noah heard the chime stop from where he sat munching his sandwich. Then silence.

"Hello? Hello? Mom?" Elizabeth said.

The receiver on the other end clicked.

"That's odd," Elizabeth said.

"You probably got a wrong number."

"Don't talk with your mouth full. I'm going to try again."

This time no one answered. Elizabeth scowled. "I don't like that. Someone is there. I'm going to call Ryan."

Wasn't Ryan somewhere in Canada doing field work? Or maybe Noah had the dates wrong. He'd only glanced at the e-mail from Ryan, accessed on a terminal at the public library. That day he'd been on sugarcane, and the temporary identity had been impatient and brusque.

"Ryan? This is Elizabeth. Do you know where Mom is? . . . If I knew her schedule I wouldn't be calling, would I? . . . Wait, wait, will you *listen* for a minute? I called her house and someone picked up and then clicked off, and when I called back a second later, it just rang. Will you go over there just to check it out? . . . Okay, yes, we'll wait. Oh, Noah's here . . . No, I'm not going to discuss with you right now the . . . *Ryan.* For chrissake, go check Mom's house!" She clicked off.

Noah wished he were someplace else. He wished he were somebody else. He wished he had some sugarcane.

Elizabeth flounced into a chair and picked up a book. *Tariffs, Borders, and the Survival of the United States,* Noah read upside-down. Elizabeth was a passionate defender of isolationism. How many desperate people trying to crash the United States borders had she arrested today? Noah didn't want to think about it.

Fifteen minutes later, Ryan called back. Elizabeth put the call on speaker phone. "Liz, there are cop cars around Mom's house. They wouldn't let me in. A guy came out and said Mom isn't dead or hurt or in trouble, and he couldn't tell me any more than that."

"Okay." Elizabeth wore her focused look, the one with which she directed border patrols. "I'll try the college."

"I did. I reached Evan. He said that three men claiming to be FBI came and escorted her to the UN Special Mission Headquarters in Manhattan."

"That doesn't make sense!"

"I know. Listen, I'm coming over to your place."

"I'm calling the police."

"No! Don't! Not until I get there and we decide what to do."

Noah listened to them argue, which went on until Ryan hung up. Of course Elizabeth, who worked for a quasi-military organization, wanted to call the cops. Of course Ryan, who worked for a wildlife organization that thought the government had completely messed up regulations on invasive botanical species, would shun the cops. Meanwhile Mom was probably just doing something connected with her college, a UN fundraiser or something, and that geek Evan had gotten it all wrong. Noah didn't like Evan, who was only a few years older than he was. Evan was everything that Noah's family thought Noah should be: smart, smooth, able to fit in anyplace, even into a country that wasn't his own. And how come Elizabeth's border patrols hadn't kept out Evan Blanford?

Never mind; Noah knew the answer.

He said, "Can I do anything?"

Elizabeth didn't even answer him.

MARIANNE

She had seen many pictures of the *Embassy*. From the outside, the floating pavilion was beautiful in a stark sort of way. Hemispherical, multifaceted like a buckeyball (Had the Denebs learned that structure from humans or was it a mathematical universal?), the *Embassy* floated on a broad platform of some unknowable material. Facets and platform were blue but coated with the energy shield, which reflected sunlight so much that it glinted, a beacon of sorts. The aliens had certainly not tried to mask their presence. But there must be hidden machinery underneath, in the part known (maybe) only to Navy divers, since the entire huge structure had landed without a splash in the harbor. Plus, of course, the hidden passage through which the sub had come, presumably entailing a momentary interruption of the energy shield. Marianne knew she'd never find out the details.

The room into which she and the others stepped from the submarine was featureless except for the bed of water upon which their sub floated, droplets sliding off its sleek sides. No windows or furniture, one door. A strange smell permeated the air: Disinfectant? Perfume? Alien body odor? Marianne's heart began to beat oddly, too hard and too loud, with abrupt painful skips. Her breathing quickened.

The door opened and a Deneb came out. At first, she couldn't see it clearly; it was clouded by the same glittery energy shield that covered the *Embassy*. When her eyes adjusted, she gasped. The others also made sounds: a quick indrawn breath, a clicking of the tongue, what sounded like an actual whimper. The Russian translator whispered, "*Bozhe moi!*"

The alien looked almost human. Almost, not quite. Tall, maybe six-two, the man—it was clearly male—had long, thin arms and legs, a deep chest, a human face but much larger eyes. His skin was coppery and his hair, long and tied back, was dark brown. Most striking were his eyes: larger than humans', with huge dark pupils in a large expanse of white. He wore dark green clothing, a simple tunic top over loose, short trousers that exposed his spindly calves. His feet were bare, and perhaps the biggest shock of all was his feet, five-toed and broad, the nails cut short and square. Those feet looked so much like hers that she thought wildly: *He could wear my shoes.*

"Hello," the alien said, and it was not his voice but the mechanical one of the radio broadcasts, coming from the ceiling.

"Hello," Desai said, and bowed from the waist. "We are glad to finally meet. I am Secretary General Desai of the United Nations."

"Yes," the alien "said," and then added some trilling and clicking sounds in which his mouth did move. Immediately the ceiling said, "I welcome you in our own language."

Secretary Desai made the rest of the introductions with admirable calm. Marianne tried to fight her growing sense of unreality by recalling what she had read about the Denebs' planet. She wished she'd paid more attention to the astronomy. The popular press had said that the alien star was a K-something (K zero? K two? She couldn't remember). The alien home world had both less gravity and less light than Earth, at different wavelengths . . . orange, yes. The sun was an orange dwarf. Was this Deneb so tall because the gravity was less? Or maybe he was just a basketball player—

Get a grip, Marianne.

She did. The alien had said his name, an impossible collection of trilled phonemes, and immediately said, "Call me Ambassador Smith." How had he chosen that—from a computer-generated list of English names? When Marianne had been in Beijing to give a paper, some Chinese translators had done that: "Call me Dan."

She had assumed the translators doubted her ability to pronounce their actual names correctly, and they had probably been right. But "Smith" for a starfarer . . .

"You are Dr. Jenner?"

"Yes, Ambassador."

"We wanted to talk with you, in particular. Will you please come this way, all of you?"

They did, trailing like baby ducklings after the tall alien. The room beyond the single door had been fitted up like the waiting room of a very expensive medical specialist. Did they order the upholstered chairs and patterned rug on the Internet? Or manufacture them with some advanced nanotech deep in the bowels of the *Embassy*? The wall pictures were of famous skylines: New York, Shanghai, Dubai, Paris. Nothing in the room suggested alienness. Deliberate? Of course it was. *Nobody here but us chickens.*

Marianne sat, digging the nails of one hand into the palm of the other to quiet her insane desire to giggle.

"I would like to know of your recent publication, Dr. Jenner," the ceiling said, while Ambassador Smith looked at her from his disconcertingly large eyes.

"Certainly," Marianne said, wondering where to begin. Where to begin? How much did they know about human genetics?

Quite a lot, as it turned out. For the next twenty minutes Marianne explained, gestured, answered questions. The others listened silently except for the low murmur of the Chinese and Russian translators. Everyone, human and alien, looked attentive and courteous, although Marianne detected the slightly pursed lips of Ekaterina Zaytsev's envy.

Slowly it became clear that Smith already knew much of what Marianne was saying. His questions centered on where she had gotten her DNA samples.

"They were volunteers," Marianne said. "Collection booths were set up in an open-air market in India, because I happened to have a colleague working there, in a train station in London, and on my college campus in the United States. At each place, a nominal fee was paid for a quick scraping of tissue from the inside of the cheek. After we found the first L7 DNA in a sample from an American student from Indiana, we went to her relatives to ask for samples. They were very cooperative."

"This L7 sample, according to your paper, comes from a mutation that marks the strain of one of the oldest of mitochondrial groups."

Desai made a quick, startled shift on his chair.

"That's right," Marianne said. "Evidence says that 'Mitochondrial Eve' had at least two daughters, and the line of one of them was L0 whereas the other line developed a mutation that became—" All at once she saw it, what Desai had already realized. She blinked at Smith and felt her mouth fall open, just as if she had no control over her jaw muscles, just as if the universe had been turned inside out, like a sock.

NOAH

An hour later, Ryan arrived at Elizabeth's apartment. Repeated calls to their mother's cell and landline had produced nothing. Ryan and Elizabeth sat on the sagging sofa, conferring quietly, their usual belligerence with each other replaced by shared concern. Noah sat across the room, listening.

His brother had been short-changed in the looks department. Elizabeth was beautiful in a severe way and Noah knew he'd gotten the best of his parents' genes: his dead father's height and athletic build, his mother's light-gray eyes flecked with gold. In contrast, Ryan was built like a fire hydrant: short, muscular, thickening into cylindricalness since his marriage; Connie was a good cook. At thirty, he was already balding. Ryan was smart, slow to change, humorless.

Elizabeth said, "Tell me exactly what Evan said about the FBI taking her away. Word for word."

Ryan did, adding, "What about this—we call the FBI and ask them directly where she is and what's going on."

"I tried that. The local field office said they didn't know anything about it, but they'd make inquiries and get back to me. They haven't."

"Of course not. We have to give them a reason to give out information, and on the way over I thought of two. We can say either that we're going to the press, or that we need to reach her for a medical emergency."

Elizabeth said, "I don't like the idea of threatening the feds—too potentially messy. The medical emergency might be better. We could say Connie's developed a problem with her pregnancy. First grandchild, life-threatening complications—"

Noah, startled, said, "Connie's pregnant?"

"Four months," Ryan said. "If you ever read the emails everybody sends you, you might have gotten the news. You're going to be an uncle." His gaze said that Noah would make just as rotten an uncle as he did a son.

Elizabeth said, "You need to make the phone call, Ryan. You're the prospective father."

Ryan pulled out his cell, which looked as if it could contact deep space. The FBI office was closed. He left a message. FBI Headquarters in D.C. was also closed. He left another message. Before Ryan could say, "They'll never get back to us" and so begin another argument with Elizabeth over governmental inefficiency, Noah said, "Did the Wildlife Society give you that cell for your job?"

"It's the International Wildlife Federation and yes, the phone has top-priority connections for the loosestrife invasion."

Noah ducked his head to hide his grin.

Elizabeth guffawed. "Ryan, do you know how pretentious that sounds? An emergency hotline for weeds?"

"Do you know how ignorant *you* sound? Purple loosestrife is taking over wetlands, which for your information are the most biologically diverse and productive ecologies on Earth. They're being choked by this invasive species, with an economic impact of millions of dollars that—"

"As if you cared about the United States economy! You'd open us up again to competition from cheap foreign sweatshop labor, just let American jobs go to—"

"You can't shut out the world, Elizabeth, not even if you get the aliens to give you the tech for their energy shields. I know that's what you 'border-defense' types want—"

"Yes, it is! Our economic survival is at stake, which makes border patrol a lot more important than a bunch of creeping flowers!"

"Great, just great. Wall us off by keeping out new blood, new ideas, new trade partners. But let in invasive botanicals that encroach on farmland, so that eventually we can't even feed everyone who would be imprisoned in your imported alien energy fields."

"Protected, not imprisoned. The way we're protecting you now by keeping the Denebs off-shore."

"Oh, you're doing that, are you? That was the aliens' decision. Do you think that if they had wanted to plop their pavilion in the middle of Times Square that your Border Patrol could have stopped them? They're a starfaring race, for chrissake!"

"Nobody said the—"

Noah shouted, which was the only way to get their attention, "Elizabeth, your cell is ringing! It says it's Mom!"

They both stared at the cell as if at a bomb, and then Elizabeth lunged for the phone. "Mom?"

"It's me. You called but—"

"Where have you been? What happened? What was the FBI—"

"I'll tell you everything. Are you and Ryan still at your place?"

"Yes. You sound funny. Are you sure you're okay?"

"Yes. No. Stay there, I'll get a cab, but it may be a few hours yet."

"But where—"

The phone went dead. Ryan and Elizabeth stared at each other. Into the silence, Noah said, "Oh yeah, Mom. Noah's here, too."

MARIANNE

"You are surprised," Ambassador Smith had said, unnecessarily.

Courtesy had been swamped in shock. "You're *human*? From Earth?"

"Yes. We think so."

"Your mitochondrial DNA matches the L7 sequence? No, wait—your whole biology matches ours?"

"There are some differences, of course. We—"

The Russian delegate stood up so quickly her chair fell over. She spat something which her translator gave as a milder, "'I do not understand how this is possible.'"

"I will explain," Smith said. "Please sit down."

Ekaterina Zaytsev did not sit. All at once Marianne wondered if the energy field enveloping Smith was weaponized.

Smith said, "We have known for millennia that we did not originate on World. There is no fossil record of us going back more than 150,000 Earth years. The life forms native to World are DNA-based, but there is no direct genetic link. We know that someone took us from somewhere else and—"

"Why?" Marianne blurted. "Why would they do that? And who is 'they'?"

Before Smith could answer, Zaytsev said, "Why should your planet's native life-forms be DNA-based at all? If this story is not a collection of lies?"

"Panspermia," Smith said. "And we don't know why we were seeded from Earth to World. An experiment, perhaps, by a race now gone. We—"

The Chinese ambassador was murmuring to his translator. The translator, American and too upset to observe protocol, interrupted Smith.

"Mr. Zhu asks how, if you are from Earth, you progressed to space travel so much faster than we have? If your brains are the same as ours?"

"Our evolution was different."

Marianne darted in with, "How? Why? A hundred fifty thousand years is not enough for more than superficial evolutionary changes!"

"Which we have," Smith said, still in that mechanical voice that Marianne suddenly hated. Its very detachment sounded condescending. "World's gravity, for instance, is one-tenth less than Earth's, and our internal organs and skeletons have adjusted. World is warmer than Earth, and you can see that we carry little body fat. Our eyes are much larger than yours—we needed to gather all the light we can on a planet dimmer than yours. Most plants on World are dark, to gather as many photons as possible. We are dazzled by the colors on Earth."

He smiled, and Marianne remembered that all human cultures share certain facial expressions: happiness, disgust, anger.

Smith continued, "But when I said that our evolution differed from yours, I was referring to social evolution. World is a more benign planet than Earth. Little axial tilt, many easy-to-domesticate grains, much food, few predators. We had no Ice Age. We settled into agriculture over a hundred thousand years before you did."

Over a hundred thousand years more of settled communities, of cities, with their greater specialization and intellectual cross-fertilization. While Marianne's ancestors fifteen thousand years ago had still been hunting mastodons and gathering berries, these cousins across the galaxy might have been exploring quantum physics. But—

She said, "Then with such an environment, you must have had an overpopulation problem. All easy ecological niches rapidly become overpopulated!"

"Yes. But we had one more advantage." Smith paused; he was giving the translators time to catch up, and she guessed what that meant even before he spoke again.

"The group of us seeded on World—and we estimate it was no more than a thousand—were all closely related. Most likely they were all brought from one place. Our gene pool does not show as much diversity as yours. More important, the exiles—or at least a large number of them—happened to be unusually mild-natured and cooperative. You might say, 'sensitive to other's suffering.' We have had wars, but not very many, and not early on. We were able to control the population problem, once we saw it coming, with voluntary measures. And, of course, those subgroups that worked together best, made the earliest scientific advances and flourished most."

"You replaced evolution of the fittest with evolution of the most cooperative," Marianne said, and thought: *There goes Darwin.*

"You may say that."

"*I* not say this," Zaytsev said, without waiting for her translator. Her face twisted. "How you know you come from Earth? And how know where is Earth?"

"Whoever took us to World left titanium tablets, practically indestructible, with diagrams. Eventually we learned enough astronomy to interpret them."

Moses on the mountain, Marianne thought. *How conveniently neat!* Profound distrust swamped her, followed by profound belief. Because, after all, here the aliens were, having arrived in a starship, and they certainly looked human. Although—

She said abruptly, "Will you give us blood samples? Tissue? Permit medical scans?"

"Yes."

The agreement was given so simply, so completely, that everyone fell silent. Marianne's dazed mind tried to find the scam in this, the possible nefarious treachery, and failed. It was quiet Zhu Feng who, through his translator, finally broke the silence.

"Tell us, please, honored envoy, why you are here at all?"

Again Smith answered simply. "To save you all from destruction."

NOAH

Noah slipped out of the apartment feeling terrible but not terrible enough to stay. First transgression: If Mom returned earlier than she'd said, he wouldn't be there when she arrived. Second transgression: He'd taken twenty dollars from Elizabeth's purse. Third transgression: He was going to buy sugarcane.

But he'd left Elizabeth and Ryan arguing yet again about isolationism, the same argument in the same words as when he'd seen them last, four months ago. Elizabeth pulled out statistics showing that the United States' only option for survival, including avoiding revolution, was to retain and regain jobs within its borders, impose huge tariffs on imports, and rebuild infrastructure. Ryan trotted out different statistics proving that only globalization could, after a period of disruption, bring economic benefits in the long run, including a fresh flow of workers into a graying America. They had gotten to the point of hurtling words at each other like "Fascist" and "sloppy thinker," when Noah left.

He walked the three blocks to Broadway. It was, as always, brightly lit, but the gyro places and electronics shops and restaurants, their outside tables empty and chained in the cold dusk, looked shabbier than he remembered. Some stores were not just shielded by grills but boarded up. He kept walking east, toward Central Park.

The dealer huddled in a doorway. He wasn't more than fifteen. Sugarcane was a low-cost, low-profit drug, not worth the gangs' time, let alone that of organized crime. The kid was a freelance amateur, and God knows what the sugarcane was cut with.

Noah bought it anyway. In the nearest Greek place he bought a gyro as the price of the key to the bathroom and locked himself in. The room was windowless but surprisingly clean. The testing set that Noah carried everywhere showed him the unexpected: The sugarcane was cut only with actual sugar, and only by about fifty percent.

"Thank you, Lord," he said to the toilet, snorted twice his usual dose, and went back to his table to eat the cooling gyro and wait.

The drug took him quickly, as it always did. First came a smooth feeling, as if the synapses of his brain were filling with rich, thick cream. Then: One moment he was Noah Jenner, misfit, and the next he wasn't. He felt like a prosperous small businessman of some type, a shop owner maybe, financially secure and blissfully uncomplicated. A contented, centered person who never questioned who he was or where he was going, who fit in wherever he happened to be. The sort of man who could eat his gyro and gaze out the window without a confusing thought in his head.

Which he did, munching away, the juicy meat and mild spices satisfying in his mouth, for a quiet half hour.

Except—something was happening on the street.

A group of people streamed down Broadway. A parade. No, a mob. They carried torches, of all things, and something larger on fire, carried high. . . . Now Noah could hear shouting. The thing carried high was an effigy made of straw and rags, looking like the alien in a hundred bad movies: big blank head, huge eyes, spindly body of pale green. It stood in a small metal tub atop a board. Someone touched a torch to the straw and set the effigy on fire.

Why? As far as Noah could see, the aliens weren't bothering anybody. They were even good for business. It was just an excuse for people floundering in a bad economy to vent their anger—

Were these his thoughts? Noah's? Who was he now?

Police sirens screamed farther down the street. Cops appeared on foot, in riot gear. A public-address system blared, its words audible even through the shop window: "Disperse now! Open flame is not allowed on the streets! You do not have a parade permit! Disperse now!"

Someone threw something heavy, and the other window of the gyro place shattered.

Glass rained down on the empty tables in that corner. Noah jerked upright and raced to the back of the tiny restaurant, away from the windows. The cook was shouting in Greek. People left the parade, or joined it from side streets, and began to hurl rocks and bottles at the police. The cops retreated to the walls and doorways across Broadway and took out grenades of tear gas.

On the sidewalk outside, a small child stumbled by, crying and bleeding and terrified.

The person who Noah was now didn't think, didn't hesitate. He ran out into the street, grabbed the child, and ran back into the restaurant. He wasn't quite fast enough to escape the spreading gas. His nose and eyes shrieked in agony, even as he held his breath and thrust the child's head under his jacket.

Into the tiny kitchen, following the fleeing cook and waiter, and out the back door to an alley of overflowing garbage cans. Noah kept running, even though his agonized vision was blurring. Store owners had all locked their doors. But he had outrun the tear gas, and now a woman was leaning out of the window of her second-floor apartment, craning her neck to see through brick walls to the action two streets away. Gunfire sounded. Over its echo off the steel and stone canyons, Noah shouted up, "A child got gassed! Please—throw down a bottle of water!"

She nodded and disappeared. To his surprise, she actually appeared on the street to help a stranger, carrying a water bottle and a towel. "I'm a nurse, let me have him. . . . Aahh." Expertly she bathed the child's eyes, and then Noah's, just as if a battle wasn't going on within hearing if not within sight.

"Thank you," Noah gasped. "It was . . ." He stopped.

Something was happening in his head, and it wasn't due to the sugarcane. He felt an immediate and powerful kinship with this woman. How was that possible? He'd never seen her before. Nor was the attraction romantic—she was in late middle age, with graying hair and a drooping belly. But when she smiled at him and said, "You don't need the ER," something turned over in Noah's heart. What the fuck?

It must be the sugarcane.

But the feeling didn't have the creamy, slightly unreal feel of sugarcane.

She was still talking. "You probably couldn't get into any ER anyway, they'll all be jammed. I know—I was an ER nurse. But this kid'll be fine. He got almost none of the gas. Just take him home and calm him down."

"Who . . . who are you?"

"It doesn't matter." And she was gone, backing into the vestibule of her apartment building, the door locking automatically behind her. Restoring the anonymity of New York.

Whatever sense of weird recognition and bonding Noah had felt with her, it obviously had not been mutual. He tried to shake off the feeling and concentrate on the kid, who was wailing like a hurricane. The effortless competence bestowed by the sugarcane was slipping away. Noah knew nothing about children. He made a few ineffective soothing noises and picked up the child, who kicked him.

More police sirens in the distance. Eventually he found a precinct station, staffed only by a scared-looking civilian desk clerk; probably everyone else was at the riot. Noah left the kid there. Somebody would be looking for him. Noah walked back to West End Avenue, crossed it, and headed northeast to Elizabeth's apartment. His eyes still stung, but not too badly. He had escaped the worst of the gas cloud.

Elizabeth answered the door. "Where the hell did you go? Damn it, Noah, Mom's arriving any minute! She texted!"

"Well, I'm here now, right?"

"Yes, you're here now, but of all the shit-brained times to go out for a stroll! How did you tear your jacket?"

"Dunno." Neither his sister nor his brother seemed aware that eight blocks away there had been—maybe still was—an anti-alien riot going on. Noah didn't feel like informing them.

Ryan held his phone. "She's here. She texted. I'll go down."

Elizabeth said, "Ryan, she can probably pay off a cab and take an elevator by herself."

Ryan went anyway. *He had always been their mother's favorite,* Noah thought wearily. Except around Elizabeth, Ryan was affable, smooth, easy to get along with. His wife was charming, in an exaggeratedly feminine sort of way. They were going to give Marianne a grandchild.

It was an effort to focus on his family. His mind kept going back to that odd, unprecedented feeling of kinship with a person he had never seen before and probably had nothing whatsoever in common with. What was that all about?

"Elizabeth," his mother said. "And Noah! I'm so glad you're here. I've got . . . I've got a lot to tell you all. I—"

And his mother, who was always equal to anything, abruptly turned pale and fainted.

MARIANNE

Stupid, stupid—she never passed out! To the three faces clustered above her like balloons on sticks she said irritably, "It's nothing—just hypoglycemia. I haven't eaten since this morning. Elizabeth, if you have some juice or something . . ."

Juice was produced, crackers, slightly moldy cheese.

Marianne ate. Ryan said, "I didn't know you were hypoglycemic, Mom."

"I'm fine. Just not all that young anymore." She put down her glass and regarded her three children.

Elizabeth, scowling, looked so much like Kyle—was that why Marianne and Elizabeth had never gotten along? Her gorgeous alcoholic husband, the mistake of Marianne's life, had been dead for fifteen years. Yet here he was again, ready to poke holes in anything Marianne said.

Ryan, plain next to his beautiful sister but so much easier to love. Everybody loved Ryan, except Elizabeth.

And Noah, problem child, she and Kyle's last-ditch effort to save their doomed marriage. Noah was drifting and, she knew without being able to help, profoundly unhappy.

Were all three of them, and everybody else on the planet, going to die, unless humans and Denebs together could prevent it?

She hadn't fainted from hypoglycemia, which she didn't have. She had fainted from sheer delayed, maternal terror at the idea that her children might all perish. But she was not going to say that to her kids. And the fainting wasn't going to happen again.

"I need to talk to you," she said unnecessarily. But how to begin something like this? "I've been talking to the aliens. In the *Embassy*."

"We know, Evan told us," Noah said, at the same moment that Elizabeth, quicker, said sharply, "*Inside?*"

"Yes. The Deneb ambassador requested me."

"Requested you? Why?"

"Because of the paper I just published. The aliens— Did any of you read the copies of my paper I emailed you?"

"I did," Ryan said. Elizabeth and Noah said nothing. Well, Ryan was the scientist.

"It was about tracing human genetic diversity through mitochondrial evolution. Thirty mitochondrial haplogroups had been discovered. I found the thirty-first. That wouldn't really be a big deal, except that—in a few days this will be common knowledge, but you must keep it among ourselves until the ambassador announces—the aliens belong to the thirty-first group, L7. They're human."

Silence.

"Didn't you understand what I just—"

Elizabeth and Ryan erupted with questions, expressions of disbelief, arm waving. Only Noah sat quietly, clearly puzzled. Marianne explained what Ambassador Smith—impossible name!—had told her. When she got to the part about the race that had taken humans to "World" also leaving titanium tablets engraved with astronomical diagrams, Elizabeth exploded. "Come on, Mom, this fandango makes no sense!"

"The Denebs are *here*," Marianne pointed out. "They did find us. And the Denebs are going to give tissue samples. Under our strict human supervision. They're expanding the *Embassy* and allowing in humans. Lots of humans, to examine their biology and to work with our scientists."

"Work on what?" Ryan said gently. "Mom, this can't be good. They're an invasive species."

"Didn't you hear a word I said?" Marianne said. God, if Ryan, the scientist, could not accept truth, how would humanity as a whole? "They're not 'invasive,' or at least not if our testing confirms the ambassador's story. They're native to Earth."

"An invasive species is native to Earth. It's just not in the ecological niche it evolved for."

Elizabeth said, "Ryan, if you bring up purple loosestrife, I swear I'm going to clip you one. Mom, did anybody think to ask this ambassador the basic question of why they're here in the first place?"

"Don't talk to me like I'm an idiot. Of course we did. There's a—" She stopped and bit her lip, knowing how this would sound. "You all know what panspermia is?"

"Yes," said Elizabeth.

"Of course." Ryan.

"No." Noah.

"It's the idea that original life in the galaxy"—whatever *that* actually was, all the textbooks would now need to be rewritten—"came from drifting clouds of organic molecules. We know that such molecules exist inside meteors and comets and that they can, under some circumstances, survive entry into atmospheres. Some scientists, like Fred Hoyle and Stephen Hawking, have even endorsed the idea that new biomolecules are still being carried down to Earth. The Denebs say that there is a huge, drifting cloud of spores—well, they're technically not spores, but I'll come to that in a minute—drifting toward Earth. Or, rather, we're speeding toward it, since the solar system rotates around the center of the galaxy and the entire galaxy moves through space relative to the cosmic microwave background. Anyway, in ten months from now, Earth and this spore cloud meet. And the spores are deadly to humans."

Elizabeth said skeptically, "And they know this *how*?"

"Because two of their colony planets lay in the path of the cloud and were already exposed. Both populations were completely destroyed. The Denebs have recordings. Then they sent unmanned probes to capture samples, which they brought with them. They say the samples are a virus, or something like a virus, but encapsulated in a coating that isn't like anything viruses can usually make. Together, aliens and humans are going to find a vaccine or a cure."

More silence. Then all three of her children spoke together, but in such different tones that they might have been discussing entirely different topics.

Ryan: "In ten months? A vaccine or cure for an unknown pathogen in ten months? It took the CDC six months just to fully identify the bacterium in Legionnaires' disease!"

Elizabeth: "If they're so technologically superior, they don't need us to develop any sort of 'cure'!"

Noah: "What do the spores do to people?"

Marianne answered Noah first, because his question was the simplest. "They act like viruses, taking over cellular machinery to reproduce. They invade the lungs and multiply and then . . . then victims can't breathe. It only takes a few days." A terrible, painful death. A sudden horror came into her mind: her three children gasping for breath as their lungs were swamped with fluid, until they literally drowned. All of them.

"Mom," Ryan said gently, "are you all right? Elizabeth, do you have any wine or anything?"

"No," said Elizabeth, who didn't drink. Marianne suddenly, ridiculously, clung to that fact, as if it could right the world: Her two-fisted cop daughter, whose martial-arts training enabled her to take down a two-hundred-fifty-pound attacker, had a Victorian lady's fastidiousness about alcohol. Stereotypes didn't hold. The world was more complicated than that. The unexpected existed—a Border Patrol section chief did not drink!—and therefore an unexpected solution could be found to this unexpected problem. Yes.

She wasn't making sense, and knew it, and didn't care. Right now, she needed hope more than sense. The Denebs, with technology an order of magnitude beyond humans, couldn't deal with the spore cloud, but Elizabeth didn't drink and, therefore, together Marianne and Smith and—throw in the president and WHO and the CDC and USAMRIID, why not—could defeat mindless space-floating dormant viruses.

Noah said curiously, "What are you smiling about, Mom?"

"Nothing." She could never explain.

Elizabeth blurted, "So even if all this shit is true, what the fuck makes the Dennies think that *we* can help them?"

Elizabeth didn't drink like a cop, but she swore like one. Marianne said, "They don't know that we can. But their biological sciences aren't much more advanced than ours, unlike their physical sciences. And the spore cloud hits Earth next September. The Denebs have twenty-five years."

"Do you believe that their biological sciences aren't as advanced as their physics and engineering?"

"I have no reason to disbelieve it."

"If it's true, then we're their lab rats! They'll test whatever they come up with on us, and then they'll sit back in orbit or somewhere to see if it works before taking it home to their own planet!"

"That's one way to think of it," Marianne said, knowing that this was exactly how a large part of the media would think of it. "Or you could think of it as a rescue mission. They're trying to help us while there's time, if not much time."

Ryan said, "Why do they want you? You're not a virologist."

"I don't know," Marianne said.

Elizabeth erupted once more, leaping up to pace around the room and punch at the air. "I don't believe it. Not any of it, including the so-called 'cloud.' There are things they aren't telling us. But you, Mom—you just swallow whole anything they say! You're unbelievable!"

Before Marianne could answer, Noah said, "I believe you, Mom," and gave her his absolutely enchanting smile. He had never really become aware of the power of that smile. It conferred acceptance, forgiveness, trust, the sweet sadness of fading sunlight. "All of us believe everything you said.

"We just don't want to."

MARIANNE

Noah was right. Ryan was right. Elizabeth was wrong.

The spore cloud existed. Although technically not spores, that was the word the Deneb translator gave out, and the word stuck among astronomers because it was a term they already knew. As soon as the clouds' coordinates, composition, and speed were given by the Denebs to the UN, astronomers around the globe found it through spectral analysis and the dimming of stars behind it. Actually, they had known of its existence all along but had assumed it was just another dust cloud too small and too cool to be incubating stars. Its trajectory would bring it in contact with Earth when the Denebs said, in approximately ten months.

Noah was right in saying that people did not want to believe this. The media erupted into three factions. The most radical declared the "spore cloud" to be just harmless dust and the Denebs plotting, in conspiracy with the UN and possibly several governments, to take over Earth for various evil and sometimes inventive purposes. The second faction believed that the spore threat might be real but that, echoing Elizabeth, humanity would become "lab rats" in alien experiments to find some sort of solution, without benefit to Earth. The third group, the most scientifically literate, focused on a more immediate issue: They did not want the spore samples brought to Earth for research, calling them the real danger.

Marianne suspected the samples were already here. NASA had never detected shuttles or other craft going between the ship in orbit around the moon and the *Embassy*. Whatever the aliens wanted here, probably already was.

Teams of scientists descended on New York. Data was presented to the UN, the only body that Smith would deal with directly. Everyone kept saying that time was of the essence. Marianne, prevented from resuming teaching duties by the insistent reporters clinging to her like lint, stayed in Elizabeth's apartment and waited. Smith had given her a private communication device, which no one except the UN Special Mission knew about. Sometimes as she watched TV or cleaned Elizabeth's messy apartment, Marianne pondered this: An alien had given her his phone number and asked her to wait. It was almost like dating again.

Time is of the essence! Time is of the essence! A few weeks went by in negotiations she knew nothing of. Marianne reflected on the word "essence." Elizabeth worked incredible hours; the Border Patrol had been called in to help keep "undesirables" away from the Harbor, assisting the Coast Guard, INS, NYPD, and whoever else the city deemed pertinent. Noah had left again and did not call.

Evan was with her at the apartment when the Deneb communication device rang.

"What's that?" he said off-handedly, wiping his mouth. He had brought department gossip and bags of sushi. The kitchen table was littered with tuna tataki, cucumber wraps, and hotategai.

Marianne said, "It's a phone call from the Deneb ambassador."

Evan stopped wiping and, paper napkin suspended, stared at her.

She put the tiny device on the table, as instructed, and spoke the code word. A mechanical voice said, "Dr. Marianne Jenner?"

"Yes."

"This is Ambassador Smith. We have reached an agreement with your UN to proceed, and will be expanding our facilities immediately. I would like you to head one part of the research."

"Ambassador, I am not an epidemiologist, not an immunologist, not a physician. There are many others who—"

"Yes. We don't want you to work on pathogens or with patients. We want you to identify human volunteers who belong to the haplogroup you discovered, L7."

Something icy slid along Marianne's spine. "Why? There hasn't been very much genetic drift between our . . . ah . . . groups of humans in just 150,000 years. And mitochondrial differentiation should play no part in—"

"This is unconnected with the spores."

"What is it connected with?" *Eugenics, master race, Nazis* . . . .

"This is purely a family matter."

Marianne glanced at Evan, who was writing furiously on the white paper bag the sushi had come in: GO! ACCEPT! ARE YOU DAFT? CHANCE OF A LIFETIME!

She said, "A family matter?"

"Yes. Family matters to us very much. Our whole society is organized around ancestral loyalty."

To Marianne's knowledge, this was the first time the ambassador had ever said anything, to anyone, about how Deneb society was organized. Evan, who'd been holding the paper bag six inches from her face, snatched it back and wrote CHANCE OF SIX THOUSAND LIFETIMES!

The number of generations since Mitochondrial Eve.

Smith continued, "I would like you to put together a small team of three or four people. Lab facilities will be provided, and volunteers will provide tissue samples. The UN has been very helpful. Please assemble your team on Tuesday at your current location and someone will come to escort you. Do you accept this post?"

"Tuesday? That's only—"

"Do you accept this post?"

"I . . . yes."

"Good. Good-bye."

Evan said, "Marianne—"

"Yes, of course, you're part of the 'team.' God, none of this real."

"Thank you, thank you!"

"Don't burble, Evan. We need two lab techs. How can they have facilities ready by Tuesday? It isn't possible."

"Or so we think," Evan said.

NOAH

It hadn't been possible to stay in the apartment. His mother had the TV on non-stop, every last news show, no matter how demented, that discussed the aliens or their science. Elizabeth burst in and out again, perpetually angry at everything she didn't like in the world, which included the Denebs. The two women argued at the top of their lungs, which didn't seem to bother either of them on anything but an intellectual level, but which left Noah unable to eat anything without nausea or sleep without nightmares or walk around without knots in his guts.

He found a room in a cheap boardinghouse, and a job washing dishes that paid under the counter, in a taco place. Even though the tacos came filmed with grease, he could digest better here than at Elizabeth's, and anyway he didn't eat much. His wages went on sugarcane.

He became, in turn, an observant child, a tough loner, a pensive loner, a friendly panhandler. Sugarcane made him, variously, mute or extroverted or gloomy or awed or confident. But none of it was as satisfying as it once had been. Even when he was someone else, he was still aware of being Noah. That had not happened before. The door out of himself stayed ajar. Increasing the dose didn't help.

Two weeks after he'd left Elizabeth's, he strolled on his afternoon off down to Battery Park. The late October afternoon was unseasonably warm, lightly overcast, filled with autumn leaves and chrysanthemums and balloon sellers. Tourists strolled the park, sitting on the benches lining the promenade, feeding the pigeons, touring Clinton Castle. Noah stood for a long time leaning on the railing above the harbor, and so witnessed the miracle.

"It's happening! Now!" someone shouted.

What was happening? Noah didn't know, but evidently someone did because people came running from all directions. Noah would have been jostled and squeezed from his place at the railing if he hadn't gripped it with both hands. People stood on the benches; teenagers shimmied up the lamp poles. Figures appeared on top of the Castle. A man began frantically selling telescopes and binoculars evidently hoarded for this occasion. Noah bought a pair with money he'd been going to use for sugarcane.

"Move that damn car!" someone screamed as a Ford honked its way through the crowd, into what was supposed to be a pedestrian area. Shouts, cries, more people rushing from cars to the railings.

Far out in the harbor, the Deneb *Embassy*, its energy shield dull under the cloudy sky, began to glow. Through his binoculars Noah saw the many-faceted dome shudder—not just shake but shudder in a rippling wave, as if alive. *Was* it alive? Did his mother know?

"Aaaahhhhh," the crowd went.

The energy shield began to spread. Either it had thinned or changed composition, because for a long moment—maybe ninety seconds—Noah could almost see through it. A suggestion of floor, walls, machinery . . . then opaque again. But the "floor" was growing, reaching out to cover more territory, sprouting tentacles of material and energy.

Someone on the bridge screamed, "They're taking over!"

All at once, signs were hauled out, people leaped onto the roofs of cars that should not have been in the park, chanting began. But not much chanting or many people. Most crowded the railings, peering out to sea.

In ten minutes, the *Embassy* grew and grew laterally, silently spreading across the calm water like a speeded-up version of an algae bloom. When it hardened again— that's how it looked to Noah, like molten glass hardening as it cooled—the structure was six times its previous size. The tentacles had become docks, a huge one toward the city and several smaller ones to one side. By now even the chanters had fallen silent, absorbed in the silent, aweing, monstrous feat of unimaginable construction. When it was finished, no one spoke.

Then an outraged voice demanded, "Did those bastards get a city permit for that?"

It broke the silence. Chanting, argument, exclaiming, pushing all resumed. A few motorists gunned their engines, futilely, since it was impossible to move vehicles. The first of the motorcycle cops arrived: NYPD, then Special Border Patrol, then chaos.

Noah slipped deftly through the mess, back toward the streets north of the Battery. He had to be at work in an hour. The *Embassy* had nothing to do with him.

MARIANNE

A spore cloud doesn't look like anything at all.

A darker patch in dark space, or the slightest of veils barely dimming starlight shining behind it. Earth's astronomers could not accurately say how large it was, or how deep. They relied on Deneb measurements, except for the one fact that mattered most, which human satellites in deep space and human ingenuity at a hundred observatories was able to verify: The cloud was coming. The path of its closest edge would intersect Earth's path through space at the time the Denebs had said: early September.

Marianne knew that almost immediately following the UN announcement, madness and stupidity raged across the planet. Shelters were dug or sold or built, none of which would be effective. If air could get in, so could spores. In Kentucky, some company began equipping deep caves with air circulation, food for a year, and high-priced sleeping berths: reverting to Paleolithic caveman. She paid no more attention to this entrepreneurial survivalism than to the televised protests, destructive mobs, peaceful marches, or lurid artist depictions of the cloud and its presumed effects. She had a job to do.

On Tuesday she, Evan, and two lab assistants were taken to the submarine bay at UN Special Mission Headquarters. In the sub, Max and Gina huddled in front of the porthole, or maybe it was a porthole-like viewscreen, watching underwater fish. Maybe fish were what calmed them. Although they probably didn't need calming: Marianne, who had worked with both before, had chosen them as much for their even temperaments as for their competence. Government authorities had vetted Max and Gina for, presumably, both crime-free backgrounds and pro-alien attitudes. Max, only twenty-nine, was the computer whiz. Gina, in her mid-thirties and the despair of her Italian mother because Gina hadn't yet married, made the fewest errors Marianne had ever seen in sample preparation, amplification, and sequencing.

Evan said to Marianne, "Children all sorted out?"

"Never. Elizabeth won't leave New York, of course." ("Leave? Don't you realize I have a job to do, protecting citizens from your aliens?" Somehow they had become Marianne's aliens.) "Ryan took Connie to her parents' place in Vermont and he went back to his purple loosestrife in Canada."

"And Noah?" Evan said gently. He knew all about Noah; why, Marianne wondered yet again, did she confide in this twenty-eight-year-old gay man as if he were her age, and not Noah's? Never mind; she needed Evan.

She shook her head. Noah had again disappeared.

"He'll be fine, then, Marianne. He always is."

"I know."

"Look, we're docking."

They disembarked from the sub to the underside of the *Embassy*. Whatever the structure's new docks topside were for, it wasn't the transfer of medical personnel. Evan said admiringly, "Shipping above us hasn't even been disrupted. Dead easy."

"Oh, those considerate aliens," Marianne murmured, too low for the sub captain, still in full-dress uniform, to hear. Her and Evan's usual semi-sarcastic banter helped to steady her: the real toad in the hallucinatory garden.

The chamber beyond the airlock had not changed, although this time they were met by a different alien. Female, she wore the same faint shimmer of energy-shield protection over her plain tunic and pants. Tall, coppery-skinned, with those preternaturally huge dark eyes, she looked about thirty, but how could you tell? Did the Denebs have plastic surgery? Why not? They had everything else.

Except a cure for spore disease.

The Deneb introduced herself ("Scientist Jones"), went through the so-glad-you're-here speech coming disconcertingly from the ceiling. She conducted them to the lab, then left immediately. Plastic surgery or no, Marianne was grateful for alien technology when she saw her lab. Nothing in it was unfamiliar, but all of it was state-of-the-art. Did they create it as they had created the *Embassy*, or order it wholesale? Must be the latter—the state-of-the-art gene sequencer still bore the label ILLUMINA. The equipment must have been ordered, shipped, paid for (with what?) either over the previous months of negotiation, or as the world's fastest rush shipping.

Beside it sat a rack of vials with blood samples, all neatly labeled.

Max immediately went to the computer and turned it on. "No Internet," he said, disappointed. "Just a LAN, and . . . wow, this is heavily shielded."

"You realize," Marianne said, "that this is a minor part of the science going on aboard the *Embassy*. All we do is process mitochondrial DNA to identify L7 haplogroup members. We're a backwater on the larger map."

"Hey, we're *here*," Max said. He grinned at her. "Too bad, though, about no World of Warcraft. This thing has no games at all. What do I do in my spare time?"

"Work," Marianne said, just as the door opened and two people entered. Marianne recognized one of them, although she had never met him before. Unsmiling, dark-suited, he was Security. The woman was harder to place. Middle-aged, wearing jeans and a sweater, her hair held back by a too-girlish headband. But her smile was warm, and it reached her eyes. She held out her hand.

"Dr. Jenner? I'm Lisa Gutierrez, the genetics counselor. I'll be your liaison with the volunteers. We probably won't be seeing each other again, but I wanted to say hello. And you're Dr. Blanford?"

"Yes," Evan said.

Marianne frowned. "Why do we need a genetic counselor? I was told our job is to simply process blood samples to identify members of the L7 haplogroup."

"It is," Lisa said, "and then I take it from there."

"Take *what* from there?"

Lisa studied her. "You know, of course, that the Denebs would like to identify those surviving human members of their own haplogroup. They consider them family. The concept of family is pivotal to them."

Marianne said, "You're not a genetic counselor. You're a xenopsychologist."

"That, too."

"And what happens after the long-lost family members are identified?"

"I tell them that they are long-lost family members." Her smile never wavered.

"And then?"

"And then they get to meet Ambassador Smith."

"And *then*?"

"No more 'then.' The Ambassador just wants to meet his six-thousand-times-removed cousins. Exchange family gossip, invent some in-jokes, confer about impossible Uncle Harry."

So she had a sense of humor. Maybe it was a qualification for billing oneself a 'xenopsychologist,' a profession that, until a few months ago, had not existed.

"Nice to meet you both," Lisa said, widened her smile another fraction of an inch, and left.

Evan murmured, "My, people come and go so quickly here."

But Marianne was suddenly not in the mood, not even for quoted humor from such an appropriate source as *The Wizard of Oz*. She sent a level gaze at Evan, Max, Gina.

"Okay, team. Let's get to work."

II: S MINUS 9.5 MONTHS

MARIANNE

There were four other scientific teams aboard the *Embassy*, none of which were interested in Marianne's backwater. The other teams consisted of scientists from the World Health Organization, the Centers for Disease Control, the United States Army Research Institute for Infectious Diseases, the Institute of Molecular Medicine at Oxford, the Beijing Genomics Institute, Kyushu University, and the Scripps Clinic and Research Foundation, perhaps the top immunology center in the world. Some of the most famous names in the scientific and medical worlds were here, including a dozen Nobel winners. Marianne had no knowledge of, but could easily imagine, the political and scientific competition to get aboard the *Embassy*. The Americans had an edge because the ship sat in New York Harbor and that, too, must have engendered political threats and counterthreats, bargaining and compromise.

The most elite group, and by far the largest, worked on the spores: germinating, sequencing, investigating this virus that could create a worldwide human die-off. They worked in negative-pressure, biosafety-level-four chambers. Previously the United States had had only two BSL4 facilities, at the CDC in Atlanta and at US-AMRIID in Maryland. Now there was a third, dazzling in its newness and in the completeness of its equipment. The Spore Team had the impossible task of creating some sort of vaccine or other method of neutralizing, worldwide, a pathogen not native to Earth, within ten months.

The Biology Team investigated alien tissues and genes. The Denebs gave freely of whatever was asked: blood, epithelial cells, sperm, biopsy samples. "Might even give us a kidney, if we asked nicely enough," Evan said. "We know they have two."

Marianne said, "You ask, then."

"Not me. Too frightful to think what they might ask in exchange."

"So far, they've asked nothing."

Almost immediately the Biology Team verified the Denebs as human. Then began the long process of finding and charting the genetic and evolutionary differences between the aliens and Terrans. The first, announced after just a few weeks, was that all of the seventeen aliens in the Embassy carried the same percentage as Terrans of Neanderthal genes: from one to four percent.

"They're us," Evan said.

"Did you doubt it?" Marianne asked.

"No. But more interesting, I think, are the preliminary findings that the Denebs show so much less genetic diversity than we do. That wanker Wilcox must be weeping in his ale."

Patrick Wells Wilcox was the current champion of the Toba Catastrophe Theory, which went in and out of scientific fashion. Seventy thousand years ago the Toba supervolcano in Indonesia had erupted. This had triggered such major environmental change, according to theory proponents, that a "bottleneck event" had occurred, reducing the human population to perhaps 10,000 individuals. The result had been a great reduction in human genetic diversity. Backing for the idea came from geology as well as coalescence evidence of some genes, including mitochondrial, Y-chromosome, and nuclear. Unfortunately, there was also evidence that the bottleneck event had never occurred. If the Denebs, removed from Earth well before the supervolcano, showed less diversity than Terrans, then Terran diversity couldn't have been reduced all that much.

Marianne said, "Wilcox shouldn't weep too soon."

"Actually, he never weeps at all. Gray sort of wanker. Holes up in his lab at Cambridge and glowers at the world through medieval arrow slits."

"Dumps boiling oil on dissenting paleontologists," Marianne suggested.

"Actually, Wilcox may not even be human. Possibly an advance scout for the Denebs. Nobody at Cambridge has noticed it so far."

"Or so we think." Marianne smiled. She and Evan never censored their bantering, which helped lower the hushed, pervasive anxiety they shared with everyone else on the *Embassy*. It was an anxious ship.

The third scientific team aboard was much smaller. Physicists, they worked with "Scientist Jones" on the astronomy of the coming collision with the spore cloud.

The fourth team she never saw at all. Nonetheless, she suspected they were there, monitoring the others, shadowy underground non-scientists unknown even to the huge contingent of visible security.

Marianne looked at the routine work on her lab bench: polymerase chain reaction to amplify DNA samples, sequencing, analyzing data, writing reports on the genetic inheritance of each human volunteer who showed up at the Deneb "collection site" in Manhattan. A lot of people showed up. So far, only two of them belonged to Ambassador Smith's haplogroup. "Evan, we're not really needed, you and I. Gina and Max can handle anything our expensive brains are being asked to do."

Evan said, "Right, then. So let's have a go at exploring. Until we're stopped, anyway."

She stared at him. "Okay. Yes. Let's explore."

NOAH

Noah emerged from the men's room at the restaurant. During the mid-afternoon lull they had no customers except for a pair of men slumped over one table in the back. "Look at this!" the waitress said to him. She and the cook were both huddled over her phone, strange enough since they hated each other. But Cindy's eyes were wide from something other than her usual drugs, and Noah took a look at the screen of the sophisticated phone, mysteriously acquired and gifted by Cindy's current boyfriend before he'd been dragged off to Riker's for assault with intent.

VOLUNTEERS WANTED TO DONATE BLOOD
PAYMENT: $100
HUMAN NURSES TO COLLECT SMALL BLOOD SAMPLES
DENEB EMBASSY PIER, NEW YORK HARBOR

"*Demonios del Diablo*," Miguel muttered. "*Vampiros!*" He crossed himself.

Noah said dryly, "I don't think they're going to drink the blood, Miguel." The dryness was false. His heart had begun to thud. People like his mother got to see the *Embassy* up close, not people like Noah. Did the ad mean that the Denebs were going to take human blood samples on the large dock he had just seen form out of nothing?

Cindy had lost interest. "No fucking customers except those two sorry asses in the corner, and they never tip. I shoulda stood in bed."

"Miguel," Noah said, "can I have the afternoon off?"

Noah stood patiently in line at the blood-collection site. If any of the would-be volunteers had hoped to see aliens, they had been disappointed. Noah was not disappointed; after all, the ad on Cindy's phone had said HUMAN NURSES TO COLLECT SMALL BLOOD SAMPLES.

He was, however, disappointed that the collection site was not on the large dock jutting out from the *Embassy* under its glittering energy shield. Instead, he waited to enter what had once been a warehouse at the land end of a pier on the Manhattan waterfront. The line, huddled against the November drizzle, snaked in loops and ox-bows for several blocks, and he was fascinated by the sheer diversity of people. A woman in a fur-lined Burberry raincoat and high, polished boots. A bum in jeans with an indecent tear on the ass. Several giggling teenage girls under flowered umbrellas. An old man in a winter parka. A nerdy-looking boy with an iPad protected by flexible plastic. Two tired-looking middle-aged women. One of those said to the other, "I could pay all that back rent if I get this alien money, and—"

Noah tapped her arm. "Excuse me, ma'am—what 'alien money'?" The $100 fee for blood donation didn't seem enough to pay *all that back rent.*

She turned. "If they find out you're part of their blood group, you get a share of their fortune. You know, like the Indians with their casino money. If you can prove you're descended from their tribe."

"No, that's not it," the old man in the parka said impatiently. "You get a free energy shield like theirs to protect you when the spore cloud hits. They take care of family."

The bum muttered, "Ain't no spore cloud."

The boy said with earnest contempt, "You're all wrong. This is just—the Denebs are the most significant thing to happen to Earth, ever! Don't you get it? We're not alone in the universe!"

The bum laughed.

Eventually Noah reached Building A. Made of concrete and steel, the building's walls were discolored, its high-set windows grimy. Only the security machines looked new, and they made high-tech examinations of Noah's person inside and out. His wallet, cell, jacket, and even shoes were left in a locker before he shuffled, wearing paper slippers, along the enclosed corridor to Building B, farther out on the pier. Someone was very worried about terrorism.

"Please fill out this form," said a pretty, grim-faced young woman. Not a nurse: security. She looked like a faded version of his sister, bleached of Elizabeth's angry command. Noah filled out the form, gave his small vial of blood, and filed back to Building B. He felt flooded with anticlimactic let-down. When he had reclaimed his belongings, a guard handed him a hundred dollars and a small round object the size and feel of a quarter.

"Keep this with you," a guard said. "It's a one-use, one-way communication device. In the unlikely event that it rings, press the center. That means that we'd like to see you again."

"If you do, does that mean I'm in the alien's haplogroup?"

He didn't seem to know the word. "If it rings, press the center."

"How many people have had their devices ring?"

The guard's face changed, and Noah glimpsed the person behind the job. He shrugged. "I never heard of even one."

"Is it—?"

"Move along, please." The job mask was back.

Noah put on his shoes, balancing first on one foot and then on the other to avoid touching the grimy floor. It was like being in an airport. He started for the door.

"Noah!" Elizabeth sailed toward him across a sea of stained concrete. "What the hell are you doing here?"

"Hi, Lizzie. Is this part of the New York State border?"

"I'm on special assignment."

God, she must hate that. Her scowl threatened to create permanent furrows in her tanned skin. But Elizabeth always obeyed the chain of command.

"Noah, how can you—?"

A bomb went off.

A white light blinded Noah. His hearing went dead, killed by the sheer onslaught of sound. His legs wobbled as his stomach lurched. Then Elizabeth knocked him to the ground and hurled herself on top of him. A few seconds later she was up and running and Noah could hear her again: "Fucking flashbang!"

He stumbled to his feet, his eyes still painful from the light. People screamed and a few writhed on the floor near a pile of clothes that had ignited. Black smoke billowed from the clothing, setting the closest people to coughing, but no one seemed dead. Guards leaped at a young man shouting something lost in the din.

Noah picked up his shoes and slipped outside, where sirens screamed, honing in from nearby streets. The salt-tanged breeze touched him like a benediction.

A flashbang. You could buy a twelve-pack of them on the Internet for fifty bucks, although those weren't supposed to ignite fires. Whatever that protestor had hoped to accomplish, it was ineffective. Just like this whole dumb blood-donation expedition.

But he had a hundred dollars he hadn't had this morning, which would buy a few good hits of sugarcane. And in his pocket, his fingers closed involuntarily on the circular alien coin.

MARIANNE

Marianne was surprised at how few restricted areas of the *Embassy* there were.

The BSL4 areas, of course. The aliens' personal quarters, not very far from the BSL4 labs. But her and Evan's badges let them roam pretty much everywhere else. Humans rushed passed them on their own errands, some nodding in greeting but others too preoccupied to even notice they were there.

"Of course there are doors we don't even see," Evan said. "Weird alien cameras we don't see. Denebs we don't see. They know where we are, where everyone is, every minute. Dead easy."

The interior of the *Embassy* was a strange mixture of materials and styles. Many corridors were exactly what you'd expect in a scientific research facility: unadorned, clean, lined with doors. The walls seemed to be made of something that was a cross between metal and plastic, and did not dent. Walls in the personal quarters and lounges, on the other hand, were often made of something that reminded her of Japanese rice paper, but soundproof. She had the feeling that she could have put her fist through them, but when she actually tried this, the wall only gave slightly, like a very tough piece of plastic. Some of these walls could be slid open, to change the size or shapes of rooms. Still other walls were actually giant screens that played constantly shifting patterns of subtle color. Finally, there were odd small lounges that seemed to have been furnished from upscale mail-order catalogues by someone who thought anything Terran must go with anything else: earth-tone sisal carpeting with a Victorian camelback sofa, Picasso prints with low Moroccan tables inlaid with silver and copper, a Navaho blanket hung on the wall above Japanese zabutons.

Marianne was tired. They'd come to one such sitting area outside the main dining hall, and she sank into an English club chair beside a small table of swooping purple glass. "Evan—do you really believe we are all going to die a year from now?"

"No." He sat in an adjoining chair, appreciatively patting its wide and upholstered arms. "But only because my mind refuses to entertain the thought of my own death in any meaningful way. Intellectually, though, yes. Or rather, nearly all of us will die."

"A vaccine to save the rest?"

"No, there is simply not enough time to get all the necessary bits and pieces sorted out. But the Denebs will save some Terrans."

"How?"

"Take a selected few back with them to that big ship in the sky."

Immediately she felt stupid that she hadn't thought of this before. Stupidity gave way to the queasy, jumpy feeling of desperate hope. "Take us *Embassy* personnel? To continue joint work on the spores?" Her children, somehow she would have to find a way to include Elizabeth, Noah, Ryan and Connie and the baby! But everyone here had family—

"No," Evan said. "Too many of us. My guess is just the Terran members of their haplogroup. Why else bother to identify them? And everything I've heard reinforces their emphasis on blood relationships."

"Heard from whom? We're in the lab sixteen hours a day—"

"I don't need much sleep. Not like you, Marianne. I talk to the Biology Group, who talk more than anybody else to the aliens. Also I chat with Lisa Gutierrez, the genetic counselor."

"And the Denebs told somebody they're taking their haplogroup members with them before the spore cloud hits?"

"No, of course not. When do the Denebs tell Terrans anything directly? It's all smiling evasion, heartfelt reassurances. They're like Philippine houseboys."

Startled, Marianne gazed at him. The vaguely racist reference was uncharacteristic of Evan, and had been said with some bitterness. She realized all over again how little Evan gave away about his past. When had he lived in the Philippines? What had happened between him and some apparently not forgiven houseboy? A former lover? Evan's sexual orientation was also something they never discussed, although of course she was aware of it. From his grim face, he wasn't going to discuss it now, either.

She said, "I'm going to ask Smith what the Denebs intend."

Evan's smooth grin had returned. "Good luck. The UN can't get information from him, the project's chief scientists can't get information from him, and you and I never see him. Just minor roadblocks to your plan."

"We really are lab rats," she said. And then, abruptly, "Let's go. We need to get back to work."

"Evan said slowly, "I've been thinking about something."

"What?"

"The origin of viruses. How they didn't evolve from a single entity and don't have a common ancestor. About the theory that their individual origins were pieces of DNA or RNA that broke off from cells and learned to spread to other cells."

Marianne frowned. "I don't see how that's relevant."

"I don't either, actually."

"Then—"

"I don't know," Evan said. And again, "I just don't know."

NOAH

Noah was somebody else.

He'd spent his blood-for-the-Denebs money on sugarcane, and it turned out to be one of the really good transformations. He was a nameless soldier from a nameless army: brave and commanding and sure of himself. Underneath he knew it was an illusion (but he never used to know that!). However, it didn't matter. He stood on a big rock at the south end of Central Park, rain and discarded plastic bags blowing around him, and felt completely, if temporarily, happy. He was on top of the world, or at least seven feet above it, and nothing seemed impossible.

The alien token in his pocket began to chime, a strange syncopated rhythm, atonal as no iPhone ever sounded. Without a second's hesitation—he could face anything!—Noah pulled it from his pocket and pressed its center.

A woman's voice said, "Noah Richard Jenner?"

"Yes, ma'am!"

"This is Dr. Lisa Gutierrez at the Deneb embassy. We would like to see you, please. Can you come as soon as possible to the UN Special Mission Headquarters at its pier?"

Noah drew a deep breath. Then full realization crashed around him, loud and blinding as last week's flashbang. Oh my God—why hadn't he seen it before? Maybe because he hadn't been a warrior before. His mother had—*son of a bitch*—

"Noah?"

He said, "I'll be there."

The submarine surfaced in an undersea chamber. A middle-aged woman in jeans and blazer, presumably Dr. Gutierrez, awaited Noah in the featureless room. He didn't much notice woman or room. Striding across the gangway, he said, "I want to see my mother. Now. She's Dr. Marianne Jenner, working here someplace."

Dr. Guiterrez didn't react as if this were news, or strange. She said, "You seem agitated." Hers was the human voice Noah had heard coming from the alien token.

"I am agitated! Where is my mother?"

"She's here. But first, someone else wants to meet you."

"I demand to see my mother!"

A door in the wall slid open, and a tall man with coppery skin and bare feet stepped through. Noah looked at him, and it happened again.

Shock, bewilderment, totally unjustified recognition—he knew this man, just as he had known the nurse who washed tear gas from his and a child's eyes during the West Side demonstration. Yet he'd never seen him before, and he was an *alien*. But the sense of kinship was powerful, disorienting, ridiculous.

"Hello, Noah Jenner," the ceiling said. "I am Ambassador Smith. Welcome to the *Embassy*."

"I—"

"I wanted to welcome you personally, but I cannot visit now. I have a meeting. Lisa will help you get settled here, should you choose to stay with us for a while. She will explain everything. Let me just say—"

Impossible to deny this man's sincerity, he meant every incredible word—

"—that I'm very glad you are here."

After the alien left, Noah stood staring at the door through which he'd vanished. "What is it?" Dr. Guiterrez said. "You look a bit shocked."

Noah blurted, "I know that man!" A second later he realized how dumb that sounded.

She said gently, "Let's go somewhere to talk, Noah. Somewhere less . . . wet."

Water dripped from the sides of the submarine, and some had sloshed onto the floor. Sailors and officers crossed the gangway, talking quietly. Noah followed Lisa from the sub bay, down a side corridor, and into an office cluttered with charts, print-outs, coffee mugs, a laptop—such an ordinary-looking place that it only heightened Noah's sense of unreality. She sat in an upholstered chair and motioned him to another. He remained standing.

She said, "I've seen this before, Noah. What you're experiencing, I mean, although usually it isn't as strong as you seem to be feeling it."

"Seen what? And who are you, anyway? I want to talk to my mother!"

She studied him, and Noah had the impression she saw more than he wanted her to. She said, "I'm Dr. Lisa Gutierrez, as Ambassador Smith said. Call me Lisa. I'm a genetics counselor serving as the liaison between the ambassador and those people identified as belonging to his haplotype, L7, the one identified by your mother's research. Before this post, I worked with Dr. Barbara Formisano at Oxford, where I also introduced people who share the same haplotype. Over and over again I've seen a milder version of what you seem to be experiencing now—an unexpected sense of connection between those with an unbroken line of mothers and grandmothers and great-grandmothers back to their haplogroup clan mother. It—"

"That sounds like bullshit!"

"—is important to remember that the connection is purely symbolic. Similar cell metabolisms don't cause shared emotions. But—an important 'but!'—symbols have a powerful effect on the human mind. Which, in turn, causes emotion."

Noah said, "I had this feeling once before. About a strange woman, and I had no way of knowing if she's my 'haplotype'!"

Lisa's gaze sharpened. She stood. "What woman? Where?"

"I don't know her name. Listen, I want to talk to my mother!"

"Talk to me first. Are you a sugarcane user, Noah?"

"What the hell does that have to do with anything?"

"Habitual use of sugarcane heightens certain imaginative and perceptual pathways in the brain. Ambassador Smith—well, let's set that aside for a moment. I think I know why you want to see your mother."

Noah said, "Look, I don't want to be ruder than I've already been, but this isn't your business. Anything you want to say to me can wait until I see my mother."

"All right. I can take you to her lab."

It was a long walk. Noah took in very little of what they passed, but then, there was very little to take in. Endless white corridors, endless white doors. When they entered a lab, two people that Noah didn't know looked up curiously. Lisa said, "Dr. Jenner—"

The other woman gestured at a far door. Before she could speak, Noah flung the door open. His mother sat at a small table, hands wrapped around a cup of coffee she wasn't drinking. Her eyes widened.

Noah said, "Mom—why the fuck didn't you ever tell me I was adopted?"

MARIANNE

Evan and Marianne sat in his room, drinking sixteen-year-old single-malt Scotch. She seldom drank but knew that Evan often did. Nor had she ever gone before to his quarters in the Embassy, which were identical to hers: ten-foot square room with a bed, chest of drawers, small table, and two chairs. She sat on one of the straight-backed, utilitarian chairs while Evan lounged on the bed. Most of the scientists had brought with them a few items from home, but Evan's room was completely impersonal. No art, no framed family photos, no decorative pillows, not even a coffee mug or extra doughnut carried off from the cafeteria.

"You live like a monk," Marianne said, immediately realizing how drunk she must be to say that. She took another sip of Scotch.

"Why didn't you ever tell him?" Evan said.

She put down her glass and pulled at the skin on her face. The skin felt distant, as if it belonged to somebody else.

"Oh, Evan, how to answer that? First Noah was too little to understand. Kyle and I adopted him in some sort of stupid effort to save the marriage. I wasn't thinking straight—living with an alcoholic will do that, you know. If there was one stupid B-movie scene of alcoholic and wife that we missed, I don't know what it was. Shouting, pleading, pouring away all the liquor in the house, looking for Kyle in bars at two a.m. . . . anyway. Then Kyle died and I was trying to deal with that and the kids and chasing tenure and there was just too much chaos and fragility to add another big revelation. Then somehow it got too late, because Noah would have asked why he hadn't been told before, and then somehow . . . it all just got away from me."

"And Elizabeth and Ryan never told him?"

"Evidently not. We yell a lot about politics and such but on a personal level, we're a pretty reticent family." She waved her hand vaguely at the room. "Although not as reticent as you."

Evan smiled. "I'm British of a certain class."

"You're an enigma."

"No, that was the Russians. Enigmas wrapped in riddles." But a shadow passed suddenly behind his eyes.

"What do you—"

"Marianne, let me fill you in on the bits and pieces of news that came in while you were with Noah. First, from the Denebs: they're bringing aboard the *Embassy* any members of their 'clan'—that's what the translator is calling the L7 haplogroup— who want to come. But you already know that. Second, the—"

"How many?"

"How many have we identified or how many want to come here?"

"Both." The number of L7 haplotypes had jumped exponentially once they had the first few and could trace family trees through the female line.

"Sixty-three identified, including the three that Gina flew to Georgia to test. Most of the haplogroup may still be in Africa, or it may have largely died out. Ten of those want to visit the *Embassy*." He hesitated."So far, only Noah wants to stay."

Marianne's hand paused, glass halfway to her mouth. "To *stay*? He didn't tell me that. How do you know?"

"After Noah . . . left you this afternoon, Smith came to the lab with that message."

"I see." She didn't. She had been in her room, pulling herself together after the harrowing interview with her son. Her adopted son. She hadn't been able to tell Noah anything about his parentage because she hadn't known anything: sealed adoption records. Was Noah the way he was because of his genes? Or because of the way she'd raised him? Because of his peer group? His astrological sign? Theories went in and out of fashion, and none of them explained personality.

She said, "What is Noah going to *do* here? He's not a scientist, not security, not an administrator . . ." *Not anything.* It hurt her to even think it. Her baby, her lost one.

Evan said, "I have no idea. I imagine he'll either sort himself out or leave. The other news is that the Biology Team has made progress in matching Terran and Deneb immune-system components. There were a lot of graphs and charts and details, but the bottom line is that ours and theirs match pretty well. Remarkably little genetic drift. Different antibodies, of course, for different pathogens, and quite a lot of those, so no chance we'll be touching skin without their wearing their energy shields."

"So cancel the orgy."

Evan laughed. Emboldened by this as much as by the drink, Marianne said, "Are you gay?"

"You know I am, Marianne."

"I wanted to be sure. We've never discussed it. I'm a scientist, after all."

"You're an American. Leave nothing unsaid that can be shouted from rooftops."

Her fuzzy mind had gone back to Noah. "I failed my son, Evan."

"Rubbish. I told you, he'll sort himself out eventually. Just be prepared for the idea that it may take a direction you don't fancy."

Again that shadow in Evan's eyes. She didn't ask; he obviously didn't want to discuss it, and she'd snooped enough. Carefully she rose to leave, but Evan's next words stopped her.

"Also, Elizabeth is coming aboard tomorrow."

"*Elizabeth*? Why?"

"A talk with Smith about shore-side security. Someone tried a second attack at the sample collection site shore-side."

"Oh my God. Anybody hurt?"

"No. This time."

"Elizabeth is going to ask the Denebs to give her the energy-shield technology. She's been panting for it for border patrol ever since the *Embassy* first landed in the harbor. Evan, that would be a *disaster*. She's so focused on her job that she can't see what will happen if—no, when—the street finds its own uses for the tech, and it always does." Who had said that? Some writer. She couldn't remember.

"Well, don't get your knickers in a twist. Elizabeth can ask, but that doesn't mean that Smith will agree."

"But he's so eager to find his 'clan'—God, it's so stupid! That Korean mitochondrial sequence, to take just one example, that turns up regularly in Norwegian fisherman, or that engineer in Minnesota who'd traced his ancestry back three hundred years without being able to account for the Polynesian mitochondrial signature he carries—*nobody* has a cure 'plan.' I mean, 'clan.'"

"Nobody on Earth, anyway."

"And even if they did," she barreled on, although all at once her words seemed to have become slippery in her mouth, like raw oysters, "There's no sig . . . sif . . . significant connection between two people with the same mitochondrial DNA than between any other two strangers!"

"Not to us," Evan said. "Marianne, go to bed. You're too tipsy, and we have work to do in the morning."

"It's not work that matters to protection against the shore cloud. Spore cloud. *Spore cloud.*"

"Nonetheless, it's work. Now, go."

NOAH

Noah stood in a corner of the conference room, which held eleven people and two aliens. Someone had tried to make the room festive with a red paper tablecloth, flowers, and plates of tiny cupcakes. This had not worked. It was still a utilitarian, corporate-looking conference room, filled with people who otherwise would have no conceivable reason to be together at either a conference or a party. Lisa Gutierrez circulated among them: smiling, chatting, trying to put people at ease. It wasn't working.

Two young women, standing close together for emotional support. A middle-aged man in an Armani suit and Italian leather shoes. An unshaven man, hair in a dirty ponytail, who looked homeless but maybe only because he stood next to Well-Shod Armani. A woman carrying a plastic tote bag with a hole in one corner. And so on and so on. It was the sort of wildly mixed group that made Noah, standing apart with his back to a wall, think of worshippers in an Italian cathedral.

The thought brought him a strained smile. A man nearby, perhaps emboldened by the smile, sidled closer and whispered, "They *will* let us go back to New York, won't they?"

Noah blinked. "Why wouldn't they, if that's what you want?"

"I want them to offer us shields for the spore cloud! To take back with us to the city! Why else would I come here?"

"I don't know."

The man grimaced and moved away. But—why had he even come, if he suspected alien abduction or imprisonment or whatever? And why didn't he feel what Noah did? Every single one of the people in this room had caused in him the same shock of recognition as had Ambassador Smith. Every single one. And apparently no one else had felt it at all.

But the nervous man needn't have worried. When the party and its ceiling delivered speeches of kinship and the invitation to make a longer visit aboard the *Embassy* were all over, everyone else left. They left looking relieved or still curious or satisfied or uneasy or disappointed (no energy shield offered! No riches!), but they all left, Lisa still chattering reassuringly. All except Noah.

Ambassador Smith came over to him. The Deneb said nothing, merely silently waited. He looked as if he were capable of waiting forever.

Noah's hands felt clammy. All those brief, temporary lives on sugarcane, each one shed like a snakeskin when the drug wore off. No, not snakeskins; that wasn't the right analogy. More like bread crumbs tossed by Hansel and Gretel, starting in hope but vanishing before they could lead anywhere. The man with the dirty pony tail wasn't the only homeless one.

Noah said, "I want to know who and what you are."

The ceiling above Smith said, "Come with me to a genuine celebration."

A circular room, very small. Noah and Smith faced each other. The ceiling said, "This is an airlock. Beyond this space, the environment will be ours, not yours. It is not very different, but you are not used to our microbes and so must wear the energy suit. It filters air, but you may have some trouble breathing at first because the oxygen content of World is like Earth's at an altitude of 12,000 feet. If you feel nausea in the airlock, where we will stay for a few minutes, you may go back. The light will seem dim to you, the smells strange, and the gravity less than you are accustomed to by one-tenth. There are no built-in translators beyond this point, and we will speak our own language, so you will not be able to talk to us. Are you sure you wish to come?"

"Yes," Noah said.

"Is there anything you wish to say before you join your birthright clan?"

Noah said, "What is your name?"

Smith smiled. He made a noise that sounded like a trilled version of *meehao*, with a click on the end.

Noah imitated it.

Smith said, in trilling English decorated with a click, "Brother mine."

MARIANNE

Marianne was not present at the meeting between Elizabeth and Smith, but Elizabeth came to see her afterward. Marianne and Max were bent over the computer, trying to account for what was a mitochondrial anomaly or a sample contamination or a lab error or a program glitch. Or maybe something else entirely. Marianne straightened and said, "Elizabeth! How nice to—"

"You have to talk to him," Elizabeth demanded. "The man's an idiot!"

Marianne glanced at the security officer who had escorted Elizabeth to the lab. He nodded and went outside. Max said, "I'll just . . . uh . . . this can wait." He practically bolted, a male fleeing mother-daughter drama. Evan was getting some much-needed sleep; Gina had gone ashore to Brooklyn to see her parents for the first time in weeks.

"I assume," Marianne said, "you mean Ambassador Smith."

"I do. Does he know what's going on in New York? Does he even care?"

"What's going on in New York?"

Elizabeth instantly turned professional, calmer but no less intense. "We are less than nine months from passing through the spore cloud."

At least, Marianne thought, *she now accepts that much.*

"In the last month alone, the five boroughs have had triple the usual rate of arsons, ten demonstrations with city permits of which three turned violent, twenty-three homicides, and one mass religious suicide at the Church of the Next Step Forward in Tribeca. Wall Street has plunged. The Federal Reserve Bank on Liberty Street was occupied from Tuesday night until Thursday dawn by terrorists. Upstate, the governor's mansion has been attacked, unsuccessfully. The same thing is happening everywhere else. Parts of Beijing have been on fire for a week now. Thirty-six percent of Americans believe the Denebs brought the spore cloud with them, despite what astronomers say. If the ambassador gave us the energy shield, that might help sway the numbers in their favor. Don't you think the president and the UN have said all this to Smith?"

"I have no idea what the president and the UN have said, and neither do you."

"Mom—"

"Elizabeth, do you suppose that if what you just said is true and the ambassador said no to the president, that my intervention would do any good?"

"I don't know. You scientists stick together."

Long ago, Marianne had observed the many different ways people responded to an unthinkable catastrophe. Some panicked. Some bargained. Some joked. Some denied. Some blamed. Some destroyed. Some prayed. Some drank. Some thrilled, as if they had secretly awaited such drama their entire lives. Evidently, nothing had changed.

The people aboard the *Embassy* met the unthinkable with work, and then more work. Elizabeth was right that the artificial island had become its own self-contained, self-referential universe, every moment devoted to the search for something, anything, to counteract the effect of the spore cloud on mammalian brains. The Denebs, understanding how good hackers could be, blocked all Internet, television, and radio from the Embassy. Outside news came from newspapers or letters, both dying media, brought in the twice-daily mail sack and by the vendors and scientists and diplomats who came and went. Marianne had not paid attention.

She said to her enraged daughter, "The Denebs are not going to give you their energy shield."

"We cannot protect the UN without it. Let alone the rest of the harbor area."

"Then send all the ambassadors and translators home, because it's not going to happen. I'm sorry, but it's not."

"You're not sorry. You're on their side."

"It isn't a question of sides. In the wrong hands, those shields—"

"Law enforcement is the right hands!"

"Elizabeth, we've been over and over this. Let's not do it again. You know I have no power to get you an energy shield, and I haven't seen you in so long. Let's not quarrel." Marianne heard the pleading note in her own voice. When, in the long and complicated road of parenthood, had she started courting her daughter's agreement, instead of the other way around?

"Okay, *okay*. How are you, Mom?"

"Overworked and harried. How are you?"

"Overworked and harried." A reluctant half-smile. "I can't stay long. How about a tour?"

"Sure. This is my lab."

"I meant of the *Embassy*. I've never been inside before, you know, and your ambassador"—somehow Smith had become Marianne's special burden—"just met with me in a room by the submarine bay. Can I see more? Or are you lab types kept close to your cages?"

The challenge, intended or not, worked. Marianne showed Elizabeth all over the Terran part of the Embassy, accompanied by a security officer whom Elizabeth ignored. Her eyes darted everywhere, noted everything. Finally she said, "Where do the Denebs live?"

"Behind these doors here. No one has ever been in there."

"Interesting. It's pretty close to the high-risk labs. And where is Noah?"

Yesterday's bitter scene with Noah, when he'd been so angry because she'd never told him he was adopted, still felt like an open wound. Marianne didn't want to admit to Elizabeth that she didn't know where he'd gone. "He stays in the Terran visitors' quarters," she said, hoping there was such a place.

Elizabeth nodded. "I have to report back. Thanks for the Cook's tour, Mom."

Marianne wanted to hug her daughter, but Elizabeth had already moved off, heading toward the submarine bay, security at her side. Memory stabbed Marianne: a tiny Elizabeth, five years old, lips set as she walked for the first time toward the school bus she must board alone. It all went by so fast, and when the spore cloud hit, not even memory would be left.

She dashed away the stupid tears and headed back to work.

III: S MINUS 8.5 MONTHS

MARIANNE

The auditorium on the *Embassy* had the same thin, rice-paper-like walls as some of the other non-lab rooms, but these shifted colors like some of the more substantial walls. Slow, complex, subtle patterns in pale colors that reminded Marianne of dissolving oil slicks. Forty seats in rising semicircles faced a dais, looking exactly like a lecture room at her college. She had an insane desire to regress to undergraduate, pull out a notebook, and doodle in the margins. The seats were filled not with students chewing gum and texting each other, but with some of the planet's most eminent scientists. This was the first all-hands meeting of the scientists aboard. The dais was empty.

Three Denebs entered from a side door.

Marianne had never seen so many of them together at once. Oddly, the effect was to make them seem more alien, as if their minor differences from Terrans—the larger eyes, spindlier limbs, greater height—increased exponentially as their presence increased arithmetically. Was that Ambassador Smith and Scientist Jones? Yes. The third alien, shorter than the other two and somehow softer, said through the translator in the ceiling, "Thank you all for coming. We have three reports today, two from Terran teams and one from World. First, Dr. Manning." All three aliens smiled.

Terrence Manning, head of the Spore Team, took the stage. Marianne had never met him, Nobel Prize winners being as far above her scientific level as the sun above mayflies. A small man, he had exactly three strands of hair left on his head, which he tried to coax into a comb-over. Intelligence shone through his diffident, unusually formal manner. Manning had a deep, authoritative voice, a welcome contrast to the mechanical monotony of the ceiling.

From the aliens' bright-eyed demeanor, Marianne had half expected good news, despite the growing body of data on the ship's LAN. She was wrong.

"We have not," Manning said, "been able to grow the virus in cell cultures. As you all know, some viruses simply will not grow in vitro, and this seems to be one of them. Nor have we been able to infect monkeys—any breed of monkey—with spore disease. We will, of course, keep trying. The better news, however, is that we have succeeded in infecting mice."

Good and bad, Marianne thought. Often, keeping a mouse alive was actually easier than keeping a cell culture growing. But a culture would have given them a more precise measure of the virus's cytopathic effect on animal tissue, and monkeys were genetically closer to humans than were mice. On the other hand, monkeys were notoriously difficult to work with. They bit, they fought, they injured themselves, they traded parasites and diseases, and they died of things they were not supposed to die from.

Manning continued, "We now have a lot of infected mice and our aerosol expert, Dr. Belsky, has made a determination of how much exposure is needed to cause spore disease in mice under laboratory conditions."

A graph flashed onto the wall behind Manning: exposure time plotted versus parts per million of spore. Beside Marianne, Evan's manicured fingers balled into a sudden fist. Infection was fast, and required a shockingly small concentration of virus, even for an airborne pathogen.

"Despite the infected mice," Manning went on, and now the strain in his voice was palpable, "we still have not been able to isolate the virus. It's an elusive little bugger."

No one laughed. Marianne, although this was not her field, knew how difficult it could be to find a virus even after you'd identified the host. They were so tiny; they disappeared into cells or organs; they mutated.

"Basically," Manning said, running his hand over his head and disarranging his three hairs, "we know almost nothing about this pathogen. Not the *r nought*—for you astronomers, that is the number of cases that one case generates on average over the course of its infectious period—nor the incubation period nor the genome nor the morphology. What we do know are the composition of the coating encapsulating the virus, the transmission vector, and the resulting pathology in mice."

Ten minutes of data on the weird, unique coating on the "spores," a term even the scientists, who knew better, now used. Then Dr. Jessica Yu took Manning's place on the dais. Marianne had met her in the cafeteria and felt intimidated. The former head of the Special Pathogens branch of the National Center for Infectious Diseases in Atlanta, Jessica Yu was diminutive, fifty-ish, and beautiful in a severe, don't-mess-with-me way. Nobody ever did.

She said, "We are, of course, hoping that gaining insight into the mechanism of the disease in animals will help us figure out how to treat it in humans. These mice were infected three days ago. An hour ago they began to show symptoms, which we wanted all of you to see before . . . . well, before."

The wall behind Jessica Yu de-opaqued, taking the exposure graphic with it. Or some sort of view screen now overlay the wall and the three mice now revealed were someplace else in the *Embassy*. The mice occupied a large glass cage in what Marianne recognized as a BSL4 lab.

Two of the mice lay flat, twitching and making short whooshing sounds, much amplified by the audio system. No, not amplified—those were desperate gasps as the creatures fought for air. Their tails lashed and their front paws scrambled. They were, Marianne realized, trying to *swim* away from whatever was drowning them.

"In humans," Yu continued, "we would call this ARDS—Adult Respiratory Distress Syndrome, a catch-all diagnosis used when we don't know what the problem is. The mouse lung tissue is becoming heavier and heavier as fluid from the blood seeps into the lungs and each breath takes more and more effort. X-rays of lung tissue show 'white-out'—so much fluid in the lungs increasing the radiological density that the image looks like a snowstorm. The viral incubation period in mice is three days. The time from onset of symptoms until death averages 2.6 hours."

The third mouse began to twitch.

Yu continued, her whole tiny body rigid, "As determined thus far, the infection rate in mice is about seventy-five percent. We can't, of course, make any assumptions that it would be the same in humans. Nor do we have any idea why mice are infected but monkeys are not. The medical data made available from the Deneb colonies do indicate similar metabolic pathways to those of the mice. Those colonies had no survivors. Autopsies on the mice further indicate—"

A deep nausea took Marianne, reaching all the way from throat to rectum. She was surprised; her training was supposed to inure her. It did not. Before her body could disgrace her by retching or even vomiting, she squeezed past Evan with a push on his shoulder to indicate he should stay and hear the rest. In the corridor outside the auditorium she leaned against the wall, lowered her head between her knees, breathed deeply, and let shame overcome horror.

No way for a scientist to react to data—

The shame was not strong enough. It was her children that the horror brought: Elizabeth and Ryan and Noah, mouths open as they tried to force air into their lungs, wheezing and gasping, drowning where they lay . . . and Connie and the as-yet-unborn baby, her first grandchild . . . .

Stop. It's no worse for you than for anybody else.

Marianne stood. She dug the nails of her right hand into the palm of her left. But she could not make herself go back into the auditorium. Evan would have to tell her what other monstrosities were revealed. She made her way back to her lab.

Max sat at the computer, crunching data. Gina looked up from her bench. "Marianne, we found two more L7 donors."

"Good," Marianne said, went through the lab to her tiny office behind, and closed the door firmly. What did it matter how many L7s she found for Smith? Earth was finished. Eight-and-a-half months left, and the finest medical and scientific brains on the planet had not even begun to find any way to mitigate the horror to come.

Gina knocked on the office door. "Marianne? Are you all right?"

Gina was the same age as Ryan, a young woman with her whole life still ahead of her. If she got that life. Meanwhile, there was no point in making the present even worse. Marianne forced cheerfulness into her voice. "Yes, fine. I'll be right out. Put on a fresh pot of coffee, would you please?"

NOAH

Noah stood with his clan and prepared to *Illathil*.

There was no word for it in English. Part dance, part religious ceremony, part frat kegger, and it went on for two days. Ten L7s stood in a circle, all in various stages of drunkenness. When the weird, atonal music (but after two months aboard the *Embassy* it no longer sounded weird or atonal to his ears) began, they weaved in and out, making precise figures on the floor with the red paint on their feet. Once the figures had been sacred, part of a primitive religion that had faded with the rapid growth of science nurtured by their planet's lush and easy environment. The ritual remained. It affirmed family, always matrilineal on World. It affirmed connection, obligation, identity. Whenever the larger of World's moons was lined up in a certain way with the smaller, Worlders came together with their families and joyously made Illathil. Circles always held ten, and as many circles were made as a family needed. It didn't matter where you were on World, or what you were doing, when Illathil came, you were there.

His mother would never have understood.

On the third morning, after everyone had slept off the celebration, came the second part of lllathil, which Marianne would have understood even less. Each person gave away one-fifth of everything he had earned or made since the last ll-lathil. He gave it, this "thumb" as it was jokingly called, to someone in his circle. Different clans gave different percentages and handled that in different ways, but some version of the custom mostly held over the mostly monocultural World. The Denebs were a sophisticated race; such a gift involved transfers of the Terran equivalent of bank accounts, stock holdings, real estate. The Denebs were also human, and so sometimes the gift was made grudgingly, or with anger at a cousin's laziness, or resignedly, or with cheating. But it was made, and there wasn't very much cheating. Or so said Mee^haoj, formerly known to Noah as Smith, who'd told him so in the trilling and clicking language that Noah was trying so hard to master. "We teach our children very intensively to follow our ways," Smith said wryly. "Of course, some do not. Some always are different."

"You said it, brother," Noah said in English, to Smith's total incomprehension.

Noah loved lllathil. He had very little—nothing, really—to give, but his net gain was not the reason he loved it. Nor was that the reason he studied the Worldese for hours every day, aided by his natural ear for languages. Once, in his brief and abortive attempted at college, Noah had heard a famous poet say that factual truth and emotional truth were not the same. "You have to understand with your belly," she'd said.

He did. For the first time in his life, he did.

His feet made a mistake, leaving a red toe print on the floor in the wrong place. No one chided him. Cliclimi, her old face wrinkling into crevasses and hills and dales, a whole topography of kinship, just laughed at him and reached out her skinny arm to fondly touch his.

Noah, not like that. Color in the lines!

Noah, this isn't the report card I expect of you.

Noah, you can't come with me and my friends! You're too little!

Noah, can't you do anything right? When he'd danced until he could no longer stand (Cliclimi was still going at it, but she hadn't drunk as much as Noah had), he dropped onto a large cushion beside "Jones," whose real name he still couldn't pronounce. It had more trills than most, and a strange tongue sound he could not reproduce at all. She was flushed, her hair unbound from its usual tight arrangement. Smaller than he was but stockier, her caramel-colored flesh glowed with exertion. The hair, rich dark brown, glinted in the rosy light. Her red tunic—everybody wore red for lllanthil—had hiked high on her thighs.

Noah heard his mother's voice say, "A hundred fifty thousand years is not enough time for a species to diverge." To his horror, he felt himself blush.

She didn't notice, or else she took it as warmth from the dancing. She said, "Do you have trouble with our gravity?"

Proud of himself that he understood the words, he said, "No. It small amount big of Earth." At least, he hoped that's what he'd said.

Apparently it was. She smiled and said something he didn't understand. She stretched luxuriously, and the tunic rode up another two inches.

What were the kinship taboos on sex? What were any of the taboos on sex? Not that Noah could have touched her skin-to-skin, anyway. He was encased, so unobtrusively that he usually forgot it was there, in the "energy suit" that protected him from alien microbes.

Microbes. Spores. How much time was left before the cloud hit Earth? At the moment it didn't seem important. (*Noah, you can't just pretend problems don't exist!* That had usually been Elizabeth.)

He said, "Can—yes, no?—make my—" Damn it, what was the word for microbes? "—my inside like you? My inside spores?"

IV: S MINUS 6.5 MONTHS

MARIANNE

Gina had not returned from Brooklyn on the day's last submarine run. Marianne was redoing an entire batch of DNA amplification that had somehow become contaminated. Evan picked up the mail sack and the news dispatches. When he came into the lab, where Marianne was cursing at a row of beakers, he uncharacteristically put both hands on her shoulders. She looked at his face.

"What is it? Tell me quickly."

"Gina is dead."

She put a hand onto the lab bench to steady herself. "How?"

"A mob. They were frighteningly well armed, almost a small army. End-of-the-world rioters."

"Was Gina . . . did she . . . ?"

"A bullet, very quick. She didn't suffer, Marianne. Do you want a drink? I have some rather good Scotch."

"No. Thank you, but no."

Gina. Marianne could picture her so clearly, as if she still stood in the lab in the wrinkled white coat she always wore even though the rest of them did not. Her dark hair just touched with gray, her ruddy face calm. Brisk, pleasant, competent. . . . What else? Marianne hadn't known Gina very well. All at once, she wondered if she knew anyone, really knew them. Two of her children baffled her: Elizabeth's endemic anger, Noah's drifty aimlessness. Had she ever known Kyle, the man he was under the charming and lying surface, under the alcoholism? Evan's personal life was kept personal, and she'd assumed it was his British reticence, but maybe she knew so little about him because of her limitations, not his. With everyone else aboard the *Embassy*, as with her university department back home, she exchanged only scientific information or meaningless pleasantries. She hadn't seen her brother, to whom she'd never been close, in nearly two years. Her last close female friendship had been over a decade ago.

Thinking this way felt strange, frightening. She was glad when Evan said, "Where's Max? I'll tell him about Gina."

"Gone to bed with a cold. It can wait until morning. What's that?"

Evan gave her a letter, addressed by hand. Marianne tore it open. "It's from Ryan. The baby was born, a month early but he's fine and so is she. Six pounds two ounces. They're naming him Jason William Jenner."

"Congratulations. You're a nan."

"A what?"

"Grand-mum." He kissed her cheek.

She turned to cling to him, without passion, in sudden need of the simple comfort of human touch. Evan smelled of damp wool and some cool, minty lotion. He patted her back. "What's all this, then?"

"I'm sorry, I—"

"Don't be sorry." He held her until she was ready to pull away.

"I think I should write to Gina's parents."

"Yes, that's right."

"I want to make them understand—" Understand what? That sometimes children were lost, and the reasons didn't necessarily make sense. But this reason did make sense, didn't it? Gina had died because she'd been aboard the *Embassy*, died as a result of the work she did, and right now this was the most necessary work in the entire world.

She had a sudden memory of Noah, fifteen, shouting at her: "You're never home! Work is all you care about!" And she, like so many beleaguered parents, had shouted back, "If it weren't for my work, we'd all starve!"

And yet, when the kids had all left home and she could work as much as she wanted or needed without guilt, she'd missed them dreadfully. She'd missed the harried driving schedules—*I have to be at Jennifer's at eight* and *Soccer practice is moved up an hour Saturday*! She'd missed their electronics, cells and iPods and tablets and laptops, plugged in all of the old house's inadequate outlets. She'd missed the rainbow laundry in the basement, Ryan's red soccer shirts and Elizabeth's white jeans catastrophically dyed pink and Noah's yellow-and-black bumblebee costume for the second-grade play. All gone. When your children were small you worried that they would die and you would lose them, and then they grew up and you ended up losing the children they'd been, anyway.

Marianne pulled at the skin on her face and steeled herself to write to Gina's parents.

NOAH

There were three of them now. Noah Jenner, Jacqui Young, Oliver Pardo. But only Noah was undergoing the change.

They lounged this afternoon in the World garden aboard the *Embassy*, where the ceiling seemed to be open to an alien sky. A strange orange shone, larger than Sol and yet not shedding as much light, creating a dim glow over the three Terrans. The garden plants were all dark in hue ("To gather as much light as possible," Mee^haoȷ had said), lush leaves in olive drab and pine and asparagus. Water trickled over rocks or fell in high, thin streams. Warmth enveloped Noah even through his energy suit, and he felt light on the ground in the lesser gravity. Some nearby flower sent out a strange, musky, heady fragrance on the slight breeze.

Jacqui, an energetic and enormously intelligent graduate student, had chosen to move into the alien section of the *Embassy* in order to do research. She was frank, with both Terrans and Denebs, that she was not going to stay after she had gathered the unique data on Deneb culture that would ensure her academic career. Smith said that was all right, she was clan and so welcome for as long as she chose. Noah wondered how she planned on even having an academic career after the spore cloud hit.

Oliver Pardo would have been given the part of geek by any film-casting department with no imagination. Overweight, computer-savvy, and a fan of superheroes, he quoted obscure sixty-year-old science fiction books and drew endless pictures of girls in improbable costumes slaying dragons or frost giants. Socially inept, he was nonetheless gentle and sweet-natured, and Noah preferred his company to Jacqui's, who asked too many questions.

"Why?" she said.

"Why what?" Noah said, even though he knew perfectly well what she meant. He lounged back on the comfortable moss and closed his eyes.

"Why are you undergoing this punishing regime of shots just so you can take off your shield?"

"They're not shots," Noah said. Whatever the Denebs were doing to him, they did it by having him apply patches to himself when he was out of his energy suit and in an isolation chamber. This had happened once a week for a while now. The treatments left him nauseated, dizzy, sometimes with diarrhea, and always elated. There was only one more to go.

Jacqui said, "Shots or whatever, why do it?"

Oliver looked up from his drawing of a barbarian girl riding a lion. "Isn't it obvious?"

Jacqui said, "Not to me."

Oliver said, "Noah wants to become an alien."

"No," Noah said. "I was an alien. Now I'm becoming . . . not one."

Jacqui's pitying look said *You need help.* Oliver shaded in the lion's mane. Noah wondered why, of all the Terrans of L7 mitochondrial haplotype, he was stuck with these two. He stood. "I have to study."

"I wish I had your fluency in Worldese," Jacqui said. "It would help my work so much."

So study it. But Noah knew she wouldn't, not the way he was doing. She wanted the quick harvest of startling data, not . . . whatever it was he wanted.

Becoming an alien. Oliver was more correct than Noah's flip answer. And yet Noah had been right, too, which was something he could never explain to anyone, least of all his mother. Whom he was supposed to visit this morning, since she could not come to him.

All at once Noah knew that he was not going to keep that appointment. Although he flinched at the thought of hurting Marianne, he was not going to leave the World section of the *Embassy.* Not now, not ever. He couldn't account for this feeling, so strong that it seemed to infuse his entire being, like oxygen in the blood. But he had to stay here, where he belonged. Irrational, but—as Evan would have said—there it was, mustn't grumble, at least it made a change, no use going on about it.

He had never liked Evan.

In his room, Noah took a pen and a pad of paper to write a note to his mother. The words did not come easy. All his life he had disappointed her, but not like this.

> Dear Mom—I know we were going to get together this afternoon but—
> Dear Mom—I wish I could see you as we planned but—
> Dear Mom—We need to postpone our visit because Ambassador Smith has asked me if this afternoon I would—

Noah pulled at the skin on his face, realized that was his mother's gesture, and stopped. He looked longingly at the little cubes that held his language lessons. As the cube spoke Worldese, holofigures in the cube acted out the meaning. After Noah repeated each phrase, it corrected his pronunciation until he got it right.

"My two brothers live with my mother and me in this dwelling," a smiling girl said in the holocube, in Worldese. Two boys, one younger than she and one much older, appeared beside her with a much older woman behind them, all four with similar features, a shimmering dome behind them.

"My two brothers live with my mother and me in this dwelling," Noah repeated. The Worldese tenses were tricky; these verbs were the ones for things that not only could change, but could change without the speaker's having much say about events. A mother could die. The family could be chosen for a space colony. The older brother could marry and move in with his wife's family.

Sometimes things were beyond your control and you had no real choice.

Dear Mom—I can't come. I'm sorry. I love you. Noah

MARIANNE

The work—anybody's work—was not going well.

It seemed to be proceeding at an astonishing pace, but Marianne—and everyone else—knew that was an illusion. She sat in the auditorium for the monthly report, Evan beside her. This time, no Denebs were present—why not? She listened to Terence Manning enumerate what under any other circumstances would have been incredibly rapid triumphs.

"We have succeeded in isolating the virus," Manning said, "although not in growing it in vitro. After isolation, we amplified it with the usual polymerase processes. The virus has been sequenced and—only a few days ago!—captured on an electromicrograph image, which, as most of you know, can be notoriously difficult. Here it is."

A graphic appeared on the wall behind Manning: fuzzy concentric circles blending into each other in shades of gray. Manning ran his hand over his head, now completely bald. Had he shaved his last three hairs, Marianne wondered irrelevantly. Or had they just given up and fallen out from stress?

"The virion appears to be related to known paramyxoviruses, although the gene sequence, which we now have, does not exactly match any of them. It is a negative-sense single-stranded RNA virus. Paramyxoviruses, to which it may or may not be directly related, are responsible for a number of human and animal diseases, including parainfluenza, mumps, measles, pneumonia, and canine distemper. This family of viruses jumps species more easily than any other. From what we have determined so far, it most closely resembles both Hendra and Nipah viruses, which are highly contagious and highly virulent.

"The genome follows the paramyxovirus 'Rule of Six,' in that the total length of the genome is almost always a multiple of six. The spore virus consists of twenty-one genes with 21,645 base pairs. That makes it a large virus, but by no means the largest we know. Details of sequence, structure, envelope proteins, etc. can be found on the LAN. I want to especially thank Drs. Yu, Sedley, and Lapka for their valuable work in identifying *Respirovirus sporii*."

Applause. Marianne still stared at the simple, deadly image behind Manning. An unwelcome thought had seized her: the viral image looked not unlike a fuzzy picture of a not-too-well-preserved trilobite. Trilobites had been the dominant life form on Earth for 300 million years and comprised more than 10,000 species. All gone now. Humans could be gone, too, after a much briefer reign.

But we survived so much! The Ice Age, terrible predators, the "bottleneck event" of 70,000 years ago that reduced *Homo sapiens* to mere thousands . . .

Manning was continuing. This was the bad news. "However, we have made little progress in figuring out how to combat *R. sporii*. Blood from the infected mice has been checked against known viruses and yielded no serological positives. None of our small number of antiviral drugs were effective, although there was a slight reaction to ribavirin. That raises a further puzzle, since ribavirin is mostly effective against Lassa fever, which is caused by an arenavirus, not a paramyxovirus." Manning tried to smile; it was not a success. "So, the mystery deepens. I wish we had more to report."

Someone asked, "Are the infected mice making antibodies?"

"Yes," Manning said, "and if we can't manage to develop a vaccine, this is our best possible path to a post-exposure treatment, following the MB-003 model developed for Ebola. For you astronomers—and please forgive me if I am telling you things you already know—a successful post-exposure treatment for Ebola in nonhuman primates was developed two years ago, using a cocktail of monoclonal antibodies. It was the work of a partnership between American industry and government agencies. When administered an hour after infection, MB-003 yields a one hundred percent survival rate. At forty-eight hours, the survival rate is two-thirds. MB-003 was initially developed in a mouse model and then produced in plants. The work took ten years. It has not, of course, been tested in humans."

Ten years. The *Embassy* scientists had less than five months left. Ebola had previously been studied since its first outbreak in 1976. And the biggie: *It has not, of course, been tested in humans.* In whom it might, for all anyone knew, not even work.

Maybe the Denebs knew faster ways to produce a vaccine from antibodies, exponentially increase production, and distribute the results. But the aliens weren't even at this meeting. They had surely been given all this information already, but even so—

—Where the hell were the aliens that was more important than this?

V: S MINUS 3.5 MONTHS

MARIANNE

Marianne felt ridiculous. She and Evan leaned close over the sink in the lab. Water gushed full-strength from the tap, making noise that, she hoped, covered their words. The autoclave hummed; a Bach concerto played tinnily on the computer's inadequate speaker. The whole thing felt like a parody of a bad spy movie.

They had never been able to decide if the labs, if everywhere on the *Embassy*, were bugged. Evan had said yes, of course, don't be daft. Max, with the hubris of the young, had said no because his computer skills would have been able to detect any surveillance. Marianne and Gina had said it was irrelevant since both their work and their personal lives were so transparent. In addition, Marianne had disliked the implication that the Denebs were not their full and open partners. Gina had said—

Gina. Shot down, her life ended just as Jason William Jenner's had begun. And for how long? Would Marianne even get to see her grandson before everything was as over as Gina's life?

Dangerous to think this way. Their work on the *Embassy* was a thin bridge laid across a pit of despair, the same despair that had undoubtedly fueled Gina's killers.

"You know what has to happen," Marianne whispered. "Nobody's saying it aloud, but without virus replication in human bodies, we just can't understand the effect on the immune system and we're working blindly. Mice aren't enough. Even if we could have infected monkeys, it wouldn't be enough. We have to infect volunteers."

Evan stuck his finger into the flow of water, which spattered in bright drops against the side of the sink. "I know. *Everyone* knows. The request has been made to the powers that be."

"How do you know that?"

"I talk to people on the other teams. You know the laws against experimentation on humans unless there have first been proper clinical trials that—"

"Oh, fuck proper trials, this is a crisis situation!"

"Not enough people in power are completely convinced of that. You haven't been paying attention to the bigger picture, Marianne. The Public Health Service isn't even gearing up for mass inoculation or protection—Robinson is fighting it with claw and tusk. FEMA is divided and there's almost anarchy in the ranks. Congress just filibusters on the whole topic. And the president just doesn't have the votes to get much of anything done. Meanwhile, the masses riot or flee or just pretend the whole thing is some sort of hoax. The farther one gets from New York, the more the conspiracy theorists don't even believe there are aliens on Earth at all."

Marianne, still standing, pulled at the skin on her face. "It's all so frustrating. And the work we're doing here—you and I and Max and Gina"—her voice faltered—"is pointless. It really is. Identifying members of Smith's so-called clan? Who cares? I'm going to volunteer myself to be infected."

"They won't take you."

"If—"

"The only way that could happen is in secret. If a subgroup on the Spore Team decided the situation was desperate enough to conduct an unauthorized experiment."

She studied his face. In the biology department at the university, Evan had always been the one who knew how to obtain travel money for a conference, interviews with Nobel Prize winners, an immediate appointment with the dean. He had the knack, as she did not, for useful connections. She said, "You know something."

"No. I don't. Not yet."

"Find out."

He nodded and turned off the water. The music crescendoed: Brandenburg Concerto #2, that had gone out into space on the "golden record" inside *Voyager 1*.

The secret experiment turned out to be not all that secret.

Evan followed the rumors. Within a day he had found a lab tech in the Biology Group who knew a scientist in the Spore Group who referred him, so obliquely that Evan almost missed it, to a security officer. Evan came to Marianne in her room, where she'd gone instead of eating lunch. He stood close to her and murmured in her ear, ending with, "They'll let us observe. You—what's that, then?"

The last sentence was said in a normal voice. Evan gazed at the piece of paper in Marianne's hands. She had been looking at it since she'd found it under her door.

"Another note from Noah. He isn't . . . he can't . . . Evan, I need to go ashore to see my new grandchild."

Evan blinked. "Your new grandchild?"

"Yes. He's three months old already and I haven't even seen him."

"It's not safe to leave the *Embassy* now. You know that."

"Yes. But I need to go."

Gently Evan took the note from her and read it. Marianne saw that he didn't really understand. Young, childless, orphaned . . . how could he? Noah had not forgiven her for never telling him that he was adopted. That must be why he said he might not ever see her again; no other reason made sense. Although maybe he would change his mind. Maybe in time he would forgive her, maybe he would not, maybe the world would end first. Before any of those things happened, Marianne had to see little Jason. She had to affirm what family ties she had, no matter how long she had them. Or anyone had them.

She said, "I need to talk to Ambassador Smith. How do I do that?"

He said, "Do you want me to arrange it?"

"Yes. Please. For today."

He didn't mention the backlog of samples in the lab. No one had replaced Gina. As family trees of the L7 haplogroup were traced in the matrilineal line, more and more of Smith's "clan" were coming aboard the *Embassy*. Marianne suspected they hoped to be shielded or transported when the spore cloud hit. She also suspected they were right. The Denebs were . . .

. . . were just as insistent on family connections as she was, risking her life to see Ryan, Connie, and the baby.

Well.

A helicopter flew her directly from the large pier outside the *Embassy* (so that's what it was for). When Marianne had last been outside, autumn was just ending. Now it was spring, the reluctant Northern spring of tulips and late frosts, cherry blossoms and noisy frogs. The Vermont town where Connie's parents lived, and to which Ryan had moved his family for safety, was less than twenty miles from the Canadian border. The house was a pleasant brick faux-Colonial set amid bare fields. Marianne noted, but did not comment on, the spiked chain-link fence around the small property, the electronic-surveillance sticker on the front door, and the large Doberman whose collar Ryan held in restraint. He had hastened home from his field work when she phoned that she was coming.

"Mom! Welcome!"

"We're so glad you're here, Marianne," Connie said warmly. "Even though I suspect it isn't us you came to see!" She grinned and handed over the tiny wrapped bundle.

The baby was asleep. Light-brown fuzz on the top of his head, silky skin lightly flushed with pink, tiny pursed mouth sucking away in an infant dream. He looked so much as Ryan had that tears pricked Marianne's eyes. Immediately she banished them: no sorrow, neither nostalgic nor catastrophic, was going to mar this occasion.

"He's beautiful," she said, inadequately.

"Yes!" Connie was not one of those mothers who felt obliged to disclaim praise of her child.

Marianne held the sleeping baby while coffee was produced. Connie's parents were away, helping Connie's sister, whose husband had just left her and whose three-year-old was ill. This was touched on only lightly. Connie kept the conversation superficial, prattling in her pretty voice about Jason, about the dog's antics, about the weather. Marianne followed suit, keeping to herself the thought that, after all, she had never heard Connie talk about anything but light and cheerful topics. She must have more to her than that, but not in front of her mother-in-law. Ryan said almost nothing, sipping his coffee, listening to his wife.

Finally Connie said, "Oh, I've just been monopolizing the conversation! Tell us about life aboard the *Embassy*. It must be so fascinating!"

Ryan looked directly at Marianne.

She interpreted the look as a request to keep up the superficial tone. Ryan had always been as protective of Connie as of a pretty kitten. Had he deliberately chosen a woman so opposite his mother because Marianne had always put her work front and center? Had Ryan resented her for that as much as Noah had?

Pushing aside these disturbing thoughts, she chatted about the aliens. Connie asked her to describe them, their clothes, her life there. Did she have her own room? Had she been able to decorate it? Where did the humans eat?

"We're *all* humans, Terrans and Denebs," Marianne said.

"Of course," Connie said, smiling brilliantly. "Is the food good?"

Talking, talking, talking, but not one question about her work. Nor about the spore cloud, progress toward a vaccine, anything to indicate the size and terror of the coming catastrophe. Ryan did ask about the *Embassy*, but only polite questions about its least important aspects: how big it was, how it was laid out, what was the routine. Safe topics.

Just before a sense of unreality overwhelmed Marianne, Ryan's cell rang, and the ringing woke the baby, who promptly threw up all over Marianne.

"Oh, I'm sorry!" Connie said. "Here, give him to me!"

Ryan, making gestures of apology, took his cell into the kitchen and closed the door. Connie reached for a box of Wet Ones and began to wipe Jason's face. She said, "The bathroom is upstairs to the left, Marianne. If you need to, I can loan you something else to wear."

"It would have to be one of your maternity dresses," Marianne said. It came out more sour than she'd intended.

She went upstairs and cleaned baby vomit off her shirt and jeans with a wet towel. The bathroom was decorated in a seaside motif, with hand towels embroidered with sailboats, soap shaped like shells, blue walls painted with green waves and smiling dolphins. On top of the toilet tank, a crocheted cylinder decorated like a buoy held a spare roll of toilet paper.

Keeping chaos at bay with cute domesticity. Good plan. And then: *Stop it, Marianne.*

Using the toilet, she leafed idly through magazines stacked in a rustic basket. *Good Housekeeping, Time*, a Macy's catalogue. She pulled out a loose paper with full-color drawings:

HOW TO TELL PURPLE LOOSESTRIFE FROM NATIVE
PLANTS DON'T BE FOOLED BY LOOK-ALIKES!

Purple loosestrife leaves are downy with smooth edges. Although usually arranged opposite each other in pairs which alternate down the stalk at 90-degree angles, the leaves may sometimes appear in groups of three. The leaves lack teeth. The flowers, which appear in mid- to late summer, form a showy spike of rose-purple, each with five to seven petals. The stem is stiff, four-sided, and may appear woody at the base of larger plants, which can reach ten feet tall. Average height is four feet. Purple loosestrife can be distinguished from the native winged loosestrife (*Lythrum alatum*), which it most closely resembles, by its generally larger size, opposite leaves, and more closely placed flowers. It may also be confused with blue vervain (pictured below), which has . . .

At the bottom of the page, someone—presumably Ryan—had hand-drawn in purple ink three stylized versions of a loosestrife spike, then circled one. To Marianne it looked like a violet rocket ship unaccountably sprouting leaves.

Downstairs, Jason had been cleaned up and changed. Marianne played with him the limited games available for three-month-old babies: peek-a-boo, feetsies go up and down, where did the finger go? When he started to fuss and Connie excused herself to nurse him, Marianne said her good-byes and went out to the helicopter waiting in a nearby field. Neighbors had gathered around it, and Ryan was telling them—what? The neighbors looked harmless, but how could you tell? Always, Gina was on her mind. She hugged Ryan fiercely.

As the copter lifted and the house, the town, the countryside got smaller and smaller, Marianne tried not to think of what a failure the visit had been. Yes, she had seen her grandchild. But whatever comfort or connection that had been supposed to bring her, it hadn't. It seemed to her, perhaps irrationally, that never had she felt so alone.

NOAH

When Noah woke, he instantly remembered what day it was. For a long moment, he lay still, savoring the knowledge like rich chocolate on the tongue. Then he said good-bye to his room. He would never sleep here, out of his energy suit, again.

Over the months, he had made the room as World as he could. A sleeping mat, thin but with as much give as a mattress, rolled itself tightly as soon as he sprang up and into the tiny shower. On the support wall he had hung one of Oliver's pictures—not a half-dressed barbarian princess this time, but a black-and-white drawing of plants in the World garden. The other walls, which seemed thin as rice paper but somehow kept out sound, had been programmed, at Noah's request, with the subtly shifting colors that the Worlders favored for everything except family gatherings. Color was extremely important to Worlders, and so to Noah. He was learning to discern shades that had once seemed all the same. *This* blue for mourning; *this* blue for adventure; *this* blue for loyalty. He had discarded all his Terran clothes. How had he ever stood the yellow polo shirt, the red hoodie? Wrong, wrong.

Drying his body, he rehearsed his request to Mee^haoj (rising inflection in the middle, click at the end—Noah loved saying his name).

Breakfast, like all World meals, was communal, a time to affirm ties. Noah had already eaten in his room; the energy suit did not permit the intake of food. Nonetheless, he took his place in the hierarchy at the long table, above Oliver and Jacqui and below everyone else. That was just. Family solidarity rested on three supports: inclusion, rank, and empathy. A triangle was the strongest of all geometrical figures.

"G'morning," Oliver said, yawning. He was not a morning person, and resented getting up for a breakfast he would not eat until much later.

"I greet you," Noah said in World. Oliver blinked.

Jacqui, quicker, said, "Oh, today is the day, is it? Can I be there?"

"At the ceremony? No, of course not!" Noah said. She should have known better than to even make the request.

"Just asking," Jacqui said. "Doesn't hurt to ask."

Yes, it does. It showed a lack of respect for all three supports in the triangle. Although Noah had not expected any more of Jacqui.

He did expect it of the three Terrans who took their places below Oliver. Isabelle Rhinehart; her younger sister, Kayla; and Kayla's son had come into the World section of the Embassy only a week ago, but already the two women were trying to speak Worldese. The child, Austin, was only three—young enough to grow up trilling and clicking Worldese like a native. Noah gazed with envy at the little boy, who smiled shyly and then crawled onto his mother's lap.

But they could not hold Noah's interest long. This was the day!

His stomach growled. He'd been too excited to eat much of the food delivered earlier to his room. And truthfully, the vegetarian World diet was not exciting. But he would learn to like it. And what a small price to pay for . . . *everything.*

The ceremony took place in the same room, right after breakfast. The other Terrans had left. Mee^hao¡ changed the wall program. Now instead of subtly shifting greens, the thin room dividers pulsed with the blue of loyalty alternating with the color of the clan of Mee^hao¡.

Noah knelt in the middle of the circle of Worlders, facing Mee^hao¡, who held a long blue rod. *Now I dub thee Sir Noah. . . .* Noah hated, completely hated, that his mind threw up that stupid thought. This was nothing like a feudal knighting. It was more like a baptism, washing him clean of his old self.

Mee^hao¡ sang a verse of what he had been told was the family inclusion song, with everyone else echoing the chorus. Noah didn't catch all the trilling and clicking words, but he didn't have to. Tears pricked his eyes. It seemed to him that he had never wanted anything this much in life, had never really wanted anything at all.

"Stand, brother mine," Mee^hao¡ said.

Noah stood. Mee^hao¡ did something with the rod, and the energy shield dissolved around Noah.

Not only a baptism—an operation.

The first breath of World air almost made him vomit. No, the queasiness was excitement, not the air. It tasted strange, and with the second panicky breath he felt he wasn't getting enough of it. But he knew that was just the lower oxygen content. The *Embassy* was at sea level; the O_2 concentration of World matched that at 12,000 feet. His lungs would adapt. His marrow would produce more red corpuscles. The Worlders had evolved for this; Noah would evolve, too.

The air smelled strange.

His legs buckled slightly, but before Llaa^moh¡, whom he had once known as Jones, could step toward him, Noah braced himself and smiled. He was all right. He was here. He was—

"Brother mine" went around the circle, and then the formalities were over and they all hugged him, and for the first time in 150,000 years, Terran skin touched the skin of humans from the stars.

MARIANNE

The security officer met Marianne and Evan in their lab and conducted them to a euchre game in the observation area outside the BSL4 lab.

From the first time she'd come here, Marianne had been appalled by the amateurishness of the entire setup. Granted, this was a bunch of scientists, not the CIA. Still, the Denebs had to wonder why euchre—or backgammon or chess or Monopoly, it varied—was being played here instead of at one of the comfortable Commons or cafeterias. Why two scientists were constantly at work in the negative-pressure lab even when they seemed to have nothing to do. Why the euchre players paid more attention to the screens monitoring the scientists' vitals than to the card game.

Dr. Julia Namechek and Dr. Trevor Lloyd. Both young, strong, and self-infected with spore disease. They moved around the BSL4 lab in full space suits, breathing tubes attached to the air supply in the ceiling. Surely the Denebs' energy suits would be better for this kind of work, but the suits had not been offered to the Terrans.

"When?" Marianne murmured, playing the nine of clubs.

"Three days ago," said a physician whose name Marianne had not caught.

Spore disease (the name deliberately unimaginative, non-inflammatory) had turned up in mice after three days. Marianne was not a physician, but she could read a vitals screen. Neither Namechek nor Lloyd, busily working in their space suits behind glass, showed the slightest signs of infection. This was, in fact, the third time that the two had tried to infect themselves by breathing in the spores. Each occasion had been preceded by weeks of preparation. Those times, nothing had happened, either, and no one knew why.

Physicians experimenting on themselves were not unknown in research medicine. Edward Jenner had infected himself—and the eight-year-old son of his gardener—with cowpox to develop the smallpox vaccine. Jesse William Lazear infected himself with yellow fever from mosquitoes, in order to confirm that mosquitoes were indeed the transmission vector. Julio Barrera gave himself Argentine hemorrhagic fever; Barry Marshall drank a solution *H. pylori* to prove the bacterium caused peptic ulcers; Pradeep Seth injected himself with an experimental vaccine for HIV.

Marianne understood the reasons for the supposed secrecy of this experiment. The newspapers that came in on the mail runs glowed luridly with speculations about human experimentation aboard the *Embassy*. Journalists ignited their pages with "Goebbels," "Guatemalan syphilis trials," "Japanese Unit 731." And those were the mainstream journalists. The tabloids and fringe papers invented so many details about Deneb atrocities on humans that the newsprint practically dripped with blood and body parts. The online news sources were, if anything, even worse. No, such "journalists"would never believe that Drs. Namechek and Lloyd had given spore disease to themselves and without the aliens' knowing it.

Actually, Marianne didn't believe that, either. The Denebs were too intelligent, too technologically advanced, too careful. They *had* to know this experiment was going on. They had to be permitting it. No matter how benign and peaceful their culture, they were human. Their lack of interference was a way of ensuring CYA deniability.

"Your turn, Dr. Jenner," said Syed Sharma, a very formal microbiologist from Mumbai. He was the only player wearing a suit.

"Oh, sorry," Marianne said. "What's trump again?"

Evan, her partner, said, "Spades. Don't trump my ace again."

"No table talk, please," Sharma said.

Marianne studied her hand, trying to remember what had been played. She had never been a good card player. She didn't like cards. And there was nothing to see here, anyway. Evan could bring her the results, if any, of the clandestine experiment. It was possible that the two scientists had not been infected, after all—not this time nor the previous two. It was possible that the pathogen had mutated, or just hadn't taken hold in these two particular people, or was being administered with the wrong vector. Stubbins Firth, despite heroic and disgusting measures, had never succeeded in infecting himself with yellow fever because he never understood how it was transmitted. Pathogen research was still part art, part luck.

"I fold," she said, before she remembered that "folding" was poker, not euchre. She tried a weak smile. "I'm very tired."

"Go to bed, Dr. Jenner," said Seyd Sharma. Marianne gave him a grateful look, which he did not see as he frowned at his cards. She left.

Just as she reached the end of the long corridor leading to the labs, the door opened and a security guard hurried through, face twisted with some strong emotion. Her heart stopped. What fresh disaster now? She said, "Did anything—" but before she could finish the question he had pushed past her and hurried on.

Marianne hesitated. Follow him to hear the news or wait until—

The lab exploded.

Marianne was hurled to the floor. Walls around her, the tough but thin membrane-like walls favored by the Denebs, tore. People screamed, sirens sounded, pulsing pain tore through Marianne's head like a dark, viscous tsunami.

Then everything went black.

She woke alone in a room. Small, white, windowless, with one clear wall, two doors, a pass-through compartment. Immediately, she knew, even before she detected the faint hum of blown air: a quarantine room with negative pressure. The second door, locked, led to a BSL4 operating room for emergency procedures and autopsies. The explosion had exposed her to spores from the experimental lab.

Bandages wreathed her head; she must have hit it when she fell, got a concussion, and needed stitches. Nothing else on her seemed damaged. Gingerly she sat up, aware of the IV tube and catheter and pulse oximeter, and waiting for the headache. It was there, but very faint. Her movement set off a faint gong somewhere and Dr. Ann Potter, a physician whom Marianne knew slightly, appeared on the other side of the clear glass wall.

The doctor said, her voice coming from the ceiling as if she were just one more alien, "You're awake. What do you feel?"

"Headache. Not terrible. What . . . . what happened?"

"Let me ask you some questions first." She was asked her name, the date, her location, the name of the president—

"Enough!" Marianne said. "I'm fine! *What happened?*" But she already knew. Hers was the only bed in the quarantine room.

Dr. Potter paid her the compliment of truth. "It was a suicide bomber. He—"

"The others? Evan Blanford?"

"They're all dead. I'm sorry, Dr. Jenner."

Evan. Dead.

Seyd Sharma, with his formal, lilting diction. Julia Namechek, engaged to be married. Trevor Lloyd, whom everyone said would win a Nobel someday. The fourth euchre player, lab tech Alyssa Rosert—all dead.

Evan. Dead.

Marianne couldn't process that, not now. She managed to say, "Tell me. All of it."

Ann Potter's face creased with emotion, but she had herself under control. "The bomber was dressed as a security guard. He had the explosive—I haven't heard yet what it was—in his stomach or rectum, presumably cased to protect it from body fluids. Autopsy showed that the detonator, ceramic so that it got through all our metal detectors, was probably embedded in a tooth, or at least somewhere in his mouth that could be tongued to go off."

Marianne pictured it. Her stomach twisted.

Dr. Potter continued, "His name was Michael Wendl and he was new but legitimately aboard, a sort of mole, I guess you'd call it. A manifesto was all over the Internet an hour after the explosion and this morning—"

"This morning? How long have I been out?"

"Ten hours. You had only a mild concussion but you were sedated to stitch up head lacerations, which of course we wouldn't ordinarily do but this was complicated because—"

"I know," Marianne said, and marveled at the calm in her voice. "I may have been exposed to the spores."

"You *have* been exposed, Marianne. Samples were taken. You're infected."

Marianne set that aside, too, for the moment. She said, "Tell me about the manifesto. What organization?"

"Nobody has claimed credit. The manifesto was about what you'd expect: Denebs planning to kill everyone on Earth, all that shit. Wendl vetted okay when he was hired, so speculation is that he was a new recruit to their cause. He was from somewhere upstate and there's a lot of dissent going on up there. But the thing is, he got it wrong. He was supposed to explode just outside the Deneb section of the *Embassy*, not the research labs. His organization, whatever it was, knew something about the layout of the *Embassy* but not enough. Wendl was supposed to be restricted to sub-bay duty. It's like someone who'd had just a brief tour had told him where to go, but either they remembered wrong or he did."

Marianne's spine went cold. *Someone who'd had just a brief tour . . .*

"You had some cranial swelling after the concussion, Marianne, but it's well under control now."

Elizabeth.

No, not possible. Not thinkable.

"You're presently on a steroid administered intravenously, which may have some side effects I'd like you to be aware of, including wakefulness and—"

Elizabeth, studying everything during her visit aboard the *Embassy*: "*Where do the Denebs live?*" "*Behind these doors here. No one has ever been in there.*" "*Interesting. It's pretty close to the high-risk labs.* "

"Marianne, are you listening to me?"

Elizabeth, furiously punching the air months ago: "*I don't believe it, not any of it. There are things they aren't telling us!*"

"Marianne?"

Elizabeth, grudgingly doing her duty to protect the aliens but against her own inclinations. Commanding a critical section of the Border Patrol, a member of the joint task force that had access to military-grade weapons. In an ideal position to get an infiltrator aboard the floating island.

"Marianne! *Are* you listening to me?"

"No," Marianne said. "I have to talk to Ambassador Smith!"

"Wait, you can't just—"

Marianne had started to heave herself off the bed, which was ridiculous because she couldn't leave the quarantine chamber anyway. A figure appeared on the other side of the glass barrier, behind Dr. Potter. The doctor, following Marianne's gaze, turned, and gasped.

Noah pressed close to the glass. An energy shield shimmered around him. Beneath it he wore a long tunic like Smith's. His once-pale skin now shone coppery under his black hair. But most startling were his eyes: Noah's eyes, and yet not. Bigger, altered to remove as much of the skin and expose as much of the white as possible. Within that large, alien-sized expanse of white, his irises were still the same color as her own, an un-alien light gray flecked with gold.

"Mom," he said tenderly. "Are you all right?"

"Noah—"

"I came as soon as I heard. I'm sorry it's been so long. Things have been . . . happening."

It was still Noah's voice, coming through the energy shield and out of the ceiling with no alien inflection, no trill or click. Marianne's mind refused to work logically. All she could focus on was his voice: He was too old. He would never speak English as anything but a Middle Atlantic American, and he would never speak Worldese without an accent.

"Mom?"

"I'm fine," she managed.

"I'm so sorry to hear about Evan."

She clasped her hands tightly together on top of the hospital blanket. "You're going. With the aliens. When they leave Earth."

"Yes."

One simple word. No more than that, and Marianne's son became an extraterrestrial. She knew that Noah was not doing this in order to save his life. Or hers, or anyone's. She didn't know why he had done it. As a child, Noah had been fascinated by superheroes, aliens, robots, even of the more ridiculous kind where the science made zero sense. Comic books, movies, TV shows—he would sit transfixed for hours by some improbable human transformed into a spider or a hulk or a sentient hunk of metal. Did Noah remember that childish fascination? She didn't understand what this adopted child, this beloved boy she had not borne, remembered or thought or desired. She never had.

He said, "I'm sorry."

She said, "Don't be," and neither of them knew exactly what he was apologizing for in the first place, nor what she was excusing him from. After that, Marianne could find nothing else to say. Of the thousands of things she could have said to Noah, absolutely none of them rose to her lips. So finally she nodded.

Noah blew her a kiss. Marianne did not watch him go. She couldn't have borne it. Instead she shifted her weight on the bed and got out of it, holding on to the bedstead, ignoring Ann Potter's strenuous objections on the other side of the glass.

She had to see Ambassador Smith, to tell him about Elizabeth. The terrorist organization could strike again.

As soon as she told Smith, Elizabeth would be arrested. *Two children lost—*

No, don't think of it. Tell Smith.

But—*wait*. Maybe it hadn't been Elizabeth. Surely others had had an unauthorized tour of the ship? And now, as a result of the attack, security would be tightened. Probably no other saboteur could get through. Perhaps there would be no more supply runs by submarine, no more helicopters coming and going on the wide pier. Time was so short—maybe there were enough supplies aboard already. And perhaps the Denebs would use their unknowable technology to keep the *Embassy* safer until the spore cloud hit, by which time, of course, the aliens would have left. There were only three months left. Surely a second attack inside the Embassy couldn't be organized in such a brief time! Maybe there was no need to name Elizabeth at all.

The room swayed as she clutched the side of the bed.

Ann Potter said, "If you don't get back into bed right now, Marianne, I'm calling security."

"Nothing is secure, don't you know that, you silly woman?" Marianne snapped.

Noah was lost to her. Evan was dead. Elizabeth was guilty.

"I'm sorry," she said. "I'll get back in bed." What was she even doing, standing up? She couldn't leave. She carried the infection inside her body. "But I . . . I need to see Ambassador Smith. Right now, here. Please have someone tell him it's the highest possible priority. Please."

NOAH

The visit to his mother upset Noah more than he'd expected. She'd looked so small, so fragile in her bed behind the quarantine glass. Always, his whole life, he'd thought of her as large, towering over the landscape like some stone fortress, both safe and formidable. But she was just a small, frightened woman who was going to die.

As were Elizabeth, Ryan and Connie and their baby, Noah's last girlfriend Emily, his childhood buddies Sam and Davey, Cindy and Miguel at the restaurant— all going to die when the spore cloud hit. Why hadn't Noah been thinking about this before? How could he be so selfish about concentrating on his delight in his new clan that he had put the rest of humanity out of his mind?

He had always been selfish. He'd known that about himself. Only before now, he'd called it "independent."

It was a relief to leave the Terran part of the *Embassy*, with its too-heavy gravity and glaring light. The extra rods and cones that had been inserted into Noah's eyes made them sensitive to such terrible brightness. In the World quarters, Kayla's little boy Austin was chasing a ball along the corridor, his energy suit a faint glimmer in the low light. He stopped to watch Noah shed his own suit.

Austin said, "I wanna do that."

"You will, someday. Maybe soon. Where's your mother?"

"She comes right back. I stay right here!"

"Good boy. Have you—hi, Kayla. Do you know where Mee^haoj is?"

"No. Oh, wait, yes—he left the sanctuary."

That, Noah remembered, was what both Kayla and her sister called the World section of the *Embassy*. "Sanctuary"—the term made him wonder what their life had been before they came aboard. Both, although pleasant enough, were close-mouthed about their pasts to the point of lock-jaw.

Kayla added, "I think Mee^hao¡ said it was about the attack."

It would be, of course. Noah knew he should wait until Mee^hao¡ was free. But he couldn't wait.

"Where's Llaa^moh¡?"

Kayla looked blank; her Worldese was not yet fluent.

"Officer Jones."

"Oh. I just saw her in the garden."

Noah strode to the garden. Llaa^moh¡ sat on a bench, watching water fall in a thin stream from the ceiling to a pool below. Delicately she fingered a llo flower, without picking it, coaxing the broad dark leaf to release its spicy scent. Noah and Llaa^moh¡ had avoided each other ever since Noah's welcome ceremony, and he knew why. Still, right now his need overrode awkward desire.

"Llaa^moh¡—may we speak together?" He hoped he had the verb tense right: urgency coupled with supplication.

"Yes, of course." She made room for him on the bench. "Your Worldese progresses well."

"Thank you. I am troubled in my liver." The correct idiom, he was certain. Almost.

"What troubles your liver, brother mine?"

"My mother." The word meant not only female parent but matriarchal clan leader, which Noah supposed that Marianne was, since both his grandmothers were dead. Although perhaps not his biological grandmothers, and to World, biology was all. There were no out-of-family adoptions.

"Yes?"

"She is Dr. Marianne Jenner, as you know, working aboard the *Embassy*. My brother and sister live ashore. What will happen to my family when the spore cloud comes? Does my mother go with us to World? Do my birth-siblings?" But . . . how could they, unaltered? Also, they were not of his haplotype and so would belong to a different clan for Illathil, clans not represented aboard ship. Also, all three of them would hate everything about World. But otherwise they would die. All of them, dead.

Llaa^moh¡ said nothing. Noah gave her the space and time to think; one thing World humans hated about Terrans was that they replied so quickly, without careful thought, sometimes even interrupting each other and thereby dishonoring the speaker. Noah watched a small insect with multicolored wings, whose name did not come to his fevered mind, cross the llo leaf, and forced his body to stay still.

Finally Llaa^moh¡ said, "Mee^hao¡ and I have discussed this. He has left this decision to me. You are one of us now. I will tell you what will happen when the spore cloud comes."

"I thank you for your trust." The ritual response, but Noah meant it.

"However, you are under obligation"—she used the most serious degree for a word of promise—"to say nothing to anyone else, World or Terran. Do you accept this obligation?"

Noah hesitated, and not from courtesy. Shouldn't he use the information, whatever it was, to try to ensure what safety was possible for his family? But if he did not promise, Llaa^moh¡ would tell him nothing.

"I accept the obligation."

She told him.

Noah's jaw dropped. He couldn't help it, even though it was very rude. Llaa^moh¡ was carefully not looking at him; perhaps she had anticipated this reaction.

Noah stood and walked out of the garden.

MARIANNE

"Thought," a famous poet—Marianne couldn't remember which one—had once said, "is an infection. In the case of certain thoughts, it becomes an epidemic." Lying in her bed in the quarantine chamber, Marianne felt an epidemic in her brain. What Elizabeth had done, what she herself harbored now in her body, Noah's transformation, Evan's death—the thoughts fed on her cells, fevered her mind.

Elizabeth, studying the complex layout of the Embassy: "*Where do the Denebs live?*" "*Behind these doors here.*"

Noah, with his huge alien eyes.

Evan, urging her to meet the aliens by scribbling block letters on a paper sushi bag: CHANCE OF SIX THOUSAND LIFETIMES! The number of generations since Mitochondrial Eve.

Herself, carrying the deadly infection. Elizabeth, Noah, Evan, spores—it was almost a relief when Ambassador Smith appeared beyond the glass.

"Dr. Jenner," the ceiling said in uninflected translation. "I am so sorry you were injured in this attack. You said you want to see me now."

She hadn't been sure what she was going to say to him. How did you name your own child a possible terrorist, condemn her to whatever unknown form justice took among aliens? What if that meant something like drawing and quartering, as it once had on Earth? Marianne opened her mouth, and what came out were words she had not planned at all.

"Why did you permit Drs. Namechek and Lloyd to infect themselves three times when it violates both our medical code and yours?"

His face, both Terran and alien, that visage that now and forever would remind her of what Noah had done to his own face, did not change expression. "You know why, Dr. Jenner. It was necessary for the research. There is no other way to fully assess immune-system response in ways useful to developing antidotes."

"You could have used your own people!"

"There are not enough of us to put anyone into quarantine."

"You could have run the experiment yourself with human volunteers. You'd have gotten volunteers, given what Earth is facing. And then the experiment could have had the advantage of your greater expertise."

"It is not much greater than yours, as you know. Our scientific knowledges have moved in different directions. But if we had sponsored experiments on Terrans, what would have been the Terran response?"

Marianne was silent. She knew the answer. They both knew the answer.

He said, "You are infected, I am told. We did not cause this. But now our two peoples can work more openly on developing medicines or vaccines. Both Earth and World will owe you an enormous debt."

Which she would never collect. In roughly two more days she would be dead of spore disease.

And she still had to tell him about Elizabeth.

"Ambassador Smith—"

"I must show you something, Dr. Jenner. If you had not sent for me, I would have come to you as soon as I was informed that you were awake. Your physician performed an autopsy on the terrorist. That is, by the way, a useful word, which does not exist on World. We shall appropriate it. The doctors found this in the mass of body tissues. It is engraved titanium, possibly created to survive the blast. Secretary General Desai suggests that it is a means to claim credit, a 'logo.' Other Terrans have agreed, but none know what it means. Can you aid us? Is it possibly related to one of the victims? You were a close friend of Dr. Blanford."

He held up something close to the glass: a flat piece of metal about three inches square. Whatever was pictured on it was too small for Marianne to see from her bed.

Smith said, "I will have Dr. Potter bring it to you."

"No, don't." Ann would have to put on a space suit and maneuver through the double airlock with a respirator. The fever in Marianne's brain could not wait that long. She pulled out her catheter tube, giving a small shriek at the unexpected pain. Then she heaved herself out of bed and dragged the IV pole over to the clear barrier. Ann began to sputter. Marianne ignored her.

On the square of metal was etched a stylized purple rocket ship, sprouting leaves.

Not Elizabeth. Ryan.

"Dr. Jenner?"

"They're an invasive species," Ryan had said.

"Didn't you hear a word I said?" Marianne said. *"They're not 'invasive,' or at least not if our testing bears out the ambassador's story. They're native to Earth."*

"An invasive species is native to Earth. It's just not in the ecological niche it evolved for."

"Dr. Jenner?" the Ambassador repeated. "Are you all right?"

Ryan, his passion about purple loosestrife a family joke. Ryan, interested in the *Embassy*, as Connie was not, asking questions about the facilities and the layout while Marianne cuddled her new grandson. Ryan, important enough in this terrorist organization to have selected its emblem from a sheet of drawings in a kitschy bathroom.

Ryan, her son.

"Dr. Jenner, I must insist—"

"Yes. Yes. I recognize that thing. I know who—what group—you should look for." Her heart shattered.

Smith studied her through the glass. The large, calm eyes—Noah's eyes now, except for the color—held compassion.

"Someone you know."

"Yes."

"It doesn't matter. We shall not look for them."

The words didn't process. "Not . . . not look for them?"

"No. It will not happen again. The embassy has been sealed and the Terrans re-moved except for a handful of scientists directly involved in immunology, all of whom have chosen to stay, and all of whom we trust."

"But—"

"And, of course, those of our clan members who wish to stay."

Marianne stared at Smith through the glass, the impermeable barrier. Never had he seemed more alien. Why would this intelligent man believe that just because a handful of Terrans shared a mitochondrial haplotype with him, they could not be terrorists, too? Was it a cultural blind spot, similar to the Terran millennia-long be-lief in the divine right of kings? Was it some form of perception, the product of di-vergent evolution, that let his brain perceive things she could not? Or did he simply have in place such heavy surveillance and protective devices that people like Noah, sequestered in a different part of the *Embassy*, presented no threat?

Then the rest of what he had said struck her. "Immunologists?"

"Time is short, Dr. Jenner. The spore cloud will envelop Earth in merely a few months. We must perform intensive tests on you and the other infected people."

"*Other?*"

"Dr. Ahmed Rafat and two lab technicians, Penelope Hodgson and Robert Chavez. They are, of course, all volunteers. They will be joining you soon in quarantine."

Rage tore through her, all the rage held back, pent up, about Evan's death, about Ryan's deceit, about Noah's defection. "Why not any of your own people? No, don't tell me that you're all too valuable—so are we! Why only Terrans? If we take this risk, why don't you? And what the fuck happens when the cloud does hit? Do you take off two days before, keeping yourselves safe and leaving Earth to die? You know very well that there is no chance of developing a real vaccine in the time left, let alone manufacturing and distributing it! What then? How can you just—"

But Ambassador Smith was already moving away from her, behind the shatter-proof glass. The ceiling said, without inflection or emotion, "I am sorry."

NOAH

Noah stood in the middle of the circle of Terrans. Fifty, sixty—they had all come aboard the *Embassy* in the last few days, as time shortened. Not all were L7s; some were families of clan brothers, and these, too, had been welcomed, since they'd had the defiance to ask for asylum when the directives said explicitly that only L7s would be taken in. *There was something wrong with this system*, Noah thought, but he did not think hard about what it might be.

The room, large and bare, was in neither the World quarters nor the now-sealed part of the *Embassy* where the Terran scientists worked. The few scientists left aboard, anyway. The room's air, gravity, and light were all Terran, and Noah again wore an energy suit. He could see its faint shimmer along his arms as he raised them in wel-come. He hadn't realized how much he was going to hate having to don the suit again.

"I am Noah," he said.

The people pressed against the walls of the bare room or huddled in small groups or sat as close to Noah as they could, cross-legged on the hard floor. They looked terrified or hopeful or defiant or already grieving for what might be lost. They all, even the ones who, like Kayla and Isabelle, had been here for a while, expected to die if they were left behind on Earth.

"I will be your leader and teacher. But first, I will explain the choice you must all make, now. You can choose to leave with the people of World, when we return to the home world. Or you can stay here, on Earth."

"To die!" someone shouted. "Some choice!"

Noah found the shouter: a young man standing close behind him, fists clenched at his side. He wore ripped jeans, a pin through his eyebrow, and a scowl. Noah felt the shock of recognition that had only thrilled through him twice before: with the nurse on the Upper West Side of New York and when he'd met Mee^haoᵢ. Not even Llaa^mohᵢ, who was a geneticist, could explain that shock, although she seemed to think it had to do with certain genetically determined pathways in Noah's L7 brain coupled with the faint electromagnetic field surrounding every human skull. She was fascinated by it.

Lisa Gutierrez, Noah remembered, had also attributed it to neurological pathways, changed by his heavy use of sugarcane.

Noah said to the scowler, "What is your name?"

He said, "Why?"

"I'd like to know it. We are clan brothers."

"I'm not your fucking brother. I'm here because it's my only option to not die."

A child on its mother's lap started to cry. People murmured to each other, most not taking their eyes off Noah. Waiting, to see what Noah did about the young man. Answer him? Let it go? Have him put off the *Embassy*?

Noah knew it would not take much to ignite these desperate people into attacking him, the alien-looking stand-in for the Worlders they had no way to reach.

He said gently to the young man, to all of them, to his absent and injured and courageous mother: "I'm going to explain your real choices. Please listen."

MARIANNE

Something was wrong.

One day passed, then another, then another. Marianne did not get sick. Nor did Ahmed Rafat and Penny Hodgson. Robbie Chavez did, but not very.

The lead immunologist left aboard the *Embassy*, Harrison Rice, stood with Ann Potter in front of Marianne's glass quarantine cage, known as a "slammer." He was updating Marianne on the latest lab reports. In identical slammers, two across a narrow corridor and one beside her, Marianne could see the three other infected people. The rooms had been created, as if by alchemy, by a Deneb that Marianne had not seen before—presumably an engineer of some unknowable building methods. Ahmed stood close to his glass, listening. Penny was asleep. Robbie, his face filmed with sweat, lay in bed, listening.

Ann Potter said, "You're not initially viremic but—"

"What does that mean?" Marianne interrupted.

Dr. Rice answered. He was a big, bluff Canadian who looked more like a truck driver who hunted moose than like a Nobel Prize winner. In his sixties, still strong as a mountain, he had worked with Ebola, Marburg, Lassa fever, and Nipah, both in the field and in the lab.

He said, "It means lab tests show that as with Namechek and Lloyd, the spores were detectable in the first samples taken from your respiratory tract. So the virus should be present in your bloodstream and so have access to the rest of your body. However, we can't find it. Well, that can happen. Viruses are elusive. But as far as we can tell, you aren't developing antibodies against the virus, as the infected mice did. That may mean that we just haven't isolated the antibodies yet. Or that your body doesn't consider the virus a foreign invader, which seems unlikely. Or that in humans, but not in mice, the virus has dived into an organ to multiply until its offspring burst out again. Malaria does that. Or that the virus samples in the lab, grown artificially, have mutated into harmlessness, differing from their wild cousins in the approaching cloud. Or it's possible that none of us knows what the hell we're doing with this crazy pathogen."

Marianne said, "What do the Denebs think?" Supposedly Rice was co-lead with Deneb Scientist Jones.

He said, his anger palpable even through the glass wall of the slammer, "I have no idea what they think. None of us have seen any of them."

"Not seen them?"

"No. We share all our data and samples, of course. Half of the samples go into an airlock for them, and the data over the LAN. But all we get in return is a thank-you on screen. Maybe they're not making progress, either, but at least they could tell us what they haven't discovered."

"Do we know . . . this may sound weird, but do we know that they're still here at all? Is it possible they all left Earth already?" *Noah.*

He said, "It's possible, I suppose. We have no news from the outside world, of course, so it's possible they pre-recorded all those thank-yous, blew up New York, and took off for the stars. But I don't think so. If they had, they'd have least unsealed us from this floating plastic bubble. Which, incidentally, has become completely opaque, even on the observation deck."

Marianne hadn't known there was an observation deck. She and Evan had not found it during their one exploration of the Embassy.

Dr. Rice continued. "Your cells are not making an interferon response, either. That's a small protein molecule that can be produced in any cell in response to the presence of viral nucleic acid. You're not making it."

"Which means . . ."

"Probably it means that there is no viral nucleic acid in your cells."

"Are Robbie's cells making interferon?"

"Yes. Also antibodies. Plus immune responses like—Ann, what does your chart on Chavez show for this morning?"

Ann said, "Fever of 101, not at all dangerous. Chest congestion, also not at dangerous levels, some sinus involvement. He has the equivalent of mild bronchitis."

Marianne said, "But why is Robbie sick when the rest of us aren't?"

"Ah," Harrison Rice said, and for the first time she heard the trace of a Canadian accent, "that's the big question, isn't it? In immunology, it always is. Sometimes genetic differences between infected hosts are the critical piece of the puzzle in understanding why an identical virus causes serious disease or death in one individual—or one group—and little reaction or none at all in other people. Is Robbie sick and you not because of your respective genes? We don't know."

"But you can use Robbie's antibodies to maybe develop a vaccine?"

He didn't answer. She knew the second the words left her mouth how stupid they were. Rice might have antibodies, but he had no time. None of them had enough time.

Yet they all worked on, as if they did. Because that's what humans did.

Instead of answering her question, he said, "I need more samples, Marianne."

"Yes."

Fifteen minutes later he entered her slammer, dressed in full space suit and sounding as if speaking through a vacuum cleaner. "Blood samples plus a tissue biopsy, just lie back down and hold still, please . . ."

During a previous visit, he had told her of an old joke among immunologists working with lethal diseases: "The first person to isolate a virus in the lab by getting infected is a hero. The second is a fool." Well, that made Marianne a fool. So be it.

She said to Rice, "And the aliens haven't . . . Ow!"

"Baby." He withdrew the biopsy needle and slapped a bandage over the site.

She tried again. "And the aliens haven't commented at all on Robbie's diagnosis? Not a word?"

"Not a word."

Marianne frowned. "Something isn't right here."

"No," Rice said, bagging his samples, "it certainly is not."

NOAH

Nothing, Noah thought, had ever felt more right, not in his entire life.

He raised himself on one elbow and looked down at Llaa^mohⱼ. She still slept, her naked body and long legs tangled in the light blanket made of some substance he could not name. Her wiry dark hair smelled of something like cinnamon, although it probably wasn't. The blanket smelled of sex.

He knew now why he had not felt the same shock of recognition at their first meeting that he had felt with Mee^haoⱼ and the unnamed New York nurse and surly young Tony Schrupp. After the World geneticists had done their work, Mee^haoⱼ had explained it to him. Noah felt profound relief. He and Llaa^mohⱼ shared a mitochondrial DNA group, but not a nuclear DNA one. They were not too genetically close to mate.

Of course, they could have had sex anyway; World had early, and without cultural shame or religious prejudice, discovered birth control. But for the first time in his life, Noah did not want just sex. He wanted to mate.

The miracle was that she did, too. Initially he feared that for her it was mere novelty: be the first Worlder to sleep with a Terran! But it was not. Just yesterday they had signed a five-year mating contract, followed by a lovely ceremony in the garden to which every single Worlder had come. Noah had never known exactly how many were aboard the Embassy; now he did. They had all danced with him, every single one, and also with her. Mee^hao¡ himself had pierced their right ears and hung from them the wedding silver, shaped like stylized versions of the small flowers that had once, very long ago, been the real thing.

"Is better," Noah had said in his accented, still clumsy World. "We want not bunch of dead vegetation dangle from our ears." At least, that's what he hoped he'd said. Everyone had laughed.

Noah reached out one finger to stroke Llaa^moh¡'s hair. A miracle, yes. A whole skyful of miracles, but none as much as this: Now he knew who he was and where he belonged and what he was going to do with his life.

His only regret was that his mother had not been at the mating ceremony. And— yes, forgiveness was in order here!—Elizabeth and Ryan, too. They had disparaged him his entire life and he would never see them again, but they were still his first family. Just not the one that any longer mattered.

Llaa^moh¡ stirred, woke, and reached for him.

MARIANNE

Robbie Chavez, recovered from *Respirovirus sporii,* gave so many blood and tissue samples that he joked he'd lost ten pounds without dieting. It wasn't much of a joke, but everyone laughed. Some of the laughter held hysteria.

Twenty-two people left aboard the *Embassy.* Why, Marianne sometimes wondered, had these twenty-two chosen to stay and work until the last possible second? Because the odds of finding anything that would affect the coming die-off were very low. They all knew that. Yet here they were, knowing they would die in this fantastically equipped, cut-off-from-the-world lab instead of with their families. Didn't any of them have families? Why were they still here?

Why was she?

No one discussed this. They discussed only work, which went on eighteen hours a day. Brief breaks for microwaved meals from the freezer. Briefer—not in actuality, but that's how it felt—for sleep.

The four people exposed to *R. sporii* worked outside the slammers; maintaining biosafety no longer seemed important. No one else became ill. Marianne relearned lab procedures she had not performed since grad school. Theoretical evolutionary biologists did not work as immunologists. She did now.

Every day, the team sent samples of data to the Denebs. Every day, the Denebs gave thanks, and nothing else.

In July, eight-and-a-half months after they'd first been given the spores to work with, the scientists finally succeeded in growing the virus in a culture. There was a celebration of sorts. Harrison Rice produced a hoarded bottle of champagne.

"We'll be too drunk to work," Marianne joked. She'd come to admire Harrison's unflagging cheerfulness.

"On one twenty-second of one bottle?" he said. "I don't think so."

"Well, maybe not everyone drinks."

Almost no one did. Marianne, Harrison, and Robbie Chavez drank the bottle. Culturing the virus, which should have been a victory, seemed to turn the irritable more irritable, the dour more dour. The tiny triumph underlined how little they had actually achieved. People began to turn strange. The unrelenting work, broken sleep, and constant tension created neuroses.

Penny Hodgson turned compulsive about the autoclave: It must be loaded just so, in just this order, and only odd numbers of tubes could be placed in the rack at one time. She flew into a rage when she discovered eight tubes, or twelve.

William Parker, Nobel Laureate in medicine, began to hum as he worked. Eighteen hours a day of humming. If told to stop, he did, and then unknowingly resumed a few minutes later. He could not carry a tune, and he liked lugubrious country and western tunes.

Marianne began to notice feet. Every few seconds, she glanced at the feet of others in the lab, checking that they still had them. Harrison's work boots, as if he tramped the forests of Hudson's Bay. Mark Wu's black oxfords. Penny's Nikes—did she think she'd be going for a run? Robbie's sandals. Ann's—

Stop it, Marianne!

She couldn't.

They stopped sending samples and data to the Denebs and held their collective breath, waiting to see what would happen. Nothing did.

Workboots, Oxfords, Nikes, sandals—

"I think," Harrison said, "that I've found something."

It was an unfamiliar protein in Marianne's blood. Did it have anything to do with the virus? They didn't know. Feverishly they set to work culturing it, sequencing it, photographing it, looking forward in everyone else. The protein was all they had.

It was August.

The outside world, with which they had no contact, had ceased to exist for them, even as they raced to save it.

Workboots—

Oxfords—

Sandals—

NOAH

Rain fell in the garden. Noah tilted his head to the artificial sky. He loved rainy afternoons, even if this was not really rain, nor afternoon. Soon he would experience the real thing.

Llaa^mohį came toward him through the dark, lush leaves open as welcoming hands. Noah was surprised; these important days she rarely left the lab. Too much to do.

She said, "Should not you be teaching?"

He wanted to say *I'm playing hooky* but had no idea what the idiom would be in Worldese. Instead he said, hoping he had the tenses right, "My students I will return at soon. Why you here? Something is wrong?"

"All is right." She moved into his arms. Again Noah was surprised; Worlders did not touch sexually in public places, even public places temporarily empty. Others might come by, unmated others, and it was just as rude to display physical affection in front of those without it as to eat in front of anyone hungry.

"Llaa^moh¡—"

She whispered into his ear. Her words blended with the rain, with the rich flower scents, with the odor of wet dirt. Noah clutched her and began to cry.

VI: S MINUS TWO WEEKS

MARIANNE

The Commons outside the lab was littered with frozen food trays, with discarded sterile wrappings, with an empty disinfectant bottle. Harrison slumped in a chair and said the obvious.

"We've failed, Marianne."

"Yes," she said. "I know." And then, fiercely, "Do you think the Denebs know more than we do? And aren't sharing?"

"Who knows?"

"Fucking bastards," Marianne said. Weeks ago she had crossed the line from defending the aliens to blaming them. How much of humanity had been ahead of her in that? By now, maybe all of it.

They had discovered nothing useful about the anomalous protein in Marianne's blood. The human body contained so many proteins whose identities were not understood. But that wouldn't make any difference, not now. There wasn't enough time.

"Harrison," she began, and didn't get to finish her sentence.

Between one breath and the next, Harrison Rice and the lab, along with everything else, disappeared.

NOAH

Nine, not counting him. The rest had been put ashore, to face whatever would happen to them on Earth. Noah would have much preferred to be with Llaa^moh¡, but she of course had duties. Even unannounced, departure was dangerous. Too many countries had too many formidable weapons.

So instead of standing beside Llaa^moh¡, Noah sat in his energy suit in the Terran compartment of the shuttle. Around him, strapped into chairs, sat the nine Terrans going to World. The straps were unnecessary; Llaa^moh¡ had told him that the acceleration would feel mild, due to the same gravity-altering machinery that had made the World section of the Embassy so comfortable. But Terrans were used to straps in moving vehicles, so there were straps.

Kayla Rhinehart and her little son.

Her sister, Isabelle.

The surly Tony Schrupp, a surprise. Noah had been sure Tony would change his mind.

A young woman, five months pregnant, who "wanted to give my baby a better life." She did not say what her previous life had been, but there were bruises on her arms and legs.

A pair of thirty-something brothers with restless, eager-for-adventure eyes.

A middle-aged journalist with a sun-leathered face and an impressive byline, recorders in her extensive luggage.

And, most unexpected, a Terran physicist, Dr. Nathan Beyon of Massachusetts Institute of Technology.

Nine Terrans willing to go to the stars.

A slight jolt. Noah smiled at the people under his leadership—he, who had never led anything before, not even his own life—and said, "Here we go."

That seemed inadequate, so he said, "We are off to the stars!"

That seemed dumb. Tony sneered. The journalist looked amused. Austin clutched his mother.

Noah said, "Your new life will be wonderful. Believe it."

Kayla gave him a wobbly smile.

MARIANNE

She could not imagine where she was.

Cool darkness, with the sky above her brightening every second. It had been so long since she'd seen a dawn sky, or any sky. Silver-gray, then pearl, and now the first flush of pink. The floor rocked gently. Then the last of the knock-out gas left her brain and she sat up. A kind of glorified barge, flat and wide with a single square rod jutting from the middle. The barge floated gently on New York Harbor. The sea was smooth as polished gray wood. In one direction rose the skyline of Manhattan; in the other, the *Embassy*. All around her lay her colleagues: Dr. Rafat, Harrison Rice and Ann Potter, lab techs Penny and Robbie, all the rest of the twenty-two people who'd still been aboard the *Embassy*. They wore their daily clothing. In her jeans and tee, Marianne shivered in a sudden breeze.

Nearby lay a pile of blankets. She took a yellow one and wrapped it around her shoulders. It felt warm and silky, although clearly not made of silk. Other people began to stir. Pink tinged the east.

Harrison came to her side. "Marianne?"

Automatically she said, because she'd been saying it so many times each day, "I feel fine." And then, "What the *fuck*?"

He said something just as pointless: "But we have two more weeks!"

"Oh my God!" someone cried, pointing, and Marianne looked up. The eastern horizon turned gold. Against it, a ship, dark and small, shot from the Embassy and climbed the sky. Higher and higher, while everyone on the barge shaded their eyes against the rising sun and watched it fly out of sight.

"They're going," someone said quietly.

They. The Denebs. *Noah*.

Before the tears that stung her eyes could fall, the *Embassy* vanished. One moment it was there, huge and solid and gray in the pre-dawn, and the next it was just gone. The water didn't even ripple.

The metal rod in the center of the ship spoke. Marianne, along with everyone else, turned sharply. Shoulder-high, three feet on a side, the rod had become four screens, each filled with the same alien/human image and mechanical voice.

"This is Ambassador Smith. A short time from now, this recording will go to everyone on Earth, but we wanted you, who have helped us so much, to hear it first. We of World are deeply in your debt. I would like to explain why, and to leave you a gift.

"Your astronomers' calculations were very slightly mistaken, and we did not correct them. In a few hours the spore cloud will envelop your planet. We do not think it will harm you because—"

Someone in the crowd around the screen cried, "What?"

"—because you are genetically immune to this virus. We suspected as much before we arrived, although we could not be sure. *Homo sapiens* acquired immunity when Earth passed through the cloud the first time, about seventy thousand years ago."

A graphic replaced Smith's face: the Milky Way galaxy, a long dark splotch overlapping it, and a glowing blue dot for Earth. "The rotation of the galaxy plus its movement through space-time will bring you back into contact with the cloud's opposite edge from where it touched you before. Your physicists were able to see the approaching cloud, but your instruments were not advanced enough to understand its shape or depth. Earth will be passing through the edge of the cloud for two-point-six years. On its first contact, the cloud killed every *homo sapiens* that did not come with this genetic mutation."

A gene sequence of base pairs flashed across the screen, too fast to be noted.

"This sequence will appear again later, in a form you can record. It is found in what you call 'junk DNA.' The sequence is a transposon and you will find it complementary to the spores' genetic code. Your bodies made no antibodies against the spores because it does not consider them invaders. Seventy thousand years ago our people had already been taken from Earth or we, too, would have died. We are without this sequence, which appeared in mutation later than our removal."

Marianne's mind raced. Seventy thousand years ago. The "bottleneck event" that had shrunk the human population on Earth to a mere few thousand. It had not been caused by the Toba volcano or ferocious predators or climate changes, but by the spore cloud. As for the gene sequence—one theory said that much of the human genome consisted of inactive and fossilized viruses absorbed into the DNA. Fossilized and inactive—she could almost hear Evan's voice: "*Or so we thought . . . .*"

Smith continued. "You will find that in Marianne Jenner, Ahmed Rafat, and Penelope Hodgson this sequence has already activated, producing the protein already identified in Dr. Jenner's blood, a protein that this recording will detail for you. The protein attaches to the outside of cells and prevents the virus from entering. Soon the genetic sequence will do so in the rest of humanity. Some may become mildly ill, like Robert Chavez, due to faulty protein production. We estimate this will comprise perhaps twenty percent of you. There may be fatalities among the old or already sick, but most of you are genetically protected. Some of your rodents do not seem to be, which we admit was a great surprise to us, and we cannot say for certain what other Terran species may be susceptible.

"We know that we are fatally susceptible. We cannot alter our own genome, at least not for the living, but we have learned much from you. By the time the spore cloud reaches World, we will have developed a vaccine. This would not have been possible without your full cooperation and your bodily samples. We—"

"If this is true," Penny Hodgson shouted, "why didn't they *tell* us?"

"—did not tell you the complete truth because we believe that had you known Earth was in no critical danger, you would not have allocated so many resources, so much scientific talent, or such urgency into the work on the *Embassy*. We are all human, but your evolutionary history and present culture are very different from ours. You do not build identity on family. You permit much of Earth's population to suffer from lack of food, water, and medical care. We didn't think you would help us as much as we needed unless we withheld from you certain truths. If we were mistaken in our assessment, please forgive us."

They weren't mistaken, Marianne thought.

"We are grateful for your help," Smith said, "even if obtained fraudulently. We leave you a gift in return. This recording contains what you call the 'engineering specs' for a star drive. We have already given you the equations describing the principles. Now you may build a ship. In generations to come, both branches of humanity will profit from more open and truthful exchanges. We will become true brothers.

"Until then, ten Terrans accompany us home. They have chosen to do this, for their own reasons. All were told that they would not die if they remained on Earth, but chose to come anyway. They will become World, creating further friendships with our clan brothers on Terra.

"Again—thank you."

Pandemonium erupted on the barge: talking, arguing, shouting. The sun was above the horizon now. Three Coast Guard ships barreled across the harbor toward the barge. As Marianne clutched her yellow blanket closer against the morning breeze, something vibrated in the pocket of her jeans.

She pulled it out: a flat metal square with Noah's face on it. As soon as her gaze fell on his, the face began to speak. "I'm going with them, Mom. I want you to know that I am completely happy. This is where I belong. I've mated with Llaa^mohį—Dr. Jones—and she is pregnant. Your grandchild will be born among the stars. I love you."

Noah's face faded from the small square.

Rage filled her, red sparks burning. Her son, and she would never see him again! Her grandchild, and she would never see him or her at all. She was being robbed, being deprived of what was hers by *right*, the aliens should never have come—

She stopped. Realization slammed into her, and she gripped the rail of the barge so tightly that her nails pierced the wood.

The aliens *had* made a mistake. A huge, colossal, monumental mistake.

Her rage, however irrational, was going to be echoed and amplified across the entire planet. The Denebs had understood that Terrans would work really hard only if their own survival were at stake. But they did not understand the rest of it. The Deneb presence on Earth had caused riots, diversion of resources, deaths, panic, fear. The "mild illness" of the twenty percent like Robbie, happening all at once starting today, was enough to upset every economy on the planet. The aliens had swept like a storm through the world, and as in the aftermath of a superstorm, everything in the landscape had shifted. In addition, the Denebs had carried off ten humans, which could be seen as brainwashing them in order to procure prospective lab rats for future experimentation.

Brothers, yes—but Castor and Pollux, whose bond reached across the stars, or Cain and Abel?

Humans did not forgive easily, and they resented being bought off, even with a star drive. Smith should have left a different gift, one that would not let Terrans come to World, that peaceful and rich planet so unaccustomed to revenge or war.

But on the other hand—she could be wrong. Look how often she had been wrong already: about Elizabeth, about Ryan, about Smith. Maybe, when the Terran disruptions were over and starships actually built, humanity would become so entranced with the Deneb gift that we would indeed go to World in friendship. Maybe the prospect of going to the stars would even soften American isolationism and draw countries together to share the necessary resources. It could happen. The cooperative genes that had shaped Smith and Jones were also found in the Terran genome.

But—it would happen only if those who wanted it worked hard to convince the rest. Worked, in fact, as hard at urging friendship as they had at ensuring survival. Was that possible? Could it be done?

Why are you here?

To make contact with World. A peace mission.

She gazed up at the multicolored dawn sky, but the ship was already out of sight. Only its after-image remained in her sight.

"Harrison," Marianne said, and felt her own words steady her, "we have a lot of work to do."

Joe Abercrombie, "Tough Times All Over," *Rogues*.
Daniel Abraham, "The Meaning of Love," *Rogues*.
Nina Allan, "Mirielena," *Interzone 254*.
——, "The Science of Chance," *Solaris Rising 3*.
Charlie Jane Anders, "The Cartography of Sudden Death," *Tor.com*, January 22.
Kelley Armstrong, "The Screams of Dragons," *Subterranean*, Spring.
Eleanor Arnason, "The Black School," *Hidden Folk*.
——, "The Puffin Hunter," *Hidden Folk*.
——, "The Scrivner," *Subterranean*, Winter.
Madeline Ashby, "By the Time We Got to Arizona," *Hieroglyph*.
——, "Coming From Away," *Upgraded*.
Paolo Bacigalupi, "Moriabe's Children," *Monstrous Affections*.
Kate Bachus, "Pinono Deep," *Asimov's*, October/November.
Kage Baker, "In Old Pidruid," *Book of Silverberg*.
Dale Bailey, "The Culvert," *F&SF*, September/October.
David Ball, "Provenance," *Rogues*.
Tony Ballantyne, "The Region of Jennifer," *Analog*, June.
——, "Threshold," *Analog*, October.
Justin Barbeau, "Nanabojou at the World's Fair," *F&SF*, November/December.
Christopher Barzak, "The Boy Who Grew Up," *Uncanny Stories*, June.
Stephen Baxter, "The Lingering Joy," *Multiverse*.
Amelia Beamer, "Lelia and the Conservation of Entropy," *Uncanny Magazine*.
Elizabeth Bear, "Madame Damnable's Sewing Circle," *Dead Man's Hand*.
——, "No Place to Dream, But a Place To Die," *Upgraded*.
——, "You've Never Seen Everything," *The End is Now*.
——, "This Chance Planet," *Tor.com*, Oct 22.
Chris Beckett, "The Goblin Hunter," *Solaris Rising 3*.
Gregory Benford, "Bloodpride," *Multiverse*.
——, "Lady with Fox," *Carbide-Tipped Pens*.
M. Bennardo, "How Do I Get to Last Summer from Here?," *Asimov's*, July.
——, "Last Day at the Ice Man Café," *Asimov's*, February.
——, "Now Dress Me in My Finest Suit and Lay Me in My Casket," *Asimov's*, December.
——, "Slowly Upward, the Coelacanth," *Asimov's*,
Paul M. Berger, "Subduction," *F&SF*, July/August.
Holly Black, "Ten Rules for Being an Intergalactic Smuggler (The Sucessful Kind)," *Monstrous Affections*.
James P. Blaylock, "The Adventure of the Ring of Stones," *Subterranean Press*.
Gregory Norman Bossart, "The Leaves Upon Her Falling Light," *Beneath Ceaseless Skies 158*.

Richard Bowes, "Sleep Walking Now and Then," *Tor.com*, July 9.

Marie Brennan, "Daughter of Necessity," *Tor.com*, October 1.

——, "Mad Maudlin," *Tor.com*, February 5.

David Brin, "Latecomers," *Multiverse*.

Keith Brooke and Eric Brown, "The End of the World," *Paradox*.

Sarah Brooks, "The Great Detective," *Strange Horizons*, 9/15.

Terry Brooks, "The Fey of Cloudmoor," *Multiverse*.

Christopher Brown, "Countermeasures," *Twelve Tomorrows*.

Tobias S. Buckell, "A Cold Heart," *Upgraded*.

——, "Ambassador to the Dinosaurs," *Book of Silverberg*.

——, "System Reset," *The End Is Nigh*.

Oliver Buckram, "A Struggle Between Two Rivals Ends Surprisingly," *F&SF*, March/April.

Karl Bunker, "Ashes," *Interzone 251*.

Pat Cadigan, "The Big Next," *Paradox*.

——, "Business As Usual," *Twelve Tomorrows*.

——, "Report Concerning the Presence of Seahorses on Mars," *Reach for Infinity*.

James L. Cambias, "Contractual Obligation," *War Stories*.

——, "Periapsis," *Hieroglyph*.

Rebecca Campbell, "Lilacs and Daffodils," *Interzone 250*.

Seth Chambers, "In Her Eyes," *F&SF*, January/February.

Robert R. Chase, "Decaying Orbit," *Asimov's*, October/November.

C. J. Cherryh, "Dancing on the Edge of the Dark," *Multiverse*.

Rob Chilson, "Our Vegetable Love," *F&SF*, March/April.

Liu Cixin, "The Circle," *Carbide-Tipped Pens*.

Eric Choi, "Crimson Sky," *Analog*, July/August.

Gwendolyn Clare, "It Gets Bigger," *Asimov's*, September.

David L. Clements, "Catching Rays," *Paradox*.

Heather Clitheroe, "Cuts Both Ways," *Lightspeed*, June.

Ron Collins, "Primes," *Asimov's*, January.

Jay O'Connell, "Of All Possible Worlds," *Asimov's*, August.

C. S. E. Cooney, "Witch, Beast, Saint: An Erotic Fairy Tale," *Strange Horizons*, 7/2.

Brenda Cooper, "A Heart of Power and Oil," *Coming Soon Enough*.

——, "Elephant Angels," *Hieroglyph*.

James S. A. Corey, "The Churn," *Orbit Short Fiction*.

Paul Cornell, "A Better Way to Die," *Rogues*.

Albert E. Cowdrey, "Byzantine History 101," *F&SF*, March/April.

——, "Out of the Deeps," *F&SF*, January/February.

Ian Creasey, "Ormande and Chase," *Asimov's*, June.

Malcolm Cross, "Pavlov's House," *Strange Horizons*, 4/21.

Kara Dalkey, "The Philosopher Duck," *Asimov's*, June.

Indrapramit Das, "A Moon for the Unborn," *Strange Horizons*, 11/10.

Rjurik Davidson, "Nighttime in Caeli-Amur," *Tor.com*, January 15.

Aliette de Bodard, "A Slow Unfurling of Truth," *Carbide-Tipped Pens*.

——, "The Breath of War," *Beneath Ceaseless Skies 142*.

——, "The Dust Queen," *Reach for Infinity*.

——, "The Frost on Jade Buds," *Solaris Rising 3*.

——, "Memorials," *Asimov's*, January.

——, "The Moon Over Red Trees," *Beneath Ceaseless Skies* 157.

Craig Delancey, "Racing the Tide," *Analog*, December.

A. M. Dellamonica, "The Color of Paradox," *Tor.com*, June 25.

——, "The Ugly Woman of Castello di Putti," *Tor.com*, March 5.

Bradley Denton, "Bad Brass," *Rogues*.

Malcolm Devlin, "Must Supply Own Work Boots," *Interzone* 255.

Seth Dickinson, "A Tank Only Fears Four Things," *Lightspeed*, May.

——, "Economics of Force," *Apex Magazine*, September.

——, "Morrigan in the Sunglare," *Clarkesworld*, March.

——, "Wizard, Cabalist, Ascendant," *Upgraded*.

Cory Doctorow, "Petard: A Tale of Just Desserts," *Twelve Tomorrows*.

Sarina Dorie, "The Day of the Nuptial Flight," *F&SF*, July/August.

Jeffifer Dornan-Fish, "Mind the Gap," *Interzone* 255.

Brendan Dubois, "Minutes to the End of the World," *Asimov's*, October/November.

Tananarive Due, "Removal Order," *The End Is Nigh*.

——, "Herd Immunity," *The End Is Now*.

Thoraiya Dryer, "Human Strandings and the Role of the Xenobiologist," *Clarkesworld*, March.

Christopher East, "Videoville," *Asimov's*, December.

Greg Egan, "Bit Players," *Subterranean*, Winter.

——, "Break My Fall," *Reach for Infinity*.

——, "Seventh Sight," *Upgraded*.

Rhonda Eikamp, "The Case of the Passionless Bees," *Lightspeed*, June.

Phyllis Eisenstein, "The Caravan To Nowhere," *Rogues*.

Warren Ellis, "The Shipping Forecast," *Twelve Tomorrows*.

Harlan Ellison, "He Who Grew Up Reading Sherlock Holmes," *Subterranean*, Summer.

Amal El Mohar, "The Lonely Sea in the Sky," *Lightspeed*, June.

Raymond E. Feist, "A Candle," *Multiverse*.

Gemma Files, "Drawn Up from Deep Places," *Beneath Ceaseless Skies* 159.

C. C. Finlay, "The Man Who Hanged Three Times," *Asimov's*, January.

Eric Flint, "Operation Xibalba," *Multiverse*.

Gillian Flynn, "What Do You Do?," *Rogues*.

Michael F. Flynn, "The Journeyman: Against the Green," *Analog*, July/August.

——, "The Journeyman: In the Stone House," *Analog*, June.

Jeffrey Ford, "*La Madre del Oro*," *Dead Man's Hand*.

——, "The Prelate's Commission," *Subterranean*, Winter.

Karen Joy Fowler, "Nanny Anne and the Christmas Story," *Subterranean*, Winter.

Nancy Fulda, "Recollection," *Carbide-Tipped Pens*.

Neil Gaiman, "How the Marquis Got His Coat Back," *Rogues*.

Stephen Gallagher, "One Dove," *Subterranean*, Spring.

David Gerrold, "The Thing in the Back Yard," *F&SF*, September/October.

William Gibson, "Death Cookie/Easy Ice," *Twelve Tomorrows*.

Greer Gilman, "Exit, Pursued by a Bear," *Small Beer Press*.

Kathleen Ann Goonan, "A Short History of the Twentieth Century, or, When You Wish Upon a Star," *Tor.com*, July 20.

——, "Girl in Wave: Wave in Girl," *Hieroglyph*.

——, "Where Do We Come From? What Are We? Where Are We Going?," *Tor.com*, February 12.

——, "Wilder Still, the Stars," *Reach for Infinity*.
Theodora Goss, "Cimmeria: From the Journal of Imaginary Anthropology," *Lightspeed*, July.
John Grant, "Ghost Story," *Interzone 251*.
Sarah Gray, "Rocket Summer," *Flytrap*, February.
Daryl Gregory, "We Are All Completely Fine," *Tachyon*.
Nicola Griffith, "Cold Wind," Tor.com, April 15.
Eileen Gunn, "Chop Wood, Carry Water," *Questionable Practices*.
——, "Phantom Pain," *Questionable Practices*.
James Gunn, "Patterns," *Asimov's*, September.
Caren Gussoff, "The Bars of Orion," *Interzone 253*.
Maria Dahvana Headley, "Dim Sun," *Lightspeed*, June.
——, "What There Was To See," *Subterranean*, Summer.
Howard V. Hendrix, "Habilis," *Carbide-Tipped Pens*.
Sarah Hendrix, "The Coin Whisperer," *Abyss & Apex*, 3rd Quarter.
Crystal Lynn Hilbert, "Soul of Soup Bones," *Lightspeed*, June.
Tory Hoke, "Lysistrata of Mars," *Strange Horizons*, 2/10.
Nalo Hopkinson, "Left Foot, Right," *Monstrous Affections*.
Kat Howard, "Hath No Fury," *Subterranean*, Spring.
——, "The Very Fabric," *Subterranean*, Summer.
Matthew Hughes, "Avianca's Bezel," *F&SF*, September/October.
——, "The Ba of Phalloon," *Lightspeed*, May.
——, "His Elbow, Unkissed: A Kalso Chronicles Tale," *Lightspeed*, January.
——, "Inn of the Seven Blessings," *Rogues*.
——, "Under the Scab," *Lightspeed*, September.
Claire Humphrey, "A Brief Light," *Interzone 252*.
Alex Irvine, "For All of Us Down Here," *F&SF*, January/February.
Pasi Ilmari Jaaskeainen, "Where the Trains Turn Past," Tor.com, November 19.
Alexander Jablokov, "The Instructive Tale of the Archeologist and His Wife," *Asimov's*, July.
William Jablowsky, "Static," *Asimov's*, January.
Xia Jia, "Tongtong's Summer," *Upgraded*.
Alaya Dawn Johnson, "A Guide to the Fruits of Hawai'i," *F&SF*, July/August.
Bill Johnson, "Code Blue Love," *Analog*, July/August.
C. W. Johnson, "The Anomaly," *Analog*, December.
Mathew Johnson, "Rules of Engagement," *Asimov's*, April/May.
James Patrick Kelly, "The Pope of the Chimps," *Book of Silverberg*.
——, "The Rose Witch," *Clarkesworld*, August.
——, "Uncanny," *Asimov's*, October/November.
Caitlín R. Kiernan, "Bus Stop," *Subterranean*, Spring.
——, "The Jetsam of Disremembered Mechanics," *Book of Silverberg*.
——, "Pushing the Sky Away (Death of a Blasphemer)," *Subterranean*, Summer.
Maggie Shen King, "Ball and Chain," *Asimov's*, February.
Ellen Klages, "Caligo Lane," *Subterranean*, Winter.
——, "Hey, Presto!," *Fearsome Magics*.
Leo Konstantinou, "Johnny Appledrone vs. the FAA," *Hieroglyph*.
Mary Robinette Kowal, "Water Over the Dam," *Coming Soon Enough*.
Nancy Kress, "Angels of the Apocalypse," *The End Is Now*.
——, "The Common Good," *Asimov's*, January.

——, "Eaters," *Book of Silverberg*.

——, "Outmoded Things," *Multiverse*.

——, "Pretty Soon the Four Horsemen Are Going to Come Riding Through," *The End Is Nigh*.

——, "Sidewalk at 12:00 P.M.," *Asimov's*, June.

——, "Someone To Watch Over Me," *Coming Soon Enough*.

Matthew Kressel, "Cameron Rhyder's Legs," *Clarkesworld*, Nov.

Naomi Kritzer, "Containment Zone: A Seastead Story," *F&SF*, May/June.

Derek Kunsken, "Persephone Descending," *Analog*, November

——, "Schools of Clay," *Asimov's*, February.

Geoffrey A. Landis, "A Hotel in Antarctica," *Hieroglyph*.

——, "The Chatbot and the Drone," *Commuications of the Association for Computing Machinery*.

——, "Incoming," *Coming Soon Enough*.

Sarah Langan, "Black Monday," *The End Is Now*.

Joe R. Lansdale, "Bent Twig," *Rogues*.

——, "The Red-Headed Dead," *Dead Man's Hand*.

Rich Larson, "The Air We Breath Is Stormy, Stormy," *Strange Horizons*, 8/11.

——, "Brute," *Apex Magazine*, November.

——, "Capricorn," *Abyss & Apex*, 4th Quarter.

——, "Ghost Girl," *War Stories*.

——, "Maria and the Pilgrim," *Apex Magazine*, "February.

Anaea Lay, "Salamander Patterns," *Lightspeed*, January.

Ann Leckie, "She Commands Me and I Obey," *Strange Horizons*, 11/10–11/17.

Yoon Ha Lee, "Always the Harvest," *Upgraded*.

——, "The Bonedrake's Pennance," *Beneath Ceasesless Skies 143*.

——, "Combustion Hour," *Tor.com*, June 15.

——, "The Contemporary Foxwife," *Clarkesworld*, July.

——, "Warhosts," *War Stories*.

——, "Wine," *Clarkesworld*, January.

David D. Levine, "The End of the Silk Road," *F&SF*, May/June.

——, "Mammals," *Analog*, December.

Michael Libling, "Draft 31," *F&SF*, March/April.

Kelly Link, "The New Boyfriend," *Monstrous Affections*.

Marissa Lingen, "The New Girl," *Apex Magazine*, November.

——, "The Suitcase Aria," *Strange Horizons*, 8/17.

'——, and Alec Austin, "The Young Necromancer's Guide to ReCapiatation," *On Spec*, Winter.

Ken Liu, "The Clockwork Soldier," *Clarkesworld*, January.

——, "The Gods Will Not Be Chained," *The End Is Nigh*.

——, "The Gods Will Not Be Slain," *The End Is Now*.

——, "Home Floresiensis," *Solaris Rising 3*.

——, "In the Loop," *War Stories*.

——, "Lecture 14: Concerning the Event-Cloaking Device.and Practical Applications Thereof," *Cosmos*, April.

——, "None Owns the Air," *Lightspeed*, February.

——, "Presence," *Uncanny Magazine*.

——, "Reborn," *Tor.com*, January 29.

——, "Saboteur," *Analog*, December.

——, "What I Assume You Shall Assume," *Dead Man's Hand*.

Karin Lowachee, "Enemy States," *War Stories*.

Karen Lord, "Hiraeth: A Tragedy in Four Acts," *Reach for Infinity*.

Scott Lynch, "A Year and a Day in Old Theradane," *Rogues*.

Ian R. MacLeod, "The Traveller and the Book," *Subterranean*, Spring.

——, and Martin Sketchley, "The Howl," *Solaris Rising 3*.

Ken Macleod, "The Entire Immense Superstructure: An Installation," *Reach for Infinity*.

Bruce McAllister, "La Signora," *Tor.com*, August 23.

Jack McDevitt, "Enjoy the Moment," *The End Is Nigh*.

Sandra McDonald, "End of the World Community College," *F&SF*, July/August.

——, "Selfie," *Lightspeed*, May.

——, "Story of Our Lives," *Asimov's*, July.

Alex Dally McFarlane, "Popular Images from the First Manned Mission to Enceladus," *Solaris Rising 3*.

Seanan McGuire, "Midway Relics and Dying Breeds," *Tor.com*, September 24.

Ian McHugh, "The Extracted Journal Notes for an Ethnography of Bnebene Nomad Culture," *Asimov's*, January.

Wil McIntosh, "Scout," *Asimov's*, April/May.

Daniel Marcus, "Albion Upon the Rock," *F&SF*, March/April.

George R. R. Martin, "The Rogue Prince," *Rogues*.

Sam J. Miller, "Songs Like Freight Trains," *Interzone 254*.

Kris Millerine, "A Word Shaped Like Bone," *Lightspeed*, June.

Judith Moffett, "Space Ballet," *Tor.com*, February 4.

Dustin Monk, "The Street of the Green Elephant," *Shimmer 18*.

Sunny Moraine, "Cold as the Moon," *Strange Horizons*, 8/18.

——, "So Sharp That Blood Must Flow," *Lightspeed*, February.

——, "To Increase His Wondrous Greatness," *Apex Magazine*, March.

——, "What Glistens Back," *Lightspeed*, November.

Linda Nagata, "Attitude," *Reach for Infinity*.

——, "Codename Delphi," *Lightspeed*, April.

——, "Light and Shadow," *War Stories*.

David Erik Nelson, "There Was No Sound of Thunder," *Asimov's*, June.

——, "The Traveling Salesman Solution," *F&SF*, July/August.

Mari Ness, "Memories and Wires," *Upgraded*.

Alec Nevala-Lee, "Cryptids," *Analog*, May.

Garth Nix, "A Cargo of Ivories," *Rogues*.

——, "Home Is the Hunter," *Fearsome Magics*.

Larry Niven, "The Far End," *Multiverse*.

Val Nolan, "Diving into the Wreck," *Interzone 252*.

Jay O'Connell, "Of All Possible Worlds," *Asimov's*, August.

——, "Other People's Things," *F&SF*, September/October.

An Owomoyele, "And Wash Out the Tides of War," *Clarkesworld*, February.

——, "Undermarket Data," *Lightspeed*, August.

Suzanne Palmer, "Fly Away Home," *Interzone 251*.

——, "Shatterdown," *Asimov's*, June.

Susan Palwick, "Windows," *Asimov's*, September.

K. J. Parker, "Heaven Thunders the Truth," *Beneath Ceaseless Skies* 157.

——, "I Met a Man Who Wasn't There," *Subterranean*, Winter.

——, "Safe House," *Fearsome Magics*.

——, "The Things We Do For Love," *Subterranean*, Summer.

Richard Parks, "The Manor of Lost Time," *Beneath Ceaseless Skies*,

——, "The Sorrow of Rain," *Beneath Ceaseless Skies* 157.

Tony Pi, "The Sweeter Art," *Beneath Ceaseless Skies* 155.

Sarah Pinsker, "A Stretch of Highway Two Lanes Wide," *F&SF*, March/April.

——, "How a Map Works," *Unlikely Stories*, June.

——, "The Low Hum of Her," *Asimov's*, August.

——, "The Sewell Home for the Temporally Displaced," *Lightspeed*, June.

——, "The Transdimensional Horsemaster Rabbis of Mpumalanga Province," *Asimov's*, February.

Gareth L. Powell, "This Is How You Die," *Interzone* 251.

William Preston, "Each in His Prison, Thinking of the Key," *Asimov's*, April/May.

Cherie Priest, "Heavy Metal," *Rogues*.

Tom Purdom, "Bogdavi's Dream," *Asimov's*, September.

Chen Qiufan, "Oil of Angels," *Upgraded*.

Hannu Rajaniemi, "Invisible Planets," *Reach for Infinity*.

Cat Rambo, "All the Pretty Little Mermaids," *Asimov's*, March.

——, "Tortoiseshell Cats Are Not Refundable," *Clarkesworld*, February.

Dinesh Rao, "The Aerophone," *F&SF*, July/August.

Robert Reed, "Aether," *Paradox*.

——, "The Cryptic Age," *Asimov's*, December.

——, "Every Hill Ends With Sky," *Carbide-Tipped Pens*.

——, "GW in the Afterlife," *Postscripts 32/33*.

——, "Pernicious Romance," *Clarkesworld*, November.

——, "The Principles," *Asimov's*, April/May.

——, "The Sarcophagus," *Upgraded*.

——, "Will He?," *F&SF*, September/October.

——, "wHole," *Clarkesworld*, June.

Alastair Reynolds, "The Last Log of the Lachrimosa," *Subterranean*, Summer.

——, "Wrecking Party," *Dead Man's Hand*.

Mike Resnick, "Bad News from the Vatican," *Book of Silverberg*.

M. Rickert, "The Mothers of Voorhisville," *Tor.com*, April 30.

Mecurio D. Rivera, "Atonement, Under the Blue-White Sun," *Paradox*.

Adam Roberts, "Trademark Bugs: A Legal History," *Reach for Infinity*.

Justina Robson, "On Skybolt Mountain," *Fearsome Magics*.

Margaret Ronald, "The Innocence of a Place," *Strange Horizons*, 1/13.

Benjamin Rosenbaum, "Fift and Shira," *Solaris Rising 3*.

Patrick Rothfuss, "The Lightning Tree," *Rogues*.

Christopher Rowe, "The Dun Letter," *Fearsome Magics*.

Kristine Kathryn Rusch, "Playing with Reality," *Asimov's*, October/November.

——, "Snapshots," *Analog*, May.

——, "Voyeuristic Tendencies," *Book of Silverberg*.

Ian Sales, "Far Voyager," *Postscripts 32/33*.

Jason Sanford, "What Is Sand But Earth Purified?," *Asimov's*, October/November.

Steven Saylor, "Ill Seen in Tyre," *Rogues*.

John Scalzi, "Unlocked: An Oral History of Haden's Disease," *Tor.com*, May 18.
Veronica Schanoes, "Among the Thorns," *Tor.com*, May 7.
Karl Schroeder, "Degrees of Freedom," *Hieroglyph*.
——, "Khledyu," *Reach for Infinity*.
Gord Sellar, "Stars Fell on Alabama," *Asimov's*, October/November.
Lewis Shiner, "The Black Sun," *Subterranean*, Summer.
Robert Silverberg, "Christmas in Gondwanaland," *Multiverse*.
Vandana Singh, "Wake-Rider," *Lightspeed*.
Emily C. Skaftun, "Diary of a Pod Person," *Asimov's*, October/November.
Doug C. Souza, "Mountain Screamers," *Asimov's*, August.
Benjanun Sriduangkaew, "Autodidact," *Clarkesworld*, April.
——, "Synedoche Oracles," *Upgraded*.
Allen M. Steele, "The Legion of Tomorrow," *Asimov's*, July.
Bruce Sterling, "Pilgrims of the Round World," *Subterranean*, Winter.
——, "Tall Tower," *Hieroglyph*.
——, "The Various Mansions of the Universe," *Twelve Tomorrows*.
Andy Stewart, "The New Cambrian," *F&SF*, January/February.
S. M. Stirling, "A Slip in Time," *Multiverse*.
Bonnie Jo Stufflebeam, "The Damaged," *Interzone 250*.
Tim Sullivan, "Anomaly Station," *Asimov's*, December.
——, "The Memory Cage," *F&SF*, May/June.
——, "Yeshua's Dog," *F&SF*, November/December.
Tricia Sullivan, "The Ambulance Chaser," *Paradox*.
Michael Swanwick, "Of Finest Scarlet Was Her Gown," *Asimov's*, April/May.
——, "Tawny Petticoats," *Rogues*.
——, "3 A.M. in the Mesozoic Bar," *Postscripts 32/33*.
Rachel Swirsky, "Endless," *Solaris Rising 3*.
Anna Tambour, "The Walking-Stick Forest," *Tor.com*, May 21.
David Tellerman, "Bad Time To Be in the Wrong Place," *Interzone 250*.
Adrian Tchaikovsky, "Lost to Their Own Devices," *Paradox*.
Natalia Theodoridou, "The Eleven Holy Numbers of the Mechanical Soul," *Clarkesworld*, February.
Karin Tidbeck, "Migration," *Fearsome Magics*.
Lavie Tidhar, "The Dead Leaves," *Black God's Kiss*.
——, "Die," *Dangerous Games*.
——, "Kur-a-lin," *Black God's Kiss*.
——, "Murder in the Cathedral," *Asimov's*, June.
——, "Selfies," *Tor.com*, September 17.
——, "The Time-Slip Detective," *Tel Aviv Noir*.
Jeremiah Tolbert, "In the Dying Light, We Saw a Shape," *Lightspeed*, February.
E. Catherine Tobler, "The Cumulative Effects of Light Over Time," *Upgraded*.
Joseph Tomaras, "Bonfires in Anacostia," *Clarkesworld*, August.
Ian Tregillis, "The Testimony of Samuel Frobisher . . .", *F&SF*, July/August.
Jean-Louis Trudel, "The Snows of Yesteryear," *Carbide-Tipped Pens*.
Harry Turtledove, "The Eighth Grade History Class Visits the Hebrew Home for the Aging," *Tor.com*, January 8.
——, "The Man Who Came Late," *Multiverse*.

Lisa Tuttle, "The Curious Case of the Dead Wives," *Rogues.*
Genevieve Valentine, "Dream Houses," *WSFA Press.*
——, "Small Medicine," *Upgraded.*
Greg Van Eekhout, "The Authenticator," *Flytrap*, February.
James Van Pelt, "My Father and the Martian Moon Maids," *Interzone 253.*
——, "This Gray Rock, Standing Tall," *Unlikely Stories*, June.
——, "The Turkey Raptor," *Asimov's*, June.
Carrie Vaughn, "Harry and Marlow and the Intrigue at the Aetherian Exhibition," *Lightspeed*,
    February.
——, "Harry and Marlow versus the Haunted Locomotive of the Rockies," *Lightspeed*, July.
——, "Roaring Twenties," *Rogues.*
——, "Salvage," *Lightspeed*, June.
Elizabeth Vonarberg, "Chambered Nautilus," *Strange Horizons*, 6/30.
Juliette Wade, "Mind Locker," *Analog*, July/August.
——, "Not Easily Thrown Away," *Clarkesworld*, March.
Kali Wallace, "Water in Springtime," *Clarkesworld*, April.
Jo Walton, "Sleeper," *Tor.com* August 12.
Peter Watts, "Collateral," *Upgraded.*
——, "Hotshot," *Reach for Infinity.*
Gerry Webb, "In the Beginning," *Paradox.*
Tracie Welsor, "A Doll Is Not a Dumpling," *Interzone 251.*
Ted White, "The Uncertain Past," *F&SF*, March/April.
Rick Wilber, "Scouting Report," *Asimov's*, September.
Ysabeau S. Wilce, "Lovelocks," *Prophecies, Libels, and Dreams.*
——, "Scaring the Shavetail," *Prophecies, Libels, and Dreams.*
Fran Wilde, "Like a Wasp to the Tongue," *Asimov's*, April/May.
Genevieve Williams, "The Redemption of Kip Banjeree," *Asimov's*, March.
Sean Williams, "The Cuckoo," *Clarkesworld*, April.
Tad Williams, "Strong Medicine," *Dead Man's Hand.*
——, "Three Lilies and Three Leopards . . .," *Multiverse.*
Walter Jon Williams, "Diamonds From Tequila," *Rogues.*
——, "The Golden Age," *Dead Man's Hand.*
Neil Williamson, "The Posset Pot," *Interzone 252.*
Connie Willis, "Now Showing," *Rogues.*
——, "Silverberg, Satan, and Me . . .", *Book of Silverberg.*
Daniel H. Wilson, "The Blue Afternoon That Lasted Forever," *Carbide-Tipped Pens.*
Kai Ashante Wilson, "The Devil in America," *Tor.com*, April 2.
Alyssa Wong, "*Santos de Sampaguias*," *Strange Horizons*, 10/5–10/13.
Peter Wood, "Drink in a Small Town," *Asimov's*, March.
John C. Wright, "Idle Thoughts," *Abyss & Apex*, 4th Quarter.
J. V. Yang, "Patterns of Murmuration, in Billions of Data Points," *Clarkesworld*, September.
Caroline M. Yoachim, "Paperclips and Memories and Things That Won't Be Missed,"
    Apex Magazine, May.
Alvaro Zinos-Amaro, "Hot and Cold," *Analog*, July/August.
K. J. Zimring, "The Talking Cure," *Asimov's*, April/May.